KU-729-831

The Critics on Nancy Taylor Rosenberg

'Incredibly fast-paced and exciting from page one until the end' James Patterson

'Puts her plots together neatly, incorporating a cunning and unexpected twist towards the end, and uses a wringer to good effect on the reader's heartstrings' *Evening Standard*

'A more than worthy contender for the John Grisham crown' *Sunday Express*

'A riveting and well-told portrait of a world in which truth and justice are sometimes opposites' *New York Newsday*

'Packed with suspense and keeping you turning pages far into the night'
Andrea Newman, *Sunday Express*

Also by Nancy Taylor Rosenberg

Mitigating Circumstances
First Offence
California Angel
Trial by Fire
Abuse of Power
Buried Evidence

Nancy Taylor Rosenberg received a BA in English and worked as a photographic model before studying criminology and joining the Police Department. She has served as an Investigative Probation Officer in Court Services for the County of Ventura, where she handled major crimes such as homicide and multiple-count sex-related offences. Nancy Taylor Rosenberg has five children and lives in New York.

To my mother, Laverne Taylor,
and in memory of my father,
William Hoyt Taylor, and to my
father- and mother-in-law, Hyman
and Doris Rosenberg.

INTEREST OF JUSTICE

Nancy Taylor Rosenberg

ORION

acknowledgments

I WOULD LIKE TO ACKNOWLEDGE ALL THE MANY PEOPLE WHO ASsisted me in the development of this novel. First, I offer thanks to my wonderful agent and good friend, Peter Miller, of PMA Literary and Film Management, for his constant support and tireless efforts on my behalf; and to Jennifer Robinson, also of PMA, who assisted me greatly. I am particularly grateful to my editor, Michaela Hamilton of Dutton Signet, who offered her brilliant editorial insight. Without her this novel would not be what it is today. Elaine Koster, my publisher, has been wonderful, as well as the entire staff at Penguin USA.

Additionally, I would like to offer thanks to Dr. George Awad for his expert advice in the field of pathology. And last, I would like to thank my wonderful children: Blake, Chris, Brett, Alex, and Nancy for allowing their mother to become a writer and follow her dream, and for handling a lot of their problems without me. Nancy, I would particularly like to thank, since she sacrificed her summer vacation to assist me in editing this novel.

Chapter 1

Judge Lara Sanderstone had a ritual. When she was pondering a complex legal matter or was about to make a judicial ruling, she would spin her high-backed leather chair toward the American flag on the left side of her mahogany desk. It seemed to give her inspiration. As for the California flag right next to it, well, she didn't put much stock in its ability to inspire her – or anyone else, for that matter, although she certainly wouldn't voice this opinion publicly.

Many of the judges didn't have flags in their chambers. She had inherited the flags, the furniture, her chambers, even her secretary from the judge she had replaced when she was appointed to the superior court bench two years prior after eleven years as a prosecutor. The weekend before her swearing-in ceremony, she had driven to the courthouse in her jeans and lovingly sanded down and refinished the marred surface of the once magnificent desk. There wasn't much she could do about the chair, however. The judge she had replaced was a heavy man, and the innersprings had collapsed with his weight. They had promised her a new chair, but it had never appeared. It was like sitting in a bucket.

She glanced at the clock. It was almost time to return to the courtroom. The matter on the afternoon calendar was a pretrial motion. These were generally routine and uneventful, carried out in an almost empty courtroom. But unfortunately, this particular motion could destroy the people's case completely, and it had carried over to a second day. The motion should have been heard at the preliminary hearing, but then the defendant had been represented by the public defender, a man sympathetic to the prosecution and buried in cases. Now the case had been taken over by Benjamin England, a Rhodes scholar, a man established enough to devote himself full-time to this case and none other.

The case involved the rape and murder of twenty-year-old Jessica Van Horn. She had left her home in Mission Viejo after a weekend visit en route to the UCLA campus in her 1989 Toyota Camry. The car was later found abandoned alongside the freeway with a flat tire. An exhaustive two-month search for the pretty blonde had culminated in tragedy. Her defiled and decomposed body had been found in a field near Oceanside, about forty miles from where her car was discovered. All those involved had hoped against reason that she was still alive. By the time the body was discovered, the officers, reporters, the entire community, had Jessica's image firmly implanted in their minds: the curly blond hair, the shy smile, the big blue eyes, even the white blouse trimmed in lace that she was wearing in the thousands and thousands of flyers they had distributed.

Judge Sanderstone was no longer facing the flag. She had her chair turned to the right side of her desk, where she had a large framed portrait of her great-grandfather, a tribal chief of the Cherokee nation. She took in the proud posture, the sculpted cheekbones, the penetrating eyes, the wisdom. This was where her eyes rested when she was looking for strength.

The courtroom was packed and noisy. Almost every seat was taken, and several reporters had been forced to bend on one knee in the aisles with their notebooks and pens ready. At least a dozen police officers were present, some in uniform, some plainclothes.

One of the clerks whispered something to the bailiff. The judge was on the way. Two additional bailiffs entered, escorting the defendant, a small, thin man in his thirties, to the counsel table. He kept his head down, holding his cuffed wrists to his face, actually sucking on one finger. He took small steps, the shackles around his ankles jangling like an enormous charm bracelet. On the top of his head was a shiny bald spot glistening with perspiration from the overhead lights. His bright yellow jumpsuit had the words ORANGE COUNTY JAIL on the back.

'All rise,' the bailiff said, stepping to the front of the bench once the defendant was deposited next to his attorney. 'Remain standing. Superior Court of Orange County, Department Twenty-five, is now in session, the Honorable Lara Sanderstone presiding.'

Lara entered the courtroom through the small door behind the bench and ascended the stairs in a swirl of black robes. People told her there was a deceptive delicacy to her face: pale, soft, unblemished skin, the kewpie doll mouth, the high protruding cheekbones, the long eyelashes that fluttered behind her glasses. Her black hair was held back in a fancy gold clip, her one attempt at femininity in what was traditionally a masculine role. Young for the bench at thirty-eight, she had to work to appear authoritative. Not too long ago, someone had commented that she looked like a member of a church choir instead of a judge.

The A.D.A., Russ Mitchell, bolted through the double doors. He was late and had jogged from another courtroom and another matter. Slightly out of breath, he rushed to the counsel table and slapped a thick file down, adjusting his tie and glancing up at the bench.

Lara's gaze was firm and her voice laced with annoyance as she reprimanded him. 'I'm pleased that you were able to join us today, Mr. Mitchell, but we are already in session and you are late as usual. I'll give you a few minutes to collect yourself, and then we'll begin.'

Her eyes found the victim's parents while Mitchell frantically shuffled papers. They were seated in the first row, side by side like two parrots on a perch, their faces somber. They held each other's hand, the man and woman, both in their early fifties. Whatever was going on around them they didn't see or hear. They stared straight ahead, waiting. What they were waiting for now was justice.

Seated next to them was a dark haired twenty-year-old boy, the victim's boyfriend. Lara recalled his face from the newspaper articles. He was wearing a black suit, probably the one he had worn to her funeral. He had dated the victim for the past three years. This was their first year at UCLA, and they had been living together in a small apartment near the campus. He'd told reporters he had been saving to buy her an engagement ring.

Finally the district attorney looked up. He was ready.

'*People* versus *Henderson*,' Lara said, immediately calling the case, accepting the file from the clerk's hand as the courtroom fell into silence, all eyes on the bench. 'We will be continuing with the defense's motion to suppress evidence. Specifically, the defendant's confession. Mr. England, I understand you have another witness.'

'Yes, Your Honor,' England said, already on his feet. His dark hair was laced with gray, but at forty-three he was still a youthful, handsome man.

Once the witness was sworn in, he stepped up to the stand. He was in uniform. Yesterday they'd heard testimony from the arresting officers. Lara felt certain they'd perjured themselves. Today she could hear more of the same – more concocted lies. After the officer stated his name for the record and his position as a correctional officer assigned to the Orange County Jail, England stepped from behind the table and approached the witness box.

'Officer White, when did you first see the defendant on the night of June fifteenth?'

'I believe it was about three o'clock in the morning. I was due to get off at three. He was in a holding cell, on a bench.'

'I see,' England said slowly. 'Was he alone in the cell?'

'Yes, he was.'

'And what was the defendant doing when you entered the holding cell?'

'He was sleeping.'

'Sleeping?' England said, cocking his head. Turning to face the spectators, he walked to the table and picked up something.

'I-I thought he was sleeping,' the officer answered.

'Is it possible he was unconscious?' England's eyebrows went up. The witness's eyes were locked on the items in his hands, tracking them as England waved them around as he spoke.

'Probably,' the officer replied. Then he scooted closer to the microphone. 'I thought he was drunk.'

'I see,' England said. 'So, you tried to rouse him?'

'Yes. When he didn't respond, I got another officer and we moved him to the cell.'

'How did you move him?'

'We carried him under his arms.'

'Did you look at his face during the time you were carrying him or dragging him to his cell?'

'Of course.' The man scanned the faces in the audience, trying to find the arresting officers and possibly some of the correctional officers he worked with, grab some moral support.

'And you didn't notice the bruises on his face, his right eye swollen shut?'

'I don't remember.'

The D.A. was squirming in his seat, tapping his pen annoyingly on the table.

England's momentum was building up like steam inside him. With the next question, Lara could almost hear the hiss. 'You didn't possibly notice that his left arm was broken, did you?'

'No,' the officer said, perspiration across his brow.

'Officer White, did you think for even one moment that the defendant was in urgent need of medical treatment, that he was in fact unconscious, that his arm was severely broken, so severely broken that it was flopping back and forth like a piece of rubber? Surely that's something you would notice?'

'No,' the officer said. 'I thought he had been in a bar fight or something. It's the booking officer's responsibility to see that a suspect gets medical treatment if he needs it. I'm just a jailer.'

England spun around. 'Officer White, did you beat the defendant, cause these injuries?'

He jumped in his seat. 'No. I didn't lay a hand on him. I simply put him in the cell bunk and left.'

'Well, that's very interesting. The arresting officers testified yesterday that he might have incurred, I quote, "a few bruises" when they were placing him under arrest, but nothing more. I guess that means you broke his arm, right? I mean, if they didn't break his arm, you must have been the one who broke it.'

The officer's face was bright red. He wasn't about to take the fall. 'No way. His arm was broken when he was booked. I certainly didn't break it.'

A flurry of commotion rang through the courtroom. The D.A. was ashen. England attacked. 'You mean by the arresting officers? Right? Not during booking but prior to booking?'

The witness became silent. He dropped his eyes. 'I guess so,' he finally said.

'And you,' England said, pointing a finger at him, 'you left this man, this injured and unconscious man, in a cell where he could have died. Why? I'll tell you why. Because you were about to go off duty and you didn't want to be bothered. You didn't want to mess with the paperwork, the trip to the infirmary, all that time-consuming stuff. Isn't that right, Officer White?'

The officer's head dropped. He didn't answer.

'Objection,' the D.A. spouted. 'He's badgering the witness.'

'Sustained,' Lara said.

'No further questions, Your Honor,' England said, taking his seat, his point clearly scored.

Lara looked at the D.A.; the tension in her neck was increasing, and she rolled her head around to relieve it. 'Your witness, Mr. Mitchell.'

The officer was gulping water from a glass placed in the witness stand. The two arresting officers were seated in the back row, their eyes black daggers. White had far more to fear now than Benjamin England, Lara thought. He had rolled over on his own. The future months wouldn't be easy.

The D.A. stood, adjusting his jacket, his voice low and soft. 'Officer White, are you absolutely certain that the defendant didn't fall out of his bunk and break his arm? Your preliminary statements were that you didn't notice any injuries. Are you now recanting that testimony?'

This time the witness met the arresting officers' eyes. He was beyond all that now. He just wanted out, off the stand

and out of the courtroom. As a correctional officer he didn't testify on a regular basis, and for him this was grueling. 'Yes. I noticed his arm. His arm was broken when I went into the holding cell.'

'And you're absolutely certain of this now? Your earlier statement was false?' Mitchell swiped the hair off his forehead, shaking his head. He knew it was bad. He didn't know it was this bad.

'Yes,' he said, blinking rapidly, more perspiration appearing on his forehead, his upper lip, little beads of it rolling down his cheeks.

'Isn't it possible, Officer White,' the D.A. said, going for the last escape hatch, 'that he could have fallen off the bench in the holding cell and incurred this injury before you arrived?'

White thought a moment. He apparently made a decision to come clean, spill his guts, make a feeble attempt to make amends in the eyes of the court and possibly his own conscience. 'I guess he could have, but he didn't. Everyone knew he was roughed up before he was booked.' He cleared his throat and continued. 'He killed and raped a girl, you know?' With this last statement he looked confidently at the spectators, as if they would all understand, that if they had been given the opportunity, they too would have wanted to make this man suffer, to break some bones, draw a little blood.

The D.A. wasn't touching this one. Actually, he'd gone too far and there was no road back. England didn't bother to object to the speculation that the defendant was guilty. 'No further questions, Your Honor,' the D.A. said. He didn't simply take his seat, he fell into it.

Mitchell turned to the victim's parents and met their gaze. Lara felt the tightness move from her neck to her chest. The parents hadn't moved. They were still sitting ramrod straight, their shoulders touching, their hands tightly clasped. They looked like statues, bronze replicas of suffering. They had as yet to realize the magnitude of what had just occurred.

From the look on the face of the young man next to them, however, he had.

'Very well,' Lara said, peering down at the witness. 'You can step down,' she told him. Then she turned to the courtroom. 'We will recess for fifteen minutes before I deliver a ruling. Mr. Mitchell, I'll see you in chambers.' She tapped the gavel one time lightly and slipped from the bench. As soon as she was through the door, she pressed her fingers down over her face, pulling her skin, wishing she could wipe the stench of this off her face and hands. It was poison – clear and simple.

She walked rapidly to her chambers. The D.A. was right behind her. She began speaking without looking back at him, and she entered her outer office with only a nod at her secretary. 'Are you going to file on Madriano and Curtis?' she said, referring to the arresting officers. Not only had they beaten the defendant within an inch of his life, they had obviously perjured themselves the day before.

The D.A. answered, 'I assume. I haven't given it much thought.' He appeared more concerned about his case, or what was left of it, than pressing charges against the officers.

They were in chambers now and Lara stepped behind her desk, taking her seat and tossing her glasses, swiveling her chair to face the young D.A. 'These officers should be prosecuted, relieved of their positions on the force, and frankly, taken out and shot. I've never seen such a fucked-up case in my life.' She was so angry that her hands were trembling as she fingered a piece of paper on her desk.

The D.A.'s chin jerked up in response, but he didn't speak. It was obvious that he'd like to do the honors himself as far as the officers went. Crestfallen, he finally said, 'He's guilty, you know?'

Lara didn't respond to this statement. Her hands were tied. Even if she was to blatantly deny the defense's motion to exclude the confession, any conviction would be overturned in appeal. 'A layman would have no trouble figuring this one out. You simply cannot beat a person and then garner a confession.' She watched as the D.A. slid farther down in his seat.

'You rule to suppress this, we're dead meat,' Mitchell said. 'He knows it,' he continued accusingly, referring to the defense attorney. 'Our primary witness died last week. Without the confession . . . well, we're looking at dismissal.'

None of this was news to Lara. They'd been agonizing over this for three weeks. In a slurred voice on tape, the defendant had admitted the crime. The tape had suddenly ended. Lara was certain the defendant had collapsed from the injuries inflicted by the arresting officers. They had worked the case all along, speaking daily with the family. They both were mature investigators with teenage daughters of their own.

They had simply lost it.

Without the eyewitness, and the absolutely vital confession, the prosecution had nothing. Lara had called Mitchell into chambers only to allow both of them a few minutes to accept the inevitable, present a unified front. The D.A. would withdraw the charges and regroup. If they took a case as weak as this to trial and ended up in acquittal, it was finished. They were better off withdrawing now and praying for more evidence to construct a more concrete case. The biggest problem was the public outrage sure to follow and the fact that a dangerous killer would be walking the streets while they built a better case. Instead of the public venting its anger on the real culprits in this case, the police officers, it would all fly in Lara's face.

'Are you going to withdraw today?' She hoped not. That

would be the worst: for her to suppress the evidence and the defendant to walk out of jail a few hours later a free man.

'I don't know. England's going to press for dismissal.' He leaned forward in his seat. Then he slapped back, throwing his hands in the air. 'We have no case. We have shit . . . nothing but dog shit.'

Lara stood to return to the courtroom. Mitchell took her cue and stood as well. A few seconds later, he was following her down the corridor.

Once back in session, Lara addressed the court. 'After careful consideration,' she said, the weight of the words she was uttering causing her to compress in her seat so that only her head could be seen from below, 'the defendant's motion to suppress is granted.' She braced herself for the onslaught and continued, looking out over the courtroom, 'From the evidence presented in this courtroom, the defendant was severely battered, the confession was issued under extreme duress and is therefore determined to be inadmissible.'

England sprang to his feet. 'We move for dismissal, Your Honor. Without this evidence the case against my client is non-existent.'

The defendant looked up, a blank look in his eyes. Lara had read in the files that he was on psychotropic medication. The noise in the courtroom was getting louder with every second. The D.A. had turned around in his seat and was speaking with the victim's family. The woman was crying, the father holding her head against his shoulder. He was whispering to her, stroking her hair, making a feeble attempt to comfort her. The victim's boyfriend's mouth fell open in shock and he jumped up. The D.A. yanked his jacket and he sat back down.

Mitchell stood. 'The people withdraw the charges, Your Honor.'

Now the courtroom was in an uproar, and the defendant's eyes were darting wildly around the room.

Who would he rape or, God forbid, murder while the D.A. scrambled for more evidence? Lara thought. Was he thinking about it right now? Was his sick and tortured mind right this very minute hungering for another kill, his eyes searching the courtroom for another victim? Lara tapped the gavel loudly again and again, standing and leaning over the railing. The bailiffs started moving toward the victim's family, eyeing them and then the defendant. Finally the noise died down and Lara took her seat. 'Let the record read that the charges have been dismissed at the people's motion,' she said, sighing deeply, keeping her eyes on the file in front of her. 'The defendant is remanded into custody; however, the sheriff will be notified to release the defendant posthaste. Monies posted as bail shall be released in the appropriate fashion through the court clerk's office. This court is adjourned.' She didn't bother with the gavel. No one would have heard it anyway.

Reporters were running from the courtroom, pushing and shoving one another to reach their editors. Lara was rooted to her seat, her eyes locking on the victim's parents, her chest swelling with compassion. The D.A. was conferring with them, sitting next to them on the bench. The woman was holding a tissue to her eyes, then blowing her nose. People were leaving the courtroom; the court reporter was folding up her machine. All the police officers had vanished before the ruling. They weren't stupid, Lara thought. They knew how it would fall. By tomorrow the D.A. would file charges against the two arresting officers. The bailiff was chatting with one of the clerks. England was packing his briefcase, his job over.

Suddenly the victim's boyfriend stood, his face a twisted mask of rage. 'How could you do this?' he screamed at Lara. 'He killed her. He raped her and killed her. He deserved to be beaten. He deserves to die.' He was panting, his face flushed crimson, leaning over the back of the seat in front of him. His eyes were enormous and blazing with hatred. A bailiff was rushing toward him, the D.A. trying to pull him back in his seat. 'You're letting him get away with this. Someone should kill you . . . rape you, strangle you. You fucking bitch . . .'

The bailiff put his hands on the boy, and the two other bailiffs were moving in that direction. They were watching both his hands for a weapon. 'Someone should kill your whole family . . . slaughter them . . . then you'd know about justice and your stupid laws. What do I have to do, kill the mother fucker myself? You're not a judge. You're no better than he is . . .'

Lara just sat there, consumed with his sense of injustice. He had looked to the courts to avenge the death of the girl he loved and had met a brick wall of law. Those that should have upheld it had destroyed it. The bailiffs looked at her, waiting for direction. One nod and they would cuff him. They had him in tow and he was twisting, saliva dripping down one corner of his mouth, trying to wrench his arms away, ready to cross the floor and rip her apart with his bare hands. She shook her head at the bailiffs and left the bench. He had every right to vent his hostility. She hit the door and once through it, she leaned against the wall in the corridor, her eyes glazed and fixed, her chest rising and falling with the hatred that had been directed at her, so intense that she could feel the heat of it even now. She glanced up and down the hall, but all she could see was a misty fog of red. Images of the victim's decomposed body appeared in her mind, and she tried to suppress them.

Pushing herself off the wall, she straightened her robe and shuffled down the hall. Twenty-five homicides had occurred the past weekend in Los Angeles. One weekend, she thought in despair. One lousy weekend and twenty-five deaths. The city was being buried in an avalanche of violence, and she had just set a murderer free in the community. 'Great,' she said bitterly. 'Just what you wanted to do all your life, Lara – set killers free, give them their walking papers.' Heading toward the door to her chambers, she stopped in front of her secretary's desk.

'Did you say something?' Phillip asked, spinning around from his word processor. He was a slender, well-groomed man in his late twenties with sandy blond hair and dove gray eyes.

'What are you doing tonight, Phillip?'

'Tonight? I-I have plans. Why?' he said self-consciously.

Lara studied his face. She didn't think she could handle eating alone tonight, going home to an empty house. All she needed was a little companionship, some light conversation, something to purge the day's events from her mind. Before she could ask him to join her for dinner, he continued.

'I'm seeing someone later, ah, about nine. But if you need something typed, I can stay late.'

His face flushed. Lara wondered if he had a new girlfriend, or any girlfriend, for that matter. She'd never heard him mention anyone. 'No,' she said, changing her mind, thinking she would try someone else, feeling foolish for even thinking of asking Phillip to have dinner with her. 'Forget it. Go on home. It's nothing.'

'What happened in there? How did you rule?'

'I suppressed the confession. The D.A. dismissed, so Henderson will walk.'

'God,' he said, arching his eyebrows and resting his chin on his hands. 'Because the officers beat him up, right? They really punished that guy, didn't they? I guess they got carried away. The crime was heinous. You almost can't blame them for what they did.'

'Well, I hope they enjoyed punishing him,' Lara said flatly. 'It might be the only punishment Thomas Henderson ever receives in this case.'

With that, she entered her chambers and closed the door behind her.

Chapter 2

For over an hour Lara had sat behind her desk and stared into space. She'd given thought to calling the victim's parents and telling them how sorry she was, explaining to them how she was left with no choice but to make the ruling she had. But she realized that would be inappropriate.

Phillip buzzed her on the intercom. 'I have the *Daily News* on line one. They'd like a statement from you about the Henderson matter.'

'Tell them I've left for the day,' she said, knowing she was only stalling. She'd have to give them a statement tomorrow.

Hanging her robe on the hook and grabbing her purse, Lara told Phillip good night and made her way down the back corridor to Judge Irene Murdock's chambers. Lara spotted her head bent over her desk. 'Still at it, I see,' Lara said, stepping into the room.

'Oh, Lara,' Irene said, 'you startled me.' She looked up and removed her glasses, tossing them on her paper-padded desk.

Irene was approaching fifty but few would ever know it. She was tall and fashionably thin. Except for a few lines that shot down from her mouth and darted across her forehead, time had been kind. She wore her muted blond hair in soft feminine curls that framed and flattered her narrow face. Her lips were always lined and coated with fresh, moist lipstick, a bright coral, but her eyes held the key to her strength. They were an emerald green. 'How did it go today?' she asked. 'You know, the Henderson case?'

'You haven't heard?' Lara didn't sit down. She leaned against the back wall. 'The D.A. dismissed.' Raising her wrist, Lara glanced at her watch. It was after five o'clock. 'Henderson should be walking out the door of the jail any minute. Free as a bird.'

Irene didn't respond. They had all anticipated that it would fall this way. She sat there studying Lara's face. She had been on the bench far longer than Lara. As Irene had told her again and again, a judge's role was to interpret and rule on the law. She couldn't allow herself to become emotionally involved.

'This was a tough one, Irene. The parents . . . the relatives . . . I can't imagine how they feel right now. She was so young. And those frigging cops – '

Irene cut her off. 'Have you heard about Westridge?'

Charles Westridge was a municipal court judge, known to be impassioned and ambitious. 'No, tell me.'

'He filed today on the sheriff for violating court orders in releasing prisoners prior to the completion of their terms.'

'But the sheriff's under court order to release or close the jail down due to overcrowding. What does Westridge possibly hope to gain?'

'Attention maybe. Press. Who knows? I've heard he wants my position, is planning to run against me next year. He reviews every one of my decisions and probably stands up and cheers every time I'm reversed on appeal.'

Lara took a seat, shaking her head. 'Don't we have enough problems around here without going after each other? And the sheriff . . . that's inane. I swear, Irene, it seems like the system is falling down around us. It's like walking in rubble. The violence, the corruption, the ambiguities in the law . . .' Lara paused and then continued, 'It gets worse by the second, and we're simply powerless to stop it. Sure, those officers were assholes for what they did to Henderson, but the cops are walking time bombs. They're just sick of it all. I mean, are we even civilized anymore? I'm not sure if you can call this civilization.'

Irene looked at a spot over Lara's head. 'Aren't you the voice of doom today?' Then she dropped her eyes to Lara's and smiled. 'Things are bad. But even at the end of the world, Lara dear, someone's got to sit in judgment.'

'Right,' Lara said, making a feeble attempt to return Irene's smile. 'I'd prefer it wasn't me, though.' She added, 'On a lighter vein, how about dinner tonight? I guess you may have plans with John, but . . .'

Irene pushed the auto-dial button on her phone. While the rapid tones rang out, she said, 'Let me call him. If he isn't home, sure, I'd love to join you. To tell you the truth, I'm starving. I skipped lunch today.' A few seconds later, she was listening to her own voice on the answering machine. She left a message for her husband, a prominent physician, and then hung up. 'John's working too many hours, Lara. I have no idea why. Last year he told me he was going to scale it down, let his new partner carry more of the load, but he seldom comes home before eight o'clock every night. He's – ' Suddenly she stopped herself. Irene Murdock did not make a habit of talking about her personal life, not even to her closest friends.

Now the roles were reversed, and Lara was watching the concern on Irene's face. John Murdock was in his early sixties, and Irene worried about him all the time. There was a long history of cancer in his family. His father and grandfather had died of it, plus several of his uncles, and just last year his brother had fallen victim as well. Even though Irene was a rock of strength and conviction, it was like she was waiting for the other shoe to fall, certain her husband would be next. A lot of people viewed her as strident and overbearing. Generally her speech was laced with all kinds of terms of endearment: honey, baby, darling, and dear. Lara knew she had cultivated this habit intentionally to tone herself down.

Her husband was as docile as a lamb, a sweet, gentle man. She even towered over him in height, particularly with heels. There was never any doubt who wore the pants in that family, Lara thought.

Irene closed the file in front of her and stood, collecting her briefcase and purse, then turning out the lights. She walked with long, rapid strides down the corridor, and Lara almost had to run to keep up with her.

'I was thinking we could eat at Bob's Big Boy,' Lara said. 'What do you think? It's only a block away, and they have this great special.'

'Lara darling,' Irene said, cracking a smile and turning to face her, 'you're incredible. No, I will not eat at Bob's Big Boy. If you insist on your disgusting diet of junk food and greasy fried food, you'll have to eat alone. I don't know how you live like that. I really don't.'

'All right,' Lara said. 'We can go to that new seafood restaurant down the street.'

'Better,' Irene said. 'I'll follow you.'

A few minutes later, they were both in their cars and heading up the ramp from the underground garage.

It was late, but Lara was still awake. She'd been thrashing about in bed for hours trying to sleep, details of the Henderson case playing over and over in her mind. First, she heard her neighbors' little terrier yelping. Then the other dogs on the block joined in, and Lara held her breath and listened, pulling the sheet up to her chin and staring at the ceiling. It was a quiet residential neighborhood in Irvine, but she was a woman who lived alone. She knew all the normal sounds of the night well: the ambulances and police sirens racing by on the nearby thoroughfares, the jets passing overhead, the occasional couple coming home from a late night and the familiar crank of their garage door. But when the dogs started howling, which they seldom did, it usually meant someone was out there prowling around.

Then she heard it: a soft tapping at the front door.

The tapping turned into a frantic pounding. Lara glanced at the clock and saw that it was after one. Thinking of calling the police, she reached over and put her hand on the phone. Then she heard a familiar voice calling her name through the bedroom window. It was a hot summer night, and she'd left the window open to get some fresh air.

'Lara, it's me. It's Ivory. Let me in.'

Grabbing her robe, she padded barefoot to the door and listened to make certain she wasn't imagining the whole thing.

'Lara, open the door. Please open the door. It's Ivory.'

She punched in the alarm code, and after releasing the double dead-bolt locks, she found herself face to face with her younger sister.

'Honey,' she said, taking her in her arms as she walked through the door, 'what's happened now?' She brushed a strand of dark curly hair off Ivory's face and looked for bruises. 'Did Sam hit you?'

Ivory kept glancing over her shoulder at the street, her chest rising and falling, gasping for breath as if she'd been running. 'No, no . . . it's not Sam. Someone's following me, Lara. Shut the door. Quick.'

Lara slammed the door and slid the dead bolts back into

place, quickly resetting the alarm, her own heart pounding now. 'Who's following you? Where's Sam?'

Ivory was agitated, her dark eyes darting around the room. 'Listen, I can't explain. I need to call Sam. I just need to use your phone.'

'Stop right here, okay?' Lara said, placing her hands on her sister's arms and holding her. 'Tell me exactly what's going on. If someone is following you or trying to hurt you, we'll call the police. Maybe he's still out there and they can pick him up. What kind of car was he driving? Give me his description.' Lara started across the room to the phone.

'Forget it,' Ivory said. 'I'm not calling the stupid cops.' Flopping down on the sofa, she grabbed the phone from her sister's hand.

Lara stared at her, thinking how beautiful she was, even now when she was frightened and upset. She was a striking brunette, with shoulder-length curly hair that framed her almost perfect face. Whereas Lara's eyes were gray, Ivory's were a brilliant blue. But it was her skin that was her finest feature. Her skin was absolutely flawless.

'Sam,' Ivory spoke rapidly into the phone, 'I'm at Lara's. Please, come and get me. Something's happened. Someone's following me.' She paused and then her voice rose another octave. 'I said I'm not leaving until you come and get me. No, I'm not driving home by myself. I don't care what time it is.' Then she slammed the phone back on the hook.

Lara turned on the lights in the living room and sat on the sofa across from her sister. 'Now,' she said, her voice firm, 'tell me what's going on. Is this about money?'

'Sam's coming,' Ivory said, avoiding her sister's eyes. 'He'll be here in about twenty minutes.'

Lara felt her anger and frustration growing with each passing minute. She'd always been the one who protected Ivory, made certain no one hurt her. Ever since they were children, only a few years apart in age, Lara had been the one she always turned to when she had a problem. But since she'd married Sam Perkins, everything had changed.

'Ivory, you must tell me what's going on with your life. Don't you understand that I'm concerned about you? You can't just bang on my door at this hour and tell me someone's following you and then refuse to tell me what's going on.'

Ivory stood and started pacing. 'I can't,' she said emphatically, tossing her long mane of hair, jerking her head around to look at her sister. 'Don't worry, okay?' she snapped. 'I won't come over here and bother you anymore. I won't even call you anymore. You can just forget you have a sister.'

Lara put her head in her hands, and then peered up at Ivory through her fingers. 'I never said I didn't want you to call me or come over here when you need something. You're not being fair, Ivory. I love you. It's Sam, isn't it? All of this has something to do with Sam.'

'Leave Sam out of this. All you ever do is bash him, tell me what an asshole he is. He's my husband, Lara.' She suddenly started tossing her arms around wildly. 'Look at you, your whole life. You want me to end up like you, alone, with no one, living for nothing but a job, a career? Sam and I are going to make it, and we're going to make it big time. Then we're going to move away from here, start all over.'

Lara tried to let her sister's words roll off her back. Every time they were together, they ended up fighting like this. What Lara wanted was to repair the relationship, help her sister put her life back on track. 'What about your child, Ivory? What about Josh? You shouldn't uproot him, make him move. He's lived in that house all his life. He lost his father. And what about the pawnshop? You said if I loaned you and Sam the money for the pawnshop, you could make it. Not only that, but you haven't made one payment. You know, Ivory, I have financial obligations too.'

'Josh is fine . . . just fine. What do you care, anyway? You haven't seen him in years.'

It had been a long day. Lara was exhausted and couldn't handle a screaming match. But the issue of Josh was a sensitive one, and with each second her control was slipping. 'And why haven't I seen Josh in years, Ivory?' she shot back, flopping back against the sofa and crossing her arms over her chest, locking them together and digging her nails into her skin. 'Because you won't allow me to see my own nephew. You've poisoned him against me for absolutely no reason.' She inhaled and her chest swelled, her gray eyes blazed. 'I thought the deal was that I loan you the money for the pawnshop and we put the past to bed. What happened to that promise?'

'You,' Ivory spat, still pacing, still frantic. 'You tried to take my kid away from me. My own fucking sister tried to steal my kid. You know what Sam said? He said you were just bribing me with that money so you could get your hands on Josh and take him away because you don't have any kids of your own.' She went to the window and peeked through the blinds and then returned to the center of the room.

Lara slumped on the sofa. No matter what she did, she couldn't get beyond this. 'We've been over this a million times. After Charley got killed, you were drinking, using cocaine, bringing one man after another into the house. I never tried to take him away. I was only concerned for him. And I was concerned for you.'

Lara had been so concerned about her nephew that she'd threatened to call Social Services if Ivory didn't get her act together. She'd only wanted to shock her, get her attention, make her realize what she was risking with her reckless behavior, but Ivory had never forgiven her.

Suddenly she noticed how Ivory was dressed. Was this the latest fashion? She looked like a tramp, a streetwalker. Once she had married Sam, Lara had thought the bar-hopping was over. When her first husband had been alive, Ivory had been a contented wife and mother. Lara knew that grief could destroy people, even strong people, and Ivory was far from strong, but her descent had been radical. Lara had arrived at the opinion that life had finally caught up with her sister and then simply passed her. Ivory was a child in a woman's body. She had been classified as learning disabled as a child, and had an emotional and mental age far below her chronological age. Within a closely structured and protected setting, she could survive. But alone, or with a negative influence like Sam, Ivory was in serious trouble. Then when alcohol and drugs were mixed in, the arrows all pointed to disaster.

Lara then noticed her sister's breasts, and her eyes expanded. Ivory had always been shapely, far more shapely than Lara, but not like this. Now her sister looked like Dolly Parton. Lara hadn't seen Ivory in two or three months. She must have had breast implants. It was complete absurdity. Sam and Ivory were always calling for money, claiming they needed it to meet the mortgage and survive, and now Ivory was sporting silicone breasts.

'If you won't tell me anything else, at least tell me why you're dressed like this,' Lara said, her eyes narrowing. 'And when did you get your breasts enlarged?'

'Fuck you, Lara. How do you want me to dress? Like you? You've never known how to dress. And look at your stupid hair. No wonder you can't get a man. You're jealous. That's what Sam says. He says you've always been jealous of me.'

Now Lara was really angry, about to explode. Ivory was immature and ignorant, but this time she had gone too far. She simply couldn't take it anymore. 'You've taken money from me,' she screamed, her body trembling, 'refused to let me see Josh, and you – you've pissed it away on cosmetic surgery and God knows what else.'

'You're a bitch, Lara. You're cold now. You're not the same person you used to be . . . You're heartless. You've turned to stone.' Ivory walked over until she was only inches from her sister's face, her breath foul with beer and cigarettes. 'I don't give a shit if I ever see you again,' she said. 'How do you feel about that? Why don't you stick that up your judicial rear?'

Lara stood there with her hands at her sides. She was beyond anger. The whole day rose up to meet her. Everything she did, everywhere she turned, she met hostility and rage. But this was her home and this was her flesh and blood. 'Ivory, let's stop this . . .' Lara paused. Someone was knocking on the door.

Ivory's face became animated. She raced over and released the dead bolts, waiting for Lara to turn off the alarm. After Lara had done so, she flung the door open and leaped into her husband's arms. 'Oh, Sam,' she said. Then she took his hand and led him outside to the doorstep, where she started whispering and gesturing.

Lara strained to hear, but it was impossible. She walked over to close the door, hoping she could go back to bed and get at least a few hours' sleep before the sun came up.

Sam Perkins stepped over the threshold. Lara back-stepped into the house.

He had dark, unkempt hair that fell over his collar and forehead and a thick black mustache. Even though he was only in his thirties, his face was heavily lined from hard living and years of drinking. He was dressed in a wrinkled red polo shirt and faded Levis, with about fifteen keys dangling from a metal clamp attached to his belt. He could have been handsome in a rugged, masculine way. To Ivory, he was handsome. But the only way anyone would agree with her was to see him in the dim light of a bar with about five drinks under their belt. To Lara, he was the scum of the earth. Even though she was several feet away, she could smell the alcohol. He put his hands together and cracked his knuckles, causing his biceps to bulge and his tattoo to appear from under the sleeve of his shirt. It said EASY RIDER. There was nothing easy about this man.

'I don't want you upsetting my wife anymore,' he said, the words hissing between clenched teeth, stained from tobacco. 'We've had about all we want of you. You may be a big-shot judge, but you ain't a fucking thing as far as we're concerned. Here,' he said, throwing a handful of bills on the floor. 'There's your payment. You happy now?'

'Get out of my house,' Lara said. 'And don't ever ask me to cover for you again, Sam, because I won't.' She glanced at the bills on the carpet. Most of them were ones. He owed her over a hundred thousand dollars, and he had just paid her back maybe ten – she was counting – no, twelve dollars of it.

Ivory was standing right next to him now, one arm flung around his shoulder, her silicone breasts spilling over the cut of the tank top. 'We don't need your money,' she said proudly. 'We're going to have plenty of our own. Soon too, real soon.'

Lara blinked back tears. She couldn't possibly let this man see what he had done to her family, to her sister. Before her mother had died, Lara had promised she would look after Ivory, make certain that she and Josh were taken care of. But they were out of her hands now.

'Get out of my house,' she said again, her voice firm.

'Come on, baby,' Sam said to Ivory. 'Let's let the old maid get her beauty sleep. Way she looks, she sure as hell needs it.'

He yanked on Ivory's arm and she followed him to the door. Then she glanced back over her shoulder at Lara.

For a moment their eyes met and the clock stopped ticking. Lara glimpsed the sadness in her sister's eyes. She saw Ivory's lips move, but no words came out. It was as if she could see the past projected on her sister's face, both of them fresh-faced little girls walking home from school together. Sam's laughter was time-delayed; it burst through the silence and the clock was ticking again, faster than before. Then the door slammed shut and they were gone.

Chapter 3

Three weeks had passed since Thomas Henderson had walked out of the Orange County Jail a few hours after Lara's ruling. But he hadn't been on the streets long, thank God, she thought now, heading briskly down the corridor to her chambers during morning recess, and as far as they knew, he hadn't raped or killed anyone. This morning Russ Mitchell had called to tell her that Henderson had been institutionalized at Camarillo State Hospital, a state-operated psychiatric facility. Maybe tonight she could sleep instead of thrashing about until one or two o'clock in the morning and then waking at four.

The prosecution's case was still in limbo. They'd dredged up one good lead, a service station attendant who thought he'd seen the victim and Henderson together. But the twenty-year-old man was an extremely poor witness. He couldn't recall the date, the time – was such a stoner that he hardly remembered his own name. They would keep at it; eventually something would surface.

Even though the defendant had signed himself in as a voluntary admission and could walk out anytime he wanted, just knowing he was behind locked doors right now and heavily medicated made them all breathe a sigh of relief.

The press had been horrendous. In the local papers, the officers had been raked over the coals and had taken the brunt of the responsibility. They were both under suspension from the force and facing prosecution. In years past, the case might have folded, but the officers would've never been held to answer for their actions. Things were different today. This incident had fallen on the heels of the Rodney King fiasco, a notorious case of police brutality that had ignited riots in south central Los Angeles – angry crowds burning down one building after another, random and senseless acts of violence. Some speculated the area would never be rebuilt.

Lara looked up and saw Irene Murdock headed in her direction. 'Are you coming to see me?' she said.

'Lara,' Irene said, trying to contain a chuckle, 'I'm going to give this to you, but only if you take it with a grain of salt and have a nice laugh over it.'

Lara looked at the other woman's hands. She was holding a thin newspaper. Lara looked closer and saw it was the *National Tattler*. 'What is it?' Lara reached out, but Irene pulled the paper away.

'Promise me you won't get all worked up over this, okay?'

'I promise. Let me see it, Irene.' She did. The headline was a story about a horse with a human head. It was the strangest-looking thing Lara had ever seen. 'Pretty funny. Is this what you want me to see?'

'Page three, Lara,' Irene said, the smile disappearing.

On the third page was Lara's picture with the caption: 'JUDGE RELEASES VIOLENT RAPIST AND MURDERER ON TECHNICALITY.' 'Gee,' Lara said facetiously, 'I'm a star. I'll go home and put this right in my scrapbook.' But it wasn't really funny. This was a national publication. Even if it was made up of sensationalism and ridiculous stories, everyone read it at one time or another.

Irene pushed a strand of hair off her forehead and

touched her friend on the shoulder. 'I guess I shouldn't have even brought this to your attention, honey. I don't know why, but I thought it was funny. I mean, the whole paper is ridiculous. Look at the cover story. Who would believe anything these people say?'

Lara looked up into those deep green eyes. 'Well, it is true, Irene. I did release him on a technicality.'

'Hey,' Irene said, stepping close and draping an arm around Lara, 'we all release people on technicalities at one time or the other. You're not still agonizing over this case, are you?'

'No, no,' Lara said softly, smiling at her friend. 'Thanks for showing the paper to me, Irene. It's better than having people gang up on me at the grocery store.'

Lara stood with the smile glued on her face until Irene had turned and headed back down the corridor. Then the smile evaporated and she too headed back to her office.

She was in between trials, something that seldom occurred. With the dismissal of the Henderson case, her calendar had been left wide open, and the presiding judge, sixty-seven-year-old Leo Evergreen, had zapped her into the felony arraignment calendar for vacation relief. Everyone called it the zoo.

Walking by Phillip, she gave him a nod. He had earphones on his head and was typing on his word processor. At least she thought he was typing. She took a few steps back and glanced at the screen. Once she had found him playing video games. But no, he was typing something. What, she didn't know. Probably his homework from law school.

Once she was inside, she slammed her door. It was a satisfying feeling. Besides, Phillip couldn't even hear it. Collapsing in her chair, she felt her buttocks slide into the hole. The least the county could do for me would be to buy me a cushion, she thought. Then she let the frustration go.

It was counterproductive. So she wouldn't go to the grocery store for a few weeks until the newspaper article was cold. Irene was right. The article wasn't something to get upset about. All she ever bought anyway at the store were TV dinners and things that could be heated in the microwave. She didn't cook. She'd never learned how and simply didn't have the inclination. She ate simply to survive. She could live on hamburgers and nachos without a second thought and never gain a pound. Maybe that was why her ex-husband had divorced her, she thought now, because he had wanted a home-cooked meal.

Everyone else might go on coffee breaks during these recesses, but most of the judges worked. They pored over briefs, motions, read probation reports, returned phone calls, conferred with attorneys. If they were fast, they could go to the bathroom. She looked around her paneled office at the bookcases crammed with law books. Even though they had as yet to replace her chair, the office itself had been recently redecorated and was actually nicer than her home in many ways, with new mauve carpeting, two studded leather chairs facing her desk, a conference table off to the side in one corner where she sometimes worked when she was in the midst of a big trial. She had to rely on artificial light since there were no windows. She hated overheads and glare. On her desk were two matching lamps with green lucite shades that she had purchased herself. They gave the room a different look, an almost surreal atmosphere, casting shadows in the corners and across the faces of those who sat in front of her. Instead of looking like an office, it looked like a study or library in a stately home.

She opened the enormous file on her desk and then closed it. She was preparing herself for a trial that she would begin next Monday, but before she did anything, she had to pay her bills. She took out her checkbook and thought about the Adams case. It was another thorn in the side of the criminal justice system. As a senior district attorney, she had handled only the most serious cases. She really preferred it that way. When things didn't go right, however, as a D.A., there were a lot of whipping boys. Sometimes she'd cursed the judge. Now she was the judge.

The only person she had to vent her frustrations on was Leo Evergreen. He assigned all the cases. He was, in effect, her boss. But the man was the essence of professional perfection, his judgment impeccable, his knowledge seemingly endless. Getting angry and shaking her fist at Leo Evergreen was seldom justified. Most of his case assignments were well thought out and fair. If he advised her on something, his advice was solid and almost always on the money.

In actuality, Leo Evergreen was one of the most intelligent men Lara had ever known. His long-term management of the Orange County superior court had earned it the lowest percentile of judicial error in the state. The higher courts thought he was a god. He could have easily won a position on the appellate court, or any other higher court, for that matter, yet he preferred to remain here. From what she could tell, he was firmly rooted in his little domain, a creature of habit. He had also told Lara one day that he would never move from Orange County. He considered it one of the most beautiful places to live in the world. In many ways Lara agreed with him. There was nothing like it.

Orange County was south of the Los Angeles city limits. The courthouse was located on Civic Center Drive in Santa Ana, not far from Anaheim and Disneyland, the crest of the county. Once into Irvine, Newport, Laguna Beach, or Mission Viejo, the population was made up of WASPs and yuppies, wall-to-wall BMWs and those little Mercedes Benzes, the ones for baby professionals who wanted to show everyone they were on their way to the big time.

Past Mission Viejo was the quaint fishing village of Dana Point, right on the ocean with a lovely marina; farther south were San Juan Capistrano and San Clemente, authentically Spanish. San Juan Capistrano was where the swallows returned each year to the mission. A few years ago, they hadn't returned. Lara thought the swallows knew what all the people building huge homes there didn't realize: Los Angeles was sprawling outward, the crime following.

Miles of uncluttered beaches stretched beneath towering glass and metal structures housing high-tech companies. Orange County was only an hour drive by freeway to Los Angeles, but the air was cooler and cleaner here, the breezes full of the salty scent of the sea. Crime, street gangs, and crack were escalating in Santa Ana, Anaheim, and Costa Mesa, but elsewhere criminal activity was still moderate. People wore shorts and polo shirts and drove convertibles. This was California suburbia at its best.

Even though Lara was in chambers, she was still wearing her robe. She liked her black robe. It was a symbol of justice. When she slipped it over her clothes every morning, usually a simple white shirt and black skirt, she felt the weight of it, the yoke of responsibility she'd undertaken. She wasn't in this position for the money or the status. The satisfaction, the sense of accomplishment, the feeling that she was making a valuable and necessary contribution to society, were her motivations. She was idealistic, stubborn, compulsive. Some people thought she was a fool, clinging to values that no longer existed, seeking reasonable and fair solutions in an unreasonable and cruel environment.

They were probably right.

She slapped the stack of bills on top of the mounds of

paper already covering the top of her desk, and started adding the columns of figures in her checkbook on an electronic calculator. Her salary was ninety-nine thousand per annum. In the beginning it had seemed like a fortune, but with taxes, retirement, insurance, it wasn't really that much. Most families relied on dual incomes while Lara was solo. And this was also Southern California, where the cost of living was particularly high. A decent house could run as high as three hundred thousand for something that would sell in the Midwest for eighty or ninety, and of course, in L.A. everyone drove a nice car, even if they lived in a shack. It was hard to plead poverty when making a hundred grand a year, but Lara's standard of living was far from the lap of luxury. Besides, she had always been a civil service employee. Most of the other judges who lived in spacious houses in the best of neighborhoods and had second homes in Palm Springs had left thriving private practices and amassed fat nest eggs before they took to the bench. Lara had been saddled with student loans from college and law school that she'd only satisfied a few years before. Her parents had been simple people. She had paid for her own education.

Thumbing through her checkbook, she saw all the checks made out to Ivory over the past two years and winced. She could kiss the savings account goodbye, she thought. No need for an IRA this year. She had also counted on the payments Sam had contracted to make on the loan she'd made for him to buy the pawnshop. She'd never see that money again.

A thought suddenly crossed her mind, and she punched numbers into the phone with her pen, getting Judge Evergreen's secretary. 'Is he in, Louise? This is Lara Sanderstone.'

'Yes, just a moment, Judge Sanderstone.'

'Lara,' an older male voice said, 'I was just thinking about you. Why don't you come down?'

'Uh, Leo, I just wanted to call and see how you were feeling,' she said in soft tones. 'I heard you were out last week with the flu.'

'Well, that's very nice of you to think of me,' he said. 'I'm feeling much better, actually. Come to my chambers and we'll talk.'

Before she had a chance to tell him that she was due back in court in less than ten minutes, he was gone. She grabbed a handful of case files for the afternoon session and rushed out of the office.

'Here,' Phillip said, 'give me those and I'll take them down in the cart with the others.'

'No,' she told him. 'I've got to review them.' Juggling the cumbersome files in her arms, she opened one and began reading as she walked.

Although D.A.'s, public defenders, and clerks roamed around in these halls behind the courts, no one else was allowed back here and the area was sealed off with closed-circuit television monitors and manned security behind locked doors. Too many times defendants went crazy and came looking for judges with a loaded gun. Still walking and reading, she glanced up and saw the placard on the door and stepped inside. Evergreen's secretary nodded and she entered his chambers.

At sixty-seven, Evergreen was well preserved. He evidently worked at it. His hair was dyed. What color he had wanted it to be really didn't matter, because it had turned out a funny artificial shade of red. It was almost blood red, but not new blood. More like old blood that tends to darken. His face was soft and fleshy. Never was there even a hint of a beard. In some places his skin had a sheen to it as though he lathered it each morning with expensive wrinkle creams.

His lips were full and his eyes small and wide-set, a watery gray. Behind those eyes was a great legal mind, a mind Lara coveted.

'How do you stand on the Adams matter?' Evergreen said. He didn't stand but swiveled his high-backed leather chair to face her. 'This is an important case, Lara. There's been a lot of press.'

'Press,' she said. 'I've had enough of that for a lifetime.' She didn't want to get into a discussion of the tabloid article even though she was certain Evergreen had heard of it. 'No one's requested a continuance yet. It should go off as planned.' A tremendous amount of coordination and organization went into Evergreen's position as presiding judge. This required real finesse, for attorneys were known for delays, and delays clogged down the system like wads of toilet paper in a toilet.

Glancing at her watch, she knew she had to be back in court any minute. 'I'm preparing now. I thought I might review it with you before we open next week. When's a good time?'

They settled on a day and time, and Lara started to leave when Leo began speaking again. 'There's a case on your calendar this afternoon. Hold on a moment,' he said, moving a few papers around on his desk while she waited, making sure they were all perfectly aligned in a neat little stack in one corner.

Unlike Lara's desk, Evergreen's was so neat she could actually see the polished surface. He was a perfectionist, and every item on his desk had a designated place. According to Phillip, he didn't allow his secretary to touch it. He even dusted and polished it himself.

Evergreen was speaking, 'Let me confirm the name. Here it is: Packard Cummings. The charge is possession of a concealed weapon.'

'Yes,' Lara said, wondering if old Packard had been

conceived in the backseat of a car. With a name like that, he had to have been. She'd seen the file on her walk down but hadn't as yet reviewed it.

Leo continued in that monotone of his, so low she had to strain to hear him. He did that on purpose. He wanted her to work, have to listen closely. 'We've been contacted by a local law enforcement agency about this individual. They informed us this man's been working for them as a confidential informant on a very large narcotics case. They alluded that this might be the reason he was armed. If I'm not mistaken, he's appearing on a bail review. As a courtesy, they've asked that we release him on his own recognizance.'

'Just a minute, Leo. I have his file right here.' She juggled the files in her arms, setting the others on the floor and dropping to a chair. Flipping through the top sheets to the computer printout of the man's criminal record, she quickly scanned it and looked up. 'My God, Leo, this man has a five-page rap sheet of extremely serious offenses. He's been sentenced twice for rape, was suspected of stabbing another inmate at Chino, and he's even on parole. The district attorney's made a note right in the file that they intend to prosecute him as a career criminal. He's a member of the Aryan Brotherhood.' This was a white-supremacist prison gang, basically neo-Nazis, extremely violent. 'We can't release him O.R. even if he's working for the CIA.'

Evergreen was silent. His mouth fell open and he breathed heavily, something he did often when he was thinking. Finally he said, the words barely distinguishable, 'Well, of course, that's your decision, but we always try to cooperate with law enforcement.'

Lara bit a corner of her lip, sucking it right into her mouth and sinking her teeth into it. One of the reasons she had fought for this appointment was to make independent rulings, decisions she felt were fair and just, but that kept men like this one off the streets. She started to speak up, but visions of another stint in the zoo should the Adams matter be continued flashed in her mind. 'Fine,' she said, pushing the words out of her mouth. 'I'll grant him O.R.'

'Very good, then,' he said, his mind shifting to something else right before her eyes. 'You handled yourself quite well with that Henderson matter, Lara. How is the prosecution's case developing?'

'Not good, Leo. Not good at all. But I'll keep you posted.'

Lara snatched the files off the floor and headed down the corridor. As to the man he wanted released O.R., Lara thought she had probably overreacted. She was a diehard. The man's parole agent should put a hold on him anyway, so the issue of bail would be redundant.

She wasn't looking where she was going and ran right into Phillip on his way to the court. The files fell from her arms and scattered all over the carpeted hallway.

'I'm sorry,' Lara said, looking at the mess she'd made and glancing at her watch. She bent down and picked up a few papers and tossed them into the cart. For a few moments, her eyes searched Phillip's face. Dark circles were etched under his soft eyes, and he seemed unusually tense. She noted a slight tremor in his hand as he picked up the remaining file off the floor. 'Are you feeling all right, Phillip?' she asked, wondering if he was coming down with the flu.

'Oh,' he said, standing. 'No, I'm fine. Why do you ask?'

For the past two years Lara had made every attempt to get to know this young man, but she had as yet to break the ice. 'I just thought . . . I mean, you look tired.'

'Law school,' he said, looking away, clearing his throat. 'It's not easy when you have a full-time job.'

'Hang in there,' she said, giving him a warm smile.

Following him down the hall, Lara unclipped the bow at the base of her neck and pulled the unruly strands back before she snapped it into place again. What she had to do was get on Leo's A-list, become part of the inner circle of judges that ruled the county. Irene had made the team years ago. She and Evergreen were close friends, but Lara was still on the outside. Then, she thought, she could make any kind of rulings she wanted.

'Get me a fucking beer,' Sam Perkins yelled from the living room, 'and put up my TV dinner.'

'Get your own beer,' Josh yelled back from the kitchen, his own dinner already in the oven. 'What do you think I am, your slave?'

'You little punk. You're nothing but a skinny little punk. Get me that beer and fix my fucking supper, boy, or I'll beat the ever living daylights outa you.'

'Go ahead,' Josh said, just as his stepfather rose from the big easy chair in front of the television and headed in his direction, his face a mask of drunken rage. 'Hit me. Go ahead.'

His stepfather met his challenge and punched him right in the face with his fist. Then he pulled back and punched him several more times, connecting with his cheek, his forehead, the strength of his blows almost knocking the boy out of the chair. Suddenly he stopped and looked at Josh. He knew just how far he could go. He didn't want the school reporting Josh's injuries to the authorities. He had other ways to punish him. Ways that didn't show.

He forced Josh to sit at the table and eat the TV dinner he'd made for himself. 'Since you're such a hot shot, too good to make your dad something to eat, I want you to eat the whole thing, even the fucking tray. Eat it,' he demanded. 'Now!'

'Don't you ever say you're my dad,' Josh blurted out,

blood trickling from his nose where Sam had slugged him. 'My dad's dead and you're nothing. You're a bum, a loser, a pervert.'

'Eat it,' Sam said, laughing. He reached over and grabbed Josh's hair and shoved his face into the TV dinner. 'Eat the foil, the tray, the whole damn thing, you wise-ass puny punk.'

Josh's entire body was shaking with anger and humiliation, his face smeared with mashed potatoes and gravy. 'I can't eat the foil. It'll kill me if I eat it. Please, Sam, I'm sorry.'

'You ain't sorry. You're nothing but a spoiled pussy boy, a momma's boy.' He leaned over and yelled at the top of his lungs. 'Eat that fucking foil. You ain't getting up from that table until there's nothing left of that dinner.'

Josh ate it.

He ripped the foil into small pieces and began swallowing them along with chunks of the food, tears streaming down his cheeks. He would run away . . . never come back. He missed his father. Since his mother had married Sam Perkins, their life had become a nightmare of humiliation so awful that he wouldn't even tell his closest friends.

Sam had returned to the chair in the living room. He yelled back at Josh, 'If I come in there and see one speck of foil, I'll put your fucking little pecker in the garbage disposal.'

Josh tore off another piece and ate it, listening to Sam's laughter from the other room. With his eyes glued on Sam's back, he grabbed what was left of the foil tray and shoved it under the waistband of his jeans to dispose of later. This was his home, had always been his home for as long as he could remember. If he ran away, where would he go, how could he survive? Before his father died, the house had been filled with laughter and the wonderful aromas of his mother's home-cooked meals. But in the past two years she'd almost completely stopped cooking, and she'd certainly stopped cleaning. Now the house was a pigsty. Beer cans and newspapers were thrown everywhere. Dishes were piled in the sink. Every night his mother went out, always telling Josh some stupid story about a club meeting, spending time with a sick friend. Tonight she'd told him she was going to the PTA meeting at his school. It was Tuesday night. Josh knew the PTA meeting wasn't until next Wednesday and his mother had never gone to one in her life.

Night after night she would leave him there, alone in the house with Sam, with nothing to eat but TV dinners. She thought he didn't know what was going on, thought he was still a dumb little kid. But she was wrong.

He knew everything.

Chapter 4

After the Henderson case had been disposed of, Benjamin England had called and asked Lara to dinner. Fluttering with schoolgirl excitement, she had rushed out and bought a new dress, got her hair cut, even fiddled with her makeup so she could be as attractive as possible. And the relationship was developing nicely. Tonight was their fifth date. They'd just finished a lovely dinner at a fine restaurant, sipped a sweet red wine over a pale pink tablecloth and fine china, chatting about books they had read and people they both knew.

'Why did you take Henderson's case?' Lara suddenly asked him. 'You haven't taken a criminal case in years.' When they had first gone out, Lara had issued a no-shop-talk policy, but they were running out of other things to talk about. She'd heard all about the sad days of his wife's illness, her death from breast cancer, heard all about his son at Stanford. Her own personal revelations had consumed no more than thirty minutes of conversation before being exhausted. Her marriage had lasted six months; she couldn't stretch it that far.

'To be honest, his mother is a client of mine and she asked me to represent him. Not only did she ask me, but she paid me. I feel sorry for the woman. She built a successful business, a chain of small hotels, but her son is a fucked-up lunatic. Besides, I love criminal law.'

'I see,' Lara said. 'Didn't it bother you to know you were involved in releasing a dangerous man, a probable killer?'

England swirled his wine in his glass and gazed at Lara with those magnificent eyes. He sat forward, leaning over the table. 'Do you doubt for one moment that even the public defender would have pushed for dismissal and suppression of that confession? Those cops beat him until he collapsed. They broke his arm. They . . .'

Lara nodded in agreement. England was right. Even though the P.D. had let it slide and the defendant was so whacko that he didn't realize his rights had been violated, it would have all come to light in the end. They were all just doing their jobs. England had done his well; the cops had not.

'I can't really believe you even asked me that,' he said, raising his eyebrows in a questioning expression. The waiters were yanking off tablecloths and setting up for the next day. They would have to leave soon.

'It's just sad for the family when something like this goes down,' Lara said. 'I feel for them, you know.'

He was a little abrupt, somewhat shocked at her emotional involvement. 'Then you might be in the wrong profession,' he said.

Lara smiled. 'Just a little feminine regression. I love my position, but that doesn't mean it's easy. Anyway, I think they're about to throw us out.'

England draped an arm around her walking to his Mercedes in the parking lot. When he suggested they continue the evening at his sprawling home in the Tustin hills, Lara eagerly agreed. Five dates was a respectable amount of time. It was obvious where the evening was heading.

He had thick candles burning around the large Jacuzzi; two chilled glasses and a bottle of wine were set on the stone ledge. Soft music filtered out of two stereo speakers designed to look like boulders positioned among the greenery. It was overcast and the air was heavy and moist. He slipped her sweater off her shoulders with thin, tapered fingers. She inhaled his scent, something musky and masculine. She really didn't need the wine; she was already intoxicated by the moment – ready, willing.

'Look at you,' he said, 'even your shoulders are beautiful. I don't know why you always cover them up.' He bent down and kissed each one, moving his mouth to her neck and tugging on her sweater until her breasts were exposed, encased in her bra. He slipped his hands behind her and unsnapped the hook. Tossing the flimsy bra to a dark corner of the patio, he quickly seized her breasts in both hands and squeezed them like lemons.

'Don't squeeze too hard,' she whispered in his ear. 'They're sensitive. Be gentle.'

He ignored her and locked his mouth on one and started sucking, moving his teeth over the nipple like he wanted to take a bite. She unzipped his pants and let her hands slide over his hips, pulling him closer to her body.

'God, you feel so good,' he said in a raspy voice. 'I want you.'

She could tell; he was eager, his eyes heavy-lidded with lust. His erection was pushing against her, strong, solid, his hand making its way up the inside of her thigh and ending up between her legs on the crotch of her panty hose. 'Are we going to get in the water?'

'What water?'

'Your neighbors will see us. Let's go inside.'

'No one will see us. I want you here.' The panty hose was down and she was exposed from the waist up, her sweater being swiftly removed and tossed like her bra. He groped under her skirt, his fingers probing inside her. She moaned, trying to let the pleasure take her, but then she jerked away.

'What's wrong?' he mumbled, undaunted, his breath hot and fast, his fingers back again, more insistent than ever.

'You have a hangnail.'

He didn't reply and removed her skirt, letting it fall to the ground. 'Bend over. I want to take you right here.'

'Protection . . .' she said. This was the nineties: safe sex, condoms.

'I have it,' he said. His arms were already turning her around, and he moved in close behind her, pushing gently but firmly on her back until she bent over and placed her hands on the cool stone surrounding the Jacuzzi. In seconds she felt him push himself inside her, and her body began to respond. The strokes were long and smooth. Her mouth fell open and she moved with him, almost in time with the music, a soulful Kenny G tune, while her long dark hair tumbled over her head and brushed the ledge, several strands floating on the water. She tried to shut out everything but the feeling, the sounds, the excitement. It was going to be good, and she needed it desperately. They would make mad, passionate love all night, and she would sleep in his arms, warm and secure, waking to make love again in the early morning hours before the sun came up. They would take vacations to Las Hades and Palm Springs and spend Christmas and Thanksgiving together. She would buy a string bikini and a dozen off-the-shoulder slinky black dresses with hems four inches above her knees. His hands gripped her around the waist and the pace quickened. She began panting with mounting desire and anticipation of the sun-filled days ahead.

Then it stopped.

He didn't cry out or moan or sigh. He just stopped. She

waited, thinking it would continue, but she could tell it was over. Inside her body he was retracting, shrinking.

'That was wonderful,' he panted, pulling her to a standing position and kissing the back of her neck. In seconds the panting stopped. 'Want to get in the Jacuzzi now?'

She stuttered, 'I . . . oh, we could . . .' She watched as he stepped into the swirling water and reached for his wineglass. It was no use suggesting that they go inside to continue this in the bedroom, continue it to the point where she too could enjoy it. Mission accomplished, she thought. Case closed. Another notch on the old belt, already heavily notched with all the willing secretaries and law clerks and divorcees that had gone before her. He was leaning his head back with his eyes closed as if she were already gone.

'Boy, today was a bitch. I'm dead. One of my clients came storming in today threatening to sue me because he has to pay fifty grand to his ex-wife. The nerve of these assholes. Never fails to amaze me. Without me, he would have paid a hundred grand. Believe me, if it weren't for the money, all my cases would be criminal. But the crooks can't pay, so . . .' He sipped his wine, opening his eyes momentarily and then closing them again. The other wineglass remained empty. He made no move to fill it.

Lara stood there naked, her arms wrapped around her breasts. It was always chilly at night in Southern California. She glanced around her. The yard was enclosed with a white picket fence – charming, probably his wife's idea, but not capable of affording them privacy. She imagined the neighbors watching them through the slats of the fence, looking at her standing there exposed. Had they seen her bending over the Jacuzzi a few minutes before?

'I think I'll go home now,' she told him. 'I had a long day too.' She started searching for her clothes. Some of them were wet, having been tossed in puddles of water splashed from the Jacuzzi. She picked up her soggy bra and shoved it into her purse.

'Now?' he said, his eyes springing open, the muscles in his face, previously relaxed, tense. 'You want me to drive you home now? Right now?'

'Well, you said you were tired. The evening's over.' She didn't look at him. She was stepping into her skirt.

'Just sleep here. I can drive you to the office in the morning. I'm too tired to drive anywhere right now.' He leaned back in the Jacuzzi and closed his eyes again.

She was frustrated and angry. 'I said I'm ready to go home, Benjamin. Will you please have the common courtesy to drive me?'

'Can't you take a cab?' he said without opening his eyes.

Impulsively she kicked the empty glass into the water and exploded. 'You're an asshole, a self-centered asshole.' She stomped into the house and called a cab, waiting on the doorstep until it arrived. So much for this fantasy, she told herself. The cab pulled up and she climbed in the backseat, giving the driver her address.

Thirty minutes later the cab pulled up to her modest ranch house in Irvine, a far cry from England's palatial spread. Lara was sound asleep in the backseat, and the cabbie had to wake her. Then she had to search the littered contents of her purse for enough money to pay him, dumping out all the change and counting it out into his palm.

The house was dark. She had her shoes in her hands, her feet were killing her, and she now had a throbbing headache. Post-coitus syndrome, she thought. Post-nothing syndrome was more like it. She was about to put the key in the door when she saw a small card stuck into the slit. She pulled it out and tried to read it, but it was impossible in the dark. Dropping her shoes on the porch, she unlocked the door and flipped on the light.

Her heart started racing and she almost screamed. Quickly she glanced at the card and saw it was from the sheriff's department. She'd been burglarized. The police had responded around seven-thirty when her alarm had gone off, only a few minutes after Benjamin had picked her up.

Her eyes took in the damage. Everything she owned was dumped in the middle of the floor, and the place was a total shambles. Even the cushions on her new sofa were slit, and the stuffing was scattered everywhere like thick balls of snow.

She just stood and stared. Although a residential burglary probably occurred every second in Los Angeles, she had never been hit. She felt violated. They had gone through her things. Her head was pounding so violently that she knew she had to sit down. But she couldn't disturb anything. She went to the garage, hoping the doorknob wasn't the only one in the house with fingerprints, and called the sheriff's office from the car phone in her Jaguar. Then she hit the garage door opener and sat in the dark until they arrived.

An hour had passed. Lara stood on the back porch with one of the police officers while evidence people were still working inside the house. One of them was hammering a piece of plywood over the broken window where the intruder had entered. Lara was picking dead white roses off a rose bush, oblivious to the thorns. 'What?' she said, glancing up at the officer, barely able to hear him over the racket. 'You really think it was more than a burglary?' It was three o'clock in the morning, and she was so tired she couldn't think.

'Well, nothing was taken of value and the place was ripped apart.' The officer was a well-groomed man in his late thirties. His uniform was tight across his midsection, almost too small. She could see the outline of his bullet-proof vest. 'Not many burglars do this type of damage and walk off without taking the TV, VCR, stereo, or something. Just doesn't make sense.' He had a bag of peanuts squeezed in his pocket and was cracking them open and tossing them into his mouth. 'Want a peanut?' he said, offering one to Lara.

'No, thanks,' she said. 'Then what were they after, what was the point?'

'How do I know?' he said nonchalantly. He had a handful of shells now and shoved them into his other pocket rather than toss them on Lara's porch. 'Looked kind of vicious to me. Like maybe someone was looking for you, didn't find you, and went a little bonkers in there. You know, cushions slit with a knife . . . stuff like that. The only time I see a crime scene like this one is in a drug deal. When they're looking for the stash.'

Lara was deep in thought. Jessica Van Horn's boyfriend came to mind and his hurled threats in the courtroom. With Henderson safely locked away, there was only her or England to strike back at. Could the boy have followed her from the courthouse one day and come here to act on his threats? She wrapped her arms around her body and shivered. A young man like that, so deeply in love, so devastated by his girlfriend's death – it was possible.

'What should I do?' she said.

'Anyone got a beef to pick with you?' He wasn't looking at her. He was looking up at the sky. Some of the fog had lifted and he could see the stars. 'Didn't you handle that Henderson case?'

So, she was notorious. 'Yes . . .' Of course, she had tried hundreds of people, both as a D.A. and as a judge. If a person wanted to count her enemies, they'd have to have a lot of free time.

'Judge Sanderstone, if I were you . . . you know,' the

officer continued, 'I'd find somewhere else to stay for a while. At least until we process the evidence and see what we can find. I'd hate to come out here one night and find you cut up like your sofa.' He had finished the peanuts, and he dusted his hands off. He was deadly serious, his eyes on Lara's face. Then his vision drifted and Lara realized she wasn't wearing a bra. With the sheer sweater she had on, her nipples were protruding. His eyes lingered on her chest, and he took a few steps closer. Lara stepped back, putting her arms around her chest again.

'I have an alarm. I even have a panic button.'

'Yeah,' he said. 'Well, those are worth jack shit. See, how it works is the alarm company calls us when they get around to it, and then by the time we get here, the perp's long gone. I'd lay low if I were you. I personally think someone's got a hard-on for you. They'll probably come back.'

'Great,' Lara snapped, jerking her head to the side in anger. That's all she needed – some off-the-wall lunatic stalking her.

'Can I go inside now?' She glanced around the yard, all the tall trees and greenery. Even with the officer beside her, she was afraid. They might still be out there, hiding. They could have a gun and start shooting any second. Even before this had happened, she sometimes got frightened in the middle of the night, hearing strange noises, letting her mind wander. She handled so many heinous crimes that they came back to haunt her, always in the twilight hours before dawn. She sometimes had nightmares of autopsy pictures, bloody crime scenes, imagined her own image in the place of the victims.

Lara didn't know what to do or where to go. 'Don't you think I'm safe here tonight? I mean, why would he come back the same night?' They went into the house. Lara stopped and made sure the sliding glass door was locked.

The other men had loaded up their equipment and left. The officer was eager to leave as well, and he moved toward the door. 'Probably won't tonight. But if I were you, I'd get out of here by tomorrow and keep a low profile.'

'Thanks,' Lara said. Once he was gone, she locked the front door and slid the dead bolt in place. Like she could really keep a low profile. She was beyond logic at this point, into the area of absurdity. I can go to work tomorrow, she thought, and wear a hood over my head. The unknown judge, they could call her.

She staggered to the bed, certain she would be asleep in minutes. She was wrong. A dog barked, and she jumped, her heart racing. A car backfired and she leaped out of the bed and fell flat on her face on the carpet. By the time the gray light of dawn filtered into the bedroom, she had decided to move out.

She went through the day in a haze of exhaustion. It was Tuesday and her night to teach at the University of Irvine. Several times she picked up the phone to cancel and then decided against it. She was going to check into a motel that night until she could figure out what to do. I might as well teach my class, she decided, and then hopefully I'll sleep through the night.

The evening was pretty disappointing. She taught a class on field officer legal liability, more or less for students majoring in police science and aiming at a career in law enforcement. She'd offered to teach the class, thinking it might be a way to stop police brutality before it even started, telling these soon to be cops what could happen if they stepped out of bounds. Tonight, only about six students showed up. Right after the Henderson matter, the class had been packed – standing room only. The students had wanted to know exactly what was going to happen to the arresting officers. Would they be sued by the defendant? Could they actually go to jail? Would they ever get their jobs back? Tonight, she thought, they must be studying for a big test in another subject.

After the last student left, Lara headed to the computer lab to pick up her friend and fellow instructor. Emmet Daniels suffered from Lou Gehrig's disease, or ALS, amyotrophic lateral sclerosis. The disease caused disintegration of the nerve cells in the spinal cord and the section of the brain that regulates voluntary muscle control. It doesn't affect the mind, thank God, Lara thought, peering into the lab and seeing the small man sitting in a wheelchair before a computer terminal. Emmet's genius was renowned, particularly in the area of computer science. UCI was extremely fortunate to acquire him, although he did require a teaching assistant to handle the class. Every year his ability to talk diminished. Soon he might not be able to speak at all and would have to rely on a voice synthesizer. His actual profession was designing computer software for major corporations across the country. Except on Tuesdays, when he taught his class, Emmet worked in his condominium not far from the courthouse. A heavyset woman who lived in his complex drove him to the campus every week, and Lara drove him home.

For a minute she just stood there and watched him, recalling the day she had met him three years before. They had both been attending their first faculty meeting and ended up sitting right next to each other. Emmet had struck up a conversation about the death penalty once he'd learned that Lara was a district attorney. He had such an analytical mind that she had followed him to his car and ended up in a heated conversation for almost an hour. Back then he had been in a wheelchair, but his ability to talk had as yet to be impaired and he was a ferocious debater. Over the past three years she had sadly witnessed this devastating disease consume him. But never once had she heard a complaint.

'Ready,' she said, bracing herself in the doorway.

He hit a button on his wheelchair and it spun around. His glasses were so thick she could barely see his eyes. They were magnified many times over – large milky orbs that seemed to hold all the mystery of the universe. Although they had really never discussed his age, Lara thought Emmet was in his early thirties.

'Yes,' he said. 'I'm . . . ready. Tired . . . tonight.'

The longer the day, the more strenuous it became for him to talk. Most of the time he spoke in short, choppy sentences, his eyes drifting here and there uncontrollably. When they were in his lab or his home, however, he used the computer, tapping out rapid-fire messages faster than Lara could read, using a metal-cage type of device that he slipped onto his head, allowing him to use a pen instead of his weakened fingers.

He already knew about the Henderson case. He knew about all her cases. Lara loved talking to him. Not only was he brilliant and sensitive, completely logical, but he was a great listener. Possibly his disease was partly responsible, yet Lara was certain he would have been a great listener anyway. He not only listened, he weighed each word. She filled him in on the burglary and the officer's belief that she was in danger.

'Doesn't . . . sound good,' he said. 'Stay . . . with . . . me.'

'Oh, Emmet,' Lara said, 'that's really sweet of you, but I wouldn't impose on you like that. Besides, I really think I'll do what the officer said. You know, lay low for a while, get another place to stay. I'm just going to check into a hotel tonight.' She pushed the chair across the campus parking lot to the Jaguar. At the car door, she opened it and helped Emmet into the passenger seat.

She shut the door and folded the wheelchair, placing it in the trunk. Once she was behind the wheel and they were on the road, Emmet turned to her again. 'That's . . . silly. Let . . . me return a . . . favor. You've . . . driven me all these months. Stay . . . with . . . me, Lara.'

She sighed. Of all the people she knew, Emmet was without a doubt the nicest. 'Just tonight, then,' she said. 'Tomorrow I'll figure something else out.'

Once they were inside his condominium, Emmet motioned for her to follow him to his office, and he slipped on the metal contraption and started tapping on the computer. Words flashed across the screen. 'There's a place for sale in this development. It's been on the market for over a year, and they're now looking to rent. We can call them and see if they'll allow you to rent it for a few weeks, a month, whatever. It's furnished . . . a model.'

'Great,' Lara said, leaning over the back of his chair. 'That would be perfect.' Emmet's complex was only a few blocks from the office, and all she'd have to do is go home and bring over some clothes. 'I'm sure this whole thing is nothing anyway. Maybe the burglar didn't take anything because he was scared off by the alarm.'

'Better to be safe than sorry,' Emmet typed.

They said good night and Lara collapsed in the little twin bed in Emmet's spare bedroom, his huge computer terminals whirring and blinking in the dark a few feet away. He had to have enough equipment in this place, she thought, to launch a rocket. It looked like NASA.

Tomorrow she'd try to rent the vacant condo. Tonight she was safe – the frail little man in the next room her sentinel. His very presence was reassuring even if he didn't have the strength to fend off an attacker. At least she wasn't alone. In minutes she was asleep, the soft tap-tap-tapping of Emmet's pen on the keyboard like a lullaby as he worked far into the night.

Chapter 5

Josh looked up the hill in front of him and sighed, letting his feet slide off the bicycle pedals to the asphalt. Every day he had to ride his ten-speed to school and back. Mornings were the best, because he could coast down the hill, wind whipping his face, and imagine he was on a motorcycle instead of a bike. His father had ridden a motorcycle, a big, roaring 450 Harley. But that didn't matter, he thought, stepping back onto the pedals and beginning the agonizing climb up the mile-long hill leading to his house. He'd never ride a Harley or any other motorcycle, for that matter. Not as long as his mother was still around. Not since the accident and his father's death. He'd be lucky if she let him drive a car in two years when he was sixteen and could get his license.

When he'd gone to the bathroom that morning, the toilet had been filled with blood from the sharp edges of the foil he'd been made to swallow. Crying to his mother wouldn't solve anything, even if he told her what Sam had made him do last night. She wouldn't do anything about Sam. All she talked about was how they were going to move away, how their ship had finally come in, or something dumb like that.

Halfway up the hill, he removed his T-shirt and tied it around his waist. It was already damp with perspiration and he was only halfway home. His mother screamed at him at least once a week because he was so thin. Maybe if she rode six miles a day, two of them up Mount Everest like he did, then she'd be skinny too. Besides, he thought, flexing his muscles by gripping the handlebars and seeing the veins and ridges, he wasn't skinny anyway, he was cut. That's what they called it in the gym – when someone's body fat was so low that the skin merely stretched over the interior musculature like a piece of transparent fabric.

Josh had trekked along to the local health club when his father was alive and watched him work out, bench-pressing twice his body weight, grunting and groaning, jostling and trading jokes with the other men. But they couldn't afford to belong to a gym anymore. Josh worked out alone in his room every night, lifting again and again the few weights he'd got for Christmas, dreaming of the day he'd be as strong as his father, strong enough to defend himself against any man.

Even a man like Sam.

Reaching his block, he froze. Sam's truck was in the driveway. Glancing back over his shoulder, he thought of coasting back down the hill and maybe hanging out with one of his friends until dinner. He just couldn't take seeing Sam this early in the day – not with so many hours left, not when he might already be drinking, cursing, and looking for trouble. But Josh knew if he rode down and goofed off until dinner, he'd just have to go back up the killer hill and then he'd be too tired to work out. Better to sneak in through the back door and try to make it to his room before they saw him.

Quietly opening the side gate, he left the ten-speed leaning against the brick wall of the house, pushed aside the two trash cans, removed the key above the ledge, and entered through the door into the kitchen. It was quiet, still. Good, he thought with relief, his eyes surveying the room. This was the biggest mess he'd ever seen. Everything was thrown out in the middle of the floor. They'd either had one of their screaming fights where they hurled anything they could find at each other, or they really were packing to move. Sam probably hadn't made the payments on the house and they were being evicted. That's all they needed right now, to be thrown out on the street.

He hated Sam Perkins. There wasn't anything in the entire universe he hated more than he hated Sam Perkins. He didn't care if the whole world blew up in a nuclear explosion as long as Sam Perkins blew up with it. 'Pow,' he whispered, seeing it in his mind: old Sam's body blown to kingdom come.

He snatched a can of Coke out of the refrigerator and headed to the back of the house. To get to his room he'd have to pass the master bedroom. He prayed the door would be closed. Sam had probably come home early to stick it to his mother. What other reason could there be? He was probably right this minute in there doing disgusting things to his mother in broad daylight. It made Josh want to puke right on the beige carpet and leave it there where Sam would step in it when he came strolling out of the bedroom.

The door wasn't closed. It was open.

Josh glanced inside the bedroom: his lunch rose in his throat and his heart stopped beating. He knew what he was seeing. His mind was screaming, trying to tell him what he knew he was seeing, but he just saw the images without thought or comprehension. Far away someone was screaming – it couldn't be him, it had to be someone else. There was a clawing, scraping wild animal inside his body, poking at his eyes through his forehead, eating through his stomach, squeezing his heart with huge hands until he knew it was going to burst. Then he heard it. His own voice. Time-delayed.

'Mom!' the scream rang out and reverberated in the air like an echo, the sound going forward and then returning. He placed his hands over his ears. He didn't want to hear it. His eyes were frozen on the scene before him, but he didn't want to hear the awful sound coming from his own mouth.

Department twenty-seven of the Orange County Superior Court was still in recess, but the clock was ticking. The fifteen-minute mark had passed, and it was now approaching almost twenty minutes since the gavel had come down. A few feet away, the courtroom was packed and noisy, everyone talking at one time, attorneys still rushing in and slamming their files on the tables, quickly conferring with their clients, some who they'd never met until that very moment. Phillip walked into Lara's chambers and stood quietly in front of her large, paper-strewn desk. Her eyelids fluttered, but she didn't look up. He stood and waited.

'Yes,' she said finally, removing her glasses and fixing him with her slate gray eyes. 'What have you got, Phillip?'

'I know you're working on the Adams matter and you asked that I not disturb you. It's Sergeant Rickerson with the San Clemente Police Department on line one.'

She didn't speak. He stood still, hands by his sides. Her eyes returned to the brief in front of her. Long moments passed.

'I'm sorry, but do you want me to tell him to call back?'

'Please, no calls,' she mumbled, eyes down, deep in thought. 'I only have a few more minutes. No calls.'

He left. Then a few seconds later, he returned, a grimace on his face. 'It's imperative that he speak with you. He says it's about your sister.' He paused, waiting for her to look up, his face a mask of concern.

She set her hands on the desk. The fingers spread and

pressed hard into the papers, her back rigid. 'Okay, Phillip, I'll speak to him.'

As he hurried for the door, she picked up the receiver. 'My secretary said this was about my sister . . . Ivory Perkins . . Is that correct?' Her voice was controlled. No need to panic. It was probably not even about Ivory. Generally it was Sam's name they mentioned when they called. 'Mr. Perkins said to call you regarding this ticket,' they would say. 'Mr. Perkins said to contact you regarding this complaint that he's receiving stolen property.'

The officer was speaking. She was looking at the second hand on the large wall clock. She was late. A few minutes could equal several arraignments. 'I'm sorry, Officer, repeat what you just said.'

'There's a problem here. It's bad. Your sister and her husband have been killed. It looks like a double homicide.'

'Double homicide?' she repeated, as though she'd never heard of such a thing. 'Ivory?' Not Ivory. Sam Perkins, yes. But not her sister.

'We're here at the house. Guess her son came home from school and discovered them. Pretty bad scene.' Sergeant Rickerson paused. 'He was hysterical when we got here, but he's calmed down somewhat and we sent him to a neighbor's house.'

'I . . . he . . . she's dead.' She stood, holding the phone, her mind blank, her hands sweating profusely. Gripping it with both hands, she stuttered, 'When d-did it happen?'

'Medical examiner won't have an exact time of death until he does the post. Maybe a few hours ago from the looks of the bodies.'

She had already started walking around the desk, heading to the door. She suddenly reached the end of the phone cord, dragging the multi-line phone over the top of her desk, knocking over her coffee and several files, which scattered on the carpet. In a state of shock she was going to walk out the door with the phone still in her hand. Finally realizing what she was doing, she dropped it and it crept back across the carpet. Then she turned around and bent over and picked it back up and said in a hoarse voice, 'I'm on my way.'

She didn't pick up her purse. She didn't speak to her secretary. She simply walked out of her chambers, still wearing her black robe, and kept walking until she reached the end of the hall, where the security console was set up. She stopped and stood, staring into space.

'You okay there, Judge Sanderstone?' the black guard said, leaning over the console. 'You look real pale.'

She slipped off her robe and handed it to the guard. 'Call Phillip and tell him to have someone bring my car keys to the parking garage and cancel my afternoon session. Hurry,' she yelled, walking fast as he pressed the buzzer on the security doors. 'My sister . . .' She walked through the doors, talking to herself. 'My sister's been murdered.'

She punched the button and got in the elevator. It was reserved for judges only and led to the underground parking garage. The doors shut. The elevator didn't move. She fell against the back wall and then screamed: 'Ivory! God, no! She can't be dead. I won't accept it.' She was screaming and spitting at the same time, her fists clenched into tight balls, the emotionalism an alien and terrifying feeling as it consumed her. Her chest rose up and down, and she knew she was on the verge of hyperventilating.

The doors opened and Phillip stepped inside, handing her purse to her. 'Is there something I can do? Has there been an accident? Do you want me to drive you somewhere?'

Pushing herself off the wall, she looked down. Tears were streaming down her face. She could feel them.

'No,' she said. 'Just cancel my afternoon session, please. My sister's been murdered.' She reached over and punched the button for the garage level, flipping Phillip's hand off the elevator door. For a moment their eyes met.

'I'm sorry . . . so sorry. Call me if there's anything I can do.'

'What could you do?' she said as the doors closed, his face disappearing an inch at a time. What could anyone do when someone was dead? Breathe life back into them? Make their heart start beating again and their blood circulate?

Nothing else really mattered.

She didn't remember the thirty-minute drive over – the traffic on the freeway, the exit to San Clemente, the steep hill to their house. She was approaching the house. It was real. It was a living nightmare.

Police cars lined the block, wheels turned to the curb so they wouldn't roll. One black-and-white, probably the first to arrive, had run up over the curb. She pulled her green Jaguar into someone's driveway four houses down and left it there, keys in the ignition, engine running, her purse on the seat, and ran the short distance. Several officers had placed a yellow police tape across the front lawn and were standing there, blocking neighbors and kids from entering. The curious were pressing against one another, trying to see, their faces flushed with excitement. One small child managed to slip his hand out of his mother's and duck under the yellow tape, jumping up and down in glee on the grass. An officer grabbed him back over the tape to the sidewalk.

Lara didn't see the tape. She walked right into it and kept walking, her eyes focused on the front door of the small adobe house, nothing else in her line of vision.

'Hey, you,' a burly voice yelled. 'You can't go in there. Get back.' A large arm reached out and managed to catch the edge of her sleeve.

She jerked her arm away and glared at him. 'My sister,' she said. She kept walking, flinging the tape aside and stepping over it. 'My sister.'

At the door she was again met with resistance. A uniformed officer placed an arm in front of her, blocking her entrance. 'Can't go in there, lady. This is a crime scene.'

'My sister,' she said again, trying to push him aside. His eyes got large and he looked behind him and then back to her face.

'Judge Sanderstone, right?' he said, standing a little straighter, adjusting his gun belt. 'Listen, wait here and I'll get Sergeant Rickerson. He's in charge here. You don't want to go in there.'

She saw the compassion in the man's eyes. It didn't help. She stepped in front of him. The tiny house was crawling with people. Some were in uniform, others in suits. A few wore dark pants and white shirts with name tags pinned above the pockets. Those were the ones from the white van that she now remembered seeing parked at the curb with the rear doors open. The van that said the dreadful words on the side: MEDICAL EXAMINER.

A good-sized man wearing a shiny gray suit with unruly red hair and penetrating eyes, his face scarred from acne, walked up to her through the sea of bodies. He came close, too close. 'Sergeant Rickerson . . . Ted,' he said. He started to extend his hand and then realized it was an inappropriate gesture and dropped it by his side. 'We met, but you probably don't remember. It was when you were still a D.A.'

'Where is she?' Lara's eyes blinked rapidly as they searched the room, seeing nothing but bodies, hearing nothing but a cacophony of jumbled words.

'Look, I don't think it's a good idea for you to go in there.' He flicked his red mustache and leaned even closer. 'Why don't we step out in the backyard and talk a minute? Let the people do their job.'

'I have to see her. Please, Sergeant, let me see my sister.' She brushed her hand over her head as though swatting a fly. Too many people were in the small room and not enough air. An officer tried to squeeze past them, and his nightstick became lodged obscenely between her legs, pushing the hem of her skirt up, exposing the top of her panty hose. She didn't notice.

Rickerson pulled her gently aside, dislodging the nightstick and giving the officer a dirty look.

'Sorry,' the man said with a slight smile, raising his shoulders and moving on, unaware who the small, dark-haired woman was or what she was doing here.

'Come on,' Rickerson said softly. 'Let's go out back. You need some fresh air.'

'Where is she?' She waited, counting seconds in her mind: one, two, three, four, five, six. It was coming. She knew it. It began somewhere in the pit of her stomach and rose with a fury as she opened her mouth and screamed, 'Get these fucking idiots out of here and let me see my sister. Now!'

Almost every noise stopped. Everyone dropped what they were doing and stared at her. Some who were kneeling down stood so they could see what was going on. Sergeant Rickerson started waving his hands toward the front of the house and whispering in people's ears. One by one, they headed for the front door, and soon the living room was empty. 'In the master bedroom,' he said. 'The medical examiner is in there now.'

She was in a black tunnel. The bedroom door was at the end. In front of her on the end table was her own image in cap and gown at her graduation from UCLA. Next to it was a picture she and Ivory had taken at one of those booths at Knotts Berry Farm years ago where they were both dressed in costumes from the Old West. Ivory was holding a toy rifle.

She saw the door frame passing over her head as she entered, almost as if she was being moved forward by a conveyor belt or a moving sidewalk at an amusement park. Somehow she had moved to this point without awareness of her body. She immediately placed her hand over her mouth to stifle her screams, digging her fingernails into the soft flesh of her cheeks. The walls were splattered with blood in strange designs like an abstract painting. Sam's body was sprawled half on, half off the bed, face down, his head an unrecognizable mass of bloody tissue. The room smelled of death: coagulating blood, human excrement. The vision of what had occurred in this tiny space hung like a cloud of ash over them all. They all saw it, felt it, denied it was real.

She didn't see Ivory at first, and her heart leaped. They'd made a mistake. Ivory was alive. Someone had murdered her despicable husband, but Ivory was still alive.

Then she saw her.

Her body was on the floor by the bed. She was nude from the waist down yet wearing a flimsy bra. Her legs were spread obscenely. Both eyes were open and bulging. Her lips had a bluish tinge. Her mouth was tightly shut with a death-like grimace. Her black hair was matted with blood. The flawless skin was gray-blue, and streaks of blood ran down her forehead, her cheeks, covered her upper torso. Lara's eyes jerked from her face and rested at her feet. She was wearing worn-out tennis shoes, the laces not tied.

A man was crouched over the body; another man was snapping photos. The first one stood. He was wearing a white mask and surgical gloves. She focused on his bushy eyebrows, bypassing his eyes. She was exhaling and then swallowing. Every time the camera clicked, Lara's body twitched, almost like a spasm. She forced herself to inhale.

She was sensitive to odors. This was death she smelled. Death and fear. Ivory's death, her fear.

'From what I can tell at this point, she was probably suffocated with a pillow. If you will note the bulging eyes, the red and blue hemorrhage streaks across the white conjunctiva, the bluish and contused lips. These are all indications of suffocation. The blood you see is his.' He glanced at Sam's body on the bed. 'I think we have the murder weapon for this fellow. Looks like someone bludgeoned him from behind with a twenty-pound free weight. Cracked his skull wide open. This cheesy stuff here is his brain tissue,' he said, picking up a glob of something off the bedspread with tweezers and dropping it into a plastic bag. To Lara, it looked like oatmeal.

He stepped over Ivory's body and moved to the other side of the bed. Lara dropped to her knees and tried to force her head down to her sister's face. She could not. She stared at the man in the mask and gloves, now bending over Sam. Ivory's hand was cold and limp, but soon it would be as rigid as a statue. Lara picked it up without looking at her and then dropped it. She had started tying her shoes laces when she felt someone's hands under her arms, lifting her slowly to a standing position.

'Let's go now. There's nothing you can do here,' Sergeant Rickerson said softly, his eyes full of compassion.

'I need to wash her face,' Lara said, seeing the splattered blood, knowing she was being irrational but powerless to stop it. Ivory had always had such beautiful skin. Since birth, actually. Most infants have ruddy complexions, but according to their mother, Ivory's was perfect from day one – smooth and white. It was why their mother had named her Ivory. Ivory wouldn't want anyone to see her this way, Lara thought. She was proud of her lovely complexion. It was one of her best assets.

'No, no,' Rickerson said. 'That's not necessary. Please,

let's go outside. Someone will get you a glass of water or a cup of coffee. Get some fresh air. You'll feel better.' He was speaking low. He placed an arm around her shoulder as if he might embrace her.

Lara looked up into his eyes and then looked away. She had to do something but she couldn't remember what. She couldn't remember anything . . . couldn't think. She walked straight out of the house, the sergeant hurrying after her, her mind completely blank. She didn't see the people still gathered in front of the house, the crowd growing larger and larger as people came home from work. Some of them had gone home and returned with cold sodas or beer cans – refreshments – as in the movie theater. She didn't see the news van and camera crew that were there shooting her very image as she walked out the front door, her blouse soiled and stained, her face wet with perspiration, her face almost as rigid as marble. She didn't hear the voice of the reporter speaking into a microphone only inches from her face.

'We're here in San Clemente, where the sister and brother-in-law of Orange County Superior Court Judge Lara Sanderstone have been brutally murdered. Judge Sanderstone,' he said, pointing the microphone at her, 'can you give us a statement?'

She walked by without even glancing in his direction and headed for her car. Rickerson stopped on the sidewalk and watched her until she drove off. Then he turned in the direction of the house. It was useless to try to interview her now anyway, he thought. She was in another world.

The collection of investigators and uniformed police officers who had been standing on the front lawn in a tight group, some smoking cigarettes, others making notes on clipboards as they waited, turned and followed the detective back into the house.

Judge Lara Sanderstone had forgotten all about her

nephew. But so had Detective Sergeant Ted Rickerson. When an officer came in from the boy's bedroom with a box of dumbbells, the same brand as the murder weapon, a matched set, all accounted for but one, the murder weapon, Sergeant Rickerson still didn't think of fourteen-year-old Josh. Affixed to the outside of the box with Scotch tape was a torn piece of Christmas wrapping paper and a little tag. 'TO JOSH, FROM MOM,' it read. One glance and Rickerson's head jerked to the officer standing closest to him.

'Get the kid,' he barked. 'Get the fucking kid.'

Chapter 6

Lara drove without thought. Finally she pulled up to the thirty-year-old cottage in Dana Point where they had grown up and parked the car. It didn't even look the same. The new owners – several, actually, in the ten years since their mother's death – had added a second story and remodeled the one-car garage, making it into some type of playroom. It looked like many different houses all pieced together into one. Gone were the beautiful rose bushes her mother had tended to every single day, wearing her wide-brimmed hat and cloth gloves. A wrought-iron fence and a padlocked gate had been installed in front of the house to keep transients out. All beach communities had their share of transients and homeless. Dana Point, San Clemente, and San Juan Capistrano, only a few miles apart, had more than their share. Inside the fence was nothing but concrete. No grass, no flowers, no walkway to the door. Everything was turning to stone: Ivory's once lovely hands, the front yard where they used to play. All stone now.

She gunned the Jaguar and sped away. The past was over. Both of their parents were dead. They had waited too long to start a family; the children had been almost an afterthought. When Lara was born, her mother had been close to forty and her father in his mid-fifties. They were up in years before Lara even graduated from college, and her father didn't live to see her complete law school. Now Ivory was dead too. There was no one to even remember the sunny days of years gone by, the happiness, the laughter, the hopes and expectations.

Ivory was going to grow up and become an actress – a movie star. Everyone really believed it, even Pop, and he barely believed Lara would make it through college when she'd made straight A's since the first grade. He was far from an optimist, but he truly believed his gorgeous younger daughter, the light of his life, would one day be on the silver screen. She was so pretty, so fun-loving, so eager to please people. She loved to pose for the camera. How could the world not love her as much as they did?

Before Charley died and after their mother had passed away, Lara used to call Ivory and suggest they meet somewhere for lunch. She wanted to stay close, keep the family together. Ivory would always say, 'I'll have to call Charley and call you back.' They had argued. Lara was so independent, so strong, so opinionated. Even though she liked Charley, had even had a big crush on him in high school before Ivory started going out with him, she couldn't tolerate the fact that her sister let him control her entire life, that the woman couldn't make a simple decision to have lunch without consulting her husband. She knew her sister was immature and not terribly bright, but every adult had to have opinions of their own, some sense of their own identity. All Ivory espoused were Charley's opinions. When Charley died, she was like a lost child, easy prey for a man like Sam Perkins – for any man, really.

In only a matter of months Sam had squandered every dime Ivory had: Charley's life insurance money, the savings account he'd had for Josh's education. He'd even taken out loans on their little house in San Clemente that

Charley had purchased when he and Ivory were first married.

Lara was now on the freeway headed north to Santa Ana. At lunch, she'd made arrangements to move into the condominium across the courtyard from Emmet's. Before she went to work, she'd gone to her house and tossed a bunch of clothes in the trunk. She hadn't even told the detective about the break-in, the threats in the courtroom. The two incidents couldn't possibly be related, she told herself. How would anyone know Ivory was her sister? Her mind was spinning, still awash in blinding sorrow and denial. She was only blocks from the congested civic center area that housed the courts and other city and county office complexes as well as dozens of private law firms.

Then she thought of Josh.

They had no relatives. An aunt maybe in Georgia, but she had to be in her eighties now, a few cousins somewhere.

She would have to take Josh.

She gripped the steering wheel until her knuckles turned white and almost rear-ended the car in front of her. The poor kid. They hardly knew each other. Ivory had forbidden her to even see the boy for at least two years. But Lara had no excuse for what she'd done. She'd walked away and left him there without so much as a word.

Her eyes searched for the exit ramp in the string of cars in front of her. They weren't moving. Traffic was so congested that they were practically standing still. She couldn't go back to the house in San Clemente. Some things a person just couldn't do, and this was one of them. She forgot the exit ramp and seized the car phone from the console. Who should she call? The police, of course. She'd tell them to bring Josh to the condo. Then she'd figure it all out tomorrow.

Funeral arrangements had to be made. People had to be

called. Plans had to be formulated. Although the sun was still out, the sky had clouded over and her vision was blurred. Like a nightmare, a case she'd handled or heard in the courtroom, Lara told herself someone else's sister had been murdered back there. Not her sister. The tears started to fall. They felt like hot acid, etching themselves into her face, the skin far from flawless, nothing at all like beautiful Ivory's.

She called the police station on her car phone, but Rickerson hadn't arrived. She asked the dispatcher to get him on the radio and find out where her nephew was. The girl put her on hold. She waited.

'He said the boy is being brought to the station here. He wants to know if you're coming to pick him up.'

'Tell Rickerson to call me.' She'd have them bring him to the condo. She gave them Emmet's phone number and the number of the car phone. 'If he doesn't reach me, I'll call him back.'

She replaced the car phone and took the First Street exit to the condo, glancing at the fast-food restaurants as she drove, her mind jumbled and unfocused. He'd have to eat. She needed food. She had nowhere for him to sleep. The place she had rented was a one-bedroom condominium. She'd have to go back to her home.

No, she thought, she couldn't go home. Not now, not after what had happened to Ivory and Sam. Fear seemed to be surrounding her. She felt trapped, paralyzed. Maybe they were after her, wanted to kill her and her entire family. It could be the boy who had threatened her in the courtroom . . . anyone. She was terrified, completely panicked. You have to stop it, she told herself. She had to find her inner strength, put her sister's pathetic body out of her mind long enough to find the condo, figure out what to do about her nephew.

How old was he anyway? She didn't remember. He was

a sweet kid. He reminded her of Charley, but she hardly knew him.

She'd always wanted a child of her own, dreamed she would someday have a family. In some ways Sam had been right when he told Ivory that Lara was jealous. She'd envied Ivory for having a child, a family. Finally, a few years ago Lara had reconciled herself to her childlessness by telling herself she was doing the things that had to be done in the world to keep it safe. Ironic, she thought. Ivory's death made it all seem like smoke. Blown away. Just like that. Gone. The whole premise she had based her life on had been eradicated. If she couldn't keep an unknown person from snuffing out her sister's life, it was all a big zero.

She crossed the parking lot to Emmet's condo. That morning she hadn't even looked to see if the place she had rented had a phone. She was certain it didn't. It was a small complex, only about forty units. Emmet's unit was on the ground floor, a quick walk to the parking lot. The one she had rented was right across the grassy courtyard. It wasn't even a security building, and the area around here was riddled with crime. She looked around her, behind her. She cursed herself for not carrying a gun. A lot of the judges did. She knocked on Emmet's door and waited.

He didn't answer. She started beating on the door. He still didn't answer. She was trembling, shaking. She didn't know whether to go to the condo across the courtyard or drive to the San Clemente P.D. Finally the door clicked open and she entered, closing the door behind her and leaning back against it. 'Emmet,' she yelled, 'are you in there?'

He appeared in the hallway. 'Sorry,' he said. 'I . . . was in the . . . bathroom.' Then he saw her tear-stained face, the look in her eyes. 'What's . . . wrong?'

Lara put her hand to her mouth. For a few moments she

couldn't say the words. Emmet hit a button on the wheelchair and crossed the room to her. Reaching out, he touched her shoulder. Then his hand fell away. 'Tell . . . me.'

'My sister, Emmet,' Lara stammered. 'My sister and brother-in-law were murdered.'

'Murdered?' he repeated. 'Oh, no . . . How . . . terrible.'

She told him all that she knew, rattling off the details in a manic series of jumbled sentences. She rushed to the window to peer outside. 'It could be over me. They may want me, Emmet. They may have even followed me here and be out there right now.' Her heart was pounding, pressing against her chest. She didn't even ask. She simply grabbed Emmet's phone and called the police station again. This time she got through to Sergeant Rickerson.

She spoke rapidly, standing in Emmet's living room, turning around in small circles. 'I didn't tell you that someone broke into my house the other day. The investigating officer thought they were looking for me, that it was more than a burglary. And I was threatened about three weeks ago . . . a case I handled. The Henderson homicide. You may have read about it.'

'Calm down,' the detective said. 'Where are you?'

'I'm at a friend's house in Santa Ana. I rented a small condo in his complex. The officer told me to move out until this blows over, not to stay at my house. I'm not sure, but this could all be related. They could have killed Sam and Ivory to hurt me.'

'If you feel you're up to the drive, you can come to the station. I have your nephew. You can give me all the details.'

'Do you think this is related to what happened to my sister and Sam?' Lara had wrapped the phone cord around her and had to turn in the opposite direction to get free. Emmet was sitting quietly a few feet away.

Rickerson answered, 'It could be, but then you might have been a victim of an ordinary burglary.' He was trying to reassure her.

'I'm coming there to get my nephew.'

'That sounds like a good idea. We have to interview him, and we'd like to interview you. I was going to wait and do it tomorrow, but if you come – '

'I'll come,' Lara said, her hands trembling on the phone, grasping it with both hands to keep it steady. 'He's just a kid. This is so terrible for him. I forgot all about him. I didn't think.'

She decided that the one place she'd like to be right now was a police station. Besides, she should have never left without Josh. This was all that was left that she could do for her sister – take care of her precious child, arrange her funeral.

'Judge Sanderstone . . .' He paused, his voice tense and uncertain. 'Do you mind if I call you something else?'

'Lara,' she said.

'Lara,' he said, pronouncing it as Laura. Everyone did. 'Let me tell you something here. Your brother-in-law was killed with a dumbbell. That dumbbell belonged to your nephew. And let me tell you something else, your nephew isn't exactly a little boy. This kid is almost as big as me. Do you know what I'm saying?'

She had no idea what he meant. So, Josh wasn't a little kid anymore. What bearing did that have on all this nightmare? 'Who killed my sister? Did the neighbors see anything? Did you find anything in the house?' Her voice started to rise, even though she tried to contain it. She had pushed these thoughts to the back of her mind, too painful to begin to deal with now. She couldn't suppress them any longer.

His voice was low and measured. 'Take it easy, Lara. I know this is a terrible time for you, and please accept my deepest sympathy – the whole department's, in fact – but surely you understand that we have to do our jobs here. We have to cover all the bases.'

She was silent, thinking. What he had tried to say diplomatically now clicked into place. He had implied, in a roundabout way, that Josh could be responsible. That was absurd. Sure, patricide wasn't uncommon. As awful as it was, it did occur. But her own nephew? Outrageous! Just the thought made her already churning stomach turn over and over like a ferris wheel.

'Why don't you come down and we'll discuss all this in person?'

'Fine,' she said.

'What . . . did . . . he say?' Emmet asked once she had disconnected. She was just standing there staring into space.

'He . . . oh, Emmet, I-I have to go and get my nephew. He thinks my nephew . . .' She just couldn't say it. She walked over to Emmet and kissed his forehead and then rushed out the front door.

The San Clemente Police Department was housed in a small, older building. It wasn't a large department. San Clemente wasn't a large town. Even if Richard Nixon had once resided here and people had heard the name, it was still what some people called the boonies, stuck in the middle between Los Angeles and San Diego. New housing tracts and shopping centers were springing to life here and there, but the town itself still looked like a small, beachy city, almost like a town found along the Eastern Seaboard.

Rickerson had a cup of coffee in one hand and a soda in the other. The coffee looked disgusting, but he needed it. As long as it still moved in the cup, it was drinkable. The soda was for Josh, waiting alone in the interview room. He hoped like hell it wasn't the kid who was responsible for the bloodbath in that bedroom. He had two kids of his own, and he hated it when he had to arrest young people on serious crimes. Oh, a little bust now and then for possession or drinking in public or a curfew violation didn't bother him, but not a crime like this one. And this one was going to be big. It was going to make all the papers. The deceased weren't notable. The female was a housewife; the husband owned a small pawnshop in the center of old San Clemente. But the relationship to a judge would do it, particularly since this judge had made all the papers already only a few weeks before. It was a red flag to the press. And if they got wind that the boy was a possible suspect, all hell would break loose.

'Hey, Josh, brought you a soda, guy,' he said, knowing his smile would not bring another from the grim young man who sat in front of him, his long sandy blond hair falling onto his forehead and almost obscuring his eyes. He was a fairly attractive kid – clear skin, nice features, blue eyes. Under the circumstances, it was hard to tell what he was really like.

The can of soda remained on the table. The boy didn't reach for it. His body was angled forward in the chair, his shoulders slumped, his eyes glazed and puffy.

'Okay, let's start at the beginning. I know this is painful, son, and I'm sorry we have to do this, but we do. As soon as we're through here, you can go home with your aunt and try to get some rest.'

Josh blinked and licked his lips. 'My aunt? I haven't seen my aunt in . . .' He stopped himself and focused on a framed poster on the wall.

'So, let's get this over with. You came home from school and saw your stepfather's truck parked in front of the house. You told the other officer that this was an unusual event –

that he didn't generally come home from the shop that early in the day. Is that correct?'

'Yeah.'

He looked at the boy with compassion. 'Sorry, kid.' He continued, 'You entered through the back door into the kitchen. Was it open or did you use your key?'

'I used my key. We hide it above the door ledge.'

Rickerson was reading from the officer's notes and looked up at Josh. His eyes were wide, his mouth open. 'You went to the refrigerator, got a soda, and then walked down the hall to your room. When you passed the master bedroom, the door was open and you saw the bodies. Is that right?'

'Yeah.' Josh leaned forward in the chair, getting even closer to the table. His hands found the soda and he popped the cap, but didn't take a drink. With a jerky movement he swiped the hair out of his eyes and continued to stare at the poster.

'Tell me about the weights?' He looked directly into the boy's eyes and tried to read his reaction. Nothing. Even the tone of his voice was almost flat.

'The weights? What're you talking about?'

'You know, the set of weights your mom bought you for Christmas last year. Do you work out, Josh? You've got a nice build there, guy.'

A small flicker of light went on in his eyes. 'My dad was a body builder. My real dad. Yeah, I work out. How'd you know my mom bought me weights for Christmas?' He swallowed, choking up at the mention of his mother, almost ready to cry.

'We found them in your room, son. One of them was missing – the twenty.'

Josh turned to the detective and spoke without blinking. 'The twenty?'

'Yep, the twenty. It wasn't with the rest of the set.'

'Oh, yeah. What does this have to do with my mom?'

'Why don't you answer my question first and then I'll answer yours. Sound fair?'

'All my weights were in the box in my room where they always are. I kept them in my closet 'cause Mom – ' He stopped and coughed, a glint of moisture appearing in his eyes.

'Please, go on.'

Tears streamed from both his eyes. He made no move to wipe them away, and Rickerson pretended he didn't see them. 'My mom didn't like them all over the floor in my room, see. She made me keep them in the box in the closet.'

'So, the twenty was in your closet this morning when you left for school?'

'Yeah, sure. I guess. I mean, I didn't look. It was there the night before.' He sniffed. 'I could have left it on the floor. I don't remember.' The tears stopped and dried on his face. His face had been dusty and now there were streaks where the pale skin showed through and the dust had changed into muddy lines.

'Well,' Rickerson said, 'we didn't find it there. We found all your weights in your closet, the twenty missing. But we found the twenty in your parents' bedroom.'

Josh's gaze was penetrating, his reply sharp. 'My mom's bedroom. That wasn't my dad. I told you. My dad is dead. That was my stepfather.'

Rickerson leaned back in the chair, rubbing his stomach. It was popping and churning. He'd have to check on how the real father died. Something about this kid was beginning to make him wish he'd taken his vacation this week like he'd planned. But no. Joyce had seen to that. After almost twenty years of marriage, she had jumped up one morning and told him that she wanted to go back to college and get her engineering degree. Then a few months later, she had moved into her own apartment and left him with the two boys. But she kept insisting she didn't want a divorce, and she called him every night and told him how much she missed him. She even made him promise that he wouldn't tell a soul at the department. Women, he thought, twirling the gold wedding band on his left hand. Fucking woman. Right this very minute he could be stretched out on a beach in Hawaii instead of sitting here facing off with this kid.

'Okay, Josh,' he said, 'just answer this for me. Why would your twenty weight be in your parents' – excuse me – your mother and stepfather's bedroom?'

'Dunno.'

'Can you think of any reason someone would do this to your mother and stepfather?' He certainly wouldn't want to use the word *parents* again. One look from this kid was enough to make a clear impression on that one.

'Because Sam was a bastard! I hated him, man. Everyone musta hated him 'cept my mom.' Now he reached for the Coke and drank half the can in one swallow, setting what was left back on the table with a thud.

'Did you kill them, Josh?' the detective said softly, knowing he was treading on shaky ground. He could question him about the murder as a witness, but he couldn't interrogate him as a suspect until a parent or guardian arrived. But the opening was there and Rickerson found the temptation irresistible.

'No,' Josh said, looking him straight in the eye. 'I wish I'd killed Sam, though.'

Rickerson sighed and leaned back in his chair. 'Your mother? Know anyone that might have wanted to hurt your mother?'

'Dunno. Sam maybe. He was always screaming at her.'

'Did you ever see anyone at the house you didn't recognize? Can you give us a list of their friends?'

'I can't remember, okay. They didn't have a lot of friends.' A dark shadow passed over his face. He refused to look at the detective.

'Did you see anything at all amiss or different when you came home today, before discovering the bodies?'

'All I saw was Sam's stupid truck. He never comes home in the middle of the day. And everything was all torn up like we were moving out or something.'

Rickerson was tired and he was hungry. He was getting nowhere fast. The poor kid either didn't know anything, or what he did know, he wasn't telling. He stood and shoved the metal chair away from the table, placing his hands behind him and stretching his aching back. 'Let's go, kid. That's it for today. Your aunt should be here any minute. She's on the way to pick you up.'

Josh stood as well. Rickerson walked to the door, then turned and glanced back. The boy just stood there. 'Come on,' he said again. 'Don't want to stay in this room all night, do you?'

'Why do I have to go to my aunt's house? She's a bitch. Why can't I go back to my house and stay there? I need my bike . . . and my clothes – my things.'

Rickerson just shrugged his shoulders. Tough situation, he thought. Nothing's going to be easy in a case like this one, not now, not later. 'It's either your aunt's house or juvenile hall until we find a foster home. Take your pick.' He didn't wait for the boy to answer. The answer was evident. He walked out of the room and waited in the hall, leaning and resting his back a few seconds against the wall. A few minutes later the boy came out and shuffled behind him to his office. Did he kill the stepfather he hated, Rickerson asked himself, and then suffocate his own mother? Hard to tell at this point. He had enough doubts, however, to generate plenty of sleepless nights in the days to come. As far as Judge Sanderstone's fears that someone was after her, he personally doubted it. A residential burglary was a far cry from a double homicide. He had officers canvassing the neighborhood, and hopefully forensics would come up with something they could sink their teeth into and run with. If not, it was going to be a bad one.

In his own little world, he startled when the young boy next to him spoke.

'That's her, isn't it?' he said, watching as a bedraggled woman made her way down the hall.

Rickerson looked up and saw Lara Sanderstone. 'Don't you even know her, son?' he whispered, wondering if the boy was okay. Surely he recognized his own aunt.

'Yeah,' he said. 'I know her. I just forgot what she looked like, it's been so long.' He cut his eyes to Rickerson. 'I told you she was a bitch. That's what my mom always said. She said we weren't good enough for her. That she thought we were white trash and that's why she stopped coming around.'

'Oh, yeah,' Rickerson said. 'Well, she's a pretty smart lady. Why don't you give her a chance?'

As Lara got closer, Rickerson looked up and shook his head. He felt sorry for the woman. Nope, he sure didn't want to be in her shoes right now. Sister and brother-in-law murdered; this gangly, bitter kid to deal with. She was a pretty woman, he thought, looking her up and down. Even under this kind of strain, there was an ethereal, unusual quality about her. But she looked small, vulnerable, broken. Not like the tough little prosecutor he remembered from her days in the D.A.'s office.

'Josh,' she said, seeing him and running to embrace him. 'I'm so sorry, honey. I'm so sorry.' Then she finally pulled back and stared at him. 'You're so big . . . my God.' She put her hand over her mouth. He looked just like his father. It was like spinning back in time, back to the days when they were all in high school, the days when . . . She stopped herself, seeing the black look in his eyes, a look that passed right through her.

Josh just stood there. He didn't say a word.

Chapter 7

At the police station, Sergeant Rickerson called Lara aside, sending Josh down the hall to look at mug shots of possible suspects, anyone that he might have seen in the neighborhood or at his parents' house. It was really just a way to diffuse the situation – the friction between the boy and his aunt. Josh had flatly refused to go home with her. 'It might have been a mistake for you to come down here,' Rickerson said. They were standing in the corridor leading to the lobby. 'This has been really tough for him, obviously. Why don't you go home and I'll talk some sense into him? Then I'll either bring him to your place later or find a placement for him.'

Lara still felt the sting of her nephew's look. What she had seen in his eyes was pure hatred. She glanced at the detective and then looked away. Maybe he was right about the placement. 'I don't know anything about teenagers,' she said. 'I'm not married, you know.'

Rickerson ran his fingers through his already unruly red hair and then braced his back against the wall. 'Yeah, well, I'm not sure I know that much myself, and I've got a few of my own. A kid's a kid. That's about it.'

Although she was tempted to turn Josh over to Social

Services, she couldn't. 'Please convince him to stay with me. Tell him I care. He's my sister's only child. I have to take him.' Lara reached into her purse for the rental receipt, gave him the address, and then something flashed in her mind – the last night she'd seen Ivory alive. 'Someone was following my sister,' she blurted out, stepping into a doorway as an officer walked by. 'She came to see me about two months ago, late at night. She was excited, frightened, but she refused to tell me what was going on.'

'Did you call the police, get a description of the car or whatever?' Rickerson was alert and standing only inches from Lara, his breath and clothing reeking of cigar smoke even though he wasn't smoking.

'No, she wouldn't tell me anything.' Lara looked down at the worn and scuffed linoleum. The floor must have been white at one time. Now it was an ugly shade of yellow. 'We had an argument. I have no idea what was going on. I asked her to leave.'

Ivory had been in trouble two months ago, the night she'd come to her house. In what way or over what she had no idea. She knew Ivory had problems. She should have understood. She should have tried to figure out what was going on. If she had, her sister might still be alive. Rickerson was staring at her. Beads of perspiration were popping out on her upper lip. She blotted them with her hand.

'I'll call the sheriff's department and see what they made of the break-in at your house,' he said, concerned about the woman standing beside him, more worried about her emotional state than any physical threats right now. 'Nothing missing, huh?'

'No, not that I could see,' Lara said, leaning back against the whitewashed wall. 'I mean, I didn't go through everything. They told me to move out, so I moved out.'

'I heard some of the details of this Henderson case, but not all. You said someone threatened you, one of the family members?'

'The dead girl's boyfriend,' Lara said, the words reverberating inside her head; she kept seeing Ivory on the floor in that room. Would someone refer to her as the dead girl's sister? 'I don't remember exactly what he said. I mean, he called me a fucking bitch . . . said someone should kill my family or me . . . something like that. We weren't on record then, so we don't have it documented, but the D.A. was in the courtroom, the bailiff. A number of people were present.' Lara paused, not looking at the detective, her voice low. 'I thought he was just distraught. It was a difficult situation.'

'The medical examiner believes your sister was sexually assaulted prior to the suffocation.' He hated to say it, but she had to know.

Lara looked up in shock. 'No . . . Jesus Christ . . . she was raped. Ivory was raped.' Then she quickly pressed her lips together into a hard, thin line. Ivory was dead. That she was raped was incidental. But it went to the suffering, the agony she had endured in her final moments of life.

'Wasn't the Henderson girl raped?' Rickerson asked.

Lara's head shot up at the big detective. 'God, yes . . . You can't possibly think that the boyfriend would rape and murder Ivory to strike back at me? That would be insanity. All I did was rule on the law. My hands were tied.' The muscles in her face were twitching. She no longer cared what Rickerson or the officers passing them in the hall thought about her. Facing the wall, she pounded it with her fists. She then thought of something and spun around to face him. 'Are they certain it wasn't consensual? Maybe she and Sam had sex before she was killed.'

Rickerson dropped his eyes. 'Lara, the medical examiner said it was a rape. Pretty brutal from what he said. Numerous rips and tears in her vagina.' He paused, his eyes full of conviction. 'Whoever did this, we'll nab them. They'll pay. Go home now. Call someone . . . a friend, a relative. There's nothing you can do here.'

Tears gathered in Lara's eyes. She thought of Thomas Henderson. He hadn't paid. He was sitting in a loony bin, free to walk out the door whenever he felt like it. She pushed herself off the wall and headed out of the building to the parking lot. All these years, all the cases, the endless faces. They were like a blur now, moving so fast before her eyes that she couldn't remember any of them. How many enemies did she have? Were there hundreds, even thousands? Was someone right this minute lying in wait for her, bent on revenge? Was someone so full of hatred that they would kill her sister and brother-in-law just to hurt her?

She heard herself arguing in court during her days as a D.A.: 'The people believe the maximum sentence is both appropriate and justified in this case, Your Honor. The defendant is a sociopath, a danger to society, an animal . . .'

These people had wives and children, mothers and fathers, brothers and sisters. For all she knew, she'd made mistakes. Could she have been responsible for sending an innocent person to prison? The system wasn't infallible.

Lara Sanderstone had a reputation for being tough, unmerciful, always leaning toward the longer terms, stacking the penalties as high as they would go. No one ever mentioned her name and the word leniency in the same sentence. Leo Evergreen had even called her into his chambers and read her the riot act only months after her appointment.

'You aren't a prosecutor anymore, Lara,' he had said. 'The bench has to consider other factors in imposing sentences. You can't send every single offender to prison.

In some cases there are calculated risks. We have to take them.'

The truth was obvious. She had enemies, probably far more than even a scum bag like Sam Perkins.

Lara glanced at the clock. It was late now, almost eleven o'clock. The little condo she'd rented looked like the typical model. Every other wall was mirrored to make it look more spacious. The furniture was small, deceptively so, also in order to create the illusion that the rooms were larger than they were. She wanted to hear noise, so she went to turn on the television. It wasn't real; it was a black plastic box that just looked like a television. She felt like she was in Disneyland.

She was still waiting for the detective to deliver Josh.

Although there was no phone, someone had placed the Yellow Pages inside the doorway. She picked up the book and flipped through the section listing funeral homes, but quickly found her fingers trembling on the thin paper pages. Dropping the large book on the floor, she decided Phillip could take care of it all tomorrow. She'd tell him what she wanted and he'd make the calls.

That's when the stark reality of death really hits a person, she thought. When they call a funeral home and purchase a casket to put their loved one in the ground, under the dirt. She stared at the door and tried to swallow the morbid thoughts like a pill without water.

On the drive back from San Clemente, she'd called almost everyone she could think of on the car phone, mostly the numbers she had committed to memory. Wasn't that what you were supposed to do when someone died? She'd called Irene Murdock. Irene was a rock of strength – just what she needed right now, she thought. Irene's machine had answered. Lara hung up.

Then she'd called Benjamin England. Even if he was a

pig in bed, he was a man and she needed someone. She got his machine too. She'd forgotten that he was going to San Francisco on business. She didn't leave a message. She wanted to, but she just couldn't get the words out of her mouth. Telling a machine that your sister had been murdered was almost obscene.

She'd called Phillip. He'd listened, tried to console her, told her not to come to the office in the morning. He'd make the notifications, he'd said, arrange things, call Evergreen. He asked her if she wanted him to come over, but she told him no.

She'd started to call her ex-husband, Nolan, a prominent entertainment attorney, but decided against it. The short-term marriage had ended in a bitter divorce a number of years ago. They didn't have the same goals. He worshiped the God of money; she had a thirst for justice. Anyway, she thought, Nolan had a new wife now and a mansion in Beverly Hills. She doubted if he was willing to drive all the way over here just to help her bury her sister.

She went to the windows and peered through the drapes. On the coffee table was a little card that said the drapes were a decorator item. They didn't come with the condo. Although a light was burning in Emmet's condo, it was close to midnight. It wouldn't be right to wake him. His illness drained him and, besides, she thought, what could he do?

She was getting scared – more so with each passing minute. She heard sounds, sounds different from the ones at her house: cars on the nearby freeway, sirens, horns honking, people talking, their voices far away but audible. Was someone out there, waiting, just waiting for her to shut her eyes so they could come in and bash her head in or suffocate her with her own pillow as they had Ivory? They could have followed her even here.

She collapsed on the sofa. It was small, more like a

loveseat. She'd sleep here, give Josh the one bed. Thank God, Rickerson had managed to talk him into staying with her. He'd called an hour ago saying that he was bringing the boy to the condo. He was big, as big physically as most men. They would be together.

Slouched on the sofa, consumed with exhaustion and grief, she vented her anger at Sam. In her eyes Perkins was a borderline criminal. Although it was mandated by law that a pawnshop operator report any property taken in to the local police, Perkins seldom did. If the police found him in possession of stolen property, he simply suffered the loss and paid the fine, claiming that the paperwork got lost in the mail. He also used his connection to Lara and the bench to escape prosecution and loss of his business license. Three times she had bailed the bastard out. She knew better – it had gone against everything she believed in – but she had done it for Ivory. Besides, all the judges granted favors at one time or another, and she had loaned him a hundred thousand of her hard-earned dollars to buy that business.

Finally there was a soft knock, and she jumped up and ran the short distance, flinging the door open without looking to see who it was. Rickerson stepped inside the condo and Josh followed.

'You're so late. I was worried,' she said, her eyes locked on Josh. Even though she knew he was fourteen, she couldn't believe how big he was, how much he'd grown since the last time she'd seen him. He had to be at least five-ten and his body was developed like a full-grown man's, with bulging biceps and broad shoulders like his father's on a lean, wiry frame. 'Are you hungry?' she said. 'Have you eaten?'

He didn't answer. After a few awkward moments at the door, he walked into the room and looked around. Rickerson asked her to step outside.

'Look, I would suggest that you don't open the door next time without finding out who's there.'

'I know,' she said, embarrassed. 'I've been waiting all this time, that's all . . .'

'And maybe you should get a gun if you don't have one.'

Lara looked up. 'You really think I need one?' He was compounding her fears, making her crazy. Why couldn't he just lie and tell her she was perfectly safe – that this had nothing to do with her?

'I think that's a definite possibility. I talked to the S.O. Your place wasn't burglarized, Lara, it was ransacked, rifled. Someone was looking for something. And they were looking for something at your sister's as well. They tore that place apart.'

'But what? . . . I don't have anything. I have nothing anyone would want. I don't even have much worth stealing.'

'How about a case?' he said. 'Do you bring work home, evidence, police reports . . . things like that?'

'Certainly,' she said, 'but not lately. I'm starting a trial next week, but even if I brought the whole file home, I can't see any reason for someone to steal it. All they have to do is walk into the records department and fill out a slip, and they can see it themselves. Unless the file is sealed, it's accessible to the public.'

He shrugged. 'Get your nephew to some type of psychologist or something. Of course, I'm sure you know that. He didn't eat. And here,' he said, giving her a halfhearted smile, 'don't say I never gave you anything.'

Lara stared at the object in his hands. Light reflected off the blue steel of a small-caliber revolver.

'Go on, take it,' he said.

'No,' she said, 'I don't want it. I hate guns. And Josh is here . . . You know how dangerous it is to have a gun in the house with a child.' Especially with this child, she thought. He was so big that even the word child was a misnomer. And Rickerson's suspicions could be valid. Josh could have come home and found his stepfather standing over his mother's body and bashed his head in. All she needed to do was give the kid access to a gun. Just the thought made her shiver.

'Yeah,' he said, letting the word linger, looking deep into her gray eyes, almost as if he could read her mind. 'You might be right.'

Rickerson stepped even closer. The detective had a bad habit of invading her personal space. If he knew what was good for him, he'd step back. He didn't. He put the small handgun back in the pocket of his jacket.

A siren was blasting on the freeway a few miles away. Lara held her breath and thought of Ivory, the last night she'd seen her. 'The night she came to my house had to have been July seventh,' Lara said. 'I thought I'd just tell you. It was the night before my birthday.' Ivory hadn't even remembered her birthday. She'd gone out to dinner with Irene and some other women in Los Angeles. 'What kind of evidence did you collect at the house?'

'We . . . I . . . we'll have to get back to you tomorrow. We've got to sort through everything, see what we've got. The crime-scene unit is still working there now, and I'm on my way back. Then we're going to start on his pawnshop. We've secured it as well.'

It was chilly and Lara wrapped her arms around her body to stay warm, but she was still freezing, her teeth actually chattering as if she were in sub-zero temperature instead of a California evening in the sixties. The chill was not in the air, she decided, it was inside her.

'That has to be it, you know?' she said to Rickerson. 'The pawnshop. Of course. What else could it be? They're not after me. If they wanted me, why didn't they kill me instead of them? Someone got pissed at Sam over something and came to his house and murdered them. He probably made the guy a loan and then sold the property out from under him. The guy could have been a criminal. Sam wasn't exactly a sweetheart, you know.'

'So I've heard. Your nephew told me.'

Lara jerked her head up. 'What did he say? Does he know anything?'

Rickerson didn't want to upset the woman by repeating his suspicions. Of course, on the other hand, if the boy was a psycho, he was putting her in a pretty risky position. 'How close were you to your sister?'

'Not very.' She cracked the door and peeked inside. Josh was on his stomach on the sofa. She closed the door again. 'Not close at all in the last two years. I didn't approve of Sam. She wouldn't leave him. Kind of like that, you know?'

'Yeah, but the kid? What do you know about the kid?'

'Nothing.' She looked away. She was embarrassed by the truth.

'Your brother-in-law was killed with a weight, a dumbbell. The weights belonged to the kid.'

'You already said that. Are you saying what I think you're saying?' Another resident of the complex walked by, and Lara and Rickerson stepped back, letting him pass. He nodded at the man; Lara ignored him, tilting her face up at the detective.

'Looks that way. Can't rule it out. Not yet.' He rubbed his fingers across his face, feeling the acne scars.

'Jesus,' she said, shaking her head, trying to convince herself as much as the detective. 'I won't buy it. That's an aberrant thing, for God's sake. Don't even think it, and listen –'

'Yeah.' He was reaching in his jacket. A few seconds later, he was rolling a cigar around in his fingers. He didn't light it.

'Please, have the decency not to spread this around about my nephew's possible involvement. He just lost his mother.'

Rickerson grimaced. 'It won't be in the press release, but it's not confidential information. I mean, there were dozens of officers at the scene today, and they all know the murder weapon was a dumbbell and the dumbbells belonged to the kid. We found them in his room.'

She was indignant. 'What kind of cops are you?' She flushed. 'I'm sorry. I just can't see the rationale behind this. Just because the murder weapon is a dumbbell and the child owns a set of dumbbells doesn't mean anything. That would never fly in any court I sit, or anywhere else, for that matter. You're grasping at straws here, Rickerson.' She turned and put her hand on the doorknob. 'I want every officer you can round up to start tearing that filthy pawnshop apart. Call every single person he's ever made a loan to and run them every which way for criminal history. There's where you'll find your killer.'

'I'm sending a man over tonight to watch your place.'

'Thanks,' she said. At least she could sleep. She opened the door and started to enter. Rickerson headed down the walk to the parking lot. He turned and spoke over his shoulder, 'No forced entry. Whoever killed them knew them or had a way to gain entrance to the house.'

She heard him. She couldn't think about it now. Seeing Josh on the sofa was something she'd have to get used to. But there were a lot more difficult things to get used to in this nightmare. That he might have been involved was one.

'Josh,' she whispered, placing her hand lightly on his back, bending down over the sofa. He didn't raise his head, but he turned his face. The sofa was so small his long legs were protruding from the other end. She could see he'd been crying. He looked grown up, but he wasn't. He was still a child. And this child had been royally screwed, she thought, by the forces that be. He'd lost his father on that blasted motorcycle, and then Ivory had brought Sam into their lives, a situation she was certain had not been pleasant. Could it have made him bitter enough to kill?

'I'm sorry, Josh,' she said. 'I know how much you're hurting. I loved your mother very much.' Instinctively she stroked his hair as her mother had done when she and Ivory were children.

He fixed her with those penetrating eyes, eyes so like his mother's. 'Just . . .' he snapped, knocking her hand away, 'leave me alone? Okay?' Then he turned his head toward the back of the sofa.

Lara got up and walked around the condo. It was so small. It was confining, like a box, like a coffin. She had to get out. 'Josh,' she said softly, 'I'm going to drive over to Taco Bell and get something to eat. They're open all night. Are you hungry?'

He sat up on the bed and rubbed his red eyes with his hands. 'I want to go home,' he said flatly. 'I'm not staying here with you.' He got up and headed for the door. 'I'll walk if you won't drive me. I've gotta get outa here.'

Lara leaped in front of him and put her body in front of the door. 'No, Josh. Listen to me. You can't go home. You have to stay here with me. The police won't let you back in the house, and you're too young to stay alone.'

'Get out of my way,' he snarled. He was looming over Lara, glaring down at her like he was going to pick her up and toss her across the room. 'You can't keep me here. This isn't a jail.'

Lara felt tears on her face and wiped them away with her hand. Keeping Josh with her wasn't going to work. He was too disturbed and she didn't have a clue how to handle him. But no matter what happened, they had to get through tonight. She took a deep breath and turned to him, her voice firm. 'Look, Josh, I know you resent me. But that was my sister that was murdered there today. It wasn't just your mother. It was my sister. I'm going to get myself something to eat. If you want, you can go with me. If you don't, you can starve. It's your decision.'

'I'm hungry,' he finally said. 'I'll go.'

'Good,' she said. She found her purse and headed to the door, mumbling to herself under her breath, 'We have to eat or we'll get sick.' That's what her mother always said.

She had planned on going through the drive-thru and then returning to the house with their food, but she couldn't face the condo now. 'Want to go in?'

He was staring out the passenger window. He didn't answer.

Lara parked the car and got out. Josh followed a good distance behind her. They got their food. He had ordered all kinds of things. 'I'm glad you came with me, Josh,' she told him. 'I didn't want to be alone.'

All he said was 'I'm hungry.'

Walking to the table, Lara noticed his face had softened somewhat. She figured it was the law of survival. They had been thrown into this situation. Neither of them could change it.

'You a real judge?' he said, unwrapping a large burrito and shoving it into his mouth.

Lara glanced at his hands and saw that his fingernails were dirty. 'Sure I am. Didn't your mother ever tell you that I became a judge?' She studied his face, his eyes.

'I didn't think hot-shot judges ate at Taco Bell.'

'Well, now you know the awful truth.' They were talking. His tone was still sarcastic, but it was a start. 'I'm a fast-food junkie. I'll probably die of a heart attack from all the chemicals and cholesterol one of these days, but I like the quick fix. No muss, no fuss. You know?'

The burrito was gone. He tossed the paper aside and

began on the taco. 'I don't like health food,' he said, his mouth full of food. 'I lift weights and I'm supposed to eat right. Never do, though. I hate that bean curd stuff. That's sick.'

'Uh-huh,' Lara said, munching her taco, thinking he'd actually managed to complete an entire sentence without lashing out at her. 'You'd think sick if you knew what was in that taco. I don't think about it. I just eat it.'

No, she thought. He couldn't be involved. If he'd done this abominable act, it would show in his face. He couldn't have killed someone and a few hours later sit here and consume a burrito, a taco, and a complete plate of nachos. What she saw was grief, disbelief. It was etched on his young face, shot from his eyes. Like her, he was struggling for strength, trying to see through the horror to the other side.

'What will I do about my school?'

Lara almost choked on her taco. She'd never thought of his school. She certainly couldn't drive to San Clemente and back to the office every morning. 'I don't know, Josh. We'll have to figure everything out. Tonight, let's not worry about anything. Tonight, let's just get by.'

'Yeah,' he said, his eyes drifting away, gazing out the window, filling with recognizable sadness.

Lara shoved the rest of the taco aside and looked at her nephew. Then she turned to the window and soaked up the night. Darkness and death were intrinsically compatible. Two spotlights illuminated the parking lot, but the vacant lot behind was completely black. The killer could be out there in the shadows, ready to pull the trigger the minute they walked out the door. Placing her hands on the Formica table, she inched her fingers toward Josh's until she finally made contact. He didn't pull away, but he didn't look at her. Lara removed her hands and slid out of the booth. 'Ready?' she said.

'Who killed my mother and Sam?' he said, finally turning to face her.

'I wish I knew, Josh.'

'But you don't, right?'

'No, I don't,' Lara answered, looking down at him. From this perspective, he looked small and helpless. His body was slouched low in the seat, his hair tumbling over his forehead and obscuring one eye. She wished she could wrap him in her arms and comfort him. What she really wanted was some miraculous way to assuage his grief and stop the pain. 'Right now, Josh, we're going to go home and get some sleep. Tomorrow I'll start searching for the answers.'

Running it through her mind, Lara decided the place to begin was with the victim's boyfriend who had threatened her in the courtroom. Then she would review her past cases to see which defendants were back on the streets possibly bent on revenge. Finally, she knew they would have to sift through the pages of Ivory and Sam's life: the pawnshop, the house in San Clemente, friends, neighbors.

Deep in her thoughts, she headed to the front of the restaurant. Josh passed her and stepped outside. By the time Lara saw him, he was halfway across the parking lot and a man in dark clothing was walking toward him from the direction of the vacant lot.

'No,' Lara screamed, lunging at the doors, completely panicked. Racing across the parking lot, she seized Josh from behind and toppled them both to the ground. 'Don't move,' she whispered, her heart pounding, her eyes jerking to the man she'd seen. The man glanced at them and then walked away.

'Get off me,' Josh yelled. 'You're crazy. You're a nut. The whole world's crazy.'

Lara stood and dusted herself off. 'I saw that man and I

became frightened,' she said quickly. 'It's late. This isn't such a good area. I don't want anything to happen to you. Anyway, I'm sorry I knocked you down.'

'You're sorry. Yeah, sure. Everyone's sorry.' Josh stood there with a sullen look on his face while Lara unlocked the car. When they were both inside, he continued, staring straight ahead, his voice as sharp as a knife. 'You know how many times I've heard that I'm-sorry bullshit? Every day, man. That's all my mom used to say to me, how sorry she was about everything. And when my dad died, that's all people said to me.' He turned and moved his face close to Lara's. His breath was hot and sour. 'Do me a favor, okay? Forget the sorry stuff.'

They rode home in silence.

Chapter 8

Lara lay on the sofa, the floral bedspread from the bedroom thrown over her. She had insisted that Josh take the bedroom. He was just a child, she had determined, and he had lost his mother. Right now all she could offer him was a bed and a burrito. In a deep, fitful sleep, she heard someone tapping gently on the door. Her pulse quickened and she rolled off the sofa to the floor, certain this was it, expecting someone to start shooting at her through the door. The clock read five in the morning. She seized it and listened to it. It was real. It wasn't just another prop.

'It's Officer Ringers,' a man yelled through the door. 'Judge Sanderstone . . .'

Her heart started pounding. Why in the world would they wake her this time of day?

'Sorry to wake you,' the young officer said when Lara opened the door, his face haggard from lack of sleep, 'but Detective Rickerson wants you to come to the house in San Clemente.' He looked away. 'You know, your sister's place. He's been there all night and he said there are some things you should see.'

'Now? You want me to drive there now?' Lara whispered. 'My nephew's asleep. Look, Officer, is this really necessary?' Her voice was sharp. She felt her sweatshirt and it was soaked with perspiration; damp strands of her hair fell across her face. Nightmares she couldn't remember, she thought, pulling the wet shirt away from her body. Even in sleep, the mind kept fighting, trying to accept the unacceptable.

'Sergeant Rickerson said so.'

'You really think I should go?'

'Yeah.' He looked around as if to say, What do I know, lady? I'm just following orders.

'There shouldn't be any traffic. Tell him I'm on my way. You're not going to leave, are you?' she asked the officer. She didn't want to leave Josh alone.

'I get off at six o'clock. They're sending a relief. Someone will be here.'

'Fine,' she said, closing the door in his face. She didn't know what to do about Josh, so she left him a note and some money on the kitchen table. McDonald's was right across the street. He could walk there for breakfast. She left him the spare key to the condo.

It was still dark when she left, but the darkness slowly changed before her eyes to a misty morning gray. The freeways were empty, particularly heading south away from Los Angeles. Bile rose in her throat. What had they found? A body. Something more gruesome than she could imagine, more gruesome than what had already occurred. Maybe Sam had killed someone and dissected them, burying their body parts under the house, and then someone had come looking for them and killed Sam and Ivory. Her mind was boggled; she was letting her imagination run wild.

From the moment she'd met Sam Perkins, she'd known he was nothing but trouble. She had an eye for things like that. But Ivory had been so alone and despondent, sliding into a haze of alcohol and drugs, dragging strange men home from bars. At first Lara had thought the marriage was for the best. One dirt bag was better than a dozen.

When she arrived at the house, three cars were in front. All the lights were still burning even though the sun was up and the day was evidently going to be a clear, sunny one. She hadn't brushed her teeth, hadn't combed her tangled hair, and she was wearing the sweatshirt and jeans from last night. She had slept in them.

Inside the living room, Rickerson pointed at the bedroom and she followed him reluctantly. The other officers continued working. Every drawer and cabinet in the house was open and everything out on the counters, the floors, everywhere. She cringed, stepping over an old photo album and a football trophy from years back, one of Charley's. Ivory's whole life was being invaded. Not only was the medical examiner about to invade her poor lifeless body, already ravaged and defiled, these strangers were snooping through every inch of her existence. They were touching her underwear, going through her toiletries: her Tampax, her Midol, her laxatives. It was disgusting, disrespectful, but Lara knew it had to be. Get yourself murdered and you're an open book, part of the public domain.

As she entered the bedroom, the bloodied walls pressed forward, surrounding her. She felt faint. Her body swayed back and forth, her stomach tumbling. Remnants of last night's taco were about to come spewing out.

Rickerson saw her and came over, extending his arm in front of her body. 'Hold on. Take some deep breaths. Don't pass out on me. I guess I should have taken these things out in the living room. I'm sorry. I thought, though, that you should see them where I found them.'

'I'm fine,' she said weakly.

He opened a panel on the floorboard of the closet that was covered by a piece of cut carpet. It led to the crawl space under the house. Then he removed a large plastic storage box filled with various items. Some were clothes, others magazines and newspapers – some were photos. She tried to look at them, but her gaze kept returning to the walls, the blood, the nightmare in living color. She reached over and picked up a photo. Rickerson had spread them out on the dresser.

Her hands started trembling. She couldn't believe what she was seeing. 'God,' she said, 'so he was taking pictures of her like this – the slimy bastard.' She picked up another one. Ivory was wearing a black corset or something and thigh-high black boots, the same silly boots she had worn that night when she came to Lara's house. She was wearing a mask and holding a riding crop. They were stupid pictures. They were disgusting. To Lara, they weren't even sexy. 'So, I don't understand the importance of this, Rickerson. Certainly not to make me drive all the way over here at five in the morning just to see my sister like this. It might be disgusting, but lots of men take suggestive photos of their wives.'

She gave him a look that said he should know about that type of thing. He was a man. Even old Nolan had once taken a picture of her naked when they were first married.

'Can you wait a minute?' Rickerson barked. 'It's far more than the pictures. Your sister and brother-in-law were evidently into bondage, S and M, stuff like that. Did you know that?'

She stepped back in shock. As appalling as it was, her mind was adjusting to the bloody walls. 'Of course I didn't know that.'

'Well, if you'll look at these magazines and pictures, you'll see that they were more than a little interested in this stuff. Your sister was working in the trade, advertising for clients.'

Lara's face turned white and her mouth fell open. The

way Ivory had been dressed that last night she came to the condo . . . the phony breasts. 'My sister was a prostitute? Is that what you're saying?' He was holding a thin newspaper, and she snatched it from his hand. He had circled a number of small ads. She tried to read them, but the print was too small and she didn't have her glasses. Her eyes were dry and scratchy from crying. She should have known. She shoved the paper back in his face. 'I can't read it. I don't have my glasses.'

Rickerson moved in close. Lara stepped back. 'She wasn't a prostitute,' he said. 'Not exactly. She was a dominatrix and a submissive. Meaning, she would be whatever they wanted for a price. If they wanted to be whipped, she'd whip them. If they wanted to whip her, she'd let them. Most working girls choose either one or the other, but some play both sides of the fence to make more money. That's evidently what she did.'

'No,' Lara said, dragging the word out in disbelief, to the point where it almost echoed in the room. 'No way. I can't believe this. She was a mother. She had a child. Surely you're not saying she brought strange men over here with her teenage son in the house and dressed up like this and whipped them.' She still had the photo in her hand and was waving it foolishly in the air in front of him.

Worse than that, Rickerson thought, avoiding her eyes. He had no doubt whatsoever that this would be the most sensational case of his career. 'Okay, let me just tell you what we've found. We've been working all night here.' He looked at her, expecting sympathy, approval. 'We found two private phone lines in this house, one of them in this bedroom with no extensions. Several of these ads had pictures of your sister with the number to call. We verified that it's this phone number. It rings in this room. Another answering machine had to be here to pick up these calls, but it's gone. We think the killer took it.'

Lara started chewing on a hangnail, her eyes darting around the room, the walls and the blood back again in full horror. 'How do you know there was an answering machine?' she asked in a small voice.

'There was a power pack and a plug that fits an answering machine. They took the machine but left the electrical cords. If you look under the bed there, you can see an indentation in the carpet where it sat. It must have been an old one, like a Record-a-Call. Big, you know. When they first came out, they were larger than they are now.'

Here they were discussing progressive electronics and Ivory had been selling her body to anyone that wanted it. More than her body, actually, she had been selling her will, her dignity. 'Then she probably did it a long time ago and then quit. The pawnshop was floundering with the economy. She told me. Possibly she did it once or twice and then stopped.'

'Doesn't fly, Lara. This ad' – he raised the newspaper in her face – 'was current. They renewed two weeks ago. We checked. And all these clothes and things . . . they're all costumes. You know, B and D costumes. I don't know if she had them over here to the house. She might have done out-calls. Or she could have serviced them while the kid was at school.'

'Don't use that word!' she spat.

'What word?'

'*Serviced.* That's disgusting. You're talking about my sister.'

'Sorry, okay. Like I told you, I've been up all night. We had to track people down on this and call them at home. The phone company, the paper . . .'

She followed him into Josh's bedroom. Clothes were strewn everywhere, and the contents of the drawers and closet were in a pile in the middle of the room. Not only was Ivory's life spread out for all to see, her son's was also.

She saw little army men from when he had been a small child, a few stuffed animals, a few toy trucks. Then there were motorcycle magazines and *Playboys*, some of the pages ripped out. Lara bent down and began picking up a few items of his clothing to take back to the condo.

She suddenly dropped the clothes back onto the floor and fell onto Josh's twin bed, on the bare mattress now that they'd stripped it. She placed her hand over her mouth. Then she began sobbing. She couldn't stop. Her shoulders started shaking. It was all too much, just too much. This was all some sort of a dream, a delusion. She was cracking up, her mind unable to absorb this . . . the whole thing.

Could the poor kid have done this horrid thing? Could he have discovered what was going on and possibly killed Sam and then had to kill his mother when she walked in and saw him? Rickerson was talking to her. She couldn't concentrate on his words; they were floating around over her head somewhere like black birds or vultures.

'. . . do you think? It could be that Josh came home and found your sister dead. He saw Sam Perkins over the body and went to his room for his weight. Or maybe he had it in his hand and heard noises and then saw the body, assuming Perkins killed her, which of course, he may have. Josh then bashed him to death in retaliation. That works.'

Rickerson was talking to her as though she were another investigator. Her sister was dead and her fourteen-year-old nephew about to be accused of murder. 'I don't know about any of this, but I know that animal she was married to was behind it all. That's all I know. Josh isn't a killer. I'd bet my life on it.' She started walking to the door. Even if she had her own doubts about Josh, she owed it to her sister to defend him. She'd never felt so overwhelmed and horrified in her entire life.

'You are betting your life in a way,' Rickerson said in a soft voice, almost taunting.

'What . . . what are you talking about now, Rickerson?' Then she saw the clothes she wanted to take and picked them up and held them to her chest.

'Well, you're living with him, aren't you?'

She didn't answer. She would probably have to pay to bury Sam Perkins. Now she might have to hire an attorney for her sister's child to defend him against a murder charge, possibly for more than just killing his stepfather, which might be feasible under the circumstances, but even his own mother, which was beyond comprehension. She shuffled to the car, tossed the handful of clothes in the backseat, and left.

Once Lara had left, Rickerson stepped outside the house and fired up his cigar. Then he reached in his pocket and took out the stack of Polaroids that he'd found inside the box in the crawl space held together with a rubber band, ones he had not shown Lara Sanderstone. One photograph was of a young boy, naked, posing suggestively with his buttocks to the camera, glancing back over his shoulder. He couldn't be certain, the boy was younger, but he'd bet his last nickel that he was looking at Lara Sanderstone's nephew. He'd found other photos as well, photos of children having sex with an adult male, his back to the camera. The man might even be Perkins himself. He shook his head and looked at the sky. He had started to tell her, but then decided against it. If the district attorney did prosecute the boy, these photos could be trump cards, and she was too close to the boy to play their hand. Judge or not, this was a criminal investigation and he was holding valuable evidence.

From the other photos he had found, along with this one, he assumed the boy had been exploited and more than likely sexually abused, how recently or to what extent he didn't know. But it was certainly a reason to kill someone, and it might not have been just his stepfather.

'Hey, Rickerson,' another officer yelled, sticking his head out the back door. 'Someone's on the phone for you. It's a reporter from the *Orange County Register*. Do you want to take the call or not?'

'I'll pass,' he said, lost in his thoughts. Reporters were a pain in the neck anyway. They were going to be crawling all over his ass on this one.

'What do you want me to tell them?'

'Tell them it's a black day, buddy. Their weather report was all wrong and I don't want to talk to them. The sun's out, but it's just not shining. Know what I mean?' He shoved the photos back in his pocket and returned to the task.

Chapter 9

Screeching into the parking lot and taking up two spaces, Lara rushed to the condo and threw open the door. Then she hurried to the bedroom. 'Are you all right?' she asked. 'I left you a note. I had to go out and take care of some things.'

Josh sat up in the bed, rubbing his eyes. They were swollen and red.

'How did you sleep?' She wanted to take that back. How did she expect him to sleep?

He glared at her. 'I slept.'

'Okay, this is the plan,' she said, trying to act like this was a normal day, a normal situation. 'You go for breakfast across the street at McDonald's and I'll take care of some things at my office. Get a pen and write down the number. If you need me, you can call me from the pay phone on the corner. I'll be home by lunchtime.' She tried not to let the strain show in her voice. It took a concentrated effort.

'I don't live here, remember?' he said sarcastically. 'I don't know where a pen is?'

'I left one in the kitchen. Forget it, I'll write it down for you.' She headed to the kitchen and then thought better of her plan. She needed to keep an eye on him. She went back to the bedroom. 'Listen, scratch that plan. You'll go with me to my office.'

'What for?'

'Don't worry about it. Take a shower now. I have some clean clothes.' Again she searched his face, his eyes.

'My clothes?' He was standing up by the bed now, holding the sheet around his waist. He must have been sleeping in his briefs. He wasn't wearing any other clothing.

'I went to the house and picked up some of your things.'

His eyes expanded. 'Did you get my bike?'

'No, I didn't. Take a shower.' They were a pair to draw to, as Pop would say. She wasn't very wordy herself. Even though she wanted to get to the bottom of this kid, she actually didn't mind his brevity. It made things easier right now.

She glanced at his sinewy chest. She'd have to get him a robe. This wasn't appropriate. He was too big to walk around half naked. She threw the handful of clothes at him, and he headed to the bathroom. She was thankful that at least there were two bathrooms. While he was showering, she ran to Emmet's and called Phillip.

'It was on the news last night. Everyone's been calling. The phone's been ringing off the wall ever since I walked through the door at seven-thirty. They all send their condolences.'

'Has Evergreen called?'

'Not yet. What can I do?'

'Call Evergreen. Explain to him what's happened and tell him that I'll need my calendar covered for at least three days, possibly five. They'll have to get someone in there today. Maybe a pro-tem.' A pro-tem was a local attorney willing to sit on the bench when the need arose. Since they had several judges out on vacation, it would be a mess. 'Do that first and I'll be there in about twenty minutes.'

Once she hung up, she turned to Emmet and let her shoulders fall. 'I can't talk now,' she told him. 'But I'll try to come by later this evening.'

'What . . . can . . . I do?' he said, his head rolling to one side in his wheelchair, gazing at her through his thick glasses.

'Just be my friend, Emmet. That's all anyone can do right now.'

She left him sitting there by the window and ran back to the condo. Josh was on the sofa, dressed and waiting. He was fast, she thought. It didn't take him an hour to take a shower and put on his clothes like a lot of people.

'Are you going to your court like that?' he asked her.

She looked down at her clothes and blanched. She was still wearing the sweatshirt and jeans. An unusual feeling filled her stomach, and she reached over and impulsively threw her arms awkwardly around Josh's neck. His body was stiff. 'That was nice that you mentioned that to me. I would have looked like a fool.' She stepped back and looked down at her feet. 'You should never let people see you when you aren't in control, not at your best. Not if you can help it. Do you know what I mean?'

'Yeah,' he said, a blank look on his face.

She went to the bedroom to get dressed. It took her only five minutes and she looked about the same as she did every day: a hint of lipstick, her hair tied back at the base of her neck in one of the identical black bows, a simple blouse and skirt, practical shoes. 'Better, huh?' she said, attempting a smile. It didn't work out well. The concrete of her face cracked only a hair.

'No,' he said. 'You look the same to me.' He raised his shoulders and then let them fall.

'Oh,' Lara said, thinking that he had expected her to walk out looking gorgeous, as his mother had when she was alive. It must be hard for him. There were resemblances, but not many. Ivory was lovely, almost glamorous without really trying. Even if her clothes weren't expensive, they were always colorful and flattering. Lara was pretty but plain, unnoticeable in a crowd. Her sister was always smiling and laughing, at least in the past, before Charley died and Sam Perkins took over her life.

She wasn't smiling now.

'We'll go through the drive-thru on the way to the office. McDonald's okay?'

He nodded. They left.

Returning to his home in San Clemente before his boys awoke, Rickerson dropped a sack on the kitchen counter and took out a loaf of bread, some lunch meat, a container of fresh orange juice, and a sack of apples that he had purchased on his way home. He threw open the freezer and removed some hamburger meat so it could thaw for dinner. Then he went to the sink and rinsed off a few dishes, placing them in the dishwasher. 'There,' he said, wiping his hands on a paper towel and looking around at the kitchen. He'd have to get one of the kids to mop the floor this week, but otherwise the place looked pretty good. Joyce had thought they would fall apart without her. They missed her, no doubt about it. But they were not about to fall apart. Not if he had anything to do with it.

Walking down the hall, he took his fist and banged one time on each boy's door. 'Time to get up,' he said. 'Rise and shine in there, guys.' Rushing back to the kitchen, he started a pot of coffee. Then he went to the laundry room and tossed a load of laundry in the washing machine.

His seventeen-year-old son, Stephen, stuck his head in the door, yawning. 'Got any clean underwear in here, Dad?'

Rickerson opened the dryer and yanked out a pair of Jockey shorts, tossing them to his son. 'Be sure to turn on both the dryer and the dishwasher when you get home today.'

'Sure,' he said. He was a tall, muscular redhead like his father. He was also an outstanding student, under consideration for a full scholarship at Stanford and a member of the varsity golf team at his high school. 'Hey, did you just get home or what?'

Rickerson leaned back against the dryer and rubbed the thick stubble on his chin. He was about to drop on his feet. 'Yep, you got it, bud. Caught a bad one yesterday. It's going to be rough sailing around here for a while.'

Stephen stepped into the doorway. 'How 'bout a clean shirt? Anything like that in there?'

Rickerson took the entire load of clothes out of the dryer and dumped it on the tile counter behind him. 'Be my guest. Looks like we mixed the whites again, kid. Got to be more careful in the future.'

Looking down at his underwear, Stephen started laughing. They were a pale shade of blue. Not only that, but everything else in the load of laundry was blue. His fourteen-year-old brother had washed his brand-new Levis with all their underwear. 'I kind of like it, you know. At least it's not pink like last time.' He started to walk away and then stuck his head back in the door again. 'Don't worry about anything, okay, Dad? I'll keep a lid on things around here for you.'

Rickerson smiled at his son. He loved this kid. Without him, he would have never made it after Joyce moved out. But together they were doing a pretty damn good job, if he did say so himself. 'I might not be home tonight. Just put that hamburger meat in the Hamburger Helper and read the instructions on the box. And make sure your brother does his homework.'

'No problem,' he said from the hall. 'If he doesn't, I'll kick his butt.'

Rickerson made his way down the hall to the master bedroom, his shoes clanking on the hardwood flooring. Sunlight was filtering in through the blinds, and the entire house had a warm yellow glow. He fell face first on the bed and then rolled over onto his back, staring at a streak of light and the minute dust particles dancing in the air. It wasn't such a bad house. It was small and it needed work, but for many years it had been a comfortable home. The kids had ridden their tricycles right outside on that sidewalk. They knew every single person on the block. They had watched the trees grow from tiny saplings to towering oaks.

But Joyce didn't want to live here anymore. She had said she wanted more from life. Evidently that meant more than he could give her. At first she'd insisted she only wanted a career, an education, and pleaded that if he could just bear with her until she graduated from Long Beach State with her degree in mechanical engineering, then they could start a new life. He didn't understand what was wrong with their old life. There, he thought, right there, that's where she had completely lost him. They'd raised two fine young sons. They owned their own home and had managed to save enough money for their children's education. He had his pension with the department, and when he retired, he could enter private security. They had planned their whole life from start to finish, and she had simply tossed it away.

'Dad,' Jimmy said from the doorway, 'can I talk to you a minute?'

Rickerson sat up and swung his feet to the floor. He wanted to light up a cigar, but he never smoked in the house. The boys hated it. 'Sure, guy. Come here. Have a seat. What's on your mind?'

'When is Mom coming home?'

Rickerson draped an arm around his younger son, and

they both leaned forward over their knees on the edge of the bed. Whereas Stephen looked like his father, Jimmy looked exactly like Joyce. He had her sandy blond hair, her full lips, her clear skin. And like Joyce, he had a tendency to put on weight. 'Jim-boy, I wish I could tell you, but I just can't.'

'But she's been gone three months now, and we never see her.'

'Well, she's in college and she's working hard. One of these days you'll be in college, and you'll see how hard it really is.'

'Is she ever coming back?'

Rickerson sighed. He asked himself the same question at least fifty times a day. 'I just don't know, son.'

'Are you going to get a divorce?'

About eighty percent of all the cops in the department were either divorced or remarried. Rickerson had always thought he would be different. His parents had been married for sixty years. In some ways he was old-fashioned. He thought marriage meant forever, thick or thin, rich or poor, until death – all that sappy stuff. 'Divorce? I-I don't think so, but we can't rule it out. Whatever your mother decides, we'll just have to accept. But look, if we do get a divorce, she's divorcing me. She's not divorcing you.'

His son cleared his throat and stood. 'I'm going to be late to school. Are you coming home tonight?'

'Maybe not for dinner, but I'll try to stop by before you go to bed.'

Jimmy stood there for a moment. He was a sensitive child. He had such a full face and soft, expressive eyes, it was almost a baby face. 'Be careful, Dad,' he said.

Rickerson stood and ruffled his hair. Then he pulled him roughly to his chest and hugged him. 'I'm always careful. Now get the hell out of here and let your old man get some sleep.'

He slept until about noon and then leaped out of bed when the alarm sounded. The house was quiet, the kids at school. He felt stiff as a board and ached like hell.

Years ago, he'd been writing a speeding ticket alongside the highway when a car came along and plowed into him, pinning him between the two vehicles and breaking his back and right leg. He could have retired on disability, but he had wanted to stay on. In retrospect, he considered it the worst mistake of his life. Now, no matter how much he complained, they'd never give him disability. He'd proven that he could work with the pain.

The number of homicides that occurred in San Clemente were nominal. This one, he thought, staggering to the bathroom, was surely going to kill him, both emotionally and physically. He hated to see women and children exploited. It did something to him, made him absolutely crazy. No matter how long he worked at the job, there were some things a person just couldn't stomach.

How many loans had that guy Perkins made anyway? Would there be thousands of tickets to dig through and try to track down? It would take them years to even make a dent. And now with the woman working the trade, turning tricks, and the implications of child pornography or sexual exploitation, the possibilities seemed endless. Judge Lara Sanderstone had demanded that every man in the department sink their teeth in this case, but that just wasn't going to happen. Someone had to cover the streets, the stolen cars, the drunk drivers, the injury accidents. The department wasn't that big, and this was a humongous case.

He stood under the shower, letting the hot water pound his aching back. All the bending and stooping last night and this morning had taken its toll, and it was only the beginning. By the time he waded through the pawnshop, he'd be hurting so bad that he would barely be able to stand upright.

After a short conversation with the medical examiner last night, they were both of the opinion that two separate killers could have been involved. It didn't make sense to bash in one person's head and not bash in the other's as well. Two distinct m.o.'s usually meant two killers. The manner in which a person committed a crime was almost as exclusive as their fingerprints.

It was simple, exactly like he'd told Lara Sanderstone. Kid came home from school, found the stepfather in the bedroom with his mother's body, and then smashed the fucking hell out of him with his twenty weight. He'd outright admitted that he hated the man, and it looked as though he had good reason.

Or, he thought, maybe after years of abuse Josh had simply gone over the edge and killed them both. All they had to do now was prove it, and once they did, the kid would probably get off with little more than a slap on the wrists and Rickerson would finally get his promotion to lieutenant.

There was no forced entry – another fact that pointed the finger at the boy. Even though Josh had said there was a hidden key, it was doubtful if they entered that way, using the key, killing the two people and then being cool enough to remember to put the key back exactly where they found it. If that was the case, he'd be dealing with a sophisticated killer, one he'd probably never catch, more than likely a person who did this type of thing for a living.

The biggest problem was the kid's clothes. Not a speck of blood on them. It was the first thing they'd checked. They'd torn the house apart and didn't find any blood-stained clothing. No one could beat someone as savagely as this man had been beaten and walk away without a speck of blood.

He grabbed the towel, wrapped it around him, and studied his image in the mirror. Seeing a blemish, he stood close and picked at it. Then he chastised himself. The dermatologist had told him years ago that the scars he had were from picking at his face. Old habits die hard, he thought. He smeared shaving cream on his face and started shaving.

Of course, the kid could have killed them and then buried or tossed the stained clothing somewhere before he called the cops at four o'clock that afternoon. They'd have to search the entire area on foot. Then they'd have to check with his school and determine if he was actually present in the last class of the day. Once they had the established time of death, they could start formally building the case. He needed help. He'd have to go to the chief today and get every possible body they could find.

They were wasting their time with the pawnshop. The boy had been exploited, sucked into the life-style of his mother and her new husband more than likely as a money-making proposition. Whether the boy was aware that they were selling his photographs or not was up for grabs, but Rickerson bet they were. With everyone cracking down on child pornography from local authorities to the feds, perversion of this type must have a high price tag.

They might have been selling more than just Josh's photographs. They could have been selling the boy himself.

Lara had Josh situated down the hall in the law library. She'd tossed a stack of magazines on the table and left him there. He'd talked her into ordering a Sausage McMuffin for breakfast, and it was burning a hole through her abdominal wall. Besides, she was running now on adrenaline: tense, shaky, but flying. And she was running on a razor-sharp edge of bitterness toward whoever had committed these heinous acts.

'Did you find Evergreen?' she asked Phillip. 'Is my calendar covered?'

'Finally,' the young man said, looking Lara in the eye. As soon as their eyes met, he pulled his away. 'He's sitting for you himself.'

In her chambers, she went over what she thought she wanted for the funeral with Phillip. 'Call the morgue and find out when they're going to release the body.' She gave him the name of the cemetery where she'd bought the other plots for Charley and their parents. 'Buy two cemetery plots instead of one.' She paused, sipping her coffee, scanning the spines of the books on the shelves in front of her, looking at anything but Phillip's face etched with sympathy and concern. This was so hard. He was staring at her and she felt like melting in an oily puddle all over the floor. Anything, she prayed, anything but tears. More tears she couldn't stand. The extra plot wasn't for Sam Perkins, it was for her. She didn't feel the need to explain that to Phillip, but she and Ivory would one day be side by side, next to Charley and their parents. Ivory would like that, just like she knew Ivory would like a white casket with brass fittings. She liked pretty things. 'I want a white casket with brass fittings. As long as it's under ten thousand, buy it. Do that and come back when you're finished.'

Lara bent down and was starting to make notes on a yellow pad when she noticed that Phillip was still standing in front of her desk, a strange expression on his face. 'Yes?' Lara said.

'I-I never realized you had a sister until the police called the day of the murders.'

'Well, we weren't very close. Not in recent years.'

'You look . . . I . . .' The young man's face turned parchment white. 'I'm sorry. I'll make those phone calls now.'

Before Lara could continue the conversation, Phillip

went out of the room and closed the door behind him. He was an extremely private person. Sometimes she wondered about him, about his social life. Today he looked awful, as if he were the one who had lost a loved one. Maybe he had, she thought, shaking her head. Possibly he had lost someone recently and had kept it to himself.

She had no earthly idea what she should do about Sam Perkins. Ivory had never mentioned family of any kind, but someone would probably come crawling out of the woodwork in the next day or two, thinking they would be inheriting a going business with the pawnshop. Thank God, she thought, she had insisted on her name on the title. Even if the business was shit, she'd have some means of covering her loss. She'd sell the damn building.

As to Sam, she'd just let him sit in a meat locker until some of his own clan claimed him. After what he'd done to Ivory, she gave thought to calling one of those cheap cremation places, where they charge only a few hundred bucks. If no one surfaced to claim him, she decided, he was on his way to the flames.

She went through the files on her desk and found those on the morning calendar were gone. Evergreen must have taken them. She wondered how long it had been since the old goat had handled the felony arraignment calendar. The position required some preparation but not much. Most of the day was consumed with the parties entering pleas, setting matters over for trial. The bail reviews required some judicial renderings, and she always read the reports generated by the probation department outlining the defendant's criminal history, if any, and at least scanned the police reports on the crime. Releasing someone into the community was a significant decision. Not only did a judge have to weigh the factors indicating whether or not the defendant would flee, but they had to determine the risk of recidivism. And the victim's safety had to be considered. In violent offenses this was particularly germane. Sometimes while suspects were pending prosecution, they went back and finished the job, actually killing someone. Lara made every attempt to keep violent or sex offenders in custody pending trial, even if she had to put her neck on the line to do it.

Most of the cases scheduled for that day she had already reviewed. She took out each file scheduled for the afternoon session and made detailed notes to Evergreen. Then she called Phillip and had him carry them to the court.

Alone in her chambers, she relished the cloistered privilege of her position. No one walked in unannounced except other judges, sometimes a D.A. Today, of all days, this mattered. She glanced at the lights on the phones and saw they were all blinking. The bell was turned off in her chambers. When Phillip was busy, the main reception center picked up the excess calls. In her hands were at least twenty pink message slips. She shuffled through them.

Irene had returned her call from the night before. She'd obviously heard the news by now. Lara tossed that slip in the trash, thinking she'd call her tonight or try to catch her in recess before she left the building.

Most of the other callers were condolences and offers to help. Benjamin had called and left a number at a hotel in San Francisco. She placed that one in her purse. The others she read, committed the names to memory, those who had taken the time to call, and then tossed them too. Nolan had called. Probably because she made the papers. Press. He loved it. If she'd thought of that aspect, he might have actually come last night. He liked that kind of thing. It was Hollywood, right up his alley. His message she didn't simply toss. She took the time to rip it up. It made her feel better.

She hit the intercom and Phillip answered. 'I'm

speaking with the funeral home now. They're on hold. The casket's going to run at least fifteen thousand or it won't be waterproof.'

She'd been through this before. She'd buried her father and mother. She had made all the arrangements when Charley was killed. She knew all the scams and sales techniques in the most unscrupulous industry in the universe. 'Tell the guy I don't care if it's watertight. She's dead. She can't drown. Ten thousand and not a penny more.'

'Fine,' he said. 'Anything else?'

'No,' she said, the word barely audible.

As soon as the light went off, Lara called Phillip back on the intercom and asked him to send for the Henderson file. She wanted him to give Rickerson the name and address of the boyfriend who had threatened her, let him track the kid down, find out where he was yesterday. She had to put some of this fear to rest or she would lose her mind, and she wanted to move out of the condo and back into the house. She couldn't spend that many more nights on that sofa.

Her mind kept returning to Ivory and the photos she'd seen. What her poor sister had been made to do. She couldn't bear to think of it. Sam must have coerced her into prostituting herself just as he coerced her into asking Lara for money. She felt like taking a match and cremating the bastard herself.

It was the only explanation, she told herself. Ivory certainly didn't think this one up by herself. It had slimy Sam stamped all over it. Of course, even before she'd met Sam, Ivory had been drinking and experimenting with cocaine. 'It makes me feel so good,' she had told Lara. 'It makes me feel smart and confident. I've never felt that way in my whole life.' Maybe having men pay her for sex made Ivory feel powerful and confident too. Possibly she actually enjoyed whipping them and degrading them.

Lara felt like taking every single paper and file off her desk and hurling it at the wall. Why hadn't she seen it? Why hadn't she stopped it? She was her sister and she was a goddamn judge. Wasn't she supposed to be intuitive and observant? Hadn't she seen what was happening to her own flesh and blood? The night Ivory had come to her house, she was dressed like a streetwalker.

Lara suddenly found herself gulping air. Quickly she spun her chair around to face her great-grandfather's portrait. When she was little, her grandfather used to come and visit and tell her stories about the past, about her ancestors. Not from history books had she learned how white men had taken away their precious land and moved them to reservations. She had learned these things as a tiny child sitting at her grandfather's feet, listening to him drone on and on in his deep voice, her eyes locked on his leathery skin. The one thing she had learned early in life was that a person sometimes had to accept the unacceptable.

It was time to get Josh and leave before people started trying to get in to see her and shower her with sympathy. Besides, she had to get him to a psychologist and start checking into schools. If he hadn't killed Sam, or anyone else, he was going to need therapy to get through this. If he had to live with her, which she was fairly certain was going to be the case, then he'd probably need a shrink until she packed him off to college. She didn't know if she had what it took to raise a teenager. It was going to be a long, long haul.

Then a thought flashed in her mind: boarding school. Perfect. She didn't know why she hadn't thought of it before. Not now, she thought, passing Phillip, still on the phone, and heading down the carpeted corridor to the law library, but soon. As soon as the psychologist thought he was ready. At least with this thought in mind, she could see an end in sight. She doubted if he wanted to be with her anyway.

'Let's go, Josh,' she said softly. He wasn't reading magazines. He was just sitting there staring into space.

Under the right circumstances, he might even be a nice companion, Lara thought as they headed down the hall. What he needed was stability, structure. He needed hot meals on the table, someone waiting when he got home from school, someone to wash and iron his clothes. Lara just didn't have the time, and unfortunately, she didn't have the inclination. What did she possibly know about raising a teenage boy? Nothing, absolutely nothing.

Again her eyes drifted to the shaggy-haired young man walking next to her. He didn't cry, he didn't complain much, he didn't say much. He seemed to like junk food. If she could find a man like him, she might consider getting married again.

They entered the security level, and he pushed the button for the garage. 'What're we going to do now?' he said.

'We're going to go home and arrange for you to see a doctor, a psychologist. Someone you can talk to. And I'm going to stop off and buy a portable cellular phone.'

'No way,' he said, his face frozen into hard lines. 'I'm not going to some crazy person's doctor.'

Lara was five-three in her stocking feet. She never wore heels. Josh was looking down on her inside the small space of the elevator. 'Well, you have to go,' she told him. 'I'm not that good a listener. You need to talk this out. Who knows, maybe I do too. Maybe we'll both go.' It was a tactic. She could see immediately that it wasn't going to work.

'You're not going,' he snapped. 'You're just saying that to get me to go. Right?'

'Right. Pretty astute there, kid,' she said and brought forth a weak smile. 'But I might, let me tell you.' The elevator doors opened and they headed to her car.

'Can I drive?' he asked, his voice echoing in the

underground garage. 'I can drive, you know. Sometimes Mom lets me drive to the store and back for things like milk.'

Both of them froze. He'd used the present tense. These were the kinds of things that took getting used to. They were like nails in a coffin. They just kept on pounding at you long after the person was gone. She knew. He started sniffing and breathing heavy. Lara didn't know what to do or say, but she couldn't let him continue. If the boy broke down, she'd break down with him. She handed him the car keys. 'Drive.' Then she narrowed her eyes and peered up at him. 'Were you telling me the truth? You really know how to drive a car? If you don't, we'll get killed.'

For the first time she saw her sister's son smile. She felt like she'd won a Nobel prize. It didn't really matter if they got killed, she thought. What mattered was that he smiled.

They went careening out of the underground parking tunnel, barely missing the concrete wall. Lara almost wet her pants, but she didn't. Instead she checked her seat belt and gripped the dashboard, preparing herself for the impact – if not the wall, the way he was driving, they were going to hit something. And they were going to hit it with the most extravagant possession Lara had: the Jaguar, her pride and joy. The smile on Josh's face was enormous. He was sitting up close to the steering wheel and licking his lips with excitement.

'A Jaguar . . . I can't believe I'm driving a Jaguar. Man, wait till my friends hear about this. How much does a car like this cost?'

So what if he bashed in the Jaguar? Lara thought. She was insured, maybe not for an unlicensed driver, but right now she didn't care. It was only a car, an expensive collection of metal and glass and chrome. And sometimes rules had to be broken, exceptions made. Just keep smiling, she said to herself, glancing at him. Just keep smiling, kid, and we'll get through this and make our way to the other side.

Chapter 10

About two blocks from the government center, Lara asked Josh to pull to the side of the road and let her drive. He'd run a red light and almost had a head-on collision.

'Why are you living in that place?' he asked her. 'There's nothing in there at all. I thought you had a house or something.'

'I do,' Lara said. She certainly didn't want to scare the kid to death, tell him someone might be stalking her after what he'd been through. She cleared her throat, preparing herself to lie. 'See, Josh, they're doing some remodeling at my house, so I rented the condo. It was close to the court.'

He was silent. That took care of that. The car phone rang and she let Josh answer it. It was Rickerson. He handed her the phone.

'Thought I would just touch base with you. We're going through the pawnshop tickets now. Then we're going to start on his books.'

She wanted to ask about the autopsy, find out if it had been completed yet and the findings, but it wasn't the type of thing to discuss in front of Josh. 'Call me later this evening when you've talked to the M.E. What about prints?' Josh wasn't paying attention anyway. He was staring out the window. The smile had been a momentary thing.

'Lab's working on it as we speak. We lifted all kinds of prints, but who knows who they belong to . . . I wanted to point something else out to you. There was no forced entry, remember? That means that either the killer or killers were inside the house to begin with, or they were known to the victims and were allowed to enter. Don't you think that rules out someone Perkins made a loan to here at the pawnshop? Just doesn't make sense that they'd open the door to someone like that and let them walk right into their house.'

'Look, Rickerson, Ted . . . you already told me that last night. Aren't you the man who informed me that we had to cover all the bases? I want every single pawn ticket checked out.'

'There's got to be at least a thousand of these tickets. Some of them go back a number of years. We're only going to follow through on the ones going back six months or so, or we'll be here digging through this shit forever. And we're in the process of tracking down all the phone records.'

Lara glanced at Josh and gripped the phone, steering the car with her other hand. 'Well, then I guess you'll be busy. Don't you agree that we should pursue this at least? The pawnshop.'

'Lara,' he answered, a touch of sarcasm in his husky voice, 'you seem to think there are hundreds of officers available to sift through this stuff. There's three of us right now. I'm trying to round up more men, but we can't produce what we just don't have. If we get another serious case in this city, there'll be two of us, and then as time goes on, there'll only be me. We also have to get over to the house again and comb the neighborhood looking for evidence the killer could have discarded, like bloody clothes – '

'Tell you what. You have someone box up the pawn tickets and bring them to my condo. I'll personally start going through them in the next few days, and your people can work on the phone records. Let's trace every call from that house and give me a list of the names after you run them through the system for wants and warrants.'

Josh was tugging on her sleeve. 'Ask them to bring my bike, okay?'

She looked at him and felt her heart melt. All he had of his old life right now was a few clothes. His parents were dead, his home was a shambles, and he was stuck with a woman he hardly knew. 'Forget that, Rickerson. I'll come and get the pawn tickets myself. But do me a favor, okay? Go to the house and get the kid's bike and meet me at the pawnshop in San Clemente. I'll be there in about forty minutes.'

She could hear Rickerson breathing. He didn't answer. The breathing was loud. She started to hang up when he finally spoke. 'I can't release evidence in a homicide.'

'Let's set things straight right now, Rickerson. I more or less own the pawnshop. My name's right on the deed of trust. I provided the funding for them to buy it. You've got to make a decision here. Are those pawn tickets valuable evidence or merely pawn tickets? You seem to think they're merely pawn tickets and that the whole thing is a waste of time. I'm offering to give you a hand.'

'I'll get the bike,' he said. 'And Lara, let me tell you something, you need to get that boy to a shrink right away. Don't wait. I'm telling you. That boy needs treatment.'

Lara glanced at Josh again. At least the detective had expressed a genuine concern. She appreciated that. 'Oh,' she said, 'did Phillip call you with the information on the Henderson case? . . . You know, what we discussed last night?'

'Yeah,' he said. 'I've got a man trying to track him down

now. Once we find him, I'll interview him.' With that, he hung up.

Rickerson was right. She'd have to find a psychologist for Josh today. She slipped onto the freeway and, for the third time in less than two days, headed to San Clemente. She wondered about Josh's friends, his school work, re-establishing his life, but it was too early for that. Now they had to tread water and deal with the sorrow, the funeral, the black days ahead of them – days Lara knew would get worse before they got better. The awful truth that his mother had been murdered would start to sink all the way to the bone soon enough. Lara already felt it coming. Her own subconscious was packed with reality as sharp as a machete, about to slice its way into her every thought and cut her heart into ribbons.

'Isn't that the exit to San Clemente?' Josh said, looking out the window. 'You just passed it.'

'Oh,' Lara said, lost in her thoughts. 'I'll take the next exit.'

'You're going to miss this exit too,' Josh said, all excited. 'Hurry, get in the right-hand lane.'

They were soon on the city streets, approaching the pawnshop. Lara felt tears gathering in her eyes and bit the inside of her mouth. If a person could only rewrite history knowing what was ahead, more or less stop the wheels of life from turning the wrong way. But of course, that wasn't reality. A child with no parents, she thought, glancing at Josh, Ivory's body in a tiled autopsy room – that was reality.

First they lugged the two huge boxes to the condo filled with records from the pawnshop, and then Lara sent Josh back down to bring his bike up from the trunk of the car. Lara took out the portable phone she had purchased and called Irene Murdock. She caught her in recess.

'Lara, darling,' Irene said, 'I've been frantic. I've been

calling your house since I heard this on the news. Are you all right? Your sister and brother-in-law. How horrid.'

'I guess you've heard it all by now,' Lara said, collapsing on the sofa.

'Well, I don't know if I've heard it all. I've heard what's been on the news. What do they have? Do they know who did this despicable thing? Do they have any witnesses, leads?'

'No,' Lara said. 'They have next to nothing.' She then gave her the cellular phone number and told her why she wasn't staying at her own house. 'What do you think, Irene? Tell me the truth. Do you think I'm in danger, that these crimes are related? Could it be the young man who threatened me?' Lara got the words out of her mouth just as Josh returned.

'Obviously, it doesn't sound good. Did you know that a man once stalked me? It was about five years ago. I had sentenced him to prison on an armed robbery. When he got out, he followed me home from the courthouse and parked outside my house. It was terrible. By the time the police unit would get there, he would flee. We finally got a restraining order. Then we had to wait for him to violate it. Eventually he ended up back in prison, but it was an agonizing ordeal. After that I bought a gun. I carry it in my purse everywhere I go now.'

'I didn't know that, Irene,' Lara said, and she really didn't want to know it either. Sometimes a person just wanted to pretend everything was all right even when it wasn't. 'So, you don't think I should go back to my house?'

'No, certainly not,' she said. 'Where are you now? You said you're staying in Santa Ana in a condo? Possibly John and I can come by tonight. Why don't you give me the address?'

'No,' Lara said quickly, 'but thanks.' She looked around and saw Josh standing there, practically breathing down her neck. 'Tell you what, Irene, I'll call you back later. I have my nephew here now. I can't really talk.'

'If we don't come over tonight, we'll come over tomorrow. I'll bring you some food – some things you can heat in the microwave. That poor child. This is just so terribly sad.'

'I'll let you know. Hold on.' Lara turned to Josh and asked him if he could step into the other room a minute so she could talk to Irene privately. Once he was in the bedroom with the door closed, Lara carried the portable phone to the kitchen and whispered, 'I need a good psychologist for my nephew. Maybe John can recommend someone?'

'I know someone myself. Wait a minute . . . I have his number right here in my Rolodex. He's a psychiatrist. That would be better, don't you think? They can prescribe medication. His name is Dr. Frederick Werner.' She rattled off the number.

'You know, Irene,' Lara said, cupping her hand over the phone and peeking around the corner to make certain Josh was still in the bedroom, 'I'm at a loss with this kid. He's bitter. He's obviously disturbed. There might even be a slim chance that he was involved in this nightmare.'

'What do you mean? Did he see the killer? Was he an eyewitness?'

'No, I . . .' Lara paused and inhaled. 'Maybe he killed my brother-in-law. It's possible. He was killed with a dumbbell and it was Josh's dumbbell. There was no love there, let me tell you.'

Irene didn't answer. At first Lara thought they had been disconnected. 'Did you hear me?' she said.

'Put that out of your mind, Lara. That's a terrible thought. Just get him to a psychiatrist and pursue this boy who threatened you. Call me later and we'll talk in greater detail.'

Lara was about to tell her about Ivory's occupation and the awful things they'd found in the crawl space when Irene said she had to return to the bench. Just as well, Lara thought. She didn't really want anyone to know.

Josh's bike was leaning against the door in the entryway. With the boxes and now the bike, the condo was beginning to feel no larger than a walk-in closet. She quickly contacted the psychiatrist and arranged for him to see Josh at six o'clock that evening. Then she clicked off the phone and leaned back on the sofa with her eyes closed. She might really have to do what she told Josh and see this man herself, she thought, maybe get some sedatives so she could sleep.

She opened her eyes and looked at the boxes. It would take her forever to go through all those pawn tickets. Not only that, but she had no idea what she was looking for. Even if the poor kid hadn't killed them, he might know a lot more than he was telling. There was only one way to find out. Start asking.

'Josh,' she said, having told him to come out of the bedroom, 'come here and sit down on the sofa with me.' She patted a place next to her. 'Let's have a little talk. There's the sodas we bought in the refrigerator and some chocolate chip cookies on the counter. Why don't you get them?'

It was almost lunchtime. Cookies and Coke would have to do. Tonight she'd try to find him something halfway healthy. Maybe she'd buy a roast chicken from the deli department at the supermarket before they went to see Dr. Werner. If the poor child had not shared her affinity for junk food, he would be starving to death. At least she didn't have to worry about malnutrition yet. Not for a few days anyway.

They were sitting side by side on the sofa munching cookies and sipping soda from cans. They weren't looking at each other. Finally Josh said, 'What do you want to talk about?'

Lara sighed, a long one. 'What were things like at home?'

'What do you mean?' He set the sack of cookies aside and brushed his hair out of his eyes.

'What were things like with your mom and Sam? Were they fighting? Was he drinking? Was your mother drinking?'

'Dunno.' His back became rigid and he stared straight ahead.

Lara touched his arm and he looked at her. 'It isn't going to work this way, Josh. You lived in that house. You're a smart boy. You would have known if they were drinking or fighting.'

He was silent and unresponsive. She could almost see the memories flashing in his eyes. They weren't happy ones. That Lara knew for sure.

'Please, Josh, for your mother's sake, you have to help us. You were there yesterday. You saw what happened, what someone did in that house. I know you want them to pay as much as I do, as much as we all do.'

'Sam was a bastard.'

'You're not going to get an argument from me on that one. Go on . . . there has to be more than that.'

Lara had not opened the drapes in the condo and it was dark. Some light was filtering through from the small kitchen window behind them, but their faces were bathed in shadows. She started to get up and open the drapes and then thought better of it. Somehow it seemed to work better for both of them to discuss this in the shadows.

'Sam drank at least a six-pack of beer every night. He'd get drunk and then start fights with us – Mom and me. They had fights over money, things like that. Sometimes Mom would tell me to go out somewhere on my bike.

Then when I came back home, they'd be in the bedroom with the door closed. The next day they'd be fine.'

'Josh, did Sam ever hit your mother? Did you ever see him hitting her or hurting her in any way? Did anyone else ever come over to the house? You know, strange men. Think hard. Anyone you didn't know?'

He looked sharply at Lara. 'I don't remember, okay? Everyone keeps asking me all these questions, and I just don't remember.' He stood and looked at his bike by the door. 'I don't want to talk about this anymore. Can I go out on my bike?' His face was set, his lips compressed. She'd touched a nerve.

'Wait just a minute and then you can go out. I'm not going to hold you prisoner here.' She paused. She'd have to let him out of the house. They'd go crazy for sure if they just sat hour after hour inside this dark hovel. Hopefully, if someone was out to harm her, they didn't know about Josh or where they were staying. He was several feet away, standing by the door, his hands on the bike.

No wonder he wanted that bike, Lara thought. It had been his only escape mechanism. When things got tough, he took off. Things were getting tough now. She spoke in a calm, matter-of-fact voice, not wanting to emphasize her words. 'Did you ever see anything that you didn't understand? Maybe something relating to your mother?' The images from this morning flashed in her mind. Her eyes quickly returned to Josh when she heard the door open and saw him pushing the ten-speed out the door onto the sidewalk.

'Josh, wait,' Lara said, heading to the front door. 'Stay right in this little area here by the condo. I don't want you wandering off. And you have to help us, tell us everything you saw or heard.'

He turned around and stared at her, his gaze intense, his eyes blazing with hatred. 'You're a fucking bitch,' he yelled. 'Now you're all concerned about my mom . . . about me. Now that she's dead. You never gave a shit about us when she was alive. I'd rather go to juvenile hall than stay here with you.'

Lara took a few tentative steps toward him. 'You're wrong, Josh. I always cared about you, about your mother.'

'Yeah, sure,' he said, flipping his head back to get his hair out of his eyes. His voice went up several octaves. It was almost the little boy voice before going through puberty. His face twisted up like he was trying to keep from crying. 'You used to come and see me, take me to the movies, buy me things. Then you just stopped coming . . . like we weren't good enough for you. We were just trash to you. You – '

His words stung. 'Josh,' Lara pleaded, 'listen to me. Your mother wouldn't let me see you. It wasn't that I didn't want to . . . She got angry with me . . . It was her way to get back.'

Glaring at her, he jumped on the seat and pedaled away, slamming the door to the condo behind him.

Lara went back to the sofa and sat there in the dark, leaning over onto her knees, her head in her hands. She'd had no idea that those earlier visits had actually meant something to Josh, that he'd missed her, even thought she'd abandoned him. He'd been a skinny, aloof twelve-year-old then. She'd always assumed he was bored silly on their little outings. She was wrong. He was bitter. Bitter at Lara, his mother and stepfather, the miserable world in general. Just how bitter she couldn't judge. Hopefully, she prayed, not bitter enough to become a killer.

For a long time she just sat there in the dark. She tried to think. She tried to rationalize. Her mind was so muddled that her thoughts were racing in a million different directions at once. She finally stood and went to the bathroom, thinking she'd take a shower, hoping it would help. Tossing the bedspread back on the bed, she saw something sticking out from under the mattress. She bent down and pulled it out. It was a backpack. She vaguely recalled Josh walking in with it last night. Starting to drop it back where she found it, she instead dropped to the edge of the bed and began rummaging through the contents. There were three textbooks, some notebook paper, a few pens. She took them all out and placed them on the bed. Then she saw it.

In her hands was a rolled-up T-shirt that had been shoved in the bottom of the backpack. On the T-shirt was blood.

Still holding it in her hand, she ran to the front door and flung it open. Why, she didn't know. Then she slammed it and went into the bathroom, sitting down on the toilet seat and staring at it. 'No, God,' she cried. 'It can't be. It just can't be.' She was shaking; her heart was pounding. Her palms were sweaty and she felt cold, really cold. She spread the T-shirt open all the way and tried to estimate how much blood there was. It wasn't much, just a long red streak. For a second she thought it might be paint. She held it to her nose and sniffed it. Then she tried to flick some of it off with her fingernails. It wasn't paint. It was blood.

She walked out of the bathroom and started pacing inside the bedroom. She felt like she was walking upside down. The room kept spinning and moving. Visions of Josh bringing the dumbbell down on Sam's head kept flashing in her mind. What was she going to do? She couldn't turn her own nephew over to the police, yet she couldn't allow him to get away with murder. No matter who Sam was, or what he had done, he was a human being. There was no way to reconcile herself to murder.

She thought of all the possible reasons for the bloody T-shirt. He could have fallen off his bicycle. That made sense. It could even be an animal's blood, like a dog's or a cat's. A lot of teenagers were into Satanism and cutting up cats. Suddenly a thought came to mind and she grabbed the textbooks, quickly reading the spines and then tossing them back into the backpack. Maybe he took biology, she thought, and he had dissected a frog. There was no biology textbook.

She was completely panicked.

Glancing at the door, she realized he could walk in at any moment. If he saw her with the T-shirt, he could even kill her. He was big enough. He could beat her to death, strangle her, suffocate her like Ivory. Terrified, she rolled up the T-shirt as she had found it and replaced all the items back in the backpack.

The phone rang and Rickerson started speaking. She'd left her new number with the switchboard operator at the San Clemente P.D.

'The S.O. just called and they lifted a few sets of prints from your house in Irvine. One set we can't match yet, probably one of your friends, but the others come back to a lowlife hoodlum by the name of Packy Cummings. He's got a record a mile long and even did a stint at San Quentin. He's been listed as a suspect on several homicides in the past. He's a bad actor, Lara. We're trying to pick him up now. No prints at the murder scene, though. They must have worn gloves.'

Lara's breath caught in her throat and she couldn't speak. She hadn't heard half of what the detective had said. She couldn't tell him about what she had found. She wanted to, but she just couldn't. Not until she was sure. She owed her sister at least that much. They'd drag the poor kid back down to the station and give him the third-degree; the press could even get wind of it and Josh would be tried and convicted even if it turned out to be nothing. Lara knew too well how these things happened. Once they accused a person in print, even after a full trial and acquittal, the rumors and innuendos sometimes persisted for the rest of their lives. 'I . . . I'm sorry,' she said, 'repeat what you just said.'

He did. She listened and then something seized her. The name Packy Cummings. 'Wait, Rickerson, don't hang up. What's his full name? Is it Packard Cummings?'

'Yeah,' he said. 'You know the guy?' Rickerson was a little shocked on that one, unless she knew him from the courts. He sure hoped he wasn't one of her boyfriends. That would be downright absurd.

'He was on my calendar . . . I think it was the day before Ivory was murdered. He's an informant on a narcotics case working with a local agency. I don't know which one, but I can find out.' Lara had all these crazy thoughts in her mind right now, like maybe they had somehow confused her house with that of a drug dealer's. The investigating officer had said it appeared they were looking for drugs. Things like that did happen. Several times the LAPD had gone out with their battering ram, a big tank, and destroyed an innocent person's house.

'Nah,' Rickerson said finally, 'this guy isn't working for anyone inside the law. One of the people he was suspected of knocking off about seven years ago was an undercover cop. They'd be out of their minds. Who told you that?'

'Leo Evergreen. You know who Evergreen is, don't you? He's the presiding judge.'

The line was silent. Rickerson was thinking. The sheriff's department had called him about this guy. They knew nothing about him. A drug case, of course, could mean the DEA or some other agency, but to use a man like this as an informant? Not unless he could help bust the Colombian drug cartel or something. Even if the man had been working as an informant, what was he doing breaking into houses?

Rickerson could smell something, and it was as rotten and foul as they came.

'I'll have to make some phone calls and get back to you.'

'Look,' she said, 'why don't I just call Evergreen and ask him which agency the man is working for? They called him and asked him to release Cummings O.R. as a professional courtesy. I didn't want to do it, but he pressed. It could be a mistake, you know. Some type of crazy mistake.'

Again Rickerson was quiet, reviewing things in his head. Judge releases a guy O.R. one day and the next day he pays her back by ransacking her house. Didn't make sense. 'Lara, I don't like the way this thing is stacking up. Not one little bit. I'm sending my man back over there to watch your place, and believe me, I wouldn't do it if I didn't feel you were in danger. The chief's gonna have a fit when he finds out. We need every warm body to work this case, not sit around in a parking lot.'

'What about Evergreen?' She looked at the door, thinking Josh would come back any minute, truly frightened now. She'd released this man. This man who had broken into her home. And her own nephew had a bloody T-shirt hidden in his backpack. What else could possibly happen? She was beside herself now. She wanted to throw herself on the floor and scream. 'Look,' she told him, talking fast, 'I don't really care who broke into my house. What I care about is who killed my sister.'

'If they are one and the same, then . . .'

Right now she prayed that they were one and the same. Anything or anyone but Josh. 'Is that possible? You know, that this Cummings man is the murderer?'

'Anything is possible,' he said. 'Keep this to yourself until I get back to you. Don't tell anyone anything. You know, even at the top, things get around. Let's just keep a lid on this until I check some things out. And listen, Lara, I had to call Social Services. They'll probably be contacting you about the kid today.'

'Ted, tell me something. When you picked up Josh from

the neighbors' house the night of the murder, was he carrying anything?'

'I don't recall. Another unit drove him down to the station. Why do you ask?'

'Forget it,' Lara said quickly. Rickerson hung up and she just sat there, listening to the dial tone. Surely the police would have searched his backpack looking for evidence. But then they might not have considered him a valid suspect at the time, and with all the confusion, searching his backpack might have slipped by them.

She'd let them take him, she decided. Then she wouldn't have to deal with him. In a way, she was relieved. Her breath was starting to come slower. If additional evidence surfaced that Josh was involved, then she'd come forward with the T-shirt.

Social Services would have to come out anyway, check out her place, make certain it was appropriate for Josh. It wasn't. She knew the rules. She had to have a bedroom for him. She didn't. Not unless she returned to her house in Irvine, which everyone was advising her not to do. And obviously, living with someone whose life could be in danger was not an appropriate placement for a child.

Of course, she thought, she could be in danger from Josh himself.

Then she thought of the Adams case set to open trial the next week. The entire Social Services department was in an uproar over it. The case was extremely controversial and had attracted extensive coverage by the media. It was a felony assault, with a G.B.I. enhancement, for great bodily injury. Victor Adams was a young white-collar professional, an Orange County yuppie, employed at McDonald Douglas as a high-level aerospace engineer. He was the father of two beautiful little girls. The victim was a female social worker. According to the police reports, the Social Services Agency had received information from the school psychologist that one of the little girls had been sexually abused by the father. On the basis of this information, the county authorities had obtained a court order and removed the minor children from the home, placing them in two separate foster homes while charges were being prepared against the father. The abuse turned out to be totally unfounded, but the family was destroyed. The defendant lost his job, his wife suffered a nervous breakdown, they lost their home, and the minor children spent six traumatic months separated from their parents, only able to see their mother during a weekly visitation.

The irony and tragedy in the case was the fact that the younger child, a five-year-old girl, was actually sexually assaulted while in foster care by an older teenage boy residing in the same foster home. On hearing this information, the father went crazy and chased the social worker to her car, punched out the window with his fist, spraying her with glass and causing severe lacerations to her face and neck. The entire case was a tragedy, a mockery of the system. The father had been wronged, the social worker who was only doing her job scarred for life, the children made to suffer, and the family destroyed. The clincher was the fact that the exact crime that was to be prevented had occurred. Sad case. Extremely interesting both legally and morally.

Lara deflated, letting her body compress on the sofa, sink lower and lower, like gravity was pulling her down. If the blood on the T-shirt was nothing – a spill from his bike or whatever – Josh would never forgive her for abandoning him again. But if Social Services took him on their own, then he couldn't blame her. She decided to wait it out.

She was vacillating.

If they did remove her sister's son and place him in a foster home, she thought, leaning in the opposite direction now, even more psychological damage might be inflicted on the boy. She just couldn't let it happen without at least trying to make it work. He might resent her, she thought, sniffing, holding back the tears, but all they had to call family was each other. And if there was any suspicion that he was involved, the way to find out would be to spend time with him, watch him, not send him away somewhere. She just couldn't wash her hands of him, no matter how much she wanted to.

The first thing she had to do was find out whose blood was on that T-shirt.

Chapter 11

Dr. Frederick Werner's offices were only a few miles down the road in neighboring Costa Mesa. As Lara steered the Jaguar into the parking lot of a large medical tower with tinted glass windows, she turned to Josh, who was silent and withdrawn. They'd had another battle. He had stayed out past dark on his bike and Lara had panicked. Then when she'd told him about the appointment and he had pitched a fit, she had taken his bike and locked it in the trunk of her car. He hadn't spoken a word since.

'This is it, Josh,' she said, cutting the ignition and placing her hands in her lap. She wanted desperately to ask him about the T-shirt, but now was not the time. 'If you don't like this doctor, we'll get another one. But let's give him a chance, okay?'

Werner's office was on the tenth floor. From all appearances, the majority of the people employed in the building had already left for the day, and the enormous skyscraper was eerily empty. They were late. Lara glanced at her watch and hoped the psychiatrist hadn't given up and gone home. Josh was standing on the far side of the elevator, as far from Lara as he could get, staring at the control panel. If he'd been eight or ten years old, she might have had some clue how to treat him, but with a teenager she was completely lost. She couldn't spank him and send him to his room when he refused to obey her. All she could do was take his one possession away – his bike.

'I didn't mean that about your bike,' she said just as the doors opened. 'You can still ride it and all. But you stayed out too long, Josh, and you simply must see a counselor.'

Six other physicians were listed on the door along with Werner. Lara stood at the reception desk and looked around, but there was no one in sight, just a labyrinth of halls and doors. Finally she yelled, 'Hey, is anyone in here?'

From the back she heard a chair squeak on plastic, and a tall, handsome man in his late thirties or early forties came out and extended his hand. 'I'm Dr. Werner. You must be Judge Sanderstone and this is Josh.' He shook Lara's hand. His hand was cold and soft like a woman's. He tried to shake Josh's hand, but the boy wouldn't even look at him. 'Come with me. We'll talk in here.'

His office was quite elaborate, with a comfortable pale blue leather sectional with a sort of metallic sheen, a glass-topped coffee table in the center, and real art on the walls. Lara didn't ask about his fees, but she could well imagine. She looked for a desk and didn't see one. This room must be his session room. There were a few certificates on the walls. Lara walked over to gaze at them. Josh just stood there, refusing to sit down.

She took a seat and brushed an unruly strand of hair off her forehead, feeling the urge to excuse herself and slip into the ladies' room to put on some lipstick or some blush, maybe comb her hair.

'Uh, thank you for seeing us, Dr. Werner,' Lara said. 'Josh, as you can see, is not too happy about this, but he's been through a terrible ordeal.' She looked knowingly at the psychiatrist.

'I see,' Werner said slowly. 'Why don't you let me speak with your aunt, Josh, for a few moments? There's some magazines in the reception area and some fruit juice. We'll come and get you in a few moments.'

Josh looked relieved as he exited the room, almost slamming the door behind him. Lara sat nervously under Werner's penetrating gaze and crossed and uncrossed her legs.

'I'm somewhat aware of what this situation involves. I've seen the papers, and Judge Murdock called me this afternoon. In case she didn't tell you, we're neighbors. I know both Irene and her husband. Why don't you give me a rundown?'

Lara started speaking, tentatively at first, and then she couldn't seem to stop. She told Werner about her relationship with Ivory, the night she'd come to her apartment, the break-in at her place. Basically, the whole sordid mess. Dr. Werner sat attentively, nodding his head off and on. Whatever kind of demeanor psychiatrists affect to get people to talk, this man obviously had down pat. Lara had just spilled her guts and probably consumed most of the hour. Finally she stopped herself.

'I'm sorry . . .' she said, embarrassed. 'It's Josh you should be talking to now. I'll go get him.' She stood and headed for the door and then stopped. The real issue was trapped in her throat. She had to tell someone. 'Dr. Werner, there is a slight – very slight – possibility that Josh could have played some part in my sister's and brother-in-law's death. I know this sounds awful for me to even mention something like this, but – '

'That's fine, Lara,' he said. 'May I call you Lara?' She nodded, and he continued. 'From what I can see, you have a lot of unresolved conflicts regarding your sister and the circumstances surrounding her death. You're harboring a great deal of guilt and maybe even demonstrating a little paranoia.' When Lara blanched, he quickly added, 'It's all perfectly normal. When someone close to you is violently murdered, it's easy to become fearful and confused. I would like to see you again, not just your nephew.'

'Dr. Werner,' she said curtly, 'I am not paranoid. I'd appreciate it if you would explore the possibility that my nephew was involved. Will you do that?'

'Of course,' he answered calmly, leaning back in his chair. 'But I would like to counsel you on another occasion.'

Lara stared at him. He was the typical shrink – more concerned with amassing an enormous bill than finding out if her nephew was a murderer. She couldn't afford twenty grand in psychiatrist's bills along with all the other expenses. 'We'll see,' she said. 'I'll get Josh.'

His eyes were penetrating, a rusty brown with flecks of yellow. Even with his comments about her being paranoid, Lara was enthralled by his eyes, his rich brown hair, a little black mole over the top of his full lips that looked like a beauty mark. Besides, he might be right. The bloody T-shirt could be a fluke. It could have been in there for months for all she knew. She asked herself if Werner was married and glanced at his hand for the wedding ring. It wasn't there.

Lara had a thick lump in her throat and tried to swallow it. Whatever attraction she had for this man suddenly vanished, and she felt all the blood drain from her face. In her mind, the Packard Cummings rap sheet appeared – the prior convictions for rape. She'd forgotten about his record when she spoke to Rickerson this afternoon. Ivory had been raped. Cummings had broken into her home. He could be the killer. That would eliminate Josh.

'Are you all right?' Werner said, a little flurry of concern in his eyes. 'Why don't you sit back down and I'll get you a glass of water?'

'No,' Lara said, heading for the door. 'I'll get Josh. I just need to use your phone.'

'There's one at the receptionist's desk.'

As soon as she was out of the door, she jogged down the long hall, sent Josh in to see Werner, and stabbed in the numbers to the San Clemente P.D., standing up behind the receptionist's console, too nervous to sit down.

'He's not in?' she repeated. 'Do you know how to reach him? This is Judge Sanderstone and I think it's urgent.'

She read the number off the dial of the phone and sat down, picking up a pen and tapping it on the counter. They'd said they could find him. A few seconds later, the phone rang and she grabbed it. 'Rickerson,' she said, hearing his voice, speaking rapidly, 'that man Cummings has a history of rape, sexual offenses. Ivory was raped, so . . . he could be the one . . . the one that killed them. We have to find him.'

Rickerson was unruffled. 'No shit,' he said. He was perfectly aware of Cummings's record. 'I've had his description broadcast to every unit in the city and across the state. We're trying now to reach his parole agent and get his last known address. The agent's out of town, but someone else is checking his files.'

The front of the reception desk was high. Lara could barely see over it. 'And that girl's boyfriend who threatened me?'

'Look, Lara,' he said, a hint of annoyance in his voice, 'I know how you feel right now, but why don't you just let me do my job? It's not like we're dragging our heels right now. For this kind of case, we're working at breakneck speed. If you hadn't been who you were, we wouldn't even have the lab reports back yet. They've got stuff backed up for months both in forensics and pathology. They don't even have enough drawers for the stiffs downtown.'

He was right. She'd been pressing, calling too much. 'I

just remembered his rap sheet. I wasn't certain you'd seen the whole thing.'

'I've seen it all.' He was abrupt, and then his voice softened. 'Take it easy, Lara. Try to get some rest. Just lay low, stay in that condo, take care of your nephew and yourself. Leave the police work to me. I'm the cop. As soon as I know anything, I'll call you. Deal?'

'Deal,' she said weakly. Then he was gone.

About thirty minutes later, Josh and Werner came out. It must have been his last appointment because Werner walked to the door of the office with them, slipping his jacket on. Then he followed them down the hall and got in the elevator with them. Josh was sullen. This time he stood next to Lara, however. Anything, evidently, was better than Werner.

At the condo, Josh told her he hated Dr. Werner, that Werner was nothing but a stuffy prick.

'Well, I don't care what you think about him,' she told him. 'You have to see him. That's all there is to it.'

'You can't order me around. You're not my mother. My mother's dead. I hate this place. I hate you. I hate that stupid doctor.'

Lara flopped down on the sofa. She was inches away from calling Social Services herself. He was standing in the middle of the room glaring at her. 'Josh,' she said, 'have you fallen off your bike lately?'

'I don't fall off my bike.'

'I see,' Lara said. 'Do you or any of your friends practice Satanism? You know, sacrifice animals or anything? Don't be afraid to tell me, but if you do, it's important that I know.' She was trying to remain calm during this discussion. It was difficult. Her hands were trembling; she shoved them under her hips and sat on them.

He looked at her like she was insane. 'You're crazy. I

can't believe you're even a judge. All you do is ask me ridiculous questions.'

Lara stood her ground. 'You didn't answer my question, Josh.'

'No,' he yelled at her, his voice booming. 'Do I look like a devil worshiper? What, do you want me to join up? Is that what you are? You look like a frigging witch.'

Things were getting out of hand fast. His chest was rising and falling, and his face was turning red. 'Okay,' she said. 'Let's have a truce.' She stood. 'It's late. We're both tired. Since you called me a witch, you can sleep on the sofa tonight.'

Lara left him standing there and went to the bedroom and closed the door. A few minutes later, he tapped lightly on the door, a solemn expression on his face. 'Can I at least have the bedspread?'

'Here,' Lara said, snatching it off the bed and tossing it to him. Then she remembered the backpack and picked it up. For a moment she stood there with it in her hands and searched his face. 'Need this?' she asked, curious as to his response.

Josh reached out and tried to grab the backpack out of Lara's hands. She stepped back and Josh sighed, dropping his hands to his sides.

'No, I don't need anything.' Wrapping the bedspread around him, he walked the few feet to the sofa and collapsed.

'Good night, Josh,' Lara said as she closed the door again. She opened the backpack and pulled out the bloody T-shirt. The only way to know for sure now was to have it tested, find out whose blood it was. She wondered if she could arrange something like that without anyone knowing. She didn't know. Back it went into the backpack. Tomorrow, she thought. Get through tonight and deal with it all tomorrow.

The room was dark and she watched the shadows, imagining flashes of the blood-spattered walls at the house in San Clemente. She held her breath, listening for Josh in the other room. He knew she had the backpack and might assume she knew about the T-shirt. He could come in while she was sleeping and bash her head in or suffocate her. Suddenly she felt desperately ill and bolted to the bathroom to hug the toilet bowl. All that was left in her stomach to vomit were the sodas she had consumed during the day. Josh had eaten; she couldn't swallow a bite without having it stick in her throat.

She finally stood and washed her face. Then she leaned her head under the tap and rinsed it with water. Dropping her clothes on the floor by the bed, she crawled under the covers and pulled them up to her chin and stared at the ceiling. She stayed that way for at least an hour, her body as rigid as an ironing board, listening for sounds in the other room, listening to the clock tick next to her on the nightstand. At two o'clock, she turned off the light, but still she could not sleep. She reviewed cases in her mind. She counted sheep. At four o'clock, her eyes closed involuntarily and her exhausted body fell into a deep, dreamless sleep.

Lara heard the phone ringing and opened her eyes. She was stiff and her head was pounding. She'd left the portable phone in the kitchen, and Josh had evidently answered it. He yelled at her from the living room, 'Phone.' Then he came to the bedroom door and stood there until Lara tossed on her robe and staggered over to take the phone.

'Lara,' a woman's voice said, 'it's Irene.'

'Irene, I took my nephew to see Werner. Not bad. But you know, Josh doesn't like him.'

'Isn't there anything I can do for you, Lara? And other people here at the courts have been inquiring. People are concerned. This is a tragedy. Such a terrible tragedy.'

'No,' Lara said, lowering her body to the edge of the bed. 'There's nothing anyone can do. I'm arranging the funeral. I hope that you'll come. We don't have any relatives.' Self-pity was evident in her voice and she tried to suppress it. 'Irene, something horrible came to light. This man – this man,' she started, stammering and gasping. Just the thought of this was more than she could bear. 'This man who appeared on a bail review in front of me the day before Ivory and Sam were murdered. He's the one who broke into my house. I released the son of a bitch. And he has a prior for rape. Ivory, bless her heart, was raped. I'm losing my mind over here. Let me tell you.'

'Why did you release this man?' Irene said. 'You mean on an ordinary bail situation, right?'

'No,' Lara said. 'I would have denied bail completely – any amount. Evergreen himself told me to grant him O.R., said he was working as a C.I. for some police agency . . . big drug case or something.'

'Well, dear,' Irene said, 'it sounds like nothing more than a terribly unfortunate situation. At least you know who he is and may see an end to this in sight. That's something, isn't it, Lara?'

'But I released the bastard. The man was standing right before me. I can still see his face.'

'Honey, get a handle on yourself. You don't know this man was involved in your sister's death. Possibly he was released from the jail, needed money, and tried to burglarize all kinds of homes in that area or even did, for that matter. He might have hit ten places and it was a coincidence that he hit yours. You're not far from the jail over there. And from what I know, there's no definitive link between these two crimes.'

'I don't believe in coincidence, Irene,' Lara said flatly. Normally when Irene, who was considerably older than

Lara, used all her little terms of endearment, Lara just sopped it up. But today it all sounded trite.

'Be rational. What kind of motive could this man possibly have? You released him O.R. You didn't sentence him to prison. When you were speaking of the Henderson situation yesterday, an outright threat, that was a different matter. This you must put out of your mind.' She paused and then continued. 'Honey, have you seen the paper this morning?'

'No, I just woke up. It was a rough night. I don't even know what time it is. What do they say? Do they have my picture in there or something?'

'Lara, it's far worse than that. I'd rather not be the bearer of bad news. Why don't you get your paper and read it and call me back? I'm reading the *Los Angeles Times*. Do you subscribe?'

'Yeah,' Lara said. 'Call you right back.' Bad news, she had said. What kind of bad news could there possibly be now? She walked into the living room and saw Josh sprawled with one leg off the sofa. He'd evidently gone back to sleep. She opened the front door and then remembered she wasn't at home. Seeing a newspaper lying next door, she took it. The people were probably at work already. She'd replace it before they got home.

Paper in hand, she carried it back to the bedroom. Removing the rubber band, she used it to tie her hair back in a ponytail and stretched out on her stomach on the unmade bed. There was nothing in the cover story. Maybe Irene was referring to a case she had handled that had been overturned on appeal without her knowledge.

Then she saw it. It was at the bottom of the front page.

'SADISTIC SEX MURDERS IN ORANGE COUNTY.'

She placed her hand over her mouth and glanced at the door. Then she ran over and closed it and returned to the bed, removing the paper and placing it on the carpet. She got on her hands and knees and read the text of the article.

'The sister and brother-in-law of Orange County Superior Court Judge Lara Sanderstone were brutally murdered yesterday in apparent sadistic sex-related homicides. Ivory Perkins, 36, and her husband, Samuel Perkins, 38, were murdered in their home in San Clemente by unknown assailants. The couple's fourteen-year-old son discovered the bodies on returning home from school. Insiders at the San Clemente Police Department advise that information has surfaced indicating the judge's sister was involved in sex-for-hire, specializing . . .'

She dropped the paper on the floor. Rickerson was to blame for this, and she was going to make certain he paid. Her eyes jerked to the clock on the nightstand, and she saw it was nine o'clock. Tossing on a pair of baggy jeans and an old shirt, she left the condo and jogged to her car in the parking lot, immediately calling the San Clemente Police Department on the car phone.

'Is Sergeant Rickerson there?' she asked the woman who picked up the phone.

'Yes, he just came in. I'll transfer you.'

Lara hung up. She punched the gas and pulled out into the morning traffic, honking her horn and screaming out the window like a madwoman when someone pulled in front of her. She didn't try to control her anger. She let it build like a wave far out at sea, knowing that by the time she got to the police station, it would be large enough to wash over the entire department and half the town of San Clemente. But it was Rickerson that she focused her rage on. He was responsible for leaking this smut stuff to the press, and she was ready to yank his head right off his body.

She parked illegally at the curb in a red zone. She flung

the door open and marched into the police station, huffing and puffing like she'd just climbed six flights of stairs. Passing the receptionist without so much as a glance, she headed directly to the back of the building, where she knew the Investigative Bureau was housed. Rickerson was standing by a file cabinet in his shirtsleeves, drinking a cup of coffee and joking with another detective. As soon as he saw her, he moved in her direction, a look of concern on his face.

'How could you do this? Leak this stuff to the press?' Lara said, her body shaking, her hand moving back like she was going to slap him.

Two other investigators were sitting at their desks. They stood, momentarily not recognizing her, and one moved toward her rapidly, his hand on his weapon. Lara turned and faced him. The look in her eyes was enough to stop him cold. Realizing who she was, he turned and walked back to his chair.

'Let's go outside,' Rickerson said. 'There's no use screaming in here and making a scene.'

Lara's chest was heaving and her face was crimson. She didn't take her eyes off Rickerson. 'Why did you do it? My God, I didn't think I even had to mention this to you. Any damn fool would know not to leak something like that to the press.' She tore her eyes away from Rickerson's and thought of Josh. Now he'd have to change schools. All his friends would know. The whole world knew now what his mother had been doing.

The detective was pulling gently on her hand, trying to lead her out the back door. She resisted, planting her feet on the ground, refusing to move.

'It wasn't me,' he whispered, inches from her face. 'If you'll just step outside with me, we'll discuss this like two civilized adults. Okay?'

Reluctantly, she followed. 'Okay,' she said, once they

were standing on a little concrete porch with steps leading to the parking lot, 'tell me and tell me fast. Who's responsible for this?'

'I don't know,' he said, shaking his head. 'One of the other officers must have said something to the press without thinking, or maybe he said something to his wife or kids and they got wind of it that way. It could have been a file clerk here. Anyone. But rest assured, it wasn't me.'

She stared at him, trying to read his eyes, detect if he was lying. Her breath was coming slower now. 'Retract it,' she ordered. 'Call them right this minute and make them print a retraction.'

The sun was bright and he was squinting in the glare. 'Do you really want me to do that? Think about it for a few minutes. If they print a retraction, which I'm not even certain they will, it'll only draw more attention. Do you really want that?'

She didn't answer. She looked out over the parking lot and the rows of police cars. It was a gorgeous day. The sun was bright, no fog. Even the air smelled clean and fresh, and there was a gentle breeze from the ocean. It didn't seem right in some way. Lara wished it would cloud over and pour.

'Mind if I smoke?' Rickerson said, reaching into his pocket for a cigar.

Lara didn't look at him. A few seconds later, she was waving the cigar smoke out of her face. He was right. The damage had already been done. Another article would simply fuel the fire. 'No,' she finally replied, 'you're probably right.' Then she pointed her finger at him. 'I want that person, Rickerson. You find the person who leaked this to the papers and bring them to me. I'll handle the rest.'

She turned and seized the door handle, yanking on the door. It didn't budge and she almost fell backward off the porch. Rickerson stepped behind her and inserted a key. 'Locks automatically,' he said, speaking with the cigar clamped between his teeth. 'Let's go somewhere and get a cup of coffee. I'll meet you at Denny's across the street. After this, it's better that we don't talk in the office.'

A few minutes later, they were sitting in a booth at Denny's. Lara was gripping her coffee cup with both hands. Rickerson had a large file folder that he placed on the table.

'We've been going over the phone records. I have a printout from the telephone company. I made an extra copy for you, in case you recognize anyone.' He slid it across the table, and Lara stared at it without seeing anything but a white sheet of paper. 'There's a lot of calls here to a lot of different people. I have records working on it now. As you can see, we've already tracked down most of the calls and listed the names and addresses beside them. Maybe we'll get lucky.'

'I want copies of the entire file.'

'I can't do that.'

'You owe me.'

'I told you I didn't leak anything to the press.' He'd been moving the cigar from one side of his mouth and back to the other. Now he removed it and placed it in the ashtray.

She slapped the top of the table, jiggling the coffee cups and silverware. 'Get me copies of that entire file. I'm not anyone off the street. I'm an officer of the court, for chrissake. I want that file.'

Rickerson's acne-scared face was menacing. He wasn't a man to be pushed.

'Then if you're an officer of the court,' he said softly, trying to calm her down, 'you should realize why I can't hand over evidence in a homicide. You could decide that some innocent person was responsible for your sister's murder and go out and shoot them. The department could be sued.'

She stood. 'I'm going to follow you back to the station and wait in the parking lot while you copy that file. You have that stuff in my hands in fifteen or twenty minutes max, or you'll be the sorriest cop to ever work in this county. I'll make your life a living hell.'

Rickerson remained in the booth and watched her stomp toward the door. 'Like my life isn't already a living hell,' he mumbled, tossing a few bills on the table.

When he looked up, he saw her marching back toward him. As soon as she reached the table, she placed her hands on her hips and glared at him. Then she reached down and snatched the cigar right out of his mouth and tossed it on the floor. 'And for your information, I hate these stupid things. I never said you could smoke.' She spun around and left.

Chapter 12

'Your suspect's on the run,' the sheriff's deputy informed Detective Rickerson by phone. 'We surrounded the place and went in ready for war. All we found was an empty room full of beer cans and cockroaches. No Packard Cummings.'

'Fuck,' Rickerson said, slapping the top of his desk. 'Can you tell how long it's been since he was there?'

'Guy across the street saw him come in early this morning. Looked like he'd been out all night. Said he went upstairs, came down with a bunch of garbage bags, probably with his clothes and stuff in it, tossed them in the trunk of his car, and split. We must have just missed him.'

'And the landlord?' Rickerson said. 'Do they know anything? You know, maybe a forwarding address.'

'Just that he owes them a couple months' back rent. This isn't the type of place that runs TRW's on their tenants, Sarge. This is a fleabag boardinghouse here. Landlord wasn't even sure what the guy's name was . . . said everyone pays in cash.'

'Think he was tipped?'

'By me, buddy. Anyway, we did our thing. Word's out on the vehicle. Unless he dumped it, he'll surface.'

Rickerson hung up and finally reached Packy's parole agent. The agent informed him that Cummings had basically absconded, had not reported for his weekly visit, and was presently in violation of parole.

'Were you aware that Cummings was acting as a snitch for some local agency?' Rickerson asked, knowing this was something a man like Packy would brag about to his parole agent.

'Not at all,' the man told him. 'Never mentioned a thing.'

After confirming the description and license number of the vehicle Packy was known to drive, the agent suggested several other possible locations he was known to frequent. Rickerson hung up, turning to the young detective who had been assigned to work with him on the case, Mike Bradshaw. Bradshaw was the son of the chief of police.

'Here we go,' he said, placing everything he had on Packy on his desk in a manila file folder. 'You want to prove yourself, kid, this is the case to do it on. Get some patrol units to follow up on these locations where Cummings might be, then call every law enforcement agency in Southern California and find out if anyone's ever heard of this guy. He claims to be working as a C.I. Check it out.'

Back at his desk, Rickerson took out the handful of Polaroids from his pocket and started shuffling them like a deck of playing cards. Then he studied each one. He'd waited long enough, he decided, stuffing the photos into a brown evidence envelope and jotting something on the front before he sealed it. It was time to go to the chief.

'Okay, Ace,' he said to Bradshaw, 'have someone get these to the crime lab downtown and fast. I want them hand-delivered to a Dr. Stewart and no one else.'

Bradshaw placed his hand over the mouthpiece of his phone. 'I'm speaking with the DEA now. What do you want me to do first?' he said, somewhat befuddled. 'Try to find him, call the agencies, or get this to the lab?'

'Everything,' Rickerson said, heading to the door. Then he stopped in the doorway and rolled a fat black cigar in his fingers. 'The way it looks right now, hot shot, Cummings is our man. He ransacked Sanderstone's house for what reason we don't know, probably did the killings, and he's on the run. Let's bring him in.'

After returning from her encounter with Rickerson, Lara was weak and shaky. She took the newspaper and shoved it in the trash can in the parking lot of the condo. How could she ever face her friends, her peers? Her parents were respectable people. Common people but respected. Thank God they were not here to see this. It was a disgrace, a complete disgrace.

She started to open the door to the condo and then decided against it. She crossed the grassy courtyard to Emmet's.

'Did you see the newspaper this morning?' she asked him.

'Yes, Lara . . . I did. I'm sorry.'

Emmet had a fresh pot of coffee. He told Lara to help herself. Bringing a cup for Emmet, she followed him to his office. 'I have a problem, Emmet. It's a serious one. I'm not certain there's anything you can do to help me, but I thought I'd try.'

He hit a button on his chair and spun around to the computer console, slipping his head into the metal contraption. 'Tell me, Lara,' he typed. 'I'll do anything I possibly can to help you. And Lara,' he continued, 'don't worry about the article in the paper. You must not concern yourself with what people think. If I worried about what everyone thought, I'd never leave my home. You have enough problems now.' He turned the chair around and looked at her.

'No one else knows this, Emmet, but I found a T-shirt with blood on it in Josh's backpack. I don't want to turn it over to the police unless I'm certain it's valid evidence. After what happened this morning with the newspapers, there's no telling what they will do if they learn about this. I thought I heard you mention a friend one time who was a biologist at Strand Laboratories. Could you get him to type it, see if it is my brother-in-law's blood? I can check his blood type from the police records.'

'Where . . . is it?' Emmet asked.

'It's in the condo, but I can get it.'

'Get . . . it,' he said.

'Then you think you can get it tested?'

'Yes,' he said slowly. 'Get . . . it.'

'I'll bring it over as soon as Josh goes out on his bike. And Emmet, I'd like you to meet him. Pray that it's nothing.'

The following morning, Detective Rickerson and Chief Bradshaw were walking down the corridor at the Los Angeles County Crime Laboratory after fighting the morning rush-hour traffic for over two hours. Chief Terrence Bradshaw was a very attractive man in his mid-fifties, with a full head of premature white hair and a deep tan. The only weak thing about him was his eyes; he wore thick glasses in heavy frames that magnified his eyes and made them appear enormous. To the men in the department, he was a diehard. The man jogged seven or eight miles a day every single day of his life, regardless of the weather, lifted weights, read every book he could get his hands on, and still managed to put in a fifty- or sixty-hour work week. As fit as a man twenty years younger, he was actually in better shape than his twenty-three-year-old son. Law enforcement was his life.

'Why in the hell did you insist on coming all the way down here for this?' the chief questioned Rickerson. 'I mean, we have our own lab in the county. Everyone thinks they do outstanding work.'

'Because of one woman,' Rickerson said, peering through the glass doors into the offices. 'She's fast and she knows her stuff.'

'Who?' the chief asked.

'Dr. Gail Stewart.'

'I think I've heard of her, but I'm not sure where.'

'She's one of the foremost criminologists in the country. She can do it all. There's not one piece of equipment in this lab that she doesn't know how to operate, and her specialty is photographic evidence.'

The woman stood when they walked in the door. Then she pumped both of their hands. It wasn't the kind of handshake you would expect from a woman. It was hearty. Everything about Gail Stewart was hearty. She'd been waiting.

'Gail Stewart,' she said to the chief. 'Follow me.'

Both men followed the heavyset brunette in the white lab coat. She was in her late thirties, at least forty pounds overweight, and walked like a storm trooper. She was also impossible to dislike. Her skin was soft and clear, her eyes round and expressive, and she absolutely loved what she was doing. She spent so much time at the lab that some people thought she lived there.

'Give something to this gal,' Rickerson whispered to the chief, 'and she'll grind it between her teeth, chew it up, and spit back the answer. The woman's dynamite.'

She marched them to a corner of the room where there was a screen and a slide projector. 'I have slides of the enlargements,' she said, 'but they were Polaroids, which means the quality is extremely poor. I'll give you the prints when we're finished.'

'Give me a rundown,' Rickerson said.

'Well,' Stewart said, 'none of these are recent

photographs. We've classified them in groupings. In group A, we estimate that these were taken approximately two years ago. We can denote age by the texture and rigidity of the photo itself, particularly instant print film. They tend to get more brittle as time goes on. Also, this is Kodak and they haven't produced this backing in at least two years. The photos in group B were taken with Polaroid SX-70 film and are probably about five years old or older.' She paused and sighed, mumbling under her breath, 'I wish we'd had the negatives.' Then she dimmed the lights as an image appeared on the screen.

'This first slide is a solitary young man, as you can see. You can't see his genitalia, but he has no underarm hair. We estimate his age to be about eleven or twelve, prepuberty.' She hit a button and the next slide fell into place. 'This is not the same young man, although they do resemble. They could even be brothers. These are from group A. He's even younger than the first young man. Our pathologist believes he's no more than nine or ten. This is based on his size, musculature, and other factors.'

'Is that your kid?' the chief asked Rickerson.

'Nope,' he said. 'I thought at first he was, but I was evidently mistaken. I'm fairly certain none of these photos are of Josh McKinley.'

Once they had stopped talking, she clicked another slide into place. 'These are from group B, so they're the oldest of the photos. Of course, it's obvious that the nude male standing behind the boy is an adult, probably in his forties or early fifties. He could be much older or much younger. We can't be certain, but his skin does appear to be sagging a little, therefore, we made a guess. As in just about everything, there are a lot of variables. The man could be a young man who had lost a lot of weight. Who knows? Anyway, the only distinguishable thing we can determine is that he suffers from scoliosis, or curvature of the spine.

He's in all the photos – the same man. He never faces the camera. Someone else is taking the pictures,' she said. 'See, there's his hand reflected in the mirror.'

'Did you enlarge that shot?' Rickerson asked. 'That could be him. Josh McKinley. He might be the one taking the pictures.'

'Certainly,' she said, flicking fast through the slides until she came to the right one. 'Here it is. From the looks of it, he's young. Note how slender and small his hand is. Of course, it could be a girl. We're just guessing it's a male because all the others are males.'

Rickerson got up and walked up to the screen, studying the image. 'Can't you do better than this? I need to know if this is the kid.'

'Sorry, Charley,' she said. 'I can't give you something that isn't there. But if you'll just be patient, Ted, I do have something.' She brought another slide into place, held it a few moments, and then replaced it with an enlargement of one section of the photograph. 'This is where you got lucky. See this right here?' she said. 'These weren't taken in a hotel room or something. They were taken in someone's home. This is an enhancement of a reflection in the mirror, probably on the dresser or something from the looks of it. What you're looking at is a photograph in a silver frame. It's a middle-aged woman and a young man. Hold on,' she said, clicking another slide into place. 'Now you're looking at the enlargement of the photograph itself. I know it's distorted, but if you try real hard you can see the similarities in their appearance. My bet is the young man is the woman's son. Looks about seventeen, doesn't he? Now, assuming the older man with his back to the camera in the photographs is the young man's father, we have even more to go on.'

Chief Bradshaw and Detective Rickerson were mesmerized. They spent a solid hour viewing slide after slide, studying each one intently. 'Had enough, gentlemen?'

She turned and faced them, leaning back against a desk and crossing her heavy legs at the ankles. The room was still dark. Only the light from a neighboring lab filtered through a glass window behind them. Dr. Stewart's voice echoed in the tiled room. 'What you've just seen is the photo collection of a pedophile. As I'm sure you both know, most pedophiles prefer prepubescent children. Once the child passes puberty, they are no longer desirable and are frequently discarded.'

She turned the lights back on and continued, 'If you find him, we can positively identify him by the spinal curvature. No one's spine curves exactly the same way, to the same centimeter. We can prove this by photographing this man's back and superimposing it over the photograph you've just seen, studying and comparing his X rays and medical records, and we can back it up with the latest computer technology.' She smiled and her full face creased with two large dimples. 'All you have to do is find him. Piece of cake, huh?'

'Sure,' Rickerson said, exchanging glances with the chief. 'Pretty impressive.'

'I saved the best for last. Follow me.' They followed her across the tiled floor to another work space and a computer terminal. 'Have a seat, guys. I've been working on this all night.' She turned around and squinted at Rickerson. 'And I mean all night, Ted. I haven't been to bed.'

By the time the men had pulled up two chairs, Dr. Stewart had the computer up and running. 'This is new software. We just recently got this whole system. It requires the use of high-speed computers.' She waved her arms around the room. Behind a glass partition was row after row of huge computers, lights blinking and tape spilling out of printers. 'I generated a computer composite of the young man in the photograph with the woman and a torso of the nude adult male. Working under the assumption that they are related, or even father and son, we developed another composite photograph of what this older man might look like. Of course, we've aged him as well.' She tapped a few keys on the keyboard and an image appeared on the screen. 'Here it is. What do you think?'

Both the chief and Rickerson leaned over and peered at the screen. The image was three-dimensional. While they watched, Dr. Stewart rolled a mouse around on the pad, tapped instructions into the computer, and the naked image actually walked, turned, and moved its arms and head.

'The technology you are seeing is called artificial reality along with computer-assisted design, or CAD. It's the latest thing. They even used something like this recently in San Francisco in the trial of that guy who murdered his brother. You know, the porno kings. They've been using it in the movies for a while now, but of course, it's extremely expensive, so we're just getting it.'

'Isn't this fascinating?' the chief said. 'It looks like a video game or an animated movie.'

'See,' the woman continued, 'this is a very rough attempt here. That's why his facial features are so generic at this point. It actually takes weeks to make it perfect. If it's complex, it can take months. We can create a crime scene, put the suspects in the picture, and then move them around like the crime really occurred. This way we can tell if someone is telling the truth, match their testimony to what actually occurred. We can also tell the exact point a bullet would strike if fired from a certain location, which way the body would fall, and basically recreate every aspect of the crime. The possibilities are endless.'

She glanced at both men and then turned back to the screen. 'Now, watch this image walk. I didn't spend a lot of time on the face yet. We have no way of knowing that the young man and the older nude male in the pictures are actually related, and therefore I thought this was a little premature. If you will notice, however, this man has a noticeable limp on the right side of his body. We developed this from data entered into the program on the scoliosis. I can print this out, but it won't be threedimensional like you're seeing.' She hit a button and a printer generated a hard copy. She handed it to Rickerson. 'I'm going to keep refining this, and eventually you'll have something pretty realistic to look at.'

'You did good, Gail,' Rickerson said, visibly excited. He turned to the chief. 'Told you she was the best. There's no one around like her.'

'Yeah,' the chief said, rubbing his chin and addressing Dr. Stewart. 'This is all intriguing, but you hit the nail on the head. Until we find him, we don't have anything. And this is all just speculation. To assume that the two people in the small picture were his wife and son is a mammoth assumption. They might not be related at all.'

'Right you are,' the woman replied, 'but you've got to start somewhere. Let's watch this man move again, officers. A person's walk is a distinctive thing, and this man's spinal curvature is quite severe, enough to have an effect on how he moves all of his limbs.' She started tapping like wild on the computer, and the figure on the screen appeared inside a room, with doors, furniture, walls. While they watched, she moved him to the back of the room and then brought him forward. 'One hip is actually higher than the other, therefore, the limp. Also, watch how he moves his arms. That swing right there – ' She stopped the figure and locked the image into place. 'That's a compensation factor, meaning in simplistic terms, that he must balance himself, particularly since his body is physically imbalanced by his deformity.'

Finally stepping away from the computer, she turned and punched Rickerson on the arm with a fleshy fist. 'Hey, big guy, you promised me a steak dinner if I shelved everything else I'm working on and delivered. I delivered. When do I get my dinner?'

'You'll get it,' Rickerson said, smiling. 'I'm not sure you need it, though. You don't look very hungry to me.'

'Asshole,' she said, shaking her head and laughing. 'Why am I so gullible? Next time you can wait your turn like everyone else.'

'Thanks a lot, Gail. We'll be in touch.' Rickerson headed for the door and the chief followed.

Dr. Stewart yelled to him, 'You know what I'd do?'

'What?' Rickerson replied.

'I'd let Lois Anderson at the FBI take a look at these pictures. She heads the task force on missing children. One of these boys might be a runaway that's since been returned to his parents. I hope you catch this bastard. You know why?'

Rickerson just stood there and stared at her. Of course he knew why. Whoever this person was, he felt certain he was involved in contracting the Perkins homicides. Cummings might have been the hands-on killer, but Rickerson's assumption right now was that it was a contracted assassination.

'In an active pedophile's career, certainly one as old as this one, he can have hundreds of victims. Maybe it's time this fellow pays the price.'

'Send them over to her now,' Rickerson said, thinking of all the young lives this man had destroyed – children so devastated that they might never be the same.

'No problem,' she said, plunking her large body down in a chair that looked like it was about to collapse beneath her and snatching a Snickers bar from her desk. She unwrapped it and then held it in the air. 'Brain food,' she said. 'Secret to my success. Person just can't think when they're hungry.'

•

'So what do you think?' Bradshaw said as they headed back down the hall, their shoes tapping on the linoleum.

'I think we've got one hell of a case on our hands, Chief. Someone killed that couple to get their hands on these photos. There's no doubt about it. I was hoping we could exclude the kid.'

'I'm not sure you can do that. If the boy was being exploited or sexually abused, your motive is right there.'

'I don't think Perkins and his wife took these pictures or even sold them as I originally thought. I think they found them. What do you think about that?'

'They just found them, huh? Interesting. Want to be more specific?'

They hit the double doors and stepped outside. It was overcast and muggy. The smog was so thick they could see it hanging like a foul cloud over the entire city. They stood for a few minutes on the steps, as officers and other law enforcement personnel passed them coming in and out of the building. 'Can you believe this place?' Rickerson tossed out to the chief. 'It's like Grand Central Station here.'

'Yeah,' the chief said, uninterested. 'Lot of crime.'

Rickerson looked at him. 'Last weekend they had twenty-five homicides in L.A. County. We're talking one weekend, Chief – one lousy weekend and twenty-five lives.'

The chief belched and looked at the detective. Every year the crime stats went up. Just thinking about it made his stomach churn. And crime was working its way out from the inner city to the suburbs, particularly since the riots. There wasn't much left in south central Los Angeles, other than burned-out buildings and rubble. 'Want to tell me about the case?'

'Okay, Ivory Perkins was working as a prostitute, see,' Rickerson said, leaning back against a spiral column in front of the building, 'with heavy emphasis on S and M. I think she had a client that was a pedophile, liked to have sex with kids.'

'Wait a minute,' the chief retorted. 'That doesn't make sense. Why would a guy who liked kids go to a hooker? That doesn't fit anything I know about pedophiles. They usually abhor sex with adult women.'

Rickerson had thought of this and was ready with an answer. 'I already talked to the S.O.'s staff psychologist. He thinks this man was masochistic, possibly out of guilt over his attraction to young boys. I mean, he could have been sadistic, but it really doesn't work as well. One day when the Perkins broad serviced him, she somehow came across his little X-rated photo collection, and that's when she and her husband decided to try their hands at extortion.'

'Sounds plausible,' the chief said, looking at the sky. 'Think it's actually going to rain?'

'Never,' Rickerson said, lighting a cigar. 'Trust me. Weather is my specialty.'

'How does Packy Cummings fit into this picture?'

'Well, that's the glue that holds this whole thing together. On September seventh, the day before the murders, Judge Leo Evergreen informed Lara Sanderstone that Packy was a police informant and insisted that she release him without bail. If he is, no agency in the state of California will claim him. And if you review his criminal history, I think you'll agree that they would've never used a guy like this one. Jesus, he was a prime suspect in a cop killing a few years ago, Aryan Brotherhood membership paid in full, prior convictions for rape.'

'Really?' Chief Bradshaw said. 'What happened to the case? The officer-related killing.'

'Got off for some reason. They couldn't put it together. Anyway, I think Evergreen was lying.'

The chief started down the steps. Rickerson followed,

puffing clouds of cigar smoke into the atmosphere. 'Go on,' the chief said. 'I don't understand why you think he was lying, but go on.'

'I think he's our man.'

Chief Bradshaw stopped halfway down the steps and looked straight at Rickerson, his mouth open, his eyes enormous behind his thick glasses. For a few moments he was completely speechless. 'The presiding judge of Orange County? Really, Rickerson, isn't that taking things a little too far? We're only in the preliminary stages of this investigation anyway.'

'Not hardly,' Rickerson said, his voice laced with conviction. Not as far as he was concerned. 'Have you ever met Evergreen?'

The chief was at the bottom of the steps and looked back up at the detective. 'Not that I recall. I think I've seen his picture in the paper sometime in the past, but to be honest, I wouldn't know him if I saw him.'

Rickerson moved the cigar to the other side of his mouth and clenched it between his teeth, the words snaking out of one corner of his mouth. 'Well, I have,' he said, his chest expanding. 'I'll never forget that bastard. Years ago, one of my first big cases to go to trial was dismissed on a technicality. Evergreen was the judge.'

'And . . .'

'Just listen, okay. What if Leo Evergreen was Ivory Perkins's client and had no idea she was Judge Sanderstone's sister? Obviously, the Perkins woman didn't broadcast this information to all her clients. Might tend to make a client a little nervous. Know what I mean? So, Evergreen sprang Packy Cummings to do his dirty work: get the pictures back, kill the people that had them. He knew from court records that Packy was down for a fall, headed straight back to prison, and this time he was going for the long haul. The D.A. was planning to prosecute him as a career criminal, tacking on all those five-year enhancements for his priors. Old Packy had nothing to lose and everything to gain.'

'Hold on,' the chief said just as a burly motorcycle cop bounded down the steps and almost knocked him down. 'Once this man was out on the streets, why didn't he just split?'

'Bucks, cash, bread,' Rickerson said, rubbing his fingers together. 'Can't go too far without it, and I never saw anyone come out of jail or the joint with an abundance of green. Not only that, before this asshole could drive two feet, Evergreen could have every cop in town after him with handfuls of warrants. He's certainly in a position powerful enough to do a man a lot of harm, particularly if you're on the wrong side of the law.'

'As I understand it,' the chief said, 'his prints were found in Sanderstone's house in Irvine. All you've got him on right now is 459, residential burglary. How do you put him into the homicides?'

The two men started walking to their car. This was typical L.A., Rickerson thought, glancing around him in disgust. Almost every building and every wall in sight were covered with graffiti. The names of rival gangs were spray-painted in fluorescent colors in large block letters.

'Let me give you my theory, Chief,' Rickerson said as they crossed the street at the light. 'Ivory Perkins came to her sister's house almost exactly two months before the murders claiming that someone was following her. Whoever it was, they were completely unaware that the house belonged to Judge Sanderstone. They probably thought Ivory lived there herself or something. Like I said, why would anyone in their wildest dreams connect these two individuals? One a prostitute . . . one a judge.'

'So your theory is that Evergreen paid Cummings to kill the couple and get the pictures back when he couldn't find them in the judge's house. But when Cummings committed the homicides, he left the pictures there. Why would he do that?'

'Possibly because the boy came home and startled him, or he just never thought of the crawl space. The carpet obscured it pretty well, and there was a box of old clothes on top of it. He went through those, he just didn't think to look for the crawl space. Anyway, he ransacked Sanderstone's house thinking they were hidden there, and when it was a no-go, Evergreen got desperate and contracted the killing.'

'A killing? You really think that's possible? A judge contracting a killing?'

Rickerson raised his eyebrows. Both he and the chief had been in this business too long not to realize that anything was possible. 'Maybe Evergreen just wanted the photos back . . . and the animal he hired – Cummings – simply went nuts in there. Pretty, sexy woman. He's a sex offender. Then the husband walked in and he had to do him too.'

'Well,' the chief said, deep in thought, 'if Evergreen is the man in the photos, he would certainly have a lot to lose. There's no doubt about that. Boy,' he said, actually shivering, 'that's a chilling thought . . . a fucking iceberg.' The chief stopped walking and turned to the detective. 'Do you have any idea, Rickerson, what it's going to take to go up against the most powerful judge in the county? Don't think for a minute you can put together a thin case and ever get out of the box.'

The chief waited until Rickerson unlocked the police unit and then opened the passenger door. He looked up at the sky and held his hand in the air, smiling at Rickerson. 'It's raining. Hope your ability to solve homicides is better than your ability to predict the weather.'

They were looking at each other over the hood of the

police unit, the sky spitting forth moisture but only enough to leave a few drops on the windshield. Rickerson drew hard on his fat cigar, and an enormous cloud of smoke appeared, almost obscuring his face. Just before it started pouring, the detective ducked inside the police car, leaving the chief standing there in the rain.

The first step in building a case against Evergreen, Rickerson thought, was somehow connecting him to the homicides. The problem was simple: lack of evidence. Once the chief was inside the car, Rickerson fired up the ignition and pulled out into traffic. 'I blew a lot of hot air out there, Chief. Even if my gut tells me it's Evergreen, I'm gonna have a hell of a time proving it.'

The chief had his glasses off and was wiping them from the rain. Rickerson stopped at the light and glanced at him. Funny, he thought, people look so different without their glasses.

'I don't think you've even broken ground with this case, Ted. What about this woman's tricks? What if this Perkins fellow was dealing in child pornography and stepped on the wrong people? That's a dirty business. These photos we just saw aren't even recent. There's no telling where they came from. And all you have to connect Judge Evergreen to these crimes is the fact that he asked Judge Sanderstone to grant Cummings an O.R. release. Why don't you interview Evergreen and find out who asked him to release this man?'

The chief had some valid points, but Rickerson certainly wasn't going to interview Evergreen and tip his hand. He liked the element of surprise, wanted his prey to move around freely while he stalked them. That way they might fall right into his hands. 'There's one thing you are right about, Chief.'

'Yeah, tell me.'

'Even if our man isn't Evergreen himself, the person

behind these killings has to be someone working inside the system: a judge, D.A., cop, someone with access to booking information and rap sheets.'

'Thousands of people have access to that kind of information,' the chief said, 'even clerical people.'

'Whoever arranged Packy Cummings's release is our killer, Chief. I might be wrong about Evergreen, but I'm not wrong here.'

Chapter 13

By the time Rickerson got back to San Clemente that afternoon, Lara Sanderstone was waiting in his office. She was sitting in the little chair by his desk in the detective bay. Her hair was down instead of pinned at her neck. It fell to her shoulders in a blunt-cut style that was extremely flattering. The jet black hair against her fair skin, the high cheekbones, the stress she was obviously under, all served to give her a look of vulnerability and touching beauty. She was wearing a tailored pants suit and little black shoes with studs on the toes. Josh was waiting outside in the Jaguar with the radio blasting. Rickerson had seen him on his way into the building.

Lara stood when he walked up, glancing at the other officer at the next desk. The man was on the phone, not paying attention to them. 'I wanted to apologize for the way I acted yesterday,' she said in a contrite voice. 'I know you wouldn't have leaked that stuff to the press. It was all just too much and I took it out on you. I'm sorry.'

He smiled at her. 'Yeah, well, we all have our bad days. You've certainly had more than your share. Forget it.'

'Do you have any news on that man . . . Packard Cummings?'

Rickerson loosened his tie and flopped into his chair, tossing his legs on his desk. 'He split, but we'll nab him. Give us time. We're working around the clock.'

'Did you find out who he's working for? What agency?'

He didn't want to tip his hand, take a chance on blowing the biggest case of his career. He looked away, avoiding her eyes. 'We're working on it.'

'Why don't I just ask Evergreen? Why all this subterfuge? You know, I want to go back to my house. The condo is too small for Josh and me. I want to go home.'

'Listen to me. I'm going to repeat myself. I already told you this the other day. Don't open your mouth about this to a soul. Not a soul, do you hear me? If you want to find out who murdered your sister, do exactly as I say and don't ask questions. And as of this minute, I don't want you anywhere near that house. Got it?'

Lara flipped a wayward strand of hair off her forehead. 'I went over there this morning and got some more clothes and things.' Rickerson was glowering at her. 'I didn't go to the condo from there, so don't give me that look. I came straight over here. If anyone followed me, they would have just followed me here. And I'm not going straight back to the condo.'

'It's your neck, Lara,' he said. 'You lead the guy back to that condo and you can kiss safety goodbye. Not only that, but I can't spare the manpower right now to have someone sit there all night. As of right now, you're on your own.'

'What about the autopsy and forensics? Is the report complete yet? I want to see it.'

'No, they're still working on it. I told you no prints in the San Clemente house.'

'No prints,' she repeated. 'Shit . . .'

'They're completely swamped down there. All the M.E. told me is that he thinks it went down this way.' Rickerson paused, picking up his cigar, and then he remembered the scene in the restaurant with Lara. He dropped it back in the ashtray, turning his chair to face her. He spoke in a low, controlled voice. 'Somehow the assailant managed to get into the house. He may or may not have intended to kill them. We can't know that for sure. All we know is that he was looking for something in that house, and from the looks of it, he didn't find it. She was there . . . he raped her, held the pillow over her face to keep her from screaming, drawing attention, and then he suffocated her. Maybe she was fighting; maybe he just likes to kill women, or maybe someone paid him to kill them both. Your brother-in-law more than likely walked into this scene. The suspect was hiding, probably in Josh's bedroom, and bashed Perkins in the back of the head as he went to your sister's side. Sam fell forward on the bed where we found him.' Rickerson sat back in his seat. 'At first we thought there were two separate killers, but now we're going on the basis of only one. Forensics has some pubic hair, not your brother-in-law's, some skin under her fingernails, and other than that, they're still looking.'

Lara was trembling, her mind filled with the horror Ivory had endured. She hadn't heard half of what Rickerson had said. She kept seeing the bloody walls, Ivory's lifeless body, Sam's cracked skull with his brain exposed. 'Isn't there something . . . that I can do?' she stammered. 'I can't let this person get away with this . . . my sister . . . I simply can't.'

'Not a thing. We're doing everything humanly possible to bring this man in and put this to bed. We've even called some men in from retirement, borrowed some men from the sheriff. We're doing it all.'

'Nothing,' she reiterated, her frustration escalating. 'Just like that, I'm supposed to sit around and do nothing.'

'Just like that, kid,' Rickerson said, his rust eyes flashing with compassion. 'I know you like to run the show, but this is one show you better stay out of or you'll end up the star. That's more or less what happened to your sister and she's dead.'

Lara's chest was rising and falling. She stood to leave but didn't speak. She kept her eyes locked on the redheaded detective. He stared right back until she looked away. 'The boy involved in the Henderson case? Have you found him yet?' she asked.

'He's coming home from UCLA tonight. I've already talked to his parents. I'm interviewing him later this evening. To be honest, I don't really think he's involved, but believe me, we're gonna give him a full tumble.'

'I'm frightened, you know,' Lara said. Her palms were sweaty and she was rubbing them on her pants legs. 'And I keep thinking they're going to get away with this. Too many people get away with these horrendous crimes.'

Rickerson came out from behind his desk. The other detective had disappeared. Phones were ringing. Outside the detective bay was a flurry of activity. He needed to get back to work. He put his large hands on her shoulders and stared her right in the eye, only inches from her face. 'One of these days you're going to have to trust someone, Lara. Why don't you start with me? They aren't going to get away with it.'

The detective dropped his hands, and Lara walked out of the police station. Packy Cummings was still out there somewhere. She tried to bring forth the image of his face from that day in the courtroom, but it was buried somewhere in her subconscious. Had he followed her here to the police station? Had someone hired him to eliminate her entire family? She saw the Jaguar and Josh still in the front seat. She should have never left him alone.

Once she was inside the car, Lara turned down the radio and smiled at Josh. 'You hungry? I'm starving. Where do you want to go to lunch?'

Josh jerked his head away and stared out the window. With each passing hour the boy became more withdrawn and morose. Today he had barely spoken.

'Yes, Aunt Lara, lunch would be terrific,' she said, hoping she might embarrass him into opening up, acknowledging how hard she was trying.

Slowly he turned toward her and stared at her with a black intensity. 'I'm not hungry,' he snapped. 'And I don't know why I have to go everywhere with you. I'm not your pet dog, you know.'

'No, Josh,' Lara said softly, trying to keep the exasperation out of her voice, 'you're not my pet dog, but you are the only relative I have now. It would be nice if we could help each other get through this, don't you think?'

Josh didn't answer. Lara felt her fingers tighten on the steering wheel. As horrid as it might seem, she knew she could not eliminate her nephew as a suspect. While the police were combing the city for the killer, the killer could be sitting right next to her.

The men were assembled in the squad room at the San Clemente Police Department. It was three o'clock, time for the regular change-of-shift briefing, and the majority of the men were uniformed officers. Chief Terrence Bradshaw walked to the front of the room to address the men.

'In a few minutes I'm going to have Detective Rickerson go over where we stand in the Perkins homicides. He's heading the task force investigating these crimes, along with my son, who you all know.' The chief paused and looked out over the men, seeing the fresh-scrubbed face of his oldest son. He'd been on the force two years now. This would be his first assignment out of uniform, his chance to prove himself to both the seasoned men on the force and his father.

'As you've all probably heard by now,' the chief continued, 'someone in this department leaked sensitive information to the press, and when that person is found,' he said, his eyes scanning the room with authority and menace, 'he will be dealt with appropriately. Now, I'll turn you over to Detective Rickerson.'

The chief took a seat in the front row and Rickerson stood. 'This is what we have,' he began. 'We have a man and a woman who were found murdered in their home in the San Simeon housing tract of our city. The medical examiner has placed time of death between 0100 hours and 0300 hours on Wednesday, September eighth. There was no forced entry into the residence, but the killer or killers could have managed entry through the rear door of the residence. There was a hidden key there. The murder weapon on the male was a twenty-pound dumbbell discovered at the scene. The female was suffocated. There are only two sets of prints on the murder weapon – the woman's and those of her fourteen-year-old son.'

Rickerson paused and took a drink of water from a glass on the table. 'We do, however, have a suspect, as you are all well aware by now. His prints were found in the residence of the murdered woman's sister, Judge Lara Sanderstone, which was ransacked only a day before the murders.'

Rickerson stopped and picked up a large stack of flyers off the table that he handed to one of the officers to distribute. 'This individual should be considered armed and dangerous. Use extreme caution if you attempt to stop him. I'm certain you've all heard earlier broadcasts and have been on the lookout for this vehicle. The suspect, a Packard Cummings, was on parole and recently arrested for carrying a concealed weapon. Right now he's wanted only for questioning and for violation of parole. If located, book him on the parole violation and contact me immediately. Do not interrogate the subject.'

A commotion broke out in the room. Officers were talking among themselves and fidgeting in their seats. So far Rickerson hadn't told them anything they didn't already know, and they were eager to hit the streets. The senior Bradshaw stood and the pandemonium immediately stopped. He then sat back down. Rickerson continued.

'The murdered woman, an Ivory Perkins, was working the trades as a prostitute, specializing in S and M. We have reason to believe that she and her husband, Sam Perkins, were extorting money from someone, possibly a high-placed government official.'

'Who? Tell us who,' a voice from the back yelled out.

'No names will be disclosed at this point.'

The younger Bradshaw raised his hand. Rickerson glanced at his father and then back to the boy. 'Yes, Mike.'

'What evidence is there implicating extortion?'

Rickerson's opinion of the chief's son was obvious from his expression, but he didn't let it show in his voice. 'Next sentence, Mike. I was getting to that. Just be patient here.'

'Sorry,' the young man said, a flush spreading over his face. The men let forth a round of laughter. It wasn't easy being an officer in a department where your father was the chief. Every time the young officer opened his mouth, someone thought it was a reason to ridicule him.

'Shortly before the murders, Samuel Perkins started throwing a lot of cash around – paying for things with a thick roll of hundred-dollar bills. He was seen at the racetrack in Del Mar, where he dropped a bundle, and there was about forty thousand in cash in the safe at the pawnshop. We know of no legitimate means for him to come up with this kind of money. His pawnshop was failing. Before this date he was being hounded by creditors. In addition, he was apparently fencing stolen property through the pawnshop. Some of it we have recovered and returned to the rightful owners.'

A burly cop in the second row spoke up. 'I tried to pop this guy a number of times for receiving stolen property. He was connected. Judge Sanderstone stepped on me hard.'

Rickerson coughed and looked at the ground. This was something he didn't want spread all over the department – that a superior court judge was using her position to cover for a small-time thief like Perkins. Of course, with the kind of cash they had found, he was evidently growing in stature and couldn't really be classified as small-time anymore. 'Let's move along, okay.'

Now the officer who had spoken up stood. His name was Connors. 'No, let's not move along. I'm getting pretty fed up with the graft and corruption in this county. We do the work and some crooked judge throws it out or tells us to take a hike.'

'As I said, Connors, let's move along,' Rickerson said, again glancing at the chief. 'We have the phone records from the residence and numerous other leads that we will be following up on. Anyone with any information regarding this case, please contact me at once.' Rickerson started to walk off and then reluctantly returned, remembering the chief was in the room. 'Or contact Investigator Mike Bradshaw if I'm not available.'

Getting that out of his mouth took a lot. It was a bitter pill to swallow, getting stuck with the chief's inept son on a case as big as this one. As soon as he was out of the squad room, he removed a cigar from his pocket, bit off the end, and shoved it between his teeth. A few seconds later, the younger Bradshaw was right by his side.

Rickerson looked down at him. He almost wanted to laugh. The man was so small. He couldn't be taller than five-six. The chief was a giant of a man. Son must have taken after the mother, he thought, in more ways than one. Everyone knew he wasn't that sharp, was borderline to even be in the department at all. Rickerson headed to the detective bureau, the younger man hot on his heels.

'Some attorney has been calling here asking a lot of questions about this case,' he said. 'Says he's a friend of the judge.'

Rickerson spun around and faced him. 'Who? What's his name? Why haven't you brought this to my attention? Are you sure it was an attorney? Maybe it was a judge?'

'Uh, I don't know, but I'm certain he said he was an attorney. He was real pushy, wanting to know about any suspects we might have had. I mean, it isn't a lead or anything. Besides, I misplaced the guy's name. I have so much junk on my desk, I guess I threw it away.'

Rickerson completely lost it and stomped right on Mike Bradshaw's foot. While the young man yelped and jumped around on the linoleum, he snarled at him. 'You incompetent little fool. I want to know everything, do you hear me? Absolutely everything. And what did you tell this man, huh? What in the fuck did you tell him?'

'Nothing . . . You stepped on my foot, man.'

Looking up at a spot on the wall, Rickerson sucked air into his lungs and then slowly let it go. That's all he needed right now was for this little shit to go running to his father. His voice became soft, as if talking to a child. 'I'm sorry, Mike. That was an accident, but don't you think you should keep me informed? Isn't that what we agreed on from the start?'

'I think the lady judge is involved. See, what I think is this was a big extortion and crime ring. She was the inside contact, the protection.'

'Yeah,' Rickerson said, turning and walking fast down the corridor on his long legs, making the little man almost run to keep up with him. 'Well, I'd keep my damn mouth shut if I were you. I think you've been reading too many crime novels or watching too much TV. She may have asked Connors to lay off a few times, but that's it.'

'Can I see the pictures? Dad said there were some incriminating pictures.'

Rickerson stopped again and the other man ran right into his back. He turned and faced him, purposely puffing cigar smoke in his face. 'No, you cannot see the pictures. The purpose is to stop this type of activity, not promote it.'

'But I'm on the case,' he said, his voice almost rising to a whine. 'Is there anyone in the pictures that we know?'

'Mike,' Rickerson barked, 'just do what I tell you and don't ask questions where you don't belong.'

While the younger man stood there with a blank expression on his face, Rickerson entered the men's room. A few seconds later, Bradshaw followed him, and Rickerson spun around and grabbed him by the lapels. 'I'm going to take a crap now. Do you mind?'

'Dad just said to stay with you at all times.'

Rickerson shook his head. As if he didn't have enough problems. 'Let me tell you something, Mike,' he said, spitting the words into the little man's face, 'I know who leaked that stuff to the press. If you give me any shit at all, I'll tell your daddy.'

'But I . . .'

'You what? You thought it was fine, huh? You thought it was fun being the big guy, giving the press some juicy tidbits. Those juicy tidbits will make that kid's life hell. How would you feel if that was your mother? Now, get the hell out of here and leave me the fuck alone.'

While Josh was out on his bike, Lara removed the bloody T-shirt from his backpack and took it to Emmet's. 'I don't have Sam's blood type yet. The autopsy report isn't finished.'

'Do . . . you have . . . Josh's?'

'Wait a minute,' she said. 'It's on his birth certificate, right? I saw it in all the documents from the pawnshop. They must have kept all that stuff in the safe.'

'Good,' Emmet said. 'Then . . . we . . . have a start.'

Lara ran back to the condo and found the birth certificate. For a few moments she held it in her hand, looking at the tiny footprints, wondering what it was like to give birth to a child. Then she walked over to Emmet's and told him the blood type. It was type AB.

He said it would take a few days. While Lara watched, he rolled the T-shirt up in a ball and slipped it inside a plastic bag. Then he addressed a Federal Express envelope and handed it to Lara, telling her to drop it in the bin when she left the condo. He'd already contacted his friend the biologist. Lara thought of driving it over herself, but she had to go back to her place and wait for Josh.

She'd set strict guidelines, telling him where he could ride his bike and how long he could stay out. He was late. The minutes clicked by and turned into hours. She kept walking to the window and looking out, then returning to sit on the sofa and stare.

Finally she got in the Jaguar and rode around the neighborhood but no Josh. She didn't know what to do. He'd gone out the other day and come back a few hours later. She was frightened, but she had no choice but to wait. Lara knew the reality of his mother's death was finally beginning to sink in. Either that or he was afraid. Afraid they were getting close to finding out what had really happened in that house.

After pacing back and forth in the condo for about an hour, she decided to leave him a note and check in at the office. No matter what Rickerson said, she had to see Evergreen. She could forgo discussing this man Packy Cummings, but Evergreen was her boss.

Phillip informed her that the funeral arrangements were complete. The funeral was to be held in three days, which fell on a Monday. The medical examiner had made a commitment to release the bodies to the funeral home today, and Phillip had prepared the obituary Lara had dictated yesterday when she was in the office. It was only a paragraph. 'What do you think?' she asked him, knowing he'd seen the newspapers this morning. 'Should I just forget the obituary after what's happened? Is everyone talking about it?'

Phillip looked down at his desk and started shuffling papers from side to side. 'I mean, that's your decision. But maybe it would be better to have a small, dignified service and forget the newspaper.'

'You're right,' she said, dropping the paper back on his desk and entering her office.

A few minutes later, Phillip came in with an enormous stack of papers. 'I need your signature on these documents. A lot of them are late. I've been holding them. I didn't want to bother you.'

'Do you know where Evergreen is right now?' Lara said, signing her name on each piece of paper without even reading it.

'I'll check. He got a pro-tem to handle the calendar. He's probably in his office.'

'Forget it,' she told him, turning another document over and starting on the next one. 'I'll just go down there when I'm finished here. Any other calls?'

The young man sighed. 'Dozens.'

'Anything pressing . . . that can't wait?'

'Social Services called. They need to see you ASAP about your nephew. I didn't give them your new number.'

'Good,' she said. 'I'll call them when I get back.'

Only a few more documents were left to sign when Lara noticed a form she didn't recognize. Grabbing her glasses, she quickly scanned it and then looked up at Phillip. What he had given her was a bank form verifying his employment and salary. Phillip's annual salary was thirty-six thousand a year. On the form he had listed his salary at fifty thousand. 'Didn't I sign another loan paper like this just a few months ago?'

'Ah, yes . . . I hope you don't mind,' he said. 'I'm having some financial problems. I really . . . need this loan. I have to pay my tuition at law school . . . and my car broke down last week.'

'Aren't you afraid they'll contact county personnel and find out we're fudging on your salary? I don't mind helping you, Phillip. I mean, we all have financial problems from time to time, but it doesn't look good for me to be caught in a lie. I have enough problems right now.'

'This bank doesn't go through personnel. They go directly to the employee's supervisor. I know, remember. I already got one loan from them.'

Lara felt sorry for the young man. She remembered all too well how difficult it was to put herself through law school. She signed her name and handed him the stack of papers. 'Just don't overextend yourself. It took me years to pay off my student loans.'

Clasping the stack of papers to his chest, Phillip said, 'I don't know how to thank you. I really appreciate this.'

'No problem,' Lara said, standing. 'If you need me, I'll be in Evergreen's office.'

She walked down the back corridor to the older judge's chambers. It was silent in the windowless, carpeted halls. She glanced at her watch. Most of the courts were still in session, for it was only a little after three o'clock. 'Is he in?' she asked his secretary. The woman got all flustered and refused to look at her. Lara assumed she'd seen the newspaper article about Ivory. She silently nodded and Lara walked in.

Evergreen stood. She could see the gray at the roots of his dyed red hair, but he was a dapper dresser and Lara admired his suit.

'Lara,' he said. 'Sit down. I heard the news and saw the

papers this morning. This is a very unfortunate situation. Please accept my condolences.'

'Thank you, Leo,' Lara said, sighing. 'It's been tough.'

She remained standing, but Evergreen sank into his large leather chair and spun around to his mahogany desk. As always, it was perfectly clean, no clutter or papers whatsoever. She tried to imagine him in here at night after everyone had gone home, with his little can of Pledge and his feather duster. After a few moments of staring at him, she took a seat.

'I had no idea you even had a sister. You never mentioned her.' Evergreen started tapping a pen on his desk and then dropped it. His eyes drifted down to the surface of his desk, and then he fixed his gaze on a picture in a mahogany wood frame. The frame was a perfect match to all the other wood in the room.

'How bad is it?' she said. 'You know, the talk and all . . . about the newspaper article.'

'Oh,' he said, sort of jumping up a little in his seat as if she had startled him. 'People are calling. They're concerned.'

'I'm going to have the services Monday . . . just for the family . . . something small.' She inhaled until her lungs almost exploded. She'd have to bury Sam. She hated him, but having him cremated was too extreme. And there was Josh – it just wouldn't look right. She exhaled and sank even further in the chair. 'I'll be back Tuesday to open the Adams trial.'

'I see,' he said. 'Why don't you take some time off? Go away for a week or so instead of jumping back into all this work. Once you open this trial, Lara, it will be almost impossible for you to bail out.'

Lara stood. She wanted to ask him about Packard Cummings, what agency had called him regarding this man, but Rickerson had insisted. She thought it was stupid. Why all the secrecy? 'I need to work, keep my mind occupied. Don't worry, I can handle it.'

'I'm not sure you are emotionally ready to return to the bench.'

'I . . . Leo . . .' Lara grabbed the back of the chair and leaned forward. She needed to work, put her life back into some semblance of normalcy. She didn't need to run off somewhere by herself. They were shorthanded anyway. 'I have my nephew, Leo. I can't leave town.'

'Isn't there another relative who could take him? Your parents or someone?'

'No,' Lara said emphatically. 'They're both dead. The kid's mine.'

'I see,' he said slowly, licking his lips. 'Social Services called this morning inquiring about you.'

'God,' she said. 'Already, huh? They already called?'

'Yes, they did,' he said, his brows knitting, 'and they were concerned about some information they learned from the San Clemente Police Department.'

'What information?' Lara said, searching Evergreen's dim eyes. Certainly, she thought, they hadn't already discovered that she didn't have a room for the kid. No one at the courthouse even knew where she was living.

'As they informed me, you evidently used your position to curtail investigations into your brother-in-law's criminal activities. I had to do some follow-up on this, and it's come to light that you are co-owner of that business – that pawnshop. Social Services expressed concern that you might be involved in this whole sordid affair. I, of course, assured them that you have an excellent record both as a prosecutor and as a member of this bench, but these are serious allegations, Lara.'

'What?' she said, blanching. 'What the hell . . .' She was shocked really, quite simply shocked. 'All I ever did was tell them to lay off him a little. I never thought he was actually involved in criminal activity, Leo. I swear. I thought he was just sloppy, forgetting to report all the property he took in. He wasn't that bright.' Lara had feared that this would someday come back to haunt her, but her statements to Evergreen were more or less the truth. Sam had never run a business before, and in the beginning she had attributed these incidents to sloppy bookkeeping. Probably by the last phone call the truth was beginning to sink in and she had simply denied it. All pawnshops took in a certain percentage of stolen goods. Everyone knew that. Even those that were scrupulously honest sometimes found themselves in that position.

Evergreen lifted his head and his chin jutted out. 'Well, we've all made mistakes now and then, but it doesn't look good, particularly in light of what has occurred and all the attention this case is garnering in the press. This is an embarrassment to the bench.' He cleared his throat and started speaking again in a firm, flat voice, one he usually reserved for the courtroom. 'If you recall the *Canons of Judicial Ethics*,' he said, pausing, picking up his reading glasses and a large leather-bound book from his desk and reading from it: ' "A judge's official conduct should be free from impropriety and the appearance of impropriety; he should avoid infractions of law; and his personal behavior, not only upon the bench and in the performance of judicial duties, but also in everyday life, should be beyond reproach." ' He snapped the book shut and peered at her over his glasses.

Lara was speechless. Her hands on the chair were trembling, and she removed them and placed them at her sides, her back rigid. 'Are you saying what I think you're saying?' He was blatantly accusing her of impropriety and unethical behavior.

'Yes, unfortunately I am. I consider it serious enough to warrant a full investigation. And of course, I'll have to relay this information to the Judicial Counsel in San Francisco.'

Lara stared at him, but he didn't flinch. She thought at first he might have been attempting to scare her, teach her a lesson like a father, but the look in his eyes was not fatherly at all. How could he have the balls to do this to her, and now of all times? Her heart raced and she placed a hand over her chest. She was seconds away from letting it all go, asking him point blank about this Cummings man.

'I'm sorry, Lara, but you have to understand my position. Once something like this is brought to my attention, I would be remiss if I didn't follow through,' he said softly, punching a button on his phone that was blinking. 'If you will excuse me, I have to take this phone call. You look quite distressed. You should go home and rest.'

Their eyes locked and lingered. A coldness was reflected there – as if she were gazing into two sheets of ice. Before this had all occurred, Lara had thought she was beginning to get to know this man, win his respect and admiration. Now she could see it all dissolving right before her eyes. Sure, she looked distressed. How else would she look when someone accused her of impropriety? Reaching her office, she walked right past Phillip and grabbed her purse off her desk and headed out the door.

'Judge Sanderstone,' Phillip said, standing. 'Don't you want your messages?'

'I'll call you later,' she said, and then remembered Sam. 'Buy another coffin, the cheapest one they have, and advise the mortuary to have my brother-in-law inside it by Monday.' She didn't look back. She just kept on walking. She might be burying more than her sister and Sam come Monday. She might be burying her entire career.

Chapter 14

Racing back to the condo, Lara felt certain Josh would be home, but he wasn't. Taped to the front door was a note from Social Services insisting that she call them at once. Rickerson must have told them where she was staying. She certainly couldn't call them now. She didn't even know where the kid was. Evergreen was accusing her of impropriety, and she'd somehow managed to misplace her dead sister's child. She went into the small kitchen and looked for a glass to get a drink of water. She was shaking and her throat was dry. There was nothing. All the cabinets were empty. She suddenly spun around in the small space, slamming all the cabinets as hard as she could, kicking the walls until she thought her ankle had broken, screaming, 'Why? Why has this happened?'

Placing her head under the faucet, she let the water run into her mouth. Then she just stuck her head under and let it soak her hair, her face. She was in a tight little box – a box she couldn't escape from no matter what she did. It wasn't the condo. It was the whole thing. She had invested everything in her career, and now it was all going up in smoke. Never once had she been called on the carpet. Her record was impeccable.

Before long, it was going to be dark. She didn't know what to do about Josh. She'd seen Emmet's van in the parking lot and crossed the courtyard to his door. 'Emmet,' she yelled through the door. 'It's Lara. Can I come in?'

She waited until he hit a button and the door unlocked. She found him in his office. Her hair was soaking wet, her eyes wild.

'Lara,' he said, his voice as always weak, his head dropping to one side. 'I called. Your nephew answered . . . and . . . hung up on me.'

Sometimes it was hard to understand Emmet. His speech was slurred due to his illness, and people just didn't give him time to say what he wanted to say. 'I'm sorry, Emmet. Have you seen him? He went out on his bicycle and hasn't come back.'

'No,' he said. 'I've . . . been . . . working out.'

Lara felt her panic subsiding. Just being here with Emmet made her feel stronger. If he could deal with the harsh reality of his illness, then she would have to find the strength to deal with her own predicament, her own sorrow. She suddenly noticed that his hair was soaking wet like her own. 'Did you say working out, Emmet? Are you all right? Your hair's all wet.'

'Yours . . . too,' he said, managing a smile. 'See, I . . . want to keep . . . my strength up, so . . . I crawl . . . from room . . . to room. Then I get . . . in my bed and then . . . out of my bed.'

'Really?' she said. 'You never told me you did that, Emmet.'

'Look,' he said, unstrapping a large pair of knee pads attached to his frail legs with Velcro, 'did you . . . think I went roller . . . skating with these? Want . . . to borrow . . . them?'

Lara laughed. She needed to get back to work. Then, she thought, she could put some of this out of her mind.

Emmet was always working, either on his physical therapy or his computers. Most people were put off by his appearance, his illness. Some even mistakenly thought he was retarded. But they were wrong, dead wrong. The frail young man with the wasted body and the thick glasses was brilliant. His software programs were unrivaled anywhere in the country. His disease was advanced but not to the point that he didn't have some muscle control. He could certainly work hour after hour, day after day, put in more hours than most healthy people.

But eventually he would die. He knew that fact well. He lived with it hanging over his head.

'Can I . . . do . . . something?' he said, his wrists jutting out awkwardly. 'I want . . . to help you, Lara.' He had spotted her distress. Emmet knew she was hurting.

Lara loved this man. There was something about him that exuded personal strength and power in the midst of physical infirmity – like a high-performance engine in an old, beat-up car. It shot right from his eyes. If people only took the time to look, they'd see it.

She looked around the room for a chair and then decided she should return to the condo in case Josh returned. 'You could give me a hug,' she finally said. She needed to touch someone, feel their body heat. She needed to borrow their strength.

She walked over to his wheelchair and leaned down and kissed his forehead lightly. He tried to raise his arm, but it fell back on the edge of the chair, too weak from his exercises even to hold her. Lara pressed her body against his and held it there. This was an Emmet hug.

'Thanks,' she said. 'I feel better already.'

Emmet smiled with his eyes. Lara smiled back.

'I'm so . . . sorry . . . about your sister.'

'Yeah,' she said. 'I'm sorry too, Emmet. About as sorry as a person can get.' For a few moments he managed to maintain eye contact, and then his eyes drifted away involuntarily. She didn't have to explain pain and sorrow to him. Emmet knew all there was to know. She quietly let herself out of the apartment as he turned back to the computer. As she walked out the door, she heard the soft tap, tap, tapping of his pen on the keyboard.

Still no Josh. Lara was beginning to get very concerned now. God forbid, she thought, what if something terrible had happened to him? Did boys his age do this all the time – just disappear for hours?

She didn't touch the boxes of pawn tickets in the entryway, but she did start reviewing the copies of the phone records that Rickerson had given her.

The list of numbers and names of people who had been called from the residence in San Clemente was extensive and varied. The investigators had managed to get the names and addresses from the telephone company, and she studied the list carefully, trying to see if she recognized any of them as old friends of Ivory's or anyone she might have mentioned through the years.

A number of the names she did recognize, or at least, she recognized the businesses where the phones were located that had been called. A lot of the numbers were to hotels, some in Orange County, some in Los Angeles. Lara shuddered. Only one reason for these calls, she thought. Clients. No names were listed next to these numbers. Once the calls were transferred from the switchboard, they were impossible to trace.

The calls to public officials were puzzling, to say the least. There was a call to the man who was superintendent of the Orange County School District and a call to a man she recognized as president of the Anaheim Chamber of Commerce.

Then she started thinking, rubbing her forehead. One

fact had to be the starting point for all speculation, a fact that Rickerson knew all too well. The fact that there was no forced entry. Whoever had killed Sam and Ivory was someone they knew well enough to allow them entrance to the residence. And she really couldn't stretch her imagination far enough to believe that Ivory had clients over and 'serviced' them, as Rickerson had called it, with Sam in the house. But then again, she might be wrong. What did she know about this type of activity? Her mind was full of unanswered questions, not just about the murder, but the life her sister was secretly leading. What kind of man would allow his wife to do something like this? A cheap, slimy asshole like Sam, she thought, wishing that he were still alive so she could kill him herself. He had taken advantage of Ivory's lack of intelligence, her lack of self-confidence, her immaturity. He had probably plied her with drugs and praised her every time she turned a trick like a damn dog. He was a parasite, a predator. All her life, people had taken advantage of Ivory. As sad as it was to consider, her sister would do anything to win people's approval. Everyone's approval but that of her own sister. After Lara had threatened to take Josh away, Ivory had never sought her approval again.

Josh still hadn't returned, and Lara walked to the window and peered through the curtains. She was about to give up and call the police when the front door opened and in he walked, pushing his bike over the door frame.

'Where in God's name have you been?' she said, almost screaming at him. 'I was worried sick. You should have left me a note or something.'

He tossed his shaggy head of hair and glared at her; his skin was glistening with perspiration. 'Well, I came back and you weren't here, so I went back out.'

'Okay,' she said, lowering her voice. 'I'm sorry I screamed at you. I was just worried, that's all. You can't go running around in this neighborhood. You could get hurt.'

'So what?' he sneered, suddenly erupting in anger. 'What's it to you?'

Lara brushed her hair off her face and walked over to him. 'Look, Josh, we have to make this work. You're all I have and I'm all you have. That's the way it is, whether you like it or not.'

'You're ugly. You look like a witch. This place is a dump. I hate it here. I want my stuff . . . my friends . . . I want to go home.'

As tough a facade as he was presenting, Lara could see his chest heaving and knew he was about to break down. 'You can cry, Josh. Don't be ashamed to cry. I know how awful you feel.' She paused, shuffling her feet around on the small entryway. 'I made an appointment for you to talk to Dr. Werner again.'

'I'm not going,' he shouted. 'I told you I'm not going to that stupid shrink. I hate him. I'm not crazy. You can't make me. I'll run away. I'll . . .'

He grabbed the handlebars of the bike and started to push it back out the open door. Lara reached for his shirt and accidentally ended up with a handful of his hair. 'Stop right there,' she ordered him. 'You're not going out again. It's almost dark. There's a lot of crime around here. I won't allow it.'

'Let go of my fucking hair. You're a bitch. You look like that horror woman . . . Elvira . . . Mistress of the Dark. Let go of me.'

Lara took some deep breaths and held onto his hair. 'I'll let go as soon as you promise me you won't go back out. Do you promise?' she said, pulling on his hair enough that his forehead fell backward and she could peer down into his eyes. If this was what it took to control a teenage boy, keep him from getting hurt, then this is the way it would have to be.

The door was still standing open and Josh was really yelling now like she was killing him. 'Let go of me,' he shrieked. 'You're scalping me. Okay, I promise. Just let go.'

Lara released him and he snapped his head back up. Then both of them stood there and stared, their mouths falling open in unison. Only a few feet away on the sidewalk, watching the whole scene intently, were two women. As soon as Lara looked at them, they stepped toward the door to the condo. One of the women had short blond hair and was as skinny as a twig.

'I'm Lucille Rambling,' she said, extending her hand, 'and this is Madeline Murphy. Judge Sanderstone, I presume?'

Lara felt her stomach do about five cartwheels and for a moment thought she was going to be sick. She shook the woman's hand and then dropped it. It was cold and limp.

'We're from the Social Services Department, Judge Sanderstone,' the woman said. 'We're here about your nephew.'

Lara hadn't taken the time to make the bed or pick up the condo that morning. Josh had most of his clothes spread all over the floor in the living room. When the two women from Social Services walked into the room, the skinny blonde turned up her nose and stepped over the mess.

'Uh, Judge Sanderstone,' Lucille Rambling said, 'we need to see your nephew's bedroom, the place he will be sleeping while he's staying with you.'

Quickly, Lara tried to think. This was it. She could let them take him. Letting them take him would certainly be easier than what she was going through. Josh was just standing there with a surly expression on his face. 'In here,' she said without even thinking. 'His bedroom is right in here. Of course, I have a large house in Irvine. We'll be moving back in there in a few days.'

The women walked into the bedroom and looked around, peeking into the small bathroom and then walking back to the living room. 'Is there another room here?' the other woman said. 'You know, another bedroom.' She was craning her neck around toward the kitchen.

'No,' Lara said self-consciously. 'This is it.'

'Humph,' she said. 'Then where do you sleep?'

'I sleep on the sofa . . . here. I let Josh have the bedroom.'

'You did not,' he said, narrowing his eyes, 'you're lying. You didn't give me the bedroom except that one night. I've been sleeping on that stupid sofa. It's a bitch, man.'

Lara's shoulders fell. If he'd just kept his mouth shut, maybe they wouldn't have known about the sleeping arrangements and would have overlooked the scene they walked into at the door. But possibly it was for the best, she told herself. The child seemed to despise her anyway, and she was a nervous wreck.

'Why don't we step outside?' Ms. Rambling said.

'Fine,' Lara said, shifting her eyes to Josh. See, she wanted to tell him, see what you did.

'Look,' Lucille Rambling said once they were outside and the door was shut. 'We're certain your intentions are good in wanting to care for your sister's child, but there are certain criteria that must be met for us to allow him to remain here. One of these is that he has his own room. He's a teenage boy and he needs his privacy.'

'I understand,' Lara said, 'but surely there's some flexibility in all rules.' She kept glancing back at the door. For some reason she felt a tug on her heart. She didn't want to let him go. 'I told you we will be moving back to my house in Irvine, and Josh will have his own room. In fact, we could do that now if that would rectify the situation.'

'I'm sorry,' the blonde continued, exchanging a knowing glance with the other woman. 'Investigator Bradshaw at the San Clemente Police Department informed us that you were hiding out here, that they feel you are in some kind of jeopardy. I don't think that you should take your nephew back somewhere where he would be at risk.'

'Of course not,' Lara said quickly, wondering who this Bradshaw was. If he kept telling everyone where she was, she wouldn't be hiding out anywhere much longer. 'I could possibly rent a bigger place in this same complex. It might take me a few days to arrange it, but I'm certain I could.'

'We can't allow the boy to stay here. We'll have to find a placement for him, and then when your situation changes, you can contact us and we'll do another evaluation. Believe me, it's far better for all concerned that he remains with you, yet it must be within our guidelines.' She paused and then continued, her face softening somewhat, her voice almost a whisper. 'The Social Services agency is under close scrutiny right now, Judge Sanderstone. I know you're aware of the Adams case. The agency director has instructed us to enforce the rules with no exceptions. And that exchange we saw between you and your nephew . . . well, maybe you could both benefit from a cooling-out period.'

Lara dropped her head. She thought of throwing her weight around, insisting that they leave Josh with her. But no, she decided, an exercise in authority would make these women even more determined to take Josh away. Lara might be a judge, but in this situation Lucille Rambling and Madeline Murphy held all the cards.

'Why don't you get his things together?' Madeline Murphy told Lara. 'We'll be taking him now.'

'Look, the funeral is Monday. Why don't you let him stay here until then, and I'll work on getting another place? Besides, they're looking right now for the man that did this. As soon as they find him, we can go home.'

'I'm sorry,' she said.

Lara refused to look at the two women, her eyes on the concrete walk. 'Thanks. Thanks a whole hell of a lot.' As soon as she said it, she regretted it.

'There's no reason for you to get snippy with us, Judge Sanderstone. We're only doing our job . . . surely – '

'Excuse me,' she said to the woman, finally raising her eyes. 'I thought possibly after all he's gone through, you might see the benefit of his being with a close relative. You know, bending the rules somewhat to fit the situation.'

Madeline Murphy had mousy brown hair and thick glasses; her eyes were so small they looked like shiny black beads. 'I wouldn't talk about bending the rules if I were you, Judge Sanderstone, not from what we've heard.'

Sirens started squealing on the street in front of the complex. First, there were black-and-whites racing by, and then an ambulance raced by. The noise was so loud, they couldn't even speak. A few moments later, a fire truck rolled by. This was real impressive, Lara thought. All she needed now was someone to go running past her doorway with a sawed-off shotgun. Great neighborhood, she thought. Super place for a kid.

Finally the sirens stopped. 'What do you mean to imply, Ms. Murphy?' Lara knew just what the woman was talking about, the fact that she'd talked law enforcement out of going after Sam, covered him inadvertently while he was involved in criminal activities. She remembered all too well her little chat with Evergreen.

'Never mind,' the woman said. 'Please, just get the boy ready and we'll be on our way. We'll wait out here. Send him out.' The woman reached into her purse and handed Lara her card. 'We are sorry about your sister,' she said. 'Call us when you get situated in a larger place.'

Lara went inside and shut the door behind her, leaning back against it. Josh stuck his head out of the small kitchen.

'Are those old biddies gone?'

Lara sighed. 'Those old biddies, huh?'

'Yeah, boy, were they ugly.' He laughed and made a face. 'Look, I'm starving. We don't have any food at all here, not even a cookie. You've got to go to the store.'

'I thought I was the Mistress of the Dark?'

'Sorry,' he said and gave her a lopsided grin. 'I was in a bad mood, okay?' As soon as the smile appeared, it fell away.

'Well, unfortunately, Josh, or fortunately for you, depending on how you look at it, since you don't want to stay with me – '

'Wait,' he said. A shadow passed over his eyes as he walked into the living room and plunked down in a chair. 'I'll stay, okay? I told you I was just upset.'

'They won't let you stay. I don't have the right situation for you . . . a room and all. And they saw the little argument we had in living color. I have to pack your things. They're waiting.'

'No,' he said, springing to his feet. 'What're they going to do to me? They can't take me away somewhere. I said I'd stay here with you.'

He was blinking rapidly and Lara saw the tears gathering in his eyes. She started toward him and he disappeared into the kitchen. He really wanted to stay with her. She was shocked. More than anything, she was touched. 'Josh,' she said softly, 'I'll take care of it. I'll figure out something, okay? You may have to stay in a foster home for a day or two, but I promise I'll get you as soon as I can. We're going to have the services Monday. Maybe I can have it arranged by then.'

Josh had his forehead pressed to the refrigerator door. 'You'll never get me. Why would you want to? I called you names. I . . . I'm not a good person.'

Lara walked up behind him. 'Josh, I understand . . . please believe me. I wouldn't give up on you simply because you called me names.'

His body began shaking and Lara reached out tentatively to touch him, stroke his hair. When he didn't resist, she moved even closer, as if she were about to pet a wild animal. Now she was so close that she could smell his hair, his skin, his sweaty boy odor. He didn't move and kept his forehead against the refrigerator door.

'I miss my mom . . .' he said, his voice weak and frail now. 'I keep having these nightmares that she's calling to me . . . begging me to help her and I can't find her. I look all over the house, in every single room, and she isn't there.'

Gently, Lara turned him around and wrapped him in her arms. She felt a powerful surge of emotion, one so strong that she had to grit her teeth and lean into it, like a person walking in gale-force winds.

'Look,' she said, pushing herself away from him, 'look at me.' She let forth a nervous laugh. She wiped her eyes with her fingers. 'And I never cry.'

All of a sudden his hand reached out for her, almost in slow motion, only touching a single strand of her hair as he studied her face. Then his hand fell away and dropped to his side.

As quickly as it had come, the moment was gone.

Josh walked out of the kitchen and started throwing the few things he had in a pile on the floor.

'I'll get you a sack or something,' Lara said, heading back to the kitchen.

'What about my bike?' he said, glancing at it in the doorway, his one possession, his one means of escape. 'They won't let me take it, will they?'

'Probably not, honey, but you can ask.'

A few minutes later, he walked out the door, suitcase in hand, his shoulders slumped. He glanced back at Lara. They didn't say goodbye. He didn't return for his bicycle.

•

As soon as they left, Lara went back to Emmet's.

The complex wasn't really such a bad place to live, she thought, crossing the courtyard with the huge weeping willow, its branches brushing the ground. That is, if you overlooked the neighborhood surrounding it. A nest of sparrows lived in that tree, and every time she walked out the front door, she could hear them chirping. Today they were silent. But mature trees were scattered all throughout the complex, making it shady and lush. She thought the trees and grounds might be what had attracted Emmet. The structures were older, steeped in character, marked by time. Lara liked that type of thing. She'd always looked back instead of forward. Most of Orange County was so new, so shiny. Row after row of tract houses lined the streets, the trees all mowed down by developers.

She'd never felt so dejected in her life. She had to get Josh back. She had seen through that tough outer shell. He was just a frightened child – so alone, so full of pain. Sure, he was bitter. Who wouldn't be bitter? She had no idea what he had been through before the murders, but she knew it wasn't good.

She'd tried to call Irene Murdock, but she was out. Everyone seemed to be out. With the ever present sunshine, the seventy-degree temperature, the ocean always only a few miles away, people in Southern California seldom stayed inside their homes.

Every time she thought about Emmet, she smiled – even now when her heart was breaking. Almost from the night she had met him, Lara classified herself as an Emmet fan; she admired him so much. He struggled with his disease without ever slipping into self-pity. He lived independently and had built a successful business. And he was a marvelous companion, far more interesting than any other men she knew. He was witty, intelligent, sensitive. Many Friday and Saturday evenings when Lara didn't have a date

– and there were many – she'd call Emmet up and come over here, have real discussions about philosophy, literature, science, Emmet typing out responses on his computer faster than she could read, Lara standing behind him sipping a glass of wine.

Emmet's condominium was sparsely furnished. When he'd purchased it, he'd had all the carpeting removed and discovered the original hardwood flooring underneath. Since the building was older, it had wide hallways and oversized doors, which made it easier for Emmet to navigate his wheelchair in and around the rooms. His front door was wired to the ever present computer. All he had to do was push a few buttons and the front door opened.

Lara plunked down in the one chair, a Lazy Boy recliner. When there was no one to help him, Emmet used a trapeze type of device to hoist himself into the recliner. Lara flipped it out of the way. Every evening between six and seven o'clock, a male nurse came to assist him.

'I don't know what to do,' Lara told him after he'd joined her in the living room. 'Even if I went against Rickerson's and everyone's advice and moved back into the house in Irvine, they still won't let me have Josh back. Of course, they probably have a point – that I would be putting him at risk. I told them maybe I could get a larger place, but I can't do it today or tomorrow, and I certainly won't be able to get one that's furnished like the model. I just have to get him back, Emmet. He needs me. He just can't be involved in the murders. I know it.'

'I . . . have . . . an . . . idea,' Emmet said, making an effort to squeeze out all four words. At the end of the day, speaking was even more strenuous. 'Come . . .' He turned his electric chair around and headed for his office, the wheels rolling over the hardwood flooring. Lara followed.

Sticking his head back into the steel cage, Emmet started

tapping out words on the computer. Lara stood behind him and read.

'You can have my place until you find another and I'll stay at your place. I have three bedrooms. We'll move some of my equipment and I'll be fine. I can come over here and work during the day when you're gone.'

'Emmet,' Lara said. 'I can't ask you to do that . . . all this' – she looked around at the room – 'this is your work. You need all this equipment. We'd have to hire someone to disconnect everything and reassemble it at my place, and my place is carpeted. No,' she said, shaking her head. 'I appreciate it, but no. I'll find something.' She thought of the house in San Clemente – the obvious choice. It was doubtful if the killers would go back there, but she knew living in that house right now would be too painful.

'Yes,' Emmet typed, 'it will be easy. No big deal. I have a firm that will set up the things I need at your place in only a few hours and I can work here during the day. I'll call the phone company and have a modem installed. Because I'm disabled, they'll do it at once. Let me help you, Lara. It will make me feel good to help someone else.'

He stopped typing and tried to look her in the eye. Every time his gaze drifted, he seemed to force it back with a concentrated effort.

'But, Emmet, I have carpet, remember?'

He spun back around to the computer and typed out another rapid-fire message. 'We can have plastic runners put down. They'll work just fine. Besides, I won't need my knee pads when I exercise.'

'All right,' Lara said, putting her hands together and clapping softly and then clasping them together tightly in relief. 'We can start making the arrangements right now. You're a hero, Emmet. You're a first-class hero.'

His head rolled far to the side, almost to the armrest of

the wheelchair. His eyes smiled behind his thick glasses. 'I . . . know,' he said. 'I like being . . . a . . . hero.'

Lara laughed. 'You know, huh? Let's call these people and start getting things set up. I'm sure it won't be for more than a few days at the most. They're trying to find the man now, and then we can go home.'

'I'll . . . make the calls,' he said.

'Don't you want me to handle the arrangements, Emmet?' Lara asked.

'No need,' Emmet said. 'Let . . . me . . . do something.'

Lara gave him an extra key and let herself out of the condo, crossing the courtyard. She'd let Social Services know that she had a place for Josh first thing in the morning.

Back in the condo, she placed a call to Benjamin England at his residence in Tustin. His message had said he would be returning this weekend. She simply could not be alone another moment. When she was alone the demons came out and stalked her. They were stalking her now.

She saw herself in a dark, deep well, clawing the walls to get out, screaming for someone to come and rescue her. Her sister's body kept appearing in her mind, Sam's exposed brain tissue, the gruesome blood-splattered walls. It should have been her, she thought. Ivory had Josh. She picked up the birth certificate and stared at the tiny footprints again. She had nothing. If she could change places with Ivory right this minute, she would. In the blackness there must be peace, she thought – an end to this chaotic existence that seemed to lead nowhere and was so full of anguish.

Even though she had never been religious, Lara fell to her knees by the little sofa. She let her head fall forward and prayed. She prayed for courage to raise her nephew, track down her sister's killer and avenge her senseless death. She'd let her sister down, failed to see the signs when her life was falling apart. By her own hand, a tap of the gavel, the man who had possibly done this had been set free. She prayed for strength and direction.

In the silence Lara listened. The answers came to her. She stood and pushed her shoulders back as a wave of calmness and resolve washed over her. Her mother used to say that you should never ask God for something you can handle yourself. Lara was the direct descendant of a Cherokee chief. She would not succumb to weakness and self-pity. Not now, not ever.

Chapter 15

Rickerson and his two sons were finishing dinner at the long oak table in the kitchen. He'd finally had to take a little time off. He was completely exhausted and besides, he had to go back out to interview the young man who had made threats to Lara in the courtroom. Big case or not, Rickerson knew he had to go home every now and then. He did have a family to raise, and unfortunately, right now he was doing it alone.

Stephen and Jimmy had prepared the entire meal by themselves. They'd made a roast chicken, a salad, some lumpy mashed potatoes. 'Not bad,' Rickerson told them. 'Next time, though, turn the oven up a little higher the last ten or fifteen minutes. That way the chicken will get nice and brown on the top.'

Jimmy had the pot of potatoes set on his plate and was scooping out every last bite. 'How'd you learn to cook, Dad? Mom never said you could cook.'

'Oh, yeah, well, I know how to sew too. Think I'm a sissy?'

Jimmy started laughing. He had a little pot belly, and when he laughed, it jumped up and down. They would never in their wildest dreams consider their rugged father a sissy. 'Tell,' Jimmy said, sticking a spoonful of potatoes in his mouth.

'When I was really young, my parents lived in Ohio. We had a boardinghouse. So, I had to help my mama with the cooking. I had to mend things that needed mending. I always wanted you guys to know how to take care of yourselves. Never know when you'll be alone in this world. Can't always depend on other people to care for you all your life.'

Stephen was listening intently. He knew the boarding-house story. He also knew his mother had walked out on his father, and he simply could not forgive her no matter how hard he tried. If he was his father, he wouldn't take her back, no matter what she said or did. She was his mother and he would always love her, but she had just abandoned them. He could handle it. He would be in college next year, but it certainly wasn't fair to Jimmy. He was immature for his age and missed her terribly. Some nights Stephen heard him crying.

Rickerson was rolling a cigar around in his fingers, about to bite off the end and shove it in his mouth. 'If you light that, Dad,' Stephen said, 'I'm leaving the room, okay, and you can clean up the kitchen. I can't stand that smell.' Just then Jimmy reached over and grabbed another roll. Stephen slapped it out of his hand. 'Stop that. What do you want to do, weigh three hundred pounds? You'll die of a heart attack when you're thirty.'

Rickerson's eyelids fluttered and he dropped the fat cigar onto the table. 'Any news on your scholarship?'

'Get up, asshole,' Stephen said to his brother. 'Now. Move it. I have to do my homework. I don't want to be stuck in the kitchen all night.' As soon as his brother started clearing the table, he turned to his father. 'My counselor said I definitely have a partial academic scholarship, but it won't cover my room and board in the dorm and all of my tuition. They're still reviewing it, so I could get more, but I don't know. It's going to be expensive, Dad. Stanford's an expensive school.'

Rickerson looked at his son. He was so serious. Too serious almost. 'What? You don't think I can afford to send you to college?'

Stephen dropped his head. 'I don't know. With Mom in school now and everything, I – I could go somewhere else. Maybe I could go to UCI and live at home. That would save a lot of money. And I could help you with Jimmy if Mom doesn't move back home.'

Rickerson leaned over until he was peering into his son's eyes. 'I've got the money, kid. Just worry about your grades, okay? Let the old man worry about the dough.'

'What about Jimmy? He can't stay here alone all the time when I go off to college. All he'll do is eat and get in trouble. He won't even do his homework.'

'Hey, what are you, the diet cop? I'm the real cop and you're suddenly your brother's dietitian. Give the guy a break. And as to next year, we'll cross that bridge when we come to it.'

Rickerson left the table to go into the living room to smoke his cigar. He flopped down on the sofa, leaned his head back, and closed his eyes, sticking his long legs out in front of him and kicking off his shoes. He let his mind wander to Lara Sanderstone. For some reason his thoughts drifted more and more to her every day. Something about her intrigued him, and it wasn't simply that they were spending a lot of time together, talking to each other several times a day.

It might be the fact that she was lonely.

Rickerson knew about that type of thing. He felt terribly alone sometimes, and the funny thing was, he'd felt that way long before his wife had left. Joyce had always had the kids, the house to keep up, her own set of friends and activities. Women married to police officers tended to get very self-reliant.

The only friends he really had were other cops, and all they talked about was the job. After all these years he just got tired of listening to the same four-letter words, the same pumped-up war stories, the constant complaints. It was hard, really, for people like him to socialize. What did he possibly have in common with a man who sold used cars like the guy next door, or a man who punched numbers in a computer all day in a room about the size of a closet? Most Friday and Saturday nights when friends got together to socialize were the nights of heavy business for Rickerson. That's when the natives really got restless, and violence and crime spewed forth like water from an untapped faucet.

Cops were a different species. Most of the time when he was with people outside the job, all they wanted to do was ask him about the job anyway. Being a police officer was like wearing a suit of clothes with no zipper, like the color of a man's skin. If you were black or brown, you were black or brown from the time you got up until the time you went to bed. That's what it was like to be a cop.

Sometimes he'd made love to Joyce and fantasized about other women. He told himself that after twenty years of marriage, even the best of things became stale. Oh, he loved his wife. In many ways she had been his closest friend, but the excitement had vanished. Both of them had felt the clock ticking. Their youth was gone. All that was left, as he saw it, was to grow old and die. Now it looked like he was going to grow old and die alone. He would have never in a million years thought he would be in this position. The past three months he had tried not to give up hope, but hope was slowly slipping away.

Last night he had fantasized about Lara Sanderstone.

He sat up on the sofa and slapped his thigh. It was those

damn suggestive pictures that got him daydreaming, started the juices flowing in a direction that he just had to put a stop to, and now, right now. When he looked at the pictures of Ivory, he imagined he was looking at Lara.

He simply couldn't look at those pictures again.

Lara Sanderstone would never be interested in a man like him. He wasn't a fool. She was a classy broad – a judge at that – and a good-looking woman. He'd never had a way with the women. Joyce was the only one he'd ever seriously dated.

Dating. Just the thought made him cringe. If Joyce didn't come back soon, he'd have to start prowling around looking for someone to spend time with, someone to have sex with now and then. He might be forty, but he wasn't dead. He was a man. He had normal desires. Women didn't just hop into bed with anyone that walked by, not today, not with all the diseases floating around. And most of the single women in his age group were looking for security, a meal ticket, a man with a fat paycheck and a fancy car. He couldn't afford to wine and dine them. He just didn't have the money or the time.

'Dad,' Stephen said, sticking his head out the kitchen door. 'It's Bradshaw . . . you know, baby Bradshaw.'

Rickerson sighed, bringing himself back to reality. 'Tell him I'm off duty. Unless he's got another stiff, it can wait for tomorrow.'

Stephen disappeared and Rickerson fired up his cigar. He was smoking way too many of these things, he decided, rolling it in his fingers. Even he was beginning to get sick of them.

A few moments later Stephen stuck his head back out. 'Says he's got a stiff.' The boy shrugged his shoulders. 'That's what he said.'

'Nah,' he said. 'He's pulling your leg. That stupid little prick. Just wants me to come to the phone. I'll kill him . . . I'll frigging kill him.'

Rickerson shuffled across the living room, looking down at all the spots on the carpet. In some places it was almost threadbare. Such is life, he said to himself.

'Bradshaw,' he barked, 'if you don't have a stiff, you better take out your gun and point it at your head.'

'I do, I do . . .' the officer said, so excited that he was panting.

Rickerson let the cigar fall from his mouth to the kitchen floor in a stream of saliva. 'Give it to me. Damn you, who and where?'

'Dad,' Stephen yelled, bending down to pick up the cigar, 'that's disgusting. We just mopped the floor today.'

'Packy Cummings,' Bradshaw continued. 'The S.O. found him a few minutes ago. In a car . . . wait . . . wait. It was his car – the red Camaro. I'm in the radio room. They're on the air now.' He paused. In the background the dispatcher was talking and the unit at the scene responding.

'Okay, okay,' Bradshaw said. 'He was shot . . . in the head. Ambulance and rescue are en route, but they're certain he's dead.'

'Where, Bradshaw?' Rickerson yelled into the phone. 'Tell me where. I can't do a damn thing if I don't know where it is I'm going.'

'Just a minute . . .' More voices could be heard in the background. 'Santa Ana . . . First Street . . . parking lot of an apartment complex near the courts. The officer doesn't know the address. It just went down.'

'I'm on the way,' Rickerson said. If Bradshaw hadn't fucked up, the location he was describing was right down the street from where Lara Sanderstone lived. 'Get me an exact location and advise me over the radio.'

When his father hung up, Stephen was wiping his hands on a dish towel. 'Guess he really had a stiff, huh?'

'Yeah,' Rickerson said, walking rapidly toward the door.

Then he turned around and returned and gave his two sons a quick hug. 'Don't look for me tonight. It looks like a long one.'

'Be safe, Dad,' they both said, almost in unison.

'Always,' he answered. In seconds he was out the door and backing out of the driveway.

The parking lot of the Sea Breeze Apartments was taped, barricaded, and surrounded by squad cars.

Rickerson leaped out of his vehicle, leaving the car door standing open, and jogged the short distance to Packy Cummings's red Camaro.

A uniformed officer stepped forward and stopped him. 'Wait a minute, bud. This is a crime scene.'

Rickerson sneered and flipped his badge, then placed it on his belt and made sure his coat was open. 'What do you have?' he asked. 'And who's the commanding officer here?'

'Lieutenant Thomas,' the man said. 'Over there.'

Thomas was a big guy, six-five or more. He was young for the rank of lieutenant and carried as much muscle around as height. His light brown hair was neatly cut, and he was standing by the vehicle as the men worked. The doors were open and several men from the medical examiner's office and the sheriff's crime lab were photographing the body and poking around for evidence. Packy was in the driver's seat, his head back on the headrest, a bullet hole a few centimeters above his left ear. Blood had gushed out in brackish rivers down his neck and onto his white dress shirt. Most of it had dried now. His eyes were open and his mouth was gaping. From the expression on his face, Rickerson bet he'd never known what hit him. He was now wearing a permanent mask of surprise.

'Didn't expect it, did he?' Lieutenant Thomas said, having arrived at the same conclusion.

'Are you sure it's him?'

'It's the car' – the lieutenant jerked his head to the side – 'and that guy over there is his parole agent. He identified him. The parole office is only five minutes away.'

'What do you have?'

'Who knows?' Thomas said. 'There's all kinds of prints in and on the vehicle, but who knows who they belong to? The killer may have never stepped foot in that car. See,' he said, walking over to the vehicle, 'the driver's window was rolled down. Shooter could have stood right here and pulled the trigger.' Thomas took out a pack of cigarettes and offered one to Rickerson. He waved them away.

'What else is in there?'

'Hey, Stanley,' the lieutenant yelled at one of his men. 'Show the sergeant here what you took out of the trunk.'

Both men walked a few feet away. On the sidewalk was what looked like most of Packy's belongings. They had been inside a large plastic garbage bag and were now spread all over the sidewalk on a canvas tarp.

'Let's see,' Officer Stanley said, picking through the stuff with gloved fingers. 'We've got some underwear – definitely not clean – a couple of white dress shirts from J.C. Penney, their own brand. And these,' he said, laughing, pulling out something in little packets.

'Condoms?' Rickerson said.

'Yep. He might have gotten himself blown away, but he didn't die of AIDS. Smart guy, huh?'

All the men around them started laughing except Rickerson. The detective failed to see the humor of the present situation.

Packy Cummings was the string of crumbs leading to the prize. Whoever had offed him had known just that.

'Any witnesses?'

'Little lady over there,' Stanley said. 'She lives in the upstairs apartment, the one overlooking the parking lot.'

Rickerson felt his dinner rise in his throat and swallowed

it. If she saw the killer, the case could come together in a matter of hours. 'And . . .' he said excitedly.

'She was a good distance away, and the car was partially obscured by these trees. She saw two people in the car about two hours ago. They might have been inside the car and they might have been outside the car. She's not certain.' The man's lip was curling. 'She was opening her curtains and casually glanced down and saw the Camaro. There was another car parked nearby that she didn't recognize as belonging to one of the tenants, and she'd never seen the Camaro before today. Good place for a homicide, huh?'

Rickerson looked at the trees. 'Right. The other car. . . ?'

'She thought it was a green Mercedes, or a blue BMW, or a black Ford.' He looked at Rickerson and smacked his chewing gum. 'Get the picture?'

'Yeah,' Rickerson said. 'Did she hear the shots?'

'Yep,' the other man said, spitting his gum out onto the concrete. 'Heard something . . . thought it was a car backfiring. We got the call when some kid saw this guy with a hole in his head inside the vehicle with the engine running. Killer was gone by then. We're just lucky he called. People don't like to get involved around here.'

None of this was worth anything, Rickerson thought, greatly disappointed. The woman was a shitty observer. Many people were. He'd had homicides in which a person was killed not more than two feet from where people were standing and they didn't remember a blasted thing.

California, he thought. The land of the proverbial airhead.

'Nothing in his pockets, his wallet?'

'*Nada*, my man, no such luck,' Stanley said. 'All the dude had in his wallet was a five spot. If he had anything else, someone could have lifted it after the killing. Won't know if the killer took it or a neighborhood vulture. Fellow with a bullet in his head is a pretty unthreatening victim for a thief.'

'Small-caliber weapon?'

'Hole's little . . . guess so.'

The lieutenant had walked back to the car and was flicking his ashes in the nearby grass. He saw Rickerson and nodded for him to come over. 'We're taking impressions of the skid marks. See,' he said, looking down where a man was working. 'I'd say the killer arranged a meet here, pulled up, and parked right next to the Camaro. Killer stood outside the window and they talked. That's when he pulled out a gun and blew him away. Cummings must have felt pretty secure with this person, because his own shooter is still in the glove box.'

'The killer's prints could be on the door handle. This might have gone down inside the car.' Rickerson knew the door handle was the perfect surface for prints. He could hope. 'You guys didn't stick a dozen prints on top of it when you got here, did you?' he said, accusing the few officers standing around of destroying evidence.

'Hold on a minute, Sergeant,' the lieutenant barked. 'We aren't a bunch of backwoods cops. We know how to handle a crime scene.'

The lieutenant was being a prick, letting him know he was the one from the small department. In their eyes, they were the pros. 'Well, I guess you've got a handle on it, then,' he told him. 'I'll be waiting for the reports. As soon as your people write them, fax them to my office.'

'No problem,' the lieutenant answered. 'Think this is your shooter?'

'Maybe you need to review the facts of this case yourself, Lieutenant,' he told the man, already heading across the parking lot, tossing the words over his shoulder. 'We never had a shooter. Cause of death was a blow to the head and suffocation.'

Rickerson smiled. Let him blow that one out his asshole, he thought. Then he marched to his unit, threw the gear shift in reverse, and burned off backward onto the street.

Alone in the condominium, Lara tried reading the newspaper, but she couldn't keep her mind focused. She thought of returning to Emmet's, but his nurse was there now. All she could think about was Josh, and then the horrid conversation she'd had with Evergreen. Was he really going to pursue this? Pull out all the stops and place her entire career in jeopardy just because of a few words on the phone over Sam's pawnshop? It seemed incredible.

The phone rang and Lara seized it, thinking it was Irene or Benjamin. She'd left messages for both of them.

'He's dead,' Rickerson said.

'Who's dead?' Lara said, her heart pounding.

'Cummings. Someone shot him this afternoon not far from your apartment.'

'My God,' Lara said, her spirits soaring. 'Then I can go home. If the man who broke into my place is dead, I'm safe.' She wouldn't have to move into Emmet's condo. She could get Josh back.

'I'm right down the street,' he said. 'Can I stop by in a few hours? I'll fill you in on all the details. But, Lara . . .'

'Yes?' she said. She was sitting up straight. There was a God, she thought. He'd heard her prayers. Everything was going to be fine now. She couldn't bring Ivory back, but she could care for her son, resume her own life.

'You can't go home just yet, and . . . well, let me tell you everything when I see you. Right now I've got to go.'

Before she could say anything, the detective had hung up. The way she saw it, this was a cause for celebration. She showered, dressed in clean clothes, sprayed herself with cologne. She went to the corner liquor store and bought a bottle of wine. Then she waited.

'You can come in,' the woman said at the door to Rickerson. 'Ian's expecting you.'

He stepped over the threshold into a picture-perfect living room. The furniture and the decorations were nice enough to be on the cover of *House Beautiful*. Mrs. Berger was still standing at the door. She was in her mid to late fifties, well dressed and still fairly attractive. Her husband was a successful businessman. Finally she shut the door.

'I'll go get Ian. He's in his room.' She turned and had started walking toward the back of the house when the detective called to her.

'No,' he said, his voice low. 'Rather than talking to him in here and disrupting the rest of the household, why don't I just speak with him in his room?'

The woman's eyes drifted up and then down. She shrugged her shoulders as if it didn't matter. She was worried sick about her son. It showed. 'First door on the left,' she said.

The door was open. Ian Berger was sitting at a small desk with several books open in front of him. He looked up. Dark circles were etched under his eyes. Rickerson let his gaze wander. At least six framed pictures of Jessica Van Horn surrounded him. On the wall was an enormous poster of the murdered girl, larger than life. Her entire presence seemed to fill the room.

Ian stood and shook Rickerson's hand. 'Sit down,' he said, indicating his bed. 'Or you can sit here if you want. I mean, we could go in the living room.'

Rickerson dropped to the edge of the bed. He'd wanted to see the inside of this room. When a person's mind was disintegrating, enough to do something rash, their surroundings generally reflected it. This room might be a shrine to the dead girl, but it wasn't the room of someone who'd gone over the edge. It was neat and appealing. The bed was made, everything was in its place. But, of course, he reminded himself, the boy lived in an apartment near the UCLA campus during the week. The lack of clutter and disorder in this room might mean nothing. His mother probably cleaned it.

'Do you know why I'm here?' he asked the boy.

'Sort of . . .' He coughed and leaned over his knees. 'It's because something happened to that judge, isn't it?'

Rickerson changed the subject. He liked to switch things around, get a subject headed in one direction and then head off in another. 'What are you studying at college?'

'Economics.' The boy's eyes were locked on Rickerson's face.

'Good subject,' the detective said. 'Tough one, isn't it?'

'Yeah.'

'I was never very good at math. There's a lot of math in economics. Right?'

'Look,' Ian Berger said, 'can we get down to what you wanted to talk to me about? I have a big test next week. I have to study or I'm not going to make it this year.'

'Where were you on Wednesday, September eighth, between say twelve and three o'clock?'

The boy thought a few moments and then turned back to his desk, flipping through a calendar. 'I was at school . . . in class.'

'The entire time?' Rickerson stood, glancing up at the poster of the dead girl. Like the *Mona Lisa*, her eyes seemed to follow him around the room. He hadn't told the boy the crime had occurred in the afternoon instead of the morning, but Ian had known it had. Of course, he probably read the papers.

'From twelve to one, I was at lunch. I think I ate in the

commissary. I eat there everyday. At one, I had a class in macro-economics.'

'I see,' Rickerson said. He took a cigar out of his pocket and rolled it around. He had no intention of lighting it. 'How long did the class last?'

'Until three. Look, why don't you quit playing around and just ask me what you want to ask me?' His face flushed and he sat up, his back rigid. 'I threatened that woman judge. That's what this is all about. I certainly didn't do anything, though.'

Rickerson stopped and glared at him, flicking the hairs on his mustache. 'You did threaten her . . . tell her someone should kill her whole family?'

The boy looked down. 'You know that. Everyone in that room heard me. I . . . didn't really mean it. I was upset, angry.'

Slipping the cigar back into his pocket, Rickerson barked at him, 'Maybe you were angry enough to carry through on those threats, make her pay?'

Ian Berger shook his head. Beads of perspiration popped out on his forehead. He was a nice-looking young man, with dark hair and penetrating dark eyes, but he looked older than his years now. He would never be a carefree young man again. 'You can check with my classes. I was there. Not only that, if I wanted to kill someone, I would kill that maniac that murdered Jessica, not the stupid judge.'

'But you didn't threaten Henderson. You threatened the judge. Right?'

'Right,' Ian said. 'I made a mistake, okay? I was acting like a fool. I know she was only doing what she had to do. It was just so hard to take . . . to accept . . . Do they have anything new, or is he still out?'

'Not my case, son,' Rickerson said, stepping toward the door. Henderson was out, but it wasn't something to tell the boy. 'Write down the name of your professor and we'll verify your story.'

The young man scribbled something on a piece of paper and walked over and handed it to the detective. 'What if the professor doesn't remember that I was in class that day? It's a big class.'

Rickerson searched Ian Berger's face. He couldn't tell if what he was seeing was grief or fear. Some of the classes at UCLA had a hundred students or more, and it wouldn't be surprising if the professor didn't keep track of attendance. Without something to substantiate his statements, Ian Berger would remain an active suspect. 'Then I guess you're gonna have a problem, Ian. What about friends, other students? Surely someone saw you that day.'

Ian's head dropped. He said without looking up, 'Jessica was my best friend.'

Could he have done it? Rickerson asked himself. The ingredients were all present. Again he let his eyes roam around the room. Thomas Henderson had taken more than one life from the looks of it. The boy standing in front of him might never recover. He could even end up in prison for murder. Rickerson hoped that wasn't the case. He felt an overwhelming sadness in the room and was anxious to leave. 'We'll be in touch.'

'Tell the judge I didn't mean it, okay? Tell her I'm sorry about her family.'

'Sure,' Rickerson said, taking several steps down the hall. Then he turned and returned to the bedroom. 'Son, let me give you some advice. Take down all these pictures. She's gone now. Let her go. Go on with your life. She would have wanted you to.'

The boy had turned back to the desk. He spoke without turning around. 'I can't,' he said in a voice laced with emotion. 'I just can't.'

As Rickerson let himself out of the house, his own words

echoed in his head. She's gone now. Let her go. Go on with your life. You're pretty good at giving advice, he told himself. Might just be time to take some of that advice for yourself.

It was almost ten o'clock before Rickerson arrived at Lara's condo. She had already consumed three glasses of wine.

She threw open the door and he strolled into the small living room. He didn't appear to be in the best of moods. 'Don't open the door, remember? One of these days you're going to open that door and get a face full of lead.'

For a moment she just stood there. 'Thanks,' she said. 'I mean, I thought this was a celebration. The man is dead. Isn't that what you told me?'

He turned around and looked at her, letting his eyes roam up and down her body. 'First, I believe this man was responsible for more than the break-in at your house. I think he might be our killer, but he was hired to kill them. The person responsible is still out there, and to be perfectly honest, the next person to go could be you.'

Lara felt her heart racing. Up to this point it had been only speculation that the two crimes were related. Now the detective was confirming her worst fears. And she had released this man. 'You think someone contracted these killings? But why? My God, why?'

Rickerson's voice was urgent, his face flushed. They were both still standing in the center of the living room, only a few feet apart. 'He thinks you know something, maybe have something incriminating.' He let his words sink in before continuing. He had to evaluate how much he was willing to reveal. 'If I'm right, he's eliminated the one man who could identify him – Cummings. He's cleaning house now, Lara, tieing up loose ends. You're a loose end or your house would have never been ransacked.'

'But I can't identify anyone. This just doesn't make sense.'

'Your sister came to your house claiming someone was following her. If the man who hired Packy Cummings was the man following your sister, then this man has to consider that you know something, that she told you something. I mean, you were her sister. If she was in trouble, why wouldn't she tell you?'

'Well, she didn't. I already told you why.'

'I know that, Lara, but he doesn't. Think about it.'

She did. The silence hung heavy.

'I see your point,' she finally answered. 'What now? And what about Jessica Van Horn's boyfriend?'

'Says he was in class at UCLA. We have to verify it.'

'Do you think he's telling the truth?'

'To be honest, it's a tough call. He loved that girl and he's crazy with grief. Just how crazy I don't know.' Rickerson paused, flicking the hairs on his mustache. 'Oh, Thomas Henderson is back on the street. One of our men spotted him in Costa Mesa yesterday on their way to court.'

'Shit,' Lara said. 'He was at Camarillo State the last time I heard. He's out?'

'You got it, kid.'

'Well, Henderson should want to kiss me, not kill me. I certainly didn't do anything to him. It was my decision that set him free.' Wonderful, Lara thought facetiously. Now she was setting all the killers free instead of locking them up.

'I agree,' Rickerson said. 'Just keep in mind that he's out there.'

'What about all the other leads . . . all Ivory's clients? One of them could have killed her and Sam. Just because this Packy person broke into my home doesn't mean he was involved in the homicides.'

Rickerson sighed. She was right on that one, even though he thought he was headed to pay dirt with Evergreen. 'We've interviewed almost everyone on the list. Most of them were at work with dozens of witnesses. Remember, this crime occurred during the middle of the day. Of course, the calls to hotels and things are impossible to trace.' Suddenly he remembered his conversation with Bradshaw. 'I'd like to ask you something. Do you have a good friend that's an attorney?'

'God, Rickerson, all my friends are attorneys. Either attorneys or judges.'

'This would be a male, Lara. It appears someone has been calling the station asking about suspects in this case. He claimed he was a close friend of yours and was attempting to pry information from the chief's son.'

Lara stood there for a moment thinking. 'The only person I can think of is Benjamin England. He represented Thomas Henderson. We've been dating, but he's been out of town and I haven't even talked to him since my sister's death. I think he's coming back tomorrow.'

Rickerson took out a small notebook and scribbled England's name down. 'I'll check it out. Henderson, huh? Lot of people connected to this Henderson case.'

'It doesn't make sense for Benjamin to call and ask about the case when he hasn't even talked to me.'

'Maybe he doesn't know where you are, Lara,' Rickerson said. The man could also be a valid suspect, he thought. As a criminal attorney he would have access to courthouse information. This boyfriend of Lara's could have called Evergreen, claiming that he was with a local law enforcement agency, and easily arranged his release. Anyone who knew what to say and who to call could have pulled something like that off. The detective shook his head. This case was like chasing butterflies without a net. As soon as he thought he had something in his hand, it fluttered away.

Lara walked over to the sofa and threw herself on it face first. The wine, the disappointment, the stress of the past few days, were taking their toll. 'I thought it was over,' she said in a thin, high voice. 'Now you're telling me I'm next . . . that someone really is out to kill me, that I released the man who killed my own sister. Jesus.'

At that moment she felt Rickerson's warm breath on the back of her neck, his cool hand on her flesh. 'Scoot over,' he said softly. 'What you need is a neck rub.'

As he started kneading her neck, Lara stiffened. 'Relax,' he said. 'I'm not the big bad wolf.' This time he whispered, 'I wouldn't let anyone hurt you, Lara.'

His thigh was rubbing against her rib cage, brushing against her breast. She could almost feel his body heat through his clothing. And she could smell him. It wasn't strong cologne like most men wore. It was a masculine, earthy scent. Cigars, coffee, sweat. Tonight it didn't smell bad. This was the way her father used to smell when he used to hold her on his lap.

As he continued to rub her neck, she wondered what it would be like to have a man like this one. A man who carried a gun. A man who wasn't afraid of anything. Then she felt something else. His hands were soft and fleshy, like he was wearing velvet-padded gloves. She felt her body responding and imagined those hands on her skin: her breasts, her hips, between her legs. She shivered. What was wrong with her? This was insanity.

'I – I'm fine, Ted,' she said, attempting to roll over. 'I acted like a baby. I'm embarrassed. Let me up.'

'Ssssh,' he said. He moved his hands to her back and massaged her through her blouse. 'Go to sleep,' he said. 'We'll talk tomorrow.'

Lara shut her eyes. Several times she almost fell asleep and then her eyes sprang open. His hand was roaming. Either that or she was imagining it. She thought for sure she felt his touch on her buttocks. She wanted to feel his touch. That was the problem. 'Ted,' she said. 'Thanks for the neck rub, but I think I'll go to bed.'

His fingers were dropping down off the side of her back and grazing her breasts. He leaned over her back and lifted her hair off her neck. She inhaled, certain he was going to kiss her. And there, right there – the one spot she was so sensitive. She closed her eyes and waited. She held her breath. Her heart was beating so fast that she was certain he could tell.

Nothing happened. She heard the door close. Rickerson had left.

Chapter 16

The following morning Lara headed to the Hall of Justice. It was Saturday and the parking lot was almost empty. She wanted to review the Adams case and make some phone calls. And she wanted to get out of that condo. All night long she had thrashed about in her bed, unable to sleep. Her thoughts kept returning to Ted Rickerson: what kind of lover he was, what he looked like without his clothes, what it would be like to have him inside her. She was certain he was married. He wore a wedding ring. She'd never known anyone to wear a wedding ring that wasn't married. Not only that, he was a cop. If she started seeking sexual gratification from the police force, she might as well kiss her career goodbye.

She was all nerve endings and quivering flesh. This morning she had felt as though she'd spent the night in an X-rated movie. If he'd just make a real pass at her, she thought, the fantasy would probably vanish. That was a funny thing about women. They always seemed to want what they couldn't have, and she for one, was normally put off by real aggression. Men never seemed to realize that about her.

But the way the detective had touched her, it was so

covert, so seductive. She shook her head, getting out of the Jaguar. She had to put this out of her mind. And fast. It was silly. She didn't have time for this type of thing. He must think she was hard up, desperate. Was she? It was one thing to deal with life alone when it was uneventful. But now she needed someone. She needed someone to hold her, to make the pain go away.

It couldn't be Ted Rickerson. She knew that for sure.

Since there was no security guard on weekends, she had to search in her purse for the key to get inside the hall leading to her chambers. On her way out this morning, she'd stopped at Emmet's and he'd informed her that he'd already made arrangements with a company that would move his things to her place today and set up his equipment. The phone company had installed his line yesterday.

The air-conditioning system in the building was either off or on some type of climate control that barely moved the air. This section of the complex had no windows, and it was stuffy and uncomfortable.

Once she was inside her office, she called the number on the social workers' card and left her number at the court. They could have at least notified her where she could call Josh, where they had placed him, she thought, feeling her frustration level rise about five notches. No wonder Victor Adams had flown off the handle and gone after one of these people. Their rules were too rigid, their attitude too superior. Yesterday she'd felt like punching them both in the face herself.

She had to buy Josh something appropriate to wear. The funeral was Monday.

The phone on her desk rang and she grabbed it. It was Rickerson. 'How did you know where I was?' she asked him.

'I know everything,' he said.

'Oh, really.'

His voice dropped to a low level. 'How did you sleep?'

She cleared her throat. She would have slept a lot better if he'd been in the bed next to her. 'Fine,' she said. 'And you?'

'Fine.' After an awkward pause he continued, his voice all business now. 'I want to ask you some questions about Judge Evergreen.'

'Evergreen? Why?'

'Evergreen asked you to release Packy Cummings. If I'm right, whoever arranged Cummings's release is our killer.'

'But not Leo Evergreen. What possible motive could he have for killing my sister and brother-in-law? And he's an old man, Ted. Ivory was raped. What you're saying is absurd.'

'Lara, I'm not saying he killed them himself. Like I was telling you last night, I think someone hired Packy to break into your house and then kill Sam and Ivory.'

Lara's voice went up several decibels. 'But why?'

'Try blackmail?'

'Ivory and Sam were blackmailing Evergreen? Over what?'

'Ivory was a prostitute,' he said. He wasn't prepared to tell Lara about the photos or the cash they had discovered in the safe at the pawnshop. Not yet.

'And Evergreen probably hasn't had sex in years. None of this makes sense to me,' Lara said, tapping her pen again and again on the desk. 'Ivory had a list of clients a mile long. She and Sam could have been blackmailing dozens of people.'

'Lara, your sister specialized in S and M. Her clients didn't always have sex.'

Lara was silent.

Rickerson continued, 'What do you know about Evergreen's personal life? Is he married? Does he have children?'

'I think his wife is dead. I really don't remember. She's either dead or divorced him years ago. I think he has a son, though.'

'How old is his son?' Rickerson asked.

'Gosh, Ted,' Lara replied, 'I don't really know. Grown, I'm sure. Come to think of it, I've seen a picture of his son on his desk. What does this possibly have to do with everything?'

'Stay right there, Lara. I'm coming over.'

Before she could tell him that he couldn't get into the building, the detective had hung up. She'd have to meet him in the parking lot.

Rickerson followed Lara down the long carpeted hallway that separated the judges' chambers from the courtrooms. 'But I told you I can't unlock the door to his chamber,' she said. 'I don't have a key. Every judge locks his door for security reasons.'

'Does your secretary have a key to your chambers?'

Lara stopped and turned around. 'Well, yes, he does. He generally unlocks it before I get here every morning. He has to have a key in case I leave a case file or something in there and someone needs it when I'm not around.' Lara stopped for a few moments. The detective was making her a nervous wreck. She was in enough of a predicament as it was, and now he wanted to snoop around in Evergreen's chambers. 'Look, I know what you're saying. Evergreen's secretary has a key too, right?'

He nodded.

She continued, 'But she probably locks her desk as well. Phillip does. I'm not going to let you break in here, Rickerson. Don't even think it.'

As soon as they got to Evergreen's office, Rickerson walked in, headed straight to the secretary's desk, and removed something from his pocket. A few seconds later, he was rifling through her drawers.

Lara stood there with her hands on her hips. 'How'd you get that open?'

'With a lock pick,' he said, holding it in the air. 'These cheap county desks are a piece of cake. The door might be harder. Let's go.' He had a large brass key ring jangling in his hands.

'Stop right there,' Lara told him. 'I don't like this at all, not at all. Now you've got me breaking into the presiding judge's chambers. They're going to throw me off the bench.'

Rickerson had the door open to Evergreen's chambers and was already inside. Lara just stood there in the outer office shaking her head. He yelled at her, 'You might get thrown off the bench, but it's better than being dead.'

She walked inside.

'Is this the picture?' he said, holding up a snapshot of a baby-faced young man in his early twenties.

Lara nodded.

Rickerson picked the lock on Evergreen's desk and started digging. He found a stack of cancelled checks on what appeared to be the judge's personal bank account and looked up at Lara. 'Don't just stand there. Do something. Take these to a Xerox machine and copy them, front and back. Do you have one that prints in color?'

'I think so,' she said. 'It's down the hall.'

'Okay, take the picture out of the frame and copy it too. And hurry. He might come down here on weekends.'

'Why do you need a picture of Evergreen's son?' Lara demanded.

The detective had been standing up. He now flopped down in Evergreen's leather chair. 'Trust me,' he said.

Lara snatched the photo and cancelled checks out of his hand and left the room, moving as fast as she could down the hall. All she needed was to have Evergreen catch her with the goods right in her hands. 'Trust me,' she mumbled, mimicking Rickerson. 'Like I've never heard those words before.' Finding the copy room, she slapped the checks upside down on the glass and hit the button. The machine whirred to life.

On Sunday, Lara drove to the address Madeline Murphy had given her. The house was a sprawling older adobe in a low-income section of Costa Mesa. Scattered all over the front yard were children's toys. Lara had to pick up a skateboard off the walk to even pass. The social worker had given Lara permission to take Josh out to purchase a suit for the funeral. He came to the door himself, pale, looking as if he hadn't slept all night, his hair dirty and limp. While he was standing in the doorway, a scruffy little boy tossed a Frisbee across the room and it struck Josh in the head.

'Knock it off, you crusted little toad,' Josh yelled, 'or I'm gonna come over there and beat the shit out of you.'

'Fuck you, asshole,' the kid yelled back. He was only about seven years old, a street kid from the word go.

They drove in silence, Josh turning his head away and looking out the window.

'Honey,' she told him inside the department store, 'by Tuesday you'll be out of that place. We're moving to another condo in the complex. It's only temporary. It belongs to a friend of mine. You know, that man I told you about – Emmet.'

'They're gonna keep me in that place forever. I hate those people. The woman is a porker and she stinks. The man wears his pants so low you can see his hairy ass all the time. I don't think they ever take a bath. There's six screaming little kids in there. I can't even sleep.'

Lara jerked her head around. 'I thought you had to have your own room. Are you telling me you're in a room with six kids?'

'No,' he said. 'I have a room about the size of a closet. I

can sit on my bed and touch both walls. I can't keep the brats out. They bang on the walls too, and they throw things.'

And these people were more suitable than she was, Lara thought. They were foster parents, people who made their living caring for kids like Josh. Unfortunately, most of them didn't do it for the kids. They did it for the cash.

Lara had been looking through the racks of suits while Josh just stood there, no interest whatsoever. 'What do you think of this one?' she said, holding up a navy blue suit with a reddish stripe.

'I hate it,' Josh said.

'Fine,' Lara said. 'Even if you hate it, will you please see if it fits?'

He snatched the suit out of her hands and headed to the dressing room. She really didn't know why she was going to all this trouble. No one was even going to be there except Irene and John Murdock, Benjamin England, if he'd received her message with the time and location, and Phillip. Then she thought of Emmet. Irene could drive his van and bring him.

The suit fit; she bought it, slapping her credit card on the counter. 'I'll pick you up tomorrow about ten o'clock,' she told him. He didn't answer.

As they were walking to the Jaguar in the parking lot, he turned to her. 'Did you go through my backpack?'

Lara froze in her tracks. A car was backing up and she stepped aside. 'I-I was looking for a pen, Josh. I'm sorry. I guess I should have asked you, huh?'

'Did you take my Metallica T-shirt?'

She couldn't lie. She unlocked the car door and got in. As soon as Josh was inside, she turned sideways in the seat. 'Look, Josh, I want to be truthful with you. I took the T-shirt because it had blood on it. Now that it's out in the open, why don't you tell me whose blood it was?'

His eyes flashed with anger and he reached for the door handle. Lara grabbed the back of his shirt. 'Don't run away. That's not going to solve anything. You've got to tell me, Josh.'

'Get your fucking hands off me. I knew you were a bitch. I don't know why I thought you were different. You think I killed them, don't you?' The muscles in his face started twitching, and he leaned over close to Lara's face.

She drew back, thinking for a moment he was going to hit her.

'It was my blood. There . . . now you know. Are you happy?'

'What happened? Did you fall off your bike? How did you cut yourself?'

He turned away and stared out the window. 'I can't tell you.'

Lara reached across the seat and touched his hand. 'Josh, please look at me. You can tell me. Honey, I have to know. This was a serious thing. I want you to be totally in the clear.'

'I can't,' he said, sniffing. 'It's embarrassing.'

Lara just sat there. Finally she started the car and made her way out of the parking lot. She had no idea what he was talking about. Why would it be embarrassing? 'I have an idea,' she said. 'Could you write it?'

'Maybe.' His voice was small. He wouldn't look at her.

They drove in silence to the foster home, both of them lost in their thoughts. Once she had pulled up at the curb, she reached into her purse and handed Josh a pen and a piece of paper. 'I'm going to take a walk. Write down what happened and leave it on the seat. I promise I won't read it until you're in the house. Deal?'

She didn't wait for a response. She walked down the sidewalk and crossed the street. As soon as she saw Josh get out of the car and go into the house, she returned to the car. She looked but there was nothing there. Thinking it had fallen between the seats, she went to the other side of the car and opened the passenger door and searched for it. She glanced back at the house and saw Josh looking at her through the window. After standing there a few minutes, Lara left.

The first thing she did was call Emmet. 'Did you get the blood type on the T-shirt?' she asked.

'Yes,' he said. 'I was . . . trying to . . . find you. It's type AB.'

Lara pulled to the side of the road and put her hand over her chest. 'Thank God, Emmet. I really appreciate this. I'm not certain why his blood was there, what he did to himself, but I guess it's all right. I mean, it's his blood type.'

'Unless,' Emmet struggled to say, 'your brother-in-law . . . has . . . AB as well. Not likely . . . though. Only about four percent . . . of the . . . population has type AB blood.'

'I'll find out, Emmet. And listen, thanks. I'll see you in a few minutes.' She rushed back to the condo. The place was a shambles, but at least he had found someone to handle the move on the weekend. Poor Emmet, she thought, heading across the courtyard to his door.

He was sitting in his office working.

'Are you all right?' she said. 'This move was a bigger job than I thought it was.'

'Fine,' he typed. 'I'm leaving my office the way it is. Look in the bedrooms. See if they put everything where you want it.'

Lara checked and saw all the bedroom furniture from the model in one room and the other was as Emmet had left it. Emmet had left his computer equipment in both rooms, and the movers had placed all her clothes and things on top of them.

She went back in and hugged Emmet from behind. 'I

can never repay you for this. Never. No one's ever done something this nice for me before.'

He didn't turn around, but words flashed on the screen as he typed. 'Most people are jerks. I'm not.'

Lara laughed. 'You got the phone line in and everything?'

'Yes,' he typed. 'I had a modem installed yesterday. I seldom use the telephone. Oh,' he continued typing, 'if you want, you can talk to me that way. Just come in here and follow the instructions on this sheet. We can talk on the bulletin board. I have a lot of friends I talk to all the time. When they send me a message, a bell rings on my console.'

Lara wheeled Emmet to her place, the chair hard to push on the grass.

'See?' he said, showing her his bed. He had a tray that moved his laptop computer back and forth from the desk to his bed. That way he could work at night when he couldn't sleep.

His nurse would be there shortly, so Lara left, going back across the courtyard. Madeline Murphy had promised they would come by Tuesday and check her new living situation. Then she could get Josh back.

Only Emmet's chair was in the living room and an end table with a lamp. It looked empty, stark. Lara sat down. She was completely exhausted. Tomorrow Ivory would go in the ground. Then it would all be real – too real.

Rickerson called her. A cacophony of noises rang out in the background; Lara wondered where he was calling from.

'I'd like to see you,' he said. 'Discuss some things. Can you meet me at that bar on the corner of Seventeenth and First Street? It's not far from your house.'

'I guess,' she said. 'I mean, if it's important.'

'I'll be there in fifteen minutes.'

Before Lara could protest or ask questions, he'd hung up. What now? she thought. Did he want to tell her that she'd released someone else who was out there killing people? Lara felt like chucking it all in, taking Josh and moving to Kansas or something, leaving this whole smelly, disgusting city behind. She grabbed her purse and headed out the front door.

She beat Rickerson to the bar. It was a dive. She didn't see his unmarked unit in the parking lot, so she slid down in the seat to wait. She'd wait right here in her car until he arrived, she decided, locking the doors.

Approximately thirty minutes later, Rickerson drove up as a passenger in a black-and-white patrol car. He stuck his head in the window of the Jaguar and then waved to the officer. The man drove off. 'Want to let me in?' he said. Lara unlocked the doors.

'What's going on? Why did you want me to meet you here?' Instead of smoking a cigar, the detective was smacking a huge wad of chewing gum. Lara looked at him and sniffed. 'Have you been drinking?'

'Few beers,' he said, his voice slurred. 'Chief had a barbecue. Left my car over there. Caught a ride.'

'Want to tell me why I'm here?'

'Your sister's trick book. We got it.'

Lara gave him a questioning look.

'You know, every working girl has a book where she keeps information on her clients. We've been looking for it. Somehow we missed it. It was in her car under the mat. Some fool just booked it into evidence. I was poking through the stuff and found it today. It might be good.'

'Well . . .'

He shrugged his shoulders. 'Have to check it out. Right now most of the numbers we already have, but you never know. One might be promising – a woman, probably another prostitute. Tried to find her, but she must be out working.'

The space inside the front seat of the Jaguar was actually very small. For some reason Lara felt funny sitting here with the big detective in the dark with only a swatch of light drifting in from the bar. He was almost larger than life, and the air was thick with his very presence.

'Is that all?'

Rickerson's red hair was standing straight up. A fierce wind had picked up in the past thirty minutes, and he had his jacket collar turned up as well. They weren't that far from the ocean and Lara could smell the salty sea air.

'I think Evergreen is behind all this – that he contracted to have your sister and brother-in-law killed.'

'Not this again,' Lara said, frowning. 'Leo Evergreen contracted to have my sister and Sam killed?'

'Yeah,' he said. 'Look, I've got to go inside. I need a bathroom.' He glanced at her. It was obvious that he'd had more than a few beers. He was smashed.

'You're drunk,' she said, disgusted. 'I can't believe you called me out tonight to continue this ridiculous line of supposition that the presiding judge of Orange County is contracting murders? What are you going to tell me next, that Mother Teresa is stealing money from orphans or the Martians are landing? Sober up, Rickerson. Go home.' She started to turn the key in the ignition.

'I have to go,' he insisted, reaching for the door handle. 'I have to take a leak.'

'Well, I'm going home,' Lara shot at him.

'I'd like to talk to you. You want me to go behind a bush or something? The beer . . .' He belched, a hand over his stomach.

'My place?' she said flatly.

'Better make it fast,' he answered.

Lara was staring at the road in front of her, her mind reeling. Rickerson was trying to talk fast through the fog of alcohol, his words almost running together like a foreign language, trying to explain to her how he had arrived at this assumption. Suddenly he yelled at her to stop the car and got out without a word and disappeared behind a building. A few minutes later, he returned. 'Sorry,' he said. 'Couldn't wait.'

Lara burned inside again. 'Leo Evergreen a pedophile? He's an asshole, but a pedophile, a child molester? Never. I can't believe it. You're out of your mind, Ted. You've had too much to drink. Besides, he was married. He even had a child. You saw his picture today.'

'Right,' he said, inching his way toward sobriety with every passing second. 'Thought you judges knew everything. Since when do pedophiles never marry and have children? You know, this is something that can surface any time in their life. It's not like the color of their hair or something they're born with. It's a sickness.'

'Sure, and Ivory was seeing Leo? Ivory stole these pictures of Leo with little boys? Sure. All of this is a stretch.' She craned her neck around to look at him. 'And I mean a *real* stretch of the imagination. What possible proof do you have to support this preposterous claim?'

They pulled into the complex and parked. It was a lousy parking job. Lara had the front wheels of the Jaguar up over the curb. 'I'm living over here now,' she told him, slamming the car door, not bothering to lock it. 'I had to move because of Josh. The social workers wouldn't let him stay with me if I didn't move.'

Rickerson ignored her and walked behind her to the door.

She stopped on the sidewalk. 'What evidence do you have? Are you going to tell me, or still keep me in the dark? Come in,' she said, unlocking the door.

Rickerson walked in, looked around, and then flopped in the one chair, leaving Lara standing. Then he jumped back up and told her to sit down. He talked as he paced, slipping his sports jacket off his shoulders and tossing it on the floor. 'You got any coffee in this place?' he said, looking around. Underneath his jacket he was wearing a blue knit shirt and casual slacks. The fabric was flat over his abdomen, then strained to cover his bulging biceps. In the neck of his shirt were tufts of strawberry blond hair. He took out a cigar and then put it back in his pocket and started working his jaws on the gum.

'I'll make some,' Lara said, going to Emmet's kitchen and trying to find the coffee in the cabinet. Rickerson was still talking.

'Here's what I have,' he said. 'The lab enlarged and enhanced the Polaroids I told you we found at the house. There was a reflection in the mirror of another photo of a woman and a young man. I think it's Evergreen's wife and son. They're working to verify this as we speak. That's why I took the picture off his desk. If it looks good, then we'll find his son and talk to him, make certain it's him. His wife is dead. I saw her death certificate in his file cabinet. She died about five years ago.'

The coffee was brewing, filling the small rooms with its fragrant aroma. One of those gourmet coffees, it smelled like cinnamon. She took a seat in the chair. 'I'm certainly listening. Keep going.'

'We found over forty grand in cash in the safe at the pawnshop. Does that smack of extortion to you?'

Lara blinked at the amount. 'Forty thousand dollars? You're kidding. Sam couldn't amass that kind of money in a hundred years. You might be right on the blackmail, but I don't see how this implicates Evergreen.'

Rickerson gave Lara a sidelong glance and then continued to pace. 'We're going through Evergreen's cancelled checks, his bank statements, looking for the payout. In addition, every month Evergreen writes a check for a thousand dollars to Miramar Properties. He also writes checks to a mortgage company that I assume are his house. We checked and Miramar owns and operates apartment complexes. We couldn't contact anyone in their office today, but my guess is that Evergreen has a secret pad somewhere. That's where he met your sister for their little rendezvous and probably where he takes the kids he molests.'

'Shit,' Lara said, shaking her head. 'You're crazy. He probably pays his son's rent or something. I can't believe any of this, can't believe you're wasting your time with this.'

Rickerson stopped pacing and looked at her. 'I think Evergreen killed Cummings. I think he's desperate now. Cummings wasn't working for any law enforcement agency we can find. Evergreen was lying or someone else inside the system arranged Packy's release. Any way you look at it, it comes back to someone with access to inmate information.'

Lara's mouth fell open and her face was ashen, almost as gray as the upholstery on the chair. For a few moments she couldn't get her mouth to work. She opened it, closed it, opened it again. He was right. Anyone at the courthouse, even Phillip, could have pulled up Cummings's rap sheet and booking information on the computer and then simply called Evergreen and conned him into believing they were police officers. Lara herself had been contacted by local officers asking for special handling on cases. She'd never once verified the callers' identities.

'Evergreen told me to release Packy Cummings so he could murder my own sister? If this was true, why didn't he have one of the other judges release the man? Why me? He would have been an outright fool to do that . . . and believe me, Evergreen is no fool.'

'He didn't know, Lara,' Rickerson said. 'Use your brain. If he was seeing your sister, a prostitute, do you think for a minute she told him about you being a judge or that he would ever in his wildest dreams link the two of you?'

Lara was silent. At least this made sense even if nothing else did. Maybe the detective wasn't out of his mind completely. 'So, what you're saying is that he didn't know we were related. They were blackmailing him and he needed a hit man, a strong arm. He went for this Packy animal for whatever reason and selected me only because I was sitting the arraignment calendar?'

Rickerson just stood there flicking the hairs on his mustache. 'Looks that way.'

'And I released the man who murdered my sister?' All roads led back to this. Lara knew she was obsessing, but she couldn't stop herself. She was about to come unglued. 'Look, you said it could be anyone in law enforcement, even a clerk. How about my secretary? He knows the system like the back of his hand. Not only that, he's been getting loans lately, even falsifying his salary. And he's younger than Evergreen. Maybe he was seeing Ivory. He didn't know she was my sister. I never mentioned her to anyone at work before her death. We didn't get along, you know.'

Rickerson started pacing again. 'The man in the photos was an older man, Lara.'

Lara was silent, thinking. 'Maybe Phillip was one of the boys in the photos? You said several young boys were in those pictures and they were taken years ago.'

Rickerson stopped and locked eyes with Lara. 'I'll check him out, okay? But don't you think a pedophile has more to lose than a victim? I mean, people don't normally blackmail victims.'

'You don't really understand this type of offense, Ted,' Lara said, leaning forward in her chair. 'What makes sexual abuse so insidious is that the victims often feel responsible. The offender convinces them that they incited their advances, even encouraged them. The victims are sometimes more contrite than the offenders.'

'So you think your secretary should be considered a suspect?'

'Why not? He's in law school. If he'd been victimized in the past, he certainly wouldn't want anyone to know, particularly since you said the boys were having sex with an adult male. Maybe that's why he's been applying for all these loans – to come up with the extortion money?'

'I'll look into it,' Rickerson said, obviously not enthusiastic. Just because he felt the killer was someone in the system didn't mean it was Lara's secretary. 'Does Evergreen limp?'

Lara thought for a moment. 'I wouldn't really say he limps, Ted. He has a distinctive walk, but so do a lot of people.'

'The lab thinks they can identify the man in the photos due to some kind of physical disability.'

Lara's mind wandered and she heard only snatches of what Rickerson was saying. Someone was playing a stereo a few doors down. It sounded like Etta James – a heavy blues tune. Cars were whizzing by on the freeway. If she didn't listen closely, she could imagine it was the ocean instead of the freeway. She'd let a vicious criminal walk out on the street, and he had killed her own sister. She leaned forward and put her head in her hands, pulling her hair straight out from her head. 'I released him. I released him. I released the very man who murdered my sister.'

Rickerson stopped pacing and walked to her chair, dropping to his knees and looking her straight in the eye. 'Stop this,' he said. 'Blaming yourself isn't going to cure anything.'

She ignored him. 'I can't believe it. I just can't believe it.

All my life I've tried to do the right thing. And now I've actually caused my sister's death.'

Rickerson reached for her, touching the top of her head gently and then drawing it against his shoulder. 'It wasn't your fault. You did what Evergreen told you to do. How could you have possibly known?'

His voice was soft and low, and he was stroking her hair. She could smell the beer on his breath and the lingering odor of cigars on his clothing, but she could also feel his masculine strength. His body was solid, as hard as a rock. She let him hold her. Then she pulled away and pushed her hair out of her face. For a few moments their eyes met and he probed there – down where it was tangled and dark, a twisted maze of confusion and grief. She was beginning to lean on this man, she thought, allowing him to get close, see a part of her few people saw. She had to stop it. Their relationship was passing the level of friendship, even fantasy. Lara was about to take his hand and lead him to the bedroom. It wasn't the sex she really wanted. Not now. Right now she just wanted him to hold her, tell her everything was okay, tell her he would protect her.

'You're married, huh?' she finally said.

'Yeah,' he said.

'Kids?'

'Two.'

'Happy?'

He stood and looked away. If he was going to tell her, he thought, now was the time to do it. But he couldn't. He didn't know why, but he simply couldn't. And what would he tell her? That he was separated. That his wife had walked out on him after nineteen years of marriage. That he might or might not be getting a divorce. She was dating this Benjamin England, a prominent attorney. 'Sometimes,' he said softly, 'but not always. No one's happy all the time, Lara. That just isn't the way it is. There are good days and bad days. You know?'

'Yeah,' she said, wiping her nose with a paper napkin off the end table. 'How well I know.'

The room fell silent. They were both uncomfortable. He belonged to someone else, Lara thought. This type of discussion held no future for either of them.

'I know how you feel,' he said. The neighbors had turned the music down, and they could now hear only the bass notes, a sort of thump, thump, thumping that almost vibrated the walls. 'I killed someone one time.'

Lara jerked her head up. 'You shot them?'

'No, it was an accident – a young kid, a two-year-old boy.'

Lara didn't know what to say. His face was etched with pain, the memories flooding his mind. They weren't good ones. With the one light on the end table, the other side of the room was bathed in shadows. He stepped to the back wall and stood there as they talked.

'I was working the graveyard shift . . . it was years ago. To be honest, I was sleeping in my unit, parked under a freeway overpass. This woman ran up to me screaming her baby was dying, that he wasn't breathing. I tried to administer C.P.R. I was determined I was going to save him. Back then I thought that was what the job was all about.' He stopped speaking and she could hear him breathing, loud, raspy breaths that were like another instrument combined with the pounding bass.

'Go on,' she said.

'He was so small, so tiny. My younger son was about the same age. The woman panicked, jumping on my back, beating it frantically with her fists. She was screaming that I was killing him, insisted that I get off. She was heavy. I was bent over the front seat of her car giving him C.P.R. I fell forward on top of the child and shattered his sternum. He died.'

'It was an accident,' Lara said quickly, not knowing what else to say. 'Things like that happen. You were trying to save him.'

'But I didn't,' the detective said. 'I killed him.'

Lara was silent. He continued, 'And I never got over it. That kid's face chased me around for years. I dreamed about it; I thought about it day and night. My philosophy back then was that a person has only one chance in life to do something great, heroic – like destiny or something. I thought you lived your entire life for that one specific moment. You know, to pull someone out of the path of a car, to save them from drowning, to tackle a man with a gun and disarm him before he hurt someone. And I was convinced that I missed that chance. I didn't think there'd ever be another one.'

'Was there?' she said, her eyelids fluttering. They were going way off track, into another realm of familiarity.

'No, there wasn't. Not yet, anyway.' He stepped out of the shadows. The past was receding. 'But maybe this is it, you know. This case . . . helping you . . .'

'Tell me,' Lara said finally, her voice weak and cracking, back to the present nightmare. 'It's hard to picture a sixty-seven-year-old judge tracking down a guy like Cummings and putting a hole in his head.'

'Picture it. That's what I think happened. I think Cummings wanted more money or saw how dirty this whole thing was – you being a judge, Ivory being your sister. Evergreen was terrified of exposure. Possibly he didn't even intend for Cummings to kill them, but just to get the pictures back. He could have gone crazy over that. You know, protecting yourself from exposure is a long way from murder. Anyway, I think he met Cummings in that parking lot and blew him away. It's only four blocks from the courthouse. He could have shot him, returned to work, and no one would have been the wiser. And it was a tree-shaded area. Perfect.'

'Phillip could have done that, shot him and driven back to the courthouse.' Lara couldn't help it, but the more she thought about it, the greater her suspicions were that Phillip might be involved. 'He's a strange man, Ted. Believe me, I wouldn't be saying this if I didn't think there was something to it. And he's been acting funny lately, like he has some kind of personal problems.'

'I keep telling you I think the killer is Evergreen, and you keep talking about your secretary,' Rickerson said, annoyed. 'Can I continue my line of thought here?'

Lara nodded.

'Okay, even if we prove Evergreen is a pedophile, we can't necessarily prove that he was responsible for your sister's death. But if he does have an apartment we may find her prints there.'

'Even that wouldn't be enough for a conviction,' Lara retorted. 'Hell, you've seen the list. Being her client means nothing. Half the county was her client.' Then she thought about it. 'The only way to prove this is a direct link between Evergreen and Cummings, and you don't have it. Not only that but you don't have any proof that Cummings even committed the murders. There weren't any prints at the San Clemente house.'

'But we may have evidence soon. Forensics is working on matching the pubic hairs we found on your sister to Cummings and the skin tissue under her nails. He had some abrasions on his face and arms. There was also semen in her vagina. And it wasn't your brother-in-law's.'

'But not yet?'

'No,' he said slowly, 'not yet. So as a judge, you don't think we have enough yet for a warrant to go for Evergreen? If it came to you, you wouldn't sign it?'

'An arrest warrant, no,' she answered. 'But a search warrant to gather evidence? Possibly. You get everything you talked about put together, and you might be able to get that.'

'You'll sign it?' he said.

'You've got to be kidding. I don't think any judge in this county will sign it, go up against Evergreen. This is serious, vile stuff we're talking about. He could sue everyone involved for every dime they have – defamation of character, false arrest, no telling what else. He's a powerful, influential man. He'll hire the best lawyers in the country. He'll . . .'

Rickerson rubbed his forehead and finally sat down on the wood floor. He looked funny there. He was so big. Lara got up and gave him the chair.

'Professionally,' she said, 'I'd say go for the child molestations. The statute of limitations has been extended on those type of offenses, so there's no problem there. But you need a victim. You can't have a crime without a victim.'

'Right,' Rickerson said, licking his lips, knowing what she was saying exactly. 'We don't have a victim.'

Lara stared at him. 'What if Phillip is your victim?'

'Then Phillip would be the murderer,' the detective said, shaking his head as if he didn't agree. He didn't say goodbye. He just walked out the door. Lara knew they didn't have anything yet. What they had was absolutely nothing.

A few minutes later, Rickerson returned and knocked on her door. Lara had already shed her clothes and tossed on a robe.

'There's a light on in your old place, the other condo. Who's there? I thought it was empty.'

'I never said it was empty. My friend is staying there.

The man who loaned me this condo.' In a way it was ironic. Lara had lived such an uneventful, sedate life outside of the courtroom, and now she was moving every day like a gypsy, living out of a suitcase. Overnight her entire life had changed.

'That isn't such a good idea,' he said. 'We have no way of knowing if you're safe here. Evergreen could know where you're staying, maybe think those pictures are hidden over here now.' His face became flushed. 'You didn't tell him, did you?'

'No, no,' Lara said. Then she recalled the social workers. 'Did you give Social Services my address here?'

He shook his head. 'Of course not. I told them to contact you at the courts. Why?'

'They came here today. They had all kinds of information. Claimed some officer named Bradshaw told them. They knew all about the pawnshop fiasco, me covering for Sam. They even knew I was hiding. Who in the hell is this Bradshaw?'

Rickerson was hot now. 'Fucking Bradshaw. I'm gonna kill that prick one of these days. He's the chief's son.'

'Well, there's nothing I can do right now.' She looked across the courtyard. There was only a small light burning in the bedroom. Emmet was probably asleep.

'I'll try to spring someone to watch the place.'

'Fine,' she said. 'Thanks, Ted.'

'Lara,' he said, stepping into the doorway again, only a few inches away. His gaze drifted to the spot where her robe opened in front and her legs were exposed.

'Yes,' she said, 'what is it?' Please, she thought, don't let him ask to come back in, don't push this any further than it's already gone. Right at this minute she had absolutely no willpower. They'd just do something they'd later regret. She had enough regrets.

Suddenly the burly detective's face flushed bright red

and he stammered, 'No – no . . . never mind. Just be careful.' After that, he left.

The bedroom Lara's furniture was in at Emmet's was the guest bedroom, and Lara had to pass through Emmet's office to get to the bathroom. It must have at one time been the master bedroom before he converted it to his office, she decided. It probably made it easier for him to get to the bathroom when he was working. Emmet was always working.

Then she saw it.

The computer screen was on and there was printing across it and a light on the console was blinking. She stopped and stared at it, thinking Emmet had forgotten to turn it off.

'Shit,' she said, her eyes scanning the text, her stomach in her throat.

'sOMEone's in here with me. Im scared to move. they don't know Im here. can't call police . . . emmet.'

Darting down the wide hall to the front door and flinging it open, Lara started screaming, hoping against all reason that the detective hadn't left. 'Rickerson . . . Rickerson.'

She saw movement in the shadows. He stepped out.

'You rang,' he said, a funny, lopsided smile on his face.

'Jesus,' she said, spurting out the words. 'Someone's in the other condo. My friend's there alone. Do something quick. He's handicapped.'

'Stay here,' Rickerson said, jerking his gun from the shoulder holster with a snapping noise and a creak of leather. 'Call 911 and have them dispatch some units. Tell them I'm here, or they'll shoot me.'

Lara rushed back into the condo and did as he told her. Then she stood outside with her arms locked around herself and watched through the tree branches, her heart racing.

Rickerson arrived at the front door. He knocked and then flattened himself against the wall. 'Police,' he yelled. 'Don't move or you're a dead man.'

After only a few seconds, Lara could hear sirens. She held her breath. She prayed. Please, God, she prayed, let Emmet be okay. She'd kill herself if anything happened to him. She'd just go right out and kill herself.

Rickerson was kicking the door in. 'Wait,' she screamed, knowing he couldn't hear her, running halfway across the damp grass in her robe. Other people were coming out of their condos. Some were peering out windows. He was going in by himself like a fool. The backup units would be here any second. He should have waited. She couldn't bear to watch. Any second she thought she'd hear gunshots and the detective would be dead. This was all her fault. Everything was all her fault.

Time stood still. The sirens were getting closer.

'No,' she screamed in total anguish. No one was coming out. Emmet was dead in there. Rickerson might even be dead.

She ran back to the condo and dialed 911 again. 'Hurry,' she yelled in the phone. 'The detective is in there and he's not coming out. Something terrible is happening. God, please come . . .'

'Calm down,' the dispatcher told her. 'The units should be there any minute. Do you hear the sirens?'

'Yes,' Lara said. They were even closer now. She dropped the receiver and ran back out into the courtyard. Still, there was nothing. She was panting now, terrified. She leaned over thinking she was going to throw up on the grass.

Then she saw him and a wave of relief washed over her. He stepped outside and waved at her to come over. She ran.

'He's okay,' Rickerson said, his chest heaving, his face flushed. 'In the bedroom. Go to him. I'll wait for the units.'

Emmet was still in his bed, in his bedclothes. His bed was low, evidently so he could get in it by himself. 'Okay,' he said weakly. 'They . . . left . . .'

Emmet's belongings were thrown out in the middle of the floor. His laptop computer terminal was broken and in pieces. She rushed to his side. 'Oh, Emmet,' Lara said, falling on her knees by the bed. 'I'm so sorry. I should have never let you stay here. I'm an idiot, a fool. Please forgive me. Can I get you anything?'

'No,' he said. 'I'm . . . fine.'

She stepped aside as Emmet scooted himself across the bed into his wheelchair and headed straight to the bathroom, the electronic chair making a funny sound on the plastic runner. The movers had installed a trapeze in the bathroom similar to the one by his chair. She didn't embarrass him by asking to help. A few seconds later, he opened the door and rolled back across the mat.

'Did you see them, Emmet?'

'Mask,' he said. 'He . . . wore a . . . mask. Big man . . . deep voice . . . very thin.'

Evergreen wasn't thin and he wasn't that tall, but Phillip was tall and thin. Lara couldn't wait to tell Rickerson, but her primary concern right now was Emmet. 'Did he hurt you? Oh, God, Emmet, I feel so bad. I don't know what to say.'

'No . . . guess . . . didn't think . . . I was strong enough to . . . hurt him.'

She pushed Emmet to the small living room, which was now filled to capacity with officers. Evidence men were checking for latent prints. Lara glanced at the front door and saw where the lock had been forced.

Rickerson was outside talking to one of the men, smoking a cigar. 'Don't touch anything,' he barked at her through his teeth, his nerves still frazzled. 'Nothing. Do you hear me?'

'Nothing,' Lara said, throwing her hands in the air. 'Who did this? Surely you don't think it was Evergreen? Not the way Emmet described him – tall and thin. Phillip is tall and thin, and he knows where I'm staying. I told you I was on to something with him.'

'I don't think it was your secretary, okay? Evergreen just got another goon,' Rickerson stated.

'God,' Lara said, pulling the robe tighter around her body, pulling on the sash. 'Thank God you were still here.' Then she raised her eyebrows and tilted her head. 'Why were you still here, by the way?'

He grabbed her arm and jerked her aside. 'Don't do anything from now on without checking with me,' he said. 'Don't loan your place out. Don't talk to anyone about anything. Don't go anywhere without telling me. Don't even take a piss without calling me. Are we straight on this, Lara? Are we perfectly straight?'

She looked down. She didn't answer. There was nothing to say. 'Why did you stay?' she said.

'Who do you think was going to sit here all night and watch your place, Lara? You think I can just pick up the phone and yank one of our men off the street and have them sit here all night?'

'You were really going to stay here all night just to make certain I was safe? That's so sweet, Ted. I mean it, that was a really nice thing to do. And you weren't even going to tell me?' She shook her head. For some reason this really touched her. 'Thanks,' she said affectionately. 'I don't know what I'd do without you, big guy.'

'Oh, yeah,' he said, yanking the cigar out of his mouth like it was poison and tossing it across the courtyard. 'I hate these stinking things,' he said, the anger gone now, a smile playing at the corner of his mouth.

Just then Lara remembered that they had driven her car

to the condo, Rickerson riding over in a black-and-white. 'I remember now, you didn't have a car.'

There was a mischievous look in his eyes. 'How'd you think I was going to get home? Walk all the way to San Clemente?'

'Oh,' Lara said, narrowing her eyes, 'so that's why you came back to the door.' He must have felt like a fool and was too embarrassed to tell her. 'That was a pretty big speech you just made,' she said, smiling coyly. 'Particularly since you just stayed because you didn't have a car. Like playing the hero, huh?'

'Just wanted to show you that you can be had, Lara. A lousy third-grader could have your pants down around your ankles in about five minutes.' He paused and cleared his throat, gazing into her eyes with conspicuous longing. 'And if you're not careful, one of these days it just might be me.'

Then he turned quickly and walked back inside with the men.

Chapter 17

As soon as the officers cleared at Emmet's, Rickerson got a ride to San Clemente and then leaped in his unit, checking his notebook for the address of Carol Montgomery. The address was an upscale apartment complex right off Pacific Coast Highway in Newport Beach, but Montgomery had a record for soliciting. No matter where she lived, she was a whore.

If he wanted to catch her, now was the time to do it. It was almost two o'clock in the morning. Even in her line of work, business was probably over for the day. Tomorrow was Monday. People had to go to work.

It was a security building, a high-rise. Rickerson called her from the phone in the lobby. At first she refused to let him in. Then he told her he was a cop and the buzzer sounded.

When she flung open the door, Rickerson felt a gush of air leave his body. She was gorgeous. The woman was tall, shapely, and blond – sort of a Nordic look. She was wearing a see-through silk robe and was completely nude underneath.

'Come in,' she said, insisting first that Rickerson show her his shield. 'I was asleep.'

The apartment was luxurious. Business must be good. Rickerson gave thought to telling the woman to put on some clothes, then thought better of it. If he had to be out pounding on doors in the middle of the night, he might as well reap a few benefits. There weren't that many to be had. He walked over to a large wine-colored velvet sectional and collapsed. The woman strolled past him, fully aware that he was feasting on her body, flaunting it. She was wearing spiked heels, and her tan, smooth legs were tantalizing.

Once she was seated on the opposite side of the sectional, she reached for a cigarette from a pack on the end table and lit up, the flimsy robe falling open and exposing an ample white breast, the skin like buttermilk, the nipple a bright shade of pink. 'So, what do you want?' she said, exhaling a thin stream of smoke.

'Uh, I . . . gosh,' he said, thinking of how long it had been since he had made love to Joyce. Was it four months now . . . or five months? 'Mind if I smoke?' he asked, pulling out a cigar.

'Not those. Want a cigarette?'

'No, I . . .' Her breast was still exposed. She was watching him squirm. 'Why don't you cover yourself?' he finally said, feeling his face flush. 'You know . . .'

She did. It didn't help much. He could see right through the fabric.

'Tell me what you know about Ivory Perkins.'

'She's dead. I know that. It was in all the papers.'

'But you knew her? Did you work together occasionally, turn tricks together?' He could smell her cologne all the way across the room. Something heavy and sweet. He wondered if it was really cologne or just her body that smelled so good. It looked good; it must smell good. No, he told himself, what he was smelling was Lara's cologne from last night and imagining what Lara would look like in a robe like that. He rubbed his eyes, thinking he needed a cold shower and a cup of black coffee.

'Yeah, we worked together a few times,' the woman said. 'Sometimes a client wanted a threesome or wanted to just watch a couple of women together. Men like that kind of thing. You know what I mean?'

He certainly did. She had those mile-long legs crossed and was swinging one up and down as she talked. He licked his lips and cleared his throat, trying to remember why he was there to begin with. 'Did you know any of her clients? Anyone that might have wanted to hurt her? Anyone that she could have been blackmailing?'

She stabbed the half-smoked cigarette out in the ashtray and walked across the room to a mirrored bar, pouring herself a glass of vodka in a cut crystal glass. 'Want a drink?' she asked. Rickerson shook his head. Then she let the robe completely fall open as she crossed back to the sofa. Her pubic hair was pale blond and sparse, inching its way between her legs.

'Ivory . . . poor Ivory. She had such an asshole for a husband. Did you know he turned her out, put her in the trade? What a prick. Chick never got to spend a dime of the money she earned. Not a fucking dime. And the nose candy, man. He fed it to her like it was chicken soup or something. When she was high, she'd do just about anything and anyone. And let me tell you something, this girl liked it. She liked it a lot.'

'Were they dealing cocaine? Anything like that?'

'No, not to my knowledge. Most of it Ivory got from her johns or I guess her man bought it for her on the street. He was a boozer. He didn't even use, but boy, did he make sure she stayed high.'

'You didn't answer my first question,' Rickerson said. 'Did you know anyone that might have wanted to kill her or her husband?'

'When I first read about it in the papers, I was certain he'd killed her, but of course, he's dead too. So . . . as to her clients, I didn't know many of them. She did a lot of B and D calls. I don't handle those. Sometimes the clients get nasty. My clients like it straight – just sex, a little fun. Most of them are professionals.'

'She never mentioned anyone in particular . . . perhaps a regular client, someone she saw all the time? Maybe someone with a big job like a judge?'

Carol Montgomery tossed her head back and laughed. It was a wonderful sound, like tinkling bells. 'A judge, huh? I don't remember her mentioning a judge, but I know she had a client she saw a lot. He was a regular. Good tipper too, from what she told me. She kind of liked him. But a judge . . .'

'I see. Know this guy's name?'

She shot Rickerson a knowing look. 'No one has names. Not real names anyway.' There was an awkward silence. 'Sorry, I can't help you, Detective . . . what was your name again?' She smiled. Her teeth were straight and white.

'Ted,' he said slowly. 'Ted Rickerson. Tell me about her other clients. Anyone other than this guy who was a regular, someone she mentioned?'

Carol Montgomery twirled a strand of her blond hair in her fingers, bringing it to her mouth and draping it provocatively across her lip. 'Let me think here a minute, okay? Sometimes these people just blur after so long. I can't remember who was her client and who was mine,' she said, leaning forward and crossing her arms at the waist so that her cleavage was even more pronounced. 'I mean, you'd think if you fucked someone you'd remember them, but believe me, Ted, after a few thousand or so, you wouldn't recognize the sucker on the street if you walked right into him. She had one real weird guy. He was also a regular.'

'Tell me about him.' Rickerson decided he didn't have to look at the woman to hear what she had to say. As soon as he looked away, he saw her pull her robe shut and slap back on the sofa. Evidently the game was no fun when no one was playing.

'White guy. Young. Skinny, she told me. He wanted her to dress him in diapers and feed him in a custom-made high chair. Then she'd spank him. He never had sex with her. Wouldn't even touch her.'

'No name, right?'

She didn't even answer him. She just glared at him.

'Know what this guy did for a living?'

'Let me ask you something, Ted,' she said. 'If you went to a hooker and had her dress you in diapers and feed you, do you think you'd tell her your life history? Give me a break here. All I know is the guy didn't have any bucks. Sometimes when business was slow, she'd do him on credit. She used to call it a student loan.'

'So was he a student? Was he in college?'

'How the fuck do I know? Look, it's late.' She stood and walked up to him, purposely spreading the robe now, moving her body only inches from his face. 'I mean, I might not be able to help you on your case, but maybe I can help you in another way.' She had stepped over his legs and was standing with her own legs on either side of them. She reached a hand down and touched her genitals.

'No,' he said flatly, standing, pushing her back. He shifted his jacket on his shoulders and headed for the door. Then he turned and glanced back over his shoulder. 'Don't think I can afford you, sweetie. But if I were you, I'd be mighty careful. Don't want that gorgeous body to end up on a slab in the morgue.'

For the first time he saw a crack in her self-confidence, a slight tremor in the slender hand that reached for another cigarette.

'Can I ask you something?' he said. 'It's something that really bothers me. I don't know why, but it does.'

'You've asked me everything else,' she said. 'Fire away. If you want to know how much I charge, it's two bills. That's for straight. Anything else is extra. Of course, I do have a police discount. For cops, I charge two fifty.' Again she laughed.

'Aren't you even a little concerned about AIDS? People are dying out there, woman. Don't you want to live?'

Carol Montgomery's brows knitted and her mouth compressed into a thin, hard line. She seemed to age right before his eyes. Flicking her ashes on the carpet, she reached under the sofa and pulled out a large box and tossed it across the floor, where it landed right at Rickerson's feet. It looked like a carton of cigarettes. 'Condoms, dick head. I buy them by the case at the Price Club. Trick doesn't wear one, he doesn't fuck.'

Now he could see how hard she really was. The curtain fell on her little performance and she was fully exposed. 'Everybody fucks, Officer,' she snarled, her lip curling, 'it's a basic instinct. And they're gonna just keep on fucking, AIDS or no fucking AIDS. As long as they fuck, I'm gonna make a living. And as long as I'm alive, I'm gonna make my living fucking.'

She didn't show him to the door. Rickerson let himself out. No one on the list had been identified as a student. Then he recalled Lara's statement that her secretary, Phillip, attended law school. Carol Montgomery had described Ivory's client as tall and skinny. Lara said Phillip was tall and thin. Rickerson stuck a stub of a cigar in his mouth and lit it, looking up at the sky. A few seconds later he was coughing and tossed the cigar in a dumpster next to his car in the parking lot. This case was going to kill him, he thought, his back aching and his head throbbing. The last thing he needed was another suspect. He got into the car and pulled the door shut.

'Damn,' he said, looking out over the parking lot and slapping the steering wheel with both hands. He wanted Evergreen, not some skinny secretary. Ever since Evergreen had dismissed that case when he was a rookie, Rickerson had been carrying a grudge against him. He didn't like the man. He was too smug, too cold. He'd raked Rickerson over the coals that day, right in the courtroom in front of his fellow officers. He'd blamed Rickerson for compromising the case. And bringing down the presiding judge – what a coup that would be. Had he slanted this investigation to fit his own agenda? Obviously he had.

'Can't bust Evergreen if he isn't guilty,' he said, taking a deep breath and then letting it out. Cranking the engine on the big Chrysler, he roared out of the parking lot and headed home.

Monday was a beautiful day. A beautiful day, Lara thought, if you were going to the beach, or roller skating, or for a nice long walk. But this was the day she was burying her sister and Josh would say his final goodbye to his mother.

There was no such thing as a beautiful day for a funeral.

What she really wanted was for the sky to open up and soak them all, make it really lousy, make it seem like what it really was: a day of death, a day of finality. From this point there was no going back. Once you went in the ground, you didn't come back up.

But no, she thought, tilting her head up, the skies seldom darkened in Southern California, not just a few miles from Disneyland. The sun was shining and the temperature was in the seventies with a gentle breeze filled with the scent of the ocean.

The cemetery was in San Clemente, high on a hill. From some spots the shoreline could be seen, but most of this property was being overrun with developers. Less than a mile from where they were standing, they were clearing for a new housing tract, and huge bulldozers like dinosaurs gobbled up the foliage, turning what was once natural and green into barren, dusty earth.

While everyone was standing around, talking in hushed voices among themselves, Lara walked over to the plots where her parents and Charley were buried and gazed down at the simple markers. 'She's with you now, Pop,' she whispered. 'You, Mom, Charley, and now Ivory. You're all together.' She stopped and inhaled deeply, knowing that one day she'd be there next to them. Except for Josh, this spot of earth would soon cover her whole family. Out of the corner of her eye, she saw Sam's casket next to Ivory's on the berm, the man from the funeral home standing there solemnly in his black suit. 'I'm sorry about Sam, that he has to be here too,' she added. 'But he was her husband.'

She faced the small gathering. Only four people were present other than herself: Irene Murdock, Benjamin England, Phillip, and Josh. Lara had decided at the last minute that Emmet shouldn't come after last night and what he'd been through. The poor man had been scared out of his wits, and the police had kept him up half the night. Irene's husband, John, couldn't spare time from his thriving medical practice.

They all stood around in a tight little circle, and Lara bowed her head and said a brief prayer. Josh stood beside her in his new striped suit. 'Lord,' she said, not really knowing what to say, 'bless these two souls. One of them was a wife and a mother, a sister. She was loved and we will miss her.' As hard as she was trying, tears were gathering in her eyes behind her dark glasses. 'They are in Your hands now.' She paused and then said, 'Amen.'

Everyone was silent.

Lara had Josh's hand in hers. He walked over and placed a letter in an envelope on his mother's white casket with the brass fittings. He didn't cry, but his hand was shaking; Lara let go of his hand and put her arm around his waist. For a few long moments they just stood there, wind whipping their hair, leaning on each other.

Finally she turned back to her friends. 'I guess that's it,' she said. 'We can go now.'

Rickerson was sitting in his county vehicle on the little paved road leading to the area where they were having the services. He'd come today fully intending to pay his respects and see Lara, but once he was there, he couldn't force himself to get out of the car. She hadn't asked him to come, and in some ways it had hurt his feelings. It was a sign that she didn't consider him a part of her life outside of the investigation. He saw the BMW and the Mercedes. Fancy cars, he thought, thinking of the ten-year-old Ford parked in front of his house with the ripped upholstery. 'She's out of your league, bud,' he told himself. He picked up his binoculars off the seat and watched the little grouping of people. Seeing a tall, thin young man, he adjusted the focus. That had to be Phillip, he thought, searching the man's face with avid interest. He'd have to get his last name and address from Lara tomorrow.

Seeing that they were about to leave, he started the car and pulled farther down where he couldn't be seen and again looked through the binoculars. The guy in the expensive suit had to be Benjamin England, the attorney she had mentioned. He watched as he embraced Lara. 'Fucking prick,' he said, feeling jealousy surge through his veins, an alien, ugly emotion. 'You're a suspect too, buddy.' Then he let the binoculars slide from his hands to his lap in frustration and locked his fingers on the steering wheel. It was time for him to leave.

Lara and Josh had driven to the cemetery with Irene

Murdock. She'd arrived at nine o'clock with her BMW filled with food in plastic containers. She was always well dressed, generally something tailored and professional, something extremely expensive. Today she was appropriately dressed in black. Unlike Lara, she looked and acted like a judge even when she was outside of the courtroom. She had a presence about her that exuded strength and purpose.

'Please come to Lara's,' she told the little group of people, taking charge of the situation as she always did. 'I've prepared some food. That would be nice, don't you think?'

Benjamin England and Phillip followed them to the condominium in their own cars. Lara was bursting to tell Irene what Rickerson suspected about Evergreen and her own suspicions about Phillip, but with Josh in the car, she knew she had to wait. 'When we get to the complex, Josh,' she said, turning around to speak to him in the backseat, 'we're going to go and get my friend Emmet so he can join us. He's in my old place now, you know. I've been wanting you to meet him.'

'Why do I have to go with you to get him? Just call him on the phone.'

'He's in a wheelchair, Josh. Didn't I tell you that?'

They rode in silence the remainder of the drive. Rickerson had said he didn't feel there was a risk right now for Emmet to stay where he was; they'd searched her house now and the condo. He doubted if they would come back. Stay maybe three more days until the evidence on Cummings was processed, and then he had told her, she could finally return to her house in Irvine. The killer, Rickerson supposed, was probably now under the assumption that Lara had done something with the photos: turned them over to the police, taken them to her safe-deposit box or the office. Whoever was behind this knew where she was and could obviously find her. Lara turned her head around and glanced at Phillip in the car behind them, feeling the icy touch of fear. Then she wrapped her arms around herself and remained that way until they arrived at the condo.

At the condo, Benjamin cornered her in the kitchen. 'Lara,' he said, 'we need to talk.'

She stared up at his face. There were dark circles under his eyes, and he looked awful. 'Late night, huh?' she said, thinking he'd had some young secretary in his bed last night, someone who'd lie and tell him what a fabulous lover he was, hoping to end up with a ring on her finger and a membership to the country club.

'Not really. I've been sick with the flu, and let me tell you, it's cold as a bitch in San Francisco. The wind goes right through you.' He stopped and Lara went back to what she was doing, transferring the food from the plastic containers to serving dishes. 'Lara, can we talk about the other night, the last night we were together? I've thought about it and know you were angry with me. I shouldn't have asked you to take a cab home. I was just so tired.'

'Forget it,' she said. 'It's done.' After all that had happened, the night in England's backyard seemed like a lifetime ago. 'Oh,' she said suddenly, 'did you call the San Clemente Police Department and ask for information on the homicides?'

He stepped back a few feet and his mouth fell open. 'How'd you hear about that?' he said. 'I was really upset when I read about the murders in the newspaper, Lara. And to tell you the truth, I think it was rude that you didn't return my phone calls. I really thought we were close, you know.'

He was right, Lara thought. She should have called him back. 'There was a lot going on, Benjamin. Surely you can understand that. I think I called you once or twice, but I couldn't reach you.'

'Are you going to see me again?'

She didn't turn around. 'I don't think so. We can be friends, though. I need a few friends.' It was almost as if she were talking to herself.

He turned her around. 'But why? Don't you think you're being childish? Did I really do something that bad?'

Lara glanced through the kitchen door. Phillip and Irene were talking and sipping coffee. She didn't see Josh. She kept her voice low, almost a whisper. 'That depends on how you look at it. I'd say satisfying yourself with no regard whatsoever to your partner is inconsiderate and obnoxious, but then I'm not a man.' Lara had always been frank. If you asked a question, you usually got an answer.

'My God,' he whispered, his lips compressed. 'What are you going to do? Sue me for failing to comply with the terms of a contract or something?' He stopped and was silent. Finally he responded, 'I'm sorry. I was inconsiderate. I didn't think.'

'I have to take this in the other room, and I want to go and get Emmet now,' she said, wanting to conclude the conversation. She started toward the living room when Benjamin stopped her.

'Can we try again? We'll go away somewhere or something, maybe to Palm Springs. Then my mind will be clear.' He laughed nervously. 'I'll read books. You can give me lessons. It's never too late to learn . . . I was a real pig, huh?'

Lara smiled at him, the first smile of the day. She set the tray down and leaned back against the kitchen counter. 'Yes, you were,' she said. She thought about this elegant man standing before her: the manicured nails, the five-hundred-dollar suit, the starched lavender shirt with his initials embroidered on the pocket. He was a far cry from

Ted Rickerson, but for some reason he just didn't stack up. The detective seemed alive, living on the cutting edge. He saw and felt her pain. And something soft rested inside Ted Rickerson, something incredibly gentle and compassionate. England was self-absorbed to a fault. 'Let's go inside.'

As soon as Lara walked into the living room with the tray of food, her eyes started searching frantically. 'Where's Josh?' she asked.

'He's sitting right there under the tree, Lara,' Irene said, looking out the window.

Lara handed her the tray and went outside to Josh. 'Want to go and get my friend now?' she said.

'Yeah, I guess. What's wrong with him anyway?'

Lara explained Emmet's condition as they crossed the courtyard. Once they were inside the condo, she introduced them. 'Emmet, this is my nephew, Josh. Josh, this is one of my closest friends, Emmet Daniels.'

Josh just stared at Emmet. Then he cleared his throat and looked at Lara as if to ask her what he was supposed to do now. Emmet hit the button on his chair and headed to his office. Lara placed a palm on Josh's back and they both followed.

'Do . . . you . . . like video games?' Emmet said.

'Sure,' Josh answered, looking around the room and then back at the terminal. He watched as Emmet stuck his head into the metal contraption and started typing on the computer.

'If you want, you can come over and play later. I have almost every game. You're welcome to use my system anytime you want. I'm deeply sorry about your mother, Josh.'

'Yeah, thanks,' Josh said. 'That's cool, you know. That thing you put on your head. And your wheelchair is cool too. Is that electric?'

They headed back across the courtyard, Josh asking

Emmet about every question he could think of and Emmet doing his best to answer him. He asked him how long he had been sick, why he had to use the metal cage to type, how he went to the bathroom, what he did for a living, how fast his wheelchair would go. Lara was thankful when they finally reached the door. She wasn't certain Emmet appreciated Josh's interrogation. Some of these questions Lara had never even asked herself.

Once they were inside, they all just sat there and looked at each other. Irene and Phillip finally started chatting about office politics and one of the cases he was studying in law school. Benjamin England was brooding and obviously bored. Funerals and grief didn't appear to hold his attention. Josh sat on the floor; Emmet's wheelchair was right next to Phillip.

'Emmet,' Lara said, 'I thought your computer was broken last night.'

'I . . . have . . . friends,' Emmet said slowly. 'They all have . . . computers.'

'Oh,' Phillip said, turning to Lara, evidently assuming that he must speak or interpret for Emmet just because he was sitting next to him. 'I guess he's saying one of them brought another terminal over for him. Is that what you're saying, Emmet?'

Emmet nodded.

No one lingered. After they ate, Lara was silent and introspective, staring out the window until people got the hint and stood to leave. There weren't a lot of memories to share, she thought, looking around the room; these people were not her family. Her family was gone except for Josh. On his way out, Phillip jumped up and said he'd wheel Emmet back to the condo.

Josh gave him a nasty look. 'It's an electric chair, dummy. He doesn't need anyone to push him.' Then he stood and looked at Lara. 'Can I go back with Emmet?'

'Sure, honey,' she said, thankful that she might have a few moments alone with Irene.

While Irene stood at the sink rinsing off her plastic containers to take home, Lara stood next to her. 'How well do you know Phillip?'

'Me?' Irene said nervously, pointing a finger at her chest and facing her friend. 'He's your secretary, Lara. Why? Isn't he doing a good job for you?' Irene seemed strained, tired. She looked at her friend with compassion.

'I don't know. He's worked for a lot of the judges. I thought he had worked for you once.'

'No,' Irene said. 'He worked for Westridge. He even worked for Evergreen for a short time about two years ago. Very competent man from what I hear.' Her face relaxed and she smiled. 'I'll trade with you in a minute. Just let me know.'

That said, Lara filled Irene in on the situation with Evergreen. She didn't tell her all the details. Rickerson had said to keep it under wraps, but she had to talk to someone and Irene was her friend.

The tall blond judge stopped and wiped her hands on a dish towel. 'Well, that's just nonsense,' she snapped. 'Evergreen is a crusty old goat, but the most respected man I know. He's certainly not . . . a pedophile.' Just the word seemed to be more than she could utter.

'What do you know about him, Irene?' Lara asked, leaning against the kitchen counter. Irene knew Evergreen well. They had lunch all the time. If anyone knew about Leo Evergreen, it would be Irene Murdock.

'What do you want me to say?' She was somewhat defensive. 'He's an intelligent, decent man. His wife died, you know, a number of years ago.'

'Do you know anything about his son?'

Irene arched her eyebrows and shoved her glasses back in place on her nose. 'His son?'

'Rickerson wants to talk to him.'

'We used to see him all the time but not lately. You know, we were all friends when Elaine was alive. He went to school at the conservatory in Santa Barbara. He's a musician. A flutist.' She paused, her face stern. 'You know, Lara, if Evergreen were a child molester, which I think is complete madness, how would he recruit his victims? He couldn't risk hanging out around schools or anything. He'd have to keep a very low profile.'

'Most child molesters can't risk exposure,' Lara quickly responded. That was the truth. In most cases they were respected members of the community, had good jobs, went to church every Sunday, paid their bills.

'Well, I can't see discussing this,' she said. 'I think it's absurd.' She paused and her face softened. 'I'm concerned about you, Lara. So is Leo. He thinks very highly of you. He would be aghast if he ever heard these insinuations.'

'Thinks highly of me, huh? Sometimes he sure doesn't act like it.' Lara didn't want to get into a discussion about her improprieties. Not today. Not the day she'd buried her sister.

'It could be Phillip, Irene. He has access to court information. He's been borrowing a lot of money lately and acting strange. What if he was victimized by a pedophile years ago and Ivory and Sam got their hands on the pictures? The man who broke into the condo last night was tall and thin.' She paused, staring out into space. 'Phillip could even be a pedophile himself. I don't know anything about his personal life. Not once has he mentioned a girlfriend.'

Irene kept looking at Lara and blinking her eyes. 'I think you're getting paranoid, Lara. The stress . . .' She stopped and cleared her throat. 'Maybe you should get Dr. Werner to prescribe a tranquilizer for you?'

Lara grimaced and looked away. Irene thought she was cracking up. Maybe she was right.

'How's it going with the boy?' Irene said, changing the subject, deep concern in her eyes.

'Josh? . . . Oh, Irene, it's been tough. And I mean really tough. It was almost a relief when Social Services took him, but I know underneath it all, he really needs me. I just don't know how to reach him.' Lara took a sponge and started wiping down the countertops. 'Hey, you raised two sons. You know all about teenage boys. Is there some trade secret or something?'

Irene smiled and her face came alive. She loved her two sons and was extremely close to them. If you ever wanted to see Irene Murdock smile, all you had to do was mention them. 'With my boys, I always tried to keep them busy, involved in something positive. You know, Little League, things like that. Matt played golf. That's a great sport for a young man. It teaches them to be polite and mannerly. There's no bad element on the golf courses. If they have too much time on their hands, they'll just get into trouble.'

Lara rubbed her chin. She couldn't see Josh playing golf or baseball. He wasn't the type. But Irene had a point about keeping Josh busy. She remembered his desire to be a weight lifter and thought they might join a health club after they moved back into the house in Irvine. 'Thanks, Irene,' she said.

The other woman looked at her and then moved close and collected her in her arms. 'Honey, I'm so torn up over what's happened to you. It just breaks my heart. You're such a good person to go through all this tragedy.'

Once Irene had stepped back, Lara shrugged her shoulders. 'Just life, I guess. You have to learn to take the bad with the good. Unfortunately, there hasn't been much good lately.'

Irene put all the containers in a grocery sack and carried them into the living room, leaving them by the door. They stood there for a while, both of them deep in thought. 'This thing about Evergreen, Lara . . . I think you have to convince yourself that this detective is leading you astray. If I were you, I would distance myself from these accusations and distance myself from this man. He could destroy your career with this foolishness.'

Lara's face flushed with emotion. 'How can I distance myself, Irene? My sister was murdered.'

'Okay,' Irene said, 'let's run through the cases we've handled. In most of mine, they've had some novel way to attract young children. I had one man who was a Boy Scout leader. Leo just doesn't fit the profile. I don't know about Philip. You might have the police look into his affairs if you think there's something questionable there, but not Leo. How in the world would an older man like Leo attract young children? Can't you see how illogical this whole line of thought is?'

It was like a million flash bulbs were popping in Lara's mind at one time. An image flashed in her mind of Josh at the computer console – the revered video games he was always talking about, the games he was playing right now with Emmet. 'I've got to go, Irene,' she told her.

The other woman looked at her as though she'd lost her mind. 'What do you have to prove this, Lara? Do you have some evidence? Let me see it and then maybe I'll take this whole thing in a more serious vein.'

'No,' Lara said, her face flushed with excitement, wishing she could tell Irene about the pictures, 'but I have an idea.' She almost pushed Irene out the door and closed it behind her. 'You go on home,' she told her. 'I'll call you later. And don't mention this to anyone. Promise me.' Irene mumbled a response, but Lara didn't listen. She was sprinting across the courtyard in her stocking feet, leaving the other woman standing there with her mouth gaping open.

The door to the model condo was open and Lara let

herself in, walking straight to Emmet's bedroom. What she saw and heard there stopped her right in her tracks. It's the little things in life that make a person think there's really someone up there surveying the damage, she told herself – like a god.

Emmet and Josh were glued to the computer screen, little flashing images darting everywhere. Emmet would tap out something really fast and the images would move. Then Josh would laugh and do the same. Laughter. She was actually hearing laughter on this gray day, this day of death. She had never even heard her nephew laugh.

'What are you two doing?' she said lightly, stepping up behind Josh and peering at the computer screen.

'We're playing Lemmings,' Josh said enthusiastically. 'Emmet's got Super NES. You know, Super Nintendo. He's good, man. He's got everything over here.' He looked up and smiled. 'Every video game in the world . . . the latest stuff. And he's got a modem too. He can do all kinds of things, get almost any kind of information you want. He's got this thing called Prodigy. It's rad, totally rad. You can get sports statistics on it, order concert tickets. You said you'd buy me a computer.'

Lara waited until the game was over and then sent Josh out on his bicycle. He didn't want to go. He wanted to stay and play with Emmet. Josh certainly didn't try to speak for Emmet. As far as she could see, Emmet's disability was nothing to Josh. They talked the language of common ground. 'Go,' she said after he ignored her first request. 'Leave us alone a minute.'

'What's going on?' Emmet typed out as soon as Josh left.

'Emmet, I have this thought. We're looking for a man who may be a child molester. He has access to a computer. Is there any way he could lure children with his computer?'

'Lure . . . ?' Emmet typed out. 'How?'

'You know, you mentioned that message board. Could

he talk to them that way, get them to meet him somewhere?'

'Anything is possible,' Emmet typed. 'How old are the children?'

'Prepuberty . . . eight to, say, thirteen.'

'If they were older, there would be more possibilities. I need to think this through,' he typed. 'Give me time. I'll work on it. What's his name?'

'There's two names, two people. One's a well-known public figure. He'd never use his own name.' Lara knew that both Evergreen and Phillip had a computer.

'I . . . see,' Emmet said, then continued typing. 'People are peculiar, Lara, even people with something to hide. I read a lot. I like true-crime stories. Many times they use part of their own name, their initials, something similar so they won't forget. If you want me to help you, please tell me his name.'

'I'll tell you,' she said, 'but you must not mention the names anywhere. No one must know, Emmet. Please, these people may be innocent and we can't be responsible for slandering them. That wouldn't be right.'

'I . . . see,' he said. 'The . . . names, Lara?'

'Leo Evergreen and Phillip Ridley.'

Emmet turned from the computer with a questioning look. 'Phillip . . . your secretary?'

Lara nodded. She expected an interrogation. But Emmet was not Irene Murdock. He simply turned back to his computer.

'I'll . . . begin now.'

As she watched, Emmet typed in the name Leo Evergreen. Then he tapped a series of letters and numbers, and the screen was covered with words containing some portion of the name. She let herself out and went to find Josh.

Chapter 18

Madeline Murphy met Lara Tuesday morning at eight o'clock at the condominium and agreed to allow Josh to return. 'We never wanted to cause a problem for you, Judge Sanderstone,' she said politely. 'We were just doing our jobs.' The woman stumbled over her words a few minutes longer, making small talk about the weather. 'You can pick your nephew up tonight. He should return to school tomorrow, however. I spoke with him and I think he's eager to be with you. See, this cooling-off period served its purpose. I told you a little time – '

'Right,' Lara said, cutting her off, rolling her neck around as she locked the door to the condo. Her neck was so stiff that she could barely move. 'Excuse me, but I must run or I'll be late for court.'

After the morning session, the jury panel on the Adams matter had risen to four people and that was because they were moving fast, extremely fast for some reason. Voir dire, the process of selecting a jury, is the very essence of courtroom monotony. A lot of the judges actually fell asleep. By noon, Lara had a splitting headache and couldn't wait to put the day behind her.

'Your friend Emmet is a nice man,' Phillip told her at lunch. Rickerson had told her to avoid Evergreen, so she'd had him bring a salad to eat in her chambers. He set down the salad and then stood in front of her desk. 'You know, I'm in the Big Brothers' program, Lara. Maybe I can spend some time with your nephew, take him to the movies or something. I'm sure this has been very difficult for him. My father died when I was twelve, so I know how he feels.'

'You never told me you were in that program, Phillip,' Lara blurted out, her fears and suspicions soaring now. Being a Big Brother was the perfect way to reach children. Her back stiffened and she dropped her hands in her lap, willing herself to appear calm. 'How do you manage being a Big Brother with law school and a full-time job?'

'It's just one day a month. Besides, it looks good on my resumé.' He smiled. 'I come from a big family. I'm the oldest of five kids.'

'Are you seeing someone, Phillip? You know, a girl?'

His eyes looked right through her as if he knew exactly what she was thinking – that he was gay. 'I was, Lara,' he said, just a touch of sarcasm in his high-pitched voice, 'but we broke up recently. I have a little too much going on with my life right now to get involved in a serious relationship.'

'So do I, Phillip. Listen,' she said, changing the subject, not wanting to be too obvious. Eager to tell Rickerson the information she had just heard, Lara said, 'Are you absolutely certain that Detective Rickerson hasn't called me?' Discounting the case, Lara couldn't get the detective out of her mind. Every night before falling asleep, she let her thoughts drift to him. It was a way to push the demons aside, she thought. But with each day her fantasies were more real, her desires more pronounced.

'No, it's really been quiet around here for a change.'

'If he does and it's something urgent, get me off the

bench,' she told him as she walked out the door to return to the courtroom.

'No problem,' he said, picking up the paper plates. 'If the man calls, I'll get you right away.'

No more than two feet from the door to her chamber, Lara ran into Irene Murdock. Right in the same corridor, walking in her direction, was Leo Evergreen.

'Lara,' Irene said, 'I was just coming to see you. Can you talk a few minutes?'

Lara glanced at Leo. He was headed her way, but his head was down. She didn't want to see him. 'Gosh, Irene, I have to be back in court right now. How about later? Call me later.' Lara was already walking off when Irene called out to her.

'Can I borrow Phillip a few minutes? My secretary is out ill and I need some things typed.'

'Sure,' Lara said, entering through the rear door to the courtroom. She quickly climbed the three steps and the bailiff spoke: 'All rise.'

The afternoon session commenced.

Lara listened to the defense attorney asking the same questions for the twentieth time that day. 'Do you have children? Has any one of them ever been injured? How did you feel about that? How would you feel if someone removed your children and placed them in a foster home? How would you feel if they were sexually abused in a foster home?' On and on it went. Then at the end of the day, after the last potential juror had been interrogated, the district attorney pitched a fit over a discovery motion that he'd filed and the defense had not answered.

'Mr. Steinfield over here is attempting to withhold evidence in this case,' the district attorney barked. 'That motion was filed three weeks ago.'

Lara looked sternly at the defense attorney. 'Mr. Steinfield, have you responded to the people's motion?'

'No, Your Honor, I haven't. For the past two months I've been in trial on another matter. The psychological evaluation is complete, but the psychologist hasn't mailed me the report yet. He promised it would be in my office by the end of the day.'

The district attorney sprang to his feet. 'This is a contrived plan to buy time and undermine the prosecution,' he said. 'Mr. Steinfield should be found in contempt for failing to comply with a court order.'

Lara glared at the D.A. 'I'll decide if someone is in contempt.' Her gaze turned to the defense attorney. 'Mr. Steinfield, you have until tomorrow at three o'clock to comply with the terms of the discovery motion.' She tapped the gavel lightly and looked out over the courtroom. 'This court's adjourned until nine o'clock tomorrow morning. Good evening, gentlemen.'

Rickerson had finally called, but when she called him back, they informed her that he was out again. It was late; Phillip had already left. As Lara was rushing out the door to get Josh, she ran right into the detective.

'We've got to quit meeting like this,' he said, giving her a big smile. Then the smile vanished. 'We have to talk.'

She spun around and was headed back inside her chambers when he seized her arm. 'Not in there. Evergreen might have a listening device. He's the big boss. Richard Nixon did, so . . .'

Lara rolled her eyes. 'That's ridiculous. Where do you want to go?'

'How about your court? No one's in there, are they?'

'No, but . . .' He kept staring at her and she gave in. 'Follow me.'

Walking quickly, she entered again through the judge's

door and they took seats in the back of the court, Rickerson tossing his long legs over one of the seats. Lara just stared out over the room. Courtrooms used to be full of wood paneling and had tile or wood flooring so the voices echoed. They also had windows, fans, and no air conditioning. Defendants would sweat, she thought, really sweat, the way they should sweat when they stood in a room like this, in front of a judge and jury. When she was a teenager, she used to ride the bus to the courthouse during summer vacations and imagine she was one of the attorneys, even going so far as to imagine she was the judge. This courtroom had bright blue upholstery on the seats, pale mauve carpeting, and the windowless space was climate-controlled. Judges didn't need booming voices that would carry; they had microphones. Lara really liked it better the old way. This way was too efficient, too pretty, too neat. In her eyes, justice had become too modern. It was losing the flavor.

This was her domain, her little kingdom, she told herself, glancing at the American flag by the bench. She didn't want to lose it if she was tossed off the bench for impropriety. She'd lost enough as it was.

'Wait until you hear what I learned today,' she said, her voice echoing in the large, empty space. Rickerson had been sitting there quietly, deep in his own thoughts. 'Phillip is a Big Brother.'

'You mean the organization that helps kids?'

'Yes,' she said loudly, emphasizing the word. 'Now do you think we should consider him a suspect?'

'I'm ahead of you, Lara. I got his personnel jacket today. He has no criminal history, but that's not surprising. He lives with his mother in Costa Mesa, not far from where you are staying at the condo.'

'His mother? He never mentioned living with his mother.'

'He never mentioned being a Big Brother before either. Maybe he just manufactured that to get his hands on Josh.'

'Why Josh?'

'Josh might know more than you think.'

'Believe me, Phillip won't get within a mile of that kid. Not now. What about the money, the loans?'

Rickerson frowned. 'Takes time – oh, I went to the D.A. today. Not too promising.'

'Who'd you see? Did you go to the top, to Meyer?' Lawrence Meyer was the actual District Attorney of Orange County. Everyone else were assistant district attorneys who worked under his supervision.

'Yep. He's an asshole.'

Lara turned to him. According to Rickerson, everyone was either a child molester or an asshole. And these were the people who controlled the criminal justice system in Orange County. 'I never encountered any problems with him when I was working there. He's an outstanding prosecutor, an excellent supervisor. His record is impeccable.'

'Told me I was out of my fucking mind about Evergreen. When I persisted, he threatened to have me removed from his office.'

'Great,' Lara said, cutting her eyes to the detective. 'You shouldn't have gone to him. I told you it was premature. You didn't mention me, did you?'

Rickerson took his legs off the back of the seat. 'No, but he did.'

'What do you mean?'

'Here's what he said, practically verbatim, okay? Lara Sanderstone released Packard Cummings. We argued against it, meaning whatever D.A. was in court that day. She was using judicial influence and privilege to cover her brother's – ' Rickerson stopped and looked at Lara. 'He thought Perkins was your real brother. Anyway, he went on to say that the next day after Cummings's release, he killed someone and you were to blame. He said we should investigate your activities instead of Evergreen's if we wanted to investigate someone.'

'That slimy bastard,' Lara spat. 'I can't believe he said that. Did he think I released Cummings so he could murder my own sister? That's horrible, that's vile.'

'Told you he was an asshole.'

'Now what?'

'We need to wait for the lab reports, something linking Cummings to the homicides. I'm pushing them, but they can only move so fast. They're completely buried.'

Lara stood and climbed over Rickerson's long legs, pacing in the aisle. 'So, that's it?' Her arms dropped by her sides and she stopped short.

'Well, we have the appointment book. It's pretty interesting.'

'How? Tell me. And Ted, I have to pick up Josh, so make it fast.' Lara glanced at her watch. As soon as they moved back to the house in Irvine, Lara was going to look into changing Josh's school. She certainly couldn't keep up this frantic pace, driving him back and forth every single day.

'Everyone uses their own shorthand or code in books like that, even people who aren't prostitutes. Whatever kind of system your sister used, however, is pretty cryptic, no real rhyme or reason. But she had regular customers, which is something to go on. There's a client booked for every Wednesday afternoon. She penciled in the letters *LS* in his time slot. There's another appointment scheduled for the evening hours of July seventh, the night she came to your apartment. That was also a Wednesday, for whatever that matters. This man is penciled in as *LW*. After that date the book just stops.'

'Really?' she said. 'Well, the *LW* could stand for Leo

something. He might have used his real first name and a phony last name.'

'I already thought of that, but then what does the *LS* stand for? I was told by an expert that *LS* meant that the trick likes sex, and *LW* that he likes whips. What do you think?'

Lara just shrugged her shoulders.

'I guess once they started extorting money, Ivory stopped turning tricks. The book just stops after the night she came to your house back in July. Also, a lot of her appointments were scheduled around the seventh, eighth, and ninth every month. I have no idea what that means.'

'Probably because the house payment was due,' Lara said. 'That's when she always used to hit me up for money. Someday I'll let you see my checkbook. Sam must have pushed her to ply her trade around then.' Particularly after she had quit giving them money, Lara thought, cupping her hand over her mouth. If she hadn't cut them off, they might both still be alive.

'Well, I talked to another hooker who worked with her. She's my expert. Maybe they all used the same shorthand.'

Lara looked up. 'Another prostitute? Ivory was working with another prostitute? What did she tell you?'

'Not much. Just that she had one regular client that might have been a student of some kind.'

'Phillip's a student,' Lara shot out. She stopped and they exchanged penetrating glances. Rickerson already knew that fact. 'I need to ask you something.'

'Shoot.'

'Are you absolutely certain Josh wasn't in any of those photographs?'

Rickerson stood, stepping close to Lara. He turned sideways and his jacket brushed against her. They both leaned back against the railing. 'What makes you ask?'

'Just a thought, that's all. I know he's been abused. I just don't know how.' This had been dancing in Lara's head ever since the day with Josh and the discussion of the bloody T-shirt. She'd held back on bringing it up to him again, but it was troubling her. He had said whatever happened was embarrassing. Lara kept thinking that he could have been involved with this child molester, even sodomized or injured in some way. Eventually she knew she had to confront Josh.

The detective leaned even closer to Lara. She knew he did it on purpose. They were now shoulder to shoulder, and she was having trouble focusing on the conversation. All she could see was the slender gold band on his left hand.

'There's a slim possibility that Josh could have been the photographer, the one taking the pictures, but I personally doubt it. Because I'm convinced your sister stole the pictures, I don't really see how the boy could have been involved.'

Lara pulled away and started to leave. Rickerson walked up to her and put two strong arms on her own. 'We're gonna get this bastard,' he said. Then he ran his finger down her nose and touched her lips. Before she could say anything, he had turned and walked off, exiting through the front of the courtroom.

That one touch of his finger to her lips had left her almost panting. It was like a kiss – a delicate, fleeting kiss.

Lara headed back down the corridor leading to her office and the judges' elevator. The building was quiet now, almost empty. She walked fast. Josh was waiting.

She punched the button on the elevator and the door opened. Lara gasped and stepped back a few feet in a state of shock.

'Lara,' the man inside said, 'my, you're working late.'

For a few minutes she just stood there, uncertain what she should do, perspiration popping out on her brow and upper lip. Then she stepped inside the elevator with Judge Leo Evergreen and the mechanical doors shut.

'Yes, I am, Leo,' Lara said. 'You know, the Adams case . . .' She felt herself trembling and willed herself to remain calm. She couldn't stop herself from staring, however. He was wearing a black trench coat and carrying an expensive leather briefcase. He looked awful. His normally plump cheeks were caved in, and there were dark circles under his eyes. 'Are you feeling better?'

As if she had given him a cue, Evergreen started coughing, removing a white handkerchief from his pocket and covering his mouth. 'Not really, to tell you the truth. This flu is a nasty one. You better drink a lot of fluids and stay warm. This one can really put you down.'

Right, Lara thought bitterly just as the doors opened and Evergreen shuffled off. He might know a lot of things that could put a person down. Someone had certainly put Ivory down. Right now she was six feet under. She jerked her head back around and watched him walk across the concrete garage floor. This man didn't limp. He was old and he walked slowly, with almost a stilted, stumbling gait.

But as far as she could tell, Judge Leo Evergreen did not have a recognizable limp.

Chapter 19

The evening traffic leading into downtown Los Angeles was almost at a standstill, the sky blanketed with smog. Rickerson had stopped after he left Lara and purchased a hot dog and a Coke to eat in the car.

'Dinner,' he said, disgusted, shoving the hot dog in his mouth and consuming it in two bites. Then he guzzled the Coke and tossed the paper cup over his shoulder into the backseat. He was meeting Dr. Gail Stewart at the crime lab. One of these days, he thought, he was going to actually have to deliver on all those steak dinners, movie passes, and long-stemmed red roses that he was always promising. But not today.

'Okay,' she said, 'sit your ass down in the chair and let's get going. Have you had dinner?'

'Yes,' he said. 'In the car.'

'Lucky boy. I'm starving. Let's get this over with so I can go home.'

She killed the lights and flicked on the slide projector. 'Here's what you've got: The man in the small photograph with the woman is the same man in the picture you had sent over yesterday. See, watch how their features match perfectly when we superimpose the two images. Of course, he's holding his head at a different angle in this photo, so we had to recreate, but there's no doubt that this is the same man. Who is he?'

'Evergreen's son.'

'Hot damn, buddy, you're on a roll now. Evergreen's the man in the photo?'

'From all appearances, he has to be. That's his son.'

Dr. Stewart took a seat next to him, reaching a chubby arm behind her to a drawer. 'Here,' she said. 'Dessert.' She tossed him a candy bar and started eating one herself while she spoke. 'If you don't eat dinner, you can eat all the candy you want and never gain a pound.'

'What kind of diet is that?' Rickerson asked, placing the candy bar in his pocket.

'The candy diet, of course. I just invented it.' Once she had finished the candy and tossed the wrapper away, her face became serious again. 'The man doesn't have to be the boy's father, you know. It could be a family friend, neighbor, anything. Just because these photographs were taken in someone's home doesn't mean anything.'

Rickerson grimaced. 'It's Evergreen. Believe me, I've never felt so strongly about anything in my life. It all fits, Gail, and every day it fits a little tighter.'

'Did you bring me a tape of him walking?'

'Nah, not yet.' He twirled the hairs in his mustache. 'I guess I could get one, though, maybe coming out of the building or something. Look, Gail, are you certain that this disease or whatever it is would make him limp? Judge Sanderstone doesn't recall him having a limp like that. She claims he has a distinctive walk, but no limp.'

Gail bristled slightly. She didn't like people to question her theories. She'd put a lot of hard work into that computer profile. 'I told you the man in that photograph limps. I guess he could have had surgery. There's a new procedure where they insert a steel rod and straighten the spine. Anything is possible.'

Rickerson was thinking of how he could get a film of Evergreen walking. The problem was, Evergreen didn't come out of the building. To tape him, they'd have to get Lara to let a cameraman hide in the underground garage where the judges parked.

Dr. Stewart continued: 'What I really need is a naked shot of him from the back. Then we'd really give you something to take to the bank. We could confirm that spinal curvature, and you'd know without a doubt that he was the man in the photographs. And if he did have surgery, we'd see the scar.'

'Sure,' the detective said, standing and shoving the small metal chair back to the desk. 'Just walk up to him and ask him to take off his clothes and pose for the camera. Give me a break, here, Gail. That's pretty stupid.'

She leaned forward in the chair and stared at him. 'Cops,' she said. 'Nothing but dummies.' Then she flopped back. 'Bet he works out at a health club or something. You know, plays golf, squash, gets massages, swims. You try hard enough, you can get a picture of about anyone naked. All you have to do is hang around in locker rooms. Everyone in this state goes to some kind of club. Californians are fitness crazy.' She stopped and smiled. 'That is, everyone but me. Dentist says I have rotten teeth. I want to die before they all fall out.'

'Good idea,' Rickerson said, shuffling to the door, deep in thought, her humor sliding right past him.

'And another thing . . .' she shouted when he was out in the hall.

Instead of returning to the room, Rickerson merely stepped up close to the window, his breath smoking circles on the glass. 'Yeah?' he said.

Dr. Stewart walked over to the glass, her voice elevated

so he could hear. 'Find the son. Bet he molested him too. They usually do.'

Rickerson tapped his forehead and smiled. 'Smart.'

'It's the candy,' she said. 'Trust me.'

Removing the candy bar she'd given him from his shirt pocket, Rickerson stood right at the window and ripped it open and then shoved the whole thing in his mouth and ate it. She laughed. Then he turned and walked away. . . . Lara couldn't keep Josh away from Emmet. After missing so much school, he had books stacked two feet high on the kitchen table, but they just sat there while he played video games with his new pal across the courtyard. Lara brought home Kentucky Fried Chicken and carried the sacks to Emmet's.

'That's it,' she said, stepping inside Emmet's bedroom and speaking to Josh. He was avidly jumping around in his seat pushing buttons on a hand-held control. 'No more games, guy.'

'But Mom . . .' Josh said without turning around. After that the room fell silent. Lara was flattered, but she quickly realized that Josh had just slipped back in time. She didn't try to stop him when he got up from the computer terminal and left the room, but after glancing at Emmet and shaking her head, she went to find him.

He was outside the condo, sitting on the grass under the weeping willow. Lara approached slowly and just stood there. Finally she said, 'You shouldn't sit there. You'll get grass stains on your pants.'

He stood and dusted himself off.

'I wish your mother was still alive, Josh – that none of this had ever happened.' He nodded. She continued, 'To be honest, I was very flattered in there – flattered that you would even accidentally call me Mom.' She turned around to head back to the condo. There was nothing more to say.

'I . . . have . . . something,' Emmet said once Lara had returned. 'Working . . . all day on it.' He hit a button on his chair and spun back to the screen, blanking off the game they had been playing and pulling up a menu.

'See,' he said, 'they . . . have . . . free services.' He selected something from the computer menu and a list of what looked like businesses with toll-free numbers flashed on the screen. He moved the cursor down until he found what he wanted and hit another button with the pen attached to his head. Lara was leaning over his shoulder, reading.

SUPER SECRETS – THE GAME MAN, it said, listing an eight-hundred toll-free number to call. The caption under the title read, 'If you want to be the best on your block, call the toll-free number on your screen for tricks and insider information on video games. No charge for this service. Nintendo, Super NES, Sega . . .' It went on to list all the different systems and games. Then it listed the person to contact: Tommy Black. The phone number was good only in the state of California.

'What are you saying, Emmet?' Lara asked him.

Emmet blanked the screen again and typed, 'There are many numbers like this, help lines and things, but most of them are provided by the manufacturers of the games or the systems themselves. First, I explored the others and found they were all legitimate. I picked this one for the following reasons: It's an independent company or individual, and I'm not sure how they profit from this unless they try to sell other things, like accessories, magazines, or something related to video games. And it is also listed in several different directories for maximum exposure, particularly the directories that young people might respond to, where they have information on sports and movies, things like that. Most of these toll-free numbers are national. Even though this one mentions the state of

California, it is really only good in this immediate area. You know, Los Angeles and suburbs.'

Lara became excited. It was feasible that a young boy might call a number like that to find out how to win at a game or improve his score. 'This is great, Emmet. But the man's name? We don't know anyone named Tommy Black.'

Emmet typed, 'I thought you said the child molester would use an assumed name. Want to call him?'

'Call who?' Josh said, entering the room. 'And when are we going to eat? It's almost eight o'clock. My stomach's growling.'

Lara looked at Josh and then had an idea. 'Emmet, wouldn't it be better if Josh called? Then we'd know how he handled a child. If I call, he might just fluff me off.'

They decided to wait until Josh had finished his dinner. Emmet's nurse had already prepared his meal before they'd arrived and Lara wasn't hungry. They sat around the table and discussed what he was to say. 'Just tell him you're calling about getting better at a game. Do you have a favorite game that you can talk about?'

'Yeah,' Josh said. 'I love Joe and Mac. My friend has it. It's great. Emmet has it too.'

'You can't give your real name, you know?' she told him. 'This is something regarding my work, a little detective work.'

Lara didn't set her hopes too high. Even if the killer was an active pedophile, it was doubtful if he was still trying to recruit victims after what had occurred. But then she ran through all the cases she'd handled in the past and knew that stress seemed to make these people's needs even greater. Some of them even molested children while they were awaiting criminal prosecution. It was a compulsion, almost like an addiction to heroin. This man might be desperate now for the companionship of a young person. It probably made him feel more powerful, more secure.

'Maybe we should wait,' she told them just as Josh was about to go to the condo for the cellular phone. She recalled Rickerson's admonition not to run off on tangents on her own. This was a dangerous game. Three people had already died.

'Why?' Josh said. 'It sounds like fun. Let me call.'

She was being silly, she decided. Nothing was going to come of it anyway, and it was only a phone call. 'Okay,' she finally said. 'Do it. Go get the phone and come back.'

Once he returned, he dialed. They waited anxiously beside him. 'It's a machine,' he said.

'Quick,' Lara said, grabbing the phone out of his hands. She wanted to hear the voice on the machine, knowing she would recognize it if it were Evergreen or Phillip. It had a strange, metallic sound. It didn't even sound human. The machine clicked off, and Lara hung up and then redialed. This time she handed the phone to Emmet. 'Listen to this, Emmet,' she said. 'Is the tape worn out or something?'

Emmet listened only a few moments and then the phone dropped involuntarily in his lap and his muscles jerked, tossing his arm off the side of the chair. 'It's . . . not a . . . real voice,' he struggled to say. 'It's . . . a . . . voice-synthesized . . . computer.'

'A talking computer?' Lara said.

'Yes,' Emmet answered.

They agreed that Josh should call back and leave a name and the number to the cellular phone. He did, using the name of his best friend, Ricky Simmons.

'Well,' Lara said, thinking that the whole thing was an exercise in futility. The chances of this working out were a million to one. 'It's time for you to hit the books tonight, Josh. No more games or you'll be repeating this grade next year.'

'Not hardly,' he said, indignant. 'I have a 3.9 average. A week's worth of work will take about four hours and I'll be caught up.'

Lara was embarrassed. She'd never even asked Josh about his grades at school, or what classes he was taking. For some reason she had decided that he was a weak student, possibly because of Ivory's learning disabilities and his lackluster appearance and demeanor. Now as she looked at him, she saw him in an entirely different light. He was an extremely bright young man, probably more so than anyone knew. More than anything, she doubted if his mother or Sam Perkins had even noticed.

'I'm impressed,' she said. 'Really, Josh. I am extremely impressed that you're such a good student, but why the 3.9? Can't we make it a 4.0?'

He smiled and there was a silent exchange between them. If he had done this well in school with no one to encourage him, they both knew he could do that much better with Lara's guidance and support. She bent down and kissed Emmet goodbye on the forehead, and they headed out the door. As they started across the grassy courtyard, Emmet appeared in the door. 'Back,' he said as loud as he could manage. 'Phone . . . ringing.'

They had left the cellular phone on the kitchen table. Josh sprinted back to the condo and seized it on about the fifth ring. Lara then ran right up behind him and whispered that if it was the game man, he should remember to use another name.

'Yeah,' he said, talking now, nodding to Emmet and Lara that it was the man. He headed to Emmet's desk in the bedroom, Lara and Emmet following behind him. 'I have Super NES. My favorite is Joe and Mac.' Josh became silent and listened to the man talking. 'Okay,' he finally said, 'you said I should save my keys and open the secret area for extra one-ups. Then what?'

Lara was frustrated. There was no line for her to listen in on and hear the man's voice. She held her breath.

Josh was cool, tossing his leg on Emmet's desk and

leaning back in the chair as though he were talking to one of his friends. 'Right,' he said. 'Then I can collect all the food and get four extra men. Wow! That's cool. That's cool . . . really.' He glanced at Emmet like the man knew his stuff. Then the caller apparently started asking Josh questions, like how old he was and where he went to school. Lara grabbed a piece of paper off Emmet's desk and scribbled some words and held them up for Josh. He nodded acknowledgment.

'Yeah,' he said. 'I'm twelve.' He sneered at Lara, hating to make himself younger. 'San Clemente Elementary,' he told the man and then gave his friend's name. 'Ricky,' he said. 'Uh, Ricky Simmons.' He fell silent, listening. 'Sure, that would be great,' he finally said. 'Free . . . really? You'd let me have those games free? Prince of Persia, Smart Ball . . . Universal Soldier too. What do I have to do?'

Lara put her hand over her chest. This was getting better every second. She was flabbergasted at how sharp her nephew really was. He'd realized that he couldn't say he was in junior high school as he actually was and had told the man he was in elementary school. That was thinking on your feet. Even she hadn't thought of that one.

'My parents?' Josh repeated, glancing at Lara and making a face. 'Yeah, I . . .'

Lara leaped right in front of him and then scribbled as fast as she could on the paper: 'Your father's dead. Live with your mother.' She knew how these people operated from experience. They looked for single family homes, particularly where the boy was deprived of a father's love and attention. These young people made perfect victims for pedophiles, and in many cases they stepped right into the family, convincing the child's mother that they were attempting to help the young boy, take them off her hands every now and then.

'No,' Josh continued, taking Lara's cue, 'my dad's dead. I live with my . . .' He paused and swallowed. This was not easy for him. '. . . my mother.' Then he listened intently and answered again. 'She works . . . yeah . . . works at the hospital.' He made an expression with his eyes to see if Lara approved. She nodded. A few moments later, he hung up.

'What did he say?' Lara asked eagerly. She wished she'd grabbed the phone and listened to the man's voice, but it was too late now. They'd call him back another time, she decided.

'He gave me some pointers on the game. Pretty good, really. Then he said he could get me a bunch of games free, like demos or something. He never really said how or when, just that I should call back when I get home from school tomorrow.'

'What about the other questions?' Lara asked. 'The personal questions. And how did his voice sound? Was he young or old?'

'I don't know. It was just a voice. I can't tell how old someone is by their voice. All the dude asked was about my family, my parents, if my mom worked, if I like movies, arcades, all kinds of things. You know . . . you heard.'

'Okay,' Lara said. 'You're out of here, guy. I'll see you in a few minutes at the condo. And I hope I don't have to tell you, never and I mean never call that man back without my knowledge.'

'What's this all about?' Josh said. 'What kind of case is this you're doing? I didn't think judges did this kind of thing. Isn't this cop stuff, trying to catch people?' He paused and then continued undaunted. 'What do you think this man did anyway? It's just a con or something. He isn't going to give me those games for free.'

'Go,' Lara said, shooing him away with her hands. 'Homework, remember?'

Once Josh left, she sat there and tried to put it all together. She sincerely felt they were on to something and thought of calling Rickerson, but then set that thought aside. The poor man couldn't work twenty-four hours a day. She'd call him in the morning. Besides, Benjamin England had called earlier and asked if he could stop by later. She'd decided to give him another chance.

What she really wanted was to purge herself somehow of her growing infatuation with Ted Rickerson. The way to do that would be to focus on someone else.

'Trace . . . number,' Emmet said at the door.

'For sure, Emmet,' Lara answered before heading back across the courtyard to the condo. 'You can bet on it. This man might not be Evergreen or Phillip, but he sounds exactly like a child molester. No matter who he is, we're going to check him out.' She paused and looked at the little man. 'This could actually be the man who murdered my sister. It sounds unbelievable, but it's possible. Thanks, Emmet. You're a genius.'

'I . . . know,' he said.

Lara laughed. Emmet might be gravely disabled and frail, but he still had a pretty big ego.

When she turned around, Josh was standing there, listening to every word they said. 'I thought I told you to go to the condo and do your homework,' she said, her voice sharp, hoping he hadn't heard what she'd said about Evergreen, that he could be responsible for his mother's death.

His eyes were dark and intense. 'I forgot my key,' he said. Then he turned around and left, waiting for Lara in the courtyard.

Josh was in bed and Lara was sitting in the living room of Emmet's condo with Benjamin England. 'I'm sorry,' she told him. 'Pretty austere, huh?' He was in the one black and gray upholstered chair with the ottoman, and she was sitting Indian-style on the hardwood floor. It was sort of stupid to call it Indian-style when she was a real Indian. She and Ivory used to laugh about that when they were teenagers. They were sipping wine. Lara wasn't really drinking hers. She was just swirling it around in the glass, lost in the past.

'It seems impossible that all this has happened,' she finally said. 'Only a few weeks ago, my sister was alive. I had no idea she was selling her body, doing the things she was doing.'

'Well,' England said, 'what she was doing for a living isn't the problem. The fact that she got herself murdered is something altogether different. And you think she was blackmailing someone? A high-placed official. Tell me, Lara, who is this man?'

'I can't tell you. We don't really know who it is anyway. I mean, we have suspects, but nothing concrete.'

'Come on, you can tell me. You know I'll keep anything you tell me in utmost confidence. I'm dying to know who this person is. Tell me.'

'No,' Lara said. 'I wish I'd never mentioned it. I'm really not in a position to tell you about it right now.'

He'd been leaning forward in his chair, thinking Lara was about to reveal the secret. When she didn't, he slapped back and looked disappointed. 'Then you shouldn't have mentioned it if you weren't going to tell me. That's like a tease.'

Although he was smiling, she knew he meant it. In a lot of ways he was like an overgrown child.

'We could go in your bedroom,' he said suggestively. 'I mean, at least there's somewhere to sit.'

'Oh,' she said, 'I guess you're right.' Even though she had wanted to see him, now that he was here, she just wanted him to leave. Her mind was reeling, filled with visions of catching the killer. And if they were right and this game man was him, they might be able to catch him red-handed – right in the act of seducing a child. But she couldn't use Josh. She'd never put him at risk, and she doubted if there was any child they could use. It was just too dangerous a game right now. She put that thought aside.

As soon as they stretched out on the bedspread in the bedroom, Benjamin reached for her and pulled her to him. 'I really desire you, you know. I've been thinking about you ever since that last night we were together. You're so small and delicate, Lara. Your body's like a really young woman's. You gonna be my little girl, huh?' he said, sliding into baby talk and stroking her arm.

He looked at her and she promptly melted, allowing him to run his fingers through her long dark hair. Then his hands started roaming, reaching under her shirt for her breasts. She closed her eyes and imagined it was Rickerson's soft, padded hands. There was no comparison. Even in her imagination, England simply wasn't desirable anymore. Besides, he was grabbing, not stroking. 'Stop it,' she whispered. 'This isn't going anywhere. Not with Josh in the next room.'

He ignored her and slipped his hand under the hem of her skirt, his eyes filled with lust. 'He's asleep. He can't hear.'

His hands were sliding up the silk of her nylons, reaching the area between her legs. It had been so long. She moaned and in seconds he was on top of her. 'Unzip me,' he said just as he shoved his hand inside her panty hose and raked his fingernails through her pubic hair.

'No,' Lara said softly, closing her legs, trapping his hand so it couldn't go any farther. 'I told you we can't do anything here. The walls are so thin. Another time. We'll go to your place next time. Just be patient.' She turned her head toward the wall where Emmet's file cabinet and computer equipment were located. 'It's too soon, Benjamin. I'm not ready for this yet. Try to understand. And Josh . . .'

His hot breath was on her neck, and he was grinding his hips into her. This was definitely not sexy, she thought. The man had not even kissed her. Besides, it wasn't her he desired. It was any woman, any warm and wet port in the storm. He had started unbuttoning her blouse when Lara pushed him off and sat up in the bed. 'I said no,' she said, her voice forceful but still low. She didn't want Josh to hear.

'Come on, Lara,' he said passionately, completely undaunted. 'What's the big deal? I want you. I want to show you that I can please you this time. I've been thinking about this all day, thinking of what I was going to do to you.' He stood and dropped his pants. 'The kid's asleep anyway.'

Lara's mouth fell open and she hissed at him, 'Stop that. Another time, I said. I have Josh now. I just buried my sister, for chrissake.'

Benjamin glared at her and then jerked his pants up and zipped them. 'Can't someone else take the fucking kid?' he said. 'Why do you have to get stuck with him? Is he going to live with you permanently?'

He was a nice date, Lara thought, seeing him standing there like a spoiled and petulant child, but it seemed to stop there. Once you passed dinner and light conversation, he transformed right before your eyes into the epitome of an asshole.

And his comment about wanting to please her was nothing but an outright lie. There was only one person Benjamin England strived to please: himself.

'Go home, Benjamin,' she said, angry at herself for ever starting up with him again. She should have known better.

She hadn't purged the detective from her mind. Just the opposite. England's inadequacies made Rickerson's strengths seem even more pronounced. 'And yes, he's going to stay here with me permanently. The kid has no one else and I care about him. For your information, I care about him a hell of a lot more than I care about you right now.'

'I see,' he said with a sneer. 'I guess you don't give a shit about my feelings . . . don't care what I want?'

Now she didn't even feel anger. This man might be a Rhodes scholar, but he was such a jerk that she could feel nothing for him at all. 'Get out,' she said, narrowing her eyes and fixing him with a cold stare from her slate gray eyes, the kind of look she used when things got out of hand in the courtroom. 'And don't call me again. Go track down your murderous client Thomas Henderson. I hear he's out on the streets again.'

'Fine,' he snapped. 'And that was uncalled for, the remark about Henderson. Once a prosecutor, always a prosecutor, Lara darling. Have you forgotten? You're supposed to be a judge.' He did a pivot turn on his expensive Italian shoes and stomped out of the condo, his footsteps echoing on the wood flooring, slamming the door behind him.

Lara jumped when the door slammed and then she fell back on the bed. She pulled the pillow to her chest and hugged it. Possibly she was looking too high up the social ladder, dating high achievers like England. Their egos were simply too inflated. They didn't need her; they were in love with themselves. She'd always identified with people who were more down to earth. Her parents were good, basic people. Rickerson was . . . she had to stop it.

She recalled all the Friday nights she'd sat home alone through the years, all the New Year's Eves that came and went. Years ago, she used to peek through the curtains and watch Ivory get into the car with Charley. Lara never had a date on Friday night, and Friday night was date night. Even when she did go out with a boy, he wanted to take her out on Monday or Tuesday, any night but Friday. Ivory was gorgeous. Ivory dated the handsome football player. Her big sister had all the confidence in the world in the classroom, and absolutely none when it came to socializing, particularly with the opposite sex.

Lara stopped herself. Ivory was dead and she was alive.

Josh came into the room in his pajama bottoms, rubbing his eyes. 'What happened?' he said. 'I heard the door slam.'

'Oh,' Lara said. 'Don't worry about it. It was Benjamin. He's gone.'

Josh turned to go back to bed and then paused in the doorway a few moments with his back turned. 'I wanted . . .' he said, and then stopped.

'Yes, Josh?'

'I just wanted to say that it means a lot to me that you got me out of that place – that foster home – and that you care, you know.' He turned his head around and looked at her over his shoulder with Ivory's piercing blue eyes. A second later, he disappeared.

Rickerson called Lara at eight o'clock the following morning, just as she was rushing out the door to drive Josh to school. It was a long drive and she'd barely make it back in time for court. She told him she'd call him back later unless it was urgent, thinking she'd fill him in on the 'game man' when they talked.

'I need you to help me,' he said quickly. 'I need to find out where Evergreen's son is, and it's not in his personnel jacket. I managed to get my hands on it, but the son was still young then and in school. None of that information is valid now. It hasn't been updated in years.'

'I don't know anything about where he is now.' Then she

recalled her conversation with Irene Murdock. 'Look, let me go or I'll be late. I'll check it out and call you, but Ted . . .'

'Yeah.'

'You've got to drop this thing with Evergreen. He doesn't limp and the whole thing is just a bunch of bullshit. I go along with you that it has to be someone at the courthouse, but it just isn't Evergreen. It could be anyone, absolutely anyone.

'Shit,' she said, hanging up on Rickerson and rushing out the door, where Josh was waiting for her. 'I'm going to be late for court.'

Then she let the tension go and walked slowly with him through the parking lot, enjoying the morning air, the sun. Let them wait, she said to herself, glancing at the young man next to her. There were priorities in life, she decided, and she'd finally captured one for herself that really mattered. A career was a career and a man was a man, but a person who really loved you as she knew Josh could, in time, and asked nothing but that you return their love was a real rarity.

Her heart swelled. She didn't really need a man anymore. She had Josh. It was almost as if she had a son.

And Josh was dealing bravely with the tragedy that had been forced down his throat. He was trying to go on with his life.

He wasn't alone in that quest. Lara was doing the same thing. Some nights she thought of Ivory and cried alone in her bed.

After she dropped Josh at school, she headed back to the government complex. She parked in the underground garage and quickly made her way into the building.

Picking up her messages and a cup of coffee from Phillip, Lara went into her chambers and closed the door. She wondered what Rickerson had uncovered regarding Phillip. Having him right outside her door was agonizing; she was having trouble concentrating on her work. A few seconds later, Phillip buzzed her on the intercom. It was already nine-fifteen and they were calling from the courtroom. 'Tell them another fifteen and I'll be there,' she said, immediately dialing Evergreen's extension.

'Louise,' she said when his secretary answered, 'this is Lara Sanderstone.'

'Yes,' the woman said with her scratchy voice. 'He's not in today. He took the day off.'

'Oh,' she replied slowly. 'You know, Louise, I was going to see his son perform, but I misplaced the date and the address. Do you have that information?'

'Just a minute,' she said, putting Lara on hold.

A few seconds later, she returned. 'I have the symphony calendar right here. He's very good, you know. A very accomplished musician. The next performance is Friday evening at eight o'clock. Of course, you know where the concert hall is in Santa Barbara, don't you?'

She didn't but she would find out. She thanked the woman and hung up and called Rickerson. 'He's a flutist with the Santa Barbara Symphony. I don't have his first name, but there's a performance on for Friday evening at eight o'clock.'

'You got a date Friday?' Rickerson said.

'You want me to go with you?' she said. 'What if Evergreen is there?'

'Hey, it's a free world. We can buy tickets and go to a concert like anyone else. Maybe it's time to make him sweat anyway. He could do something rash.'

'Right,' Lara said, her hand flying to her neck. Something rash could mean her career. 'I don't know if I like that.'

'Look, it's doubtful that Evergreen travels all the way to Santa Barbara for every performance. I want to try to talk to his son, and he might be more willing to talk if there's a woman there. When he learns I'm a cop, he might clam up and we'll be wasting our time.'

'Why do you want to talk to him? I thought you just wanted to confirm he was the person in the picture.'

'Tell you Friday,' he said. 'I'm about to get the address to that apartment he rents. It's a tough one. They're going through all their cancelled checks to see what apartment they apply his money to every month. Evergreen must have leased it under another name, but has the balls to pay for it with his own checks. Guess he thinks he's invincible. Never thought anyone would start looking under his bed. Kinda know what I mean?' The whole time they were talking, Rickerson was smacking gum in her ear.

'God,' she said, 'that gum is annoying.'

'Better than cigars,' he tossed out. 'We got a date or not?'

'We've got a date,' she said. She started to hang up and then thought of something. 'Didn't he write the apartment number on his check? If he didn't, how would they know how to apply the funds?'

'How the hell do I know? But he didn't. You saw the checks. There was no apartment number on them. Maybe he encloses a note or something.'

'I guess that's possible,' Lara said. 'Did Evergreen's account reflect any large withdrawals?'

'*Nada*,' Rickerson said, 'but he might have a safety deposit box somewhere loaded with cash. Or he could have an out-of-state bank account.'

Lara lowered her voice to a whisper and kept her eyes glued on the door. 'Did you find out what Phillip was doing with the money he borrowed? The name of his bank is Orange National. I just remembered.'

'Lara, I wasn't going to tell you this until Friday, but it was Evergreen's son in the photograph. We verified it yesterday.'

'No,' she said, shocked.

'I told you he was involved in this mess. I've been telling you all along.'

'No,' Lara said again. After taking a few moments to digest what she had heard, she continued, whispering, 'Even if it was his son in the pictures, that doesn't mean Evergreen is a killer – or even a pedophile, for that matter. Phillip could have been one of those young men in the photos like I've been saying all along. Maybe he and Evergreen's son were both victimized by this unknown man in the pictures. You said the man would have a limp and Evergreen doesn't limp. Also, Phillip used to work for Evergreen. That's not such a wild assumption that he knew Evergreen's son.'

Rickerson was silent. 'Orange National Bank, right?'

'Right.'

He hung up and Lara raced to the courtroom.

Chapter 20

During noon recess, Lara bought a sandwich and walked into the park across the street, sitting there and eating it alone, enjoying the sunshine. No matter what was going on right now, she decided, she was going to stop and smell the roses. Life was too damn short. Look what had happened to Ivory.

Before her sister's death, Lara had worked through most of her lunch hours. But then she had worked through most of her life, coming down to the courthouse on weekends, staying late every single night, taking work home all the time. What did she think would come of it – that someone would give her a medal, pat her on the back? In San Francisco, members of the Judicial Counsel were probably right now deciding her fate. But these fears were not the ones haunting her, causing her to wake up in the middle of the night in a cold sweat. Even the suspicions about Evergreen she could handle. There was only one thing that Lara could not accept, would never accept. She'd released a man who had murdered her own sister.

'This arrived today,' Phillip said, handing Lara a letter when she walked through the door.

'Shit,' Lara said, reading the text. It was a letter from the

Judicial Counsel stating a review date in two weeks on the charges of impropriety. Her breath caught in her throat. She had prayed it would just go away. She had been wrong. 'You read this?' she asked. She knew he had.

'Uh, yes . . . I'm sorry,' he said. 'But look, I'm sure everything will be fine. They might issue an official reprimand or something, but they're not going to remove you from the bench. I mean, you didn't do anything everyone else doesn't do. I know. I've worked for a lot of judges, remember?'

Lara glanced at the clock. 'There's only one thing you don't know, Phillip. The budget came out last month and it doesn't look good.'

'What do you mean?'

'Next fiscal year, we'll be minus one position. It calls for substantial cutbacks, even on the bench.'

'Really?' he said. 'We're already shorthanded. How can they do that?'

'Easy,' Lara said, staring down at the paper in her hands. 'They can get rid of me. I'm the low man on the totem pole anyway. Now, with these charges, I don't know if I stand a chance.' She walked past Phillip, reached for her robe on the hook, and then stopped. 'And do me a favor please. Here's my keys. Get my briefcase. It's in the trunk of my car. I need it to take some files home tonight on this case.' They now had a full jury panel, and the Adams trial was well underway. Lara needed to review all the details.

'Gonna burn the midnight oil, huh?' Phillip said.

'You got it,' she said, heading out into the corridor. 'If I want to keep my job, I better be damn good at it.'

'I object,' the district attorney said. 'He's leading the witness.'

'Sustained,' Lara said quickly.

The witness was the school psychologist who had first

reported the sexual abuse of the Adams child. The district attorney tried a different approach.

'Mrs. Mendelson, can you tell the court the circumstances around your report that Amy Adams was being sexually abused by her father?' the D.A. asked.

'The child told me her father spanked her the night before. I asked her how he spanked her and she said, "With his hands." I went on to ask her where on her body he had spanked her, and she pointed to a place between her legs.'

'Her genitals? Is that correct?'

'Correct. I even showed her an anatomically correct doll we have just for situations like this, and she again indicated her genitals.'

'In your eyes, you fully believed this child had been sexually abused and was at risk for additional abuse? Is that correct?'

'Yes, it is.'

'No further questions,' the D.A. said, sitting back down at the counsel table.

Lara leaned over the bench to the woman, who was standing to leave. 'You're not excused yet. Please remain seated.' She turned to the defense attorney. 'You may begin your cross.'

'Mrs. Mendelson, isn't it true that you showed Amy Adams this doll prior to her telling you that her father had touched her genitals? Didn't you actually hand her the doll and point to the doll's genitals, saying, 'Is that where your daddy touched you?'

'No, I didn't,' the woman replied flatly.

'Mrs. Mendelson, isn't it true that you have reported over fifty cases of possible sexual abuse at your school, and of those fifty cases, only eight have been substantiated?'

'Yes, that's true, but there were – '

Lara leaned over and peered at the witness. 'Please confine your answers to the questions. Answer yes or no.'

'Yes,' she answered, her mouth compressed in a line.

'We have no further questions, Your Honor.'

Lara felt she could have rendered a ruling now, but this was not a court trial. They had a jury impaneled. It had gone faster than Lara had ever imagined, primarily because the defense had used up their peremptory challenges the first day and the people appeared satisfied with just about anyone. Even the D.A.'s office appeared to be sympathetic to this man and his plight, and they were the ones charged with prosecuting him.

Other than instructing them and overseeing the attorneys, ruling on specific points of law, Lara's greatest impact on this case would occur at sentencing. Adams had committed the crime under great duress, but he had no means to deny it. There were, however, numerous mitigating circumstances. Lara knew the case would fall under the interest-of-justice section of the law, allowing her substantial leeway in imposing sentence. The system had fucked up and their fuck-up had destroyed many lives. The school psychologist had been overzealous and had led the small child in her statements. She was either lying or didn't remember. This kind of mistake was not an easy one to admit.

'Will counsel please approach the bench?' Lara said while the witness stepped down.

When the two attorneys were standing there, she leaned forward and whispered, 'I'm going to call recess now. I want to see both of you in my chambers.'

'Why?' the district attorney said. They were just getting started, had just this morning delivered their opening statements.

Lara glared at him until he turned and walked back to the table. 'This court's in recess for thirty minutes,' she said, tapping the gavel lightly and slipping from the bench. The jurors filed out of the courtroom and were escorted by the bailiff to the jury room.

The attorneys followed Lara into her chambers. 'Gentlemen,' she said once they were all seated facing her desk, 'I think this trial is a waste of the taxpayers' money as well as Mr. Adams's money. As he is presently unemployed, I don't see the point of this.' She turned to the district attorney. 'From what I've read and heard so far, this case should be disposed of by means of a negotiated deposition. Adams is going to be convicted and I'm going to suspend his sentence. This whole thing has been nothing short of a disgrace. We all have egg on our faces – the whole system that allowed this to happen.'

Parker Collins, the district attorney, was a hyperactive young man. He sprang from the chair in an uproar, his voice a high-pitched whine. 'We already approached them with a plea agreement. We even offered a suspended sentence and they refused. Even the victim in this case just wants it to go away. Steinfield here wants a new Mercedes and doesn't give a shit who pays for it.'

'You're out of line, Collins,' Lara said, giving him a stern look. It used to be people worked for recognition, honors. Now everyone worked for expensive toys. 'Mr. Steinfield, can you tell me why your client failed to accept the people's offer?'

'My client worked in the aerospace industry with a top-level security clearance before the state snatched his children and destroyed his life. If he ends up with a felony conviction, he'll never get another job.'

'I see,' Lara said, leaning back in her chair and removing her glasses, rubbing her eyes. 'Did you advise him of the likelihood of conviction?'

'Of course I did,' Steinfield said, insulted by her implication that he hadn't fully informed his client, or had exaggerated their chances for acquittal.

She turned to the district attorney. 'Are you prepared to reduce to a misdemeanor battery?'

'Never,' the D.A. said emphatically. Lara's small lamps with the green shades had bathed his face in shadows, giving his skin an almost greenish cast. 'This woman is permanently scarred. I mean, we sympathize with what Adams has been through, and yes, it was a royal fuck-up, but Adams went crazy out there. A misdemeanor is totally unacceptable.'

Lara sighed. 'I guess we have nothing more to discuss,' she told the attorneys. The trial would continue and Adams would suffer both the conviction and the staggering legal fees. Everyone wanted their day in court, it seemed, no matter what the penalties. The D.A. wandered out into the outer office, but the defense attorney lingered.

Raymond Steinfield was a distinguished man in his late forties with neatly trimmed brown hair, a thick mustache, and a face like Tom Selleck's. But he looked a lot better seated than standing. He was short and squat. Once he stood, any resemblance to Tom Selleck vanished.

'Yes,' Lara said, looking up and seeing Steinfield. 'Is there something else, Ray?'

He was leaning in the doorway. 'Do you know they're trying to take his kids away again?'

Lara fell back in her chair and it squeaked on the plastic mat. 'No,' she exclaimed. 'Social Services, you mean? Why would they do that? The abuse charge was unfounded as I understand it.' For a moment she thought she was losing her mind. She'd read all the medical and psychological reports, but she'd been under a great deal of stress. 'After all this, why would they try to take his children away again?'

'His wife was committed to Community Psychiatric Hospital last week. The woman's completely destroyed. They're medicating her, but no one knows when she will be released. They think she may have suffered a psychotic break or something.' Steinfield paused a moment, frowning. 'I mean, they had the poor woman convinced her husband was a child molester and that she had to divorce him to get her kids back. If she had continued to live with him, she could never have her children. She loved the man. It's been horrid for these people, just – '

'Go on,' Lara said. 'That still doesn't explain why Social Services feels they must remove the children again.'

'Because Adams is on trial, pending almost certain conviction, and he's unemployed, a nervous wreck . . . well, you know . . .' He looked hard at Lara.

How well she knew. After what had occurred with Josh, she was beginning to think these people did more harm than good. 'Their actions are unconscionable. Why are they harassing this man?' she said, consumed with the injustice of the whole situation, shaking her head. 'Are you saying that they don't feel he's psychologically stable enough to care for the chilren?'

'Basically.' Steinfield paused. 'And of course, he did lose his cool that day.'

Lara bit the corner of her lip. That was an understatement. The reports indicated the social worker would need extensive plastic surgery, but Steinfield knew that. 'What about relatives?'

'His mother is alive but infirm. Her parents reside out of the state in a retirement village in upstate New York where they don't allow small children.'

Lara felt for the man. She placed her head in her hands, thinking. A few seconds later, she looked up. 'What about a live-in homemaker? Surely that would work?'

'He's had three. They've all quit. Evidently, the little girl who was abused in the foster home is seriously disturbed and acting out, screaming for her mother every day, tearing up the house. And no one wants to live with a single male. In addition, there's been tons of press. People think the man is violent. He *is* terribly despondent right now. I'm actually quite concerned.'

'I can imagine,' Lara said thoughtfully. 'And you've fully discussed this with him, attempted to get him to accept a plea?'

'Believe me,' Steinfield said, 'I don't need another Mercedes. I already have one. Not only that, I'm handling most of this case gratis.'

'Well, if he accepted a plea agreement, he could go on with his life, put this behind him, and possibly get Social Services off his back. Do you want me to speak with him personally? I will if you think it will help.' This would be a highly unusual tactic, but Lara was a highly unusual judge.

'We'll see,' the attorney said, glancing at the outer office, noting that the D.A. had already left and returned to the courtroom. 'Maybe tomorrow. He just can't afford a felony conviction. He'll never get another job like the one he had. His career will be over.'

They walked together to the courtroom, and Lara studied the man at the counsel table next to Steinfield. He was pale and drawn. As she watched, the muscles in his face twitched and he blinked his eyes about every five seconds. From all appearances, she thought, he was about to have a breakdown himself. As tragic as it was, Social Services might be doing the right thing by removing the children. The whole case was nothing but a nightmare.

By the end of the day, Lara was completely exhausted, both emotionally and physically. At least she didn't have to run to the school to get Josh. Ricky Simmons's mother had agreed to drive him home every day until they moved. She called him at the condo and told him she would be a few minutes late, then remained in her chambers reviewing the facts of the case. If only she could convince the district attorney's office to reduce to a misdemeanor, these people could resume their lives. The social worker, the victim in this case, wasn't the one pressing for the felony conviction. It was the D.A.

As much as she hated to do it, she picked up the phone and called Lawrence Meyer, the district attorney. How he could have said the things he did about her yesterday, she didn't know. But regardless of the mud-slinging and back-stabbing, many lives were on the line and she had to give it her best attempt.

Luckily, she caught him in the office. 'Can I come over?' she asked him. 'I need to discuss a case with you.'

'Certainly,' he said. He couldn't very well deny a judge. 'I could come over there if you need to speak to me.'

'No,' Lara said. 'I'll walk over now. I'm tired of sitting.'

Unlike the courts, the district attorney's office was far from empty. Dozens of attorneys were still moving about the offices, and phones were ringing off the walls. Most of the D.A.'s spent so much time in court during the day that they had to utilize the evening hours to play catch up, prepare arguments, dictate motions, return phone calls.

Lawrence Meyer stood when Lara arrived, extending his hand but shifting his eyes down to his desk. 'Have a seat,' he said. 'What can I do for you?'

He was intelligent and well groomed, but needed exercise badly, Lara thought, noting that he had a pot belly that made it impossible for him to close his jacket. They'd once been fairly close when Lara was a D.A., and he was the second man in the agency. His harsh comments to Rickerson had stung.

'I think you should reduce to a misdemeanor battery on the Victor Adams matter and let this one go. The poor man is completely destroyed and about to lose his children again. I think he's been pushed as far as he can go.'

Meyer bristled, staring hard at Lara. 'When did you get

to be such a bleeding heart? When you were a prosecutor, you were into nailing people to the wall.'

Lara pressed back in her seat and didn't flinch. 'Look, Larry, I'm about as far from a bleeding heart as a person can get and you know it. But enough is enough. The system has to take some responsibility for what happened in this case and make some concessions.'

'We are not prepared to reduce,' he said flatly. 'If we reduce on this, we'll look like fools. I don't care what the circumstances are, a person can't viciously attack someone and scar them for life and end up with nothing more than a misdemeanor on their record.'

Lara stood. This had been a waste of her time. She started to leave and then turned around. 'Why did you attack my reputation the other day?' she said impulsively. 'I thought we were friends.'

'Oh,' he said, blanching, 'that detecive – what's his name – he repeated our conversation?'

'His name is Rickerson and yes, he did.'

'Hey,' he said, 'talk to Evergreen. He's the one who called me and accused you of improprieties. He wanted our investigator to check out all your affairs, even on a personal level . . . and provide him with a full report.'

'What personal affairs?' Lara said, trembling with anger. She felt perspiration breaking out on her upper lip and blotted it with her hand.

'How do I know? You know, the usual dossier we prepare on any subject: associates, finances, romances, etc.'

'Have you given him this report? Has it been completed?'

'Some time ago. Let me see.' He rubbed his forehead, thinking. 'A week ago, maybe two . . . something like that.' His face turned bright red. 'I'm really sorry, Lara. And yes, I do consider you a friend. I simply became enraged with this man Rickerson the other day, barging in here demanding that we get him a search warrant to gather evidence on Evergreen himself. Hell, he's the presiding judge. I thought it was some type of war between you and Evergreen, and we'd get caught in the middle. I bowed out, that's all.'

'Thanks,' Lara said facetiously. He certainly didn't bow out gracefully, not the way Rickerson had explained it. 'And for your information, Rickerson might be a little rough around the edges and overzealous about Evergreen, but he's a fine investigator. I'm not completely convinced as to his suspicions about Evergreen either, but I don't think it's wise for either of us to simply discount them.'

'Fine,' Meyer said, standing to follow Lara out, grabbing his briefcase. 'Bring me something concrete and we'll go after Evergreen with everything we've got. We don't care who he is; we'll get our sharp knives out without a problem.'

He offered to walk Lara to her car, but she was parked in the underground garage. She left and trudged back to the courts by herself.

Lara packed her briefcase with the court file on Hobson, thinking she'd review it that night in greater detail, and headed down the elevator to the car. She might be able to dismiss on a technicality. The victim could always sue Adams for damages. That was the latest rage. Women sued rapists, families sued child molesters, sons sued fathers. Recently a child had sued his parents for divorce and actually won. Now they had three cases filed already in Orange County of children who wanted to dump their parents. It was absurd.

Certainly enough lawyers around, she thought. That was part of the problem. They could tie up the courts with litigation for the next fifty years.

She had nothing for Josh's dinner, her head was

pounding, and she was still riddled with anger over Evergreen and the pending matter before the Judicial Counsel. With the proposed budget cuts, Evergreen could have decided to railroad her. She knew he would have a strong voice in this decision, and it was a difficult one. A number of judges would be competing for the same slot next year.

Only one car was left in the garage, and her footsteps echoed in the empty space as she walked across the concrete floor to the Jaguar. Digging in her purse for keys, she had a strange feeling and glanced behind her. She'd heard something, like a brush of a broom across the floor. And it was close, the sound – very close.

No one was there. She craned her neck and squinted, trying to see into the shadows of the garage, but still she saw nothing; it was completely silent. It was probably a rat or something, she thought, just wanting to get in the car and leave.

Fumbling with the keys and the briefcase, she finally dropped it on the ground and unlocked the car. Just as she put one leg inside and started to reach back for her briefcase, a hand snaked from underneath the car and her leg was locked in a steel vise. She fell forward, slamming her head on the roof, one leg out and one leg inside, her legs spread apart like a wishbone, the muscles in her groin stretching like salt water taffy. Pulling her leg out of the car before she was split in two, she suddenly found herself on her back on the concrete floor.

A huge man in dark clothing scurried out from under the car and kicked her onto her stomach. Seizing her leg again, he pulled her across the floor, like an animal taking his kill back to his lair.

'God,' she screamed, her heart in her throat, trying to keep her face off the concrete with sheer strength of will, trying to wrench her head around, kicking out with her other leg. Her elbows scraped against the rough surface. She couldn't see his face, but he was tall enough to play professional basketball.

'Help me,' she screamed, her heart beating even faster, the sound hammering in her eardrums, so loud that she felt she was under water. Her bladder emptied; warm urine spilled inside her panty hose.

She screamed again in terror. 'God, someone help me. He's going to kill me. Help me.' This couldn't be happening, she told herself. It just couldn't be happening. She was going to die just like Ivory.

As soon as she was out of range of the car, the man stopped and peered down at her. She quit breathing. She was so completely terrified, she thought her heart had stopped as well.

His face was distorted. He looked grotesque, like something from a nightmare, a horror movie. His nose, eyes, and mouth were squashed inside a woman's stocking, which was knotted on the top of his head. She saw his leg move back to kick her again and rolled across the concrete to escape. She couldn't.

The blow struck near her ribs, and a enormous gush of air left her lungs. Blinding pain seared through her body.

'Where are the pictures?' he yelled, his voice laced with venom, his lips barely moving under the tight stocking mask. 'Give me the fucking pictures, bitch.'

'In my briefcase,' Lara said, panting. 'Over there.' Then she shrieked again, hoping someone, anyone would hear her. Her voice echoed in the underground garage, and she was surrounded by her own shrill screams.

In his hands was a large knife – a hunting knife or carving knife. Light bounced off the gleaming blade in the overhead light.

'No,' she yelled again, completely panicked. 'God, no. Please. Don't kill me. I'll do anything.'

The knife was at her throat and she dared not move. His breath was hot and foul on her face, filtered through the stocking mask. He pressed down and she felt the cold edge of the blade on the delicate tissue of her throat. She was terrified beyond all reason. She gulped and gagged, certain he'd already cut her throat, imagining the perspiration dripping from her face and dampening her shirt was her own blood. The man was reeking in body odor. To Lara it smelled like death.

I'm dying, she thought. I'm going to die just like Ivory, and Josh will be alone. I'm going to die right in this garage – right underneath the courts. She prayed, her lips moving silently. She tried to think. She waited for death to take her or the man to plunge the knife into her heart. Her eyes darted back and forth frantically. She looked to the ceiling, the pipes crisscrossing and disappearing into the dark corners. She remembered that one car had been left in the garage. She prayed that someone might still be coming. But everyone had gone for the day. She'd never seen the car that was parked in the far corner before. There was no one – no one to help her, save her.

'If those pictures aren't there, you're fucking dead,' the man spat in her face, removing the knife from her throat and standing, flipping her over on her side with the tip of his shoe like a sack of garbage.

Lara's hand went to her neck. She tried to get up and fell back down on the hard surface beneath her. For a second she thought she was going to pass out. Everything went black and then returned in blazing color. He was more horrifying than ever, larger than life, a monster sent from the bowels of Hell to destroy her, kill her, cut her into tiny pieces.

'Don't move,' he ordered, panting. 'Don't move or you're dead. There's nowhere for you to go and no one's coming, so you can stop all the screaming.'

Lara was consumed with rage. It was vibrating, pulsing. She was a fighter. She wasn't going to let this man get away with this. She sprang off the garage floor and lunged at him, trying to stick two fingers in his eye sockets and poke his eyes out. Her fingers just struck the panty hose and the man laughed, knocking her back to the ground. Again she leaped up and managed to jump on his back. She tried to press her arm against his carotid artery in a choke hold, something she'd seen police officers do. She even let alll her weight go, actually hanging from his body, but he didn't budge. While she was holding onto him, the man started walking off. Lara fell to the concrete floor, landing on her feet, feeling impotent and helpless. The man was a giant. She could never take him down.

'You're a stupid bitch,' he said. 'Get down and stay down or I'm going to slice your pretty pussy.' He turned around and lashed out with the knife, almost connecting with her body. She started to reach for the knife and then realized it was sheer madness. She had felt the blade. It would cut right through her hand. He kept swinging the weapon at her, bent over, reaching out from the level of his waist. When she screamed and stepped back to avoid the knife, she fell backward to the floor. He started cackling again.

This time she did as he said, holding her body rigid, her arms locked at her side, her legs straight out in front of her. The man's digusting laughter was echoing in the empty garage. Don't fight, she told herself. Don't fight or he'll kill you right now. What she had to do was stall for time. Her nose was running, but she dared not move. She watched out of the corner of her eye as he dumped the contents of the briefcase all over the garage floor and began sorting through them, tossing the papers in the air, searching the side pockets, snarling, growling, cursing.

Locked inside those few moments, memories from the past flooded her mind. She saw herself walking home from school with Ivory, her chunky little legs struggling to keep up with her older sister, her face beaming. She could almost smell her, smell the bubble gum she was always chewing, blowing big bubbles and letting them pop all over her face. Lara closed her hand, thinking she could feel her little sister's hand in her own. Then she saw herself at her graduation from law school, searching for her mother's and Ivory's faces in the crowd, consumed with pride and accomplishment. She saw herself when she was sworn in as a judge. Even though she'd had no family present that day, it had been the proudest moment of her life. She was going to change things, she had thought, actually make a difference. If she'd never become a judge, she would have never released Ivory's killer.

The man was making horrid noises now. Guttural sounds were emitting from the stocking mask. Lara knew he was going to kill her. She could sense it, feel it. Death was swirling all around her. When he'd held the knife to her throat, she had seen his excitement. He sounded and smelled like a wild animal. For a second she let her eyes drift to him and wondered if he was real or some terrible creature spawned from the filth of the city.

She asked herself what had gone through Ivory's mind those few moments prior to death.

Josh's face appeared before her and she tried to freeze it, lock it in. She whispered to him, hoping in some magical way that he could hear her, 'I love you, Josh. All my life I wanted a child. Don't be bitter. Try to go on.' Tears were stinging her eyes and dampening her face. Her time was evaporating. Soon it would all be over. She crawled inside herself. She prepared herself to die.

'They're not here. Fuck. You lying fucking bitch,' he yelled, his voice booming. He kicked the papers away in a fury, heading in her direction with his shoulders squared and his head down like a bull on a rampage. Then he froze in his tracks.

The electronic gate opened with a loud cranking sound, and a white panel van headed down the ramp. The man turned and quickly disappeared into the shadows.

Lara sat up and screamed, 'Help me. Over here. Please help me. God, someone please help me.'

Just as the white van pulled up beside her and two men in white uniforms leaped out, another car roared past them up the ramp, its tires squealing. It was an older model blue Corvette, one side bashed in, the windows tinted so she couldn't see inside. Lara locked her eyes on the license plate and narrowed her vision so it was the only thing in sight. She committed it to memory, repeating the letters and numbers over and over. '347PJG . . . 347PJG . . . 347PJG.' The men were beside her, trying to help her to her feet. She glanced at the name on their shirts: ORANGE COAST JANITORIAL.

'Call the police,' she yelled. 'Hurry, he's getting away. Call 911 and tell them someone tried to kill me. Blue Corvette,' she stammered, gasping, 'license number 347PJG.'

The men stared at her and shook their heads.

'Hurry. Please. He's getting away. Run. Call the police. I'm a judge.' She was standing now, wobbling, weak. 'Didn't you hear me?' she yelled again. 'He tried to kill me. Call the police. What's wrong with you? Are you idiots?'

Finally the smaller of the two men spoke, '*No habla Inglés. No comprende*,' he said in Spanish. '*Policia. . . ?*'

Lara shoved them aside and staggered to her car. She used the car phone to call 911, repeating the vehicle description and her location. Razor-sharp pains shot through her side, and she leaned over the steering wheel gasping for breath. She was alive, she kept telling herself. It wasn't meant for her to die now, not when Josh needed her. There was a God, she thought. No one else could have saved her. She had prayed and somehow He had heard her. She could still taste her own demise on the tip of her tongue. She had been so close.

He was probably gone. She should have taken the gun when Rickerson offered it. If only I had, she thought, gritting her teeth against the pain, seeing his distorted face in front of her. If only I'd taken the gun, she kept repeating, imagining the gun in her hand, her finger on the trigger, the explosion reverberating inside the underground garage. Finally, after all the years of dealing with violent crimes and violent offenders, Lara fully comprehended how a person could reach that point beyond reason. If she had taken the gun, she knew what the outcome would have been. There was absolutely no doubt in her mind.

She would have killed him.

Chapter 21

Detective Rickerson didn't show up until the other officers were almost ready to clear the scene. Lara was sitting in the front seat of her car, turned sideways, the car door open, her feet on the garage floor. Her forehead was bruised and scraped, her blouse torn and her stockings ripped. On her neck was a thin red line where he had pressed the knife to her throat. In one spot the skin had actually been broken. The paramedics had treated the scrapes on her elbows and knees with antiseptic and covered them with bandages.

'Are you okay?' the detective said, rushing to the car. 'I'll take you to the hospital. They should check you out.'

'No,' she said. 'I have to go home. Josh is with Emmet, but I want to go home.' She touched her side and winced in pain, lifting her blouse to look. There was an already darkening bruise right under her rib cage where he had kicked her. 'The bastard kicked me,' she said, still breathing hard. Every time she took a deep breath, her body was racked with pain.

'You might have a broken rib. Let me take you to the hospital. Josh will be fine.'

'No,' she said emphatically. 'It's just a bruise. I'm fine. All I wish is that I'd had a gun. I want that gun now,' she said, searching his eyes. 'If I ever see that man again, I'll kill him. I promise I'll kill him.'

'You did good, kid,' Rickerson said, patting her gently on the shoulder. 'You got the license plate. We'll get him. He's probably the same man that broke into your place when Emmet was there. The plate comes back to a Frank Door. If Frank Door was actually driving that car, he got out of jail the day of the break-in.'

Lara's eyes grew wide. 'What was he in for?'

Rickerson looked away. He'd hoped Lara wouldn't ask that question. 'Attempted murder.'

'Shit,' she said. 'Who did he try to kill?'

'Oh,' Rickerson said, realizing she would find out anyway, trying to make his recitation casual instead of alarming, 'just an ex-wife. He tried to put her in the crematorium at the mortuary where he worked. Nice guy, huh? Guess he didn't want to make alimony payments.' He let forth a nervous chuckle.

'Not funny, Ted,' Lara said. 'Lord, he tried to put her in a crematorium? Really? I've never had a case like that in my life.' Just thinking about it made her entire body shiver, and she wrapped her arms around herself. She'd certainly sized her attacker up accurately. If the janitors had not come when they did, she would almost certainly have been killed. 'How'd he get out, then? Did the victim refuse to press charges or something?'

'Nope.'

'Then he was out on bail?'

'Nope.'

She glared at him. 'All right. Want to tell me about it and quit playing games? I'm not in the mood, believe me.'

'According to the jail, they received a court order the other day to release him. So they released him. We had someone check the court file, and the preliminary hearing is scheduled for tomorrow. There's nothing whatsoever in the file to explain his release. The charges weren't dismissed. He was being held without bail.'

Lara was getting the picture. It was beginning to smack of the situation with Packy Cummings. Not only that, but it was beginning to give credibility to the detective's suspicions about Evergreen. 'So it was probably Evergreen? Right? Whose name was on the order?'

'The jail says it came from Division Twenty-seven.'

'That's the arraignment calendar. Hector Rodriguez is in there now. You think Evergreen called him, told him to release this guy like he did Packy Cummings?'

'I just don't know, Lara. It wasn't Hector Rodriguez's name that was on that order.' He paused and his voice lowered. 'It was yours.'

She was shocked. All the blood drained from her face and she leaned against the door frame. 'Mine? T-that's not possible,' she stammered. 'I didn't sign an order to release this person.'

'Then I guess someone forged your name. Since the order was sent by computer from the court to the jail, I don't even know if there was an actual signature.'

'My God, every day this gets more bizarre. Evergreen must have done it and put my name on it. That fucking bastard. If you'll give me that gun, maybe I'll just shoot him and get it over with.'

Rickerson looked away. This man's record was far worse than Packy's. This man had been convicted five times on felony assault charges and once for rape. Lara was lucky, more so than she realized. If the janitorial service hadn't shown up, he might have raped her. With his last victim he'd said goodbye by biting off one of her nipples. They'd convicted him by his teeth marks. He had an overbite.

'We tried to talk to Judge Rodriguez. He wasn't at home, but we'll get him in the morning and find out the particulars. Since the order came from his courtroom, he should know something about it. Pray that he does, Lara. Otherwise, we'll be up shit creek on this one.'

'I'm praying,' Lara said. 'Believe me, I'm praying.' She locked eyes with the big detective and filled her lungs with oxygen, then exhaled in one long, painful whoosh. 'I can't take much more of this, I just can't, Ted.' She fought back the tears. She didn't want the detective to see her crying. Then she thought of something: the budget cutbacks. 'Ted, there's another possibility. I mean, it's farfetched, but no more so than your ideas about Evergreen.'

'What?' he said, defensive.

'Just that there's going to be one less slot on the bench next year. Someone has to go.'

Rickerson's eyebrows arched and he flicked the hairs in his mustache. 'You mean someone would do this to get your position?'

'Possibly.'

'That's dumb, Lara. Just plain dumb. They might want to destroy your credibility or something like that, but they wouldn't send a goon like Frank Door over here to beat the shit out of you. I'm right about Evergreen.' He glared at her and his voice rose a few octaves. 'When are you going to believe me? When he walks up to you and blows you away like Packy Cummings?'

Lara didn't answer. She looked away.

He bent down to help her stand. 'How did this go down? Did he simply assault you? Did he say anything, give you any indication why he was doing this? Did he rob you?'

'He wanted the pictures. I guess whoever put him up to this told him I had the pictures. I lied and told him they were in my briefcase. When they weren't, he was going to rip me apart. I think he would have killed me with his bare hands. I don't think this man even needed a knife. I think he liked it. You know, the killing, the brutality.' Her eyes rose to the detective's. The muscles in her face were twitching. Her voice dropped to a whisper, 'I've never been that close . . . you know, to dying.'

'Scary, isn't it?' he said. 'I've looked down the barrel of a few guns in my life. It's not something you forget, let me tell you. But think about it. It's all related. The pictures, your sister's murder, the break-ins. This couldn't possibly have anything to do with budget cutbacks.'

For a few moments they just gazed into each other's eyes. Lara felt a sense of camaraderie. She knew now what it was like to be a cop. It was no wonder so many of them went off track, became brutal and hardened. Having someone you'd never even met try to end your life was the ultimate injustice.

The silence was shattered. Rickerson slapped his thighs. 'It's obvious that this was Evergreen's doing. If the attacker demanded the pictures, then this certainly wasn't a random act. Now that they've searched both your house and the condo, they have to assume you have those pictures on you somewhere – that you're holding them yourself. Has Evergreen been in your office? He could have searched your office and didn't find them. Where do you generally keep your briefcase?'

Lara was silent for a few moments, thinking. The other officers came over and told Rickerson they were clearing. He stepped aside and said a few words to them and then returned to Lara.

'I generally keep my briefcase in my office,' she said. 'It's one of the big ones, a litigation case. You know, it's a pain to drag around. But lately, since all this has happened, I haven't been taking any work home, so I had it in the trunk of the car. I just brought it in today. I was going to review the Adams case. And as far as Evergreen getting in my office, it wouldn't be a problem. But what about Phillip, Ted? He could have sent that order to the jail and forged my signature.'

'I don't think so. It's Evergreen's son in the photographs, not Phillip. Look, get out and let me drive. I'll call for a unit to pick me up at your house.' Then he tilted her head up and peered at her forehead, touching it gently with the tips of his fingers. 'This one isn't that bad. It'll go away in a few days, but that one on your side looks pretty nasty.'

He helped her to the passenger seat and they took off, Rickerson gunning the Jaguar up the ramp and down the street.

Josh was still at Emmet's. Lara was thankful. As soon as she walked through the door, she'd typed out a message on the computer telling him to come home for bed in an hour. She didn't want him to see her this way. The poor kid had been through enough as it was. She didn't want him to know that someone had almost killed the only relative he had left in the world.

She washed her face. She sniffed her clothes and tossed them in the trash can. Fear smells, she thought, trying to cover the place on her forehead with makeup. Rickerson wrapped a bunch of ice cubes in a towel. He handed it to her when she came out.

'Here,' he said, 'put this on your side. It will keep the swelling down.'

Then he returned to the kitchen and poured them both a stiff drink from Emmet's cabinet. Lara was leaning back in the gray and black chair, her feet resting on the ottoman, her shirt hiked up and the ice pack on her side. Rickerson was wired, tossing the drink down in one swallow, going back to refill it, returning to pace back and forth in front of her chair.

'We're getting close, Lara, really close. Evergreen's got to know that we're on to him now. He's just got to know. And my guess is that he believes Ivory told you something. We know he thinks you have the photos, so he has to have come to this assumption as well. Maybe Frank Door was hired to do more than break into your car. He could have been hired to kill you.'

Lara removed the ice and let it fall to the floor. Her blouse had become wet and she hugged herself to keep from shivering.

Rickerson continued, 'I think Evergreen is trying to erode your credibility. By spreading rumors that you were using your position to protect your brother-in-law, and initiating an investigation, he's protecting himself. He figures by the time you come forward, no one will believe you. They'll just think you're retaliating in anger, trying to implicate him because he implicated you. He's setting this whole thing up like a pro.'

'Yeah,' she said. 'He is a pro.' Presiding Judge Leo Evergreen knew more about the ins and outs of crime than the majority of criminals, Lara thought. He'd been a member of the California State Bar Association for over forty years: sixteen years as a prosecutor, twenty-four as a judge. And he was a master manipulator with tremendous power to get what he wanted.

'You know what I think he's doing?' she told Rickerson, finally falling into sync with him on his suspicions of Evergreen. 'I think he's shopping for these goons like a person shops from a mail-order catalog. He has a computer in his office and he can pull up anyone's rap sheet, court date, release date, cases. You name it. Any agency in the country will tell him anything he wants to know. Nothing is beyond his reach. With a push of a button, he can manage anyone's release. He could have an army of these guys working for him, doing his dirty work. Not only that, he knows just how dirty they will get. You know, which ones are violent and which ones are not. Once he springs them, they need cash to get out of town before the court dates comes up and we issue a warrant, enter it in the system. It's the perfect situation.'

'Pretty scary,' Rickerson said, looking hard at Lara. She knew that all too well after tonight. 'But listen, we're getting close.'

'Yeah,' she said. 'We're getting close, all right. I almost got killed tonight. I thought you weren't going to let anyone hurt me.'

The detective's face flushed and his mouth fell open. Then he just shrugged his shoulders.

So much for the hero stuff, Lara thought. 'Did you find out anything on the apartment?'

'Not what I wanted to find out. Seems Evergreen owns part of the building. It's an investment . . . something like a syndicate, they said. You know, a group of investors. I don't know a lot about that type of thing, but it sounds like a tax shelter to me. Anyway, he made an initial investment and then pays a certain amount every month.'

'Shit,' Lara said, sipping her drink and then setting it on the floor. Reaching up, she touched her neck where the knife had been. She could still feel the blade there, feel the cold edge against her skin. 'What are we going to do now? We have to connect all these crimes to build a case. I don't want him on some minor charge. I want him for the whole ball of wax.'

'I'm sending an undercover officer to his club tomorrow. He gets a massage every week. We're trying to get photos of him naked to match up with the pictures we have, to ID him from the spinal deformity. My man's going to hide in the ceiling, try to film through the air-conditioning vent. We could have gone for his medical records, but that would be a dead giveaway and we'd need a court order. Listen, his son is performing in a concert in Los Angeles tomorrow night. If you're up to it, we'll go then. I don't want to wait until Friday.'

'Sure,' Lara said. 'Josh can stay with Emmet. He adores Emmet. They're inseparable.'

'Oh,' the detective continued. 'Write me a consent to pick Josh up from school tomorrow. I'm going to take him down to the station and show him a photo lineup with Packy Cummings in it. He might have seen more than he knows. Maybe he saw the guy leaving or something that day and can't remember what he saw.'

'Sure,' Lara said. 'Anything . . .'

Lara started thinking. If they could put Packy Cummings at the murder scene, then they would have a connection to Evergreen on the homicides. She suddenly thought of the game man. She went over the events of the previous night and told Rickerson what they had learned, explaining that she hadn't gone any further.

His face instantly flushed with excitement. 'Emmet figured this out?' he said, remembering the frail young man. 'This is brilliant, fantastic. Hot damn. He should go to work for us. I can't believe it. It could be him, Lara. Jesus fucking Christ, this game guy could be Evergreen himself.'

He was smiling, slapping his thighs, practically coming out of his skin. Lara remained in the chair, reserved. 'We don't know for sure it's him. Aren't you going a little overboard with all the enthusiasm?'

'You said his name was Tommy Black, right?' he said, a smile stretching his pockmarked face and making him look almost handsome, his rust eyes beaming.

'Right,' she said, leaning back down to pick up the ice pack and finding nothing but a puddle of water and a wet towel. 'So what does that mean?'

'Guess whose name is on the list of Ivory's clients? You know, calls made from that house. Guess, Lara. Just guess.'

'I don't feel much like guessing. Why don't you just tell me?' she said, staring at him. His excitement was contagious. Her breath was coming faster.

'Tommy Black.'

Lara's mouth fell open, and for a moment she couldn't say a thing. She was speechless. Then she let out a whoop and a holler that could be heard all over the complex, and Rickerson came over and picked her right up out of the chair and hugged her until she screamed.

'Put me down,' she said, laughing in spite of the pain. 'My side, remember.'

Evergreen was not at the courthouse the following day. Lara called his office and his secretary said he was still out ill but might come in later. 'Good,' Lara said, hanging up the phone. 'Hope you have a heart attack, you bastard.' He was scared, too scared even to come to the courthouse. He had to know they were close. They had him on the run. For the first time since Ivory's death, Lara felt in control. Even with what had happened last night, she felt powerful. It could be, she thought, the very fact that she'd faced this Frank Door and survived that had given her renewed strength. With the threat of violence hanging over her head since Ivory's death, Lara had lived with tremendous fear. Although she had tried to suppress it, she had felt it growing with each day, about to consume her. Now that she'd met her worst nightmare, nothing could bring her down.

While she was in a ten-minute recess from court, Judge Hector Rodriguez stuck his head in the door to her chambers. He and Lara were about the same age, and he was a pleasant man, diminutive in size, his skin a dark brown, his mustache thin and wiry.

'I heard you were attacked in the parking garage last night,' he said, rubbing his chin. 'How in the world did they get in? Crawl under the gates? It's terrifying. Nothing is safe anymore.' He paused and looked at her self-consciously. 'The sheriff's office called me. They thought I released the man who did this.'

Lara took a deep breath and tried to remain composed. 'And did you, Hector?'

'Well, no, of course I didn't. I didn't even sit the arraignment calendar that day. I had to take care of some business in Los Angeles.'

Lara had heard rumors that Hector was looking for an appointment on the L.A. county bench. Most of his family were up there. He wanted to transfer. She hoped he did before the budget cutbacks were implemented. That would mean a vacant slot. It could mean her job. 'Then who covered for you?' She was holding her breath and felt her chest expand. Please, God, she prayed, let it be Evergreen himself. She waited.

'Irene Murdock,' he said.

Lara was shocked. 'Irene? Why would she release someone like this? My God, if anyone's a stickler for things like that, it's Irene. She would never have made this type of mistake.'

'Uh, I don't know.' Rodriguez was getting antsy, seeing the tension on Lara's face. 'Why don't you ask her yourself?' He ran his hands through his dark hair and looked out over the room. 'Anyway, I'm sorry. I'm sorry for all your problems. If there's anything I can do, let me know.'

'Don't worry about it, Hector. It certainly wasn't your fault.' She inhaled deeply. 'I'll talk to Irene. Don't tell her about this conversation. We're friends, you know.'

As soon as he turned and started walking out of the room, Lara saw him favoring his right leg and almost leaped right out of her skin. 'Hector,' she yelled at him without thinking, 'what did you do to your leg?'

'Oh,' he said, looking down, 'that . . . I pulled a muscle on the handball court a few days ago. Guess I'm not as young as I used to be.'

She was getting completely paranoid. If she kept this up,

she would end up in the funny farm. She was blanketing the entire courthouse with her suspicions. As soon as he'd disappeared from the door, she put in a call to Rickerson. With the throbbing pain in her side and now learning that her best friend had released this animal, she was about to put her face down on the desk and cry. 'Look,' she said when he came on the line, 'Irene Murdock was sitting the felony arraignment calendar that day. I'm getting ready to call her and ask her if Evergreen was the one who told her to do it. The whole thing is pretty strange.'

Rickerson sighed. 'How do you explain your name being on the order?'

'Evergreen could have called and told her to release him. Then when the clerk prepared the order, they accidentally put my name on it. I was in that division a few weeks ago. I'm a female judge and so is Irene. Maybe they just weren't thinking.'

'Doesn't something like that have to be signed?'

'Of course. Generally, we send it over on the computer and then follow up with the hard copy for their files – you know, the original, with the signature and all. A lot of times they release before they get the hard copy. They've been doing that for years. They can tell it's valid if it comes from our terminal. When we're really busy, we sometimes don't get the original over there for days.'

'Then that's probably what happened. Evergreen called her, she cut the order, and then the clerk just made a mistake on the name. There you go.'

Lara was silent. The door to her chambers was shut, so she put the detective on the speaker phone and put her head in her hands. 'I told Irene that we suspected Evergreen. I don't know why she didn't call me or something. She knew I released Packy.'

'You what?' Rickerson yelled in the phone. 'Repeat what you just said?'

Lara felt her heartbeat quicken. She was about to be blasted. She grabbed the phone, taking him off the speaker, certain he was going to yell again. 'Look, I didn't tell her about the pictures or anything. I just told her we thought Evergreen was a pedophile and possibly involved in my sister's death. God, Rickerson, she's my best friend and she's a judge. She knows Evergreen well. I thought she could give us some information.'

'Judge or not, you're a fucking idiot,' he said and slammed the phone down.

Lara listened to the dial tone and then called him back. Now she was angry too. 'Don't you ever – and I mean ever – hang up on me again. Do you hear me?'

'Calm down,' he said. 'I'm sorry, okay, but what happened to everything I told you about keeping this to yourself? Christ, Lara, she might have run straight to Evergreen. You've compromised the whole case.'

'I have not,' she insisted. 'Irene would never do that. She was genuinely concerned. I'm going to call her right now and see if Evergreen called her about Frank Door. And I've asked the jail to send me a copy of the court order. I'm going to get to the bottom of this.'

'Go ahead,' he barked. 'Why don't you tell the whole fucking courthouse? Maybe you should run down there and tell Evergreen himself.' Again he slammed the phone down in her ear.

Lara decided not to call. She was almost certain Irene was in chambers. She always took recess at this time of day. She marched down the hall and let herself in. Her secretary was evidently out somewhere.

'Lara,' Irene said, peering at her over her glasses. 'Come in . . . have a seat. My God, what happened to your face? Were you in an accident?'

'Someone attacked me in the underground garage last night. His name was Frank Door. Ring a bell?' Lara didn't sit down. She remained standing in front of Irene's desk.

The woman looked away as she spoke, avoiding Lara's eyes. 'Frank Door . . . name sounds familiar, but I can't recall from where. I think I sentenced him one time years ago.'

'Well, according to records, Irene, he was released the other day when you were sitting the arraignment calendar for Hector. The jail received an order from Division Twenty-seven. The man is a certifiable maniac.' Lara grimaced. 'You should hear the circumstances of this man's crime. God, Irene, he tried to cremate his ex-wife alive. Can you believe it? He actually tried to put her into the crematorium where he worked. He was supposed to be in court for a preliminary hearing today on an attempt 187. He certainly wasn't supposed to be released. Did Leo call you and ask you to do that, because if he did – '

Irene cut her off. 'No, no, I don't think so.' She thought about it a few seconds and then changed her mind. 'I mean, he might have said something. I could have forgotten. Things were furious in there – a real zoo. I didn't do this, Lara. I swear. At least I don't think I did.' She rubbed her forehead in dismay. She looked tired and strained. 'If I did, it was a horrid error.'

'Right,' Lara snapped back, oblivious to her friend's distress. 'A horrid error is an understatement. The man almost killed me.'

Irene looked extremely distressed now. She was blinking and Lara could see her chest rising and falling. 'I'm not used to the pace of the arraignment calendar. I just don't recall. I'm so sorry. What a terrible error. Did they catch the man?'

Lara didn't know what to say. 'No, they didn't catch him,' she finally told her. Then her face softened. Irene certainly hadn't meant to do something that would have caused another person harm. 'Not yet. Anyway, forget it,' she said.

The phone on Irene's desk started ringing. She looked at it and started to ignore it and then decided not to. 'I guess I have to take that call,' she told her. She punched the button and picked up the phone. Then she held the receiver away from her ear and whispered to Lara, 'We'll talk later.'

Lara headed to the door. She had to be back in court. She was already late. She headed straight to the courtroom. Once again she had lashed out when she should have remained silent. Irene was her friend. Everyone made mistakes. Maybe Evergreen was responsible for this anyway, she thought. He could have put a note in the file and Irene just forgot about it. About to enter the rear door to the court, she changed her mind and headed back to her office.

'Did that order come over from the jail?'

'Yes,' Phillip said, handing it to her without looking up.

'Call the court and tell them I'll be another five minutes.' With the computer printout in her hand, she made her way to the arraignment calendar. They were in session, Judge Hector Rodriguez on the bench. Lara crept in and bent down to talk to the clerk. Rodriguez glanced at her and then turned back to the courtroom. He was in the midst of an arraignment.

'Do you remember this order?' Lara whispered to the clerk, putting the paper right in front of her.

The girl looked at it and then looked at Lara. 'No. Why?'

'Well, it was issued from this courtroom. It says Division Twenty-seven right there.'

'But it's not our terminal. See?' She pointed to a series of numbers in the corner of the document. 'That's not ours. I don't know who that terminal belongs to. Our number is 45892. This was transmitted on 45891. It's got to be someone in superior court, but it's not us.'

Lara snatched the document away and crept back out of the courtroom. As she rushed down the hall, she repeated the number to herself. Then she remembered.

Terminal 45891 was on her own desk.

Evergreen must have entered her office, probably while she was out and Phillip was at lunch, and transmitted that order from her terminal. If she tried to do something about it, no one would believe her. They would assume she'd staged the entire event, possibly to attract people's sympathies, or to take the heat off herself because she was under investigation. Leo was smart. Every step he made was carefully orchestrated.

Bringing the court order up to her face as she walked, she stared at the typed lines. If she had typed this document, with her limited skills, it would have taken her hours. Could Leo Evergreen type? The words were all aligned perfectly. Not only that, what she was looking at was a form stored on the county's computer software with the specifics of Door's case entered in the blanks. Would the presiding judge know how to find this form on the county's massive computer system and execute it himself?

Lara exhaled and hit the back door to the court.

'All rise,' the bailiff said as Lara took her seat on the bench.

She didn't hear the bailiff's words. She looked right over the heads of the spectators and attorneys as if they weren't present. Evergreen might not know how to operate the computer software, but Phillip certainly did.

Chapter 22

Rickerson left Josh at the station in the hands of baby Bradshaw for the photo lineup and rushed home for an early dinner with the family. He had promised Lara he would pick up something for Josh and Emmet to eat on the way to the complex. As soon as he wolfed down his food, he got up to shower and dress for the concert.

After he cleared the table, Stephen followed his father into the bathroom and watched him shave. 'Mom called today,' he said, leaning back against the door frame.

'Oh, yeah?' Rickerson answered.

'She wants you to send her some money, and she's pissed that you haven't called her lately.'

'Sure,' he said, frowning in the mirror, 'I'll rush right out and print some up. If she calls again, tell her we've got about fifty bucks until payday. She'll have to get a part-time job or a loan.'

'I filled out an application at Baskin and Robbins today. They think they can use me a few days a week after school.'

Rickerson dropped his razor in the sink and faced his son, hitching up his towel. 'I don't want you working. First, I need you here in the house, and second, your grades are more important than the twenty bucks or so you could earn. It won't hurt your mother to get a job. She's the one who insisted on this whole thing.' He rinsed his face and splashed on aftershave. 'Besides, this next paycheck will put us over the top. I've been putting in a ton of overtime.'

Heading to his closet, he took out his best sports jacket and laid it out on the bed, turning to the dresser for a dress shirt. 'What tie would look best with this?' he asked his son, holding two or three ties in front of him.

'The brown paisley. Hey, Dad, where did you say you were going tonight?'

Rickerson looked at his son and saw the gleam in his eyes. 'I'm working.'

Stephen smiled broadly. 'Really? You're working, huh? You're getting all dressed up like this to go to work? You've got a date, don't you? You're finally getting off your duff and going out on the town. Hot damn, Dad. 'Bout time.'

Rickerson's face fell. 'I'm working, okay? I'm working undercover. Who would go out with me anyway?'

'A lot of women. Leslie thinks you're a hunk. She even told me that the other day.'

Leslie was a divorced neighbor three doors down. She was one of the few people that knew Joyce was gone. She was always coming over with casseroles and food for the kids. The woman weighed about two hundred pounds, was about four feet nine, and had four screaming little kids. 'Thanks,' Rickerson said, 'but no thanks, kid. I'm hard up, but I'm not that hard up.'

A few seconds later, Rickerson went in and spoke with Jimmy, gave him a hug and left.

Lara glanced at her watch and was relieved that the day was over. They had run past six o'clock. Poor Victor Adams looked more strained today than yesterday. He was teetering on the brink, but no one could save him, no one but the D.A. and he had refused. She instructed the jurors, tapped the gavel, and adjourned for the day, slipping from the bench. Rickerson had taken Josh to the police station for the photo lineup. She'd told him to drop him at Emmet's and then come and get her at the condo.

Back in her chambers, she was about to grab her purse and leave. Phillip had already left. Then she looked up and saw Leo Evergreen standing in her doorway.

'Leo,' she gasped, completely startled. 'I thought you were ill.'

'I was,' he said, taking a seat in front of her desk. 'I came in after lunch. I've been fighting this flu for a month now. I think the whole courthouse has it.'

Lara walked backward to her desk. She felt safer there. Her heart was racing. She couldn't stop herself from staring. This man, she thought, her whole body trembling, could be the person responsible for her sister's death. Here he was – only a few feet away, in the same room, breathing the same air.

She forced herself to sit down and started moving papers around. 'Uh, what can I do for you?' she finally said.

'I heard you were attacked yesterday. Terrible . . . bad business.' He was shaking his head, not looking up. 'You shouldn't stay late and go to your car alone. I know you do that a lot.'

She didn't say anything. What could she say? Someone had let Frank Door into the underground garage. A person could crawl through the gates, but Frank Door had managed to get a car down there. For that he needed a connection. That connection might be sitting comfortably in a chair right in front of her.

He continued, 'Something else has come up. I really hate to even mention it to you after what you've gone through, but I feel I must. Are you dating Benjamin England?'

Lara tried to read his eyes. They were expressionless –

dark, watery pools that went nowhere. Her hands were trembling. She placed them in her lap so he would not see. She couldn't bear for him to know that she was frightened. Even in her lap, her fingers were dancing and fluttering. One foot started tapping involuntarily, and she held her knee with her hands. He was waiting for her to answer. His question had disappeared from her mind. 'I'm sorry,' she said. 'What did you say?'

'England . . . have you been dating Benjamin England?'

'I've had a few dates with him,' she said. 'What's this about?'

'Oh,' he said, pausing for a long time, breathing heavily. 'I – I was hoping it wasn't true. The D.A. is filing a grievance. They heard you were dating England and believe you were prejudicial in your ruling on the Henderson matter.'

Lara slapped back in her chair so hard that she slid across the plastic mat and had to use her heels to bring herself back to the desk. Then she couldn't contain herself and exploded, the tension racing from her stomach to her mouth. 'That's insane. First, I wasn't even dating England at the time of the Henderson ruling. I would never date a defense attorney on a case I was hearing. Second, I would have made that ruling even if I'd been sleeping with the damn D.A.'

'I see,' Evergreen said, letting his mouth fall open and remain that way. Finally he closed it and said, 'Relax, Lara. This is the type of thing you must deal with when you're on the bench. You have to watch every step you make. I've tried to tell you that ever since your appointment.'

Lara's eyes were blazing, but she didn't speak. Perspiration was popping out on her brow, her upper lip, trickling down between her breasts.

'They want the ruling overturned and the matter brought back before the court,' Evergreen continued. 'I may have to oblige them. Are you lovers?'

Lara spun her chair around to the wall. This couldn't go on. She picked up a paperweight and held it in her hands, thinking in another second she was going to hurl it at him. 'I don't think I care to continue this conversation any longer, Leo,' she said in a firm, flat voice, one she hardly recognized as her own. 'Whether England and I are lovers or not is no one's business but mine. I repeat, I wasn't dating him at the time of the Henderson ruling. We started going out a week or so after. I'm no longer seeing him. If they want to open up a full-scale investigation, then so be it.'

She didn't turn around until Evergreen was almost out the door. Then she slammed the paperweight down on her desk as hard as she could, and the older man glanced back at her before stepping through the door.

Tears were gathering in her eyes. She'd felt so strong earlier, so self-assured. Now she was shaken, enraged. Everywhere she turned, everything she did was now suspect. Somehow she had gone from being a respected professional to teetering on the edge of losing it all. She grabbed her purse and stood to leave, glancing around at her chambers, wondering if she'd be here much longer. There was only one good thing about it.

Right now she didn't really care.

The traffic was light and the condo close. Lara rushed back and jumped in the shower. When she got out, she stood there naked and studied her reflection in the mirror. She didn't really have a bad body. She was slender and her breasts had yet to start drooping. They would. She knew that. It was all just a matter of time. She turned around and looked at her backside. That would be drooping too before she knew it. Taking out all her makeup, she dumped it on the countertop and started painting. Tonight she wanted to look good. She wanted to look pretty and feminine. What she really wanted was to look like Ivory, but that was impossible. Sometimes she thought Josh's resentment stemmed from the fact that she did resemble his mother. He looked at her and maybe got angry – that she was alive and his mother was dead.

As she applied blush to her cheekbones, she stared into her own eyes. 'You're going to sleep with him,' she said.

Rickerson made her temperature rise, her pulse quicken. She darkened her eyebrows and then tossed the pencil onto the counter. Her sudden attack of vanity, the man constantly in her thoughts – she knew it was going to happen. She resigned herself to it. So he was married. She didn't want to wreck his home or steal him away from his wife. She certainly didn't aspire to marry him. She just wanted to borrow him for one night, one day, a few stolen hours. Was that so despicable? After everything she'd been through, didn't she deserve a few minutes of pleasure?

'Yes,' she said out loud, 'you're despicable.' She didn't know when it would happen, but she knew she was willing.

'What will one little tryst with a cop do?' she asked her mirror image. 'They're ready to fry me. Might as well go out in a puff of smoke.'

'I want that gun,' she told Rickerson in the car. When he'd walked through the door, he'd looked quite dapper. He was wearing a nicely tailored rust-colored sports jacket that flattered him considerably and looked great with his red hair.

'No problem,' he told her, reaching down where he had the gun strapped to his leg with a few pieces of leather. He handed her a small-caliber pistol, the same one he had tried to give her before. 'Be careful. It's loaded. It's my spare.'

Lara turned it over in her hands, feeling how light it was. Such a small thing, she thought, wondering how much it weighed. But this little item was enough to end someone's life in a matter of seconds. It was amazing. She opened her purse and dropped it inside. They were stalled in traffic headed into Los Angeles. The concert began at eight.

'Rodriguez is a pretty straight shooter,' she told him. 'If you're a Hispanic judge in Orange County, you've got to be. I think he'll sign a warrant when we put everything together. I don't think he'd hesitate for a minute if the evidence is substantial.'

'Sounds good,' Rickerson said, a smug expression on his face. 'Is that all you've got for today?'

'Guess so,' she said. She'd already told him about the court order, the fact that someone had issued it from her own terminal. And she'd told him about her conversation with Evergreen just before she'd left for the day. 'I was really excited. I thought you would be too.' She was disappointed. What she'd told him didn't seem to impress him at all. Getting a judge to cooperate would be a big accomplishment.

'Oh, I'm excited, lady. Let me tell you, I'm fucking about to piss in my pants.'

She turned and leaned forward, bracing herself against the dash. 'You look like the cat that swallowed the canary. Want to share it with me?'

He slapped the steering wheel. 'We got lucky. I don't know why I didn't think of this a week ago, but I didn't. Josh identified Packy Cummings. Picked him right out of a photo lineup.'

'No . . . really? How? He said he didn't see anything that day.'

'That's because he didn't know what he was seeing. Evidently, he saw Cummings's face in a car coming down that hill. Every day he stopped and took a breather before going up. Packy was flying, speeding, burning up the roads. And guys like Josh love Camaros. They're hot cars, and a red one – not a teenage boy around isn't gonna take note. He looked, but of course he had no reason to remember. After he got to the house and saw the bodies, he forgot all about the man in the car. But today he remembered.'

Lara put her hands together like she was praying and looked at the top of the car. 'Thank you, God,' she said dramatically. 'I didn't think You were there, but I guess I was wrong.' She then turned to Rickerson. 'More, tell me more. This is better than sex.'

'He might have seen him loitering around your street, over at the McDonald's. From what he said, it was around the time Cummings was shot. He said he saw a man on the phone and recalled seeing him somewhere before, but he couldn't remember where.'

'Now he's made,' Lara said. 'Right?'

'Right, kid. Now he's made. If Evergreen talked you into letting Cummings out O.R., which he did, then there's the connection we've been looking for. Not only that, but forensics put the finishing touches on it this evening. The skin samples found under your sister's fingernails came from Packy Cummings, and the semen sample is a match.'

Rickerson saw an opening in the traffic and stomped on the accelerator. Then the line of cars braked. Not wanting to wait, he raced down the off ramp and then headed back up the on ramp. For the remainder of the drive, he repeated this technique, bypassing the traffic.

'Do we have enough for an arrest?' she asked, her spirits soaring, about to go right through the roof of the car into the stratosphere.

'Hey, you're the judge.'

'What about Phillip?'

'Bradshaw says he looks clean. He did make two loans.

One for ten grand a few months ago and a recent one for fifteen. We didn't match his phone number to any on the list. I think that rules Phillip out.'

'I'm not so sure about that, Ted. He might have an apartment somewhere. Maybe he simply lists his mother's address on his employment records. A lot of people do that – young people who move from apartment to apartment.'

'Lara, he made loans totaling twenty-five grand. Where'd he get the other fifteen? We found forty thousand in the safe, remember?'

'I don't know,' she said. 'Borrowed it from his mother.'

Rickerson rolled his eyes around, giving Lara a look that said let it go. Before she could stop herself, she broke out laughing. Just being here with him, all dressed up and on their way to a concert, made Lara feel giddy.

'Does Josh get the forty grand?' she asked. 'I mean, I could use it for his education. The killer's certainly not going to come back and claim his money.'

Rickerson smiled at her. 'I think you're right. I didn't give it any thought. Do you think we have enough for an arrest warrant for Evergreen?'

'Yes,' she said. 'I say we do. I think we can go to Rodriguez in the morning unless you think we should wait until you trace the game man's phone number. I thought you were going to do that today.'

'I let baby Bradshaw – you know, the chief's son – handle it and as usual, he fucked it up, had them trace the wrong number. Before I knew it, it was too late. We have the address, an apartment, for this Tommy Black, but we can't get in without a search warrant. I'm sure that's where the phone number will come back to – that apartment.'

Lara sat back and closed her eyes. Rickerson was silent. Then she felt something. He had let his hand drift across the seat to hers and was lightly touching her fingers with his own. She didn't move; she didn't open her eyes. She relished the contact, the exchange of energy. She felt a rush of affection for this man. It wasn't even physical desire. It was real: genuine emotion and admiration. He was strong but sensitive. He had old-fashioned values. He was the kind of man who would make a great father for Josh. She stopped herself. She could reconcile her conscience to a brief affair. The way she was thinking now was completely off base. He had two kids, for God's sake. As if he could read her thoughts, the hand disappeared and the moment was gone. Rickerson steered the car into the parking lot of the concert hall and parked.

'This is it, kid,' he told her, explaining his theory that Evergreen had molested his own son. Then he told her what he planned to do. 'After the concert we'll go backstage. Watch the section he's in and see if you can spot him. We'll tell him something. I don't know. That we're music critics and we want to interview him. How does that sound?'

'I don't know a thing about music, Ted,' Lara said. For a moment she leaned against the car, her bruised side throbbing from the long drive down. 'I don't know if I can pull something like that off. Can't we think of something else? And why would he tell a music critic or a reporter that his father molested him? That's absurd.'

It was dusk and people were walking past them, heading to the doors of the concert hall. Lara caught whiffs of cologne and men's aftershave. Rickerson joined her, standing right next to her and taking out a pack of gum. He offered it to Lara, but she waved it away. She sniffed. Even the detective smelled good. He was actually wearing cologne. And he wasn't smoking a cigar.

'You look really pretty tonight, Lara,' he said. 'I don't think I've ever seen you look this pretty.'

She smiled. It was the makeup. She'd have to start wearing it every day. 'I didn't really have much to wear at the condo,' she said, looking down at her modest black jersey dress.

'I like it,' he said. He glanced at her legs. Then his eyes rose to her chest. The dress was snug. It made her look more shapely than she really was.

She turned and touched his jacket, running her fingers along the lapels. 'Nice jacket.'

'You like, huh?'

'I like you,' she said. As soon as she had said it, she wanted to take it back. She started walking across the parking lot to the concert hall. In seconds, he was next to her and another moment had vanished. 'Go over again what we're going to do?'

'Look,' he said. 'We'll tell him this story – the music critics thing, get him to go for coffee with us, and then tell him another story. You plead and beg. Don't tell him about your sister. Make up another story about how your son was molested by his father. You know, something like that. Got it?'

'Got it,' she said. 'Hope this works.'

Lara spotted Evergreen's son immediately. She had seen his picture on Evergreen's desk many times. She actually enjoyed the concert, sitting next to Rickerson, their thighs touching, everyone around them seeing them as a couple. On several occasions during the concert, he turned and just stared at her. She kept waiting for him to say something, but he never got the words out of his mouth. Once he picked up her hand and actually put it in his lap. She chickened out and pulled it away. She didn't even think he was aware that he had done it. Maybe he held his wife's hand like that, she thought. That was enough to put a damper on her feelings.

As soon as the concert was over, they scooted backstage. 'Robert Evergreen,' Rickerson said, pumping his hand.

'This is my associate Shirley Brown. We're with *Music Today*. Can you give us a minute?'

He was in his early twenties, and it was obvious that he was painfully shy. Not once did he look either of them in the eye. '*Music . . . Today*?' he stuttered. 'I've never heard of that. Is it a magazine?'

'Yes, a new magazine. We want you for our first edition . . . want to do an interview. You were outstanding tonight. Tremendous performance. Inspired, actually. Didn't you think so, Shirley?'

The young man didn't speak. He shuffled his feet around and gripped his instrument in his right hand. 'I – I don't think so,' he finally said, his voice so low they had to strain to hear it. 'Please, excuse me.'

'Wait,' Rickerson said, touching the sleeve of his tuxedo. 'Come on, give us a chance. We're a new magazine. We need the interview. Hey, it will advance your career.'

The young man took a few steps forward and then stopped. Rickerson was blocking his way. 'What do I have to do?'

'Great,' Rickerson exclaimed loudly, turning to Lara. 'Isn't this great? We're going to get an interview with Robert Evergreen. Boy, the boss will be impressed.' He turned back to the man. 'All you have to do is go and have a cup of coffee with us. We ask you a few questions and that's it. Then you're immortal – in print. Your father will be thrilled.'

There it was. Both of them saw it. The moment they mentioned his father, he completely froze and all the blood vanished from his face.

'What . . . are you talking about? Do you know my father? Did he arrange this?'

'We've heard of him, of course. He's an important man. I know he'd be pleased.'

'I have to go,' he said and again tried to walk away.

'Please,' Rickerson said, looking to Lara for help.

'Yes,' she said. 'Please, they hired me on a trial basis. If I don't get an interview tonight, I could lose my job.'

His eyelids fluttered and he finally looked up. 'All right, give me a minute.'

'No problem,' Rickerson said. 'We'll wait right here.'

The man vanished into the crowd of musicians, and Rickerson took out another stick of gum. 'Quiet, nervous man, huh?'

'Yes,' Lara said. 'Too quiet. You might just be right about Evergreen molesting him. He fits the profile.'

They waited. Ten minutes turned into twenty. The lights went off on the stage, and most of the musicians had filed past them, exiting through the rear doors. 'Think he went to take a piss and fell in?' Rickerson said. Then he stopped one of the musicians. 'There's not another door around here, is there?'

'Yes,' the man said, carrying a large cello case. 'Right over there behind the curtain. It goes to the east parking lot.'

'He skipped.' The detective grabbed Lara's hand and pulled her behind him as he rushed to the back of the building. They looked in every room. Rickerson even checked the men's room.

Robert Evergreen was gone.

Chapter 23

On the drive back to Santa Ana, Lara's side was throbbing, her elbows smarting from the scrapes, and she was exhausted. More than anything, she was annoyed that Rickerson had made her come on what had amounted to a wild goose chase. She should have known better.

'Why would Evergreen's son tell us anything?' she said sharply. She kept moving around in the seat, trying to get comfortable. 'This was nothing but a waste of time.'

Rickerson was silent. Rolling down the window, he punched his unmarked police car up to eighty miles an hour. The wind beat against his face. He wished he had a cigar and felt in his pocket even though he knew he hadn't brought one.

'I don't really feel like going home right now,' he said. 'Want to go for a little ride?'

She didn't answer. She was looking out the passenger window, lost in her thoughts.

'I guess that means yes. Right?'

Still she didn't answer. He took the next exit and headed for the beach. There was this one stretch of road, high on a hill near Long Beach, that looked out over the ocean and the city. He hadn't been there for years.

They climbed a winding, narrow road and Rickerson strained to see if they were headed in the right direction. Everything changed so fast around here. Sometimes he couldn't recognize a place in only a matter of months with all the building. The views were breathtaking up here, particularly on a clear night like this one. He wanted to stand there and look out at the lights, the moon reflecting on the water.

And he wanted to do it with Lara Sanderstone.

He pulled up near the edge and parked, cutting the ignition.

'I'm sorry I snapped at you,' Lara said, turning to him. 'I guess everything's been too much. You know, last night . . . Evergreen today . . . the whole thing. And then with this Frank Door . . . I think I'm handling it and then suddenly I realize I'm not handling it at all. Do you know what I mean?'

He did. 'Let's get out. It's gorgeous up here.'

When they were standing near the edge of the ravine, gazing out over the lights and the ocean, he reached for her, touching her fingers lightly and then letting the contact go.

'It is beautiful up here, Ted,' she said, reaching her own hand out and lacing her fingers in his. 'It's so peaceful, so calm.'

He clasped her hand and pulled her closer. Then he draped his arm over her shoulder. Neither of them moved. They didn't look at each other. It was an awkward moment. They both knew it was the first step: a small gesture but a momentous one. Lara felt strange standing there with the detective's arm around her. She had wanted it, but now she was a bundle of nerves and apprehension. After untold moments had passed, he casually pulled her even closer, sheltering her under his arm. Even with the wind blowing, she could hear him breathing. It was heavy, labored. He was nervous too.

'I panicked yesterday when I heard you were attacked. I wrecked the car.' His voice was soft and low. Lara had to strain to hear him.

'The police car?'

'You got it. I ran right into the back of a woman with three kids in the car. Damn. Thank God, there were no injuries.'

He wasn't looking at her while he was talking. His eyes were locked on the ocean, the view. Lara couldn't believe it. He was actually that concerned for her, shook up enough to wreck his police unit. He must be terribly embarrassed, she thought. Then she wondered if he'd have to pay for the damages. She pressed her head down to his shoulder and felt the coarse grain of his jacket. Someone really cared about her.

Suddenly he faced her and gathered her in his arms. She didn't resist. He didn't kiss her. It was an emotional embrace, the way a person hugs a long-lost child, a husband coming home from the war, a parent they haven't seen in years. He squeezed her even tighter, placing his own cheek next to hers. Except for his mustache, his skin was soft and smooth, clean-shaven. She forgot all about the acne scars. Right now he was the most attractive, masculine, and appealing man she'd ever known. Right now he was a long-lost love finally returning.

Her breasts were against his chest. She inhaled his cologne, the scent of his hair. They were up quite high and the wind was blowing, the evening air chilly. But she was warm, protected.

'Ted,' she said softly.

'Don't say anything,' he said, his voice scratchy. 'Please, just let me hold you. I've wanted to hold you like this for days now . . . almost since the first day I saw you in that house in San Clemente.'

They stood there in each other's arms. Moments passed.

With his hands he turned her around and pulled her back against his body and wrapped his arms around her waist, trying not to touch her bruised side. He didn't want her to see the look on his face, in his eyes. He didn't want her to see the acne scars. What he wanted was for her to imagine that he was handsome, rich, and successful. More than anything, he wanted her to want him.

'Lara,' he whispered, his face next to hers, 'I've never cheated on my wife. Not once. Believe me. Not once in all these years.'

'Then you shouldn't start now,' she said softly.

'I only want to hold you, be close to you for a few minutes. Then we'll go back.'

'Do you love your wife?' Lara asked, leaning even farther back against his body, feeling his genitals through his pants, asking herself if he was already aroused or if what she was feeling was normal. Whatever it was, it felt good. She moved her hips around. He grew. Her heart was racing. She wanted him. It was obvious that he felt the same. She was tempted to reach behind her and just grab him. She couldn't wait much longer.

'I loved my wife, Lara, and I tried to give her a good life, but she wanted more. She – she left me.'

Lara jerked out of his arms and turned to face him. 'You're divorced?' she said, her heart in her throat.

'No,' he said, 'I'm not actually divorced, but my wife moved out over three months ago. The way it looks now, she's not coming back.'

'But you – you wear a wedding ring,' she stammered. The wind was whipping her hair in her face. She took the clasp off and let it fly free. What she wanted to do was take all her clothes off and let them just blow away in the wind, then stand there completely naked with this man only an arm's reach away. Her heart was soaring. He was separated. He was on the verge of a divorce. 'If you're lying to me, Ted, I swear to God I'll kill you.'

'I'm not lying,' he whispered. 'Why would I lie about something like that?'

They were facing each other, the moonlight throwing shadows over their faces. His hair didn't even look red. It looked dark brown. The shape of his face, the slant of his nose, his large expressive eyes, all made him look unbelievably handsome.

'I want you, Lara.' His voice was not the voice she recognized. It was softer, deeper. It was crackling with emotion and desire.

'Ted,' she said, throwing herself into his arms, practically knocking him to the ground. He started kissing her face, her nose, her cheeks. His mustache tickled. She loved it.

'You're so beautiful,' he said, lacing his fingers through her dark hair, placing his face there so he could smell it, taking a strand and twirling it around his finger.

'No, I'm not,' she said softly, pecking again and again at his face with small, delicate kisses. She felt sixteen again; she felt like screaming and jumping up and down. She had never been this excited and stimulated in her entire life. She latched onto his earlobe and almost took a bite. She'd wondered what his skin would taste like; it tasted salty and sweet at the same time.

'Yes, you are. Maybe because you don't realize how pretty you are is what makes you beautiful.'

This time his mouth connected with hers. His lips were so soft, the inside of his mouth so clean. She slid her tongue over his teeth. Briefly she asked herself if he had quit smoking cigars in anticipation of this one moment. He didn't reach for her breasts or grope between her legs as most men would. He just engulfed her body in his arms and held her as tightly as he could.

'Just tell me one thing,' he said, panting with desire. 'Tell me you feel the same way – want me as much as I want you.'

'Yes,' she said, her caution gone. 'God, yes. Can't you tell? Are you blind? I've been dreaming about you. I thought you were happily married. I thought – '

Instantly he picked her up in his arms and carried her to the car. He placed her on the hood, her legs open, positioning himself between them, running his hands from her ankles to the top of her thighs along her nylons. She sighed. He lifted her around the waist in the air with one hand and pushed the hem of her skirt up around her waist with the other. Then he put her back on the car and started tugging on her panty hose. When he couldn't get them off, Lara pulled them off herself. She could feel the cold metal of the car on her skin, on her buttocks. 'Here,' she said, reaching for his crotch, wanting to please him, touch him.

'No,' he said, breathless. 'Not yet.'

She could barely see his eyes in the moonlight, but she glimpsed the passion there. They were dark, fluid.

'I've waited too long for this to make it go fast,' he panted, moving closer into the center of her legs, spreading them even wider. 'I want it to last. I want to explore every inch of your body.'

His hand came from out of nowhere and was suddenly between her legs. The soft, padded fingers slowly stroked her, arousing her, making her wet. Her head fell over onto his shoulder and she closed her eyes, let her arms hang limp. She only wanted to feel the sensation, block out the pain of the past week. It was as if he was playing a musical instrument – one he knew well. With his other hand he touched her hair, lifting it off her neck and tickling the tender spot with his fingernails.

'God,' she said. Between her legs, she was on fire. He was so gentle, his touch delicate and sensuous. It was torture and pleasure at the same time. She pushed him back. She wanted to please him as much as he was pleasing her.

'No,' he said, shoving her back onto the hood of the car, pulling on her dress until it was over her head and gone somewhere on the ground. He unsnapped her bra and tossed it as well. Now she was completely naked, staring up at the stars. Rickerson buried his head between her legs.

She was embarrassed. This was brazen. She tried to sit up, but he pushed her back down. The cool, moist air brushed across her nipples. They were hard. His hand found them and caressed them – delicately, tenderly. Lara was floating; between her legs was throbbing now. Never had she felt such exquisite pleasure, such passion. It was more than she could bear. Everything disappeared: Ivory, Josh, Evergreen, Phillip, England. She didn't want it to stop; she wanted it to go on forever.

It almost did.

Finally she sat up and jerked him to her chest. Then she slid off the car and unzipped him, taking him in her hand and relishing the feel of him. She had wondered about this part of his anatomy. Would he be small? Would his pubic hair be as strawberry red as the hair on his chest? In the darkness she couldn't tell. But what she felt in her hands was the essence of this man's masculinity. His skin there was as soft as a baby's skin. She dropped to her knees on the ground and took him in her mouth. He was clean, almost delicious. She was impervious to the gravel on her scraped knees. She was impervious to anything but pleasure.

He tried to pull her to her feet, but she knocked his hands away. She let him slide in and out of her mouth, completely into it. He moaned. Then he cried out, 'Oh, my God . . . that feels so good.' He put his hand on her head and pressed her even closer to his body.

When she could tell he couldn't wait a moment longer,

he pulled her up with his arms and leaned back against the car. Then he lifted her in the air and let her slide down until he was inside her, kissing her mouth, probing with his tongue. She wrapped her legs around his waist, her arms around his neck. With his hands he moved her body. But it was slow, an inch at a time. And it was good. He started pushing her buttocks up until they had almost disconnected, and then he let her slide down again until he was deep inside her. She felt small, delicate, weightless. She felt wanton, without a care in the world.

Again and again he moved her up and down. His big, padded hands were on her buttocks. 'Oh, Ted,' she said. She suddenly opened her eyes and saw nothing but flashing white light. She flung her upper body backward, arching her back in pleasure, feeling her own hair grazing her back. He had to hold her tight to keep her from falling. She was impervious to the ground beneath her, secure in his grip. His own face was twisted with passion. 'Now,' she panted. 'Now, Ted. Right now.'

'No,' he said. 'Not yet.'

Carrying her in his arms, he placed her in the backseat of the car and moved on top of her, his long legs sticking out the car door. She wrapped her legs around his waist. Then he pulled his body up and she placed them around his shoulders, lifting her pelvis up high, as high as it would go, wanting to feel him push right through her.

Outside she could suddenly hear the ocean, the waves crashing on the shore beneath them. It was as though they were on an island somewhere. She couldn't contain herself any longer. She was seconds away, holding back, not wanting it to end. He stopped. Withdrawing from her, he again put his mouth between her legs, holding her upper body down with his strong arms. She was writhing, moaning, crying out. Then in an explosion of pleasure, it was over. Her arms fell off the side of the seat, her body melted in satiation. She couldn't speak.

He was on top of her again and moving faster, harder now. Her arms and legs were like rubber, but the feeling began building again and she couldn't stop it, control it.

'Jesus,' he cried in a voice from the center of his throat. He was sweating. Their stomachs were wet with perspiration, slick. There were funny smacking noises as he moved even faster, like they were stuck together, like suction.

Lara cried out again, tossing her head, never having felt such intense pleasure in her life. Just at that moment he plunged deep inside her and his body froze like a statue. He didn't cry out. He appeared to be holding his breath, locking the pleasure deep inside him. A second later, he collapsed on top of her.

'I love you, Lara,' he said.

Tears started to fall from her eyes. He couldn't love her. As wonderful as it was, it was only sex. She didn't answer. She just held him, smelled him, let herself swim in the sensations. 'You're the best lover I've ever had,' she whispered. 'And I mean that, Ted. The best.'

'You're the most exciting woman I've ever known,' he said.

They sat up. He got out and left Lara there while he found her clothes and brought them back to her. He leaned against the car door and watched as she dressed. 'I'll never be able to look at another judge without wanting to undress them,' he said lightly.

'Oh, yeah,' she said, smiling. 'Better make sure it's a female.'

'You've redefined the law,' he said. He was watching her struggle to get her clothes back on in the backseat of the car. He was grinning from ear to ear. 'You're pretty cute too.'

Then he repaired his own clothing: his shirt was unbuttoned, his jacket gone; he'd kicked his pants off by the car. Lara didn't think he had worn underwear. If he had, it was gone now.

He turned on the headlights and found the last remnants of their clothing: his jacket, her shoes; the panty hose had evidently blown away.

They stood for a long time in silence at the edge of the cliff looking out over the ocean, he with his arm around her, she leaning into him. The fantasizing was over. It had been better than she'd ever dreamed. Never had a man thrilled her, titillated her, completely satisfied her like this one. And the words – the words of love – they played in her mind again and again. Could it be real? Did she dare to let herself go, let herself really care about this man?

'Tell me about your kids, Ted,' she said, pulling away. 'Tell me everything.'

'My kids . . . well, Jimmy is fourteen and Stephen is seventeen. They both go to St. Catherine's Catholic school in San Clemente. They live with me, Lara.'

'Why?' she said. She was hungry for information and she wanted it fast. She felt like a prosecutor with a witness on the stand.

'Because Joyce – my wife – went back to college. She attends Long Beach State. She's studying engineering.'

'Must be smart,' Lara said. 'Have you filed for divorce?'

'There wasn't a reason. Before tonight, before I met you, I was actually hoping she'd come back.' He looked over at her, but she was staring out over the ocean, the lights.

'Are you going to file now?' She couldn't look at him, but she had to know. She couldn't afford to climb on an emotional roller coaster.

'Yes,' he said softly, reaching his hand out to her. 'I'm going to file now.'

Both their hands were sweating even though it was almost cold. He wasn't stupid. He knew what this conversation was all about. 'Does it bother you that I'm just a cop? I mean, a judge is a pretty lofty position.'

'Hell, no,' she said, not having to think about it for more than a second. 'And you're a damn good cop. You're a damn good cop, a damn good lover, and a wonderful man.'

'I know,' he said, laughing nervously. 'I'm also a good father. Wonder why my wife didn't figure that one out?'

'She's dumb,' Lara said, facing him.

'You just said she was smart.'

'I was wrong. Ted,' she said, serious now, 'did you really wreck the police car when you heard I'd been attacked?'

'No,' he said. 'But it worked, didn't it? Sounded awfully good to me.'

Lara punched him on the arm with her fist. 'You little shit.' Then she started laughing. Rickerson began laughing and neither of them could stop. Their laughter echoed in the canyon below and returned to surround them. Tears started rolling down Lara's face, but still she couldn't stop. She was the sophisticated judge. He was the street cop. And the man had completely seduced her, set it all up every inch of the way. All these days she had wanted him and thought she couldn't have him. 'You know, lying to me could be considered perjury.'

'Not hardly,' he said. 'Didn't I tell you the other night that you could be had?'

She was still laughing. She knew he was only joking. Besides, he was right. She had been ripe for the taking. The irony was that she had actually planned to seduce him. He had just been smarter and quicker.

'Let's go,' he said once they both stopped laughing.

She stepped up to him, gazed into his eyes, and again he took her in his arms. He was so big; she was so small. While the chilly air whipped around them, they stood there together in silence. For those few moments, time stood still. 'I think I love you too,' Lara finally said.

'You think? You don't know for sure?'

'No,' she said. 'Not yet.'

He yanked her arm playfully and she stumbled along behind him to the car. He opened the door and she stepped inside. 'You'll know soon,' he said, closing the door.

Once he was in the driver's seat, they headed down the hill.

On the ride home, Lara fell asleep. At first she faked it, leaning back and closing her eyes, wanted to savor everything that had happened and commit it to memory, sort through her thoughts. Then exhaustion overtook her and she fell into a deep slumber, slipping even farther down in the seat, her head rolling to the side against the window. Rickerson turned the volume on the police radio up where he could hear it, glanced to see if Lara would awaken, but she was oblivious to anything now.

He listened to the dispatcher. They were dispatching an officer on a barking dog. Having been out of patrol for years, he couldn't imagine sending officers out on such stupid calls. But that was a part of the job, like it or not. He'd done his time, handled the family fights, the loud parties, the neighborhood squabbles. It wasn't all action and excitement. He kept glancing at the woman next to him. Her hair was tousled, her makeup smeared. He felt exhilarated.

Then he heard something that made his hair stand on end. An officer came on the air, screaming, his siren blasting in the background. You could even hear the roar of his unit's big engine as he raced through the night. He was in pursuit.

The car he was chasing was Frank Door's Corvette.

Rickerson, almost in Santa Ana, looked quickly at the freeway off ramps. He wasn't that far away.

•

Lara had no idea where they were when she opened her eyes. The car was barreling down the road, Rickerson sitting up close to the steering wheel, gripping it with both hands. The police radio was blasting, the volume turned all the way up.

'Seat belt on?' he asked Lara, having to yell over the radio. She nodded, rubbing her eyes. Then the detective slapped the steering wheel and almost lost control of the speeding car. 'I should have never left the freeway. Fuck. I think we've lost him now.'

Lara was dazed, just trying to figure out what he was all excited about. He cut through a dirt lot, dust churning in clouds, the unit bouncing up and down like a jeep, the windows rattling and shaking. 'What the hell?' Lara screamed. 'Tell me what's going on.'

'Shut up,' he barked. 'Just hold on . . .'

'Shut up? You stop this car . . .'

Out of the dirt now, he flew over the curb, the front fender scraping against the road, fishtailed onto a side street, and again he stepped on the accelerator. 'There,' he said, 'see it – there it is. Got the sucker. Hot damn. Snuck right up on him.'

About two car lengths ahead of him was a blue Corvette with dark tinted windows. 'My God, the car,' Lara said, grabbing the dashboard and seeing if she could make out the plate. 'That's it,' she yelled, her heart beating faster and harder. 'It was 347PJG. That's it. How did you find it?'

Rickerson was closing the distance. 'I didn't find it,' he screamed. 'Another officer spotted it and went in pursuit . . . Then he lost him and we were nearby. I found him. Good thing I drove the police unit tonight.'

Rickerson grabbed the microphone. 'Station One, this is 654. I have the vehicle. I repeat, I have the vehicle in sight. We're northbound on . . .' He paused, looking frantically at the street signs. 'We're on Harbor . . . passing

Orangewood. Get me a backup. Advise them to take the Harbor exit off the freeway.'

The Corvette was exceeding the speed limit, but still wasn't aware they were following him. Then when they were practically on his bumper, the Corvette took off in a burst of speed, making a sharp right turn down a side street.

'Hurry,' Lara screamed, totally into it now. 'Get him. Get the bastard.'

'I need a backup,' Rickerson screamed into the radio again. 'I have a civilian in the unit.' He gripped the steering wheel and turned to Lara. 'Shit, that 'Vette is souped. There's no telling what's under the hood.'

He glanced at the speedometer. They were flying down a residential street at about eighty-five miles per hour, Rickerson desperately trying not to hit the parked cars in front of the houses and get them killed, maybe even run over some poor soul crossing the street in the dark.

Down another street they raced, this one a divided roadway with two lanes. Rickerson kept trying to pull up alongside the man on the left. While Lara's eyes were peeled on the road in front of them, he yanked his gun out of his shoulder holster and steered the car with one hand. 'Get down in the seat,' he ordered her. 'And don't get up, no matter what happens.'

For a moment, she didn't move.

He yelled again, 'Get down.' Then he shifted the gun to his left hand and shoved her head down with his right. The engine roared, the car vibrated. 'Here it is,' he yelled. 'Put your face into the upholstery. Hold on.'

No sooner had the words left his mouth than the car jerked violently to the left and smashed into the other car, metal jarring metal with a loud metallic crunch. Then the police unit started spinning out of control, making a complete circle backward at tremendous speed. Rickerson wrestled with the steering wheel, trying to steer into the skid and bring the car to a stop. Lara dug her fingernails into the seat and screamed.

The car stopped.

Rickerson bailed out, leaving the door standing open. She could hear him yelling, 'Police. Stop right there, you mother fucker. I'd just love to blow you away.'

Lara unfastened her seat belt and crawled to the passenger window, only her eyes and the top of her head showing as she peered out at the scene. The detective had a gun trained on a man on the ground. The Corvette was upside down and the wheels were spinning, the engine still running, steam and smoke rising from the hood. Keeping her head down, she cracked open the car door and yelled, 'Can I get out?'

'You okay?' he said, never taking his eyes off the man.

'I think so,' Lara said, standing. Her legs were wobbling and her knees knocking, but she didn't think she was injured. 'I'm fine. Is it him?'

'Take a look,' Rickerson said, stepping closer to the man. He was on his face on the asphalt. Rickerson kicked him with his foot, and the man rolled onto his side. Blood was streaming from a cut on his chin, and his arm was bent at an unnatural angle.

'My fucking arm's broken,' the man said. Then he spat on the sidewalk. His mouth was full of blood.

Since he didn't appear to be armed, Lara took a few steps closer. 'That's him,' she said. He didn't look as menacing without the stocking, but she knew it was him. He was tall and thin; his legs looked like stilts. She recognized the black polyester pants. They were about two inches too short.

'You bastard,' she hissed at him. 'You fucking bastard. I should shoot you myself.'

'Want to rough him up?' the detective said, his shoulder twitching, the strain of holding the gun in front of him causing it to move up and down in his hand. He hadn't even brought a set of cuffs. He'd gone out to a concert, not expecting to end up in a pursuit. 'You've earned it,' he urged her. 'Go ahead. Kick him or something. Kick him in the balls.'

Lara froze.

She'd never purposely hurt another human being in her life. He was vile and contemptible, but she couldn't do it. She just stared at him, watching the blood drip from the cut on his chin. He started laughing at her. A few seconds later he was coughing and hacking, then rolling over and spitting up more blood.

'I'm fucking dying, man,' he said. 'My arm . . . my arm.'

Rickerson looked back at Lara. 'Do it. Do it now. Kick his arm and see how he likes it. See how he likes to be on the receiving end.'

Lara continued to stand motionless. She finally took a few steps forward. Every second of that horrible night in the garage returned and she moved her foot around, started to pull it back and kick him. She was breathing hard. This was her chance for revenge. She could hurt him. She could kick in his face, kick him in his balls.

'Go on,' Rickerson said. 'We haven't got all night.'

Stepping close to the detective, she whispered, 'I can't. I just can't.'

'Didn't think so,' he said, smiling. 'To be honest, I'm not into that type of thing myself, but thought I'd offer.'

'I'm in pain, man,' Frank Door screamed.

'Go to the phone and make certain they're sending a black-and-white. The radio's disabled.' He looked around, trying to spot a street sign. 'Take your purse and the gun. This isn't the best area. Check the street sign on the corner and give them the cross streets. Hurry.' He paused and then added, 'I guess you better get an ambulance too.' He yelled at the man on the ground. 'That is, unless you want to make a run for it, asshole, and let me put a hole in your fucking back.'

Lara grabbed her purse and started jogging down the street toward the street light. On the opposite corner was a Stop 'n' Go. They should have a phone.

Lara stayed with Rickerson while they waited for a tow truck and then had to go to the police station to give her statement and make a positive ID that Door was the man who had attacked her. Rickerson still had to complete his report and transport Frank Door to the county jail. He arranged to have a patrol unit drive her home. Having consumed about five cups of black coffee, he was wide awake and wired. Before Lara left, he snuck her into the captain's empty office and closed the door. He kissed her, held her.

'Tonight was probably one of the best nights of my life,' he told her. 'I don't want to let you go.'

'You're not going to let me go, Ted,' she said, running her fingers through his hair. 'But I do have a trial tomorrow. I have to get a few hours' sleep.' She started for the door and he jerked her back.

'I could make love to you again – right here, right now.'

'No, Ted,' she said, pulling away forcefully. 'Not here. Don't worry, I'm not going to disappear. Believe me, this meant as much to me as it did to you. Next time we'll try a bed. I'm a little too old for the backseat of a car.'

'Tomorrow,' he said. His eyes tracked her as she left the room, leaving him standing there in the dark.

A few seconds later, she stuck her head back inside and whispered, 'Tomorrow. Better rest up.'

Then she found the patrol officer and he took her home.

It was four in the morning before Lara fell into bed. Josh had slept on the floor at Emmet's in his sleeping bag.

When she didn't get up in time after he'd returned, dressed, and had his breakfast, he went and woke her. 'Are you sick?' he said, concerned that she was still in bed.

'No,' she told him, forcing herself to put her feet on the floor by the bed. 'I'll be ready in five minutes.'

They walked to the parking lot together, her mind replaying the events of last night. They'd certainly chopped Frank Door down to size. In a way it had been quite gratifying, even if she didn't have the gumption to kick his face in or rupture his balls. Just seeing him bleed had been worth it. She thought of Ted Rickerson. Just thinking about their lovemaking on the bluff gave her a warm, satisfied glow. Everything was a little brighter, sharper: the sun, the smell of the flowers planted near the front of the complex, the soft, warm air on her face.

She drove Josh to school. There was no reason to tell him what had really transpired last night with Frank Door. Josh didn't even know about the assault in the garage. She glanced in the rearview mirror, checking her face. The bruise on her forehead was fading, and she had covered it with makeup.

Frank Door was safely in jail; he'd refused to waive his rights and had demanded an attorney. Unless the D.A. offered him a deal, Rickerson doubted he'd ever talk. Was it really Leo Evergreen behind her sister's death? With Josh's ID, they now had a connection between Packy and the murders. Evergreen had told her to release him. Additionally, Evergreen's son was in one of the obscene photos. Even though she found the whole thing incomprehensible, she had to admit the evidence was beginning to stack up. The one thing that kept appearing in her mind was the court order to release Frank Door. She couldn't see Leo sneaking into her office and figuring out how to produce and transmit that document. He could have had another secretary or clerk do it for him, she thought, even though that would have put him at risk of exposure.

A thought flashed into her mind. If Evergreen was the game man, he'd be proficient in computers. Then another thought surfaced. Phillip loved video games. Several times she had walked into her office and found him playing games on his terminal. Phillip could be the game man.

Clearing her mind of these thoughts, she made an attempt to converse with Josh.

All he talked about now was Emmet. Lara really felt she could have moved back into the house in Irvine several days ago, but she had stalled, hating to take Josh away from Emmet. They had bonded, became fast friends. In many ways they had merged into something similar to a family. And Lara knew Josh needed this companionship – to be surrounded by people. As far as she was concerned, Emmet had done more for the child than Dr Werner could have done in a hundred sessions. He was talking more. He wasn't hurling insults at her. She was beginning to see the fine young man that he really was surface – the angry young man was finally fading away.

'Emmet's so smart,' Josh said. 'He's a genius. And he never complains. I mean, he never complains about anything.'

Lara reached over and clasped his hand. 'You don't complain a lot yourself, Josh. Guess you and Emmet have a lot in common. Neither one of you has had a lot of breaks in life, but you're a fine young man.'

'Yeah,' he said, his eyes clouding over, his fingers tightening on Lara's. 'Way I see it, you have to take whatever comes along and make the best of it. That's what Emmet says. Did you know his mother dumped him when he was diagnosed? She just up and left. He hasn't seen or heard from her since.'

Lara sighed. She hadn't known. In reality, she wasn't

even certain how old Emmet was. From what he'd told her, she'd estimated his age in his late twenties or early thirties. He'd graduated from MIT. Then he'd gone on to get a master's degree at Long Beach State. But the way Josh was talking, she might be mistaken. Emmet might be only in his early twenties. He was probably a child prodigy who had gone to college at fourteen. In many ways the little man seemed ageless. One moment he seemed like a child, almost helpless, and another he seemed to know all there was to know in the universe.

'Emmet says he gets scared sometimes,' Josh continued. 'He's afraid he's going to die alone. Sometimes in the middle of the night, he told me, he wakes up and thinks about it – about what happens when you die. You know what Emmet believes? He believes he will come back after he dies in a different body, a healthy body. Because God has made him suffer so much in this life, he thinks he will have a much better life next time. But his mother? . . . How could she leave him like that?'

'Well, Josh, some people can't handle illness. Some people are weak, but that doesn't mean they're bad. Possibly it's because they haven't had enough love or people have hurt them. I don't know.'

'Is that what happened to my mother?' Josh said in a soft voice, his eyes turned to Lara. They were exiting the freeway, almost in San Clemente.

'No, no, your mother was very loved, at least before she married Sam. Our parents were loving people and your father certainly loved her. But she was insecure, afraid. She wasn't that sophisticated, and I think sometimes the world was too complex for her, had too many sharp edges. But she was a good person, Josh. No matter what happened, what she did there at the end, she loved you very much.'

He was silent. He turned the radio on and tuned in a

rock station. Then he started talking again over the noise. 'I hope Emmet is right,' he said.

Lara turned to him. They were stopped at a light, almost at the school. 'About what?'

'About people coming back when they die. I hope my mom came back in a new body – that she's happy now.'

'I do too, Josh,' Lara said. 'I do too.'

'Some people at school said some nasty things to me.'

Lara gasped, locking her fingers on the steering wheel. She had been afraid of this, but until now Josh had sworn everything was okay at school. 'What did they say?'

'That my mother was a dirty whore and I was a bastard.'

She didn't know what to say. She pulled up in front of the school and parked. 'Honey, whoever said that is the one with the problem. They have to make other people feel small so they can feel big.' She paused. 'Can you handle it? If it persists, I can go to the principal. Or we could change your school. We'll probably transfer you anyway once we move back to the house in Irvine.'

'No,' he said, his hand on the door handle. 'I can handle it. Are they about to arrest the man who killed my mother? I picked out this guy last night from a bunch of pictures. I saw him coming down our street that day . . . the day it happened. But Detective Rickerson told me the man was dead, that someone else was behind what happened to my mom and Sam.'

'We're close, honey. Everything is getting close. We just don't have quite enough evidence yet to make an arrest, but soon.'

After stepping outside, he turned back and gave her a weak smile that moved only the corners of his mouth. She watched as he walked away. Kids were congregating, laughing, jostling with one another. How could they be that cruel? she thought. Then she saw Josh walking back to the car and her heart jumped. Was there a problem? Did one of those stupid kids say something else to him? He opened the car door and climbed back in. 'What's wrong?' Lara said, her voice full of concern.

'Nothing,' he said. 'I forgot something.'

Lara tried to remember if she'd given him money for lunch. She had. 'What? I gave you lunch money. Did you forget your books?'

For a long moment he looked straight ahead. Then suddenly he jerked his head to the side and leaned over and kissed her on the cheek. 'That . . .' he said, smiling nervously.

Lara blushed. She felt her entire body surge with pleasure. Here – he had kissed her right here where all the kids could see. Teenagers didn't do that type of thing.

No man in the world could make her feel the way she felt right now, infused with such pride and joy – not even Rickerson.

She didn't say anything. She was lost in the moment, flooded with warmth. 'I – I . . . Josh,' she started stammering.

He got out and leaned back in the window, a wide smile on his handsome face. 'In all my life,' he said, the smile vanishing as he spoke, 'my mom never once drove me to school.'

Then he pulled his head out of the window and disappeared into the crowd of kids.

When Lara got to the courthouse and parked, she saw something white lying on the passenger seat. It must have fallen out of Josh's notebook. It was a piece of paper. She opened it and read. 'I wanted to tell you about the T-shirt,' it said in his small, neat handwriting. 'I was too embarrassed to tell you before, but I want you to know. Sam made me eat a TV dinner. He made me eat the foil tray. I tore it up in little pieces and ate it with the mashed potatoes. The next day I started bleeding at school. I didn't know what to do, so I put my extra T-shirt in my pants. I didn't want the kids to see blood on my pants. They would have teased me. They would have said I was a girl. You know, having what girls have every month. So that's it. Don't worry. I'm fine now. Foil isn't that good to eat, though. In case you ever wonder.' He signed it, 'Josh. Your nephew.'

Lara put her head on the steering wheel and cried. In his short life this young man had suffered more than she had in all of her thirty-eight years. And he had suffered alone – just as Emmet suffered alone. She would never complain again. Last night Ted had given her more love in one night than Nolan had in their entire marriage. And today Josh had kissed her, a clear indication that he cared. Even if they tossed her off the bench, she decided, she would just have to deal with it. That was her commitment.

Chapter 24

Detective Rickerson arrived at the San Clemente police station at eight o'clock that morning. What with the evening with Lara, apprehending Frank Door, the pending investigation, he'd had less than three hours of sleep, but he was infused with energy. A natural at stalking his prey, he had the scent of the kill in his nostrils.

Pouring himself a cup of black coffee in the detective bureau, he thought of the magnitude of their undertaking. It was one thing to haul in small-time hoodlums. Arresting a man like Evergreen was a real coup. As he saw it, it was his one chance to climb the mountain all the way to the top. It was the chance he'd been waiting for all his life.

His task force had risen dramatically since the onset of the investigation. He had several officers from patrol working full-time on the case in plainclothes, baby Bradshaw, who did more harm than good, along with numerous reserve police officers. Reserves were men who wanted to be cops but had been smart enough to pursue other, more lucrative occupations. They were trained, given uniforms, weapons, and allowed to ride with regular officers so many days per month. If they ever had a disaster such as an earthquake, a flood, a major fire, they called on these men. Some of them were professionals, like doctors, dentists, accountants. And some of them were outright fools, wanting to play cops and robbers like children.

He couldn't afford to be picky. He'd taken whatever he could get, and the extra help had paid off.

Even though there were many leads left to follow and the investigation was in no way complete, he felt time was of the essence. Lara had already been attacked once. The next time she might end up in the morgue. He couldn't take the chance. They had to make their move.

He'd informed Lara that she should set up a meeting with Judge Rodriguez for twelve o'clock the next day. He didn't want to do it at the courthouse right under Evergreen's nose, so the meeting would take place at the police station. He contacted Gail Stewart at the lab, and she agreed to drive down and make a presentation.

Now that Frank Door had been arrested, they had to move fast. They had him in isolation at the jail, but they couldn't deny him phone access. The first person he'd more than likely call to spring him would be the good judge himself.

Lara made an appointment to see Judge Rodriguez during the lunch-hour recess. As soon as she got out of court, she called Evergreen's office and his secretary advised Lara that the judge had suffered a relapse of the flu and was out ill again. She was beginning to get frightened, afraid he was going to skip town. 'Did he tell you when he thought he would be back?' she asked the woman. 'I have something important to discuss with him. Is he at home?'

'Well, yes,' she said curtly. 'Where else would he be? He's sick.'

Maybe on a plane to New Zealand, Lara thought, replacing the phone in the cradle and heading down the corridor to Judge Rodriguez's chambers. Either that or he was at home watching the shopping network, maybe looking for a few new goons.

'Hector?' she said at the door. The small man stood and waved her in, indicating she should take a seat.

Hector Rodriguez was far from neat. His desk was covered with papers, open files, law books, coffee cups. The credenza behind him was even worse, with periodicals and files stacked at least two feet deep. Cardboard boxes with personal effects he'd never got around to unpacking stood gathering dust in the corners of the room. Only three months ago, he'd been appointed to a position on the Superior Court. Prior to that, he had been in Municipal Court – traffic court, to be specific. And he was already looking to get out, transfer to L.A.

Lara went over everything with him slowly, repeating many facts several times. Rodriguez listened, nodded, made notes on a yellow pad of paper. If he was shocked, he was keeping it under wraps. The telling over, Lara leaned back in the seat and waited. The next move was his.

'Tomorrow?' he said tentatively. 'You want me to go to the police station?'

'Yes,' Lara said, sitting forward in her seat. 'I don't expect you to make a decision on the basis of my statements. Detective Rickerson is preparing a presentation, bringing in experts to outline the evidence. I want you to see it all with your own eyes.' It was really more than that, Lara thought. She wanted it to be Rodriguez's call instead of hers. If he thought the detective had compiled enough evidence for a warrant, then so be it.

He swiveled his chair sideways, staring at the flag by his desk. 'I think we should call the Judicial Counsel, have someone fly down for this presentation. This is serious business, Lara. Extremely serious business . . . and it affects all of us. Think what the press is going to do with this when we go public. It won't just be Evergreen who suffers.

Public opinion of the legal system is at an all-time low. We'll all look bad.'

'That's fine with me,' she said. 'You can have the Pope come if you want. I just want to get this thing moving, get a warrant and serve him with it before he leaves town.'

Judge Rodriguez turned his chair back to his desk and opened a law book, bending down and flipping the pages until he found what he wanted. 'If you review section 1029 of the penal code, it states clearly that the Judicial Counsel must be notified whenever a judge is charged with a criminal act. And, of course, if the D.A. agrees to prepare the case, file a complaint, it will have to be transferred to another jurisdiction. None of us can sit the trial.'

'Okay,' Lara said, standing. 'I'll call Lawrence Meyer and advise him, have him come tomorrow, and you contact the Judicial Counsel.'

When Lara was at the door, she looked back. Rodriguez was still deep in thought. 'Listen, Lara, maybe we should even call the FBI in on this due to the child pornography. They have extensive records on this type of thing.'

'Good idea. I'll handle it. And Hector,' she said, 'thank you for being so receptive. Some people would back off, want to keep their hands clean. They'd be afraid to go head to head with Evergreen.'

The little judge smiled. His front teeth were crooked. Obviously, his family couldn't afford an orthodontist when he was a child. 'Where I come from,' he said, 'basically the streets of south central L.A., the barrio, going up against anyone without a gun or knife in their hand is nothing.' He paused and smiled again. 'Besides, I never liked Evergreen that much. Something about him just rubbed me the wrong way. I think underneath that slick veneer, he's prejudicial against minorities. That's one of the reasons I want out. I think when the slot is eliminated next year, I'll be the one to go.'

Lara smiled back and left. He might be small in stature, but Judge Hector Rodriguez looked pretty big right now.

Josh got a ride home with Ricky Simmons's mother. The first thing he did was drop his books in the condo and head to Emmet's, grabbing a bag of cookies on his way out the door and the cellular phone in case Lara called him. He knocked, but Emmet didn't answer. He had a key. Emmet had told him he could come over any time he wanted. Then he remembered. Today was the day Emmet went to the physical therapist. They were trying desperately to maintain his condition, keep the strength he had in his muscles from deteriorating further.

Josh sat down in the bedroom and loaded up the computer. He munched cookies and played video games. He was playing Wanders from Y's. He couldn't seem to get the hang of it and his points were low. The following night he was spending the night at Ricky's, and he wanted to beat him. Of course, Ricky was much better. He had his own computer and tons of games. Never once had Josh beaten him. On a piece of paper by the console was the number to the game man. On a lark, he dialed it and a man answered.

'Hi,' he said. 'Uh, this is Ricky Simmons. I called you the other day. I thought you could give me some pointers on Super NES's Wanders from Y's.'

The man began talking and Josh listened intently. He blanked the screen and started over. He repeated the man's instructions. 'Okay, I have the manufacturer's name up. It's American Sammy. Press up, down, up, down, select. I did that. Now what?' Josh had the phone clamped between his ear and his shoulder. 'Start on the second controller? Okay. It looks just the same. This is just the beginning of the game.' He was a little disappointed. The man continued giving him instructions. 'Okay,' he said, 'I have the status screen. Press select on the second controller? Yeah. Did it. It says "Debug." '

'Now when you're damaged,' the man's voice said, 'and your hit points drop to zero, you can still come back to life.'

'Cool,' Josh said. He couldn't wait to show Ricky. 'Thanks.' He was staring at the computer screen, ready to hang up when the man began speaking again.

'I have all those demos for you,' he told Josh. 'They're new . . . all the newest games.'

Josh was getting nervous. Lara had told him not to call this man, but he couldn't see what harm it would do, not just one quick phone call. But if she found out some way, he thought, she would be angry. 'Hey, I have to go. I have homework.'

'Wait,' the man said, a tinge of panic in his voice, 'don't go yet. Let's talk a few minutes. You called me, remember, and I helped you. It's not very nice just to hang up on me.'

'Sure,' Josh said. 'Sorry. We can talk.' He had no idea what the man wanted to talk about.

'Do you have a girlfriend, Ricky?' he said in a wispy voice, almost childish.

'I like this one girl in my math class, but she won't even talk to me.' He thought of Heather Reynolds with the long blond hair and the big blue eyes. He'd almost fallen over his shoelaces when he'd seen her this year. During summer vacation she'd grown breasts. It was incredible. Heather Reynolds had been great just the way she was, but Heather Reynolds with tits was heaven on earth.

'I see,' the man said slowly, a little smacking noise coming over the phone line.

'Look, I said I have to go,' Josh said.

'Will you call me again, Ricky? Don't you want those demos?'

'Yeah, sure,' he answered. Then he quickly hung up the phone and left Emmet's condo, crossing the grassy courtyard to Lara's place and beginning his homework.

Once he had done his math and his English, Josh called Ricky and made sure they were all set for tomorrow night. 'I could get you some free games,' he told him. He was certain the game man didn't have anything to do with his mother's murder. The man was really pretty cool. He knew everything there was to know about video games, even more than Emmet knew.

'And how are you gonna do that?' Ricky asked. 'Hey, are you gonna rip them off from the store?'

'Do you want Smart Ball?'

'Shit, yes. I've been saving my allowance to buy it.'

'I'll see if I can get it.' Josh clicked off the phone. He was bored. Emmet had taken his TV to the model condo. Once his homework was done, he usually went over to Emmet's and stayed there until Lara got home. He thought about going out on his bike and then decided against it. After about an hour of sheer monotony, he called the game man back.

'I'd like those games, man,' he told him. 'What do I have to do to get them? I don't have any money. You said they were free.'

'Yes, Ricky, they're free just like I said. All I have to do is fill out this questionnaire about you. The company I represent likes to know what their buyers are like . . . sort of a profile.'

He started asking Josh questions. Some of them he'd already asked, like where he lived, if his father was alive, where he went to school. Then he asked him physical things: what color was his hair, his eyes, did he have bad skin? Josh answered them all. Some of them he lied about. He felt bad about that, but he had lied the first time he'd called him. He couldn't tell him the truth now.

'Do you like movies, Ricky?'

'Sure,' Josh answered.

'Do you like to play miniature golf?'

'Yeah, sure.'

'What about bowling? Do you like to bowl?'

'I don't know how.'

'I see,' the man said. 'Have you ever had sex with a girl?'

'What?' Josh asked. He didn't know what this had to do with video games.

'You know, put it to her, stuck it to her.'

'No,' Josh said, completely mesmerized, lulled by the man's soft voice, thinking what it would be like to do that to Heather, to actually touch her breasts. She had this one white blouse. Every time she wore it to school, he could see her bra through the thin fabric. Last year she hadn't even had a bra. This year it was filled.

'I have some movies at my place,' the man said in that same funny voice. 'You know, dirty movies. What does this girl look like?'

Josh felt himself perspiring. He moved around in his seat. His jeans were pinching between his legs. He was getting turned on. Normally, this only happened to him late at night, in his bed. Sometimes he touched himself, had nasty thoughts. This guy on the phone didn't even sound like a grown-up anymore. He sounded like Bart Miller at school. Bart always had dirty pictures of girls ripped from his father's *Penthouse* magazine. 'She's got this long blond hair. It's really shiny.'

'You should see this movie, Ricky. I'm looking at it right now. There's this girl in it with long blond hair and huge tits.' The man giggled like a child. 'She's touching herself. You should see her. She's putting her fingers right inside there. I bet she looks just like your girlfriend.'

Josh snapped out of it. He felt dirty and disgusting. What was wrong with this man, anyway? He shouldn't be saying these things to him, offering to let him see dirty movies and all. That just wasn't right. 'I've got to go, man,' he said quickly and slammed the phone back. Now he'd have to tell Ricky he couldn't get the game. Ricky would be pissed. He looked out the window and saw Emmet's wheelchair at the front door of the condo.

He crossed the courtyard and waited while Emmet said goodbye to the lady who always drove him, and then called to him. 'Hey, Emmet. Can I come in?'

Josh and Emmet played video games for about an hour. Josh couldn't concentrate and Emmet beat him every time. All he could think about was the man's funny voice, how he'd giggled so silly like a kid or something, the things they had talked about. Finally he turned and faced Emmet. 'I'm going to tell you something, Emmet, but you have to promise you won't tell Lara. If you don't promise me, I won't tell you.'

'I . . . promise,' Emmet said.

Josh related his experience with the game man, and Emmet listened quietly. Then Josh told him what he thought. 'This is a sick man, you know. I'm not a retard. Adults aren't supposed to talk about sex and stuff with kids. He's a pervert, isn't he? One of those child-molester people everyone's always talking about.'

'Yes,' Emmet said. 'Do . . . not . . . call this man.'

'He's a bad man.' Josh got up and started walking around in small circles. He stopped and swiped his long bangs off his forehead. 'You've got to tell me the truth, Emmet. We're friends. Did this man have something to do with what happened to my mom and Sam? Is that why Lara wants to catch him?' Suddenly the conversation he'd overheard between Emmet and Lara came back, and he knew he was right.

At first Emmet didn't answer. Then he said, 'Maybe.'

Josh flopped down in the chair again. It was one of those little chairs on rollers, and it slid a few feet on the hardwood floor. 'I don't believe it,' he kept saying. 'I just don't believe it. They know it's him, but they don't have enough evidence.' His eyes clouded over and he started thinking. They sat there without talking for a long time, maybe fifteen minutes, Emmet thinking too. Josh would look at Emmet and then look away. A few minutes later, Emmet would eye Josh and then his eyes would drift away involuntarily.

Outside, a couple of little kids were fighting over a Big Wheel and screaming at each other. Josh went to the open window and yelled at them. 'Shut up, you little creeps. We're trying to think in here.'

He sat back down and continued staring at the wall. 'I've figured this whole thing out. They have to catch him, don't they? They have to catch him doing something bad. Otherwise, they would have already arrested him. Right?' he said, looking straight at Emmet. 'Right?'

Emmet pushed a button and the chair spun around. He blanked the game off the screen and stuck his head in the wire contraption. A second later, words were flashing across the screen, Emmet tapping like mad. 'I will not tell Lara that you called this man. I made a promise. But you cannot call him again. They are not certain he was involved in your mother's death, but he could be a very dangerous man. Let the police handle this. Now, you make a promise to me. Promise me you will not call this man again.'

Emmet stopped typing and spun around to face Josh. He was about to walk out of the bedroom, leaning against the door frame. 'I can't promise you that, Emmet. It was my mother. You understand, don't you? It was my mother.'

Before Emmet could speak, Josh was out the door. Emmet hit the high speed on his electronic chair, but by the time he got to the living room, Josh had closed the front door. 'Shit,' Emmet said. He pushed the controls and his chair moved forward. Then he pushed it again and it moved backward. Back and forth he moved, the chair squeaking on the plastic runners.

'Shit,' the little man said to the empty room.

At eleven-thirty the following morning, Rickerson walked into the squad room and checked everything. They had a slide projector, a screen, and a video setup. Next to the screen were two blackboards where they had outlined the facts of the case in chalk. There was also a cork board and baby Bradshaw had placed all the photos found in the San Clemente house on it with push pins. While he was standing there, one of the reserve officers came in carrying a large coffeepot. Another followed behind him with paper cups.

They were ready.

He took a seat and stared at his own writing on the board. Was it enough? He couldn't be sure, but they were not charged with gaining enough evidence to convict him, just enough to get a warrant for this arrest and start the wheels of justice rolling.

Gail Stewart was the first to arrive. 'Too bad we don't have a computer set up,' she said.

'You think we need it?'

'Nah, we got enough.' She walked over and poured herself a cup of coffee. 'You should have brought in lunch or something,' she told him.

'If all goes well, I'll buy you the best lunch of your life, doll,' Rickerson told her.

'Sure,' she said, sipping the coffee, holding it with both hands up close to her face. 'Where have I heard that line before?'

Lara and Judge Rodriguez walked in at twelve-fifteen. Right behind them was a tall, thin man in a suit and tie. Rickerson didn't recognize him, so he assumed he was the justice from San Francisco. A few minutes later, the FBI agent arrived and took a seat, first stopping to pour himself a cup of coffee and chat with the chief. Lara was dressed in a plain white blouse and a black skirt, her hair again tied back in a clasp with a bow. She smiled at Rickerson and took a seat in the front row. Someone offered Rodriguez a cup of coffee, but he declined.

'Let's begin,' Rickerson said, standing. As soon as everyone stopped talking and moving around in their seats, he began. 'Okay, we are going to try to put this together chronologically. On July seventh, Ivory Perkins, Judge Sanderstone's sister, came to her residence in Santa Ana in the early morning hours claiming that she was being followed. She refused to tell her sister any more than that and left some time later with her husband, Samuel Perkins.

'On September seventh, Judge Leo Evergreen approached Judge Sanderstone and suggested that she release a man named Packard Cummings on his own recognizance, even though the man had an extensive record, advising her that he was working as a confidential informant for an unidentified law enforcement agency. She complied. As of this date, no agency in the state of California, or any federal agency, has been able to verify this information.'

He waited, scanning the faces in the audience before continuing.

'The photos on the bulletin board behind me were found in the crawl space at the residence in San Clemente where Ivory and Sam Perkins were murdered on September eighth.' He noted the small judge leaning forward and squinting to see the pictures. 'If you bear with me, we'll show you slides of the enlargements of these photos.'

He paused and then continued, 'Only a day prior to the homicides, Judge Sanderstone's place was ransacked, as was the murder scene, the killer evidently looking for what you see on the board behind you. Prints lifted from her residence by the sheriff's department's crime-scene unit subsequently came back to Packard Cummings.

'On September twelfth, Packard Cummings was shot and killed in the parking lot of the Sea Breeze Apartments in Santa Ana, only a few blocks from Judge Sanderstone's residence. There were no prints on the vehicle, but it appeared that he knew his assailant. His own weapon was found in the glove box.

'Three days ago, Judge Sanderstone was attacked in the underground parking garage at the courthouse, the suspect demanding that she give him these photographs. She copied down the license plate and vehicle description, and the suspect was apprehended last night. His name is Frank Door. He's in custody. Judge Evergreen must have entered Judge Sanderstone's chambers and typed out the order to release this man on her own computer terminal. He was a serious violent offender.

'Yesterday, Josh McKinley, the murdered woman's son, positively identified Packard Cummings from a photo lineup as the man he saw leaving the scene of the murders on September eighth in a red Camaro. We also have forensic evidence such as tissue and semen from the victim that matches samples from Cummings. This is an important fact, since it connects Judge Evergreen to the homicides.

'Ivory Perkins had a client that went under the name of Tommy Black. The phone records of calls from the house in San Clemente revealed this, and the phone number comes back to an apartment, also rented under this name. A search of DMV records, however, reveals about fifteen Tommy Blacks in this immediate area. We've eliminated most of them. One got killed in a traffic accident, one's in jail, another in a nursing home, and another is a seventeen-year-old boy, et cetera. Therefore, we believe this is a fictitious name adopted by Leo Evergreen. We need a warrant to search this apartment. Ivory Perkins's fingerprints could be inside.

'Tommy Black also advertises himself as a video game expert and lists a toll-free number for young people to call for tricks and pointers. This phone number has been traced to that apartment. It appears that he lures young people this way, offering them free video games and other enticements. Then he gains their confidence, befriends them, and molests them.' Rickerson paused, facing his audience.

'Gentlemen,' he said, 'what we are dealing with is a desperate man who has now become a dangerous man. To be in a position such as Evergreen and be exposed and ultimately prosecuted for sexually abusing children, especially young boys, would be a certain disgrace. In addition, a fact Evergreen knows all too well is that child molesters do not fare well in prison. They are the scum of the prison system, the lowest of the low, and they are many times brutalized and even murdered inside the prison walls.'

Rickerson let his eyes fall and then looked back up. 'We intend to prove to you that Judge Leo Evergreen and Tommy Black are one and the same, that Judge Evergreen is a pedophile, and that Judge Evergreen conspired to murder Sam and Ivory Perkins.' He nodded to Gail Stewart. 'This is Dr Gail Stewart of the Los Angeles County Crime Lab. She's going to take it from here.'

Someone in the back dimmed the lights, and Rickerson took a seat next to Lara. 'How am I doing?' he whispered.

'Great,' she said. 'You sound like a prosecutor. You've almost convicted the bastard.'

The slide projector clicked and the first slide fell into place. 'What you are seeing,' Dr Stewart said, 'are enlarged and enhanced images of the photographs on the board, the ones taken from the San Clemente house. As you can see, some of these are solo photos of nude prepubescent males. We have not identified these boys.' She stopped and another slide clicked into place. 'This is the back of a nude male fondling the genitals of a young boy while someone else operates the camera. Although you may not be able to see it with the naked eye, this man suffers from scoliosis or curvature of the spine. Watch this next slide and you can see it better in enlargement. See,' she said, 'note how the spine curves. If we had Judge Evergreen in custody, we could render a positive ID.'

A few moments later, Dr Stewart was flicking through the slides until she came to the one she wanted. She stopped for a moment and took a sip of her coffee. 'The next slide was developed from a mirror image enlarged from one of the photos found in the residence in San Clemente. What you are looking at is a photo on someone's dresser, enlarged from one of the shots with the man we think is Evergreen and the boy. The man and woman in that photograph are Leo Evergreen's wife and son.' That slide vanished and another dropped down. 'This is a recent picture of Robert Evergreen. He's several years older, but obviously it's the same individual as in the first photo. Hit the lights,' she said. 'That's all I have.'

When Gail Stewart had taken a seat, Rickerson stood. 'What this all adds up to should be evident by now. Judge Evergreen was seeing Ivory Perkins. Ivory Perkins was a prostitute. She called on him, somehow came across the compromising photos, and then she and her husband proceeded to blackmail him. He must have paid them some money, at least over forty thousand, because this is the sum we found in the safe at the pawnshop. Then they must have demanded more and he decided to put a stop to it. That's when Evergreen arranged to have Cummings released and contracted the murders. We believe he killed Cummings himself, meeting him in that parking lot, probably for a payoff. Exactly why he killed him we aren't certain, but it was more than likely to cover his tracks. Possibly Cummings was trying to raise the stakes and he feared exposure.

'Evergreen had to get the photos back. Even though his back was turned to the camera, he has to fear we will identify one of the victims and implicate him in that manner, or he is aware that his own home is reflected in those pictures. So after he eliminated Cummings, he shopped for another offender to spring, met him outside the jail, and hired him to break into Judge Sanderstone's residence again, this time the condo she was hiding in. When he still didn't recover the photos, he had Judge Sanderstone attacked in the underground garage, thinking the photos were in her car or briefcase. If the janitorial service had not arrived when it did, it is my belief that Judge Sanderstone would be dead right now.'

Rickerson turned to speak directly to Judge Rodriguez. His signature on a warrant would be the green light they needed. 'We are seeking an arrest warrant for Judge Leo Evergreen for a violation of section 187, first-degree murder in the death of Packard Cummings, for contracting a murder for hire in the deaths of Ivory and Sam Perkins, for conspiring to commit assault with a deadly weapon in the beating of Judge Sanderstone. This could even fall under section 217.1 of the penal code, in that he was attempting to murder or impede Judge Sanderstone in proceeding with her duties, and for conspiring to commit two residential 459's or burglaries of Judge Sanderstone's residences.' He stopped and took a deep breath, his eyes locking with Lara's.

Rickerson sat down next to her. Gail Stewart chatted a few minutes and left. Judge Rodriguez, the justice from San Francisco, the D.A., and the FBI agent all stood in the corner of the squad room and conferred among themselves in hushed voices. They walked up and studied the pictures pinned on the cork board. They read again the facts of the case outlined in chalk on the blackboard. The justice from San Francisco glanced at Lara and then back to the other men. He was shaking his head. Then he shook Rodriguez's hand and left the room, walking fast like he had to catch a plane, his head down. A few minutes later, the FBI agent broke from the group and left. Now there was only Lawrence Meyer and Rodriguez in the huddle. Finally they arrived at a decision.

By five o'clock that evening, Rickerson was told, he would have the warrants in his hands.

Rickerson turned to Lara and smiled. They were on their way. For Presiding Judge Leo Evergreen, the most powerful justice in Orange County, it was to be the beginning of the end.

Chapter 25

Josh went to Ricky Simmons's house after school. No one was there but the two of them. Ricky's mother was out.

They grabbed several cans of sodas and some potato chips and headed to Ricky's room. Josh had always envied his friend. He had it all. A nice home, always neat and clean. He had a mother and father that loved him, were even active in school activities. Ricky also had a huge collie named Viceroy that Josh adored. He dropped to his knees in the hall and hugged him, letting him lick his face with a red sticky tongue.

'I can't believe you let him do that,' Ricky said. 'He licks his balls, you know. He even licks his asshole.'

Ricky had rock posters plastered all over the walls, two twin beds with brown chenille bedspreads, a desk covered with books and papers, and of course, the computer. He had told his mother he needed it desperately for his schoolwork. All he'd ever used it for was games. When he wasn't vegetating in front of a video game, Ricky lifted weights like Josh. He wanted to build up his body, but not to beat someone up. He wanted to do it to attract girls. Ricky was almost fifteen. He was in heat. There was only one problem with that, Josh thought, glancing at his friend. Ricky was a nerd. He was short and skinny, wore thick glasses, and in the past year his face had erupted in angry pimples. There wasn't a girl in school who would even look at Ricky Simmons, much less let him touch her. Even Josh knew that and the boy was his best friend.

The curtains were drawn in the room. Ricky liked it that way. Dark. When he wasn't playing video games, he was reading Stephen King books. In one corner he had a big tank filled with exotic fish, and the pump made a constant gurgling sound. Every day his mother made his lunch and cleaned his room. She even ironed Ricky's clothes. Anything he wanted he got. But Ricky took all this for granted, Josh thought, looking around him. He'd certainly never take it for granted. But then, he'd never had the chance.

'You really going to do this? Call that man and everything?' Ricky said, tossing a handful of chips in his mouth and crunching them. 'I want to listen when he talks dirty. He talks about tits and everything? Wow. What else did he say to you? Tell me, man.'

Josh gave him a nasty look. 'This is not a game, dick head. This is serious stuff.'

'Fuck you,' Ricky said, tossing a few chips at Josh. 'Since when did you turn into some kind of Sherlock Holmes?'

'Since someone murdered my mother.' Josh had the phone in his hands. There was a black look in his eyes. Since his conversation yesterday with Emmet, all Josh had thought about was the game man and how they could catch him.

'I'm sorry,' Ricky said quietly, shoving his glasses back on his nose. 'Sometimes I forget. I mean, you never used to talk about them, so I just forget.'

'Well, either shut up or get out. Go in the bathroom and jerk off or something.'

He shut up.

With Ricky sitting on the edge of one twin bed and Josh stretched out on the other, Josh called the toll-free number and the game man answered.

'Hey,' Josh said, sitting up straight and avoiding Ricky's eyes, 'this is Ricky. You know, from yesterday. Say, I've been thinking and I'd really like those free games. My mom's gone today, so I could come and get them if you tell me where you live.'

'Did you have a wet dream last night, Ricky?' the man said slowly. 'Did your little pecker stand up?'

Josh turned bright red and Ricky leaned farther over his knees. 'Let me hear,' he whispered. 'Shit, you used my name.' Josh glared at him and he was silent again.

'Y-yeah,' Josh stammered. 'You gonna let me see that movie you were talking about? The one with the blonde?'

The man's voice became almost businesslike, the suggestive tone of before vanishing. 'Do you have transportation?' he asked.

'I have a bike,' Josh answered, glancing at Ricky. He didn't, but Ricky did.

'I see,' the man said slowly. 'If you come over, this has to be our little secret. When do you have to be home?'

'Anytime I want, man.' Josh held his breath, hoping the man would agree to see him. 'I can come to your house.'

'No, that would be too far. You live in San Clemente, don't you? Why don't you come to the corner of Avenue Palizada in San Clemente? Isn't there a convenience store there?'

Josh thought for a moment. That was a long street. 'You mean right near the freeway? That one?'

'Yes,' the man said. 'I'll be in a gold Lexus. How will I recognize you?'

Josh looked at his clothing. 'I'm wearing a blue T-shirt with Iron Maiden on the back. You know, the band. And I've got long hair.'

'Oh,' the man said, his voice laced with excitement, almost breathless. 'Is it as long as a girl's hair, Ricky? I like that. I like long hair. Did you bathe today?'

Josh's stomach was flopping around like he'd swallowed a bowl of goldfish. He answered, 'Yeah, I bathed. Why don't I meet you in about thirty minutes?' This guy was sick, he thought, really sick. He'd seen bad things before, but never had he heard anything as sick as this. It sounded like the man wanted to cook him for dinner. Asking him if he'd taken a bath and all. When he talked, he made these little smacking sounds. It made him want to throw up. The line was silent and then the man spoke.

'I'll be waiting, Ricky.'

The Adams trial was still in session and Lara was watching the clock, counting the seconds. She'd made Rickerson promise that he wouldn't arrest Evergreen without her. Because they were late beginning the afternoon session, they were running past five o'clock. It was now after six. In the front row behind the defense table were two lovely little girls. Lara knew they were Victor Adams's daughters. She'd watched as a baby-sitter had delivered them to the courtroom about an hour ago. They were unruly and disruptive, jumping up and running down the aisles, pulling each other's hair and screaming. Their father turned around on several occasions and tried to subdue them, but they were bored and tired of sitting. Lara felt such compassion for the man that she had let the disruption continue. As soon as the witness stepped down, Lara addressed the courtroom. 'This appears to be a good stopping point for today. Let's adjourn and resume at nine o'clock tomorrow morning.' She tapped the gavel.

Lara glanced at the defendant. His mental condition seemed to be deteriorating a little more each day. His hair looked unwashed, his shirt was wrinkled, and he didn't appear to be following the proceedings. One of the little girls leaped in his lap while the other dumped a cup of coffee on the counsel table, soaking all the papers. Adams sat there motionless, as if they weren't even there, his eyes empty and unseeing. The attorneys were packing their cases and the jurors had already filed out, but Lara didn't leave the bench.

'Mr. Steinfield,' she said. 'Could you approach the bench a moment?'

Once he had, she leaned over and spoke in hushed tones. 'Your client cannot bring his children to my courtroom. They're cute, but extremely disruptive.'

'Believe me, I know that.' He glanced over his shoulder. 'That soggy stack of paper over there is a brief I need for another case. He's having trouble with baby-sitters.'

'I see,' Lara said thoughtfully. 'I have a thought. Would your client be willing to submit to a competency test?'

'I don't know,' he said. 'Why?'

'Well, I'm not certain he's mentally competent to stand trial right now. Perhaps we could suspend the proceedings and get him some type of treatment. Then he could get his life together and return at a later date. It makes sense. I could refer him for a court-ordered psychological evaluation.'

Steinfield stood there a few moments and then glanced back at his client. 'He's not going to go for it. We're halfway there, you know. He just wants to get it over with.'

'I understand,' Lara said, her voice still low, the D.A. eyeing her suspiciously, wondering what she was discussing with the defense. 'But is he able to cooperate in his defense, Counselor?'

'Probably not,' he said, glancing back at the defense table. 'He's hardly speaking lately, and when he does, he's incoherent.'

Lara noticed that the clerks, the bailiff, the court

reporter, and the D.A. were standing around waiting, uncertain if they were adjourned or were about to continue. The court reporter had started to put away her machine and then stopped.

'We're no longer on record,' Lara told them. 'Mr. Steinfield and I are just discussing something. You may all leave.'

Now there was a lot of shuffling of papers and people started spilling out of the courtroom, ready to hit the rush-hour traffic, go home to their families.

'Well, Mr. Steinfield,' Lara said, 'what do you think?'

'I'll ask him.'

'Fine,' she said. 'Advise me tomorrow before we resume.'

Lara left the bench and headed to her chambers. Rickerson was waiting. His face was flushed and his eyes wild with excitement.

'You go with me,' he told her, smacking an enormous wad of gum. 'The others will meet us at Evergreen's house. He lives in Anaheim Hills. The traffic's going to be murder.'

'Did you get the warrants?' she asked, tossing her robe on the hook. Phillip had already left.

'Right here,' he said, patting his jacket pocket. 'Hot off the presses. D.A.'s coming too. And, of course, we have a warrant to search the residence and to search that apartment. You know, the one rented in the name of Tommy Black.'

Lara faced Rickerson, her hands at her sides. 'This is it, huh? I can't believe it. I know it's happening, but I just can't believe it. I can't wait to see his face when we walk up. God,' she said, her eyes glued on the detective's, 'I'm so nervous. I want this so bad. You'll never know. You'll just never know.'

The detective stepped up close and brushed a strand of

hair off her forehead. Then he bent down and kissed her gently on the lips. 'When this is over, we'll celebrate.'

Lara smiled at him. 'I want to meet your boys. Jimmy is the same age as Josh. That's nice, you know? Think they'll like each other?'

'Sure,' Rickerson said, dragging out the word. He knew a lot more about kids than Lara did. His boys would be jealous of Lara. Josh would be suspicious and jealous of him. Jimmy and Josh would more than likely hate each other the moment they met, but other than that, everything would work out fine.

'Just let it ring,' Rickerson said when Lara's phone started ringing. 'We've got to get moving. Everyone's waiting.'

'It could be important,' she said, seizing the phone. It was Emmet.

'Where's . . . Josh?' he said.

'Oh, I'm sorry, Emmet. He went to his friend's house. I should have told you.'

'What . . . friend?'

'Ricky Simmons. Why? Is something wrong, Emmet? Do you need something?'

'I . . . need to . . . call . . . him,' he said. 'He . . . messed up . . . my computer.'

'Oh, Emmet, I'm sorry. Hold on.' Lara looked at Rickerson. He was pacing and anxious to leave. She dug Ricky Simmons's phone number out of her purse and went back on the line with Emmet. Once she had given him the number, she disconnected and headed to the door.

'You were great up there today,' she said affectionately to the detective as they walked down the empty corridor. 'Really, Ted. I mean it. I was very impressed.'

His chest swelled with pride and his eyes flashed. 'Nah,' he said. 'You're the one, Lara. You've been a trooper through this whole thing. Even with the threats on your life and your nephew to deal with, not once have you backed down or turned into a sniveling female. That asshole attacked you and you never missed a day of work. I admire you, you know.' He stopped for a moment and cleared his throat. His face flushed bright red. Just then the doors to the elevator opened and they stepped inside. They were alone. 'What are you going to do about Josh's school?'

'I don't know,' Lara said, sighing, leaning against the back wall. 'I guess I'll transfer him to a school in Irvine.'

'Shouldn't really do that, you know. At least not right away. Everything else has changed in his life. Leave him there with his friends.'

Her eyes drifted down. He might be right. 'I'll think about it. Thanks.'

They emerged from the building and walked to his police unit. 'And Emmet,' he said, changing the subject once they were at the car, 'I owe that fellow a cup of coffee.'

Rickerson's tie was crooked. Lara stepped closer and fixed it. 'Coffee, Rickerson?' she said. 'You owe him a dinner. Got that? Let's not be cheap here.'

'What are we waiting for?' he said, throwing the car door open. 'Let's go get that big fish and reel him in. I think he's beginning to smell.'

As soon as Emmet hung up with Lara, he dialed Ricky Simmons's number. He was in his own condo, so he had access to a phone. At first Ricky couldn't understand him and thought it was a wrong number. Then he told Emmet that Josh was gone. 'You're Emmet, huh?' Ricky said. 'Josh said you have Prodigy. That's so cool. I wanted my mom – '

'Where . . . did . . . he . . . go?' Emmet said, cutting the boy off. He was nervous and having even more difficulty speaking. He was tremendously concerned about Josh. He had given thought to telling Lara what he knew, but he had promised the boy.

'To get some free video games, man. Hey,' he told Emmet, 'that's all I know. Some creepy guy is gonna give them to him.'

'Ricky,' Emmet said, his words coming faster, using every ounce of strength he had, 'you must tell me . . . where Josh is. This man . . . is . . . dangerous. Please.'

'All I know is he was supposed to meet him at the 7-Eleven by the freeway. The one off Avenue Palizada. He took my bike.'

After thanking the boy, Emmet hung up. His fears were confirmed. This was bad, extremely bad. He had to do something. No matter what he had promised, he simply couldn't let Josh get hurt. He tried to call Lara back at the court, but there was no answer. His frail body was shaking. He dialed the police.

'I . . . I . . . need to report . . .' Emmet said.

'Sir,' the dispatcher said, the recorded line beeping every few seconds, radio traffic in the background. 'You'll have to speak up. I can't understand you.'

'I . . . boy . . . San Clemente.' It seemed the harder Emmet tried to make himself understood, the less he could say.

'I'm sorry,' the dispatcher said. 'We must have a bad connection.'

Emmet was in the throes of frustration now. 'Help him. He . . . will . . . be . . . hurt.'

'Did you say your name was Burt? I need your last name and your address. Then I'll dispatch an officer. Is there someone else there I can talk to? Your mother maybe, because – '

Emmet dropped the phone in anger. The stupid woman thought he was a child. By the time he got her to understand what he was saying, it would be too late. He hit the high speed on his chair, heading toward the front door. There wasn't much time. He had to stop Josh. He couldn't afford to wait another second. Moving fast down the walkway, he stopped at the door of the woman who normally drove him, but she wasn't at home. Then he headed straight to his van in the parking lot. It had hand controls. Until last year Emmet had been able to drive. He put the key in the rear door and activated the lift. He was counting seconds under his breath. Finally he was inside and behind the wheel. Sweat was dripping off his face and his wasted muscles were twitching with fatigue. He mustered up strength he didn't know he still had, seizing the hand controls with one hand, the steering wheel with the other. In seconds he was on the road to San Clemente, his head braced on the door window, his eyes straight ahead.

Josh pedaled as fast as he could. Ricky Simmons lived near his old house, in the foothills, and the location where he was meeting the game man was in downtown San Clemente. He tried not to look at the familiar surroundings as he hit the hill and coasted down, the wind blowing his hair. His life had split into two separate sections. One was his life before the murders and now there was his life since. When he thought of his old life, when his mother was alive, he tried to imagine that Josh McKinley was not him, that those people were not his relatives, his loved ones. Those people whose bodies he had seen that day.

It wasn't that he didn't love his mother, because he did. But sometimes he was angry at her, even now, even after her death. Once she had married Sam, she had almost stopped being his mother. And she had gotten herself killed – did things that were wrong, things he just couldn't understand. She had been so beautiful when his father was alive. It was more than the way she looked on the outside. It was something inside her. It was the way she laughed, the way she smiled – the way she smelled when he was young and she used to bend down over his bed to kiss him good night. She smelled like baby powder. It was fresh and clean. He could never forget that smell. Once his father died, she hadn't kissed him good night anymore. When she got close to him, he could smell beer on her breath and a sickening too-sweet perfume.

He would always miss her, dream about her, cry for her. But she was gone and nothing would change that. No amount of crying or pleading or screaming would ever change that.

He had a system. Every day he tried to let a little of the past go, let it run through his fingers like water. All the bad times particularly. They were the first ones to go. He worked at it, sitting in study hall during the day talking to himself under his breath, telling himself that he must not think of the bad times. All he wanted to remember were the days when his father had been alive, the days when they were all happy and together.

He was beginning to love Lara Sanderstone. He couldn't tell her yet, but he was. Not like his mother, but different. Maybe he loved her the way he would love his grandmother if she'd been alive, or an older brother or sister. He wasn't sure, but he knew the feeling. It was love built on respect. She was so smart, so sure of herself. She was determined in everything that she did. Sometimes he watched her, studied her face and saw her features settling into an expression he knew all too well.

He'd seen that expression in the mirror.

They were alike. He didn't know exactly how, but he knew they were alike. They crawled inside themselves, braced themselves against the bad times. They went on when they thought they couldn't go on.

That's how they were alike.

When he'd first come to live with Lara, after his mother and Sam were murdered, he'd hated her. Every time he looked at her, he saw his mother in her face, her hair, her eyes. And she wasn't quite as pretty as his mother. She was also sterner – a far more serious person. It had annoyed him for some reason that she was so like his mother and so unlike her at the same time. But lately those feelings had disappeared. Sometimes he actually pretended that she *was* his mother.

This game man had something to do with his mother's death. He didn't know what, but he knew he did, knew Lara was after him for exactly that reason. He was a dirty pervert. His mother had been a prostitute. There was a connection there, even if he didn't understand it.

He stopped and rested, checking his pocket and removing a piece of paper. He had the number of the police department written down – the number where that Detective Rickerson worked. He wasn't afraid. He wouldn't allow himself to be afraid. He was going to do something brave, something important. It would be his final gift to his mother.

Climbing back on the bike, he continued. He was almost there. Off in the distance he could see the freeway. Right past the freeway was the convenience store.

He watched television so he knew what he had to do. Almost every station had a cop program or a true-crime program. He liked *Top Cops* and *America's Most Wanted*.

What he had to do was get this creep to do something wrong. He had to let him do something wrong, something bad. Then they could arrest him. He drew lines in his mind as to just what he'd let him do. He could touch him. That Josh felt certain he could handle, as long as he wasn't totally gross and scary, didn't look like he'd cut him up and eat him. Lots of bad guys did that now. He saw it on the news. He'd seen one guy who had heads of people in his refrigerator. They'd carried out the heads and things in boxes.

And that guy had liked teenage boys too.

Josh was perspiring. His hair was soaking wet, and sweat was dripping down onto the handlebars. He didn't think it was just from the exertion of riding a bike. He knew he was scared. Stopping by a bunch of shrubs, he went behind them and urinated. He was so nervous that he couldn't hold it even though he had gone at Ricky's right after school. Then he wiped his hands on his jeans and started off again. He crossed under the freeway and rode straight to the convenience store.

He waited.

The black-and-white police units were parked a block down from Evergreen's residence. The FBI had insisted on being present, wanting to search the residence to see if there was any child pornography inside or any reason to believe that Evergreen had been producing his own films. Lawrence Meyer, the district attorney, was present in an unmarked car. He'd brought another D.A. and one of their investigators. The chief and his son were present. They were all waiting for Rickerson.

'I think we should go in now,' the chief said, having got out of his own unit and walked down to the others. He was antsy. It wasn't every day they arrested a presiding judge. 'He could destroy evidence, attempt to flee. Let's go.'

Meyer spoke up from inside his car. Several of the other officers had stepped out onto the street. 'Why don't we wait for Rickerson?' he told the chief. 'He's probably tied up in traffic. Hell, this is his case. Let's not steal his thunder.'

The chief stood there a moment, thinking, running his hands through his white hair. 'You're right.' He turned and walked back to the police unit, his son right behind him. Then the other men returned to their vehicles, and they all continued to wait.

*

About twenty minutes after Josh arrived at the 7-Eleven, a gold Lexus with a man at the wheel pulled up. He glanced at Josh and then his eyes scanned the parking lot. Josh had the sleeves of his T-shirt rolled up and his muscles were bulging. Even though he hadn't been lifting, he thought with pride, he was still pretty buffed. If the guy tried anything really weird or looked like he was going to eat him, cut him up or something, he'd beat the shit out of him. He watched him through the windows of the Lexus. He could take him. He didn't look like Sam or anything. He was a lot older. And there was something soft and weak about his face.

'Hey,' he said, pushing the bike up to the car window once he felt confident, 'are you the game man? I'm Ricky.'

The man's face turned white. He stared at Josh, a funny milky look in his eyes like he'd been sleeping. 'You're Ricky?'

'Yeah,' he said, 'didn't you hear me? I'm Ricky.'

'You're not twelve,' the man said indignantly, his face turning a bright red. This was a mature boy, with developed musculature. He was past puberty. It was obvious.

'Yeah, I am,' Josh insisted. 'I'm just big for my age. Aren't we going to your place? You told me you'd give me those games.'

The man was silent, staring out the window. Josh didn't know what was wrong with him. He seemed to be in another world. He'd asked him to come here and now he was acting like he had seen a ghost or something. Finally the man turned to him. 'Get in the car,' he barked.

'What about my bike, man?'

They both turned back to the convenience store at the same time. There was a bike rack there and Ricky had a lock. Josh walked over and chained it to the rack and got in the passenger side of the Lexus. The man pulled out into the street, but he didn't speak. He acted disappointed.

'What's wrong?' Josh asked. 'Don't you like me or something? Did I say something wrong?'

'No, no,' he said suddenly, as if his mood had changed. He let his hand roam across the seat and touched Josh's hand. 'I think you're a fine young boy. You just look a lot older than I expected.'

Josh remembered Lara making him tell the man he was only twelve. He had no idea why. It didn't make sense. He studied the man's face. Josh inhaled and then let it out, allowed his body to sink deeper into the leather seat. He didn't look like a killer. But he did look spooky. It was just something about him. He was dressed nice, in a sports jacket and knit shirt. He smelled of strong cologne. His hair was neatly styled, but he still had a strange look. He seemed nervous, tense. Josh thought he saw his body trembling and thought perhaps he was excited instead of tense – terribly excited. And he was breathing heavily, his nose expanding and contracting, his tongue coming out almost like Ricky's dog. If the man had a tail, Josh thought, it would probably be wagging.

'Where do you live?' Josh asked as the man entered the freeway and headed north, back toward Los Angeles. Suddenly Josh felt the fear climb from his stomach to his throat. What if he took him somewhere far away, somewhere where there was no phone and he couldn't call for help?

The guy could kill him.

'Look,' he said, his voice cracking no matter how he tried to steady it, 'I made a mistake. I do have to be home tonight. I should be home by eight o'clock or my mom will go crazy and start looking for me. She might even call the police.'

'Fine,' the man said without looking at Josh. His hands were tight on the steering wheel.

Josh couldn't see his eyes for his dark glasses. They rode

in silence, the only noise inside the Lexus the man's raspy breathing.

'Can I call you Rick?' the man finally said. 'You seem more like a Rick to me than a Ricky.'

'Yeah,' Josh said. 'You can call me anything you want.' When the man turned his head, Josh forced a smile.

Emmet was panting, struggling to keep the van on the road. Thank God, the traffic was light, for he was headed away from Los Angeles. Even when he had driven, he had always traveled slowly and used the side streets. Now he was flying down the freeway, pushing the hand control for the speedometer and holding it down all the way. He saw the exit for San Clemente and steered the van down the ramp. Then he saw the 7-Eleven. His eyes started searching for Josh. A car was pulling out of the parking lot. Emmet stared at it. His heart leaped in his throat. He saw Josh in the passenger seat, a man at the wheel. He tried to turn the van around and ended up with the rear wheels on the curb.

He was going to lose them.

Chapter 26

Although it wasn't that far from Santa Ana to Anaheim Hills, they hit rush-hour traffic on the 405 freeway. Rickerson tried to contact the chief and advise them that they were on the way, but he was out of radio range. 'Let's try the sheriff's frequency,' he said, punching buttons on the police radio. 'The chief usually monitors their radio when he leaves the city just in case something heavy goes down and he's sitting right on top of it. They can relay a message to him. Let him know we're running late.'

They listened to the radio traffic. It was fast and furious. Before Rickerson could try to transmit, he had to wait his turn. They were dispatching ambulances and paramedics. 'They've got something going on,' he told Lara. 'Probably a big accident with bodies all over the road. Glad I'm not working traffic.'

Lara heard something she recognized. She sat up straight in the seat and strained to make out exactly what they were saying. The voices were crackling with static. 'Ted,' she said quickly, 'did you hear the address they just mentioned, where they're sending all the emergency vehicles?'

'Nah,' he said, 'I wasn't listening. Why?'

'I thought they said Fairmont – 820 Fairmont. Can you check? It's important.' She held her breath. If she wasn't mistaken, 820 Fairmont was Victor Adams's address. She prayed she was mistaken.

Finally Rickerson found a lull in the air traffic and seized the mike. 'Station three, this is unit 654, San Clemente. Repeat the location you are responding to. We're in the area.'

'Eight-twenty Fairmont,' the dispatcher said. 'We have a triple 187 working. Adult male and two small children. One may be a suicide.' Before the words were even out of her mouth, she was dispatching a crime-scene unit and other units to direct traffic, seal off the area.

'Oh, my God,' Lara exclaimed. She was ashen and beads of sweat appeared on her forehead. 'That's Victor Adams's address. He has two children. Please, Ted, find out what happened. They said a triple homicide . . . possible suicide. Jesus, he must have killed himself and the children. He just left my courtroom. I knew something terrible was going to happen. I just knew it.' An hour ago, the precious little girls had been alive.

Rickerson got the dispatcher on the air and asked her to scramble the transmission. He knew she couldn't advise names of victims over the air. He flipped the button on his console and activated his own scrambler. Then they waited until the woman had a free moment of air time.

'San Clemente 654,' the dispatcher said. 'We have a Victor Adams at that location and his two daughters. All three are DOA. Nothing further at this time. Units are at the scene.'

While tears streamed down Lara's cheeks, Rickerson continued. 'Cause of death?'

'Shotgun wounds. Neighbor called it in. Occurred about ten minutes ago.'

Lara couldn't believe it. She felt sick to her stomach,

about to throw up on the floorboard of the car. Sensing something horrid hanging like a dark cloud over the courtroom, she'd had a terrible feeling when she'd looked at Adams sitting there today. He was at the end of his rope, completely destroyed. And the system had done it. They were the actual murderers. They had taken his life and ripped it apart, a virtual annihilation. Those two darling girls, dead, at their own father's hands. Lara looked out the window at the string of cars ahead, the tacky billboards, the debris by the road, the thick layers of smog hanging on the horizon. It was still light outside, only about seven-thirty, but all she saw was blackness and blood red death. She saw wasted dreams: two beautiful little girls who would never wear makeup, never go to a high school dance, never get married. She saw them running down the aisles, so full of life, giggling and laughing.

'Shit happens,' Rickerson said, taking the next off ramp and speeding down the surface streets. He reached his hand across the seat and clasped Lara's. 'This was the guy on trial, right?'

'Right,' she said, sniffing, reaching into her purse for a Kleenex. 'Why didn't Evergreen shoot himself instead of Victor Adams? And why did he have to kill the children? Good Lord.'

'Never works out that way, doll. The bad ones live to be a hundred and the good ones die.'

A few minutes later, they pulled up alongside the units and Rickerson leaned out the window. The chief walked over. The other officers remained in the car.

'Let's go,' Rickerson said to the chief. 'Let's get this show on the road.'

Lara was sitting quietly beside him. Evergreen didn't really matter to her right now. All she could think about was Victor Adams and his little girls.

The man in the Lexus pulled into a parking lot. Josh

leaned forward in the seat and tried to figure out where they were. From what he could tell, they were somewhere in Irvine and the building looked like an apartment complex. They weren't far from the freeway. Most of the buildings around there were skyscrapers housing technical companies and medical offices.

The man glanced at Josh lovingly and filled his lungs with the essence and odor of youth. The boy had been perspiring. He could catch the delicious scent floating by his nostrils. The boy might be older than he thought, but he didn't yet manufacture foul body odor. It was warm and clean and fresh, this scent. If he took his tongue and pressed it to his flesh, it would be slightly salty.

This young man was only beginning his life, he thought. He envied him. Sometimes he believed his desires were actually a longing to return to his youth. By loving these young men he was traveling back in time, capturing some of their youth for himself. It was almost like a mystical experience, as if their life force, their vitality, became his own. When he was with them, he felt young again. He felt alive.

He pulled to the back of the complex and parked in his assigned spot. 'Come on,' he told the boy. 'I have a wonderful surprise for you.'

'What's wrong with your leg?' Josh asked, watching the man hobble across the parking lot. 'Did you hurt it or something?'

'No,' the man said, glancing back over his shoulder at Josh. 'I have a spinal deformity.'

'Oh, yeah?' Josh said, genuinely sympathetic. 'I have a friend who has ALS. Do you know what that is?'

'Lou Gehrig's disease,' the man tossed out without a second thought, trying to find the right key on his key ring. 'That's unfortunate. He's not a young boy like you, is he? That disease usually strikes when a person is older.'

'No,' Josh said. 'He's older, but he's still my friend.'

The man opened the door to the apartment and hit the light switch. The room came alive. He'd recently purchased a fortune in computer equipment, had it installed right in the apartment. No one knew about this place. He'd paid a year's rent in advance.

He was seeing a psychiatrist. He was even taking medication. But it only made him sleepy. It didn't take away his desire to be with young men. Nothing would take that away.

He knew that. He'd fought this alone for years. Finally he had learned to accept it. At first he'd thought he was homosexual and had been filled with self-loathing. Then he realized this was something totally different. He had no desire to have sex with men. He only desired sex with young boys – boys so tender and fresh that they were untainted by life. Boys who looked up to him, admired him.

Besides, he didn't hurt these young men. He loved them. To him, it was real – the love. He became their friend and confidant; he taught them about life. Most of the boys he had been involved with over the years had no father in the home. He was their role model. He gave them gifts, took them on wonderful outings, counseled them about their future. And then, at last, he pleased them. That's where his own pleasure was derived: from giving them pleasure, seeing that expression of bliss on their bright young faces for the very first time.

Sometimes he didn't even need the sex. Just being around these young men was enough to give him real pleasure. Their very presence chased the demons away – his ever present fear of death, his fears of inadequacy.

He couldn't stop. It was a compulsion, an addiction. The only way he could stop was to kill himself, and he didn't have the courage. In the past he had been consumed with guilt, even attempted to take his own life on several occasions. Some nights he prayed that someone would kill him, end it for him, do what he couldn't find the strength to do.

He had reconciled himself that he would never be cured. For the illness he suffered, there was no such thing as a cure.

Most of the equipment was on and lights were flickering on the consoles. Quickly he walked through the room turning on the television monitors. 'Well,' he said, putting his hands together in pleasure, 'what do you think?'

For a moment Josh didn't speak. He'd never seen a room like this one except on television, or in war movies when they showed command posts. 'Wow,' he said, truly awed, 'it's great, man.'

On every monitor was a different channel. One whole wall was computer equipment. 'My friend Emmet would go crazy in a place like this.' The man was smiling. Josh turned around and looked at him.

The man placed his hand over his mouth and giggled. When he removed it, he said, 'I knew you would love it. But you haven't seen the best.'

Strolling across the room, looking back over his shoulder at Josh, he suddenly pulled a sheet off a large object. '*Voilà*,' he said with a little wave of his hand. 'Meet Henry.'

Josh couldn't believe it. The man had a real little robot. While he was crossing the room, the man did something behind the robot's back and it sprang to life, lights blinking on top of its head, its eyes a funny shade of red.

'My name is Henry,' the robot said. 'How may I serve you?'

'This is so cool,' Josh exclaimed. 'My God, this is the coolest thing I've ever seen. How much does something like this cost? What can it do? Where did you get it?'

'I got it at the Consumer Electronics Show in Las Vegas last year,' the man told him. 'It was a gimmick. You know, they built it to attract people to their booth. I convinced them to sell it to me.'

Josh was so impressed with the whole setup that he couldn't believe it. Maybe they were all wrong about this guy, and he was just a high-tech nut or something. He seemed nice enough. He had a problem walking. It reminded him of Emmet. Sometimes people didn't understand people with problems. He knew that now.

But the hand-holding stuff in the car had to go, he told himself. That was weird.

The robot started walking across the floor like a giant vacuum cleaner. 'Would you like a cold drink or something?' the man said. 'Or maybe a nice cold beer? I also have wine coolers.'

'Yeah,' Josh said. 'I'll take a wine cooler.' He'd always wanted to try one of those things. They were real popular with all the kids in high school.

The man disappeared and the robot scooted across the floor behind him. A few minutes later, the robot appeared in the door with the wine cooler on a little tray. 'Your drink,' it said in that strange computerized voice.

Josh laughed and picked up the wine cooler. His throat was parched from the long ride from Ricky's to downtown San Clemente. It tasted like Kool-Aid. He drank it in almost one gulp. When the man came back into the room, he was wearing a velvet smoking jacket and a little pair of silk shorts. Josh stifled a laugh. He looked so funny. Although his upper body was almost chunky, his legs were real skinny and white.

The man saw the empty bottle set on one of the tables and immediately picked it up, checking to make certain it had not left a ring. 'Young men should always put their glasses on coasters. See,' he said, holding up a coaster, 'there was one right here. Do you want another?'

'Yeah, sure,' Josh said. He was still thirsty. Either that or his throat was dry from nerves. 'Do you have Smart Ball?' he asked. 'You said you did. I promised my friend.'

'Certainly,' the man said. 'All the games are right in that box by the computer. Go ahead, start playing and I'll give you some pointers. Then when you leave, you can take the games.'

Josh loaded up the computer and the game began. The man leaned over close to him and told him how to raise his score. Josh was enthralled. Wait until Ricky sees this, he thought. The game finished, Josh looked at his score. 'I can't believe it,' he told the man. 'Wait, I want to enter my name. I bet my score's right up at the top.'

'I can teach you a lot of things, Rick,' the man said. He pushed his chair even closer to Josh and leaned toward him. He put his hand on his thigh. Josh didn't even notice it.

'Can I play again? I bet the next time my score will be even better.'

'I'll get you another wine cooler,' the man said.

The man returned and handed Josh the wine cooler, his fingers making contact with Josh's and a funny, silly look in his eyes, as though he had a secret and was about to tell. 'Want to see that movie?' he said, arching his thin eyebrows.

Josh would have preferred just to play the games, but he remembered why he had come to begin with. 'I guess,' he said. The man headed off toward the back of the apartment and Josh followed him. He stopped in the door to a bedroom. It was dark in there. He wasn't going in there in the dark with this guy. No way.

Josh remained in the doorway as the man fiddled with the VCR and the movie came on the screen. Then the man walked over to Josh and Josh stepped aside, letting him pass. 'I have some things to take care of right now, so you just enjoy the movie.' He walked down the hall into another section of the apartment.

Josh flopped down on the bed and began watching the movie, tossing the new wine cooler down his throat in almost one gulp.

Stopping in the living room, the man started to turn the computer off. He hated to waste electricity. That was one of his good points. He'd always been frugal. Then he saw it. The boy's name was flashing on the screen next to the name of the game distributor.

'Josh,' he said, repeating the name, panic setting in.

The boy had lied to him. He'd said his name was Ricky. The man felt sharp pains in his chest. His breath was shallow. This boy lived in San Clemente. The horrid prostitute and her husband who had stolen the photos and blackmailed him lived in San Clemente. Even the name sounded familiar. He fell forward over the computer terminal and held his chest. He waited for the pressing pain signaling a heart attack, but it didn't come. Finally he sat up and with trembling fingers opened a drawer and took out the newspaper article he had saved on the deaths.

There it was: Josh McKinley was the surviving son of Ivory and Sam Perkins.

Emmet managed to catch up to the gold Lexus at the stoplight. He stayed at least one car length behind as he followed them to Irvine. If he stopped to call the police, he thought, they would get away and he had no idea where the man was taking Josh. When the car turned into the apartment parking lot, Emmet couldn't navigate the van fast enough.

He lost them.

'Shit,' he muttered, feeling desperate and angry, cursing

his weakened body, wishing he was strong and normal. 'Shit,' he said again. Around and around he circled in the parking lot, wrestling with the steering wheel, his exasperation rising with each second, consumed by exhaustion yet determined to go on. Something was going to happen to Josh, and he would be responsible. He should have told Lara the truth.

He found the Lexus, but it was empty. They were already gone. He fell forward against the steering wheel. His glasses slid off and ended up on the floorboard where he couldn't reach them. He had no idea what apartment the man lived in or where he had taken Josh. There was only one thing to do. He needed help and he needed help fast.

He simply had to call the police.

Josh sat on the bed in the dark room and watched the adult movie. He was beginning to get drowsy and almost fell asleep several times. But he sure wasn't going to fall asleep in this house with this man, he told himself. He set the empty wine cooler on the end table. Even though it tasted like Kool-Aid, Josh was beginning to feel the alcohol. He was dizzy and almost felt like he was going to be sick to his stomach.

The movie was dumb. He'd seen these kind of things before anyway. Sam had always had a whole drawer full of them in the bedroom.

All of a sudden the video clicked off and soft music started playing. It was old-timer music, with lots of violins and things. It gave him the willies. Sometimes they played music like this in horror movies, he thought. The room was completely black since the movie had gone off. Josh tried to see in the dark. This was turning into a horror movie as far as he was concerned. He was about ready to split. This whole thing might not have been such a good idea, he told himself, his fear escalating. He might have bit off a lot more than he could chew.

Then he saw the man in the doorway.

He was naked. He appeared for only a second and then disappeared inside the room. Josh held his breath; his heart pounded in his ears. He had to get out of here, call the police. Then he heard rustling near the bed and saw the outline of the man.

'You lied to me, Josh,' the man said. His voice was not at all the voice of before. Now he sounded like his school principal. He sounded stern and angry.

'I didn't lie to you, man,' Josh said, getting up, ready to bolt from the room.

'Ricky Simmons? You're not Ricky Simmons.'

Shit, Josh thought. How did the man find out? And what was he doing without his clothes? 'Sure, I am. I told you I was. Anyway, I have to go home. My mom will be looking for me.'

'Your mother won't be looking for you, Josh. Your mother is dead.'

Sweat sprang from every pore on Josh's body. He was terrified. This had to be the man who had killed his mother and Sam. He rolled off the side of the bed and started crawling in the dark to the door. Then he heard a flurry of rapid movement and felt a sharp pain in his hand. He tried to keep moving, but he couldn't. It was as if his body was nailed to the floor. The man was standing over him and had stepped on his hand. 'Please,' Josh cried. 'Let me go. You're breaking my hand.'

'And you,' the man said, 'you think it's just fine to lie to me, trick me, deceive me. People are always doing that to me. Boys like you, in fact. They take all the gifts I give them and then they turn against me, ridicule me, call me disgusting names. They use me, Josh. They don't appreciate me.'

'No,' Josh pleaded. 'I didn't mean to trick you. Please, let me up. I won't call you names. I won't do anything. I promise.'

'You're just like your mother, little Josh. Like mother, like son. She used me and then demanded I give her money. Even when I did, it wasn't enough. She wanted more, more, more. She was greedy. You know what happened to her, don't you? You know what happens to people who lie and cheat, who use people, don't you?'

Josh was crying. His hand was killing him and he was consumed by fear. 'Please, just let me go home. I won't tell anyone. I promise. Please.'

'No,' the man yelled. 'No. Because of you, because of what you've done, you can't go home. I can't let you go home.' He bent down and pulled Josh up by his hair. 'You must pay me back, Josh. You must do exactly as I tell you. Then we'll talk about you going home.'

'I'll do anything, man,' Josh said, rubbing his hand, glancing furtively around the room for something he could use as a weapon. 'Just don't hurt me anymore.'

'Get on the bed,' the man ordered Josh. Then his voice dropped to a low rasp. 'Be still and close your eyes. Unzip your pants. I won't hurt you. I'm going to love you.'

It didn't matter what he did with this boy, the man thought. He could indulge his every desire. Josh McKinley knew far too much ever to walk out of this apartment alive.

Before they pulled up in Evergreen's driveway, Rickerson had flipped the radio back to the San Clemente frequency. They were close enough to pick up the signal. Almost the second he did, the dispatcher advised him that Dr. Gail Stewart had called from the crime lab.

'Station one,' he responded, 'did she advise the nature of the call? I'm tied up right now.'

'Unit 654, she said it was urgent. I've been trying to raise you. She's in her office waiting.'

'Damn,' Rickerson said, turning to Lara. Then he radioed the chief and told them to stand by. They were only a few feet from the entrance to Evergreen's driveway. He tried to contact Gail Stewart on his cellular phone, but she had already left for the day.

Calling the chief back and telling him they were ready, they drove into Evergreen's driveway. Just as Rickerson was getting out of the car, a white county car roared up and screeched to a halt. Gail Stewart leaped out and jogged toward Rickerson's vehicle on her stubby legs, her breasts jiggling, her face flushed.

'God,' she said, panting, leaning over and holding her side. 'I found you. You don't know the strings I had to pull to get Evergreen's address. You haven't gone in yet, have you?'

'This better be urgent, Gail,' he told her. 'We're about to arrest the S.O.B. He's probably watching us through the window right now.'

'Well, you be the judge. I'm just the conveyor of fact. Your man finally came through with the film of Evergreen nude. They shot it in the locker room at the Sports Club in Irvine. He went there for a massage yesterday.' She paused, then spat it out. 'Evergreen's not the man in the photos.'

'What the fuck?' Rickerson exclaimed. Lara was standing next to him and placed her hand over her chest.

'Evergreen's not the man?' Lara repeated, incredulous. 'Then who is? My God . . . what's going on?'

Rickerson ignored Lara and glared at Gail Stewart. The other men were out of their units and standing around on Evergreen's circular driveway, waiting for Rickerson to give them the signal. He spoke low, stepping to a corner of the yard under a big tree. Lara followed them. 'Okay, Gail, want to tell me how you manufactured this atomic bomb?'

'He doesn't have scoliosis. He's simply not the man in the pictures, the man with the boys.' Gail shoved a tree branch out of her face.

'But that's his son. You verified that was his son and his wife. It has to be him. You must be mistaken.' Rickerson was sweating. His eyes took in the string of police cars. They were about to come down like the marines on the presiding judge of Orange County, and now she was telling him he wasn't the right man.

'I can't believe this,' Lara said, glancing first at Gail Stewart and then back to Rickerson. 'I thought you were certain.'

'Gail,' Rickerson barked, 'are you going to tell me what's going on? We were all set, I thought. This was the guy. Remember?'

She became indignant. Her chunky cheeks froze into solid rocks. There were no dimples now. 'Look here, Rickerson, I told you the man in the pictures might not be related to the people reflected in the mirror. And I told you that on several occasions. You're the one who kept insisting that he was. He might have just used their house, be a friend or something. It was Evergreen's son. There's no doubt about that, so I guess he has to be involved in some way. And he did release that Cummings guy.' She was breathing heavily. She paused before continuing, becoming defensive. 'Hey, don't jump all over me. You're the cop. I'm just a criminologist.'

'Fuck,' Rickerson said, stomping on a snail as it inched its way across the driveway and listening to it crunch. Then he just stood there, staring out at the men, trying to comprehend what he'd just heard, his chest heaving. He was flustered and angry.

'My God,' Lara said, 'what are we going to do now?' She waved her arms around, on the verge of outright hysteria. 'They're going to throw me off the bench for sure. I'm going to look like a fool. And what about all these men . . . the warrant?'

Rickerson was silent, trying to collect himself, regroup. For a few moments he didn't answer. Finally he spoke, the decision made. 'It was Evergreen's son in the pictures and Evergreen gave the order to release Cummings. If he didn't contract these killings, he knows who did.'

He paused and looked over at Lara. 'We're going in.'

Emmet opened the rear door to the van. Not wanting to wait for the lift, he shoved his wheelchair out. Then he climbed down from the van and fell the rest of the way onto the concrete. That's when he saw the number painted on the curb in front of the gold Lexus. It read 212. Instantly he realized that was the apartment number, that the man had an assigned parking spot.

He managed to get the chair open and hoisted himself into the seat. Hitting the high speed, he took off across the parking lot, his eyes scanning the numbers on the doors, leaning forward to go even faster, searching frantically for unit 212. He had to get Josh out of that apartment. If he called the police, it would take forever just to get them to understand him. Then he would have to wait for an officer to arrive. All the while Josh was in grave danger.

Emmet decided he had to rescue Josh himself.

If the man attacked him, it might give Josh a chance to escape. And Emmet had little to lose. If the man beat him, it would be nothing new. Life had already taken that shot, beat his once strong body to only a shell of his previous self. If he killed him, well, Emmet thought, he was going to die in the near future anyway. Josh was young and healthy. Emmet was not. And Josh had brought something into Emmet's life: laughter, friendship, a sense of belonging. Josh accepted him completely as he was, overlooked the ravages of his illness.

Finally Emmet saw unit 212. His eyes drifted up and his body compressed even farther in the wheelchair. What Emmet saw in front of him was the icy north face of Mount Everest. He looked for an elevator, but there was none. Then his eyes returned to the obstacle: steep, despicable stairs.

Unit 212 was on the second floor.

They knocked and announced that they were the police. Then they rang the doorbell and waited. If Evergreen didn't answer in a few seconds, they were prepared to kick the door down. Lara was sitting in Rickerson's unit in the driveway, looking out the window. A few seconds later, Evergreen came to the door. He was in his robe – an old motheaten brown and green flannel. An odor assaulted their nostrils. It was Vicks. Rickerson moved closer to the door. 'Judge Leo Evergreen,' he said, knowing it was him, having to go through the motions, make the identification.

'Yes,' he said, pulling his robe closed in the front and peering out at the police units. 'What's wrong? Has something happened to my son?' He blanched and looked as if he was about to faint, grabbing onto the door to steady himself.

'Uh, no, Judge Evergreen,' Rickerson said. 'Your son's just fine. We have a warrant for your arrest and a warrant to search your residence. May we come in?'

What they were saying didn't appear to register. Evergreen looked old and tired. He began coughing. 'A warrant for my arrest?' he repeated once the spasm passed, stepping farther inside the house. 'What in the world is going on, Officer? Yes, come in. There must be some type of mistake. Do you know who I am?'

Evergreen stepped back and they entered. The men flared out and started heading for the back of the house to conduct the search. Evergreen watched them in dismay.

Rickerson read him his rights. 'I'm sorry, but we're going to have to take you down to the station,' he told him once he was finished and the little card he'd read from was back in his pocket. He stood to handcuff them.

'But – but I can't believe this. This is an abomination. What in the heavens is this about? This has to be a mistake . . . some dreadful error.'

Rickerson read off the charges and then faced the judge. 'Do you waive your right to an attorney?' he asked him. 'Because if you do, we can discuss this right here.'

'Yes – yes,' Evergreen stammered. His body was racked by another fit of violent coughing. 'I've done nothing to need an attorney. I have nothing to hide. Explain this situation to me right now, Officer.'

Rickerson did. They took a seat on the living room sofa. It was a yellow brocade, probably twenty years old. On the end table were pictures in small silver frames, the silver tarnished. Evergreen was speechless, deep in thought. His voice was low and thin when he answered. 'I've never molested a child. I'm a judge of the superior court. I've never in my entire life even broken a law. This is ludicrous. Who made these accusations?'

'Judge Evergreen,' Rickerson said in a consoling voice, 'didn't you ask Judge Sanderstone to release a Packy Cummings, telling her he was a confidential informant?'

Evergreen thought hard for a few moments, rubbing his forehead. Then he looked up at Rickerson. 'I remember that name. I believe that was the man Irene Murdock called me about, telling me that he was a police informant and asking that I arrange his release, which of course I did.' His pale, watery eyes searched the detective's. 'We always try to accommodate you fellows in your work.' From the look on his face, that wouldn't be the case in the future.

Rickerson stood. Things were spinning in his mind. 'So

Judge Murdock is the one who wanted this man released? Packy Cummings. You're absolutely certain?'

'Well, yes, I am. I have a very good memory, Officer.' He paused and looked up at the detective as if wondering if Rickerson thought he was senile. 'Really, I do.' Then he began coughing again.

'Fine,' Rickerson told the judge, walking straight out the door to the police unit where Lara was waiting. He got inside and sat there, trying to put it together in his mind.

'They've been calling you on the radio. I didn't know how to work it, so I didn't answer.'

Rickerson picked up the mike.

Emmet was waiting at the foot of the stairs right by the trash container, praying that someone would walk by and he could get them to call the police. If not that, they could help him get up the stairs to unit 212. He saw people pulling into the parking lot, but they all headed in other directions. He tried yelling, but his voice was too weak and no one heard him. Peering into the trash can, he picked out an empty aluminum can of peas, ripping the sharp-edged lid off. He would use it as a weapon. Someone had thrown away an old, stained T-shirt, and he tore it and then wrapped the round jagged lid in it and stuck it into his shirt pocket. 'I've never asked for much, God,' he said in his mind, 'but just this once, give me the strength I need to do this and I'll never ask for another thing.' He propelled his body out of the wheelchair onto the walkway, his eyes on the steep flight of stairs. He had to get to Josh. His illness wasn't going to stop him. This might be the last thing he ever did in this world, but he was going to do it.

Taking a deep breath, Emmet started crawling, pulling his frail body a step at a time up the stairs, oblivious to the pain as his elbows scraped against the concrete, only one image in his mind: Josh.

Josh was on the bed in the darkened room. He had unzipped his pants as the man had told him. Then the phone started ringing and the man stepped into the other room. Josh sprang from the bed, picking up a statue off the dresser. He could hear the man talking in the other room. He heard him mention his name. He was telling someone about him. Josh positioned himself behind the door and waited. When the man walked back in, Josh was going to bash him.

He waited. His hands were sweaty and he was afraid the statue was going to slip out. He was trembling with fear. He peered out from the door and saw the man walking back in his direction, wearing the smoking jacket again. He raised the statue over his head and held his breath. Suddenly the man stopped. There was a funny sound at the front door. It wasn't a knock. It was like a cat scratching or a dog. The man glanced at the bedroom and then back at the door. The scratching turned into a pounding. He stepped a few feet forward.

'Stay in there,' the man said at the door to the bedroom, not realizing Josh was no longer on the bed. 'Don't come out until I tell you. Don't make a sound.'

Josh was ready to bring the statue down on his head just when the man spun around and headed for the front door. Josh stood in the shadows and watched.

The man looked through the peephole. Then he called through the door, 'Who's there?' After waiting a few more seconds, the man shoved the dead bolt aside and opened the door. He stared out and started to close it when a hand reached out toward his leg.

It was Emmet.

'What the . . .' the man yelled, seeing Emmet on the ground to the right of the door. He started kicking his foot, but Emmet held on. Then he screamed, 'My ankle. What have you done to me? What are you anyway, some kind of filthy beggar?'

Josh raced toward the front door. He ran right into the coffee table and jabbed his thigh on the sharp edge. The statue fell from his hand and shattered, but he just kept going. He had seen Emmet. No way was this man going to hurt Emmet.

Josh growled and tackled the man from behind, both hands around his lower body, his legs. The man fell forward over the doorstep, landing on his face right next to Emmet. Blood was oozing out of a deep cut in his ankle, staining the landing. He tried to get up, but Josh pulled back and slugged him right in the face. He fell back down. Josh then threw himself on the man's side and pressed his entire body weight down to hold him.

'Emmet,' he panted. 'Are you okay?'

'Josh,' Emmet stammered. 'I . . . was . . . so . . . scared.'

The man was silent, a glazed look in his eyes. Both Josh and Emmet looked at him and then looked away. 'Here,' Josh said, reaching for Emmet's hand, pulling him closer. 'Want to give me a hand here, Emmet? Shit, you didn't look scared to me. I was the one who was scared, man. Believe me, you never looked so good, Emmet. Thought I might want to kiss you right on the mouth.' Josh took a breath and then continued, 'What did you cut him with?'

Emmet was sitting on the man's legs while Josh sat on his chest. He smiled with pride. 'This,' Emmet said, holding up the bloody rag containing the lid to the can of peas and showing it to Josh.

'Cool,' Josh said. 'Totally cool, Emmet. You took this guy out with a tin can lid. Wait until I tell Ricky. That's wild. I love it.'

Seeing a woman staring up at them from the downstairs apartments, Josh yelled at her, 'Hey, call the police. Can you do that, huh? Can you call the police? We've got something for them. We need a little help up here.' He paused and then yelled again, 'And tell them to make it fast. We don't want to sit on this guy all night. We've got other things to do, you know.'

Then he turned to the little man and smiled.

Detective Rickerson finally raised the dispatcher and she began speaking. 'The S.O. has been trying to reach you. They're at an address in Irvine and would like you to 11-98 with them there. They have a Josh McKinley there and he was asking for you. The call came through their switchboard as a suspect in custody being held by a civilian – a citizen's arrest.'

'Josh,' Lara started screaming, hearing nothing other than his name. 'Josh is supposed to be in San Clemente with his friend. Something must have happened.' She punched Rickerson's shoulder. 'Quick, find out if he's okay. Find out what's going on.'

'Station one,' Rickerson continued, ignoring Lara. He was in the middle of the biggest mess of his life, and now he had to deal with some kid playing cop. 'Get a phone number. I'll call them.'

A few moments later she returned with the number, and Rickerson called the sheriff's deputy on the portable phone. He listened and then his eyes got wide and his mouth fell open. 'You're shitting me?' he said.

Lara yanked on his sleeve, about to rip it right off. 'Tell me,' she yelled, completely beside herself. 'Is he okay?'

'Yes,' he snapped at Lara. 'For God's sake, calm down.' Then he returned to the conversation. 'John Murdock, huh? The man was John Murdock? What's his wife's name?' He listened and then answered, 'That's what I thought. Judge Irene Murdock. We'll be there as soon as we can. Keep the boy there. An Emmet Daniels? Yeah, I know who he is. He's there too. Shit, this is a fucking carnival here.' As soon as he hung up, he hurled the phone against the dash. It struck and tumbled to the floorboard.

'Irene and John,' Lara repeated. 'Tell me what this is about! Now, Rickerson. Has something happened to Irene and John? And you said Emmet . . . did something happen to Emmet?'

'Stay here,' he barked, his composure gone, his case against Evergreen dissolving right before his eyes. 'Josh is fine. Emmet is fine. And I wouldn't worry right now about your good pals the Murdocks,' he said sarcastically. Then he took a deep breath and looked at Lara. 'I need to check something and then we'll go get them.'

Rushing into the house again, he found Leo Evergreen still sitting on the yellow sofa. 'Judge Evergreen,' he asked, a lot more politely than he felt, 'did you ever loan your house to someone? You know, possibly John Murdock?'

Evergreen lifted his head and his chin jutted out. 'That's Irene's husband. He's a physician. They're very good friends. Why would I loan anyone my home?'

'Yes, that's Irene Murdock's husband,' Rickerson said. He knew who the man was. He didn't need Evergreen to tell him. 'Did they ever house-sit when you were away – you know, look after things?'

Evergreen looked down at his hands and thought about this for some time. Then he said, 'Well, yes, I believe they did, but it was many years ago. I went to Europe after my wife passed away, took a leave from the bench. Everyone told me to do it. I didn't want to go.' He was regressing, returning to those sad days of grief. 'Irene and John took care of my dogs and watered the plants, things like that. They looked after our son. He was only sixteen then. He was adopted, you know? My wife loved that boy. She wanted children so badly.' His breath seemed to catch in his throat. 'She would be brokenhearted if she knew how things have turned out. We're not very close – my son and I.'

Rickerson suddenly felt sorry for the man sitting before him. From the look on his face, he didn't have a lot to live for. He seemed so alone in this huge house. He was nothing but a sick old man still grieving for his dead wife.

'What's this all about?' Evergreen said, searching the detective's face, regaining a measure of authority. 'Officer, I demand you explain this to me this second or leave my home.'

'Look, Judge Evergreen, we've made a serious mistake here. I can't divulge all the details now, but we'll inform you of everything in time.' Rickerson started yelling at the men, trying to get their attention. They were rifling through everything, tearing the house apart. 'We were only trying to do our jobs,' he said to the judge as he left the room.

He found the chief in the bedroom. He wasn't going to be happy. Rickerson told him. 'Evergreen's not our man. It's John Murdock.'

The chief looked up. 'Who in the hell is John Murdock?'

'He's married to Judge Irene Murdock. The S.O. has him in custody. Let's clear. Just leave some of the guys to smooth things over, try to put the place back together.'

The chief glared at him, tossing some of Evergreen's property back into the drawer where he had found it. 'This better be good, Rickerson,' he said, his mouth a thin, hard line. His eyes flashed behind the thick glasses. 'This better be damn good.'

Three hours later, Josh, Emmet, and Lara were waiting in the lobby at the San Clemente Police Department. John Murdock had been sequestered in an interview room for over two hours with Detective Rickerson and his attorney. The chief had called Irene Murdock and instructed her to come to the police station, where they were holding her husband. They informed her he had a minor injury, refusing to tell her anything more. As yet, she had not arrived.

Josh and Lara were huddled together in a corner in the lobby. Emmet was exhausted and sitting quietly across the room, his head drooping to the side of the wheelchair. On several occasions he had dozed off.

Lara was guzzling black coffee and chastising Josh. 'I can't believe you did that. You went against what I told you and got yourself in a terrible mess. There's no telling what he could have done to you. You could have been killed.'

He smiled, unfazed by Lara's ranting. She'd been saying basically the same thing for hours. 'We got him, though, didn't we? Wasn't Emmet cool? Can you believe he cut the guy with the lid from a can of peas?'

Lara sighed. 'Yes, we got him. And yes, I'm totally impressed by what Emmet did, but Josh, if you ever do anything like that again, I'll ground you for the rest of your natural life.'

'Oh, yeah,' he said, the smile a permanent part of his face. 'Emmet and I are heroes. You can't ground a hero.'

'Oh, yeah,' she said. 'You're a hero, all right. But I can still ground you anytime I want and don't think for a minute that I won't either.' Then she set the coffee cup down and seized him, locking him in a bear hug. 'I couldn't stand it if something happened to you.' She whispered in his ear. 'Do you understand? Do you know how much you mean to me?'

'Yes,' he whispered back. 'I love you too, Aunt Lara.'

When she finally pulled away, her eyes were filled with tears. But she was smiling.

They waited for another hour, but Irene Murdock didn't appear. Finally Rickerson came out of the interview room and approached Lara and Josh. 'He spilled his guts, even though his attorney advised him not to. I think in some ways he was relieved it was over. He's been under a psychiatrist's care – a Dr. Werner.'

'Werner?' Lara said. 'That's the psychiatrist that Irene recommended for Josh. Christ, you think he knew about this?'

'He certainly knew Murdock was a pedophile, but I doubt if he knew about the crimes. Even if he did, he was in a bad position. You know, patient confidentiality and all. He couldn't come forward.'

'What about Irene?' she said. 'Don't tell me Irene knew what John was doing. It's hard enough to believe that John was who he was, but Irene . . .' Lara played it over in her mind. She walked to the wall and looked at the pictures there. They were portraits of the officers who had died in the line of duty. Then she turned and faced Rickerson.

'Tell me everything,' she said and then glanced at Josh. 'I guess he can hear too. I mean, he's involved up to the hilt.'

All three sat on the sofa in the lobby, Rickerson sitting on the edge turned sideways. Emmet pushed a button on his wheelchair and joined them, all eyes and ears. 'Murdock's been molesting young boys for years. How many we can't possibly venture to guess. For quite some time, he's only seen patients in his medical practice in the mornings. The afternoons he spends in that apartment, taking calls from young kids.'

'I've known Irene and John for years,' Lara said, shock and disbelief registering on her face. 'Naturally, I knew Irene better than John, but still I would have never known. He was a doctor, for God's sake. They were pillars of the community.'

'Yeah, well, he claims he had nothing whatsoever to do with Packy's killing. He's sort of pussy-whipped. It's obvious Irene wears the pants, wields the power. When your sister started blackmailing him, he tried to handle it alone. But there was a problem. All of their assets were in joint accounts, requiring both their signatures, and all the banks knew Irene was a judge. They certainly didn't want to make a mistake with her money. Murdock said he managed to withdraw the first fifty thousand without Irene knowing, but when he went back for the next fifty, the bank contacted her.'

'The next fifty?' Lara said. 'Want to explain that?'

'First, your sister and Perkins demanded the fifty G's. Then once he paid, they must have decided to press for another fifty. The bank got nervous because Murdock was asking for a huge sum of money in cash and with all the divorce cases – you know, one spouse cleaning out the bank account – they notified Irene. Murdock said he had to tell her. Your sister and Sam were threatening to take the pictures to the police. I guess she was pretty shocked, even threatened to divorce him. She insisted he enter therapy with Werner. But according to John, she was mortified that their sons would find out and it would destroy them, that her career would be ruined and her standing in the community. She told him she'd handle it. Evidently one son's in medical school, the other in Harvard. She dotes on them, I guess.' Rickerson paused. Her efforts had been in vain. The young men would know it all now. 'She must have sprung Packy, and from what Murdock says, Packy just went wild in there. He raped your sister and then ended up killing them both. When the Murdocks figured out Sam and Ivory were related to you, Lara, and Packy raised the stakes, demanding more money, it's my guess that Irene killed him.'

'Irene?' Lara said, completely shocked. 'No. That's not possible. Irene is my friend. She would never have killed someone. Not Irene. No, you must be mistaken.' Lara walked over to the wall and leaned her forehead against it. 'Then it was Irene who came into my chambers and typed up that order to release Frank Door? God, he could have killed me and she didn't even care.'

Rickerson continued, 'John Murdock doesn't know for sure, but it's my guess that Irene herself met Packy that day and shot him through the window of the car. Her husband didn't even know he was dead. That is, if we can believe what he's telling us. Anyway, that's why Packy was caught off guard. Irene made John hire him and arrange everything – to get the photos back. All she did was make the phone call to Evergreen. It's my guess Packy knew nothing about Irene, only that someone high-placed in the system was involved. When she showed up that day, he probably had no idea who she was.'

'Jesus,' Lara said, turning around, facing both Rickerson and Josh. 'This is beyond belief. I would have never dreamed . . . never in a million years. And John used Evergreen's house to molest children?'

'At one time. He did more than that, Lara. He molested Evergreen's own son. According to him, it was Robert Evergreen who took most of the pictures. He started molesting the boy when he was about eleven, even before Evergreen's wife died. He used to go over and get him, take him out to play miniature golf, things like that. Evergreen was older. The boy was adopted. He didn't spend a lot of time with his son. John Murdock became like a substitute father, having raised two sons of his own.'

'What about his own sons? Did he molest them?'

'He says no. One boy was in college when this all started. Another in high school. My guess is they were too old to be appealing. Once Robert Evergreen passed puberty, Murdock stopped molesting him. Then he had him be the photographer. He helped Evergreen recruit other victims. It's really very sad. From what he says, Robert Evergreen is a homosexual now and lives with another man, a musician. He and his father seldom speak. The old man couldn't handle it.'

'Does Leo know about this . . . the child molests? Does he know what happened to his son?'

'I'm sure Leo Evergreen knows nothing about this,' Rickerson said.

'Should we tell him?' she asked, thinking of all they had already put the poor man through. They surely owed him an apology. 'It could kill him.'

'No,' Rickerson said. 'Not unless we have to. What we have to do now is find and arrest Irene Murdock. We sent a unit to the house, but she was gone. We've notified the airports. My guess is she's trying to leave the country. When John Murdock learned who Josh was, he called Irene. She was on her way to the apartment, evidently to decide what to do about it, when Emmet came.' He paused. His eyes met Lara's. They were both thinking the same thing – that the Murdocks might have taken drastic measures. They had everything to lose at that point. Those drastic measures could have meant killing Josh.

Rickerson continued, 'We probably should have never called her, tipped her, but then at the time, I wasn't certain of her involvement. A woman . . . I never figured the killer to be a woman. I think after Packy killed your sister and brother-in-law, Irene Murdock went completely insane. They only wanted the pictures back. I don't think for a moment she arranged to have them murdered. Realizing how dangerous Packy was, what he had done, she became incensed and decided to kill him. She certainly couldn't call the police and have him arrested. That would have been suicide. And if he was arrested, he would have surely implicated her husband and herself. I mean, she arranged his release. She had to fear it would come back to her eventually.'

Lara was silent. It was so hard to comprehend. 'How did this Packy person get into the house? Remember, you kept driving that point home to me, that there was no forced entry.'

'Oh,' Rickerson said. 'I forgot to tell you. We figured that one out about three days ago. Under the front seat of his Camaro, the S.O. found a phony badge. He must have bought it at a police supply store or a novelty store. We assume he just flashed it at your sister, told her he was a cop, and she let him in. It's my guess that she somehow managed to call Sam at the pawnshop, thinking she was about to be arrested, and when he came home, Packy killed him. From what the coroner says, Ivory was already dead by then.'

Emmet was shaking his head. Josh was looking at the ground. Lara put her hand on his shoulder. She was sorry now that she'd allowed him to listen. It wasn't easy hearing these things about his mother.

'Oh,' Rickerson said, 'guess who suffers from scoliosis?'

'Murdock, right? I never saw him limping. Explain that, Rickerson. You and your people kept telling me that whoever the man was, he would limp.'

The detective stood. He needed to return to the interview room. They were typing Murdock's statement and he was ready to take it in for his signature. 'Up until a week or so ago, Murdock wore special shoes with a lift. Then he developed a problem with his heel, a bone spur or something, and stopped wearing them.'

'This is still so hard for me to swallow,' Lara said. 'I mean, Irene should have known it was me. She knew I bought a house in Irvine.'

'Did she ever come over there?' Rickerson asked.

'No, we usually spent time together at the office or at her house in Newport. She had dinner parties now and then. Come to think of it, I don't think I ever even told her the address. I didn't entertain much. But you would have thought . . .'

'What? That she looked up your address, got it from personnel or something? Think, Lara. She had no earthly reason to connect you to this situation.'

'I guess you're right.' Lara sighed and stood. 'You mean we can finally go home? To my house in Irvine? We don't have to stay at the condo anymore?'

'You got it, kid,' Rickerson said with a smile. 'And rest assured, we'll get her. Every cop in the city's been alerted. She can't get far.' He paused. 'It's over. You can finally go home. Like Dorothy in *The Wizard of Oz*, huh? There's no place like home.'

'That's for sure,' Lara said, draping an arm around Josh and turning to Emmet.

Rickerson walked up to the little man and pumped his hand. 'I guess I owe you more than a dinner now, Emmet. You're quite a man. My hat's off to you, buddy. It was a lid off a can of peas, huh?'

'I . . . try,' Emmet said modestly. Then he smiled with pride. 'You know . . . a person . . . has to be resourceful.'

'And Lara,' he said, turning to her, 'if you had never asked Emmet to work on this, we might have never known it was Murdock. Leo Evergreen would be in jail right now, faced with defending himself against these charges.'

Lara didn't say anything. She didn't want the detective to feel worse than he already did. But it was a horrifying thought: that Evergreen might have faced prosecution for a crime he hadn't committed. They were about to leave. Rickerson couldn't take his eyes off Lara. He would turn toward the hall and then stop and face her again.

'Oh, by the way, Lara,' he finally said, as if he had forgotten something, 'can I speak to you a moment in private?'

'Sure,' she said. She followed him down the hall to a

vacant interview room. He closed the door and they stood there staring each other in the eye. A lot of things were said in those moments, things they couldn't say with words. 'Thank God it's over,' Lara said, looking away. 'I mean, Irene isn't in custody, but just knowing . . . you know?'

'Yeah,' he said pensively. 'Still think I'm a great cop? Right now I feel like an idiot.'

Lara reached over and hugged him, grinning up into his face. 'Yes, you're a great cop. I was certain it was Phillip, remember? How much longer do you have here before you can leave?'

'I just have to get Murdock to sign the statement. I'll get a unit to transport him to the jail. Why?' His eyes were twinkling. 'You got something in mind?'

Lara pulled back and played with his lapels. 'I thought you could join us for dinner. Then later . . . who knows?'

'I'll have to meet you when I finish.'

'No problem. We'll wait,' Lara said. 'Carl's Junior right down the street? Can you live with that?'

He held her in his arms. He didn't kiss her. He just held her. After a time he said, 'Yeah, I can live with that.'

She slowly pulled away and headed for the door, glancing back over her shoulder for one more look at the detective. 'What? About fifteen minutes?'

'You got it,' he said.

Then she walked out of the interview room into the lobby.

'You ready, fellows?' she said to Emmet and Josh. It was time to get on with the process of living. At least she didn't have to worry about the budget cutbacks. Irene had taken care of that. 'Hey, are you hungry? How about Carl's Junior for dinner? You know, a really good bacon cheeseburger with an enormous mound of fries?'

'You're on,' Josh said, snaking his arm around her waist as they walked side by side to the front door of the police station, Emmet rolling along right beside them. 'We're going to move back into your house in Irvine, right? Does that mean you're going to actually cook one of these days? I mean, I don't mind fast food, but don't forget, Emmet and I are heroes.'

Lara laughed, tossing her head back and letting it all go. The nightmare was over. 'Who knows, Josh, maybe we'll get you that motorcycle you want so bad. You know, like a reward. And Emmet, you just might get a real award of some kind, maybe something from the city.'

'Not . . . me,' Emmet said.

Lara looked at Josh.

'Nah, I don't want a motorcycle,' he said thoughtfully. 'I've decided I want a dog. Then we'll be a real family. All we need is a dog. I never had a dog.'

'A dog?' Lara said. This was the first time she'd heard this one. All he'd ever talked about was the motorcycle.

He looked up, completely serious. 'That's how my father got killed – on a motorcycle.'

Josh helped Emmet into the front seat of the Jaguar and climbed in the backseat. So, Lara thought, Josh has learned what most young people don't learn until it's too late: the value of that fleeting thing called life. Three lives had ended this evening in senseless tragedy: Victor Adams and his two daughters. Her closest friend had been responsible for her sister's death. A man she had known for years, had respected, had been a practicing pedophile. Lara looked up at the sky. She wondered why these horrid things happened, how people could go so far off track. But there were no answers. She knew that. All a person could do was struggle toward acceptance, keep fighting the fight. As her father used to tell her, you just had to keep marching.

Lara opened the trunk and hoisted Emmet's wheelchair inside and then glanced through the rear window of the car. Josh and Emmet were chatting and laughing. No, she thought, nothing would bring back Ivory or Victor Adams and his little girls. But somehow in the midst of it all, Josh, Emmet, and Lara had stumbled upon a new beginning. And she had found Ted Rickerson. The powers that be had somehow moved them all into position, moved them where they were supposed to be. She thought briefly of the pending hearing on charges of impropriety. All they could do was officially reprimand her; the charges couldn't possibly be deemed serious enough to remove her from the bench. It was a mark on her record, but after all she'd been through, she decided it was nothing to lose sleep over. Getting into the Jaguar, she pulled out onto the street.

An hour later, Judge Irene Murdock was arrested and charged with murder as she was attempting to catch a flight at John Wayne Airport. In her purse was the tiny .25-caliber handgun she had used to kill Packy Cummings, purchased years before to protect herself from irate defendants. She had tried to carry it through a metal detector.

In her haste to avoid apprehension, Irene Murdock had completely forgotten the gun was in her purse.

They handcuffed her and walked her through the crowded terminal. It was just about the time Josh, Lara, Emmet, and Rickerson got their cheeseburgers.

6/4/18

Newport Library and
Information Service

NEWPORT COMMUNITY
LEARNING & LIBRARIES

Meet Kitty & her Cat Crew

Kitty

Kitty has special powers but is she ready to be a superhero just like her mum?

Luckily Kitty's Cat Crew have faith in her and show Kitty the hero that lies within!

Pumpkin

A stray ginger kitten who is utterly devoted to Kitty.

X080979

'Don't let fear hold you back.
You're **braver** than you think!'

Join Kitty for an **enchanting adventure** by the light of the **moon**.

Kitty can **talk to animals** and has **feline superpowers**.

KU-636-106

to my parents

and to Esther

CONTENTS

Preface ix

Part I: By Right of Memory 1

1. The Forest Coup 3
2. A Stalinist Childhood 10
3. To Be Preserved, Forever 24
4. The Return of History 36
5. Widows of Revolution 52
6. Ninotchka 70
7. The Doctors' Plot and Beyond 86
8. Memorial 101
9. Written on the Water 120

Part II: Democratic Vistas 141

10. Masquerade 143
11. The Double Thinkers 162
12. Party Men 180
13. Poor Folk 198
14. The Revolution Underground 216
15. Postcards from the Empire 234
16. The Island 248
17. Bread and Circuses 256
18. The Last Gulag 264

Part III: Revolutionary Days 277

19. "Tomorrow There Will Be a Battle" 279
20. Lost Illusions 290
21. The October Revolution 306
22. May Day! May Day! 324
23. The Ministry of Love 341
24. Black September 357
25. The Tower 372
26. The General Line 398
27. Citizens 412

Part IV: "First as Tragedy, Then as Farce" 431

Part V: The Trial of the Old Regime 491

Afterword 531
Acknowledgments 541
Notes on Sources 543
Bibliography 559
Index 563

PREFACE

Long before anyone had a reason to predict the decline and fall of the Soviet Union, Nadezhda Mandelstam filled her notebooks with the accents of hope. She was neither sentimental nor naive. She had seen her husband, the great poet Osip Mandelstam, swept off to the camps during the terror of the 1930s; she described in ruthlessly clear terms how the regime left its subjects in a permanent state of fear. The people of the Soviet Union had been made, as she put it, "slightly unbalanced mentally—not exactly ill, but not normal either." But Mandelstam, unlike so many scholars and politicians, saw the signs of the Soviet system's inherent weakness and believed in the resiliency of the people.

On August 20, 1991, a rainy, miserable afternoon, I walked among the crowds protecting the Russian parliament from a potential invasion by the leaders of a military coup. We all saw that day what so few could have predicted: Soviet citizens—workers, teachers, hustlers, children, mothers, grandparents, even soldiers—all standing up to a group of ignorant men who believed themselves yet another improved version of the Bolshevik regime and possessed of a power to freeze, even turn back, time. In their hurried calculations, the conspirators assumed "the masses" were too exhausted and indifferent to fight back. But tens of thousands of ordinary Muscovites were ready to die for democratic principles. It was said then and is said even now that the Russians know little or nothing of civil society. How strange, then, that so many were willing to give up their lives to defend it.

I do not usually have a great memory for the things I have read, but that afternoon of the coup, hours before it came clear that there would be no attack and the putsch would fail, I thought of a short passage, bracketed in black, in my paperback copy of Nadezhda Mandelstam's *Hope Against Hope:* "This terror could return, but it would mean sending several million people to the camps. If this were to happen now, they would all scream—and so would their families, friends and neighbors. This is something to be reckoned with." The leaders of the August coup had not reckoned with the

development of their own people. They understood nothing. They were jailed for the miscalculation, and the struts of the old regime collapsed.

As I write, the euphoria of those August days is past and Russian democracy is a delicate thing. There are days when it seems that little has changed, that the fate of Russia hinges, once more, on the skills, inclinations, and heartbeat of one man. This time it is Boris Yeltsin: heroic during the coup, flexible, clever, but also, at times, reckless with language, careless with the bottle. No one knows what would happen should Yeltsin fall from power, the result of a stroke or an uprising of the hardline nationalists, neofacists, and nostalgic Communists who dominate parliament. As this book goes to press in April 1993, the power struggle between Yeltsin and parliament is unresolved and has underscored the lack of a clear and workable constitution, legal system, and system of authority. The institutions of this new society are embryonic, infinitely fragile.

In January 1993, Yeltsin's program of economic shock therapy has resulted in only fitful progress, much pain, and, everywhere, anxiety. Food and other supplies are in some places more plentiful, but prices are out of control. The inflation rate is beginning to look Latin American. The heads of the vast military plants show little interest in converting to a peacetime economy, and the absurd subsidies they receive make a mess of Russia's finances. A brash new class of young hustlers and even some honest businesspeople are thriving, but the old, the weak, and the poor are despondent. The crime rate is out of control. And everywhere there is a new demagogue—Communist, nationalist, or simply mad—ready to exploit the failures, vanities, and misfortunes of the elected government. The danger of the authoritarian temptation still lurks in Russia. So far, nearly all the potential successors to Yeltsin promise to be less inclined to radical economic reform and more likely to carry out an aggressive anti-Western foreign policy.

Elsewhere in the former Soviet Union, the situation is at least as worrisome. There are unlovely little wars in the Caucasus, coups d'état in Central Asia. Moldova, Latvia, Estonia, and Lithuania charge Russia with imperialism for leaving behind its troops. The Russians, for their part, complain that the leaders of the Baltic governments treat non-Balts as second-class citizens. Armenia is broke and on the edge of breakdown, Georgia is consumed in civil war. Despite a series of historic treaties with the United States, the unresolved conflicts over arms stockpiles between Russia, Ukraine, Belarus, and Kazakhstan trouble our sleep with dreams of what James Baker once called "Yugoslavia with nukes."

Despite it all, I am partial to Mandelstam's brand of hardheaded opti-

mism. This book, after all, chronicles the last days of one of the cruelest regimes in human history. And having lived through those final days, having lived in Moscow and traveled throughout the republics of the last empire, I am convinced that for all the difficulties ahead, there will be no return to the past. In the West, we cannot afford to look away from this process. To refuse help will endanger Russia, the former Soviet Union, and the security of the globe.

It will take many books and records to understand the history of the Soviet Union and its final collapse. We are, after all, still debating the events of 1917. To write history takes time. When asked what he thought of the French Revolution, Zhou Enlai said, "It's too soon to tell." To understand the Gorbachev period will require a new library covering an immense range of subjects: U.S.-Soviet relations, economic history, the uprisings in the Baltic states, the Caucasus, Ukraine, and Central Asia, the "prehistory" of perestroika, the psychological and sociological effects of a long-standing totalitarian regime.

I went to Moscow in January 1988 as a reporter for *The Washington Post* and saw the revolution from that peculiar angle. Like a lot of reporters in Moscow, I was filing three and four hundred stories a year to editors who would certainly have taken more. Even then, in the midst of that feverish work, it seemed that the multiple events of the Gorbachev-Sakharov-Yeltsin era followed a certain logic, a pattern: once the regime eased up enough to permit a full-scale examination of the Soviet past, radical change was inevitable. Once the System showed itself for what it was and had been, it was doomed. I begin in Part I with that essential moment—the return of history in the Soviet Union—and then move on in Part II to the beginnings of democracy and in Part III to the confrontation between the old regime and the new political forces. Part IV is an attempt to describe, from multiple points of view, the August putsch—that most bizarre and climactic of episodes—and its aftermath. In Part V, we see the final attempt of the Communist Party to justify itself while, all around, a new country is being born. Throughout, I tell the story largely through the eyes of a few representative men and women, some well known, others not.

I am sure if Nadezhda Mandelstam were alive today she would not dwell long on celebration. She would be ruthlessly critical of the inequities and absurdities of politics in post-totalitarian Russia. She would warn of the problem of expecting an injured and isolated people to make a rapid transfer to a way of life that no longer promises cradle-to-grave paternalism. She would, despite her own love of Agatha Christie novels, warn against the new tide of junk culture—the sudden infatuation with Mexican soap operas and American sneakers. She would not ignore the difficulties, even disasters,

ahead. But she would, I think, remain optimistic. Optimism is a belief in a gradual and painful rise from the wreckage of Communism, a confidence that the former subjects of the Soviet experiment are too historically experienced to return to dictatorship and isolation. Already there are signs all over Russia and the rest of the former Soviet Union of new generations of artists, teachers, businesspeople, even politicians on the rise. People "free of the old complexes," as Russians say. A day may even come soon when getting from one day to the next in Russia will no longer require the sort of miracles we witnessed in the last several years of the old regime. Perhaps one day Russia might even become somehow ordinary, a country of problems rather than catastrophes, a place that develops rather than explodes. That would be something to see.

PART I

BY RIGHT OF MEMORY

The struggle of man against power

is the struggle of memory against forgetting.

MILAN KUNDERA

CHAPTER 1

THE FOREST COUP

On a dreary summer's day, Colonel Aleksandr Tretetsky of the Soviet Military Prosecutor's Office arrived at his latest work site: a series of mass graves in a birch forest twenty miles outside of the city of Kalinin. He and his assistants began the morning digging, searching the earth for artifacts of the totalitarian regime—bullet-shattered skulls, worm-eaten boots, scraps of Polish military uniforms.

They had heard the alarming news from Moscow on television and radio before coming to work that morning: Mikhail Gorbachev had "stepped down" for "reasons of health." The GKChP—the "State Committee for the State of Emergency"—had assumed power, promising stability and order. But what to make of it? Kalinin was several hours north of Moscow by train and a long way off the trail of rumor and information. And so like almost everyone else in the Soviet Union on the morning of August 19, 1991, Tretetsky set to work, an almost ordinary day.

The digging in the woods outside Kalinin was a merciless project. A half-century before, at Stalin's direct order, NKVD executioners slaughtered fifteen thousand Polish military officers and threw the bodies into rows of mass graves. The month-long operation in Kalinin, Katyn, and Starobelsk was part of Stalin's attempt to begin the domination of Poland. The young

officers had been among the best-educated men in Poland, and Stalin saw them as a potential danger, as enemies-in-advance. For decades after, Moscow put the blame for the killings on the Nazis, saying the Germans had carried out the massacres in 1941, not the NKVD in 1940. The Kremlin propaganda machine sustained the fiction in speeches, diplomatic negotiations, and textbooks, weaving it into the vast fabric of ideology and official history that sustained the regime and its empire. The Kremlin took history so seriously that it created a massive bureaucracy to control it, to fabricate its language and content, so that murderous and arbitrary purges became a "triumph over enemies and foreign spies," the reigning tyrant a "Friend to All Children, the Great Mountain Eagle." The regime created an empire that was a vast room, its doors locked, its windows shuttered. All books and newspapers allowed in the room carried the Official Version of Events, and the radio and television blared the general line day and night. Those who were loyal servants of the Official Version were rewarded and pronounced "professors" and "journalists." In the Communist Party citadels of the Marxist-Leninist Institute, the Central Committee, and the Higher Party School, the priests of ideology swerved from the dogma at their peril. There were secrets everywhere. The KGB was so keen to keep its secrets that it built its vacation houses in the village of Mednoye near Kalinin, where the Polish officers had been executed and buried in mass graves, the better to keep watch over the bones.

But now something had changed—changed radically. After some initial hesitation at the beginning of his time in power, Gorbachev had decreed that the time had come to fill in the "blank spots" of history. There could be no more "rose-colored glasses," he said. At first, his rhetoric was guarded. He spoke of "thousands" instead of tens of millions of victims. He did not dare criticize Lenin, the demigod of the state. But despite Gorbachev's hesitation, the return of historical memory would be his most important decision, one that preceded all others, for without a full and ruthless assessment of the past—an admission of murder, repression, and bankruptcy—real change, much less democratic revolution, was impossible. The return of history to personal, intellectual, and political life was the start of the great reform of the twentieth century and, whether Gorbachev liked it or not, the collapse of the last empire on earth.

For decades, the massacres at Kalinin, Starobelsk, and Katyn had been a symbol for the Poles of Moscow's cruelty and imperial grip. For a Pole merely to hint that the Soviet Union was responsible for the massacres was a radical, even suicidal act, for it made clear the speaker's point of view: the "friendship of peoples," the relationship between Moscow and Warsaw, was one based on violence, an occupier's reign over its satellite. Even Gorbachev

knew that to admit the massacres would be to undermine the Polish Communists. But by 1990, with Solidarity in power, Gorbachev saw little to lose. While General Wojciech Jaruzelski was visiting Moscow, Gorbachev finally conceded Moscow's guilt and turned over to the Polish government a huge packet of files on the massacres at Katyn, Starobelsk, and Kalinin.

Soon after the Kremlin's admission of guilt, the excavations began. Working with Soviet army soldiers and Polish volunteers, Colonel Tretetsky started work in Mednoye on August 15, 1991. Tretetsky, a career officer in his mid-forties with a thin mustache and sunken cheeks, had spent several months uncovering graves in Starobelsk. With every new grave, he felt himself more deceived. He had believed deeply in Communism and the Soviet Union. He served first in the navy and then, after studying law in Ukraine, signed on in the military for life. He served nearly four years in East Germany and even volunteered to be sent to Czechoslovakia in 1968, the year the Soviet Union crushed the "Prague Spring."

"I was dumb," Tretetsky said. "I believed in it all. I would have given my life for the Motherland on a moment's notice."

He petitioned the military for a commission to Afghanistan and served there from 1987 to 1989. Tretetsky came home to Moscow only to get a bitter taste of the real history of the country he knew so little about. He was assigned to the Military Prosecutor's Office, which was conducting massive investigations into the rehabilitations of people who had been repressed over the past seventy years. Slowly, he began to learn about some of the ugliest incidents in Soviet history: the purges, the massacre of the Polish officers, the army's bloody attack on peaceful demonstrators in 1961 at Novocherkassk.

Put in charge of the excavations, first in Starobelsk and now in Mednoye, Tretetsky attacked his work with passion and precision. In Mednoye, he knew perfectly well where to dig and what to look for. He had already interrogated a local man, a retired officer of the secret police, who had helped carry out the orders from Moscow in 1940. Vladimir Tokaryev was blind and eighty-nine years old by the time history caught up with him, but his memory was clear. Sitting with Tretetsky and a videocamera, he described how in April 1940 his unit of the secret police shot Polish officers in the woods outside Kalinin—two hundred and fifty a night, for a month.

The executioners, Tokaryev said, "brought with them a whole suitcase full of German revolvers, the Walther 2 type. Our Soviet TT weapons were thought not to be reliable enough. They were liable to overheat with heavy use. . . . I was there the first night they did the shooting. Blokhin was the main killer, with about thirty others, mainly NKVD drivers and guards. My driver, Sukharev, for instance, was one of them. I remember Blokhin saying: 'Come on, let's go.' And then he put on his special uniform for the job: brown

leather hat, brown leather apron, long brown leather gloves reaching above the elbows. They were his terrible trademark. I was face to face with a true executioner.

"They took the Poles along the corridor one by one, turned left, and took them into the Red Corner, the rest room for the prison staff. Each man was asked his surname, first name, and place of birth—just enough to identify him. Then he was taken to the room next door, which was soundproofed, and shot in the back of the head. Nothing was read to them, no decision of any court or special commission.

"There were three hundred shot that first night. I remember Sukharev, my driver, boasting about what a hard night's work it had been. But it was too many, because it was light by the time they had finished and they had a rule that everything must be done in the darkness. So they reduced the number to two hundred and fifty a night. How many nights did it last? Work it out for yourself: six thousand men at two hundred and fifty a night. Allowing for holidays, that makes about a month, the whole of April 1940.

"I took no part in the killings. I never went into the execution room. But I was obliged to help them by putting my men at their disposal. I remember a few individual Poles. For instance, a young man. I asked him his age. He smiled like a young boy. I asked him how long he had been in the frontier police. He counted on his fingers. Six months. What had he done there? He had been a telephone operator.

"Blokhin made sure that everyone in the execution team got a supply of vodka after each night's work. Every evening he brought it into the prison in boxes. They drank nothing before the shooting or during the shooting, but afterward they all had a few glasses before going home to bed.

"I asked Blokhin and the other two: 'Won't it take a lot of men to dig six thousand graves?' They laughed at me. Blokhin said that he had brought a bulldozer from Moscow and two NKVD men to work it. So the dead Poles were taken out through the far door of the execution room, loaded onto covered trucks, and taken to the burial place. [The site] was chosen by Blokhin himself. It was near where the NKVD officers had their country homes, near my own dacha, near the village of Mednoye, about twenty miles from Kalinin. The ditches they dug were between eight and ten meters long, each one being enough to hold two hundred and fifty bodies. When it was all over, the three men from Moscow organized a big banquet to celebrate. They kept pestering me, insisting that I should attend. But I refused."

On and on the blind man droned, pointing his finger at "the others," denying the importance of his own role, no less a cruel, bland beast than Eichmann in Jerusalem. But Tokaryev was hardly the issue now. Nor were the executioners themselves. Blokhin and three of the others had long ago

gone mad and committed suicide. The point was that nearly everywhere they went, historians, prosecutors, archivists, and journalists discovered that the legacy of Soviet power was at least as tragic as everything they had heard from "forbidden voices": Solzhenitsyn's *The Gulag Archipelago,* Varlam Shalamov's *Kolyma Tales.* Now no book, no voice, was forbidden. To regain the past, to see plain the nightmares of seventy years, was a nearly unbearable shock. As the return of history accelerated, television routinely showed documentary films about the slaughter of the Romanovs, the forced collectivization of the countryside, the purge trials. The monthly literary journals, the weeklies, and even the daily newspapers were crammed with the latest historical damage reports: how many shot and imprisoned; how many churches, mosques, and synagogues destroyed; how much plunder and waste. Under this avalanche of remembering, people protested weariness, even boredom, after a while. But, really, it was the pain of remembering, the shock of recognition, that persecuted them. "Imagine being an adult and nearly all the truth you know about the world around you and outside your own country has to be absorbed in a matter of a year or two or three," the philosopher Grigori Pomerants told me. "The entire country is still in a state of mass disorientation."

The men of the Communist Party, the leaders of the KGB and the military and the millions of provincial functionaries who had grown up on a falsified history, could not bear the truth. Not because they didn't believe it. They knew the facts of the past better than anyone else. But the truth challenged their existence, their comfort and privileges. Their right to a decent office, a cut of meat, the month of vacation in the Crimea—it all depended on a colossal social deception, on the forced ignorance of 280 million people. Yegor Ligachev, a conservative figure in the Politburo until his forced retirement in 1990, told me ruefully that when history was taken out of the hands of the Communist Party, when scholars, journalists, and witnesses began publishing and broadcasting their own version of the past, "it created a gloomy atmosphere in the country. It affected the emotions of the people, their mood, their work efficiency. From morning to night, everything negative from the past is being dumped on them. Patriotic topics have been squeezed out, shunted aside. People are longing for something positive, something shining, and yet our own cultural figures have published more lies and anti-Soviet things than our Western enemies ever did in the last seventy years combined."

When history was no longer an instrument of the Party, the Party was doomed to failure. For history proved precisely that: the Party was rotten at its core. The ministers, generals, and apparatchiks who organized the August coup of 1991 met secretly at KGB safe houses outside Moscow many times

to discuss the ruin of their state. They talked of the need for order, the need, somehow, to reverse the decline of the Party. They were so deluded about their own country that they even believed they could put a halt to the return of history. They would shut it down with a decree and a couple of tank divisions. The excavations at Mednoye and the other sites of the Polish massacre were no exception. The putschists would try to undermine the work as well as they could. Long before the coup, Valery Boldin, Gorbachev's chief of staff and one of the key plotters in the August coup, tried to control the damage by secretly transferring many key documents on the case from Division Six of the Central Committee archives to the "presidential archive," which he controlled. But that small step did very little. Boldin and the rest of the plotters were now prepared to eliminate everything that aggrieved them. They would end the return of history. They would turn back time. Once more, fear would be the essence of the state.

On the day of the putsch, Tretetsky's men, both the Soviets and the Poles, tried to keep their minds on their work. They dug up old graves and washed the bones and skull fragments in battered bowls. But as the news of the coup reached them, piece by piece, it became harder to concentrate. The soldiers under Tretetsky even heard that the troops deployed on the streets of Moscow were from their own division: the Kantemirovskaya Division. They turned on a television in one of the tents near the work site and saw familiar faces, friends sitting on armored personnel carriers near the Kremlin, outside the Russian parliament, and on the main streets of the capital.

"The weather was wretched," Tretetsky remembered. "It rained nearly all the time, and so to dry the fragments of uniforms, we had to put them in tents, fire up a furnace, and keep the tent open to circulate the air." The team worked until late in the afternoon, when Tretetsky told them all, "The work for today is over." He told them nothing more.

All day long, Tretetsky had been getting calls from the headquarters of the KGB command in Kalinin. The KGB general there, Viktor Lakontsev, warned Tretetsky that the excavation "was no longer necessary," that work should stop and that he must come immediately to headquarters. Tretetsky refused, saying work would go on as planned. He said he would come to KGB headquarters only at the end of the working day. Despite his brave front, Tretetsky was frightened. "I knew there was trouble," he said.

That evening Tretetsky was driven under KGB guard to Lakontsev's office in Kalinin.

The work must stop, Lakontsev insisted. "If it does not," he said, "we cannot guarantee your safety or the safety of the Polish workers."

Tretetsky had to laugh. Throughout his work in Starobelsk and Mednoye

there had always been KGB men at the sites—"observers," they called themselves. "Our United Nations observers," the workers called them.

Tretetsky would not back down. "Over my dead body," he thought to himself. To Lakontsev, he put the refusal more subtly. He told the KGB general that if it was a question of the Poles, he would take responsibility for their safety. The Poles could live together in the tents with the Soviet army troops instead of in the city.

"The investigation cannot stop," Tretetsky said. "What would I tell the Poles? I need to talk to my own chief. This is not an easy question." All the same, Tretetsky thought, "Lakontsev is a big boss, and who am I?"

When he returned to his camp, Tretetsky called Moscow and was told that there had been no stop-work order. He was relieved. Exhausted, he went to sleep in his tent. But not long after, the commander of the army troops woke him saying that an order had come from Moscow: the soldiers had to return to the Kantemirovskaya base in the town of Naro-Fominsk outside Moscow.

"Listen, Viktor," Tretetsky told the commander, "this is an oral order, isn't it?"

"That's right."

"And to bring your men here, you had a written order."

"Yes, I did."

"So why should you obey?"

The troops stayed where they were. The KGB had tried to trick Tretetsky and they had failed. There never had been an order from the Military Prosecutor's Office in Moscow.

At nine the next morning, Tretetsky went before the men and said, "The work goes on. Let's begin now. Everyone is to work intensively, with enthusiasm. And that's it!"

The KGB sabotaged the tractor the men had been using for the excavation. But by now Tretetsky had connections with people in the area, and a collective farm lent him one of its tractors. The Polish workers were especially grateful and pounded Tretetsky on the back. For two more days, the Soviets and the Poles worked at the graves and listened to the radio reports coming from Moscow. Slowly, the news improved. When the men heard that the coup was on the verge of collapse, they seemed to work even harder. Finally, on the morning of August 21, after the plot had failed and troops had returned in relief and triumph from Moscow to their bases, Tretetsky went before his men. He would not live the lie any longer. He refused to return to the past, except to study its bones.

"The criminal investigation ordered by the president of the Union of Soviet Socialist Republics, Mikhail Sergeyevich Gorbachev, goes on!" he cried out. Then the colonel gave the order and his men began to dig.

CHAPTER 2

A STALINIST CHILDHOOD

Not long after my wife, Esther, and I moved to Moscow in January 1988, I was having tea and cake with Flora and Misha Litvinov at their apartment on the Frunzenskaya Embankment, where many families of Communist Party officials, active and retired, lived. The Litvinovs were a dazzling couple in their seventies, dazzling in their kindnesses and the unassuming way they seemed to know everyone and everything going on in Moscow. Misha was the quieter of the two. His reserve, I supposed, was the result of a lifetime sandwiched between a father, Maksim, who served in Stalin's inner court as foreign minister and a son, Pavel, who helped strike one of the first blows against the regime as a dissident. Surrounded by history and its actors, Misha made an art of listening. He listened patiently, with nearly imperceptible amusement. There was not much that would surprise a man whose father slept with a Browning automatic under his pillow in case of attack and a son who flipped the bird to the men of the Politburo. In a room of friends or strangers, however, it was Flora who took the lead, provided the family positions, made the polite inquiry.

She asked what I'd be writing about in Moscow.

"I'm looking for Kaganovich," I said.

Flora's face tightened. She and Misha had known more than one Ameri-

can reporter in the past, and they had undoubtedly heard more reasonable journalistic ambitions: a mastery of arms control, human rights, Kremlin politics. Strange boy, she must have thought, but she was too kind to say so.

At the time, Lazar Moiseyevich Kaganovich was in his mid-nineties and the last living member of Stalin's inner circle. As the people's commissar, he was once as close to Stalin as Goering was to Hitler. He helped direct the collectivization program of the 1920s and early 1930s, a brutal campaign that annihilated the peasantry and left the villages of Ukraine strewn with an endless field of human husks. As the leader of the Moscow Party organization, Kaganovich built the city subway system and, briefly, had it named for himself. He was responsible as well for the destruction of dozens of churches and synagogues. He dynamited Christ the Savior, a magnificent cathedral in one of the oldest quarters of Moscow. It was said at the time that Stalin could see the cathedral belltower from his window and wanted it eliminated.

Did Kaganovich still believe? I wanted to know. Did he feel any guilt, any shame? And what did he think of Gorbachev, the current general secretary? But that wasn't it, really. Mostly I wanted just to sit in the same room with Kaganovich, to see what an evil man looked like, to know what he did, what books he kept around.

Misha listened, but with a certain ethereal inattention. As I talked, he was twisting and folding a napkin into . . . something. He had lately become a master of origami, the Japanese art of paper folding. He had filled an entire room with his paper menagerie: octagons, tetrahedrons, storks, bugs.

"You know," he said, mashing out a crease with the butt of his palm, "Kaganovich lives downstairs."

Downstairs? I already knew that he lived on the Embankment, probably in one of the better buildings still stocked with the descendants of Old Bolsheviks and the Stalinist guard. But here, downstairs? In old photographs, Kaganovich was a huge man with a Prussian mustache and onyx eyes. In retirement, he had been the champion of dominoes in the Frunzenskaya Embankment neighborhood. He would play all comers in the courtyards. Once, when Brezhnev was still in power, Kaganovich made a call to the local Party committee and demanded that his courtyard be equipped with spotlights so he could play dominoes on summer nights. He still had the right to use the plush Kremlin hospitals—the "fourth administration"—and he was very much alive. Here, downstairs.

"It's apartment 384," Misha said. "We used to see him once in a while in the elevator or in the courtyard. The thing is, we never see him anymore. He never goes out, they say. He never answers the door. Maybe he has a nurse. I'm not sure he can walk. He is completely blind."

With that, Misha took a pair of scissors and made the slightest incision in

his napkin. Slowly, he unfolded the paper. A turkey ruffled its feathers in his palm.

Afternoons in Moscow, when I had a spare hour or two, I would visit Misha and Flora's building—50 Frunzenskaya Embankment, entrance 9—looking for Kaganovich. Over many months, I rang the bell at apartment 384 hundreds of times, sometimes for a half hour or more. I slipped notes under the door and into his mailbox. I rang and knocked and listened, my ear pressed against the door. Sometimes I could hear a kind of mumbling inside, other times a shuffling sound, slippers padding along the floor.

Kaganovich's daughter, Maya, an old woman herself, came evenings to check on her father and prepare his dinner. She would not talk to me, and whenever I called her at home she passed the phone to someone else. "Look, he is too old to see anyone," one relative told me. "We don't want people coming here and bothering him with unpleasant questions about the past. It might upset him."

I'd hang around in the courtyard mostly talking to people about Kaganovich. "He doesn't let anyone near him," one of the neighbors, a young engineer, told me as we sat on one of the benches in the courtyard. "I think he's afraid of the world now. One of these days, he'll just die, and he'll be lucky if they mention his name in *Pravda.* The bastard once had the power to kill every one of us."

Another day in the courtyard, one of Kaganovich's oldest neighbors, a woman with a Byelorussian accent and eyes as blue as cornflowers, was taking her daily walk. Children were jumping rope and playing hopscotch, and the old men and women watched them. "Not long ago," she said, "you'd see Kaganovich out here all day, playing dominoes or sitting off by himself with his daughter. Everyone knew who he was, what he'd done under Stalin. There are a lot of people in these buildings along the embankment who were big shots in the Party, but nobody like Kaganovich, no one still alive. Me, I always stayed away from him. Where I come from they have a saying: 'The farther away you keep from the czar, the longer you stay alive.' "

I had Kaganovich's phone number—242-6751—but he never answered. A Russian journalist who had spent years trying to talk to Kaganovich later explained to me there was a code: dial the number, let it ring twice, hang up, and dial again. I tried, and an old man came on the line.

"Hello?"

"Hello, Lazar Moiseyevich?"

"Yes?"

"Lazar Moiseyevich, my name is Remnick. I am a reporter for an Ameri-

can newspaper, *The Washington Post,* and I would like to come visit you, if possible."

"It is not necessary."

"I've heard your health is not very good, but I—"

"It is not necessary. I feel awful. I can't see anything. I feel awful."

"Perhaps, on a day you are feeling a bit better, we could—"

"I always feel awful. No interviews. I don't do interviews. Why should I do interviews?"

His voice, weak at first, was beginning to pick up a little, as if just the use of it was a kind of exercise.

"Lazar Moiseyevich—"

"I said no interviews. That's it!"

"Well—"

The line went dead. In the months ahead, he must have changed the code. The old one no longer worked, and playing with new codes of the same sort didn't work either. Doorstepping was again the only hope. Reporting is often foolish work, but there was something especially shaming about knocking endlessly on a tyrant's door. It raised insane questions of etiquette, such as what the rules of harassment are where a mass murderer is concerned. One afternoon I went up the elevator to see Flora, and with a motherly smile she listened to my complaints about the closed door downstairs.

"Well, what if he does open it, what would you learn?" Flora said. "Do you think he'd break down and apologize?"

"Well, not exactly."

"He's an old man," she said. "What does it matter?"

Then Flora told me a story.

On a winter's night in the time of Stalin—1951 or 1952—Flora opened the door to her son's room and bent low to kiss him good night. Pavel rolled toward her, the bedclothes rustling. In the dark, there was a shine to his face. He'd been crying, and his breathing had a wheezy jump to it. Pavel was a big child, self-assured and smart, but now it seemed that he was lost, scared even to speak.

"What's wrong?" Flora said. "What is it?"

Pavel was quiet a long time and turned away, turned into himself somehow.

"Please, tell me. What's wrong?"

"They said I can't tell you," the boy said. "I gave my word."

"Why not?"

"It's a secret."

"A secret?"

"Yes," he said. "A secret."

"You can tell me," Flora said. "It's right that you keep your word, but you can always tell your parents everything."

Pavel's grandfather Maksim Litvinov was Stalin's foreign minister in the first years of the regime. He'd died just a few months before, but the family still lived, by the standards of the time, in privileged circumstances. Their legacy included an apartment in the House on the Embankment, a magnificent outpost for the Communist Party elite overlooking the Moscow River with huge rooms and special cafeterias and theaters. For the families of the elite there were foreign books, competent doctors, marmalade for the toast, tomatoes in wintertime. The Litvinovs even had their own cleaning woman—a lieutenant in the KGB. In the summer they spent much of their time at a dacha in the town of Khimki outside Moscow. Surrounded by birches and pines, the house had originally been built for Stalin's family. Many of Pavel's schoolmates were the sons and daughters of the Communist Party hierarchy, or what was left of it after the first wave of purges. At school, they all joined the Timur Society, a band of zealous young patriots, the Bolshevik Cub Scouts.

"Tell me. Please," Flora said once more to her son. "What is it? What could be so secret?"

Pavel was frightened. He had sworn his silence to the Timur Society, and he knew enough to be afraid. But, still, he could not deny his mother.

There was a new hunt on for "enemies of the people," he said. One of his best friends had told him so. Flora recognized the boy's name. He was the son of an officer in the KGB.

"He said there can be enemies of the people anywhere," Pavel went on. "Anywhere. Even in our own homes!"

Flora felt a rage gather inside her. She knew the adults who supervised these groups were doing nothing less than training children to work as informers, as traitors against their own families. She was terrified—for her son most of all—but not completely surprised. These were children, after all, who were taught to revere Pavlik Morozov, the twelve-year-old Young Pioneer who was made a national hero and icon for all Soviet children when he served his collective by ratting on his own father for trying to hide grain from the police. These were children raised in schools designed according to the "socialist family" theories of Anton Makarenko, an ideology officer of the KGB. Makarenko insisted that children learn the supremacy of the collective over the individual, the political unit over the family. The schools, he said, must employ an iron discipline modeled on that of the Red Army and Siberian labor camps.

Now the story was pouring out of Pavel. He said that two strange men had

told him that soon he would have a "special task." Flora knew pretty well what that meant. They wanted the boy to report on the family.

Stalin and his circle had always been wary of Maksim Litvinov and his odd family. Although Maksim had served the regime impeccably as foreign minister and as ambassador to the United States, he was nothing at all like the most loyal of Stalin's gray henchmen. He was a man of the world. He spoke foreign languages. He had foreign friends. Maksim had also married a foreigner, an eccentric Englishwoman named Ivy who wrote fiction, had heterosexual and lesbian affairs, and preached C. K. Ogden's gospel of Basic English, an 850-word system for learning the rudiments of the language. When her husband gave her George Bernard Shaw's *Intelligent Woman's Guide to Socialism* to read, she gave him volumes of Austen, Lawrence, and Trollope.

Especially after his forced removal from the Central Committee in 1941, Maksim Litvinov was possessed of a certain sympathy for the political interests of foreigners. In 1944, he told reporters that Stalin had imperial designs on Eastern Europe and wondered aloud why the West did not intervene. In an article for *Foreign Affairs* in 1977, the historian Vojtech Mastny described Litvinov as the "Cassandra in the Foreign Commissariat," a diplomat unafraid to complain about the "rigidity of the whole Soviet system." Stalin, of course, was listening. Khrushchev wrote in his memoirs that the secret police drew up an elaborate plan to "ambush" Litvinov while he was on the road to the dacha in Khimki. Litvinov, however, was a lucky man. For years he slept with his revolver close at hand, but in the end he escaped arrest. Miraculously, he died of old age. "They didn't get him," Ivy remarked to her daughter just after Maksim's death. The family and historians could only guess why. Stalin undoubtedly valued Litvinov's contacts in the West, and he may have thought the foul publicity abroad was not worth the execution.

But even after Litvinov died on December 31, 1951, his family still lived in fear of Stalin's whim, of a knock on the door. Pavel's parents, Misha and Flora, and his aunt Tanya were more subtle characters than Ivy, more attuned to the risks of their time and country. But they, too, behaved in a way that could have landed them in jail or in front of a firing squad. Misha was a celebrated young engineer at the Aviation Engines Institute and a self-made Hero of Soviet Recreation: a mountain climber, a jogger, a dabbler in game theory. Surely this was suspiciously eccentric behavior. Pavel's aunt Tanya was thrown out of an art institute for an "excessive interest" in "decadent Western art." At home, at least, they all spoke their minds. Once Pavel brought a book home from the library about the derring-do of Pavlik Morozov. He was entranced by the boy's great service to the Bolshevik state, his heroic betrayal of his father. Flora spun off into a rage. She tore out the pages

and said that Pavel should never, never betray his parents. No child should, no matter what such foolish books said.

"Even if the parents are bad?" Pavel said.

"Yes. Even if they are bad."

Now Flora had to decide what to do about her boy and his "special task." She would not allow Pavel to become another Pavlik Morozov. In the morning, Flora put on her finest dress and went to the apartment of Pavel's friend, the son of the KGB man. She would try to bluff the officer, scare him into thinking that someone "on high" supported the Litvinov family. She tried to dress the part of a powerful Bolshevik matron and wore an elegant scarf and a pompous hat.

"You have no right to carry on negotiations with my son!" she told him. "You will stop at once!" She left immediately, still shaking with anger and a giddy sense of her own daring. Only a little later would she begin thinking about what she had risked.

In the next few weeks, Misha and Flora talked long about what they should do about their children. They decided they could no longer hold back as much as they had. It was not enough to tear up a book once in a while and then retreat again into a baffling silence. If they were to prevent Pavel and Nina from becoming the sort of young Stalinists that the schools were so eager to create, then they had to speak the truth whenever possible. They had to describe what had happened to so many of the parents and grandparents of Pavel's friends at school, how they had been thrown into the vans known as Black Marias and shipped off to camps in Kolyma, Vorkuta, and Kazakhstan, where they had vanished. They had to begin to impress upon their children that Stalin, the Mountain Eagle, was a lowly beast. Pavel must learn somehow to think outside of a system that engulfed him all day long.

Flora and Misha could not afford to be too direct too often. Such were the times and the dangers. Nor could they compete very well with the immensity of the Stalin cult in all its forms: the parades celebrating Stalin as a god on earth, the newspapers describing his heroic deeds, the radio addresses, the history books written by the Kremlin ideologists, the rallies and paramilitary drills of the Young Pioneers. Pavel had learned to love Stalin the way other children in other places learn to love God. Stalin was a kindly deity, omniscient, a gentle father. He rarely appeared in public. Instead his image was painted on banners, zeppelins, billboards, and icons. His words filled the schoolbooks, the newspapers, the airwaves. "It's not easy to compete with that," Flora thought. "Perhaps it is impossible."

On the day Stalin died, in March 1953, Pavel was thirteen years old and inconsolable. He cried for days. In the schoolyard, he got into fights with the

children who failed to mourn Stalin as deeply as he did. At home, he was furious when he discovered his parents and their friends laughing and joking about Comrade Stalin. He saw them in the kitchen, not mourning but celebrating. Pavel reddened, stormed out of the kitchen, and went off to bed, angry and confused.

It was not easy for any of the Litvinovs in those years after Stalin's death. Misha and Flora were young parents, and they were often at a loss in dealing with Pavel. He struggled in school. He married at seventeen and quickly divorced. He drank a bit, played in marathon card games, and gambled on the horses at the Hippodrome. "The horses were an obsession with him," Flora said. "We were scared that Pavel would end his life a broken-down gambler."

But Pavel was growing up, and he was in no way immune to the "thaw," the wave of anti-Stalinist sentiment, history, and ideology encouraged by Khrushchev in the middle and late 1950s. Hundreds of thousands of prisoners returned home from the labor camps, and all of them had stories to tell. The Litvinovs knew many intellectuals who had been in the camps: writers, artists, scientists, even Party officials. It was a time of revelation for Pavel. He sat at the kitchen table and heard for the first time the real history of the years under Stalin. One of his parents' closest friends, a physicist named Mikhail Levin, came home from prison in 1955 and described the conditions there, the senseless deaths of countless innocents. "It was the experience of waking up after years and years of sleep," Pavel would say a long time after. "All the fantasies of childhood and Stalin were suddenly painful and ridiculous."

In the early 1960s, Pavel got a job teaching physics at the Lomonosov Institute and eventually became friendly with a group of intellectuals who monitored the first celebrated dissident trial—the trial of the "anti-Soviet" writers Andrei Sinyavsky and Yuli Daniel. Among the older writers and scientists, Pavel was a kind of pet: a charming young man of intelligence and curious pedigree. He immersed himself in this new world, reading the underground manuscripts known as samizdat, taking part in the endless kitchen-table discussions that were the center of all intellectual life. Pavel read Solzhenitsyn, the camp stories of Varlam Shalamov, Robert Conquest's *The Great Terror.* He helped draft letters in support of political prisoners and released them, at great peril to himself, to Western journalists. He also married into one of the best-known intellectual families of Moscow. He married Maya, the daughter of the literary scholars Lev Kopelev and Raisa Orlova. Kopelev, who had been one of Solzhenitsyn's cellmates and the model for one of the characters in his novel *The First Circle,* was also a model for Pavel Litvinov. Kopelev had grown up a committed Communist, a true

believer, and then "got an education." Kopelev's life, for Pavel, was living proof of a man's ability to see and think clearly, to act honestly, even in the conditions of a nightmare.

—

On August 21, 1968, Pavel and six of his friends reacted with horror to the shortwave reports coming out of Czechoslovakia. For months they had been listening for every detail of the Prague Spring, cheering on Alexander Dubček's attempt to create a "socialism with a human face." They waited to see how Khrushchev's conqueror and successor, Leonid Brezhnev, would deal with the rebellion of a satellite state. Would he show the same ruthlessness Khrushchev showed Hungary in 1956, or would there be a new sense of tolerance? Now the answer was clear. The voice on the underground Czechoslovak station was brittle and choked: "Russian brothers, go away, we have not asked you to come," the voice said. Pavel's close friend among the early dissidents, Larisa Bogoraz, was crushed. Her husband, Anatoly Marchenko, was in jail for his political activities, and now she saw that the regime itself was prepared to stamp out large-scale dissidence with soldiers and tanks.

"We need a bold act, a movement," she thought. "We need it now."

Pavel, Bogoraz, and five others met to talk it through. They planned a brief noontime demonstration for August 25 against the invasion of Czechoslovakia. They knew well the consequences for such an "anti-Soviet" activity: a prison term, internal exile, or a long stay in a psychiatric hospital. They prepared themselves for nothing less than that. Pavel began to gather his possessions and give his books away to friends. His fate was inescapable.

On the night before the demonstration, Pavel went to the Kopelevs' apartment for a party where the famous bard Aleksandr Galich was singing. The mood was funereal, and the vodka did nothing to lighten it. The Prague invasion was surely the end of the "thaw" and all hopes of a "socialism with a human face"; Brezhnev had begun a movement of blatantly neo-Stalinist politics. For all its hesitations and half-measures, the Khrushchev era would soon seem like a paradise lost. The invasion, the novelist Vasily Aksyonov said, "was a nervous breakdown for the whole generation." At the party, they spoke of their anger, how they were ashamed before the Czechs, the Hungarians, and the Poles—before the entire world—to be a Soviet citizen. They were not citizens at all, they felt; they were subjects.

Then Galich began to sing a song of the Decembrists, the rebels during the reign of Nicholas I:

Can you come to the square?
Dare you come to the square
When that hour strikes?

Pavel felt Galich's eyes on him as he sang. The double meaning of the lyrics, their reference to the dissent of another century and the clarion call to a new generation—it was lost on no one, least of all on Pavel. When Galich put down his guitar, Pavel was tempted to announce the plans for the demonstration, but he decided against it. He was afraid that the older people in the room would feel compelled to come. For them, years in internal exile or prison could mean death.

The next day, at a few minutes before noon, Pavel, Larisa Bogoraz, and their friends gathered at Lobnoye Mesto, the spot on Red Square where the czar's executioners once chopped off the heads of heretics against the state and the church. At the sound of the noon bell on Spassky Tower, they unfurled a series of banners. In Czech: "Long Live a Free and Independent Czechoslovakia." In Russian: "Free Dubček" and "Hands off Czechoslovakia" and "Shame on the Invaders." The poet Natalya Gorbanevskaya brought her three-month-old son to the square. When the others showed their signs, she reached into the baby carriage and pulled out from under her sleeping son the flag of Czechoslovakia.

The demonstration would not have lasted long under any circumstances. KGB men had followed Litvinov and the others to the Kremlin. But a special contingent of KGB officers was also stationed on Red Square that day. They were there waiting for the end of a meeting inside the Kremlin between Brezhnev and the leaders of the Prague Spring, who had been brought to Moscow in handcuffs on the night of the invasion. When the officers saw the banners, the guards pounced on the demonstrators, shouting, "These are all dirty Jews!" and "Beat the anti-Soviets!" Pavel's face was badly bruised, and the art critic Viktor Fainberg lost a few teeth. The officers packed the protesters into unmarked cars and headed for the police station.

After a few moments, the square was quiet once more. The summer tourists went back to watching the changing of the guard at the Lenin Mausoleum. They gaped at the candy-striped whirl of St. Basil's Cathedral. The old women peddled vanilla ice-cream bars and the old men sold snapshots to the visiting comrades from Sofia, Budapest, and Hanoi. Suddenly, guards blew their whistles and ordered people to clear the lane coming out of the Spassky Gate from the Kremlin. A line of official black cars drove through at terrific speed. Then the guards blew another signal. The coast was clear. No one

knew it then, but one of the men in the caravan was probably Alexander Dubček, the leader of the Prague Spring and now a prisoner of Moscow.

"It would have been wonderful if Dubček and the others had seen the demonstration of support for what they had been doing. They didn't," Andrei Sakharov told me later. "But most important was that somewhere in this country there were some people who were willing to uphold its dignity."

The trial of the Red Square protesters, of course, was a sham, a totalitarian theater piece. On October 11, 1968, Pavel was given the chance for a last statement before the sentencing:

"I will not take your time by going into legal details; the attorneys have done this. Our innocence of the charges is self-evident, and I do not consider myself guilty. At the same time, that the verdict against me will be 'guilty' is just as evident to me. I knew this beforehand when I made up my mind to go to Red Square. Nothing has shaken these convictions, because I was positive that the employees of the KGB would stage a provocation against me. I know that what happened to me is the result of provocation.

"I knew that from the person that followed me. I read my verdict in his eyes when he followed me to the metro. The man who beat me up in Red Square was one I had seen many times before. Nevertheless, I went out into Red Square. I shall not speak of my motives. There was never any question for me whether I should go to Red Square or not. As a Soviet citizen, I deemed it necessary to voice my disagreement with the action of my government, which filled me with indignation. . . .

" 'You fool,' said the policeman, 'if you had kept your mouth shut, you could have lived peacefully.' He had no doubt that I was doomed to lose my liberty. Well, perhaps he is right, and I am a fool. . . .

"Who is to judge what is in the interest of socialism and what is not? Perhaps the prosecutor, who spoke with admiration, almost with tenderness, of those who beat us up and insulted us. . . . This is what I find menacing. Evidently, it is such people who are supposed to know what is socialism and what is counterrevolution. This is what I find terrible, and that is why I went to Red Square. This is what I have fought against and what I shall continue to fight against for the rest of my life."

No one escaped punishment. Pavel Litvinov was sentenced to five years in internal exile. He was sent to live in a remote village in Siberia—not far from where the rebel Decembrists had been imprisoned more than a century before.

After he returned home to Moscow, Pavel saw that he faced an unavoidable choice: jail or exile abroad. If he continued his human rights work—and he could not do otherwise—he would be sentenced this time to a prison camp, a far more severe fate than he had known in Siberia. An application

for emigration, a KGB officer suggested to him, would likely meet with a "positive response." Pavel said his farewells to his friends and family at a bleak party in 1973.

"I thought that when I left the country it was forever and that I would never see my parents again," Pavel said. "This was a typical experience for many people. You left, and for you the people you were leaving behind were as good as dead. They were alive, but you lost them the way you lose people when they die."

Pavel and Maya Litvinov began a new life in the United States. Pavel found a job teaching at the Hackley School, a small private school in Tarrytown, New York. They traveled, they met new friends. But for years they lived in a painful limbo. Pavel Litvinov had gone through a transformation, from obedience to independence, that had cost him his family, his home. Most of those he had left behind did not have the means or the chance to win their independence. The Soviet Union was no longer what it was under Stalin. But even with the prison camps in ruins, the system survived. The fear remained, and no one was free.

In nearly four years of living and traveling in what was once the Soviet Union, I often found myself wandering accidentally into old prison camps. During the first strikes in the Siberian coalfields in 1989, some miners in the Siberian city of Kemerovo told me to look over a fence and into a field—that low set of buildings to the left of the cows. Barracks. In a working prison outside the city of Perm in the Urals, I had tea and cookies with the commandant. He had buried a few dissidents in his time and now he was thinking about his pension. At one time the entire country was part of the camp system—the gulag archipelago, as Solzhenitsyn called it—and you did not have to travel far from home to see it. One evening I was drinking tea and visiting an old man in an apartment house on Leninsky Prospekt just down the street from where I lived in Moscow.

"I've always felt honored to live here," the man said.

The apartment was just one room, and the heat was off and the plumbing was rotting.

Why? What honor can there be in living here? I asked him.

"Solzhenitsyn helped build this dump," he said, his gold incisors flashing. "He was on the prisoners' crew when they put this place up."

At every one of these meetings, it was not hard for me to feel at once connected to the place, and lucky to have escaped it. Both my grandfathers, Alex and Ben, were born around the same time and in the same sort of place. They lived in muddy villages around the turn of the century: Alex outside

Vilna (now Vilnius), Ben outside Kiev. Neither village, so far as I have been able to determine, still exists. Neither of my grandfathers knew much, or wanted to know much, of his boyhood in the Russian empire. They were bewildered in old age by the craze for "roots." There was no nostalgia in them. They were lucky to have escaped. Upon hearing the rumors of pogroms they fled Russia on foot, on horseback, on wagon, and finally on a ship. They came to Castle Garden and Ellis Island. Alex sold "notions" in New York: girdle snaps, nylons, hairpins, all of it out of wooden barrels and cardboard boxes at a corner store on Prince Street and Broadway. Ben worked as a salesman in clothing stores in Paterson, New Jersey. When I began learning Russian in high school, my grandfathers smiled with curiosity and let it go at that. If they knew seven or eight words of Russian, it was a lot. For them, Russia was a burning house they had fled in the middle of the night. Just before I left for Russia, I flew to Miami Beach. Ben had managed to trade in his house in Paterson for a small room with a view of the Atlantic Ocean and an ambulance in the basement garage. He was one hundred years old. When I told him I was planning to live in Moscow for three or four years, he said, "You must be crazy. We almost got killed going out and you, meshuggah, you want to go back in."

My wife's family was even more suspicious of our going to Moscow. And with good reason. They were less successful at escape. Esther's grandfather Simon was a renowned rabbi, born in Byelorussia. After taking a pulpit in Poland, he married Nechama, the descendant of seven generations of rabbis. Robinson was her maiden name: son of rabbis. Eventually he moved back to Byelorussia, where he was both a rabbi and a teacher of philosophy in the local gymnasium. In 1939, an officer of the NKVD secret police came through the town of Diesna looking for Simon. The townspeople and congregants refused to give him up. But when Simon found out about the agent, he sought him out and invited him to his home. When the agent arrived at the door, he said something strange. "If you don't mind," he said to the terrified family, "I'd like to pray with you first."

When they were finished praying, it became clear that the NKVD man was a kind of double agent, or at least an agent with a hint of mercy. He told Simon that the police were after him. "You must leave," he said. "Leave now with just the clothes on your back."

Simon fled to independent Lithuania, and his wife and children soon followed. But in June 1940, just days after the Soviet occupation of Lithuania, he was arrested and jailed for six months in Vilna. Then he was deported to a labor camp in the town of Sukhobezvodnoye—meaning "Dry, Without Water"—in the Urals. He was never heard from again.

As relatives of an "enemy of the people," Nechama and her children,

Murray, Rita, and the baby, Esther's mother, Miriam, were all deported to Siberia. Nechama was put to work on a collective farm. When she refused to let her son go into the army—she claimed Polish citizenship—the two of them were arrested and jailed. Rita, at fourteen, was left to fend for herself, and Miriam was put into a children's camp in western Siberia. After the war, Miriam and her sister, brother, and mother fled Russia.

For the longest time, Esther's grandmother refused to speak of the past. By the time Esther began to insist that she needed to know what had happened, Nechama could no longer think clearly. Her mind moved in and out of time, from one language to another. Three months after we were married, Esther and I moved to Moscow. "I hope you come home once in a while," Miriam said, "because I don't think I could visit you there."

CHAPTER 3

TO BE PRESERVED, FOREVER

In the years after Stalin's death, the state was an old tyrant slouched in the corner with cataracts and gallstones, his muscles gone slack. He wore plastic shoes and a shiny suit that stank of sweat. He hogged all the food and fouled his pants. Mornings, his tongue was coated with the ash-taste of age. He mumbled and didn't care. His thoughts drifted like storm clouds and came clear only a few times a year to recite the old legends of Great October and the Great Patriotic War. Sometimes, in the gathering dark of his office, he would set out on the green baize table all the gifts that foreigners had given him: the gold cigarette dispenser, the silver Eiffel Tower, the colored pens, the crystal paperweights. The state was nearly senile, but still dangerous enough. He still kept the key to the border gate in his pocket and ruled every function of public life. Now and then he had fits and the world trembled.

But how the state kept alive, how it got from day to day, was a mystery. History was a fairy tale and the mechanisms of daily life a vast Rube Goldberg machine that somehow, if just barely, kept moving. If not for the plundering of Soviet oil fields and the worldwide energy crisis, the economy might have collapsed even before it did; and by the early 1980s, KGB reports declared that the cushion of oil profits was all but gone. The abyss awaits us, the most trenchant of the secret police reports declared. The economy was

doomed. Nothing, and no one, worked in any recognized sense of the word. I saw the serfs of a collective farm outside Vologda in northern Russia herded onto buses to buy their food in the city. Their own harvest had rotted in the rain. In the steel town of Magnitogorsk, I saw miners spending their breaks at a local clinic sucking on "oxygen cocktails," a liquid concoction infused with oxygen and vitamins. On Sakhalin Island north of Japan, I saw a few hundred thousand salmon, fish that could have sold on the Ginza or Broadway for a fortune, writhe and rot in the shoreline nets while the trawlers sat rusting in port. Sakhalin is closer on the map to Hollywood Boulevard than Red Square, but the fishermen couldn't "make a move until they get the telegram from Moscow," a local politician told me. The order from the ministry came a week after the salmon had gone white and belly up.

But somehow the state never completely collapsed. There was bread, at least, and parades marked the triumph of the state's persistence. Even the May Day parade of 1988 was not much different from those before them. I stood in the reporters' section just to the right of the Lenin Mausoleum and watched the leaders come out looking faintly embarrassed, but pleased as well that it was all hanging together: Lenin's edgy portrait still hung on the side wall of GUM, the state department store; strongmen heaved dumbbells and gymnasts skipped through hoops in a show of "physical culture"; the workers of the Moscow automobile plants carried the banners they received in the morning and drank down the vodka they got at parade's end. Only the music changed: Pete Seeger songs boomed out of the Kremlin loudspeakers as the workers of the ZIL automobile factory marched by the reviewing stand. As Sergei Ivanov, a Soviet scholar of the Byzantine period, wrote, the rites of Communism had their roots in Constantinople, when the leader's rare appearances "before the people were accompanied by thoroughly rehearsed outbursts of delight, specially selected crowds who chanted the officially approved songs."

It was Oz, the world's longest-running and most colossal mistake, and the only way to endure it all was the perfection of irony. There was no other way to live. Even the sweetest-seeming grandmother, her hair in a babushka and her bulk packed into a housecoat, even she was possessed of a sense of irony that would chill the spine of any absurdiste at the Café Flore. One morning I was sitting in a courtyard in Moscow talking with an ancient of the city, a sweet wreck of a man. He needed help desperately, and it was still a time when a foreigner seemed the last recourse for everything from KGB harassment to this man's problem: his wife was dying of leukemia. How could he get to the Mayo Clinic? He'd heard the doctors there were "beautiful." They could save his wife. As he talked, I happened to glance up over his shoulder and saw a woman on the tenth floor hurl a cat out her kitchen window.

"Animal!" she screamed. "No room for you here! Be gone!"

The cat hit the pavement, and it sounded like the soft pop of an exploding water balloon. Now the two of us, the old man and I, were watching: the woman at the window, her face twisted into an angry knot, the cat struggling to get up on its broken legs.

"Ach," the old man said, turning away, "our Russian life!"

His smile was like the smile on a skull. He went on talking.

In an era of rot, the laureate was a genius of irony and part-time drunk named Venedikt ("Benny") Yerofeyev. In the seventies, Yerofeyev's friends circulated his masterpiece, a modern *Dead Souls* called *Moskva-Petushki,* the name of a train route between the capital and a town where many people lived after they returned from the camps. Yerofeyev's book, published in English as *Moscow Circles,* is a novel of wandering that goes nowhere except down, deep into the soul of man under socialism. His greatest relief is in the mastery of the binge. He is an artful mixologist. When there is no real vodka at hand, he conjures, with nail varnish and lavender water, the "Tears of the Komsomol Girl": "After one glass your memory is as strong as ever, but your mind just goes blank. After the second glass the brightness of your mind amazes you, but your memory goes blank." His best recipe, the "Finis coronat opus," is Cat Gut: 100 grams of Zhigulev beer, 30 grams of "Sadko the Rich Merchant" brand shampoo, 70 grams of anti-dandruff shampoo, and 20 grams of insect repellent. And now, "your Cat Gut is ready. Drink it from early evening in large gulps. After two glasses of this, men become so inspired you can spit at them from five feet for half an hour and they won't take the blindest bit of notice."

Yerofeyev made his living at any job he could keep. He didn't keep them long, generally, but he did rise to the post of foreman. He commanded a small brigade of men who were laying cable, or pretending to, in the town of Sheremetyevo outside Moscow. "This is what we would do. One day we would play poker, the next day we would drink vermouth, on the third day we'd play poker, and on the fourth day it was back to vermouth. . . . For a while everything was perfect. We'd send off our socialist pledges once a month and we'd get our pay twice a month. We'd write, for example: 'On the occasion of the coming centenary we pledge ourselves to end production traumatization.' Or: 'In honor of the glorious anniversary we will struggle to ensure that every sixth worker takes a correspondence course in a higher educational institution.' Traumatization! Institutions! . . . Oh, what freedom and equality! What fraternity and freeloading! Oh, the joy of nonaccountability! Oh, blessed hours in the life of my people—the hours which stretch from opening to closing time! Free of shame and idle care we lived a life that was purely spiritual."

The state, of course, did not allow this sort of thing. *Moskva-Petushki* was published only in 1988, and then only by a temperance journal. But the state never got the joke with Yerofeyev; otherwise he would have been jailed or exiled. Let him laugh. What it could not tolerate was a challenge uncomplicated by irony. When Brezhnev shoved Khrushchev out of power, the state still had the means to squash what little freedom it had allowed. The censors went through the libraries with razor blades and slashed from the bound copies of *Novy Mir* Solzhenitsyn's *One Day in the Life of Ivan Denisovich.* Then they slashed Solzhenitsyn from Russia, hustling him from a prison cell to a jet and finally to his exile. It could not tolerate Solzhenitsyn's sneer, Brodsky's impudence, or Sakharov's superiority. The regime would rather kill its brightest children than give way. A magnificent life-support system, with millions of agents, informers, police, wardens, lawyers, and judges all working at its bedside, kept the old tyrant breathing. Their watchfulness was admirable.

"Every life has a file, if you will," Brodsky told me in his basement apartment, his New York exile. "The moment you get a little bit well known, they open a file on you. The file begins to get filled up with this and that, and if you write your file grows in size all the faster. It's sort of a Neanderthal form of computerization. Gradually, your file occupies too much space on the shelf and, quite simply, a man walks into the office and says, 'This is a big file. Let's get him.' "

They got him. At his trial in Leningrad, Brodsky encountered the soul of the regime, its peculiar language.

JUDGE: What is your profession?
BRODSKY: Translator and poet.
JUDGE: Who recognized you as a poet? Who has enrolled you in the ranks of poets?
BRODSKY: No one. Who enrolled me in the ranks of human beings?
JUDGE: Did you study for it?
BRODSKY: What?
JUDGE: To be a poet. Didn't you try to take courses in school where one prepares for life, where one learns?
BRODSKY: I didn't believe it was a matter of education.
JUDGE: How is that?
BRODSKY: I thought that it came from God.

Just before he left the country in 1972, Brodsky adopted an old Russian tradition and wrote a letter to the czar.

"Dear Leonid Ilyich: A language is a much more ancient and inevitable

thing than a state. I belong to the Russian language. As for the state, from my point of view, the measure of a writer's patriotism is not oaths from a high platform, but how he writes in the language of the people among whom he lives. . . . Although I am losing my Soviet citizenship, I do not cease to be a Russian poet. I believe that I will return. Poets always return in the flesh or on paper."

Brodsky's letter, Sakharov's manifestos, all the broadsides and masterworks of the dissidents carried with them the air of futility. The idea of change, of the resiliency of the word against the state, seemed a kind of dream, a conceit to live out the day and get to the next one. Just before his exile, Solzhenitsyn wrote his "Letter to the Soviet Leaders." "Your dearest wish," he informed them, "is for our state structure and our ideological system never to change, to remain as they are for centuries. But history is not like that. Every system either finds a way to develop or else it collapses." And with that, Solzhenitsyn was gone.

Lydia Chukovskaya, who wrote a novel about the purges while she waited in vain for her husband to return from a prison camp, got up at a meeting of the Writers' Union at the height of the anti-dissident campaign and said: "I can prophesy that in the capital city of our homeland there will inevitably be an Aleksandr Solzhenitsyn Square and an Academician Andrei Sakharov Avenue."

Inevitably! Who believed it? Even the bravest of the brave—and Chukovskaya was among them—had their doubts. When I met her she was in her nineties and living with her daughter Yelena on Gorky Street. Yelena greeted me at the door and asked me to wait a moment until Lydia Korneievna was ready to receive me. There was nothing royal about this, nothing vain, but rather a woman gathering herself. Yelena led me into the room and Lydia Korneievna was seated at a small table. There was a teapot and two cups with chipped saucers and a plate of cookies. Her hand was already on the handle of the pot.

Lydia Korneievna had not been well. Her wide, light eyes were glazed with rheum. The skin of her face was fine, a kind of papery white, as if it would burn if you touched it. Like all Moscow intellectuals of a certain kind and class, she had photographs of well-known poets and writers stuck behind the glass of her bookshelves. In many apartments this is both a vanity and a connection, a way of announcing one's sense of quality and aspiration. Lydia Korneievna had no vanity and no one deserved the portraits of Solzhenitsyn and Sakharov more than she did. She had risked all to defend them. She had lost the right to publish. Probably all that kept her safe in her bed was her age and the fact that she was the daughter of Kornei Chukovsky, a children's writer as revered in Russia as Dr. Seuss is in America.

For a while, she talked about her friends, her walks with Anna Akhmatova in Leningrad, her love for Sakharov. Her sentences were formal and clear, and her voice, though weakened with age, had a liquid sound. Then the lights went out in the entire apartment block. It was night and there was no moon and the room was black. Lydia Korneievna could hardly tell. To her it was like the slight change of light in a room when the fire settles into itself. And not noticing, she kept talking. After a while she did sense some difference, a change in the air, a certain coolness and quiet. Her mood changed. For a moment she paused, as if she were finally going to mention the darkness. Then she said, "You know, when we talk about all these people, I know now that they are all gone. It is horrible to say, but you must imagine a state that used every means to kill the best among us. All dead or all gone."

After a while, Lydia Korneievna said, "The lights. They're out. How strange!"

Yelena came in with candles and we continued talking until Lydia Korneievna announced, "I suppose I'm tired."

On the way out, I told Yelena a little of what her mother had said. She nodded. She had heard this many times before.

"But you must remember," she said, "even Lydia Korneievna has hope. She adores that young boy. Dmitri Yurasov. She adores him. You should meet him if you can."

While the world spent 1987 and 1988 waiting for Gorbachev's newest initiatives, his shifts in ideology, the boldest ideas for the creation of a civil society were debated on Saturday mornings in Moscow. At first small groups of young intellectuals—the "informals"—met at home and even typed out their declarations on onionskin paper. But after a while, the older voices gathered. Sakharov had returned from exile, and Moscow Tribune, a loose amalgamation of scholars and writers who all had lived through the promise of the thaw, was one of his regular platforms.

The first time I saw Dmitri Yurasov was at a Saturday-morning session of Moscow Tribune at Dom Kino, the headquarters of the Filmmakers' Union near the Peking Hotel. The scene was nearly always the same. Moscow Tribune's sessions would begin at ten or eleven with speeches by the best-known of the group: Yuri Afanasyev, a bearish-looking historian of the French Annales school, who had been put in charge of the Historical Archives Institute; Yuri Karyakin, a journalist and Dostoevsky scholar who nearly drank himself to death during the Brezhnev years; Nikolai Shmelyov, an economist and short-story writer who had once been a member of the Khrushchev family by marriage; Leonid Batkin, a scholar of the Italian

Renaissance whose slight heresies and refusal to join the Party prevented him from teaching in Moscow; Galina Starovoitova, a demographer, an expert on Armenia; Len Karpinsky, the son of revolutionaries, a journalist who had once been blessed by the Kremlin as "our great hope" and later betrayed it by becoming what he called a "half-dissident." And always, there was Sakharov, off to the side, sleeping through the speeches at times, clearly weakened by his years of forced exile in Gorky but ready to perform when it came his turn.

Yurasov was sitting in the back rows. He was twenty-four years old and the youngest person in the hall. He was a tough-looking kid in ratty jeans and a bleached jacket. His hair was cropped close; he looked like an army recruit on leave. When one of the speakers said something not to his liking, he sneered, as if rehearsing to be James Dean. Dmitri, or Dima as everyone called him, was known as the young kid who collected information on people who had been imprisoned or executed under Soviet power. He kept the names on index cards, and he had about 200,000 of them—that is, 200,000 out of tens of millions.

Moscow Tribune meetings never really ended. Instead, after a few hours, they sort of trailed off like smoke. The first-string speakers had left for home and even Afanasyev, who was the radical left's master of ceremonies, was getting ready to leave.

I offered Yurasov a ride home.

"Wait here, just a second," he said when we got to his apartment.

I heard him inside, frantically throwing papers into order. This was a futile effort. He led me to his room, a tiny place with journals and magazines in five-foot stacks on the floor. On the wall there were a few posters of rock stars and a calendar with a photograph of a sexy girl from Brazil who looked as though she had just had three drinks and a bad meal.

"Before we start," Dima said, "you should read this."

He handed me a short stack of letters.

"Respected Dmitri Gennadiyevich!

"My father Afonin, Timofei Stepanovich, lived in the town of Tolmachevo in the Novosibirsk region. As I remember it, he was a member of the local military party committee and was chairman of the farm council. In 1930 he was arrested by the NKVD together with other residents of the village and taken to Novosibirsk. In the court documents of the military intelligence he was judged guilty of Article 58-8-10 and 73-1 of the Russian criminal code and sentenced to be shot. On February 13, 1930, the sentence was carried out. . . ."

There were many such letters in his files: people now in their forties, fifties,

and sixties telling the stories of their parents who had disappeared, the sketchy details of their arrests, the open questions.

Finally, Dima handed me a short note, a testimonial from a woman who had written to him asking if he knew anything at all about her dead father:

"In his catalog, Dima found my father's name. He named the place of his imprisonment and, evidently, his death. Dima showed me that one of the investigators into my father's rehabilitation had said my father was a librarian. Was this some arbitrary thing he did in his camps or his real profession, I don't know. But something changed inside me. From the anonymous gray mass of pea jackets, my father had emerged as a particular man, a special man. Not all were called librarians! A father! I have a father!"

"Now maybe you can see what I do," Dima said, taking back the letters.

Dmitri Yurasov was born in 1964, the year that hard-line forces and Stalinist revivalists in the Kremlin toppled Khrushchev for the heresy of "voluntarism." Next to the Litvinovs, the Yurasovs were an unremarkable family. They lived in a cramped apartment on Leninski Prospekt and worked as midlevel engineers. They read no samizdat and did not care to. Dima's mother, Ludmila, grew up singing paeans to Stalin ("I'm a little girl, I dance and sing,/I've never seen Stalin but I love him so"). She joined the Communist Party, not so much out of an overwhelming sense of conviction but rather as a mark of distinction, a way to advance at work.

Like every other Soviet schoolboy, like Pavel Litvinov, Dima grew up outside of history and deep within the mythologies of his time. He was trained from the earliest age to become a "Soviet man." This was a matter of policy, one that had altered very little since Stalin's death. "The Communist Party of the Soviet Union proceeds, and has always proceeded, from the premise that the formation of the New Man is the most important component of the entire task of Communist construction," said Mikhail Suslov, one of the leaders of the plot to overthrow Khrushchev and Brezhnev's ideologist. In their first year of medical school, students were informed that there were two species of human beings: *Homo sapiens* and *Homo sovieticus.* As a schoolboy, Dima sat through his lessons in the latter. He learned to read using primers that substituted "Grandpa Ilyich" Lenin for Dick and Jane. His history lessons were a litany of garlanded triumphs beginning with the revolution and ending with record harvests in the Black Earth Zone. Summers, Dima went to Young Pioneers camp, outposts that taught the virtues of military discipline and the supremacy of the group over the individual.

But Dima Yurasov also had a young mind that was somehow, innocently,

subversive. Even in the fifth and sixth grade, he read constantly in the sixteen-volume *Soviet Historical Encyclopedia,* books written by Party historians and ideologists and approved by a hierarchy of censors. There were approved articles on the Revolution, the Civil War, the Great Patriotic War—each one an instruction in the pseudo-theology that the study of history had become decades before. On rare occasions, evidence of the thaw under Khrushchev washed up on the page. The censors, it turned out, could not catch everything. One day when he was eleven years old, Dima was reading about a scholar who had been, the encyclopedia said, "illegally repressed and rehabilitated after his death." Dima had never seen such a phrase. It was as strange to him as a sentence of Burmese.

Dima asked his mother for an explanation. She brushed it off. This was nearly two decades after Khrushchev's secret speech denouncing the crimes of the Stalin era, and yet the atmosphere of neo-Stalinism was so pervasive that ordinary people, even in the relatively sophisticated city of Moscow, were not prepared to talk to their children about the nightmares of the past. They themselves knew so little about it. Khrushchev's speech, after all, had never been published in the Soviet Union, and much of the literature that came out during the thaw period had been pulled from library shelves.

And so Dima set out to learn history on his own. He went slowly through the volumes of the *Great Soviet Encyclopedia* and wrote down the names of all those generals and politicians and artists who had died in 1937, 1938, 1939, 1940, the years of the Great Terror. The cause of death was almost never listed. For each name, Dima set up an index card and filled out the most rudimentary information. It was a game, a mystery. "A little like stamp collecting," he said. "Like the way kids imagine they've gone to Yemen or the Sudan when they've found the stamp. It was a sense of connection to something I had only the vaguest ideas about. And what was strangest, I couldn't really talk to anyone about it."

During the day, Dima was a good enough student and excelled in history as it was taught. He could recite with ease the mythology of the country he lived in. He was obedient and enjoyed the teachers' praise that his good memory won for him. In the evenings and weekends, Dima filled out his cards with the names of the disappeared. He had little idea what to make of this strange phenomenon, but his catalog of the disappeared continued to grow.

"Then there was this breakthrough," he said. "While I was in the eighth grade, I read in the papers the minutes of the Twenty-second Party Congress," where Khrushchev gave more body and detail to his denunciation of the Stalinist terror. "When that happened, the game changed. It wasn't a game. At first it was just these strange names that seemed to disappear at a

certain point in history. Then it became a matter of their fates. It was becoming more obvious to me what had happened to these people."

In high school, Dima signed up for the history Olympiad, an academic contest sponsored by the Young Communist League. "A lot of the questions were on the order of 'Who was the first boy to join the YCL?' and 'How many medals and honors did he win?' Stuff like that. But there were questions that went a little deeper. I decided to win." He went to study at the Central State Archive of the October Revolution. Dima met one of the directors there and asked about a few issues related to the contest. He had also brought along his stack of index cards, a stack that was growing by the hundreds as he made his way through the encyclopedias. He was hoping for more information.

"What do you want to know?" asked the director.

"I want to know whether these people were 'repressed' or killed," Dima said.

The woman lowered her eyes. Her voice dropped nearly to a whisper. "We'll answer questions about the Komsomol," she said, "but we needn't talk of these people you are talking about. It is unnecessary."

The woman was in her mid-forties and not at all cruel in what she said or how she said it. Instead, it seemed to Dima that she knew only that these were forbidden things and must not be spoken of. She was terrified.

When Dima was seventeen, he decided to apply for both work and study at the Historical Archives Institute. His mother was baffled and wondered why he didn't try for a more prestigious place. Dima said very little. He kept his passion well hidden, not so much because he enjoyed the secret but rather because he was no longer a boy; he knew how dangerous his interest could be for those around him.

To win a post at the institute, Dima had to take an entrance exam. Around that time he had read in samizdat Solzhenitsyn's essay "Live Not by the Lie." The essay recognized the difficulty, even the impossibility, of outright rebellion in a totalitarian state; instead, it implored the reader at least to refuse cooperation in the lies of the state. Better not to be a journalist than to write the lies of *Pravda.* Better not to teach history at all than to read *The Short Course* to young minds. Preserve yourself even if you cannot save the world.

But at his entrance exam, Dima found himself writing an essay that extolled the sham autobiography of Leonid Brezhnev, *The Little Land,* which was filled with heroic exploits that had never actually taken place. Brezhnev never even wrote the book, and yet he rewarded himself with the year's top literary prize, a spectacle not unlike Ronald Reagan awarding himself the Pulitzer Prize for his own ghost-written book. "What can I say? I was one more Soviet person who faced a choice and humiliated himself," Dima said. "And you know what? I got a top grade. How wonderful."

Dima's job at the institute was mainly clerical: organizing boxes of documents, counting pages, sorting files. But it was paradise. Alone in a closed room, he had enough time to comb through secret documents and copy out as much information as time allowed on his file cards. Once, when all his fellow workers in the department went out to cash their weekly paychecks, he stayed behind and scanned the files of the NKVD for 1935. He shuddered remembering the stark sight of those papers: one execution after another.

"Sometimes they would send me to the basement to find a file and I'd take five minutes to find it and twenty to copy it out. I tried to copy at least one hundred files every day. It all proved to me very soon that the *Great Soviet Encyclopedia* was a multivolume lie. The documents testified that people were tortured, that their tongues were burned with cigarettes, people were forced to stand sixty hours in a row just facing a wall. Prisoners were beaten so badly that they had to be carried to the firing squad. There were descriptions of the theater director Meyerhold, how he was forced to drink his own urine, how his interrogators broke his left arm and forced him to sign his 'confession' with his right. I remember being in shock when I read about how 208 people were shot down in the Dmitrov Camp for an alleged attempt on the life of Yezhov, who was on an inspection trip to the camp. There were women, old people. The information was like a nightmare, like being caught in a huge avalanche and it goes on and never stops. But I didn't make the connections. I couldn't hook it all up with ideology, policy. It was all on the level of the raw accumulation of data about this person and that and not much more."

Dima lost paradise when he was drafted into the army. But even during his two years of service, he continued his explorations. He even began writing a novel, "The Brothers Kaganovich." The book was based on a well-known incident in Lazar Kaganovich's life. One day Stalin told Kaganovich that there was evidence against Mikhail, Kaganovich's older brother and the head of the defense industry. Lazar Moiseyevich did not hesitate. "What has to be done must be done," he said. Mikhail Kaganovich was arrested. He killed himself in his jail cell.

Late at night, Dima read parts of his manuscript of "The Brothers Kaganovich" to his buddies. A few days later, he discovered the manuscript was missing from his drawer. His officers had confiscated the papers. The next morning he was accused of "insulting Soviet power," a charge, the officers said, that could lead to a trial and a prison term. Never mind that it had been more than a decade since Kaganovich had been thrown out of the leadership by Khrushchev and reduced to running a concrete factory in the provinces. Never mind that the story of the two brothers was based on fact. These were facts that a young soldier like Private Yurasov had no business knowing. They were, for him, nonfacts. The only way out, the officers said, was to write a letter

admitting guilt and begging forgiveness. The Soviet system's lust for confession had not changed much since the days of the Terror. Dima wrote the letter and considered himself lucky that the incident ended there.

Back in Moscow, it was not easy at first finding a job once more in the archives. The officials at the Historical Archives Institute never actually accused Dima of a crime or wrongdoing, but they had their suspicions. Dima knew he could not go back there and be allowed access to the *spetskhran*—the restricted archives. But friends tipped him off to an opening at the archive of the Supreme Court. Somehow, because the secret police apparatus was never quite as efficient as it seemed, he got the job. It was a trove of information that only the highest officials—and the archive workers—could see. In the basements of the Supreme Court were files on two and a half million criminal cases after 1924. Most of the files had not been touched since the moment they had first been shelved.

"This was it!" Dima said. "These documents were the only proof that a man or a woman had died or lived!"

Dima worked mainly in a room designed to prevent just the sort of research he had in mind. There were four desks crammed into a tiny office all facing one another; that way no one could do anything without three other people seeing. But still, Dima tried. He accumulated names, facts, the fates of thousands of the lost. After eighteen months he had accumulated 100,000 cards and established a standardized form:

1. Last name
2. First name
3. Middle name
4. Year of birth
5. Year of death
6. Nationality
7. Party status
8. Social background
9. Education
10. Last place of work and status before arrest
11. Facts of arrest, repression
12. Facts of rehabilitation

But the workplace system of *stukachi*—informers—finally caught up to Dima. One of the bosses found a book of lists in his desk, and there was a search. Once more, Yurasov's quest to recover the lost names of history was over. He was fired.

CHAPTER 4

THE RETURN OF HISTORY

Dima had good reason to worry. The new Soviet leadership did not come into power with much public daring.

Two months after Mikhail Gorbachev took office in March 1985, he delivered a speech celebrating the fortieth anniversary of the victory over Nazi Germany. There he proclaimed that "the gigantic work at the front and in the rear was led by the Party, its Central Committee, and the State Defense Committee headed by the General Secretary . . . Iosif Vissarionovich Stalin." This passage inspired ringing applause from the members of the Central Committee. In February 1986, Gorbachev told the French newspaper *L'Humanité* that "Stalinism is a concept made up by opponents of Communism and used on a large scale to smear the Soviet Union and socialism as a whole." The Party, Gorbachev assured *L'Humanité,* "had already drawn the proper conclusions from the past." And finally, in a meeting with Soviet writers in June 1986, Gorbachev said, "If we start trying to deal with the past, we'll lose all our energy. It would be like hitting people over the head. And we have to go forward. We'll sort out the past. We'll put everything in its place. But right now we have to direct our energy forward."

Communist Party officials across the country were simply in no mood for full disclosure, even if Gorbachev was. In mid-1987, the local Communist

Party boss in Magadan, a city that was once the gateway to the notorious Kolyma labor camps in the far east, told a group of visiting Western reporters that the issue of the Stalinist purges "does not exist here for us. There is no such question."

"We lived through that period, and this page in history has been turned," the official, Aleksandr Bogdanov, said. "It's not necessary to speak constantly about that." Nearly three million people were killed in Kolyma alone.

Gorbachev, who grew up inside the Party bureaucracy, knew well that to lose completely the support of such dinosaurs as Bogdanov—to say nothing of the dinosaurs of the Central Committee, the KGB, the military, and the police—would have meant an immediate end to his leadership. Years later, the liberal mayor of St. Petersburg, Anatoly Sobchak, wrote, "A totalitarian system leaves behind it a minefield built into both the country's social structure and the individual psychology of its citizens. And mines explode each time the system faces the danger of being dismantled and the country sees the prospect of genuine renewal."

Whether he relished the task or not, Gorbachev was acting as the keeper of the secrets, the chief curator of the Party's criminal history. Just as the Soviet regime combined brutality and the technology of the totalitarian state to leave behind tens of millions of corpses and a perverse social order, it also used the completeness of the state, the pervasiveness of every institution from the kindergartens to the secret police, to put an end to historical inquiry. Stalin was not the first leader to enforce a myth of history, only the most successful. As the scholar Walter Laqueur points out, modern historiography, with its demands of integrity and evidence, is less than two hundred years old. Pariscop Villas of the Incan Empire was perhaps the first of many to assemble an official state history on the order of his dictator. In Russia, Nicholas I not only crushed the uprising of the Decembrists, he also tried, with some success, to expunge the threat to his authority from the history books.

Stalin inherited the tradition of manipulating human memory, and came closest to perfecting it. For the first ten years after the Bolshevik Revolution, there had been a degree of coexistence among historians, a debate between orthodox Marxists and their "bourgeois" opponents. That all came to an end at the first—and last—All-Union Conference of Marxist Historians held in 1928, the same year that Stalin became the unchallenged leader of the Bolshevik state. As the conference made clear, Stalin's consolidation of power gave him absolute control over history. In 1934, the Communist Party Central Committee issued a decree calling for a strict ideological version of history to become doctrine in all textbooks, schools, universities, and institutes. Stalin himself supervised the writing and publication in a run of fifty

million copies of the famous *Short Course,* an angry ideological tract that was, in the words of historian Genrikh Joffe, "like a hammer pounding nails of falsehood into every schoolboy's and schoolgirl's brain." *The Short Course* was a textbook of determinist history with all events leading, necessarily, inexorably, to a glorious conclusion: the rightness and might of the present regime. In such a text, history is free of inner struggles, of ambiguity and choice, of absurdity and tragedy. The Big Lie always has an unfailing internal logic. Opponents are revealed as enemies of the state, slaughter as necessity. All is clear, all is expressed in the language of myth and epithet. Stalin's rivals for power—Bukharin, Trotsky, and the rest—were "White Guard pygmies whose strength was no more than that of a gnat." This was how history—the only history—of the regime was handed down to its subjects. An entire people's understanding of themselves was meant to dwell within this text. To question or defy the dogma was to admit guilt before the criminal code.

After Stalin's death in 1953 and the start of Khrushchev's attacks on the "personality cult," *The Short Course* was no longer the catechism. There was a new text, the revised *History of the Communist Party,* which made sure to play down the titanic role Stalin had assigned himself. A few historians even seized on the thaw as an opportunity to write more open appraisals of the crimes that Khrushchev had only touched upon. Viktor Danilov, for one, went ahead with work on a pioneering study of the collectivization campaign.

But when Brezhnev overthrew Khrushchev in 1964 and slowly began to institute a neo-Stalinist movement, the "gray cardinal" of ideology, Mikhail Suslov, turned his attention to history. The pendulum swung hard once more to dogma. Brezhnev and Suslov appointed Sergei Trapeznikov, a Party historian-apparatchik, as the head of the Central Committee's Department of Science and Educational Establishments, putting him in charge, in effect, of every history textbook and school lesson from Estonia to Sakhalin Island. To make sure the "thaw" had been thoroughly eliminated from historical studies, Trapeznikov banned Danilov's study of collectivization from publication. In the true Stalinist tradition, Trapeznikov saw collectivization as necessary and just. Trapeznikov decided that the glory of collectivization required a responsible historian. He appointed himself.

So complete was the Communist Party's hold over the study of history that nearly all the historical works of any value written in the Soviet Union were by dissidents: Roy Medvedev's Marxist study of Stalin, *Let History Judge;* Mikhail Gefter's essays on Stalinism; and, far greater, Aleksandr Solzhenitsyn's "literary investigation" of the camps in *The Gulag Archipelago.* Medvedev and Gefter, despite their devotion to the Revolution and Lenin, were cast to the margins of Soviet society and put under constant watch by the KGB. Brezhnev's attempt to return to Stalin a measure of his former stature

would not tolerate apostasy. Solzhenitsyn's trespasses were far greater. He exposed the inherent illegitimacy of the regime and every Soviet leader including Lenin. This could not be tolerated. In 1974, Solzhenitsyn became the first man forcibly exiled from the country since Trotsky.

The repression of dissident writing and study was but a small part of the state apparatus that controlled history. Trapeznikov made sure that the Academy of Sciences, the Institute of History, the Institute of Marxism-Leninism, the universities, the journals, and the schools were all free of "other-thinking people." Balts or Uzbeks or Ukrainians could not dare suggest that their histories or cultures were somehow different from Russian and Soviet history. That would undermine the myth of a common Soviet fate and Soviet man. All potentially explosive issues, from Lenin's dissolution of the popularly elected Constituent Assembly just after the Revolution to the invasion of Czechoslovakia in 1968, required a stock fairy tale and a neutralized nonlanguage to prevent even the hint of debate or "other thinking." When it came to the invasion of Afghanistan, for instance, historians wrote of "internationalist duty" and the "invitation" from "socialist brethren"—or they did not write at all.

"Only a fool or an ideologue would even think about making the study of Soviet history his profession," said Sergei Ivanov, the Byzantine scholar. "Anyone with a genuine interest in history and a sense of honesty made sure to stay as far away from the Soviet period as possible. That's why the only hints of criticism you could read in our scholarship were analogies or metaphors, historians writing about the fall of Constantinople or the French Revolution or the rise of fascism and at the same time providing a subtle undertone that maybe a few people would understand. But if you really made Soviet history your field, you were sure to lose—one way or another." Small wonder then that the most effective spokesman, later on, for a radical reform in the study of Soviet history would be Yuri Afanasyev, who had been schooled almost too well in Party politics but whose specialty had been the history of France.

Moscow was home to many scholars of the Soviet period—not only Medvedev and Gefter and Afanasyev, but also professional ideologues, cynics, and liars. I spent an astonishing evening at Moscow State University with the head of the history department, Yuri Kukushkin. For hours, Kukushkin, one of the most celebrated time-servers in his profession, a man with close connections to the Central Committee and unusual access to Western books and Soviet archives, went on about how he had had "absolutely no idea" that Stalin's collectivization campaign had been so "costly." Everything in his voice and manner appealed for sympathy, as if he, too, had somehow been a closet dissident.

"I am afraid if I try to speak about what I feel inside, I will fail," Kukushkin said. "Bitterness prevails. If only one man could do it all. If we had access to the documents. We worked in a situation that was like a chemist assigned to make a discovery, cure a disease, but he is only allowed to use the chemicals assigned to him by the keeper of the laboratory. The truth is, I didn't know anyone who knew the real facts and consciously twisted them."

But for all his righteous desire to do the right thing, Kukushkin still wanted controls, he wanted the "right people" to do the scholarly work. "Of course we need balance in our studies, but now we are pouring nothing but sewage on Lenin's bald head," he said. "I am sure our state will survive this. I'm sure Lenin will, too. But if a people no longer believe in the future, if they can only see darkness in their common past, then they will go into a state of spiritual dystrophy, and I am not sure we can cure this. In order to inspire faith, we have to show not only the filth and the crime and the blood in our history, but also what there was to be proud of. We are a great and mighty state. We repelled foreign assailants. We must be proud of this. As a man and as a historian, I am concerned that we do not annihilate ourselves spiritually."

Courtesy of Trapeznikov, the academies and universities had been stocked with countless Kukushkins. But there were also men and women like Genrikh Joffe, who saw themselves somehow as honest though they knew all too well that the system was too strong, that it mocked their petty attempts to undermine or fool it. Joffe, the author of many books about the February Revolution and the Romanov dynasty, was in his early sixties, "so I was too young to have suffered through the worst, deadly assaults on historians under Stalin." But he did receive the standard Stalinist education, the endless drilling in *The Short Course* by scared and ignorant teachers.

"That was our world, the structure we lived in," he said one afternoon. "There was a slight euphoria in the postwar years, a slight thaw, but in 1949, 1950, they accused me of being a 'preacher of bourgeois ideology.' Whatever that meant. It turned out that two friends of mine—friends!—had stolen a couple of my notebooks. And in my notes on some lecture, I had written in the margin saying, 'They must think we are idiots to believe all this.' Nothing more. Just a private moment of frustration and doubt. Later on, I couldn't find my notebooks and thought I'd probably lost them somewhere. I didn't pay it much mind. But the next time I saw them was when I had to appear at a public meeting in front of one hundred people, students and friends at the university, the Komsomol committee people and all the rest. All my so-called friends were suddenly avoiding me as we walked into the hall. And then, from the podium, the Communist Party secretary pointed at me and cried out, 'Look who sits here before us! Joffe! He thinks you are all idiots!' "

For his sin, Joffe paid a relatively small price. He was sent to teach in the provincial city of Kostroma until after Stalin's death.

Back in Moscow, Joffe worked at the Lenin Library and began working on his books. "There were certain small things you could do to make yourself feel at least a little honest," he said. "One technique was to introduce foreign sources and then make sure you criticized the 'bourgeois falsifiers.' I am not sure now that I am ashamed of that. I did manage to amass a lot of material on the February Revolution. Maybe, if I'm very lucky, some readers might have gotten the sense that there was more to the February Revolution than just being an opening act for the October Revolution. Maybe they got the sense that it was the moment that overthrew the monarchy and flirted with a kind of democracy, however weak. But I doubt it.

"Unfortunately, I compromised too much, and this is hard to bear now. Truthfully, I don't know if the way I negotiated my way through life was a completely conscious choice. I think it was just my nature. By nature I am a man of compromise, not an extremist. I am not a young man, and to live through these changes, this flood of information, is not easy. I sometimes feel guilty for changing my view of history so quickly. But how can it be otherwise? How can one fail to see what's what? Should I ignore it all for some sort of foolish consistency? I remember the historian Eduard Burdzhalov, who had been perhaps the most important historian on the liberal side of things when Khrushchev made his revelations about Stalin in 1956. Before that, Burdzhalov had been an inveterate Stalinist, the editor of *Culture and Life,* which had attacked the Jews, the so-called cosmopolitans. I asked him, 'How was it possible for a Stalinist, a party careerist, to turn around and change so abruptly?' He couldn't answer at first. But then he said, 'If someone has the chance finally to express himself, to speak the truth, why should he miss the opportunity?' "

The return of history first began with Khrushchev's "secret speech" denouncing Stalin in 1956. But the "thaw" was extremely limited and, as it turned out, reversible. Without a full and careful assessment of the past, one that could not be crammed back into the genie's bottle, real reform, much less democratic revolution, was impossible. Dmitri Yurasov and the democrats knew it, and Gorbachev knew it, too. The return of history to the intellectual and political life of the people of the Soviet Union was the foundation of the great changes ahead.

After two years of hesitation and the language of avoidance, Gorbachev used 1987 as his moment to begin what Khrushchev had started. He opened the door to history, and he did it first with a movie, then with a speech on the seventieth anniversary of the October Revolution.

Tengiz Abuladze, a small and elegant man with piercing eyes, lived and made his films in the Georgian capital, Tbilisi. By 1980, he had established his reputation as a filmmaker of extraordinary intelligence with two allegorical works: *Supplication,* which appeared in 1968, and *The Wishing Tree,* in 1977. Meticulous in manner and in his style of work, he spent years thinking and writing, letting his ideas mature, before he shot a single frame.

Unlike the musty cave-apartments of most Moscow intellectuals, Abuladze's airy house in Tbilisi was a fine place "to live and breathe," he said. Over a lunch of Georgian red wine—"Stalin's favorite"—and the local variation of pizza called *khachapuri,* Abuladze talked of how he came to make *Repentance,* a film about the legacy of evil and the moral need—for both nation and individual—to confront the past. Although television and newspapers were the principal means of the glasnost explosion, Abuladze's film was the bridge to the recovery of historical memory. More than any other work of the period—Mikhail Shatrov's historical plays, Anatoly Rybakov's and Vladimir Dudintsev's novels—*Repentance* stunned a people into a state of awareness. The national screenings of *Repentance* in 1987 and 1988 had such a powerful effect that they can be compared to Lenin's "agit-prop" trains that traveled throughout the provinces, bringing with them portable theaters to show propaganda films on the glory of the Bolshevik Revolution. As an artist or theorist, Abuladze might not be on the same level as the greatest of the early Soviet directors, Sergei Eisenstein, Dziga Vertov, and Aleksandr Dovzhenko. But because of its political resonance, *Repentance* was the most important work of subversive art in the country since the publication of *One Day in the Life of Ivan Denisovich* during Khrushchev's "thaw."

Abuladze did not have to travel far to get the spark for *Repentance.* "I got the inspiration from a true story, an incident that took place in a village in western Georgia," he said. "A man who had been sent unjustly to prison was finally released. His entire life had been broken, destroyed. And when he came home, he found the grave of the man who had sent him to jail. One night he went into the graveyard and dug up the coffin. He opened the coffin, took out the corpse, and leaned it up against the wall. This was his act of revenge. He would not let the dead man rest. This awful fact showed us that we could show the tragedy of an entire epoch by using this device. That was the spark for the treatment and then the script."

With his daughter-in-law, Nana Dzhanselidze, Abuladze wrote an eighteen-page treatment and then a script in 1981 about a kind of Every-Dictator, a tyrant named Varlam who destroys one life after another in a time mirror-

ing the late 1930s under Stalin. Varlam, a provincial mayor, promises to build a "paradise on earth" for his people. Instead he ravages them in fits of paranoia and sheer indifference. As an old man, he even tries to shoot down the sun with a pistol.

"The people need a great reality!" Varlam says, echoing the twisted paternalism of Lenin and Stalin. Later, he defends his own paranoia, saying, "Of every three people, four are our enemies! Yes, do not be shocked. One enemy is greater in quantity than one friend!"

Varlam is so ruthless that in one scene he befriends an artist named Sandro and then sends him off to die in the camps, declaring him guilty of "individualism" and friendship with "anarchist poets." Sandro's daughter, haunted for decades by the memory of the martyrdom of her Christlike father, eventually digs up the grave of Varlam and leans the corpse against the wall. She will not forget, and she will not let those around her forget.

The film, which is filled with the sort of allegorical devices and local grotesques common in Fellini, is about the necessity of memory, the need not only to battle tyranny of the present, but also to deal with the insanities of the past. Varlam's son Abel is little better than the father. He temporizes; he repeats the sins of the father. He has no conscience, no memory. And he prosecutes Keti, the daughter of Sandro, the woman who has repeatedly dug up the grave of the tyrant.

Tornike, Abel's son, cannot comprehend the life he has inherited. He rages against his father. In perhaps the most important scene in the film, Tornike confronts Abel, a battle that can be read not only as the conflict of generations, but as the singular struggle of man against power, the struggle of memory against forgetting.

"Did you know all that?" Tornike asks his father.

"All what?" Abel says.

"About Grandpa."

"Grandpa never did anything wrong. Those were complicated times. It is difficult to explain now."

"What do the 'times' have to do with it?"

"Plenty," Abel says, getting angrier. "The situation then was different. It was a question of national survival. We were surrounded by enemies who wanted to crush us. Should we have just patted their heads?"

"Was the artist Sandro Barateli an enemy?" the boy asks.

"He was. Perhaps he was a good artist. But he failed to understand many things. I'm not saying we didn't make any mistakes, but what are a few lives when the well-being of millions is at stake? We had so much to accomplish. Look at it from that perspective."

"So you applied mathematics to human lives, with proportions paramount?" the boy says in disgust.

"Don't be sarcastic," Abel says. "It's time you understood that a public official places the public interest above private considerations."

Tornike's contempt for his father has deepened. "A person is born human," he says, "then he becomes an official."

"Your head is in the clouds," Abel says. "Reality is different. Varlam was guided by the interests of society, and sometimes what happened was not his doing."

"Tell me," says the son, "would he have destroyed the entire world if so ordered?"

At the end of the film, Tornike shoots himself in despair.

—

The year was 1981 and Leonid Brezhnev was general secretary and Eduard Shevardnadze was the most powerful man in Georgia. Abuladze brought the script to Shevardnadze. "Shevardnadze read the script and said we must find a way to do this," Abuladze said. "He told me, 'The year 1937 was in my home, too.' He was a witness to all that happened. His own father was among those arrested. I remember it all, too. I was a child, and though I cannot remember all the specifics, I remember the emotion, the fear. My father was a doctor, and he always had a suitcase ready with some clothes in it. He had nothing to do with politics, but he knew there could be a knock at the door at any time. They made the arrest and you never returned.

"So Shevardnadze told us we must find a way to do something on this topic, by all means. But he said it had to go through Moscow. We went to Rezo Chkheidze, the manager of the film studios, and he told Shevardnadze that there were film programs for the republics and for the entire Soviet Union. For the republican program all we had to do was specify the topic of the film and the name of the director. So we sent a telegram saying, 'Director Tengiz Abuladze wants to make a film on a moral and ethical problem.' That was all. Moscow gave its permission, saying only that the film sounded 'interesting.' Then Shevardnadze had a good piece of advice. He told us, 'The more general you keep it, the better.' And so in a way he was an extra author to the film."

Abuladze made sure that Varlam was not simply a direct analog for Stalin. Varlam, as played by the brilliant Georgian actor Avtandil Makharadze, had a Hitlerian mustache and wore a pince-nez that immediately evoked the image of Stalin's secret police chief, Lavrenty Beria. Abuladze dressed Varlam's guards in medieval armor to deepen the sense of time. Finally, he gave Varlam the last name Aravidze, which is a bit like Kafka's semi-anonymous

K. In Georgian, there is no name Aravidze, but the root of the word, *aravin,* means "no one."

"We wanted even the name to hint at Varlam's being the very image of the totalitarian, the dictator, anywhere or at any time," Abuladze said. "They are all in there: Stalin, of course, but also Khrushchev and Lenin, too. A friend of mine met Molotov before his death and he told Molotov, 'You know, it's a pity that Lenin died so early. If he had lived longer, everything would have been normal.' But Molotov said, 'Why do you say that?' My friend said, 'Because Stalin was a bloodsucker and Lenin was a noble person.' Molotov smiled, and then he said, 'Compared to Lenin, Stalin was a mere lamb.' "

Abuladze shot the film in five months in 1984. But Konstantin Chernenko, a protégé of Brezhnev, was still in power, and so the film simply remained "on the shelf," along with the works of dozens of other filmmakers.

Soon after Chernenko died and Gorbachev came to power in March 1985, Abuladze's old friend Shevardnadze was appointed to a position on the Politburo. The prospects for *Repentance* brightened. In the spring of 1986, Abuladze called Shevardnadze in Moscow and asked him if he could use his influence with Gorbachev to get the film shown in May at a big film festival in the capital. Shevardnadze felt a certain pang of guilt or obligation and met with Gorbachev.

"I owe a lot of people back home and I can't repay them all now," Shevardnadze told Gorbachev. "But there is one debt I must pay no matter what happens, and you can help me."

Shevardnadze arranged a screening of *Repentance* for Gorbachev. When the film was over, Gorbachev, whose grandfathers had both been imprisoned during the Stalin era, gave his approval to release the film.

But a crisis intervened: the nuclear disaster at Chernobyl. The decision had to be put off.

At around the same time, Elem Klimov, a director and the new head of the Filmmakers' Union, set up a "conflict commission" as a way to move some of those many films that had been banned under previous Soviet leaders off the shelf and onto the screen. Klimov realized that the themes of Abuladze's *Repentance* were so explosive that it would require a decision at the highest level. He went to the liberal ideologist of reforms Aleksandr Yakovlev. Yakovlev was astonished by *Repentance* and called Abuladze into his office and revealed his plan. They would "leak" the film, showing it first to limited audiences in carefully selected venues. Then they would slowly increase the number of screenings, creating a certain inevitability about *Repentance.*

As it turned out, the interplay between the screenings of *Repentance* and the timing of major political events was uncanny. In October 1986 there were several showings of the film, mainly for audiences of well-connected intellec-

tuals in Moscow, Tbilisi, and other major cities. Then in January 1987, Gorbachev presided over a breakthrough plenum of the Central Committee at which he gave the clearest indication yet that he was preparing a radical reform of the political and economic systems. Filled with self-confidence now, Gorbachev returned to the public stage a month later, this time telling a gathering of journalists and writers at the Kremlin that the "blank spots" of history must be filled in. "We must not forget names," Gorbachev said. "And it is all the more immoral to forget or pass over in silence large periods in the life of the people. History must be seen for what it is."

Repentance played in thousands of theaters. Millions saw it—including the young man named Dima Yurasov.

After he'd been fired from his job in the archives of the Supreme Court, Yurasov had been working as a laborer, unloading trucks at a printing plant. The film helped raise his spirits. Now it seemed to him that change was no longer an empty promise. Yurasov discovered that he was not alone in his quest to learn more about the past. Groups of Moscow intellectuals, most of them old enough to remember the promise and the collapse of the thaw, began organizing discussion groups and public forums. With the sponsorship of Aleksandr Yakovlev, Yuri Afanasyev was appointed rector of the Historical Archives Institute. Afanasyev quickly launched a public campaign arguing for a radical revision of Soviet history and organized a series of lectures on the Stalin era. He invited scholars and the survivors of the purges to come forward at last and speak.

Yurasov, for his part, began thinking that he might "legalize" the work he had begun long ago in the stacks of the archives. He wanted to show people what he had done so far; he wanted their help to expand his collection of the names of the lost. He started going to these lectures and discussion groups, if only to be closer to people who had lived the life he had been reading about in the archives.

On April 13, 1987, Yurasov went to an "evening of remembrance" at the Central House of Writers. The first few speakers gave guarded talks about the crimes of the past. This was an older generation, one accustomed to using a language that hinted at truth, then retreated. They were trained in the art of euphemism and allegory. Their most direct complaint was about the lack of information.

Dima felt frustrated, stifled. Just before people got ready to leave, he asked for the floor and got it. With the angry, put-upon look of a petulant rock-and-roller, Yurasov described his work. He said he had collected 123,000 file cards of information from his own subterranean research. He said he knew

from experience that there were at least sixteen million files in the archives covering arrests and executions. When he was rummaging in the files, Yurasov told the audience, he had discovered a confidential letter from the chairman of the Supreme Court of the USSR to Khrushchev reporting that between 1953 and 1957, 600,000 people, who had been executed during the Stalin era, had been rehabilitated posthumously. Another 612,500, Yurasov said, were rehabilitated between 1963 and 1967. He described how from 1929 on, all "anti-Soviet" crimes—the general term used during the purges and after—were recorded on a huge index card file in the archives of the Interior Ministry.

"I have statistical material," Yurasov said. "Not complete, of course, but it gives a general idea."

The crowd was astonished, not only by the numbers but by Yurasov's access to them and his precision. One of the evening's main speakers, an older historian, took the microphone after Dima sat down and said the young man clearly "knows much more than I do and, I expect, more than anyone else in the hall. I am very grateful to him."

As the crowd was leaving the hall, one member of the audience asked Yurasov if he really thought his "sincerity" would lead to anything.

"Well," he said, "it will soon become clear whether a perestroika has begun, or whether it's merely words again."

In the summer of 1987, Gorbachev and Aleksandr Yakovlev began drafting a speech on history that would be delivered at a jubilee celebrating the seventieth anniversary of the October Revolution.

This speech would involve one of the most difficult rounds of political and rhetorical maneuvering in Gorbachev's career. To begin with, Gorbachev himself was still convinced of what he called the "rightness of the socialist choice." He continued to see Lenin as his guiding intellectual and historical model. There is absolutely no evidence to suggest that Gorbachev was out to undermine, much less destroy, the basic tenets of ideology or statehood of the Soviet Union. Certainly not in 1987. He also knew well that the Central Committee, the Politburo, and regional Party committees were dominated by men whose careers and very being were based on the persistence of a fossilized view of the world, one that did not challenge too hard the official version of Soviet history: the "necessity" of the brutal collectivization and industrialization campaigns, the "glory" of Stalin's leadership in the war. To keep his hold on power, Gorbachev could begin with only small doses of truth.

In the summer and fall of 1987, the Politburo held numerous sessions on how best to approach the Revolution Day speech. Gorbachev had little

choice but to play a game of strategy and euphemism. The Communist Party was not only the most powerful political constituency in the country, it was the only one. What later became known as the democratic opposition hardly existed. The broad range of pro-reform forces, from the former dissidents like Andrei Sakharov to the early "informal" groups like Democratic Perestroika, all put their hopes in Gorbachev. That was where the power was, and they wanted to keep it that way. Gorbachev faced a Politburo in which the committed reformers were a minority of four: Gorbachev, Yeltsin, Yakovlev, and Eduard Shevardnadze. Hard-liners like Yegor Ligachev and moderate conservatives like Nikolai Ryzhkov were in the clear majority. "It would be foolish to think that the conservatives then were any less conservative than the people who led the August coup," Shevardnadze told me. Every word of the history speech was a potential battle, a political war. Yakovlev told me that when Gorbachev passed around a proposed draft, a majority of the members of the Politburo insisted that Gorbachev not call Stalin "criminal." On that question, Gorbachev exercised his option and overruled his colleagues.

In October, Gorbachev went before the entire Central Committee in a closed plenary session for a trial run of the November speech. Like Khrushchev in 1956, Gorbachev gave specific figures to describe the Stalinist terror: how ten of the thirteen Old Bolshevik revolutionaries who survived until 1937 were purged; how 1,108 of the 1,966 delegates to the 1934 Party Congress and 70 percent of the Central Committee were "eliminated"; how "thousands of Red Army commanders, the flower of the army on the eve of Hitler's aggression," were killed; how the triumphs of the war came in spite of—and not because of—Stalin's leadership. As he recited this bloody litany, Gorbachev noticed a kind of disturbed murmuring in the crowd. Breaking off from his text, he retreated slightly.

"Comrades," he said, "please bear in mind that not everything I have stated here will go into the jubilee speech in detailed form. It will include only general, overall assessments of the complex periods in our history."

Some time before the anniversary and the public speech, Ligachev rang Gorbachev on the phone. Ligachev told me that his and his wife's families had been "wounded" by the Stalinist purges, and, yes, he, too, supported the screenings of *Repentance*. But now he was beginning to fear that a strong speech from the general secretary would "blacken" Soviet history.

"This would mean canceling our entire lives!" Ligachev told Gorbachev in a rage. "We are opening the way for people to spit on our history."

Gorbachev knew his prerogatives, but he also recognized the delicate balance of power. At the end of the Central Committee plenum one of the strongest supporters of reform, Boris Yeltsin, resigned in a fury, accusing

Ligachev of "bullying" and even Gorbachev of creating a "cult of personality" that permitted too little disagreement within the Politburo. Yeltsin's resignation, and the furious, ritual denunciations that followed, made it clear that Gorbachev was operating in a political environment that he would one day compare to a "lake of gasoline." In the coming months, as minutes of the plenum became public, people would learn just how volatile, even vicious, the atmosphere in the Party leadership could be. Even Yakovlev and Shevardnadze felt compelled to join the hard-liners in heaping abuse on Yeltsin. Gorbachev, too, showed little mercy. One day, Yeltsin's bravado would be made to order for the historical moment. One day, the hard-liners would refuse to be manipulated and would launch a counterattack, first political, then military. That would be Yeltsin's moment. But now as Gorbachev tried to manipulate the historical debate, subtlety and compromise were required. Yes, Gorbachev would spit on Stalin—but carefully.

On November 2, 1987, at the Kremlin's Palace of Congresses, Gorbachev delivered his speech to a national television audience and the great relics of the Communist world. Erich Honecker of East Germany, Wojciech Jaruzelski of Poland, Fidel Castro of Cuba, Daniel Ortega of Nicaragua, Milos Jakes of Czechoslovakia, Nicolae Ceauşescu of Romania, Gorbachev's own Central Committee: they were all there to hear what would, and would not, be said about the history of the regime. Soon, all of them would fall to revolution and election—all but Castro—and in large part, the reason was this speech. Bland, hedged, filled with the Communist Party Newspeak imagined by George Orwell and perfected by committees of cowardly men, Gorbachev's speech nevertheless opened the gate. And the lion of history came roaring in.

To read it now, just a few years later, the speech seems like a relic from another world, an ideological incantation in which the descendants of the tyrant pay annual tribute to the past and the rightness of the Party's course.

"Dear Comrades! Esteemed foreign guests! Seven decades separate us from the unforgettable days of October 1917, from those legendary days that became the starting point of a new epoch of human progress and the true history of mankind. October is truly mankind's hour of genius and its morning dawn. . . .

"The year 1917 showed that the choice between socialism and capitalism is the main social alternative of our age and that there is no way to advance in the twentieth century without moving toward a higher form of social organization, to socialism."

Only many paragraphs and rounds of applause later came the hint of real purpose, an almost apologetic break with the tone of ritual celebration.

"If today we look into our history with an occasionally critical gaze," Gorbachev said, "it is only because we want to get a better, a fuller idea of our path into the future."

Gorbachev was in a pathetic patch here, and when he turned explicitly to Stalin, he promised even-handedness, a balanced view. "To stay faithful to historical truth, we have to see both Stalin's indisputable contribution to the struggle for socialism, to the defense of its gains, and the gross political mistakes and the abuses committed by him and his circle, for which our people paid a heavy price and which had grave consequences for society." Gorbachev even paid tribute to the notion of a determinist course of history and the very kind of historical thinking in *The Short Course.* "Looking at history through sober eyes and taking into account the totality of domestic and international realities, there is no avoiding the question: Could a course have been chosen in those conditions other than that put forward by the Party? If we wish to remain true to historic method and to life itself, there can be only one answer: No, it could not."

Only one answer possible! The applause was deafening.

But then came the reason for all this bilge, a moment of candor that Khrushchev in 1956 could only venture in secret. Finally, a Soviet leader had come before the public, before millions watching on television, to speak a few paragraphs of truth:

"It is perfectly obvious that the lack of the proper level of democratization of Soviet society was precisely what made possible both the cult of personality and the violations of the law, arbitrariness, and repressions of the thirties—to be blunt, real crimes based on the abuse of power. Many thousands of members of the Party and nonmembers were subjected to mass repressions. That, comrades, is the bitter truth. Serious damage was done to the cause of socialism and the authority of the Party, and we must speak bluntly about this. This is essential for the final and irreversible assertion of Lenin's ideal of socialism.

"The guilt of Stalin and those close to him before the Party and the people for the mass repressions and lawlessness that were permitted are immense and unforgivable. . . . even now we still encounter attempts to ignore sensitive questions of our history, to hush them up, to pretend that nothing special happened. We cannot agree with this. It would be a neglect of historical truth, disrespect for the memory of those who found themselves innocent victims of lawlessness and arbitrariness."

A few paragraphs submerged in this great stew. As if to save himself, to

avoid going too far, Gorbachev quickly retreated to the tone of celebration and absolute self-confidence.

"Neither the grossest errors nor the deviations from the principles of socialism that were committed could turn our people and our country from the path they embarked upon in 1917. . . .

"The socialist system and the quest and experience which it has tested in practice are of universal human significance. It has offered to the world its answers to the fundamental questions of human life and appropriated its humanist and collectivist values, at the center of which stands the workingman. . . . In October 1917 we departed the old world and irreversibly rejected it. We are traveling to a new world, the world of Communism. We shall never deviate from this path."

And, the transcript tells us, "[prolonged and stormy applause]."

At the time, many historians in the West called the speech a huge disappointment, if not a sellout. But for all the glaring insufficiencies of the speech—its unwillingness to criticize Lenin, its praise of the brutal collectivization campaign—Gorbachev opened the most important discussion of all. Intellectually, politically, and morally, the speech would play a critical role in undermining the Stalinist system of coercion and empire. The Kremlin's reluctant "discovery" in 1989 of the secret protocols to the Molotov-Ribbentrop Pact, which signed over control of the independent Baltic states from Nazi Germany to Moscow, accelerated the liberation of Latvia, Lithuania, and Estonia. A roundtable discussion published in *Pravda* simply arguing the merits of the 1968 invasion of Prague came just as hundreds of thousands of Czechoslovaks were demonstrating in Wenceslas Square. The *Pravda* article confirmed the Kremlin's shifting attitude toward its own past and helped rob the Czech Communist Party of its last shred of "legitimacy." The Polish people would learn the truth about the massacres in the forests of Kalinin, Katyn, and Starobelsk and the origins of their country's subjugation to Moscow. There were dozens of other examples. History, when it returned, was unforgiving.

CHAPTER 5

WIDOWS OF REVOLUTION

Two months after Gorbachev's history speech, my wife, Esther, and I moved from Washington to a two-room apartment on October Square in central Moscow. No. 7 Dobryninskaya Street was a titanic L and had the hulking gravity of Co-op City in the Bronx, but little of its charm. Except for the foreign cars in the parking lot and the armed guards protecting them, the building looked like most others in the city. It was a ruin the day it went up and it was always threatening to come down. Concrete fell away from the walls in chalky little chunks. The elevator slammed shut like a cattle-car door. At $1,200 a month, my masters at *The Washington Post* were paying hundreds of times more in rent than the average Muscovite did for a similar place. This may be counted as the last vestige of state socialism. The Communist Party bureaucracy that ran the building—an agency of harpies and spooks called UPDK—gouged foreigners for hard currency whenever they could. I once asked if I might have a phone line capable of calling abroad, a maneuver that should cost about $15. This would cost $20,000, UPDK replied. So you had to love them for that.

Across the street from us was the city's biggest statue of Lenin, a bronze behemoth that had run the workers' state more than $6 million. It was a glorious thing to see. A mythic wind bulged Lenin's bronze coattails and billowed his trouser legs as he pointed toward the "shining future."

The city was littered with horrific monuments, and each had its own nickname and local following. The husky statue of the poet Mayakovsky was known as "Mr. Big Pants," and the soaring, silver phallus paying tribute to the Soviet space program was known as "The Impotent Man's Dream." But Lenin was ours, our rendezvous, as in "Let's meet near Lenin's left shoe." He was irresistible. Tourists were forever coming to stare up the great man's skirts and take a picture. Nearly four years after we arrived, local engineers were measuring Lenin for destruction. The best strategy, they felt, was to saw him off at the ankles and bring him down with a crane. But that's getting ahead of the story.

The weather when we arrived was filthy: a drizzly cotton-wool sky, muddy snow humped along the curbs. The ancient cars slogged like hippos along the swampy streets, their movement barely perceptible through the fog. The world of Russia moved in slow motion. A light snow or rain would fall and the sidewalks would be iced for days. Just to stay upright, you had to walk with a certain slide and push, your feet never quite leaving the ground. Here and there you would see someone—invariably a block-sized babushka, knees sore and numbed from hours waiting on lines, her nerves frayed with the rub and bump of shopping in stores with nothing in them—suddenly slip fiercely, flipping a couple of feet in the air and landing square on her hip. A fall like that could kill you. Usually it just left black-and-green bruises the size of dessert plates. Soon I had two myself, one for each side, the insignias of arrival.

I had imagined a winter out of David Lean's (not Pasternak's) *Doctor Zhivago,* a CinemaScope vista of whiteness and cold. But real winter was endless and foul, a gray slog that began in late September and ended with the even uglier spectacle of late April, known euphemistically as spring. The melting snow, the dun-colored landscape, the buses so caked in mud that you could not see out the windows, the sudden appearance of defeated-looking weeds, all reminded one Russian friend of "an old whore disrobing." If the sky was blue over Moscow ten or fifteen days between September and May it was a lot. Living without light was like living on another planet, another realm, and by the time we'd been there a year, we both felt like mushrooms, mushy and beige. I once asked a painter I knew why he did not emigrate when his work was starting to sell for thousands of dollars in Europe and America. "For the light," he said.

The rooms were bugged, of course. Not that we ever saw the mikes. But doubting their existence was both stupid and bad form. Stupid, because I didn't want to say anything that would get a Soviet friend in trouble; bad form, because I felt that if our offices did not think we were under "psychological pressure" we might lose the cost-of-living allowance. No successor

would forgive me that. In the bad old days, a foreigner's apartment was pretty much off-limits to ordinary Soviets. Our predecessors, "pre-Gorbachev," would never have dreamed of having Soviet friends over for dinner. The only Soviets you had as guests were people you couldn't stand: low-level officials, shady institutentiks, and hack journalists, all of whom were spooks, or at least extremely cooperative with "the organs." They were safe. But the prospect of having a real friend show his documents to the militiaman stationed at the compound gate was too grim. Now, under Gorbachev, that was gradually changing. Friends now pointed to the chandelier and said, "I hope the microphone is on, because I have something very important I want to say. Gorbachev sucks." Or doesn't suck. Whatever. Fear was slowly on the way out.

—

As a resident of the October Region—a cigar-shaped ward running south along the length of Leninsky Prospekt—I thought it wise to visit the men who ran the place. This was something no reporter would ever have dreamed of doing before. But glasnost, this curious striptease of ideology and language, was now at center stage. With each week another taboo fell to the floor. It hardly mattered that Gorbachev's committee-written speech on history had been an exercise more in evasion than revelation. One day it was all right to know that Stalin was "rude," as Lenin put it in his last testament; then it was all right to know he had slaughtered millions during the collectivization of Ukraine. Gorbachev was also making political performance a form of glasnost. In foreign capitals and Soviet cities, he ordered his limousine to stop, got out on the streets, and worked the crowds. No one had ever seen such a thing: a modern Soviet leader who walked without an aide at each elbow.

"Who is Gorbachev's chief supporter?" the joke went.

"No one. He can stand up all by himself."

The puffy gray men in the lower ranks of the Communist Party, men who had run the cities and towns like feudal princes, were beginning to get the idea that a little contact with the serfs they commanded just might prolong their dominion. And so it was that I was extended a warm welcome to the Regional Communist Party Committee of the October Region.

"Please come by," Mikhail Kubrin, the Party secretary, said over the phone in that extra-casual tone so in vogue in 1988. It was a tone, at once nervous and flip, that wanted you to get the idea that these fellows had been doing nothing but chatting up the constituents since the days of Lenin. Then, as a flourish of confidence, Kubrin said, "Bring a notebook."

I arrived at the October Regional Party Committee, a gray concrete hulk. In the lobby, an old woman with legs wrapped in elastic bandages mopped

the floor with filthy water. She kept missing the same spot, over and over. There was the overpowering smell of disinfectant, bad tobacco, and wet wool. This was the winter smell of Russia indoors, the smell of the woman in front of you on line, the smell of every elevator. Near an abandoned newsstand, dozens of overcoats hung on long rows of pegs, somber and dark, lightly steaming, like nags in a stable.

Suddenly, Kubrin appeared, all smiles and handshakes, a real glasnost man.

"Welcome, Comrade Resident!" he said.

Kubrin led me up a flight of stairs to his office. He was a New Age sort of Soviet leader with a European tie and a good haircut. He was at that middle rank in Moscow where loyal service to the state might bring a trip to the Bulgarian coast in summer. And there, too, was Yuri Laryonov, the head of the municipal government apparatus, a meaty fellow with Gorbachevian rhetoric and a Brezhnevian brow. Laryonov spoke sweetly enough, but his handshake made it clear that he was capable of crushing a Volga sedan or at least a petty bureaucrat when and if the occasion demanded. His face was as worn and gray as steel wool.

We sat down at a huge table of polished blond wood. A secretary, jittery and quick, served tea and cookies all around. She set down a chipped amber bowl filled with the wrapped candies produced down the road by the Red October chocolate factory.

"Well, what is it you would like to know?" Laryonov said, smiling and rolling his candy wrapper into a tight little spear.

"To tell you the truth," I said, "I come as a resident as well as a reporter. I'd love to know why every year you shut off the hot water in the district for a month. A whole month at least. The heat is nothing to write home about, either."

This tack was known at the time as "exploring the limits of glasnost."

Laryonov leaned forward in his chair and smiled the smile of a hungry cheetah spotting a gazelle with a sprained ankle. "I'm glad some of our foreign friends live in our district," he began, "but, sir, if you write a lousy article, we'll not only turn off your hot water, we'll turn off your lights and turn your sewage pipes around."

We all laughed, but it was clearly time to change the subject. The talk turned to the trials of running a city district of 230,000 people, forty-four schools, eleven technical colleges, the Academy of Sciences, the Gubkin Institute of Oil and Gas, the Red Proletariat machine-tool factory. To say nothing of the chocolate plant. Like every politician I have ever known, the men of the October Region wanted you to feel sorry for them, to feel for a moment their terrible burden. And for the next hour or so, the two of them,

Laryonov and Kuprin, whined about their common plight. For the first time, people were calling them on the phone and complaining about the garbage pickups that never came, the ten-year waiting lists for a phone, the fifteen-year waiting list for an apartment. There was a couple, divorced for more than five years, calling to say that they were forced to live together in a one-room apartment and if the Party couldn't find them another room somewhere the Party would have "blood on its hands, as if it needs more of it. You pigs. Goodbye."

The two of them, Laryonov and Kubrin, sighed magnificently. I mentioned that there had been a great many articles in the press about the privileges of the party apparatus—the cars, the apartments, the vacation retreats.

This was not the right thing to say, apparently.

"The only privilege we have," Laryonov said angrily, "is working weekends. And the privilege of people calling us on the phone and telling us we are petty bureaucrats. And that is not the worst thing they say!"

"Not the worst," Kubrin said, his head in his hands. "Not the worst thing at all."

—

It was not easy getting the feel for Moscow that winter of our arrival. One freezing morning, Esther and I decided to visit the Kremlin churches. We took the metro to the Lenin Library. As we were coming out of the train, I saw a man with no legs pushing himself along on a dolly cart. What hell it was to live disabled in Moscow: no ramps, elevators that gave out every other day. You hardly saw anyone on crutches or in a wheelchair, though. The state packed most of them off from childhood and stuck them in "internats," dismal homes outside of town. And now this man was wrist-deep in slush, the commuters rushing around him or bumping him with their knees and net shopping bags stuffed with potatoes and beets. His face, angular with a slight gray beard, seemed familiar. I thought I remembered his picture from an old book about the dissident movement.

I badly wanted to write something about the disabled and began to introduce myself. But before I could go on much further, he said, "Help me up these stairs, would you? There is a demonstration in fifteen minutes." As Esther and I helped him, he said he was in fact the man in the book: Yuri Kiselyov, the founder of the Initiative Group for the Defense of the Rights of Invalids.

When we got to the top of the stairs, Kiselyov pointed to the front of the library and a small crowd milling around. "Well, there they are," he said. "The demonstrators. And the rest of them. This should be something to see."

I had no idea what he was talking about. All I could see was some students and passersby, a few buses parked on the street.

"What demonstration?" I said.

Yuri rolled over to a slight young man with a black beard who was passing out a mimeographed newspaper.

"This is Sasha Podrabinek," Yuri said. Podrabinek had been jailed twice for his protests against the regime's use of psychiatric hospitals as prisons. Now he was editing a unique newspaper called *Express-Khronika,* a mimeographed weekly paper filled with short news items: a taxi drivers' strike in Chekhov, an emigration case in Kharkov, a mass rally in Yerevan. It was as if Podrabinek had developed an underground Associated Press in a country that had never had such a thing. All week long, he and his staff took dictation from their far-flung correspondents. On Saturday mornings, when the police were not too much in evidence, Podrabinek passed out his paper on the Arbat and in Pushkin Square.

"You see those people on the top step?" Podrabinek said now. "They're Crimean Tatars. At noon they're going to unroll a banner." It was a strange feeling, as if we had wandered onto a backlot at Universal or MosFilm and we were waiting for the crew to fix the lights before the big scene.

Podrabinek turned to the street.

"Now. See those yellow buses?" he said. "With the tough guys sitting in them? They're all KGB and hired goons. Just before noon they'll come out and try and stop the whole thing."

We were all standing on the library plaza, glancing from one side to the other. I checked my watch. It was 11:58.

The KGB made the first move. An officer in an enormous blue overcoat and black felt boots climbed out of the first bus, three others trailing behind him.

Surrounded now by KGB men, Podrabinek lowered his voice and continued narrating for my education this sidewalk guerrilla theater: "Watch how they circle behind the Tatars. . . . Notice the cameras. . . ."

The lead officer tried to dip his head closer to listen. One of the other agents lifted his lapel to his mouth and started muttering.

"Would you like me to talk a little louder for your microphone?" Podrabinek said.

The agent did not smile. He looked down and spotted Kiselyov on his cart.

"You are anti-Soviet, aren't you?" he said. We all waited for Yuri's answer.

"It's you who are anti-Soviet," he said.

Then the officer pointed to the Tatars waiting for the noon bell on the

library steps. They were just a few of the many thousands who had been deported during the Stalin era, all under the pretense that they had supported Hitler during the war. Stalin wanted to destroy any sort of national movement or feeling in the Soviet Union in his quest to create a "Soviet man." He was prepared to kill him to do it. Gorbachev, for his part, told his comrades on Revolution Day that all this had been a triumph. Multinational harmony had been achieved.

"Why do you bother with them?" the officer asked me, this time using a confiding between-us sort of tone. "It's their problem, not yours."

At noon, the KGB plainclothesmen, goonish young men with strips of orange cloth tied around their sleeves, poured out of the buses. A few started snapping pictures with Instamatics, and one guy panned the scene with a Sony videocamera.

Now the protesters took their cue as well, unfurling a banner that read: "Let Us Go Back to Our Homeland." The officer told them they were in violation of a recent order of the Moscow Communist Party banning demonstrations without authorization.

"They denied us permission," one of the Tatars said.

"Then that's it," the officer said, throwing up his hands and signaling to his charges. The KGB men ripped the banner to shreds. The Tatars did not put up much of a fight as they were led away to the buses.

Meanwhile, another officer demanded our passports and documents and wrote it all down. Then the officers with the cameras took our pictures.

The whole demonstration lasted no more than three minutes. Esther and I tried to flag down a cab with Podrabinek and Kiselyov. We waited a long time and no taxi. After a while one of the KGB officers came up behind us and, sweet as could be, said, "You might have better luck getting a cab on the other side of the street." Then he walked away.

Kiselyov laughed and said, "The KGB want us to think they're just people with a job to do."

The protesters were kicked out of Moscow. Most of them went back to Tashkent, the capital of Uzbekistan, where their families had been shipped in railroad cars in 1944. They were planning another series of demonstrations for the spring.

But for all the demonstrations and local politics in those early days of glasnost, the greatest changes so far were not on the streets, but on the pages of the weeklies *Moscow News* and *Ogonyok,* the thick journals *Novy Mir* and *Znamya,* and in those tentative but startling speeches of Mikhail S. Gorba-

chev. Reading was the thing. Every day, the papers were filled with the ghoulish and the heartbreaking; novels were serialized in the monthly journals after a wait of decades; history and literature were now breaking news. It would be a mistake to think that the outpouring of articles, the publication of long-banned books and poems, was a phenomenon limited to the Moscow and Leningrad intelligentsia. "The truth was that by the time *Zhivago* and Brodsky and all the rest came out, the intellectuals had already read them in samizdat editions," the fiction writer Tatyana Tolstaya told me. For Tolstaya, glasnost meant that she no longer had to hide her foreign books in her ground-floor flat in central Moscow. "Glasnost," she said, "is wonderful for the intelligentsia, but, first and foremost, it is a revolution for the proletariat." What was really incredible in 1988 and 1989 was to ride the subways and see ordinary people reading Pasternak in their sky-blue copies of *Novy Mir* or the latest historical essays in the red-and-white *Znamya.* For a couple of years, stokers, drivers, students, everyone consumed this material with an animal hunger. They read all the time, riding up escalators, walking down the streets, reading as if scared that this would all disappear once more into the censor's black box. A people that had been deprived for so long of all that was best in their language consumed classics on the installment plan: Anna Akhmatova's *Requiem* one week, Andrei Platonov's *Chevengur* the next. So many people would read one copy of *Novy Mir* that they would have to wrap it in a makeshift bookcover to protect it from fraying. Often they used *Pravda,* giving it, at last, a worthy purpose. A few foreigners also had places in that early pantheon, especially the British historian Robert Conquest for his work on the purges and, most of all, George Orwell for his uncanny description of the totalitarian state. "People read *Nineteen Eighty-four* for the first time and they discovered that Orwell, who got his education at Eton and on the streets of colonial Burma, understood the soul, or soullessness, of our society better than anyone else," the philosopher Grigori Pomerants told me.

In the dailies, there were articles on prostitutes, drug addicts, KGB informers, hippies, motorcycle gangs, nudists, mass murderers, rock stars, faith healers, and beauty queens, and all of it was new. No one had ever read anything like it. The weekly *Ogonyok* was publishing startling stuff on the war in Afghanistan by Artyom Borovik, a journalist in his late twenties who used his connections to get to the front. His father, Genrikh, had a more than passing relationship with both the KGB and Gorbachev himself. While his father was working as a "journalist" in New York, Artyom was prepping at the Dalton School. Artyom's English was as good as it gets. He said his models for his reports on the troops in Afghanistan were Michael Herr's

book on Vietnam, *Dispatches,* and Hemingway's journalism from the front. Eventually, he wound up with free-lance assignments from *Life* and an on-air job with *60 Minutes.*

For a reader, the hardest business was dealing with political prose. Until the very end, the prose of the Communist Party and its journalistic organs was clogged with the "Novoyaz"—the Newspeak—formed over dozens of years, great clots of language that had no purpose other than meaninglessness, the putting off of meaning, the softening of meaning. Gorbachev had given his crucial speech on history showing an uncanny ability to go on and on, for paragraphs, in the language of ritual: ". . . unforgettable days of October . . . a new epoch of human progress and the true history of mankind . . . mankind's hour of genius and its morning dawn . . . the rightness of the socialist choice made by October . . . a higher form of social organization . . ." This was language from the Newspeak appendix of Orwell's novel, gobs of pseudo-elevated language that expressed the sentiments of almost no one. Gorbachev was still operating in the hermetic culture of the Communist Party, a world in which the Leader had only to communicate to the members of the Party and, especially, its leaders. To speak directly and honestly to the people about the true state of deterioration in the Soviet Union would have been to risk the fury and revenge of the nomenklatura. The people hardly listened anymore to the old clichés. Who, after all, still believed that a new "epoch of human progress" began in October 1917? Certainly not the farmers of southern Russia humping hay on their backs while their tractors lay rusting in the mud. Who believed this was a "higher form of social organization"? Certainly not the workers and patients at the hospital in Krasnoyarsk, where the head physician said that the only way to get needles was to "scrape the rust" off the old ones and use them again. No, this was the old ritual in which the leadership spoke a dead language—a colorless, lying Latin—and the people spoke the vulgar tongue. The Party language had a ruinous effect on Russian, so much so that when people heard a speech by Sakharov, one of the first things they would comment on—even before the inevitable wisdom of it—was the purity of his Russian. Orwell would have loved that.

In the history speech, Gorbachev was also capable of self-deception. "Comrades," he said, "we justly say that the nationalities issue has been resolved for our country." That sentence alone reflected the Party's most suicidal illusion, that it had truly created a Soviet man, a multinational state in which dozens of nationalisms had all dissolved. Within a year, events in Yerevan, Vilnius, Tallinn, and beyond would prove otherwise. At least in public, Gorbachev seemed to have no idea of where events would lead, no

idea, even, what the general movement of history was. "In October 1917 we departed the old world and irreversibly rejected it," he said. "We are traveling to a new world, the world of Communism. We shall never deviate from this path. [prolonged and stormy applause]"

In retrospect, it appears that the speech was a crucial moment in the intellectual and political history of the empire's decline and fall. But at the time, Gorbachev seemed intent on replacing a clearly odious, untenable official history with a more liberal one, a model that proposed revised catchwords and icons for his stated goal: reforming socialism. Looking at the period after Lenin's death, Gorbachev saw an opportunity lost, a dream betrayed. His rejection of Stalinism and embrace of socialist "alternatives" was the basis of his original vision as well as the long-held hope of an entire generation of party officials and intellectuals who became idealists during the Khrushchev thaw.

These *shestidesyatniki*—"men of the sixties"—were half-brave, half-cynical careerists, living a life-in-waiting for the great reformer to come along and bring Prague Spring to Moscow. While they took few of the risks of the dissidents, the best of them refused to live the lie and found subtle ways of declaring at least a measure of independence from the regime. Some hurt their careers by refusing to join the party. Others joined research institutes or publications in the provinces or Eastern Europe where they could express themselves a bit more freely. They kept something alive within themselves. When Gorbachev took power, he put members of this thaw generation in positions of power. They edited key newspapers and magazines, led influential academic institutes, and even made policy recommendations to the leadership.

For about a year after the speech, Gorbachev was the country's principle historian, and he wanted to control the flow of revelations, keep them within certain bounds. Yuri Afanasyev, the rector of the Historical Archives Institute, soon discovered that while archives on the Stalin era were forthcoming, papers critical of Lenin and other first-generation leaders were not. A popular documentary released in early 1988, *More Light,* made a demon of Stalin but trod lightly around Lenin and the Red Terror. Later, Gorbachev's Party ideologist, a dense character named Vadim Medvedev, told reporters there was no way the Politburo could allow publication of Solzhenitsyn, especially considering the anti-Leninist heresies in *The Gulag Archipelago* and *Lenin in Zurich.*

In its way, Gorbachev's schematic view of the Soviet past was as ideologically driven—though not nearly as pernicious—as the old Party version. To legitimize his plans for a liberalized socialism, Gorbachev and his generation in the Party intelligentsia even created a new set of icons. They emphasized

the "late Lenin" of the less draconian New Economic Policy of the early 1920s; Khrushchev, as the initiator of the anti-Stalinist thaw; Yuri Andropov, as a general secretary of the Party and technocratic reformer who "died too soon"; and, perhaps most of all, Nikolai Bukharin, the relatively flexible Bolshevik ideologist who was executed by Stalin in the purges.

Gorbachev, as general secretary of the Party, had no choice but to find a Lenin of his own. But if Gorbachev intended to appear the humanist Party man, a Soviet Dubček, he could not look to the fury of Lenin's *State and Revolution* or his bloody-minded letters and cables ("We must kill more professors!") after the Bolshevik coup. To highlight a slightly more forgiving spirit in the Leninist canon, Gorbachev's circle leaned on a few late essays such as "On Cooperation" and "Better Fewer, but Better," in which Lenin seemed willing to endorse a less centralized, coercive economic and political system. Gorbachev's Lenin was represented perfectly in the historical plays of Mikhail Shatrov, *Dictator of Conscience* and *Onward, Onward, Onward.* In those plays, Lenin was the infinitely wise and patient revolutionary, humane, willing to change; Lenin as both *Mensch* and *Ubermensch.*

Khrushchev represented good intentions betrayed by political stupidity. He was the bumptious peasant who dared to undercut the Stalin cult but then lost his way in the 1960s with a series of capricious decisions that so upset the conservatives in the Politburo that they overthrew him. Until the moment of the August coup, Gorbachev remained obsessed with the example of Khrushchev, repeating to his aides, as if it were a mantra, that "the most expensive mistakes are political mistakes." He would try to balance forces, stay in the middle, and survive. He would be wiser than Khrushchev and finish the vague, improvisational reform he had begun.

Andropov, the KGB chief before he became general secretary, was important to Gorbachev for two reasons. First, Andropov believed that the first step toward an efficient, working socialism was to eliminate cheating, loafing, and double-dealing in the workplace and the bureaucracy. As a KGB man, he knew just how deep the problem was, and he was prepared to do something about it. In his short reign, Andropov upset the hard-core Brezhnevites by firing the lazy and arresting a few of the corrupt. The second reason was Andropov's unstinting promotion of the career of Mikhail Gorbachev. Andropov greased Gorbachev's graduation from provincial secretary to the Central Committee, and he never stopped campaigning on Gorbachev's behalf. As he was dying of kidney disease at a hospital for the Kremlin elites, Andropov even dictated a testament to be read to the Central Committee asking that his protégé assume his powers in his absence. But, as Andropov's aide Arkady Volsky told me, the party elders made sure that the testament was never revealed at the Central Committee plenum, and another Party

mummy, Konstantin Chernenko, won the post instead. "Kostya will be easier to control than Misha," one of the Politburo members said as he left the room where they had settled the issue.

For Gorbachev, the most meaningful new icon of all was Nikolai Bukharin. While Gorbachev was on vacation and writing his history speech, one of his aides sent him a copy of a biography of Bukharin written by a historian at Princeton University, Stephen Cohen. (There was no Soviet biography of Bukharin at the time; his name was mentioned officially only as a criminal, a backslider.) Cohen's book takes the view that Bukharin represented the road not taken—a more liberal alternative to Stalinist socialism. Such a figure could only be attractive, even an inspiration, to Gorbachev and many other reformers of his age in the party and among the intellectuals. The Bukharin alternative showed that all was not lost, that the line from Marx to Lenin did not lead necessarily to economic failure and genocide—to Stalin. Bukharin had forcefully rejected Stalin's "Genghis Khan" plans and endorsed a far less brutal collectivization, a more mixed economy, and a limited pluralism. He was no democrat, but no butcher, either. His ascent (unlikely as it was) would not have led to a civilized state, necessarily, but it might have saved countless lives. Although he spoke of mass-producing "standardized" socialist intellectuals "as if in a factory," Bukharin was also remembered as the one Party leader willing to protect the poet Osip Mandelstam from the secret police.

In his Revolution Day speech, Gorbachev broadcast what seemed to be a series of mixed signals on Bukharin: "Bukharin and his supporters, in their calculations and theoretical attitudes, effectively underestimated the significance of the time factor in the construction of socialism in the thirties. . . ." Meaning that Stalin was right to enforce an accelerated push to collectivize the farms and build gargantuan industrial plants in the Urals, northern Kazakhstan, and elsewhere.

But then, later in the speech, Gorbachev said, "In this connection it is worth recalling the description of Bukharin given by Lenin: Bukharin is not just a most valuable and major theoretician of the party. He is also legitimately considered to be the favorite of the whole party. But his theoretical outlook can only be regarded with very great doubt as being fully Marxist, for in him there is something of the scholasticist. He has never learned dialectics, and I don't think he has ever fully understood it."

There it was: the breakthrough compliment, appropriately outfitted in Leninist language, and then the ridiculous modification. As if there were more than a dozen men in the Palace of Congresses who had an idea—or gave a damn—what "dialectics" meant.

In a cramped apartment in south Moscow, a woman in her seventies watched the history speech on television. She listened carefully to Gorbachev's every word, and when she heard the word "Bukharin," she edged closer to the set. Anna Larina, who was Bukharin's young wife when he was sentenced to death at the 1938 Moscow show trials, had been waiting a half century for this moment. She hoped for justice. When Gorbachev finished, Larina leaned back, exhausted and feeling let down. Would Bukharin be rehabilitated? There was no clear signal at all.

"I felt like I was back in limbo again," she said.

When I first met her that year, Anna Larina seemed improbably young for a woman whose life spanned nearly all of Soviet history. Her face was deeply lined, her hair a gray nimbus, but she moved easily and her eyes had the shine of polished stone. In pictures from the 1930s, she was stunning. She poured out the tea and served a plate of biscuits as she ruffled through the old photographs.

"I grew up among professional revolutionaries," she said, showing me a picture of her father, Yuri Larin, a close comrade of all the Old Bolsheviks. "Life was very intense and they all believed in their own saintly ideals. I'd even say they were fanatics. That's what brought them to their deaths." When she was a child, Larina's father was sick, so weak he could not lift a phone receiver, and so the old revolutionary received Lenin, Bukharin, Stalin, and other Bolshevik leaders in his rooms at the Metropole Hotel. Little Anna met them all.

"Of course, I saw Lenin when I was a little girl," she said. "There was one episode when Bukharin and Lenin were both in my father's room. After Nikolai Ivanovich left the room, Lenin said that Bukharin was the golden boy of the Revolution. I didn't know what this meant and said, 'No, no, he's not made of gold, he's alive!' "

What seemed so strange to me was how Larina remembered those years as an intimate arrangement, the way one might remember childhood Thanksgivings. When Larina was ten, she watched Bukharin and the rest weeping at Lenin's funeral. She remembered standing in the Hall of Columns, near the coffin and Lenin's sisters, across from all the makers of the Revolution. Outside it was incredibly cold. There were fires burning on the streets, funeral marches everywhere, huge crowds coming to see Lenin.

Larina and her family lived in room 205 of the Metropole. Bukharin lived just upstairs. By the time she was sixteen and Bukharin was forty-two, she had a terrific crush on him. One day she wrote Bukharin a love letter finally confessing her feelings. As she climbed the stairs to slip the letter under

Bukharin's door, she saw Stalin's boots ahead of her. He was clearly headed for Bukharin's room. She gave Stalin the letter and asked him to deliver it; for a moment, at least, one of the great murderers of the twentieth century played mailman for a young girl in love.

For three years, Bukharin saw Anna all the time but worried that she was too young, that to marry her would ruin her life. Anna had her father's blessing: "Ten years with Nikolai Ivanovich would be more interesting than a lifetime with anyone else."

Anna never got ten years. She married Bukharin, and they lived in the Kremlin in an apartment that Stalin had abandoned after his wife committed suicide. Bukharin soon admitted to his bride that for the past few years he had considered Stalin a monster bent on destroying the Party of Lenin and ruling through sheer force of terror and personality. Though she had grown up around Stalin, Anna now tried to keep her distance from him. She remembered hearing how one day Bukharin had taken a stroll with Stalin's wife and Stalin hid in the bushes, watching the two of them. Suddenly, he darted into the clear, screaming, "I'll kill you!"

For years, Stalin kept Bukharin off-balance, as he did everyone else in the Party hierarchy. Many of the major Bolsheviks opposed Stalin, but never quite at the same time. At a Party meeting in the late 1920s, Stalin said, "You demand the blood of Bukharin? Well, you shall not get it." Then, in 1935, Stalin once more pledged his friendship to Bukharin at a banquet. Raising a glass, he said, "Let's all drink to Nikolai Ivanovich."

"It was strange," Larina said. "As late as 1936, it looked as if Bukharin's position was more stable. He was appointed editor of *Izvestia,* he was on the constitutional commission, and it even looked as if there could be a democratization process going on in the country. But Stalin played his chess game very cleverly. Bukharin figured that Stalin might kill him politically—that was fine, but Nikolai Ivanovich figured he was a talented man and he would survive. Or so he thought. He thought he could work as a biologist. It didn't scare him." Perhaps the only one who anticipated Bukharin's fall was a fortune-teller in 1918 in Berlin who told him, "You will one day be executed in your own country."

It was increasingly clear by the end of 1936 that Stalin was about to wage a mass purge against his enemies, a campaign that would wipe out millions of political rivals (real and imagined), military leaders, and ordinary people. Bukharin's illusions about his own survival dissolved. After a Party meeting at which it became evident that his arrest was imminent, Bukharin sat at his desk and wrote a letter, eight paragraphs long, and brought it to his wife.

"He read it to me very quietly. We knew the rooms were bugged," Larina said. "I had to repeat the words back to him and to learn it by heart, because

he was afraid that if the letter was found during a search, I would be hurt. He couldn't imagine that they would persecute me all the same."

With tears in his eyes, Bukharin dropped to his knees and begged Larina not to forget his appeal. Read today, it gives an eerie sense that it was addressed directly to Mikhail Gorbachev:

"I am leaving life. I bow my head, but not before the proletarian scythe, which is properly merciless but also chaste. I am helpless, instead, before an infernal machine that seems to use medieval methods, yet possesses gigantic power. In these days, perhaps the last of my life, I am confident that sooner or later the filter of history will inevitably sweep the filth from my head. . . . I ask a new young and honest generation of Party leaders to read my letter at a Party plenum, to exonerate me. . . . Know, comrades, that on this banner, which you will be carrying in the victorious march to Communism, is also a drop of my blood."

Larina was terrified as she listened, but she memorized the letter and never forgot it.

Bukharin's trial was an exercise in the surreal. The Central Committee had already condemned him thirteen months before with a simple instruction: "Arrest, try, shoot." Stalin's lead prosecutor in the purge trials, Andrei Vyshinsky, compared Bukharin to Judas Iscariot and Al Capone, a "cross between a fox and a pig," and accused him of leading a bloc against Stalin, of working as a foreign agent, of organizing a plot to murder Lenin. "The weed and the thistle will grow on the graves of these execrable traitors," Vyshinsky said in the courtroom. "But on us and our happy country, our glorious sun will continue to shed its serene light. Guided by our Beloved Leader and Master, Great Stalin, we will go forward to Communism along a path that has been cleansed of the sordid remnants of the past."

Larina could not attend the trial. She had been arrested as a "wife of an enemy of the people" and sent off to Astrakhan, the start of a twenty-year odyssey of prisons and exile all over Russia. The Bukharin's thirteen-month-old son, Yuri, was put in the care of relatives. It was the last time Anna saw Yuri as a child. And as for Bukharin, Anna knew he was dead from the day he was arrested.

In court, Bukharin played an astonishing linguistic and moral game with Vyshinsky, admitting to generalities but denying every specific trespass. Bukharin at once confessed and conducted his own countertrial of the Stalinist regime, all in the accustomed Party language of indirection and euphemism. Fitzroy MacLean, then in the British embassy, attended the trial, and believed then that Bukharin meant his general confession as a "last service" to the party. The same assumption is the basis for Arthur Koestler's novel

Darkness at Noon. Cohen, however, makes the case that Bukharin confessed to the general charges to save his wife and child but made it clear to everyone in his testimony that he was not guilty at all.

While Larina sat in a cell in Astrakhan, MacLean observed the drama from the Hall of Columns: "On the evening of March 12, Bukharin rose to speak for the last time. Once more, by sheer force of personality and intellect, he compelled attention. Staring up at him, row upon row, smug, self-satisfied and hostile, sat the new generation of Communists, revolutionaries no longer in the old sense, but worshipers of the established order, deeply suspicious of dangerous thoughts. . . . Standing there, frail and defiant, was the last survivor of a vanished race, of the men who had made the revolution, who had fought and toiled all their lives for an ideal, and who now, rather than betray it, were letting themselves be crushed by their own creation."

Bukharin was sentenced to die after a six-hour "deliberation" at 4:30 A.M., March 13, 1938. According to the death certificate, the date of execution was March 15, 1938. No place or cause of death was given on the document.

In her apartment, fifty years later, Larina's eyes filled with tears as she talked about those hellish days. She had no idea how her husband died or where he was buried, but it was probably safe to say that, like so many victims of the purge in Moscow, he was shot in the Lubyanka prison and cremated at the Donskoi Monastery.

From prison, Anna wrote a letter to Stalin: "Iosif Vissarionovich, Through the thick walls of this prison, I look you straight in the eyes. I don't believe in this fantastical trial. Why did you kill Nikolai Ivanovich? I cannot understand it." The letter may never have reached Stalin. Larina's wardens told her she would be set free if she would denounce Bukharin. She refused. She spent eight years in prison and was in internal exile until the late 1950s, well after the rise of Khrushchev. For years she lived adjacent to a Siberian pig farm.

When the authorities finally agreed to let her son visit her in exile, Yuri was already twenty years old and had never been told who his father was. Anna and Yuri arranged to meet on a railway platform near the Siberian village of Tisul. On the platform that morning, Larina looked all around for a face she could recognize, a sign of her own face, of Bukharin's. But Yuri recognized her first. Only seconds after they embraced, he wanted to know who his father had been.

"I put the answer off one day after another," Anna told me, smiling now. "Then he said, 'I'll try to guess, and you just say yes or no.' "

Yuri's grandparents had already told him he was the son of a revolutionary leader. But who? Trotsky? Radek? Kamenev? Zinoviev? When he finally guessed Bukharin, Larina said, simply, "That's it."

"I told Yuri he couldn't spread this news around," Anna said. "When necessary, he told his friends that his father had been a professor."

While she was in jail, Anna had never dared write down her husband's last testament. Instead, she lay awake at night in her cell reciting it "like a prayer." But by the time she returned home—weak and sick from tuberculosis—Khrushchev had delivered his speech denouncing the Stalinist "cult of personality." At last, she wrote down the testament. "Finally," she said, "I had to get rid of this burden."

Larina lived in Moscow with her mother, who herself had been in prison and was now very sick, and Yuri, who was suffering from a life-threatening tumor. They all lived on Anna's tiny pension. "Despite my sufferings and the camps, I always thought we would live through this, that this terrible business was just something on the surface and the real thing, socialism, would prevail in the end. I always felt that Bolshevism had been liquidated by one person, Stalin."

Larina tried to win rehabilitation for her husband under Khrushchev. Years later, dictating his memoirs in retirement, Khrushchev said that he regretted rejecting the application. In the late 1960s and 1970s, Bukharin became a kind of banner for relatively liberal Communist parties in Europe, especially in Italy. But in Moscow, Brezhnev and his neo-Stalinist ideologists held out no hope. Once more, Anna Larina would have to wait.

—

On February 5, 1988, the foreign ministry announced that the evidence for the 1938 purge trials had been "gathered illegally" and the "facts had been falsified." Bukharin and nineteen other Bolshevik leaders were rehabilitated. The Party was immensely proud of itself. "I do think we are witnessing a grand and noble deed," said Gennadi Gerasimov, the spokesman who made the announcement at the foreign ministry press center.

This was front-page news around the world, and for good reason. Bukharin's rehabilitation was not so much an act of kindness or justice as it was a theoretical justification for the reformist principles of Gorbachev's perestroika. Trotsky, with his call for "world revolution," provided nothing of the kind, and to the day of the regime's collapse, Trotsky was never officially rehabilitated.

Bukharin's name, which once carried with it the awful ring of "Nicholas II" or "Hitler" in official Soviet history books, was now glorified. Bukharin's essays and Cohen's biography were published officially. Anna Larina emerged from obscurity with a series of interviews to the press and appearances at "Bukharin evenings." One afternoon at the Museum of the Revolution on Gorky Street, I saw Larina and Cohen walking together through the

latest exhibit: the world of Nikolai Bukharin. The rooms were filled with Bukharin's papers, his mementos, even his watercolors.

"I believed," Larina said. "I believed. I wrote letter after letter. I kept going. But I was never sure that this would happen in my lifetime. Nikolai Ivanovich suffered so much because he thought that he had destroyed my life. It was awful for him. He loved me so."

CHAPTER 6

NINOTCHKA

The season of Anna Larina's euphoria turned quickly into the season of a coup. Not a coup with soldiers and tanks. That would wait. This was a quiet counterrevolution that the public hardly noticed, a struggle at the highest level of the Communist Party over the most vital questions of ideology and history. The only visible evidence of the coup was scraps of paper: a very dull play about Lenin, a pair of conflicting newspaper articles. But if this "silent coup" had succeeded, the drive for reform could have been stifled once more, perhaps for years. The process was still, as it had been thirty years before during the Khrushchev thaw, reversible.

The conservatives in the Communist Party did not pounce on the high art of the season. Their targets were not Joseph Brodsky's lyrics or Andrei Platonov's prose. They worried more about the transmission of heresy through cartoons, tabloid journalism, television, and dramatization. They worried, in short, about what they still called so lovingly "the masses."

In their January 1988 issue, the editors of the monthly journal *Znamya* published Mikhail Shatrov's play about Lenin and Stalin, *Onward, Onward, Onward.* To a Western ear, *Onward, Onward, Onward* seems yet another example of the classic "Lenin play," a form of staged ideology and glorification that had been described and endorsed by a meeting of the Party Central

Committee as early as 1936. It was a Bolshevik version of the miracle and passion play, a ritualized epic of a savior's arrival, his life and afterlife. In Shatrov's work, as in all such plays, the characters take center stage and give long speeches; they are cardboard.

But now it was clear to the ideologues of the Party, led by Yegor Ligachev, that millions of Russians would see the subtle heresies within Shatrov's version. They would read the play as a total denunciation of Stalin as a destroyer of all that was fine and good in Lenin. They would understand contemporary Soviet life as a tragic failure and the men who ruled them as inheritors of a tyrant's system. They would see the play as an endorsement of the "liberal Lenin," the gentler revolutionary figure who died "too soon." The critical moment in *Onward, Onward, Onward* comes when Rosa Luxemburg steps center stage and reads a letter she wrote from a German prison cell in 1918. She celebrates the Bolshevik Revolution but then predicts disaster ahead:

"Without general elections, without unrestricted freedom of the press and assembly, without a free struggle of opinion, life in every public institution dies out, becomes a mere appearance, and bureaucracy alone remains active. Public life gradually falls asleep; a few dozen extremely energetic and highly idealistic Party leaders direct and govern; among them, in reality, a dozen outstanding leaders rule, and an elite of the working class is summoned to a meeting from time to time to applaud the speeches of the leaders and to adopt unanimously resolutions put to them. In essence this is the rule of the clique, and of course their dictatorship is not the dictatorship of the proletariat but the dictatorship of a handful of politicians. . . . Socialism without political freedom is not socialism. . . . Freedom only for active supporters of the government is not freedom."

When Luxemburg finishes, Shatrov has his Lenin cry out, "Bravo, Rosa!"

An incredible moment. Shatrov had given theatrical shape to the new, approved, Gorbachev-version of things. If only Lenin had lived! A life of tolerance, the shining future! Historically, it was preposterous. While Luxemburg's prophecy could not have been more accurate, Lenin's approval of a Bolshevik Bill of Rights is, and was, pure fantasy. Lenin was a theoretician of state terror. In January 1918, he sent sailors from the Baltic fleet to put down the elected Constitutional Assembly—the Bolsheviks had lost in multiparty elections. And in 1921, Lenin eliminated official opposition, even within the Communist Party. But those were facts, details. They hardly mattered. Interpretation of history had always been politics in the Soviet Union, and Shatrov and Gorbachev bent the facts as long as the narrative had a pleasing conclusion. There was a noble end: to discredit Stalin and Stalinism. Other questions would have to wait.

Shatrov, a man of Gorbachev's generation, not only sympathized politically with the idea of a socialist "alternative," he was related to it by blood. He was five years old in 1937 when his uncle Aleksei Rykov, the former premier, was arrested and later sentenced to death alongside Bukharin. Shatrov's father was also arrested and shot, and twelve years later his mother was jailed as a wife of an "enemy of the people." Because of his own status as son and nephew of discredited Bolsheviks, Shatrov studied at a mining institute rather than at a more prestigious university. When he began writing, it was with a definite political purpose. Using the powerful vehicle of the ritual Lenin play, he would ever so slightly expand the form, drop hints, make rehabilitations and accusations of his own. Like the poet Yevgeny Yevtushenko, Shatrov was vain, at times rather loud about his moments of genuine daring; and like Yevtushenko, he had his privileges and patrons within the Party. Shatrov lived in a vast apartment with antique furniture in the famous House on the Embankment, once a stronghold of the Party elite. His dacha was next door to Pasternak's house in Peredelkino, a village just outside Moscow where the cultural elite spent weekends and summers. But for all his privileges, Shatrov was a figure the gray apparatchiks despised. He was a wooden writer and an unexceptional thinker—next to him, Neil Simon is Euripides—but he had the political skills to make himself a presence, the dramaturge of a threatening new script.

On January 8, at a meeting of Party leaders and newspaper editors, the editor of *Pravda,* Viktor Afanasyev, attacked Shatrov's play, telling Gorbachev that the text was filled with "inaccuracies" that "blackened" Soviet history. Afanasyev, like the majority of the members of the Central Committee, was a relic of the Brezhnev era, a self-proclaimed Marxist philosopher with an aristocratic passion for water skiing. He was not an editor in the Western sense. As editor of the Party daily, Afanasyev was an immensely powerful figure in the Communist hierarchy, a member of the Central Committee who often attended meetings of the Politburo. "Of course, I don't vote," he told me. But on his desk there was a cream-colored phone which provided the ultimate access. There were no buttons or dial on the phone, only the printed word "Gorbachev." "All I do," he said, "is pick it up and I'm connected."

But Gorbachev was clearly not in synch with Viktor Afanasyev. Two days after the meeting, *Pravda* published an attack on Shatrov, excoriating the playwright for "mistakes" and unthinkable "liberties."

On February 1, the letters department of *Sovetskaya Rossiya,* a particularly conservative Party paper, received a letter from a reader named Nina Andreyeva, a chemistry teacher in Leningrad and a Party member of two decades' standing. The letter approved the paper's own negative review of

Shatrov's play and said that an "internal process in this country and abroad" was out to "falsify" the "history of socialism." Andreyeva wrote that the play proved that the author had "turned away from Marxist-Leninist theory" and ignored the "objective laws of history" and the "historic mission of the working class and its role in a party of the revolutionary type."

Sometime in the first week of March, the editor of the paper, Valentin Chikin, came to Vladimir Denisov's office with a small stack of papers. Denisov was the science editor, but lately he had been handling ideology. He had good connections, too. Denisov had spent years working in the Siberian city of Tomsk when Yegor Ligachev was the party secretary there.

"Read this," Chikin said, giving Denisov a photocopy of the original Andreyeva letter. "Let me know your opinion."

Denisov knew Chikin had undoubtedly made up his mind. Chikin was not the sort to care about an underling's opinion.

The letter began with a scathing critique of Shatrov. Nothing unusual on the face of it. *Sovetskaya Rossiya,* which clearly spoke for the most conservative wing of the Communist Party, had been getting many such letters since the publication of *Onward, Onward, Onward* in *Znamya.* But Chikin came clean, according to Denisov's account. He told Denisov that he had been forwarding the letters to Ligachev at the Central Committee's ideology office. One morning, Chikin said, Ligachev called him on the Kremlin's secure phone-line system—the *vertushka*—and said, "Valentin, what are you planning to do with this letter? It must be used in the paper!"

Ligachev, for his part, would deny this. Years later, he made a great show of being honest about his role in what came to be known as the "Andreyeva Affair." Speaking imperiously in the third person, Ligachev lied like a thief. "Okay, I'm ready to answer everything," he told me. "The first thing is, as for the publication of this material, Ligachev had nothing to do with it. . . . Ligachev learned about Nina Andreyeva's article like all readers—from reading *Sovetskaya Rossiya.*"

But not only did Ligachev "advise" Chikin to print the letter, Denisov recounted, he also sent him an annotated copy with certain passages underlined.

Still, the piece needed improvement, sharpening, expansion. Chikin ordered Denisov to go to Leningrad and meet Andreyeva to work further on the letter. On March 8, Denisov called Andreyeva and arranged to meet her the next day. She told him to meet her on a square outside the institute where she taught.

"How will I know you?" he said.

"I'll find you," she said.

On the 9th, Denisov's train pulled into Leningrad station ahead of sched-

ule early in the morning. He was exhausted. Not to worry. Someone had reserved a room for him at the plush Smolenskaya Hotel, the hotel of the Party bosses. It would not have been in the power of an obscure chemistry teacher to make such a reservation. The Central Committee apparatus was on the case and leaving nothing to chance.

Rested now, Denisov came to the square at the appointed hour. Then he heard a voice behind him.

"Are you Denisov?"

"I'm Denisov."

"Then let's go," said Nina Andreyeva.

For the rest of the day, they worked on expanding the ideas in the original letter. Denisov was no great liberal, but he was shocked to discover the depths of Andreyeva's conservatism.

"I'm a Stalinist," she told him in the matter-of-fact way an American might say she was a Democrat.

"Well, what about the Stalinist economic system?" he said. "Hasn't it shown its lack of viability?"

"Just the opposite. The system hasn't had a chance to show its real capabilities."

Denisov decided not to argue. It was going to be Andreyeva's name on the piece, not his, he figured.

The next day, on the 10th, Andreyeva gave Denisov additional material in typescript. He was surprised at how quickly she had come through. He should not have been. Nina Andreyeva was, after a fashion, a woman of letters. Years before she had been thrown out of her institute's Party cell for writing a stream of anonymous letters condemning her colleagues for various ideological shortcomings. More recently, she'd written letters to *Pravda, Sovetskaya Kultura,* and other papers condemning the drift of the Gorbachev line. Just before he left for Moscow, Andreyeva told Denisov, "I trust you and the editors to make whatever changes you think are necessary. *Sovetskaya Rossiya* is not the sort of paper that would meddle with my thoughts." Then she asked whether the piece really would be published.

"I am sure of it," Denisov said. He did not reveal the source of his confidence.

The next morning at the newspaper's offices in Moscow, Chikin said, "Have you brought it?" Chikin seemed as excited as a schoolboy on his birthday.

"I've got it," Denisov said.

"Good. We'll put it in Sunday's paper." That was just two days away, March 13, just as Gorbachev would be preparing to leave for an important

trip to Yugoslavia. Aleksandr Yakovlev, Ligachev's ideological opponent, would be leaving for Mongolia. In Gorbachev's absence, Ligachev was the first among equals in the Politburo. His influence in the Central Committee was, perhaps, even greater. Gorbachev had put Ligachev in charge of personnel, and there were dozens of men in the Central Committee who owed their jobs to Yegor Kuzmich Ligachev.

Chikin himself came up with the headline for the piece: "I Cannot Forsake Principles." With unguarded irony, Andreyeva had used the phrase in her piece. It came from Gorbachev's speech to a Central Committee plenum in 1987: "We must act, led by our Marxist-Leninist principles. Comrades, we can never forsake our principles under any pretext."

At the Saturday-afternoon editorial meeting, Chikin told the staff he'd be putting the Andreyeva piece on page three of the Sunday edition. No one gave it much thought. It was a relatively lazy day at the office, a day to chat, drink tea, and keep the paper moving along. Some of the editors did not bother even to read the proofs. They should have. The text, a full page in the paper, was a complete contradiction of everything Mikhail Gorbachev, Aleksandr Yakovlev, and the liberal intelligentsia had been saying for more than a year. The Andreyeva article, Yakovlev would say later, was "nothing less than a call to arms, a counterrevolution."

"The subject of repressions," Andreyeva wrote, "has been blown out of all proportion in some young people's imagination and overshadows any objective interpretation of the past." Stalin may have made some "mistakes," but who else could have built the country so quickly, prepared it for the great victory against the Nazis? The country, she said, was suffering from "ideological confusion, loss of political bearings, even ideological omnivorousness." Shatrov, of course, came in for scathing criticism for daring to deviate "substantially from the accepted principles of socialist realism."

"They try to make us believe that the country's past was nothing but mistakes and crimes," Andreyeva wrote, "keeping silent about the greatest achievements of the past and the present."

There were also some less-than-subtle anti-Semitic remarks, especially to carve up Trotsky, émigrés, and the intelligentsia. "There is no question that the [Stalin era] was extremely harsh. But we prepared people for labor and defense without destroying their spiritual worlds with masterpieces imported from abroad or with home-grown imitations of mass culture. Imaginary relatives were in no hurry to invite their fellow tribesmen to the 'promised land' turning them into 'refuseniks' of socialism."

The piece ran on Sunday, March 13, and within hours, telegrams of support started pouring into the *Sovetskaya Rossiya* offices from war veter-

ans and local Party offices. Chikin boasted to Denisov that even Gorbachev's own military adviser, Marshal Sergei Akhromeyev, had phoned to say that he "fully supported" the piece.

On the same day, in Ligachev's home city of Tomsk, Shatrov's play had its national stage premier. A great battle for history had begun.

—

On the morning of the 14th, with Gorbachev in the air to Belgrade, Ligachev used his position as ideologist to call a meeting of the leading editors and broadcast agencies. He did not invite the two best-known liberal editors, Yegor Yakovlev of *Moscow News* and Vitaly Korotich of *Ogonyok* magazine. Chikin came back from the meeting at the Kremlin beaming. He told Denisov and other editors that Ligachev had told everyone to read the article by Nina Andreyeva, which "in all respects," Ligachev had said, "is a wonderful document." Ligachev also told the head of the Tass news agency to put out the word to all provincial papers across the country that the leadership "recommended" they reprint the Andreyeva letter. By the by, Ligachev said, he was hoping that the Central Committee would soon pass a resolution "not allowing destabilization in the country."

"I was in Mongolia and Mikhail Sergeyevich was in Yugoslavia," Yakovlev recalled years later on Russian TV. "They phoned me from Moscow that the article had appeared. It was quickly sent to me; my aide telephoned Irkutsk, and they sent it and I read it. Well, my reaction was understandable. . . . I know the ways of the apparatus—and I knew it had been clearly sanctioned. Such an article could not appear without being sanctioned by the leadership, because this was indeed an anti-perestroika manifesto. It was meant to overturn everything that had been conceived in 1985. What especially surprised me was the form in which it was done. . . . It had a firm, sort of Stalinist accusatory form as in the style on the front pages of our old newspapers. In other words, there was a shout of command. You know, if this had been an average article based on this theme, I would not have paid any attention. But this was a harsh bellow of a command: 'Stop! Everything is over!' I returned to Moscow the same day. . . ."

For the next three weeks, as the infighting within the Politburo developed, the liberal intelligentsia fell into a state of despair. *Ogonyok*'s editor, Korotich, half in jest, but only half, told friends he was keeping a packed bag handy in case there was a knock at the door. A few editors went to Aleksandr Yakovlev saying they wanted to respond. Cryptically, Yakovlev told them to wait.

There was really only one instance of outright protest. On March 23, a friend of Shatrov's, the playwright Aleksandr Gelman, stood up at a Party

cell meeting at the Filmmakers' Union and said the neo-Stalinist attack in *Sovetskaya Rossiya* was designed to prolong the current system and its millions of Party bureaucrats. The Party apparatchiks, Gelman said, wanted only a slight tinkering with the system, a moderate, technocratic liberalization instead of a genuine democratization which would redistribute power. Such a liberalization, he said, was merely an "open fist," a kinder, gentler version of business as usual. The Filmmakers' Union, by far the most liberal in Moscow, endorsed Gelman's statement and sent it on to the Central Committee.

Provincial editors, though, understood the Andreyeva letter to be an official change of course, and very few dared ignore it. As Ligachev had hoped, the article ran in papers across the Soviet Union. One signal that the old Communist guard was on Ligachev's side came from as far away as East Berlin. East Germany's version of *Pravda, Neues Deutschland,* published "I Cannot Forsake Principles" in its April 2 edition. The Party apparatus in Moscow also gave signs of waging an underground agitprop campaign. *Moscow News* reported that conservatives were passing out unsigned leaflets, including one called "Information for Reflection" that said that perestroika would lead to "economic disaster and social upheaval and then to the country's enslavement by imperialist states."

"It was a terrifying time," said Yegor Yakovlev, the editor of *Moscow News.* "Absolutely everything we had ever hoped for and dreamed of was on the line."

Lost in all of this was the woman herself.

Nina Aleksandrovna Andreyeva lived on Komintern Street in the Leningrad suburb of Peterhof. All day tour buses roared to and from the czar's summer palace about a mile away. On Komintern Street, though, it was quiet. The shops were empty. The air was still and redolent of gasoline.

I knocked at her door.

Andreyeva opened the door and invited me in. Somehow she did not fit the role of a polemicist, not physically anyway. With her hair swept up in a loaf, her eyes narrow and darting deep within the plump meat of her face, she looked rather more like a head nurse, a starched and angry woman of fifty trying, when the occasion demanded, to be nice. I'd called ahead, but she seemed to have forgotten my last name. I reminded her. Smiling stiffly, she repeated the two syllables, sifting through them for ethnic clues, shifting the accent fore and aft, searching for a nugget of recognition. She was too polite, though, to ask any questions. Finding nothing, she smiled and invited her guest to sit down to tea and a box of candy.

I had decided on the way that it was best not to break with the custom of foreigners visiting Russians. Nina Andreyeva was nothing if not a traditionalist. And so I presented her with a box of German chocolates and a $7 bottle of Bordeaux.

"How lovely," Nina Aleksandrovna said.

She lived in the smallest apartment I had ever seen. There was a minuscule kitchen and, next to it, a room the size of a king-size bed that served as living room, dining room, and bedroom. There were books all over, Party histories and the like, and a huge box of letters. Seven thousand of them, she said, and nearly all in support.

For a while, the discussion buzzed this way and that, confused, frenetic, like a wasp caught between double-paned windows. The train trip from Moscow. The weather. The remarkably low price of books. The train trip again. Finally the talk alighted, somehow, on rock-and-roll.

"Do you like it much?" I asked.

Nina Aleksandrovna's eyes widened just a bit, scandalized. Rock was "mindless rhythms," she said, songs that were "half-animal, indecent imitations of sex." She'd read in the Leningrad magazines about a singer named Yuri Shevchuk. "He sings a song called 'Premonition of a Civil War.' What in God's name is that? I saw this picture of him, showing him dancing, and he's wearing a pair of cutoff jeans and a waistcoat with his belly button showing. Okay, let him do it, but excuse me, everything was unbuttoned so his chest was showing and, down below, his male dignity was protruding! He is dancing with his male thing jutting out in front of all those young girls. How can you talk about purity anymore after that?"

The question seemed to ring in the air, unanswered. Then Nina Aleksandrovna enlarged on her point. "The thing is, we may not need an iron hand, but in any state there must be order," she said, her voice rising to meet the higher theme. "This is not a state we have now, it is like some anarchistic gathering. When there is such a gathering, there is no state, no order, no nothing. A state, above all, means order, order, order."

The labels of public life had long ago become meaningless in the Soviet Union. If Mikhail Gorbachev had been a politician in the late 1920s and had gone around Moscow peddling privatization of farms, democratization of the government and the Communist Party, free markets, and the rest of the pretty-colored bottles in the sales case called perestroika, he would have been branded, with Bukharin, a right-wing deviationist. And then they would have put him up against a wall.

"Now 'right' is left and 'left' is right and no one knows what anything means anymore. Who is who?" Nina Aleksandrovna said. She rolled her eyes like an exasperated teenager.

Her husband, Vladimir Ivanovich Klushin, a whey-faced scholar of "Marxist-Leninist concepts," sat across the small card table, interrupting every so often until his wife resumed her train of thought and cut him off. He tried to put in his two cents on the left-right problem, but she would not hear of it.

"Volodya, quiet. I'll tell it, thank you," she said.

"You see, if Bukharin had been our leader," she went on, "there would have been no Soviet Union today. The Soviet Union would have been destroyed completely during World War II. Bukharin as a personality was fine, a good man. He went skiing with his students in the hills, and anyone could talk with him. But he lacked character and principles. He was for collective farms, but only step by step. He would have dragged it out until the fifties. But if there'd been no collective farms in the beginning of the thirties, then in 1941 we would have been destroyed. Demolished."

And with that, Nina Aleksandrovna smiled queerly and poured out tea and a few tiny glasses of cognac.

Since 1985, she said, the country had been awaiting the results of Gorbachev's reforms. Where were they? "During four years of Lenin, the country succeeded in revolution and won the Civil War and we were saved from foreign invaders. In four years under Stalin, the people rebuffed the Nazi attack and became a part of the vanguard of nations. Approximately the same amount of time was needed to heal the wounds after the war and achieve the prewar levels of production."

And what of perestroika, the "brainchild of the liberal intelligentsia"? Humbug. "The political structure of an antisocialist movement is taking place in the form of democratic unions and popular fronts. The number of ecological disasters is growing. There is a decline in the level of morality. There is a cult of money. The prestige of honest, productive labor has been undermined. We have also aggravated the situation of our socialist brethren. Poland and Hungary are running ahead of us, straight toward the abyss."

It was these feelings of horror, the fearful sense that the country had lost its way and was sprinting hellbent for oblivion, that caused Nina Aleksandrovna Andreyeva to write her famous letter. In her way, she was a defender of "traditional values"—the homey Stalinist verities of collectivization, central authority, the dictatorship of the proletariat. She said she had begun thinking about writing after reading two articles on politics and Afghanistan by Aleksandr Prokhanov in the conservative tabloid *Literaturnaya Rossiya* and the labor paper *Leningradsky Rabochy*. Prokhanov romanticized the Afghan adventure, made it seem like a great imperial quest. She approved, but found them "wanting."

—

Nina Aleksandrovna left me with her husband, tied an apron around her thick waist, and retreated to the kitchen. She prepared an enormous lunch of salads, roast potatoes, vegetables, and meat and only occasionally ducked her head into the sitting room to punctuate her husband's sentences.

While Nina Aleksandrovna cooked, the windows steamed and Vladimir Ivanovich came to life once more. He had been mostly silent in her presence, having learned the price of his wife's celebrity and severity. In her absence he was unbound. As he unleashed a great tirade on the "tremendous value of Stalin," I had the feeling that he was speaking for them both. Where she would temper her comments about Stalin, Vladimir Ivanovich was unapologetic. His lack of fame loosened his tongue.

"What is the younger generation learning from the liberal magazines like *Yunost* and *Ogonyok*? That Stalin was a paranoiac, a sadist, a skirt-chaser, a drinker, a criminal. They try to equate him with Mao Zedong, as if there were no achievements under Stalin.

"As for the repressions, I cannot talk about their scale. Because now people just feel free to present any old figure. Khrushchev, when he was working on the commission about those times, found that eight hundred and seventy thousand were repressed in this country. This is a lot, but it is not a million, not twenty million or fifty million as some people are trying to say it was. Everything now is based on inventions and concoctions.

"Look," Klushin said sternly, "in a struggle there are always victims. But I was at the front in 1943. I knew common soldiers, officers. And they treated Stalin differently. . . . The majority of our farmers and intellectuals respected Stalin. At any holiday, people drank their first drink to the commander in chief, to Stalin. No one was forced to do that.

"My own father was repressed according to Article 58 of the criminal code. So what of it?"

Vladimir Ivanovich told the story of how his father, an engineer, had lost "some kind of state secret or another" during the war. He was sent to a labor camp for ten years. It was harsh punishment for "a slip-up," he conceded, "but, after all, he was to blame for something."

"You," he said, pointing at me with a wagging finger, "you represent a younger generation. Ask your parents who might have fought in the war. During that time, man's life was not as valuable as it is now. In this country, we had war from 1914 to 1917, then again in 1918 to 1921. In wartime, when perhaps a simple punishment is enough, people are executed. This is very cruel . . . but had there not been such cruelty, everyone would have just run around in different directions. Sometimes brutality can be justified."

The lunch was hot, long, and filling. Russian reactionaries, I had been discovering, were fine cooks. Nina Aleksandrovna was exceptional. Considering Leningrad was almost empty of food and the provinces were worse, the lunch was a miracle of shopping and preparation.

As she savored her own meal, Nina Aleksandrovna sat back in a hard chair and talked of her life.

"I was born October 12, 1938, in Leningrad to a simple family," she began. "I was baptized and still remember the church bells at Easter. They elevated you to great heights. But I believe in reality. Religion is just a wonderful fairy tale that while we suffer here, tomorrow will be better. Communism is based on your real actions, on what you have done today.

"My parents were peasants from the Kalinin region of central Russia. In 1929, when the famines started, they escaped to the city. My father, my mother, and my elder brother all joined the ranks of the proletariat. My father had only four years of education and my mother less. My mother's family had been considered middle-class. They had ten children, they had a horse and a rowboat with a little motor. There was a cow, too, but the children were always half-starved.

"At the start of the war, my mother dug trenches in Leningrad. She and one of my sisters worked in a hospital where the wounded soldiers came. I was three years old when I was evacuated from the city with two of my brothers and their school class. Mama left Leningrad on the very last train out of the city. After that, all links with Leningrad were broken.

"My eldest sister went to the front and was killed in 1943 at Donbass. Her husband, a commissar with an antitank battalion, was killed a week after she was. My father was at the Leningrad front, and my eldest brother was also at war.

"My sisters and mother and I lived in a place called Uglich until 1944. It was a communal apartment, twenty-two or twenty-four square meters, that we shared with two other families. There was a table—I always wondered why it wasn't used for firewood—and an empty bed and nothing else. No bowl, no spoon, no glasses. Absolutely zero. We were loyal and kept a 'red corner,' a place for a portrait of Lenin; the same place where Christians used to keep their icons. One day they came and told us that my brother and my father, who had been in the artillery battalion, had been killed at the front.

"In 1953, back in Leningrad, we heard the news that Stalin had died. I was in the sixth or seventh form. It was a time of total mourning. All the children stood in a line as the director spoke to us about Stalin. All the teachers were crying. The deputy master of the school was sobbing so hard she could not

speak. We all stood there, holding back our own tears. It was a gloomy day, a spring day without sun. We put on our coats and went out onto Nevsky Prospekt to the monument of Catherine the Great. Funeral music was playing on all the radios. Everyone was sad, and everyone was thinking about the same question: What will we do now?"

There was a catch in her throat. For a moment, Nina Aleksandrovna could not go on telling the story of her life. Then she raised her head and waved it all off, half angry, half sad. Why continue the story, after all? It seemed that nothing would fulfill Nina Aleksandrovna's hopes. Khrushchev was a failure, a debunker of Stalin. Brezhnev was corrupt and a fool. Now she was living through an age when dissidents were suddenly dominant, legal voices, and Stalin was compared to Hitler on national television. When Nina Aleksandrovna considered it, her eyes narrowed; a stony anger overtook her.

"Stalin is the leader under whose leadership the country built socialism for thirty years," she said. "We were poor, illiterate people shod in slippers. The majority of the peasants were so poor they could hardly exist from harvest to harvest.

"Our media are lying about Stalin now. They are blackening our history and erasing the world of millions of people who were building socialism in terrible conditions. We are saying, 'Look at how awful our lives were.' Well, our lives were hard, but everyone had the belief that we would live better and our children and grandchildren would live better still. People with nothing could achieve something. And now what? Now do we have such trust and faith in the future? I think in the four years of perestroika, they have undermined the trust of working people—I emphasize working people, decent, normal people—because they have spit on our past.

"An unpredictable future cannot be a basis for a normal working existence of the current generation. In the past, a person going to bed at night knew that in the morning he'd go to work and have free medical care—not very skilled care, but free nonetheless. And now we don't even have these guarantees."

We cleared the dishes and took a walk along Komintern Street. The meal had been fine, the talk clear and frank, but by now something had gone very wrong. For a while Nina Aleksandrovna's opinions seemed mainly those of a woman of her particular age and circumstances. She had been poor, she'd lost a brother, her father. She had survived, and all in the name of Stalin. Guarded from real accounts of history, Nina Aleksandrovna made sense to herself, just as so many people had made sense to themselves for so long. But now she was faced with an avalanche of contradictions, an army of "pseudo-

intellectuals" telling her that the history of Bolshevism was a litany of horror, and this she could not, and would not, accept. Although she was merely a tool, a curiosity, in a greater political struggle, Nina Aleksandrovna seemed to think that she herself was the lead crusader of the party, its Saint Joan.

Late afternoon was coming on, the long-shadowed moment in the day. But just before the conversation turned into the timeworn suburban ritual of helping the guest figure out the quickest way back to the city—the electric train? the ferry across the gulf?—Nina Aleksandrovna somehow slid into the subject of Jews. She had not been asked. She knew there were subjects to avoid with a stranger, especially an American journalist. It was as if she had been driving and had suddenly fallen asleep and lost control:

"Switch on Leningrad TV," she said. "If you watch it you see that they are mainly praising Jews, whether you like it or not. They may call the person 'Russian,' but that is only for naive people. If they show a Russian on TV, they'll always find a fool with horrible bug eyes and protruding teeth. A caricature. Then they'll show an artist, a painter, who is supposedly a representative of Russian art. But excuse me, he is not Russian. He is a Jew.

"In our society there are less than one percent Jews. That's just a very few. So then why is the Academy of Sciences in all its branches, all the prestigious professions and posts in culture, music, law—why are they almost all Jews? Look at the essayists and the journalists. Jews, mostly. At our institute, people of all different nationalities defend their theses. But Jews do it illegally. We can see that the work they hand over is a simple dissertation, but they insist that they have made a world-class discovery. And there's nothing in it at all. This is how the department is formed.

"Certain Zionist organizations are carrying out their work here. You have to take that into account. They are clever conspirators. I know that our Leningrad professors—I got this information from someone who is no longer at the institute—they go once a month to the synagogue and give them money on the day they get their salary. This goes on. This is constant mutual aid. In such a way, the Jewish people keep getting into the institute.

"You are not even allowed to say someone is a Jew. You aren't even supposed to pronounce the word! You can say Russian, Ukrainian, so why not Jew? Does it diminish the person? Why hide him behind some other nationality? 'Jew' and 'Zionist' mean different things, but all Zionists are Jews. Life has proved this, and not just to me.

"Among our friends, there are some wonderful Jews. In our society, there are some interesting Jews, clever professors, economists, and they don't accept the political positions now being advertised. Do you understand?"

Of course, I said. I understood.

Nina Aleksandrovna looked around a bit. At first she seemed a bit sur-

prised by her own outburst, and then she gave a quick nod, as if to say, "Well, so I said it. So what?"

We kept walking. In the czar's summer gardens, no one knew Nina Aleksandrovna. They knew her name, perhaps, but not her face. In high heels and a white outfit that made her seem even more the head nurse, she had a proud strut, and her husband kept pace, describing this fountain, that historic bench. At one point the talk was of beauty and then beauty contests in the Soviet Union, a new phenomenon. Nina Aleksandrovna made a face that one would have thought she saved specially for rock-and-roll.

"The most beautiful thing in a woman is her charms and femininity, the richness of her soul, her purity. She must clean and purify a man, to lead and raise him to something higher, to take away from him all that is wild and animal. In the sex act, she must enrich him, raise him above animal desire. These girls, they strip themselves down to their God-knows-what, and wiggle their backsides."

After that, we walked along in silence. What more could be said? This was the woman, I thought, who was the ideologist's ideologist. She was both pawn and theoretician, no more ignorant than her sponsors, just less of a politician. At last, we reached the ferry dock. As I climbed into the boat, Nina Aleksandrovna waved and then turned toward home, her face to the palace of the czars and her back to the West.

—

By the beginning of April, Gorbachev and Yakovlev were beginning to win their battle. Perhaps for the last time, they were able to rely on the key authoritarian principle of the Party—Party discipline—to bring the conservatives to heel. Even though the reformers were in a minority in both the Politburo and the Central Committee, Gorbachev was able to manipulate the situation so that defiance of the general secretary would be impermissible. They still had control over the main party newspaper, *Pravda,* and they began to prepare an article that would make it clear that the "Andreyeva coup" and its sponsors had lost.

"The Politburo spent two days going over this article," Yakovlev said. "All the members of the Politburo had their say and expressed their views. Mikhail Sergeyevich's opening remarks were very harsh—he gave a severe assessment of the article—and as a result, as it always happens with us, with our very high sense of principle and probity, everyone agreed with his view!"

Ligachev recalled that two-day-long session of the Politburo as a "witch-hunt in the spirit of [Stalin]." He said that before the meetings began, several members of the Politburo expressed support for the Andreyeva article, but folded under pressure from Yakovlev and Gorbachev.

Gorbachev's article, as drafted by Yakovlev, denounced those who would "put the brakes" on perestroika or indulge in "nostalgia" for the old order. It ran on page three of *Pravda* on April 5. As they read the text that morning, the liberals in Moscow, from Dima Yurasov to Yuri Afanasyev to Yegor Yakovlev, all breathed a little easier for the first time in three weeks.

"It has proved harder than we had presumed to rid ourselves of old thoughts and actions, but there is no turning back," Yakovlev wrote in the *Pravda* piece. "The [*Sovetskaya Rossiya*] article is dominated by an essentially fatalistic perception of history which is totally removed from a genuinely scientific perception of it, by a tendency to justify everything that has happened in terms of historical necessity. But the cult [of Stalin] was not inevitable. It is alien to the nature of socialism and only became possible because of deviations from fundamental socialist principles."

Just after the affair was over, Gorbachev and Yakovlev pretended it had never happened. When asked about Ligachev, they said that all was well and unanimous in the Politburo. To state otherwise would be to mouth the lies of the Western press and its intelligence organs. But long after, Yakovlev would be more candid. "Did you notice that the article against Nina Andreyeva in *Pravda* didn't even mention her name? That's not by chance," he told me. "It was all part of a process that snowballed. Besides, we knew how the whole thing had been organized, who was behind it, who revised the article, who went to see her in Leningrad. Had it been just some lady named Nina Andreyeva writing an article that somebody published, it would have been different. The article in response did not mention her because it was not addressed to her."

In private, Yakovlev urged Gorbachev once more to reconsider his attitude toward the Communist Party. In December 1985, Yakovlev had written a confidential memo to Gorbachev asking him to consider splitting the Communist Party and then siding with the more liberal faction. After all, the Andreyeva affair had already proved just how deep the splits actually were. There could be no acceleration of change while the dead weight of the Party apparatchiks hung on the shoulders of the reformers. Eventually, Yakovlev insisted, they would have to consider the idea not only of two or three Communist parties but of a true multiparty system.

Sooner or later, Yakovlev knew, the Party would have to break with its own history, or it would collapse entirely. The Party was filled with ministers and apparatchiks who swore their fealty to the general secretary, but they were always prepared to betray him in the name of the System. Years later, in retirement, Gorbachev would admit that even he did not understand fully the "monster" he was trying to transform. "At least Ligachev was out in the open," he would say. There were others who would pretend loyalty and then send tanks into the streets of Moscow.

CHAPTER 7

THE DOCTORS' PLOT AND BEYOND

Sometime between the Andreyeva affair and the start of the Nineteenth Party Conference in June 1988, the anti-Semitic incidents began. In a suburb of Moscow where Jewish intellectuals often rented dachas for the summer, vandals burned one house to the ground and broke into a few others, smashing windows, knocking over furniture, and spray-painting swastikas on the walls. Members of Pamyat and other hate groups toppled Jewish headstones and tacked up handbills signed "Russia for Russians: The Organization of Death to Yids."

Judith Lurye, a longtime refusenik, called me one night and said that she and her friends were terrified. That night they had gone to a hall they'd rented at the Yauza Club for a meeting of their new Jewish cultural organization. When they arrived, the door was padlocked and a pair of KGB officers were on guard. A leaflet was nailed to the door.

"How long can we tolerate the dirty Jews?" it said. "Scoundrel Jews are penetrating our society, especially in places where there are profits to be gotten. Think about it. How can we allow these dirty ones to make a rubbish heap out of our beautiful country? Why do we—the great, intelligent, beautiful Slavs—consider it a normal phenomenon to live with Yids among us? How can these dirty stinking Jews call themselves by such a proud and heroic name as 'Russians'?"

Many of the same Jews who were calling to warn me were also publishing their literary or scientific work for the first time and getting visas to travel abroad. Some were getting permission to emigrate. They had high hopes for perestroika, but they could not let down their psychological guard. A historic dislocation had begun. The economy was in serious decline. If things got much worse, the Jews understood, they would be among the first ones blamed. Far-right intellectuals writing for *Nash Sovremenik* ("Our Contemporary") and *Molodaya Gvardiya* ("Young Guard") were already shaping a fanatic Russian nationalist ideology that made all Jews devils, and all enemies Jews. If they came to despise a Russian, they then wrote that the person in question had obviously changed his name from Goldshtein or Rabinovich.

Igor Shafarevich, a world-renowned mathematician who joined both Sakharov and Solzhenitsyn in the seventies in a number of dissident causes, turned out to be one of the most dangerous of the intellectual anti-Semites. His long essay "Russophobia" proposed that "the Little People"—mainly Jewish writers and émigrés—had ruined the self-respect of "the Big People"—native Russians—by describing them as a nation of slaves who worship power and intolerance. Jews, he wrote, had managed to create an image of themselves as reasonable, cultivated, and European and of Russians as barbaric.

I visited Shafarevich one evening at his apartment on Leninsky Prospekt. He eyed me suspiciously and denied he was an anti-Semite. His enormous hound circled the floor of the study, never stopping. Such accusations, he said, were the result of Jewish "persecution mania."

"There is only one nation whose needs we hear about almost every day," Shafarevich had written in *Nash Sovremenik.* "Jewish national emotions are the fever of the whole country and the whole world. They are a negative influence on disarmament, trade agreements, and international relations of scientists. They provoke demonstrations and strikes and emerge in almost every conversation. The Jewish issue has acquired an incomprehensible power over people's minds and has overshadowed problems of Ukrainians, Estonians, and Crimean Tatars. And as for the Russian issue, that is evidently not to be acknowledged at all."

When I read this passage back to Shafarevich, he nodded in agreement, enthusiastically, as if hearing it for the first time. Then he said, "The term 'anti-Semitism' is like an atom bomb in our heads. Against the background of violence against Armenians or Russians, it is impossible even to speak of anti-Semitism. I haven't heard about a single quarrel or of people being beaten in the face because of anti-Semitism. It is absolutely incompatible with the real problems present now. I am just amazed to hear such things."

Shafarevich was not alone. While many leading Russian writers spoke out

against anti-Semitism, the Russian Writers' Union leadership promoted a nationalist ideology steeped in hatred of Jews. In an open letter signed by seventy-two of its leading members and published in the house organ, *Literaturnaya Rossiya,* the union declared: "It is precisely Zionism that is responsible for many things, including Jewish pogroms, for cutting off dry branches of their own people in Auschwitz and Dachau."

For months, Jewish friends called saying they were convinced that there would soon be pogroms. Not more abuse, not the occasional attack, but pogroms, a word that evoked the memory of massacres of Jews a century ago in Kishinev, Odessa, and Kiev, a word that implied the tacit participation of the state. The Kremlin did nothing to help the situation. The official Tass news agency ran an item saying that Natan Shcharansky, who had spent eight years in the camps on trumped-up charges before he was allowed to leave the Soviet Union for Israel, was now "scrambling back into the news" as an army conscript. "As he was issued his brand-new Israeli uniform, Shcharansky declared pompously that he had finally found his place in life," Tass reported. "Walking on Palestinian corpses is indeed a logical and natural campaign in the life of that sham advocate of human rights."

It was hard to judge what all this amounted to. One of the older leaders of the Jewish community in Moscow told me he had not seen such threatening signs of anti-Semitism in Moscow since Stalin's time.

I had been complacent about all this until the first night of Passover the previous spring. After all, hadn't vandals desecrated Jewish cemeteries at home? Why was this more of a threat? Esther and I went to evening services at the Choral Synagogue, itself a depressing sight. Outside on the steps, KGB goons kept a careful watch on who went in the building. In a way both cloying and threatening, the agent of the evening (dressed in the easily recognizable black plastic topcoat and red-and-brown plaid scarf) asked questions as if he were taking a poll: "Do you believe in almighty God? Have you ever been to Israel?" Usually, a couple of his buddies waited in a car across the street. Inside, on the main floor of pews, where the men prayed, there were only a few dozen ancients gossiping in Yiddish and some curious tourists from New York and Buenos Aires. The young had long since written off the synagogue as an impossible place to meet or pray. The few observant Jews who had not already gone to Israel or the West prayed in their homes. Even those who didn't care much about the KGB presence outside felt the rabbi had been too compromised over the years.

Upstairs, sitting with the women, Esther got into a discussion about Passover rituals and discovered that they knew next to nothing.

"My grandfather used to do all this," one old woman said, casting back her memories to the last century, "but I forget: how many cups of wine must we drink?"

Esther, who was raised in an Orthodox home and knew the language and rituals as second nature, was astonished. She explained as well she could, but it broke her heart to see how desperate they were to know. "Can you really not eat bread on Passover?" another woman said.

We left the services early to get back and prepare the seder at home for a half-dozen Soviet friends. But when we got to the car I noticed that someone had written on the grimy door a huge Y with a circle around it. Y for Yid. If the leaflets and vandalism had not focused my attention, the writing in the dust certainly did.

As it turned out, there would be no pogroms. But the anxiety was real. As the state structures began to disintegrate, so too did the old facade of a "friendship of peoples." The glasnost that had begun to encourage genuine historical debate also, inevitably, revealed the depths of historical resentments and hatred in Stalin's empire. In Tallinn, I heard Estonians describe Russians as cretins and brutes, and Russians describe Estonians as Nazi collaborators. In Yerevan, Armenians were sure that Azerbaijanis had deliberately "set off" the earthquake that killed at least 25,000 people with an underground nuclear test and were about to carry out an Islamic crusade against them more bloody than the Turkish massacre of Armenians in 1915. In Baku, Azerbaijanis knew with absolute certainty that the Yerevan government was preparing to grab all its territory and assert an Armenian kingdom with the help of émigré millionaires in Los Angeles.

For Jews in cities like Leningrad, Moscow, and Novosibirsk, the new street-level face of hatred was the group known as Pamyat, "Memory." Pamyat began in the early 1980s as a group attached to the Aviation Ministry and was organized by a few cultural activists to help preserve Russian monuments and buildings. But after years of expansion, infighting, and splits, the most vocal group still calling itself Pamyat turned out to be a band of anti-Semitic fanatics, a motley bunch of Russian factory workers, Party members, teachers, career military officers, and street thugs. Their feeling for imagery was impeccable and historically resonant. They wore black T-shirts, a symbol that linked them to the Black Hundreds, the anti-Semitic mob that carried off dozens of pogroms under the last czars.

While he was still in the Politburo, Boris Yeltsin met with representatives from Pamyat on the grounds that as Moscow Party secretary he should get to know a broad range of public groups. He went away from the session disgusted. "Pamyat began as something interesting and then turned out evil," he said. He never had anything to do with it again.

I met leaders of Pamyat at various apartments and rallies in Moscow, Leningrad, and Siberia, and they were uniformly, and not surprisingly, supreme dolts. Dmitri Vasiliyev, a former photographer and bit player in the movies, boasted of having only an eighth-grade education, a claim that did not stretch credulity. At one small rally, this doughy little man barked into a megaphone for a couple of hours, berating Zionists and "those who would humiliate the Russian people." He said that Russian children were being turned into alcoholics because "sinister forces" were slipping alcohol into the yogurt supply. Jewish editors were guilty of subliminal conspiracy because they used six-pointed stars in their papers. Jewish architects "by no coincidence" designed Pushkin Square so that Pushkin's back was to the movie theater, the Rossiya. It was unclear whether Vasiliyev was the most dangerous of the Pamyat leaders. His rival Valery Yemelyanov, after all, spent a few years in a mental institution after murdering his wife. He left the institution just in time to enjoy the fruits of the new glasnost.

The clearest and most comprehensive representation of Pamyat's "ideas" I saw was contained in a twenty-four-page manifesto that had been passed along to me. The document was written in a less hysterical tone than Vasiliyev's rants, but, all the same, it attacked the "satanic" cultural influence of the West and a "genocide of the Russian people." Jews and Zionists were responsible for the ills of Russia. Jews, homosexuals, and Masons were responsible for rock music, drug addiction, AIDS, and the dissolution of Russian families. Brodsky's poems, Chagall's paintings, and Pasternak's "antipatriotic" novel *Doctor Zhivago* were all worthless, a blot on "true Russian culture." The Russians, the manifesto said, "saved" the Jews in World War II, but the Jewish media only mocked and degraded Russians and their suffering: "It's as if the mass media told us that only Jews were killed on the front during the war."

Pamyat members circulated copies of the "Protocols of the Elders of Zion" and won support from *Literaturnaya Rossiya, Molodaya Gvardiya,* and other right-wing magazines. In Leningrad, one of the most active centers for Pamyat, the group denounced Isaak Zaltsman, a Jew who headed the production of Soviet tanks during World War II, for organizing "a chorus of sixteen-year-old Russian virgins" and then seducing them. Elsewhere, Pamyat blamed Jews for food shortages, sex on television, and the nuclear accident at Chernobyl.

Compared to what was going on elsewhere in the empire, the real threat to Jewish life was relatively slight. Yet the rise of glasnost, the loosening restric-

tions on emigration, and the atmosphere of tension and fear of an uncertain future all helped to produce the moment that Jews around the world had awaited for many years. An exodus had begun. Soviet Jews who wanted to leave now for Israel, for the most part, could. In 1989, 100,000 Soviet Jews left for Israel and the West. Hundreds of thousands more were waiting for visas, invitations, and tickets. A people that had once seemed destined for oblivion were getting visas for a new life.

There would be no second "Doctors' Plot." In fact, the only living survivor of that ugly affair, Yakov Rapoport, declared he would not join the new wave out. "My time is past," he told me. "I'm ninety-one years old. It's too late for me. I'll be buried here." And yet his story, and his family, seemed an emblem of the history and the future of the Jews of Russia.

Yakov Rapoport, like many Jews of his generation, well understood that the purges of the 1930s were not an aberration of the moment. Cruelty had preceded 1937 and cruelty was sure to follow. Stalin was indulging his hatred of the Jews. In 1948, Stalin ordered the execution of Solomon Mikhoels, the legendary director of the Jewish State Theater and the leader of the Jewish Anti-Fascist Committee as a presumed enemy of the state. After the murder of Mikhoels—called a car accident by the authorities—the KGB arrested the leading members of the Anti-Fascist Committee, citing a "postwar return to normalcy." Almost as a warm-up to the Doctors' Plot and the coming purge, the KGB killed twenty-three Jewish intellectuals in 1952 on trumped-up charges of spying and treason. Then, in the first weeks of 1953, Stalin ordered the arrest of a group of nine prominent doctors, six of them Jewish; the Party papers claimed the doctors were poisoning the Kremlin leaders and covering up the conspiracy. Stalin's murderous paranoia appeared ready to soar once more. Most historians now agree that Stalin's order to arrest the doctors was similar to the Kremlin-ordered assassination of the Leningrad Party chief Sergei Kirov in 1934—a prelude to a wave of mass terror. Khrushchev said as much in his speech at the Twentieth Party Congress in 1956:

"Stalin personally issued advice on the conduct of the investigation and the method of interrogation of the arrested persons. He said that Academician Vinogradov should be put in chains, another one should be beaten. Present at this Congress is the former minister of state security, Comrade Ignatiev. Stalin told him curtly, 'If you do not obtain confessions from the doctors, we will shorten you by a head.'

"Stalin personally called the investigating judge, gave him instructions, advised him on which investigative methods should be used. These methods were simple—beat, beat, and, once again, beat. Shortly after the doctors were arrested, we members of the Politburo received protocols containing the

doctors' confessions of guilt. After distributing these protocols, Stalin told us, 'You are blind like young kittens; what will happen without me? The country will perish because you do not know how to recognize enemies.' "

Of the nine doctors arrested, only Yakov Rapoport lived to see the advent of glasnost. I got to know him, his daughter Natasha, and his granddaughter Vika and visited them several times at Natasha's apartment. The old man was long retired, but his memory was good, his voice as clear as that of a man half his age. "I thought I was finished, a dead man," he said, remembering his despair in prison. "Then one day they let me out of jail—for no reason at all, it seemed. I didn't understand what had happened until I came home and my wife told me that Stalin was dead. It was just dumb luck, for me—and probably for hundreds of thousands of other Jews."

The furious anti-Semitism of the Stalin era and the Doctors' Plot itself were merely two of countless "blank spots" in official versions of Soviet history. The first official publications on the period were Yakov Rapoport's memoir in the magazine *Druzhba Narodov* ("Friendship of Peoples") and Natasha Rapoport's memoir in *Yunost* ("Youth")—both in April 1988. Both father and daughter began writing years before the rise of Gorbachev. But it was only in 1987 that either one thought it might soon be possible to tell the story of the Doctors' Plot. Natasha visited her friends Irina and Yuli Daniel in the country and read them her manuscript. She could not have chosen a better audience. Yuli Daniel, along with Andrei Sinyavsky, had been jailed for seven years in the sixties in one of the very first dissident cases. Daniel's father was Mark Meyerovich, a celebrated Yiddish writer. When Natasha finished reading, Daniel told her it was time to publish.

At Daniel's suggestion, Natasha took her manuscript to *Yunost,* a monthly famous for publishing young talents during Khrushchev's thaw. The new, relatively liberal editors were impressed, but she was told there were "too many Jewish names" in the story, too much explicit discussion of anti-Semitism. Natasha laughed and said, "I told them it reminded me of the joke about the boy who asks his grandfather, 'Is it true Christ was a Jew?' And the grandfather says, 'Yes, it's true. At the time, everyone was a Jew. Such were the times.' Well, during the Doctors' Plot, such were the times." The editors said they would try to publish, but they didn't want to "irritate" the audience. They asked Natasha if she could remember any "good Russian people who had helped" her. The meetings ended vaguely, with no promises, no rejection. The editors had not yet gotten the necessary signal from above, and so they waited.

"Then came November and Gorbachev gave the history speech," Natasha said. "He even mentioned the Doctors' Plot. Two days later there was a telephone call from *Yunost* congratulating me. They had decided to publish.

And then they said, 'Only don't think that it is in any way connected to Gorbachev's speech.' Well, no, of course not! They got Yevtushenko to write the preface. He wrote rather a lot about anti-Semitism, but they cut that, insisting, after all, that Russians, too, had been arrested. There was also a sentence saying that there were rumors of pogroms in 1953, that concentration or labor camps were being prepared to accept Jews after the doctors were executed on Red Square. We fought over that, but what could I do? They cut that, too."

Despite the cuts, the appearance of both Rapoports' memoirs marked the first attack in the press on anti-Semitism. "We took a walk in the forbidden zone," Natasha said.

The generations of Rapoports were tied to one another in an easy, undramatic way. Their stories, even their sentences, elided into a single line of thought and memory. Their family narrative was nothing less than the Jewish experience in the Soviet Union in this century. "There is a whole age behind these eyes," Yakov said, "from Nicholas II to Gorbachev." Natasha smiled and put her hand over her father's knobby wrist.

There was great love between them, but tension as well. "I've wanted to emigrate since the sixties, but my parents refused to go," Natasha said. "They were afraid, and I couldn't persuade them. They decided it was too late for them and that they should die here. My mother is gone now. I cherish her memory and I love my father very much. But still, I cannot forgive them this."

As he listened to this, no doubt for the thousandth time, Yakov Rapoport's left hand trembled slightly. He said nothing, just stared at the teapot and let it pass. He feigned a kind of nonchalance that his hands betrayed. When Natasha began talking about her fears that a worsening economy would provide "openings" for groups like Pamyat, he said bravely, "I've seen this before. I'm not afraid," but his hands shook once more.

It must have seemed to him that little had changed. Weekend mornings sometimes, Yakov Rapoport looked out his apartment window and saw the Pamyat boys in their black T-shirts carrying placards around All Saints Church. "Yids Out!" "Down with the Judeo-Masonic Conspiracy!"

"I have seen this before, too," Yakov said.

Rapoport grew up in the Crimea. His first memory was of a pogrom in 1905. "I was six years old. My father was teaching Russian and mathematics where I went to school. We were having a science lesson when the Cossacks rushed in. The school was destroyed. I remember the globes were smashed, there was broken glass everywhere, and my father was badly injured. The

police brought the bodies to the morgue, and my father along with them because they thought he was dead. One of our friends saw my father there, only by chance, and they could hear him moaning. He was unconscious, covered with blood. His fingers and hands had been broken by the truncheons. He had tried to guard his face, so they just broke the arms. It took months for him to heal.

"This friend of ours tried to drag my father through a gate to a cab. The school principal was there, and he was shouting, 'Go away, you Jew!' When my father finally returned to the school weeks later, the other teachers shunned him. They would not speak to him, and he finally had to leave the school. This is what was first imprinted on my memory as a child."

As a boy, Rapoport was also caught up in reports of the Beilis case in Kiev. For the Jews under the czars, the case had an impact equal to that of the Dreyfus affair in France. In 1911, police in Kiev found the corpse of a thirteen-year-old Russian boy. His mother, a poor prostitute, accused "the Jews"—that scheming mass—of murdering her son to use his blood to make Passover matzoh. The "Blood Accusation" was rooted in anti-Semitic folklore in Ukraine—and was, of course, preposterous. Nevertheless, the czarist police arrested a Jewish factory worker, Mendel Beilis, and thought they were sure to win a conviction. With the world press watching, the prosecution brought in witnesses to testify that such ritual murders were widespread. "It was an accusation against all Jews, not just Beilis," Rapoport said. "In our school, about half the class believed the accusations, and half did not." But the jury, made up mostly of illiterate Ukrainian peasants, rejected the Blood Libel and set Beilis free.

"It was a great miracle," Rapoport said. "One of the jurors was asked why he had voted for acquittal, and he answered, simply, 'My conscience.' I found out later that those peasants in the jury were seen praying before they brought in the verdict. So religion, at least in this case, was a carrier of conscience."

From one year to the next in Rapoport's life, there were attacks on the Jews in schools and in the courts. There were always pogroms and the threat of pogroms. Discrimination, life-threatening and petty, touched every facet of ordinary life. Jewish students like Rapoport even paid extra fees to study in the state schools. "My family was never religious, but my whole life in the czarist times let me know who I was," Rapoport said.

A keen student of natural sciences, Rapoport set off to study medicine in Petrograd, the city of the czars that would soon be the city of revolution and renamed Leningrad. Petrograd was outside the Pale of Settlement, the only region where Jews were allowed to live, but for some reason the university officials let Rapoport study there. "All in all," he said, "I think the czars were

somehow more liberal than the Bolsheviks were." Rapoport arrived in 1915 and rented the corner of someone's room.

Those years were for him a mix of laboratory study and street revolt. After mornings in class and autopsy rooms, he sat in the gallery of the Duma, the Russian legislature, listening to the charges of repression and incompetence gather against the czar. Later he stood on the street and watched Lenin preach workers' revolution from the apartment balcony of the city's richest ballerina. Soon there were food riots and student protests. "When the first—the February—Revolution took place and the czar fell, I was there," Rapoport said. "I was armed with a rifle and a pistol. Together with the workers I helped arrest the czarist ministers. It was a real bourgeois revolution. . . . We thought we would have a constitutional state, as in France and other parts of Western Europe. I don't think that was a naive hope.

"At first, I was taken by the ideas of the revolution, but then I became much more realistic. I had no admiration for the Bolshevik Revolution. I saw it as a terrific threat because of the mass of illiterates inside it who hated intellectuals. That spelled the elimination of the intellectuals. I thought there would be chaos, and I turned out to be right.

"Lenin was surrounded by both Russians and Jews. There was not such a differentiation then. They were just members of the Party, and this ethnic question was not raised there. But there is an interesting detail which quite often evades many people. I remember reading in the complete works of Stalin, where Stalin describes the Third Party Congress, where there was a split between the Bolsheviks and Mensheviks. At the Third Congress, Stalin wrote, the majority of the Mensheviks were Jews and the majority of Bolsheviks were Russians. Malinovsky, a friend of Lenin's, said there should have been a Party pogrom. For Stalin that was no joke. Stalin understood that suggestion as guidance for action.

"In the Crimea after the Revolution, I saw terrible things happening to the White officers. Zemlyachka and Bela Kun came to the Crimea and started to gather lists of people who had taken part in the White movement. They promised not to kill them, just to register them. And then they killed everybody, many young men among them. Those who did register were shot. Those who did not survived. I realized what was going on by then, and who was who."

Rapoport quickly became a prominent pathologist in Moscow. He tried to avoid politics as much as possible. But the better known he became in his field, the harder it became to stand apart. With Stalin in power, Rapoport was constantly being asked to join the Communist Party. Over and over again he refused. He got into trouble in the late 1930s when, as the head of the admissions committee at a medical institute in Moscow, he would not

discriminate against children of the "enemies of the state"—those who had been arrested or shot for no reason by Stalin's secret police. Rapoport guessed that the only reason he himself had avoided arrest and execution in the camps was that the country could ill afford to wipe out all its best doctors. "But the truth is I really don't know why I got through the purges," he said. "Good luck, maybe?"

During the Battle of Stalingrad in 1943, the pivotal point in the war for the Soviet Union, Rapoport finally gave in and joined the Party—"for patriotic, not political reasons. At that time the Party was the only force that held the country together. What I will always remember is the interview I had at Party headquarters. The first thing they asked me was 'What is Zionism? What do you think of it?' I was angry with this, but I answered: 'Zionism is the national liberation movement of Jews aimed at the organization of their own territorial state.' They were stunned."

Natasha Rapoport was fourteen when the doorbell rang. It was the night of February 2, 1953. One of the family's closest friends, Dr. Myron Vovsi, had already been arrested, and the newspapers and radio had begun a crude propaganda campaign against the "murderers in white smocks," the Jewish doctors.

"There were rumors that, for the sake of 'protecting' the others—the 'innocent' Jews—from the mass hatred, camps were being set up for them in Siberia. All of them would be sent there soon," Natasha said. "The question of how to execute the criminals was widely discussed. Informed circles in my class contended that they would be hanged in Red Square. Many were worried whether the execution would be open to the public or only to those with special permission. Someone consoled the disappointed: 'Don't worry. Surely they will film it.' I had nightmares about Vovsi on the gallows."

Now, with the doorbell ringing incessantly, the secret police had come for her father. The agents rifled through every drawer and book, noting a few volumes of Freud as further evidence for the court protocols against Yakov Rapoport. During the search, one of the agents happened to cut his finger. Terrified that Natasha's mother would poison him with contaminated iodine, he refused treatment. "They phoned somewhere for a car," Natasha said, "and the suffering one was taken away—most likely to a special clinic where his scratch would be treated by a trusted, dependable Russian surgeon."

The arrest was, for Natasha, what the 1905 pogrom in the Crimea had been for her father—the pivotal memory of what it means to be a Jew in a hostile place. "Stalin is a bastard and a criminal," Natasha's mother told her, "but never say this to anyone. Do you understand?" Natasha's friends scorned

her, stared at her in class. The children in the courtyard mocked her, telling her that her father had taken pus from cancerous corpses and rubbed it into the skin of healthy people. They hurled rotten tomatoes, stones, and dead mice at her. The police confiscated all the family's money, bonds, and bank passbooks. Natasha's mother sold the family's copies of Tolstoy, Pushkin, and Hugo to buy bread and milk. Natasha lay awake nights wondering when the police would come for her mother, too.

An anti-Semitic hysteria engulfed Moscow. Party committees met in every school, institute, and factory to denounce the doctors and instruct "the workers" to be "on the lookout" for other Jewish plotters. At Moscow State University, Mikhail Gorbachev sat through a painful session of his Komsomol organization and heard a colonel, a decorated veteran of the war, denounce Gorbachev's close friend Vladimir Lieberman. Many years later, at a class reunion, Lieberman told a reporter, "Some comrades sniffed the wind, tried to criticize me. I was the only Jew at the law faculty's Communist Party meeting. Gorbachev had entered the Party right before this event, but it was he who tried to prevent the attack on me and did so very sharply, using some unparliamentary words. He called one of our old and respected veterans a 'spineless animal.' That just stopped them."

But very few rebelled, and few did not believe the Doctors' Plot was a prelude to something more ominous. Within a few weeks of the arrest, the Rapoports were convinced that Yakov was dead. The prison officials said it was no longer "necessary" to deliver food parcels to the jail. Hundreds of thousands of families during the purges recognized this as a sign that their loved ones were already dead.

On March 5, the director of Natasha's school gathered all the students in a huge recreation hall. Comrade Stalin was no more, she told them. For forty-five minutes, Natasha looked around her and saw everyone crying, her teachers, the students. She could not cry but tried not to seem too obvious. "Finally they let us go home," Natasha recalled. "My friend and I were walking home and we started to discuss some absolutely other problems and we started to laugh. We had forgotten completely that Stalin had died and we should be mourning with all the others. As we laughed, the people around us on the street were furious, they were shocked. We had to run home because we were afraid we'd be beaten right there on the street."

Three days after Stalin's death in March, there was a phone call, a stark male voice: "I am calling at the request of the professor. The professor asked me to tell you that he is healthy, feels fine, and is concerned about his family. What should I tell him?"

He was alive! Yakov Rapoport came home on April 4. Before coming up to the apartment he called from a phone downstairs: "I didn't want them to have a heart attack at the sight of me," he said. Every year thereafter, the survivors of the Doctors' Plot gathered for a party on that day as an anniversary of freedom. Around thirty people—the doctors who had been arrested and a short list of other "suspects"—celebrated their own survival and the survival of the Jews in Russia.

"Now there is only me," Yakov Rapoport said. "My family and I, we celebrate alone."

Yakov Rapoport came home a grateful man. Even now it was hard for him to find much fault with Nikita Khrushchev—"not after he freed hundreds of thousands of people and gave them back their good name." But for Natasha, the Doctors' Plot was a great divide between childhood and adulthood, innocence and alienation. The end of the plot meant freedom for her father, but a different quality of mind and trust for the daughter: "I began to see all the lies around me. I began to have a double life, one outside of my circle when I had to be careful what I did and said, and one inside my circle of family and friends, when I could have my own thoughts, my real life, the times when I could be myself.

"My attitude toward people had changed. There were so many who had betrayed us, people I never would have suspected. I stopped trusting people. And I began to understand—really understand—that I was Jewish. I understood that to be Jewish was to be persecuted. Years passed until I understood that, and maybe I don't have a full understanding even now. After all, I am deprived of Jewish history, Jewish culture, Jewish language.

"For all of us, this is the saddest thing. We know nothing of ourselves. We have had in here in our building a Jewish boy, with a Jewish face and appearance. A funny little boy. Another boy came from Central Asia. And there was a fight between the two boys. One mother asked the Jewish boy why he was fighting the Central Asian. The little Jewish boy said, "Because he is not Russian!" The poor child didn't even understand that he was not Russian either. The first time he'll understand it is when a Russian comes after him, with a leaflet, or a club."

State anti-Semitism followed Natasha Rapoport throughout her life and career as a chemist. After graduation she and the rest of her Jewish classmates were sent off to work in factories while others got far better work at academic institutes. Eventually she won a spot at a prestigious institute, but she was told she could not advance very far. "I don't have anything against

you or your abilities, Natalya Yakovlevna, but there are just too many Jews in your department," said one of the institute chiefs. "The regional Communist Party committee is already angry with your lab boss for hiring too many Jews. Do you want him to have more problems?"

In 1978, she watched with astonishment as a less deadly version of the Doctors' Plot was played out at her father's institute. Local authorities received an anonymous "tip" that Russian patients were dying while Jewish patients were being cured. The letters charged the Jewish doctors at the institute with carrying out Nazi-style experiments on the Russians and that the crimes were being covered up. "Instead of throwing the accusations in the garbage, the authorities made a thorough investigation," Natasha said as her father smiled weakly at the absurdity of it all. "Can you imagine? Ancient history all over again. And guess what? It turns out that there had been no experiments after all.

"There is something special in *Homo sovieticus,* in this special nation of people, and the scale of anti-Semitism here is unique," Natasha said. "Here, anti-Semitism is political, it is a weight on the political balance. Our government will sell Jews or not sell Jews, will let them go or not, depending on what it gets in return. Jews are a card in the political game. And this makes anti-Semitism more dangerous, because you never know how politics will change and what they will do with us the next time around."

Natasha was thwarted in her attempts to leave the country for Israel or the United States. Israelis promised her an immediate post at the Chaim Weizmann Institute in Jerusalem, but she could not persuade her parents to move. And her husband, Vladimir, was also hesitant. "He is a very indecisive man," she said. "This issue almost broke up our marriage. I think my life would have been different in Israel. As a scientist I could have worked as far as my talents could bring me. Here I am trapped, kept in a cage."

Natasha was determined that at least her daughter, Vika, would learn to live and think like a free woman. At first, when the little girl came home humming and singing the Bolshevik hymns she had been taught in school, Natasha was furious. "I told her to shut up," Natasha said, "but she loved those songs. When I tried to counter the lies she was being told in school and I told her to look around at the real life around her, she started crying and shouting, defending what she was told in the second and third grade. She was struggling for the sake of these beautiful lies."

But as Vika grew older, she began to understand the deep contradictions between the textbooks in school and everything she knew about the real history of her own grandfather and the world around her. Like so many, she grew cynical, alienated from anything that smacked of official Soviet life. She

decided she would emigrate if she could. "By the time I was thirteen I already knew that I could no longer live here," Vika told me. "I was still in the Soviet Union, but I knew it was temporary. Just thinking that way set me free.

"I'm not scared of the latest wave of anti-Semitism. They are pathetic people, and they will always be around. I'm leaving because I cannot stand it here any longer: the rules, the psychology, the gray sameness of everything. If I stay here, I will suffocate. Unless a brick were to fall on my head, I could predict every moment of my life here until I die. I want to have children one day, but I will not have them here. I will miss everyone, but I am gone."

A few nights before she was to leave for Israel, Vika and her mother staged an extraordinary puppet show for all their friends and relatives. Around seventy-five people were packed into a single tiny room. The puppets, with voices supplied by Vika's friends, played out her own personal history and coming exodus. When it was over, and the puppets lay in a heap, some people were still laughing, the rest were in tears.

Until the last minute, Vika was reminded of just why she was leaving. On the night of her departure, she and Natasha were driving through their neighborhood in north Moscow in Natasha's tiny orange Lada. Natasha glanced in the rearview mirror and noticed they were being followed. She pulled into the local police station and said, "What the hell is going on? Why are you having me followed?"

"It's for your own protection," the police captain said.

Natasha was furious, but her daughter smiled, as if in justification of her decision to go. That night, Vika flew to Budapest, then switched planes for the flight to Tel Aviv. When Vika left, Natasha said, "it was the first time in weeks that I had a good night's sleep."

A little while later, I visited Natasha Rapoport once more. With her daughter in Jerusalem and her father still in Moscow, Natasha said she felt like a "woman in the middle." Whenever we talked, she did everything she could to avoid the inevitable question of her father's death and her long wait to emigrate. Finally, she brought it up herself.

"I know what you are thinking," she said. "And the answer is yes. When he is gone, I will be gone, too."

CHAPTER 8

MEMORIAL

Esther has no idea where her grandfather died or where he is buried. Most likely, he was shot in the back of the head. Probably he is buried in a mass grave somewhere near the city of Gorky. She can guess, but she does not know.

In the Soviet Union, an empire of holocaust survivors and the children of survivors, this gnawing uncertainty was the usual condition of life. As Hannah Arendt writes, "The concentration camp, by making death itself anonymous (making it impossible to find out whether a prisoner is dead or alive), robbed death of its meaning as the end of a fulfilled life." I am not sure we met anyone who did not have a grandparent, a parent, a sibling, a friend, someone who still wandered through his dreams, still ghostly because there was no way to fix the dead one's end in time and place. The survivor can usually imagine the death in a generic way—the executioner's rubber apron, the ditch dug in frozen mud. But the suffering continues because there is no closure. It's as if the regime were guilty of two crimes on a massive scale: murder and the unending assault against memory. In making a secret of history, the Kremlin made its subjects just a little more insane, a little more desperate.

Awake, the people lived in the ruins of their nightmares. In their daily lives

they lived in apartment buildings that had been built by prisoners, sailed through canals dug by slaves of the state. One afternoon in Karaganda—an industrial city in central Kazakhstan that, seen from the air, looked like an ashtray stuffed with cigarette butts—I wandered into the woods and discovered an abandoned school. The coal miners showing me around pointed to the bars in the windows. "It was a pretty good school, but it was a wonderful prison camp," one miner said bitterly. His father spent a year for "anti-Soviet activity" in a room that later became the second grade. The rooms were dank, and a bitter wind blew through them. In the basement playrooms, the miner said, the guards carried out their nighttime executions. There were drainpipes in the floors to catch the blood, zebras and wildebeests on the walls to amuse the children.

Much later on, I took another trip, this time to Kolyma in the Russian far east, the old prison camp region just across the water from Alaska. At least two million prisoners died in Kolyma. The survivors went home years ago, but the place was still haunted. The Russian north was once the region of "little peoples," hunters and nomads, Eskimos, Yakuts, Chukchis, Yukagiris. A friend told me that one hundred or so Eveni people lived in the village of Godlya an hour north of Magadan. Would I like to see them?

We arrived in Godlya at about eight-thirty in the morning. The village was a sea of mud, a few heaps of garbage, an empty store, a couple of wooden houses tilting into the mud, and the sort of poured-concrete barracks you'd see on the outskirts of almost any Soviet city. We saw a young woman—a beautiful woman, with a round Eskimo face—stumble drunkenly through a puddle. She sort of squinted at us and dropped to one knee. Farther on, we saw a few more people, some leaning against a wall, a couple more passing a bottle back and forth and saying nothing. Half the town was smashed before breakfast. It was always this way in the morning, and by sundown hardly anyone was awake, my friend told me. They drank vodka, bathtub gin, hair tonic, eau de cologne, even bug spray. It had been that way for years. The Eveni had been herded into these villages after centuries of hunting reindeer in the forest; once they ceased to wander, they were lost. The regime, in order to create a more perfect Soviet Eveni, or Chukchi or Eskimo, took children away from their parents and villages and "educated" them in state boarding schools, sickening little places in the middle of nowhere. By the time the schools got done with them, there was no Eveni left in them at all. Now they spoke Russian miserably and Eveni not at all.

One of the few sober men around, a squat young man with a withered arm, introduced himself. He said his name was Viktor, and I asked him my earnest questions. "The Eveni are dying out," he said. "They have nothing to do and they drink until they can't drink anymore. I spoke Eveni until I was four

years old. That's what they tell me. Then they sent me off to the schools. It wasn't school really. They just let us sit there and made sure we spoke only Russian. So most of us didn't say anything at all."

I asked him what chances he thought he had in life and whether the changes in Moscow might help. By now a small crowd of drunks had circled round us. Their eyes were glassy and their heads swayed slightly, like dandelions in a breeze.

"We are done for," Viktor said, looking at his neighbors. "It's too late. They killed us."

Viktor led us over to two other Eveni men. They were wearing cheap Soviet coveralls and University of Alaska baseball caps that must have floated across to Siberia on the Bering Strait. They were the only two men in town working. They had a curious job. With huge blowtorches they scorched the skin on a huge dead hog until it was pink and dry. Then, they cut the skin in strips and fried and salted them. "Very tasty with vodka," one said. Bar food, Eveni potato chips.

Another man, Pavel Trifonov, came over and watched this strange ritual with us for a while. "This is the sort of thing we do now," he said. "The state won't let us fish. And there are no reindeer left. They call this village a state farm, but there hasn't been any farming here in a long time. It's way below zero most of the time. What are we supposed to raise? Lemons? Most of the time, this place is a sheet of ice."

I asked him what his family had done before they settled here in Godlya.

"My grandfather was a trapper and a hunter and he traded with the Japanese," Pavel said. "And what am I? I stand around and watch this. I don't feel like an Eveni and I am not a Russian. I don't feel like anyone. They are killing us. No, they already have. This is slow genocide, and it's almost at its end."

How to put a limit on these stories, this sense of hauntedness? On a winter afternoon in Leningrad, I paid a call on Dmitri Likhachev, a distinguished scholar of medieval Russian literature at the Leningrad institute known as Pushkin House. Likhachev was eighty-four at the time, and his office seemed designed to ignore all things Soviet. The feeling of entering that room was the reverse of what happens to the pitiful exile in Nabokov's story "The Visit to the Museum," who wanders through a museum in France and magically finds himself "not in the Russia I remembered but in the factual Russia of today." One entered Likhachev's study as if into another time. There was Dal's great dictionary of the Russian language, a prerevolutionary clock, a stunning portrait of Pushkin where the dull face of a general secretary might

have been. But it somehow avoided fakery. This was not fantasy, but rather an act of attention and defiance. In a city where thousands of volumes in the main library had been burned and ruined from neglect, where Rembrandts faded needlessly on the walls of the Hermitage, Likhachev created an idealized room in which to read and think.

"Most of all, I like the quiet," he told me that winter afternoon. "Russia is a noisy state." When he was a boy, Likhachev watched the February and October revolutions from his window. A decade later he had an even closer view of the rise of Soviet civilization, courtesy of a five-year term in a labor camp. Likhachev was arrested in 1928 for taking part in a students' literary group called the Cosmic Academy of Sciences. The club posed about as great a threat to the Kremlin as the *Harvard Lampoon* does to the White House. For election as an "academician," Likhachev presented a humorous paper on the need to restore to the language the letter "yat." The Bolsheviks banned the letter as part of a campaign to "modernize" Russian after the revolution. Later, one of Likhachev's interrogators railed at him for daring to waste his time on such things.

"What do you mean by language reform?" the interrogator shouted. "Perhaps we won't even have any language at all under socialism!"

Likhachev spent most of his term in Solovki, a labor camp established by Lenin in 1920 on a White Sea island. The monastery on the island had been used as a prison before, but a single statistic gives some idea of the difference between the czarist repressions and the Bolshevik Terror. From the sixteenth century to the end of the Romanov dynasty in 1917, there were a total of 316 inmates at Solovki. On a single night—the night of October 28, 1929—Likhachev listened to gunfire as three hundred men were executed.

"It was autumn and my parents had come to visit me. We had rented a room from one of the guards," he once said. "A man came running to see me on that night saying the wardens had just been to the barracks to get me. Well, I told my parents that I had to go because I was being summoned for night work and that they shouldn't wait up for me. I could not tell my parents that they were coming to take me away and shoot me. I hid myself behind stacks of firewood so they would not see it happening.

"Meanwhile the shooting was in full swing. I was not found. It meant that I was also included in that number, I was also meant to be one of those three hundred. So they took somebody else instead of me. And when I emerged from my hideout the next morning, I was a different man. So many years have passed since then, more than half a century, sixty years in fact, and I still cannot forget it. Exactly three hundred people were mowed down just like that, as a warning. . . . Three hundred shots, one per man. The executioner was drunk, so he did not manage to kill them all immediately. But all the

same, they threw all the bodies in a big pit. The executioner is older than me, and he is still alive."

A little while after the Nina Andreyeva affair in the spring of 1988, I was walking along the Arbat, the pedestrian mall in downtown Moscow, and saw a young woman in her twenties collecting signatures. This was still dangerous business in 1988. I'd seen people arrested on the Arbat and near Pushkin Square for handing out petitions or organizing an "unauthorized" demonstration. Sasha Podrabinek regularly got himself arrested when he passed out his underground paper, *Express-Khronika,* on the street.

There were about a half-dozen people huddled around the woman. A couple signed; the others kept a step back and listened, passing the time. She said her name was Elena and her petition, a sheaf of onionskin sheets riffling in the wind, was for a new "historical, anti-Stalinist" group called Memorial.

Memorial, Elena said, wanted to "give a name" to the victims of the Stalin era; they wanted to build monuments, research centers. The more she explained the group, the more it seemed to me their goal was to build a kind of Soviet Yad Vashem, the memorial center in Jerusalem dedicated to the memory of the six million Jews killed in the Holocaust. She kept talking about "the names," giving people back their names, and as I stood there, I remembered going to Yad Vashem nearly twenty years before and walking into a vast, dark library, a room filled with immense volumes containing the names of the lost. I had never even begun to understand the immensity of the Holocaust until that moment. I'd had teachers who had asked us to imagine four of the five boroughs of New York gassed to death. But it was only in that simple room, surrounded by the names of all of them, that I felt it. And what had Solzhenitsyn written? What was his count of the victims of the Soviet regime? Sixty million?

The woman told me how I could find out more about Memorial. She said I should find Lev Ponomarev or Yuri Samodurov, a human rights activist and a friend of Sakharov's. Lev Ponomarev lived on the very outskirts of Moscow, a neighborhood that had apartments on one side and miles of birch forest on the other. He was in his forties but looked many years younger. Unlike the shaggy Russian intellectual of legend, Ponomarev looked like an astronaut, fit, clean-cut. With his daughter running in occasionally with a shriek and announcements about the weather ("huge snow!") or dinner ("coming soon!"), Ponomarev brought me up to date on the start of Memorial. He said that he and most other intellectuals in their twenties, thirties, and forties viewed the advent of Gorbachev skeptically. But when Sakharov was released from internal exile, he said, "We began to come around."

"Like a lot of people," Ponomarev said, "I thought that what had to be done at the start in order to dismantle the system was to tell people how many victims there have been, to plant the idea that monuments should be erected to those who had perished, archives should be published. This is the real start of perestroika. The truth. And with that, the process can become irreversible. Without that, without everyone acknowledging that the system is discredited and guilty, a crackdown can always succeed.

"In the winter of 1987, I got together with Yuri Samodurov. We formed an action group of about fifteen people. This was at a time when many informal groups were being launched. A general meeting was held in someone's apartment. We started drafting a one-page-long appeal in order to begin a petition campaign. To get the language of it just right was very tricky. For example, we knew that millions of people had been killed, no one doubted it, and yet we didn't know whether we ought to include the word 'millions' in our document. We still had no legal proof to substantiate it. We were afraid of turning people off."

The Memorial founders, a group of mainly young unknown scholars and writers, first tried to collect signatures at their various offices. That seemed to be the safest route. But Ponomarev and the others found that even close friends they had known for many years were refusing to sign.

"A lot of them agreed with what we were after," he said, "but they were suspicious. You could see they were wondering if their friends had suddenly become agents and the petition was some kind of trap. So then we decided to take the more anonymous route and go to the streets and ask passersby to sign. And since we wanted our appeal to have legal force, we asked people for both their names and their addresses. We all had our doubts about this. This is something that is terribly dangerous in our country. The levels of suspicion run so deep. But people responded! After all these years, people were just ready for this. It was such an amazing sociological experience. We discovered that there were people willing to give a name and an address and yet they had no idea that we were not KGB agents. They trusted us."

The Memorial people usually went to the streets in groups of threes. One held a poster saying "Sign this appeal," another collected signatures, and the third held up a quotation from Gorbachev's speech saying there should be no "blank spots" in history. Gorbachev still had tremendous authority and popularity; what's more, Lev said, Memorial hoped that a quotation from the general secretary would ward off the police. It did not always work. The petition groups were often arrested, until, finally, mysteriously, they found themselves getting hauled into the police stations less and less often. Divine—or Party—intervention, they supposed.

If the Memorial group was to become the preeminent historical preserva-

tion society, it needed historians to help. This was an almost impossible order. The field of Soviet history had become so degraded over the years that the Memorial people felt they could not trust anyone; the ones they could trust, people like Dima Yurasov, were not professionals.

There was one exception at first, a young scholar named Arseny Roginsky. Roginsky's father was arrested twice in the Stalin era and died in 1951 at a camp near Leningrad when his son was five years old. But, typically, the KGB did not bother to tell the Roginsky family about the death. Month after month, until 1955, Arseny's mother sent parcels to her husband in the camps, all the while planning for his eventual return. The family learned about the death only when they received a telegram informing them that the "packages are no longer being received." Later on, the Roginskys were given a packet of documents that claimed the cause of death had been a heart attack. "When I saw that document I was eight or nine years old," Arseny told me one afternoon at the Memorial headquarters. "I saw the stamp and the seal of the Soviet Union, and yet I knew it was false. They were telling us lies and they didn't care how absurd they were. That's when I decided to become a historian."

Roginsky took his university degree in Tartu, a university town in Estonia that had about it the air of the Berkeley academic underground in the sixties. The most influential teacher there—and Roginsky's mentor—was the cultural historian Yuri Lotman. While it was impossible to conduct courses and draw up reading lists on subjects considered "anti-Soviet," Lotman and his students looked at the structure of literary texts and cultures in a way that they all understood as a thinly veiled critique of the society they were living in. Their refusal to use Newspeak and channel everything into Marxist-Leninist categories was a form of dissidence. At Tartu, Roginsky's classmates included Natalya Gorbanevskaya, who joined Pavel Litvinov on Red Square for the 1968 demonstration, and Nikita Okhotin, another future leader of Memorial.

After graduating and moving to Leningrad, Roginsky took a tremendous risk. He founded an underground group called Pamyat, or Memory (not to be confused with the racist Russian nationalist group of the same name). Roginsky's Pamyat was a forerunner to Memorial. Working secretly and with friends in the dissident movement, he began building an archive of Western and Soviet documents on the Stalin period. Roginsky followed Solzhenitsyn's lead in *The Gulag Archipelago* and interviewed dozens of camp survivors about their experiences. "More than anything, I wanted to prove that the study of history actually could exist in this country," he told me. It was not long before the police and the KGB were on to him. They searched his apartment seven times, bugged his telephone, and called him in for

questioning. But while the KGB obviously knew what Roginsky was up to, he made it difficult for them, carefully burying his tapes and papers. The KGB never found that evidence. Then in 1981 the KGB ended all pretense toward the legal niceties. They arrested Roginsky and he was sentenced to four years in the camps. They moved him from camp to camp in order to prevent him from "infecting" the other inmates with anti-Soviet ideas and to make sure he never got too comfortable. When Roginsky finally returned to Moscow in August 1985, Mikhail Gorbachev was in power. He was ready to try the same crime again. "I had to assume that history would outlast stupidity and cruelty," he said.

Through the spring of 1988, Memorial was adding thousands of names to its petition lists. Gorbachev planned on holding a special conference at the end of June to plant the seeds of a more democratic political system, and Memorial wanted to find some way to use the historic meeting to establish itself. For that it needed support at a higher level; it needed backing from people who would command the attention of at least the reformist flank in the Party leadership. The activists needed a core of names that would lend some political heft to Memorial. Most of the names were obvious: Sakharov, of course, writers such as Ales Adamovich, Dmitri Likhachev, Daniil Granin, Lev Razgon, Anatoly Rybakov, and Yuri Karyakin; the editor of *Ogonyok,* Vitaly Korotich; and Boris Yeltsin, who had become a mythic figure of defiance after his ouster from the Politboro in 1987.

And there were two historians on the list. The first was Roy Aleksandrovich Medvedev. Throughout the Khrushchev and Brezhnev eras, there had been other scholars who tried to work honestly, to conduct research outside the system of Party rules and guarded archives. Mikhail Gefter, another of Arseny Roginsky's mentors, was well known to historians in the West for his essays on what he saw as the Stalinist "aberration." Viktor Danilov's groundbreaking first attempts to describe the scope and brutality of the collectivization campaign had also won respect abroad.

But while Western historians trying to piece together the scale of the Soviet catastrophe relied almost solely on published Soviet documents, literature, and émigré sources, only one historian still living in Moscow played a major role in deepening the world's understanding of Stalin and his successors. The publication in the West of Medvedev's *Let History Judge* in 1971 astonished foreign scholars with its unstinting denunciation of Stalin and the sheer accumulation of evidence.

I came to Moscow thinking that Roy Medvedev was the man to know. Dozens of my predecessors—especially the American and Italian correspon-

dents—depended mightily on him for analysis and high-grade gossip: who was fighting whom, who had a fatal cold in the Politburo. The same sources in the world of Communist Party politics, bureaucracy, and journalism who had informed *Let History Judge* also provided Medvedev with nuggets of information that, for foreigners, could be mined almost nowhere else.

Roy and his wife, Galina, lived on Dybenko Street in a distant part of town not far from Sheremetyevo Airport. Medvedev's tiny study was a meticulous arrangement of books and files, a masterly use of space imposed by necessity. File cards peeked out of the shelves announcing "early Leninists," "Beria," or "Brezhnev." Roy's twin brother, Zhores, who had lived in a middle-class section of London called Mill Hill since his exile in 1973, had arranged his own office in the same fashion. London street life murmured outside, but inside, Zhores had recreated Russia. All through their separation, Roy and Zhores exchanged necessities with the help of obliging Western diplomats and journalists. For Zhores's books on Soviet agriculture and the Chernobyl nuclear disaster, Roy sent clippings and source materials; Zhores handled Roy's foreign-language publication rights and sent him packages of books, rubber bands, envelopes, folders, and underwear, socks, and shoes.

Before Gorbachev came to power, Roy Medvedev was considered a dissident. After years of study and teaching school in the provinces, Medvedev took Khrushchev's "secret speech" in 1956 at the Twentieth Party Congress and the further anti-Stalinist mood of the Twenty-second Party Congress in 1961 as a signal of permission. Year after year he accumulated source materials and interviews with Party officials, camp survivors, and other witnesses to the era. As a scholar he pushed the limits of the possible. But Medvedev's timing was dangerous. By the time he finished *Let History Judge* and sent it to the West for publication, Khrushchev was out of office and Brezhnev had already begun a movement to rehabilitate the reputation of Stalin.

Medvedev, who had maintained his membership in the Communist Party, was soon banned from its ranks. But while he was rejected by officialdom, he was also never really accepted by the dissidents. In his memoirs, Sakharov rarely levels any personal attacks, but in several spots he makes it clear that by the early seventies he not only disagreed with Medvedev's Marxism but also did not entirely trust him. Without saying so directly, he wonders if Medvedev did not have at least the tacit support of, or some kind of unsavory relationship with, the KGB. Other dissidents were far less guarded in their conjectures.

I find it hard to believe the worst. In the early eighties, a KGB guard sat outside Medvedev's door, and I doubt he was there to give out flowers to foreign guests. The specter scared off some visitors, but not all, and by the time I arrived, Roy still gave help to anyone who asked for it. I think his

fallen reputation among the dissidents and then, later, among the liberal intelligentsia as a whole had more to do with his refusal to shed Marxism than with any shady dealings with the Party and its organs. It seemed strange to me that people who had never made a peep for thirty years could forgive themselves rather quickly for their cowardice, but were brutally critical of Medvedev's constancy. This was a man who first made sense of his life as a scholar during an interrogation at Lefortovo Prison in the mid-seventies.

"Comrade Medvedev, tell me, please," the KGB officer had said, "would you have written your books about Stalin if your father hadn't been sent away to the camps?"

For nearly two decades before the start of glasnost, the KGB had regularly shown its interest in Roy and Zhores Medvedev. Zhores was Roy's equivalent in the scientific world, a biologist and gerontologist who wrote about the abuse of genetics under Stalin and the use of psychiatric wards as prisons for dissidents under Brezhnev. In 1970, the authorities declared that Zhores suffered from "paranoid delusions of reforming society" and threw him into an insane asylum. Only Roy's intervention, his rallying of Soviet and Western scholars, forced the Kremlin to release Zhores within three weeks.

The KGB officer at Lefortovo had surely asked Roy the right question. "Why?" No one had ever posed it to him quite so directly or with such perverse intent. "I realized then just how closely my destiny was intertwined with my father's," Roy told me one day in his tiny study. "I was sitting there in that prison room, and it all came back."

On an August night in 1938 there was a knock on the door. The familiar scene had begun. Working with their uncanny efficiency and speed, KGB men introduced themselves and went to work. The twins, fair and thin, sat up in bed and tried to make out the muffled commotion outside the bedroom door.

"Why do you come so late, comrades?" they heard their father say.

They could not make out the answer.

For weeks the boys had noticed that their father was depressed, eating almost nothing. It was a mystery to them why their father, Aleksandr Medvedev, a respected officer in the Red Army and a professor of philosophy and history at the Tolmachev Military-Political Academy, had been fired from his job. And why had they been sent home early that summer from Pioneer camp? Some of the family's friends had been arrested, but the boys could not understand what their father understood only too well, that the defining principle of the terror was its randomness. There was no reason for any of this except the ruthlessness, perhaps the pathology, of Josef Stalin and the system he had built.

When the boys woke the next morning, the visitors were still there, opening

and slamming cabinets, pushing aside furniture, rummaging through everything. The bedroom door opened and the boys' father walked in. He was dressed in a military tunic, but wore no belt. He looked as if he'd gone days with no sleep. Without a word, he sat down on the bed and embraced his sons. There was something final and desperate about his grip. Zhores told me he still remembered the feel of his father's prickly, unshaven face scratching against his cheek, how his father's wordless terror was so obvious, so physical, that all three began to cry at once.

A few minutes later, the visitors left with Aleksandr Medvedev.

In the first months after the arrest of their father, Roy and Zhores and their mother received a series of letters from Aleksandr Medvedev. He was writing from Kolyma, the camps of the far east. Some of the letters from their father were addressed for forwarding to the Communist Party Central Committee, the Supreme Court, the secret police. They all protested his innocence.

"There was always the sense that this was odd, a mistake that could not have happened to us," Zhores said. "Of course, everyone in the country, when it touched them, felt that way."

Roy and Zhores had idolized their father. He had been a strict teacher and a scholarly example to them, urging them to read everything from Jack London to the Russian classics. His letters to them from Kolyma betrayed none of his own suffering. They concentrated instead on the boys' future.

My dear Roy and 'Res:

At last, spring has come, a rare guest in this part of the country. I am very far from you, but in my thoughts and in my heart, I am very close, closer than ever. You fill my everyday thoughts, and you are the aim and essence of my life. You are on the threshold of becoming young men. I so want to be beside you and give you all my experience and deliver you from youth's mistakes. But destiny has decided otherwise. I do not want my absence from your lives to sadden your youth.

The main thing is that you must study persistently and not limit yourselves just to the school program. Use your time when your perceptiveness and memory are especially keen. Try to be disciplined in your work, for even a mediocre man can accomplish a great deal if he is disciplined. You are talented capable boys. You must learn to think and be well organized. What you need above all is patience. You must learn to overcome difficulties no matter how large. I am sorry for the preaching tone . . .

Love,
Your Father

In the winter of 1941, the Medvedev family received a letter from Aleksandr saying he was in the hospital and needed vitamins. A few months later,

a letter they had sent to him in Kolyma came back unopened and stamped: "The money is returned on account of the death of the addressee." For a while, the family could not accept this all too obvious reality and continued sending parcels. But each time they were returned with the same dark stamp.

When he was just a teenager, Roy's mother told him, "Don't be a philosopher or a historian. It's too dangerous." And too painful. When Roy was studying at Leningrad State University in the forties, he began to do some independent research. He slowly uncovered who had betrayed his father. At the height of the terror, Boris Chagin was both a military officer and an intelligence agent of the NKVD, the precursor to the KGB. He was the author of numerous letters slandering his fellow officers. Those letters helped send many men, including Aleksandr Medvedev, to the camps. In Leningrad, Roy discovered that Chagin held a prestigious position in the same history department in which Roy was studying. Chagin was a professor of dialectical materialism.

The Medvedev brothers stood off to the side, observing the man who had betrayed their father. Zhores especially made a thorough study of Chagin's books: *The Struggle of Marxism-Leninism Against the Philosophy of Revisionism* and *The Struggle of Marxism-Leninism Against Reactionary Philosophy.* They took no action. They did not confront him. They learned. "I felt disdain for him, but not hatred or the desire for revenge," Zhrores said.

Decades later, when Roy was interviewing camp survivors for *Let History Judge,* a woman called him at home. "Are you the son of Aleksandr Medvedev?" she asked. Roy said he was, and the woman invited him to visit her at her apartment, which she shared with several other survivors from the Kolyma camps. There, for the first time, Medvedev heard the story of his father's death, how he had injured his arm in an accident while working in a copper mine and was sent to work in a greenhouse. He developed cancer and was admitted to the camp infirmary. The inmates knew their friend was gone only when they saw the camp foreman walking like a peacock around the muddy yard. He was wearing the dark wool jacket Aleksandr Medvedev had had on his back when he arrived in Kolyma.

For all his credentials as a scholar, Roy Medvedev was not for Memorial, and Memorial was not for him. Although he was nominally a member of the group's "public committee"—its council of well-known senior figures—Medvedev did not attend meetings and even doubted the value of the group. Roy believed in Gorbachev and in the Party as the only legitimate body of power. Memorial, to him, seemed ragtag, beside the point.

The man who quickly took the lead as Memorial's chief scholar-politician

and was an admitted hypocrite, a calculating man who had been on the editorial board of *Kommunist* and was an instructor in the Higher School of the Young Communist League. Yuri Afanasyev had no illusions about his past. "For more years than I care to remember," he said one night on television, "I was up to my neck in shit."

His ascendance was astonishing. In my first year in Moscow, Afanasyev was already the democratic movement's master of ceremonies. At nearly every meeting you'd go to—at the Saturday-morning sessions of Moscow Tribune, at the lectures on Stalin—Afanasyev was invariably the man at the microphone, mediating, introducing, lecturing. He was a specialist in French historiography, and yet he looked, with his bullfrog neck and barrel chest, like a high school football coach. He had the gruff confidence of a man who had led many a committee meeting, first in the Young Communist League (the Komsomol), later in the radical opposition.

His metamorphosis was not so much laughable as pitiable. Here was a man who never would have dared defend Roy Medvedev in the seventies and then scorned him as "hopelessly reactionary" in the late eighties. But I found that for all his presumption, his gall, Afanasyev's analyses of what was happening in the country and where the situation was leading were uncanny. There were times when Afanasyev, with his supreme confidence, reminded me of Norman Mailer. He knew he had lived a life full of mistakes but he insisted on being heard. His campaign for the "return of history," his early attacks on the "Stalinist-Brezhnevite" Supreme Soviet and on Gorbachev himself, always preceded fashion. He was not much loved—he had none of Sakharov's subtlety or carriage—but he was often right. In contrast, Medvedev's predictions now were not nearly as reliable as his gossip had once been. Typically, the day that Eduard Shevardnadze resigned as foreign minister in December 1990 predicting the rise of a dictatorship, Medvedev declared to all who would listen that Shevardnadze was stepping down because of trouble in the Georgian Republic.

Afanasyev grew up in Ulyanovsk, the town where Lenin was born. His father, a household repair man, was sent to jail for several years in eastern Siberia on the usual false pretense: he had pilfered a few kilos of flour from the collective farm to give to a poor family. "But the strange thing," Afanasyev told me one afternoon at his office at the Historical Archives Institute, "is that we did not experience it as a grief or tragedy, because literally every other person we knew then was in prison for collecting leftovers on the farm or for missing a day of work. We never had any conversations about Stalin and I had no doubts about him."

Like Gorbachev, Afanasyev was a provincial boy whose grades were good enough to gain him admission to the best university in the country, Moscow

State University. As a student, Afanasyev said, "I was like everyone else. I memorized *The Short Course* like any good Komsomol boy, like any other Communist." On the night before Stalin's funeral in March 1953, Afanasyev wandered the streets near the Kremlin. Tens of thousands of people jammed the streets headed for the Hall of Columns, where Stalin lay in his coffin. People were hysterical, wracked with fear after the death of their living god. Dozens, perhaps hundreds, of people suffocated to death in the mad crush to get to the hall. Afanasyev broke free of the crowd. As he walked, he could hear some drunks singing in an alleyway. He had never heard such joyous singing. The drunks were celebrating the death of Stalin.

"I suppose once or twice in a lifetime you have those moments when you see something or hear something that tilts your life just slightly in another direction. When I heard those men, well, suddenly the purity of my political consciousness was stained," Afanasyev said. "I felt the first moment of doubt. It wasn't until Khrushchev's speech three years later that I really started to rethink things more thoroughly, but it was this drunken celebration in the dark corners of Moscow that made me start to doubt. I was never quite the same."

After graduation, Afanasyev worked as a Komsomol leader in Krasnoyarsk, not far from where his father had been in jail. He certainly was no radical. He believed in the "infinite possibilities" of the Party. He and his friends talked about the great vistas of Leninist ideology, the great hydroelectric power station they—or at least the workers—were building.

"That enthusiasm," he said, "lasted until the late sixties, when Brezhnev tried to reanimate Stalinism."

Back in Moscow, Afanasyev worked in the national leadership of the Komsomol organization and then took his graduate degree in history, specializing in French historiography. Afanasyev knew enough to stay away from Soviet history as a field—"That's where all the real idiots and time-servers were"—but even in his own work he made sure to glorify the obvious and denigrate "foreign influence." For years his published works set out to prove that the "bourgeois" historians had grossly misinterpreted the October Revolution. Basically, he said, "I scoured the texts for their 'glaring insufficiencies.' "

But like so many others of his generation, Afanasyev developed a kind of two-track mind. Because he was such a loyal servant of the official line, he was sent abroad several times to study in France. In Paris, Afanasyev read books by the dissidents and émigrés. He lived in an academic atmosphere where he could speak a little more freely. So by the time he returned to Moscow, Afanasyev had changed just a little more. Once more he had heard the shouting from the dark corners, and he responded—or at least part of

him did. Little by little, it became harder for him to resist the evidence. His faith—what little there was of it—eroded. Polish students at the university told him about Stalin's massacres of Polish officers in the Katyn Forest. Afanasyev saw how senior professors of history at the university were arrested, or at least fired and silenced, when they strayed too far from doctrine.

In the late seventies and early eighties, Afanasyev was a resident scholar of "the critique of bourgeois historiography" at a Moscow institute and was an editor at *Kommunist,* the Party's chief theoretical journal. When Gorbachev came to office, Afanasyev wrote him a series of daring letters about the situation in Soviet historical science, calling on him to use his position as general secretary to end restrictions on academic study and open the archives of the Party and the KGB. Afanasyev got no direct answers. But he did win the key appointment in 1986 to take over as rector of the Historical Archives Institute and quickly used that position to give the first public lectures criticizing Stalin and introducing to the public several new faces—Dima Yurasov included.

Afanasyev was determined to use his new post to help open up the study of the Soviet past. Exploiting his new access to at least some Party archives, he reviewed the letters of Olga Shatunovskaya, a woman who had been a member of the Communist Party Control Committee under Khrushchev. In those letters Shatunovskaya wrote that she had collected sixty-four folders of documents saying that according to KGB and Party data, between January 1935 and 1941 19,800,000 people had been arrested; and of these, seven million were executed in prisons. Her statement was supported by specific data describing how many were shot and where and when. But the files Shatunovskaya described were declared "missing." By reading such letters, Afanasyev began to realize that the Party and the KGB had probably destroyed many of the most incriminating documents in the archives.

Afanasyev got into some of his first battles with the Party hierarchy when he began to insist that professional scholars and not the Central Committee—not even the general secretary—should be the country's principal historians. Although Gorbachev's 1987 history speech helped open the process, Afanasyev said that there could no longer be such speeches. "As long as such things still exist," he said, "there will still be the idea that history should be made not in the archives and universities and by writers, but rather at Party conferences and committees. That way history remains a handmaiden of propaganda and an extension of policy rather than a sphere of knowledge on the level of science or literature. If power wants to gain authority, then it has to say honestly, 'We are not linked in any way with the previous regime.'

"When we talk about perestroika, we see it in the following way: the former model of socialism was no good, so let's work out a new model and

put it into life. Again, we have it backward. We must give up this idea of a conscious construction of a more perfect society, the whole culture of belief in the limitless capabilities and opportunities of the human mind, and the ability to construct a model of socially engineered society and then realize it all.

"Educators and utopian thinkers used to think that the opportunities were endless. That the idea of a just society could be formed by the human mind, that it could be discovered on a theoretical basis; and it seemed to them that those theories could be realized in practice. In other words, a society of universal justice and prosperity could be built by thinking things out. We are now living through the final stages of that culture. Marx and Lenin are vanishing. They are being swept away in the same way that the 'truth' of Newtonian mechanics was swept away by Einstein and relativity."

—

By June 1988, Gorbachev's victory in the Nina Andreyeva affair had given the Memorial leadership a sense of hope and expectation. Afanasyev and the liberal head of the Filmmakers' Union, Elem Klimov, decided to seize on the Nineteenth Party Conference as Memorial's moment. Both men had been elected delegates to the conference and here was a chance to propose the Memorial platform to the top officials of the Communist Party.

Afanasyev had already helped to lay the political and intellectual groundwork for Memorial's plan. A few weeks before the conference, he produced the most important political book of the Gorbachev era: *Inogo ne dano* ("There Is No Other Way"), a collection of thirty-five essays by the leading intellectuals of the "thaw" generation, men and women who had become the torchbearers of the glasnost era. While Gorbachev's own book, *Perestroika,* was sodden with Party cliché, "There Is No Other Way" provided dazzling clarity and a sense of possibility. Published by the huge state-run firm Progress and edited by Afanasyev, "There Is No Other Way" read like an underground manifesto but it was printed officially and on good paper. Afanasyev, Mikhail Gefter, the renaissance scholar Leonid Batkin, and the journalist Len Karpinsky all wrote essays on the persistence of Stalinism and the need to evaluate the past in order to create a humane future. In one way or another, the need for truth, for a clear-eyed view of history, was behind every piece in the collection, among them Vasily Selyunin's analysis of the Soviet bureaucracy, Aleksei Yablokov's survey of ecological disasters, Yuri Chernichenko's essay on the "agro-gulag" of the collective farm system, Gavriil Popov's piece on the absurdity of the centralized economic system. Nearly all the authors were scholars and journalists who had, for years, pulled their punches, spoken in euphemism, or spoken not at all. The presence of one

author, however, honored the entire project. The simple addition of Andrei Sakharov, and his essay "The Necessity of Perestroika," showed that an alliance existed between the dissidents and a much wider category, the liberal intelligentsia. Sakharov's article was not much different from his underground manifestos; what was different now was the audience. The first printing alone was 100,000. Until Sakharov's release from exile there were probably not ten thousand people in the country who knew the name Sakharov as anything other than an odious figure in the pages of *Pravda* and *Izvestia.* In his essay, Sakharov wrote that perestroika "was like a war. Victory is a necessity." To even begin to win that war, he wrote, the leadership had to end the folly in Afghanistan, sponsor a thorough rewriting of the criminal code, endorse freedom of speech, and agree to a radical reduction in strategic and conventional weapons. In the next two years, Gorbachev would follow Sakharov's prescriptions almost to the letter.

A few days after buying my blue-and-silver copy of "There Is No Other Way," I went to a demonstration organized by Memorial outside a sports arena in Moscow. It was a brilliant sunny day, and the people on the streets outside the arena took obvious delight in their freedom to chant slogans and carry signs reading "No to Political Repression," "Death to Stalinism," "Stalin's Boot Still Endangers Us." A half-dozen of the contributors to "There Is No Other Way" gave speeches on the steps. But one moment struck me above all. Not far from Sakharov, a young man carried a sign saying, in Russian, "I would like to call you all by name," the famous line from Anna Akhmatova's long poem *Requiem.*

During Stalin's Terror, Akhmatova spent seventeen months, day after day, waiting in long lines to find out what had become of her son, who had been arrested at the height of the purges. "One day someone 'identified' me," she wrote in a preface to the poem. "Beside me, in the queue, there was a woman with blue lips. She had, of course, never heard of me; but she suddenly came out of that trance so common to us all and whispered in my ear (everyone spoke in whispers there): 'Can you describe this?' And I said, 'Yes, I can.' And then something like the shadow of a smile crossed what had once been her face."

I quote a few lines here (in a translation by D. M. Thomas) because, in them, Memorial found its voice and credo:

> Again the hands of the clock are nearing
> The unforgettable hour. I see, hear, touch
>
> All of you: the cripple they had to support
> Painfully to the end of the line; the moribund;

And the girl who would shake her beautiful head and
Say: "I come here as if it were home."

I should like to call you all by name,
But they have lost the lists. . . .

I have woven for them a great shroud
Out of the poor words I overheard them speak.

I remember them always and everywhere,
And if they shut my tormented mouth,

Through which a hundred million of my people cry,
Let them remember me also. . . .

And if ever in this country they should want
To build me a monument

I consent to that honor,
But only on the condition that they

Erect it not on the seashore where I was born:
My last links there were broken long ago,

Nor by the stump in the Royal Gardens,
Where an inconsolable young shade is seeking me,

But here, where I stood for three hundred hours
And where they never, never opened the doors for me.

Lest in blessed death I should forget
The grinding scream of the Black Marias,

The hideous clanging gate, the old
Woman wailing like a wounded beast.

And may the melting snow drop like tears
From my motionless bronze eyelids,

And the prison pigeons coo above me
And the ships sail slowly down the Neva.

A few days after the demonstration, Afanasyev and Klimov hauled their huge sacks of petitions through the gates of the Kremlin. It was the opening day of the Nineteenth Party Conference, and the Party apparatchiks eyed them suspiciously. Afanasyev and Klimov presented the petitions to Gorbachev and his aides and waited for a response.

On the last day of the Nineteenth Party Conference—after Boris Yeltsin's dramatic appeal for rehabilitation, after a war over the direction of reform—Gorbachev took the podium and delivered a long speech. Just before he finished, he said that an idea had been "introduced," one that echoed a similar suggestion in 1961 by Khrushchev—to build a memorial to the victims of the Stalin era. Now the Party, he said, must finally approve the idea. Gorbachev's words had a tacked-on feel to them; they sounded like an afterthought. In fact, it was one of the most critical moments in the political and emotional life of the perestroika era. Although the Party would later try to block Memorial, although it would try to deny it funds and meeting places, the group had sown the first seeds of a struggle far deeper and more unpredictable than anyone had imagined.

CHAPTER 9

WRITTEN ON THE WATER

Just as Memorial's demonstration outside the sports area was ending, Arnold Yeryomenko's plane was landing. Yeryomenko lived in Magadan, the city that had once been the "capital" of the Kolyma region of the gulag archipelago in the Soviet far east. The rest of the passengers were worn out from the ten-hour flight to Moscow aboard Aeroflot's cramped and creaky liner. The one meal served had been a Dixie cup of green mineral water and a greasy chicken wing. Somehow, Arnold bounded off the plane "refreshed," he said. He'd come to Moscow on a mission.

Yeryomenko was the leader of Democratic Initiative, the first non-Communist political group ever in Magadan. The group's membership decided to send him as a "delegate" to the Nineteenth Party Conference. "We figured that if democracy is starting in this country, then we ought to be heard, too," he said. The membership passed a hat and collected his 800-ruble round-trip airfare.

Before he left, Arnold called me in Moscow. He said he had heard my articles read in Russian on Radio Liberty. Could we meet? Of course. Not only had Yeryomenko managed to sound engaging at a distance of six thousand miles, I was also eager to talk to someone from Magadan. Magadan had always defined distant to me, an almost mythical outpost, closer to

Los Angeles than Moscow, where the winters are ten months long and a mild day in January is forty degrees below zero. Magadan is the setting for two of the best books ever written about Stalinism: Yevgenia Ginzburg's memoirs *Journey into the Whirlwind* and her son Vasily Aksyonov's novel *The Burn.* Magadan "was, in a sense, the freest town in Russia," Aksyonov wrote. "In it there lived the special deportees and the special contingent, which included those categorized SHE (Socially Harmful Elements) and SDE (Socially Dangerous Elements), nationalists, social democrats, Catholics, Muslims, Buddhists . . . people who recognized themselves as the lowest slaves and who, therefore, had challenged fate." In June 1988, Magadan was still closed to foreigners. The only way to get there was on an official Potemkin-village tour with the Foreign Ministry. It was on such a trip in the summer of 1944 that Vice President Henry Wallace decided that Kolyma was wonderful and the regional secret police chief, the infamous General Goglidze, was "a very fine man, very efficient, gentle and understanding with people."

I met Arnold at the Lenin statue on October Square near my building. He was in his early fifties with the silver hair and fine features of Cesar Romero, quick and jaunty as a bantamweight.

"You are Remnick?" he said. "Well, come, I've got great things to show you."

Arnold spoke such good English that when we switched to Russian I had the odd sensation that he had an American accent. Probably he was just dumbing down his Russian for my sorry self. He told me he had learned his English in school "but mostly from listening to 'the foreign voices,' " Radio Liberty, the Voice of America, and, especially, the BBC. Evidently the jamming system had been less efficient in Magadan than in Moscow. On the short walk to my apartment, Arnold told me he was born in 1937, the year the purges really began. His father was an engineer who had been assigned to Magadan for his technical expertise. In those days, Magadan was still short on barracks and ports for the slave ships that came in every few days from Vladivostok.

"It was kind of a gulag boomtown," Arnold said with a terrific smile; it was the "gateway to hell." Even in late spring, the ice was thick near the shore. It was on days like those that the tramp steamers could not make it through to the docks. The prisoners, many of them barefoot and dressed in rags, had to walk on the ice for the last mile to shore. A camp orchestra would assemble on the ice and play for the new prisoners, usually a march or a waltz.

In a way, arrival was a relief, the journey had been such hell. The train trip to the far east from Moscow and European Russia was in cattle cars, and it took a month at least. The prisoners were packed together so tightly that it

was said there were those who starved to death and were found still upright at the end of the journey. At the embarkation points on the Pacific, inspectors went up and down the line looking for slaves. Like horsemen before an auction, inspectors checked the prisoners' teeth and eyes. They pinched their biceps and buttocks to see how much muscle tone there was left after more than a month in the cattle cars. At Vanino in the late 1940s the NKVD had a contract to supply some state firms for 120,000 slave workers a year.

The rest of the prisoners were then packed into the holds of tramp steamers headed for Magadan. As the purges became a permanent condition of state in the thirties and forties, rumors of the sea journey reached Moscow and the other big cities on the "mainland." But no rumor could capture the horror of the voyage itself. Michael Solomon, a Romanian prisoner, wrote of his shock as he was herded into the hold of the ship *Sovlatvia* headed north to Magadan. It was a scene, he said, "which neither Goya nor Gustave Doré could ever have imagined": thousands of men and women, dressed in rags, half-dead and covered with boils and blisters. "At the bottom of the stairway we had just climbed down stood a giant cask, on the edges of which, in full view of the soldiers standing on guard above, women were perched like birds, and in the most incredible positions. There was no shame, no prudery, as they crouched there to urinate or empty their bowels. One had the impression that they were some half-human, half-bird creatures which belonged to a different world and a different age. Yet seeing a man come down the stairs, although a mere prisoner like themselves, many of them began to smile and some even tried to comb their hair."

Later, the officers would load on board even more prisoners—not more "politicals," but murderers, thieves, rapists, whores: "When I saw this half-naked, tattooed apelike horde invade the hold," Yevgenia Ginzburg wrote, "I thought that it had been decided that we were to be killed off by mad women. The fetid air reverberated to their shrieks, their ferocious obscenities, their wild laughter and their caterwaulings. They capered about incessantly stamping their feet even though there appeared to be no room to put a foot down. Without wasting any time, they set about terrorizing and bullying the 'ladies'—the politicals—delighted to find that the 'enemies of the people' were creatures even more despised and outcast than themselves. Within five minutes we had a thorough introduction to the law of the jungle." Feeding time came and the warders dumped a cartload of bread down the hold and into the gaping mouths of the beasts.

The killing went on and on, day after day, and in every form. The ships would often get caught in the ice far from any shore, and the crew had no choice but to wait out the weather and keep the rations for themselves. The wait could go on for weeks, even months. Thousands of prisoners would die

of hunger and disease. Sometimes the guards left the corpses in the hold with the living. Sometimes they pitched the dead over the rails onto the ice, where they stayed, day after day, rotting, until the thaw came and the sea swallowed them and the ship sailed on, to Magadan.

That was the world Arnold Yeryomenko grew up in, the landscape of his childhood and youth. "The ships would come in to shore all the time," he said as we sat down to some coffee in my kitchen. "I remember seeing the prisoners in huge lines, five, six thousand men and women in rags, exhausted, being marched from the ships and onto the shore and up to the barracks. The guards were always beating them in the street, and sometimes you heard the pistols going off. Sometimes you'd see a dead man in the street. Maybe no one had time to cart him off."

Arnold's professional life never really got going. He studied engineering and foreign languages in the early 1960s. But he was broke, and, to make some extra money, he tried to trade on the black market. He was arrested and put in jail for ten years. When he was freed, he was not allowed to live in Moscow, and he moved back home to Magadan. The humiliation of his arrest and imprisonment and his growing sense that the cruelty he had seen as a child was still an essential part of the social order of the Soviet Union helped make Yeryomenko an angry man, a political man. In 1981, he wrote a book condemning the Communist Party and circulated it in samizdat editions. For that he got two more years in prison.

When perestroika finally started in Moscow, Arnold was impudent enough to think that reform ought to come to Magadan as well. He started Democratic Initiative. He stood outside KGB headquarters—he and a few kids and housewives—shouting slogans into a bullhorn. He was summarily fired from his construction job. The local Party committee and the KGB began to treat this out-of-work engineer and his younger friends in Democratic Initiative like an invading army. They bugged, harassed, and occasionally jailed the members on false charges.

Arnold said I should come see for myself. I told him I'd always wanted to go to Magadan, but it was still a closed city.

"Well, you don't have to go," he said. "I can show it to you on television." He took a videocassette out of his briefcase and said, "Do you have Beta or VHS?" He explained that one of the members of Democratic Initiative had bought a videocamera on a trip to Alaska. "It's better than having a newspaper, which of course, we can't," he said.

The tape flickered and jerked and then finally found its focus on a crowd of about 2,500 people on the city's main square. Lenin Square, of course. There were signs protesting that the city's leading Communist Party officials had grabbed up all the delegate seats to the Party conference in Moscow.

There was Arnold shouting into a bullhorn, demanding that the Party, the "sole possessor of power in this country," let representatives from outside the Party apparatus represent Magadan in Moscow. Another speaker pointed to the "White House," the relatively elegant-looking building that was the Party headquarters, and asked why the "Communists always hogged all the wealth."

"That's where the mafia lives!" the speaker shouted. "That's why they have to be guarded day and night by the militia! They're criminals!"

Another speaker demanded that a special hotel for visiting Party officials be converted into a kindergarten. It wasn't easy to make out all they said. The police had hooked up a set of speakers near the demonstration and played deafening Soviet pop music to drown out democracy.

The most dramatic moment came when Ludmila Romanova, a local Party official, accepted Arnold's invitation to address the crowd. The young woman spoke with a kind of hyped-up spirit, but she could only talk in the old Party way. She told the anti-Party demonstrators that they had assembled "without proper permission from the Party." But she did say that workers would be "invited to participate" in discussions about new schools and other civic improvements.

"We're sick of your promises!" "We don't want your words!" came some of the more polite replies.

Then Romanova ended with a prim reminder of "Soviet legality."

"You must know," she said, "that according to the Constitution, the political rights given to the people should not damage the rights of others." The crowd was less than impressed with her insinuation and booed her off the platform.

Now Arnold was laughing. He got up from his chair and pointed to a building and a set of windows in the top right-hand corner of the screen.

"There," he said. "Look at that building. You can see the KGB guys in the windows taking our picture."

The next day, Arnold tried to deliver Democratic Initiative's manifesto and petitions to the Party conference. We stood about half a mile from the Kremlin and watched one black limousine after another ferry the visiting Party hacks to the conference.

"They won't let me near the place," Arnold said.

After he dumped off his documents at a Party "reception hall," he booked a seat back to Magadan. Back at my place, we watched some of the conference on television. We were like football fanatics on New Year's Day. We

could not take our eyes off the set. Arnold hissed the hacks and cheered on the liberals.

"You know what will bring these people down?" he said. "Embarrassment. One day they will just slink off the stage."

Like most of the liberals in Moscow, Arnold was all for Gorbachev's scheme to create a new legislature, but suspicious that it would be rigged and loaded with Party leaders. He loved watching Yeltsin's confrontation with Yegor Ligachev, his plea to the Party for rehabilitation and his call for a faster, more radical, program of democratization. Looking dazed by the task ahead, Yeltsin jutted his jaw and barged on, evoking in speech if not in manner nothing less than the return of Nikolai Bukharin and other Old Bolsheviks who had been shot in the purges and restored to the Party ranks under Gorbachev:

"Comrade delegates! Rehabilitation fifty years after a person's death has now become the rule, and this has a healthy effect on society. But I am asking for political rehabilitation while I am still alive."

Yeltsin also lambasted Ligachev for trying to railroad him and obstruct reform, in general. Ligachev had his chance at the podium and replied, "Boris, you are wrong!" To Yeltsin's barrel-chested, hangdog heavyweight, Ligachev came across on television as a street-tough middleweight. He was furious, accusing Yeltsin of sitting mute at Politburo meetings. The nomenklatura in the hall roared their approval while most of the country made a hero of Yeltsin.

Yeryomenko reveled in this liberating theater. Like millions of others, he was delighted to see the Party begin, at last, to feed on itself, to expose its corruptions and splits, live on television. But most of all, Arnold was thrilled that Memorial had won its great victory at the conference. By allowing the construction of a memorial to the victims of the regime, the Party, largely in spite of itself, had begun a period of national repentance.

"At least the conference wasn't a complete loss," he said from the airport. I told him I still wanted to come to Magadan. "I'll see you soon," I said. We both laughed. The possibility still seemed very far away.

Memorial's victory at the Party conference was sweet, but even its leaders knew that there was something too easy and superficial about it. "Stalin Died Yesterday" was the title of Mikhail Gefter's contribution to the "There Is No Other Way" collection and by that he meant that Stalinism infected everything and everyone in the Soviet Union. Every factory and collective farm, every school and orphanage was built on Stalinist principles of gargantuan

scale and iron authority. In every relationship—in trade, on buses, in almost any simple transaction—people treated each other with contempt and suspicion. That was Stalinism, too. Only now were people beginning to wonder out loud about the efficacy of such a life. Only now were they permitted to express those doubts in the papers, in books, on television. "Stalinism is deep inside of every one of us," Afanasyev told me after the Party conference. "Getting rid of that spirit is the most difficult thing of all. Next to that, getting the Party to permit a monument is nothing."

I met a filmmaker named Tofik Shakhverdiyev, an Azerbaijani who had made a documentary called *Stalin Is with Us.* He interviewed Stalinists all over the country: a Cossack on the Don River, a cab driver in Tbilisi, the man who was Bukharin's guard during the purge trial. At one point in the film, a group of veterans is sitting around a table singing songs in praise of Stalin. The old soldiers seem transported.

I told Tofik about my Kaganovich obsession, and instead of giving me a patronizing look, he laughed and said, "Me, too. But he just won't answer the door." Lately, *Moscow News* and a few other papers had been trying to figure out, through interviews and polls, how people felt about Stalin. Just the idea of political opinion was new. But the polls were primitive, and I thought Tofik would have as good a sense as anyone what it meant now to be a Stalinist. Who were they? What did they want?

"The number of people who openly defend Stalin, really admire him, is limited," Tofik said. "But if you talk about people whose first instinct is a passion for order, then I think you are talking about not less than half the people in the Soviet Union. You see, we use fashionable words like 'democracy' and 'pluralism' now, but so few people can really live without the security of complete order and control.

"In a perverse sense, the dissidents and the nonconformists of today are Stalinists. We democrats have become like-minded in a way. We ignore or ridicule what's really out there. But off to the side, the Stalinists are going against the current, and this halo of being dissidents, strange as it seems, gives them a sort of dignity. They believed in their great cause and the creation of a great society, of Communism. They see democracy and capitalism as a matter of the rich exploiting the poor, while in our system, we are all poor. For them, the lack of an iron hand means prostitution, AIDS, emigration to the West. Stalinists derive their sense of themselves from their connection to the memory of the great man himself. When a slave kisses the hand of the master who whips him, he is getting some of the power of the master. A belief in his greatness appears."

That spirit remained on view, at least physically, in the Republic of Georgia, among other places. Like all reporters in Moscow, I eventually made a trip to

Gori, Stalin's hometown. As if that would tell me much. Gori was about an hour's drive through the mountains from the Georgian capital, Tbilisi.

The centerpiece of the town was one of the most spectacular bits of kitsch on earth. The Gori Party authorities, with some funding from Moscow, had moved Stalin's ancestral house—a tiny two-room structure—to the center of town in 1936. In an attempt to make a hut into Olympus, the Party had built neoclassical columns to frame the great man's childhood home. The rooms themselves were intended to speak for Stalin's Leninist modesty. One room had a simple wooden table, the other a portrait of Stalin with his beady-eyed, black-shrouded mother. Next door, the vast Stalin Museum, as grandiose as the columns, was closed—"pending reconsideration," the guard told me.

People who had finished looking around the Stalin house sat outside in the park under the trees eating sausages and apples. Not a single visitor I spoke to said he had any problem with Stalin. They said the country needed someone just like him to put an end to all the "confusion." A factory worker I talked with showed me the tattoo on his chest. It was an impressive double portrait of Lenin and Stalin. I asked the worker about Gorbachev. Was there room for him?

"Gorbachev?" he said. "I wouldn't tattoo his name on my ass."

Stalin was born Iosif Vissarionovich Djugashvili on December 21, 1879. His father was a drunk and beat his wife. He died young. When he was a boy, Stalin's favorite story was Aleksandr Kazbeg's *The Patricide,* the tale of an avenging hero of Georgia named Koba. After he read the book, Stalin demanded that all his friends call him Koba. "That became his ideal," wrote a childhood friend. Stalin's closest comrades in the party called him Koba—sometimes until the day he had them shot.

Stalin studied at a Russian orhthodox seminary. The monks said he was "rude and disrespectful." His mother always wanted him to enter the clergy. When he visited her in 1936—by then he was already the Soviet leader and planning the Great Purge—she said, "What a pity you did not become a priest."

In 1895, Stalin wrote:

> Know this: He who fell like ashes to the ground
> He who was never oppressed,
> Will rise higher than the great mountains,
> On the wings of a bright hope.

In 1926, Stalin's wife, Nadezhda, left him. He begged her to return, and at the same time had her followed by the secret police. Six years later they

fought over Stalin's brutal treatment of the peasantry in Ukraine. When the row was over, Nadezhda left the room and shot herself. Her daughter, Svetlana, later said, "I believe that my mother's death, which he took as a personal betrayal, deprived his soul of the last vestiges of human warmth."

Stalin lived for years by himself in the Kremlin. One of his guards said that Stalin bugged the phones of all his advisers and spent long periods of the day listening in on their conversations. Aleksei Ribin, a secret police officer and Stalin's guard, wrote in *Sociological Research* magazine that Stalin loved to tell his limousine driver to pull over to the side of the road to give old women rides home. "He was just that kind of man," said Ribin.

In the Homeric tradition, *Pravda* used countless titles to refer to Stalin: Leader and Teacher of the Workers of the World, Father of the Peoples, Wise and Intelligent Chief of the Soviet People, the Greatest Genius of All Times and Peoples, the Greatest Military Leader of All Times and Peoples, Coryphaeus of the Sciences, Faithful Comrade-in-Arms of Lenin, Devoted Continuer of Lenin's Cause, the Mountain Eagle, and Best Friend of All Children.

There were Western intellectuals who adored Stalin. In the midst of a state-imposed famine in 1932, George Bernard Shaw looked up from his plate at the Metropole Hotel and said, gaily, "Do you see any food shortages here?" Later he added that he "took his hat off" to Stalin "for having delivered the goods." In a meeting with Stalin, Shaw's traveling companion Lady Astor asked, "How long will you go on killing people?"

"As long as necessary," Stalin replied.

Lady Astor quickly changed the subject, asking Stalin if he could help her find a good Russian nanny for her children.

After his own audience with Stalin, H. G. Wells reported he had never "met a man more candid, fair and honest." The American ambassador in Moscow, Joseph Davies, wrote of Stalin that "a child would like to sit on his lap and a dog would sidle up to him."

Stalin, who was five feet four, wanted a court portrait done showing him as a tall man with powerful hands. The painter Nalbandian complied by portraying Stalin from a flattering angle with his hands folded, powerfully, across his belly. Stalin had his other portrait painters shot and their paintings burned. Stalin rewrote the official *Short Biography of Stalin*, personally adding the passage "Stalin never allowed his work to be marred by the slightest hint of vanity, conceit, or self-adulation."

Stalin died of a stroke on March 5, 1953. He once said that those revolutionaries who refused to use terror as a political tool were "vegetarians." According to Roy Medvedev, Stalin's victims numbered forty million.

Solzhenitsyn says the number is far greater—perhaps sixty million. The debate continues even now.

—

It was the trial of the season. Since the rise of Gorbachev, a retired lawyer from Kharkov named Ivan Shekhovtsov had filed repeated lawsuits against various intellectuals and newspapers for "slandering Stalin." He made a career of these suits. Sixteen so far. This time his opposition was *Vechernaya Moskva,* the city's evening newspaper.

STALIN IS THE FATHER OF OUR PEOPLE.

SLANDER IS THE DIRTY WEAPON OF THE ANTI-STALINISTS.

"Get those signs out of here," said the judge.

At the witness table, Shekhovtsov sat taking notes. He wore a suit and a row of military medallions. He had been a tank gunner on the Baltic and Ukrainian fronts in the war and had lost part of a lung in a firefight. There were a half-dozen benches, all crammed with Shekhovtsov's supporters. Most of them were older men and women, and nearly all wore ribbons and medals from the war. They were angry that they had to get rid of their banners, but they made up for it with loud gossiping. There were some nasty remarks about the Jews and Armenians, about Raisa Gorbachev, about Memorial. They carried copies of right-wing journals, *Nash Sovremenik* ("Our Contemporary"), which was hard-line Russian nationalist, and *Molodaya Gvardiya* ("Young Guard"), which was hard-line Stalinist. There was a lot of whispered speculation about whether the representative from *Vechernaya Moskva* was a Jew. Of course, they concluded. She must be.

"We spent our lives building socialism, and now these people—Afanasyev, Adamovich, Korotich—they are getting rid of socialism and they are succeeding," a woman named Valentina Nikitina told me as we waited through the lull in the proceedings.

She, too, was a decorated veteran of the war. She said she had lost many friends and relatives in the war—"half the people I knew," she said—and the idea of reforming, much less dismantling, the system was unconscionable. "These people are like the Hungarians in 1956. They are staging a counterrevolution. The majority of our people support Stalin as a builder of socialism. The kulaks, most of them, were Jews. The secret police at the Belomor Canal were Jews. The leader was a Jew! The chief engineer was a Jew! If the Jews would only move to an autonomous region, they would have a wonderful life!"

I thanked her for sharing her thoughts with me and turned to Shekhovtsov himself. He looked imperious and bored. He drummed his fingers on the

witness table, making sure the three judges could observe his superiority even as they conferred. Shekhovtsov had no lawyer. He was his own advocate.

A few yards away, the woman from *Vechernaya Moskva* finally stood and told the judges that her lawyer could not make the session. Could she have a continuance?

"He's on vacation," she said uncertainly.

Shekhovtsov rolled his eyes. The crowd chuckled and hissed. The judge set another court date.

"A lot of rubbish that is!" my seatmate muttered. We all stood to leave. As the woman from *Vechernaya Moskva* left the crowded little room, she kept her head down and took quick, purposeful steps toward the door.

"Slanderer!" the crowd hissed at her. "Shame on you!"

Out in the parking lot, Shekhovtsov's supporters unfurled their banners and celebrated. I introduced myself to Shekhovtsov.

"Then I suppose you want to interview me," he said. "Well, I could use a lift to the train station. And maybe something to eat, if you don't mind too much."

I asked Shekhovtsov why he bothered. Why was he spending all his money and energy filing suits and always losing? He looked at me, not angrily, but with a sort of kindly eye. I was a foreigner and didn't know any better.

"It is I who is restoring the historical truth," he said. "I didn't know anyone who was repressed. In the press now they are saying that in every house everyone at least knew someone who was repressed. In Kharkov, I investigated one hundred and fifty households and not one said it was waiting for a knock on the door. These numbers you are hearing are all sensations, pure libel. During collectivization in 1929, my grandfather was kicked off his land and exiled. But people gave us clothing and food, and after six months we returned to the land. During the exile, my brother died of an inflammation of the lung, but my mother never blamed Stalin. It was the local officials! My mother is eighty-six and she understands this with her woman's mind!

"From the point of practical deeds, Stalin did more than even Lenin. But that, of course, is probably a matter of longevity. I get letters all the time from people nostalgic for the life under Stalin—their joy in labor and love of the Motherland, how they lived with heads raised high and sang patriotic songs. Right now we don't hear anyone singing. And it's not that there is an absence of songs to sing. There is an absence of faith. You see, people forget. They need to be reminded. In the thirties, when I was in the Young Pioneers and in Komsomol, there was unprecedented patriotism in this country. There was a willingness to sacrifice personal needs for the good of the nation. People had in mind great aims and a wonderful future, and so they endured. Stalin is with us and Stalin will come. That is the mind-set of a generation. We went

into battle with his name on our lips. He took Russia, which had a wooden plow in its hands, and he left it with an atomic bomb. Such a man cannot be slandered. The young should learn their history."

In his most celebrated suit, Shekhovtsov charged that Ales Adamovich, the Byelorussian writer and one of the leaders of Memorial, had slandered Stalin in a film called *Purification.* To Shekhovtsov, Adamovich represented the "worst kind of liar," a "man old enough to know better" who was trying to lead the youth of the Soviet Union astray.

"People have lost the ability to learn the truth for themselves," Shekhovtsov said. "They listen to Korotich and Yevtushenko. They don't read the truthful histories that have been published by the Institute of Marxism-Leninism."

And what about Sakharov? After all, Sakharov was now the nominal chairman of Memorial. Could he not be trusted either?

"Under Brezhnev, Sakharov was exiled to Gorky so that he would not have the chance to talk about nuclear secrets or slander the system," Shekhovtsov said. "Now, under Gorbachev's instructions, he has been returned. But in revenge, Sakharov is trying to slander us, and he is guiding the greatest power in the country—Memorial. Memorial can one day turn into an alternative party."

Shekhovtsov said he knew Nina Andreyeva and thought her a "good worker." Their acquaintance seemed confirmed when he said he was quite convinced that "the majority of people who slander Stalin and the homeland are Jews."

A few weeks later, Shekhovtsov called to tell me he had some news. He'd won his suit against *Vechernaya Moskva.* Not that it had slandered Stalin. But the court did rule that the paper had libeled Shekhovtsov when it said that he had used "Stalinist methods" when he was working as a prosecutor. The paper printed a long apology, and Shekhovtsov said he had won a great victory for himself and, most of all, for "Stalin's good name."

"The day I stop my fight," he said, "is the day I die."

In the courtroom, I'd gotten a dinner invitation from a woman who described herself as a "great lover of Stalin," Kira Korniyenkova. She was a matronly woman in her late fifties. Plump and stern, she wore wire-rimmed glasses, and her hair was done up in a bun. She looked like a teacher who specialized in handwriting and never gave an A. Her apartment was dim, dowdy, crammed with books. She lived with her two parakeets, Tashka and Mashinka. "My children," she called them as she poked the cage. She had never married. Never wanted to. "I wanted to be free," she said. "When you have close

relatives living with you, they get in the way. They are a hindrance. I've got my plan and I am fulfilling that plan."

If she ever had a passion, it was Stalin. "I have always loved him. I have dedicated my life to him and his memory." Kira Alekseyevna was a woman unstuck in time. She spent countless days at the Lenin Library researching the "scandalous" charges of Western and Soviet scholars writing on Stalin. Medvedev, Solzhenitsyn, Afanasyev, Roginsky—they were all "enemies" to her. She wanted to disprove "everything they say about how Stalin killed millions. He didn't. He only attacked enemies of the people." Sometimes she wrote letters to the Central Committee to complain about one point or another in the avalanche of articles in the liberal press.

"Feel right at home," she said, and left me in the dining room with the parakeets. She went off to cook. The room was decorated with dozens of pictures of Stalin. Stalin as a boy. Stalin with Lenin in Gorky. Stalin on the front page of *Pravda.* Stalin in white military dress. She had hundreds more photographs in albums and shoeboxes. She had stacks of photos wrapped with purple silk ribbons.

"I've never seen anything like this," I said, shouting politely down the hall as if I were admiring my hostess's Matisse.

"Oh, I've got lots of them!" she said, shouting back from the kitchen. "Look, look . . ."

She came running down the hall, flushed. She started shuffling through a stack of pictures.

"Look!" she said, thrusting them a few inches from my eyes. "Each one shows a different emotion, every stage of that great man's life." Kira glowed.

Like a lover of Wagner who goes every year to Bayreuth, Korniyenkova took an annual pilgrimage to Gori. Sometimes, she said, she went twice a year: once on the anniversary of Stalin's death, once to celebrate Victory Day. "There are a lot of people who think as I do. In 1979, we gathered there for the centenary of his birth. I think more than thirty thousand people visited the Stalin Museum that day. People who want to build a monument to the so-called victims of Stalin should think about that a little. It's not necessary to build a monument to people who were imprisoned. They had something to answer for. It's not necessary to build monuments for rich peasants who were purged. They should build monuments to the Communists. Traitors don't deserve monuments."

Kira served pot roast and potatoes. By the by, it seemed, she said that two of her relatives had been sent to the camps during the purges. Their crime had been being late to work.

"They were properly judged," Kira said. I didn't say anything at all. Tashka and Mashinka twittered in their cage. Kira's voice rose in anger.

"Was it Stalin's fault that my uncles were out late drinking and came in late for work? They had to be punished for that. I am a person who loves order. I am for real order, an iron hand or some other kind of hand. I am for a situation in which people are answerable for their deeds."

The food was delicious, but Kira Alekseyevna did not eat. She lectured. She swooned. She ascended to rapture. "I only wish we could be living in such merry days as we had then," she said. "When you see the documentary films, you can see how animated people were, how happy they were. Their faces glowed. They had poor tools, but they worked and they loved working. And now we are supposed to think that labor is 'monkey's work.' It was always so wonderful for the people to tell Stalin about their successes. I was only eighteen when Stalin was alive, but I could see how my mother worked in those years. She didn't work because she was afraid of anything, but for the sheer pleasure of it. Those parades on Red Square were some of the happiest days of our lives."

I asked her if she had ever actually seen Stalin. Kira's eyes watered as if she had suddenly been swept by a wave of memory, love recalled. "The last time I saw Stalin was in 1952. I remember the mood of the workers when, at first, Stalin could not be seen standing on the Lenin Mausoleum. They mourned. But then he appeared, and you cannot quite imagine the happiness we felt. He was quite old by then, and we greeted him with such joy. We were all fulfilling the tasks he had set out for us. We were ready to go to the moon for him. We loved Stalin, we believed in him with all our hearts."

When I asked Kira how she had reacted to Stalin's death, she told me, and cried all the while. After she heard the news, she said, she felt ill and would not leave the apartment for several days.

"On the day of the funeral I went out into the street, and you could hear all the factory sirens wailing," she said. "They used to do that when a worker left a plant forever, and now they were wailing for Stalin. Nowadays we have no such passion for our leader. Everyone gets his salary, but there is no food. How can I believe in these rulers? I believe in real things."

After dinner, Kira told me that she had once been friends—"oh, well, not friends, but comrades"—with a few of Stalin's relatives. She had even visited Molotov at his dacha. Molotov, she said, had "the eyes of wisdom." Until he died in his nineties, Molotov would tell all his visitors that Stalin had acted rightly. There had been enemies, and enemies, he said, had to be eliminated.

But hadn't there been mistakes? I asked Kira Alekseyevna. Did Stalin never commit a mistake?

"Mistakes?" she said. "Yes, he made one. He died too soon."

—

There was one other visitor to the Stalin trial I wanted to see: Stalin's grandson, Yevgeny Djugashvili. There were four Stalin grandchildren still living in Moscow: a housewife, a surgeon, a theater director, and Djugashvili. The first two begged off from a meeting. I spoke with the director, a slender and quiet man named Aleksandr Burdansky, at his office at the Soviet Army Theater, a vast building shaped like a star. All his life, he had done what he could to distance himself from Stalin. He changed his name. ("I think Burdansky sounds better than Stalin. Don't you agree?") He quit military school and always tried to look at Stalin "the way an artist would."

"I have to carry a burden, but I am not to blame for having such a grandfather. I think and act like a normal man. I have no extreme views about Stalin. I try to understand him as a phenomenon. Shakespeare's *Richard III* helped me understand Stalin. Not the play so much as Richard's biography. Richard was born a hunchback, but he had talent and a quick mind. So the man wanted to prove his right to be on an equal footing with everyone else."

If Burdansky had not pushed Stalin off to the boundaries of his mind, then he certainly liked to think he had. I had never known anyone to talk about Stalin with such an air of boredom and abstraction. "Looking at it from a civilized point of view," he said professionally, "it would be naive to regard Stalin as pure evil after he was portrayed by everyone as the friend of all peoples, children, and animals, the most outstanding personality of the age, and so on. I think he correctly translated Marx's ideas into life. It was the only way to carry them through, alas. . . ."

Burdansky did have one public moment of pique—an appearance on television in which he made it plain that he despised his grandfather. He outraged the Stalinist wing of the Stalin family. When I called Yevgeny Djugashvili on the phone, he said, "Just one thing. Don't talk to me about that faggot half brother of mine. He betrayed Stalin. His grandfather."

Djugashvili was the son of Yakov, who was captured by the Nazis and, when Stalin refused or failed to win his release, was executed. The day I met him, Djugashvili was preparing to retire from his job in the Defense Ministry in Moscow and retire, at the age of fifty-five, to Tbilisi. The man who opened the door looked exactly like Stalin: a little thinner, perhaps, his mustache more a pencil line than a hairbrush, but, still, the resemblance was chilling. He was in full military dress and, at first, conducted himself with the formality of a Politburo member. We entered a room that had several portraits of Stalin on the wall and a bookcase crammed with Party and military histories published in the Stalin era. There was a simple table and on it a stack of fresh paper and several sharpened pencils.

"So, what is question number one?" he said as he stared hard at me across the table. This was not a naive man. He was not so foolish as to think that an American reporter was visiting in order to do anything other than harm—and, in this, I suppose, he was right. But there was no point in confronting him. I simply asked him what he thought about his grandfather, what he thought of the attacks in the press and within the Party. It was the question he had expected.

"I always adored Stalin," he said. "No congress, no book or magazine article is ever going to change that and make me doubt him. He is my grandfather, first of all, and I adore him."

Solzhenitsyn was "an immoral scum," and, as for Gorbachev, "The Party's authority has fallen, this is obvious. They say the fish rots from the head. And when the fish is rotten, people throw it away. Everything is moving in that direction. In the end, I think the party will be disbanded."

Djugashvili had a nasty word to say for all the obvious people—Shatrov, Afanasyev, Sakharov, Yeltsin, the leaders of Memorial. He went on for a while, too, about the latest plays and television programs that had slandered his grandfather. He clearly kept up with it all. The only thing that seemed to lift his mood was his own recent appearance, as Stalin, in a Georgian film production.

"They say I'm a real chip off the old block!" And then he stopped and stared at me once more. For a moment it really felt as if Stalin were there. But Djugashvili broke the spell.

"Enough!" he said, slamming his hand down on the table. His face broke into a weird grin. "I like you! I have decided that! Now I will make you my real guest!"

In Georgia, a good host usually shows his guest around the farm and the farmhouse. Stalin's grandson showed me his kitchen, then his bathroom shelves.

"I built these myself!" he said, waving his hand across them lovingly as if they were a prize in a game show.

"And here is the bedroom . . . and over here . . . the living room! . . . By the way, you know, I never got anything out of being Stalin's grandson. But, of course, when I needed an apartment I wrote a letter to Brezhnev. They gave me this place. And they jumped me ahead on the waiting list for a car, too. So it hasn't all been bad.

"And this," he said, entering the kitchen, "is the kitchen again."

Djugashvili yanked a jerry can out from under a table. "Here is cha-cha," he said, lifting the moonshine. Then he put a watermelon in my arms, and we marched back to the living room.

"Pour out two glasses of cha-cha," he said. Djugashvili cut thick slices of the watermelon with a curved dagger and salted them. He stood and lifted his glass and waited. I stood.

"We shall drink to friendship between nations!" he said. Fair enough, I thought, and we both downed the cha-cha, a home brew from Tbilisi. On first gulp, the drink did not seem as obvious or as strong as Russian vodka.

Djugashvili stood again. "In a Georgian house," he said, "the host makes all the toasts, and in my house, the second toast is always to Stalin!"

I felt a wave of nausea sweep through me and weaken my knees. But I kept my glass high and my eyes fixed on my host's. "The Soviet Union took on the brunt of the war, and Stalin was at the head of all that," he went on. "He took a backward country, with peasants in felt boots, and made it great. And yet we still curse him. These people should be punished and their lies exposed! I think there will come a day when the Soviet people will give their evaluation. And so . . . to Stalin!"

"To Stalin," I said. And may God forgive me.

By the end of 1988, there were chapters of Memorial in over two hundred Soviet cities. A debate was beginning between members who wanted to limit Memorial's attention to the repression during the Stalin period and those who thought it should widen to include all acts from the first arrests and executions under Lenin to the death of the dissident writer Anatoly Marchenko in a prison camp in December 1986. In other words, some Memorial members were beginning to speak not merely of the "aberration of Stalin" but of a criminal regime.

Novy Mir, Neva, and other journals began to publish articles critical not only of Stalin, but of Lenin and even the Revolution. In January 1989, Yuri Afanasyev presided over a two-day constituent congress of Memorial. Vadim Medvedev, a leading member of the Politburo, tried to shut down the session before it ever began, citing obscure reasons of "permission" and "sanction." Sakharov called Medvedev and informed him that the Politburo had no business getting involved. "If you shut us out of our meeting hall, we will hold the congress in apartments all over Moscow," he said. Medvedev gave up, and the congress went on. The Communist Party was beginning to lose control of history, and a Party that could not be sure of its hold on the past had to be nervous about its future.

But even as Memorial expanded its definition of the past, its essential purpose remained the same: to honor the dead, to give them back their names. Some of the younger historians and volunteers worked on their own to accumulate more information on arrests, executions, exiles. Others made

careful studies of existing history textbooks and won a series of critical victories when the Party decided to rewrite the schoolbooks, eliminate high school ideology exams, and make mandatory university courses in Marxism-Leninism and scientific socialism as optional as basket weaving.

No one took the mission of Memorial more literally than Aleksandr Milchakov. A journalist whose father had been the general secretary of the Young Communist League and head of one of the industrial ministries, Milchakov grew up in the House on the Embankment. When he was a child, he saw guards in the courtyard carrying what seemed to be violin cases. "In reality, they were cases for their machine guns," he told me. "They were ready for action at all times."

Milchakov was in his fifties and still lived in the apartment of his childhood when I got to know him. As one of the leading figures of Memorial, he decided to narrow his journalism to a single investigation. According to Roy Medvedev's *Let History Judge,* around one thousand people per day were killed during the height of the purges in the late thirties. Milchakov wanted to know where the dead of Moscow were buried.

Milchakov's own father was arrested and spent fifteen years in internal exile. "During those arrests I was only around eight or nine, but I was a curious boy and liked to hang around the courtyard. I saw the reaction of the other boys when their parents were taken away. It was a time when you could hear the clomp of high boots on the staircase. The police were in the habit of never using the elevator. I remember clearly how they took my father down the stairs, not the elevator. And so we all listened every night for footsteps.

"Most of the parents truly believed that there were enemies in the Party and that there was a genuine political struggle going on. They were always surprised when someone was arrested. But their surprise was that someone who they thought was honest turned out to be a traitor. When my father was arrested and our belongings were confiscated, I remember how we children were ousted from our own apartment and we sat in the courtyard on wooden sleighs and no one, none of our old friends, would come near us or talk to us. To talk to a relative of an enemy of the people was the gravest sort of sin."

Using Western and Soviet published sources, Milchakov began researching the location of the biggest mass graves in the Moscow area: the Donskoi Monastery, the grounds of a KGB colony in the village of Butovo, the Kalitnikovsky Cemetery near the city pet market, the fourteenth-century Novospassky Monastery, the banks of the Moscow-Volga Canal.

Early one morning, my friend Jeff Trimble of *U.S. News & World Report* and I met Milchakov outside the House on the Embankment and headed for the Donskoi Monastery. The flower ladies in their blue canvas jackets sat

near the entrances selling carnations, 5 rubles a bunch. Milchakov led us toward the main building on the cemetery grounds, the crematorium. We walked to the back of the building where an old man, an attendant, was watching over a small bonfire of garbage. A few broken tombstones lay on the ground.

"See this gate?" Milchakov said. "Well, every night trucks stacked with bodies came back here and dumped the dead in a heap. They'd already been shot in the back of the head—you bleed less that way—at the Lubyanka prison or at the Military Collegium. They stacked the bodies in old wooden ammunition crates. The workers stoked up the underground ovens—right in through that door—to about twelve hundred degrees centigrade. To make things nice and official they even had professional witnesses who countersigned the various documents. When the bodies were burned they were reduced to ash and some chips of bone, maybe some teeth. Then they buried the ashes in a big pit."

We walked for a few minutes up and down rows of tombs, elaborate monuments that would not have seemed out of place at Père Lachaise Cemetery in Paris. We stopped at a tomb marked "The Grave of Unidentified Corpses, 1930–1942." There were four white plastic tulips stuck in the ground and a stack of rotting carnations that smelled like spilled wine. Someone had also put a tiny icon of Saint George near the base of the monument. Milchakov said that the pit had been five yards deep and twenty feet square and when it was filled completely with ashes—"hundreds and hundreds of pounds of ash"—the secret police paved it over with asphalt. He said there were rumors that Bukharin was buried at Donskoi, but he was not sure.

"When the purges were at their peak," he said, "the furnaces worked all night and the domes of the churches and the roofs of the houses here were covered with ash. There was a fine dust of ash on the snow."

We drove to Kalitnikovsky Cemetery, a dumping ground for thousands of corpses. There was a sausage factory nearby, a fetid place, and Milchakov said, "In the purges, every dog in town came to this place. That smell you smell now was three times as bad; blood in the air. People would lean out their windows and puke all night and the dogs howled until dawn. Sometimes they'd find a dog with an arm or a leg walking through the graveyard."

At the Novospassky Monastery, Milchakov showed us the steep bank near the pond where the NKVD buried the bullet-riddled corpses of foreign Communists: John Penner of the American Communist Party; Herman Remmele, Fritz Schultke, Herman Schubert, and Leo Fleig, leaders of the 842 German antifascists arrested in April 1938; Bela Kun and Laiosh Madyr

of the Hungarian Communists; Vladimir Chopich of the Yugoslavian Party; Marcel Pauker and Alexander Dobrodzhanu of Romania.

"There used to be apple trees along the bank," he said. "They burned them off. They took the prisoners to the monastery church to a room they called 'the baths.' They stripped the prisoners, weighed them, and shot them in the back of the head. In the records, this was called the 'medical process.' They had them shot in a sitting position. A little window would open behind the prisoner's head and the executioner reached in and fired. They used that method so they could avoid strokes, heart attacks, and hysteria. They stacked the bodies like pencils in a box and carried them off in a horse-drawn cart to a crematorium."

Milchakov struggled constantly with the KGB to get permission to carry out excavations on all these sites. The "glasnost" KGB, under Vladimir Kryuchkov, was engaged in an extraordinary public relations maneuver. Kryuchkov tried to humanize the secret police, declaring to the press that he was a great lover of theater and dogs and children. At the same time, the KGB did what it could to deflate the likes of Aleksandr Milchakov. They rebuffed his requests for documents, denied him access to Butovo, and made sure he was followed and harassed when he went on one of his field trips. But the better-known Milchakov became, the more he publicized his findings in a series of articles in *Vechernaya Moskva,* the more he accomplished. The KGB didn't help him much, but they did not stop him either.

A couple of weeks later, we went together to the very edge of town near a water-treatment camp on the banks of the Moscow-Volga Canal. Stalin ordered the construction of the nearly useless canal in 1932, and it was finished in 1937. The workers were slaves, prisoners, most of them peasant farmers who, because they owned a horse or a cow, were declared kulaks and arrested. Genrikh Yagoda, the secret police chief at the time, worked the prisoners to death.

Milchakov said that around 500,000 prisoners died working on the canal, most of them from cold and exhaustion. Even in winter they were given nothing more to wear than a thin jacket. The prisoners lived in shabby barracks next to the construction site. They built the 127-mile canal using shovels, picks, and wheelbarrows. Their diet was dismal. Scientists have done analyses of the teeth of the prisoners. From the way the enamel has worn off, it appears that many of the prisoners ate bark, roots, and grass to supplement the bread and thin gruel they were given.

Milchakov was not prone to superstition, but in order to find the graves along the canal he resorted to divining rods when witnesses and guesswork proved unavailing. He had arranged for us to meet with an expert diviner

near a certain row of birches. Milchakov assured us that in the past he'd been able to dig up several long mass graves with this man's help. And so for a couple of hours we watched in silence as the diviner paced and weaved through the woods and a flock of jays rioted in the trees.

"Someone else is meeting us here, too," Milchakov said. He led me to a monument in the woods: a towering cross wrapped in barbed wire. Memorial had constructed it to honor the prisoners who died building the canal. Next to the cross stood an old, stooped man who introduced himself as "Sergei Burov, pensioner."

He said that when he was a child of ten or eleven, he had lived near the barracks. Every morning, on his way home from the store, the workers would call out to him to throw them pieces of bread.

"I'd wrap the bread in newspaper and throw it," he said. "Sometimes I saw the guards catch them and beat them. I saw the burial teams, too. They were prisoners, and for their work they were given bottles of vodka to keep them drunk. I remember running around, quite innocently, playing, and seeing these men in their prison clothes throwing bodies into the ground. Our parents told us about it and they would say, 'There is some sort of wildness going on.' They just had no idea. They did not want to know."

One morning, years after the canal had been completed, Burov said, he was walking beside it and saw some families on the bank. They were all crying. They folded pieces of paper, letters, and put them in bottles. They corked the bottles and threw them into the water.

"I asked them what they were doing and they told me they were sending messages to people they had lost on the canal," Burov said. "They said they hoped that sometime in the future people would find the bottles and read the letters and remember. They said they were sending the names of their loved ones into the future. They cast their names on the water."

PART II

DEMOCRATIC VISTAS

CHAPTER 10

MASQUERADE

After the Bolsheviks sacked the Winter Palace and seized power in 1917, they still had an empire to win. To help conquer the hearts and minds of the people, Lenin declared cinema the most important of the arts and sent propaganda films and projectionists by train across Russia to advertise the Revolution. Stalin, too, saw the value of the new art. Though his preferred instrument of enculturation was the pistol, he told the Communist Party that cinema was "the greatest means of mass agitation." And so for years after the Great October, workers and peasants in makeshift tent-theaters and railroad cars watched *The Extraordinary Adventures of Mr. West in the Land of the Bolsheviks, Strike, October,* and *Kino-Eye,* imbibing all the while the spirit of revolution.

But with new revolutions come new media. When Gorbachev rose to power in 1985, his chief ideologist and propagandist, Aleksandr Yakovlev, declared, "The television image is everything." Yakovlev had been for ten years an ambassador in Canada, and he often sat at home in Ottawa, watching the Canadian and American networks. Yakovlev also studied television in Moscow. For years he worked in the Central Committee's ideology department. Better than anyone around him, he understood the potential of television as an instrument of persuasion, coercion, and homogenization in an empire as vast as the Soviet Union.

Though the Soviet Union was poor and primitive, nearly everyone had a television. Everyone watched. Yakovlev understood that if there was one ritual that could unite Baltic intellectuals and Siberian peasants, it was television. Above all, he understood the essential value of *Vremya* ("Time"), the official evening news program, a prime-time ritual for nearly 200 million people every night of the week.

—

Stalin had been an untelevised tyrant. He was like some magical Eastern god, unseen, rarely heard. The media technology of the day allowed him easy control of his own cult. To a great extent, Stalin's cult was a phenomenon of print: histories, newspapers, textbooks, posters. It was so easy to manipulate. His photographs in *Pravda* were retouched. Pockmarks disappeared. He grew a head taller. It was impossible to tell he had a withered arm.

But as the system loosened somewhat and technology advanced, the people of the Soviet Union came to know the leaders of the post-Stalin era—Khrushchev and Brezhnev—more intimately, mainly through television and the evening news. *Vremya* was an invention of the Central Committee in the sixties. It was a product designed to be the high mass of a closed, atheist state. The Party ideologists shaped the look and sound of the program with painstaking care. After a long search, they discovered their Big Brother in Igor Kirillov, an unassuming actor of deceptive skill. For twenty years, Kirillov would anchor *Vremya.* He was slender and wore serious glasses, giving him the unthreatening look of a kindly teacher of mathematics. Such was the public face of the Kremlin.

Kirillov was the master of his own voice and presence. Using the slightest gesture or shift in intonation, he made the declarations of the Central Committee seem the revealed wisdom of heaven; he could also report the most ordinary events in the capitalist West as if they were scandals against humanity, a mockery of all that was good and decent. Above all, he commanded attention. "Today, in the Politburo . . ." Kirillov would begin gravely, and every subject would listen, waiting for instruction.

Kirillov, like so many servants of ideology, went through a conversion experience born of necessity under Gorbachev. When I saw him at the state television studios in 1991, Big Brother wore a sweater and the hound-dog look of repentance. He was grateful for a second chance, and now introduced various youth programs. He apologized for himself constantly and wore his cardigan as if it were sackcloth. "The sweater shows I've changed," he said. "The system survived as long as it did thanks to the ideological service of the Communist Party and television. It was a kind of mass hypnosis." For that Kirillov seemed genuinely sorry.

Kirillov had been chosen for his great role thanks to his training in the Stanislavsky Method. "I had the ability to make people believe," he said. Kirillov remembered being overcome with emotion in 1961 when Khrushchev declared on television that the Soviet Union would achieve Communism in his lifetime. "And as Khrushchev spoke those words, the sun came out—and the entire Hall of Congresses seemed to light up. See, we told each other, even nature believes in our cause. That's when my wife and I decided to have our first daughter. We hoped that she would live under Communism. Now I am ashamed that I was used as a marionette and that, through me and through television, a fog was created in the minds of the people."

The producers of *Vremya* knew precisely how to create an imagery of empire and to win over, or at least befuddle, the people. They surrounded Kirillov with the aural and visual symbols of Bolshevik grandeur. When the question arose about what music to use for the opening of the show, the TV ideologists immediately ruled out Mozart and Beethoven. To use German music would have violated the Russian imperial spirit.

"The opening showed the Kremlin as the symbol of empire. The idea was for information to flow from this mighty pinnacle downward," said Eduard Sagalayev, who ran *Vremya* for a while under Gorbachev. "*Vremya* was a medium not only to convey information but also to give instructions, especially to provincial Party leaders and to the most ordinary person. It was the singular connection between supreme authority and the people. I personally saw letters from old ladies addressed to Igor Kirillov saying, 'Please, dear Igor Leonidovich, tell Gorbachev to do such-and-such.' Kirillov was for many people right between general secretary and the Lord God. In fact, he was higher than general secretary, because, after all, it was *Vremya* that prescribed precisely how to live. Kirillov would read the decrees of the Central Committee without any editing or compression, for such decrees were on the order of the Ten Commandments. It was a biblical phenomenon. How could Moses compress the commandments God had handed down to the Israelites?"

The rituals on *Vremya* were always repeated precisely. Even during the Gorbachev era, there was little room for improvisation. If the general secretary was leaving for a trip abroad, the producers of *Vremya* knew precisely how to portray the scene. First, the establishing shot at the airport with a red banner reading "Long Live the Party"; then the Politburo members in their hats and overcoats coming out of the building to wait by the plane; then the general secretary himself saying good-bye, kissing each of his comrades on the cheek; then the general secretary at the top of the airplane stairs, waving farewell.

"Faith was the issue," Sagalayev said. "People swallowed the stereotypes

they were fed, they believed everything was all right, everything was fine, as long as the rituals were in place. Even the kisses at the airport were a cause for pride and joy. Provincial Party secretaries watched and dreamed of the day when they'd be shown on television, leaving for Zimbabwe."

In Brezhnev's dotage—an interminable stretch on the critical list—*Vremya* began to work against him. For a man who could barely function in office, television was a cruel medium. Leonid Parfyonov, a popular television host in the glasnost era, told me with just a touch of irony that after Andrei Sakharov, the most effective dissident of the 1970s was *Vremya.* "It was only then that people could see how decrepit our leaders were," he said. "They'd watch Brezhnev talking, losing his place in his speeches, mumbling like an old man falling apart, and they began to think: 'This is the leader of our great state?' It had never been like that." Not a few viewers understood Brezhnev's deterioration as a new symbol: the symbol of the deterioration of the Soviet Union itself.

—

Gorbachev knew that he could use *Vremya,* and television in general, to create a public image of himself as new kind of czar. His image, and no other, would embody his policy. Television was still his tool, his to use as he liked. In his first major public appearance as general secretary, a speech in Leningrad, Gorbachev was so vigorous compared to his predecessors, so critical of the status quo, so informal and unembarrassed by his southern accent and grammatical slips, that he was quickly dubbed "the chairman of the collective farm." On television, Gorbachev dove into crowds. No one had to know that the KGB had carefully screened those crowds or that the producers had carefully edited the footage to the general secretary's own specifications. The entire state media apparatus was dedicated not to reporting the news but rather to the evolution of a personality and the promotion of a policy, a new way of doing things.

The Kremlin inner circle was obsessed with Gorbachev's television image. Just before airtime, Sagalayev said, Gorbachev himself frequently called the *Vremya* producers at the studio to go over the details of his appearance. No editing, no visual image or remark, was left to the judgment of anyone but Gorbachev and his aides. "Gorbachev's image," Sagalayev said, "was carefully planned and organized with the help of the KGB, Gorbachev's staff, and the ideology department of the Central Committee. And most of all, Yakovlev and Raisa Maksimovna helped develop the new image of the general secretary—open, democratic. They wanted him to resemble Lenin, for Lenin's image was that of a simple man who received ordinary people and peasants and drove in a car with no bodyguards. They wanted perestroika to

be a return to Leninism, a purification of the Party from Stalinism and totalitarianism."

Every night, people would turn on *Vremya,* and, inevitably, Gorbachev would be up to something: speaking off the cuff at a provincial Party meeting, wading through crowds in New Delhi or Bonn, greeting a foreign delegation in a room with a green baize table and a red runner carpet. Gorbachev was never interviewed in the conventional Western sense. A nervous state broadcaster, carefully briefed, would ask a fuzzy, open-ended question ("Mikhail Sergeyevich, what hopes do you have for your trip to London?"), and then Gorbachev would go on for fifteen or twenty minutes. By mid-1987 at the latest, urban intellectuals especially sat in front of the television watching this new figure, captivated, a little bit in love. The intellectuals were like film critics who, after sitting through years of depressing schlock, were suddenly shown a print of *Citizen Kane.*

Probably the height of Gorbachev's television career, in Soviet eyes, was his performance at the Nineteenth Party Conference. Not only did he read his own part well, he also directed "spontaneity" to his advantage, sending up obscure speakers to excoriate and embarrass hidebound Politburo members, setting Ligachev up against Yeltsin to enhance his own stature as the wise, liberal center flanked by ideological and emotional extremes.

Never again would Gorbachev's mastery be so complete; never would he be as in control of the spectacle of politics. But for several years, Gorbachev not only was the lead actor, producer, and director in his nightly drama, he also had no competition. *Vremya* played on all the main channels. The educational channel's Italian lessons were not exactly an ideological challenge. For nearly four years, there were no competing political actors to speak of. None, that is, who had access to prime time. Yeltsin did not really appear until June 1988, and even then the focus of his attack was Ligachev, not Gorbachev. Sakharov also did not get much airtime until mid-1989. And the right wing was still too bound by the traditions of Communist Party discipline to go on television in the spirit of contradiction.

Gorbachev was a lecturer, a cajoler. At conferences and in his meetings on the street, he was a relentless pedant. But for all his power and self-possession, Gorbachev did allow a bit of humor about himself. This, too, was revolutionary. Political humor had always been a staple of private life in the Soviet Union, starring Brezhnev as the doddering fool or the corpse of Lenin as *kopchushka,* the "smoked fish." But such jokes were never permitted in official publications. In the March 1988 issue of *Teatr,* the satirist Mikhail Zadornov adopted the voice of a resident of a town Gorbachev had just visited. He writes a letter to the general secretary telling him how the once dingy town had been transformed. "It is true that you informed our local

authorities about your visit just three days in advance," the mock letter to Gorbachev says, "but even in those three days they managed to do more for our city than they had in all the years of Soviet power. All the buildings that you were supposed to pass were painted, but then someone said that you like to swerve off your planned course and so our authorities were obliged to paint all the other houses in the city. They worked so hard that they painted the windows, too."

The joke was less on Gorbachev than on the vanity of the Communist Party and the Russian tradition of Potemkin villages. But a year later, as glasnost expanded farther beyond the strict control of the Politburo, the humor cut deeper and Kremlin patience wore a bit thin. The Gorbachev family was no longer amused. On the stage of the Satire Theater, one of the actors starring in Vladimir Voinovich's political satire *The Tribunal,* Vyacheslav Bezrukov, spun out a long and hilarious imitation of Gorbachev, complete with his signature hand motions (karate chops, raised index finger), odd grammar, and accent. Gorbachev's daughter, Irina, was sitting in the third row, and she had been laughing throughout the show. But when Bezrukov started his Gorbachev imitation, Irina scowled. The moment the curtain fell, she headed for the exit, unsmiling, not applauding.

Gorbachev did not shut down any theaters, but he did guard his image, and his life, jealously. Despite his policy of democratization, he never suffered the scrutiny of a real political campaign, much less the assault of a hungry press corps in search of his "character." Gorbachev's climb to power took place inside the Soviet Communist Party, an institution that valued aggressive obedience and secrecy. The initiator of glasnost revealed little of himself except through political performance. When it came to unsanctioned exploration of his personality and his past, Gorbachev was not, at first, much more forthcoming than his predecessors. Even the most liberal papers and magazines did not dare publish what a Westerner would call a profile. Gorbachev insisted on communicating directly with the Soviet people, and the only filter permitted would be the one that he and his staff designed and approved.

For all his support of glasnost, for all his talk of the need to fill in the "blank spots" of history, Gorbachev kept to himself a central fact of his early life for more than five years after coming to power. It was only in December 1990, when he was alienating the entire liberal intelligentsia, including Shevardnadze and Yakovlev, by cooperating with the hard-liners in the Party, that Gorbachev revealed that both of his grandfathers had been repressed under Stalin. You had to be listening carefully to catch it. Late one night, Central Television broadcast a tape of one of Gorbachev's meetings with a large group of leading writers and journalists. Somehow, Gorbachev was

trying to justify his swing to the right but at the same time to win back the respect of the intelligentsia.

"Look at my two grandfathers," Gorbachev said. "One was denounced for not fulfilling the sowing plan in 1933, a year when half the family died of hunger. . . ."

Why now? Why hadn't he said anything in 1988 when the battle for history had been raging?

". . . They took him away to Irkutsk to a timber-producing camp, and the rest of the family was broken, half-destroyed in that year. And the other grandfather—he was an organizer of collective farms, later a local administrator. This was quite a figure for those times. He was from a peasant family, a peasant of average means. He was in prison for fourteen months. They interrogated him, demanded that he admit what he'd never done. Thank God, he survived. But when he returned home, people considered his house a plague house, a house of an 'enemy of the people.' Relatives and dear ones were not able to visit him, otherwise 'they' would have come after them, too."

It was as if Gorbachev's family was a paradigm of the Stalinist era: one grandfather was punished for failing to fulfill the absurd and brutal demands of collectivization; the other, a leader of collectivization, suffered for no reason other than to be a victim of Stalin's scheme of organized, random terror. "When I was up for membership in the Communist Party, I had to answer for all this," Gorbachev told me later, in an interview. "It was a very painful moment." Throughout the speech, Gorbachev made plain that he himself was the leader of a particular generation with a particular vision: a man of late middle age, born into a system that betrayed his family, but one who is convinced nevertheless that "genuine" socialism was possible and still "my banner." The tragedy of the Stalin era and the farce of the Brezhnev period represented for Gorbachev not the failure of ideology, but rather its perversion.

But Gorbachev had not finished. There was a reason for his revelation. It turned out that he had saved his confession for traditional ends. "I've been told more than once that it is time to stop swearing allegiance to socialism," he was saying now. "Why should I? Socialism is my deep conviction, and I will promote it as long as I can talk and work." By late 1990, political opinion polls showed that only a minority of Soviet people—not more than 20 percent—still shared Gorbachev's faith in the efficacy of socialism. But attempts to turn away from the "socialist choice" were inconceivable to Gorbachev—a betrayal, a "counterrevolution on the sly." The Baltic independent movements were a threat to his notion of the Soviet Union as "one people"; he saw the calls for private property as a threat to the psychology of a people

who spent years being taught to despise it. The opposition to such foreign ideas, he said, were "last stands," comparable to the battles of Moscow and Stalingrad.

"Am I supposed to turn my back on my grandfather, who was committed to the [socialist] idea? . . . And I cannot go against my father, who defended Kursk, forded the Dnieper River knee-deep in blood, and was wounded in Czechoslovakia. When cleansing myself of Stalinism and all other filth, should I renounce my grandfather and my father and all they did?"

—

In 1989, I traveled to the scene of Gorbachev's youth, the southern Russian city of Stavropol and the farming villages nearby. When I showed up at the Hotel Kavkaz, a forbidding old woman with bandaged legs sat squat on a stool, her gaze set on me, barring the door. I tried to get an explanation from her but I could not.

"You'll have to excuse us, but we're having a mass killing in there," said a voice over my shoulder. The local tourist guide, Valentin Nizin, as it turned out. "We're wiping out the cockroach population. But don't worry. When you get to your room, I'm sure you won't be disappointed."

Nizin was right. Roach platoons raced down the linoleum in columns.

Nizin, who seemed like something more than a tour guide, was extremely interested in why I had come to Stavropol "when there are hundreds of other places for you to go in the Soviet Union." Except to protect friends and sources, I did not conceal much when reporting in the Soviet Union, even in conversations with people I took to be informers. I printed nearly everything I knew anyway. So I told Nizin that I was there to learn what I could about Gorbachev's past. I was not the first, and Nizin kindly helped me find a few of Gorbachev's old friends in town. But when I said I wanted to go to Privolnoye, the village nearby where Gorbachev was born and raised, Nizin stiffened. He would get back to me on that, he said, and disappeared into his office.

Within an hour, he told me I could not go.

"There is a quarantine in Privolnoye," he said. "It is forbidden to you."

"What sort of quarantine?"

"The cows are diseased, apparently. They do not want any foreigners to come and get sick."

"The cows are against it?"

"No," Nizin said. "Not the cows."

I knew very well what this meant and could guess with even more accuracy with whom Comrade Nizin had just been talking. But I was tired and angry, and so I pushed things a bit too far.

"Mr. Nizin, I do not plan to interview any cows, nor do I plan to exchange fluids with one. I told the Foreign Ministry I was going to Privolnoye and they had no objections, and I don't believe there is any quarantine."

"Oh, but there is," he said. "Hoof and mouth disease."

Or whatever. Nizin smiled and shrugged in a way to let me know that he knew that I knew, but that was too bad, you'll have to limit yourself to the city, where we can keep a good eye on you. It was no use, and we both knew it. I gave up, bought Nizin a drink, set my alarm for 5:00 A.M., and went to bed.

When I woke it was snowing, fat flakes that whitened the grim city. I dressed quickly and walked past the concierge, who was slumped in her chair and snoring. The halls still stank of pesticide, and there were still roaches, thousands of them skittering along the linoleum.

On the street, I got lucky. I was looking to hire a car, and I found one after only fifteen minutes or so. A tiny orange Zhiguli with bald tires and a smashed windshield pulled over. Perfect. It would not have been so smart to go to Gorbachev-land in a bright yellow taxi. I got in the car and quickly explained to the driver, a young farmer out to make some extra money before breakfast, where I wanted to go. When he squinted quizzically, I added that I was willing to pay $25 in hard currency, a sum that would surely put him in feed until harvest time. Off we went.

The driver and I figured that it would be best if we just drove through Privolnoye to get a quick look and then went to Krasnogvardeiskoye, a much larger town where Gorbachev went to high school, entered Communist Party politics, and fell in love. If I was still undetected after talking to people there, we'd stop in Privolnoye on the way back to Stavropol. With so many KGB men around, my luck would surely run out; it was just a question of when.

The road was among the most beautiful I'd ever seen in the Soviet Union, including the Georgian Military Highway through the Caucasus and the flat road through the Kara Kum desert in Turkmenia. Snow dusted the rich fields like confectioner's sugar over a Black Forest cake. In two hours of driving, we passed more horse carts than automobiles. Peasant women with silver teeth, humped backs, and mud-covered boots led cows down the side of the road. The lushness of the farmland seemed to me the very soil of Gorbachev's optimism. "You could shove a stick in the ground around here and you'd get a harvest," people told me in Stavropol, and now I could believe it.

Privolnoye was not much different from the village before it and the one after. Peasant huts, livestock, fields. The air was cold and sweet with the smell of fertilizer, hay, and loam. There was one paved road and some dirt ones,

all near the muddy stream known as the Yegorlik River. A black bull was tethered to the green fence surrounding Gorbachev's first schoolhouse. Ducks and geese waddled down the road.

Privolnoye, which is roughly translated as "free and easy," could no longer be called an entirely typical village. Not when the KGB was in town keeping a close watch on the white brick house with blue-green shutters where Gorbachev's mother, Maria Panteleyevna Gorbacheva, lived. Gorbachev's mother was in her late seventies, a stout and friendly-looking woman in support hose. Her accent was southern, a peasant's accent. The KGB took great pains to shield her from journalists, but she did appear on television on one of Gorbachev's birthdays, informing the nation that young Misha had worked hard on the farm, read all the books in the collective farm library, and played a mean balalaika. "And my how he could sing!" According to people I met who have lived in the village and in villages nearby, Maria Panteleyevna rarely went out anymore. A few years later, when her son was on the brink of resignation, she said perhaps that might not be so bad, since he'd had no time to visit her in years. Accustomed to the pace and the faces of the village, Maria Panteleyevna had always refused Gorbachev's requests to move to Moscow. She did have a few modern conveniences that had not been around when her son lived there: television, indoor plumbing. She was too old to care for the animals anymore. "She said, 'At least let me keep the rooster so I'll get up in the morning,' " Georgi Gorlov, an old family friend, told me.

At the very moment when Gorbachev was born in March 1931, southern Russia and Ukraine were living through the collectivization campaign and the starvation that went along with it. According to Western studies, more than thirty thousand people in the Stavropol region died during the terror-famine of 1931–32. Despite the horror of those years, Gorbachev, like so many "reform Communists," believed in the idea of collective farms, but abhorred what Bukharin called the "Genghis Khan" methods of Stalin.

Without plunging into the puddle of psychohistory, one might fairly say that Gorbachev's early sense of himself as a success was tied to the collective farm. Working with his father and the family of fellow farmworker Aleksandr Yakovenko, Gorbachev spent his teenage summers on a rickety S-80 combine harvesting grain. It was hard and filthy work, usually under a broiling southern sun. To cool off, the two boys, Gorbachev and Yakovenko, stripped and sat in barrels of river water. The Gorbachev-Yakovenko team was a local success, so much so that they earned a banner headline in the June 20, 1948, edition of the *Road of Ilyich,* the local newspaper: "Comrade Gorbachev Is Ready to Harvest."

The next year, while Gorbachev was in high school, the team won a coveted honor, the Medal of the Red Banner. Such an honor was the first step toward a life in the Party. Many years later, when he was the regional Party leader in Stavropol, Gorbachev would visit the farms in the region and stun his traveling party when old farming friends like the shepherd Vasily Rudenko would greet him with a bear hug and "Hey, Misha! Have you eaten?" With that, they would march into Rudenko's hut for a plate of jellied innards and a bowl of borshch.

After the brief and unnerving driving tour of Privolnoye, we headed for the town of Krasnogvardeiskoye, or "Red Guard." Gorbachev knew this stretch of road well. Four decades before, he woke early in his parents' house, a two-room hut made of mud, manure, and straw with pigs and chickens and an outhouse in the yard. The harvest was over. The village schools were opening. Gorbachev tucked a package of home-grown food under his arm, met up with his friend Dmitri Markov, and began the walk to Krasnogvardeiskoye's High School No. 1. Gorbachev rented a bed in the house of an old retired couple there. Weekends he returned home to Privolnoye to work in the fields.

The two-story brick high school fast became the center of Gorbachev's universe. He was the classic small-town overachiever, a class-president type who scored high marks, starred in the school plays, and won the heart of the best-looking girl in the school. For half a day, I buzzed around the town, talking to teachers, old friends, people on the street. There was, of course, something preposterous about the entire mission, something straight out of the old television series *This Is Your Life.* Yekaterina Chaika, Gorbachev's old chemistry teacher, was one of several people to deliver twinkling remembrances and boilerplate as if on cue. "He is a man of his time," she said, "and there are countless factors of history that come into play. But if you want to understand him better as a man, it doesn't hurt to know where he came from. Like anyone, he has roots. And those roots are right here." Others who probably did not know him at all conjured visions of the ideal. "You know," one man told me, "I don't think Mikhail Sergeyevich even had that birthmark on his head when he was here."

But there were others in town who had something to show me. The high school principal was Oleg Sredni, a man at least fifteen years younger than Gorbachev. He seemed unfazed by the prospect of helping an uninvited foreigner find out more about the general secretary of the Communist Party.

"You want to see Mikhail Sergeyevich's grades?" he said. "I think we have them here in the safe."

Plump and graceful, Sredni darted across his office to the safe and brought out a musty, Dickensian ledger. He opened to 1950, the year of Gorbachev's graduation, and there, in a formal hand and cloudy ink, was "Gorbachev, Mikhail Sergeyevich" and a line of numbers. On a grade scale with 5 being the highest to 1 the lowest, Gorbachev had a nearly uninterrupted row of 5s: algebra, Russian literature, trigonometry, history of the Soviet Union, the Soviet Constitution, astronomy, and so on. The one blemish was a 4 in German. "Apparently his class in Privolnoye refused to take German after the war, so he was a bit behind when he got here," Sredni said in a tone of churchly reverence. "That is why he got the silver medal here, not the gold."

Except for the portrait of Gorbachev on Sredni's office wall, the school had not paid much attention to honoring their native son. In the school's hall of fame, Gorbachev was listed as just one medal winner among many, a future general secretary next to Gennadi Fateyev, the class poet. I had been to high schools in the United States where third-rate quarterbacks have been honored more grandly. Sredni had made sure there would be no personality cult in the halls of his school.

"In our day there were lots of pictures of Stalin, of course. I remember one especially, a portrait of Stalin and Mao called *The Great Friendship,*" said Yuri Serikov, one of Gorbachev's classmates and now a history teacher at the school. "It was absurd, but what did we know?"

Gorbachev was a Soviet Best Boy, with conventional ambitions and ideas. He was the leader of the school's Komsomol organization and became a candidate for membership in the Communist Party when he was only eighteen. He was no high school rebel. "We were told that Stalin was doing everything perfectly, and we believed it all," Yuri Serikov said. "That was our level of understanding, and Mikhail Sergeyevich was no exception. None of us ever thought twice about it."

After interviewing fifteen or twenty people in town, the inevitable happened: the KGB caught up with me. Sredni, the school principal, took a phone call while I was in his office. "*Da,*" he said grimly. And *da* three or four times more, all with the same dead tone of obedience. He hung up the receiver and, lifting his eyes to me, said, "I'm afraid I can't talk with you anymore. Please wait here."

Someone had obviously called the authorities, and I was soon summoned to the office of the deputy Communist Party chief, the head chief being out of town on business. The deputy chief had a caveman brow and never smiled. When I told him that I had heard no objections from the Foreign Ministry

in Moscow to my coming to the countryside, the deputy chief did not betray the slightest emotion.

"You will get in your car, and proceed directly to Stavropol," he said.

"What about Privolnoye?" I said. "I told the foreign ministry I'd go there, too."

"As you know, there is a quarantine."

"What quarantine?"

"You know very well. You were told."

"And how do you know that?"

The deputy chief blinked once, slowly, to indicate annoyance. I was not to be childish, he seemed to say. He had no time. He had an entire town to run into the ground before the year was out.

Before leaving Krasnogvardeiskoye, I had asked a dozen people if Gorbachev had a girlfriend when he was in school. Everyone remembered the same name: Yuliya Karagodina. "Very pretty, if I remember." "Played the Snowgirl in the play with Mikhail Sergeyevich." When I asked one local Communist Party official if she had Karagodina's number, she smiled girlishly, conspiratorily, and gave it to me.

Yuliya Karagodina, it turned out, had long ago moved to Moscow, where she was divorced, living with her mother, and teaching at a chemistry institute. When I called and asked to see her, Yuliya, as she asked me to call her, was nervous, but quickly agreed. "Make sure you use 'Karagodina,' my maiden name, and don't tell any other reporters my number. I knew this would happen sooner or later. I'll tell you everything and that'll be it."

A few days later, we met in a basement laboratory at her institute. Yuliya was no longer beautiful, not even a match for the woman she faintly regarded as the victor, Raisa Maksimovna. She was middle-aged, matronly, and sweet.

"Was it love?" I said.

"It was love, yes it was, for both of us," she said. "I was attracted to him, he was magnetic. But I'd be upset if you thought that our relationship was like those that young people have now. It just wasn't that way. We were close friends, and we cared for each other and helped each other. It was—what would you say?—a specific kind of friendship, not just a Komsomol thing. Young love, you might call it. We met for the first time in the September he arrived at school, and after a few months we grew closer. He once told me that he had liked a blond girl named Talia in Privolnoye, but that was more a child's affection.

"You know, it's funny, but whenever I watch him now on television

leading the Supreme Soviet, I think of Misha in school, playing the Grand Prince in Lermontov's *Masquerade* or heading the morning gym class, shouting into a big megaphone: 'Ready, class! Hup, two, three, four! Hup, two, three, four!' He was fearless for someone that age. I remember him correcting teachers in history class, and once he was so angry at one teacher he said, 'Do you want to keep your teaching certificate?' He was the sort who felt he was right and could prove it to anyone, be it in the principal's office or at a Komsomol meeting."

Yuliya said she had grown up in a village much like Privolnoye a few miles down the road. Her mother was a widowed schoolteacher, and so their circumstances were more modest than Gorbachev's. Yuliya put her briefcase on the table and took out a huge sheaf of old photographs. In pictures of the young drama costars, Gorbachev was dark and regal in his homemade costume and fake mustache. Karagodina was wide-eyed, delicate, a bit faraway. She looked like Lillian Gish in *Broken Blossoms.*

As Yuliya leafed through the pictures, slowly, like a child dealing cards, she said, "Once we were rehearsing Ostrovsky's play *The Snowgirl.* And there is a point when the Snowgirl—that was me—says, 'Dear Czar, ask me a hundred times if I love him, and I will answer a hundred times that I do.' I said those lines in open rehearsal, with the principal sitting right there in the audience. Suddenly, Gorbachev leaned over and whispered in my ear, 'Is it true?' My God! I was shaken. I could hardly go on with my monologue. Everyone was asking what had happened, and there was Gorbachev off to the side, smiling. Sometimes we spoke rather roughly to each other, but I was so dumbfounded, I couldn't answer.

"The truth is, he was a very good actor. There was a time when he even talked with me, and his friends Boris Gladskoi and Gennadi Donskoi, about trying for a theatrical institute. But I think he really always wanted to be a lawyer.

"We never really spoke about the future, except that we would go to Moscow and study there together. I'll tell you the truth. If we had been well dressed, well fed, and had everything like this generation, then maybe we would have talked about such things. But they were hard times, and we concentrated on our studies. . . .

"I was very proud and poor. Gorbachev was better off. He was better dressed. During the war, my family had been evacuated from Krasnodar to the Stavropol region. Gorbachev's family were living in their own house on their own soil. They always had enough to eat. He once invited me to come meet his parents in Privolnoye. I said that I had been brought up in such a way that I could not do such a thing. I was too proud. I think I must have

felt that his parents would feel that I was offering myself to them. . . . I just imagined how they would look at me, a simple little girl.

"But Misha did visit my own home. At first we lived in a dugout hut, and then in a small house that we built ourselves. He had the bravery to tell my mother he liked me, but I kind of lied to my mother and said the two of us were just solving the problems of the Komsomol together. He spent the night on a little bed in the house, and I stayed with neighbors.

"He could be so cool and businesslike sometimes. Once at a Komsomol meeting, in front of everyone at the local cinema house, he was angry with me for not finishing on time a little newspaper we put out. And despite our friendship, he reprimanded me in front of everyone, saying that I'd failed, that I was late. He was shouting a bit, disciplining me. Then afterward it was as if nothing had happened. He said, 'Let's go to the movies.' I was at a loss. I couldn't understand why he did what he did, and I said so. He said, 'My dear, one thing has nothing to do with another.'

"That reminds me: Years later I was living way outside of the city with my mother, and the commute was very long and we had hardly any room. By then Gorbachev was in the Central Committee. And so I wrote him a letter, asking him to help me. I wanted to get permission to move into the city center and get an apartment. I reminded him who I was, in case he had forgotten. I got the letter back soon after, and on it he had written simply that it wasn't his area, it wasn't his job, and that I should apply to the city authorities, not him. Just like that, so businesslike. Not one warm word. Deep in my heart I had hoped he would help me, but I suppose he wanted to avoid even the appearance of favoritism.

"In school, it was all very innocent. We never said things like 'I love you' to each other. He would never say such things. And on the rare times he put his arm around my shoulder, as if to say, come, let's go to the movies or somewhere, I would kind of glance over at his hand. No, it wasn't like our young people today. I finished school first, and went off first to Moscow. But I had no money and could not find any place to live. Remember, this was still a hard time, and so I returned to my village to work as a teacher. I've always thought that Gorbachev somehow thought I was weak for having come home.

"When he went off to the law faculty of Moscow State University, he wrote letters to me telling me how much he liked Moscow and the abundance of things and the fascinating people. There was never a sense in his letters that he felt any lack of confidence because he was a village boy. There were many letters, and later, when I was married, my husband was so jealous he burned

them all. I suppose he didn't know Misha would be general secretary. I'm so sorry those letters are all gone.

"I'll tell you how it was. I think in the end I felt I was not really good enough for him, or we didn't really fit. He was too energetic, too serious, so organized. And he was smarter than I was. He was the center of attention. We drifted apart. Things were getting lost. But he did send me a letter at the end with his picture, and on it he wrote 'Dum spiro spero,' Latin for 'While I am breathing, I am hoping.' I suppose I didn't want to acknowledge that he was getting farther than me in life, so I said to myself, 'Okay, Misha, live and write as you like, but as for me . . .' I accepted a job in the Soviet far east, but even before I got there, on the road so to say, I was married.

"The few people now who know that Misha and I were good friends sometimes ask me about Raisa Maksimovna. I like Raisa. She plays her role very well. She's intelligent, and there's obviously a lot of love there between the two of them. She helps him greatly, that's clear enough. I'm not envious of her. I cannot say I am glad, just that my destiny is my destiny. I see things as a realist. When I do think back to those days, I see it as a pleasant island of time. Sometimes when I watch him on television I think to myself, 'Poor Mikhail Sergeyevich. He is so tired, and he has the weight of the world on his shoulders. If he could only take out ten minutes and just be Misha for a while.' I think of how nice everything was back then. I see that moon in the country sky, and the little river and everything was so lovely."

Gorbachev came to Moscow in September 1950. At Moscow State University, where he would study law until 1955, he took a room with six others at the Stromynka student dormitory. The crumbling, overcrowded dorm had once been a barracks for the soldiers of Peter the Great. Gorbachev had one jacket and one pair of decent pants to put in his closet. "Gorbachev was a villager, and you might have expected him to seem worse off than the city boys, but we were all poor then, and our new surroundings were no better," said Rudolf Kolchanov, an editor at the labor newspaper *Trud,* who roomed with Gorbachev for three years.

Zdenek Mlynar, a Czech Communist and another of Gorbachev's college friends, arrived at the same time in Moscow as an exchange student from Prague and recalled a Moscow of "poverty and backwardness . . . a huge village of wooden cottages" where people had barely enough to eat, where "most families lived in one room and instead of flush toilets there was only an opening leading directly to a drainpipe." In his memoir of the Prague Spring, Mlynar wrote that in Moscow at the time "what you didn't hold on

to tightly would be stolen from you in a crowd, drunks lay unconscious in the streets and could be dead for all the passersby knew or cared."

Dressed in his baggy, hayseed clothes, Gorbachev tried doggedly to catch up with students who had gone to superior schools in the city. He often returned from the library at one or two in the morning and then stayed up another couple of hours talking with his roommates. Mlynar, Gorbachev, Kolchanov, and six war veterans would lock the door, turn a portrait of Stalin to the wall—revealing on the back an amateur portrait of a czarist-era courtesan—and drink and talk the night away. "Yes, it could be grim and wild even," Kolchanov said. "But Gorbachev seemed to avoid drinking too much. He was fastidious that way. That dorm room may have been the greatest classroom for all of us. We talked about everything from girls to more serious things: the latest exhibition or the latest artistic awards or historical event. Of course, one subject that was never mentioned was Stalin himself. That was too risky, even with the door closed."

The law class was dominated by some older vets and younger men, like Gorbachev, who had won academic medals in high schools. Unlike the politics or history departments, the law departments provided their students, by the standards of the time, with a relatively wide reading list. Along with the standard diet of Marx, Lenin, and Stalin, students read many of the essential works of Western thought: Roman law, Locke's treatises on government, Rousseau's *Social Contract,* and even the U.S. Constitution. But those texts served mainly as relics of bourgeois liberalism, and the core readings, the holy writ, were Stalinist textbooks.

Gorbachev, who as general secretary would campaign for a "law-base state," was steeped in the theory of its opposite: Stalinism. "The theme of political crimes was touched upon only in very brief and general terms," according to Mlynar. "There was nothing complex about it, as long as you accepted the fundamental principle that political activity upsetting to the government was comparable to any other form of criminal activity." Dissidence among the students was a crime; dozens of students were arrested for ideological missteps and sent to labor camps.

Mlynar, who returned to Czechoslovakia and eventually helped lead Alexander Dubcek's ill-fated Prague Spring reforms, now lives in Vienna. Some biographers have found a pleasant irony in what they see as Mlynar's influence on the man who would become the most powerful reformer in the Soviet Union and Eastern Europe. But Kolchanov said that "the influence is overrated. Gorbachev was intellectually curious, he was tolerant, but there were no signs of radicalism. You can't make those leaps. Remember, Stalinism

was something deep inside us. We were only lucky that we were young enough and flexible enough to change later on."

But there was in Gorbachev and some of his friends a tendency toward independence, toward questioning authority, that was surprising, considering the times. Once, in 1952, as a professor teaching "Marxism and Issues of Language" droned on—he was reading straight from the works of Stalin—Gorbachev rose from his chair and said, "Respected professor, we can read for ourselves. What is your interpretation of the reading, and why don't we discuss it?" Gorbachev was summoned to the dean's office. But he was not punished. Probably his position in the Komsomol helped him avoid a suspension.

But at the same time, Gorbachev was a leader of the law department's Komsomol group, and in this position, he took no risks. Two émigrés now living in the West who were in Gorbachev's class remembered him as a hard-liner in the Komsomol who made speeches scolding the shortcomings and improprieties of fellow Party members. Writing in the émigré journal *Possev,* Friedrikh Neznansky recalled hearing "the steely voice of the Komsomol secretary of the law department, Gorbachev, demanding expulsion from the Komsomol for the slightest offense, from telling inappropriate political jokes to trying to avoid being sent to a collective farm."

Midway through his five-year course, Gorbachev met Raisa Titorenko, a philosophy student from Siberia. A few of Gorbachev's friends were taking a ballroom dancing class, and one day Gorbachev and Kolchanov dropped by with the expressed purpose of mocking their buddies. "We were ready to say, 'You call yourselves real men and look at all this,' " Kolchanov said. "But then one of our friends in the class, Volodya Kuzmin, introduced Mikhail Sergeyevich to his dance partner. It was Raisa Maksimovna. I think for Gorbachev it was love at first sight. Just like in the movies. She was just so striking. And, as I think he discovered later on, she was extremely smart." Raisa, for her part, liked Gorbachev, according to Mlynar, for his "lack of vulgarity."

The marriage may have been the crucial personal event of Gorbachev's youth, but the signal political event for nearly everyone of his generation came in March 1953: the death of Joseph Stalin. In the years to come, Khrushchev would set free hundreds of thousands of prisoners and begin to tell the truth about Stalin. Although Gorbachev would choose the path of the Party apparatchik, scaling his way up through the hierarchy, flattering Brezhnev and his superiors, he would be one of thousands who would be changed by the Twentieth Party Congress in 1956 when Khrushchev gave his "secret speech" denouncing Stalin. Through a long process of personal and

historical change, Gorbachev would recognize the need to transform the country and its relationship to the world. "Really, we have no alternative," he would say, decades later.

But at the moment Stalin died, there was for Gorbachev and his friends only stunning confusion. "There are a lot of things you could say about Mikhail in the old days that you could say now," Rudolf Kolchanov said. "He was hardworking, a good listener, tolerant, decent, but he was also much like the rest of us. In fact, he was not the most impressive student in our class by any means. And he believed what he was taught about Stalin. It's not as if he were always a great reformer and world leader just waiting to happen. Most of us were out all night in the freezing cold trying to see Stalin's body at the Hall of Columns. When we all got back to the room, in the early hours of the morning, we were sitting on our beds. We tried to talk, but mostly we were just silent, thinking. Some were crying, though I remember that I wasn't, and neither was Mikhail Sergeyevich. We were so accustomed to life under Stalin. We might find it strange and terrible now, but that was how it was. And then someone spoke the question that everyone had on his mind: 'What are we going to do now?' "

CHAPTER 11

THE DOUBLE THINKERS

A very popular error: Having the courage of one's convictions; rather, it is a matter of having the courage for an "attack" on one's own convictions!

—FRIEDERICH NIETZSCHE, *notebooks*

On a winter's night in 1986, two electricians and their KGB escort installed a "special telephone" in the apartment of Andrei Sakharov. For six years, Sakharov and his wife, Yelena Bonner, had been living in the industrial city of Gorky under government edict, and the phone seemed at first just another Orwellian moment in the day of exiles. Maybe the Soviet press would call for an interview, Sakharov thought. Two magazines had already put in requests. Turning the moral equations in his mind, Sakharov arrived at a finely calibrated stand of principle: he would refuse all interview requests until there was no longer a "noose around my neck." The KGB agent merely turned to Sakharov and said, "You will get a call around ten tomorrow morning."

The next day, the phone rang. A woman's voice said, "Mikhail Sergeyevich will speak to you." Now Gorbachev was on the line, telling Sakharov that he and Bonner could return home to Moscow.

"You have an apartment there," Gorbachev said without a word of apology or regret. "Go back to your patriotic work!"

Sakharov said a brief word of thanks, then wasted no time in going back to his "patriotic work." He told Gorbachev that for the sake of "trust, for peace, and for you and your program," the Kremlin was obliged to release the political prisoners included on a long list he had mailed to the leadership from Gorky. The Soviet leader said he did not quite agree that all the prisoners Sakharov was speaking for had been tried illegally. Then the two men said their awkward good-byes.

One week later, Sakharov arrived by overnight train at Moscow's Yaroslavl Station, an event of such moral and political importance that it evoked another homecoming decades earlier—that of Lenin at the Finland Station. But no one could have predicted what was ahead for Sakharov in the three years left to him. Exile had worn him down. KGB threats, a painful hunger strike, forced feedings, random attacks, thefts of his diaries and manuscripts—all of it had taken a toll on his health. Now, as he answered questions into the swarm of tape recorders and television lights, his voice was mumbly, hesitant at times. He walked with a stoop and had to catch his breath every few steps on flights of stairs. Bonner said at the time that Sakharov would limit his activities. He would read up on developments in cosmology and work on specific human rights cases. That seemed like more than enough.

A few days after his return to Moscow, Sakharov was sitting at the kitchen table of his close friend the human rights activist Larisa Bogoraz. Another of the guests, the historian Mikhail Gefter, turned to Sakharov and said, "How are you feeling, Andrei Dmitriyevich?"

Sakharov said sadly, "It is difficult to live now. People write me, they visit, and they are all hoping that I will be able to help somehow. But I am powerless."

For months Sakharov mulled over his role, tried to find his political voice. Some younger dissidents were impatient with Sakharov's hesitation and what they saw as his naive, uncritical support of Gorbachev.

Those young dissidents probably should have known better, but the rest of the country knew Sakharov hardly at all. They could not have known what sort of man he was. Until Sakharov returned from exile, most people knew nothing more about him than the slanders they had read for years in the press. Even intellectuals with some connection to the human rights movement knew little about him. "We knew he was out there, but for years Sakharov was almost like a myth," said Lev Timofeyev, one of the political prisoners freed shortly after Sakharov's return from Gorky. But when Sakharov did return home, his gift for judgment became an open secret and a

public trust. Many ordinary people who had been instructed to despise Sakharov came to love and trust him. Through him they saw the hollowness of the old propaganda and the system itself. There was a sense of the uncanny about Sakharov. In 1988, at a discussion sponsored by and published in *Ogonyok* magazine, a group of Soviet and American intellectuals went around the table trading opinions on the myriad issues of perestroika. For nearly an hour, Sakharov seemed half asleep, but when it came his turn, he found all the inherent faults in the latest wave of political reforms. He zeroed in especially on the "unhealthy" way Gorbachev continued to control both the government and the Communist Party. No one had ever said that before, and yet, as we all left the room, Sakharov's brief exposition seemed like sense itself.

For anyone living in Moscow in those years, Saturday mornings were a time to listen to this voice. Sakharov was everywhere. He inevitably became either the chairman or the spiritual leader of all the key groups to the left of Gorbachev: first Moscow Tribune, then Memorial, and, later the Interregional Group of radical deputies in the parliament. Nearly every Saturday morning, Sakharov would sit in some dim auditorium, usually the House of Scholars on Kropotkinskaya Street, or the Filmmakers' Union near the Peking Hotel, and for half an eternity he would doze, his great dome of a head nodding off as the speeches went on. When it was his turn at last, Sakharov would take the lectern, and in a few minutes of very formal, incisive Russian, he would make the point that most needed making, invariably pushing public thinking ever closer to the creation of a civil society.

With the authority of his life and the clarity of his thinking, Sakharov became a one-man loyal opposition, a moral genius who was now, at last, able to speak directly to the people. "Sakharov was the only one among us who made no compromises," said Tatyana Zaslavskaya, a leading sociologist whose views helped shape the early reforms. "For us, he was a figure of the inner spirit. Just the bare facts of his life, the way he suffered for all of us, gave him authority that no one else had. Without him, we could not begin to rebuild our society or our selves. Gorbachev may not have understood it quite that way when he let Sakharov come home, but he would understand it eventually."

What made Sakharov unique was not his suffering alone. Others had suffered much more. And what made him unique was not his ideas. He shared his ideas with men and women who were dissidents even before he was—Larisa Bogoraz, Pyotr Yakir, Pavel Litvinov, Solzhenitsyn, and, for that matter, the first opponents of Russian totalitarianism, Aleksandr Herzen, Nikolai Berdyaev, Vladimir Solovyov. "My father's ideas were not original," Sakharov's son Efrem told me. "His ideas of morality and liberty had all

been said before. It was his fate to bring received wisdom to a place where it did not yet exist." The story of the perestroika years—the years between the rise of Gorbachev and the collapse of the Soviet state—was, to a great extent, the story of change inside the hearts and minds of individuals. Sakharov's life and thought prefigured that change in such a dramatic way that I would not hesitate to call him a saint. He was the dominant moral example of his time and place.

Sakharov was a scientist whose metaphors and sense of truth were rooted in an understanding of cosmology, the "magic spectacle" of a thermonuclear explosion, the calculus of the Big Bang. His unerring sense of rightness, like that of scientist-moralists from Galileo to Oppenheimer, was steeped in his understanding of the scientific problems of light and time, his firsthand appreciation of both the laws of the universe and man's tragic tendency to turn progress into catastrophe. He held in mind, it seemed, a picture, even a music, of eternity. Sakharov once turned to his wife and said, "Do you know what I love most of all in life?" Later, Bonner would confide to a friend, "I expected he would say something about a poem or a sonata or even about me." Instead, Sakharov said, "The thing I love most in life is radio background emanation"—the barely discernible reflection of unknown cosmic processes that ended billions of years ago.

Sakharov was a man inclined toward the purities of theoretical physics but who became the conscience of the Soviet Union, a political actor in spite of himself. His physics and his politics grew out of the same mind, the same sense of wholeness and responsibility. "Other civilizations, perhaps more successful ones, may exist an infinite number of times on the preceding and following pages of the Book of the Universe," Sakharov wrote in his Nobel Prize lecture. "Yet we should not minimize our sacred endeavors in the world, where, like faint glimmers in the dark, we have emerged for a moment from the nothingness of unconsciousness into material existence. We must make good the demands of reason and create a life worthy of ourselves and of the goals we only dimly perceive."

For almost every young man and woman who would one day join the circle of Communist Party liberals around Gorbachev, the death of Stalin was the pivotal event of moral and intellectual life. The same was true for Sakharov. Like Gorbachev, Sakharov knew well the horrors of the age. When he was a boy, his aunt Zhenya received news of her husband's death in the camps when one of her letters was returned "Addressee relocated to the cemetery"; later one of Sakharov's friends died in the gulag, the authorities announced, owing to a "chilling of the epidermal integument."

And yet, Sakharov's response to the death of Stalin was utterly typical. He heard the news while he was working on the Soviet bomb project and wrote home to his first wife, Klavdia: "I am under the influence of a great man's death. I am thinking of his humanity." Even in his memoirs, written three decades later, Sakharov could not pretend to understand his own reaction: "I can't fully explain it—after all, I knew quite enough about the horrible crimes that had been committed—the arrests of innocent people, the torture, the deliberate starvations, and all the violence—to pass judgment on those responsible. But I hadn't put the whole picture together, and in any case, there was still a lot I didn't know. Somewhere in the back of my mind the idea existed, instilled by propaganda, that suffering is inevitable during great historic upheavals: 'When you chop wood, the chips fly.' . . . But above all, I felt myself committed to the goal which I assumed was Stalin's as well: after a devastating war, to make the country strong enough to ensure peace. Precisely because I had invested so much of myself in that cause and accomplished so much, I needed, as anyone might in my circumstances, to create an illusory world, to justify myself."

Sakharov's sense of patriotic urgency after the American attack on Hiroshima and also the sheer seduction of the scientific world involved left him "no choice," he once said, but to move to a desolate weapons research center in Kazakhstan known only as the Installation, the Soviet Los Alamos. Even though he was immersed in what he called the "superb physics" of nuclear weaponry—"the sustenance of life on Earth but also the potential instrument of its destruction were taking shape at my very desk"—Sakharov still saw the gulag through the fence. The Installation, where Sakharov lived for eighteen years, was near a slave labor camp, and every morning he watched long lines of prisoners trudge to and fro, guard dogs at their heels.

Nevertheless, there was a determined innocence about Sakharov in those first years at the Installation. The prisoners and the guard dogs were a background that could be overlooked. But five months after Stalin's death, Sakharov began a personal and political conversion ignited by nothing less than the explosion of the first Soviet thermonuclear bomb. On August 12, 1953, twenty miles from ground zero, he watched the explosion, his eyes protected by dark goggles. The test was a success, and in his memoirs Sakharov describes the vision only in its incandescence, without a trace of regret: "We saw a flash, and then a swiftly expanding white ball lit up the whole horizon. I tore off my goggles and though I was partially blinded by the glare, I could see a stupendous cloud trailing streamers of purple dust." The government awarded Sakharov and his partner, Igor Tamm, 500,000 rubles each, dachas in the countryside outside Moscow, and the title of Hero of Socialist Labor. Marshal Kliment Voroshilov spoke for the state at the

awards ceremony in the Kremlin: "I have been told that Sakharov's work was especially outstanding," he said. "Let me kiss you."

In the months to come, Sakharov grew more and more concerned about the effects of nuclear fallout. Secretly, he was beginning to make calculations, trying to figure out how many innocent people would likely be hurt by every nuclear test. Roald Sagdeyev, the former head of the Soviet space program, visited Sakharov at the Installation after the test and noticed how "this young, distant god of physics" drew little offhand doodles of airplanes dropping bombs as he talked. "Those were the first real doubts," Sagdeyev told me. The accidental deaths of a young girl and a soldier at the test site also startled Sakharov. Then, after another successful test in 1955, Sakharov's sense of complicity in these few accidents began to torture him.

At a banquet after the test, Sakharov gave the first toast, and said, "May all our devices explode as successfully as today's, but always over test sites and never over cities."

The table fell silent, Sakharov recalled, "as if I had said something indecent." Marshal Mitrofan Nedelin, the ranking military man at the banquet, rose to give a countertoast, the rebuke.

"Let me tell a parable," he said. "An old man wearing only a shirt was praying before an icon. 'Guide me, harden me. Guide me, harden me.' His wife, who was lying [in bed], said, 'Just pray to be hard, old man, I can guide it in myself.' Let's drink to getting hard."

Sakharov turned pale. He understood well that Nedelin's joke was a parable. "He wanted to squelch my pacifist sentiment, and to put me and anyone who might share these ideas in my place," Sakharov wrote. "The ideas and emotions kindled at that moment have not diminished to this day, and they completely altered my thinking."

Finally, Sakharov understood. His moral protests were nothing to the men of the Communist Party. The Party was way beyond the control even of a Hero of Socialist Labor. So gradually, Sakharov became a dissident, and the ideas of his dissidence, which crystallized in his 1968 manifesto *Reflections on Progress, Peaceful Coexistence, and Intellectual Freedom,* anticipated the ideas of perestroika.

But while Sakharov was the moral leader of the era, he was not a man of raw political power. There may have been no Gorbachev without Sakharov, no perestroika without the efforts of the dissidents to keep the idea of truth alive in a dead time, but there were other figures, less easy to love, more ambiguous, who had the political power to make something out of ideas.

Gorbachev and the most influential people around him were contradictory

men, politicians, academics, and journalists whose lives were filled with doubt, small victories, and sorry compromises. They had done things of which they were ashamed or should have been. For the sake of ambition, they told themselves lies and half-truths. They served brutal masters and tried not to care too much. There was Vitaly Korotich, the crusading editor of *Ogonyok,* who had once been only too glad to write a scurrilous book about America called *The Face of Hatred.* There was the poet Yevgeny Yevtushenko, preternaturally vain, slippery, periodically brave. And there were the Gorbachev advisers who had worked in the Central Committee staff under Yuri Andropov and still remembered it as an oasis of free thinking: the Americanist Georgi Arbatov, the policy advisers Anatoly Chernayev, Georgi Shakhnazarov, and Oleg Bogomolov, the journalists Aleksander Bovin and Fyodor Burlatsky.

These were the *shestidesyatniki*—those who came of age during the thaw under Khrushchev, and grew disillusioned when Soviet tanks crushed the Prague Spring in 1968. They were the generation that woke to the horror of the Stalin era after Khrushchev's "secret speech" of 1956 denouncing the "personality cult." They harbored the dream of a humane socialism in Russia. They did not dare take the risks of full-blown dissidence, as Sakharov had, but they found a measure of independence and sanity in their work. There were scholars, like Abel Aganbegyan and Tatyana Zaslavskaya, who fled the oppressive scrutiny of Moscow for the relative academic freedom of Novosibirsk. There were journalists like Yegor Yakovlev and Yuri Karyakin who fled *Pravda* for Prague and wrote for the slightly liberal magazine *Problems of Peace and Socialism.* The *shestidesyatniki,* especially those from Moscow and Leningrad, were like an enormous floating club in which everyone had a nodding acquaintance with everyone else. They scrutinized each other's compromises and drew fine distinctions that would appear to be nonsense to anyone outside. The gossip in this crowd was as thick as it is in official Washington or the studios of Hollywood. Whether they worked in academia, for the press, or inside the Central Committee, it was all the same: every day they were faced with questions of what to say, whom to protect, when to withdraw. They thought one thing and said another, and sometimes, after speaking lies long enough, they believed them and were beyond redeeming.

"Gorbachev, me, all of us, we were double-thinkers, we had to balance truth and propaganda in our minds all the time," said Shakhnazarov, an elfin intellectual who was at Gorbachev's side from start to finish. "It is not something I'm particularly proud of, but that is the way we lived. It was the choice between dissidence and surrender."

Westerners were often fast to judge these people. They came from countries where liberty was almost a given, and still they mocked men and women in the Soviet Union who looked foolish in the act of trying to save both their families and their souls. The system made beasts of them, and it was a sorry sight. When the atmosphere of fear began to fade under Gorbachev, there were those who grabbed the public stage shamelessly, as if all that they had done in the past was of no matter. Some had trimmed their ideological sails for so many years that it was hard to take them seriously. They were indecent. But there were also quite a few who not only relished their new power, they understood their contradictions. They were complicated men and women who had done the best they could and knew their best was far from exemplary. Len Vyacheslavovich Karpinsky, a columnist and later editor in chief of *Moscow News,* was among the most likable because his case was one of the most complicated and tragic.

Len Karpinsky's parents were Old Bolsheviks. He was named in honor of his father's mentor and friend Lenin. "The name Len was pretty common then and so was Ninel, Lenin backward, or Vladilen for Vladimir Ilyich Lenin," Karpinsky said. "I'm just glad I didn't get a name like Elektrifikatsiya or some others my friends got stuck with."

Karpinsky's father, Vyacheslav Karpinsky, belonged to a generation of revolutionary romantics, the *fin de siècle* Communists. He joined the Communist Party in 1898, and in 1903, after his activities as a political organizer got him into trouble with the police in the Ukrainian city of Kharkov, he went into exile. In Switzerland he was Lenin's aide and copy editor. In Moscow, after the Revolution, he helped Lenin assemble his personal archives from exile and held various posts at *Pravda* and the Central Committee's Department of Propaganda. He received three Orders of Lenin and in 1962 became the first journalist ever named a Hero of Socialist Labor.

For the Karpinsky family, a life in revolution provided an elevated sort of existence. From 1932 to 1952, they lived in the House on the Embankment with the Kremlin elite: generals, Central Committee members, agents of the secret police. There were billiard halls, swimming pools, and, for the children, Special School No. 19. When Len Karpinsky was a boy, he was even friendly with a couple of Stalin's nephews. At a birthday party once, the playing stopped as the runty, pockmarked man with the withered left arm—the Mountain Eagle, the Friend of All Children—stood in the doorway. "Children!" one of the adults announced. "Iosif Vissarionovich is here!" Stalin

waved and smiled. The children all waited in silence until he left, and then resumed their games.

That was in 1935. In the coming years, Len watched dumbstruck as one acquaintance after another in the building lost parents, aunts, uncles, grandparents, and friends to the great furnace of Stalin's purges. Nearly every night, secret police vans would arrive and there would be arrests—an admiral, a lecturer on Marxism-Leninism, the sisters of a spy in a foreign embassy. "There was a knock and then they disappeared," Len said. It had been the world of Yuri Trifonov's novella *The House on the Embankment*—a world where "a life went on that was utterly different" from the life of ordinary people. Now it was a world where the most devoted revolutionaries, the most obsequious ministers, suddenly found themselves declared "plotters" and "infiltrators" and "enemies of the people." Karpinsky's family was, by the standards of the building, not hard hit. One of his aunts and her two brothers were sent off to the camps. To this day, Karpinsky does not quite understand why his father, the very sort of Lenin loyalist who so threatened Stalin, was never arrested and executed. The only reason he can think of now, he said, is that by 1937 or 1938, his father was semiretired and out of politics.

—

From the moment that the leadership installed Karpinsky's old friend Yegor Yakovlev as editor in chief, *Moscow News* became the paper of the thaw generation, subtly breaking taboos formed over seventy years. From time to time I visited Karpinsky at the *Moscow News* office, on Pushkin Square, and he always seemed to me an honest man, if a limited writer—a representative figure whose life had been, as he put it to me, "the inner conflict between the ambition to be a boss in the Communist Party and the almost involuntary development of a conscience." His appearance, waxen and drawn, spoke of that struggle. He looked exhausted at every minute of the day. His face was long, lined, and worn. The fingers of his right hand were yellowed up to the first knuckle from tobacco. More often than not when I called and asked how he was, he would say dryly, "My health is awful. I'm spending the week in a sanatorium. I may die."

Karpinsky was so unassuming, so ironic about his own failures and hesitations, that it was hard to believe he was once, in the culture of Soviet politics, as ambitious as any flaxen-haired kid who takes a job as a Senate intern and starts talking about "the day I run for office . . ." He believed deeply in Communism and in himself, in his entitlement to success. After entering Moscow State University in 1947, he began working as a "propaganda man" at factories and construction sites during the days before the Party's single-candidate elections. "My assignment was to make the workers get up at six

in the morning and go to the polls," he told me. "There was a competition among the propaganda men over whose group would be the first to finish voting. The limit was midday, by which time the whole Soviet people was supposed to have voted. That was a decision of the Party. We eighteen-year-olds were supposed to conduct propaganda among the workers, and the only tool was the promise to improve their housing conditions. They lived in horrible slums, railway cars with no toilets, no heat. I loved the work, thought it was a great service and, yes, a stepping-stone. At the university, Yuri Levada, who is now a well-known sociologist, wrote an article about me called 'The Careerist.' And it was true. I did it all with the idea of getting to the top. That was what it was all about: to be one of the bosses.

"But having said that, I have to say a few words in self-defense. Society during the Stalin era left open no real opportunities for self-realization or self-expression except within this perverted system of the Communist Party. The system destroyed all the other channels: the artist's canvas, the farmer's land. All that was left was the gigantic hierarchic system of the Party, wide at the base and growing narrower as one climbed to the top. You had to have a Party membership just for admission. That was the only opportunity. When you are engaged in that work, you forget about the social and political implications, and just do it. Gradually, this sort of life bifurcates your mentality, your intellect. You can begin to understand that life is life and it's better to do something good for thy neighbor than to climb upward stepping on their bones. But it all depends on moral principles. I suppose my first doubts came when I went to Moscow State University in 1948. A Jewish friend of mine named Karl Kantor was attacked at the university's Party committee at the start of Stalin's anti-Jewish campaign. That was just the start of a long transformation.

"After graduation, I was sent to the city of Gorky for Komsomol work. It was in 1952 and Stalin had one more year to live. I got to know the working class and the peasants there. I saw the utter degradation, the ruin. I saw Soviet society as it had really emerged. This 'intellectual conscience' that I talk about began to emerge. Some people still think, erroneously, that the life of the apparatchik breeds only conformists and subjects loyal to the regime. Actually, the regime splits people into two opposing factions: those who believe they can make it only through conformism and time-serving, and those who, thanks to a different structure of mind, dare to question the surrounding reality.

"So when Stalin died, I realized perfectly well what he had been all about. Still, I went to the funeral in Moscow out of curiosity. I felt like one of those prisoners in the camps who threw his hat in the air and cried, 'The man-eater has finally kicked the bucket!' My father's reaction to Stalin's death was

interesting. By then he was retired, working for the Central Committee only as a consultant. He sat there in his office typing on an old Underwood which he had brought from the offices he had in Switzerland with Lenin. He called me into his study and said, 'Son, Comrade Stalin has passed away. And having been an epigone of Lenin, he created all the necessary conditions for our cause to triumph.' It was so strange. My father had never talked so formally before to me in his life. I think he talked that way because his generation had always carried a burden to promote at all times the Party line and he felt it was his duty to pass that down to his children. But in a way, this was a man, eighty years old, who had conceived of his idea of the Party before the Revolution and while living in exile. He had to convince not me, but himself. He was talking to himself."

When Karpinsky returned from Gorky to Moscow for good, in 1959, the thaw was in full swing. *Novy Mir,* Aleksandr Tvardovsky's monthly journal of literature and opinion, was publishing texts critical of the old regime. Khrushchev himself read a manuscript copy of Solzhenitsyn's *One Day in the Life of Ivan Denisovich* and sanctioned its publication in *Novy Mir.* Karpinsky's friends Yevgeny Yevtushenko and Andrei Voznesensky were winning a following with their lyrics and public performances. In various pockets of the Central Committee apparatus, young apparatchiks wrote proposals and outlines of economic and political reform—though all within certain boundaries of ideology and language. For his part, Karpinsky worked as head of the Komsomol's Department of Propaganda and Agitation and as the editor of *Molodoi Kommunist* ("Young Communist"). Then in 1962 he joined the empyrean of the adult Communist world. He was promoted to *Pravda*'s editorial board heading the department of Marxism-Leninism. He had made it.

"Once I was back in Moscow from Gorky, my critical approach weakened somewhat," Karpinsky said. "I was part of the elite again, and not merely as my father's son but as a real member. I was part of the top nomenklatura, and the nomenklatura is another planet. It's Mars. It's not simply a matter of good cars or apartments. It's the continuous satisfaction of your own whims, the way an army of boot-lickers allows you to work painlessly for hours. All the little apparatchiks are ready to do everything for you. Your every wish is fulfilled. You can go to the theater on a whim, you can fly to Japan from your hunting lodge. It's a life in which everything flows easily. No, you don't own a yacht or spend your vacations on the Côte d'Azur, but you are at the Black Sea, and that really is something. The issue is your

relative well-being. You are like a king: just point your finger and it is done."

Karpinsky's potential as a man of the Communist Party elite was unlimited. It is conceivable that he could have won election to the Politburo one day. He was a Soviet Ivy Leaguer: bright, ambitious, a legacy. One afternoon, at a Kremlin ceremony, two of Khrushchev's most powerful partners in the leadership, Mikhail Suslov and Boris Ponomarev, complimented Karpinsky as their golden boy, their comer. One of them said Karpinsky was like a "son of the regiment" to them and they saw for him a great future in the ideological department of the Communist Party. "We are pinning our hopes on you," Suslov said.

Working in that rarefied atmosphere, Karpinsky got to know nearly every figure who would make a difference (one way or another) during perestroika. He was friendly with Yegor Yakovlev, the Lenin biographer who became the editor of *Moscow News;* Yuri Karyakin, a Dostoevsky scholar who was among the leading radical deputies in the Congress of Peoples Deputies; Aleksandr Bovin, the gargantuan journalist at *Izvestia* who promoted the "new thinking" in foreign policy; the reform-minded economists, Gavriil Popov and Nikolai Shmelyov and the sociologist Yevgeny Ambartsumov; Otto Latsis, the son of an Old Bolshevik and an editor at *Kommunist;* Gennadi Yanayev and Boris Pugo, who helped lead the August coup; and even the leading triumvirate of reform, Eduard Shevardnadze, Aleksandr Yakovlev, and Gorbachev himself.

"I first met Gorbachev in the sixties when I was working at *Pravda* and he was in Stavropol working in the Komsomol organization there," Karpinsky said. "He was not very well known at the time, but I must tell you that Gorbachev was saying the same things then that he did at the beginning of perestroika. He was in Moscow on some business trip or another—I forget what it was all about—but we met for a couple of hours, and I was impressed. He talked about the outrage of paying combine operators by the mileage and not their output. In a nutshell, he spoke about the absurd system of incentives, or lack of them, in the economy. He was excitable, but somehow very rational. And for the first two or three years of perestroika, Gorbachev was the same sort of innovator he was when he was young. The innovative projects were always limited, within certain boundaries, and that, of course, was telling later on. Well, I understand him. Like all of us, Gorbachev had to have a dual nature. It was in his mind and soul. He knew well that the idea of reward for work well done was considered out of the ordinary but not quite heretical. You could experiment with something limited like that. But we were not allowed to make any political or philosophical conclusions that the system itself was a failure. In your mind you avoided such conclusions.

You were simply incapable of thinking that way. To think that way was not only career suicide, it was a form of despair. And so, like the rest of us, Gorbachev hedged—outwardly, and within himself."

—

Karpinsky and his friends were, at first, not greatly upset with Brezhnev and Suslov's overthrow of Khrushchev in 1964. When Karpinsky heard the news, he and Yegor Yakovlev celebrated over a bottle of cognac. Khrushchev had long since tightened restrictions on the press and the arts, and he had become prone to unpredictable decisions—a manic "voluntarism," as the Party language had it. It was only years later, when Khrushchev was a sad old man living in the exile of his dacha, that Karpinsky called him to wish him well on his birthday. Karpinsky said he was calling on behalf of the "children of the Twentieth Party Congress" and that Khrushchev should know that one day history would make clear to everyone the importance of that session, in 1956, at which he leveled his first attacks against Stalin's "cult of personality."

"I have always believed this and I am very pleased that you and your relatively young generation understand the essence of the Twentieth Congress and the policies I initiated," Khrushchev replied. "I am so happy to hear from you in my twilight years."

It did not take Karpinsky or anyone else long to realize that Brezhnev had no intention of instituting reforms. Just the opposite—a neo-Stalinist movement was in the works. One night at dinner with Yevtushenko and Otto Latsis, Karpinsky began to pronounce aloud what was happening to his generation, to its way of thinking. "Our idea was this: when one has an education in philosophy and a certain intellectual background, one begins to understand the inner properties of reality, something I termed 'intellectual conscience.' It's not a natural, inborn conscience, yet a conscience that stems from a kind of thinking that links you with a moral attitude to reality. If you understand that everything in this society is soaked in blood, that society itself is heading toward collapse, that it is all an antihuman system—if you understand this instinctively and intellectually—then your conscience cannot remain neutral. Look, I never really took any risks, and didn't want to. I was sort of compelled to take the steps I did by my conscience. And once compelled to take those steps, I could never foresee the bad consequences. Every time I thought I'd get away with it. And every time I didn't."

Karpinsky made his first real foray into the netherworld of what he called "half-dissent" in 1967, and it was a personal disaster. He and a friend at *Pravda,* Fyodor Burlatsky, wrote an article in *Komsomolskaya Pravda* calling, in a euphemistic way, for an easing of censorship in the theater. Kar-

pinsky now says the piece was "half rotten," especially its solipsistic arguments that the best way to eliminate anti-Soviet sentiments from the theater would be to let the people, and not the official censors, decide. That way, the authors said, the playwrights would have no right to complain about the government, and so would be deprived of a source of anger and subject matter. But the article, "On the Road to the Premiere," contained one idea, plainly stated, that caused an uproar when it appeared: the personality cult, Karpinsky and Burlatsky said, had been criticized only lightly, and the censors were preventing anything deeper.

Brezhnev, who had already begun the ideological rehabilitation of Stalin, was furious when his aides brought the article to his attention. He took it as a personal attack. By chance, the article appeared on the same day that a member of the Central Committee criticized the country's enormous arms industry, which had been Brezhnev's province before he became general secretary. Karpinsky, Burlatsky, and the editor of *Komsomolskaya Pravda* were all fired. Karpinsky was quickly appointed to a job at *Izvestia,* but after he made a few critical remarks at a meeting of that paper's Communist Party committee, he was eased out of that post, too.

Despite his inherited romantic view of Bolshevism and his own pleasure in the perquisites of power, Karpinsky could no longer hide his disaffection. The invasion of Czechoslovakia, in August 1968, was, for Karpinsky and many of his friends, a breaking point. He did not join the seven young protesters who went to Red Square. Nor did he form any close links with Sakharov or other leading intellectuals who had decided, once and for all, to give up their lives in the hierarchy for the dangers of political dissidence. But he did act. Under the pen name L. Okunev, Karpinsky wrote a long article titled "Words Are Also Deeds," for circulation only among a select group of friends and would-be reformers within the world of the Party and its official academies. (The pseudonym was an inside joke—"Karpinsky" derives from "carp," and "Okunev" from "perch.") In the article, Karpinsky argued that free thought—and not "rows of armed soldiers, insurgent crowds, columns of revolutionary sailors, or a volley from the cruiser *Aurora*"—would one day challenge the Soviet system. Furthermore, the state structures and ideological machinery would not be able to resist, for the system "lacks any serious social basis. It cannot convince anyone of its viability and only hangs on by the instinct of self-preservation. The face of neo-Stalinism we are passing through is just the outward expression of the 'uneasy forebodings' the petty tyrants feel. They long for the old regime, the 'Stalin fortress,' but they find only decrepit foundations too weak to support such a structure."

The article, like nearly all of Karpinsky's writings, is clogged with indirection and filler, great clots of undigested verbiage typical of a Party ap-

paratchik. But this piece was remarkable not only for its points of clarity and daring but also for its prescience. Here was an apparatchik ("We are pinning our hopes on you," Suslov had said) who now believed no more in the viability of the Bolshevik state than did Sakharov himself.

"Our tanks in Prague were, if you will, an anachronism, an 'inadequate' weapon,' Karpinsky wrote. "They 'fired' at—ideas. With no hope of hitting the target. They 'dealt with' the Czechoslovak situation the same way that at one time certain reptiles 'dealt with' the coming age of mammals. The reptiles bit at the air, gnashing their teeth in the same ether that was literally seething with the plankton of renewal. At the same time, fettered by their natural instincts, they searched for 'hidden stocks of weapons' and diligently occupied the postal and telegraph offices. With a fist to the jaw of thinking society, they thought they had knocked out and 'captured' its thinking processes."

Karpinsky also provided an insider's view, identifying within the monolith of the Party structure "a layer of party intellectuals." He went on to say, "To be sure, this layer is thin and disconnected; it is constantly eroded by cooption and promotion and is thickly interlarded with careerists, flatterers, loudmouths, cowards, and other products of the bureaucratic selection process. But this layer could move toward an alliance with the entire social body of the intelligentsia if favorable conditions arose. This layer is already an arm of the intelligentsia, its 'parliamentary fraction' within the administrative structure. This fraction will inevitably grow, constituting a hidden opposition, without specific shape and now aware of itself, but an actually existing and widely ramified opposition at all levels within the administrative chain."

It was this "layer" that made itself known when Gorbachev came to power. The dissidents were the bravest and most clear-minded of all, but in the early Gorbachev years they did not constitute, in numbers or in force, an adequate army. As if from nowhere, intellectuals within the Party, the institutes, the press, and the literary, artistic, and scientific worlds slowly took a Soviet leader at his word when he said that this would be a different age. For once, the purposes of a Kremlin leader and the liberal intelligentsia intersected.

The tragedy was that by the time Gorbachev came to power there were so many broken lives: great minds lost to emigration, drink, suicide, despair, or sheer cynicism. It was a miracle, after seven decades of murder and repression, that there was any intelligentsia left at all. "So many people had been destroyed," Karpinsky said. "One can behave in that split way of thinking for a while, but then you begin to degenerate and start to speak only what is permitted and the rest of the conscience and soul decays. Many people did not survive to perestroika. We had to create an internal moral system, and not everyone could sustain it indefinitely. Solzhenitsyn spoke about this in his

essay 'Live Not by Lies.' I understood his viewpoint, and we tried not to live by lies, but we couldn't always manage it. If you ignore the regulations of the state completely, and go into complete dissidence, then you can't have a family, you don't know where you will get rent money, and your children would have to go into the streets to scrape up money. To fulfill this principle of living not under a lie in every aspect is just impossible, because you live in a certain time.

"Compared to the people who were not afraid of prison, my friends were not heroes. We abstained from direct acts. This position was itself a compromise. But it was like the sort of compromises you make when you are in the same cage with a lion. It is understandable, though nothing to be proud of. When I myself was in the position of having to say what I felt, I said it. I just didn't deliberately try to put my head in a noose. I used Aesopian language. I had to use hints about progress, but nothing more. What we did publish only hinted at our real thoughts."

But Karpinsky's "Words Are Also Deeds" went far beyond Aesopian language. In 1970, Karpinsky gave a copy of his text to Roy Medvedev, the Marxist historian. One night, Medvedev called Karpinsky and told him that the KGB had ransacked his apartment and taken every manuscript in sight, including "Words Are Also Deeds." For a few years, Karpinsky was oblivious to the trouble he was in. He bounced around from job to job, from a sociology institute to editing Marxist-Leninist works at Progress Publishers. But in 1975, when he was caught working on the manuscript of his friend Otto Latsis's book *On the Eve of a Great Breakthrough,* an analysis of collectivization and Stalinism, the KGB called him in. Naturally, the interrogator was an old friend: a Komsomol buddy named Filipp Bobkov, who had become one of the most infamous figures in the Soviet secret police. Karpinsky tried to soften up Bobkov. "When you came to me there was tea and cookies," he told him. "You don't even offer me tea. It's not very polite." Bobkov was not amused. He had passed along the damning documents to the Communist Party Control Committee, and Len Karpinsky, son of Lenin's friend and the Party's great hope, was expelled. Suslov, for one, viewed Karpinsky's transgressions as a personal betrayal.

Now Karpinsky did whatever he could to make a living—among other things, commissioning paintings and monuments for a state agency, for which he received a minuscule salary. He kept up his friendships, talked politics, lived awhile at the dacha he had inherited from his father. The moment of reckoning he had written about in "Words Are Also Deeds," the advent of dissent as a cultural and political fact of life, seemed years and years off.

—

Even after Gorbachev took power, Karpinsky never dreamed change could come so quickly. And at first it did not. Although the liberals in the Politburo secured the editorship of *Moscow News* for Karpinsky's friend Yegor Yakovlev and told him to transform this tourist giveaway sheet, published in Russian and several foreign languages, into a "tribune of reform," glasnost was initially a process of hints, insinuations. To read now through a stack of *Moscow News* issues from 1987 and 1988 is to get lost in a blur of nonlanguage. The barriers were immense at first, the victories almost unbearably difficult. When the editors of *Moscow News* wanted to print a simple obituary of the émigré poet Viktor Nekrasov, the Politburo itself had to give permission, and did so only after long debate.

"But, still, the change was tremendous," Karpinsky said. "The difference between 'the thaw' and 'glasnost' was a difference in temperature. If the temperature under Khrushchev was two degrees above zero centigrade, then glasnost pushed it to twenty above. Huge chunks of ice just melted away, and now we were talking not only about Stalin's personality cult, but of Leninism, Marxism, the essence of the system. There was nothing like that under Khrushchev. It was just a narrow opening, through which only Stalin's cult could be seen. There were no real changes. And as we saw, it could all be reversed. The bureaucracy, the Party, the KGB, all the repressive apparatus in charge of the intelligentsia and the press, remained in place."

For Karpinsky, *Moscow News* provided the opening to a public hearing and a rehabilitation. In March 1987, he published a long article, "It's Absurd to Hesitate Before an Open Door." Like his other liberal pieces of the past, it was a mixed performance. Karpinsky made sure to blast the West for what he thought was its phony concern for the Soviet dissidents, but he also made a crucial point that was getting close consideration within the government but was rarely voiced in public: the critique of Stalin begun in 1956 would have to go deeper. Reform without a thorough consideration of the country's "core" problems, the rottenness of its history and foundations, would be meaningless.

Karpinsky wanted to rejoin the Party not only as personal vindication but also to play a role in what was still the central institution of political power. At a meeting with the chairman of the Party's Control Commission, however, the hard-liner Mikhail Solomontsev mocked Karpinsky. From a thick stack of papers that had obviously been compiled by the Party and the KGB, Solomentsev pulled out a copy of "Words Are Also Deeds" and, holding it up, he shouted, "You still have not disarmed ideologically! Nothing has changed in our party!"

But things had changed. The sharp ideological divisions within the Party had now become an open secret, an open struggle, and the trick was to get the support of powerful liberals within the structure. Three old friends—Yuri Afanasyev, Nikolai Shmelyov, and Yuri Karyakin—brought to the Nineteenth Special Party Conference, in June 1988, a petition demanding Karpinsky's rehabilitation. With the help of his old acquaintances Aleksandr Yakovlev and Boris Pugo, the tactic worked. By the next year, Len Karpinsky was in the regular rotation as a columnist at *Moscow News*—a golden boy, he says, "of a certain age."

CHAPTER 12

PARTY MEN

Geidar Aliyev was humiliated. After two decades as the Communist Party boss of Azerbaijan, he had been dumped in 1989 from Gorbachev's Politburo, vilified for corruption in the news columns of *Pravda,* and reduced to sharing the backseat of a dismal Volga sedan with an American journalist. The upstarts in the Party—the Karpinskys, the Yakovlevs, even Gorbachev himself—had all betrayed him. "When we made Gorbachev general secretary we had no idea what it would lead to!" he said. The pressures of Aliyev's decline wore on him. He had suffered mild heart attacks; his complexion had turned the shade of a votive candle. He complained of poverty to all who would listen. But Aliyev was still possessed of a certain unctuous charm, a parody of William Powell's parody of a regal smoothie. "You should feel quite honored," he told me as we drove to Moscow from his posh dacha in the village of Uspenskoye. "It's not often that I give an audience."

When he was a young man, Aliyev's ambitions were almost derailed when he was accused of sexual assault. He avoided expulsion from the Party by a single vote at his disciplinary hearing. There were, of course, no further "legal" proceedings. The Party's judgment was all. In 1969, as the republic's KGB chief, Aliyev launched a "crusade against corruption." He intended

only to purge his enemies and elevate himself and his clan, and he succeeded spectacularly. Once installed as republican Party chief, Aliyev ruled Azerbaijan as surely as the Gambino family ran the port of New York. The Caspian Sea caviar mafia, the Sumgait oil mafia, the fruits and vegetables mafia, the cotton mafia, the customs and transport mafias—they all reported to him, enriched him, worshiped him. Aliyev even practiced hegemony over the intellectual life of Azerbaijan. He appointed his relatives chairmen of various institutes and academic departments, enabling them, in turn, to charge tens of thousands of rubles to scholars in search of meaningful employment.

The structure of state in Azerbaijan—and everywhere else in the Soviet Union—was itself a mafia. The Communist Party's dispensation of power and property was unchallenged by election or by law. Administrators of "socialist justice" were duplicitous props intended by the Party to give the appearance of civil society. These judges, police captains, and prosecutors were generally well fed and not meant to stand up for anything more than their share of the booty.

There had been, of course, some honest men in the Party structure. In one famous incident in Azerbaijan, a prosecutor named Gamboi Mamedov tried to investigate corruption in the Communist Party leadership. Aliyev had him fired and denounced. Later, at a session of the republican legislature, the inflamed Mamedov managed to grab the microphone, shouting, "The state plan is a swindle, likewise the budget—also, of course, those reports of economic success are a pack of lies, and . . ." Police hustled Mamedov off the speaker's platform and into a back alley of obscurity. Seventeen loyal legislators quickly lined up to defend Aliyev. "Who are you fighting against, Gamboi?" Suleiman Ragimov, a hack writer and deputy, cried out. "God sent us his son in the form of Geidar Aliyev. Are you then opposing God?" The legislature rose as one in a standing ovation.

When Gorbachev came to power in 1985, he became the boss of bosses, the leader of a Communist Party Politburo in which most of the leaders were unabashed mafia sultans, men like Aliyev of Azerbaijan, Viktor Grishin of Moscow, Grigori Romanov of Leningrad, Dinmukhamed Kunayev of Kazakhstan, Vladimir Shcherbitsky of Ukraine. In Russia, the principle of blood ties did not mean as much as it did in Azerbaijan or Central Asia, but the Party hierarchy, and the way it controlled all economic activity, was just as powerful. The Central Committee, too, was filled with "dead souls," Party hacks whose sole mission was the protection of the Party as a privileged class. They had all long ago turned the poverty of Leninist ideology to their own advantage. In a state in which property belonged to all—in other words, to no one—the Communist Party owned everything, from the docks of Odessa to the orange trees of Georgia.

Aliyev, like the others, knew that the only real imperative of stability under Brezhnev had been to grease the don. Leonid Ilyich did not require the genuine prosperity or happiness of his people to please him. He needed only reports of same. As long as the official-looking documents that crossed his desk informed him of record successes and overfulfilled plans, he was well pleased.

Of course, the traditions of tribute pleased him even more. When Brezhnev came to the Azerbaijani capital, Baku, in 1978, Aliyev gave him a gold ring with a huge solitaire diamond, a hand-woven carpet so large it took up the train's dining salon, and a portrait of the general secretary onto which rare gems had been pasted as "decoration." For an official visit in 1982, Aliyev built a palace for Brezhnev's use, an edifice with all the kitsch grandeur of the Kennedy Center in Washington. The great man slept there for a couple of nights and then the palace closed. To commemorate the same visit, Aliyev gave Brezhnev yet another ring that symbolized the worldview of the Kremlin better than any map. One huge jewel, representing Brezhnev the Sun King, was surrounded by fifteen smaller stones representing the fifteen union republics. "Like planets orbiting their sun," as Aliyev explained. This masterpiece of the jeweler's art was given the title "The Unbreakable Union of Republics of the Free." When he received the ring and listened to Aliyev's careful explication, Brezhnev, in full view of the television cameras, burst into tears of gratitude.

This system of shadows and gilt served the Party well while it lasted. But now Aliyev, who had grown accustomed to long Zil limousines while he was in power, found himself with his knees jammed into the seat ahead of him.

"Ach, I live badly," he said as we sped along the highway linking Moscow to the villages where the Party elite kept their dachas. "My pension is tiny. Believe me, you would never work for such a sum. The driver? The car? Not mine. I just have the right to order them up once in a while."

In office, Aliyev had grown used to ordering suits from the Kremlin tailor, to regular deliveries of Japanese electronics, American cigarettes, and delicacies from the special farms and shops run by the KGB. Now his world was confused and threatening. "Gorbachev says he is for the renovation of socialism and against capitalism," Aliyev said. "Fine. But what sort of renovation? What does it mean? Is it social democracy? That's not socialism. What exactly is his socialism? No one knows. They don't know what socialism is anymore, and they are all living in a fog. You Americans want everyone to follow your way, and the more things here are to the liking of George Bush, the better. But is Bush Jesus Christ or something?"

We rode on a while in an agreeable silence toward Pushkin Square. Then,

suddenly, through the evening fog, the gleaming apparition of the future: a pair of yellow arches, a winding line of hungry Russians. Aliyev sneered.

"McDonald's!" he said. "There's the perestroika you all love so much."

The Communist Party apparatus was the most gigantic mafia the world has ever known. It guarded its monopoly on power with a sham consensus and constitution and backed it up with the force of the KGB and the Interior Ministry police. There were also handsome profits. The Party had so obviously socked away money abroad and sold off national resources—including the country's vast gold reserves—that just after the collapse of the August coup, the Party's leading financial officer took a look into the future and threw himself off a high balcony to his death.

The Party's corruption under Brezhnev was not a matter of exceptions, of rotten apples fouling the utopian barrel. No thorough prosecution could stop with a single indictment. "If it were a question of just one of the former leaders, the new government could easily give him up to be destroyed, presenting him as the black sheep—a sad exception to the general rule," according to Arkady Vaksberg, the top legal writer for the weekly paper *Literaturnaya Gazeta.* "But since it is a question precisely of all (or nearly all) of the members of the previous administration of autocratic old men, their exposure would lead to only one possible and inescapable conclusion from a historical perspective, that is, of the criminal character of the Party and the whole political system which enables criminals to make their way into positions of power and fanatically protects them from exposure."

In many ways, Stalin's Terror mirrored the tactics of the mafia. He used violence as an instrument of coercion and discipline; he fostered an atmosphere of secrecy and universal suspicion; there were "made" men (Party apparatchiks) and the outward appearance of legitimate business (embassies, diplomats, trade, etc.). As terror faded under Khrushchev and then Brezhnev, the Communist Party's business became business. "Sometimes you gotta get rid of the bad blood," Richard Castellano tells Al Pacino in *The Godfather.* But after an all-out war, the mafia always dreams of an Arcadian period of cooperation, of relations that are profitable, stable, and, always, "just business." Ideology in the post-Stalin era was not so much a system of beliefs or behavior as a kind of language, a password among the "made" men; if you could speak the language without deviation, you might be trusted to share in the loot. "More than anything else," the Yugoslav dissident Milovan Djilas wrote a few years after Stalin's death, "the essential aspect of contemporary Communism is the new class of owners and exploiters."

It was only in the post-Stalin era, after the violent period of collectivization and industrialization was over, that the Party-mafia structures took shape. Vladimir Oleinik, a famously honest investigator in the Russian prosecutor's office, published excerpts from his diary in *Literaturnaya Gazeta* that described the rapid growth in the 1960s of the trade mafia, a pyramid of corruption that began in the Communist Party Central Committee and the top ministers and went all the way down to butchers, bakers, and gravediggers, with everyone getting a piece. Oleinik wrote of how one Central Committee member filled his bank account by selling midlevel positions in the ministries for 50,000 rubles a spot.

The trade mafia worked thousands of scams. Even the small-time jobs had a certain beauty to them. In Central Asia, I was told about the fruit juice scam. Workers paid enormous bribes to get jobs servicing carbonated juice machines throughout the warm, southern republics. When the workers serviced the machines, they skimped on the syrup and then sold it elsewhere. They also skimmed some of the money out of the cash boxes. The workers used part of their gains to pay the foremen; the foreman, in turn, paid off the assistant minister; the assistant minister paid the minister . . . and all the way up the line and to the top of the Party structure.

In the same region, even high Party positions and awards were for sale. The magazine *Smena* ("Change") reported that the position of regional Party secretary in Central Asia cost a bribe of $150,000, and an Order of Lenin, the Soviet Union equivalent of the Congressional Medal of Honor, cost anywhere from $165,000 to $750,000.

It wasn't as if this swamp of corruption were a secret to the Soviet people any more than the existence of the mafia is a secret to the New York storekeeper forced to pay protection money. The mafia made itself known at every turn. You literally could not leave this earth without feeling its heavy hand on your shoulder. One afternoon, the nanny who took care of our son came to work exhausted and depressed. Her mother had died, but what had run her down most was the enormous effort and expense of getting the woman buried—a process that drained her as much as it enriched the "cemetery mafia" and its Party patrons.

"I knew immediately this was going to run into big money for us," Irina said. "We were supposed to get a free funeral and burial. But that is a joke. The first stop was the bank. First, Mother's body had to be taken to the morgue. We were told that the morgues were all filled up, and they wouldn't take her. But when we paid two hundred rubles to the attendants, they took her. Then there was the fifty rubles for her shroud.

"Then the funeral agent said he had no coffins my mother's size and that

we could only buy something eight feet long. My mother was five feet tall. For eighty rubles he came up with the right size. Then the gravediggers said they could not dig the grave until two P.M., even though the funeral was set for ten A.M. So that took two bottles of vodka each and twenty-five rubles each. The driver of the funeral bus said he had another funeral that day and couldn't take care of us. But for thirty rubles and a bottle of vodka we could solve the problem. We did. And so on with the gravesite and the flowers and all the rest. In the end, it took two thousand rubles to bury my mother. Three months' income for the family. Is that what ordinary life is supposed to be? To me, it's like living by the law of the jungle."

In the West, the mob historically moves in where there is no legal economy—in drugs, gambling, prostitution—and creates a shadow economy. Sometimes, when it can buy the affections of a politician or two, the mafia meddles in government contracts and runs protection schemes. But in the Soviet Union, no economic transaction was untainted. It was as if the entire Soviet Union were ruled by a gigantic mob family; virtually all economic relations were, in some form, mafia relations. Between a government minister's order for, say, the production of ten tons of meat and Ivan Ivanov's purchase of a kilo of veal for a family dinner, there were countless opportunities for mischief. No one could afford to avoid at least a certain degree of complicity. That was one of the most degrading facts of Soviet life: it was impossible to be honest. And all the baksheesh, eventually, ended up enriching the Communist Party.

"Look, it's all very simple," Andrei Fyodorov, who opened Moscow's first cooperative restaurant in 1987, told me. "The mafia is the state itself."

Before opening his restaurant, 36 Kropotkinskaya, Fyodorov worked for twenty-five years in the state restaurant business. Over a cup of tea one morning in his empty dining room, Fydorov described how it all worked at his old place of business, the Solnechny Restaurant, a huge state banquet hall. "The game started at nine o'clock on Friday mornings when the inspectors came by. I soon realized they were not really interested in the state of things in the restaurant. Very soon we established good contacts in terms of giving them various foodstuffs, providing tables in the restaurant, arranging saunas. The director of the restaurant would just tell me which services I had to arrange for them. You see, every person working in services is always on a hook. The restaurant director's salary is one hundred ninety rubles a month, say. You can't live on that, and so he is forced to take bribes. But there is a system of bribing in the USSR. You can't get too greedy. A restaurant director cannot take more than two thousand or three thousand rubles per month. If he starts taking more, the system grows worried, and in

the next five or six months new people will come around to inspect your place, which means that you can be arrested for violating the unwritten code of bribery.

"It goes from the bottom on up. From waiters, the bribes go to the maître d', and then on to the deputy director, to the director of the restaurant, and upward to various Party officials and auditing bodies. The same system applies to cafés, tailor shops, taxi depots, barbershops. A man who does not give bribes for more than six months is doomed."

Until his untimely arrest a few years ago, the most flamboyant mafia figure in the country was Akhmadzhan Adylov, a "Hero of Socialist Labor" who ran for twenty years the Party organization in the rich Fergana Valley region of Uzbekistan. Adylov was known as the Godfather and lived on a vast estate with peacocks, lions, thoroughbred horses, concubines, and a slave labor force of thousands of men. Anywhere Adylov went, he was accompanied by his personal cooks and a mobile kitchen. For lunch, he always ate a roasted baby lamb. He locked his foes in a secret underground prison and tortured them when necessary. His favorite technique was borrowed from the Nazis. In subzero temperatures, he would tie a man to a stake and spray him with cold water until he froze to death.

Adylov insisted he was a descendant of Tamerlane the Great. Considering his taste for ritual and cruelty, his blend of ancient and Bolshevik cruelty, it seems fitting. Adylov often sat in judgment, as if on a throne, under a portrait of the state deity, Lenin. When a Party hack named Inamzhon Usmankhodzhaev was nominated for high office in Uzbekistan, he had to appear before Adylov for approval. As a test of loyalty, Adylov ordered Usmankhodzhaev to execute an informer, but he could not bring himself to pull the trigger. Adylov could not excuse such a pathetic show of weakness and relented only when Usmankhodzhaev begged for forgiveness and, on his knees, licked clean the shoes of the Godfather.

From the Uzbeks, Brezhnev wanted only cotton and, more important, wonderful cotton *statistics.* The cotton scam was gigantic, yet elegant. Brezhnev would call on the "heroic peoples" of Uzbekistan to pick, say, 20 percent more cotton than the previous year. The workers, heroic as they were, could not possibly fulfill the order. (How could they when the previous year's statistics were already wildly inflated?) But the local Party leaders understood the overriding issue. They assured Moscow that all had gone as planned. If not better! The central ministries in Moscow would, in turn, pay vast sums of rubles for the record crop. The republican leaders would pocket the extra

cash. Brezhnev, for his part, smacked his lips anticipating the gifts that would come, air freight, from Bukhara, Samarkand, and the other centers of Uzbekistan.

Of all the most famous Party mafias in the Soviet Union—the Kazakhs, the Azeris, the Georgians, the Crimeans, the Muscovites—the Uzbeks showed a certain flair. Sharaf Rashidov, the republican Party chief, was a soft-spoken sybarite with literary pretensions. He fancied himself a novelist. To fulfill his ambition, he hired two Moscow hacks, Yuri Karasev and Boris Privalov, to do the writing. The resulting potboilers were published in editions that would cause Judith Krantz profound envy. Rashidov also knew how to satisfy his appetites. After hours of waving to the masses from the podium on May Day, he would descend into the basement beneath the podium, where, as Vaksberg reports, there were tables "piled with festive fare and delightful young ladies ready to put the spring back in his step." Rashidov was awarded ten Orders of Lenin, and when he died in 1984 he was buried with pharaonic ceremony in the center of Tashkent near the Lenin Museum. For years, people brought mounds of roses and carnations to the tomb. Finally, the Uzbek leaders recognized the shift in political winds from Moscow and moved the grave to a remote village. But Rashidov's legacy lived on. In 1988, regional Party officials summarily pardoned 675 people who had been sentenced for their roles in the corruption scandals of the Brezhnev era.

These were the go-go years under Brezhnev, and Uzbekistan did not, by any means, hold a monopoly on the grotesque. In the Krasnodar region of southern Russia, a mafia stronghold, ordinary membership in the Party cost anywhere from 3,000 to 6,000 rubles. Vyacheslav Voronkov, mayor of the resort city of Sochi, hired an Armenian architect to construct a musical fountain in the foyer of his state mansion. Tourists were permitted to pay a few kopecks to hear their Party leader's fountain in full aria. When Communist Party chiefs in Russia went fishing, scuba divers plunged underwater and put fish on the hooks. When they went hunting, specially bred elk, stag, and deer were made to saunter across the field in point-blank range. Everyone had a wonderful time. When the king of Afghanistan visited the Tajik resort of Tiger Gorge, he blew away the last Turan tiger in the country.

The mutual congratulations, the feasts and wedding parties, the piety and self-righteousness all smacked of mafia culture. At a conference of the Soviet Writers' Union in 1981, Yegor Ligachev, who would later serve as Gorbachev's nominal number-two man and conservative nemesis, said, "You can't imagine, comrades, what a joy it is for all of us to be able to get on with our work quietly and how well everything is going under the leadership of dear

Leonid Ilyich. What a marvelous moral-political climate has been established in the Party and country with his coming to power! It is as if wings have sprouted on our backs, if you want to put it stylishly, as you writers do."

—

In Kazakhstan, a republic bigger than all of Western Europe, Dinmukhamed Kunayev showed a certain kindliness to his relatives and (a rare feature in mafia men) to his wife. Arkady Vaksberg confirmed a story about Kunayev's connubial bliss that I had first heard when I was in Alma-Ata.

It seems that Kunayev's wife became jealous after learning that the wife of the Magadan Party secretary had been given as a gift an extremely expensive Japanese tea service. Magadan, the former labor camp center in the far east, had unique access to Japanese goods, but Mrs. Kunayev would not be soothed. She had to have these cups and saucers. Party etiquette did not allow Kunayev simply to order the tea set from Japan or even Siberia. That was somehow too obvious. Even dispatching an aide to Tokyo was deemed unseemly.

"A way had to be found, of course," Vaksberg writes. "And such was its originality and refinement that it deserves its own little page in the history of the Soviet mafia." Kunayev could not merely send his private plane, a Tupolev 134, on the mission. Party rules dictated that a Politburo member's plane always had to be on the ready for emergency sessions in Moscow. So Kunayev told his aides to draw up an official report saying the plane's engine required repair. This would allow him to order another plane while the first was being "fixed."

Rules also dictated that after the repair, a Politburo member could not fly on the plane until it had been flown twenty thousand kilometers. "The point of this brilliant move is clear," Vaksberg writes. "Some of Kunayev's closest associates were happy to take on the 'kamikaze' role. They worked out a route which, there and back, would clock up the required distance of twenty thousand kilometers. There would be stopovers in Krasnoyarsk, Irkutsk, and Khabarovsk. They would return via Petropavlovsk-Kamchatsky, for it would have been unthinkable to visit the Soviet far east and not gawk at geysers and an active volcano. Everywhere they were received at the highest level—after all, they were emissaries from Kunayev himself. Those that have clawed their way to power have an astonishing passion for recording their pleasure on film. Thanks to this hobby we can today see with our own eyes how their trip went. Lavish picnics everywhere with the traditional shashlik and variety of vodkas, saunas, and royal hunting of boar, elk, and deer especially put up in front of them for easy shots.

"The first lady herself did not take the trip, needless to say. Like her

husband, she was not allowed to take chances with her life. However, the jolly kamikazes came back with the passenger cabin and baggage hold crammed with gifts from the Soviet far east and Siberia. They brought not only dozens of Japanese tea sets but also Japanese sound and video equipment, furs, carvings on rare deer horn—the finest art of indigenous craftsmen—thousands of jars of Pacific crab and other fruits of the ocean. All these things were brought back to Alma-Ata like trophies."

After three decades as the Kazakh Party chief, Kunayev had been forced to retire for "reasons of health" in 1986. In retirement, he lived across the street from a park named in his honor. The focal point of the park was an enormous monument, a huge plinth with the great man's granite head perched on top. The building at 119 Tulebayeva Street looked like a second-rate Miami Beach motel. In addition to Kunayev, the two top-ranking Party leaders also lived there.

The first time I went to meet Kunayev, I tried to "doorstep" him, to show up and hope for the best. This was not a wise maneuver. A KGB guard in the courtyard stopped me and made it clear, as his hand flashed lightly to his holster, that one further step toward the Kunayev residence would be inadvisable. So I tried a more conventional tactic. Through a Kazakh journalist, a particularly obedient one whom I knew from Moscow, I asked to see Kunayev and sent along a list of questions of the "What are the key achievements of Kazakhstan under Soviet power?" variety. While we waited for word back from Kunayev, we ate a multicourse dinner at the apartment of the journalist's in-laws. It was a long evening. His father-in-law got badly hammered on the cognac I brought as a gift and spoke lovingly for some hours of Stalin's "iron hand." We all ate heartily of a dish that I was later informed was "delicious noodles" mixed with shredded horse heart. Tastes like chicken, my hosts assured me. They were wrong.

Finally, the call came from Kunayev. He was ready to see us the next morning at eleven.

We arrived, four of us, at the house five minutes early.

"Where are you going?" the guard asked us.

"We have an appointment with Kunayev."

"Impossible," the guard said.

"We do. An interview at eleven. He is expecting us."

"Documents!"

We all showed our various papers, and the guard went to his special phone. He talked for a while and came back smiling in triumph.

"The American is forbidden," he said. This seemed nonnegotiable.

Clearly, the ministers of Moscow had no interest in giving Kunayev a public platform, especially not in an American newspaper. They were prepared to let Kunayev live in relative splendor amid his beloved collections of cigarette lighters and foreign shotguns, but they did not want to be the agents of a resurrection. Gorbachev had already suffered once from Kunayev. When he fired Kunayev in 1986, Gorbachev made the mistake of appointing in his place an outsider and a Russian, Gennadi Kolbin. This was just what Kunayev needed. By all accounts, Kunayev's clan encouraged anti-Russian, anti-colonial riots, using a latent nationalism to do his own work. Gorbachev soon corrected the mistake, replacing Kolbin with a Kazakh, Nursultan Nazarbayev. But it was that incident in Alma-Ata that should have demonstrated to the Kremlin that, contrary to myth, the Soviet Union had not solved its national problems; instead, the abuses of a half-century had created an empire of resentments. Alma-Ata was prelude to a series of national movements Moscow never expected.

I waited on the street. An hour later, the Kazakhs came out of Kunayev's place, beaming. "Kunayev seemed sad that you couldn't come," one of them said. "He said, 'It seems I'm powerless in my own house.' "

It seemed I would never meet the fallen don. But later the same day, while I was with another Kazakh political official, one of the journalists walked into the room, tapped me on the shoulder, and told me to "wrap things up." He had called Kunayev and we were all set to meet—on the street, outside the gates of the Communist Party's House of Rest.

A half hour later, a Volga, not unlike Aliyev's modest car, pulled up. Kunayev unfolded himself from the backseat. He was enormous, silver-haired, and dressed in a chalk-striped suit. He wore dark glasses and carried the sort of carved walking stick that gave Mobuto his authority. He had a fantastic smile, all bravado and condescension, the smile of a king. Without my asking a thing, he launched into a monologue about the such-and-such anniversary of Kazakhstan and wheat production and the need to preserve the monuments of the Bolshevik state. "I've never swayed," he solemnly reminded us. "I am a man of the Leninist Party line. Never forget that." We swore we would not.

When I finally asked my earnest questions—about Gorbachev, about politics—Kunayev laughed them off, fiddled with the mahogany knob of his stick, and set back on the course of his monologue.

There were, I said, interrupting, still many Kazakhs who wanted Kunayev to return to politics. "Are you ready to make a comeback?" I asked.

"I wouldn't be against it," he said. "Let the people decide. But tomorrow, I should tell you, I'm busy. I'm going hunting for ducks. I love hunting for ducks."

The decline of the Party mafia began with the death of Brezhnev and the brief reign of Yuri Andropov. Although Andropov was guilty of many things—most notably his brutally efficient campaign against the dissidents while he ran the KGB—he was a throwback to a tradition of Leninist asceticism. Andropov was profoundly corrupt, a beast. No man who ran the Budapest embassy during the Soviet invasion of Hungary in 1956 can be declared an innocent. "In a way I always thought Andropov was the most dangerous of all of them, simply because he was smarter than the rest," Aleksandr Yakovlev told me.

But Andropov's main virtue was that he was appalled by the kind of corruption and rot that had become endemic under Brezhnev. While he was KGB chief, Andropov conducted a wide-scale, independent investigation into Party business and the general state of the country's economic system. After Brezhnev's death, in his few months as general secretary, Andropov ordered arrests of some of the most obvious Party and police mafiosi. He frightened the worst elements in the apparatus so badly that a series of high-ranking officials in Brezhnev's old circle shot, gassed, or otherwise did away with themselves.

The remaining Brezhnevites at the top were not much grieved when Andropov became seriously ill. The Party mafia could not bear the thought of reforms that would endanger its comfort. As Solzhenitsyn wrote in 1991, "The corrupt ruling class—the many millions of men in the party-state nomenklatura—is not capable of voluntarily renouncing any of the privileges they have seized. They have lived shamelessly for decades at the people's expense—and would like to continue doing so."

Had it not been for that primal urge to power and privilege, Gorbachev might well have taken over as general secretary more than a year earlier than he did. Arkady Volsky, a former aide to Andropov and a leading figure in the Central Committee, told me how the Brezhnevites in the Politburo steered power away from Gorbachev, an Andropov protégé, to "their man," the moribund apparatchik Konstantin Chernenko. By December 1983, Andropov was in the hospital with kidney problems and blood poisoning. His aides would take turns visiting him in the hospital with important matters and paperwork. On a Saturday preceding a Tuesday plenum of the Central Committee, Volsky came to Andropov's room at the Kremlin hospital on the outskirts of Moscow to help him draft a speech. Andropov was in no shape to attend the plenum, and he would have one of his men in the Politburo deliver the speech in his name.

"The last lines in the speech said that Central Committee staff members

should be exemplary in their behavior, uncorrupted, responsible for the life of the country," Volsky said. "We both liked that last phrase. . . . Then Andropov gave me a folder with the final draft and said, 'The material looks good. Make sure you pay attention to the addenda I've written.' I didn't have time to look right away at what he had written. Later, I got a chance to read it and saw that at the bottom of the last page Andropov had added in ink, in a somewhat unsteady handwriting, a new paragraph. It went like this: 'Members of the Central Committee know that due to certain reasons, I am unable to come to the plenum. I can neither attend the meetings of the Politburo nor the secretariat [of the Central Committee]. Therefore, I believe Mikhail Sergeyevich Gorbachev should be assigned to preside over the meetings of the Politburo and the secretariat.' "

Volsky knew well what this meant. The general secretary was recommending that Gorbachev be his inheritor. Volsky made a photocopy of the document and put the copy in his safe. He delivered the original to the Party leadership and assumed, naively, that it would be read out at the plenum. But at the meeting neither Chernenko, Grishin, Romanov, nor any of the other usual suspects in the Brezhnev circle made mention of Andropov's stated wishes. Volsky thought there must have been some mistake. "I went up to Chernenko and said, 'Sir, there was an addendum in the text.' He said, 'Think nothing of any addendum.' Then I saw his aide Bogolyubov and said, 'Klavdy Mikhailovich, there was a paragraph from Andropov's speech . . .' He led me off to the side and said, 'Who do you think you are, a wise guy? Do you think your life ends with this?' I said, 'In that case, I'll have to phone Andropov.' And he replied, 'Then that will be your last phone call.' "

Andropov was furious when he heard what had happened at the plenum, but there was little he could do. Even Lenin did not have the power to name his successor, and the Brezhnevites in the Politburo were just too powerful. When Andropov died in February 1984, Chernenko became general secretary, the ventriloquist's dummy of the Party mafia.

As a concession to the Andropov faction and over the objections of some of his own confidants, Chernenko made Gorbachev the nominal number-two man in the Politburo. This turned out to be a serious tactical mistake. Chernenko held office for only thirteen months, and much of the time he was sick and powerless. As Chernenko wasted away, Gorbachev was carefully consolidating power. He ran Politburo sessions and won the support of two critical figures—the foreign minister, Andrei Gromyko, and the KGB chief, Viktor Chebrikov. He also took his famous trip to Britain, where he made a lasting impression on Margaret Thatcher and the world press. When Chernenko finally died in March 1985, Gorbachev had the backing of the younger

Party secretaries and a few key members of the old guard, including Gromyko. He was in a position to head off any potential opposition from the mafia dinosaurs.

Gorbachev, for his part, took office without taint of blood or corruption, a first for a leader of the Soviet Union. But even this was relative. As the Party leader of a resort region in the Caucasus, a neighbor of the notorious Krasnodar region, he must have known about the Party way of doing business, both with Moscow and within the local structure. At best, it is unlikely that he could have avoided toadying to Brezhnev either as the Party chief of the Stavropol region in southern Russia or in Moscow as a member of the Central Committee. Roy Medvedev, a Gorbachev loyalist to the last, told a reporter for *La Stampa,* "I believe that presents for Brezhnev even arrived from Stavropol."

"Did Gorbachev give Brezhnev diamond rings the way Aliyev did? Of course not," Arkady Vaksberg told me. "But on the other hand, no provincial Party secretary could survive, much less advance, by ignoring the birthdays and so on of those superior to him. Even an 'honest' Party secretary coming to Moscow would have to bring gifts for his superiors: a few cases of good wine. You couldn't get away from that. Gorbachev included. That was life in the Communist Party."

On New Year's Eve 1989, the censors canceled an installment of the popular television program *Vzglyad* ("View") for "aesthetic reasons." Vaksberg claims that the aesthetic reason in question was that Brezhnev's daughter, Galina, had told an interviewer that Raisa Gorbachev had tried to curry favor with the Brezhnev family when Leonid Ilyich was in power and had given them a number of presents, including an expensive necklace. But Vaksberg is also quick to recount how after publishing a piece called "Spring Floods" in *Literaturnaya Gazeta* about the negligence of ministers while the harvest rotted in the fields, the paper got a dressing-down from the Ideology Department of the Central Committee. Just as the editor was instructing Vaksberg to print a retraction, Gorbachev called the paper to express his compliments for its crusade against corruption.

But Gorbachev knew that he could not conduct a genuine investigation into the Party's corruption. First, the Party, of which he was the head, would sooner kill him than allow it. Second, even if he could carry out such an investigation, Gorbachev would be faced with the obvious embarrassment: the depths of the Party's rot. Instead, taking a page from Andropov's style manual, he made a grand symbolic gesture. Yuri Churbanov, Brezhnev's son-in-law and a deputy chief of the Interior Ministry, was indicted and tried for accepting more than $1 million in bribes while working in Uzbekistan. At his trial, Churbanov admitted accepting a briefcase stuffed with around

$200,000. "I wanted to return the money, but to whom?" he said. "It would have been awkward for me to raise the question with Rashidov," the Party chief of the republic. Churbanov was sentenced to twelve years in prison at a camp near the city of Nizhny Tagil. Brezhnev's personal secretary, Gennadi Brovin, was sentenced to nine years in prison, also for corruption.

Like Andropov before him, Gorbachev believed in his ability to master the Party and reform it. Over a five-year period, he fired and replaced the most obvious mafiosi in the Politburo: Kunayev, Aliyev, Shcherbitsky. But just as he could never distance himself enough from a discredited ideology, Gorbachev's inability to jettison the Party nomenklatura and his political debts to the KGB spoiled his reputation over time in the eyes of a people who had grown more and more aware of the corruption and deceit in their midst.

—

In the meantime, a new wave of politicians saw Gorbachev's equivocations as an opportunity. Telman Gdlyan and Nikolai Ivanov, investigators who helped convict Churbanov, became two of the most popular legislators in the parliament purely on the strength of their public attacks on the Party. In their investigations of corruption under Brezhnev, Gdlyan and Ivanov were known for mistreating witnesses, manufacturing evidence, and committing other illegalities. They dismissed such charges with a smirk. Gdlyan, especially, was a wild man. He told me one day that Yegor Ligachev, the number-two man in the Politburo, had "definitely" accepted at least 60,000 rubles in bribes from an Uzbek official. When I asked for proof, Gdlyan laughed, as if such things hardly mattered.

Boris Yeltsin was the master of the populist attack, using the issue of Party perks and corruption as a way to discredit everyone at the top, Gorbachev included. In his memoir, *Against the Grain,* which was terrifically popular in Russia, Yeltsin writes about the "marble-lined" houses of the Politburo members, their "porcelain, crystal, carpets, and chandeliers." For an audience living in cramped communal apartments, he described his own house when he was in the Party leadership, with its private movie theater, its "kitchen big enough to feed an army," and its many bathrooms, so many that "I lost count." And, he wrote, "why has Gorbachev been unable to change this? I believe the fault lies in his basic cast of character. He likes to live well, in comfort and luxury. In this he is helped by his wife."

At times, Yeltsin seemed the Huey and Earl Long of Soviet politics, a theatrical populist. Relying on the politics of resentment, he won an angry public's affection. After he'd been fired from the Politburo for daring to confront the leadership in October 1987, Yeltsin was still a member of the Central Committee, with all the privileges that entailed. But in an interview

with me at his modest office at the Ministry of Construction, Yeltsin swore that he had voluntarily given up his dacha, his grocery shipments, and his car. "All finished!" he said with the pride of the converted. For a very short while Yeltsin made sure that Muscovites saw him tooling around the city in a dinky sedan. Later, when he returned to power, however, Yeltsin lived no worse than Gorbachev did. He commandeered a splendid dacha, organized a regal caravan of limousines, and made a public show of his love for that proletarian game—tennis. Yeltsin's new double-breasted suits and silk ties were also, one supposed, not available for rubles.

Like Gorbachev, Yeltsin was an ambitious provincial who made good in the Communist Party. Like Gorbachev, he made absurd speeches at various meetings praising the wisdom of Leonid Brezhnev and the eternal goodness of the Party. But while Gorbachev spent all his working life in the Party, Yeltsin began late. He became a member of the Party to get ahead at the state construction agency in Sverdlovsk. In his autobiography, Yeltsin recounts with a brand of irony foreign to Gorbachev the preposterous oral exam at the local Party committee required for membership:

"[The examiner] asked me on what page of which volume of *Das Kapital* Marx refers to commodity-money relationships. Assuming that he had never read Marx closely and had, of course, no idea of either the volume or page number in question, and that he didn't even know what commodity-money relationships were, I immediately answered, half-jokingly, 'Volume Two, page 387.' What's more I said it quickly, without pausing for thought. To which he replied, with a sage expression, 'Well done, you know your Marx well.' After it all, I was accepted as a Party member."

After his fall from the Politburo, no statement, no amount of bombast, was out of bounds. In interviews, Yeltsin would suggest with a burlesque arch of the brow that the KGB could yet kill him with a high-frequency ray gun that would stun his heart. "A few seconds," he told me, "and it's all over." His paranoia was comic, but understandable. The Kremlin leaders despised him. They formed a commission within the Central Committee to investigate him and ordered wild stories in the state-run press to disgrace him.

As the man who would not go away, Yeltsin was, for the Communist Party, an intolerable dissident. Such was his vital importance, his first important contribution to the collapse of the regime. Despite the Kremlin's best efforts, the history of Soviet politics will show it was Yeltsin—vain, comic, clever, crude—who accelerated the essential step in political reform: the shattering of the Communist Party monolith. From the moment Yeltsin attacked Yegor Ligachev at the Party plenum on October 21, 1987, and rumors of this assault became the talk of Moscow, the facade of unanimity and invincibility, the hermetic code of Party discipline and loyalty, began to

crumble. Although the proceedings of the plenum remained secret for months, Yeltsin quickly became an underground martyr. An actress performing in a hit play about the cleaning of the Augean stables, *The Seventh Feat of Hercules,* stepped center stage, abandoned her script, and accused the audience of sitting idly by as a new Hercules, come to purify the city, had been disgraced and persecuted. There were demonstrations at Moscow State University. Small independent political groups such as the Club for Social Initiatives petitioned the government for more facts on the Yeltsin case. Club members reported they were followed around town by men in small cars.

After failing to win back his position or good name within the Party at the Nineteenth Party Conference, Yeltsin took his campaign for revenge and rehabilitation to the public. His barrel-chested fury, his awkward candor, had an almost narcotic appeal for a people who saw the Party that ruled them for seven decades—the Party of Aliyev and Kunayev—as an ominous secret. To any reporter or crowd who would listen, Yeltsin insulted Gorbachev's "timidity and half-measures" and Ligachev's "dark motives."

The Communist Party, for its part, well understood not only the meaning of Yeltsin's attacks but also the much wider issue of what his political success would mean to its future. Yeltsin's ascendance embodied the threat to the Party's control of the economy and the Party mafia's system of tribute.

From the first appearance of cooperative businesses in 1987, the Party did everything it could to destroy the new movement it had ostensibly endorsed. One leading conservative in the Central Committee, Ivan Polozkov, made his name fighting the rise of semiprivate cooperative businesses in the Krasnodar region. He closed down more than three hundred co-ops in the region, calling them "a social evil, a malignant tumor." The KGB, under Vladimir Kryuchkov, waged a campaign against private business, all under the pretense of rooting out corruption. But Kryuchkov never got around to investigating the barons of the state military plants, men who would soon become his closest allies in the struggle against radical reform. The conservatives also knew they could play games with the psychology of a people grown accustomed to "equality in poverty." They knew they could arouse bitter jealousy in millions of collective farmers and workers by advertising cases of abuse under the new "mixed" economy. They portrayed the new wave of businessmen as hustlers (invariably Jewish, Armenian or Georgian hustlers) who made millions by buying products at low state-subsidized prices and then reselling the same products for three or four times more.

Undeniably, the first wave of private businessmen in Russia were no angels—no more than the first Rockefellers or Carnegies were. Racketeering, theft and bribery soared. But to the Party and the KGB, what these entrepreneurs and hustlers represented was not so much evil or capitalism as competi-

tion. This was intolerable. Lev Timofeyev, the journalist and political activist who spent 1985 to 1987 in a labor camp for writing a book describing rural corruption, wryly demanded that the Party men "transform themselves into men of property, landowners or shareholders.

"Let them make profits and reinvest them, let them outrun competition and become rich. Let them be useful at last. They have a right to do that. The only requirement is that they do not prevent others from doing the same," he wrote. "Unfortunately the party officials will hardly become successful owners of land or industries. They lack the qualities needed for becoming honest entrepreneurs and this is why they are so terrified of those who have them. They will stop at nothing trying to prolong the days of their rotten power and they are still strong enough to do it."

CHAPTER 13

POOR FOLK

There in some smoky corner which, through poverty, passes for a dwelling place, a workman wakes from his sleep. All night he has been dreaming of a pair of boots. . . .

—FYODOR DOSTOEVSKY, Poor Folk, 1845

When I first came to Russia in 1985, I rode through Moscow on a tour bus packed with a gaggle of British socialists. They were spindly fellow travelers who wore orthopedic shoes and plastic raincoats that folded away into envelopes "no bigger than the palm of your hand." They felt like complaining about the rotten breakfast—cold kasha, bad coffee, surly waiters—but they knew they should not.

We settled into our seats, and with a noxious wheeze, the bus headed north for the monastery at Zagorsk. The tour guide, who spoke English with the clutzy formality of a movie spy working undercover, chirped on about the "utterly ideal" marriage of atheism and freedom of religion in the Soviet Union. "It is epitome of social and spiritual," she said obscurely, but with a smile. The passengers had neither the strength nor the inclination to press

her. They all wiped little circles in their misted windows and watched Moscow go to work on a dun-colored morning. Somewhere along the Avenue of Peace, we stopped at a red light. Through the gloom, I noticed a woman in a brown tattered coat begging in a doorway. She was hunched over and kept her gaze on the sidewalk so no one would see her face. She thrust her hand into the foot traffic. There were, I could see, a few 5-kopeck coins in her palm, though judging by the way everyone streamed by her, she probably had put them there herself, as a hint. A woman in the row behind me on the bus raised her hand and asked the guide what was going on. "Unlike in London," the woman said, "doesn't the state care for the poor?"

"This is quite unusual," said the guide without looking out the window longer than she had to. "It is quite likely, in fact, that precisely the woman you see is a foreigner. Or gypsy." Enough said. The guide was rattled and we were all a bit embarrassed for her. We rode the rest of the way to the center of Russian holiness in silence.

Those were the last days of illusion in the Soviet Union. Under Brezhnev, Andropov, and Chernenko, the regime floated on an immense sea of oil profits. At the height of the world energy crisis and its aftermath, the state plundered its vast oil reserves in Siberia, Azerbaijan, and Kazakhstan, giving Moscow the cash it needed to fund the vast military-industrial complex. The rest of the economy was a wreck and ran on principles of magic and graft, but so long as world crude prices remained high, it hardly mattered to the Kremlin. There was still enough wealth to fill the stores with four kinds of cheese, cheap boots in wintertime, and 3-ruble vodka.

But by the time Gorbachev took power in March 1985, the oil boom had vanished. The economy of illusion was dead. The Soviet Union entered the era of high tech with none of its own and could not hope to compete. It could barely hope to survive. The state of affairs was best summarized in the chestnut "The Soviet Union makes the finest microcomputers! They are the biggest in the whole world!" Although the West was slow to notice, its great enemy of the cold war was dangerous and broke. "Upper Volta with missiles," as the *Daily Telegraph*'s Xan Smiley put it.

At first it was hard to make any sense of the poverty, to quantify it. In 1988, there were still far more articles in the press about Stalin's mental health than about homelessness, infant mortality, or malnutrition. It was as though the press were in vague agreement with Edmund Wilson's observations of Moscow a half-century ago: "One gradually comes to realize that, though the people's clothes are dreary, there is little, if any destitution; though there are no swell parts of the city, there are no degraded parts either.

There are no shocking sights on the streets; no down-and-outers, no horrible diseases, no old people picking in garbage pails. I was never able to find anything like a slum or any quarter that even seemed dirty." But decrepitude was everywhere now. Every sign of poverty that Wilson could not, or would not, see was now general and could not be overlooked. You wandered into poverty at every corner, in every city and village.

On a winter afternoon, I drifted away from a small street demonstration outside the offices of *Moscow News* and into a run-down cafeteria on Gorky Street. I was cold and hungry, and so I bought a bowl of watery borshch and sat down at one of the communal tables.

"You want a spoon with that?"

The woman next to me was smiling, her mouth filled with steel teeth. She gave me her spoon, a flimsy thing, and filthy, too, but a spoon. She said her name was Yelena and that for the past eight years she'd been living in train stations and airports. In summer she slept in some of the more obscure parks on the perimeter of Moscow. "Sometimes I get five rubles a day scrubbing the floors on the train after they pull in to Moscow," she said. "Right now I'm broke, and everything I have is what you see—the coat and the clothes I'm wearing." Yelena said that some of her friends had been thrown out of their apartments by husbands and boyfriends and they had nowhere to go. She wrote letters appealing for help to the Communist Party at every level and never got a response.

A friend of Yelena's, a homeless man named Leonid, joined us. "I've written Mikhail Gorbachev, Andrei Gromyko, everyone," he said. "I want my right to work and live guaranteed by the Constitution of the Soviet Union."

Yelena nodded. "You know," she said, "there are thousands like us in this country. Thousands."

"To tell you the truth, I probably make more money out here collecting empty bottles for twenty kopecks apiece than I would on a construction job in town," said Vitya Karsokos, who made his living searching garbage dumps. "My biggest problem is I have to sleep in the train station or out in a dump in a box somewhere. I'd get a job in town if I could, but good luck."

For years, while state television was still broadcasting documentaries about the street people of New York as an advertisement against capitalism, the Moscow police tried in vain to keep their own homeless out of sight. But as the number of homeless grew, their efforts collapsed. Moscow *bomzhi*—the acronym for "without definite place of residence"—slept in cemeteries, railway stations, construction sites, and basements. A favorite spot was the empty top floor of Moscow high rises with their ventilation pipes and heating ducts. There were drunks, abandoned children, the mentally ill—people who

had fallen into the bureaucratic abyss and no longer had any right to a place on the apartment waiting list. *Bomzhi* sometimes worked, sometimes for money, sometimes for a bottle of vodka. You'd see them afternoons helping the local liquor store unload the vodka delivery truck. They'd collect empty bottles in the park and on garbage heaps and cash them in for change. At airports and train stations, *bomzhi* helped the drivers hustle fares and then took a small cut. In Moscow they might hold a place for you in line at a store; in Central Asia they'd take on migrant work at harvest time in the cotton fields.

At the Kazan Station in Moscow a wanderer named Alik said he'd talk my ear off if I'd only buy him a bottle. I suggested we go to a store and join the vodka line. When he stopped laughing, he said, "Just give me thirty rubles." He snatched the bills from my hand and set off down the sidewalk. We walked ten feet before Alik found what he was looking for. A ghostly woman in a ratty coat reached into her pocket and the silent exchange was done. Alik quickened his pace and we headed toward a place marked CAFÉ. Three feet inside the door, he screwed off the bottle cap and downed the entire liter bottle in a few magnificent swigs. "Usually, in the morning, I like some potatoes," he said and then stormed out the door, singing.

Alik was a sawed-off man with a two-week beard. He kept a change of clothes stuffed in a ventilation duct at the station. He said he refused to work collecting empties. "Too humiliating. What am I, a dog?" he said. "I'll tell you what I do. When I need money, I take it. Like, one minute you've got your rubles, then you don't!" For his adventures in pickpocketing, Alik had spent the better part of twenty years in prison camps and exile. Whenever he was released, he returned to "the station life." He had no residence permit—"In Moscow, I'm no one"—and hospitals and drunk tanks couldn't bear him for long. He didn't make it easy. He was a nasty drunk. Sometimes he went three or four days without eating—"just 'cause I can't stomach it." He was irritable, manic. In a moment, he would turn sentimental, an autodidact who recited the poems of Pushkin and sang the songs of the great bard Vladimir Vysotsky, screaming them all in your face as if they were a curse.

"My father and mother worked morning till night just to support us kids," Alik said, sitting in a deserted courtyard. "My brother was killed in Hungary in '56. He was nineteen. Sometimes I think if he had survived I might not have started the way I did. I ran away when I was sixteen or seventeen, went off to Kazakhstan. I was going hungry, and so I lifted my first purse. That's how my prison career started. I got five years in the Tashkent camp for teenagers. I've been all over the prison zone ever since. You sit in a rank cell and get twenty minutes' exercise a day and you're hungry, lying there on the cold concrete. I started getting sick that way. We *bomzhi* stay in these places

twenty-four hours a day and we're always worried we're gonna get clubbed by the cops, day and night. We have nowhere to go. I'm telling you this on behalf of the Soviet homeless, who are punished for their destinies. No rights, no residence permit, no nothing. It's tough when you get out of jail. It's like you're a third-class citizen and nobody needs your life."

At times, Alik stopped talking and began humming and singing a Vysotsky song about a man going off to jail and never seeing his beloved again. Then he'd break it off and stare out into space and take another swig on a new bottle.

"So how do I break this cycle? I just don't know. One of my buddies comes up to me the other day, yesterday maybe, and says he'll smash my face if I don't stop drinking, and I said, 'You son of a bitch, I can't stop. I can't.' I worked some in Uzbekistan, but it didn't last. Never got along with the bosses. Worked on an oil rig once, too. I've never worked a single day in Moscow. For me, three hundred rubles a month and a flat, and I'd make it all right. But I don't have it. So where should I go? You tell me."

To describe the Soviet Union in terms of overwhelming national poverty was, by 1989, no longer the work of fire-breathing ideologues from abroad. Even the news organs of the Communist Party took up the survey of the wreckage of everyday life. *Komsomolskaya Pravda,* the Party's youth newspaper, blamed the Soviet system, pointing out that before the 1917 revolution, Russia ranked seventh in the world in per capita consumption and was now seventy-seventh—"just after South Africa but ahead of Romania."

"If we compare the quality of life in the developed countries with our own," the paper said, "we have to admit that from the viewpoint of civilized, developed society the overwhelming majority of the population of our country lives below the poverty line."

The people themselves began to make the connection between the grimness of their circumstances and the failure of the Communist Party leadership. In the streets, "the mafia" became the muttered explanation for every shortage and inequity, and only foreigners made the mistake of thinking the term referred exclusively to the hustlers at the bottom of the criminal structure.

For a while the Kremlin ministries set the poverty line at 78 rubles a month—a level fit for dogs. But no one, not even the government itself, took the official poverty line seriously. Most officials and scholars in Moscow and in the West argued that the figure should be doubled. Even then, about 131 million out of 285 million Soviet citizens would have been registered as poor. "For decades we were striving to translate into life the idea of universal equality," economist Anatoly Deryabin wrote in the official journal *Molodoi*

Kommunist. "So what have we achieved after all these years? Only 2.3 percent of all Soviet families can be called wealthy, and about 0.7 of these have earned that income lawfully. . . . About 11.2 percent can be called middle-class or well-to-do. The rest, 86.5 percent, are simply poor. What we have is equality in poverty."

Poverty in the Soviet Union did not look like poverty in Somalia or Sudan; it did not necessarily mean bloated bellies and famine, but rather a common condition of need. The self-deception and isolation of the Soviet Union had been so complete for so long that poverty felt normal. Even so, almost no one, save the government elite, could ignore the widespread misery. "Even the 'millionaire' farm chairmen don't have hot water out here," a cotton farmer told me in the Turkmenian countryside. Or as Joseph Brodsky writes, "Money has nothing to do with it, since in a totalitarian state income brackets are of no great variety—in other words, every person is as poor as the next."

Miners in the northern region of Vorkuta did not have enough soap to wash the coal dust from their faces; mothers on the far eastern island of Sakhalin gave birth in rented rooms for lack of a maternity hospital there; Byelorussian villagers scavenged scrap metal and pig fat to pay for shoes. A few early published figures began to give some sense of the scope of the problem: the average Soviet had to work ten times longer than the average American to buy a pound of meat; the riggers in Tyumen, a Siberian oil region with greater resources than Kuwait, lived in shacks and shabby trailers despite winter temperatures of forty degrees below zero; even Party officials estimated that there were between 1.5 and 3 million homeless, more than a million unemployed in Uzbekistan alone, and a national infant mortality rate 250 percent higher than in most Western countries, about the same level as Panama.

There was also the sheer crumminess of the things that you could find: the plastic shoes, the sulfurous mineral water, the collapsible apartment buildings. The decrepitude of ordinary life irritated the soul and skin. Towels scratched after one washing, milk soured in a day, cars collapsed upon purchase. The leading cause of house fires in the Soviet Union was television sets that exploded spontaneously. All of it kept people in a constant state of frustration and misery.

Glasnost meant admitting to all this, too. Sometimes the admission came in the shape of an earnest article in the paper, sometimes with a certain flair, a Russian irony that deflated Soviet pomposity. The Exhibition of Economic Achievements, a kind of vast Stalinist Epcot Center near the Moscow television tower, had for years put on displays of Soviet triumphs in the sciences, engineering, and space in huge neo-Hellenic halls. Vera Mukhina's gigantic

statue *Worker and the Collective Farm Girl* (jutting breasts and biceps, bulging eyes) presided at the entrance, providing citizens with the sense that they were now part of a socially and genetically engineered breed of muscular proletarians. But with glasnost, the directors grew humble and put up an astonishingly frank display: "The Exhibit of Poor-Quality Goods."

At the exhibit, a long line of Soviets solemnly shuffled past a dazzling display of stunning underachievement: putrid lettuce, ruptured shoes, rusted samovars, chipped stew pots, unraveled shuttlecocks, crushed cans of fish, and, the show-stopper, a bottle of mineral water with a tiny dead mouse floating inside. All the items had been purchased in neighborhood stores. "It was time to inject a little reality into the scene here," one of the guides told me. The exhibit was unsparing, a vicious redefinition of socialist realism. In the clothing section, red arrows pointed to uneven sleeves, faded colors, cracked soles. One piece of jewelry was labeled, simply, "hideous," and no one argued.

"Let me tell you a little secret," a transport worker, Aleksandr Klebko, said as we filed past the display of rotten fruit. "This isn't so bad. I've seen worse. Most stores have less than this. Or nothing at all."

ASHKHABAD

Stalinism was still lethal a quarter century after Stalin was dead. In the mud-brick hovels on the outskirts of Ashkhabad, the capital of Turkmenistan, children were the first casualties of poverty. Every year, thousands of infants throughout the republic and the rest of Soviet Central Asia died within twelve months of birth. Countless others suffered more slowly, weakened by the heat and infected water, the pesticides from the cotton fields, a diet built on bread and tea and soup. "I consider myself fairly lucky. I've given birth five times, and only one child died," said Elshe Abayeva, a woman of thirty-one who looked twenty years older. Some of her children played on a hillock of mud and garbage as she cut grass with a blunt scythe. Farther up the road, Abayeva's neighbors, the Karadiyevs, were not so lucky. "Five children are alive and three died—two at birth and one after a month," the father said. "In Turkmenia, it's like this all the time. Worse in the villages."

Inside the Abayevs' two-room hut, the bare bulbs were furred with dust, flies buzzed around the children's faces. The children were filthy, their clothes in tatters. Only heavy stones kept the tin roof from blowing off the outhouse and the rusted chicken coop. Aba Abayev, Elshe's husband, earned 170 rubles a month as a video technician for state television—less than 6 rubles

a day to support a family of six. The Abayevs had been waiting since 1975 to be assigned an apartment in the city. "When that child was born, it was a cold winter morning," Aba Abayev said. "No one has phones here, and there are no hospitals or doctors around. I ran two or three kilometers to the pay phone and called. It looked like the baby was dying—or was dead already, maybe—and it took the doctors more than an hour to get here. By then the child was dead. This is the way our lives go out here. I have no hope, to be honest. And for my children, I don't think things will change, unless they get worse somehow."

In Turkmenistan, the official infant mortality rate in 1989 was 54.2 infants per 1,000 births, ten times higher than in most West European countries and more than two and a half times that of Washington, D.C., the city with the highest rate in the United States. Turkmenistan was about on a level with Cameroon. In especially poor regions, such as Tashauz in the north, the rate soared to 111 deaths in every 1,000 births. Many experts in Moscow and the West said that even these statistics understated the problem. The Central Asian republics, they said, regularly underreported their infant mortality rates by as much as 60 percent.

Children fell sick for many reasons, but mainly they suffered from the effect of the cotton "monoculture," the obsession with a cotton crop at all costs. Working in the cotton fields, the children often drank from irrigation sources poisoned with pesticides and toxic minerals. In the regions near the Aral Sea, which had been ruined and drained through a mad scheme to irrigate the cotton fields by diverting the rivers that flow into the sea, the poisons in the drinking water were so intense that children were taking them in through their mothers' breast milk. Even seeing a doctor proved dangerous at times. In the first year of their lives, Turkmenian children were given an average of two hundred to four hundred injections, compared to three to five for American children. It was nothing systematic. The doctors threw everything they had at the children. Within a few years the effect of the vaccines was close to zero.

Everything that went wrong with the Soviet system over the decades—the centralization of authority, the vacuum of responsibility and incentive, the triumph of ideology over sense, the dominance of the Party and its police—was magnified in Central Asia. The system was known as "feudal socialism," a Soviet-Asiatic hierarchy led by Communist Party bosses and collective-farm chairmen.

At the Institute of Health Care for Mothers and Children in Ashkhabad, the head pediatrician, Yuri Kirichenko, treated dozens of patients every day. Outside Kirichenko's door, Turkmenian women, many of them pregnant, paced the hall and waited hours for treatment for themselves and their

children. Some of the pregnant women were in their late forties and had already had a dozen or more children. Because of the tribal legacy, there was a high rate of marriages among close cousins and other relatives. Many Turkmenian men refused birth control, and women frequently gave birth twice in one year, believing that more children would bring greater wealth—"more hands, more rubles." The state, of course, encouraged the high birth rate, figuring that could only mean a boon for the cotton crop.

Kirichenko said he was a Communist Party member of twenty-five years' standing, but he was thinking about quitting after reading about what the Party hierarchy had done to the region. "We had always been brought up to believe that our system was the best, that our lives were the best, and now we find just the opposite," he said. "This is not Africa—children are not starving to death in the same blatant way—but there is no way to hide it anymore: we are poor and we are suffering. Of course, we need to educate people on birth control and all the rest. But as a Party member—and it hurts me to say this—the truth is that poverty here is tied to politics. Ninety percent of the blame lies with the system, the bureaucracy, the command system, the centralization of control. There is no escaping that."

In Ashkhabad, government and health officials did all they could to convince me that their horrifying infant mortality rate was "temporary" and had nothing to do with politics. They were furious that I had come to write about the problem at all. I asked local officials for permission to visit several of the collective farms west of Ashkhabad. They refused most of my requests on the grounds that they were too close to the Iranian border. Finally, I was granted permission to visit Bakharden, which was also close to the border, but, evidently, not so close that I would be tempted to make a run for Teheran.

The Mir Collective Farm was a pathetic sight. A mother and her dirt-caked, vacant-eyed daughter stood by the gate. A ragged dog slept curled in the road, flies buzzing around its sores. The "office of administration" was a shed with a few ancient desks, a half-empty bookshelf, and a portrait of Lenin framed in gold. At a small hut nearby, I struck up a conversation with a young woman named Aino Balliyeva. She was twenty years old and unmarried. She picked cotton in the fields and said she knew there were dangers in the work, that she was undoubtedly taking in pesticides and defoliants that would one day hurt her children. "But what can I do about it?" she asked. "I want to have children, because that is life. And as for the rest, I just don't know what to do."

As if on cue, a police car, lights flashing, pulled up. Two uniformed police told me and my friend—a Russian photographer, Edik Gladkov—that we were in a "restricted area" and that we should "come along." At the police station, we were interrogated by a couple of officers and then by a blond

Russian official who was clearly KGB. Like a fool, I told the KGB officer that if he called the officials in Ashkhabad he would find out that I had their permission to go to Bakharden. He called, and, of course, the very same official said no such permission had been granted and, in fact, he could not recall our ever having met. Edik pointed to one of the wall posters: under a portrait of Lenin, it read, "Socialism—is control." After a few hours, we rode back to Ashkhabad, this time with a police escort.

—

I did meet a brave man in Turkmenia. His name was Mukhamed Velsapar, a young writer who had grown up in a family of eight children near the town of Mary, east of Ashkhabad. He said he never knew, until long after he was a young man and had seen the relative wealth of Moscow, that he had been raised in poverty. "And that is the mind-set of nearly all Turkmenians: 'We have bread, we have tea, we have a roof, we are alive—therefore, we are not poor,' " he said one afternoon. "These people have no basis for comparison. There are seventy-three newspapers in the republic, and not one of them has any degree of freedom."

In 1989, Velsapar, along with a few hundred other writers, journalists, and workers in Ashkhabad, organized Ogzibirlik, a democratic advocacy group with two key aims: to bring glasnost to Turkmenistan and to encourage radical economic change to end what one member called "the cycle of poverty and the colonization of our resources." Members of Ogzibirlik met with nationalist leaders in the Soviet Baltic republics for crash courses on developing a mass movement. The Ogzibirlik activists believed that the ruin of Central Asia had been the decades-old demand from economic planners in Moscow that the republics turn most of their farmland into cotton fields. The cotton monoculture, directed by Moscow planners and Central Asian overlords, brought the region everything from the tragic infant death rate to the drying up of the Aral Sea. The rulers of the Russian empire had never been as cruel. Ogzibirlik was seemingly powerless to challenge the Communist Party boss, Saparmurad Niyazov, and his well-organized apparatus. Velsapar said he was often interrogated by party officials. "They'll just blatantly say they have been listening to my phone conversations and then make some wild accusation," he said.

Velsapar did succeed, however, in stirring up the Party. His weapon was a short article in *Moscow News.* "It is hard to believe," the piece began, "but the majority of Turkmenian children in our time are permanently undernourished." The article was merely a summary of the infant mortality crisis, but for local authorities it was a humiliation. Not so much because it exposed the horrific details of infant mortality in the region—there had been other such

articles in local papers—but because it appeared outside Turkmenistan in a paper read by the liberal intelligentsia and Gorbachev himself.

"It was a libel on all of us!" Geral Kurbanova, vice president of the republic's Children's Fund, shouted at me. "No one goes hungry here. The Turkmenian people love to eat! And poor? Oh, they have lots of money, cars—two cars sometimes. They could buy proper food if they wanted, but instead they buy carpets and expensive dresses." Comrade Kurbanova was a Turkmenian version of those American demagogues who go on about welfare queens who buy Cadillacs with food stamps.

What intensified the furor over Velsapar's article was the accompanying photograph of an emaciated two-year-old child named Guichgeldi Saitmuradov. The image was hellish, like something out of the worst African famines—hollow, desperate eyes, a skeleton barely alive. Several sources corroborated the boy's fate: After repeated trips to a hospital near his parents' collective farm in the Tashauz region, the child died in 1988. Before Guichgeldi's death, however, Khummet Annayev, a physician and senior researcher at the Institute for the Health of Mothers and Children, made a research trip to the region. He reported dire shortages of meat, butter, chicken, and other foodstuffs over a ten-year period, abuse of pesticides and defoliants, miserable medical facilities. And when he saw Guichgeldi in a clinic, he asked someone to take the photograph that would eventually be published in *Moscow News.*

"An aberration," said the republic's deputy health minister, Dmitri Tessler, who pronounced Velsapar an "adventurer" and Annayev "out of his depth." The republic's newspapers never reprinted Velsapar's article, but they did run countless denunciations triple its length.

—

After the Bakharden incident, the republic's foreign ministry said I ought to see what a "typical" collective farm looked like. They sent me to a farm called Soviet Turkmenistan just outside Ashkhabad. The head of the farm looked like Burl Ives playing Big Daddy in *Cat on a Hot Tin Roof.* Broad-bellied and wearing a crisp suit and a panama hat, Muratberd Sopiyev was one of the most powerful men in the republic. He had been "elected" chairman of Soviet Turkmenistan thirty years running. "We have democracy here on the farm," he told me. "Every so often I'll tell the people they can nominate an alternative candidate, but they say, 'Oh, no! Never! No need!' and that's that."

Sopiyev said the rate of infant mortality on his farm was "not so bad" as in the rest of the republic—"forty-five out of a thousand"—but that is still more than double that of Washington, D.C.. Like the rest of the Turkmenian

leadership, Sopiyev saw the "triumph of Communism" as the road out of poverty.

"We have to keep fulfilling, even overfulfilling, the five-year plans," he said. "We don't need private property. Not in this country. That will only bring exploitation. No one wants it. We know that in capitalist countries they have very, very poor people. We don't have that. We provide free apartments, gas, education, medical care. We don't need a multiparty system, either. We don't need the chaos that would bring. We need the Communist Party, and we have to follow the Party line. That is the way to wealth."

With that, Sopiyev got into his car, and his driver took him to a ministry in Ashkhabad where the republic gets its instructions from Moscow.

SPASSKAYA

At the height of spring planting, Edik Gladkov and I visited the farm villages outside Vologda in northern Russia. At midday, with the sun high and the weather ideal, we drove past one field after another—all empty, all unplowed and unplanted. There were tractors and trucks leaning at crazy angles, stuck in the mud. We stopped at the gates of one of the biggest state farms in the Vologda region, the Prigorodni Sovkhoz, which allegedly grew vegetables and raised livestock.

The usual cheap irony greeted us at the entrance: a faded portrait of Lenin and a tattered banner—"We Shall Witness the Victory of Communist Labor." We drove down the long road to the farm center, its headquarters, its store, and its three-story concrete barracks. Everything looked abandoned, the fields, the road. Where had everyone gone? Certainly not into the fields. In the store, the shelves were bare of everything except some canned eggplant and pickled tomatoes.

"Most people go on the buses and buy food in Vologda," the counterman said. "Probably they're off in the city now."

And where does the food in Vologda come from? Why weren't there any vegetables in the store here?

The counterman rolled his eyes. He explained patiently, as if to idiots, the problems on the farm. The ministry still hadn't delivered seed. Wages were low, so no one wanted to work. They couldn't get spare parts for the machinery. And so on for a half hour. "So you see," he said, "there is no point."

The farmers and their families who were not in Vologda standing in grocery lines were in their concrete apartments. They all had televisions and they were all watching the same game show.

One member of the farm who showed both anger and initiative was a young man named Yuri Kamarov. He said that of the hundreds of people on the farm, he was the only one who thought the idea of giving some land back to the peasants would come to anything good. Everyone on the farm had parents and grandparents who had been jailed, starved, or deported for their dreams of ownership and prosperity. "I guess I'm the only true believer here, the only one," Kamarov said. He was twenty-seven and dreamed of raising livestock and vegetables on a plot that was now little more than a swatch of mud and rubble. Every day after work, Kamarov worked alone, building a house for his wife and daughter. The neighbors came by sometimes and laughed. Others made threatening remarks about destroying his project. Kamarov was suffering from that terrible envy born of years of serfdom under czars and general secretaries, an envy embodied in a classic Soviet joke: A farmer's cow dies, but a great spirit grants him one wish. And what is the wish? "Let my neighbor's cow drop dead, too," he says. Kamarov persisted, nonetheless. He took out a 24,000-ruble loan, which meant, he said, "I'm up to my eyeballs in debt for the rest of my life. That's the gamble. Let them laugh. Maybe they're right, and nothing will ever change," the true believer said, "but it's time I started living a real life, a life like my grandfather had long before the disasters began."

The legacy of collectivization was everywhere in the Soviet Union. In the Vologda region alone, there were more than seven thousand "ruined" villages, ghost towns of collapsing houses and untended land that had once been working farms. For decades, the young had been abandoning the wasted villages in droves, searching for a decent wage in the textile and machine-tool plants of Vologda. Like others before them, their search for the industrial utopia turned out to be fruitless. They found only miserable work in textile plants and lived in vast dormitories.

Edik and I spent a few days at one of the villages near Vologda, a row of two dozen houses called Spasskaya. Behind an abandoned church, the cemetery was filling up. Every six months or so, a workman arrived from the city, borrowed a shovel, and dug a grave. No one had been born in Spasskaya in twenty-five years. A prosperous village before the Revolution, it was now little more than a few collapsed cabins, a graveyard, and wheel ruts in the mud.

Mariya Kuznetsova, a stooped old woman with fierce, squinting eyes, spent her days tending her chicken coop and gossiping with her neighbors along the rails of a rotten pine fence. There were seventeen people left in Spasskaya. Once there had been hundreds. At seventy-five, Mariya was among the youngest. "On winter days," she said, "we check the other houses.

If there's no smoke coming out of one of the chimneys it usually means another one of us is dead."

Mariya Kuznetsova said she lived on a pension of less than 3 rubles a day. Not long ago, before new pension levels were adopted, retired farmers got a ruble a day. Kuznetsova's meals were mainly bread, milk, macaroni, cabbage soup, potatoes, and salted fat. If she needed to see a doctor or go to the store, she had to walk two miles down a road of mud and stones to catch a bus that "comes when it comes." During the winter, when temperatures hit thirty and forty degrees below zero and the snow piled up, she said, "we are prisoners."

"We listen to the radio and hear all that talk about 'Land for the Peasants' and private farming, but who's going to do the work?" she said. "Who is going to save the countryside? One generation should hand down what it knows and what it has collected to the next. But all that is broken. Everyone has long since left for the cities. The collective farms are a disaster. There's nothing left. It's all lost."

One of Kuznetsova's neighbors, Anatoly Zamokhov, leaned out the window of his cabin and cackled viciously. He spit at the sound of the word Moscow. "I'll tell you about Moscow," he said, taking an angry drag on a foul cigarette. "Before the Bolsheviks, my parents and their parents lived decently. They weren't rich—not by any means, God knows—but they had food and a cow and a table to call their own. We were all supposed to be one big family after collectivization. But everyone was pitted against everyone else, everyone suspicious of everyone else. Now look at us, a big stinking ruin. Now everyone lives for himself. No one visits anyone on Easter. What a laugh, what a big goddamn laugh."

During collectivization, people in Spasskaya told me, police crammed countless peasants into a complex of labor camps that was just north of the village. The police ripped the crosses and icons out of the churches and used the transepts and basements as holding cells. In the Vologda region, 25,000 children died in the churches over a three-month period. In a matter of a few years, an entire fabric of social relations, of village life, was in shreds. The "masters of the land" were suddenly servants of the state, stripped of their religion, their traditions, and their will.

The Bolshevik contempt for the peasant was rooted in the works of Lenin, who called them *myelki khozyaichiki*—roughly, "little landlords." Before the Revolution, Solzhenitsyn has estimated, the peasantry constituted more than 80 percent of the Slavic population. Today, many of those "little capitalists" not already in mass graves, urban bunkers, or dying villages live in the "inter-nats," state-run homes for the aged.

Not far from Spasskaya, about a hundred villagers lived at the inter-nat in

the town of Priluki, near an abandoned monastery. The place was run by a well-intentioned, kind woman named Zoya Matreyeva. She and her small staff did what they could to keep the place clean, care for the sick and dying, and arrange decent burials when the time came. She had lived in the area for many years and said that the old people yearn only for the village life before the ruin began. Soviet and Western historians have described the harsh conditions, drunkenness, and bigotry of the prerevolutionary villages in such stark terms that it seems impossible for anyone to be nostalgic for them. Impossible, that is, until the surviving villagers describe what came afterward, in the early 1930s.

"We even have a few old Communist Party members here, people who worked half their lives and more on the collective farms, but you won't find one who believes in collectivization," Matreyeva said. "They talk about the cows and chickens they had, how it was theirs and they cared about it. Then it was all stripped away."

The inter-nat dining room was a dim place of buckled linoleum, fluorescent light, and Lenin's portrait. The old women, plump and toothless, peasant scarves tied around their heads, shuffled to their seats. The men ate in a separate room, and there were only a few of them—nearly all the men in the area were killed in World War II. Each place was set with a bowl of soup, a tin spoon, and two small pieces of brown bread. Zoya Matreyeva, for forty years a loyal employee of the state, had a point she wanted to prove.

"Grandmothers!" she said. "Maybe you can tell our visitor about what you remember about the old days. The old days before you were on the collective farms."

The old women stopped stirring the sour cream into their soup and looked up. "These gigantic state farms killed the villages and put nothing in their place," said one, and then they all began to chime in.

"Six of the families from our village were dragged away and we never saw them again."

"In my village, there were one hundred and twenty houses. Now there are ten, and the only people who live there now are people who use the houses on weekends to get out of the city. They garden, they don't farm."

"I had to spend my life feeding something called the state. Now at least the state feeds me."

"My grandchildren wouldn't know what to do with a piece of land. Even my own children have a hard time telling the difference between a horse and a cow. Are these the new 'masters of the land'?"

"One generation is supposed to show the next how to live. One generation is supposed to build something so the next can carry on. That was all cut off. Destroyed. Do they think you can rebuild that in a day? In five years?"

After a while, the old women quieted down. In a way they seemed happy for a moment to have a visitor ask a question or two, but as the memories rushed forth, the women grew sullen and tired, and they ate.

MAGNITOGORSK

At the height of the Depression, John Scott, a young socialist from Philadelphia, decided to quit his academic work and join in the creation of what *The Nation* was then calling "the world's most gigantic social experiment." Scott arrived in Moscow in 1932, desperate to find a future that worked. Stalin's bureaucrats promptly sent Scott, and hundreds of other young American socialists, to one of the "hero projects" of the first five-year plan, to "Magnetic Mountain," the steel town of Magnitogorsk in the Urals.

In Magnitogorsk, Scott discovered a city that was one massive construction site: workers pulling eighteen-hour shifts, families living in tents and ramshackle barracks. The vast majority of the Soviet workers at Magnitogorsk had come not out of any ideological commitment to the "shining future" of socialism, but because they were forced to. Many of them had been peasant farmers, forced off their private plots during the collectivization campaign. Scott saw priests in their cassocks digging coal with picks and wheelbarrows, workers killed by falling girders. But in his memoir of working at Magnitogorsk between 1932 and 1938, *Behind the Urals,* Scott noenetheless remembered a "city full of vitality and life. . . . Tens of thousands of people were enduring the most intense hardships in order to build blast furnaces, and many of them did it willingly, with boundless enthusiasm, which infected me from the day of my arrival."

Magnitogorsk became a legend of the war. Because it produced the steel for half of the tanks and one third of the artillery used to defeat the Nazis, people began referring to the mills as "Hitler's grave." But Magnitogorsk never stopped running on a wartime mentality. The ultimate bosses, the ministers in Moscow, measured success in sheer quantity. Never mind that other countries were beginning to produce modern steel alloys that brought the weight of a refrigerator down to a hundred pounds, not four hundred; never mind that pollution got so bad that the clouds of poison above the city decreased sunlight 40 percent. But the Lenin Steel Works, the biggest mill in the world, kept churning on in ignorant isolation. And always the command was "More steel!"

"Magnitogorsk is a classic Stalinist city," Aleksei Tuplin, a correspondent for the local paper, the *Magnitogorsk Worker,* told me. "We built an autonomous company town here that pushed away every cultural, economic, and

political development in the civilized world. We existed, and still do exist, for the sake of a machine that doesn't even work." When Premier Aleksei Kosygin proposed a massive retooling project in the 1960s that would have put an end to Magnitogorsk's antiquated open-hearth mills in favor of more efficient conversion techniques used elsewhere in the world since the 1950s, Brezhnev and the rest of the leadership pronounced the project too expensive. "All they ever wanted was more steel," Dmitri Galkin, the plant director during the Brezhnev era, told me. "That's all they ever cared about."

I stayed a week in Magnitogorsk as a guest of the city coroner, Oleg Yefremov. Oleg was in his early forties, and he had a smoker's cough that plagued him without end. He did not smoke. He suffered, as did most of the citizens of Magnitogorsk, from the habit of breathing.

"I should quit inhaling," he said.

We woke early and drove to the top of a hill to get a sense of the biggest company town I'd ever seen. The Lenin Steel Works stretched seven miles along the left bank of Factory Lake. The plant was in full operation day and night, grinding out sixteen million tons of steel every year. The smokestacks never stopped pumping poison, a sickly mix of yellow, gray, green, and bluish smoke that shifted in color, depending on the light. According to a report by the local environmental protection committee, the city's industries dumped one million tons of pollution annually. "There's four hundred and thirty thousand of us, so that means more than two tons for everybody," said Yuri Zaplatkin, the committee's chairman. Satellite pictures show that the mills have produced a zone of ruined air and soil 120 miles long and 40 miles wide. In winter, the snow was crusted black; in summer, the grass grew in sad, brownish tufts.

Oleg said that at one time or another in their lives, 90 percent of the children of Magnitogorsk suffered from pollution-related illnesses: chronic bronchitis, asthma, allergies, even cancers. The local environmental protection committee reported that birth defects in Magnitogorsk doubled between 1980 and 1990. At the city morgue, Oleg surveyed the morning's corpses. A worker with collapsed lungs. A little girl dead from asthma, a weakened heart, or both.

Oleg lived on the "good side" of Magnitogorsk; the bad side being downwind from the plant, the "left bank." One of the worst neighborhoods in the city was one of the oldest, Hardware Square. The air there was especially foul and gassy; you could taste the dust on your tongue. In room after room in one of the barracks, old women stared blankly out windows, children were as filthy as any street kid in the barrios of Lima. At eight o'clock in the morning at the health clinic on Hardware Square, groups of a dozen children got ultraviolet treatments and drank their daily "oxygen cocktails," a viscous

soup of fruit juice, herbs, and sugar infused with pure oxygen. Older patients came in just to take a few pulls from an oxygen tank.

Down the road at the steelworks' own pulmonary ward, one of the doctors, Natalya Popkova, said that she had seen thousands of workers and their children who came in for a few days suffering from "what the plant provides us." "The patients, all of them, become permanently angry at the mills," she said. "They know why they are sick, but what choice do they have? Where can they go?"

The apparatchiks who ran the mill and the city were masterful in the way they headed off any potential political conflicts with the work force. The mill owned everything in town, from the sewer system to the streetcars; the mill directors had an iron grip on food supplies and distribution of the goods they earned in barter deals with the West. When companies from West Germany or Japan offered televisions, washing machines, and vacuum cleaners in exchange for scrap metal, the bosses used the goods to bribe the workers. "We are a poor people," said Viktor Seroshtanov, a judge in the municipal court. "If you throw us a little piece of meat, a VCR, something, we'll be happy. In a way, the foreign companies that do business with the mill are contributing to a kind of colonial system." When the Communist Party organization in the mill sensed there might be a strike coming in 1989, they tipped off the factory bosses, who quickly sold barrels of cheap beer to the workers. When the threat of strikes disappeared, so did the beer. "What am I supposed to do about it?" a mill worker named Viktor Oyupov told me. "Should I rebel and not eat? Then what?"

The trap seemed inescapable, as inescapable as the system itself. For all the excitement in the big cities over glasnost and the new parliament, the great majority of the people in the Soviet Union felt trapped, cogs in a system that not only oppressed them, but also failed to provide a decent, minimal standard of living. "Our workers are soldiers, shock troops who serve a machine," said Oleg Valinsky, a liberal member of the Magnitogorsk city council. "They wear the shoes the factory gives them. They kill themselves working and they go home. All the spirit is drained out of them. We created a city of robots."

CHAPTER 14

THE REVOLUTION UNDERGROUND

The life of the underworld was now rumbling around them, with deputies continually running to and fro, trains going up and down, drawn by trotting horses. The darkness was starred by countless lamps.

—EMILE ZOLA, *Germinal*

For the first few years of the glasnost era, *Moscow News, Ogonyok,* and the rest of the liberal press had only hinted at the connection between the seventy-year rule of the Communist Party and the disastrous state of the country. The year of miracles in Europe, 1989, began with the first opportunity for the people of the Soviet Union to make that connection for themselves. On March 26, the people would vote in multiparty elections for the new Congress of People's Deputies. Despite Aleksandr Yakovlev's advice to split the Party, to separate the progressives from the conservative majority, Gorbachev believed that by strengthening the government, by creating this new Congress, he could gradually diminish the role of the Party regulars.

In the months before the balloting, I spent many nights at election meetings and debates—in Moscow, Leningrad, the Baltic states, in provincial

Russia. The issues varied somewhat. In the Baltics, of course, the emphasis was on sovereignty, on gaining greater distance from Moscow; in the Russian provinces, the emphasis was on empty stores, ground-level economics. But everywhere the talk was of freedom, of learning democracy. Confronted for the first time by the prospect of political choice, people were both confused and exhilarated. They had no prior experience of genuine debate or choice, and yet they seized the opportunity immediately. Nowhere was that more the case than in my own precinct—Gorbachev's district—the October Region of Moscow.

On a January afternoon, after the first shift had let out, the bureaucrats and workers of the Red Proletariat machine-tools factory filed into their auditorium and saw their boss and director, Yuri Ivanovich Kirillov, waiting onstage to greet them. For once, Kirillov was all smiles, saccharine and ingratiating. He looked like a game-show host in a bad suit. With his seigneurial handshakes and shoulders-back posture, he showed every sign of expecting the 325 "electors" for the six thousand workers to fall into place, to rise as one and nominate him as their candidate for the March 1989 elections.

The workers stashed their heavy wool coats under their chairs, settled down, and quickly chose a secretary and a chairman. Then the chairman called a factory foreman named Nikolai Blinkov to the rostrum. Blinkov read a long, formal speech, talking of the "grave responsibilities" of political reform. "There were so many mistakes in nominating candidates in the past," he said. "This is why we are so nervous now." Then, "without further ado," Blinkov proposed the nomination of Yuri Ivanovich Kirillov. Surrounded by his deputies in the first row, Kirillov crossed his legs suavely and smiled, the master of all he surveyed. The election meeting was going splendidly, just as he had planned it. The birth of democracy was going to be wonderful.

"This man," Blinkov said, pointing to Kirillov, "this man is a simple Soviet worker. He is not spoiled by applause." Blinkov praised Kirillov's "magnificent" two years as factory director, his "extraordinary facility with problem-solving," his "superlative" relations with the workers, his "uncanny" ability to remember everyone's name. The applause was furious in the front rows near Kirillov, and softened out in the rear.

Then someone on the aisle rose and asked Blinkov the first impertinent question of the afternoon.

"Are there any other candidates proposed?"

There followed a moment of tense silence. Clearly, this question was not part of the script. Blinkov blinked, then scanned the first row, a rabbity panic in his eyes. But the denizens of the first row could not help him, Kirillov least of all. They had not anticipated the messiness of democracy any more than Blinkov had.

Blinkov conceded the obvious. "On my way over here," he said, "I was told that in all the work collectives there were no other names suggested."

The chairman edged Blinkov away from the podium and called on a succession of Red Proletariat employees to sing the praises of Yuri Ivanovich. "From the day he walked in the door, our director was already a well-formed organizer," said a worker named Sergei Khudyakov. "And thanks to him, our factory has a resort home for the workers in the Crimea." A Komsomol leader pledged the "fealty of our youth to Yuri Ivanovich." A foreman described the director's "generosity of spirit" and "high intelligence."

And so it went. For nearly an hour, the meeting seemed like a grass-roots version of Brezhnev's Central Committee circa 1978, a mix of oleaginous praise and muggy boredom. Through it all, Kirillov relaxed in his seat and smiled his kingly smile.

But in the transitional moment between the last speech and what would have been the call for a voice vote of acclamation, all hell broke loose. A balding engineer named Viktor Oskin asked for the floor.

"You are not on the schedule," the chairman scolded him.

But after some catcalls and shouted comments about "learning democracy," Oskin got the microphone.

"I've just got one question," he said. "Yuri Ivanovich already has so many duties. When will he find the time to work as a deputy in the legislature?"

No one could quite believe this display of impudence.

"Get off the stage!" one person shouted.

"Who asked you to speak? Get off!"

"Away with him!"

But Oskin was unafraid. He dipped his face closer to the mike and shouted over the noise.

"You all say Yuri Ivanovich is such a good man," he said. "You act as if there are no problems at all in our factory. This man has too many duties. He should refuse some. They've been telling us all along that we should have two or three candidates, and once again we've only got one. We are supposed to be talking about democracy, but we only have one candidate."

There was some hissing and booing, but just as many workers in the audience were quiet or nodding slightly, as if in agreement. Something had happened; there had been a breakthrough. Oskin plopped down in his chair, and his friends around him eyed him nervously.

Now a younger man asked for the chance to speak. He said his name was Konstantin Yasovsky and he represented a work collective. "Our collective doesn't want to approve this man Yuri Ivanovich!" he said.

Yuri Ivanovich, for his part, was now squirming in his seat in the front row like a man with the bends.

Yasovsky went on: "We don't know his program or what he'll do. What is he for? What is he against? Our opinion is that we need him as a factory director, but only that."

The boos rolled over Yasovsky like a wave, and the undertow of hostility brought him sliding back to his seat. But then there were some cheers, here and there. Then catcalls, and arguments in patches of the crowd. The meeting had gotten distinctly out of hand. With a nod from one of the assistant directors in the front row, the chairman snatched the microphone off its stand and said, "Well, I guess it's time for a vote."

But by now there were enough voters in the hall who knew something was wrong. The present seemed too much like the past. This time they would not be deceived. They would not be fooled or ignored. There were insults from every direction. Of course, no one had any illusions. There would be no alternative candidates, no rebellions, certainly. But there was at least a feeling, an insistence, that the appearance of democracy had to be served.

"A vote?" one man shouted from the back of the hall. "All our lives we've been raising our hands. Let the man tell us who he is and what he stands for before he gets our vote."

And so, finally, Yuri Ivanovich Kirillov spoke. This was his magnificent concession to the democratic process. He said he didn't mind the criticism, "though it wasn't very pleasant to sit through it." He made no mention of a platform in his long, rambling speech. His only idea for reform at the national level was his "firm intention to build a recreation center for the workers of the Red Proletariat machine-tools factory."

The applause was polite. The chairman got his way, and there was, at last, a vote: 308 for Kirillov, 10 against, and 7 abstentions. The hands went up slowly, more in concession than affirmation. After all, what choice did they have? No one was prepared to rebel. The idea did not yet exist. At least not here, and not yet. The catcalls, the insistence on hearing the candidate, had been rebellion enough. The electors filed out of the auditorium in silence, guilty and downcast, as if they knew they had not gotten things right and did not yet know what it was they had to do.

The Communist Party, of course, wrote the election laws for the 1989 elections to ensure that it would have the vast majority of seats, and that is the way it turned out. More than 80 percent of the 2,250 deputies were Party members, the vast majority of them local secretaries, military officers, and

other loyalists. The reason was simple. Every imaginable Party front group, from the Komsomol to the Union of Stamp Collectors, was guaranteed a raft of seats. Only one third of the deputies would come from open races. In conservative regions, especially Central Asia, single-candidate races were the rule, not the exception. "This was not a democratic election," Sakharov told me. "It was rigged quasi-democracy. The only oases of democracy were where the system was somehow imperfect." In those few spots where the elections were imperfect—meaning open—the establishment Party candidates invariably lost. Central Committee members, admirals, generals, apparatchiks of every sort suffered the humiliation of public rejection.

Such was the case in the October Region when Comrade Kirillov was one of a half-dozen apparatchiks who didn't even come close. The runoff came down to a popular, and not very intelligent, television commentator and Ilya Zaslavsky, a textiles engineer, not quite thirty years old, who walked on canes and spoke in a barely audible mumble. Zaslavsky, running on a platform of general reform with an emphasis on the rights of the disabled, won easily.

When the Congress opened in May, Zaslavsky was one of dozens of young liberals who had gotten into politics only because they had finally seen a leader they thought they could trust. Zaslavsky, Arkady Murashev, and Sergei Stankevich of Moscow, nationalists from the Baltic states, Armenia, and Georgia, environmentalists from Ukraine, Byelorussia, and Siberia—they all had seen the elections as an opening. That period just before and after the first Congress was a time of euphoria. These were days when radical democrats thought that reform of the Party was not only possible, but the only route to change. Somehow the chance of a reactionary counterrevolution seemed academic, remote.

That first session of the Congress was an endless series of astonishments. In the opening minutes of the Congress, Sakharov ambled to the podium to make the first speech. Later on, Sakharov would make specific proposals about the creation of a multiparty system and a "decree on power" that would lead to constitutional democracy, but now he kept his remarks general, trying, it seemed, to serve simply as a model of patience and openness. But the Congress quickly became something hotter, as if the crises of seventy years could wait no more; what followed was an explosion of public debate and revelation. A former Olympic weightlifter, Yuri Vlasov, blasted the KGB, saying that the secret police ran an "underground empire" in the Soviet Union and had not reformed at all. A law professor from Leningrad, Anatoly Sobchak, attacked the generals and Party officials who had sanctioned and led the assault in Tbilisi against a peaceful demonstration in April 1989 which left at least nineteen people dead. Yuri Karyakin, the Dostoevsky scholar, called for the removal of Lenin's remains from the mausoleum on

Red Square and for their "decent burial." The liberals in the Congress also were beginning to make clear they would criticize Gorbachev, even oppose him, when they thought it necessary. When Gorbachev was put up for election by the Congress as chairman of the legislature, an obscure and slightly woolly delegate from northern Russia, Aleksandr Obolensky, nominated himself. "It's not a question of winning," he said. "It's a matter of creating a tradition of political opposition and competition."

The action in the hallways during the frequent recesses was almost as dramatic as the speeches inside. At first, the young Soviet reporters watched with amazement as the Westerners walked up to the most powerful men in the country and pestered them with cameras, tape recorders, and notebooks. Within a few days, the Soviets were getting the hang of it. For the first time in their careers, members of the Politburo and leaders of the military and the KGB were subjected to embarrassing questions. For decades, no one had dared ask them about the weather, much less the erosion of the Communist Party. Now they were being chased to the bathrooms and the buffet tables for their opinions, for accountings of themselves.

Gorbachev quickly mastered the art of spin control. Accidentally on purpose, he would wander into a huge crowd of journalists just after the lunch breaks, make his case, and disappear. *Vremya,* of course, would run his comments in full, giving him the role as both chairman and media commentator over his political creation.

Sakharov, for his part, endured interviews with a wistful patience. The camera lights, he must have understood, were part of modern democracy. Everyone talked, and talked. Or almost everyone. Day after day I stalked Viktor Chebrikov, the head of the KGB until 1988, a man with a gnarled face and the posture of a Roman emperor. As he paced the halls, very few deputies dared approach him. Those who did say hello were grasped by the elbow and taken off to a private corner. Chebrikov would not talk where other deputies or foreigners could overhear him. I kept after Chebrikov, and at first he shooed me away as if I were a small cloud of gnats. When I would not go away, he said, "We'll talk tomorrow." Or "after the next break." Finally, toward the end of the session, he said, "Mr. Remnick, there will be no interview." Strange, but I had never told him my name.

No one in the country could tear himself away from these televised sessions of the Congress of People's Deputies. No newspaper, no film, book, or play had ever had such an immediate political effect on the people of the Soviet Union. The sessions were broadcast live for two weeks, and factories and collective farms reported that no work was getting done. Everyone was gathered around television sets and transistor radios. People simply could not believe what they were hearing. Though the reform-minded deputies were

in a distinct minority—no more than three or four hundred out of 2,250—they were much more savvy about getting to the microphone, and Gorbachev was usually eager to hear from them. It was only when someone went beyond the barriers of the official conception of perestroika—most famously, Sakharov's demand for a repeal of the Party's hold on power—did Gorbachev grow impatient and call for the next speaker. Gorbachev ruled his Congress with the swiftness and guile of Sam Rayburn in his House of Representatives. When Sakharov's criticism exceeded Gorbachev's tolerance, he dropped all pretense of democracy; he switched off the microphone and sent Andrei Dmitriyevich to his seat.

The reformers were overcome with a sense of triumph and possibility. While the session was on they had seen the Chinese leadership order the slaughter of hundreds of peaceful demonstrators in Beijing, and they had the sense that for once, the leader of the Soviet Union was not the same sort of butcher. Vitaly Korotich, the sly editor of *Ogonyok,* walked with me toward the Kremlin gates talking of how the conservatives were in for a "crash," how the country had changed in just two weeks. "The people in this country have always been afraid of power," Korotich said. "Now, maybe, the powerful are becoming a little afraid of the people." By the end of the session, the conservatives in the Politburo were impossible to find. They were finally embarrassed and tired of all the criticism and challenges. They made liberal use of their private, guarded entrances and exits and were rarely seen on the way from the Hall of Congresses to their waiting limousines.

But for all the exhilaration of the elections and the catharsis of the Congress, no one had any idea what it would lead to. From start to finish, the Gorbachev era was an improvisation, with alternating dull spots and high-wire periods. Until now, the politics of the country had gone unseen. Politics had been a matter of the Kremlin, the closed, untelevised sessions of the Politburo and Central Committee. The gulf between the state and the individual was unbridgeable. Even the huge street demonstrations in Yerevan and the Baltics went nearly unreported in the main Party newspapers.

But now almost everyone had seen the accumulated anguish of seventy years broadcast live. They had become familiar with the ideas and personalities not only of the country's leaders, but of Sakharov, Zaslavsky, and Afanasyev of Moscow. They had seen a bookish Estonian woman, Marju Lauristan, challenge Gorbachev's authority as if it were almost . . . normal. They had even seen a half-articulate cabdriver named Leonid Sukhov take the podium and warn Gorbachev that, "like Napoleon," he was being led by the nose by his own "Josephine," his wife, Raisa. Another deputy demanded that Gorbachev answer for his new expensive dacha on the Crimean coast. Until now, Kremlin power had run on mystery as well as might. The Con-

gress had ended all that in one two-week-long television extravaganza. The Congress hinted at something new, a revolution from below. But what form would it take? Who would lead it, and when?

Little more than a month after the Congress closed and Moscow shifted into its mode of summer torpor, perestroika spun out of control, first in the coal mines of Siberia, then in mines all across the country, from Ukraine to Vorkuta to Sakhalin Island. After July 1989, the Kremlin could never again have any confidence at all that it was the master of events. After July 1989, the illusion of a gradual, Gorbachev-directed "revolution from above" was over.

The "revolution from below" began when a group of coal miners in the Siberian town of Mezhdurechensk walked off the job at the Shovikovo mine, led by their shift leader, Valery Kokorin. The main issue was soap. The miners were angry, too, that their equipment was pitiful, that the work was wretched and underpaid, that food supplies were meager and benefits nonexistent. But what galled them most was the grit in every crevice of their bodies, the inability to come home from work and wash themselves clean. There was no soap.

All around the Kuznetsk Basin (the Kuzbass) of Siberia—in Mezhdurechensk, Prokopievsk, Novo-Kuznetsk, and Kemerovo—miners had been grumbling for years among themselves. They had never dared take their protests outside a small circle of friends and family. Their poverty—like the poverty of the farmhands in Turkmenia or the steelworkers of Magnitogorsk—was, simply, the way things were. But within twelve hours of the walkout in Mezhdurechensk, nearly every mine in the Kuzbass was on strike. "You cannot imagine how off-the-cuff this was. It became so enormous so quickly, but it started from almost nothing," one of the miners at the Severovo mines, Ilya Ostanin, told me. Soon the strike spread to Vorkuta in the far north, to the Don Basin (the Donbass) in Ukraine, to Karaganda in northern Kazakhstan, to Sakhalin in the far east.

Gorbachev went on television looking stricken and exhausted, but still pretending to complete mastery. He had no choice but to try to make the strikes his own, to describe them as a healthy manifestation of a very young democracy and then pray they would end before the railway workers, collective farmers, or oil riggers got any ideas in their heads. He could not control an entire nation in rebellion. Even the conservatives in the leadership could not ignore the miners. The miners had the ability to shut down heavy industry and force the Kremlin to contemplate what a long, cold winter could mean.

After a five-hour flight and a half-hour ride through the Siberian taiga to the city of Kemerovo, I got my first glimpse of the working-class rebellion. In Armenia I had seen hundreds of thousands of demonstrators on the streets and almost as many in Lithuania, Estonia, and Latvia. But there had never been anything quite so dramatic as this, nothing that had so vividly illustrated the disintegration of the workers' state and the changing mind of a broad sector of the people.

In a hard afternoon sun, miners dressed in their work gear, tens of thousands of them, sat in the main square of Kemerovo outside the headquarters of the local government and Communist Party. "Get Up and Show Your Anger!" one sign read. "The Kuzbass Is Not a Colony!" said another. When some of the local Party officials took the microphone to tell the miners that the strikes were hurting old people and schoolchildren, they were shouted down and booed off the podium. The local Party press denounced the strikes, but one local television host, Viktor Kolpakov of *Kuzbass, Day by Day,* read straight, informative reports on the strikes around the country every night at eight.

The Siberian miners had an instinctive sense of media and imagery. They made for great television, and they knew it. Though they were not working, they came to the meetings dressed as "miners," smeared with coal dust, wearing their helmets and gritty work clothes and boots. At dusk, they created an even more spectacular image when they turned on their Davy lamps. It seemed as if tens of thousands of huge fireflies had invaded the square and gone into a frenzy. The speakers, of course, took their turns under the feet of the city's biggest statue of Lenin. The irony was lost on no one.

At first, only a few strike committees called for a Solidarity-style union. The initial demands were economic: more soap, detergent, toothpaste, sausage, shoes, and underwear, more sugar, tea, and bread. Vacations and a regular work week were at stake, not Gorbachev. He still represented, for the miners, a shining possibility, a figure of integrity. Almost everyone was careful to praise him, or at least show a measure of respect. One of the speakers, Pyotr Kongurov, a member of the strike committee in Prokopievsk, said that while ecological conditions and the standard of living remain "a focus of despair" in the mining town, "people are not blaming Gorbachev. They know they are able to strike because of Gorbachev. But on the other hand, they are waiting—and we can't wait forever."

There had been strikes before in the Soviet Union: bus drivers in the city of Chekhov, airline pilots who refused to fly until safety standards were improved. But the symbolism of the miners' strike was extraordinary. The miners embodied the vanguard of the proletariat, a bastion of Bolshevism in the old days. To look out at the great crowd of them in Lenin Square was to

see a kind of poster for what had once been called "the masses." And now the masses were walking off the job and declaring that socialism had not delivered anything—not even a bar of soap.

Soon the word came to Siberia from Moscow that the Coal Ministry was ready to promise more supplies, higher salaries, and other benefits. At a huge public meeting in the Kemerovo city square, the miners gathered to hear the details and vote. They heard promises from Moscow's emissaries that planes would soon land loaded to the ribs with soap, meat, lard, cooking oil, and detergent. Salaries would be increased, vacations lengthened. Most of the miners were relieved. At least for now they had reached the limit of their daring and were ready to go back to work. They were ready to believe Moscow. Some miners warned that the deal would fall apart, that Moscow was "up to its old tricks," but when it came time for the vote, nearly everyone agreed to end the strike. Tens of thousands of hands shot into the air to vote yes, to accept the deal.

That night, workers arrived at the Yagunovsko mines for their first shift. They seemed happy to be back, but wary, as if they were already losing conviction in their decision to return. "I'm down in these mines for thirty-nine years, and I'll walk out again without any hesitation if Moscow tries to go behind our backs," said a tunneler named Leonid Kalnikov. "I believed in Communism, once our great dream, and now I believe in the power of our strike. We're not very experienced with this, but we are ready to learn." Kostya Doyagin, who had worked in the mines near Kemerovo for seven years, said that with the thirty-five-point settlement worked out between the Kremlin and the local strike committees, "we've won a small victory. But it's still small. We have to wait and see if they deliver." The miners did not get much done that night. Mostly they stood around in the offices and down in the shafts talking through what had happened in the days before.

Even in the beautiful summer weather, the villages near the Yagunovsko mines were dismal places, more miserable than anything I had seen in West Virginia or the north of England. The miners and their families lived either in tiny wooden houses, shacks with a tin chimney, or, more often, two- and three-story apartment flats known as barracks. Families were packed into these dwellings, and somehow they could not keep them clean. No one took the garbage away. There was no hot water. Indoor plumbing was rare; in winter, that meant a trip to the outhouse in temperatures forty degrees below zero. Men confided that they and their wives were humiliated that they had to make love in rooms while their children were sleeping, or pretending to sleep. They had not been able to buy contraceptives of any kind for months.

"The abortionist is the busiest man outside the mine," one woman told me. The children in the villages seemed to have no toys and wandered through the streets, playing army, hurling sticks and stones. They were filthy and their teeth were already yellowing. Their parents' teeth were rotten, and the lucky ones had caps made of brilliant silver or gold. They all looked older than they were. Men in their fifties who had just gone on pension were hunched over and sinewy from crawling through the mines and swinging a shovel since they were fifteen. They wore greasy jackets and caps. When you shook their hands, they felt like a fighter's hands, rough and pillowy, swollen from too much work. Their eyes were vacant and filmed with rheum. The women, at least the ones who worked above ground, seemed to have more spirit in them, but not much. They were women who, after a certain age, had seen their husbands fall sick or break down and die.

It was a miserable life. Near the mines, I saw a ten-year-old runaway begging for coins. There were ration coupons for cooking oil, butter, vodka, meat, macaroni, and fat. There were coupons, but not always the products themselves. The main grocery store near the Yagunovsko mines had nothing but canned tomatoes, oatmeal, and rotting cabbages. People didn't go hungry, but they did not have enough. Many people told me they got by mostly on bread and macaroni. Sausage was a twice-monthly treat. One morning my cabdriver swerved crazily, nearly plowing into a tree. He pulled over to the side of the road. He was disoriented and knew it. He apologized, saying, "I haven't eaten much in a while."

The drugstores were empty unless you counted the bottles of leeches and the jars of aspirin. An old woman named Irina Shatokhina, who worked twenty years underground as a ventilator specialist, told me that one of her friends had had a mild stroke and could not get the medicine he needed. "Because of that," she said, "he is now a vegetable."

If there were pleasures in the life of the miners beyond those of good talk and family, I did not see them. The most obvious pleasure killed them: in the morning, retired miners lined up at a vodka truck, and seconds after they'd made their score, they drained the bottles. When they could not get the real thing, they made moonshine out of everything from hair tonic to canned peas. I saw one drunk lying in the street drinking water out of a puddle.

Everywhere, the air was thick with gas. Around the mines, the leaves on the trees were filmed with a gray dust. One pond in Kemerovo was so thoroughly contaminated with toxic waste that municipal workers got rid of dead stray dogs by throwing them in the water. After a few days, even the bones disintegrated.

The mines themselves pretended to be offices. Blocking the view of the elevators and the open pits, there was invariably a brick office building where

the engineers and administrators had their cubicles and the workers had their lockers and showers. There was the illusion of "going to work" instead of plunging straight down to hell.

I met a few men outside the headquarters of the Yagunovsko mines one afternoon and asked where I could find the director. I wanted permission to go down the coal shaft.

"Why do you want to bother with the director?" one of them said. "He'll just tell you a lot of shit and send you on your way. Come with us."

The miners took me inside to the locker room. I stripped to my underwear and T-shirt and they gave me a full set of gear. Without a moment's condescension or mockery, they showed me how to wrap my feet in long white bandages and pull on black rubber boots. The miners' suits were made of heavy, fireproof cloth, a thick canvas, and felt strangely light; there were thick rubber gloves that made your hands sweat, a plastic helmet, an emergency oxygen supply, and an extra flashlight. The miners flipped on their suits easily; they had spent most of their waking hours dressed like this and underground since their mid-teens.

We walked clunkily down a set of stairs and outside to the elevators for mine No. 6. The iron door slammed shut, and, packed shoulder to shoulder, we began our descent a quarter mile into the Siberian earth. Thirty miners dressed in greasy coveralls stared at their boots, then at the dents in the ceiling. Irritable, still half asleep, they shuffled and fidgeted. It took a while to get to where the coal was. Their helmet lamps darted nervously in the dark. There was no talk, only coughing and a few long yawns. The elevator went down and down, and my ears ached, then popped. The iron walls rattled against the shaft. Finally, we hit bottom and the door opened onto a labyrinth of dark halls of stone. A blast of cool air from the ventilators hit us in the face. It was the freshest air I had smelled since arriving in Siberia.

"Sometimes this town stinks so bad that the air down here is better than the air up there," said Leonid Kalnikov. Even before the day's mining had begun, his face was black, and I supposed mine was, too. As we walked through a long tunnel, Kalnikov said he was sixty years old and kept working because his family could not survive on his pension. There was no other way for him. He had no illusions; "I'll probably drop dead down here one of these days," he said, without self-pity. Forty years before, he had been a young, muscular man and had helped build this shaft, digging through the stone and putting up steel struts. "Now almost all the coal is gone," he said. "It's got some years left, but it's just about dead. I'm not so eager to stick around for the last lump. But I may have no choice."

During the strike, the mine had been neglected. The labyrinth of alleys and tunnels and chutes had filled with water, which made the walking all the

harder. As we made our way down the main shaft we began to stumble along through water a foot deep. The bottom was like the muck at the bottom of a pond, and after a few minutes my boots were filled with bits of coal, sharp-edged chunks that began to slice my ankles and blister the soles of my feet. Not one of the miners said a word about it. Along the way, we passed men, many of them in their fifties and sixties, tucked into crevices and cracks only a couple of feet high. They lay on their backs, or in some other contorted position, chipping at the coal face or repairing some part of the support structure. When they opened their mouths, coal dust would fall in. The men who had been working for an hour or more were completely black, and all you could see in the half-dark was their flashlights, their eyes, and their teeth. I glanced into one corner and saw three miners, black figures in shadow-light, and they did not move or speak. They were on their ten-minute break.

After a long walk—how far I could not tell—we reached a tiny railcar, a steel contraption that rides on tracks through the mine shafts. The "metro" took us another four miles farther along the mine, rumbling and rattling along like the Seventh Avenue local in New York. "It's about the last chance you get to relax all day," one of the workers said as he slumped in his seat and caught a nap. He slept soundly and then woke with a start when the brakeman put an end to the reverie.

Once the work began there could be no relaxing. To relax, to let attention drift, could mean a horrendous accident, an explosion or a collapse. The miners lived with this fear all the time. Each year a few men died at every mine in "minor" accidents, the sort that are never reported in the news, the undramatic kind. It was November when the mine last blew up. Vladimir Gaponyuk, who put in twenty-four years "underground," told me he remembered the strange muffled sound of it. "It was close to silence, but you knew exactly what had happened." Someone broke a safety rule, then a stream of methane caught a spark, and, in the end, four miners were crushed to death. "We've got accidents like that all the time," Gaponyuk said. "We lose a couple every year." Outside the mine shaft there were two posters: "Hail to the Work of the Twenty-seventh Party Congress" and "We Need Your Hard Work, But What We Need Most Is You Alive."

Valentina Alisovna, a member of the mine's Party committee, was one of my guides. She watched me listen and take down the long, numbing litany of complaints: the horrible work conditions, the danger, the disgust with a life that goes nowhere. Party leader or not, she seemed ashamed, and at one point her eyes filled with tears. "We live like pigs, I'm sorry to say it, but it's true," she said. "The mine is a century behind the times. When we go home we can't count on electricity. The water goes out on us. I'm no capitalist, but it's obvious this system has done nothing for us." All the miners were listening

and nodding. Alisovna's comment hung in the dank air. I had thought this had not been a political strike. That is what I had been told. No one said anything, and we got down on our knees and crawled through another tunnel. The ventilator wind whistled across the stone.

—

In the afternoon, while more teams of miners tried to clear the shafts of water and sludge and to get production moving once more, the Yagunovsko strike committee met in a wooden shack where the Communist Party committee had its offices. Across the country, the strike committees had become the center of political power at the mines. The Party and the official unions were doomed. Six men and Valentina Alisovna sat down to a table, the inevitable portrait of Lenin staring down over them. A poster on the wall read: "The Party is the mind, honor, and conscience of our epoch." Everyone was anxious. They had some sense that all of the Soviet Union, and all of the world, had seen the images from the mines of Siberia, Ukraine, and beyond, but the strike committee had no idea of what would come next. There was no pleasure in their voices, only the suspicion that they were about to be betrayed, the conviction that there were more strikes, more trouble ahead.

"Look, it's a long time before we have any real money in our pockets from this strike," one of them said. "We have to watch out."

The talk bounced around the room, picking up speed and fury all the time.

"No one's paying any attention to the fact that this mine is the worst around the Kemerovo region. It's exhausted. There are two villages to feed, and we're going to be out of coal in a few years. Some of the mines have no coal left in them at all."

"We've got to talk about redundant work. Sixty percent of us are working, and forty percent are standing around 'supervising' or smoking cigarettes upstairs."

"Not true. People are breaking their backs down there."

"We need a united front. Obviously, our union is nothing. And we can't stand alone, we're just one little committee. We miners have to unite, form a real union or something."

"The Politburo can't do everything for us. Perestroika has to move faster. Maybe we need new tires."

"It's time to get rid of the bosses. We don't need them."

"We have to answer two simple questions: 'How are we going to live?' and 'What do we do now?' "

The meeting lasted an hour.

—

Afterward, I walked with the shift leader of mine No. 6, Anatoly Shcheglov, a huge man with a broad smile and mouth filled with gold teeth. The day had begun for him at five forty-five in the morning. He woke in his izba, a small log cabin two miles from the mine, and took a look at the *Kuzbass,* the morning paper, for more news about the mines still out on strike. His address was 2 Second Plan Avenue. In the summer, Shcheglov said, it was easier to get out of bed. The sun was already high. "At least you can walk outside without snow up to the waist in the dark," he said.

Now the kitchen garden outside his door was rich, green with basil and cucumbers. Shcheglov said he ate a lot of cucumbers, "raw or pickled, there's not much else." He opened his refrigerator, a squat primitive thing that buzzed, and searched it for something for dinner. It was filled with food that he was lucky to have: a grayish roll of sausage, a few eggs, a cabbage, a cut of pork that was no less than three-quarters fat, a half-bottle of vodka. Lucky, because the stores were nearly empty. Nearby, at Fruit and Vegetable Store No. 6, known as the best in town, Anatoly went looking for something more to eat. The groceries available were these: half-brown cabbages, rotten tomatoes, cans of tomato juice and sardines, salt, and jars of pickled cabbage. And at the state "products" store off Johann Sebastian Bach Street there were more half-brown cabbages, more rotten tomatoes, smelts, five wan chickens, bins of white bread, and sacks of dried corn. To do better, they say here, you need *blat,* or connections. The only way to do better was to make a deal, to trade a bottle of home brew for a bag of decent carrots, an auto part for a cut of meat.

"The only other way is to buy from the private market," Anatoly said, "and the prices there are impossible for anyone but a Party big shot, the guys who have the dachas down the road."

About a half mile from Shcheglov's place was a prison camp: Prison 1648-043. Every day the convicts—thieves, rapists, murderers—were shuttled in railway cars between their cells and the "zone," the work camp. People in town despised the prison, mainly because when the convicts were released, they said, they took jobs at the mines and the factories nearby, and many of them went back into crime. "But I'm not so sure it's a bad thing," Shcheglov said. "We have three guys down in our mine who were prisoners there. One of them stabbed his wife in the stomach. Another beat someone over the head. I think he killed him. And another guy's wife was involved in some sort of scandal, and so he beat her to death. But they served their time. They work all right."

During the Stalin years, Shcheglov's father was thrown in a labor camp for ten years for no crime at all. Anatoly remembered the day Stalin died, and how everyone around, even those with parents and friends in the camps, wept,

as if the world were lost. "It was March 1953," he said. "I was a Young Pioneer, and we always wore those orange scarves. They gave us black ones to wear. And when the teachers started crying, we cried, too. Children always imitate the emotions of their parents."

Shcheglov was no radical. He heard the news that the miners in Vorkuta in northern Russia were still on strike and demanding an end to the Party's constitutional hold on power. "I'm not sure that's right," he said. He was a trusting man who spoke with only the slightest bit of irony when I asked him about the effect the dust had on him after working in the pits for so long. "My lungs?" he said, taking a long drag on a cigarette butt. "The doctors always tell us our lungs are fine. They give us a checkup every year. And why shouldn't I trust the doctors? If you can't trust them, who can you trust?"

For years, his dream had been simple: finish working at fifty or so, take his pension, and move outside of town to the taiga, the vast Siberian forest. What he wanted from the strike, he said, was just the chance to live "decently," to have a cake of soap or toothpaste when he needed, to eat a cut of meat worthy of the word, to wear a pair of shoes that could last six months, and to have the chance to earn a profit if, by some miracle, his work brigade could squeeze some extra coal out of mine No. 6. And then, when it was time, he'd move out to the forest, where the fishing was good, the air was clear, and life was lived above ground. "I'm used to the dark," he said. "But enough is enough."

The Siberian miners had no single leader, no Lech Walesa. The unions were a farce. They did not protect the workingman so much as they ensured his passivity and obedience to the Party. That had been Lenin's design. Lenin declared Western-style labor unions "narrow-minded, selfish, case-hardened, covetous, petty bourgeois." The unions under socialism, he said, would be "conveyor belts" of the Party. One of the first thing the miners did during the strike was to box out the union leaders and set up strike committees. Taking their cue from the miners, all kinds of laborers set up "workers' clubs" in the Baltics, Byelorussia, and Ukraine, and in Russian rust-belt cities like Magnitogorsk, Sverdlovsk, and Chelyabinsk.

But there was no Walesa. Probably, Walesa had been a particularly Polish phenomenon, a figure able somehow to unite workers, Catholic clergy, and urban intellectuals. Anatoly Malikhin was as close as it came to a Walesa in the Soviet miners movement, but because of the vastness of the country, his influence was mainly in western Siberia.

Malikhin was an eloquent tunneler from Novo-Kuznetsk. He had the muscular, squashed-down, weary look of a man who had played fullback for

one year too many. He was in his early thirties and looked ten years older. All that was left of his hair was a kind of monk's tonsure. Malikhin said he was a "congenital enemy of the people," a bitter joke. His grandfather, a Cossack, was arrested in the purges of 1937, and his father, as a child of an "enemy of the people," was deported to Siberia. Malikhin's mother, a Ukrainian, was also a political deportee.

For years, he said, he had led the same "unconscious existence" his father had, that everyone around him did. There was never any thought of protest, much less mutiny. Miners were serfs in a patrimonial system in which the lord was the Communist Party and its instruments were the schools, the trade unions, the mine directors. "Our system and our propaganda didn't allow people to grow as individuals, to ask questions. We were raised to be uninterested," Malikhin told me. "We had no idea how the state was run. We went to elections having no idea what they were about. They told us, 'You are a small man, a punk, and why should you care? You just do what your boss tells you.' The principle was this: 'I am the boss and you are an idiot.' If you tried to argue, even slightly, you were immediately thrown to work in the worst spots. You were crushed, humiliated. We are still dogs with three different kinds of collars: green, yellow, and red. They are the colors of the passes to the mine, and they can be changed or taken away for the slightest violation. Everyone violates the rules sometimes—that is the only way you can work with the equipment we have—so if they don't like you, they seize on that and you'll never work again. People who tried to preserve their dignity were crushed and thrown away.

"This is not a life for human beings. We have no time for leisure. We have no decent clothes. We spend our entire lives making just enough to feed ourselves and our children. The shift starts at six A.M., so you have to be up at four-thirty. You go to the mine, work eight hours underground, and all your life is work. When you come home you are too exhausted to do anything but collapse. On the weekend there are chores to do at home. About the only leisure we have is a mug or two of beer in the morning after the night shift. That's it. And then you quit—if you haven't already been killed in an accident. A few years later, your lungs give out, or your heart goes. Bye-bye. You're dead."

In the coming months, I went to mines in Ukraine, Sakhalin, and Kazakhstan. As it became clear that Moscow would not—and, probably, could not—come through on the economic deal, I heard more and more miners and other workers talking about a political strike. They were giving up on the system. But I had also heard those very things on the afternoon before I went

back to Moscow from Kemerovo. Another of the workers at mine No. 6, Ivan Narashev, invited me home. His hut, at 6 Krupskaya Street, was smaller and even plainer than Shcheglov's. He could barely control his anger. He had voted against going back to work. "We should have stayed out until there was money on the table," he said. "We should have been like bulls and waited until we got exactly what we wanted." Hunched forward in his pine chair, Narashev talked about how the "party big shots" were trying to break the strike with "sweet words and no deeds." He remembered being on the town square in Kemerovo one afternoon at the height of the general strike meetings and seeing the local KGB chief hovering near the speaker's platform.

"I'll tell you, I'm only thirty-seven but I'm ready to go for early pension," he said. "I've had it. Ten years underground is enough for me. I'd like to get a car and put my wife and kids in it and drive away from here, somewhere where the air doesn't burn your eyes. We should have had these strikes years ago. We've been destroyed by Stalinism and Brezhnev's cronies. I'm ready now for a leader other than Gorbachev. Someone more like Boris Yeltsin. Yeltsin's a man of concrete deeds. How is it possible that until now our leaders eat all the pork and we chew on the bones? If Yeltsin were sitting where Gorbachev is, maybe it would be different."

What seemed to burn in him most was the feeling that the strike would turn out to be not the glorious victory that everyone at mine No. 6 was saying it was, but another humiliation, like gray sausages and no electricity. It was not yet clear that the miners' strike of July 1989 was the first and most dramatic step in the creation of a link between the revolt of the intelligentsia in the cities and the nationalists in the republics with the political uprising of workers across the country. "Think about this country for a minute," Ivan Narashev said as the room began to darken. "Our leaders have always divided us, kept us down. I think they're doing that now, and they will rule again."

CHAPTER 15

POSTCARDS FROM THE EMPIRE

Valentin Falin, a rumpled, weary man high up in the Central Committee apparatus, was always prepared to serve the Party. But now he had an impossible task. With Eastern Europe beginning its democratic revolution, with evidence of the same in Lithuania, Latvia, and Estonia, he was instructed to go before the press and deny the existence of a Soviet empire.

The Kremlin had long since given up trying to rein in Eastern Europe. "We made that decision in 1985, 1986," Yegor Ligachev, of all people, told me. "We already had the example of Afghanistan before us." That is not to say the Kremlin was overjoyed with the triumph of Solidarity or other non-Communist parties in Eastern Europe. Officials in the Kremlin simply could not believe that the Eastern Europeans were rebelling on their own. Ligachev told me that had it not been for Western "provocateurs," the Eastern Europeans would have chosen "reformed socialism" and not "bourgeois" democracy. The leadership had hoped for Eastern Europe what it hoped for itself: the victory of the Communist Party's liberal wing. "I am confident," Gorbachev said in an interview with *The Washington Post* in the spring of 1988, "that the vast majority of people in Poland favor continuing along the path on which the country started after World War II." But no matter how

disappointed the Soviet Communist Party was in the nature of the Eastern European revolution, it could not afford intervention—not if it was going to get Western support for rebuilding the Soviet economy.

Moscow, however, was absolutely determined to hold together the union, the "internal empire." The preservation of the union, Gorbachev said repeatedly, was "a last stand," and yet his strategy was all muscle-flexing and expulsion of wind, the threat of force and a fraudulent argument that all the republics, including the Baltics, had joined the Soviet Union willingly and happily. For all his democratic pretensions, Gorbachev never saw the Soviet Union as an empire, a product of czarist and Bolshevik conquest, but rather as a "multinational union." He saw the union as inexorably linked not only by economic ties, shared history, and intermarriage, but by an ineffable sense of commonality. Gorbachev portrayed himself as a kind of Soviet one-worlder and the proponents of republican independence as retrograde nationalists doomed to the tribal battles of centuries past. "We are looking ahead," he told the Lithuanians, "and you are looking to the past."

To preserve the union, the Party was still willing to use its airbrush on history. The leaders of the Baltic independence movement, backed up by nearly every reputable Western historian, argued that Latvia, Estonia, and Lithuania came under the Soviet sphere of influence as the result of a secret deal between the Kremlin and the Nazis. The Molotov-Ribbentrop Pact of August 1939 surreptitiously divided Europe into Soviet and German spheres of influence. One of the secret protocols gave Moscow control over Latvia, Estonia, and parts of Poland and Romania. A second protocol, signed a month later, gave the Kremlin control over Lithuania. In 1940, Stalin annexed the Baltic states and forced their puppet legislatures to "request admission" into the union. And now Valentin Falin, chief of the Party's international department, was on the stage of the Foreign Ministry press center telling us that even if there had been such protocols, so what? They had nothing to do with "present realities." Falin's excuses would have shamed a schoolboy. The dog, he seemed to say, had eaten the secret protocols of the Molotov-Ribbentrop Pact.

When perestroika began, Gorbachev had at least some sense of the deterioration of the national economy and the difficulty of creating semidemocratic politics in a totalitarian state. But he and his colleagues started out nearly oblivious to the nationalities question. In December 1986, Gorbachev fired the Kazakh Party chief, Dinmukhamed Kunayev, and replaced him with an ethnic Russian, Gennadi Kolbin, never anticipating that the people of the republic would object. The ensuing riots in the republic's capital, Alma-Ata, eventually forced Gorbachev to replace Kolbin with a Kazakh, but the incident did not seem to impress the Kremlin very strongly. Even the massive

demonstrations in Armenia and Azerbaijan in early 1988 seemed to Gorbachev a matter of local interest, a petty squabble over Nagorny Karabakh that could be resolved by replacing the local Party leadership. He saw no threat there. After all, hadn't the protesters in Yerevan carried portraits of Gorbachev?

But the Balts spoke more clearly; their demands were easier to discern. They began with demonstrations about the environment, then about the need to preserve Baltic languages and cultures. Step by step, the Baltics grew more political, more self-confident. By early 1989, the most popular politicians in the region were non-Communists, and by May the parliaments of Estonia, Latvia, and Lithuania had all declared their sovereignty. It was unclear what sovereignty meant, or could mean. Even the leaders of the main opposition groups—Sajudis in Lithuania, the popular fronts in Estonia and Latvia—were careful not to talk of outright independence as anything other than a remote goal; when they spoke of independence it was in the wistful tones of scientists planning on the colonization of Mars. "We cannot afford illusions," said Marju Lauristan, a leader of the Estonian Popular Front. Lauristan least of all. Her father had been a leader of the Estonian Communists who welcomed Stalin's annexation in 1940 with open arms.

At first, the Kremlin had not seemed so threatened by the Baltic republics. They were, after all, a "special case," minuscule states absorbed into the Soviet Union more than twenty years after the Bolshevik Revolution. And just as important, there was the matter of temperament. The Balts were calm and measured, reasonable. Their demonstrations—next to the huge and noisy marches in Yerevan, Baku, or Tbilisi—were as gentle as a Save the Whales march on a summer's day in Sausilito. The Balts were "more European" somehow than the rest of the Union, and their traditions of small-scale farming and business, Gorbachev supposed, might even set a healthy example in Russia.

But the Baltic example became the model not for the revitalization of the Union, but rather for its collapse. In the three years it took to win independence, the Balts were never violent, only stubborn. It was that very temperament—Sakharov's calm confidence on a mass scale—that characterized their revolution. None of the other republics organized quite so well or thought with such precision and cool.

At first glance, the idea of Lithuania standing up to Moscow sounded like an episode from *The Mouse That Roared.* It was too comic to consider. Sajudis headquarters, a small building near the main Catholic cathedral in the capital city, Vilnius, was filled with well-scrubbed volunteers. They had a couple of PCs, a fax machine, satellite phones, and sweet wall posters showing Balts holding hands and singing songs. One afternoon I watched as

a young woman, wearing Birkenstock sandals and humming a Tracy Chapman song, pumped press releases through the telex machine and sent them to news bureaus all over the world. She was announcing a demonstration for August commemorating the fiftieth anniversary of the Molotov-Ribbentrop Pact. I thought of how blithe she seemed next to the traditional Bolshevik image of "real" revolutionaries: sweaty, bearded men in the Smolny denouncing "factionalism," Lenin speaking from an armored car, the stink of bad cigarettes. And yet she was their master; here she was, playing a vital role in the creation of a mass movement that would eventually liberate Lithuania and give the rest of the Soviet Union . . . ideas.

In their public statements, the leaders of the Baltic popular fronts had a knack for echoing Gorbachev's own rhetoric and then applying the principle to their own situation. When the Central Committee issued a threatening statement directed at the Balts, the popular front groups in the region issued a counterstatement that sounded much like Gorbachev's address to the United Nations: "The time when military force can solve everything has long since passed. Tanks are not only an immoral argument, they are no longer omnipotent. The main thing is that such a turn of events could once and for all put the Soviet Union back into the ranks of the most backward of totalitarian states." The Latvians, Estonians, and Lithuanians were keenly aware that for Moscow, the price of violence would be much higher than it had been in 1956 or 1968; this time Moscow made no secret that it needed the help of the West to survive. A bankrupt empire would be forced to shrink. That equation gave the Balts their confidence, a confidence that was shaken only when the governments of the West were weak, or tardy, in their support. "How can there be a 'threat' of tanks when there have already been Soviet tanks in the Baltic states for fifty years?" said Trivimi Velliste, president of the Estonian Heritage Society. "Tanks will not help them, even if they do move them into our city streets. The only thing they will do is cause a lot of trouble for our road repairmen. India used a passive resistance and India became independent in the end. In terms of that kind of strategy, we can learn a lot from India."

In Lithuania, especially, you could see with the greatest clarity the Baltic strategy. The Estonians, the saying went, were the brains of the movement, the Latvians the organizational spine, and the Lithuanians the heart, the moral force. The key leader of Sajudis, and eventually the president of the republic, was Vytautas Landsbergis, a man of almost infuriating confidence and righteousness, a moody academic who drove Gorbachev and even George Bush to distraction with his disdain for "playing politics" and moral compromise. A musicologist at the Vilnius conservatory, Landsbergis was no less a pedant than Gorbachev himself. When the Lithuanian parliament—in

what seemed like a moment of fantasy—took up the question of a national anthem, Landsbergis went into a long discourse about how the song could not be sung, as it had been traditionally, in the key of F sharp. "No one can sing that high," he said, and thus launched into a long disquisition.

Like many other intellectuals in the Baltic states, Landsbergis had not lived the dangerous life of an outright political dissident. But unlike the older Moscow intellectuals who worked within the Party and saw its reform as the only avenue of change, Landsbergis kept his distance from officialdom. In the years before Gorbachev, he saw the preservation of the Lithuanian culture as the only possible political act. "If we could keep alive the language, our religion, the culture, everything Moscow was trying to kill, then we had a chance," he said. Landsbergis's cultural dissidence was a family trait. His maternal grandfather, Jonas Jablonskis, was a linguist who fought for the primacy of the Lithuanian language after it was banned by the czars; his paternal grandfather, Gagrielus Landsbergis, was arrested and deported by the czarist government for the crime of writing for an underground newspaper; his father, Vytautas Landsbergis, Sr., was an architect during Lithuanian independence who fought in the resistance against the Nazi occupation. In the "years of stagnation" under Brezhnev, Landsbergis himself tried to preserve Lithuanian culture by studying the music of the composer Mikalojus Ciurlionis.

When the political opportunity came in 1989, Sajudis and Landsbergis led a cultural revolution, a revival of historical memory. I was in Vilnius to see a political act that would, in the next few years, become the ultimate symbol of the return of history. I saw members of Sajudis, after a vote of parliament, ripping down the signs reading "Lenin Street" along the main drag in Vilnius and replacing them with signs reading "Gediminais Street," named for one of the great dukes of Lithuanian history. The highway between Vilnius and Kaunas was changed from Red Army Avenue to Volunteer Avenue, celebrating the volunteers who fought for Lithuanian independence in 1918. On Sunday mornings, Lithuanian television broadcast Catholic mass on a new program, *Glory to Christ.* The young quit the Komsomol and the Young Pioneers. The Lithuanian Communist Party even conducted its sessions in Lithuanian, a great departure from the days when sessions were held in often clumsy Russian, the "Soviet language."

Western visitors, still flush with Gorbymania, would, with increasing frequency, come to Vilnius and hope that they could bridge the differences between the Kremlin and Sajudis. No matter how distinguished the visitor, Landsbergis would greet such attempts only with weary condescension. "We are an occupied country," he told me once. "To pretend we are grateful for a little democracy, to go through some sort of referendum to prove our

commitment to independence, to talk with Mr. Gorbachev as anything other than a foreign leader, is to live a lie. . . . It is very simple. We are an occupied land. Only now we can say it, of course, but we have never considered ourselves a genuine part of the Soviet Union. That is something that Gorbachev does not quite understand. We wish his perestroika well, but the time has come for us to go our own way."

In the end, the Baltic strategy was excruciatingly simple. They would speak the truth and then press the Kremlin to make good on its own moralistic rhetoric. As Gorbachev himself had done, the Balts defined their direction by first clarifying the facts of history. The secret protocols of the Molotov-Ribbentrop Pact made clear that the Baltic states were occupied as part of a geopolitical deal with the Nazis. The second step was a matter of logic: if the occupation was illegal in 1939, then it had always been such; therefore the Baltic states need only reaffirm their independence. Once they had established this logic of revolution, the other Baltic leaders followed Landsbergis's strategy and spoke of Moscow as a foreign state. Nearly all the Baltic representatives in the Soviet parliament suddenly declared themselves "interested observers" rather than deputies. They also played a kind of moral game with Gorbachev, insisting on his goodness, his distinctiveness. "We in the Baltics look on Gorbachev as the 'good czar' and try to pretend that the 'czar doesn't know,' it's his ministers who are up to mischief,' " said Andres Raid, a television journalist in Tallinn. "In a way, we are playing a political game, using Gorbachev's name. He is an anchor for us, a shield, a shelter. Of course, we disagree with him on some things, but we try not to be too harsh about it. We have no one else looking out for us in the political hierarchy. We have nowhere else to go for help."

The Balts were determined to prove that they were tougher than the Kremlin, that their moral certainty would result in either victory or annihilation. Perhaps what gave them their confidence, and what distinguished them from most of the rest of the Soviet Union, was that the Lithuanians, the Estonians, and the Latvians enjoyed and remembered a legacy of at least intermittent independence. The Lithuanians, for example, had been dominated by the Danes, the Teutonic Knights, the Swedes, the Russians, and the Nazis, but there were periods of freedom, most lately between 1918 and 1940. In the most recent period of domination, under the Soviet Union, Stalin deported hundreds of thousands of Lithuanians to Siberia and "replaced" them with Russian workers. But now the Baltic leaders would not accept a middle ground, for the middle ground meant continued occupation. And they were right. The Kremlin capitulated, slowly, step by step. On July 23, Aleksandr Yakovlev, as chairman of a legislative investigating committee, conceded the obvious: the secret protocols existed. Landsbergis could not

help but be amused. "This announcement," he said, "comes to us as a great shock." History had once more been returned.

—

A few months after Yakovlev's announcement, I had a chance to see glimpses of the worst nightmare of those who had once dreamed of an eternal Soviet empire.

In early October 1989, Gorbachev visited Berlin, ostensibly to help celebrate the anniversary of East German statehood. The cracks in the wall were already visible. Thousands of East Germans were fleeing across border points for West Germany, Hungary, Czechoslovakia, and Austria. But the East German leader, Erich Honecker, was as obstinate as any of the Eastern European dictators; he was the sort of tyrant who could begin a proclamation, "If I die . . ." He had every intention of outlasting Gorbachev and the pressure to change. To make himself understood, Honecker orchestrated a grand ceremony of state in Gorbachev's presence: a day of speechmaking in the main government palace, a goose-stepping military parade, fireworks. One night, tens of thousands of the Party youth league members marched through the streets of Berlin carrying flaming torches and singing songs of socialist brotherhood. (In a few weeks, they'd be marching through the Berlin Wall to buy steaks and singing praises of the gods Nike and Reebok.)

The Berlin visit was one of Gorbachev's finest moments, the sort of subtle exchange that he was made for. A year later, when blunt decisiveness was needed at home, when democratic politics demanded an end to backroom maneuvering, Gorbachev would hesitate and fail. Boris Yeltsin would fill the vacuum. But Gorbachev was the man for this moment. In public, he played along nicely with the East German leadership. In his own speeches and comments, he never drifted far from his host. He kissed Herr Honecker firm on the lips. But in the end that kiss was the kiss of farewell. In private, Gorbachev hinted broadly that the leadership could either begin its own massive reforms or end up defeated and defunct. Gorbachev trotted out one of his favorite aphorisms for the occasion: "Life itself punishes those who delay." He repeated it here and there, and his spokesman made sure to emphasize it at a press conference.

Such hints can spark a revolution. As the East German folksinger and dissident Wolf Bierman said of Gorbachev's phrase, "the tritest common places, launched into the world at the right moment, become magic spells." Many factors led to the collapse of the East German regime—the action along the border, dissension in the ruling Politburo, the rise of opposition groups—but Gorbachev's hint surely let the people know where the Kremlin, the center of the empire, stood. Within hours after he left for Moscow, an

uprising had begun, angry confrontations between demonstrators shouting "*Freiheit! Freiheit!*" and the Stasi police on the Alexanderplatz. According to reports on the radio, the demonstrations were far bigger in Leipzig. Erich Honecker may not have been listening to Gorbachev, but the people of East Germany were. On November 9, just one month after Gorbachev's visit, the Berlin Wall collapsed.

—

To live anywhere between Bonn and Moscow in 1989 was to be witness to a year-long political fantasy. You had the feeling you could wander into history on the way to the bank or the seashore. Esther and I had bought cheap tickets to Prague for Thanksgiving week, thinking we'd have time to see the city and some friends and relax. There was little chance of that. The day we arrived, we checked in at the hotel and walked to Wenceslas Square, where there were no fewer than 200,000 people marching for an end to the Communist regime. A couple of days later at an even bigger demonstration, I was leaning out a window watching Alexander Dubček, fifty feet away, declare his return to Prague after two decades of shame.

Dubček's return was remarkable enough—he was the living personification of the 1968 Prague Spring—but it was even more extraordinary that he now seemed antique. The crowds roared for him when he walked out on the balcony, but the enthusiasm faded steadily as they listened to him. His was still the old dream of "socialism with a human face." The tens of thousands of students who led the 1989 revolution, who were pouring into factories and bringing the workers out to join them on the city squares, looked on Dubček as a well-intentioned but slightly out-of-it grandfather. Dubček sounded as if he had been frozen in time from the moment he was arrested by the Soviet authorities in 1968. His language was still stiff, his cadences metronomic. Like Len Karpinsky's articles, Dubček's speech could not quite dispense with the Communist Party habit of euphemism, pomposity, and cliché. By the time he finished that day on Wenceslas Square, the applause was only polite.

With each demonstration Václav Havel's voice grew more and more hoarse, but his expressions of liberty and passion transcended the dead language of the official newspapers and Party pronouncements. It was as if by writing and speaking clearly, honestly, Havel helped keep alive principles and a language that would inevitably triumph over the regime. His opposition was to act outside the system, to act decently. How lucky the Czechs were to have such a voice among them! Havel was no less a hero than Sakharov or Walesa, and his greatness, like theirs, was in his absolute belief in himself and the rightness of his cause.

In Prague I read a collection of letters Havel sent to his wife, Olga, from

prison. They were filled with philosophical discussion, abstract exploration of the reasons for existence and faith, but I found myself just as moved by "overhearing" Havel describe the routine of prison life, his reading of Max Brod's biography of Kafka and Bellow's *Herzog;* his progress in English and German; his hemorrhoids; the pleasure of smoking two cigarettes a day and intensifying that pleasure by smoking slowly in front of a mirror; his reasons for living, his reasons for hope. Most of all, I found myself nodding with admiration at Havel's description of the insidious way the Prague regime (or the Moscow or Beijing regimes) had made language "weightless" by twisting it, pacifying and corrupting it.

"Words that are not backed up by life lose their weight," Havel wrote, "which means that words can be silenced in two ways: either you ascribe such weight to them that no one dares utter them aloud, or you take away any weight they might have, and they turn into air. The final effect in each case is silence: the silence of the half-mad man who is constantly writing appeals to world authorities while everyone ignores him; and the silence of the Orwellian citizen."

A man of the theater, Havel held his press conferences onstage during those weeks of revolution. On November 24, after Dubček's speech on the square, he and Dubček answered the nightly questions from the press at the Magic Lantern Theater and even got into a mild debate on socialism. Dubček was all for a "purified" socialism, once rinsed of Stalinist "deformations." A familiar, Gorbachevian theme. Havel said he could no longer discuss "socialism," that it was a word and idea that had been rendered meaningless. After about an hour of this meeting of the generations, Havel's brother walked on the stage, which was still set for a production of Dürrenmatt's play *Minotaurus.* He whispered in Havel's ear. Havel smiled, a radiant smile. Dubček was talking, and Havel interrupted with a polite gesture.

"The entire Politburo has resigned," Havel announced.

Suddenly there was a bottle of champagne and glasses all around.

Havel and Dubček rose and toasted a free Czechoslovakia.

Curtain.

In the epilogue a few weeks later, Havel appeared not onstage, but on state television. He was now president of Czechoslovakia. Citizens, he declared, "your government has been returned to you!" This was not theater. This was really happening.

Inside the Soviet Union itself, republican independence leaders celebrated the end of the external empire. Except for Romania, where the revolution ended in bloodshed and political ambiguity, the liberation of Eastern Europe

seemed almost effortless. But they were careful not to let themselves believe that their own freedom would come soon. The Kremlin gave them every reason to think otherwise. Writing in *Sovetskaya Kultura,* the Kremlin's arch spokesman, Gennadi Gerasimov, said that the West was showing "malignant pleasure" in the Baltic independence movements. Such movements, he wrote ominously, "threaten our reforms and are provoking use of the 'iron fist.' "

In early 1990, after the string of revolutions in Eastern Europe had come to an end, an American historian, Eric Foner, conducted a seminar with his history students at Moscow State University. Foner was a specialist in the American Civil War, and the afternoon I sat in on his class, he and his students discussed the parallels between Gorbachev and Lincoln and their quests to keep together a union. For a while, Foner and his students compared the two leaders, but soon the students began to talk about what they thought their country would look like in a few years. Every one of them predicted collapse, and every one was frightened that the old regime would resist to the end.

The Soviet Union is a great empire, and we are now watching its disintegration, Igor, a student from Byelorussia, said. "Assuming that by my early thirties I have not been killed in a civil war, I think what will be left will be Russia—the original core territory. And that is what happened to the Roman Empire, isn't it? It shrank. I just hope that it all happens without haste, and peacefully."

"I'm frightened," said another student, a Russian, Aleksandr Petrov. "Power is still in the hands of the Communist Party and the KGB. They can stir it all up if they want. And if there is violence, they'll say they had to do it all to preserve peace."

Their fears and visions of the future differed, but all of Foner's students fully expected the Union to collapse. "The old regime," Petrov said, "is not just old. It's dead."

As I traveled around the Union, opinions varied on when and where the old regime died. Uzbeks in Tashkent and Samarkand told me that the exposure in around 1988 and 1989 of the callous way Moscow had turned all of Central Asia into a vast cotton plantation—in the process destroying the Aral Sea and nearly every other area of the economy—was the turning point. In the Baltic states, the official "discovery" of the secret protocols to the Nazi-Soviet pact was the key moment. But it was in Ukraine that I found the most unifying event, the absolute metaphor for the explosion of the last empire on earth.

On a trip to the western Ukrainian city of Lvov in 1989, I met with small

groups of nationalists who promised that "one day" their republic of over fifty million people, the biggest after Russia, would strike out for independence and do far more damage to the union than the tiny Baltic states ever could. They knew their history. "For us," Lenin once wrote, "to lose the Ukraine would be to lose our head." Bogdan and Mikhail Horyn, brothers who had spent long terms in jail for their pro-independence activities before Gorbachev took power, said that while an independent, post-Soviet Ukraine may be years off, the old regime collapsed, practically and metaphorically, at 1:23 A.M., April 26, 1986, the moment of the nuclear accident at Chernobyl. That devastating instant had from the start been wrapped in a mystical aura. Within weeks of the accident, people realized that "Chernobyl" meant "Wormwood" and then pointed to Revelations 8:10–11; "A great star shot from the sky, flaming like a torch; and it fell on a third of the rivers and springs. The name of the star was Wormwood; and a third of the water turned to wormwood, and men in great numbers died of the water because it was poisoned."

The accident at Chernobyl embodied every curse of the Soviet system, the decay and arrogance, the willful ignorance and self-deception. Before leaving for Chernobyl, I arranged to see Anatoly Aleksandrov, the physicist who designed the reactor model at Chernobyl. Aleksandrov was in his nineties, the dean of Soviet science. He was the former head of the Academy of Sciences and the head man at the Kurchatov Institute of Nuclear Energy. During the Brezhnev era, Aleksandrov had written that nuclear power plants were 100 percent safe and ought to be built as close to population centers as possible, the better to solve the country's heating problems during the winter.

Aleksandrov's office was grander than any I had seen before, grander even than most of the palatial offices at the Kremlin. He and a group of his top aides and engineers sat in a semicircle and he talked of the accident. No, he felt no remorse. Yes, the reactor was sound and reports of future accidents were absurd. "If there was a defect or two, we've fixed it, you see." And as for reports that hundreds, if not thousands, of people would die over the years from the effects of radioactivity unleashed at Chernobyl, Aleksandrov lifted his enormous, aged hand and flapped it in derision.

"Oh, really now," he said. "That's wild exaggeration. Stop worrying so much!"

There remains every reason to worry. The Chernobyl explosion released a radioactive cloud ten times more deadly than the radiation following the blast at Hiroshima. There were children in the region who absorbed radiation equivalent to a thousand chest X rays. More than 600,000 workers took part in the cleanup, a deadly job; more than 200,000 people were evacuated from the region, but only after a thirty-six-hour delay and after absorbing danger-

ous amounts of radioactivity. There are thousands of people in Ukraine, Byelorussia, and other republics who eat food grown in radioactive earth and drink contaminated water. At the Petrovsky Collective Farm in Narodichi, the farm directors reported that sixty-four farm animals were born with serious deformities in 1987: calves without heads, limbs, ribs, eyes; pigs with abnormal skulls. In 1988, the rate continued to rise. They recalled only three or four such instances before the accident. *Moscow News* said that the radiation readings in the area were thirty times greater than normal, but that local farm animals were still fed fodder from the contaminated fields. People in the region received 35 rubles a month from the state as a subsidy—money the people called the "coffin bonus." The various bureaucracies seemed not to care about, or believe in, the perils of radiation. As late as 1990, more than 180 tons of contaminated meat was shipped to stores in Siberia and northern Russia from a processing plant in Bryansk where the sausage was being made from beef and pork with radiation levels ten times normal.

"Chernobyl was not *like* the Communist system. They were one and the same," said Yuri Shcherbak, a physician and journalist who led the fight in Ukraine to publicize the medical and ecological hazards of the accident. "The system ate into our bones the same way radiation did, and the powers that be—or the powers that were—did everything they could to cover it all up, to wish it all away."

From the moment that the engineers in the control room of reactor No. 4 at Chernobyl reported a disaster beyond imagining, their superiors refused to act. The top bureaucrats at Chernobyl kept repeating the same fiction: that there had been a "mishap," but nothing terrible, the reactor had not been destroyed. They quickly passed on this fiction to the leadership in Moscow. The next day, the people of Chernobyl, Pripyat, and the neighboring villages acted out their lives under a radioactive cloud. Children played soccer in radioactive dust. There were sixteen outdoor weddings sponsored by the Young Communist League. Old men fished in a contaminated river and ate the contaminated fish. When he was told by his engineers that the radiation at the plant was millions of times higher than normal, the plant director, Viktor Bryuchanov, said the meter was obviously defective and must be thrown away. For more than a day, Boris Shcherbina, a deputy prime minister, refused suggestions to carry out a mass evacuation. "Panic is worse than radiation," he said. The world got word of the seriousness of the accident only when Scandinavian scientists reported dramatic increases in radiation levels. Even as they were evacuating their own families, Ukrainian Communist Party officials insisted on holding the annual May Day parade; the children of Kiev kicked up radioactive dust to celebrate the victories of socialism. After a long filibuster in the Politburo and strict controls on public

information about the disaster, Gorbachev went on television to discuss Chernobyl a full sixteen days after the accident, and much of his talk was taken up with denunciations of the Western press.

"Meanwhile the reactor was burning away," wrote Grigori Medvedev, an engineer who once worked at Chernobyl. "The graphite was burning, belching into the sky millions of curies of radioactivity. However, the reactor was not all that was finished. An abscess, long hidden within our society, had just burst: the abscess of complacency and self-flattery, of corruption and protectionism, of narrow-mindedness and self-serving privilege. Now, as it rotted, the corpse of a bygone era—the age of lies and spiritual decay—filled the air with the stench of radiation."

In the aftermath of the accident, Shcherbina, the deputy prime minister, issued a secret decree in force from 1988 to 1991 telling Soviet doctors they could not cite radiation as a cause of death. Shcherbina, who had himself been exposed to high doses of radiation, died in 1990. The cause of death was marked "unspecified."

One morning in Kiev, an official from Spetsatom, one of the cleanup bureaucracies, picked me up in a van and we drove north for Chernobyl. I had visited cities that were often described as "frozen in time": Havana, with its faded hotels from the era of gambling and Battista; Rangoon, with its stopped clocks, reworked English cars, and the battered English silver at the Strand Hotel downtown. Usually it was a matter of faded colonialism matched against the poverty of the native regime. Chernobyl was something else again, a kind of ruin of the Soviet system, a horrible metaphor for the era that began with the Revolution in 1917 and was now ending. We passed a series of checkpoints, changed into a "dirty" radioactive van, and headed into the haunted "zone." In the town of Pripyat there were abandoned apartment buildings, dilapidated as any other buildings in the Soviet Union. The workers and administrators of the power plant lived there. It was a moonscape of abandoned playgrounds, half-buried cars, buses, railroad wagons, abandoned fields. After the accident, people desperate for cash would dig up the buried cars and sell the radioactive parts or just drive the whole car off to Kiev. I met older people who had been evacuated but now had come back to the "zone" to live and die. They had never believed anything the state had told them, and why should they begin now? They drank poisoned tea and ate poisoned potatoes. A few hundred yards away was reactor No. 4, now encased in layers of concrete. Engineers were still trying to work out how they would finally eliminate the near-eternal danger posed by the core. The concrete would not hold forever.

Most of the people still living in "the zone" were cleanup workers, and most of them stayed "inside," working for fifteen days, and then went home

to Kiev and other towns for fifteen days of recuperation. That was the rule. But there were also some who were so dedicated to the cleanup project that they rarely left "the zone" except to visit family for a day or two every month. The Spetsatom director, Yuri Solomenko, and the chief engineer, Viktor Golubyev, spent nearly all their time in the zone and vowed to stay on until the Sarcophagus—the nickname for reactor No. 4—was "cleaned out." Once, while I was interviewing the two men, Golubyev excused himself. He had another meeting. As soon as he left the room, Solomenko told me his friend "was all but finished." After getting news of the Chernobyl accident while working at a reactor site in Cuba, Golubyev had volunteered to help put out the fire. In those rescue operations, he absorbed so much radiation that his skin turned deep brown and had to be peeled away. Solomenko explained that his friend's body had been "utterly degraded." And yet he would not leave Chernobyl until the damage was cleared away.

"Chernobyl was like everywhere else in this empire," Yuri Shcherbak said. "The only thing that stood between us and total oblivion was a few good people, a few heroes who told the truth and risked their lives. If it weren't for the danger, they should leave the Chernobyl plant standing. It could be the great monument to the Soviet empire."

CHAPTER 16

THE ISLAND

I met a free man on the island of Sakhalin. His name was Nikolai Batyukov, a would-be intellectual turned itinerant fisherman, and he knew only vaguely of the political fervor thousands of miles to the east in Moscow. He did not have much to say about Gorbachev or Yeltsin or any other figure in the political life of the capital. "As you can see, I keep my distance," he said.

Batyukov was one of the few men or women I had encountered in Russia who seemed at ease with what he had made of his life. He was in his fifties, and many years before he had been, in the loose, Russian sense, an intellectual, a serious student, but he saw "no future at all" in a life of the mind. "Not in this country, not in the Soviet Union." He gave it all up to live as a "half-legal, independent" fisherman. "In this country, the only way to be free was to run away from it," he said. "I couldn't run to Tokyo so I ran for the hills."

In the warmer months, Batyukov set up camp in the pine woods overlooking the Sea of Okhotsk, a landscape as jagged and beautiful as the coast of northern California. He fished mainly for salmon and spiny crab and sold his catch at markets in the capital city, Yuzhno-Sakhalinsk. Batyukov had a hermit's wild gray beard, and today he said he felt more worn out than usual.

All day he had been hauling nets heavy with salmon; it was the summer run. There were more fish around than he could possibly catch. What made him furious was to see the "government nets"—the nets set out along the shore by the state fishing boats—filled with rotting fish, big, glorious salmon going gray and belly up while the captains idled at sea, waiting for Moscow to give them the order to bring the fish on board. Those fishing nets held at least 150,000 pounds of salmon, Batyukov reckoned, but because the local bureaucrats had to wait for orders from the central bureaucrats of the "central command system," a million-dollar catch would soon be little more than rotting guts, bones, and scales. "Can you imagine anything so stupid?" he said.

As if to make his guests taste the loss, Batyukov set out one of the most splendid seafood feasts I have ever eaten. He cooked it all outside over a fire, in dented tin pots and an ancient fry pan. He worked with speed and skill; he was the fifteen-minute gourmet. There was a fish soup as fine as any in Marseilles, a mound of steamed spiny crabs, glossy red salmon caviar smeared on fresh bread, glasses of home-brewed vodka, and mugs of hot *chaga,* a chocolaty tea made from the sap of birch trees. Most people in the Soviet Union got fat on bad sausage, potatoes, and butter. Batyukov had clearly built his magnificent pot on finer things.

"I live the way I want to live," he said, "but the only way I do it is to keep low and out of sight. In your country, I'd be a worker, maybe a businessman. Here, I'm like an outlaw. An outlaw fisherman. So, sure, I like what I'm hearing on the radio about Sakharov and glasnost. Fine. But I'll believe it when I can see it. Tell me. You've been in Yuzhno-Sakhalinsk. Do you figure everything's different? You figure there's a place for a free man like me?"

In 1890, Chekhov left behind his literary triumphs in Moscow and traveled by rail and riverboat to the prison colonies and fishing villages on Sakhalin. "This seems to be the end of the world," he wrote in his journal as he approached the coastline, "and there is nowhere else left to go." In Chekhov's day, Sakhalin was Russia's Australia, a penal colony so distant that it seemed the very definition of exile. The camps were places of arbitrary cruelty and violence; one prisoner finally murdered a sadistic guard by suffocating him in fermenting bread dough. Working conditions were miserable. Migrant coal workers ate candles and rotten wood while the czar's ministers sold the island's salmon and caviar abroad. Chekhov visited Sakhalin to work as a census taker, to talk with prisoners and vagrants, and to write a long, and strangely dispassionate, account of life there, *The Island.* Sakhalin seemed to him as remote as Patagonia; Sakhalin, for Chekhov, was as much

an idea as a place, a representation of Russia's vastness and the czar's reach across it. In his census, he discovered a people who took on names that somehow reflected their remoteness and conditions. "The most common surname is Nepomnyashchy [Unremembered]. Here are some of the vagrants' names: Mustafa Nepomnyashchy, Vasily Bezotechestva [Without Parents], Franz Nepomnyashchy, Ivan Nepomnyashchy 20 Years, Yakov Bezpozvaniya [Nameless], Vagrant Ivan 35 Years . . ."

The czar's prison camps closed long ago. Stalin favored the slightly closer, but less accessible, Kolyma region as his favorite murder site. The Soviet regime did what it could to Sovietize Sakhalin, building squat, shabby apartment houses in Yuzhno-Sakhalinsk and crabbed collective farms in the ports and provinces. The government populated the island by offering extra pay for miners, fishermen, and farmers.

Sakhalin was considered a border frontier, and so, until just a few months before my visit in the summer of 1989, the island was closed to foreigners and even to nonresident Soviet citizens. Even when I was there, Sakhalin was covered with concrete guard shacks. The KGB border troops were the age of college sophomores and wore daggers in their belts. They were stunned by the presence of foreigners: a reporter from *The Washington Post* one day, a Korean computer salesman the next. It seemed to them an invasion, but they were under orders now to let us through.

I went to Sakhalin to see if the political reforms going on in Moscow had taken root at the edge of Russia. By the time I got to the island, there had already been an awakening. The first sign of trouble for the local Party apparatus came in May 1988 when a few hundred men and women staged a demonstration outside the Chekhov Drama Theater in the capital to accuse the Party chief, Pyotr Tretyakov, of doling out apartments to his relatives and generally padding his own patronage rolls. The police and KGB circled the small demonstration but were too stunned, too confused, to act. The Party tried to wish it all away. To acknowledge the demonstration would have been "a situation." That was impermissible, unthinkable. The next morning, the official papers made the requisite noise about "a handful of extremists," then ignored the issue entirely.

But soon, as if sensing the Moscow breeze at their backs, the local democrats staged even bigger demonstrations on the squares and streets of Yuzhno-Sakhalinsk. The island's Party leadership was suddenly, and unalterably, on the defensive. A triumphant banner appeared over Lenin Avenue: "Get Rid of the Bureaucrats and Give Them a Shovel." Tretyakov, the Party chief, would have fought back if he could have, but he got no support from Moscow. He was fired by the Central Committee and fled Sakhalin for Moscow on a military transport jet. He never returned to the island. In the

meantime, the new Party leaders knew well enough to halt construction of an expensive new headquarters and said they would let the people of Sakhalin decide whether to make a hospital or a school out of the building. In fact, everywhere I went in the Soviet Union in 1989 and 1990, the Communist Party was always in a state of "halted construction." Dozens of expensive headquarters never opened, were turned into schools and hospitals, or, more often, sat empty, dark, haunted.

This tiny revolution became an instant legend on the island. It was known as the "May events," a distinct echo of the legendary "July events" that led to the Bolshevik uprising of October 1917. Gorbachev was so pleased with the sign of an awakening in the hinterlands that he told reporters, "Finally, perestroika has come to Sakhalin."

But for all of Gorbachev's triumphalism, the Party still could not grasp the depths of people's anger with the old structures of power and the hegemony of Moscow. The Central Committee replaced the old apparatchik, Tretyakov, with a new one, Viktor Bondarchuk. Sakhalin Island had to wait only a few months before it showed its opinion of Comrade Bondarchuk. In the race for the Yuzhno-Sakhalinsk seat in the Congress of People's Deputies, an obscure and dyspeptic journalist named Vitaly Guly trounced Bondarchuk. Guly had been an ardent Komsomol boy, dutifully traveling the island preaching ideology. But he had changed radically by the mid-eighties. Now in his late thirties, he wrote many of the opinion pieces and embarrassing investigative pieces that led to the "May events."

One afternoon, we rode around in Guly's tiny Moskvich "looking for constituents." He wanted to talk with workers about the Congress and the miners' strikes. "I can't exactly say all I need to say in my paper—*Sovetsky Sakhalin*—so they have to hear it from the horse's mouth." The roads were generally miserable, but suddenly we found ourselves on a strip as fine as a German autobahn. Guly laughed and said, "You want to know why the road is so smooth? This is the road from Party headquarters downtown to where all the Party big shots had their dachas. They wanted a good road for themselves, and that's all there was to it. Presto! It was built! As for the rest of us . . ."

We headed toward a fishery and caviar-processing plant on Freedom Peninsula. To get there, we had to get through yet another KGB checkpoint, which consisted of a crumbling concrete shack, two teenage guards, and a boom box booming "I Saw Her Standing There." The guard poked his head inside. He asked for our documents. While he checked them over he was still tapping his foot to the music.

"Okay," he said. "We were expecting foreigners. Go ahead through."

After I got over my awe at the sight of the caviar—women in white

fingering their way through bucketfuls of wondrous, slick goo—I could concentrate on how easily Guly mixed with the workers. He had the knack of listening to their complaints, remembering their names, and laughing at their jokes. Many of the workers referred to the first session of the Congress simply as "the show," the "great show in Moscow," and they wanted to know much more about immediate things: their salaries, housing. One woman told Guly with no embarrassment that "the main method of birth control on this island is abortion and the only way you can get one is to hire a doctor and rent a hotel room."

Guly said he would look into the possibility of building a clinic and making birth control available on the island. But there was also a grim understanding between the woman and Vitaly Guly: only the Communist Party had the power to do anything. And it would do nothing. Guly and his constituent smiled thin smiles at each other and parted.

Guly headed for the car, boiling. "Sakharov is right," he said. "I'm a member of the Party, but the Party has to go. The rest is details."

—

But the Party remained and the Party was still all-powerful, especially in a distant province like Sakhalin. The Party had rigged the elections so that it could stock the Congress with obedient servants. These were, in the main, dim-witted hacks who had very little idea at all what words like "perestroika," "glasnost," or "democratization" meant. Since the days of Stalin they had been hearing the Kremlin boast of its democracy, its constitutionalism; the Constitution written under Stalin, after all, sounds no less glorious than the American version of 1789. But it hardly mattered. Words, much less slogans, had long ago lost their meaning. What really meant something was belonging. Membership in the Party apparatus was all.

During my stay in Sakhalin, I shuttled back and forth between one host and the other, between Guly and a happy lug named Anatoly Kapustin. Both were deputies in the Congress, but they could not have been more different. Kapustin was elected not by people in his territory, but rather to a seat specially reserved for fellow Party and labor union officials. According to the more polite critics in town, he was a time-server, a low-rent apparatchik who had worked his way up from the coal mines to a soft office job in the union bureaucracy. He was in no way nasty, and friendlier even than Guly. Kapustin was eager to please. He had voice like a bassoon and a crushing handshake. He smiled constantly, like a maniac. But now he was in deep trouble. After the triumph of his election, he was having a very bad summer.

"Things are out of control," he said, "and that's not good."

There had been strikes at the Sakhalin coal mines, and in their aftermath

Kapustin wanted badly to show us that he was "working closely with the working class." One morning we watched him try to negotiate his way through a meeting with about 150 miners at union headquarters in Yuzhno-Sakhalinsk. Kapustin did the best he could. He pledged "openness" like Gorbachev. He chopped the air and wrapped the lectern like Gorbachev. But his moves were unconvincing. The poor man was too weighed down by his own meager talents, his dubious résumé and election, his habits of thought and speech. He was a cliché, an earnest windbag of the apparat. His new role as a "man of perestroika" was beyond him. He was no more convincing to the miners than he was to himself. Kapustin was like a dinner-theater extra asked to play Hamlet at the Old Vic with an hour's preparation. He knew some of the lines—"We will work together, hand in hand!"—but he fooled no one. The miners rolled their eyes and hooted like a flock of owls.

Afterward, Kapustin was embarrassed and sad. He thought he was getting it. He thought he'd been brave. "I used to toe the line all the way," he said. "The big guys would say what to do, and I would do it. It was just 'Kapustin do this' and that was that. Now I think if something is wrong, I try to speak up." But it wasn't enough.

Nearby, in the hallway, one of the strike leaders, Vitaly Topolov, said he was trying hard to work with Kapustin, but the prospects were not good at all: "I suppose he was an apparatchik, but Gorbachev was an apparatchik under Brezhnev, too. I keep hoping."

Kapustin bumbled on. We drove through the hills to Sinegorsk, a tiny mining town built by the Japanese when they were in control of the island in 1905. There, in the mine director's office, Kapustin was suddenly at ease. These were his friends, the midlevel bureaucrats who were marginally competent in their jobs, marginally honest. They all regretted the passing of time and apologized for the meager spread of ham sandwiches and fizzy water.

"Too bad this isn't the Brezhnev era," one of the mine directors said. "Back then we really would have laid out a banquet for you."

It wasn't their arrogance that hampered them so much as their complete lack of comprehension. When it came to simple economics, they could not connect the dots. The mine director complained that production had fallen at the mine by half, but at the same time he launched into a glorious paean to the central planning system and the web of state orders and subsidies. The fact was that his mine was badly equipped, primitive, and probably defunct. It was a dangerous place to work and an ecological disaster, and would never be profitable in a normal economy.

After lunch, Kapustin led us on an expedition of the mine, and it was worse than anything I'd seen in Siberia, Ukraine, or Kazakhstan. The mine was a horror. There were no elevators, and the shafts were brutal and tight. It took

some of the miners two hours of sliding and creeping along stone just to get to their work stations. Later, my back and legs were covered with bruises and I was more sore than I would have been if I'd run ten miles. Until the strike, the miners had not been paid for this "commuting" time: they tore themselves up, four hours every day, for free. "And we've taken you down the best mine we've got here," the director said. "This one's dry. In the others, you've got water running down your back all day."

Outside, in the daylight at last, Kapustin wiped the soot from his eyes and put on his Gorbachev face again. Two dozen miners, exhausted and instantly bored, circled around. They wanted to go home but had been told to wait. "I'm here to listen to your problems," Kapustin said clumsily. "Please, tell me your problems." The men wore the bemused expressions of high school students watching their teacher trying too hard to be hip. They could not wait to go home and soak in a bath. They were in no mood to perform for a union hack like Anatoly Kapustin.

—

And yet, for a few days, I liked him. Kapustin was trying so hard to be admired, and the rewards for toadying were next to nothing: a slightly better salary, a better summer vacation. As a member of the Congress, he was the Soviet equivalent of a congressmen, and yet no American—much less a member of the House of Representatives—could have lived the life of Anatoly Kapustin. He lived just about as badly as anyone else in the Soviet Union.

A couple of days after our trip to the mine, Kapustin took us out to a huge fishing trawler. I thought we'd get a chance to see how a state boat operated, why it was that so many tons of salmon were rotting in the nets a few hundred feet away. But Kapustin had no interest in that. He was a close friend of the ship captain, and, as Kapustin said, "It's time we kicked back and relaxed. You relax sometimes in America, don't you?"

He led us to the captain's stateroom, a wood-paneled affair of surprising elegance. The table was already set with china, decent silverware, dishes heaped with food, and a half-dozen bottles: Georgian champagne, Ukrainian beer, pepper vodka. There was no way out. We were in for a time of it, and I prayed only that the seas would stay calm.

Amazingly, Kapustin was a worse drinker than I am. After three vodkas he was expressing his eternal fealty to Yegor Ligachev and the "wisdom" of the Party hard line. The strikes were an outrage, private property impermissible, the independence movements in the Baltic states treason. After just one more drink, he was making horrible sport of Sakharov, calling him "self-righteous," "anti-Soviet," and "useless."

"Just who does he think he is?" Kapustin said, his face darkening. "The man talks too much for his own good. He's a slander-monger."

It was a nasty performance, and I was—to my surprise—surprised. So many Party apparatchiks in so many situations had performed prettily for me, the foreign journalist. But now Kapustin was unbound. The vodka and the days of proximity had worked on him like a key. He was a man who instinctively felt the moral and political threat that Sakharov posed to him and the Party. Sakharov and his followers were challenging the very existence of the Party, the power of the Kremlin, the way of doing business. "Sakharov and his bunch think we don't understand them," Kapustin said, lifting his glass one last time, "but we do. We understand them. All too well."

CHAPTER 17

BREAD AND CIRCUSES

When Gibbon wrote the saga of Rome's decline and fall, he relied on the written word, on memoir, epic, and history, for his source material. But the scholars of the collapse of the Soviet empire will go not to the library so much as the videotape. And in this video revolution, Anatoly Kashpirovsky played the role of Rasputin, the crazy wisdom man.

In a thousand years of Russian history, there have always been healers, mystics, and "holy fools." Usually they came to prominence in periods of rapid change, disaster, and disorientation. The sixth-century historian Agathias recalled "charlatans and self-appointed prophets roaming the streets" after an earthquake in Byzantium. "Society," he wrote, "never fails to throw up a bewildering variety of such persons in times of misfortune." In the last years of the czarist regime, Rasputin, an illiterate Siberian, convinced the Romanovs of his magical powers. The royal family was sure Rasputin was curing the heir to the throne of his hemophilia.

But while Rasputin's mesmerizing influence was limited to the czar's family and high society, Kashpirovsky was a man of the global village and the world tour. His healing "séances" captured television audiences of 300 million in the Soviet Union and Eastern Europe and filled huge concert halls and football stadiums. Kashpirovsky's medicine show had been kicking around

for years, but it was at the end of 1989, when the economy was plummeting and people began talking about a new "Time of Troubles," that the Communist Party officials who ran state television decided it was time for a grand diversion, a video healer.

I saw the first of Kashpirovsky's broadcasts, and, like everybody else, I was hooked from the opening credits:

A logo announced the "tele-séance." Kashpirovsky came on the screen dressed all in black. He had the hyped-up glare, the scissors-and-a-bowl haircut of Brando in *Julius Caesar.* He started talking about his method of reaching the "bio-computer" inside his "patients," how he had healed "hundreds of thousands, perhaps millions" of people of their tumors, hernias, and heart pains. His voice was 16 rpm, low and even, like a threat. He claimed medical successes never known in "human history," successful cures of impotence, frigidity, blindness, baldness, emphysema, ovarian cysts, kidney stones, psoriasis, eczema, varicose veins, scars, tuberculosis, asthma, diabetes, allergies, stuttering, astigmatism, and, in four "documented" cases, the AIDS virus. He was at once God and Ponce de León: amputated limbs and extracted teeth regenerated at his mere suggestion; gray hair turned glossy and dark. Thanks to him, a woman of seventy began menstruating again and Mikhail Gorbachev's mother got over her arthritis. And then there was the Kashpirovsky Diet: one of his patients dropped 350 pounds, "and without the skin hanging off or anything." Or so the doctor said . . . so he said.

The soundtrack picked up now, a great wash of synthesizer music, switched-on baroque.

"Rid your mind of everything," Kashpirovsky purred. "Get rid of all those goals and ambitions. Everyone, close your eyes. No matter what emotional reactions you have, don't suppress them. And you will have different kinds of emotional reactions. Our silence is like a pause, a pause without words. Words don't matter. There's no work involved in this. It's hard to understand, because all their lives people have been taught to try and understand. . . . Forget everything. . . . Listen to the music. . . . Don't be afraid of the process that's starting within you. . . . If something is moving, pay no attention."

The man seemed never to blink. He glistened, and for long periods he said nothing, just stared and smirked a little, the way a tyrant dinner guest does when he is half soused and certain you should be fascinated by everything he says.

". . . Some of you are seeing forests, mountains. One . . . two . . . three. . . . Others are having very sad memories. Five . . . six. . . . Others are making plans for tomorrow, weighing, weighing everything. Seven. . . ."

By "ten" Kashpirovsky was gone.

"The séance," he said, "is over."

We were healed.

Since his first televised séances, Kashpirovsky's popularity—his cult of personality—went unmatched. Everyone knew his name and thought him either a genius or a confidence man. He told me once that he had an archive of more than a million telegrams and letters mainly from grateful viewer-patients. Schoolgirls and pensioners wrote in hinting they would do anything to be near him, learn from him, sleep with him. Older women wrote saying they had redecorated their *krasny ugol*—"red corner"—by taking down the traditional portrait of Lenin and replacing it with his. In the provinces, street vendors sold picture postcards of Czar Nicholas II, John Lennon, Jesus Christ, and Anatoly Kashpirovsky. He may have been the only man in the city of Kiev with three cars in his garage and a bank account to match. Newspapers that debunked his legend did so at their peril. After the weekly *Literaturnaya Gazeta* printed an article calling Kashpirovsky a dangerous charlatan, the protest mail grew into such an avalanche that the editor canceled a second article.

There were those who thought of Kashpirovsky as a healer not only of stretch marks and wens, but of nations as well, and he was loath to dismiss the claim. "If I were president, people would kiss my footprints after I died because I would go out among the people and work for their interests," he told me. His constituency was uncertain, but, he insisted, it was vast. "Ukraine is too small for me."

Kashpirovsky first appeared on the scene with a series of six nationally televised séances in the last few months of 1989. With the rise of independence movements and a workers' revolt, perestroika was spinning out of Gorbachev's control. The health care system was a shambles, with officials saying that only 30 percent of all basic medicines were available; even aspirin and penicillin were impossible to find. There were constant reports of hospitals without running water, doctors operating by candlelight. Kashpirovsky's rise came precisely at the start of this extreme uncertainty, confusion, spiritual search. And, as happened so often in Russian history, disruption gave rise to an increased interest in black magic, prophecy, and wizardry. *Bogoiskatelstvo,* the search for God, in Russia led not only to the church, mosque, and synagogue, but to such frauds as Rasputin and Kashpirovsky.

Always, even during the purges, there were village healers and mystics in Russia. In his dotage, Leonid Brezhnev secretly invited the healer Dzhuna Davitashvili to the Kremlin to work her magic. But now there were no taboos, no hiding. During the Gorbachev era, old women sold copper brace-

lets in city parks swearing they would work as a vaccine against AIDS; horoscopes ran in Communist Party newspapers; the official news agency Tass announced that "humanlike" giants and a midget robot flying in a "banana-shaped object" had landed in the city of Voronezh. Witnesses described the craft in question as a "large shining ball" and the "one, two, or three" creatures as being "three or four meters high but with very small heads." In Moscow, a healer named Alan Chumak opened shop on the program *120 Minutes,* the Soviet version of the *Today* show. Waving his hands as if he were petting an invisible cat, Chumak "charged" glasses of water and tubes of cold cream that people put in front of their television sets with "healing energy."

"I am in touch with another world," Chumak told me. He dug his hand into a garbage bag and pulled out one of his "countless" telegrams: SINCERELY GRATEFUL STOP HAD CHRONIC TACHYCARDIA AND GASTRITIS STOP DOCTORS COULDN'T CURE ME STOP NOW THANKS TO YOU I LIVE WITHOUT MEDICINE STOP THANKS SERGEI OF NOVOCHERKASSK

I followed Chumak as he rode the elevator downstairs and stepped out into his building's parking lot to heal a crowd of a few hundred people. This was a biweekly event, weather depending. A big crowd had gathered. Some of the people held up pictures of their sick children or parents, in hopes that the healer could radiate his energy through the photographic medium. Chumak stood on the steps and invited all to gather around and feel his aura. He had only one warning: he could not cure any former functionaries of the Communist Party.

"Their souls are already too hardened," he said.

Kashpirovsky, of course, regarded Chumak as "a quack" and himself as above all this common magic. He was the *über* doctor, a secular priest of mind and body. "I've outgrown the title of 'doctor,'" he said one night backstage before a séance. "That's child's play. It's not healing. I have a Great Idea. But I'm not pushing religion. What good does it do if Jesus walked on water two thousand years ago? What does it do for these people?" He rubbed his chin and wondered where his marvelous gift came from. "The spiritual power that drove Jesus Christ very possibly exists within me," he said, "and, in fifty years, I think I will be remembered as a saint."

Kashpirovsky trained as a psychologist in Vinnitsa, a provincial city in Ukraine, and worked in a hospital there for twenty-eight years. He earned a tiny salary, and to earn 100 rubles a month extra, he worked at night loading trucks with cement and lumber. For a while he was a fanatical weight lifter and boxer, and even now, in his early fifties, he was physically vain, claiming,

"I can beat any champion of the world." But in 1975, Kashpirovsky said, he had severe pancreatic disorders and nearly died. He spent a year in a hospital in Ukraine and then decided to go to Sakhalin, where he wandered the island, like Saint John the Baptist, eating one cookie a day. "Thanks to my hunger," he said, "I was cured."

It was only in 1988 that Kashpirovsky began his public experiments in hypnosis and mass healing. He held five tele-séances in Kiev and, he claimed, cured thousands of children of bedwetting. His technique was as obscure then as now, a talking cure in which the healer somehow sets right the organic balance of the body. "Happiness and sadness have some sort of material basis, biochemical substances behind them. When I am afraid, I have a lot of adrenaline. When I'm depressed, I have more," he said, beginning a lecture of sorts. "The gates open up inside of you and you accept information. You don't know how those gates open—that's my method—the information comes in, but because you don't know how it comes in, it can't get out. I reach beyond the mind, into the innermost being, to heal the body. The mark is left."

In 1988, the head of Soviet television was Mikhail Nenashev, a doltish apparatchik who told his aides that the primary aim of television was to soothe and reassure the troubled masses. In Kashpirovsky, who had strong support from people high up in the Ukrainian Communist Party organization, Nenashev found his soothing and reassuring voice. He signed him up for séances that were broadcast in 1989 not only in the Soviet Union, but in Bulgaria, Poland, Israel, Czechoslovakia, and Scandinavia. "In a country where you can't even find aspirin, you begin hoping for a miracle," said Yelena Chekalova, a television critic for *Moscow News.* "Then along comes this man and he offers you an easy way out, a miracle. It's a phenomenon inherent in a poor and miserable country." Leonid Parfyonov, a well-known broadcaster, said, "Kashpirovsky's role has been similar to Gorbachev's role in '85 and '86. They even have common gestures. They both come up with tremendous patches of meaninglessness in their speeches, and yet they were mesmerizing and inspired confidence."

Kashpirovsky's most theatrical bit of psychic trickery came in a "telebridge" between Kiev and the Georgian capital, Tbilisi. A woman named Lesya Yershova needed a major abdominal operation at a Tbilisi hospital. Rejecting ordinary anesthesia, she allowed Kashpirovsky to hypnotize her, via television from Kiev. The resulting tape, a split-screen extravangnza, was grotesque.

"Just close your eyes and sing 'The Poplar Tree,' " Kashpirovsky tells the poor woman. The poor woman actually squeezes out a few wobbly notes.

"Close your eyes! You're floating!" Kashpirovsky says. "You have no pain

from your stomach to your spine! Close those eyes! . . . Yes, yes, you do feel the surgical instruments in your body, but you feel normal. Soon everything will be all right! People will ask me later if you are asleep. Are you?"

"No," she says meekly. "I feel someone doing something to my body." Indeed they are. The operation requires a forty-centimeter incision.

When it is over, Kashpirovsky tells the audience, "Now all of you who have watched me can go to the dentist and get a tooth pulled. There will be no pain at all. I assure you."

Kashpirovsky claimed he had made medical—"no, spiritual!"—history with that performance. But then the patient rebelled. Lesya Yershova told reporters that, in fact, she had been in "monstrous pain" during the operation and had cooperated only because she "didn't want to let Kashpirovsky down."

Yuri Savenko, the president of the Independent Psychiatric Association, said the Ministry of Health's cooperation in Kashpirovsky's broadcasts was an outrage and part of a broader bread-and-circuses conspiracy engineered by the Communist Party. He was far from alone in believing that the Party was using the broadcasts to divert the attentions and sorrows of the people. "With the Russian people," he said, "Christianity is superficial. They are largely pagan. They observe rituals without understanding the essence. Under the political situation today, mysticism increases, and with such a low cultural level it acquires outrageous forms." Savenko said that one of his colleagues had "firm data" proving that Kashpirovsky's séances had not only done nothing to heal people of their ills, they also caused some Russians to have psychotic episodes. But there was no investigation. Journalists and doctors alike had a difficult time attacking a figure so popular that he won Man of the Year honors in various newspapers in 1990 and had a following no politician or movie star could match. Savenko said that some of his psychologist and psychiatrist "friends" were reduced to pranks: "I know some people made fun of Kashpirovsky by sending him cables saying things like 'Thanks to you, my amputated stump has grown five centimeters longer.' Then they waited for him to read them out in public as a testimonial."

On tour, Kashpirovsky packed concert halls, factory courtyards, and even soccer stadiums. His videocassettes were passed hand to hand the way Solzhenitsyn's manuscripts once were. In the provinces, where very few people had VCRs, video salons and movie theaters organized Kashpirovsky Nights and showed the great man's tapes. As a businessman, he was not altogether happy with this underground trafficking. At the beginning of one tape put together in the United States, the usual FBI warning that it is a crime

to copy the tape dissolved into Kashpirovsky's own message: "Warning! Duplicating this tape will result in losing its medical properties!"

I saw Kashpirovsky in Moscow and on his world tour in the West. It was always the same scene, a mix of spooky New Age and Beatlemania. One night in New York, at a school in the Pelham Parkway section of the Bronx, Kashpirovsky hid in a corner, trying to avoid the stares of the bulky, perfumed émigré babushkas as they filed into the auditorium. The healer was in an awful mood. A few nights before in Queens he had had a good time of it. The adulation level was just right. "I believe in you like a god," one woman told him. "Someone should blow up your enemies. Thank God that you were delivered to us. You are a god on earth." Another man threw away his cane and started limping joyously around the apron of the stage, yelping his thanks in Russian. Kashpirovsky accepted all this as his due. He feigned boredom. Sure there was a "cult of Kashpirovsky," Kashpirovsky allowed, but it wasn't "as if I'm going to tell them to blow up a nuclear power station. . . . You shouldn't be afraid of a repeat of Stalin or something."

But now, Kashpirovsky wore the collapsed look of the doomed. He was sure everything would go wrong. His manager, Mikhail Zimmerman, darted around like a wasp, frantic to know why the microphone crackled with static, why his star was so riddled with gloom. "Anatoly Mikhailovich is like a great instrument," Zimmerman said. "Sometimes he is just not in tune."

Kashpirovsky was feeling the despair of all self-declared prophets. The world, the very universe, was not prepared for his wonderfulness. "Humankind is not ready yet to be saved," he said. "There is not yet the technique. Imagine that everyone is healthy, no one is dying, and people keep reproducing. Where will they go? The other planets aren't inhabitable yet. It's some kind of law."

Once he was on stage, Kashpirovsky gave it a valiant try but never caught the groove. Never mind the inadequate universe; hell, as Robert Frost said, is a half-filled auditorium. He was angry at the middling ticket sales. He was used to 300 million on TV and 25,000 live, and now he had three hundred, if he was lucky. He recited his accomplishments and theories with all the tricked-up enthusiasm of a guy selling toupees on late-night television. Then the testimonials began. A woman's neck no longer had its crick. Hallelujah. Another woman's rheumatism was gone, her gray hair had darkened. "I feel like thirty, not sixty," she said. She looked seventy. Kashpirovsky hardly acknowledged the miracles he had wrought. He had his eye on the clock on the back wall, and, after a decent interval, he declared it time for the real séance, the synthesizer music and the purring into the microphone, the healing. But even this, his centerpiece, wilted.

As he strolled up and down the aisle, Kashpirovsky spotted people who had not closed their eyes, others who fidgeted in their seats.

"Don't look at me!" he shouted at one woman. "You're irritating me! Turn away from me!"

As he turned away, the music swelled, and Kashpirovsky reddened: "Where did you get that music?!" he barked at his assistant at the mixing board. "This is not human music! This is the sort of music they play at the May Day parade! Quieter! Turn it down!"

When it was over, Kashpirovsky waited at the lip of the stage as grandmothers and mothers and children all rushed at him in a frantic grab for the star's handshake and his healing glance. A few tried to corner him and describe their cancers, their migraines and tumors. "Look, I'm not an ordinary doctor," he answered in a huff. "Don't address me with your concrete illnesses." Sometimes when the ailing and the weak approached him with their ills, their pains, Kashpirovsky was even more specific.

"Take a couple of pills," he said.

CHAPTER 18

THE LAST GULAG

The country in which my books are printed will not be the same country that exiled me. And to that country I will certainly return.

—ALEKSANDR SOLZHENITSYN

On a summer afternoon in 1988, Yelena Chukovskaya was leading a tour through the small museum in the village of Peredelkino dedicated to the life and work of her grandfather, the children's-book writer and eminent literary scholar Kornei Chukovsky. One of the tourists fixed on a small photograph of Solzhenitsyn, a friend of the family. "Why doesn't Solzhenitsyn just come home?" the tourist asked. "What is he waiting for?"

Yelena was stunned. "I could not believe how naive, how unknowing, the question was," she told me. "And the younger people, they just had no idea who Solzhenitsyn was. A generation had already gone by since his exile, and he'd become little more than a legend to them, almost forgotten in his own country."

By that summer, Gorbachev's glasnost had already opened the door to

many of the "anti-Soviet" classics: Anna Akhmatova's *Requiem,* Mikhail Bulgakov's *Heart of a Dog,* Boris Pasternak's *Doctor Zhivago,* Vasily Grossman's *Life and Fate.* After a comic court case, the government even let Nabokov's *Lolita* go through. But nothing of Solzhenitsyn. The Politburo would not sanction it. I asked Yegor Ligachev, Gorbachev's conservative rival, about Solzhenitsyn, and he made it plain that the Politburo felt, for a long time, that it could not tolerate a writer—especially a living, exiled writer—who considered the entire reign of the Communist Party an unmitigated crime and catastrophe. Ligachev wanted me to know that he was no critic but he knew obscenity when he read it. Ligachev was in charge of presenting a report to the Politburo on Solzhenitsyn, and he portrayed himself as the put-upon Party apparatchik, staying up night after night at home reading through the entire oeuvre, from *One Day in the Life of Ivan Denisovich* to the historical volumes known as *The Red Wheel.*

"You know that adds up to a lot of pages," he said proudly.

It was Solzhenitsyn's merciless portrait of Lenin as a fanatical revolutionary, as the originator of a system based on state terror, that most disturbed Ligachev and, for a time, Gorbachev himself. "After all, Lenin is ours!" Ligachev said. "We adhere to his viewpoint, to Leninism, and we must defend him."

But why should the Politburo decide instead of the reader? I asked.

Ligachev grimaced and waved the question away in disgust. After all, it had always been so. It was Khrushchev himself, after a long day's reading in 1962, who gave the word that *One Day in the Life of Ivan Denisovich* could be published in *Novy Mir.* And it was also Khrushchev who led the campaign against Pasternak. It was the Party's absolute right to decide.

"We have sacred things, just as you do," Ligachev said dryly.

But why use censorship to enforce it?

"Okay, pardon me, but we have a different psychology, a different worldview," he said, his voice rising. "I respect you and you should respect me. For me, Lenin is sacred."

A few days after the incident at the museum in Peredelkino, Yelena Chukovskaya sat down at her desk determined to "do something—and fast." She wrote a brief article outlining the facts of Solzhenitsyn's life and appealing to the government to return his citizenship. Then she sent it to *Book Review,* a weekly with a good reputation among the intelligentsia. The act seemed natural to Yelena, an extension of family tradition. Her mother, Lydia Chukovskaya, set an example in the 1970s when she went before the Writers' Union and, at great risk, swore to it that despite its evil denunciations,

Solzhenitsyn would return to Russia. For her troubles, Lydia Chukovskaya was denounced and *Sofia Petrovna,* her extraordinarily personal novel about the purges, banned. Now Yelena was picking up the battle. Just hours after receiving the piece, the editor of *Book Review,* Yevgeny Overin, took an enormous risk. He accepted the article for the August 5 issue on "editor's responsibility," an extraordinary step meaning that he did not wait for clearance from the censors.

Yelena Chukovskaya's piece was an immediate sensation. Thousands of letters and telegrams of support arrived at her door and at *Book Review*'s ramshackle offices. Officials in the Central Committee reported that they, too, started getting more and more mail demanding the rehabilitation of Solzhenitsyn and his works. Chukovskaya's article and the response to it were signals, hints of what was politically possible and morally necessary. Other publications quickly took the cue. The editors of *Rabochoye Slovo* ("Worker's Word"), an obscure newsletter for Ukrainian railway workers, acted first, becoming the first aboveground publication to print Solzhenitsyn for nearly three decades. On October 18, the paper's 45,500 subscribers heard the old vatic voice, Solzhenitsyn's appeal to the young from 1974, the year he was exiled, to "Live Not by Lies":

"Let us admit it: we have not matured enough to march into the squares and shout the truth out loud, or to express openly what we think. It is not necessary. It is dangerous. But let us refuse to say what we do not think. This is our path, the easiest and most accessible one, which allows for our inherent, deep-rooted cowardice."

From his home in Cavendish, Vermont, Solzhenitsyn tried to manage the terms of his return. The editors of *Novy Mir* talked with him by phone and telegram and asked for permission to publish the two early novels, *Cancer Ward* and *First Circle.* Solzhenitsyn refused, insisting instead they they publish *The Gulag Archipelago* before any other of his books. Not only was *Gulag* his monument to the millions of victims of the Soviet regime, it was also the book, when it was published abroad, that hastened his arrest and his forced exile to the West. Solzhenitsyn's demand was also a way of attacking in the quickest way possible the latest official version of the Soviet past. Unlike the Gorbachevian scheme of socialism-gone-errant, of blaming all sins on Stalin, Solzhenitsyn's three-volume "literary investigation" argued that the forced labor camp system was no aberration, but began instead with Lenin.

The editors agreed to Solzhenitsyn's demand. Now they had to deal with something only slightly less intimidating: the Communist Party. At first, *Novy Mir*'s editors thought they could somehow ignore the Party and slip Solzhenitsyn into the pages of the magazine, as if through a hidden door.

On the back cover of *Novy Mir*'s October 1988 issue, the editors printed

a cryptic announcement, saying merely that Solzhenitsyn had given them permission to publish "some of his works" beginning in 1989. But the Central Committee's ideological department, which certainly had its informers at the *Izvestia* plant where *Novy Mir* was printed, quickly suppressed the plan. In the middle of the night, the printers got a firm "stop work" order from an anonymous official in the ideological department of the Central Committee. "The printers were indignant," said Vadim Borisov, the editor at *Novy Mir* who was working most closely with Solzhenitsyn. "They felt great respect for glasnost, democracy, and the name of Solzhenitsyn. They were furious and invited reporters from the newspapers and television to come to the print shop to see what had happened. But no one came." The printers were forced to pulp more than a million covers and print new ones—without the Solzhenitsyn announcement. Only a few subscribers, mainly in Ukraine, got the journal as it was originally printed.

Not long after, Vadim Medvedev, who had replaced Ligachev as the chief Party ideologist in a shift in the leadership, attacked Solzhenitsyn for his "disdain" of Lenin and the Soviet system. *The Gulag Archipelago* and *Lenin in Zurich,* he told reporters at a news conference, "undermine the foundations on which our present life rests."

That foundation, however, was crumbling fast. The momentum of glasnost, fueled now by the publications of Solzhenitsyn in *Book Review, Worker's Word,* and other journals, as well as by rumors of the *Novy Mir* incident, could not be contained or ignored. *Novy Mir* was well positioned to press the issue. The editor in chief, Sergei Zalygin, was a contradictory figure, an elfin man in his seventies who had "played the game" in the Brezhnev years, constantly compromising principles to stay afloat. Like Len Karpinsky at *Moscow News* or Vitaly Korotich at *Ogonyok,* Zalygin had much to regret. But he saw glasnost "as my last chance," he told me. He would try now to right a great wrong. Zalygin adopted a strategy of defiant persistence. For six months running, he kept including Solzhenitsyn's Nobel Prize lecture in the galleys for the next issue—and for six months, the censors kept removing it. Aleksandr Tvardovsky, a legendary figure during the thaw, had used the same strategy when he ran *Novy Mir* in the sixties. Zalygin also made his rounds, campaigning quietly for publication with various members of the Politburo, including Gorbachev himself. Zalygin knew there were sharp ideological divisions in the leadership—especially on questions of history and glasnost—and he was prepared to wait for his opportunity. He knew, most of all, that Gorbachev was in an extremely difficult position. Many members of his earliest constituency, the middle class and the intelligentsia, were growing impatient, disillusioned with reform. Any further resistance to publishing Solzhenitsyn could only damage his popularity further.

But as an avowed Leninist, a "committed Communist" dependent on the support of the Party apparatus, Gorbachev also had to find a graceful way to change the policy and, at the same time, keep his distance from a writer who despised the system.

On a June afternoon in 1989, Medvedev summoned Zalygin to his office at the Central Committee. The meeting, *Novy Mir*'s Vadim Borisov told me, was "extremely unpleasant," and gave Zalygin the distinct impression that the delay in publishing Solzhenitsyn could be indefinite. The next day, the Politburo gathered for its usual Thursday meeting. To the surprise of some Politburo members, Gorbachev broached the "Solzhenitsyn problem." He suggested that the Soviet Writers' Union meet and decide the issue for themselves.

The *Novy Mir* contingent did not know what to expect of the union, an organization famous for its cowardice. Many of the leaders who still ran the union headed the smear campaigns against Solzhenitsyn in the early 1970s which led to his exile. Zalygin and Borisov settled uneasily into their seats at the Central House of Writers.

The first speaker was the union first secretary, Vladimir Karpov, a veteran toady of the regime. Karpov was one of those hack novelists who, in return for unstinting obedience, won huge printings for his books, a large apartment, and a dacha in the shade. Just a year before, Karpov had told reporters at a news conference that Solzhenitsyn would never be welcomed back in the Soviet Union if he did not renounce his views: "If someone wants to come back to take part in our reform process, then he is welcome. But if a person has lied through his teeth and slandered our country from abroad and wants to come back and do the same from here, then there is no place for him." Surely, Karpov would do the Kremlin's bidding, Zalygin thought. But what would that bidding be?

"Comrades," Karpov began, "we used to think one way about Aleksandr Isayevich, but now things have changed. . . ."

Borisov felt his entire body lighten with happiness. The long wait was over. Solzhenitsyn's Nobel lecture appeared in the July 1989 issue of *Novy Mir* along with an announcement that the first of several installments of *The Gulag Archipelago* would appear in August. The state-run publishing house, Sovetsky Pisatel, announced that it would issue a multivolume *Collected Works.* After long exile, Solzhenitsyn had returned.

A few days after I got the first "Solzhenitsyn issue" of *Novy Mir* in the mail, I went with my friend Lev Timofeyev to see a theatrical version of *One Day in the Life of Ivan Denisovich* at the Independent Studio. There were no ads,

no posters around town. The Independent Studio group was a poor, obscure troupe working out of a dank basement just around the corner from one of the most ominous buildings in Moscow: 38 Petrovka, the headquarters of the Interior Ministry police.

Backstage, I met with the lead actor, Yuri Kosikh. His head was shaved clean and he was dressed in his costume, the filthy padded jackets that prisoners wore in the camps throughout the Stalin era. Could it be that labor camp prisoners, like eccentric English colonels or French roués, were now "characters" on the Moscow stage?

Kosikh was quick to say, however, that the play was not distant to him. In rehearsals, he heard the voice of his father ringing in his head. His father had spent ten years in the labor camps of Kolyma. "I've played Chekhov, Shakespeare, every kind of role," Kosikh said. "But never has it come so smoothly. It's as if I'd internalized the being of Ivan Denisovich through my father."

Like the novella, the play began with five-o'clock reveille and ended with Ivan Denisovich falling asleep "fully content." And as in the novella, Kosikh's Ivan spends a day—one of hundreds—filled with petty humiliations, brutalities, and small triumphs of the spirit. The set was dreary, barbed wire draped over heating ducts, dirt scattered in clumps on the concrete floor. The light flickered weakly, even at "midday," like winter afternoons in Siberia.

The production was sometimes overwrought, but, all the same, Lev was deeply moved. He idolized Solzhenitsyn. Lev spent more than two years in the labor camp at Perm in the Urals—more than six months of that time in an isolation cell. He was a Gorbachev-era prisoner who was released only during the "amnesty wave" following Sakharov's return to Moscow from Gorky and the superpower summit in Reykjavik. No writer meant more to him than Solzhenitsyn. He had read *Gulag* in an underground edition, and just the memory of certain passages about the spiritual life of the prisoner helped sustain him throughout his own term. "Aleksandr Isayevich leveled the telling blow against the system," he said. "*The Gulag Archipelago* is the criminal and spiritual indictment of a sick society."

Onstage, Ivan Denisovich was falling asleep. There was darkness for a while, then the dawn of the house lights at half power and a stunned, desultory applause. The people in the audience finally rose to their feet, everyone weary and stretching, stunned to be in a theater and thinking, suddenly, of ordinary things: the walk home and how to buy some milk and bread for breakfast. But the feeling stayed with Lev for hours. As we walked down the street, he said, "That smell. Even that smell of wet leather and wet wool and sweat is the smell of the camps. It takes me back."

By 1990, political prisoners became a new breed of politician. In Ukraine, nationalists looked to former "politicals" to lead them: Bogdan and Mikhail Horyn, Stepan Khamara, Vyacheslav Chernovil. I met the philologist Levon Ter-Petrossian in Yerevan a week after he was released from prison; two years later he was elected president of Armenia. Georgia adored the former political prisoner Merab Kostava, and then mourned him endlessly after he was killed in a car crash. A far lesser man, Zviad Gamsakhurdia, filled the gap. Gamsakhurdia was a paranoiac, an untrustworthy fool, but he was, after all, a comrade to Kostava. That was his selling point. He would be elected Georgian president and then chased out of Tbilisi in a coup d'etat. Sakharov's protégé the biologist Sergei Kovalev, a prisoner in the Urals for many years, became a key leader in the Russian parliament. As a deputy, he suddenly found himself in a suit touring prison sites and instructing the commandants in the rudiments of decency and human rights.

According to the main human rights organizations in the Soviet Union and in the West, the last island of the gulag, the last outpost for political prisoners, was a camp in the Ural Mountains called Perm-35. Anatoly Shcharansky, Vladimir Bukovsky, Sergei Grigoryants, Timofeyev, and Kovalev had all spent time in Perm. Now the number of political prisoners had become so small that some of the Perm camps closed and were consolidated into just one, Perm-35.

Perm was a classic Soviet city—that is, an urban mass indistinguishable from hundreds of others, with a Lenin Avenue and broad and pitted streets and apartment blocks so ugly and uniform that you could weep looking at them. For a long time, Perm was closed to foreign journalists. Like many cities in the Urals, it was a center for military production. But now Perm was open, and getting to the camp turned out to be no problem at all. Accompanied by a local journalist I had gotten to know in Moscow, I paid a call on the chief of police. The Interior Ministry in the region was thoroughly bored by then with occasional visits by journalists or members of Congress. Colonel Andrei Votinov, the man in charge, was just a harmless wise guy. He wanted me to tell him why "in God's name" I wanted to drive for hours to see "a rathole." And after I explained my worthy reasons, I asked what conditions were like at Perm-35.

"You'll see," he said. "It's just like Switzerland."

I was told to return to my hotel and wait.

At eight the next morning, Major Nikolai Dronin, an unsmiling officer of the law, rapped on my door.

"So now we go to prison," he said.

It was a four-hour drive to Perm-35 from the city, but I was happy for the boredom. In Moscow, and even on trips to other republican capitals, it was easy to lose the sense of the vastness of the country. Out here it was easier to understand how so many hundreds of islands in the gulag archipelago could go unseen, tucked away in forests and mining villages and on mountaintops. All the banalities of the size of the Soviet Union—the eleven time zones, the number of times you could fit France into Kazakhstan, etc.—took on real meaning just by driving hour after hour. In the Urals, as in so many other places, Russia seemed like an unending frontier, wild and huge with only occasional settlements, hastily built towns, unlivable places where tens of millions of people lived, not villages so much as population clusters, work forces built around workplaces: lumber works, chemical plants, coal mines. All along the road, we saw peasant men riding wooden carts heaped with coal, humpbacked women carting their heavy sacks down the road. We could have driven for a week or more to the east and seen little else.

Finally there was a turnoff, primitive and unmarked. "The road to Perm-35," the major said.

My host would be Lieutenant Colonel Nikolai Osin, who had been running the camp since it went up in 1972. Shcharansky, Bukovsky, Marchenko, Stus, Orlov, Timofeyev: they all knew Osin. Shcharansky, especially, remembered his eyes, the dull gleam in the ruddy meat of his face. "Osin was an enormous, flabby man," Shcharansky wrote, "with small eyes and puffy eyelids, who seemed to have long ago lost interest in everything but food. . . . But he was a master of intrigue who had successfully overtaken many of his colleagues on the road to advancement. . . . I could see that he enjoyed his power over the prisoners and liked to see them suffer. But he never forgot that the zeks—the prisoners—were, above all, a means for advancing his career, and he knew how to back off in a crisis."

Once, when Shcharansky was refused permission to celebrate Hanukkah, he went on a hunger strike. Osin didn't want a scandal and cut a quick deal: if Shcharansky would end the hunger strike, he could light his Hanukkah candles. Shcharansky agreed, but demanded that while he said the appropriate prayers, Osin would stand by with his head covered and, at the end, say "Amen."

"Blessed are You, oh Lord, for allowing me to light these candles," Shcharansky began in Hebrew. "May you allow me to light the Hanukkah candles many times in your city, Jerusalem, with my wife, Avital, and my family and friends."

Inspired by the sight of Osin, Shcharansky added, "And may the day come when all our enemies, who today are planning our destruction, will stand before us and hear our prayers and say, 'Amen.' "

"Amen," Osin repeated.

Shcharansky quickly spread the word in Perm-35 of Osin's "conversion." This meant a freezing stint in the isolation cell, but Shcharansky could not resist. Today, Shcharansky lives in freedom in Israel. After his release, his mother sorted through photographs of her son in Jerusalem. She wanted to send a little memento to Lieutenant Colonel Nikolai Makarovich Osin.

Perm-35 was a tiny place, five hundred yards square, a few barracks, guard towers and razor wire everywhere. Osin was there to greet us, and he was much as Shcharansky had described him, enormously fat with dull, pitiless eyes. We went up a flight of stairs, past a few Party propaganda posters—"Socialism Is Order!"—to his office. Osin had a broad desk and a well-padded armchair, and he affected the pose of a contented chief executive officer. He was humbled only by the size of his work force. Just sixteen men remained in his charge. The Interior Ministry was planning to get rid of the "politicals" and bring in a "full population" of common criminals: rapists, murderers, thieves.

"So it's time to retire," the commandant said, leaning back as if waiting for the gold watch. "I'll be on a pension by the end of the year."

Osin tried, but failed, to conceal his disdain for the latest turn of Soviet history, the fitful lurch toward a civil society that was making him a relic of the totalitarian past. For years, he had inflicted punishment on dissident poets, priests, and mathematicians. He was, to use the Stalinist accolade, an exemplary "cog in the wheel." He did what he was told, "and all the prisoners were the same to me." Equal under lawlessness.

"You know, they talk about political prisoners, but there were never any political prisoners here," Osin said. "There were laws, and they were convicted on those laws, and that was it. They betrayed their Motherland. Later, the laws changed, but that's something else." There was no hint of repentance, or even self-doubt. "What do I have to regret?" he said. "People were sent here under the law, and I did what I was told to do. This was the work I chose, and I did it. This is what was required of me. I think the prisoners here have better living conditions than some people who are free. They have meat, after all." At this, Osin grabbed his belly and shook with laughter. He was a card.

Osin was not completely out of work, of course. The courts were still capable of indulging the political intrigues of local and regional Communist Party bosses, and, of all the branches of government, the judicial system has probably been touched least by reform. But most of the remaining cases were not, in the jargon of monitoring groups, "pure" political cases. In fact,

Gorbachev and the administration at Perm-35 claimed that there were no political prisoners in the country at all. "Most of the remaining cases are mixed—people who tried to flee the country illegally, people with ambiguous contacts with foreign groups," said Sergei Kovalev, a former political prisoner who eventually became the chairman of the human rights committee in the Russian parliament. "What I'm mainly working on is the length of their terms. People with ten, fifteen years in a camp for trying to row a raft to Turkey is absurd."

Like a good host at a housewarming party, Osin rose from behind his desk and said, "So! Let's give you the tour!"

Osin's tour, with an emphasis on the quality of the paint job and the cleanliness of the floors and toilet, was significant insofar as we saw no prisoners.

"They're off at work," Osin said.

When will they be back? I asked.

"Let's have lunch," Osin said.

And so we did, a meal beyond the imagination of the prisoners—cabbage soup, brown bread, salad, chicken, mashed potatoes, fruit juice. Then, like hurried tourists, we were off for more touring. We saw the infirmary. We saw the barracks where the men slept. But suddenly, as Osin was demonstrating the firmness of the camp beds, a pasty, middle-aged man with a shaved head and wearing prisoner coveralls burst through a door and down the hall, screaming.

"I must talk with you! They are beating me!"

"Yasin," Osin said glumly, his eyes still on the mattress. The commandant pursed his lips. His neck turned crimson.

"I must talk to you!" Yasin said. The guards tried to wrestle him back down the hall and into a room where they had been keeping the prisoners. I asked Osin if it would be all right to talk to the man, fully identified later as Valery Yasin. The commandant rolled his eyes and made a signal with his hand to suggest that Yasin was mentally unbalanced and not worth listening to. Still, Osin said, "Bring him back in."

The guards led Yasin back into the room. He was out of breath and his skin was pale and damp. He had been in and out of prisons, mental hospitals, and camps like Perm-35 for more than fifteen years. He had been accused of fleeing the country illegally, consorting with foreign intelligence. His term was set to run until the year 2003. Yasin's case, according to an official at Helsinki Watch, was murky—"the political and the criminal aspects are all tangled, confusing." There was, however, no doubting Yasin's fury. His words tumbled out between gasps for breath.

"For seven years I refused to go out for walks or to go out to the street.

This was my protest. I also demanded to stay alone in a one-man cell. I was in despair, sure I would be killed. They beat me. They demanded evidence that the KGB needed. They wanted me to cooperate with them and said that otherwise I'd be left to die here.

"I was desperate and slashed my arm. I was beaten and put in an isolation cell. This was in February. I lost one and a half liters of blood. I was half dead, and in this state I was dragged into the isolation cell, which was extremely cold, and they threw me in there naked. This was the order of Lieutenant Colonel Osin."

Osin, sitting nearby, rolled his eyes. He said nothing. A guard near the door spoke: "Let him say why he cut his veins!"

"I have a written document stating why I cut my veins," Yasin said. "They did barbaric things. On December 10, Human Rights Day, they forcibly shaved off my hair. I was beaten, my hands were twisted, my arms were twisted. This is how they celebrate Human Rights Day here."

The guard said, "You can only grow hair three months prior to release. How long until your release?"

"My hair was already short," Yasin said.

"If someone passes a new law, then maybe we won't shave your hair," the guard said. "Until then, if you don't get it cut voluntarily, then we'll do it by force."

Osin was silent.

Yasin was sweating. "So, this is how they abide by the law," he said. "They put handcuffs on people and beat people, under the pretext that the guy will resist. People are forced to submit to this humiliating procedure. All over the world, when your head is shaved bald, it is considered a humiliation."

With an imperial wave of the hand, Osin signaled the guard to lead Yasin out of the room. I asked to talk to a few more of the prisoners. Osin rolled his eyes, but agreed. The first man I asked to see was Yuri Pavlov, who had been sentenced to seven years on charges of espionage for the United States. The man I met did not seem capable of dialing the United States on the telephone. He was lethargic and distant and admitted to some sort of "brain injury." I asked him about the treatment of prisoners in Perm, and he said mechanically, "There are changes for the better. I remember how it was before, and I can compare with the present. When I was in Perm-36 with Timofeyev it was much worse. Now my complaints are mostly medical." Pavlov asked to be remembered to Timofeyev and walked slowly out the door.

Then the guard brought in the last prisoner on my list, Vitaly Goldovitch, a physicist who had worked in defense research and had been charged with treason and other crimes when he tried to row a rubber raft across the Black

Sea to Turkey. Goldovitch was nervous, his hands fluttering at his sides. Months passed with no visitors, no company except the guards and his fellow prisoners. No one had told him a reporter was coming, and now the words, half-pronounced, flew out of him. To try to calm him, I repeated what Pavlov had told me, that the treatment had gotten better lately. But Goldovitch said that was nonsense, that he was still manhandled and berated.

All the same, he said, "I'm trying to see the human being under the guards' uniforms. I can see that some of them may be good people, but they are crushed psychologically. There are almost no free people in the Soviet Union." Osin listened to all this with bored amusement. Once more he twirled his index finger around his ear, signaling that the charge was mere fantasy, craziness. Who would believe such a thing could happen in Perm-35?

As we left Goldovitch, I asked Osin to see the "isolators," the punishment cells. Nearly everyone in Perm-35, nearly every political prisoner in the history of the Soviet Union for that matter, had spent time in such places.

"Is this really necessary?" Osin asked.

Still, Osin walked outside in a huff, opened a huge gate, and pointed to a small field covered with snow and mud. There were rusted soccer goals at either end of the field. "Recreational facilities," he said angrily. "Here we let them play soccer, volleyball, whatever. I don't suppose they have that in prisons where you live, do they?"

Osin opened the door to a shed with a narrow hall and a series of tiny cells—the punishment cells. For now—perhaps for the benefit of the day's visitor—they were empty. Each one had a wooden plank for a bed. "See?" Osin said. "Not so terrible." In our talk, Goldovitch had said he spent more than a year in a punishment cell after a rebellion in Perm-35 in 1989. Some prisoners had refused to work, attend roll calls, or wear their names on their shirts. "We refused to do everything that was required as if we were soldiers of the army," he said. "We wanted to make this revolt in compliance with the law, in the framework of the law. Nine people ended up in the isolation cells after that.

"It is very hard but you get used to it. The cell is three meters long, one meter wide, two meters high. The cell is like your clothes. You are very cold, but in three days your body heat keeps you warmer. You walk around all day, don't sleep, look for some trifles, like filling the cracks with paper, to avoid going crazy. Or you wash your handkerchief over and over again. You think a lot and it helps."

Osin slammed shut the door to the cell and led me to our car. He said good-bye and did not smile.

During the ride back to the city, Major Dronin got to talking about politics, about the "lawlessness" in the country these days.

"There will be a dictatorship soon," he said with a certain relish in his voice. "It won't be the Communist Party organs, it will be the real organs—the KGB. They will try to develop the economy, but there will be a strict discipline."

As in Stalin's day? I asked.

"No, that was too harsh," he said. "But maybe as it was under Brezhnev or Andropov."

Dronin stared out the car window as the camp disappeared into the milky fog behind us. His eyes were open, but he seemed to be dreaming.

PART III

REVOLUTIONARY DAYS

CHAPTER 19

"TOMORROW THERE WILL BE A BATTLE"

The facts of history evolve into the mythologies of history, but I had never realized just how quickly. Everything I was watching in Moscow, Vilnius, Siberia, and beyond instantly transcended "the facts"—the meetings, the demonstrations, the newspaper accounts, the transcripts and videotape. No part of the narrative, no conflict or uprising, was without its mythic dimension: the revenge drama of Gorbachev-and-Yeltsin, the David-and-Goliath drama of Lithuania-and-the Kremlin, the ironic drama of the coal miner proletariat. Most mythic of all was the presence of a saint among the foolish and the vain, among the insulted and injured. Sakharov was the founder of fire (the hydrogen bomb) who renounced his gift; who dedicated himself to the rescue of the Land of Nod when rescue seemed quixotic; who returned from exile to reveal his wisdom and prod the czar.

But there was the man, too, and, by the end of 1989, Sakharov looked as though he had wrung the last ounce of blood and energy from his body. He was sixty-eight and his face was delicate as parchment. He spoke in a slurred mumble. He had trouble walking up more than seven or eight stairs before gasping for breath; he was stooped, listing a little to the right. And yet the demands on his time and energy only increased. There were more visitors now to the apartment on Chkalova Street than there had been in the seventies

when Sakharov's kitchen table was the crossroads of the human rights movement. Now no one had reason to be afraid to come, and so they all did, reporters, filmmakers, friends, foreigners on the make, acolytes, deputies, scholars from abroad.

In bringing home Sakharov from Gorky, an act that met with much grumbling in the Party nomenklatura, Gorbachev felt himself to be the kind and benevolent czar. He was proud. But Sakharov refused to indulge Gorbachev's vanity. Even in that first telephone conversation from Gorky, he quickly reminded Gorbachev of the death of one political prisoner, his dear friend Anatoly Marchenko, and then pressed for the release of a long list of others. Sakharov did what saints do; he lightly complimented the czar when he did right, but never let him relax. Sakharov's support was conditional; his decisions were based not on intra-Party realities—though he understood them well—but on a set of moral standards that could be etched on two small tablets of stone.

Sakharov respected Gorbachev as a brave politician, but he was not in awe of him. During the first session of the Congress, Gorbachev had given Sakharov the floor immediately and often, but when Sakharov tried to press Gorbachev into endorsing a "decree on power" that would end the Communist Party's guaranteed ascendancy, Gorbachev's response was haughty disdain. Saints annoy, and Sakharov annoyed Gorbachev profoundly. Even the transcript, devoid of the glares, the peremptory, bullying tone of Gorbachev's voice, showed that much:

GORBACHEV: Anyway, finish up, Andrei Dmitriyevich. You've used up two time allotments already.

SAKHAROV: I'm finishing. I am leaving out arguments. I have left out a great deal.

GORBACHEV: That's it. Your time, two time allotments, has run out. I beg your pardon. That is all.

SAKHAROV: [Inaudible]

GORBACHEV: That's all, Comrade Sakharov. Do you respect the Congress?

SAKHAROV: Yes, but I respect the country and the people even more. My mandate extends beyond the bounds of this Congress.

GORBACHEV: Good. That's all!

SAKHAROV: [Inaudible]

GORBACHEV: I ask you to finish. I ask you to conclude. That's all! Take away your speech, please! [Applause in the hall] I ask you to sit down. Turn on the other microphone.

There was part of Gorbachev that could not help but respect Sakharov, even envy him; but it rankled him, too, that the man he had deigned to release was, somehow, untouchable, uncontrollable. Sakharov seemed, somehow, to float above politics even as he was engaged in the most critical debates. When an Afghan vet attacked him and Sakharov was booed and whistled at by the hard-line majority, some viewers called in worried that Andrei Dmitriyevich would suffer a heart attack. But he was serene, absolutely serene. Perhaps it was that quality that helped drive Gorbachev to distraction. When the weekly tabloid *Argumenti i Fakti* published a poll showing that Sakharov was, by far, the most popular politician in the country, Gorbachev was incensed. He even threatened to fire the editor.

It was very simple: Sakharov represented the hard and inescapable truth. One evening during that first Congress session, Sakharov requested a private audience with Gorbachev. In his memoirs, Sakharov remembers waiting for the meeting:

"I could see the enormous hall of the Palace of Congresses, semidark and empty. There were guards at the distant doors. Finally, around a half hour later, Gorbachev came out with [his deputy, Anatoly] Lukyanov. Lukyanov had not been part of my plans, but there was nothing that could be done about it. Gorbachev looked tired, as did I. We moved three chairs to the corner of the stage at the table of the Presidium. Gorbachev was very serious throughout the conversation. His usual smile for me—half kindly, half condescending—never appeared on his face.

"I said, 'Mikhail Sergeyevich! It is not for me to tell you how serious things are in the country, how dissatisfied people are and how everyone expects things to get worse. There is a crisis of trust in the country toward the leadership and the Party. Your personal authority and popularity are down to zero. People cannot wait any longer with nothing but promises. A middle course in situations like these is almost impossible. The country and you are at a crossroads—either increase the process of change maximally or try to retain the administrative-command system with all its qualities. In the first case you must use the support of the 'left,' you can be sure there will be many brave and energetic people you can count on. In the second case, you know for yourself whose support you will have, but you will never be forgiven the attempt at perestroika."

In other words, side with the radicals, who you know are right; the Party apparatchiks, the military-industrial complex, are enemies no matter what you do. They will betray you no matter how long you coddle them. Do not delude yourself. But Sakharov could not break through to Gorbachev.

Just after the strikes broke out in Siberia, Sakharov, Yeltsin, Yuri Afana-

syev, and the economist Gavriil Popov put together a radical opposition faction in the legislature, the Inter-Regional Group. That development only increased the tensions between Gorbachev and Sakharov at the next session of the Congress in December 1989. To his credit, once more Gorbachev made a point of calling on Sakharov to speak, but when the speech was too radical, he dismissed him summarily. "That's all!" Gorbachev barked as Sakharov tried to present him with tens of thousands of telegrams sent him in support of eliminating the Party's monopoly on power. At home, Sakharov despaired so of Gorbachev's "half-measures" that he wrote out in a thick spiral notebook his own proposed constitution envisioning a Eurasian commonwealth in which participation was voluntary and the Communist Party was one among many. Just as his essays in 1968 anticipated the ideas of perestroika, his constitution envisioned what would one day seem like sense itself. ("If we had only listened more carefully to Andrei Dmitriyevich, we might have learned something," Gorbachev would say three years later.)

Late in the afternoon of December 14, the Inter-Regional Group held an open caucus at the Kremlin. Sakharov looked worn out, and he dozed off during some of the other speeches. Yeltsin would say later that Sakharov was "obviously suffering," but no one said a word at the time and the session dragged on. Sakharov delivered a typically understated speech. He said he despaired of the current policy of half-measures and an opposition force was the only way to accelerate the reform process. Gorbachev's government, he said, was "leading the country into catastrophe and dragging out the process of perestroika over many years. During this period it will leave the country in a state of collapse, intensive collapse. . . . The only way, the only possibility of an evolutionary path, is to radicalize perestroika." Once more he pressed Gorbachev to repeal Article 6 of the Constitution, which gave the Communist Party a guaranteed monopoly on power. Instead of heading home when the session was over, Sakharov agreed to meet with some Kazakh journalists at a hotel near the Kremlin for a long interview.

Back at his apartment, Sakharov told his wife, Yelena Bonner, that he was going downstairs to his study. He wanted to take a nap and then get up to write another speech. He asked Bonner to come wake him at nine. He had a lot of work to do before morning. "Tomorrow," he said, "there will be a battle."

When Bonner went downstairs to wake her husband, she found him in the hallway on the floor, dead. "The totalitarian system probably killed him," Vitaly Korotich said later. "I'm only glad that before he died Sakharov dealt the system a mortal blow. If God sent Jesus to pay for the sins of humankind, then a Marxist God somewhere sent Andrei Sakharov to pay for the sins of our system."

By nine in the morning of the 15th, as the deputies milled around in the vast foyer of the Palace of Congresses, everyone knew, was finding out, or was about to know. The men and women closest to Sakharov looked stricken. They stood alone or with friends, saying nothing, smoking and staring through the windows that looked out on the churches and spires of the Kremlin. Yuri Karyakin, the Dostoevsky scholar who had helped found the Moscow Tribune study group with Sakharov, told me the country had lost its "perfect moral compass." Yeltsin wandered the hall, loose-limbed and aimless, until a few of us asked him about Sakharov. Yeltsin seemed relieved to have a task, to deal with the cameras and the notebooks. "We must come to the end of the path that Sakharov began. Our duty is to Sakharov's name, to the persecution he suffered," he said, sounding very much like a man talking to himself.

Gorbachev, in his constant need to appeal to the majority of deputies in the room, played politics. It would take him years to admit fully to Sakharov's influence, and now he chose not even to announce the news himself or comment from the rostrum. He expressed his regrets to the liberal weekly *Moscow News,* but would not do the same in front of this audience. He lost the moment. Instead, one of the thickest men in the Politburo, Vitaly Vorotnikov, was in the chairman's seat and his gavel came down at ten o'clock. Vorotnikov stood and droned that "one of the country's greatest scientists and a prominent public figure," Andrei Dmitriyevich Sakharov, was dead. "His contribution to the defense capability of the state was great and unique," he allowed. But when it came to politics, Vorotnikov was all euphemism: "The objective analysis of various aspects of his activities is the province of history." No mention of the dissident movement or the new opposition, nothing of his moral leadership or example.

Then we all rose for a minute of silence.

From there, Gorbachev just let Vorotnikov go on with business. Members of Sakharov's circle found it astonishing that the session was not called off for the day or that the day of the funeral was not declared a day of national mourning. Ilya Zaslavsky, the thirty-year-old engineer crippled by a childhood blood disease, hobbled on his crutches to the podium. He represented the October Region of Moscow. Before the session, Zaslavsky had approached Gorbachev and asked that he declare a day of mourning in honor of Sakharov. Gorbachev refused, telling him it was "not the tradition." And so now Gorbachev knew very well what Zaslavsky wanted to say, and before the young deputy could open his mouth, Gorbachev said firmly, "Sit down!" But Zaslavsky would not move. Again, Gorbachev told him to sit. And again Zaslavsky stood his ground and waited only for the deputies to stop their murmuring and hear him out. From the side of the stage came a flunky who

tried deftly to "help" Zaslavsky down the steps. Zaslavsky cast him a withering look, the look of a boxer staring across the ring at a presumptuous opponent. The flunky slunk away. And so now Gorbachev had the choice of either forcing a young cripple to his chair for the crime of wanting to speak out for a fallen saint, or to give in. It was an amazing standoff, and even from my gallery seat, I could see (with a pair of binoculars) the fury in Gorbachev's eyes. But he gave in. Zaslavsky demanded a day of mourning, and the chairman said the suggestion would be taken under advisement. It never was.

Later, Zaslavsky told me about the encounter. "I considered it my duty not to sit down," he said. "Sometimes a person has to say his piece. Sakharov was the conscience of our country. I have admired him since childhood and I felt this was my duty to him. At the beginning of the session I approached Gorbachev and asked him to call for national mourning, but he said he could probably not do that because it would defy tradition. We have a procedure, it seems, for this: a general secretary gets three days of mourning, a Politburo member one, and none for an academician. Gorbachev said that according to precedent, there should be no such mourning. But all the other countries will be in mourning. What about us?"

Meanwhile, the hard-liners in the Congress could not restrain their scorn for Sakharov. They, too, played their part in the mythic narrative, the unbelievers, the heathen raging against the saint. They had jeered him when he was at the rostrum and now they disdained him in death. Tatyana Zaslavskaya, a sociologist who had given Gorbachev invaluable advice on public opinion before he came to power, told me she was filled with shame and disgust hearing the "mocking, filthy remarks made by the apparat" about Sakharov. When it was finally announced that the session would be suspended for a few hours on the day of the funeral, the conservatives hissed. There was hypocrisy everywhere. Tass, which had slandered Sakharov in his lifetime as a "foreign agent" and "moneygrubber," was now spitting out shameless tributes over the wires. And by the way, came one announcement, exclusive videotape of Sakharov's last days is available to foreign television stations—for $1,500, hard currency only. There were other squalid moments, too. Yevgeny Yevtushenko scurried around the Congress buffet, handing out to correspondents (in Russian and English) a copy of the poem that he had written, instantly, in honor of Sakharov. "Maybe you will print it on your editorial page?" he said.

The people of Moscow were fast turning 48 Chkalova Street into a shrine. They came alone and in groups and heaped carnations at the doorstep. Someone tacked a photograph of Sakharov to the wall, and, as if this were not icon enough, others put lighted candles and flowers around it. One of the first mourners at the building put out a thick notebook for the people to write

out messages of farewell. "We are orphans," one entry said. "Without you, there is no one to defend us and our children." "Shame on the murderers," said another. "Forgive us for all the misfortune that we caused you. Forgive us for the fact that now only good things will be said of you by those who did not do so while you were alive. Words will not help, and we did not safeguard your life. But I believe we will safeguard your memory. Forgive us."

Upstairs, Bonner was frantic with grief. With her husband's body still in the apartment, she had to go through the ordeal of planning the funeral with Gorbachev's man, Yevgeny Primakov. Finally, an ancient and humpbacked ambulance pulled up in the slush near Primakov's limousine. Three medics in dirty smocks went up to Sakharov's place. They strapped the body to a stretcher and carried him down seven flights of stairs to the car. Then Bonner had to deal with the reporters out on the stairs. She stuck her head out the door and lost it: "You all worked hard to see that Andrei died sooner by calling us from morning till night, and never leaving us to our life and work. Be human beings! Leave us alone!"

Bonner did have a terrifying temper, but she, too, had to be admired deeply. She was indispensable to Sakharov, his lion at the gate. She protected him, inspired him, and he loved her ferocity. In their human rights work, Sakharov and Bonner were a team. They suffered, physically and psychologically, as equals. The KGB harassed the Sakharovs every way they could, even mailing them "Christmas cards" with grotesque images of mutilated bodies and monkeys with electrodes stuck in their skulls. There were threats against their children and grandchildren. Tass, *Izvestia,* and *Pravda* spewed reams of slander. In Gorky, thugs broke into the apartment waving pistols. After threatening to turn the apartment "into an Afghanistan," one of the men turned to Sakharov and said, "You won't be here long. They'll take you to a sanatorium where they have medicine that turns people into idiots." A "historian" named Nikolai Yakovlev wrote a book insulting Bonner as a "sexual brigand . . . who foisted herself on the widower Sakharov." In the most memorable moment in the history of Russian chivalry, Sakharov—good, gentle Andrei Dmitriyevich—confronted Yakovlev and slapped him square in the face.

"A year ago, Yelena Georgiovna and I went to Paris together for a conference on human rights," Lev Timofeyev told Esther at the wake. "Andrei Dmitriyevich was coming from the States and had met us at the airport. They hadn't seen each other for a month and a half, and when they saw each other, their faces lit up like young newlyweds. Such clear young faces. They saw nothing except one another. All the journalists who were waiting there seemed out of place, and I felt like an interloper at a meeting of two lovers."

Primakov offered Bonner a general secretary's funeral for Sakharov. He could lie in state at the Hall of Columns across from the Kremlin—the same place where the corpses of the various Bolshevik leaders had been put on display in their time. Bonner said no. She wanted something less official, and unique to Sakharov. She chose the Palace of Youth, an enormous hall on Komsomolsky Prospekt.

The next morning it was so desolate and cold that it hurt to breathe. Esther and I picked up Flora and Misha Litvinov and some of their friends and walked along the ice to the Palace of Youth. We were an hour early for the wake and were stunned to see that a line of thousands of people had already formed. We found people in line who had flown from Leningrad, Armenia, and Siberia. There were Azeris and Crimean Tatars, teenagers and children, old men and women who suffered terribly in the cold. Some of them waited three or four hours, their faces red and chapped—but they waited.

Inside, Sakharov was laid out on a coffin festooned in red and black crepe. Within moments after the doors had opened, mountains of flowers accumulated at his feet. Yelena Georgiovna sat off to the side with her children and other family from Russia and the United States. Yeltsin, Timofeyev, Sergei Kovalev, and many others stood near the coffin as honor guards. And for the next five hours the long flow of people streamed by at a slow, unceasing step.

"Forgive us!" one woman cried out as she passed. "Forgive us, Andrei Dmitriyevich!"

Yelena Georgiovna walked over to the coffin and bent over her husband, kissed his forehead, smoothed his cheek with the back of her knuckles. She stood a long time there, her elbow draped over the coffin and her face buried in her hands.

If the day of mourning at the Palace of Youth had shown the general grief set off by Sakharov's death, the next day made clear the political dimension of his loss.

At nine-thirty on December 18, a string of black limousines pulled up to the front entrance of the Academy of Sciences building on Leninsky Prospekt. Gorbachev and a half-dozen other Politburo members got out of their cars and walked up the stairs past a banner of Lenin that read: "Under the Banner of Marxism-Leninism, the Leadership of the Communist Party, Forward Toward the Victory of Communism! Proletarians of the World, Unite!" It had gotten slightly warmer, and there was a mix of drizzle and fat snowflakes that melted when they hit the ground. A few minutes later, the funeral train arrived, a police Mercedes leading a few decrepit yellow buses. As

Sakharov's coffin was unloaded from the back of one of the buses, Bonner spoke briefly with Gorbachev and the other members of the Politburo. She told Gorbachev that with the death of Sakharov he had lost his most loyal opponent. He asked if there was anything he could do for her. Yes, she said. Memorial had still not been registered as an official national organization. It will be done, Gorbachev said.

A member of the honor guard lifted the lid of the coffin. Gorbachev took off his gray fur hat and stepped to the foot of the casket. The other members of the Politburo took off their hats and flanked their general secretary. They stood in silence for two or three minutes, all of them staring at Sakharov's pale and regal face. Someone held a black umbrella over the coffin. Then, with two quick nods of the head, as if to say, "Okay, enough," Gorbachev signaled that the moment was over. The group went inside the Academy of Sciences and signed a memorial book. The general secretary wrote "M. S. Gorbachev" in a bold script and the rest of the Politburo signed below in more modest hands.

Before Gorbachev left, a reporter asked him a question about Sakharov's Nobel Prize for Peace in 1975, an event that the Brezhnev regime had taken as a humiliating international endorsement of state treason.

"It is clear now," Gorbachev said, "that he deserved it."

Early in the afternoon, the funeral cortege slowly wended its way from the physics institute where Sakharov had once worked to the parking lot of the Luzhniki sports complex near the Moscow River. I was just a few yards behind the lead bus. The back door was open and Bonner sat on a bench next to the coffin. Yeltsin was walking just ahead of me. Even then it was clear that if anyone was going to take the lead of the political opposition, it was Yeltsin; and yet he knew that Sakharov and the people closest to Sakharov regarded him with apprehension. Yeltsin was not one of them. He was, after all, a former member of the Politburo. But while Yeltsin already had tremendous support as a populist, he wanted badly to widen his appeal, to learn from the radical democrats and to get their support. By walking just behind Sakharov's casket he was not so much grandstanding as he was keeping himself as close as possible to everything he was not, but wanted to be.

The march went on for hours. It was not until we reached Luzhniki that I could see how many people had come to say farewell to Sakharov. No fewer than fifty thousand people had packed into a vast parking lot. And there was something far more striking about the crowd than its mere size. It was the first time that I got any sense that there could ever be a unified democratic movement in the Soviet Union. Until now, the miners, the Baltic independence groups, the Moscow and Leningrad intelligentsia had all seemed spread out, loosely knit at best. But now I saw Baltic flags, a Russian tricolor,

banners supporting the Rukh independence movement in Ukraine, miners from Vorkuta, students. There were placards with a huge "6" crossed out—meaning that Article 6 of the Constitution, which guaranteed the Party's "leading role" in society, should be eliminated.

Oginsky's "Farewell to the Motherland" played through the loudspeakers. The speakers included former political prisoners—Kovalev and dissident priest Father Gleb Yakunin among them—and the politicians who would now have to begin filling in the enormous vacuum: Yeltsin, the Lithuanian independence leader Vytautas Landsbergis, the Leningrad law professor Anatoly Sobchak, Ilya Zaslavsky, Yuri Afanasyev, Gavriil Popov. Sakharov's casket was hoisted up in front of the flatbed truck where the speakers stood, and Bonner, wearing Sakharov's gray fur hat, stood near the microphone smoking cigarettes. She stepped up to speak only once, asking everyone to make room so that the ceremony would be peaceful and safe. Only a non-Soviet would have missed the reference: in the days after Stalin's death, the crowd outside the Hall of Columns was so dense and emotional that hundreds of people were crushed to death—a fitting tribute.

Dmitri Likhachev, the scholar of Russian literature and the oldest of all the deputies in the Congress, was the first to speak: "Most respected Yelena Georgiovna, relatives, friends, colleagues, and students of Andrei Dmitriyevich! Respected comrades! We are gathered here to honor the memory of a very great man, a citizen not only of our country, but of the whole world. A man of the twenty-first century, a man of the future. This is why many did not understand him in this century.

"He was a prophet, a prophet in the ancient sense of the word. That is, he was a man who summoned his contemporaries to moral renewal for the sake of the future. And like every prophet, he was not understood. He was driven from his own city."

Afanasyev said that in the future the union of democratic forces should be named for Sakharov. Father Gleb Yakunin compared Sakharov to a holy man; others mentioned Martin Luther King, Gandhi, Tolstoy. Landsbergis said that on Cathedral Square in Vilnius, church bells were ringing out in tribute to Sakharov. As they listened to the speeches, many people held candles and wept. As darkness gathered, the service broke up. The huge crowd shuffled to the metro stations and the bus stops. I have never heard so many people be so quiet.

The burial was an hour later on the outskirts of Moscow at Vostryakovskoye, a cemetery cut out of a pine forest. The snow was falling once more, and everywhere was the smell of pine and snow. A military band played Chopin's "Funeral March" and Schumann's dirge "Traumerai." Sakharov's grave, fresh and deep, was dug out next to two straight pines and the grave

of Bonner's mother, Ruf. Bonner let a cigarette drop from her hands into the wet earth. She pulled back the thin white cloth that covered Sakharov's face, kissed him one last time, covered him, and stepped away. But she could not bear it. She came back, kissed him once more, and lingered there. I was near Timofeyev, who stood at attention, tears flowing into his beard. Finally the music stopped. Two workmen closed the coffin and lowered it into the grave. Bonner threw a bit of dirt down onto the coffin. Others did the same, with dirt and pine branches still dusted with snow, and everywhere there was quiet except for the thud of the dirt and the branches on the coffin. The gravediggers filled in the hole and Bonner watched, smoking. Soon the mourners, carrying candles, covered the grave over with flowers, red carnations and yellow roses. Then they stepped back and lingered. There was nothing left to do. Once more the rain began to fall.

I felt hollow that day and for days after. I have never felt that way about anyone's death except the death of those whom I have loved. Many people I knew in Moscow felt the same, and even more strongly for having lived their lives under the regime. In March 1953, the bewitched people of the Soviet Union learned of Stalin's death and asked themselves, "What now?" Now, the spell was finally gone, but the question was the same. "What now?" Sakharov was just better than the rest of us. His mind worked on an elevated plane of reason, morality, and patience. Valentin Turchin, one of Sakharov's closest associates both in physics and the human rights movement, remembered one typical episode:

"It was September 1973, soon after the infamous letter of forty academicians condemning Sakharov. I was sitting with the Sakharovs—in their kitchen, as usual—and discussing the letter. The Sakharovs had just returned from a Black Sea resort, and Yelena told me about a funny occurrence which took place a couple of days before they left. They were taking the sun at the beach when a short man ran up to Andrei Dmitriyevich, said how glad he was to meet him, shook his hand, and several times repeated how fortunate it was that such a person was among them.

" 'Who was that?' Yelena asked when the short man departed. Andrei Dmitriyevich answered that it was Academician so-and-so. Three days later, when the letter of forty was published, that academician was among the signers. Yelena, who is generally emotional, spoke with contempt and indignation, which were certainly well justified. I looked at Andrei Dmitriyevich: what was his reaction? It was very typical of him. He was not indignant about the episode. He was *thinking* about it."

The Soviet Union could ill afford to lose such a man.

CHAPTER 20

LOST ILLUSIONS

Aleksandr Yakovlev thought he was a dead man. He lay on a swampy battlefield outside Leningrad, his body and legs riddled by Nazi machine-gun fire. It was dark and cold and he was terrified. He was a village boy, so sickly as a child that his mother waited two years before she registered his birth. Now he was eighteen and a lieutenant in the Baltic marines' 6th Brigade and he was going to die. His only chance for survival was the tradition of the Soviet marines: no one was to be left on the battlefield, not the wounded, not even the dead. Tradition saved him. Five of Yakovlev's buddies sprinted onto the field to get him. The first four were shot down and killed. The fifth scooped Yakovlev up in his arms and ran. They made it. Yakovlev came home to his village outside Yaroslavl on crutches. His mother was so horrified at her son's condition that he felt as if he had failed her. There were three younger sisters to feed and the country was a ruin. What was he going to do with his life?

A half century later, after he had become known as Gorbachev's closest adviser and the intellectual architect of perestroika, Yakovlev told a group of students at Moscow State University how he, a wounded teenaged veteran of war, became a man of the Communist Party. He went to a pedagogical institute and dreamed of a career in teaching. But he had also become a Party

member in 1944. With millions of Party activists dead or still in battle, the local bosses scrambled to train young Communists, to fill up the ranks. They urged Yakovlev into political work and out of academia. "Then, after a number of years, enrollment began for the Higher Party School," Yakovlev told his audience. "I was invited for an interview to the regional Party committee. I didn't know what they wanted of me. In those times, everything was done in an atmosphere of utmost secrecy. I was asked to sit for exams, which I passed to become a trainee of the Higher Party School. That was how I started."

For liberal students in Moscow in February 1990, Yakovlev was about the only figure in the Politburo who could be trusted—Gorbachev included. The Communist Party was, for them, a dead issue. No one took the old exams in Party history anymore; those who specialized in Party history did so with the dispassionate interest of anthropologists studying the lives of cannibals and fire-eaters. Downstairs, in the main lobby of the university, students pinned up the most notorious quotations of Lenin and Stalin; they started clubs in honor of the Beatles, Iron Maiden, banned Russian authors, and American baseball. But they were young and still wanted to know what it was like to have lived through a nightmare.

Yakovlev told the students he was a typical member of his generation. He and his buddies had run into battle shouting, "For Stalin! For the Motherland!" They believed in the "shining future" promised by the Party. In Korolyovo, the tiny village where Yakovlev grew up, no one could even begin to understand the great tragedy the country was living through. When one of Yakovlev's great-uncles was thrown off his land and deported in the twenties, no one understood that this was part of a far greater collectivization campaign in which millions would die. There were few newspapers around, and the ones that could be found were filled with lies. Many of the people in the region, including Yakovlev's mother, were illiterate; his father had four years in a Russian Orthodox school, his mother no schooling at all. It was only through an accident of kindness and loyalty that Yakovlev's father did not disappear into the meat grinder of the purges.

"Our district military commissariat was headed by a man named Novikov. As it turned out, he was the commander of my father's platoon during the Civil War. He was an extraordinary person. I remember how he would ride through our village high on his horse, talking with all the kids and conscripts. He was the only one we knew from the district leadership. One day he came and knocked on the window with his whip handle. My father was not home, and Novikov told my mother, 'Tell him that he should go to the conference, which—only be sure to get this right—will last three days at least. I'll come later.'

"Mama didn't understand. When she went to tell my father, he questioned her several times—especially about that last phrase, 'I'll come later.' My father packed some things in a bag and went to a neighboring district, to mother's sister Raya—'to the conference.' He told mama where he could be found, just in case. Mama was a quiet woman, a peasant.

"That night, there was a knock at the door and they asked where my father was. Mama said, 'He went to the conference.'

" 'What conference?'

" 'I don't know,' she said. 'He didn't say.'

"They left. They came again the next night. . . . And after three days, Novikov showed up. That's what the friendship of the front meant. Not everything was inhuman. Then Novikov told Mama it was time to tell her husband to come home. The 'conference' was over! Mama sent me off to get him."

As Yakovlev well understood years later, the local Party committee probably had a "plan" to fulfill: kill X number of people in Y number of days. When Nikolai Yakovlev could not be found, they just found someone else.

By 1956, Yakovlev was living in Moscow and working at the Central Committee headquarters. As a young instructor—in fact, the youngest in the building—he received an "observer" invitation to attend the Twentieth Party Congress in the Kremlin. He sat in the balcony and listened to Khrushchev deliver his breakthrough report on Stalin's personality cult. As Khrushchev described the purges of the Party and military ranks, the delegates sank into a state of shock. The complicit were humiliated, the ignorant stunned. "There was a deathly silence," Yakovlev recalled. "People did not look at one another. I remember sitting in the balcony and from up there you could hear just one word spoken, the same word, one after the other: 'Yes.' You could hear only that: 'Yes.' There were no conversations. People went around shaking their heads. What we had heard did not quite penetrate right away. It was very hard, very hard. It was especially hard for those of us who had not become hardened by cynicism, who still had ideals and yet did not know the truth."

Khrushchev committed a heroic deed at that Twentieth Congress, Yakovlev told me. But the tragedy was that "he never could take the next step toward democratization. . . . Instinctively, he understood it was necessary to move forward, but he was thigh-deep in the muck of the past and he couldn't break free. When he grew older in his memoirs he regretted that he had not gone forward. But memoirs do not make up for a man's life."

By his early thirties, Yakovlev was the deputy head of the Central Committee's Department of Science and Culture, and there he began to learn about "that cruel force" the Party apparat. He arrived an ideological romantic, a

believer in Leninism and the new thaw. But he found himself inside the most Orwellian world of all, one of whispered threats, hermetic codes of behavior and privilege, black comedy. He was at one meeting at which a department chief accused someone of "Trotskyism" as it related to his supervision of animal husbandry. Yakovlev, too, was subject to the "petty brutalizations" of a life in the apparat. "For example, I once received a prize for a review of a film I never saw," he said, recalling an incident in the Yaroslavl Party organization. "There came an order from 'the center' to publish in all the papers a review of the movie *The Battle of Stalingrad.* They called the editor and said the review had to be in the next day's paper. The film hadn't come to our region and no one had seen it. We called the local film purveyor and it turned out that he had a list of the actors and the plot of the film. I wrote off of that. I knew some of the actors from other films, and I could say how they had 'profoundly revealed their characters' or some such. It goes without saying that the review was positive."

Yakovlev's career before 1985 was a mix of the academic and the apparatchik. After he won an advanced degree in history and philosophy, the Party thought him reliable enough to send to New York for a year of study at Columbia University. Yakovlev's classmates in New York remember him as doctrinaire and defensive, but intellectually curious. He traveled around the northeast and midwest and wrote a thesis on the politics of the New Deal, a program that he would later take as a kind of inspiration for perestroika. Yakovlev enjoyed the experience, but he was also haunted for years by the ignorance of Americans about the Soviet Union. For many years to come he would tell people a story about a New Yorker who asked him if all Russians had horns.

As Brezhnev took power, Yakovlev's work back in Moscow took a curious turn. He was highly valued in the propaganda department of the Party—the department that ran television and the press—but he was increasingly thought of as not quite reliable. In 1966, when the writers Andrei Sinyavsky and Yuli Daniel were arrested, Brezhnev's "gray cardinal," Mikhail Suslov, asked Yakovlev to handle the "propaganda side" of the trial. The Sinyavsky and Daniel affair was one of the first major dissident trials, and Yakovlev, repulsed by the incident, found a way to keep his distance. He did not have rebellion in mind. He valued his career and comforts too much for that. But Yakovlev did tell Suslov that the trial should be handled by the some other department. "I said that I was not sufficiently 'in the know' to take part," Yakovlev told me. "I wouldn't exactly call that bravery of the highest order." After that and similarly subtle "defenses" of dissidents such as Sakharov and

Lev Kopelev, Yakovlev said, "the Brezhnev leadership treated me with the utmost distrust" and refused to make him head of the department instead of acting head.

In the 1970s, Yakovlev even helped protect a young Party leader in southern Russia, Mikhail Gorbachev, who was carrying out experiments by hiring student brigades during harvest time. "He was organizing these brigades and paying them, and this was thought to be ideologically unsound," Yakovlev said. "He was obviously an impressive man and I did what I could for him."

As a polemicist for the Central Committee. Yakovlev wrote his share of agitprop monographs and books, wooden diatribes mainly about the American "empire" and "imperial ideology." He even edited a volume of the Pentagon Papers. These labors were all greatly appreciated by the Central Committee. But Yakovlev ended his career as a Party propagandist by writing a long, and unusually pointed, article directed against Russian nationalism. In November 1972, the weekly *Literaturnaya Gazeta* splashed the article, "Against Anti-Historicism," across two full pages. Yakovlev lashed out at the hard-line nationalists for making a "cult of the patriarchal peasantry," for romanticizing the prerevolutionary past. The article was directed especially at writers for the journal *Molodaya Gvardiya* ("Young Guard"), who saw the rise of Western intelligentsia both inside and outside the Party as a grave threat to Russia's "national spirit." Yakovlev couched his argument in the ritualistic language of Leninism, attacking the writers for their "extra-class and extra-social approach," but he also made a veiled defense of "intellectualism," a term understood as thinking outside the boundaries of official dogma.

Brezhnev and his ideological guard dogs did not like the article at all. Yakovlev knew now for sure that he no longer had a place in the Central Committee apparatus. As if to head off the punishment from above, he invented his own. He asked about diplomatic work, perhaps in an English-speaking country. Within hours, it was done. Yakovlev was sent to Canada, and there he stayed for ten years, an ambassador and an exile.

At the embassy in Ottawa, Yakovlev improved his English and marinated in the books, articles, and pop culture around him. He met regularly with Canadian officials, diplomats, and intellectuals. And he continued to write. "Canada was wonderful for me. It was a way out," Yakovlev told me. It was in Canada that Yakovlev also forged his relationship with Gorbachev. In May 1983, Gorbachev was a leading member of the Politburo. He came to Canada and traveled with Yakovlev across the country, from Niagara Falls to Calgary, in an old Convair prop plane. They visited farmers and businessmen, but the most important talks they held were with each other. According to both men, they spent hours talking about the disasters awaiting the Soviet

Union, the rot at the core of the economic system, the self-crippling lack of openness in the press, the cultural and scientific worlds. "The most important common understanding," Yakovlev told me, "was the idea that we could not live this way anymore. . . . We talked about absolutely everything, openly, and it was clear to me that this was a new kind of leader. It was a thrilling experience politically and intellectually."

Yakovlev wanted to return to Moscow, and Gorbachev had the power to give him his wish. Within a month, Yakovlev became the director of one of the most prestigious and liberal-minded think tanks in Moscow, the Institute of World Economy and International Relations (IMEMO).

For Western Sovietologists trying to figure out the thinking of the team forming around Gorbachev both before and after he took power in March 1985, Yakovlev was a beguiling figure. Cold warriors took one look at Yakovlev's book of the early Reagan era, *On the Edge of an Abyss,* and decided he was a hard-liner, a figure who would do nothing at all to ease Soviet-American relations in the near future. Scholars searching for flexibility in the nascent Gorbachev team found none in Yakovlev's opus. *On the Edge of an Abyss* reads like the sort of tract the Young Spartacus League might have been passing out on college campuses twenty years ago. In a voice of rage inherited from *What Is to Be Done?* Yakovlev lit into the United States as a smug, soft, and warped country sporting a "messianic ideology" and the urge to police and "dominate the world." John Wayne, TV evangelists, the "bourgeois press," and Norman Podhoretz all made him sick. For Yakovlev, the United States was "a miserable sight. A miserable democracy. Unfortunately, many Americans still harbor illusions. They are used to believing that they elect law-givers, benefactors and defenders and are shocked to discover that some of them sold themselves out long ago. This is an indisputable fact. However, the bourgeois propaganda media go out of their way to prove the contrary. . . . The romanticizing of brutality, approval of violence, the relishing of sex exploits and the portrayal of murder as an ordinary and normal phenomenon are characteristic features of the mass media and culture. . . . The main hero Americans see everywhere—in the movies, on television, in books, magazines and newspapers—is a gangster, sleuth, or sadist."

And yet, read in retrospect, *On the Edge of an Abyss* showed Yakovlev was a consumer of rigorous books and articles about the United States. He read everything from *Foreign Affairs* and *International Security* to the memoirs of Henry Kissinger. He also had a better sense of humor than most ideological warriors: "Some say, for example, that of all the superficial roles Reagan played while a film actor, the most successful one was as the sidekick to a chimpanzee named Bonzo. This film has not been forgotten by the public.

Demonstrators in Toronto, Canada, who came out to protest Reagan's militarist policies, carried placards admonishing Americans for having chosen the wrong chimpanzee."

Years later, when I asked him about his pre-perestroika books, Yakovlev said that they, like their author, were "prisoners of the time." "Had I not been in the U.S.A. and Canada, I would never have written such books about America," he said. "But being an impulsive man, when I read newspapers and books criticizing my country, well, this hurt me deeply. For example, I know that I am crippled. But when every day people tell me, 'You are crippled, you are crippled,' I get furious! And then I answer back: 'You are the cripple! You yourself are the fool!' "

—

From the moment Gorbachev took power, Yakovlev was an essential, if not lead, player in every progressive idea, policy, or gesture coming from the Kremlin. Yakovlev was a peculiar animal in the Communist Party leadership. Unlike most of the men in the Politburo, he never ran a republic or a region or even an industrial plant; he was never at the head of one of the major institutions like the army or the KGB. "The truth was he didn't know anything about ordinary life or practical politics," Yegor Ligachev, Yakovlev's nemesis in the Politburo, told me.

Yakovlev was simply the man at the leader's side, the homely intellectual with twitchy brows and goggly glasses whispering into the ear of the general secretary. "Seneca to Gorbachev's Nero," a Russian friend said. "Or maybe Aristotle to Alexander the Great?" In any case, it turned out that the obligatory language and fury of *On the Edge of an Abyss* masked a unique intelligence and a powerful urge to remake the Soviet Union. Yakovlev explored the New Deal, Kant's *Critique of Pure Reason,* the early socialists, and far less exalted texts for answers. One afternoon, Vitaly Korotich came to the Kremlin to see Yakovlev about an issue of *Ogonyok* and was amused to discover that the Communist Party's chief ideologist had his team of aides spend the afternoon "studying" a video of *Raiders of the Lost Ark*—presumably to understand the peculiarities of American media and self-image. It is not known whether Yakovlev's antipathy toward John Wayne extended to the more politically correct adventures of Harrison Ford.

Between 1985 and 1990, Yakovlev's accomplishments were legion. He helped draft the foreign-policy principles of "the new thinking." Because it dispensed with the classic Leninist approach of a class-based approach to foreign affairs, "the new thinking" gave an ideological rationale for everything from the withdrawal from Afghanistan to the rapprochement with the United States to the policy of noninterference in Eastern Europe.

Yakovlev engineered the cultural revolution known as glasnost by using his power to appoint liberal editors to publications like *Ogonyok* and *Moscow News.* Republican leaders from Armenia to the Baltic states found in Yakovlev a sympathetic ear. At one Politburo meeting in 1988, the KGB chief, Viktor Chebrikov, said that the Baltic national fronts were conspiring to create a counterrevolution, while Yakovlev, just returned from the region, said that there was no threat, "only the manifestations of perestroika and democratization." As the Politburo's house historian, he headed the commissions which rehabilitated political exiles and prisoners, investigated the Kirov murder of 1934, and "discovered" the secret protocols of the Molotov-Ribbentrop Pact.

As an ideologist, Yakovlev's predecessors had been men like Mikhail Suslov, dogmatists, enforcers of the faith. Yakovlev was charged with changing that faith. He and Gorbachev began with the idea of "cleansing" socialism and the Party, but they had precious little idea of how they would do it and where it would all lead. The truth is that Yakovlev, Gorbachev, and Shevardnadze—the lead reformers in the Politburo after Yeltsin resigned in 1987—were flying almost blind, and against a terrific conservative headwind, from the start.

"Speaking generally," Yakovlev said, "our baseline principle was that some things could be improved: more democracy, elections, more in the newspapers—limited, but slightly more open—the management system should be improved, centralization should be less strict, power should be redistributed somewhat, maybe the functions of the Party and the government should be divided. But you can find all of these democratic axioms since 1917, even under Stalin. 'Socialist democracy' was talked about as an ideal even then. But speeches are speeches. In 1985, for the first time, we started implementing things so that our words were matched by deeds. But as soon as these words became reality, a logic of development began to develop, and that dictated the next steps. Perestroika acquired its own logic of development, which dictated what to do. This logic of development led us to the 'conclusion' that the concept of improvement will not do us any good. One can fix up a car, add some oil, tighten some bolts, and you can drive on. But with a social organism you cannot always do this. It is not enough. It turned out that everything had to be made over.

"The ideological disputes began right away, in 1985. We clashed openly on questions of glasnost. The reformist wing had their own understanding of perestroika from the start. The conservative wing thought only that something needed to be changed. They thought we had to change a little bit, but always relying on the Party apparat. It was then that the tributes to the conservative spirit appeared: state factory inspections, the anti-alcohol cam-

paign. They were all administrative methods and had nothing to do with a real economy. For example, we tried that—what did we call it?—*khozrashchet* . . . regional, or local, cost-accounting . . . whatever! It was rubbish!

"After losing two and a half years we began searching for new types of society, radical restructuring on entirely new principles, and we realized that it was a more formidable task than we had anticipated. . . . It was not the Party, it had nothing to do with the concept of perestroika. It was a limited group of people who started that."

By 1989, Ligachev and the orthodox wing of the Communist Party came to blame Yakovlev, Gorbachev, and Shevardnadze for radicalizing perestroika to the point of creating a "bourgeois" state, for abandoning the "class approach" to politics, for failing to provide a blueprint for the future. "Some of our conservatives now say that a group of adventurists began to restructure things without a concept," Yakovlev replied. "But imagine what would have happened if we'd just gone into an office and created an entire scheme. Marx did that and look what it led to! One should take things from life, and adjust them every day. Our whole trouble is that we are inert, we think in dogmas. Even if reality tells us to change things, we always check first in a book.

"Let's imagine if Ligachev had come to power. Would he have started perestroika? Yes. But it would have been of the Andropov sort: restore law and order in the economy, but only with administrative methods. But he would have done it. The result might even have been better. There might have been better conditions, more bread, more grain. But the old system of fear would have remained, the same lack of democracy and antihuman relations."

In the first years of perestroika, Yakovlev was careful about his terminology. As a political loyalist, he did not want to go too far beyond Gorbachev's own public expressions. But still, there were times when Yakovlev played the role of stalking horse and outraged the Party apparat. "I was under constant attack beginning with those first careful speeches," he said. "It was enough for me just to mention the word 'market' [in 1988] and there was an attack. Now everyone talks about the market. But back then you had to put your words in a special sort of wrapping paper."

Yakovlev's most radical proposal in the early days of power was to dismantle the one-party system. In his secret memo to Gorbachev dated December 1985, Yakovlev suggested as a first step toward the creation of a democratic, multiparty system that the Communist Party be divided into progressives and conservatives. Such a split would acknowledge the obvious: the Party was unified by nothing but its pretenses and camouflage. Yakovlev

hoped that such a move would either eliminate or silence the most hidebound elements in the Party. In the time-honored Russian tradition, it would show who was who. But Gorbachev knew the Party at least as well as Yakovlev, and he rejected the idea as out of the question, too dangerous. We could lose everything, he told Yakovlev. You'll see, he said. The Party can be reformed. But slowly.

By July 1989, the Party was proving unchangeable. The leading reformers still in the Party talked about quitting; hundreds of thousands of members did just that. Komsomol chapters were closing or dying out. Yakovlev, for his part, was under constant attack in *Pravda, Sovetskaya Rossiya,* and the rest of the Party press. So he finally decided that it was time to dispense with the wrapping paper. It was time to deal with the Party's dismal history and its dubious future. Yakovlev chose an extraordinary occasion for his "coming out": a July 1989 speech given in honor of the bicentennial of the French Revolution.

Before an audience of Party members, intellectuals, and foreign guests, Yakovlev deepened his scrutiny of the past. Gorbachev had already denounced the "crimes" of Stalin, but now his intellectual alter ego was launching a public attack on the founding myths of the Soviet Union. The Bolshevik Revolution, he told his audience, quickly dissolved into a reign of terror, one that far outstripped the Jacobin use of the guillotine.

"The idealization of terror was starkly evident during the October Revolution," Yakovlev said. The Bolsheviks looked back on the terror of 1793 as a model and "faithfully believed in violence as a cleansing force . . . a salvation for the country and the people. . . . The edifying thirst for freedom degenerates into the delirious fever of violence which ultimately extinguishes the flames of the revolution."

Then Yakovlev made a connection between Lenin and Stalin that was still considered radical even for non-Party intellectuals. To hear it from the main ideologist of glasnost, perestroika, and the "new thinking" in foreign policy was absolutely stunning: "Today, when we are asking ourselves the excruciating question of how it was possible for this country and Lenin's Party to accept the dictatorship of mediocrity and put up with Stalin's abuses and the shedding of rivers of innocent blood, it is obvious that one of the factors that nurtured the soil for authoritarian rule and despotism was the morbid faith in the possibility of forcing through social and historical development, and the idealization of revolutionary violence that traces back to the very sources of the European revolutionary tradition."

In other words, the appearance of Stalin was no aberration, but rather the direct result of Lenin's "revolutionary romanticism" that idealized violence as an instrument of class struggle and a force of purification. Until pere-

stroika, even the most radical underground historians in the Soviet Union denied this. Roy Medvedev saw Stalin only as a pathological rupture with Leninism. Some Western historians tended to play down, or deny, Lenin's ruthlessness. But the evidence was undeniable, and no one knew it better than Yakovlev, the chairman of the Politburo's commission on history. As the émigré scholars Mikhail Heller and Aleksandr Nekrich point out, it was Lenin and Trotsky who were the first Europeans to use the term "concentration camp" and then use the device to such effect. Three months after Trotsky used the term, Lenin sent a telegram to the Penza Executive Committee on August 9, 1918, demanding the local Red leaders carry out "ruthless mass terror against the kulaks, priests, and White Guards; confine all suspicious elements in a concentration camp outside the city."

Yakovlev demanded that the Party recognize its past and renounce the old methods. "History cannot be different but we must be different," he said. "The idea of violence as the midwife of history has exhausted itself, as has the idea of dictatorial power based on violence."

It was a terribly difficult speech for Yakovlev to make. He had been working in one capacity or another in the Communist Party since just after the war. He said his first doubts about the Soviet leadership came when he saw how Stalin greeted returning prisoners of war by sending them directly to labor camps for fear of their "foreign influence." His thinking had developed radically since those days, and so had the thinking of many men and women of his generation; but he knew all too well that the majority of Party officials had changed only slightly. Despite their outward obedience to the vocabulary of the Gorbachev era—"perestroika," "acceleration," "democratization," and all the rest—they were deeply resistant to a fundamental change in the political system. In the French Revolution speech, Yakovlev acknowledged as much. "The need for radical renewal is born of the times, but, on the other hand, is always ahead of them," he said. "A rise to a new spiral of civilization does not occur without pain. Acute dramas are generated by the inertia of the outgoing social structures, the refusal to accept the new things, and revolutionary impatience."

Yakovlev even tried, in an oblique way, to address "the problem" of how revolutions consume their children, to reassure the right-wingers that there would be no hunt for enemies. He did not lash out at his antagonists; rather, he warned them. "A party that revels in myths and vain illusions," he said, "is doomed."

By the beginning of 1990, the collapse of the Communist Party monolith was at hand. Sakharov was gone, but his demand to eliminate the Party's guaran-

teed hold on power had become a banner of the growing democratic opposition. Nevertheless, Gorbachev needed convincing. The proposals of Sakharov or Yakovlev—and the rise of dozens of new parties across the country—were not enough for him. He had to be beaten over the head before he dared make a move on the Party. Lithuanians, as usual, were only too pleased to provide the drubbing.

In January 1990, Gorbachev went to Vilnius, confident that he could find a way to finesse the alarming developments there. He was sure he could slow down the sprint to independence and convince the republic's Party organization to come back into the fold. Yakovlev had already been to Vilnius and said it would be "immoral" to deny the Lithuanian argument that Moscow was still running a coercive empire. Gorbachev plainly disagreed. He berated the Lithuanian Party leader, Algirdas Brazauskas, for splitting with the all-union organization and for letting the "romantic professors" of the Sajudis popular front assume such power there. In Vilnius, Gorbachev's fury and confusion were obvious at every meeting and encounter. As long as the progressive elements of the country followed him, Gorbachev had been happy; but now his erstwhile followers were in the lead, and this was intolerable. Gorbachev had lost control of the political world.

At one point on the trip, Gorbachev confronted an elderly factory worker who was carrying a sign reading "Total Independence for Lithuania."

"Who told you to write that banner?" Gorbachev asked angrily.

"Nobody. I wrote it myself," the worker said.

"Who are you? Where do you work?" Gorbachev said. "And what do you mean by 'total independence'?"

"I mean what we had in the 1920s, when Lenin recognized Lithuania's sovereignty, because no nation is entitled to dictate to another nation," the worker replied.

"Within our large family, Lithuania has become a developed country," Gorbachev said. "What kind of exploiters are we if Russia sells you cotton, oil, and raw materials—and not for hard currency either?"

The worker cut off Gorbachev. "Lithuania had a hard currency before the war," he said. "You took it away in 1940. And do you know how many Lithuanians were sent to Siberia in the 1940s, and how many died?"

Gorbachev finally could not bear this impudence. "I don't want to talk to this man anymore," he said. "If people in Lithuania have attitudes and slogans like this, they can expect hard times. I don't want to talk to you anymore."

Raisa tried to calm down her husband.

"Be quiet," he snapped.

On the last day of his trip to Lithuania, Gorbachev finally conceded the obvious. A year before he had called the idea of a multiparty system *chepukha*—rubbish. Now, he said, "We should not be afraid of a multiparty system the way the devil is afraid of incense. I don't see a tragedy in a multiparty system if it serves the people."

By now, Gorbachev knew that tragedy might come if he did not make his run at the Communist Party. From a distance, he watched what had become of Jaruzelski in Poland, Honecker in East Germany, and, most vividly, the Ceauşescus in Romania. Gorbachev did not need to strain very hard to see the same rage gathering at home. Everywhere there was an urge to clean house. In the northern Ukrainian city of Chernigov, crowds gathered around a car crash and discovered that the drunken driver of one car was a leading Party official. It turned out the official was carrying around a trunkload of various delicacies that had not been seen in the city in years. The official resigned. In Volgograd, the entire Party leadership was forced to quit when tens of thousands of people protested the construction of special housing for the local officials. In the Siberian city of Tyumen, the entire Party leadership resigned after it was accused, en masse, of corruption. And in Leningrad, the former Politburo member and local Party chief Yuri Solovyov was expelled from the Party after hundreds of people demonstrated outside his home demanding to know just how he was able to buy a Mercedes-Benz sedan for 9,000 rubles when the usual price was more like 120,000.

On February 4, 1990, a bitter cold day in Moscow, around a quarter-million people marched halfway around the Garden Ring Road, down Gorky Street, and toward the Kremlin for a rally on Manezh Square that could only have scared the wits out of the denizens behind the great brick walls. It was the biggest demonstration in Moscow since the rise of Soviet power, and there was nothing polite about it. The banner "Party Bureaucrats: Remember Romania!" was just one of the helpful reminders they provided. While the crowd clapped their gloved hands and stamped their feet to keep warm, Yuri Afanasyev climbed onto the bed of a flatbed truck and shouted into the microphone, "All hail the peaceful February revolution of 1990!" The reference was lost on no one: it was the February Revolution that toppled the established order, the czar, in 1917. The Central Committee was scheduled to gather for a plenum a few days later and a vote on the fate of Article 6, the clause guaranteeing the Party primacy in public life. For the first time, the opposition seemed sure of a great victory. "When the [members of the Central Committee] show up at the Kremlin Monday morning they had better have in mind the image of hundreds of thousands of people you

see here today," Vladimir Tikhonov, the head of the Union of Cooperative Businesses, said. In his speech, Yeltsin barked that this would be Gorbachev's "last chance." And the crowd—the vast brew of democratic socialists, social democrats, greens, monarchists, Hare Krishnas, veterans, housewives, and students—roared its approval.

At the plenum, Ligachev and various other members of the Central Committee complained about the "loss" of Eastern Europe, the "chaos" on the streets. But then they fell into line. On February 7, 1990, the Central Committee passed a platform that effectively opened the way for a multiparty system. They really had no choice. They had seen the crowds. They had read the placards and the future they promised.

Yakovlev never gave up his loyalty to Gorbachev, but now they were clearly split over matters of ideology and tactics, especially where the Party was concerned. "I am a convinced Communist," Gorbachev kept saying. But for Yakovlev, socialism meant little more than the idea of a welfare state, a government that could "protect people against calamity and misfortune." His attitude toward Lenin also grew more and more critical. "Oh, yes, it did change," he told me. "As the Bible says: there is much grief in wisdom. . . . [Lenin] was an extremely talented politician. There is no question about it. But he was geared only toward power and power alone. Everything else was subordinate to that. He thought morality was of no value in the proletarian revolution."

The Party scheduled a congress for July—a congress that Yuri Afanasyev predicted would be its "funeral." In the weeks before the event, the Party press steadily increased its attacks on the reformers in the Party, describing them as "traitors" to socialism and the state. Invariably, the named targets were Yeltsin and Yakovlev. At the congress itself, deputies were handed leaflets allegedly reporting Yakovlev's comments at a meeting with the radical and conservative factions. The "answers" made Yakovlev seem disloyal to Gorbachev, insulting to the army, and even more radical than he was. Later, an investigating committee discovered that the organizer of the leaflet was General Igor Rodionov, the military commander who won national fame for leading the assault in Tbilisi against a crowd of peaceful Georgian demonstrators.

Yakovlev had rarely stepped out in public over the years, preferring to stay at Gorbachev's side and influence events with his advice. But at the congress he took the rostrum in his own defense, and his performance was devastating. After debunking the leaflet attacking him, he held up yet another leaflet that had been circulating among the Party delegates, a photocopy from the news-

paper *Russky Golos* ("Russian Voice"). It said, "We need a new Hitler, not Gorbachev. We are badly in need of a military coup. There is still a lot of undeveloped space in Siberia waiting for the 'enthusiasts' who have buried perestroika."

"My name is there," Yakovlev said. "So, Siberians, await the arrival of new gulag inmates. That's what's happening, comrades. A massive attack has been launched and all means, including criminal ones, are being used in this campaign. True, all this leaves scars on the heart, but I want to say this to the organizers of this well-orchestrated campaign and those who are behind it: you may shorten my life, but you can't silence me."

Yakovlev's despair over the Party led to even more probing about the viability of Marxism itself. Soon he would be telling all who would listen that Lenin's intolerance was matched by Marx's irrelevance. "A great deal has been rejected by life," he told the newspaper *Rabochaya Tribuna* ("Worker's Tribune"). "Marx said, for instance, that revolutions would take place in several industrialized European capitalist countries at the same time. That did not happen. A revolution took place in Russia, but even there it resulted from a queer concurrence of circumstances. Marx said that capitalism was a rotting society that impeded scientific, technological, and social progress. He was wrong about that, too. . . . But this is not even the main point. Life corrects many a theory. The problem is that a rash experiment was performed on Russia. An attempt was made to create a new model of society and put it into practice under conditions that were unfit for socialism. No wonder the new way of life was imposed by terror."

On August 20, 1990, Gorbachev had signed a decree rehabilitating all those who had been repressed in the twenties, thirties, forties, and fifties and repealed any orders that had stripped dissidents of their citizenship. The Party, of course, thought it was being awfully generous in this. But then Yakovlev came on the evenings news program *Vremya* and made a short statement worthy of Sakharov or Havel.

The president's two decrees, he said, "are, in my view, acts of repentance. . . . When we say that we are rehabilitating someone, as if we are mercifully forgiving him for the sins of the past, this smells of cunning and hypocrisy. We are not forgiving him. We are forgiving ourselves. It is we who are to blame that others lived for years both slandered and oppressed. It is we who are rehabilitating ourselves, not those who held other thoughts and convictions. They only wanted good and freedom for us, and the leadership of the country answered with evil, prisons and camps.

"As we breathe the air of freedom, it is already becoming difficult today

for us to remember what happened in the distant and not so distant past. There were hundreds of thousands of brutal trials, people who were shot and killed, people who killed themselves, people who did not even know what they were charged with, but who were destroyed. . . .

"For us, they are not a reproach but a harsh reminder to all those who still have a yearning nostalgia for the past, for those who would turn everything back to the fear. . . . I want to pay special attention to the tragic fate of our peasantry, which paid the price in blood for the criminality of the Stalinist regime. This is not only an unprecedented reprisal against the peasantry, which disrupted the flow of the society, but it also brought the development of the state into crisis. History has never known such a concentrated hatred toward man."

CHAPTER 21

THE OCTOBER REVOLUTION

As the Party was collapsing, I got to know one of its last high priests. Vyacheslav Shostokovsky, an ally of both Yakovlev and Yeltsin, ran the Moscow Higher Party School, the ultimate training ground for young Leninists. In a matter of months, he undid the work of a thousand ideologues, firing faculty, bringing in new, younger teachers, revising the curriculum to include every possible idea and thinker. Suddenly, the students were reading Mill and Locke along with Marx and Lenin. Much of what they read of Soviet history came from foreign and underground editions; there was no time to wait for the Party publishing houses to catch up with the world. It was a desperate mission. Either Shostokovsky would revive the Party with a new crop of young social democrats, he told me one afternoon, "or we die."

"We're moving toward a multiparty democracy, to a political marketplace, and the Communist Party is just not ready for that," he said. "I'm afraid even Gorbachev himself is not ready for this marketplace."

After my meeting with the dean, I headed for the exit. On my way out, I noticed a handwritten sign advertising a showing of "an American movie tonight in Lenin Hall." No title given, but I went anyway. Lenin Hall was

packed. The lights dimmed and the familiar faces of Michael Douglas and Charlie Sheen flickered on the screen: the Communist Party Higher Party School presents *Wall Street.*

If I hadn't known then that Communist ideology was dead, I knew it by the final credits. The young acolytes, presumably the next generation of Leninist priests, reacted to this morality play of American finance in a way that would have made poor Oliver Stone weep. They did not see it as a warning about the perils of greed, not a propaganda cartoon meant to steer the best and the brightest toward a life of goodness and social work. Not at all. They audibly lusted after the goods on display: the stretch limo (with bar and TV), the sushi-making machine, the steak tartare at "21," the fabulous cuffs on Michael Douglas's Turnbull & Asser shirts. God, they loved those shirts. When Charlie Sheen, the young stud stockbroker, first checked out his new East Side apartment, with the wraparound windows and the view to die for, you could hear the sighing of the young Leninists.

"Models are out. Dogma is out," Shostokovsky had told me. "Now we can only speak about goals." Precisely. It was pretty clear what the goals were here. The climax of the film came when Douglas, doing his best Ivan Boesky imitation, delivered the killer line: *"Zhdanost—eto khorosho!"* ("Greed is good!") The Communists went wild. There were whoops of approval. Unironic whoops.

As we were all leaving Lenin Hall, the student next to me, Muen Tan Kong, an exchange scholar from Vietnam, said, "All I can tell you at this point is that Communism is the contradiction of capitalism—I think," he said. "And the Party is the vanguard. We're studying that now. It's all very confusing. But the movie was good, wasn't it?"

Local elections were scheduled for early March 1990, and they held out the promise of a new vanguard of mayors and ward heelers. Such a sudden test of a multiparty system still in swaddling clothes seemed unfair. The Communists had the resources, the money, and, when all else failed, the KGB to keep them afloat. Most of the new parties consisted of a few dozen people in a rented auditorium making terrifically dull speeches. Sometimes there were sandwiches.

But the democrats were confident of victory. In those first weeks after the collapse of the one-party system, one young politician, Moscow's Ilya Zaslavsky, made a startling campaign promise. He told the voters of the October Region that if he was elected to the local council and made its chairman, he would do nothing less than reverse seven decades of economic disaster. "We

will build capitalism in one district," he declared. The reference was clear. Zaslavsky would counter Stalin's greatest ambition to build "socialism in one country."

It was quite a campaign promise. All anyone could do was wish him the best of luck. The same Communist Party apparatchiks I had visited not long after moving in two years before were still running the October Region with singular incompetence. Like everyone else in the neighborhood, I was appalled at the decay: the heaps of uncollected garbage, the empty shops and decrepit buildings, the abandoned construction sites. The district looked like a slum. In this way it looked like almost everywhere else in the country. Now Zaslavsky was proposing as a remedy the very sort of free enterprise that Lenin had long ago declared "parasitism . . . a thing of the past."

The leaders of the democratic opposition—Zaslavsky included—had all but given up on the national parliament as anything more than a televised debating forum. They knew well that the majority of deputies were at best obedient to Gorbachev and at worst potential followers of a harder line. After that initial burst of drama and glasnost during the first session, the radicals despaired that the Congress did not have the means to push the program of economic or political changes faster or further. And so now the leading reformers of Russia had shifted their focus from national to local politics. Democratic Russia—an alliance of everyone from Memorial to the latest social democratic party—hoped to fill the city halls and regional soviets, or councils, with their people. Popular-front groups in the Baltics, Central Asia, and the Transcaucasus hoped to do the same. Just as Yeltsin wanted to win a seat in the Russian parliament and turn that institution into a power base, Zaslavsky wanted to do the same "at the sidewalk level."

As a Democratic Russia organizer, Zaslavsky advised candidates not only for the October Region, but for the entire city. In a country that had little experience of elections and none at all of the gimmickry of the West, Zaslavsky hired pollsters, ran seminars on campaign techniques, and even found psychologists to help draw up effective campaign literature. He called on well-known writers, who used their own connections to get leaflets printed when the main Party printing plants refused.

Disabled, a little snide and condescending, Zaslavsky was not a natural politician. His teachers, his bosses at the textile plant where he worked, even his parents could not comprehend his becoming a politician—much less one of the most famous new names in Russia. He was just thirty years old. But the voters never forgot it when he insisted on calling for a day of national mourning when Sakharov died; and they never forgot that when Gorbachev told him to sit, he did not. Now all the reform candidates for the Moscow city

council or the regional councils wanted his endorsement and his organizing talent.

Zaslavsky won his race in the October Region easily. The local council was filled with Democratic Russia candidates, who quickly made Zaslavsky the regional chairman. His personal victory was one among hundreds for Democratic Russia and other reformist groups throughout the union. Many people had, as they put it, "voted a straight democratic line." Yeltsin was elected to the Russian parliament, and it was obvious that he would try to become its chairman. Gavriil Popov, the economist, went to city hall and became the mayor of Moscow. Anatoly Sobchak, the law professor who became a star of the Congress, was now mayor of Leningrad. Once more, there was a brief wave of euphoria in the most politically active pockets of the Soviet Union, a sense of possibility and confidence. When I went to see Sobchak in Leningrad, he had commandeered an enormous office in the Mariinsky Palace. And yet I could not get past the fact that he still kept an enormous painting of Lenin hanging behind him.

As I was leaving the office, I whispered to an aide, "What's the painting doing there?"

He laughed. "Pay it no mind," he said. "We tried to take it down, but we found a huge stain on the wallpaper. We don't have the money for new wallpaper."

In his first months in office, Zaslavsky came to an even deeper understanding of the Communist Party's legacy. The Party, which had complete control over every store and factory, every police station and fire brigade, had let the October Region fall into a state of economic decay—a typical situation throughout the Soviet Union. Food supplies were erratic; there were days when even the bread shops were empty. The housing shortage was pitiful. Many people lived in studios the size of walk-in closets or in communal apartments with fifteen or twenty people to a bathroom. By reading district documents, Zaslavsky also discovered that the huge showpiece statue of Lenin on October Square had cost 23 million rubles—7 million of which had come from the local budget. In the meantime, garbage lay rotting for days on the streets, uncollected; doctors at the local state hospitals were paid half as much as bus drivers.

One night a week, Zaslavsky sat in a dismal office near October Square listening to residents' complaints. Widows, pensioners, drunks, and young parents would sit on narrow benches in the hall and wait their turn. To sit next to Zaslavsky from six until long past midnight was to hear a catalog of the failings of "socialism in one separate country":

"Ilya Iosifevich, my husband and I are divorced, but we still have to

share the same one-room flat. We've been in line for a new apartment since 1978. . . ."

"Ilya Iosifevich, my mother died this week, but they say the only way they will bury her is if I pay bribes to the cemetery manager. I have no bribe money. . . ."

"Ilya Iosifevich, my son has leukemia, but the doctors say they can do nothing. They say the only place he can get treatment is in the West. We have no visa and no money. . . ."

Zaslavsky slumped in his chair, not so much from the specific complaints—everyone knew the problems—but from the sheer number of them, the weight of his responsibility. The self-confidence was slowly draining out of him. He was powerless and sad. After he began his comeback in the Congress of People's Deputies, Yeltsin had also allowed me once to sit in on his office hours, and while the complaints were similar, he was often able to do something. The apparatchiks may have despised Yeltsin, but they had to listen to him. He was still a former Politburo member and a member of the Central Committee. Yeltsin could make a quick phone call and get his constituent just about anything: an apartment, a wheelchair, a visa to see a daughter in Warsaw. But that was mainly because of his immense authority and connections as a former member of the Kremlin leadership. Zaslavsky could only leaf through the growing stacks of papers and complaints his constituents brought him. He would look into the problems, he told them all, he would do what he could. He wrote letters, he made phone calls. But the system he relied on considered him its enemy.

Zaslavsky knew real change would come only with political and economic reform far beyond the boundaries of the October Region. In the meantime, he could hardly look his constituents in the eye. "They think of me as their last hope," he said one night between visitors, "and there is so little I can do. How do I tell them it will take years?"

—

At first, Zaslavsky's only successes were symbolic. New parties were required by law to register, and every new party in the city and Russia itself, it seemed, registered in the October Region because it had the most accommodating regulations. Nearly every Saturday another party would hold its founding congress in the October Region. "It got a little absurd. We'd already registered three different Christian Democratic parties before we ever made a move on economics," said Grigori Vasiliyev, a thirty-two-year-old economist who was Zaslavsky's choice to head the region's *ispolkom,* or executive committee.

Zaslavsky also recognized that glasnost was still far from free speech, and

so he registered and helped fund newspapers that were too small or too radical to get help from the Party bureaucracy and its printing presses. Sergei Grigoryants, an underground editor whom Gorbachev, in an interview with *The Washington Post,* described as a parasite, was able to take over a small building and run his magazine *Glasnost* without government or Party interference. Zaslavsky also opened a book and magazine store in the lobby of the regional headquarters on Shabolovka Street where you could buy émigré journals like *Kontinent* and *Posev.* Later he sponsored the openings of newsstands in the metro stations.

The October District also began to wage war on the Communist Party organization that had run things for so long. Zaslavsky stripped the Shabolovka Street headquarters of all its Communist trappings—the busts of Lenin, the hammers and sickles—and then pushed the Party bureaucracy out of the way. He gave them a few bad offices on a high, drafty floor and took away their internal phone lines.

"Let them fend for themselves," he said. "These people have no more right to this building than the Christian Democrats or the local bird-watchers' association."

Zaslavsky and his colleagues knew what they wanted to do, but they wanted at least the pretense of consensus before they did it. I went along and heard Zaslavsky tell the local police force that the city, and not the Interior Ministry bureaucracy, should be hiring and firing police officers. I saw him try to describe to a room filled with befuddled factory workers how it was time that they had shares in their own workplace, that inefficient or polluting plants should be shut down and replaced with factories that "worked cleanly and made things that people need." Zaslavsky also knew that the creation of a real market would lead to higher prices, unemployment, bankruptcies, and the end of relatively equal incomes, and he said so. He was cold and honest, and the reception he got was never easy or enthusiastic. At a machine factory one afternoon, Zaslavsky sat on the podium under a huge banner—"The Name and Work of Lenin Will Live Forever!"—and, once more, got an earful:

"What are you going to do about all those Azerbaijanis selling in our markets?"

"These kebab salesmen are making a fortune on our backs! They buy up all the meat and they sell it for three and four times the original price!"

"Don't make us your lab rats for capitalism!"

The workers were understandably more concerned with their daily disasters than with grand designs and new October revolutions. Zaslavsky tried to explain the difference between the black market and a real market, the need for competition, regulation, incentive. He was getting nowhere. "If I had

known about all this, I never would have voted for you!" one worker shouted.

By the end of the session, Zaslavsky and Vasiliyev were depressed. The euphoria of the election campaign was fading fast. "We never understood just how deep the psychology of Bolshevism is in every one of us," one aide, Ilya Gezentsevei, told me. "The harder we try to push, the harder that psychology pushes back."

For months, they floundered. But slowly, Zaslavsky and Vasiliyev's economic planning began to pay off. Their first stroke of genius was to make the October Region the Delaware of Moscow. The regional council passed measures making it easy for private businesses to register in the region. With no Party bureaucracy to impress or bribe, the businesses came in droves. More than 4,500 small enterprises registered in the region within twelve months—nearly half of all the new private businesses in Moscow. Restaurants, brokerages, commodities exchanges, private research labs, construction firms, law firms, and an electronics store opened. Taking in a percentage of the business profits as tax, the October Region raised its annual income from 73 million rubles to 250 million rubles in one year.

In the October Region you could see the first signs of a market economy: the ambition, the fast profits, the crime, the bewildering greed. The "October Revolution," as the local papers called it, was a gold rush for a hustler like German Sterligov, a twenty-four-year-old college dropout and one of the self-proclaimed pioneers of Soviet capitalism. He set up a private commodities brokerage and named it after his dog, Alisa. Just like that. And within six months, he told me, he was worth "tens and tens of millions of rubles." Sterligov made his fortune in the vacuum left by the collapse of the old command system. As the system deteriorated, it was becoming impossible for builders to get bricks, for truckers to get oil and gas. Alisa filled in where the old ministries would not, or could not. When I visited him at the brokerage house on Leninski Prospekt, he acted like a child sultan. Everywhere there were pretty young blond women wearing spandex miniskirts: Sterligov's angels. "They are assisting me," Sterligov said with a leer. He had big dreams and, what was more, he was fulfilling them. Sterligov was the owner of the country's first professional hockey team and the founder of the Young Millionaires Club, a place where like-minded tycoons could get together and make big plans. "Oh, and another thing," he said as his secretary stooped to light his Marlboro. "We're going to take over the Moscow racetrack and bring in the Kentucky Derby people to set up some big-time international racing."

As he grew rich, Sterligov developed a stony heart. "Why should I pity the

poor and the lazy?" he said. "Pity the sick and the weak, okay, but if the rest want to live in poverty, God help them. If they want to be slaves—well, then, every slave has his dignity before God. But history is made by the individual, not the crowd. It is only when the ignorant crowd takes part in the historical process that it turns into a mess.

"My generation despises the system. It killed everyone and everything it touched. This was the richest state in the world and they destroyed it all down to the bone! But older people don't understand us. Their psychology is all screwed up. They are so used to being equal in poverty that they assume if you have any money, you are a crook."

Sterligov was not a lonely robber baron. The newspaper *Tochka Zreniya* ("Point of View") reported that there were at least 150,000 "ruble millionaires" in the Soviet Union by the end of 1990. "But look, a million rubles on the open market is now twenty-five thousand dollars. Is that really so much?" Sterligov said. "And I don't have a single free ruble. Everything is tied up in the business."

After our talk, one of Sterligov's men showed me around the trading floor, which was buzzing with brokers and angels. "Welcome to the future," said Yevgeny Gorodentsov, an Alisa broker who had just put together a brick deal that brought him 750,000 rubles in commissions. He was twenty-one years old. The brokers all talked of Sterligov as if of a god—a slightly mad deity. His people reminded me of the inner circle around Citizen Kane. They knew he would crash, but they wanted to be next to something transcendent and new. Sterligov's ambitions were boundless and wild, a mix of Thatcherian free-market zeal, Chicago in the twenties, and P. T. Barnum mythmaking. When I last saw him, his newest scheme was to buy a huge tract of land 150 miles from Moscow and build a self-contained "mini Western country," with factories and accredited schools and universities, airports and heliports, satellite dishes and a "Japanese TV for everyone."

Perhaps the singular feature of Sterligov's wealth was the envy, and the harassment, it attracted. Once a week, police inspectors showed up at Alisa demanding to see his books. The KGB dropped in too. To avoid racketeers demanding protection money, Sterligov, his wife, and their infant daughter moved from apartment to apartment. The same dangers appeared to await anyone who succeeded in the new marketplace. Of the twelve new members of the Young Millionaires Club, only Sterligov would reveal his name. Dozens of others told him they wanted to join but feared kidnapping and attacks. The Communist Party weekly *Glasnost* printed an article accusing Sterligov of a "pathological hatred of Communism," a history of racketeering, and a "real lack of intelligence." The attacks came from all sides. So successful was

Alisa in its first six months of existence that rival entrepreneurs told me that they were sure Sterligov had a working relationship with the KGB. There were rumors that one of his uncles was a minister.

Sterligov, like most plutocrats, immunized himself from criticism and convinced himself that everyone was simply jealous. "It's still a sin to be rich in this country," he said. "But we're going to change all that. It won't take long."

Liberals in their late thirties and forties were not so much angered as amazed at this new, younger generation. My friend Alex Kahn, a music critic from Leningrad, grew up in semi-dissident circles reading samizdat and listening to pirated tapes of John Lennon. Now the young seemed entranced by money and the possibility of money. "Every month, every week, you see more of these guys around town," he said. "My generation, in our late thirties and forties, worshiped the ideas and ideals that were forbidden to us. We looked to the poets and the bards. These guys are sick of all that. What they want most is a society that works."

The young millionaires were an arrogant lot, young men (never women) acting without a developed code of behavior or common language. Primitive capitalists, as Marx called them. The hard-liners despised the new breed, and the liberals saw them only as a necessity, a first step toward a decent material life. "Some of them are a crude bunch, but to develop wealth, you need these people. We can't wait for angels to do the spadework," said Igor Svinarenko, a reporter for the leading newspaper of the Soviet business world, *Kommersant*. "These businessmen who make their money selling rotten meat or lousy computers or patched-together trade deals, they'll accumulate money and build things and set up factories and stores. Some of them may do ugly things or act like barbarians. But they'll also educate their kids, maybe send them overseas to Harvard. And then the kids will come back with their high-minded ideas and they'll say, 'Dad, you are a scoundrel.' And so they'll do things in a more refined way. They'll act on their guilty conscience. And so society will develop from there."

If there was a Soviet model for the young millionaires it was Artyom Tarasov, a high-tech and trading magnate in his forties who was a constant target of KGB and police investigation for the allegedly illegal export of capital. Tarasov was the first of the Soviet millionaires to flaunt his wealth publicly, even describing his real estate deals and foreign trips at a press conference at the Foreign Ministry. He once suggested publicly that Gorbachev might sell the disputed Kuril Islands back to the Japanese for billions of dollars. Infuriated, Gorbachev threatened to sue, and the KGB investiga-

tions increased. By 1990, Tarasov was spending most of his time on the French Riviera, fishing and waiting for the right moment to come back home. "I've been fascinated watching this generation—these young Tarasovs—and it's clear they love the game more than the money as an end in itself," said Vladimir Aleksanyan, an émigré who ran an import-export business with offices in Palo Alto, California, and Moscow. "They work sixteen, eighteen hours a day. Their mentality is completely different from anyone I ever knew before I left twelve years ago. They speak foreign languages. They come to the States and they rent cars, move around. They are absolutely fearless. They talk about renting military transport planes from the army to fly over some product, and they don't even realize how mind-boggling this sounds to anyone over the age of thirty."

An example of the breed was Anton Danielets, a twenty-four-year-old information services and real estate czar in Leningrad. He was a moon-faced naïf with the bovine grace of a young Jackie Gleason. He claimed by 1991 a fortune of 20 million to 30 million rubles and $1.5 million in foreign banks. Danielets used a dying Communist institution, the Komsomol, to build his nascent empire. In the first rush of cooperative businesses in 1987 and 1988, he opened a video theater with Komsomol help and made 500,000 rubles in personal profit within a year. He learned management from a pirated copy of a business text published abroad. One of the first things he did next was to hire lawyers to "guide me through the thicket of laws." The key to business amid the "war of laws" between Moscow and the republics, between cities and districts, he said, was to know just who owns what, who has the right to issue licenses.

Racing around Leningrad from morning till night in a dilapidated Soviet Fiat, he quickly used his savings to rent and buy valuable properties and put some of his long-held ideas to work. He rented a run-down indoor pool and gym that the city had left for dead and turned it into a profitable sports center, popular with his fellow Soviet millionaires and the foreign community. He saw business on the rise and started a financial information center, a kind of Dow Jones in Leningrad. He started a popular newspaper, *Nevskoye Vremya* ("Neva Times"), and bought a printing press that had once belonged to the local Communist Party. In Siberia, the Urals, and Karelia, he traded in raw materials "whenever the deal looks good." He had more than a thousand people working for him. After a while, Danielets finally decided that the backseat of his car was not quite adequate as a corporate headquarters, and so, for 300,000 rubles, he bought the glorious three-story mansion at 47 Herzen Street—Vladimir Nabokov's childhood home.

"My forebears too were business people, gentry, and we're going to make this place look like it once did," Danielets said, pointing to rooms immortal-

ized in Nabokov's memoir *Speak, Memory.* "I think of this place as our connection to what we lost and what we want to regain. People forget that there was something known as a Russian business life before the Revolution. Now we are nothing more, nothing less, than a Third World country—at best. I want to restore what we had. So when people come to me with interesting projects, I invest, maybe with cash, maybe with equipment or space.

"Everyone knows that the smart guys in the Communist Party are trying to grab up as much as they can before they finally leave the stage. My attitude is this: Let them. Most of them are so stupid they don't even know what real business is. It's the young who are going to do the work over the years. We're building empires, but not evil ones."

In classical Marxist theory, the initial stages of the accumulation of wealth produce "morbid symptoms." Chief among them in the Soviet Union was the rapid rise of thuggery: protection rackets, Ponzi schemes, the occasional murder and night of arson. Zaslavsky and the police faced problems with crime all over the district, especially on blocks with new private businesses. For some reason, though, I had better luck meeting the mob in Leningrad.

Alex Kahn said he knew someone who knew someone who sold computers "and whatnot" out of a storefront in the Vasilievsky Region of the city. The businessman, who was named Aleksandr, told us just to bring a bottle or two of Scotch—"Johnnie Walker if you've got it"—at two in the afternoon and we "might meet some interesting people." Happily, the hard-currency store in the Astoria Hotel was well stocked with Johnnie Walker.

The office was a shambles, a room filled with spiderwebs, scrap lumber, dust, and a desk and a phone. Aleksandr quickly said the Scotch was not for him and, "under the circumstances," he would prefer I didn't print his last name. It was soon clear why.

Within five minutes, four brawny types arrived. "The Charity Society," they called themselves. It was time to collect the weekly 5,000-ruble "donation" from Aleksandr. I handed over the Scotch, Aleksandr handed over a paper bag, and the Charity Society boys seemed happy. They were only too pleased to talk, they said brightly.

"Some people call us gangsters," an ex-athlete named Sergei explained as he popped a knuckle. "We like to think of it this way: we protect people. We persuade them to let us protect them." Sometimes, Sergei said, they used pistols and Uzis bought on the black market as their instruments of persuasion. Pasha, a wiry hood who "went a little crazy" fighting in Afghanistan, explained how he and his partners did their business during what economists

in the press were now calling "the transition period" from a centralized, socialist economy to a free market, and what the punks referred to as "the Wild West" and "Chicago in the thirties":

"First, everything is explained to the businessman in question. Very slowly and carefully. Then if he doesn't seem to understand the kind of payments he has to make, he's beaten up. But professionally. A couple of broken ribs, a few nights in the hospital. The next step is, he's hustled into a car, driven out to the woods, and given a shovel. We tell him to start digging his own grave. That's usually when they crack."

There was no way to know whether their stories were fact or cheap bravado. But such rackets did exist, such murders went on all the time, and Aleksandr, a Nordic-looking man in his late thirties, tried hard to keep from trembling as he listened. Occasionally he shot me an anxious glance. To make everyone just a little more nervous, Sergei broke into the sort of half-mad giggle that Robert De Niro used to great effect in the film *Mean Streets.* The mannerisms, it turned out, were as imported as the Reeboks on their feet. Sergei admitted that he had seen the films *Once Upon a Time in America* and *GoodFellas* on the Charity Society's video system. "We learn a lot of what we do that way," he said.

With private business growing by the day here, life was good for the Charity Society. They shook down everyone from the owners of newspaper kiosks to department stores selling foreign goods.

"Just the price is different," Sergei said.

"When I get about two or three million for myself, then maybe I'll go out and get some principles," Pasha said. "I've got plenty of time later on to buy a farm and live quietly."

After the Charity Society left, Aleksandr said paying protection money was "just part of doing business nowadays." His only other expense was his phone bill. "This country is in a state of transition, a wild time, and so there are no rules, no stability. It's open season," he said. "I know of one guy who couldn't make his payments and they tortured him with a soldering iron. Ninety-nine percent of the businessmen in town—me included—violate a lot of rules. Taxes, hard-currency restrictions, the laws on hiring people. We have to break the law if we want to get anything done. And so the racketeers know we can't resist. Calling in the police is hopeless. That is, unless you want to spend the rest of your life in a fortress. Or dead in the canal."

During the Brezhnev era, the personification of sleazy business dealings was the *tolkach,* the weary factory representative who would travel the country to make sure he got the supplies his firm needed. Bribes and gifts were his

stock in trade. If he was from Moldavia, he would bring cases of wine to sway his clients; if he came from Astrakhan, it would be quart-size tubs of black caviar. But the *tolkach* was only the comic face of a degraded, dishonest system. Corruption permeated the centralized economy from the bottom to the top: from the state butcher shop manager who sold his best beef on the black market to the members of the Council of Ministers who lied about production levels to curry favor with the general secretary.

That legacy of cynicism and lawlessness, despite all the talk of reform, still lingered. "The standard of 'dual honesty' for seventy years here has led to a deterioration of ethical standards," said Vladimir Aleksanyan, the émigré import-export executive. "You rob your workplace. You cut in line. You skip out on contracts if it's convenient. Dishonesty is deep-rooted. When a person in business is honest, it is because he has made a conscious, and usually temporary, decision to be honest. There is not a deep-rooted sense of ethics."

Corruption was a matter of course. In Leningrad's Kirov District, officials and businessmen said, merchants quickly discovered that to do a simple remodeling job on a building or to get a decent location for a kiosk they had to pay off the district government's architect. Finally, the local police caught the architect, Timur Kuriyev, taking a 9,000-ruble bribe in a public bathroom. One of the great scams of the Gorbachev era was known as the "convenient collapse." In an effort to encourage semiprivate cooperative businesses, the government issued huge start-up loans at low interest rates. Some cooperators used the funding to open stores or services. But others, who did not believe the period of liberalization would last more than a few months and wanted to make a quick fortune, grabbed the money and, when the loan came due, said, "Sorry, the business failed." The bank could do little more than put a 12 percent lien on the debtor's meager state salary. Every time a new form of commerce began, it seemed, a new racket appeared alongside it. After Sotheby's held its first auction of modern Soviet paintings in Moscow in July 1988, black marketeers discovered a source of quick income. Soviet artists told me that a man identifying himself as Oleg Petrovich—alias "the Gypsy"—showed up with his henchmen at various artists' studios demanding works that he knew would bring in big money when sold abroad for hard currency. "Friends of mine were hit bad, and they told me that I was on the guy's list for four or five paintings—specific ones that they saw in the Sotheby's catalog," said Lev Tabenkin, a Moscow painter who had sold many of his canvases abroad. "They're very systematic. So far they haven't gotten to me, but I haven't been working very much in my studio these days either."

Lieutenant Nikolai Mirikov, chief of the Moscow police investigations

department, said the "evolving economic situation," the conversion to a market economy, will keep the rate of crime soaring for years. He said that while he needs five thousand police to cope with rising crime rates, he has lost more than a thousand officers in the past two years. "They mainly go off to work in cooperatives, where their salaries are a lot higher," he said. KGB officers, some of them at the highest levels, often took an early retirement to use their connections in the official and underground economies and make a killing as businessmen. Sometimes the police went into business without turning in their uniforms. A Moscow detective was caught shaking down street vendors for bribes of 10,000 rubles a month, the business newspaper *Kommersant* reported. In 1990, the same officer had been voted the city's Detective of the Year.

Businessmen in the October Region and elsewhere told me it was easy to make millions of rubles. Step One: Get a short-term loan of, say, 10 million rubles. Step Two: Launder the rubles. That is, convert them into dollars. One of the most common back-channel methods is to buy from a third party a paper obligation for money owed in "semihard" currencies: Indian rupees, Chinese yuan. The paper obligation, for which you have paid dearly, makes the transfer to dollars much easier. Step Three: Buy goods—Japanese VCRs, Hong Kong computers, American blue jeans. Volume and a foreign label matter far more than quality. Step Four: The easiest part—sell the goods to a middleman or a commission store or a workplace. Make sure your prices are absurd; Soviet consumers are desperate, and the demand curve knows no bounds. Step Five: Collect your money and pay off the bank. In three or four months, if all goes smoothly, you will be several million rubles richer.

It seemed painless. But then I met Oleg Falkovich.

A plump man with a heavy measure of guile, Falkovich worked for twenty-five years in the state economy in Siberia and the far east before he began dealing privately in construction materials, clothes, and video equipment. Eventually, he became a buyer for a company called ARTO, which was looking to obtain millions of rubles' worth of video equipment for resale on the Soviet market. Falkovich contacted another firm, Terminal, which agreed to get the televisions and VCRs from Japanese suppliers. A few weeks later, however, Terminal said the deal in Tokyo had fallen through, and Falkovich had to give the bad news to ARTO. But ARTO said it was going to suffer losses in the millions as a result of the deal's collapse because it had taken out short-term loans with high interest rates. The ARTO bosses told Falkovich that the burden for getting back the money was on him.

One spring afternoon, Falkovich said, and other sources confirmed, three

men forced him into a car and drove him to the Rossiya Hotel near the Kremlin. "Once we were in a room, they started threatening me, saying that unless I signed a contract handing over to them five million rubles, they would rape me, kill me, kill my wife and daughter. This went on for days. But when they got to my family, I signed. I would have signed anything."

Falkovich managed to reach one of his partners by phone, and the partner called some members of their acquaintance in the Uzbek mafia to come to Moscow and set their boss free. The team flew to Moscow and knocked on the door of the hotel room. But Rustam, the Uzbek leader, recognized one of the three men as an old friend and colleague. "It was a nightmare," Falkovich said. "Instead of freeing me, Rustam turned to one of the others and said, 'Once you beat the five million out of him, we'll beat out another million.' "

Eventually, the police arrived at the Rossiya and sent everyone home. Later, they arrested the three men whom Falkovich accused of kidnapping him. But the men were released after three days of questioning; the police said there was insufficient evidence to prosecute. "Falkovich claims the men were extortionists and the three said they were not. The whole situation was a blur," said Genri Reznik, the lawyer for ARTO.

In the meantime, Falkovich said he is sure he is "a hunted man." He has moved his family from their home in Magadan to a secret location, and he is hoping to emigrate to the United States. With no relatives there, his chances for an entrance visa are not good. "I can't live this way any longer," Falkovich said. "In a normal world, they settle these things with contracts or, if it comes to that, with lawsuits. This kind of thing will go on and on in this country until we have real laws, real business, and not the kind of insanity we have now."

Despite the "morbid symptoms" of the new capitalism, Zaslavsky and Co. had no intention of scaling back their ambitions. They were world-beaters. Dmitri Chegodayev, the twenty-seven-year-old chairman of the district's media committee, began holding meetings with foreign investors about setting up a thirty-two-station cable television system featuring an "October channel." "We want to hook into Europe via cable TV," he said. There were meetings about how best to attract foreign investors—the "capitalist leeches" of Stalinist legend. The most ambitious plan—one that smacked of megalomania to Communist Party loyalists—was to create a huge business center on Gagarin Square modeled on the La Defense complex in Paris. Important-looking documents were drawn up. The center would include luxury hotels,

office buildings, underground parking lots, an exhibition center, a computer and communications center, a trade center, and a medical complex.

But by the summer and fall of 1990, something else was happening. The Communist Party newspapers were beginning to hint at a counterrevolution. Suddenly, the most prominent free-market advocates in the country were under attack—Zaslavsky included. Like the Soviet Union itself, Zaslavsky was flying into the heavy weather of a market economy without a flight plan or a radar screen. His vision of the future—a world of stock markets, computer centers, and shopping malls—met head-on with the endless barriers of habit and instability: the obstinate psychology of a people grown used to "equality in poverty." Perhaps a little sooner than the rest of the country, the radical free-market leaders of the October Region encountered the limits of people's tolerance. Some workers in the district were growing angry with the new businesses. There were small demonstrations. Some of Zaslavsky's supporters began to turn on him. "Many people in the district saw businesses like Alisa succeeding very quickly while they still had to stand in lines for food. It outraged them, and they started screaming, 'Give us! Give us!' " said Zaslavsky's aide, Gezentsevei. "Many people could not understand that the idea of government is not to provide, the way parents provide for a child. What we were trying to do was set up the structures, the possibilities for everyone to have the chance to work and succeed."

It came as no shock to Zaslavsky that a lot of the negative letters he got in the mail, to say nothing of the articles in the nationalist press, were anti-Semitic. As the business explosion intensified and the average wage bought less and less, resentment eventually made its way toward that fine end. Anyone with a little extra was a Jew. You heard the grumbling on the buses, on the streets, on park benches. Sometimes it became the stuff of public meetings and demonstrations. On June 6, 1990, at the Red October cultural hall in Moscow, seven hundred members of something called the People's Orthodox Movement met, and the level of hatred was startling. "We declare that the Jews bear collective responsibility for the genocide of the Russian people and other peoples of our country!" said one speaker, Aleksandr Kulakov. "And we demand that Jews be forbidden to leave the country until a tribunal of the Russian people decides their fate. We express solidarity with the Arab world, which struggles with this evil! We also express solidarity with the German people. The Jews were never victims of the German people. The Germans were the victims of Jewish deception!"

Groups like the United Workers' Front, Motherland, and Unity all emit-

ted similarly horrifying grunts, all in the name of "proletarian justice" and the call for a class war. Zaslavsky showed me some of his mail, where the word *Zhid*—Yid—appeared more frequently than commas. It was as if he had ended up on the wrong side of a perverse class war, a focus of class resentment. *Nash Sovremenik, Moscow Worker,* and *Molodaya Gvardiya* were the main publications supporting this strange amalgam of nationalism, neo-Stalinism, and pure resentment that was fast becoming known as National Bolshevism. "We face a paradox," wrote Richard Kosolapov in the *Moscow Worker.* "An actual ban on the class approach and its false contrast with universal human values is happening at a time when the gap between rich and poor is widening. We are stubbornly being told that there is a need for fraternization between striking coal miners and the growing ranks of millionaires . . . despite the fact that our entire historical experience is literally crying out about the inevitability of conflict."

Zaslavsky had begun his term in early 1990 with the support of more than a hundred of the 150 October Region deputies. But by winter, he could rely on only forty or so. The rest, with help from various Communist Party organizations, began to plot against him. Articles began appearing in the Russian Communist Party paper *Sovetskaya Rossiya* accusing Zaslavsky of incompetence, of "aggressive anti-Communism," of taking power out of the hands of the people and putting it in the hands of a few young millionaires. "Zaslavsky was not the man we thought he was," said Alla Vlasova, a conservative on the council. "He turned arrogant. He would only listen to the inner circle around him. He has to go."

Inexperience and a measure of arrogance also gave Zaslavsky's enemies ammunition for the approaching political battle. Some members of the city's executive committee, it turned out, were also businessmen. Vasiliyev's deputy, Shota Kakabadze, for one, was president of the law firm Assistant, which did legal work for the region. Although the lawyers said they did their municipal work free, the impression of a conflict of interest became indelible. "We started falling victim to our own stupidity and inexperience," Chegodayev said.

The biggest mistake was in the way Zaslavsky handled the privatization of several thousands parcels of land and new enterprises. The Municipal Property Board was in charge of holding auctions and selling off land in order to help create businesses, hotels, or plants that fit in with the October Region's plans for the future. Zaslavsky saw the dilemma of mixing the state and the private sectors, but he argued that this was often done in other developing countries. "And that," he said, "is what we are, let's face it. A developing

country that happens to have nuclear weapons." Upper Volta with rockets. Zaslavsky's enemies pounced all over him, accusing him of funneling profits to his cronies. And while the charge was never proved, it hurt him badly. Suddenly, the young politician who had started with a pristine image was stained.

To make matters worse, Zaslavsky took a hit from a powerful corner. For months, Zaslavsky had been telling the press and even audiences abroad that Gorbachev was a "lost cause" who was getting far too much credit for even beginning perestroika. He said that it was Ronald Reagan's strategy of negotiation through strength that brought the Kremlin to its knees. "I will never forget what Gorbachev did at the start," Zaslavsky said, "but it would be a mistake to put all our hopes in one man anymore. Thank God, we're beyond that." Gorbachev, who was then turning sharply to the right, went before a meeting of the Moscow Communist Party organization and railed against the "so-called democrats." It was one of his most conservative speeches during a conservative winter in the Kremlin. Zaslavsky in particular, Gorbachev said, had "disappointed" him.

On the bitter cold afternoon of February 13, 1991, Zaslavsky's opponents called a council session and put a no-confidence vote on the agenda. To bring down Zaslavsky, however, they needed a quorum of ninety-nine deputies. Zaslavsky's only remaining strategy was to block the quorum, to keep his people outside the hall. As he sat in his second-floor office, his opponents hammered him in the auditorium.

"All summer Zaslavsky was in the United States. He is learning to destroy our political, economic, and ideological system!" said Alla Zhokina.

"Zaslavsky's emissaries took their training in the United States!" said Gennadi Markov. "All his people now have cushy jobs." Yuri Mazenich said Zaslavsky's team "tried to establish a totalitarian regime based on the arbitrary seizure of regional property."

The denunciations went on from five to nearly midnight. Although the deputies were five short of a quorum, they held a no-confidence vote anyway, with seventy-eight voting for Zaslavsky's resignation. It was beginning to look as though the October Revolution would not lead to the shining future of "capitalism in one district." Zaslavsky sat in his office exhausted. He was surrounded by the mementos of his rise to fame: the bric-a-brac from his trip to the United States, the aides who doted on him, the map of the future—the gleaming region he saw in his mind's eye. The revolution was at a stalemate. "It turns out this is going to be a very long game," he said.

CHAPTER 22

MAY DAY! MAY DAY!

I woke early on May Day, 1990, the annual festival of labor, sunshine, and kitsch. The weather was perfect, a sweet astonishment in the perpetually dreary city of Moscow. Rumor had it in the past that the Communist Party, in its constant attempt to tame the heavens and the earth, seeded the clouds so it would rain before and after—but never on—the parade.

May Day was a cartoon of what was happening in the country. You could just plant yourself on Red Square and watch it all go by. Under Stalin, May Day raised the cult of personality to the level of communal entertainment. Every float and billboard, every song and banner was devoted to the worship of his greatness. Under Khrushchev and Brezhnev the atmosphere was still grotesque, but more jolly. Unsurpassed achievements of the workingman at least equaled the unsurpassed wonderfulness of the Leader.

By 1988, there were still some portraits of the Politburo leaders and Central Committee–approved slogans ("Acceleration!") floating by, but Gorbachev had reduced the ceremony mostly to a bit of tacky fun, a production worthy of halftime at the Sugar Bowl: strongmen flinging golden dumbbells into the air, gymnast-nymphets jackknifing at the waist in honor of the working class. Harmless Sovietiana. The banners were more in the spirit of self-help than national vanity. The country was collapsing, after all, and

everyone knew it. It was in the papers every day. That year I also managed to run into Yeltsin as he wandered toward his modest car. He had not been seen around Moscow since his fall from power nearly a year before, and this was probably his last moment of shyness. Oh yes, he said with a fantastically broad smile, he was quite healthy. We would hear from him soon.

By 1989, the slogans had turned to a sugary mush. "Peace for Everyone!" one said. Or the touching "We're Trying to Renew Ourselves!" It was all so innocent, a Fourth of July barbecue without the hot dogs. Ideology had disappeared. There were no "our rockets are bigger than your rockets" signs anymore, no boasting of magnesium production rates, no Uncle Sams stepping on the neck of the Third World. An empire with thousands of nuclear warheads was eager to show just how toothless it had become. The Soviet Union was in the midst of a self-actualization craze.

For 1990, Gorbachev decided to account for the new wave of young politicians in the various legislatures, city halls, and town councils. The Kremlin announced that the liberal mayor of Moscow, Gavriil Popov, would be on the reviewing stand of the Lenin Mausoleum along with the Politburo and a few selected government honchos. Yuri Prokofiyev, the astonishingly dense leader of the Moscow Party organization, also declared that factory workers would no longer be compelled to celebrate. This year May Day would be "completely voluntary," he said. Only banners bearing "anticonstitutional" slogans would be discouraged. "What a gesture!" everyone was supposed to think. "What a kind and liberal leadership!" But, as usual, the Party was acting more out of anxiety than generosity. They opened up the parade only in exchange for an agreement from Democratic Russia, Memorial, and other opposition groups that there would be no embarrassing "countermarches" across town. In Leningrad, the Party was taking no chances; it canceled the parade altogether.

The morning was reliably gorgeous—a hard bright sun and a cool breeze washed along faces that had turned the lightest shade of pale after the long winter. Along the walk north from October Square to Red Square, I saw a few people carrying a Lithuanian flag and some rolled-up banners. I didn't think much of it. I got to the reviewing stand early, bought an ice cream, and gossiped with some of the other reporters. The public address system pumped out some treacly Soviet pop tunes and Pete Seeger's "We'll See That Day Come Round."

Finally, it was time for the ceremonies to begin. As always, the reporters took careful note of the order in which the various leaders walked up the stairs of the Lenin Mausoleum to the reviewing stand. Yeltsin and Geidar Aliyev had told me how Gorbachev, like a baseball manager, would give everyone his place in the order just before showtime. "Usually, it was written

on a little card or piece of paper," Yeltsin said. He also said that at lunch breaks during Politburo sessions, everyone sat in his usual May Day order.

For the reporters, it was still considered slightly important who chatted with whom, who wore a fedora, who a homburg, and, above all, who was missing. This was called "Soviet watching." At least for me, the ritual lost its aura with the discovery that underneath the mausoleum there was a laboratory charged with monitoring the temperature and rate of deterioration of "the living Lenin." Below that, there was a gymnasium where the guards could work out on off hours. The idea of some pimply kid from Chelyabinsk doing squat thrusts in the bowels of sacred territory somehow erased all mystery from the grand procession and the leaders who watched it.

For about an hour, May Day was as calm and uneventful as the Macy's Thanksgiving Day parade. One merely had to substitute images of heroic labor for Underdog and Bullwinkle. Gorbachev watched with a bored, kingly smile, as if he were pleased to live through this hour of his life without crisis. The first marchers were mostly factory workers and members of official unions, and the signs they carried reflected their fear that a market economy would leave them without money or a job. "Enough Experiments," one said. "A Market Economy Is Just Power to the Plutocracy," said another. "Down with Private Property." Even while they mouthed the slogans of the right wing, those workers demanded our sympathy. They had lived for decades in a world of guarantees (however meager) and absolute truths (however false), and now everything had been denounced, undercut, found out. They felt threatened to the core.

The crowd moved from left to right, from the brick Museum of the Revolution across the cobblestones of Red Square then down the slope past St. Basil's Cathedral and toward the steely Moscow River, glinting now like the oiled barrel of a .38. But suddenly, the march seemed to run out of marchers. We all looked left and saw that another wave had gathered, but they were waiting, and they looked . . . different. What was this? There were red, yellow, and green Lithuanian flags, black, blue, and white Estonian flags, Russian tricolors from the czarist era. There was shouting, more young people, an entirely different feel. Something was about to happen. You could feel it. Everyone could. These were the very people who would have gone off to "counterdemonstrations" had the Party not cut a deal with them. Soon the Party would wish it had never had this stroke of genius.

The democrats started marching onto the square, and now their placards became visible from the reviewing stands. I'd seen the same ones at other demonstrations, but on Red Square? With Gorbachev watching?

"Socialism? No Thanks!"

"Communists: Have No Illusions. You Are Bankrupt."

"Marxism-Leninism Is on the Rubbish Heap of History."

"Down with the Politburo! Resign!"

"Ceauşescus of the Politburo: Out of Your Armchairs and Onto the Prison Floors!"

"Down with the Empire and Red Fascism!"

There were no portraits of the Politburo members, but there were numerous posters featuring Yeltsin ("Tell 'em, Boris!") and Sakharov ("Conscience of the Nation"). Then came the most chilling symbol of all: red Soviet flags with the hammer and sickle ripped out—an echo of the opposition flags on the streets of Bucharest during the uprising of December 1989. The demonstrators all stopped and turned toward the Lenin Mausoleum. The square was filled with tens of thousands of people now, waving their fists, chanting "*Doloi KPSS!*" ("Down with the Party!") "*Doloi Gorbachev!*" "*Doloi Ligachev!*" I borrowed a pair of binoculars and glimpsed the faces of the men on the reviewing stand. (Later I got a closer look on television.) Ligachev glared and nodded, his face hard as a walnut. Yakovlev was impassive, Yoda-like; Popov looked utterly serene, even pleased, though hesitant to let it show in such company. Gorbachev, as always, was a master of his emotions. As tens of thousands of people denounced him, he never let the minutest flicker of anger crease his face. I remembered other men in similar situations, how confused and frightened Ceauşescu had looked when he listened to those first demonstrators from his balcony in Bucharest. Gorbachev's performance was as amazing as the demonstration itself. He watched and watched and occasionally chatted with those next to him, as if this were the most common May Day parade in memory. As if it were normal!

The confrontation seemed as if it might go on endlessly. The demonstrators were ready to stay in Red Square all day. We all stood there, watching, still as lizards in the sun. The men on the mausoleum did not move. They merely stood there, as if they were watching something else, some other parade, instead of their own last judgment. Finally, someone ordered the Kremlin loudspeakers turned up and they started churning out patriotic slogans and marching music. But it was no match for the chanting on the square, a surge that grew louder with every minute. This was their square and there was not a goddamn thing anyone could do about it. At the center of the crowd stood a Russian Orthodox priest, his beard from the pages of Dostoevsky; he carried a seven-foot-high crucifix and shouted, "Mikhail Sergeyevich, Christ Has Risen!"

Finally, after a full twenty-five minutes of this, Gorbachev nodded, turned on his heels, and walked off the tribune. What else could he do? Everyone, Popov included, followed. Later, I visited Popov at city hall and asked him how he and Gorbachev had felt standing there on the mausoleum.

"For me, it was interesting," he said. "For Gorbachev? I would say the word is . . . uncomfortable."

I also spoke to Yegor Ligachev, who told me that he had been deeply disturbed by the incident. "Not just me, but Mikhail Sergeyevich, everyone had this feeling," he said. "On the one hand, we gave the chance for any force to march on Red Square and express themselves. On the other hand, we witnessed such extremist outbursts, such blatant aggressiveness, that if they would come to power and we would organize such a demonstration, we would be sent directly to jail from Red Square. No doubt about that. I watched for a long time and Mikhail Sergeyevich came up to me and said, 'Yegor, probably it's time to finish it.' And I said, 'Yes, it's time.' And we left, with me walking beside him. It was uncivilized. I said to Mikhail Sergeyevich, 'Once again we are seeing what a deplorable state the country is in.' These were my exact words."

After Gorbachev and the rest left the reviewing stand on Lenin's tomb, I walked into the square and joined the march at its tail end. Everyone was jazzed with a sense of power. "The leadership may try to dismiss what happened here today as just some extremists blowing off a little steam, but it runs deeper. Gorbachev has done a lot of good, but when it comes to us, the radical, he turns away from his natural allies," one demonstrator, Aleksandr Afanasyev, told me. His face was streamed with sweat, flush with the thrill of the standoff. A young man named Vitaly Mindlin, who was carrying a pro-Lithuanian banner, told me, "I've been forced to go to these rallies for years, and this is the first time I've come voluntarily, acting from my own soul. Gorbachev may have been insulted by our openness, but we have to take that risk. We can't afford to act as if we were someone's subject. We are our own masters. The people dictate the moment now, not Gorbachev."

The Party, of course, tried to make sure the country did not hear about the demonstrations. Official television gave blanket coverage to the first hour of the parade, but once the radicals crested the hill and entered Red Square, the broadcast ended. Of course, glasnost subverted any attempt to control the information. The more liberal papers were filled with accounts of the May Day events, and the public read not only about Moscow, but about the anti-Communist demonstrations in Eastern Europe and the "anti-empire" demonstration in Ukraine. The Party had been humiliated nearly everywhere. In Lvov, the center of the Ukrainian independence movement, demonstrators carried icons of the Virgin Mary and signs saying, "USSR: The Prison House of Nations." The mayor of Lvov, Vyacheslav Chernovil, could not help but applaud. He'd spent the better part of his adulthood as a dissident and political prisoner. "Happy May Day," he told everyone. "Happy May Day."

A few days later, Aleksandr Yakovlev had the pitiable job of facing the press. Playing against type, the most liberal man in the leadership denounced the May Day demonstrations as "insulting" and "freakish." Yakovlev turned demagogue as he singled out the few kooks in the march, war veterans with pictures of Stalin, monarchists with icons of Nicholas II. He made out this lunatic fringe to be the main current of the demonstration itself and then pompously declared that what we had witnessed that day were "anti-reform" forces trying to frighten the goodly men of the Kremlin. What a strange and terrible thing it must have been for Yakovlev to carry out such a task. Yuri Prokofiyev, the Moscow Party chief, was more honest in his anger. The crowds, he said, "carried insulting slogans exceeding the limits of decency. They smeared the leaders of the country, the Communist Party, and the president and chanted rude, almost obscene words and whistled. The goal of these people was explicitly clear: to spoil the holiday with the poison of confrontation." What a phrase! "Almost obscene words!"

The Party press scolded the "tastelessness" of the demonstration, as if the demonstrators had used the fish fork for the steak. Gorbachev, for his part, just kept away from the subject. What could he say? What he felt standing there on the mausoleum? What had Lyndon Johnson felt as he sat in the Lincoln bedroom or the Oval Office and heard the great throbbing coming from Lafayette Park: "Hey! Hey! LBJ! How many kids did you kill today?" In his own perverse way, Johnson had started out thinking of himself as doing good, raising up the poor, giving black folks a chance. And now he was a baby-killer, a demon. Gorbachev's indignation on May Day must have gone even deeper. He had challenged institutions and a system many times more monstrous than anything a modern American could imagine. His maneuvering, his attempt to erode the power of the Party and slowly build up democratic institutions, was the political feat of an age. No czar or general secretary had ever put himself and his power in such jeopardy. And now it had all gone wrong. Day by day, the people of the Soviet Union were developing minds of their own. Gorbachev cheered that—at least in principle. But the reality of a new psychology, independent and defiant, confused him, sent him running to the reliable bases of traditional power. He ignored those who told him what he did not want to hear. The only men who would flatter him were precisely those who would one day betray him. His tragedy had begun.

The liberal press was forever wringing its hands over the lack of young people in politics. I found that strange. Red Square that May Day was filled with men and women in their thirties, twenties, and teens. Unlike Karpinsky,

Afanasyev, Yakovlev, and Gorbachev—men who had been raised as true believers and then begun the long process of awakening after Stalin's death—the young had never believed for a minute. They did not believe in Communism, the Party, or the system. They did not believe in the future. As a secret Politburo analysis dated May 19, 1990, described the phenomenon, there was now in Soviet society an utter "disrespect for the organs of state power."

The Gorbachev years were not a negation for the young, but rather a chance to fill a void, to move from a despairing cynicism toward something resembling normal modern life in all its multiplicity. For the young, the instructions and pretensions of the existing system constituted a separate world of the absurd, a realm of lies so funny you could die laughing.

The official indoctrination had started in the first grade. On the first day of school, the principal would gather all the children in an auditorium and tell them, "You are so lucky to be living in this country where all childhoods are happy ones!" The first words in their readers were "Lenin," "Motherland," and "Mama." The flyleaf bore a picture of the Lenin Mausoleum, and in the sixties the last page of all textbooks had a portrait of Khrushchev with the caption "Nikita Sergeyevich is a fighter for peace. He says to all peoples, 'Let's live in peace!' " On Revolution Day, the children were declared *Oktyabritsti,* "Children of October," and they wore star-shaped badges bearing little pictures of Lenin as a cherubic child. In the essay "Less Than One," Joseph Brodsky captures the experience of school under the regime in two sentences: "It is a big room with three rows of desks, a portrait of the Leader on the wall behind the teacher's chair, a map with two hemispheres, of which only one is legal. The little boy takes his seat, opens his briefcase, puts his pen and notebook on the desk, lifts his face, and prepares himself to hear drivel."

In summer, the luckier children went to Pioneer camps, where they played war games with balsa rifles and acted out "The Siege of Sevastopol" in evening song competitions. They were raised on a quaint prudery. During the Brezhnev era, the weekly *Ogonyok* magazine advised that "girls should learn self-respect, then there won't be any need to pass laws prohibiting kissing and hugging on the street. A woman's modesty increases the man's sexual energy, but a lack of modesty repels men and brings about total fiasco in their intimate relations." In 1980, an American researcher published *Sex in the Soviet Union* and cited one article in the official press declaring that premarital sex caused neurotic disorders, impotence, and frigidity; another article said that the "ideal duration of the sexual act" was two minutes, and a man who delayed ejaculation for the pleasure of his partner was doing something "terribly harmful" which could lead to "impotence, neuroses, and psychoses." All this while many Russian girls, in the absence of effective birth control, were having one abortion after another.

Those who grew up under Brezhnev were slowly crushed by a great, invisible weight. "Most conformed out of laziness, hopelessness," the music critic Alex Kahn told me one night. "When I was eighteen and in my first year of college, I was picking apples on a collective farm and I was talking to a friend of mine every day in the field. And I remember how we concluded that we were living in the most sophisticated dictatorship that has ever existed on this planet. The force of the propaganda was so strong that there could never be a revolution from below. I knew all about Sakharov and the other dissidents, but they were a tiny island off by themselves. The system had permeated society at every level. It was everywhere. No one was being tortured, as in the Middle Ages or under Stalin—or, at least, not many. But the system was unshakable because it penetrated society so thoroughly. You could talk openly only with your closest friends, and even that was not always safe."

But people of Alex's generation and younger grew up without the same sense of ever-present fear that their parents had known. The "era of stagnation" demanded obedience, but usually not your neck, not even your soul. For the first time, a generation began to distance itself from the system and look at it with disdain; it saw the strangeness and horror in all that had gone on before. Its relation to the state and its institutions was purely ironic.

What seemed to save people was the cocoon of friendships, the feeling of independence and intimacy that long nights of talk could provide. My tutors in this were, above all, a quartet of friends in their mid-thirties so close to one another for so many years that I feel presumptuous even now saying I was part of their circle. At least I was a kind of tangent to the circle of Masha Lipman and her husband, Seriozha Ivanov, and Masha Volkenshtein and her husband, Igor Primakov. They were the sort of people you'd see in the audience at meetings of Memorial or Moscow Tribune or, joking and paying half attention, at a rally somewhere on the outskirts of Moscow. Seriozha was a historian, Igor a seismologist, Masha Lipman a translator, Masha Volkenshtein a pollster. They were not famous, but they knew people who knew this well-known artist or that reform politician. Of the four, I knew Masha Lipman best, because she eventually came to work for the *Post.* When we finally had the nerve to stop hiring the KGB-approved informers that the Foreign Ministry had always sent us, Masha went to work as a researcher and translator, finally displacing a harpy of the higher organs.

Most nights when we got together, the talk was about politics. I supposed that was always the way in a city of revolution. But after a while Masha and Seriozha talked about their families, typical stories for educated people of their generation.

"My maternal grandfather, David Rabinovitch, was born in Kharkov, in the Pale of Settlement, and he became enthralled with proletarian ideas,"

Masha told me. "He was a typical Jewish intellectual, enthusiastic about a new era, a new art. He was a musician. When he came to Moscow and graduated from the conservatory, he taught Marxist political economy and was a member of the Russian Association of Proletarian Musicians. He wanted a new proletarian culture, loved Mayakovsky. For Jews, the Revolution meant the idea of an end to the Pale of Settlement. Grandmother was an actress who studied with Meyerhold, worked in his Theater of the Revolution. My grandfather knew Shostakovich, and my grandmother played a vendor who sold fur-lined brassieres in a Mayakovsky play.

"It was incredible. They and their friends developed a revolutionary style even in the way they lived at home. They had no dishes, no real furniture. They decided it was all too bourgeois and left it all in Kharkov. Birthday parties, weddings, and New Year's trees were also gotten rid of. Bourgeois. To make a table, my grandmother found a few boards, scrap wood, and asked the super to make a table. They thought that traditional Russian felt boots, *valenki,* were also bourgeois, so the children walked through the slush and the snow in their thin leather shoes, crying of the cold. They just mocked all traditions of the old order. So they had my mother call them by their first names and they ate their meals off of butcher paper."

Nevertheless, Masha's maternal grandfather was sent to the camps for espionage. He had met a few times with an American reporter. He survived, returning home after Stalin's death. Her paternal grandfather was not as fortunate. Aleksandr Levit was a revolutionary who worked in the Komintern and attended the Seventeenth Party Congress in 1935. He used the pseudonym Tivel. The year after the congress, he was arrested and disappeared. During the Moscow purge trials, Masha's grandmother turned on the radio and heard the voice of one of the accused, Karl Radek, testifying. "It was Tivel who came to me suggesting we kill Comrade Stalin," Radek said. Masha's grandmother fainted straightaway: "She knew it was the end."

Seriozha's family history was less dramatic and, perhaps, more typical. "My first clear memories can be easily dated. My parents had sent me to bed. Guests were coming over. My uncle brought a typewritten copy of *Paris Match,* which had run excerpts of Khrushchev telling the story of Stalin's death. I was in bed, trembling with curiosity. I had the door opened slightly and listened. I remember I was incredibly interested, even though my parents tried to fight this interest. They knew it was vaguely dangerous.

"When I was thirteen I had some very sharp political discussions with my parents, about history, about Bolshevism, about conformity. I was insisting that Bolshevism was a mistake that had caused incalculable suffering. I knew it from the beginning. I listened to the 'foreign voices' even though they were jammed. You had to sit out those long *wooo wooo* sounds. But you could

hear the stations better out in the country where the jamming wasn't quite as good as it was in the center of Moscow."

At about the same age, Masha said, she was in a ninth-grade class that was reading *Crime and Punishment,* and the discussion turned into a political event, a moment when Masha realized that she was growing slowly and inexorably away from the mythical Soviet childhood. "I raised my hand and said I thought the killing of another human soul was prohibited, and what's more, there was nothing more precious than a human life. No one in the class agreed. There were those who said, 'What if the person is an enemy?' The teacher accused me of sharing an 'abstract concept of humanism.' At the next parent-teacher meeting, this teacher told my mother with great assurance, 'Don't worry. I will struggle with her.' "

As a teenager, Masha listened carefully to the talk at her kitchen table. Her parents were on the margins of dissident society. They knew people who knew Solzhenitsyn. They visited Nadezhda Mandelstam, the great memoirist; as always, Mandelstam greeted her guests in bed, in her nightgown and covered with the husks of sunflower seeds and cigarette ash. Masha listened to her parents' underground music tapes—the *magnitizdat*—of Aleksandr Galich and Bulat Okhudzhava. "The tapes were a big secret. Not all of my friends had a tape recorder, and my friends would come and listen to other things. Once a girl opened a drawer and saw the tape marked 'Galich' and I will never forget the terror of that moment. I was sure that we'd end up at the KGB."

Masha and Seriozha traveled in the same circles during the Brezhnev years. When they first met, they discovered that they both adored the same book: Venedikt Yerofeyev's comic epic *Moskva-Petushki.* "That was the book of what our lives were, the pain of it and the irony, too," Masha said. "It was a book about trying to escape when no escape was possible." Their friends were students, young men and women who lived on the edge of dissidence, who were absorbed in books and talk. "In school and university, to be an intellectual meant that you got together all the time, talking and drinking and talking about how drunk you got the night before," Masha said. "I think of it now as a life of meaninglessness. It was considered the height of good taste to disdain your studies, to skip classes. A job was valued insofar as how often you could call in sick without losing it."

"My choice of occupation was a form of escape," Seriozha said. "I really wanted to be a diplomat, but I realized what that led to. Then a journalist. I was sent by my school in 1971 to sort of hang around the paper *Moskovski Komsomolets,* and I realized very quickly that it was impossible to be a journalist and a decent person. The means of escape for intellectuals were ancient history, theoretical physics (if you could avoid military research),

structuralism. Or you could be a *dvornik,* a caretaker or an elevator operator, and spend your vast amounts of spare time reading. It was a bit easier to be a scientist, but in the humanities you always had to be on the watch for the dead hand of ideology. So that's what I did. I raced into the past, far past the Bolsheviks, to Byzantium."

The circles of urban intellectuals whom Masha and Seriozha knew so well played at escape, at separateness, through style as well as substance. Unlike their Bolshevik grandparents, who affected the lives of ascetics, these Westernized intellectuals made a point of having good manners, of an almost stylized politeness, with men holding open doors and helping women on with their coats. They used a slightly ornate vocabulary, one as distant as could be imagined from the crude, politicized speech of *Pravda* and *Izvestia.* "There was a time when you would even kiss a woman's hand as a greeting," Seriozha said. "What could be more opposite from 'Greetings, comrade!' "

Real escape was possible only through emigration. And even though Masha and Seriozha both saw many of their friends off at the airport, they could not bear the idea of leaving, of living a life outside the Russian language and culture, of forcing their children to imagine their Russianness from a tremendous distance. "I went many times to get the forms and applications, but finally I just could not imagine myself stepping off a plane in another country and saying to myself, 'Where I am now is where I will be for the rest of my life.' I could not do it."

And so they staked their lives on a new Russia and tried to understand the pathology of the old. "Igor would quote Paul Tillich, who said there are two great fears: the fear of death and the fear of vastness, senselessness," Seriozha said. "Death and suffering are the same for all, but senselessness means different things in different cultures. Europe chose the undeniability of death as a principle, refusing to construct anything everlasting, so life ends with the end of life and is senseless. Previous old cultures and modern Oriental cultures chose another explanation. One possibility is to create something that lasts forever, a form of eternity. So we are together and there is no death. When some cells in an organism die in one organ, the organism still lives on, because it is social and not individual. The problem of death is solved. The idea that the ego has borders that are the same as the borders of the self is a new idea; it began with Descartes's idea 'I think, therefore I am.' If you ask a representative of old Roman culture or European medieval culture, 'Does human life coincide with the life of one man?' he'd say no.

"This was the case with Russian culture. And in Russia, this medieval mind-set has lasted until very recently. The serfs in Europe were liberated in the mid-fifteenth century, but it happened in Russia in the mid-nineteenth century. The idea of community was more important; that way the physical

unit lasted eternally. The idea that the individual was of absolute value appeared in Russia only in the nineteenth century via Western influences, but it was stunted because there was no civic society. This is why human rights was never an issue. The principle was set out very clearly by Metropolitan Illarion in the eleventh century in his 'Sermon on Law and Grace,' in which he makes clear that grace is higher than law; you see the same thing today in our great nationalists like Prokhanov—their version of grace is higher than the law. The law is somehow inhuman, abstract. The attempts to revise this principle were defeated. The Russian Revolution was a reaction of absolute simplification. Russia found its simplistic and fanatic response and conquered its support. What we are living through now is a breakthrough. We are leaving the Middle Ages."

The young people in Red Square on May Day had changed not only in intellectual terms. Many of them were fairly ordinary, if being a worker or a student or running an elevator is ordinary. Simply because the intellectuals and the articles and books they wrote might have given the best expression of the times, the perestroika phenomenon was also a matter of the pleasure principle, the Id unleashed. The Id of sex, of self-expression, of rock and roll, of materialism, of even the junkiest impulse. The Id of tabloid accounts of the murderous past, the ruined landscape.

The war in Afghanistan, for example, was just one reason among many that the young had come to despise anything that smelled of official Soviet life. More and more, the worst insult you heard was *sovok,* a slang word for Soviet. If you called someone *sovok* you were saying he was narrow-minded, officious, weak, lazy, obsequious, a hypocrite. After years of reducing the West to a swampy hell of imperialism and homelessness, Soviet television and the press now romanticized "over there" as an attainable paradise. The movie *Little Vera,* with its brutally realistic view of Soviet family life, was a hit, but eventually people tired of putting the mirror to their own sorry selves. The state film industry quickly realized that the way to fill the theaters was to buy up Hollywood movies—surf movies, second-rate police thrillers, *Porky's II,* anything smacking of dumb pleasure.

In Leningrad, I met a man, no longer young, named Kolya Vasyn. He was a genuine dissident in the Brezhnev years, but his dissidence consisted of his worship not of Jefferson or Mill, but of Chuck Berry, Keith Richards, and, above all, John Lennon. "Lots of things can liberate people," he told me as we listened to a tape of *The White Album.* "For me it was the freedom in John Lennon's voice." Since the early sixties, he and his friends had been collecting pirated tapes of Western rock and roll and listening to them with the same

furtive pleasure and sense of revelation as the intellectuals who read Sakharov in onionskin underground editions in one night-long sitting. He told me that when he first started listening to rock and roll, it was impossible to get records and it was before the era when audio cassettes were easy to find. "We had friends who worked in medical clinics and they would steal used X rays," Kolya said. "Someone would have a primitive record-making machine and you would copy the music by cutting the grooves in the material of the X rays. So you'd be listening to a Fats Domino tune that was coming right off of the X ray of someone's long-forgotten broken hip. They called that 'on the bones.' "

Kolya Vasyn's closet-sized apartment, decorated with Beatles memorabilia and a massive reel-to-reel tape recorder, became the equivalent of Sakharov's kitchen for the rock-and-roll set. Every major rock and jazz talent in Leningrad—the Soviet Union's Liverpool—came through, talked the night away, and, inevitably, collapsed in a corner. The native rock scene there was interesting enough: Kolya, Alex Kahn, and a bunch of others started a rock club on Rubenshtein Street, and Boris Grebenshikov's group, Aquarium, was as innovative as many of the top bands in the West. But what was most important was not the Soviet version of rock and roll, but the way that rock and roll brought kids into the greater world.

The Soviet regime had long worried about the lures of Western pop culture. Even the dullest ideologues, men who had never traveled much farther west than Minsk, knew that somehow James Brown and the Rolling Stones were nearly as dangerous as Helsinki Watch and the Voice of America. "The enemy is trying to exploit youthful psychology with dubious programs," Konstantin Chernenko declared at a 1983 plenum of the Central Committee. The Party's youth paper, *Komsomolskaya Pravda,* said of rock and roll, "Those who fall for this bait are playing into the hands of ideological opponents who sow in immature minds the seeds of a way of life alien to our society." But by 1989 and 1990, *Komsomolskaya Pravda* was earnestly reporting the latest news about Pink Floyd, the Talking Heads, and the *kheep-khope* (hip-hop) phenomenon. On my trip to Perm to visit the prison camp, I heard an odd throbbing sound coming from a vegetable stand. It was the first time I had ever heard a Russian rapper.

Rock and roll brought along with it sexier clothes, Reeboks, commercials, McDonald's. To the ideologues and nationalists nostalgic for an imagined Russian past, *Purple Rain* and Metallica were more of a threat than the idea of a stock exchange on Revolution Square. Now even the conservatives admitted that the country needed wealth, but in any issue of *Molodaya Gvardiya* or *Nash Sovremennik* you could read raving polemics about the evils of rock music, the encroachment on traditional Slavic music. "Live rock

has become the scourge and poison of our lives," wrote Valentin Rasputin, Vasily Belov, and Yuri Bondarev, all prominent novelists and cultural conservatives. "Pop music, with its stupefying, monotonous, hollow pulsation, absurd texts, completely lacking in poetry, is kicking every new stream of youngsters into a spiritual void." I was even told that the Politburo would frown severely upon the rise of a rock culture in the Soviet Union. Alexsandr Yakovlev's view is what passed for liberalism. "It's not exactly my sort of thing, but I don't think banning it is the answer," he said. Ligachev, for his part, wanted to prevent Elton John from getting an entry visa. I am not sure what dire order Yegor Kuzmich would have given had it been Ice-T and Public Enemy on the passport line.

Most of the men who ran the Kremlin had never been to the West, or when they had been, it was in the "bubble" of an official visit. It was not by chance that the two men who had traveled in the West extensively before coming to power were also the two main figures of official reform: Yakovlev and Gorbachev. God only knows what the hard-liners thought the Soviet Union would look like if the West moved East. But you could guess. When a young activist named Roman Kalinin registered a gay newspaper with Moscow City Hall in 1990 and published personal ads and some fairly tame articles on gay life in Moscow, *Pravda* accused the paper, *Tema,* of telling necrophiliacs where they could find corpses and pedophiles where to buy children for sex. Kalinin seemed unfazed. He started passing out fliers for a gay rights demonstration: "Turn Red Square into the Pink Triangle."

For the older generation that had finally given up the Communist dream, the West was the land of their defeat, a smug and garish landscape of success. It was as if all the dreams of utopia had evaporated and they were stranded between McDonald's and the gulag. What could they do but order a Big Mac?

But for the young, the West was the dream itself. Compared to the hole they were in, the problems of the West seemed laughable. The West was romanticized, sure enough, but why not? How could you begin to talk about the decline of the American economy with a thirty-year-old woman who still had to live with the husband she had divorced five years before because there was nowhere to move? By 1990, one of the fastest-selling books in the street kiosks was *How to Find Work in America,* followed quickly by *How to Find Work in Europe.* This lust for all things Western could break your heart. For a couple of weeks, I watched the making of *Russia House.* The director, Fred Schepsi, set John le Carré's novel against all the most predictable postcard backgrounds. Off to the side, dozens of young Russians worked in odd jobs,

as translators, stand-ins, technicians. I talked mostly with a young woman named Kira Sinyeshikova, who helped the Americans communicate with the Russians in the crew. I watched her watch Hollywood; I watched her bask in the glow of Michelle Pfeiffer. Kira could not get over the organization, the equipment, the treatment of the stars. And after a while she giggled at the way the Americans thought they were "capturing the true Russia" as they filmed Red Square, the Zagorsk cathedrals, the radiant parks of Leningrad. A few weeks after the production closed, Kira was back in her regular job as a tour guide at the Museum of the Revolution in Leningrad. We had agreed to meet for dinner, and I joined one of her tours. It was late morning and she was leading around a bored group of tourists from Voronezh and Siberia. She told them all about the "wondrous" documents stored there, the "unique" memorabilia of Lenin. The tourists did not care, and Kira cared less. I have rarely seen eyes so blank.

Things Western opened the world up. That spring and summer of 1990, I spent a couple of afternoons a week in Lenin Hills, where the Japanese had built a pretty decent baseball park for Moscow State University. I sat in the dugout with a kid from Sioux City named Bob Protexter who had come all the way from Iowa to coach baseball.

"I read this was happening in *Sports Illustrated,*" he said. "I wanted adventure, but what the hell would I do in Tahiti? So I figured I'd teach Russians how to turn a double play."

When the baseball craze began in 1986, traditionalists were gravely concerned. Somehow it never occurred to them that the country had also gone basketball-mad in the seventies without causing the sudden implosion of the Soviet nuclear force. Nevertheless, *Izvestia* published a frenetic editorial claiming that baseball was a foreign intruder and that, anyway, Russian *lapta* was a superior game that gave America the idea for baseball in the first place. Sergei Shachin wrote that *lapta,* which dates back to the days of Ivan the Terrible, came to California when Russian émigrés settled there in the nineteenth century. Hence, baseball. "It was a guess," Shachin admitted later.

The Soviets were getting an all-star team ready for an American tour, and they looked raw but not without talent. The field was filled with former javelin throwers, former water polo players, and former hockey players. Protexter's friend Richard Spooner was the Johnny Appleseed of the game in Moscow. He worked days at an American business consortium and spent weekends preaching the wisdom of the infield fly rule. Spooner managed to supply the Chemists, his team at the Mendeleyev All-Union Chemical Society, with gloves, balls, helmets, and even videocassettes of Los Angeles Dodgers highlights. The more they watched the tapes, the more the Russians

developed the tics and affectations of their American brethren. Scratching, spitting, bubble-blowing. It took a while to get them all down pat. In one game, a guy took his gift of Red Man chewing tobacco and gobbled it down like chocolate. He threw up and spent the rest of the game in a hopeless daze. He struck out three times, looking.

"Now they chew and spit all right, but so far they haven't caught on to the tradition of grabbing your balls before the pitch," Protexter said.

Vadim Kulakov, Spooner's catcher at Mendeleyev, was a fanatic devotee of Gary Carter, later of the Mets and Expos. "If I ever have a son," Kulakov said, "I shall call him Gary, after the great Gary Carter." Kulakov used a curling iron to affect the cherubic look of Gary Carter. On the field, he had the same frenetic style, the same showy sense of hustle as "Mr. Hustle." And when he went on road trips with the team, Vadim Kulakov gave his girlfriend a Gary Carter 1988 Topps baseball card "so she will remember me."

So far, no Russian had ever hit a home run at the Moscow State University park. The Big Bear was still a nation of spray hitters. So far, no one had thrown a proper curve, and the slider was as distant a dream as shopping malls and microwaved tacos. But the fielding was surprisingly good. The country boys, the kids from the collective farms, had a good sense of outfield play. The only thing that seemed a little precarious was the decision-making. Billy Martin–Reggie Jackson-like squabbles were a common sight in the Moscow dugouts, and I was told that was likely to last a good while. "We decide everything together," said the leading Soviet manager, Vladimir Bogatyryov. "Despite all that's happened, we still have more of a collective mentality here in Russia."

It was nice to see that the Russian ballplayers had developed a sense of style despite the obvious impediments. Most of the players wore caps from major-league teams, though one wore a Minute Maid model and another, as if in the worst nightmare of the KGB, sported a model with the bold logo "Radio Liberty." In the other dugout, one of the coaches was writing a new lineup combination on the pale-blue cover of an old copy of *Novy Mir.* For a while I watched the action with Bill "the Spaceman" Lee, late of the Boston Red Sox. Lee was entranced with the players, the way they strived equally for mannerism and real skill, as if they knew, instinctively, that the quirks of the American game were not irrelevant, but the beauty part. He tried to show the pitchers that they had to "respect" the mound, to care for it "like your home, your office." And they loved the Spaceman.

"I'll tell you this, speaking as a red-blooded American who has no beef with the Russians: I hope they get this game down," Bill Lee said. "Because if they learn how to play, they'll discover it beats the shit out of working.

Take anything. Take music. When they can turn on the TV and they can see Joe Cocker singing 'Civilized Man' with fifty thousand people going apeshit and everybody's got their tops off and their tits jiggling, well, they'll say, 'You know, I want that! I gotta have that!' The same with baseball. They want what we have. And why the hell not?"

CHAPTER 23

THE MINISTRY OF LOVE

Until I got to Moscow, I never caught the spy bug. In college, there were rumors that a professor might tap you for the work, the way the Communist dons of Cambridge had done for Philby, Burgess, and Blunt. I never heard of it happening, though I suppose that was the idea. As a reporter in Washington, I felt ridiculous the few times I was called upon to write about espionage and its entertainments. Inevitably, someone was feeding you a hunk of fakery: a "scoop" that won an obscure political point, an alluring narrative cooked up in some embassy basement. Once I wrote a story about a Soviet defector, the wife of an embassy official. She betrayed her country and fled into the arms of a used-car salesman. She was known, in the headlines and elsewhere, as "the Woman in the Blond Wig." On television, she wore her wig and big sunglasses. Later she signed a six-figure book contract. I knew I was somebody's fool. But whose?

In Moscow, it was understood that we, the foreigners, were under careful watch by the KGB. People talked about other reporters making graceless exits from Moscow after having been shown eight-by-ten glossies of themselves in sexual rapture with someone not their spouse. No matter how dramatic events became in Moscow, our friends and relatives at home wanted to know most of all what it felt like to be listened to, to be watched. After

it became an instinct to avoid any mention of our Soviet friends, a life overheard felt like nothing at all, or almost nothing, like a slight numbness on your forearm that you forget until you touch it. Mostly, you stopped caring. Stupidly, arrogantly, you felt invulnerable. Go ahead. Let them listen. The cold war was over, wasn't it?

Vladimir Kryuchkov, who took over as KGB chief in 1988 from Viktor Chebrikov, tried hard to convince the world that he had created a kinder, gentler secret service. The Ministry of Love, as Orwell called it. Taking a page from Gorbachev's own stylebook, Kryuchkov tried to "personalize" himself and the institution he represented. He described for the press his great love for Bellini's *Norma.* If only Van Cliburn would move to Moscow, he said, the KGB would build him a wonderful apartment. Kryuchkov even begged for the workingman's sympathy. "The KGB chairman's life is no bed of roses," he told the editors of *New Times.* So much work, and so little time. He gave press conferences. He fielded (carefully screened) questions on a television talk show. He met with foreign visitors. There were even tours of Lubyanka on which guides would point to display cases filled with preposterous spy equipment—telephones in the heels of shoes, things like that. Kryuchkov never mentioned that he took part in planning the invasion of Budapest in 1956 and Prague in 1968. This did not quite fit with the new image.

Without cutting his forces by a single spy or border guard, Kryuchkov had embarked on one of the most curious public relations campaigns in history: trying to portray the spy apparatus of Dzerzhinsky, Yezhov, Beria, and Andropov as an earnest government servant of legality and democratic reform. One evening, the press was invited to the Foreign Ministry press center and treated to a documentary about the "new KGB," in which officers swooned over the food ("Can I have the recipe?") and generally acted like the corn-fed careerists in a U.S. Army recruiting film. Kryuchkov was eager not only to gild the present, but also to whitewash the past. "Violence, inhumanity, and the violation of human rights have always been alien to the work of our secret services," he told the Italian paper *L'Unità.* Although the Brezhnev era was "not the best in our lives," Kryuchkov said the KGB acted at the time in "compliance with existing legislation."

Kryuchkov's self-advertising was born of necessity. For the first time in its existence, the KGB was subject to public criticism. The former Olympic weight lifter Yuri Vlasov took the podium at the Congress of People's Deputies in May 1989 and denounced the KGB as a vast "underground empire" that had been using its troops and prisons to slaughter the best and brightest of every Soviet generation since the Revolution. Vlasov, a Hercules with

horn-rimmed glasses, said the KGB was the "most powerful of all the existing tools of the apparatus" and must be put under strict control of the new, elected legislature. Needless to say, such a thing had never happened before, especially not on live national television. Kryuchkov admitted he had an "unpleasant" reaction to Vlasov's speech, "but then I asked myself: I must think about what is taking place. . . . He is just not aware of the many things we are now engaged in and what we are planning to do. If all Soviet people are as ignorant as he is, then many of them must think along the same lines." After all, he said, Western reports that the KGB somehow represented a reactionary, antireform force in the leadership were "unsubstantiated. . . . The KGB and the army both are closely connected with the people. They entirely accept the program of perestroika worked out by the Communist Party and are ready to support it and defend it."

Kryuchkov really must have thought he was fooling everyone. There was no shame to his public relations schemes. A man of the old order, he was sure he could master the new. He had the arrogance of a man who watched television once and was convinced he understood it. By 1990, the KGB even opened a press office and put a general in charge of "facilitating press relations." At one affair, Kryuchkov invited all the female correspondents in Moscow for an "interview," where he treated them with all the courtliness a scoundrel can muster. Waiters in formal dress brought the ladies their parting gifts: bottles of sweet Soviet champagne and a red, ersatz-leather-bound two-volume history of the Soviet secret services, autographed by Kryuchkov himself. What did he want out of this? Did Kryuchkov expect the reporters to rush to their keyboards and tap out feature stories comparing the KGB to the League of Women Voters?

One morning, on *Komsomolskaya Pravda*'s front page, under the headline "MISS KGB," there was a photograph of a pretty young woman named Katya Mayorova, the holder of the world's only "security services beauty title." It was a curious pose. She was making erotic work of strapping on a bulletproof vest. The article said that Comrade Mayorova would soon appear on the television program *Good Evening Moscow* to make "announcements" about KGB operations. It said that Katya wore her bulletproof vest with "an exquisite softness, like a Pierre Cardin model." Beyond "mere beauty," among her many charms was an ability to "deliver a karate kick to her enemy's head."

I called the press center and asked if I might interview Miss KGB. I thought everyone at the KGB's Lubyanka headquarters would get a good laugh out of that. But ten minutes later a call came back, confirming an interview appointment at the headquarters of the KGB.

"May I bring a camera?" I said.

"We would expect you to," came the answer.

At the appointed hour I parked in front of one of the auxiliary buildings just off Lubyanka Square. I gave my name to a receptionist and sat down to wait for my audience with the reigning queen. In the meantime, I noticed that every so often an ordinary person off the street would come in and shove an envelope or even a packet of documents into a large mailbox. This was where people came with their appeals and their complaints. It was a bitter reminder of what this place was—still was. I thought of Lydia Chukovskaya's novel *Sofia Petrovna,* her fictionalized account of her days spent trying to get the secret police to tell her what had happened to her husband; I thought of Akhmatova's days in line, waiting to know the fate of her son. And I imagined the scene downstairs at the end of the day, a few agents sitting around the furnace, laughing and emptying the mail into the fire.

"Mr. Remnick?"

It was Katya Mayorova, splendidly turned out in an angora sweater and a pair of tight Italian jeans.

In the presence of a KGB "press officer," Katya answered my questions—or didn't. She said the contest had taken place "in private" and even the number of contestants was a secret. That there obviously had never been any contest at all was, I supposed, a given and did not bear mentioning. But Katya, for someone trained in "kill methods" and marksmanship by the most feared organization in the world, was charming. She was making terrific work of this. With her combination of Miss America sweetness and a veiled sense of danger, she was satisfying some base fantasy that I could not quite identify. What? The Rosy Executioner? Mata Hari? No, she said she doesn't "necessarily only date KGB men." Yes, she had been getting quite a number of calls since the *Komsomolskaya Pravda* item appeared. "Men are the same everywhere," she said, rolling her eyes like a true Valley Girl. When I asked her to pose for a picture, she sidled up to a statue of "Iron Feliks" Dzerzhinsky, the founder of the secret police, and cooed.

—

It was getting late, and I wanted to stop by Lubyanka Square outside. The city's leading democrats were going to unveil the first major monument to the victims of the regime: a huge stone taken from Solovki, a labor camp established on a White Sea island by Lenin. I asked Katya if she would be going to the ceremony. She blushed, but then recovered with an answer that I imagined was highlighted in the daily briefing book of the KGB's public relations campaign. "Tens of thousands of innocent KGB men were also killed," she said. "And so I'll go to the monument tonight. I think of it as my monument, too. All of ours."

Outside it was snowing lightly and a small group of demonstrators had already begun to gather. They carried signs saying "The KGB Can Never Wash the Blood from Its Hands" and "Bring the KGB to Justice!" Slowly, several hundred people assembled around the stone as darkness fell. The ceremony began. Yuri Afanasyev, representing Memorial, took the microphone and in a voice that rang out across Lubyanka Square, he said, "Never before has a regime spent seventy years waging such a brutal war against its own people. Blessed are those who died in the camps and were hungry and cold." Oleg Volkov, a former prisoner of Solovki, pointed across the traffic to the statue of Dzerzhinsky and declared that the time had come for "false idols to be toppled." Priests in dark cassocks chanted prayers over the rock. People laid flowers on the stone and wept. Others carried candles and shielded the flames with their hands from the wind. The cars coming around the traffic circle slowed to catch a glimpse of this strange ceremony, and the snow fell harder, and then one of Sakharov's closest friends, the human rights champion Sergei Kovalev, warned everyone. He said what everyone really needed to hear, that "nothing has changed yet, that we the people are still down here, and they, the KGB, are still over there."

No lie was too big for Vladimir Aleksandrovich. When a *New Times* correspondent asked whether the KGB kept files on Soviet citizens, Kryuchkov was adamant: "Ask a KGB man that and he will laugh. You might find such things in other countries, but not here."

The "new KGB" under Gorbachev fed the correspondents spy stories as if they were bird seed, and they were impossible to resist. Even before Kryuchkov's arrival, they let a British journalist spend a few days debriefing the defector Kim Philby. Philby, a rat forever pretending to be a mouse, did his Honorable Englishman routine to perfection, waxing on about his service to ideals and complaining about the delay in getting copies of the *Times* and the *Independent.* Actually, Philby was a terrible drunk and the KGB treated him like a pathetic dependent whose bedpan needed constant changing. When Philby died in 1988, the KGB managed to leak very selectively the time and place of the funeral. Some of the British papers played the story as if it were the signal event of the century.

With Kryuchkov, the public relations campaign widened. An official in the Foreign Ministry press department—a KGB man himself, to be sure—let me know that if I wanted, I could have "a cup of tea and a chat" with Yevgeny Ivanov. In British tabloid language of the time, this was Yevgeny Ivanov, the "Slavic Mystery Man," who slept with "Good Time Girl" Christine Keeler, who "Coaxed Valuable Secrets" from John Profumo, the minister of war,

who "Toppled Tory Government." In setting up the meeting with Ivanov, the KGB showed a New York publicity agent's sense of timing. *Scandal,* a breezy reenactment of the 1963 Profumo affair, was, at that very moment, playing in theaters in Britain and the United States. The film had a lot of yuppie appeal, what with its orgies and *Decline and Fall* accents.

I sat waiting for Ivanov in the dim Foreign Ministry café, wondering what this spy-novel figure would look like, how he'd behave. He'd been the Red Rogue in a story hardly anyone remembered anymore. The year was 1963. Under the tutelage of the society osteopath Stephen Ward, Christine Keeler and her friend Mandy Rice-Davies were well acquainted with some of the members of the Macmillan government and Burke's Peerage. The war minister, Profumo, who was married to a movie actress named Valerie Hobson, had his affair with Keeler and fell into disgrace after he lied to Parliament about it. He fell lower still when Keeler claimed that she had also slept with Ivanov, a KGB agent working undercover in the London embassy as military attaché. Ward, her mentor, killed himself. And so on.

A rumpled older man approached my table. He moved with a shy shuffle and seemed vaguely sad, as if he had gotten terribly lost and was too embarrassed to ask directions to the exit door.

"I am Yevgeny Ivanov," he said. "Sit down? Yes?"

In the legend of the Profumo affair, Ivanov had fluent English and public-school manners. Lord Astor liked to have him around. The man at my table could barely speak English and was very grateful when we switched to Russian.

"Slava Bogu," he sighed. Thank God.

I told him the critics in the West thought *Scandal* was a pretty good movie and had stirred interest once more in the Profumo affair and the name Yevgeny Ivanov. "Your name is in the papers. You're famous again," I said.

"Ach, ach, why is everyone so interested in this?" he said. "Why bring up this whole dirty story again? Our relations with the English are getting better. There was just a summit meeting with Thatcher and Gorbachev. We're waiting for Queen Elizabeth, to see and listen to her. And against this background, to stir up mud from twenty-five years ago? What forces can gain from that?"

Ivanov said he had worked for the Defense Ministry "analyzing documents" until 1982 and then for Novosti, the press agency that was also a well-known center for the KGB. He was vague about what he had done at Novosti, yet everyone knew that it was a holding pen for agents. Despite Ivanov's stagy lack of interest in the headiest days of his life, he said he was thinking of writing a memoir.

In that spirit, I asked him if he had ever slept with Keeler. And had he coaxed her to give up Profumo's whispered confidences?

"Never, never, never," Ivanov said. "My relationship? None at all. I never paid any attention to her. I say this honestly. Never. What kind of star was she? Okay, she had long legs, but that kind of girl exists even in Moscow.

"Some people say I gave her the task of pumping Profumo on where and what kind of nuclear weapons would be delivered to West Germany. That's nonsense. I could have done that better myself, just asking. It wasn't a secret that I, as a military man, as a Soviet man, am interested in those nuclear weapons and when they'll be delivered to Germany. And they called me a spy!"

Ivanov said he thought that he'd been trapped in a conspiracy that had nothing whatever to do with him or the Soviet Union. When the news broke, he said, he quickly realized that all his "old friends" in the British Parliament and the dinner party circuit would no longer talk with him or be seen with him. It was time to close up shop.

"I left London and a week later Keeler's 'life story' was in the press," Ivanov said. "I don't know if she ever went to college, but she could never have written that stuff herself. It was all prepared beforehand. Some sort of group was interested in Profumo's downfall. What group, I don't know. He had enemies and they needed material to compromise him."

Ivanov shrugged. His whole physical bearing was a shrug. He reminded me of a retired ballplayer who had ended his career on a missed shot, a dropped pass in the ultimate game. He was famous when he would have been happier in obscurity. He was there eating with me because someone told him he had to, because it would serve an interest. "I guess I may be able to travel now to Britain, but I don't want to," he said. "And why? Because there is so much press in England. And if I go to England, and if Christine Keeler hears I'm there, she might just call in the press and say, 'I slept with him,' once again. It's just not worth it."

And so I wrote my story. Months later, Ivanov got a fat advance from some foreign publishers. He was ready to tell all. Had he slept with Keeler? Had he pirated secrets from the War Department? Of course, Ivanov wrote. Of course!

—

A few months later, at an interminable press conference at the Foreign Ministry, I was tapped on the shoulder and told there was a very important phone call for me. It was General Karbainov, the KGB's press officer, asking

phone call for me. It was General Karbainov, the KGB's press officer, asking whether I would like to meet Edward Lee Howard.

Howard was the first CIA operative ever to defect to the Soviet Union and the KGB. He had been forced out of the CIA in 1983 as a bad security risk for failing a series of polygraph tests about his private conduct. The CIA was also convinced Howard had sold out a number of key "assets" in Moscow, including one aviation expert who was eventually executed for espionage. Howard defected in 1986, a "walk-in" at a Soviet embassy in Eastern Europe—probably Budapest.

Karbainov told me to go home and expect a phone call "confirming everything" at noon.

I was at the apartment in five minutes. The phone rang precisely at noon.

"You know the cuckoo clock at the 'Mezh'?" the voice said, using the foreigners' nickname for the Mezhdunarodnaya, the International Hotel. "I'll meet you under the cuckoo clock tomorrow at ten-thirty in the morning."

I said a quick okay and the line went dead. (As it always does in these stories.)

So once more, life would imitate trash fiction. Or the other way around. No doubt, by arranging a meeting with *The Washington Post,* Howard and probably the KGB itself were playing yet another clever game of "international intelligence." And yet it all seemed so . . . dumb.

On Saturday morning, at the appointed hour exactly, under the monstrous cuckoo clock with a squawking copper rooster on top, a man neither short nor tall, neither skinny nor fat, neither handsome nor ugly, tapped me on the shoulder.

"Hi. I'm Ed Howard," he said. "Good to meet you. Why don't we go?"

The International Hotel was the one place in the entire Soviet Union in the glasnost era that resembled Business-Class America. There were upholstered "conversation areas," an atrium with glass elevators, shops with goods in them, restaurants with food in them. Nothing like Russia.

"I like it 'cause it looks like one of those malls back home," Howard said. "Sometimes I eat upstairs at the German beer place, and I like the ice cream parlor a lot."

Howard headed toward the door, walking in that quick two-step that hit men use after they've finished a job. He seemed nervous, jumpy. But he never ran, never hid his face. The lobby was filled with Westerners, businessmen mainly, tired-looking men who roamed the lobby waiting for the next meeting, aimless as guppies in a bowl. Possibly one or more of them knew who Howard was, if only vaguely, as a distant scandal in a newspaper story, a man who humiliated the FBI and CIA when he slipped through their surveillance

in New Mexico and left for Soviet sanctuary. Possibly—possibly not. No one seemed to be paying him special attention.

How was it that a defector—one suspected of selling secrets to the KGB—could roam around in public? I asked him. Wasn't he afraid that someone from the CIA station at the U.S. embassy here might try to grab him? Wouldn't he be recognized by some computer-chip salesman from Tacoma who all of a sudden would point and say, "Hey you, aren't you . . . ?"

"No way," Howard said. "If you asked a thousand people on the streets in Washington, D.C., or in a normal American city, say Cleveland, Ohio, 'Who is Ed Howard?' nine hundred and ninety-nine would never know who I am, much less what I look like."

And the CIA?

"They have better things to do with their time."

Outside in the driveway, Howard opened the rear door of a black Volga, the preferred car of countless midranking Communist Party, military, and KGB officials.

"We're going to the dacha," Howard said in terrible Russian, and the KGB driver, whose English was undoubtedly fluent, headed out Kutuzovsky Prospekt toward the southwest outskirts of Moscow. After leaving the main road, the driver took a deliberately circuitous route toward Howard's place. He took every curve at stomach-turning speed and kept glancing at us in the rearview mirror.

Howard rolled his eyes.

"On the way back, don't bother going this way," he told the driver. "After all, what's the point?" The driver was clearly not just a driver, but he indulged Howard with a nod just the same.

Dachaland, at least Howard's neck of it in the town of Barvikha, was a mix of ordinary peasant huts and the soaring brick-and-glass cottages of the Soviet power elite. Not far away from Howard's place, the notoriously anti-Semitic and unconscionably popular painter Ilya Glazunov lived in a multistory brick monstrosity; elsewhere there were KGB officials, Communist Party men, retired generals.

We pulled up to a smart, two-story brick house surrounded by a fence. There were two car sheds in the yard, one for the Volga, the other for Howard's own Volvo. A retired couple lived in a small cottage on the grounds; the woman cooked and cleaned for Howard and the man tended the garden, growing apples, strawberries, roses, and potatoes. The couple called Howard "Ivan Ivanovich," Mr. Nobody. In the backyard there was a guard booth where two young KGB men kept a round-the-clock watch on Howard. Inside the gate there were infrared devices to signal the presence of intruders. Howard, who also had a spacious apartment just off the Arbat in downtown

Moscow, was quick to mock his landlords as poor, shiftless Russians. He pointed to the second-floor window. "They never finished the construction up there. Typical. They probably ran out of money three quarters of the way through."

Inside, the house was set up with well-made, if wan, Soviet furniture and top-of-the-line Western video and audio equipment. There were two bedrooms, a large living room, a deck, and a study. The living-room ceiling was twenty-five feet high. Howard's library was slim: *Lenin: His Life and Work,* the Bible, *Russian for Everybody,* and a Len Deighton thriller. He said he picked up *USA Today* and *Newsweek* on his trips downtown, and the KGB bought him subscriptions to *National Geographic, Money,* and *Computer World.* To pass the time, Howard played chess with his guards or watched one of his three hundred videocassettes. In his study, an aerie that overlooked the living room, Howard kept two computers. He used them for his "economic consulting work" at a Soviet bank, he said. He also loved to play computer games for hours: "My favorite is this one, SDI," he said. "It's American-made software. The premise is that the KGB has taken over the country and is going to attack the West. So you fight the KGB. I always win. But my friends always lose."

In a country of general poverty, Howard lived like a pasha, mainly at KGB expense. "Oh, I'm comfortable," he said, sounding like a periodontist trying to downplay the expense of his new rec room. Howard said he earned 500 rubles a month at his institute job and some "paltry" hard-currency commissions at the bank. He had access to the well-stocked diplomatic stores where Westerners bought their groceries. But he denied the KGB ever paid him major sums of money for information or for his simple presence as a defector-trophy.

"When I got here I had one suitcase of clothes," he said. "Basically, when I got to work, they said make sure the boy has some good clothes. That's what Kryuchkov said. They gave me an allowance to buy clothes. Maybe a couple thousand rubles. Also, the first three months until I could work out my situation they gave me some money, some rubles. It wasn't a big amount. I don't want to specify how much."

All the guards and tails didn't seem to bother him. "The KGB is responsible for my security. They take it seriously. Sometimes I get lectures from them about why do you not take your security seriously and so on," he said. "But it's my decision. I made the decision on my own to take you out to the dacha today. Kryuchkov said, 'It's your decision.' They don't like it but they said I was responsible. We have a good relationship and I respect them in regard to the security they are providing. . . . As long as they give me the freedom

to operate—well, 'operate' is a bad word—but the room to move around, to associate with who I want, to do what I want, it's okay. And they do."

Howard said he was even free to make his own travel decisions. In the past four years, he said, he had wandered Eastern Europe, Nicaragua, Cuba, Mexico, France, and Canada—"for fun." He said he had visited his wife and son in Minnesota and even gone to Cuba. I guessed he was lying, bragging for some complicated spy-versus-spy reason. And when I told him so, he got testy in a weird sort of way.

"Cuba's got some awfully nice beaches," he said. "Have you ever been to Cuba and seen those beaches?"

Howard was a small-town boy from New Mexico who grew up reading James Bond novels. Working for the Peace Corps in Colombia and the Agency for International Development in Peru, he got a taste for travel (and a bit for cut-rate cocaine). In 1980, when he was twenty-eight, he had a job interview with the CIA. "I must admit there was the aura of adventure," he said. At first Howard remembered his original image of the CIA. "But then, after meeting some agents in the Foreign Service, I thought, hey, they're human just like us. They like to party."

With his graduate degree in business administration from American University, Howard thought he'd spend his career abroad as an intelligence officer specializing in economics, "finding out what's in people's accounts and stuff." Instead, in 1982, the CIA put Howard in the "pipeline" for the Moscow station. "When I told my classmates that I was going to Moscow, everybody kind of opened their mouths. 'Ah, the Big M!' I thought, well, I'll put up with it and then I can name where I want to go next, like Zurich." For months, Howard trained in Virginia and Washington, learning "dead drops" and countersurveillance techniques, putting little pieces of film in tree stumps and not blinking. He learned terms like "wet assets" (Russian terminology for liquidated spies), "honey pots" (women used as sexual lures), and "ravens" (male homosexual lures). He learned of how the agency kept the names of its "live assets" in Moscow in separate black envelopes in a basement safe. Howard loved the memory of it: "Ah, very holy and all that sort of thing."

But then Howard failed the polygraph tests and was forced to resign. According to CIA sources quoted in David Wise's book *The Spy Who Got Away,* Howard began acting strangely, phoning the U.S. embassy in Moscow and leaving messages for the CIA station chief. He also admitted later that he stood outside the Soviet consulate in Washington and contemplated "going over." There were unexplained trips to Vienna—practically an espio-

nage playing field because of its position in Central Europe and its former status as a divided city in the days of *The Third Man.*

When the CIA forced Howard to resign from the agency, they had uncovered evidence of his personal problems, especially his history of heavy drinking. When he showed up at the hotel to meet me he was carrying a shopping bag with two bags of liquor, but, he said, "that's just for the guests."

"I think my drinking problems came from a lot of stress factors, especially when I was in the CIA," he said. "And there were some adjustment problems here. No doubt about it. And now I am mainly a beer man. I admitted to myself that I can't handle hard liquor. And that's the big step. I got depressed the last time I drank too much."

It was only after the Soviet spy Vitaly Yurchenko defected to the West and reportedly told the CIA about Howard that the CIA let the FBI in on the secret and the surveillance began. Howard was living at the time in Santa Fe, working in the New Mexico legislature. Trained by the CIA in countersurveillance, Howard soon realized he was being followed and watched. He said his shadows were "incompetent" and "fools." "I'd see the same guy all the time riding around the house. I mean, really. And then I took a trip to Seattle. I see people on the flight with me to Los Angeles, then on the flight to Seattle, and then all of a sudden back in Santa Fe."

Howard denied he ever had contact with the KGB until he finally defected in June 1986. Under pressure and drinking heavily at times, Howard felt he could no longer stay in the United States. In September 1985, he made his escape. Once more he used the techniques he had learned in CIA training. With his wife behind the wheel of their Jeep on the night of September 21, Howard rolled out of the passenger door. A dummy popped up in his place. Then he was gone. While her husband began a half-year odyssey through Latin America and Europe, ending with defection to the Soviet Union, Mary Howard went through a long interrogation by the FBI. According to David Wise, she admitted that her husband had collected $150,000 in a Swiss bank account and buried a small cache of Krugerrands and silver bars in an ammunition box. She also admitted that the Soviet Union had paid for her husband's trip to Vienna in September 1984. All of which reflected rather badly on Howard's claim that he had never had any relationship at all with the Soviet Union or the KGB until he defected. Every time the subject of that period came up, Howard looked away and said, "Let's please get off the subject of '85."

Where the United States was concerned, Howard enjoyed an exquisite sense of *Schadenfreude.* He was delighted with the KGB's bugging of the U.S. embassy in Moscow and the celebrated incidents of marines romping around with Soviet spies with names like Big Raya. Howard said, "I thought it was

comical, funny. I think it turned out that only one guy went to jail after all that. The rest of the guys were just normal, young, red-blooded, horny Marines. And they were having some fun with some Soviet girls. Ha! Ha!"

At times, Howard acted as though the interview was a painful task done at someone else's beckoning. But at other times he rose to the subject, especially that of his own innocence. It was strange to hear him discourse on one of the other spy cases of his time, the Walker family of U.S. Navy spies who sold the Soviets codes and other key military secrets. His views were one part gall, one part moral relativism. "Oh, they should answer for their crimes, but in the intelligence business it's very difficult to say what is a crime and what isn't. Maybe I'm trying to back off here a bit, but God, it's a land of mirrors. I mean, it's very hard to moralize. . . ."

The long gray Saturday shoved on outside. At first, Howard played his character nicely, waxing cynical even about the KGB's current "kinder, gentler" public relations campaign: "Oh, Americans should believe that about as much as they believe the CIA press campaign." But as the day went by, the character seemed to drain out of Howard. He seemed to get bored with himself, bored with his story. Here was a man, after all, who was a bit player, a waterfly, in the great drama of the superpowers. And after all, wasn't the cold war over? Who needs Ed Howard? He was no Kim Philby or George Blake; there was no romance, no matter how perverse, about the Howard case. He didn't "come out" for ideals or fortune. He defected, and probably sold secrets, mainly out of panic and anger.

We drove back to Moscow and had lunch at the German beer hall on the second floor of the International Hotel. Howard hacked away solemnly at his roast chicken. All around him businessmen were laughing and hoisting their steins of beer and talking about their flights to Copenhagen and Paris and London. They were relieved to be going home.

Howard said he was thinking of living one day with his family in a "neutral country." "The Soviets haven't stopped me from seeking that alternative," he said. "I still consider it a viable option." In the meantime, from "a material point of view, I have pretty much everything I want." Including free court time at the Central Committee tennis courts.

At the dacha, his second bedroom was cluttered with huge stuffed animals and other toys. They were for his son, Lee, he said. So far, Lee Howard knew only that his father did "financial work" in Moscow. "I suppose one day I'll explain it all to him. I don't know at what age, but I will," Howard said. "He'll evaluate the situation against what he knows of me as a person, whether I've treated him well, whether I've raised him well, whether I love

him. And eventually, after the shock, I think it will settle down into a relationship. I mean, you look at Kim Philby's sons. They used to visit him here regularly. They came to his funeral and everything."

Finally, Edward Lee Howard had nothing more to say. It was time to go back to the dacha. "I suppose they'll call tonight and ask how it went," he said. They probably already knew. But why did they care? I called a few days later and Howard was stone drunk. He had no idea who I was.

Sakharov had always said that compared to the hierarchy of the Communist Party, the men of the KGB were relatively honest and well educated, even a possible breeding ground for reformist tendencies. KGB analysts and agents, he reasoned, traveled and read widely, and they knew far better than anyone else the true picture of desperation within Soviet borders and the realities beyond them. Sakharov's thinking made sense, but it did not hit home with me until I spent a Saturday at the October movie theater on Kalinin Prospekt where the liberal wing of the Party, Democratic Platform, was holding its founding congress.

All morning the speeches had been predictable and by predictable people. By June 1990, with the Twenty-eighth Party Congress just weeks away, it was no longer a novelty that there were democrats in the Party. In fact, in Russia, most of the key reform leaders were still Party members, including Yeltsin. But an odd thing happened. One of the Democratic Platform leaders asked everyone to pay special attention because a special guest—Oleg Danilovich Kalugin, a former major general of the KGB—had decided to speak. Kalugin had the razor-sharp features and icy glare of a movie spy. In fact, he looked like a younger Zbigniew Brzezinski. His speech was untheatrical, but stunning all the same. He described his career as a KGB operative, including stints as the press attaché in the embassy in Moscow and as the chief of foreign counterintelligence in Moscow. He did not give many details then, but later he told me how he had helped run the famous Walker spy ring and was Kim Philby's designated "conversational partner" in Moscow: "I did not get all these medals for my good works as a Boy Scout, after all."

Kalugin's message was simple: the KGB, despite any public relations campaigns to the contrary, continued to infiltrate every workplace, church, artistic union, and political group in the Soviet Union. At the same time, many KGB officers, especially younger ones, could be called "dissidents," or at least in fundamental disagreement with the policies and ambitions of Vladimir Kryuchkov.

"The role of the KGB hasn't changed. It's got a new image, but it's the same old horse," he said after the speech. "The KGB is everywhere—om-

nipresent—and this is true today. As long as they are an instrument of the Communist Party, they are going to do this. We do not murder anyone on political grounds, but we can murder a person with character assassination. Thousands and thousands of human lives and careers are broken because of the manipulation of the KGB."

As a specialist in foreign intelligence, Kalugin learned to speak fluent English, Arabic, and German. As an exchange student at Columbia University in 1958, he became friends with another fellow Russian—Aleksandr Yakovlev. When he was in New York, Kalugin even scored a publicity coup in *The New York Times.* Max Frankel, who became executive editor many years later, wrote a "man in the news" profile of Kalugin in which he was described as a "real personality kid" who liked to sneak backstage at Lincoln Center and take photographs of the ballerinas "sometimes in ungraceful poses."

A few days after the speech, I went to see Kalugin at his apartment in Kuntsevo, a relatively tranquil district of Moscow. He and his wife, Ludmila, lived in a special KGB building, and outside there were several black Volgas ready to take their charges to work at Lubyanka and God knows where else. It was one of the more comfortable apartments I had seen in Moscow, filled with Western appliances, a brass dog, a ceramic Cinderella, and countless souvenirs from a lifetime with the KGB.

"Be careful of that ashtray," Kalugin said. "One of the best African dictators gave me that."

Kalugin counted himself a great bibliophile. "Look at this," he said, pointing to a copy of Solzhenitsyn's *The Cancer Ward* bound in red leather. "I've always loved him. I had it specially bound. Look at the gold lettering." There were also spy thrillers, *Europe on Five Dollars a Day,* Akhmatova, Gumilyev, and a good selection of old KGB disinformation books, including the notorious *White Book,* which was used in the eras of Brezhnev, Andropov, and Chernenko to spread lies about the personal and political lives of the refuseniks. Moving farther along the shelves, Kalugin said that in 1971 he became the KGB's "caretaker" for Kim Philby. "Kim had been drinking heavily. His life was going to the dogs. It was Yuri Andropov's idea for me to help Philby. I used to go by and see him maybe once a month. I was responsible for his safety and well-being until he died in 1988. I was the first to lay a wreath on his grave." He showed me his copy of Philby's memoir, *My Secret Life.* On the flyleaf it was inscribed, "To Ludmila and Oleg, With deep gratitude and happy memories . . . Best, old boy, Kim."

The neighbors, of course, were "rather upset" at Kalugin for speaking out at the Democratic Platform meeting. Kryuchkov, who lived in an even more exalted building, had been angry with Kalugin for years. In 1987, Kalugin

sent a letter to Gorbachev warning him that the KGB was out of control. The personnel of the KGB, he wrote, ought to be cut in half at the very least and ought to be put under strict legislative watch "as they do in civilized countries." In 1989, he wrote an article for the journal *International Life* criticizing the KGB for its foreign operations. The article identified its author only as a major general "formerly occupied for a long period of time with questions of diplomatic activity." Three months before his "coming out" at the October Theater, Kalugin received notice that he was being retired at the age of fifty-five.

What Kalugin was saying now about the KGB was no more a secret to the world than what Yeltsin had said about the Communist Party. His description of the close relationship between Gorbachev and Kryuchkov as a "bad omen" was nothing original. But Kalugin's position gave him a certain authority, and it humiliated the men in power. Here was a major general of the secret police telling virtually anyone who asked that the KGB was still the backbone of a totalitarian state. Sure he could be playing a game. But why? What was in it for him?

Two weeks after the speech at the Democratic Platform convention, the Tass wire ticked out the announcement: Oleg Kalugin had been stripped of his military rank and decorations by order of President Mikhail Gorbachev. The military men who had ordered the slaughter of peaceful demonstrators had gone unpunished, but Kalugin was out. It was a chilling moment—in a year that was going to get a lot colder. Either Gorbachev was acting on his own or he was under pressure from the KGB. It was hard to say which was worse. Either way, the Ministry of Love was still in business.

CHAPTER 24

BLACK SEPTEMBER

What is written with a pen cannot be hacked away even by an ax.

—RUSSIAN PROVERB

In the morning twilight, the village priest opened his front gate and headed for the train platform a half mile away. It was Sunday, and Father Aleksandr Men always caught the 6:50 train from the village of Semkhoz near Zagorsk to his parish church in Novaya Derevnya, a small town thirty miles outside Moscow. He had a full day ahead of him: confessions to hear, baptisms, a lecture in the evening.

Father Aleksandr, a robust man of fifty-five with a thick beard of black and gray, was an emerging spiritual leader of the Russian Orthodox Church. Some of his followers compared him to Sakharov, "a spiritual Sakharov." Unlike countless other priests and church leaders, Men had kept his independence through the Brezhnev years. He refused to cooperate with the KGB. He taught underground Bible classes and published his theological works abroad under a pseudonym. He endured the harassment, sat through long searches of his home and interrogations, came home to open his mail and

read death threats, threats against his wife and two children. All because he was an honest priest and served his flock honestly. But he had survived. Now, he told his brother, Pavel, he felt like "an arrow finally sprung from the bow."

In the old days, Father Aleksandr's meetings with intellectuals like Solzhenitsyn, Nadezhda Mandelstam, and Aleksandr Galich were more or less a secret. Now he had become, in spite of himself, a central figure in the rebirth of a degraded church. In the past couple of years, he'd been able to preach and lecture in churches and auditoriums, even on radio and television, all without fear. Just the night before, Men had given a lecture in Moscow and spoken of the spiritual quest as an endless ascent: "We climb breathlessly. Truth is not given easily. We look back down and know there is a great climb ahead. I remember the words of Tenzing, who climbed Mount Everest with the British. He said that you can only approach a mountain with respect. The same is true with God. Truth is closed to those who approach it without respect."

Father Aleksandr never seemed to tire, and he was intent now on getting an early start on Sunday. He kept walking along the asphalt path through the Semkhoz woods toward the train. The narrow macadam path had proved dangerous at times. There had been rapes, a few beatings. Drunks in town sometimes took their bottles into the woods and harassed the passersby. Not long ago, the local authorities had cleared away some of the trees to make the path to the train platform less forbidding. Still, a couple of weeks before, Men asked his young assistant, Andrei Yeryemin, to help find him a place to stay in the city on nights when he was teaching or lecturing late. He said it was getting dangerous to walk too late at night. "I was amazed to hear him say it after all the things he'd been through in 1981 and 1982 when he could have been hauled off at any time," Yeryemin said. But it wasn't just that. Lately, the priest had betrayed a tone of fatalism in his voice. He told one friend that he hadn't much time to live. He gave no explanation.

Suddenly, from behind a tree, someone leaped out and swung an ax at Aleksandr Men. An ax: the traditional Russian symbol of revolt, Raskolnikov's weapon in *Crime and Punishment,* one of the symbols of the neofascist group Pamyat. The ax hit Men on the back of the skull. The killer, police said later, grabbed the priest's briefcase and disappeared into the woods. Father Aleksandr, bleeding terribly, stumbled toward home, walking a full three hundred yards to his front gate at 3A Parkovaya Street. Along the way, two women asked if he needed help. He said no and continued on. From her window, Natasha Men saw a figure slumped near the gate, pressing the buzzer. She could not quite make out who it was in the half-light. Then she

did. *"Gospodi!"* Good Lord! She called an ambulance. Within minutes, her husband was dead.

The murder of Aleksandr Men on September 9, 1990, was an ominous, almost supernatural portent of a time of troubles, and it had come just when political expectations seemed once more on the rise.

All summer it appeared as if Gorbachev was preparing to accelerate the pace of reform, if only to keep up with the events around him. As one republic after another, including Russia, took its cue from the Baltic states and declared itself sovereign, Gorbachev made the dramatic step of joining with Yeltsin to draw up a radical economic program that would encourage the creation of a market and, even more important, redistribute power from "the center" to the republics. In a government dacha outside the city, a witty old economist named Stanislav Shatalin and a plump wizard of market principles named Grigori Yavlinsky plotted, in civil tones and bureaucratic language, the dismantling of the System. On the face of it, the "500 Days" plan was an ambitious and amazingly facile prescription to begin the cure of a ruined economy. Few had any illusions about the 500 Days part. It would certainly be more than a year and a half before the empty lots of Moscow were transformed into shopping malls of plenty. When I asked Shatalin how long it would be until the Soviet Union had what passed for a modern economy, he said, "My optimistic scenario?" Yes. Be optimistic, I said. "Generations," he said. No, it would be a good while before there was a Silicon Valley in the Urals and the people of eastern Siberia were cruising the supermarket aisles choosing among Tide, Ajax, and Solo. It was the set of principles behind the 500 Days that made it so revolutionary, so immediate. Realization of the plan would mean the shutdown or conversion of hundreds of defense plants, the rise of private property, radical cuts in the budgets of the army, the police, and the KGB. What could that mean for the lords of the System? It was very simple. It meant the end.

When Gorbachev returned from his annual summer holiday on the Black Sea he told the legislature he was "inclined" to support the plan. That was all the hard-liners had to hear. The fight for their political life, a war that would rage for the next eleven months, had begun. The KGB chief, Vladimir Kryuchkov, piled dozens of reports on Gorbachev's desk insisting that the 500 Days plan was nothing more than an attempt, supported by the West, to crush socialism, destroy the Party, and weaken the country. At various meetings, leaders of the Party and the military-industrial complex threatened to revolt against Gorbachev if he gave his final support to the plan. A

creeping coup was under way, but Gorbachev was so vain, so sure of his ability to master both the machinations of the System and the passions of the people, that he thought he could control it all, finesse it as easily as he had the Nina Andreyeva affair in 1988.

One Politburo document, dated March 12, 1990, revealed the dark sense of foreboding in the Communist Party leadership and the attempt to exaggerate the situation in order to encourage emergency tactics. "The popular consciousness is being radicalized," the memo said. "Distrust in official structures and administrative structures grows. The criticism of the 'partocracy' and the local and central apparatus is more acute. . . . The opposition forces are attempting to exploit the situation. In fact, plans are being made to seize power by clearly antidemocratic means—through pressure, rallies, and the 'roundtable' tactic, which is completely antidemocratic." The "healthy forces in society," the memo added, want "decisive measures based on the law. . . . Use all means of propoganda to stop the discrediting of the army, the KGB, and the police. . . . Disarm the [opposition] ideologically and undermine them in the eyes of society."

For thousands of believers and nonbelievers in the city of Moscow, the first portent of the grim year ahead came with the swing of an ax in the village of Semkhoz. When I first heard about the murder of Aleksandr Men, I did not understand the importance of the event or of the man himself. He was a village priest whose church was an hour's drive from Moscow. And yet within days of the murder, I heard over and over how much he had meant.

In theory, at least, perestroika liberated the realm of the spirit as much as it did political and economic life. After seven decades of dogmatic atheism, the regime ended the persecution of religious believers and the institutions of worship. Suddenly, the word *bogoiskatelstvo*—"the search for God"—was the vogue. There were plenty of frauds around like Anatoly Kashpirovsky, but there were good signs as well. The churches were no longer the domain only of ancient women with childhood memories of a czarist world. Religious classes were no longer dissident activities. Gorbachev returned to the Russian Orthodox Church its ruined monasteries and cathedrals. Synagogues and mosques reopened. But just as the attempt at political reform slammed into one wall of resistance after another, the revival of spiritual life could not, in an instant, transcend a history of political repression. The nomenklatura of the Russian Orthodox Church, put in place by the ideologists and intelligence operatives of the Party, was at least as strong as the nomenklatura of the Party.

The history of the spirit's subservience to state authority goes back centuries before the first Bolshevik. As opposed to the Catholic Church, which developed its independent structures after the fall of the Roman Empire, the

Byzantine Church was always dependent on the state. The Byzantine emperors presided over all the synods of the church and were considered "God on earth." In a sign of things to come, the great dukes of the early Moscow period urged the clergy to reveal the mystery of confession, especially if state security was at issue. Ivan the Terrible tortured priests and jailed one metropolitan for life. The word "czar" is a Slavic form of the word "Caesar," but Iosif Volotsky, a great religious philosopher, wrote that the czar was simply the highest of all priests. When Napoleon met Aleksandr I in East Prussia, Napoleon said, "I see that you are an emperor and a pope at the same time. How useful."

The Bolsheviks despised the Russian Orthodox Church as an embodiment of old Russia. Lenin planned a soulless utopia. But when the Revolution needed to mobilize millions of illiterate people, it couldn't preach Marx to them. As the spiritual inheritor of Russian statehood, the Party needed to co-opt, not destroy, the church, bring it to its knees but not cut off its head. Stalin knew well how deeply the appeal of the church echoed in the Russian soul. To gain the allegiance of the population during the war, he appealed not so much to Communist ideology as to a mystical sense of Russianness, to Holy Russia and its warriors Nevsky, Suvorov, and Kutuzov. In his radio addresses to rally the country, Stalin would put aside the language of atheism. He returned some priests from prison camps and gave them decent positions and salaries. He was their emperor and pope. How useful. And when the war on Germany ended, the war on religion resumed. The dynamiting of churches, the imprisonment of priests, rabbis, and muftis, the prosecution of believers as "enemies of the state"—it all resumed.

Aleksandr Men was born a Jew. His father was a nonbeliever, and his mother converted to Russian Orthodoxy. In a country where Jewish religion and culture had been assaulted even more severely than the church, many families of the intelligentsia gravitated to Russian Orthodoxy, if only because they were able to feel their Russian identity more closely than their Jewishness. Men's mother, Yelena, saw the church as a place apart, a refuge. "In our family there was a personal religious search," said Men's brother, Pavel, a computer programmer. "Like so many people disgusted here by the life around them, our family tried to look within themselves for a religious way out." Yelena Men took her sons to pray under the guidance of an honest priest named Serafim who evaded the authorities by moving from apartment to apartment. The "catacomb church," they called it. Most of the parishioners were believers who had been in the prison camps, people who had lost relatives and friends for their faith.

"And so Aleksandr saw around him a kind of elevated moral life, God's people," Pavel Men said. "He made a decision when he was just twelve to study for the priesthood. He went to the local priest and asked what he would have to do to get into the seminary one day. The priest said Aleksandr was not 'one of ours.' Meaning he was Jewish. But Aleksandr set out to overcome that kind of thinking." As a boy and young man, Men found religious books in ramshackle country stores, "there among the nails and the guinea pigs." He began reading the great religious philosophers of the early part of the century, such writers as Vladimir Solovyov, Sergei Bulgakov, and Nikolai Berdyaev, who wrote in spiritual opposition to the Bolsheviks. Such reading, Men once said, "inoculated me against the cult of Stalin. I trembled as I read them."

As a young man, Men went off to study biology at an institute in Irkutsk, a Siberian city on the shore of Lake Baikal. His closest friend there was another Orthodox believer, a temperamental redheaded student named Gleb Yakunin. Men and Yakunin lived together in a tiny wooden house. Men brought with him huge trunkloads of books and kept Yakunin up nights at their rickety kitchen table talking about issues forbidden or, at least, discouraged by Soviet law. They talked about the sham that Soviet biology had become, about questions of Christian ethics and the way they contradicted the rules they lived under. "The Russian character, as you may have noticed, can be very lazy and unambitious," Yakunin told me, "but Aleksandr knew just what he wanted to do. He was interested in all subjects, and he had a purpose. Unlike me, he always knew he was meant to serve God, no matter the consequences."

One day the two city boys wandered into a village church looking, as Yakunin said, "like a couple of white elephants." Someone told the local KGB about these strange creatures. For making their religious faith so public, the two men risked their academic careers. The institute director barred Yakunin from finishing his studies and wanted to throw Men out, too. But the students, feeling the first flush of the post-Stalin "thaw," went out on strike in support of Men, refusing to go to lectures or classes. Men completed his degree.

Yakunin and Men returned to Moscow to follow their varying paths. Yakunin became Father Gleb, a priest and an unabashed political dissident who wrote letters to the Kremlin and the church hierarchy calling for religious reforms. For that he got nine years in prison camps and internal exile. Under Gorbachev, Yakunin returned home from exile and in 1990 was elected to the Supreme Soviet of the Russian Republic.

Men became a spiritual dissident, a less dangerous path than Yakunin's, but still perilous. "Each man has his own talent, his own way, and I moved

toward the politics of religion," Yakunin said. "Aleksandr had another kind of gift. In a church that suffered from inaccessibility, he had the ability to explain, to make the teachings of the church available to people." Men's form of dissidence meant being an honest, uncompromising priest; it meant providing the means for internal, spiritual rebellion in individuals. While his friend Yakunin organized political groups to defend the rights of believers, Men tried to instill a kind of spiritual dissidence in his parishioners, an independence of soul. He was a man of faith, but his own man, and God's. Especially for urban intellectuals, Men became a link to turn-of-the-century religious thinkers and philosophers such as Bulgakov and Solovyov who stood apart from this tragic tradition of subservience and obscurantism. Even in the darkest moments under Brezhnev, Moscow intellectuals made Sunday pilgrimages to the village of Pushkino to hear Aleksandr Men. The crowds only increased with the gradual erosion of fear under Gorbachev.

"In general, I think politics is a transitory thing and I wanted to work in a less transitory way," Men told the newspaper *Moskovski Komsomolets* just before he was killed. "I consider myself a useful person in society, which like any society needs spiritual and moral foundations." Men once said, "Dissent is the individual's way of protecting his right to perceive reality in his own way, not to yield to the views of the mass. When an individual calls such views into question, he shows his natural independence, his freedom. It is only when such a personal appraisal is lacking that the law of the mob prevails and an individual turns into a particle of a mass which can easily be manipulated."

After such a long period when he was called in for interrogations by the KGB, Men suddenly found himself a very public theologian in the Gorbachev era. He gave lectures in meeting halls and spoke on the radio. He taught courses on religion at the Historical Archives Institute, Yuri Afanasyev's outpost for nonconformist academics in Moscow. Young people who attended his lectures taped them and then circulated the tapes throughout the country. Just days before the murder, officials at the Russian Republic's new television station were discussing ways to give Men airtime at least once a week to speak on religious topics.

"This was a man who could speak to all of us, from Sakharov to the simplest person," said the writer Yelena Chukovskaya. The literary critic Natalya Ivanova said, "In a country where the regime managed to eliminate, in a sort of grotesque genetic engineering, its best minds, its most honest souls, Men survived to teach, to be an example."

All that was cut off in the woods of Semkhoz. Andrei Bessmertni, a young filmmaker and "spiritual child" of Father Aleksandr, said Men "could have reached millions of young people." Men, he said, saw how at a time when

faith in the "bright future of Communism" had faded away, young people had begun a spiritual quest. To overcome their profound cynicism, their sense that history had provided them nothing to rely on or believe in, younger people had turned inward, more in search of themselves than the next political sensation. "These times are not just about getting blue jeans and a McDonald's hamburger," Bessmertni said. "Some people actually want meaning in their lives, spiritual food."

On the day of the funeral, thousands of people, including religious leaders from the West, crowded the grounds of the village church in Novaya Derevnya. In Men's hand was placed a small Bible and a golden cross. People wept, and some sank to their knees in prayer. Several of the Orthodox priests who did their best to ignore or suppress Aleksandr Men in his lifetime made sure to speak his praises in eulogy. "My stomach turned as I listened to it all," Yeryemin said.

The eulogy that seemed to speak most eloquently for Men's followers and admirers was published a week later in *Ogonyok.* The article, written by a young journalist named Aleksandr Minkin, revealed that Men, as an honest, charismatic, and, not least, Jewish-born priest, had scores of enemies: the anti-Semites of Pamyat, the conservative zealots in the Russian Orthodox Church establishment, the police, the KGB. Minkin was convinced that the murder was not simply a random disaster, a mugging that went too far, the grotesque folly of an angry drunk. He was sure that this was an assassination intended to scare anyone else who would dare to challenge the System. A thief, Minkin wrote, "goes after a woman wearing jewels on the street or a well-dressed man with a fat wallet. But rich people don't go to work at 6:00 A.M. on a Sunday morning. The rich don't live in Semkhoz. . . . Humanization and democratization are one side of our system. The other is murder. We have been freeing ourselves from fear, but the ax is an instrument to remind us of our fear. They are reminding us that we are defenseless." Minkin compared Men's murder with the Polish secret police's assassination of the pro-Solidarity priest Jerzy Popieluszko in 1984—"an event that once and for all set the people against the forces of power in Poland." But in the Soviet Union, Minkin wrote, "people are standing in lines talking about other things. They have fallen lower into the muck than our brothers in the 'socialist camp' in Eastern Europe. So much the worse for us. We have not revolted, we have not become indignant. . . . This is a turning point in our history and we do not realize it yet. When we do become aware, what will we do?"

On the fortieth day after the murder, the day in the Orthodox faith on which the soul of the deceased either ascends to heaven or descends to hell, I drove out to the church in Novaya Derevnya. Even now, weeks after the funeral, people walked down the muddy road to the church to stop awhile at the grave, to lay down fresh flowers. The rotting flowers smelled like old wine, fruity and sour. I met a woman, eighty-six years old, named Maria Tepnina near the grave. She had known Aleksandr Men since he was a child; she knew the whole family. She stared a while at the grave and her face darkened with grief and confusion. After we stood there a while in silence, a light rain slowly soaking us, Tepnina invited me to her house. She lived just up the road from Father Aleksandr's church. Half the floor was covered with just-harvested potatoes, the walls were covered with family pictures and small icons.

For many years, Tepnina said, she helped Men with his secretarial work. "He'd get threatening letters all the time. He just threw them all away, never paid any attention. They accused him of everything from insulting the church, to being a 'rotten kike,' to serving the powers that be. Awful things, and they meant nothing to him."

From 1946 to 1954, Tepnina was in a prison camp near the Siberian city of Kemerovo and then in exile in Krasnoyarsk. In the camps, she met priests and believers, "real holy men." She saw people baptized secretly in their cells, priests shot muttering their thanks to God. But, she said, she had never met anyone with Men's gift for sympathy. And so she made sure, in her old age, to live near his church. Now, she was trying to make sense of the murder. "I think he was a genuine apostle, and all apostles end their lives as martyrs," she said. "So maybe there is a certain justice in this. All his life, Father Aleksandr prepared himself for this, daring to speak from his soul."

Another of Men's parishioners, Tatyana Sagaleyeva, came in and sat down with us. She had just moved from the nearby village of Abramtsevo to Tepnina's house. She also came to be closer to Men's church and to care for her aging friend. And now she was crying, and angry. "The murder of Father Aleksandr is a mystical event, not just a simple killing, an accident," she said. "God has taken this man from us, a spiritual leader who was at the prime of his life. His appearance was a miracle, a man who could, despite it all, despite an aggressive atheistic state, penetrate the sufferings of a great writer like Solzhenitsyn or of a simple woman like me. And suddenly he disappears. How to understand it? Why did God take him from us? Why now?"

The day after the murder of Aleksandr Men, a convoy of paratroopers from the Ryazan Airborne Division headed north for Moscow, 125 miles away. It was 3:00 A.M. Hours later, three dozen military transport planes carrying two

regiments in full battle gear landed at airstrips in Ryazan. The KGB's elite Dzerzhinsky Division was also put on full battle alert.

For days after the newspaper *Komsomolskaya Pravda* broke the story, there were rumors that the military had staged a rehearsal for a coup d'état. Yeltsin appeared before the Russian parliament and said, "They are trying to prove to us that these are peaceful maneuvers connected with the November 7 Revolution Day parade. But there are strong doubts about this." A spokesman for the military, of course, declared the maneuvers were not maneuvers at all. The soldiers were merely helping out in the fields collecting the potato harvest. Which led *Komsomolskaya Pravda* to ask why soldiers gathering potatoes required the use of AK-47 machine guns and bulletproof vests.

By now, I had spent many nights in Moscow listening to the dark forecasts of one Russian friend or another. Every unpromising development, every hint of difficulty, was somehow part of a larger pattern, a murderous conspiracy. For a long while, I felt like Earl Warren at an unending convention of Kennedy-assassination theorists. What it took me a long time to realize was that in Moscow, being paranoid doesn't mean doom is not on the way. To live in a totalitarian world and not be paranoid—or at least pessimistic—was itself lunacy. When had events ever been benign in this twisted Oz?

As we would soon find out in the coming months, first in Vilnius and Riga, then in Moscow, there was indeed a conspiracy under way, and it was the most open, unguarded conspiracy imaginable. The hard-liners' struggle for power started with pressure, fleeting signs, random moments of psychological terror. Perhaps we would never know who had killed Aleksandr Men . . . but we could guess. We would never know what the troops were doing in Ryazan . . . but we could guess.

What was so strange about the times we were living in was that the press was free to guess, too. Political talk was no longer a dark parlor game among trusted friends. The week after the Ryazan "rehearsal," a well-known writer, Andrei Nuikin, published a piece in *Moscow News* called "Military Overthrow." Nuikin quoted a leader of the radical servicemen's group "Shield," who told him that "the leadership of the armed forces already had a clear plan to take control of the situation in the country." Nuikin said the plan was to start the coup, perhaps in the far east, with the seizure of television stations and newspapers and with the "neutralization" of foreign journalists and their ability to get information out of the country. The Shield supporter said the military would justify the coup not by campaigning directly against Gorbachev's reforms, but by claiming that ethnic tensions had gotten out of control, the economy was collapsing, and socialism was endangered and that the situation required emergency measures. Nuikin wrote that he had no evi-

dence that the military actually had plans for such a coup but he added that the liberals had "grounds to consider means of responding."

The third omen of September arrived on the 18th with the morning mail. *Komsomolskaya Pravda* contained a special insert: a sixteen-thousand-word essay called "How Can We Revitalize Russia." The author was Aleksandr Solzhenitsyn, and the essay marked the first time in three decades that he had been able to publish a new work in a Soviet journal.

The article seemed like notes from the dead, as if Herzen or Dostoevsky had suddenly published from the Great Beyond a manifesto on the current state of things. Solzhenitsyn was being published everywhere now, but they were works from the sixties and seventies, historical works about twentieth-century tragedy written in an eighteenth-century language. Some readers were interested; some were bored with later works, especially the "Red Wheel" cycle of historical novels. But in either case, Solzhenitsyn himself was a gigantic absence, a legend living a ghostly life in a place that might as well have been a mountain palace in Brunei. And that mattered. In Russia, the presence of the writer was almost as important as the presence of the work. One writer after another—Vasily Aksyonov, Sasha Sokolov, Yuz Aleshkovsky, Vladimir Voinovich—came back, at least for long visits, to make contact with the audience and the language they had lost. Even in emigration they had always written for "home."

But Solzhenitsyn was secluded and mum. He was a legend. Russian intellectuals, especially, were alternately fascinated and repelled by the odd life the writer led in the woods of Cavendish, Vermont. Each new detail intrigued them. Solzhenitsyn lived in a good, but not indecently opulent, house, and he put up a chain-link fence to keep away unwanted visitors and snowmobiles. But in Moscow, I often heard people talk of Solzhenitsyn's "castle" and the "great wall" that surrounded it. When he first moved to Vermont, he spoke for twenty minutes at a town meeting and apologized to the people of Cavendish for the fence. He told them that when he lived without it, scores of uninvited visitors "arrived without invitations and without warning. . . . And so for hundreds of hours I talked to hundreds of people, and my work was ruined."

That Solzhenitsyn would insist on such a monkish life seemed incredible, especially in America, where publicity was the coin of the realm. Solemn, imperious, even righteous beyond measure, Solzhenitsyn had the nerve to make much of the contemporary literary scene look vaguely frivolous. He wrote gigantically (if not always well), as if from another age. He lacked the modernist leveler of irony. Instead, his rare public pronouncements were

chillingly sarcastic. In political argument, disdain was his most common thread. He thundered against the "cowardice" of the West and the "liquid manure" of pop culture in the fierce voice of another era. Jeremiah was heroic, no doubt, but hard to love. He made no apologies. "The writer's ultimate task is to restore the memory of his murdered people. Is that not enough for a single writer?" Solzhenitsyn told his biographer, Michael Scammell. "They murdered my people and destroyed its memory. And I'm dragging it into the light of day all on my own. Of course, there are hundreds like me back there who could drag it out, too. Well, it didn't fall to them; it fell to me. And I'm doing the work of a hundred men, and that's all there is to it."

To me, Solzhenitsyn had a perfectly accurate sense of his mission and place in the world. No matter how dull some of the later work on the Revolution might be, *The Gulag Archipelago* would never fade from the history of Russian literature or the history of Russia. No single work, including Orwell's novels, did as much to shatter the illusions of the West; no book did more to educate the Soviet people and undermine the regime. So who cared if he had a fence? Who cared if some of his books were beside the point? But the price Solzhenitsyn paid for his sense of mission and its immodest expression was mockery. Both in America and in the Soviet Union, there were jokes about Solzhenitsyn's "gulag complex," speculations that he craved the isolation of prisons and prisons-of-his-own-making. He was a monarchist, an anti-Semite, a paranoiac. Voinovich wrote a satirical novel, *Moscow 2042*, that featured a Solzhenitsyn-like character who seemed a cross between a fundamentalist imam and a West Virginia hermit. Solzhenitsyn felt wounded. "They lie about me as they would about a dead man," he once said.

Aleksandr Isayevich, for his part, kept to his schedule. He worked twelve to fourteen hours a day at his desk filling notebooks with the tiny handwriting he learned while trying to conceal his drafts in prison. He also worked on assembling archives on the Revolution and the development of a fund to help the survivors of the gulag. In August 1990, he got back his citizenship. The Russian prime minister, Ivan Silayev, practically begged Solzhenitsyn to return home "in the interests of the state and its future destiny. . . . Your return to Russia is, in my view, one of those moves that our homeland needs as much as air." It seemed strange that Solzhenitsyn still had nothing to say about what was going on in the Soviet Union. When he caved in and granted an interview to *Time* magazine, he set down firm conditions: no questions about Gorbachev or politics, only literature.

"How to Revitalize Russia" came as a shock. After such long silence, Solzhenitsyn worked all summer on his essay and then published it in a paper with a circulation of between twenty-five and thirty million readers. (The next

day it also ran in the weekly *Literaturnaya Gazeta,* which went out to another four million.)

The text began in prophetic voice:

> The clock of communism has tolled its final hour.
> But the concrete structure has not completely collapsed.
> Instead of being liberated, we may be crushed beneath the rubble.

That opening, and the essay as a whole, had much the same rhythm as his "Letter to the Soviet Leaders," which he sent to the Kremlin the year before his exile. "Your dearest wish," he had written to Brezhnev, "is for our state structure and our ideological system never to change, to remain as they are for centuries. But history is not like that. Every system either finds a way to develop or else collapses." He was now addressing a country that was doing both at once, though the collapse was ruthless and the development erratic. After a ringing restatement of the "blind and malignant" Bolshevik disaster—the murder of tens of millions of people, the destruction of the peasantry, the poisoning of the environment, the moral and spiritual degradation of the country—he provided what he called a "tentative proposal" but what sounded more like the vatic prescription of a convinced prophet:

"This is how I see it: We should immediately proclaim loudly and clearly: The three Baltic republics [Estonia, Latvia, and Lithuania], the three Transcaucasian republics [Georgia, Armenia, and Azerbaijan], the four Central Asian republics [Kirgizia, Uzbekistan, Turkmenia, and Tajikistan], and also Moldavia, if it is drawn more to Romania, these eleven—indeed!—definitely must be separated for good. . . .

"We do not have the energy to deal with the periphery, either economically or spiritually. We do not have the energy to run an Empire! And we do not need it, let us shrug it off: It is crushing us, it is draining us, and it is accelerating our demise. . . ."

The essay did not mention Gorbachev by name and gave him credit for nothing. Instead, the criticism, resounding and heavy with sarcasm, began in the third word of the title: *obustroit'* was a play on the word "perestroika." Gorbachev and the Communist Party used "perestroika" to mean the "rebuilding" or cleansing of socialism after Stalin's "deformation" of Leninism. Solzhenitsyn's verb, *obustroit',* could be translated as to reconstitute, fix, fix up, make comfortable, organize, or, more loosely, revitalize. The ironic echo of "perestroika" and the use of "Russia" instead of "Soviet Union" made it clear from the start that Solzhenitsyn's program had little to do with Gorba-

chev's idea of a "humane democratic socialism" or the maintenance of the "multiethnic state." Indeed, Solzhenitsyn showed little else but disdain for Gorbachev's efforts. The events of five years were reduced almost to nothing: "What have five or six years of the much-celebrated 'perestroika' brought us? Pathetic reshuffling in the Central Committee. Slapping together of an ugly, artificial electoral system, with a view solely to the Communist Party's clinging to power. Slipshod, confused, and indecisive laws. . . ."

Immediately after publication, there were varied complaints about the essay. The language, so full of archaic words, felt artificial, dusty. The Kazakhs were furious that Solzhenitsyn felt the northern part of the republic was, essentially, Russian. Ukrainians, especially, made it clear that independence, not a Slavic union, was their goal. Then there was the cranky side of Solzhenitsyn, the prig worrying that Russia would mindlessly pursue the road to Gomorrah because it couldn't find the off switch on the TV set: "Our young people, whom families and schools have overlooked, are growing in the direction of mindless, barbaric emulation of anything enticing coming from alien parts, if not in the direction of crime. The historic Iron Curtain protected the country superbly from everything good that exists in the West. . . . However, this Curtain did not reach all the way down, and this is where the liquid manure of debased, degraded 'mass pop-culture,' most vulgar fashions and excessive public displays seeped through. It was this waste that our impoverished, unfairly deprived young people swallowed greedily."

This old-mannish side of Solzhenitsyn seemed to me as marginal as Tolstoy's retrograde views on women and sex in *The Kreutzer Sonata.* But more important was that the right-wing fanatics, the monarchists and black-shirted nationalists, the anti-Semites of Pamyat, were deeply disappointed by the essay. They were looking for an endorsement of authoritarian rule, and what they got was a peculiar, but distinct, support of democracy and private property. What they got was a call for the breakup of the empire they worshiped.

There were serious mistakes and misjudgments in the essay. Solzhenitsyn did not recognize just how deeply Ukrainians, for example, had come to believe in their own distinctiveness, how much they wanted a capital in Kiev, not Moscow. And, as always, Solzhenitsyn created problems for himself with the pitch of his voice, its hyped-up grandeur. Somehow, the strength of his own hopes for a Slavic state drowned out the admission that he also makes: that, yes, of course, it must be the Ukrainians themselves who decide if they want to join Russia.

Solzhenitsyn's most curious critic turned out to be Gorbachev himself. A few days after the publication of "How to Revitalize Russia," a member of the Supreme Soviet asked the president to comment. (The idea of it! The

general secretary responds in parliament to Solzhenitsyn!) To a hushed chamber, Gorbachev said he felt "contradictory" emotions after reading the essay twice through. Solzhenitsyn's views "on the future of the state," he said, "are far from reality and are being constructed out of the context of our country's development and bear a destructive character. But nonetheless there are interesting thoughts in the article of this undoubtedly great person." A splendid backhanded compliment. But then Gorbachev felt the need to distort Solzhenitsyn, to exploit the recurring stereotype of his views. Solzhenitsyn, Gorbachev said, "is all in the past, the Russia of old, the czarist monarchy. This is not acceptable to me." It was self-serving, a moment of demagoguery designed to present himself as the singular modern democrat.

—

On October 15, Gorbachev received the Nobel Prize for Peace.

On October 16, after the leaders of the KGB, the police, the army, and the defense industry made it quite clear that they would not tolerate a radical reordering of political and economic power, Gorbachev withdrew his support for the 500 Days plan. Gorbachev had caved in to the people who had everything to lose from the reform of the country. When he did that it was clear to everyone in the Soviet Union that Gorbachev had begun listing to the right. Soon he would reject all the reformers in his team, he would begin to speak, with a sneer, of the "so-called democrats." He would ignore one grab for power after another, ever confident that he was serving the cause of reform. The counterrevolution, which began with the swing of an assassin's ax, was now ascendant.

"When Mikhail Sergeyevich rejected the 500 Days program he was rejecting the last chance for a civilized transition to a new order," Aleksandr Yakovlev told me. "It was probably his worst, most dangerous mistake, because what followed was nothing less than a war."

CHAPTER 25

THE TOWER

On the December morning in 1990 that Eduard Shevardnadze resigned as foreign minister, I was in Riga to learn more about a strange series of dirty tricks aimed at the Baltic independence movements. There had been explosions near monuments and war memorials, the sort of incidents the army and the KGB could blame on the "radicals" and present as reasons to take "emergency measures" to "reassert an atmosphere of stability." They already had the language down pat. And why not? All they had to do was reach up to the shelf and bring down the handbook and look under "putsch, cf. Prague '68, Budapest '56, et al." The scenario was all there. All they needed now was the dossier, the pretext.

Shevardnadze, of all people, knew perfectly well what was going on. For months he saw how the military were trying to deceive him, how they tried to embarrass him before the West with their games in the Baltic states and ruin his arms negotiations by moving their tanks and missiles in just such a way that the Americans would catch it on their satellites and blame Moscow for bad faith. He and Yakovlev both saw how the Supreme Soviet chairman, Lukyanov, and the KGB chief, Kryuchkov—those gray Siamese twins—would sit in Politburo meetings and try to unscrew Gorbachev's head, try to convince him that the "so-called" democrats and Baltic independence people

were going to take over with armed insurrections Vilnius, Riga, Tallinn, Tbilisi, and even the Kremlin. And Gorbachev would listen to every word, nodding sagely. These were the men he trusted, the Party men, the men he'd known since the early days. Sure, they were a little more conservative, but they spoke the same language, the language of the Party, and they knew what discipline was.

I spent the morning of Shevardnadze's resignation at the editorial offices of *Diena* ("The Day"), the main pro-independence paper in Riga. The rightward swing had already started, and so the reporters had no shortage of anecdotes about provocations and intimidation. It was an anxious newsroom. The place had the nasty edge of the family waiting room in intensive care. Something awful was going to happen, they said. It had to.

Then it did. One of the typists, who'd tuned in to the Congress broadcasts on the radio, slowly took off his headphones. He opened his mouth and nothing came out. He was ashen.

"Maybe I got it wrong," he said in a whisper. "Let me listen again."

Then he closed his eyes and listened.

"Shevardnadze," he said. "He's resigned. He said dictatorship is coming. He is sure of it."

Shevardnadze had warned that "dictatorship is coming" and that the democrats had scattered "to the bushes." Shevardnadze had not told anyone that he would make his speech except his family and a couple of his closest aides. As he spoke, his Georgian accent made thicker by the anger in him, the sense of moment, Gorbachev sat at the Presidium as shocked as anyone else in the hall. It was one thing for Moscow intellectuals at the kitchen table to talk about a nascent dictatorship, quite another for Shevardnadze, the second-most-recognized face in the leadership, to put an end to his career. What did this man, who was in a position to know so much, really know?

Everyone in the newsroom at *Diena* was shattered. Ever since the three Baltic states declared their independence a half year before, they had tried to sustain the conceit that they were already independent. They did not need to ask permission or hold a referendum or in any way pay much attention to the politics of Moscow, because Moscow was elsewhere, a foreign power. Now that conceit was finished, untenable. The Baltic leaders could always trust Shevardnadze (or at least as much as they trusted anyone in Moscow), and now he was telling them that their worst midnight fears were true. Dictatorship was coming, and a conceit of attitude and language, no matter how inventive or assured, would do nothing to stop the brutal charge.

—

I flew back to Moscow the next morning and went straight to the Kremlin. At the Palace of Congresses, military officers strutted in packs, back and forth across the main foyer. Before, the generals and admirals had always seemed to caucus down near the coatroom, away from the cameras and the reporters. They'd linger by the door in little crowds of olive green and navy blue. They seemed to laugh more than other deputies. After all, they were comrades. They had known each other for years. This democracy stuff, well, it was a lark, a sideshow. But now they were all over the main lobby, dumping one-liners off to the press, confident stuff about how they respected Eduard Amvrosievich, but, my dear American friend, not to fear, everything is under control, don't go worrying about coups and turns to the right. Everything is fine. Gorbachev's military adviser, Sergei Akhromeyev—a marshal much beloved by Admiral William Crowe at the Pentagon—chuckled through his teeth when I asked him about a military coup.

"How many times do we have to tell you people?" he said. "Relax! Stop inventing fantasies!"

Upstairs at the buffet tables, Communist Party hacks were stuffing themselves sick with state-subsidized caviar, smoked salmon, sturgeon, cream cakes, and tea. When they thought no one was looking, they bought ten sandwiches more and stuffed them in their briefcases, the better not to be hungry later on.

Meanwhile, the radicals did the death march, up and down the halls. Vitaly Korotich, with that ate-the-canary smile of his suddenly gone, said his friends and he had started making plans "for the trip to Siberia." He was only half kidding. Afanasyev was more bleary-eyed than usual. The Balts, those who hadn't left for home already, smoked furiously near the lavatories. Shevardnadze had said in his speech that "democracy would prevail," but he warned that the democrats, the radicals, were disorganized and dyspeptic, divided, egocentric, petty. They were risking everything. His language was cryptic, but he made it clear that they could no longer depend on the moral authority of Sakharov—he was gone—or the political strength of Gorbachev—that was in doubt.

Finally, toward the very end of the Congress, one of the democrats had a moment of eloquence that helped make sense of Shevardnadze's great gesture. Ales Adamovich, a war veteran, the best-known writer in Byelorussia, and a founder of Memorial, got up from his first-row seat, walked up the stairs to the stage, and took hold of the lectern, as if for balance. Gorbachev, Adamovich said, "is the only leader in Soviet history who has not stained his hands with blood, and we would all like to remember him as such." Then he turned for an instant behind him, as if to address Gorbachev directly: "But a moment will come when the military will instigate a bloodbath, and later

they will wipe their bloodstained hands against your suit. And you will be to blame for everything. In the West, you are known as a political genius. I would like you to exercise your wisdom again. Otherwise, you will lose perestroika."

The truth was, it looked lost already. Day by day, the hard-liners made their moves, and there was nothing secret, nothing tricky, about them. Gennadi Yanayev, a witless apparatchik, philanderer, and drunk, was now vice president. Shevardnadze was replaced as foreign minister with Aleksandr Bessmertnykh, a liberal, but without any of the strength or authority of his predecessor. The KGB and the Interior Ministry gave themselves the right to patrol the streets of all major cities. Yazov went on the air complaining about provocations and warned that he would strike back whenever and however he deemed necessary. Kryuchkov announced that he might have to spill a little blood to keep the peace in the republics. And Anatoly Lukyanov, "Lucky Luke," the creepy chairman of the Supreme Soviet, was always eager to give the floor of the standing parliament to the colonels and crazies from Soyuz ("Union"), the right-wing faction that called, on a daily basis, for Gorbachev's neck and a state of emergency.

It was an ugly time, and everyone expected it to get uglier. Yakovlev said that the right wing was off on a "vengeful and merciless" counterrevolution, an echo from Pushkin's *The Captain's Daughter*. But Yakovlev, instead of resigning, quietly moved out of Gorbachev's orbit. Gorbachev would no longer listen to him anymore. What could he do? When I asked Yakovlev what he thought of Gorbachev's appointment of Yanayev, Yakovlev smiled wearily and said, "The president is a wise man, so I am sure it is a wise decision." But much later, when he could afford to be less cryptic, Yakovlev told me he saw an "eerie quiet" developing around Gorbachev that winter, as if all his ministers were merely pretending to obey the president, but then went off and did as they pleased. Slowly, they were making a hostage of Gorbachev, and they were counting on the man's powerful desire to stay in office to keep themselves in control.

Sobchak, the liberal mayor of Leningrad, was the coolest head among the democrats, and when I saw him at the Mariinsky Palace, the headquarters of the city government, he made perfect sense of what was going on. "We are living now through a transition from a totalitarian system to a democratic one, and the forces of dictatorship and democracy live side by side," he said. "Under these conditions, the danger of a new dictatorship, of military coups or the use of military force against the people, is absolutely real." It was all so ominous. And nothing had really happened yet.

By the winter of 1990–91, Moscow had become a newspaper fanatic's dream. Len Karpinsky's columns and *Moscow News* were only a part of the morning haul. Having started from nothing, from the wet wash of the Communist Party press, Moscow became the most exciting newspaper city since New York after the war. The Khrushchev "thaw" was a liberalization from which emerged a few works of real literature, but glasnost was a period of journalism, of investigation, sensation, commentary, and scoop.

At first, the most obvious mainstays of glasnost were *Moscow News* and the weekly magazine *Ogonyok.* But as glasnost evolved into more genuine freedom of the press, the democratic vista widened. There were breathless papers that rushed to the aid of the radical cause, especially *Komsomolskaya Pravda* with its circulation of twenty-five million. *Literaturnaya Gazeta* printed a blend of high-minded cultural criticism, political analysis, and Yuri Shchekochikhin's startling investigative work on the KGB. *Argumenti i Fakti,* with a circulation of thirty million, was a kind of bulletin board of two-hundred-word articles and factoids. *Izvestia* was solid, and for tabloid sensation there were *Top Secret*'s true crime stories ("Murder on Kutuzovsky Street!") and *Megapolis-Express*'s local muckraking. The puckish *Kommersant,* edited by Yegor Yakovlev's son Vladimir, covered the emerging business world, letting young entrepreneurs know which mafia clan ruled which district and how to find cheap computers on the black market. In the train stations and street corners, hawkers did a brisk business in Baltic sex papers, neo-Bolshevik mimeograph sheets, and copies of Dale Carnegie's *How to Win Friends and Influence People.*

For the hard-liners there was *Sovetskaya Rossiya,* which published the Nina Andreyeva letter in 1988 and the key manifestos leading up to the coup still to come, and *Dyen* ("The Newspaper of the Spiritual Opposition"), edited by Aleksandr Prokhanov, a theocratic-militarist wacko known affectionately as "the Nightingale of the General Staff." Among the wire services, the old Big Brother of the ticker, Tass, was as much a fossil as the evening news program *Vremya* or *Pravda,* while Interfax and a few others in some of the republics developed the manic intensity of the Associated Press on a good day. Interfax's leading reporter, Vyacheslav Terekhov, was a breeder reactor in a brown suit, badgering politicians and filing dispatches from breakfast till midnight.

Until 1988 or 1989 at the latest, *Moscow News* remained the iconoclast, always smashing idols just before the reformers in the leadership did. Ligachev called *Moscow News* an "ersatz" paper, and small wonder. *Moscow News* was clearly the voice of the liberals in the Politburo. But it was this lack

of real independence at *Moscow News,* its obvious link to Gorbachev himself, that began to work against it in 1990 and 1991. As the country grew more diverse, as the liberal intelligentsia's ideas about the future of society and politics grew far more radical than Gorbachev's own, *Moscow News* under Yegor Yakovlev began to look a bit timid and almost comically protective of its original patron.

"Without realizing it, Yegor was turning *Moscow News* into *Pravda,*" said Vitaly Tretyakov, who was Yakovlev's deputy at the time. "Just as *Pravda* was the tribune of the old powers, he wanted *Moscow News* to be the tribune of the new power, the left-of-center position, the Gorbachev position in the Politburo. When I became Yegor's deputy, I began to see how many visitors and calls there were from the Central Committee and it was obvious the paper was not operating independently. Len Karpinsky was much more radical than Yegor, but *Moscow News* could only be as radical as Yegor would allow it to be. Yegor has the personality of a dictator, which may be necessary, but he always wanted to be in possession of ultimate truth, he claimed to know all the answers. None of us could take a step at *Moscow News* without Yegor's say-so. You couldn't mention Lenin, for instance, because Yegor thought he knew all there was to know. And then there was Gorbachev: we could not criticize him directly. And what could someone like Len Karpinsky do? After all, it was Yegor who pulled Len out of obscurity and got him a job."

By the summer of 1990, millions of people were quitting the Communist Party. The Party that called itself the "initiator of perestroika"—an appalling bit of self-congratulation considering the blood on its hands—had lost the power to convince many of its own members that it supported radical change. At *Moscow News,* Tretyakov proposed that the paper's Party committee all quit as one. But Yakovlev said no, they should "stay the course." As usual, Yakovlev had the votes—Karpinsky's included.

Vitaly Tretyakov was feeling more alienated from his colleagues at the paper by the day. At thirty-nine, he was not a man of the Gorbachev generation and he had none of the Old Bolshevik background and Party connections of so many of the *shestidesyatniki.* His parents were laborers. Tretyakov had worked for years on the sort of glossy propaganda magazines that the government printing organs ground out like sausage meat: *Soviet Life, Études Sovietique, Soviet Woman,* and the rest. His time at *Moscow News* was "a gift," but the time had come to quit, he decided. "My idea," he said, "was to start something new, a better *Moscow News.*"

Tretyakov had very little idea of what he wanted when he began his first planning sessions in the summer of 1990. He knew only that he did not want to tie the fate and tone of his paper to the fate of Mikhail Gorbachev or any

other political personality. At first, he tried to lure some of the best-known writers in Moscow to join him, but they all turned him down. No one with a family and an established position was prepared to risk it all on an experiment, a notion. Tretyakov's one essential break came with the election of liberal democrats to the Moscow City Hall. The new mayor, Gavriil Popov, and his deputy, Sergei Stankevich, were intrigued by Tretyakov's idea and gave him a start-up grant of 300,000 rubles. No strings attached, Popov said. Remarkably, the city officials kept their word. They have never considered the paper their own and have not interfered in editorial or business policy. "It was just a small investment in the transition to a free press," Stankevich said.

I had heard about the paper a half year before its first issue appeared. One summer afternoon, I drove to the country town of Peredelkino to visit Andrei Karaulov, a young theater critic, and his wife, Natasha, the daughter of the playwright Mikhail Shatrov. Karaulov was a journalist-hustler the likes of whom I never had seen before or have since—at least not in Moscow. Even in the early days of perestroika he managed to get interviews with one Politburo member and spymaster after another. He somehow made patently evil and slimy men feel comfortable, then tortured them with his combination of unctuous charm and barbed questions. Andrei's knack was so uncanny that some of his rivals moaned that he must have "dark connections." At the Peredelkino dacha that afternoon, one of the other guests was a man in his early forties named Igor Zakharov. Zakharov, it turned out, was an extreme cynic who despised himself most of all. He worked for years at the Novosti press agency editing its propaganda sheets. "I am a born functionary," he said. "I never believed in anything official: not in Communism and not in the possibility of perestroika. I may have published all that shit, but I never believed it. You know that expression 'Life is elsewhere'?" Somehow this willingness to work with odious bureaucrats while believing "otherwise" seemed to wear less well on him than on an older idealist like Karpinsky. It was touching that Karpinsky actually did believe in something when he was young and then believed in something else later on. Zakharov believed in nothing but the hopelessness of just about everything, and the sudden advent of radical changes in the country made his cynicism seem worthless. There were times when Karaulov and Zakharov both made my skin crawl. So when they began telling me about their work with Vitaly Tretyakov on a new newspaper to be called *Nezavisimaya Gazeta*—"The Independent Newspaper"—not only did I think it would fail, I hoped it would.

I forgot about that discussion and *Nezavisimaya Gazeta* until six months later when I was flying back from Riga to Moscow on the morning after Shevardnadze's resignation. On the plane I borrowed two copies of an unfa-

miliar broadsheet—the first and second issues of *Nezavisimaya Gazeta*—and I was startled. The front page of the first issue featured little mug shots of the country's leading ministers—a loutish bunch who looked like the comic thugs in "Dick Tracy," Flattop, Mumbles, and the rest. Above the pictures was a triple-stack headline: "They Rule Us: But What Do We Know About Them, the Most Powerful People in the Country? Almost Nothing. . . ." On page five, Yuri Afanasyev published what was surely the most incisive and prescient piece of political commentary of the year: "We Are Moving to the Side of Dictatorship." In details that proved absolutely accurate, Afanasyev described Gorbachev's "tragedy," how his own internal and political limitations left him open to the pressures of the hard-line Communists in the regime. It was just the sort of pointed political critique of Gorbachev that *Moscow News* could not bring itself to publish. Then on page eight of the first issue—the back page—Tretyakov printed a manifesto declaring that there had never been "in the history of the Soviet Union" a paper independent of political interests. He promised *Nezavisimaya Gazeta* would be such a paper. The second issue led with the headline "Eduard Shevardnadze Leaves. The Military-Industrial Complex Stays. What Choice Will Gorbachev Make?" A few pages later, Karaulov weighed in with a fascinating interview with the number-two ranking man in the KGB, Filipp Bobkov—the same man who interrogated Len Karpinsky two decades before.

One day during those first weeks of *Nezavisimaya Gazeta*'s life, I went to the paper's offices with Karaulov. As we walked along the muddy streets near the KGB buildings on Lubyanka Square, he was trying to sell me—literally—some crackpot spy-story documents involving the Bolshoi Theater. Information was constantly for sale now in Moscow. When asked for interviews, some Kremlin officials had no shame. "How much?" they would say. When I refused Karaulov's "tip" on the Bolshoi and explained the rules about not paying for information, he seemed alternately bemused and hurt. "Besides, you'd never find the place without me," he said. "You owe me for that, at least." *Nezavisimaya Gazeta*'s offices were tucked away in an obscure courtyard building not far from Lubyanka Square. At the time, the paper shared the building with the Voskhod (Sunrise) printing company. Expansion eventually eased the printers out. The paper originally had twenty staffers and appeared three days a week, then built up to two hundred employees and five issues a week. When I first visited the office, the place was a sea of paper and ironic memorabilia—faded portraits of old Politburo members a specialty. No one looked as if he had slept, showered, or shaved in days.

Tretyakov wanted nothing more than to mimic the traditional model of a Western newspaper. His staff looked *Village Voice,* but he yearned for the style and substance of *The New York Times.* "It may seem boring to you,"

Tretyakov told me during one of our talks, "but I want to create the first Western-style, respectable, objective paper of the Soviet era."

Turned down by the older stars, Tretyakov got his journalists wherever he could find them. Most of them had worked at second- and third-tier publications, at movie and theatrical quarterlies, Baltic underground sheets, Komsomol dailies. Some had no experience at all. They were biologists, secretaries, workers, students, diplomats, anything. Whatever skills they did or did not have, they had a unanimous contempt for all things *sovok*—the slang term for "Soviet." (The staff's favorite early fan letter read, "Congratulations: You are neither pro-Soviet nor anti-Soviet. You are simply non-Soviet.") All were young, and they did not bother to struggle with the questions of their elders. The ideological ruminations of a man like Len Karpinsky were for these kids irrelevant and just a little bit sad.

Mikhail Leontyev, the paper's economics editor, was a typical hire. He had studied economics at the Plekhanov Institute in Moscow, but to avoid doing "idiot work for the regime," he quit the academic world and worked for years restoring old Russian furniture. He hardly ever wrote, he told me: "Why bother?" He did publish one prescient essay for the Latvian paper *Atmoda* in 1989 titled "The New Consensus," about the growing front of fascists, nationalists, and military leaders. "That was about all I could do," Leontyev said. "I just couldn't work for any of the old papers. Coming here, discovering *Nezavisimaya Gazeta,* was the revelation we were all waiting for. The coverage of economics in our paper starts from the principle that we don't need to tear our hair out about whether Marxism-Leninism or capitalism is the right way to go. That debate is dead as can be. Do we really have to go crazy over whether it is good to find a healthy balance between efficiency and social welfare? About whether the rules of the market are ultimately correct? I don't think so. I don't cover Communism or any other religions in these pages. That's not my business."

The darkening political mood that winter, the ominous sense that the army, the KGB, and the Communist Party now formed an open alliance against a radical reform of the country, had given *Nezavisimaya Gazeta* an immediate sense of purpose. Muscovites reading *Nezavisimaya Gazeta* in that first month or so had a sense of understanding and foreboding about the political earthquake to come. Not so with *Moscow News,* which still kept its reports within certain bounds. *Moscow News* was no longer responding to government censors—they had been either removed or rendered completely benign—but, rather, to an internal sense of propriety and caution, a lingering reverence for Gorbachev and the old hopes of the thaw generation.

Week after week, *Nezavisimaya Gazeta* was reinventing the newspaper in Moscow, and a twenty-seven-year-old reporter named Sergei Parkhomenko

was consistently the paper's most incisive political commentator. The son and grandson of journalists, Parkhomenko first won a name for himself at the quarterly *Teatr* when he covered the first session of the Congress of People's Deputies in May 1989, a job he called the "ultimate in theater criticism." Gorbachev played the Great Reformer, Sakharov was the Conquering Saint, and the Communist Party hacks were the Evil Chorus. "Imagine if you in America had held the Constitutional Convention live on television," he said. "The old order died a little every day. No play ever changed an audience more thoroughly."

One night, I went with Sergei to the presses at *Izvestia* where *Nezavisimaya Gazeta* was printed. He was the duty editor, acting as a liaison between the printers and the editors back at the office, who were constantly trying to shove late items into the paper. He had already written a column in the morning and had called in a few items for his after-hours job as a stringer for other publications. Like many good young reporters in Moscow, Parkhomenko discovered he could make some hard currency on the side by working for a foreign news organization—in his case, Agence France Presse, the official French wire service. As it turned out, the experience expanded his sense of journalism. "With the French, I got a taste of real reporting," he said. "It was a new sort of game. Who can be the first to get the information? Who can get sources? Before it was all 'I think this,' 'I think that.' Now the game had changed and I loved it and the skills were just what I needed. You see, I somehow always knew I would work at a place like *Nezavisimaya Gazeta.* I knew it instinctively. I wanted a place that was born without any complexes. There are more radical publications, but I'm not interested in the contest for who can be the most radical or liberal. I can't stand unity and consensus."

Parkhomenko was best known in Moscow for his commentaries—mainly because he refused to shill for any one politician or party line—but he was also an instinctive investigative reporter. He caused a terrific scandal when he discovered that the Central Committee had been running for years a huge fourteen-room workshop for manufacturing fake Western passports. He reported that there were fake stamps, blank passport forms for dozens of foreign countries, and even false mustaches and beards and hats for the passport photos.

Investigative work was a signature of the front page at *Nezavisimaya Gazeta.* A married couple in their twenties at the paper, Anya Ostapchuk and Zhenya Krasnikov, enraged the Party when they scooped everyone by printing a copy of the Communist Party's proposed new platform endorsing a "democratic, humane socialism." Anya's methods were "quite simple and un-Soviet." She went to the apartment of a Central Committee member,

Vasily Lipitsky, and asked about the platform. He gave her the twenty-three-page document written by Gorbachev's aide, Giorgi Shakhnazarov, and said she could read it, "but no notes and no tape recorders."

"Then something odd happened," Anya said. "Lipitsky said he had to take a phone call in the next room. As soon as he left, I got out my tape recorder and read the thing as fast as I could. He didn't come back in time to stop me. I finished. But I'm sure he wanted me to do just that. It was terrific fun."

Presented with the scoop, Tretyakov was stunned. At *Moscow News,* his bosses would never have permitted such a thing. Too dangerous, a distinct lack of respect. But Tretyakov immediately published the piece. In a wry note to the readers, he wrote that ordinarily *Nezavisimaya Gazeta* did not print party manifestos and platforms "because that would be a form of advertising," and added, "but from such a party we would rather not take any money."

The next day, as every newspaper in Moscow scurried to catch up with the platform story, Parkhomenko got a swift lesson in the sensibilities of the powerful. At a small late-night press conference in the Moscow suburb of Novo-Ogarevo, Gorbachev looked at the reporters and said, "Okay, so who here is from *Nezavisimaya Gazeta*?"

The reporter from state television, a whinnying time-server, blanched and panicked.

"No, no, it's him," he said, pointing at Parkhomenko.

"Where did you steal it from?" Gorbachev said.

"I can't say," Parkhomenko said.

"And why not?"

"Because that's the way we work."

After the press conference, two of Gorbachev's aides tried to weasel the information out of Parkhomenko. "Oh, come on," one of them said. "You can tell me. I won't tell another soul!"

Shakhnazarov, for his part, told me he was shocked to see his work in the paper. "Woodward and Bernstein—that is not exactly something we're used to," he said.

Sometimes Tretyakov and Zakharov, the village elders at the paper, were scared by their own reporters, their relentlessness, their giddy fearlessness. They were well aware of just how inexperienced the reporters were, how little they knew about degrees of reliability and balance. Often, reporters turned in stories that were merely rumors that seemed a bit too good to check. But while the top editors often demanded more reporting and numerous rewrites, they seldom killed any stories. The only story that Tretyakov refused to run without further question was the rubbish about the KGB and the Bolshoi Theater that Karaulov had tried to peddle to me.

"The reason these kids do things like investigative work is that they not only don't fear the system, they don't even respect it," Zakharov said. "These kids are arrogant, silly, uneducated, undisciplined; they live only in the present. They don't care about yesterday and have no idea that there is nothing new under the sun. But they have no prejudices. They don't think ahead and wonder if someone at the Kremlin will think this or that. They just go ahead and do it."

The young reporters also changed the language of newspapers. They dispensed with the wooden bureaucratese and fanatic sloganeering of the Soviet period. "We don't talk *Pravda* language," Parkhomenko said. The change was incredible. Before I left for Russia, I took a course at George Washington University in something called "Newspaper Russian." For weeks, we memorized endless lists of political clichés: "The talks were held in a warm and friendly atmosphere"; "The peace-loving comrade-nations of the world will face the imperialists in a round of negotiations next week"; and so on. It was the language of Novoyaz, or Newspeak, and nowhere had it reached such a level of absurdity as in the Soviet Union. But *Nezavisimaya Gazeta*'s younger reporters had never had to write that way—or at least not for long. While someone like Len Karpinsky still had trouble clearing the Novoyaz from his prose—"I try, but I can't always get it clear"—the *Nezavisimaya Gazeta* crowd had no such handicap.

"Right away, we tried to imitate Western language," Parkhomenko said at the print shop. "In Russian, there had never been political language of a civilized country."

It took a while, but I was getting a better sense now of who was leading the right-wing counterrevolution. One night I went to the Red Army Theater for what the right-wing press promised would be an evening of "patriotic celebration." It was a full house, and nearly everyone was in uniform: army drab, priests' black, and, here and there, a writer in a pilled chocolate-brown suit. Onstage, one Father Fyodor, his robes festooned with military decorations, droned on about the greatness of Russia's warriors, "her Aleksandr Nevsky, her Dmitri Donskoi, her proud knights."

"God is our greatest general!" he cried out, and God's seconds, the teenage recruits who'd been bused in for the show, applauded dutifully.

"But what about Yazov?" one of these teenagers whispered to me. "Isn't he our general?"

Valentin Rasputin, a Siberian novelist well known for his moral indignation and attacks on the ecological ruin of Lake Baikal, sat off to the side of the stage, nodding solemnly at all the speeches. Rasputin was a writer of real

talent. His stories about the degradation of the countryside and Communism's damage to the spirit were respected even by those critics who despised his right-wing politics. But he was not merely conservative. Rasputin was a hater, a brooding anti-Semite who blamed the Jews for the crimes of the Bolsheviks. And that was when he was giving an interview to *The New York Times*. He was less discreet at gatherings of the Russian Writers' Union.

For years the right-wingers lived in comfort. They controlled the unions, lived decently. But now, with the barbarians at the gate, they were ready to form even the strangest of coalitions. Rasputin's literary nationalists and the official priests of the Russian Orthodox Church aligned themselves with men like Akhromeyev and Yazov of the Red Army and Kryuchkov of the KGB, avowed Communists and party leaders. It was a confusing picture. But as I sat there that night in the Red Army Theater, I could see that they had forged a common language, one that had nothing to do with Communist ideology or theocracy. The unifying banner of this alliance of "patriots" was the imagery of empire, vast and powerful, unique and holy. Democracy, rock and roll, stock markets, foreign businesses, independence movements, uppity Jews, Balts, and Asians all undermined the empire.

After the priest blessed the military, and Rasputin blessed Mother Russia, Lieutenant General Gennadi Stepanovsky, one of the leaders of the army's Communist Party organization, gave the final benediction. The democrats, he said, were "auctioning off our tanks, destroying our monuments, destroying our ability to fight for freedom in the Baltics. But they will not win. They cannot wipe out our great history." Like Stalin during the war, Stepankovsky hoped a mystical stew of great-power nationalism would form the common bond. This time the enemy was not the Nazis, but the greater world itself, and its vanguard, the democratic infidels.

After the ceremonies that night I glanced through the latest issue of *Molodaya Gvardiya* ("Young Guard"), one of the exemplars of the new ideology. It was filled with the usual claims: "[Yeltsin's] Russia is a marionette of Western Zionism without a single shot being fired. One clearly sees a plan to draw the world into yet another world war in which Russians and other Slavs will be the cheap cannon fodder. A new spiral of historical genocide is being plotted against us." Another article warned against "strangers bearing gifts" and "cancer-causing shampoos" from Poland, "contaminated bread boxes and shopping bags" from Vietnam, and, of course, the American Big Mac ("too fast and very unhealthy").

The most powerful of the hard-liners—Kryuchkov, Pugo, Yazov, Lukyanov—knew better than to announce their leadership of the creeping, milita-

rized coup d'état that Shevardnadze had warned of. They made threatening gestures and issued chilling proclamations, but, in general, they let others do the dirtiest work. In those winter months, the man who gave a face to the coup was an army colonel from Latvia, Viktor Alksnis. With his high black pompadour and black leather jacket, Alksnis was known in the liberal press as the "black colonel," the Darth Vader of the hard-line set. He loved his role and fairly chewed the scenery every time he appeared on the public stage.

"Before you stands a reactionary scum!" he once told the Congress. (Who would doubt him?) Then he pushed up his lower lip and affected the glare of Mussolini. Caricature, the picture of outsized badness, was just what the part required, and Alksnis played it beautifully. By comparison, men like Supreme Soviet Chairman Lukyanov and Kryuchkov thought they would look like the soul of sweet reason.

As a deputy, Alksnis represented the Soviet military bases in Latvia. He was not much liked. His own aunt went door to door campaigning against him. But Alksnis won, promising to restore the "honor of the military" after the "humiliations" of the withdrawal from Afghanistan and Eastern Europe, the arms reduction treaties with the West, and the cuts in the defense budget. As Party elders like Geidar Aliyev and Yegor Ligachev faded from view, Alksnis, and his counterpart from Kazakhstan, Colonel Nikolai Petrushenko, organized the Soyuz faction under Lukyanov's subtle patronage. Soyuz was a remarkably effective weapon for the right. It was Soyuz that pressured Gorbachev to fire his liberal interior minister, Vadim Bakatin, and replace him with a hard-liner, Boris Pugo. And it was Soyuz that constantly denounced Shevardnadze's foreign policy as treasonous. When he resigned, Shevarnadze angrily wondered why no one had defended him against the "boys in colonel's epaulets."

Alksnis's grandfather, Yakov, was head of the air force in the 1930s. In May 1937, at the height of the purges, Yakov Alksnis was a member of the three-man military tribunal that ordered the conviction and execution of Marshal Mikhail Tukhachevsky, the most brilliant military man of his time, on trumped-up charges of espionage. Alksnis then fell to the logic of the era. Eight months after Tukhachevsky's trial, he was arrested and shot.

"Those were complicated times," the grandson said blandly.

I met "the black colonel" at his suite at the Moskva Hotel, the vast home to out-of-town deputies in the Supreme Soviet. After looking me up and down, Alksnis said, "If you want to call me a reactionary, go ahead." A strange greeting, but then he was not an ordinary man. Even in his overheated room, Alksnis never took off his black leather jacket. He was like a teenager who could feel the length of his hair and the cut of his jeans at every moment like a second being. His look was his statement. He affected at all

times an expression of bored disgust and quickly pronounced himself disgusted to meet me, a representative of the "lying bourgeois press." But, at the same time, he was eager to convey the greater disgust he felt with the way the Kremlin had gone all fuzzy and pusillanimous on him. "We are like Cupid: armed, naked, and we impose love on everyone," he said. "Sad as it may be, the reality of today's 'new thinking,' the priority on 'common human values,' well, the reality of it is that the Soviet Union has lost its status as a superpower. It is treated as if it should know its place. We are bullied now!"

And this weakness, I asked, was all the fault of Shevardnadze?

"The last myth of perestroika is collapsing: the myth of our wonderful foreign policy," he said, and then launched into an account of grievances, of being "sold out" by a government willing to debase itself before its rival, to grant every concession, to withdraw from every "interest"—all to get economic help that never came. It was humiliating! And now, he said, Washington was backing a Baltic independence movement that would tear apart the union and lead it to civil war. "Look at the technical equipment of the popular front of Latvia, the number of fax machines, computers, video machines. That kind of stuff can only be bought for foreign currency, and they had none of their own. It was all received from the West under the cover of various charities. I am acquainted with documents gathered by Soviet intelligence, and it is clear what measures the West has taken to support the separatists in the Baltic states. These are government organizations. They actively support them.

"The West," he went on, "has an official plan to break apart the Soviet state. Doesn't Bush's statement indicate that when he says he supports separatist movements in the Baltics? Doesn't the pressure indicate this? I think it does. This is called arm-twisting, and it's a policy. . . . The West wants to remove the Soviet Union from the political arena as a superpower. They have already managed to remove the Soviet Union as an ideological enemy. Now they want to remove them from the world arena. It is all being achieved without the use of force, just through exploiting the processes going on inside the Soviet Union. The West now thinks it can talk down to us. They used to think of the Soviet Union as Upper Volta with missiles. Now they just think of us as Upper Volta. No one fears us."

More than anything else, Alksnis wanted to be feared. This was his role, to give a face to intimidation. He wanted the democrats and the independence movements to fear the possibility of violence; he wanted the West to fear its own attempts at intervention. Fear, which had been so undercut by five years of reforms, was still the only weapon left to the hard-liners. Everything else—ideology, the promise of a shining future—was lost, forgotten.

Alksnis even had a prescription for the near future, and it went like this:

disband the democratically elected parliaments, arrest all resisters ("Landsbergis, Yeltsin, whatever it takes"), take control of the press, and install in power a "national salvation front." I said that sounded a lot like the scenarios for Prague in 1968 or, even more, the martial law in Poland.

"Yes," he said, "and you should not forget that martial law in Poland prevented a civil war there. It preserved the internal political stability in Poland and allowed a peaceful transition to reforms." Gorbachev, he said, could play the role of General Jaruzelski. "And then everything will be okay. There will be stabilization of the economic situation, the internal political situation. Gorbachev may not want it, but he is not in a position to dictate the situation. Events have gone too far, and Gorbachev is hostage to his own policy. It's gone beyond his control. It's a grass-roots policy. These processes will splash out into the streets in the next few months. It will be very hard to take any specific actions then. The situation is such that it will all happen in the next few months."

The tanks rolled in Lithuania on January 13, 1991.

For more than a year, the KGB and the army had been running operations in Lithuania designed to terrify the popularly elected government and the people. They arrested and beat draft dodgers; they seized various public buildings, institutes, and printing presses; they embarked on a propaganda campaign designed to convince the Russians, Poles, and Jews living there that the Lithuanians would turn them into third-class citizens; they ran military "exercises," including sending dozens of tanks rumbling past the parliament building in the middle of the night; they established a National Salvation Committee led by the few Communist Party officials in Lithuania still loyal to Moscow.

For more than a year, they hinted at an all-out offensive to unseat the Lithuanian government. On January 13, at around 2:00 A.M., the operation began. The National Salvation Committee declared itself in power and tried to take over all means of communication. With the KGB and ground forces commander General Valentin Varennikov in charge, soldiers fired on demonstrators at the Vilnius television tower. At least fourteen people were killed and hundreds injured: they were shot, beaten, or crushed under the tank treads.

But it was a botched job. Even as thugs, the organizers of the coup were miserable failures. The violence did nothing but intensify hatred toward Moscow. The attempts to control the media were halfhearted. The newspaper *Respublika* continued publishing daily eyewitness reports. The television station in Kaunas, a city two hours from Vilnius, jacked up its signal and

broadcast the same footage that was going out on CNN, the BBC, and other foreign stations. The men who planned the operation had figured that the Western media would be too preoccupied with the war in the Persian Gulf to care much for Lithuania. They figured that the Bush administration would be too grateful for Moscow's support of the allied coalition against Saddam Hussein to show much public outrage. There was some truth in this. Americans were spending hours "watching the war" on CNN. The Lithuanians despaired that the West would overlook a series of events that could well mean the end of the revolutionary attempt to transform the Soviet Union.

"Of course, it depends on where you are sitting, but I am convinced that in the long run, what you are seeing now in the Soviet Union will prove more important historically than the war in the Persian Gulf," Algimantis Cekoulis, a leader of the Sajudis front in Lithuania, told me. "I don't think anyone doubts that the allied coalition will win in Iraq, but who will prevail in the Soviet Union? How much blood will be shed? This is not some isolated issue for the tiny Baltic states, or even for the Soviet Union. The course of events in this country will have a dramatic effect on the fate of Europe and even of the United States."

My colleague Michael Dobbs finished dictating his first eyewitness account to me from Vilnius at around four-thirty in the morning. I got a couple hours' sleep and went to Manezh Square. If there was going to be any demonstration at all, it would be outside the Manezh, an exhibition hall near the Kremlin gates. A few hundred people had gathered in the cold. Those with radios kept them tuned to the BBC or Radio Liberty. The main Moscow television and radio stations were broadcasting no news about what had happened in Lithuania except to say that there had been some sort of "incident," and it was all the fault of the sitting government, of course. But Radio Liberty and the BBC were reading back essentially what the Western reporters in Vilnius had put into the Sunday-morning papers.

The reaction was furious: "Gorbachev Is the Saddam Hussein of the Baltics!" one sign said. "Down with the Executioner!"

I ran into Sergei Stankevich, a charming baby-faced politician, and now the deputy mayor of Moscow. I'd first met him when he was campaigning for the Congress of People's Deputies wearing jeans and a T-shirt. He was furious. He had joined the Party because of the promise of Gorbachev and spent one night after another in political argument trying to defend the general secretary to his friends. "Now, that's over. No more," he said. "I'm finished with Gorbachev. There are just so many times you can let yourself be deceived."

Yuri Afanasyev climbed a platform and told the crowd that they would

march toward the Central Committee buildings, the Party headquarters in Old Square. "The killings in Vilnius are the work of a dictatorship of reactionary circles—the generals, the KGB, the military-industrial complex, and the Communist Party chiefs," he told the small crowd. "And at the head of that Party dictatorship stands the initiator of perestroika, Mikhail Sergeyevich Gorbachev."

We marched up Marx Street toward the Central Committee, a series of dreary and imposing buildings around the corner from the KGB. A line of police had already cordoned off the area with sawhorses and a row of parked buses. But the crowd was in no mood to behave, and the people simply walked around the barriers and headed toward the entrances to the headquarters of the Communist Party. One man rushed by the cops and planted a six-foot crucifix at the front door. For a while, the people shouted up at the windows of the building and at the occasional apparatchik coming in to work. Then the police regrouped and cut off the marchers once more. Another charge could have led to blood. Stankevich and the other Democratic Russia leaders stepped in and said it was best to disperse, "to go home and figure things out."

The failed coup attempt in Lithuania changed everything for the middle-aged intellectuals who had remained loyal to the idea of a reformed Communist Party. They were the Gorbachev generation, the *Moscow News* generation, and they had lost a dream that many of them had held since the end of the war and the Twentieth Party Congress. While the young staff at *Nezavisimaya Gazeta* reported the story of the Lithuanian coup attempt as if it were the logical extension of the events of the months before, the writers and editors at *Moscow News* suddenly went through an ideological conversion. With the bloodshed in Vilnius, they lost all faith in Gorbachev. Len Karpinsky, Yegor Yakovlev, and a long list of *shestidesyatniki* including Vyacheslav Shostokovsky from the Higher Party School and Tengiz Abuladze, the director of the movie *Repentance,* signed a front-page editorial in *Moscow News* saying the regime, now in its "death throes," had executed a "criminal act" in Lithuania: "After the bloody Sunday in Vilnius, what is left of our president's favorite topics of 'humane socialism,' 'new thinking,' and a 'common European home'? Virtually nothing."

For so long, most of these men and women had hoped for a socialism made humane. They felt comfortable with the idea of the traditional power structure—the Party—leading the way. After all, weren't they all members? The idea of other parties was something foreign, bourgeois. The impudence of such people as Boris Yeltsin and Vytautas Landsbergis made them uncomfortable. Yegor Yakovlev, especially, had never liked Yeltsin, never liked the

way he attacked Gorbachev or conducted himself. Now the men of *Moscow News* and their generation had nowhere to go but to the people Gorbachev had called, so venomously, the "so-called democrats."

"The Lithuanian tragedy must not fill our hearts with despair," the editorial continued. "While opposing the onslaught of dictatorship and totalitarianism, we are pinning our hopes on the leadership of other Union republics."

The crowd at *Nezavisimaya Gazeta* viewed the conversion of *Moscow News* with pity and condescension. "The truth is, I could never understand why those people only decided to make their split when the tanks rolled into Vilnius," Igor Zakharov said. "It's like trying to figure out why a woman who hates her husband for twenty years finally decides one day, after one little incident, to get up, walk out the door, and never come back."

Maybe the young could never understand. The editors at *Moscow News* sat a long and painful wake for their own dreams and delusions. Not long after the attack in Lithuania, Yegor Yakovlev invited Karpinsky and a few other friends to his apartment for a sixtieth birthday party. "It was a meeting of people who didn't know what to say to one another," said Yakovlev's son Vladimir, the editor of the business paper *Kommersant*. "The energy they used to have was gone, and the world around them was no longer their world. And, most important, they didn't know how to relate to this new world. It was the feeling you see at the gatherings in Russia forty days after someone dies. No one is crying anymore, but no one knows quite what to say. These birthday gatherings had always been such celebrations. Now it was just silence, a complete breakdown."

—

While the newspapers played out their generational drama, the most brutal struggle was the war for television. It was fitting that the scene of violence in Vilnius was the concrete television tower on the edge of the city, for this revolution was a battle for the minds of every person in the Soviet Union. "The television image is everything," Aleksandr Yakovlev had said, and now both sides knew it. For the reactionaries to recapture television would be far more than a symbolic defeat for democracy. It would be the beginning of the end.

When I got to Vilnius a week after the killings, young Red Army soldiers were still camped around the tower, guarding it as if it were the most precious property in all of Lithuania. And it may have been. The soldiers had AK-47s slung over their shoulders and wore tight, frightened expressions. These were kids, eighteen, nineteen, twenty years old, many of them unaware of what had happened. The crack troops who had carried out the assault had already been evacuated.

Outside the chain-link fence, on an incline leading away from the tower, a Lithuanian sculptor had carved out of wood a weeping, haggard Christ, a figure out of the paintings of Goya. People had made a shrine of the Christ, surrounding it with candles and flowers. Teenagers came and sat on the muddy hill and played tapes of Lithuanian folk songs and stared off into the pale winter sky.

Down the road a couple of miles, thousands of pro-independence Lithuanians had surrounded the parliament building with makeshift barricades, the better to guard against the next assault. They used huge blocks of poured concrete, steel scrap, sandbags, buses, trams. Outside the building, people sat in the cold, some of them around oil-drum campfires. One man made a fire for himself out of a dozen copies of *The History of the Communist Party of the Soviet Union.* Along the barbed wire that cut off access to the front entrances to the parliament building, people had thrown the symbols of their fury: plastic machine guns, water pistols, watercolors of the tanks painted by schoolchildren; there were portraits of Gorbachev as a killer, Gorbachev kissing Stalin on the lips, Gorbachev shoving Lithuanians into a meat grinder; some had spiked their red Party membership cards along the top of the razor wire, giving the fence a leafy, autumnal look. Inside the parliament building, everyone was waiting for the next move. Why would they stop at the TV tower? Landsbergis stayed in his office and slept a few hours a night on his couch. He refused to go home for fear of kidnapping, or worse. Kids who had run away from the Red Army acted as a makeshift guard. They carried ancient hunting rifles, rusty knives, and the sort of clunky revolvers you saw in Hollywood westerns. In the press room upstairs, young volunteers sent out faxes and telexes to news bureaus around the world: bulletins, appeals for help, official pronouncements of the president. Always, the televisions played. We watched the British Sky Channel and CNN to see what the world was seeing and *Vremya* in the evening to get a fix on the Moscow propaganda line. The Lithuanians despaired when the Gulf War news completely overwhelmed their own crisis on the Western stations. Rumors inside the building gave everyone a bad case of the jumps: "Tonight's the night." "They're going into Latvia tomorrow morning." "The roof's been rigged up so they can't land the helicopters." Lithuania was on the edge of a nervous breakdown, but there was no retreat.

"Why should we not win?" Landsbergis said.

At first, there were some heroic attempts in Moscow to bypass the censors and deliver the news. The cheeky late-night program *Television News Service* (*TSN*) broadcast footage of soldiers beating Lithuanians near the tower. The

Leningrad magazine show *The Fifth Wheel* also showed tape of the beatings and shootings.

But the Kremlin's new television czar, a fearsome hack named Leonid Kravchenko, quickly clamped down on all information broadcast about Lithuania. As the head of Gosteleradio, the huge bureaucracy that ran central television and radio, Kravchenko wiped out nearly all the major programs that had dared to report the news independently. In short order, Kravchenko banned *Vzglyad* ("View"), the most heroic of the glasnost magazine shows; he censored the reports on *TSN;* he darkened whatever glimmer of independence *Vremya* was beginning to show and returned it to the glory days of the Brezhnev era.

In the halls of the Supreme Soviet one afternoon, a reporter asked Kravchenko what he wanted in his broadcasts.

"Objectivity," Kravchenko said.

"And who decides what is objective?"

"I decide," he said.

Kravchenko said plainly that central television should reflect the view of the president and not attack him. "State television does not have the right to engage in criticism of the leadership of the country," he told *Nezavisimaya Gazeta.* What replaced much of the censored shows was even more insidious and cynical. Just as the Party had used the faith healer Anatoly Kashpirovsky to soothe a hurting country, they now filled the airwaves with other diverting junk. *Field of Miracles,* a rip-off of the low-rent American show *Wheel of Fortune,* was the new sensation. Contestants lined up to win such wonders as a rhinestone ring and a box of Tide. Kravchenko put on professional wrestling, Geraldo Rivera's interviews with dwarf transvestites, the *Death of Elvis* miniseries, schmaltzy World War II documentaries, and a Czech soap opera, *Hospital on the Edge of Town.* Kravchenko was willing to try whatever opiate on the masses that seemed to work. On the day after the bloodshed in Vilnius, while there were solemn marches in cities across the country honoring the dead, Kravchenko aired the *Aleksandr Show,* a variety hour so sleazy that Wayne Newton would have cringed.

In their front-page editorial, the *Moscow News* editors and their supporters echoed Solzhenitsyn's essay "Live Not by Lies" and put out the call to their colleagues: "We appeal to reporters and journalists: If you lack courage or opportunity to tell the truth, at least abstain from telling lies! Lies will fool no one anymore. They are evident today."

But because state controls were still relatively tight, television journalists had a much harder time following their consciences than print reporters. On *TSN,* Tatyana Mitkova ran a tape of Interior Minister Boris Pugo's fantastical testimony about Lithuania in the Supreme Soviet. Pugo's defense of the

operation in Vilnius was a transparent lie. When Mitkova came back on the screen, she said, "Unfortunately this is all the information *TSN* has found it possible to provide." That was the best she could do.

In Kaunas, the Lithuanian television producers set up a relay system so that their broadcast could go to all the Baltics, southern Finland, and eastern Poland. When the Kaunas Party chief went on the air to defend the attack, the host stared him down and said, "After what's happened in Vilnius, how do you even look people in the eye?" The Kaunas station director, Raimondas Sestakauskas, told me, "Look, we don't have tanks, we don't have much at all to win our war for independence. But we're going to resist, and the resistance now is a matter of strength of character . . . and television."

—

No matter what the *Moscow News* appeal said, the Communist Party still thought it could lie to the people and get away with it. Their designated con man was Aleksandr Nevzorov, the right wing's video warrior. A former movie stuntman, he hosted *600 Seconds,* an immensely popular program on Leningrad television that featured gruesome true-crime stories and propaganda in the service of the Motherland. Like his friend Colonel Alksnis, Nevzorov was into leather. He always wore a black leather jacket and a matching sneer. As a journalist, he was equal parts Geraldo Rivera and propaganda minister, a master of the basest instincts of schlock and vengeance. For a couple of years, *600 Seconds* had been a semi-harmless distraction for hard times, the Soviet equivalent of a few minutes with the *New York Post* or one of the "real cops" shows on American television. Nevzorov won huge popularity by exposing his audience of around eighty million people to the world of corruption and vice. His was the scream in the agitprop cathedral, and the people loved it. Night after night, as the clock ticked away frantically in the corner of the screen (600 . . . 599 . . . 598 . . .), Nevzorov showed police dragging bullet-riddled corpses from the Neva River, cajoled rapists and murderers into "live on tape" confessions, and exposed the dalliances and secret luxuries of the Communist Party elite. Nevzorov was constantly sticking his camera in the snoot of some greedy apparatchik who'd just been caught getting a deal on a car or a house. "I'm probably responsible for the heart attacks of about forty apparatchiks," Nevzorov boasted when I went to see him at his studios in Leningrad.

Despite Nevzorov's attacks on the Party, few people ever had any illusions that he was a knight of liberal reform. He described himself as a monarchist and occasionally wore a czarist-era military uniform, thoughtfully sewn for him by his girlfriend. He bragged about his extraordinary rapport with the police and, especially, the KGB. "I have good relations with the KGB,"

Nevzorov said. "This is natural. They give us a lot of help and I highly value that organization. . . . They are incorruptable and not for sale." As the counterrevolution began to show its head, first in the Baltic states and then everywhere else, Nevzorov quickly became the televised face of Gorbachev's allies in the defense of the empire: the army and the KGB. As the semioticians might have said, he was the sign of the times.

One night when I was in Leningrad, *600 Seconds* showed a tape of a city council liberal frantically combing his bald spot. "So this is the last hope of the city?" Nevzorov growled in the voice-over. Then, armed with a minicam, Nevzorov and his crew stormed the headquarters of the Movement of Civil Resistance, one of the council's more radical factions, as if they had uncovered Hitler's bunker. "The place is a pigsty," Nevzorov said. Next, in a move that would have earned him an immediate libel suit in the West, he showed file footage of a pile of guns and said, "It's difficult to imagine how many arms these people have." There was never any proof that the guns belonged to the movement. But too late. It was time for the next item. On other nights, Nevzorov accused Leningrad city council deputies of welshing on their alimony payments, wandering drunk through the streets, and conducting shady business deals. And as for Sobchak, Nevzorov said, "His sole policy is survival at any cost. If the Germans attacked Leningrad again, he'd start learning German just to stay in power."

After years of grain harvest assessments, intermediate Polish lessons, and "Boy Meets Harvester Combine" movies, Soviet television may have needed Nevzorov badly. He was pugnacious, malicious, and wonderfully crude. He provided a thrill-hungry country with a nightly video *frisson* and his libels were somehow easy, or convenient, to overlook. Even Sobchak tried hard not to mind too much. "Nevzorov is a journalistic cowboy from the Wild West who does what he can to stay in the saddle" was about the worst thing the mayor would say.

—

But what was once a sordid amusement now became a centerpiece of the Kremlin's turn toward authoritarian politics. At times it seemed as if Nevzorov's role in the shift to the right ranked just below the ministerial level. *Vremya,* of course, tried to do what it could to stanch the propaganda wound of the Lithuanian assault with some bogus account of how the independence movement had itself caused the tragedy. Gorbachev waffled, and said the first he had heard of the assault was when he was wakened by his aides the next morning. Was he lying? It was hard to know which was worse: that he was telling the truth, and therefore not in control of the army and the KGB; or

that he was lying, and at the head of a coup attempt against the Lithuanians. Later, when I asked Gorbachev's former economic adviser, Nikolai Petrakov, whether Gorbachev truly "slept through" the Vilnius events in ignorance, he said, simply, "Don't be naive."

The Kremlin and Kravchenko knew they needed a new form of public relations. Enter Nevzorov. If *Vremya* was Lawrence Welk, Nevzorov was Ice-T, the hip-hop artist of Soviet television. He didn't wear those mouse-gray suits like the announcers on *Vremya.* He was cool. When he lied, he did not sweat. His lip did not even twitch. And he had fantastic ratings. Boris Gidaspov, the conservative head of the Communist Party in Leningrad, told the city that "our Sasha Nevzorov" would soon deliver the "objective truth" on the situation in Lithuania.

The day after the shootings, Nevzorov and his crew piled into one of those tuna-can-sized Ladas and raced from Leningrad to Vilnius, where they quickly shot a ten-minute piece. Nevzorov called his film *Nashi*—"Ours," or "Our People," meaning . . . Russians. The idea was that the military was the defender of "Ours" and the Lithuanians an unruly—no, treasonous!—mob. Nevzorov called Landsbergis's pro-independence government "fascists" who had "declared war" on the state. In other words, the message was the same as Gorbachev's, the same as *Vremya*'s. But it was the imagery that did it. With a Kalashnikov slung over his shoulder and snippets of *Das Rheingold* booming on the soundtrack, Nevzorov inspected the fierce and sturdy faces of the troops inside the television center. They were defenders of the faith, defenders of the holy airwaves. They would save us all against the hordes of ungrateful Lithuanian college professors. Didn't they understand what an empire was? And as for the dead, Nevzorov had an answer for that, too. They had not died from the soldier's bullets; no one was crushed under the treads of the tanks or beaten to death with the butt-end of a rifle. No, they died in "car accidents" and of "heart attacks."

The funny thing about *Nashi* was that Nevzorov never interviewed a single Lithuanian. I asked him about that later in Leningrad. "I could have shown sweet Lithuanian flags waving in the air," he said, "but I didn't." Why should he? This was the army's show—with production credits to the KGB and the CPSU.

Nevzorov's broadcast and the endorsement it won from the Kremlin leadership were almost as chilling as the violence in Vilnius itself. The omen was nasty. The Supreme Soviet, with a push from Lukyanov, ordered Nevzorov's film shown three times on national television. The Communist Party daily, *Pravda,* which for years had suffered the scorn of *600 Seconds,* now praised Nevzorov as a "brilliant professional . . . an intrepid man." The paper said

that Nevzorov's film was convincing proof that "the responsibility for the deaths of innocent people lies with the chief Lithuanian 'democrat'—Vytautas Landsbergis."

The broadcast cut into Nevzorov's ratings a little. Some of the democratically inclined said it made them just sick to watch him now. But that was all right with Nevzorov. His cubicle office at the Leningrad studios had turned into a political headquarters for local reactionaries. Every day, right-wing members of the city council, retired cops, and leaders of groups like Motherland and the United Workers' Front piled into the room to get a glimpse of him, to ask him to get their grievances (the Jews! the co-ops! Yeltsin!) on the air. To make everyone feel at home, Nevzorov decorated the place with some czarist memorabilia, a bulletproof vest, and a classic Bolshevik recruiting poster from the Civil War period that he'd doctored to read: "Have You Killed Any Democrats Today?"

In the weeks after the Vilnius affair, Nevzorov intensified his nationalist campaign in other films. In Riga, he hailed the decision of the shadowy Black Berets to storm the local police station, an incident that left at least five dead. He tirelessly promoted the career of Colonel Alksnis, who was now busy egging on Gorbachev to "finish the job he started" in Lithuania.

In all his reports, Nevzorov's methods were simple. He meant to scare the hell out of his viewers—all in the service of the Motherland. If the Baltics became independent, he warned, Leningrad would suddenly be overrun with hundreds of thousands of refugees: "There will be tent cities, hunger, fights, deaths, and with all those weapons we have!" Those who were with him were "ours." Those who were not were "radical scum."

Nevzorov insisted he was his own man, but at the same time he was quick to sing the praises of the KGB and the army—"the only institutions holding the country together." The local paper *Chas Pik* ("Rush Hour") reported that the "Public Committee for the Support and Protection of the TV Program *600 Seconds*" included eight directors of huge defense plants and leaders of the local military-industrial complex. Nevzorov made it a point to brag about a hunting rifle that the defense minister, Dmitri Yazov, had given him, and he went on and on about his grandfather who had been a KGB officer—in Lithuania. "They say I am the spitting image of my grandfather. He was a hero, wounded many times in the line of duty. This is a source of great pride for me," Nevzorov said. "The KGB is a great group of guys."

Nevzorov said his alliance with Gorbachev was probably only a temporary "coincidence of positions." He felt more at one with the men who carried the hardware, the soldiers who "bore the ideals of Peter the Great and Aleksandr Nevsky. These are our great Russian defenders. Look, there is chaos in the country. It's better to bring in the tanks now when we are not talking about

hundreds and thousands of deaths. . . . A military coup, a military dictatorship, will be around for a while. It's only logical. If there are no healthy forces in society and everything is headed for chaos, then it is only natural that power should be seized by a structure that can maintain authority and order."

Nevzorov said he found my questions about television "whiny and pathetic." He was a pragmatist, he said. "Television and newspapers are nothing more than weapons," he said. "They brainwash the people. A journalist is always serving someone. I am serving my Fatherland, my Motherland. *The Fifth Wheel* is sophisticated propaganda against the state and order. I have no problems with censorship. If the head of Leningrad TV calls me up and tells me to do this or that, you just say, 'Fuck off.' "

And with that he stormed off to do battle for the Motherland. On the way out, I stopped off at the offices of *The Fifth Wheel,* where everyone was trying to figure out ways to beat the censors and undermine Nevzorov's broadcasts. Nothing was working and they were desperate. Viktor Pravdiuk, one of the lead reporters, told me, "They haven't strangled us yet, but their fingers are tightening around our throats."

CHAPTER 26

THE GENERAL LINE

May the god of history help me.

—STALIN, 1920

As 1991 dragged on, the fury of the hard-liners deepened with every week; with every victory they won, the more brazen their demands became. There was no mystery about what was going on. In meetings public and private, Gorbachev was hearing the full-throated cry of the generals, the military-industrial complex, the Communist Party apparatus, and the KGB. They demanded he turn away from his most reform-minded advisers, and he did. They blamed him for the "loss" of Eastern Europe, the "triumphs" of Germany and the United States, the "ruin" of the union and the Communist Party, and the "degradation" of the armed forces. The KGB chief, Vladimir Kryuchkov, made speeches asserting that the policies of perestroika had evolved into a road map for the destruction of the Union, plans that were no less anti-Soviet than the darkest designs of the CIA. In a meeting in Moscow with Richard Nixon, Kryuchkov said, "We have had about as much democracy as we can stomach."

There was an acrid smell in the air, a sense of panic, fear of the past returning. The Moscow Spring of 1988 was long gone. Privately, Aleksandr Yakovlev told his friends that they would soon see each other in Siberia, "against a wall somewhere." There may have been something to his gallows humor. The press printed rumors that the KGB had even ordered the "reconstruction" of labor camps in eastern Siberia.

Gorbachev counseled calm, but you could see he was thoroughly spooked. At an afternoon session of the Congress that winter, I saw him mounting a short flight of stairs and, in the hasty, idiotic way of such encounters, I blurted, "Mikhail Sergeyevich, they say you are moving to the right."

Gorbachev stopped walking and fixed his eyes on me. His mouth clenched in a pained, ironic grin. The truth is, he said, "I feel as if I am going around in circles." It was the impish explanation of the confused schoolboy, the harried parent. But in Gorbachev's mouth, it was sad. What more was he willing to do to mollify these people? While Gorbachev may well have thought he was finessing the hard-liners and playing for time, he was ruining himself forever. The more he attacked Yeltsin and Landsbergis, the more he made cult figures of them. The man who had mastered his own personality and the tactics of the Communist Party now found himself unable to master the new form of politics he had set free. Gorbachev's compromises, his ugly language, betrayed him. A great man now looked weak, mean-spirited, and confused. There he was, in prime time, railing against the "so-called democrats" who got their marching orders from "foreign research centers." What fresh hell was this? Yeltsin accused Gorbachev of betraying the people, and who now was rushing to the defense of Mikhail Sergeyevich?

The generals, for their part, were so confident of their hold on power and the flow of events that they were ready at last to turn back history. They would reassert a "balanced" version of the past and rescue history from the historians. The hard-liners even had a new icon. Colonel Alksnis, Ligachev, and conservatives of all varieties wrote articles and gave interviews extolling the late KGB chief and general secretary Yuri Andropov for seeing the need for technocratic reform and for modernizing the economy. Andropov, they all said, had been a man of stability, one who never challenged the principles of socialism or the state.

To chart a new historical orthodoxy would not be easy for the hard-liners. The debate on Soviet history had long since gone beyond the boundaries set out by Gorbachev in 1987. Every leader, not merely Stalin, was now under question. The taboo against criticism of Lenin had weakened to such a degree that now even conservatives like Ligachev had to admit, with the gravity of sudden revelation, "Vladimir Ilyich was a man, not a god." Even Khrushchev and Bukharin were no longer held out as "alternatives."

At street demonstrations, however, there were signs calling for the criminal indictment of the Party and the KGB. The slogans of the old order gave way to a new irony and sense of repentance. "Workers of the World Forgive Us!" one banner read. The liberal intellectuals no longer debated whether the seventy-year history was a disaster; the argument was over the roots of that disaster. Igor Klyamkin, a leading economist, blamed Lenin for setting the tone of Soviet power with the Red Terror and the first labor camps. Aleksandr Tsipko, a former Central Committee official, argued that Marxism was the cause.

—

Of all the major events in Soviet history since 1917, the one that was preserved the longest as an unquestionable victory of the regime was the Great Patriotic War against Nazi Germany. Not even the Revolution held such an important place in the collective psyche of the Soviet people.

The May 9 victory parades were just one element in the cult of the war. Even in the mid-eighties, you could turn on the television any day of the week and there was a better than even chance that a group of veterans, old and festooned with medals and ribbons, would be talking about the Battle of Stalingrad to a group of theatrically interested schoolchildren. The war was the touchstone, the regime's lingering reason for being. When Gorbachev defended his allegiance to socialism in early 1991, he said, yes, his grandfathers had been persecuted, but how could he betray his father, who fought bravely at the Dniepr and was wounded in Czechoslovakia? Gorbachev recalled his train ride in 1950 from Stavropol to Moscow and looking out the window at mile after mile of devastation and misery. If he abandoned socialist principles now, he asked, would he not be betraying the memory of the twenty-seven million Soviet citizens killed during the war?

For the hard-liners, the meaning of the cult of the war went even deeper. Victory in the war served to legitimize the brutal collectivization and industrialization campaigns that went before it. Although these men no longer celebrated Stalin, at least not in public, their view of history was surely Stalinist. In textbooks and on television, the Party's propagandists portrayed the war as proof of the system's ultimate strength—the system that saved the world! Of course there had been excesses, the Stalinist pamphleteer Nina Andreyeva once told me, but without collectivization "we would have starved during the war," and without industrialization "where would the tanks have come from?"

Even as late as 1991, the military leadership held on to the habit of sponsoring official histories, and few projects were more important to the hierarchy than the writing of a new history of the war. This would be the

third multivolume official history of the Great Patriotic War since Stalin's death. But the Ministry of Defense, which was in charge of the project, knew that this time, several years into the glasnost era, a completely bogus history was out of the question. The committee-written project would have to address the Molotov-Ribbentrop Pact and the purge of the officer corps in the late thirties. The new official history would have to answer the question why the Nazis were able to invade the Soviet Union in June 1941 with such ease.

The man in charge of the first volume, tentatively titled *On the Eve of the War,* was General Dmitri Antonovich Volkogonov. Marshal Dmitri Yazov, the defense minister, Marshal Sergei Akhromeyev, the leading military adviser to Gorbachev, General Valentin Varennikov, the commander of all ground forces, and the other hard-liners at the top of the army accepted Volkogonov as editor knowing they would not get a warmed-over version of the old histories of the war. His biography of Stalin, *Triumph and Tragedy,* published with the encouragement of the Gorbachev leadership in 1988, was the first objective study not written by a dissident. As the director of the military's main history institute, he had had access to all the major archives of the Party, the KGB, and the military while they were still closed to almost everyone else. He was the logical man for the job. They were prepared for a history that was more critical than those published under Khrushchev and Brezhnev. But they were not prepared for what they got.

In late 1990, Volkogonov's team turned in a draft that coolly assessed the relative evils of Stalin and Hitler and described in full detail the "repressive command system" which carried out, at Stalin's direct order, the wholesale slaughter of thousands of officers before the war. The draft explored the roots of Stalin's Terror and its origins in the Red Terror that followed the Revolution. They wrote critically of Stalin's negotiations with the Nazis that allowed Moscow to annex the Baltic states and other key territories. Most appalling of all to the hard-liners, Volkogonov's draft concluded that the Soviet Union had won the war almost "by chance"—despite Stalin, not because of him. They implied that perhaps the death of twenty-seven million Soviet people was in vain, that the victory of the Soviet Union represented the victory of one brutal regime over another.

The Ministry of Defense sent copies of the draft history around to various "reviewers": generals, admirals, officials in the Communist Party, and the heads of the major institutes. Their reaction was angry and quick. Akhromeyev gave an interview to the reactionary *Military Historical Journal* that accused Volkogonov of acting as a "traitor."

"Had Volkogonov succeeded in publishing the work, with its obviously false positions as set out in the first volume, it would have done great harm, and not only to history," Akhromeyev said. "The lies about the war would

have been used for undermining the integrity of our country and the socialist choice, and for the constant defamation of the Communist Party. This could not be allowed." Volkogonov, he said, was an anti-Communist "turncoat" serving just one master: the equally anti-Communist Russian president, Boris Yeltsin.

—

The denunciations had only just begun. On March 7, at an elegant meeting hall in the Ministry of Defense, fifty-seven generals, Central Committee officials, and official academics gathered to review Volkogonov's work. The chairman of the editorial committee, General A. F. Kochetov, opened the session by reminding everyone that "when the original conception of the ten-volume work was discussed, everyone agreed with the idea that the driving force [of the victory] was the Soviet people, the people's army, the toilers, all led by the Party. But today, proceeding from the interests of the moment, everyone insults and blames the Party. Suddenly the people are to blame. . . . Many of the reviews asked the question: 'If things were so awful before the war, why did we win?' "

Kochetov pointed out incredulously that in the book there was an implicit (and intolerable) comparison of socialism with fascism. He said that some of the reviewers had also complained that Volkogonov betrayed the intentions of the volume by discussing the origins of the system leading up to the war, and others simply objected to the titles of chapters such as "The Political Regime Grows Stricter" and "The Militarization of Spiritual Life."

Kochetov then opened the session for "general discussion": an invitation to a beheading. General Mikhail Moiseyev, chief of the general staff, attacked Volkogonov, saying that he was merely out to inspire "today's destructive forces"—meaning Yeltsin and the pro-independence activists in the republics.

"Defend the army!" came the calls from the hall.

Later, Valentin Falin, the head of the Central Committee's International Department, took the floor. "We must point out the insufficiencies of this volume, its thousands of mistakes," he said. "I have not seen such fantastical stuff in thirty or forty years. . . . To waste government money on this is out of the question!"

Volkogonov turned pale. He had grown away from these men, but he was only now aware by how much. After more than an hour of denunciations, he finally demanded the floor.

"Respected comrades!" Volkogonov began. "My voice in this hall will no doubt be a lonely one. There is not likely to be a real scholarly discussion here. This is a tribunal on scholarship, on history, on a large group of writers.

Instead of an analysis of the issue, there is just unbridled criticism. . . . In the atmosphere that has been created here I cannot write a new history. To write only about the victory of 1945 means to talk nonsense about 1941, about the four million prisoners, about the retreat to the Volga. It is impossible to reduce history to politics."

Volkogonov had only begun, but now Varennikov, one of the most reactionary generals in the Ministry of Defense hierarchy, broke in, shouting, "There is a suggestion to deny him the floor!"

Volkogonov refused to back down.

"I am no less a patriot than Falin and love the Motherland no less than he," he said. "But you cannot change the consequences of history. I agree with those who say there are many faults in this volume. . . . But let's discuss and debate them. We'll give our points of view. But, no, Comrade Falin and some others do not engage in scholarly debate, but rather make accusations about a lack of patriotism."

"Enough!" one general shouted. "Listen to this!"

Somewhere in the hall came the shout "Stop his speech!"

Volkogonov kept going, arguing that unless the book and the Soviet people dealt with all the cruelty and misery that had preceded the war, there could be no understanding of what happened after the opening volleys of the Nazi invasion.

"How else can we look at the fact that forty-three thousand officers and other army officials were purged?" he said. "And what of the other victims? We don't need blind patriotism. We need the truth! . . . Mine is a lonely voice in this hall, but I want to see what you say about it all in ten years."

The chairman was appalled. He took personal offense.

Finally, the swarm overtook Volkogonov. The generals shouted him down, and he did not speak again. But the ritual was far from over. Two and a half hours after the session had begun, Marshal Yazov, the minister of defense, arrived. Yazov, with his lumpy face and bulbous nose, was none too bright. When it came time to appoint a new defense minister after a German teenager, Mathias Rust, managed to land his little plane on Red Square in 1987, Gorbachev went way down the ladder and found Yazov, the chief of military operations in the far east. The man had a reputation for mediocrity. But that was the point. Gorbachev wanted a man utterly without cunning. He wanted a pleasant mutt, a loyal friend.

But that was years ago, and now, with the conservatives in the midst of a full-fledged counterrevolution against radical reform, Yazov was showing his strength. He despised the direction perestroika had taken. Hundreds of thousands of young men in the Baltic states, the Caucasus, and other regions were ignoring their draft notices. Gorbachev was cutting troop levels and other

liberals wanted even more reductions. Meanwhile, officers returning from Eastern Europe and Germany were living in crowded dormitories and even tents.

Yazov quickly addressed the group, and there was no doubt that his anger went far beyond any rough draft or a three-star general named Volkogonov. The battle over the book represented to him nothing less than the overall struggle for power in the Soviet Union.

"The 'democrats' now have made it their goal to prepare and carry out a Nuremberg II on the Communist Party," Yazov said. "The volume has in it the outlines for an indictment for such a trial."

"This book has at its foundation a libel of the Party," Varennikov pitched in.

"In this hall," Yazov continued, "I think, everyone is a Communist. And Communists cannot spit on their Party."

It was over. Volkogonov was dismissed from the editorial committee and his draft was "returned to the board for fundamental reworking." Another victory for the hard-line coalition. Five months later, in August, Yazov, Varennikov, Moiseyev, and other men in the room would go even farther and attempt a coup d'état.

—

I first met Volkogonov in 1988 when he was still in the official fold and about to publish his biography, *Stalin: Triumph and Tragedy.* (The English translation did not appear until 1991.) The publicity flaks around the foreign ministry were pitching him as their "breakthrough historian"—which caused immediate suspicion. For the liberal intelligentsia in Moscow and Leningrad, Volkogonov was not an inspiring choice. He had published dozens of books and monographs on military ideology, and none of them even hinted at independence, rigor, or critical thought. Here was a military man who had played the game; if he harbored dissident thoughts, he had not yet committed a whisper of them to paper.

But at a meeting with journalists at the Foreign Ministry, Volkogonov was impressive. He spoke without bluff or euphemism. He was familiar with all the major Western scholarship on Stalin, making detailed and admiring references to a number of books, especially Robert C. Tucker's multivolume biography-in-progress. As a way to defend himself against official Party historians who would attack his use of foreign scholars, Volkogonov wrote in the introduction, "Without realizing it, Stalin did far more to blacken the name of 'socialism' than anything written by Leonard Schapiro, Isaac Deutscher, Robert Tucker or Robert Conquest." Volkogonov clearly had full access to the *spetskhran*—the "special shelves" of Soviet libraries where

banned books were secreted away. In his bibliography, he cites books that were, until glasnost, unavailable for ordinary Soviets: Adam Ulam's biography of Stalin, Deutscher's biography of Trotsky, Richard Pipes's *Russia Under the Old Regime,* Milovan Djilis's *Conversations with Stalin,* and the memoirs of Stalin's daughter, Svetlana Alliluyeva. In addition, Volkogonov read and made reference to the works of Stalin's enemies, the men he defeated and executed: Bukharin, Trotsky, Rykov, Kamenev, Zinoviev, Tomsky.

If Volkogonov had merely cribbed the Western biographies of Stalin and published the result under his name in the Soviet Union, his book would have had a certain notoriety. The mere notion of a Red Army general laying bare the awful facts of the Stalin era would have been an astonishing advance in the Soviet Union's attempt to recover its historical memory. But he did much more. Volkogonov will be remembered not so much as a great thinker or writer but rather for the uniqueness of his access, the way he made scholarly use of his political position. Volkogonov alone had the chance to exploit the paperwork of the totalitarian regime, and he went everywhere: the Central Party Archives, the USSR Supreme Court Archives, the Central State Archives of the Army, the Ministry of Defense Archives, the Armed Forces General Staff Archives, and the archives of several important museums and institutes, including the Institute of Marxism-Leninism.

On those shelves, Volkogonov found no definitive answers to the remaining riddles of history. For example, he did not come up with a "smoking gun" in the 1934 murder of the Leningrad Party chief Sergei Kirov. Nearly all Western scholars assume, with good circumstantial reason, that Stalin ordered Kirov killed in order to eliminate a potential political threat and to set the stage for the Great Terror. Volkogonov assumed the same and wrote: "The archives that I have searched do not provide any further clues for making a more definitive statement on the Kirov affair. What is clear, however, is that the murder was not carried out on the orders of Trotsky, Zinoviev, or Kamenev, which was soon put out as the official version. Knowing what we now know about Stalin, it is certain that he had a hand in it. The removal of two or three layers of indirect witnesses bears his hallmark."

But while *Triumph and Tragedy* made no sensational advances, while it did not "solve" the enigma of Stalin's motives or produce a definitive death toll for the repressions of the era, the book was in no sense a failure. By providing excerpts from hundreds of memos, telegrams, and orders that had never been seen by scholars before, Volkogonov allowed the reader a terrible intimacy with the Soviet despot; *Triumph and Tragedy* gave new texture, at once horrifying and bland, to our knowledge of one of the worst passages in human history.

In his portrayal of Stalin, Volkogonov was more critical than many of his

liberal critics might have expected. *Triumph and Tragedy* showed Stalin to have been a coward, a miserable commander in chief during the war, a "mediocrity but not insignificant," as Trotsky once put it. Volkogonov provided the conclusive documentary evidence that Stalin, using blue or red pencils, personally ordered the deaths of thousands in the same offhand tone as a man ordering a drink at a bar.

". . . According to I. D. Perfilyev, an Old Bolshevik who had spent many years in a concentration camp and who told me the story, once, in Molotov's company, while discussing a routine list with [secret police chief Nikolai] Yezhov, Stalin muttered to no one in particular: 'Who's going to remember all this riffraff in ten or twenty years time? No one. Who remembers the names now of the boyars Ivan the Terrible got rid of? No one. . . . The people had to know he was getting rid of all his enemies. In the end, they all got what they deserved.'

" 'The people understand, Iosif Vissarionovich, they understand and they support you,' Molotov replied automatically."

In Moscow, I got to know Volkogonov fairly well, first in his incarnation as a military historian, then as a political outcast, and, finally, when he became a radical deputy in the Russian parliament in 1990 and a top military adviser to Russian President Yeltsin. Even early on, when he had to take great care in how, and with whom, he talked about his work, Volkogonov never concealed just how deeply his days in the archives had moved him.

"I would come home from working in Stalin's archives, and I would be deeply shaken," Volkogonov told me. "I remember coming home after reading through the day of December 12, 1938. He signed thirty lists of death sentences that day, altogether about five thousand people, including many he knew personally, his friends. This was before their trials, of course. This was no surprise. This is not what shook me. But it turned out that, having signed these documents, he went to his personal theater very late that night and watched two movies, including *Happy Guys,* a popular comedy of the time. I simply could not understand how, after deciding the fate of several thousand lives, he could watch such a movie. But I was beginning to realize that morality plays no role for dictators. That's when I understood why my father was shot, why my mother died in exile, why millions of people died."

Volkogonov was born in the Siberian city of Chita in 1928 and later moved to the Pacific coast of Russia. His father was an agrarian specialist and his mother cared for the three children. In 1937, at the height of the purges, Anton Volkogonov was summoned to the local Party committee, where he was arrested for the crime of possessing printed matter of a "politically

questionable" origin—a pamphlet by the "right deviationist" Nikolai Bukharin. Volkogonov's father was never seen again. "He just disappeared into the meat grinder of the purges," Volkogonov said. "When I was older, my mother whispered to me, 'Your father was shot. Never, never speak of it again.' "

This family of an "enemy of the people" was exiled to the village of Agul in the Krasnoyarsk district of western Siberia, near an ever-growing complex of forced-labor camps. When he was a child, Volkogonov saw long columns of prisoners marching from the rail stations fifty miles away to the camps. Guard dogs, barbed wire, and watchtowers were all part of his childhood landscape. With each passing month, NKVD workers cordoned off more land and built more camps. The guards dug huge trenches in the pine forest and carried the corpses to the trenches at night on old-fashioned Russian sleds. Schoolchildren would go looking for pine nuts in the forest and they would hear gunfire, Volkogonov recalled, "like the sound of canvas being ripped apart."

Volkogonov's mother died just after the end of the war. Like many other orphans, Dmitri Antonovich entered the military as a draftee and never left. His brother and sister were adopted by other families. As a young private and officer during the late forties and the fifties, Volkogonov got a thorough education in political orthodoxy. He learned quickly that no diversion was too small to be noticed. Toward the end of *Triumph and Tragedy,* Volkogonov let himself enter the portrait of the system, here as a student of military equipment and state ideology:

". . . Students were tested first and foremost for their ability to summarize Stalin's works. I remember being kept back by the teacher when I was attending the Orel Tank School. He was a lieutenant colonel, no longer a young man, and was very much liked by the class for his good nature. When we were alone he handed me my work, which was a summary of sources, and said to me in a quiet and fatherly voice: 'It's a good summary. I could see right away you hadn't just copied it down and had given it some thought. But my advice is, summarize the Stalinist works more fully. Understand, more fully! And another thing. In front of the name Iosif Vissarionovich, don't write "Com." Write "Comrade" in full. Got it?' That night one of my roommates told me they'd all had similar conversations with the teacher of Party history. The exams were coming up and there were rumors that in a neighboring school 'they had paid attention' to the sort of 'political immaturities' I had shown in my summaries."

As an officer, Volkogonov was prepared to do anything for the Motherland. At a nuclear test site, he was ordered to drive a new-model tank straight through the area that had just been the epicenter of an atomic bomb test. And

he did. "There was nothing I would not do," Volkogonov told me. "I was a young lieutenant when Stalin died and I thought the heavens would fall without him. The fact that my father had been shot and my mother died miserably in exile, that didn't seem to matter: it was destiny, incomprehensible. My mind was contaminated. I was incapable of analyzing these things, of putting the pieces together."

In the Komsomol and the Communist Party organizations of the Lenin Military Academy in Moscow, Volkogonov became such a master of the standard texts of dogma that he gained a reputation among the senior officers as an especially reliable *polit rabotnik,* a political propagandist. Volkogonov got a doctorate in philosophy—which, in those days, meant Marxist-Leninist philosophy—and in 1970 was transferred to the army's Department of Propaganda. There he climbed the ladder steadily; he was promoted to general at forty, won a professorship at forty-four, and made it to deputy chief in charge of political instruction. Along the way, he also earned a doctorate in history.

With his high rank and credentials, Volkogonov was allowed access to all the most important—and closed—archives in the capital. "But make no mistake about who I was," Volkogonov said. "I was not a closet radical. I cannot distort history to suit my needs. The fact is, I was an orthodox Marxist, an officer who knew his duty. I was not part of some liberal current. All my changes came from within, off on my own. I had access to all kinds of literature. You know there were many people, especially young officers of the KGB, who thought liberally because they had more information than anyone else. That's why there have always been a lot of thinking people in the KGB, people who understand the West as it really is and what our own country really was.

"I was a Stalinist. I contributed to the strengthening of the system that I am now trying to dismantle. But latently, I had my ideas. I began asking myself questions about Lenin, how, if he was such a genius, none of his predictions came true. The proletarian dictatorship never came to be, the principle of class struggle was discredited, Communism was not built in fifteen years as he had promised. None of Lenin's major predictions ever came true! I confess it: I used my position. I began gathering information even though I didn't know yet what I would do with it."

While working in a KGB archive during the thaw, Volkogonov even read his father's file and learned that what his mother had whispered had been true. Anton Volkogonov had been shot in 1937 just after his arrest.

Almost as a dream, Volkogonov decided he would write a trilogy on Stalin, Lenin, and Trotsky. By the late seventies, Volkogonov was secretly working on the Stalin volume. His apartment was crammed with tens of thousands of

photocopied documents and books, many of them banned. As time passed and times grew a bit more liberal, Volkogonov made little secret of what he was doing. The military hierarchy, however, decided that Volkogonov's historical research was not "consistent" with his position as a propagandist. He was shunted aside and installed at the Institute of Military History, a move that represented a demotion, Volkogonov said, of "three steps down the ladder." For a soldier, perhaps. But for a historian, the demotion was a gift. Now Volkogonov had more time and access to the archives. When the leadership finally came looking for a biography of Stalin, Volkogonov was there, ready to write.

Using his position as a general, Volkogonov was able to realize the dreams of such outsiders as Dima Yurasov. Volkogonov's work in the archives not only provided him international fame, it also shattered whatever last illusions he might have had about Soviet history. Now Volkogonov, like so many other intellectuals throughout the union, saw the roots of catastrophe in the ideology itself, in Leninism. "Abstract ideas give rise to fanatics, and such was Trotsky," he wrote. The utopianism, the ferocity, of Bolshevism gave rise to the totalitarian state.

In the spring of 1991, Volkogonov invited me to meet with him in his hospital room. He was exhausted by his battle with Yazov and the other generals. The hospital was tucked away on a side street off Kalinin Prospekt. Compared to other Soviet hospitals I'd seen, with their filthy floors, their crowded rooms, this special clinic for the military elite was a wonder. There were private rooms, wood-paneled hallways, a clean and efficient staff. Volkogonov told me he was ill and not sure how long he had to live. He had stomach cancer and would go for surgery to Western Europe. But he did not seem shocked or sad and wanted only to pick up on what we had talked about in his various offices.

"You see, I am now convinced that Stalinism created a new type of man: indifferent, without initiative or enterprise, a person waiting for a messiah, waiting for someone to come alive and solve all of life's problems. The most awful thing about it is that this cannot merely be shed, like taking off an old raincoat and donning a new one. There are many aspects of this mentality still inside me, and I lose them only slowly. This whole period we are living in now is about scrubbing this mentality from our minds. We are all becoming revolutionaries when it comes to our own individual way of thinking. For you it is so hard to understand. You are indifferent as to who will be in power in your own country. Democrats or Republicans, America is America. Only some nuances of the system change. For us, a mutiny is going on. The

Revolution was one sort of mutiny, and we are on the threshold of another. We are making our way through an intellectual and spiritual fog and all around us is collapse.

"The generals in the army reproach me for being a chameleon. They say I am a traitor or a renegade. But personally I think it is a more courageous stance to abandon honestly something which has been devalued by history instead of carrying it to the end in your soul. There are people among them who criticize me in public and in private say I am right but they can't say so.

"Now I am in complete isolation. I get support from the grass roots, from junior officers, and a couple of generals even support me secretly. The majority despise me. Even when I meet generals here in the hospital they pretend not to notice me. Others want to talk to me, but they fear the consequences.

"These people are frozen in the past. Even truth will not change them. Stalin died physically, but not historically. The image of Stalin lives because it has so many allies. No less than fifteen percent of the letters I get are from Stalinists, and the worse the situation gets, the more of those I get. The Party has sixteen million people in it. Thirty percent are like Akhromeyev or Nina Andreyeva. They won't change. Another thirty percent see the Party as a modus vivendi. They can't advance in their careers if they are not members. And the rest could leave at any moment.

"The army and the KGB were never for real perestroika. They were for minor repairs of the system, a little camouflage. They wanted to preserve the system intact by getting rid of the most obviously odious features: superbureaucracy, corruption, and so on. Yet none of them wants to question the essence of the system. The Party ought to be in control, they say.

"Totalitarian systems usually absorb people absolutely. As I have come to realize, very few people have been able to transcend such a system, to tear themselves away from it. Most people of my generation will die imprisoned in this system, even if they live another ten or twenty years. Of course, people who are twenty or thirty are free people. They can liberate themselves from the system quite easily. The only thing I have to offer is my experience. Maybe my example will be valuable in tracing the crisis, the tragedy, and the drama of Communist ideas and utopia played out over the generations."

Volkogonov was getting tired. And at the same time, his mood was changing. The full weight of the news he had just gotten was beginning to hit him, and he began to talk about working "at full speed" to finish the volumes on Lenin and Trotsky and perhaps write a memoir. When we got to talking about the dark mood in Moscow, I finally asked him what he thought was ahead.

"Democratization is irreversible on the historic, strategic scale," Volkogonov said. "But on the tactical plane, in the short run, the right-wing forces still have a chance. They may even come to the head of the country and hustle us all back into the barn for another five or ten years. They could try. They are that crazy and that angry."

CHAPTER 27

CITIZENS

YAGUNOVSKO

In the summer of 1989, when the miners brought the revolution to Siberia, Anatoly Shcheglov walked me back from his village to the tram for Kemerevo and invited me back. "I'll take you fishing in the taiga," he said. Now, a year and a half later, the miners were on strike again and I was back in Siberian coal country. Most of the government's promises had been broken and conditions were as dismal as ever. Along the road to Shcheglov's hut on Second Plan Street, the snow was crusted black, the air was cold and gassy.

Anatoly Shcheglov had no phone. I just assumed he'd be at home. When he opened the door, he greeted me as if I'd been away a week and coming back to Yagunovsko were the most ordinary thing in the world for an American. He looked cleaner, more relaxed, but a good deal older. A lacework of wrinkles ate deep into his face. "I'm retired now," he said. "The expected happened." He said that the winter after we'd met, as he settled his huge frame into a chair one night after dinner, he had a heart attack. Like a horse kicking him in the chest, he said. He was fifty years old. "It's the usual

thing for us underground men," Anatoly said. "You quit at fifty and you're lucky to make it to fifty-five. I doubt if I'll be around much longer."

Shcheglov now spent his days standing in lines at empty village stores, shuttling from one filthy hospital to the next looking for doctors, aspirin, glycerin pills. "An old man's life," he said. But what brightened him, he said, was the nerve and determination of his fellow miners across the country. The strikes now had nothing to do with the issues of July 1989. "It's not about soap or vacation pay anymore," he said. The miners wanted nothing less than the resignation of Gorbachev's government and the dismantling of the system of state socialism. "There are no more illusions left, no more socialist dreams," Shcheglov said. "The first strikes were for a crust of bread, a cut of meat. We got nothing that was promised us. Life just got worse. Now we know the secret. The system has to go."

Since the beginning of March 1991, over 300,000 miners had gone out on strike. The remaining 900,000 miners worked only to avert a complete collapse of the national economy. The strike leaders figured they would gain no supporters if it came to that. Their strategy was measured and effective. In the coming weeks there were warning strikes by machinists in Leningrad, electricians in Samara, Black Sea dockworkers in Odessa.

The strikes terrified the Kremlin hard-liners. They knew that the radicalization of the workers—the proletariat's evolving consciousness, to borrow from the Marxist phrasebook—could be the finishing blow to a tottering regime. Soviet power seemed able to withstand the demonstrations of urban democracy movements, but the workers had the power to turn the lights out in the Kremlin. And they were not kidding. "No more games," Shcheglov said. "No more games." At a session of the Russian Republic's legislature, most of the deputies did little more than echo softly Yeltsin's latest demands for Gorbachev's resignation. But late in the session, the Kuzbass strike leader, Anatoly Malikhin, took the floor and announced, "We are prepared to flood the mines." The miners, he said, had lost all tolerance for the system that had bled them white. Lead the attack, he told the Russian deputies, or the miners will.

A few days after the speech, I met Anatoly Malikhin at the Rossiya Hotel in Moscow. There were remnants everywhere of late-night strategy sessions: leaflets, stuffed ashtrays, and dirty glasses. Strike headquarters was wherever Anatoly Malikhin happened to be. His phone rang incessantly: strike committees from Siberia, Ukraine, the far east, and Vorkuta in northern Russia called with congratulations, questions, advice, more plans.

"Well, then fuck 'em," he said at one point on the line to the Kuzbass. "We'll go back when the demands are met. Not sooner."

Malikhin showed more certainty, more sense of purpose, than any of the liberal intellectuals in Moscow and Leningrad. He was absolutely serious; there was no theater to him, no veneer of irony. He and the other strike leaders had taken Gorbachev at his word when they negotiated a settlement to the strikes in 1989, and they would not repeat the mistake. Simple as that.

"No one is belittling what Gorbachev has already done, but every person has his moment, his moment of peak operation, like a machine," Malikhin said. "But Gorbachev thinks he is unique. At the beginning, he really did do a lot, and we take our hats off to him. But he should have changed the system radically a year or more ago. Then he could have found himself a place for himself in that new structure. But he didn't. He was stuck with his socialist principles. Now he is doing more harm than good. If Gorbachev is so smart, why is he still trying to protect the Party? There is a rumor that he is getting ready to send army troops to the mines. Well, believe me, if he does that the soldiers will die there by the thousands."

NOVOCHERKASSK

No one knew where the dead were buried. There were rumors: the KGB had pushed the corpses down a mine shaft or into a swamp, or the police had brought the bodies to a series of unmarked graves in cemeteries spread across the Black Earth zone of southern Russia. But no one knew.

For nearly thirty years, the story of the Novocherkassk rebellion was a secret of the state. The strike in June 1962 over price rises and wage cuts at the city's Electric Locomotive Works was the first workers' uprising in Russia since the fitful years immediately after the Revolution. At Moscow's orders, the military turned its machine guns on the unarmed demonstrators in Novocherkassk. At least twenty-four were killed, dozens more injured. Not long after, the Kremlin's judges ordered the execution of seven "ringleaders" who had survived. Within three days, all mention of Novocherkassk disappeared from the state-controlled press. Even Western specialists knew almost nothing of the bloody affair. Solzhenitsyn published a few pages of rough description in the third volume of *The Gulag Archipelago,* but that, of course, was considered "anti-Soviet propaganda" and banned until 1990.

Now, with the miners on strike once more, with the KGB, the army, and Gorbachev himself feeling threatened by nationalists and political opponents, in a time of increasing food shortages and ethnic division, there was constant talk of conflict, of civil disobedience, of the possibility of bloodshed. The massacre of demonstrators in Tbilisi, Baku, and Vilnius made it clear that the regime, despite all the reforms, could be expected to bring out the

tanks and machine guns, even poisonous gas, if that was what it took to survive. What had changed, if anything, since that summer afternoon in southern Russia in 1962?

In addition to the twenty-four people killed in Novocherkassk, the massacre claimed at least one more victim: Soviet Army General Matvei Shaposhnikov, a true believer in the Bolshevik ideal who was awarded the title of Hero of the Soviet Union after leading a tank division to victory in some of the bloodiest fighting in World War II. Years before the emergence of Sakharov and the dissident movement, Shaposhnikov had done the unthinkable. Ordered to attack the demonstrators at Novocherkassk, he refused.

When I met him, the general was eighty-four years old. His political superiors forced him to retire three years after the Novocherkassk massacre, but he was active and strong. With his grip he could have crushed a walnut. His apartment in the city of Rostov-on-Don, which he shared with his daughter and son-in-law and their children, was military-neat, his books and memorabilia perfectly arranged and dusted.

"Let's talk, face to face," Shaposhnikov said, lifting a heavy chair and setting it down for his guest. He was older than the regime. "I remember clearly singing revolutionary songs as an eleven-year-old boy in 1917: 'Oh, march, march forward, working people . . . !' I believed all my life in Soviet power, and now I was being told to shoot at my own people, unarmed people. I had to pay for my decision with everything. They stripped me of my rank, my decorations, my membership in the Communist Party. They told me to retire for 'health reasons.' And my wife, my dear, dear wife, finally paid for it even more deeply. She died a few years ago, and I am convinced she died from the attacks on us. Finally, she just could not bear it."

There was not one hour, even now, the general said, when he did not think back to the days of the massacre. On the morning of June 1, 1962, the Communist Party press in Novocherkassk announced that the prices of meat and butter would go up at least 25 percent. When workers at the Electric Locomotive Works arrived at the plant, they discovered that their wages would be cut by as much as 30 percent. Both local newspapers, the *Hammer* and the *Banner of the Commune,* assured the people that these were merely "temporary measures," all in the name of "social progress." Somehow, the workers were not prepared this time to believe the usual doublespeak. Their anger was so intense that they forgot themselves. They forgot for a moment their "party discipline" and confronted the plant director, an odious bureaucrat named Kurochkin.

How would they live now? the workers demanded.

"You're used to wolfing down meat pies," Kurochkin replied. "Now you can stuff them with jam instead."

The workers were enraged. They blew the shop floor whistles and started gathering in the courtyards. There they talked of a strike and drew up placards: "Give Us Meat and Butter," "We Need Places to Live." They ripped down portraits of Khrushchev and burned them. Terrified, the plant managers locked themselves in their offices. The local Communist Party officials refused to meet with any of the strike representatives.

Meanwhile, the regional military command had been on alert for weeks in anticipation of the announcements of price hikes and wage cuts. According to Shaposhnikov, the regional military commander, General Issa Pliyev, received a stream of coded orders from the Ministry of Defense and Khrushchev himself. That first night, KGB officers and police arrested some of the most outspoken factory workers in an attempt to head off a potential strike.

Two members of Khrushchev's inner political circle, Anastas Mikoyan and Frol Kozlov, were already in the city. Shaposhnikov, who had been put in charge of the armed detachments stationed near the locomotive factory, told the two Politburo members that he was "gravely concerned" that the troops were carrying guns. A confrontation, he said, could lead to bloodshed.

"Commander Pliyev has been given all the instructions he needs," Kozlov replied angrily.

On the morning of June 2, at around eleven o'clock, seven thousand workers and other demonstrators began their protest march from the locomotive plant to the center of Novocherkassk. They ignored the troops and tanks that surrounded the plant. As they marched, some workers tried to block the railway line leading into town as a further show of protest. "But people were unarmed, peaceful. They even carried portraits of Lenin," said Vladimir Fomin, one of the region's deputies in the Russian parliament. The greatest offense of the marchers was their willingness to question Moscow. "Khrushchev for sausage meat!" the protesters chanted.

Anticipating violence, Shaposhnikov told all his soldiers to empty the ammunition from their guns and for the tank brigades to do the same. As the column of demonstrators passed, Shaposhnikov stopped one worker and asked where they were going.

"Comrade General," the worker said, "if the mountain will not come to Muhammad, then Muhammad will go to the mountain." They were headed for the police station and Communist Party headquarters. Shaposhnikov radioed ahead to Pliyev and told him that the column of protesters was now moving across the Tuzlov bridge and into town.

"Stop them! Don't let them pass!" Pliyev shouted into his radio.

"I haven't got enough men to stop seven thousand people," Shaposhnikov said.

"Send the tanks! Attack them!" Pliyev said.

Shaposhnikov said, "Comrade Commander, I see no enemy that our tanks ought to attack."

Pliyev slammed down the receiver in a rage. In that moment of dead air, Shaposhnikov sensed disaster, but he thought he might be able to head it off. He jumped in a jeep and tried to catch up with the protesters. But by the time he neared the city's central square, the marchers were at the gates of the police station, demanding that the strike leaders be let out of jail. Suddenly, soldiers started firing into the crowd. Some witnesses said the troops were issued dumdum bullets, which expand on impact. In a panic, the crowd turned and started to flee up Moskovskaya Street. The troops continued firing at their backs. One woman lay in a flower bed bleeding to death. Her arm had been shot off.

By the time the crowd was gone, Solzhenitsyn wrote, "the soldiers looked around for trucks and buses, commandeered them, loaded them with the dead and wounded, and took them to the high-walled military hospital. For a day or two afterward these buses went around town with bloodstained seats."

News of the killings spread to other factories. Workers left the plants and staged an even bigger rally in the center of town. "Trucks full of workers arrived from everywhere," one witness recalled. "It was a torrent of human bodies. No force on earth could have stopped them."

"Khrushchev! Khrushchev! Let him see!" the crowd chanted.

Soon Mikoyan was on the radio. He spoke of "hooligans" and "the tragic accident." The police issued a curfew order and sent the crowd home. The army left its troops and tanks in the city for weeks. Within two days, the official press ceased all mention of the Novocherkassk affair. And so it stayed for decades.

General Shaposhnikov was a loyal Party member with memories of the first days of the Revolution. He could not understand why the local Communists had not simply met with the workers as "comrades" and negotiated with them. He thought that he should write a letter to the Central Committee of the Communist Party. Maybe they would understand. After all, he thought, the Soviet army simply did not attack its own people. You could read it in Lenin, in all the Party rulebooks! He remembered how the Party always referred to "Bloody Sunday" when the czarist police in 1905 attacked a

crowd of peaceful petitioners. The Party and its army would never act that way.

Shaposhnikov asked to speak with the Party officials. He was refused. Even after a few months went by, the general could not let the killings pass. He began sending anonymous letters to the Soviet Writers' Union in Moscow in the naive hope that their "great humanism" would be of help to him. And so Shaposhnikov, a Hero of the Soviet Union in his sixties, wrote: "The Party has turned into a car which is steered by a reckless, drunken driver who is always breaking the traffic rules. It's high time to take away the driver's license and prevent a catastrophe. . . . Today it is extremely important that the working people and the intellectuals should see clearly the essence of the political regime under which we live. They must realize that we are under the rule of the worst form of autocracy which rests on an enormous bureaucracy and an armed force. . . . It is necessary that people learn to think. Our blind faith is turning us into mere living machines. Our people have been deprived of all political and international rights."

Once more Shaposhnikov's idealism was betrayed. The Writers' Union was a hopelessly corrupt organization, a swamp of toadies, and its officers turned Shaposhnikov's letters over to the KGB. Shaposhnikov said his intentions were never "anti-Soviet" but rather "anti the bureaucrats and their arrogance." Somehow the KGB did not see it that way. The general began noticing that his mail was arriving already opened. He soon confirmed that he was under surveillance. In 1966, with no explanation, the army forced him out of active duty. In 1967, police searched his apartment and confiscated his archives. Without even pretending to secrecy, they also installed a listening device in the bedroom wall. "I was basically under house arrest, and I was followed by men in dark glasses all the time," Shaposhnikov said. "There was nothing I could do. Some friends remained loyal, but it was very hard for them, especially in a provincial place like this. They saw what was happening. People tried to avoid me. They would actually cross the street just to avoid saying hello to me in town."

Finally the KGB called Shaposhnikov to local headquarters for a prolonged interrogation. Over and over they demanded that he confess to "anti-Soviet" activities, and Shaposhnikov always described his work in the countryside teaching illiterate workers to read, his work in the mines for 20 kopecks a shift, his long and celebrated career in the army. "How could I have been anti-Soviet when I gave Soviet power everything?" he said. "If anyone had been dedicated to building Communism, it was me." He was stripped of his army rank and his membership in the Communist Party. Only by writing an impassioned letter to the KGB chief, Yuri Andropov, did Shaposhnikov save himself from jail.

Through the Brezhnev, Andropov, and Chernenko years, there was not much for the general to do except live in shabby retirement. While other Soviet generals had generous benefits—dachas, special food orders, generous pensions—Shaposhnikov lived no better than a retired factory worker. To pass the time and make a few extra rubles, he wrote memoirs of the war, about the tank assaults on the Nazis on the Ukrainian front. The books were published, but, of course, they had nothing to do with the massacre at Novocherkassk.

Throughout the sixties and seventies, the general never connected with the underground political ferment in Moscow and Leningrad. The truth was, the dissident movement confused him. It seemed directed not only at the leadership, but also at the foundations of Leninist ideology. "I could never understand that," he said.

When Gorbachev came to power in 1985, Shaposhnikov wrote five letters to the Kremlin. They all went unanswered. Finally, in 1988, he got an imperious letter from the Supreme Court: "Your case has now been dismissed in view of the absence of corpus delicti. . . . The acts perpetrated by you in the sixties provided ample grounds for bringing charges of anti-Soviet propaganda against you. It is only in the context of perestroika and the democratization of all spheres of life in the Soviet Union that it has become possible to find you not guilty."

It would be hard to find a more egregious example of indirection and self-righteousness in the service of simple justice. But Shaposhnikov was only relieved. He began going once more to his local Party meetings—"I am sixty years a Communist!" But his faith is of a certain kind. In 1990, when a group of young officers in the army scandalized the generals by forming the reformist group called Shield, they made Shaposhnikov their honorary chairman. They even asked him to speak at a huge antigovernment rally in Moscow just as troops were killing Azerbaijanis on the streets of Baku. "I thought a long time about what I wanted to say that day," Shaposhnikov said. "I thought about that afternoon in Novocherkassk and everything that is going on now, and so I said the army has to vow that they are always with the people and not against them. We can never shoot at our own people. Otherwise we are nothing. Otherwise, we have no future. We'd better remember that."

MOSCOW

Even after "Bloody Sunday" in Vilnius, the hard-liners wanted still more blood. They wanted to provoke a confrontation with the opposition forces that would *require* force; they wanted an incident so ugly that they would

finally have the pretense they needed to step in, declare a state of emergency, and put an end to the strikes and the defiant leaderships in the Baltic states, Moldavia, Georgia, Armenia, and, most of all, Russia.

Gorbachev was showing no signs of relaxing his position. In early March 1991, he proclaimed victory in a referendum to preserve the union, but he knew well that he had been trumped by Yeltsin. Yeltsin added a second question to the ballot asking voters of the Russian Republic if they wanted direct elections for a Russian president. They voted overwhelmingly for a June election. Until now, Yeltsin had been the Russian leader, but only because he had been elected chairman of the republican parliament, and then only by a narrow margin. But Yeltsin knew two things: first, that he would run and win; second, that such a victory would force Gorbachev, who had never been elected to anything by the people, to deal more seriously with the opposition.

But for now, as president of the country and general secretary of the Party, Gorbachev still thought his power was with the Party, the KGB, and the military. He listened to them almost unquestioningly, even to their wildest deceptions. Shevardnadze, whose instincts and judgments had proved uncanny since the day of his resignation speech, saw in his friend Gorbachev a man who was a prisoner "of his own nature, his conceptions, and his way of thinking and acting." All through 1991, Shevardnadze wrote in his memoir, it was "none other than Gorbachev himself [who] had been spoon-feeding the junta with his indecisiveness, his inclination to back and fill, his fellow-traveling, his poor judgment of people, his indifference toward his true allies, his distrust of the democratic forces, and his disbelief in the bulwark whose name is the people—the very same people who had changed thanks to the perestroika he had begun. That is the enormous tragedy of Mikhail Gorbachev, and no matter how much I empathize with him, I cannot help but say that it almost led to a national tragedy."

Yakovlev told me that Gorbachev believed the chiefs of the KGB and the Interior Ministry police when they informed him that the reformers were actually planning to storm the Kremlin walls using "hooks and ladders." To tighten the screw, *Pravda*'s deputy editor, Anatoly Karpychev, repeated the same rumors in print, writing that the radicals were making "preparations for the final storming of the Kremlin." Yakovlev exploded, telling Gorbachev that these so-called intelligence reports were sheer nonsense and that he was making a fatal error in listening to all the sycophants and double-dealers around him. But Gorbachev was sure he knew better.

"You exaggerate," he told Yakovlev.

Against Yakovlev's advice, Gorbachev ordered a ban on demonstrations in Moscow from March 26 to April 15 and gave Boris Pugo's Interior

Ministry control of the Moscow police force, taking it out of the hands of the liberals who ran city hall. Gorbachev authorized all law enforcement bodies to "use all necessary measures to ensure appropriate public order in the capital."

The battle had reached a point of no return. Yeltsin called a demonstration for March 28. In his own legislature, he was facing a vote of no confidence from the orthodox Communist deputies. In February, Yeltsin had gone on television blaming Gorbachev for driving the country "to the edge of the abyss" and for flirting with military dictatorship. Gorbachev, he said, had to step down and power must be transferred to the collective rule of the republican leaders.

By March 27, the center of Moscow looked like an armed camp. Like the czars who once kept a cavalry unit stabled near Red Square in case of an uprising by university students, the Soviet police meant to deny the center of the capital to the pro-democracy demonstrators. More than fifty thousand Interior Ministry troops positioned water cannons and tear-gas launchers along the streets. Row after row of empty buses and troops cut off all access roads to Manezh Square outside the Kremlin.

The hard-line press and Tass ran ominous warnings, including the threat to use "all means at our disposal" from the KGB chief of Moscow, Vitaly Prilukov. Democratic Russia's leaders realized that they would never get to the Manezh, where they had held so many rallies before, but they did not call off the demonstration. Instead, they said, people should gather at two alternative spots: the Arbat metro station and Mayakovsky Square near the Tchaikovsky Concert Hall.

On the morning of the 28th, I walked with my friends Masha and Seriozha to the statue of Mayakovsky. We were more than an hour early, and while we waited to meet some other friends, we saw people selling pro-Yeltsin and anti-Gorbachev buttons; others listened to the new pro-opposition radio station, Echo of Moscow, which was describing the troop positions along Gorky Street and all around the Manezh. Like the Chinese demonstrators at Tiananmen Square in 1989, the demonstrators were going out of their way to seem casual, as if pretending that the worst could never happen. A bunch of teenagers were taking the afternoon as a *tusovka,* a hangout, and they were listening to a tape of *Exile on Main Street* on their boom box. For once, Mick Jagger's voice of threat seemed like more than puffed-up theater. As more and more people crowded onto the square, I was getting jumpy. What would prevent these generals from picking a fight? They had made a mess of their coup in Vilnius, it was true, but the KGB still had the means to provoke a conflict, to make it seem as if the demonstrators were out of control, and then "restore order." It hadn't been many weeks before that I was talking to

General Boris Gromov, the last Soviet commander in Afghanistan and now Pugo's deputy, and he was telling me that one "can stand back and be polite for only so long. But sooner or later, you have to take action." Not long before that I interviewed fifteen generals and admirals at the Congress of People's Deputies one afternoon, and all fifteen said they thought Viktor Alksnis, the "black colonel," had the right idea.

The demonstration began. The usual speakers—Afanasyev, Popov—spoke. There were the usual banners—"CPSU to the Ash Heap of History!"—and the usual chants. We marched a little this way, a little that way, but mostly we stood still. The simple fact that so many people had ignored the threat of violence was demonstration enough. We heard from other marchers, and even from an American senator who happened to be there, David Boren of Oklahoma, that plainclothes police, probably KGB, had punched and beaten a few demonstrators who had ventured too close to the armed cordon near the Manezh. But the incidents were few. The demonstration turned out to be boring, blissfully boring.

On the face of it, the day had been a political draw. The soldiers held their ground and the demonstrators marched in defiance of Gorbachev's order and avoided any serious provocations. But in this case, victory belonged to the opposition. The whole stew of opposition forces—urban intellectuals, teenagers, pro-independence people from the republics—proved that they were willing to face down a threat with their bodies as well as their slogans. As we walked home, my friends and I noticed that the crowd was full of itself. They were celebrating a great victory. If the attack on the Lithuanian television tower was the rehearsal for a coup, the protection of the Lithuanian parliament and now this demonstration were rehearsals for the resistance. The resistance looked far more impressive. How could the KGB ignore that? What's more, how could Gorbachev?

MAGADAN

For the first time in their thousand-year history, Russians were about to elect a president. In those last days of the old regime, in the last few days of the June 1991 campaign, I went to the farthest shore of the empire, to Magadan, where Stalin's slave ships docked and the labor camps of Kolyma began. I had never seen a city so desolate. In the days of the Great Purge and for years after, prisoners called the rest of the country the "mainland," as if Magadan and the wastes of Kolyma beyond were an island in the sea of nowhere. Even now it seemed to me a ghostly place, a landscape of the dead. Mornings, the water was the color of iron, the sky the color of milk. The black-green hills

were shrouded in a dense mist and long wisps of smoke trailed into the sky from the tin-shack slums known as Shanghai. Even in the center of town, the loudest sound was from the desultory passing of beat-up cars, Ladas, Volgas, and Zhigulis, their tires smearing the slush.

I was also here to visit my friend Arnold Yeryomenko. We'd first met in Moscow during the Nineteenth Party Conference in 1988, and we saw each other whenever he returned to the capital. I sent a telegram to Arnold telling him I was on the way, but I knew he'd never get it. He was still a marked man in his hometown. The Party press in Magadan wrote denunciations of him as if he held it in his power to topple the regime and steal all its daughters. He was still the anti-Soviet devil.

After the nine-hour flight, I walked to Arnold's building and stuck a note under the door telling him where he could find me. The building was appalling. The concrete looked wet and ancient all at once and the yard outside was a sea of mud and abandoned construction junk. Kids had nothing at all to play with. They threw rocks against a wall, and when they tired they just sat down on a thick stick stretched across a sheet of abandoned concrete.

The next morning, Arnold found me at the Hotel Magadan. We took a long walk to the sea, and then headed back up the hill, the same path the prisoners took fifty years ago. "You see where that ship is now?" he said, pointing down a hill into the port. That was where the lines of prisoners began their march from the sea to the holding camps. Many of them would be marched hundreds of miles to camps throughout Kolyma. Arnold said, "Our house was fifty meters from a labor camp—now it's a movie theater. I could see them from my room, from the kitchen. None of it was ever out of my sight, and it went on from the time I was a baby until I was a young man. And I remember every day in school we ran to the windows and watched the prisoners go by in their chains: the Russians, later the Japanese POWs and the Vlasovites. I remember we'd come up to them and one might say, 'Boy, go get me some fish.' And he'd slip us a few rubles to buy it. But everyone knew they'd soon be dead. Getting them fish: it was like some horrible joke."

Magadan really was the history of the Soviet Union, its proper spiritual capital. Magadan and the vast territory of Kolyma had been all but wild, unsettled before the Revolution. Magadan was an invention of the Kremlin and the NKVD, an administrative center for mass murder throughout the Kolyma region in eastern Siberia. As a project of centralized planning, Magadan fulfilled and overfulfilled its five-year plans. In the one hundred camps of Kolyma, an area six times the size of France, around three million people were slaughtered between 1936 and 1953. They were shot, stabbed, beheaded, thrown into pits, or starved. Three million in just one corner of a

country that was itself a vast network of concentration camps. There was no way to shove it out of the mind; in Magadan, the dead were everywhere, in the abandoned mine shafts, under the taiga, under the seabed. One of the roads to the northern camps was built on a bed of bones. The main street, Lenin Prospekt, was a road to oblivion. Starting from the center of downtown, the prisoners walked to their camps, sometimes to an outpost a thousand miles away. You could walk all the way to Yakutia, where the reindeer run. And now nearly all the living in Magadan slept in the houses of the dead. Eighty percent of the standing structures in Magadan were once barracks or headquarters for the secret police administration or "shooting halls."

Varlam Shalamov was the poet of Kolyma. He survived seventeen years in a camp there, all for the crime of declaring Ivan Bunin, who had won the Nobel Prize, a "classic author." Shalamov's own classic stories, quick narratives, sharp and glinting as mica, so pierced Solzhenitsyn that the younger man invited Shalamov to help him with the massive project of *The Gulag Archipelago*. Shalamov was too old and sick. He declined. But the work he did leave behind provided the clearest picture of the Kolyma nightmare that exists. In one story, he described the officer Postnikov, who made a blood sport of hunting down escapees:

"Drunk with murder, he fulfilled his task with zeal and passion. He had personally captured five men. As always in such cases he had been decorated and received a bonus. The reward was the same for the dead and the living. It was not necessary to deliver the prisoners complete. One August morning a man who was going to drink at a stream fell into an ambush set by Postnikov and his soldiers. Postnikov shot him down with a revolver. They decided not to drag the body to the camp but to leave it in the taiga. The signs of bears and wolves were numerous.

"For identification, Postnikov cut off the fugitive's hands with an ax. He put the hands in his knapsack and went to make his report on the hunt. . . . In the night the corpse got up. Pressing his bleeding wrists to his chest, he left the taiga following the trail and reached the prisoners' tent. With pale face and blue eyes, he looked inside, holding himself at the opening, leaning against the doorposts and muttering something. Fever devoured him. His padded coat, his trousers, his rubber boots were stained with black blood. They gave him warm soup, wrapped his chopped-off wrists in rags, and took him to the infirmary. But already Postnikov and his men came running out of their little hut. The soldiers took the prisoner. He was not heard of again."

As late as 1988, the Communist Party allowed no monument to the dead of Kolyma. In fact, the Party chief, Aleksandr Bogdanov, did unveil one monument in 1988: a bust of Reingold Berzin, the founding director of the Far Northern Construction Trust and the concentration camps of Kolyma.

Berzin himself was purged after Stalin's Central Committee decreed in 1937 that prisoners could no longer be "coddled."

But by June 1991, times had changed. For one thing, foreigners were allowed to visit, and I saw Russians on the streets wearing their old plastic overcoats and the new trucker caps that the exchanges across the water had brought: "Alaska Airways," "I Love Anchorage." There was a video store renting *Terminator* and a complete line of Bruce Lee movies. I saw one man wandering in an empty butcher shop wearing the official jacket of the Seattle Seahawks.

Perhaps most alien of all, this Russian city, this museum of brutality, was taking part in a presidential election. On the streets, there was something otherworldly about standing near a building that was once a camp barracks and listening to sidewalk political arguments that in spirit, if not content, sounded like primary-year debates on the street corners of Nashua or Sioux City. It did not take a computer poll to figure out where the votes were. Boris Yeltsin was going to win, and, more important, the Communist Party was doomed. Outside a shoe store, people milled around in the cold and debated the election. A few young men in leather jackets and scarves handed out Yeltsin leaflets printed by the Democratic Russia group in Moscow. Another kid held up the red, white, and blue tricolor, the flag of czarist Russia. "The point is to get rid of the Communists in Russia, once and for all," Tamara Karpova, a housewife who was with the Yeltsin group, told me. "My parents and grandparents lived in the Ukraine until the Communists sent them here to the camps," Karpova said. "Why should I vote for anyone in the Communist Party?"

Bogdanov had been replaced as head of the Magadan Party organization, but his successors were no smarter. Their only cause was survival. They printed one article after another in their newspapers describing Yeltsin as a "wrecker" and his Communist Party rival in the race, Nikolai Ryzhkov, as the voice of "unity" and "justice, honesty and order." Ryzhkov was the man to help the Party men keep their jobs. Without Ryzhkov, they would lose their offices with the baize tables and red runner carpets at Party headquarters. Without Ryzhkov, they would lose their dachas in "Snow Valley" outside of town. Yeltsin represented a new order and, most likely for them, unemployment.

In totalitarian society, habit replaces happiness, and habits were in jeopardy. "My father was a Party member, my husband is a Party member, and that is how I will vote. The rest are all adventurists," said Svetlana Murashkina, a woman who passed out Ryzhkov leaflets on the same street corner.

In the village of Palatka, I spoke to Boris Sulim, who had worked in one of the camps when he was a teenager and was now serving on the local

raikom, the Party committee. Sulim was a sawed-off shotgun of man with a broad, meaty face. He was a Ryzhkov man—"fast and firm." But the longer we talked, the sadder he got. He seemed exhausted, uncertain. All he had believed in, all he had worked for, was finished, and he knew it. His local Party committee, which had always ruled Palatka, had no influence now, "and I guess I know that."

Under Stalin, Sulim worked in the Omsuchkan camp, about four hundred miles from Magadan. "I was eighteen years old and Magadan seemed a very romantic place to me. I got eight hundred eighty rubles a month and a three-thousand-ruble installation grant, which was a hell of a lot of money for a kid like me. I was able to give my mother some of it. They even gave me membership in the Komsomol. There was a mining and ore-processing plant which sent out parties to dig for tin. I worked at the radio station which kept contact with the parties.

"If the inmates were good and disciplined they had almost the same rights as the free workers. They were trusted and they even went to the movies. As for the reason they were in the camps, well, I never poked my nose into details. We all thought the people were there because they were guilty. Why should I have believed anything else? In 1936, when I was still in the first grade, our teacher made us blot out the pictures in history books of the generals Tukhachevsky, Blucher, and Yegorov, and we had to cover them over with swastikas and write in the margin, 'enemy of the people.' "

Sulim said that after watching a few television documentaries on the Stalin era he would admit there had been "mistakes" and "abuses." I asked him if he had ever seen any of the prisoners executed or any of them die from the cold and the endless work in the mines. "Deaths?" he said. "I don't know. I wasn't interested then. But I think death is a natural phenomenon under any circumstances. Look, I was not part of the gulag system, so I have no intention of repenting."

MOSCOW

Sulim was a man of the old regime: ignorant, angry, unrepentant. But even in his worst moments, Gorbachev held firm to his better self, his ability to change, if only to survive. On April 23, with Yeltsin clearly headed for victory and his own percentage in the popularity polls nearing single digits, Gorbachev had yielded to the obvious. Despite the bad information he was getting, despite the betrayals around him and his own tragic vanity, even he could look out the window and see. He could see that the people were no longer his. They were Yeltsin's, and Landsbergis's, and Nazarbayev's in Kazakhstan

. . . but not his. And so Gorbachev moved once more to the left. He did not announce a favorite candidate—many people assumed he would vote not for Yeltsin or Ryzhkov, but for Vadim Bakatin, the former interior minister—but he did sign a "nine plus one" agreement. The document, drafted jointly by Gorbachev and the republican leaders, was an agreement to agree: republican leaders (so far, the Baltic states, Georgia, Armenia, and Moldavia declined to participate) were announcing their intention to form a new Union Treaty, under which the republics would acquire vastly more political power.

In June, Yeltsin won the election, as Gorbachev and everyone else knew he would. For his inauguration at the Kremlin's Palace of Congresses, Yeltsin planned a ceremony, both moving and pompous, clearly intended to distance the new office from Soviet history and align it with a kind of liberal Russian nationalism. He stripped away all signs of the Bolshevik state in the Kremlin hall. In place of the massive picture of Lenin that had always been the backdrop for ceremonies of state, there was simply a red, blue, and white Russian flag. Priests, rabbis, muftis, and ministers sat in the front row. Patriarch Alexy II, with his flowing robes and Tolstoyan beard, blessed Yeltsin with the sign of the cross and said, "By the will of God and the choice of the Russian people, you are bestowed with the highest office in Russia. . . . We will pray for you." Russia, the patriarch said, "is gravely ill." An actor from Leningrad, Oleg Basilashvili, read a long speech describing the degradation of the country through seventy years of Bolshevik rule.

Introduced by regal trumpeters and a blaring fanfare, Yeltsin swore himself in. At times he seemed overwhelmed by the occasion, and his voice broke once or twice with nervousness. He did not begin with the traditional *tovarishchi,* "comrades." "Citizens of the Russian Federation . . . Great Russia is rising from its knees . . ." he began. "The president is not a god, not a monarch, not a miracle worker. He is a citizen . . . and in Russia, the individual will become the measure of all things."

Gorbachev, for his part, tried to appear gracious at the ceremony, but he did not quite bring it off. He made a clumsy speech and even clumsier attempts at humor about the strangeness of a country with two presidents. At one point he said, "People on all continents are watching with great interest what you and I are doing." The intonation was such that people in the hall understood it to mean that the two men were up to some sort of shenanigans. The hall fairly buzzed with discontent until Gorbachev moved on.

But even as he was trying to assert his power, Yeltsin was hoping that his presidency would help Gorbachev realize that there could be no future in an alliance with Kryuchkov, Yazov, Pugo, and the old guard. He needed to seduce and bully Gorbachev at the same time. And so when Gorbachev was

finished with his speech, Boris Yeltsin was the first out of his seat to lead a standing ovation.

But in 1991, nothing was stable. You couldn't relax for a moment, you could never think for an instant that all would be well. As Sobchak had said, the side-by-side existence of a totalitarian regime (no matter how subdued compared to the Stalin era) and a fledgling democracy was impossible. Something would have to give.

In June, there were clues once more that the hard-liners were prepared to act, no matter what sort of marriage—of convenience or conviction—existed between Gorbachev and Yeltsin. The Soviet Prosecutor's Office, backed up by a report by Marshal Yazov, said, "In the course of the examination of the events [in Novocherkassk in 1962], it was established that arms were used by the military in accordance with the law, in order to defend state property from criminal attack and for purposes of self-defense. . . . The shooting started only after the unruly crowd attacked the soldiers and tried to seize their weapons." To most Soviet readers, the report was a justification not only of an event thirty years past, but of the assaults in Tbilisi, Vilnius, and Baku. And perhaps they were a threat, too; a threat of more violence to come.

Yeltsin answered that veiled threat with a veiled warning. He sent a representative to Novocherkassk with a message from the Russian president: "The truth about the tragedy of Novocherkassk is a stern warning to anyone who tries to resolve social problems by means of military force." Like General Shaposhnikov, the people would resist.

Two weeks later, on June 17, the Soviet prime minister, Valentin Pavlov, went before the parliament and asked to be given many of Gorbachev's powers. Pavlov, who clearly had the backing of Supreme Soviet Chairman Anatoly Lukyanov, said he was making the proposal out of consideration for Gorbachev's onerous schedule. "There are just not enough hours in the day," Pavlov suggested sweetly. What he forgot to say was that he was acting without Gorbachev's knowledge.

"I heard about it and told Gorbachev," Aleksandr Yakovlev told me. "Gorbachev was outraged. It was the first he had heard about it." But before Gorbachev had a chance to act, Pugo, Yazov, and Kryuchkov all went before a closed session of the Supreme Soviet and read out speeches accusing the leadership (they would not say "Gorbachev") of selling out the Party and leading the country to ruin. Yazov complained that hundreds of thousands of young men were refusing to obey their draft notices. Pugo railed on about "disorder" and "lawlessness." Kryuchkov was most vicious of all, saying that the reforms of the leadership and the fondest wishes of the CIA seemed

to coincide. He was charging treason. That gave the delegates from the Soyuz faction the cue to rise from their chairs and call for resignation.

"Away with Gorbachev! And away with his clique of liberals!" cried Leonid Sukhov, a cabdriver from Kharkov and a deputy in the Soyuz faction.

"A great power has been reduced to the lowly status of a beggar standing by others' doors with outstretched hands instead of working out its problems here where its problems are," charged Yevgeny Kogan, a Russian speaker from Estonia and another member of Soyuz.

Gorbachev was slow to react, but when he finally came to the Supreme Soviet to respond on June 21, he was able to summon for the occasion one of his vintage performances, full of indignation. Still he could not go all the way. Just as he would never admit to any conflict with Yegor Ligachev in 1988, he said he had no differences with Pavlov. The prime minister's proposals, he said, were "not well thought out."

When the session was over, Gorbachev came out of the chamber to meet the press. He was surrounded by none other than Messrs. Yazov, Pugo, and Kryuchkov. The three ministers were stone-faced and silent. "The coup is over," Gorbachev said. He was laughing. He meant it as a joke. And it was.

[illegible] He was changing [illegible]. [illegible] the [illegible] from the [illegible] and call for restoration.

"Away with Gorbachev!" And away with [illegible] [illegible]

[illegible]

[illegible]

[illegible] too [illegible]

When the [illegible] the press. He was surrounded by none other than [illegible] and Kryuchkov. The [illegible] were [illegible] and silent. "The coup is over," Gorbachev said. He was laughing. He meant it as a joke. And it was.

PART IV

"FIRST AS TRAGEDY, THEN AS FARCE"

Evil has great momentum, but the forces of good are inert. The masses . . . have no fight in them, and will acquiesce in whatever happens.

—Nadezhda Mandelstam, *1970*

Boris Yeltsin was twelve when he had his first run-in with the Communist Party. He'd had a mean childhood. His father was a construction worker who beat him with a belt. The family lived in a hut near a building site in the Urals, and the six of them, and their goat, lived in one room. Everyone slept on the floor. Once, when Yeltsin was six, he woke in the middle of the night to see his father being led out of the hut by strange men. The family was lucky that the arrest did not lead to a long jail term or the camps.

As a boy, Yeltsin was a good student and a troublemaker. "I've always been a bit of a hooligan," he told me. In the fifth grade, he encouraged the entire class to jump out the first-floor window while the teacher was out of the room. He took part in gang fights and got his nose broken when one of his friends took a swing at him with a club. When he was eleven and the war was on, Yeltsin and a few of his friends broke into an arms depot in a local

church. They climbed through three layers of barbed wire and stole a couple of hand grenades: "We just wanted to see what they were made of." Yeltsin, of course, decided that he would take charge. Without removing the fuses, he tried to open the grenades with a hammer. The explosion mangled the thumb and forefinger on his left hand, and when gangrene set in, the fingers had to be removed. "Wouldn't you say that was brilliant?"

Yeltsin's troubles with the Communist Party began at his graduation ceremonies from primary school. As one of the best students in the school, he had the honor of being allowed to sit on the stage. When it came his turn to give a short speech, Yeltsin grabbed the microphone and turned his ceremonial moment into an outrageous harangue. He launched into an attack on a certain homeroom teacher, a hated shrew who cursed the children, smacked them with a thick ruler, and made them clean her house. "She was a horror and I had to say what I had to say," Yeltsin said. The parents and the staff in the audience listened for a while in shock. The principal finally jumped out of his chair and snatched away the microphone and sent Yeltsin back to his seat. The day was ruined. And what was more, instead of a diploma, Yeltsin received a "wolf's ticket," a certificate forbidding him from getting a high school education. At home, Yeltsin's father came at him with the strap. It was the usual punishment. But this time, Yeltsin grabbed his old man's arm and fended him off. No more, he said, and then went looking for retribution at the local headquarters of the Communist Party. For weeks, Yeltsin heard nothing from the local bureaucrats but rebuke. Finally, he got one official to listen to his complaints against the teacher, how she had humiliated her students. A board of inquiry was established. The teacher was fired and Yeltsin was reinstated as a student in good standing. He had won his first battle inside the "horror house" of the Soviet system.

By the middle of 1991, Yeltsin was hoping to transform himself from an executioner of the sacred cow, a political figure who made his name by attacking Ligachev, the Party, Gorbachev and all the rest, into a statesman of the "new Russia." As Russia's first elected president, he hoped to rebuild the bridge to Gorbachev and move into a new era in which the sovereignty of the republics would allow for greater wealth and liberty. Yeltsin knew that real power still lay elsewhere: with the army, the KGB, the police. He, like Gorbachev, had heard rumors of a coup, and while the two men negotiated a new Treaty of the Union that would give far greater powers to the republics, Yeltsin warned Gorbachev that he was surrounded by reactionaries who could eventually betray him. Yeltsin had seen what had happened in Lithuania in January and then in the Supreme Soviet when Pavlov and his sponsors made their grab for power. He had no reason to expect that these men would go quietly.

It must have been the first coup d'état in world history to have been announced in advance, and in the national press.

The first to plow the rhetorical earth were the military ideologists, the men of the lunatic fringe who saw the army as the sainted institution of the Russian empire, the bulwark of a great world power. With Defense Minister Dmitri Yazov's blessing, Major General Viktor Filatov edited the monthly *Military-Historical Journal,* which featured excerpts from *Mein Kampf,* attacks on Sakharov, and, most prominently of all, the collected works of Karem Rush, a full-throated booster of the Soviet imperial idea. "The military," Rush wrote, "should consider itself the backbone and sacred institution of a thousand years of statehood." By publishing such stuff, Filatov boosted circulation from 27,000 in 1988 to 377,000 in 1990. He was a lovely man, Filatov was. He published the famous anti-Semitic forgery *The Protocols of the Elders of Zion,* and told *The New York Times* that he regarded the document "as a normal piece of literature, like the Bible or the Koran." He was an ardent supporter of Saddam Hussein and wrote pro-Iraqi propaganda during the Gulf War. Perhaps his favorite target was the liberal press. Once, Filatov wrote, "It's a pity we have no Beria now; if he had read today's *Ogonyok,* he would have shot half [the staff] and sent the remaining rubbish to rot in a camp." *Nash Sovremenik,* another journal of the nationalist right wing, seconded that emotion, declaring the army "not only has the right, but also the duty, to become extremely involved in internal affairs."

For a long time, the country's most important reactionaries, ministers like Yazov, Kryuchkov, and Pugo, hid behind figures like Filatov, Rush, and the editors of *Nash Sovremenik.* They did not risk the appearance of outright treason. But, eventually, such niceties faded. On May 9, 1991, Aleksandr Prokhanov's paper, *Dyen* ("The Day"), published a roundtable discussion with some of the most hard-line figures in the military: Valentin Varennikov, the general in charge of all ground forces and the leader of the charge on Vilnius; Igor Rodionov, the general most responsible for the 1989 massacre in Tbilisi; and Oleg Baklanov, the head of the country's military-industrial complex. Only the naive could have read what these men had to say and not come to the conclusion that they wanted nothing less than a coup d'état. Baklanov spoke with touching modesty about the military's ability to rule the country. But rule they could, and would: "The defense industry has much greater organizational experience than, say, the newly appointed politicians who are incapable even of ensuring garbage collection on the streets of Moscow."

If Gorbachev needed greater proof that the rhetoric of the hard-liners matched their real intentions, he got it at the end of June.

On June 20, the foreign ministers of the United States and the Soviet Union were holding talks in Berlin in preparation for a Bush-Gorbachev summit a month later in Moscow. Secretary of State James Baker and Foreign Minister Aleksandr Bessmertnykh had already spent a long day with each other in meetings on a wide range of issues. But when Bessmertnykh returned to his embassy in the late afternoon, Baker was on the phone saying they had to meet again.

"Jim, what's the matter? What's happened?" said Bessmertnykh, who spoke English fluently.

"It's something very urgent," Baker said. "I'd like to meet you very much."

Bessmertnykh said that he had a meeting. Couldn't it wait?

Baker tried to find the words to convey the gravity of the matter and yet not give away any detail on a phone line that was probably not secure.

"It's a somewhat delicate matter," he said. "If I go, a lot of cars will follow with guards, and there will be a lot of commotion in town. The press will be on to us. If you can, I'll wait for you at the hotel room where I'm staying, but please let everything be quiet!"

"Is it really that urgent?" Bessmertnykh said. "I have a scheduled meeting."

"If I were you, I would, perhaps, put off all my affairs and come over."

In an unmarked car, Bessmertnykh rode cross town to Baker. He brought with him one of his policy advisers, a specialist from the USA-Canada Institute, but Baker said he would prefer to meet alone with Bessmertnykh.

When they were alone, Baker said, "I've just received a report from Washington. I understand it may come from intelligence sources. It seems that there may be an attempt to depose Gorbachev. It's a highly delicate matter and we need to convey this information somehow. According to our information, Pavlov, Yazov, and Kryuchkov will take part in the ouster. . . . It's urgent. It must be brought to Gorbachev's attention."

The initial report had come from Moscow's Mayor, Gavriil Popov, who told the American ambassador in Moscow, Jack Matlock, that the KGB and the military were preparing a coup.

Baker asked if it was possible to call Gorbachev on a direct line from the Soviet embassy in Berlin. Bessmertnykh said that such lines were under KGB control and, therefore, useless. Baker suggested instead that they set up a

direct, private meeting between Gorbachev and the American ambassador in Moscow, Jack Matlock. Bessmertnykh agreed.

On June 22, Gorbachev, Kryuchkov, Yazov, and the rest of the Soviet leadership took part in an annual ceremony in Moscow—laying a wreath at the Tomb of the Unknown Soldier outside the Kremlin gates. In retrospect, it was a tableau out of a Shakespearean tragedy: the monarch surrounded by his men, his deferential advisers, his betrayers.

After the ceremony, Gorbachev held a short private meeting with Bessmertnykh.

How had the session gone with the American ambassador? the minister asked.

It had gone well, Gorbachev said. Once he had the information, he said, he had had a "tough talk" with those concerned. And that was all.

In a document dated June 20, 1991, the same day as Baker's secret meeting with Bessmertnykh, the KGB quoted a source in Gorbachev's "inner circle" coolly analyzing how to push Gorbachev out of power or, at least, into an increasingly conservative position. The document, uncovered later by the Russian prosecutors, said that the Bush administration held Yeltsin in disdain and considered the possibility of his ascension to supreme power as "catastrophic" for U.S.-Soviet relations. It also said that the Bush circle was beginning to wonder if Lukyanov was positioning himself as a successor to Gorbachev. The document said that the "most logical and sensible" course would be to force Gorbachev to abandon a radical course in the same way he was "persuaded" to abandon the 500 Days program. The source of the analysis was not named.

It was a season of deception. Little by little, the conspirators were undermining the authority of the president. The attempt to grab Gorbachev's powers in parliament in June had failed, but they were still chipping away, humiliating the president in a hundred different ways.

Despite promises to the contrary, the military carried out nuclear tests in Semipalatinsk and Novaya Zemlya without consent of the republics or national authorities. The Ministry of Defense and the general staff came close to scotching the Conventional Forces in Europe treaty that they despised so much by playing games with the rules on the counting of weapons. While Gorbachev was in Oslo to collect the Nobel Prize in June, the General Prosecutor's Office released a report exonerating troops involved in the Vil-

nius violence; on the same day, troops in Lithuania set up fifteen checkpoints and made two arrests. All this assured that Gorbachev would have to answer some embarrassing questions at what would have otherwise been a triumphant press conference. While Gorbachev was trying to get himself invited to the summit of industrialized nations in London, the commander of Soviet forces in East Germany sent a letter to the German Foreign Ministry threatening to slow down troop withdrawals if Bonn did not move faster to build apartments in the Soviet Union for the returning soldiers.

With every new incident, the leading officials denied any political meaning, and each time they tugged a little on the trigger.

It was easy to look away. Despite all the ominous signals to the contrary, most of the talk in Moscow in the early summer of 1991 was reasonably optimistic. Gorbachev seemed to have shifted course once more, this time making his peace with Yeltsin and the other republican leaders. Negotiations on the Treaty of the Union appeared to be moving along without the usual disasters.

But three days after Yeltsin issued a decree barring Party cells in government institutions, and just one week before George Bush landed in town for a summit with Gorbachev, the leading paper of the reactionaries, *Sovetskaya Rossiya,* published a stunning appeal called "A Word to the People." Signed by leading right-wing generals, politicians, and writers, the appeal, dated July 23, declared that Russia was in the midst of an "unprecedented tragedy":

"Our Motherland, this country, this great state which history, Nature, and our predecessors willed us to save, is dying, breaking apart and plunging into darkness and nothingness. . . . What has become of us, brothers?" The language was apocalyptic, the imagery of a ship of state "sinking into nonexistence," evil forces selling out a great power. "Our home is already burning to the ground . . . the bones of the people are being ground up and the backbone of Russia is snapped in two." It even condemned the Communist Party for giving power to "frivolous and clumsy parliamentarians who have set us against each other and brought into force thousands of stillborn laws, of which only those function that enslave the people and divide the tormented body of the country into portions. . . . How is it that we have let people come to power who do not love their country, who kowtow to foreign patrons and seek advice and blessings abroad?"

The key signatories were General Boris Gromov, the last Soviet commander in Afghanistan and now Pugo's deputy in the Interior Ministry; General Varennikov, again; Vasily Starodubtsev, the head of the conservative agricultural lobby; and Aleksandr Tizyakov, the head of an association of military plants. For months, Tizyakov had been carrying around documents in his briefcase outlining the shape a military coup could take. But the

main author of the appeal was Aleksandr Prokhanov, the editor and novelist whose ode to Soviet empire in *A Tree in the Center of Kabul* led him to adopt the sobriquet "the Soviet Kipling." He waited for the coup as if it were Christmas. "Get ready for the next wave, my friend," he once told me. "Get ready." Prokhanov, with likely help from two other writers and signatories, Yuri Bondarev and Valentin Rasputin, managed to capture the tone of apocalypse in every reactionary's heart. As the critic Natalya Ivanova pointed out in a stunning essay in the monthly journal *Znamya,* the July 23 appeal, with its vulgar nationalism and self-pity, matched almost perfectly the language of the doomsday declarations issued on the first morning of the August coup. The conspirators envisioned a new vanguard, not of Communists, but of soldiers, priests, workers, peasants, and, of course, writers. "I also can't help but be reminded," she wrote, "that on the eve of the coup, the military state publishing house issued in the millions a brochure called 'The Black Hundreds and the Red Hundreds' which laid out in detail the program of the national party in 1906." The nationalists of 1906, like the putschists of 1991, wanted to dissolve parliament, declare military, emergency rule, and ban all left-wing newspapers and journals. "A Word to the People" was a blatant call for a coup d'état.

"We were making no secret of what we wanted," Prokhanov told me. "Why keep secrets? We live in a democracy, don't we?"

Even if Gorbachev was not paying much attention to the smell of a storm, Yeltsin was. On July 29, Yeltsin went out to Gorbachev's dacha to finish negotiations for a new Treaty of the Union. Gorbachev had already agreed to language that would give the republics far more power and make it possible for the Baltic states to become independent very quickly. Yeltsin wanted more. He wanted the power of the purse, and he made it his goal at this meeting to convince Gorbachev that the republics, and not Moscow, should have the ability to levy taxes and distribute the funds as they saw fit.

The talks went on for hours. Yeltsin, Gorbachev, and the Kazakh president, Nursultan Nazarbayev, went back and forth over the taxation issue so long that they had to break for dinner and then come back at it.

At one point, the two republican leaders could not hold back. Yeltsin told Gorbachev that the right-wingers in the Union leadership were doing everything they could to undercut a transition to genuine democracy and a market economy. Kryuchkov and Yazov were clearly against the Treaty of the Union, he said. Nazarbayev agreed with Yeltsin, and added two more names to the list of "resisters": Prime Minister Valentin Pavlov, and Gorbachev's great friend of forty years, Supreme Soviet Chairman Anatoly Lukyanov.

These people realized that the treaty would rob them of power, Yeltsin said. In a Union led mainly by the republican leaders, Yazov and Kryuchkov must be fired and sixty or seventy Union ministries would have to be liquidated.

Gorbachev said, well, yes, of course. He was not blind, after all. "Everything will have to be reorganized, including the army and the KGB," he said. But let's wait until after the treaty is signed, he said. And, you know, he added, Lukyanov, Kryuchkov, and the rest are "not as bad as you think."

At this point, Yeltsin got out of his chair and stepped out onto the balcony.

Nazarbayev and Gorbachev were dumbfounded. What was Yeltsin looking for?

"To see if anyone is eavesdropping," he said.

Nazarbayev and Gorbachev laughed. What a card Yeltsin was. Imagine. Bugging the president and general secretary of the party. How absurd!

After all, how could a man like Anatoly Lukyanov, the chairman of the Supreme Soviet, betray a friend he had known since university days? The man was a lawyer, just like Gorbachev, an amateur poet, just like Andropov, and his friendship was a matter of immortal verse.

> Safeguard your conscience for your friends.
> A friend seeks neither gain nor flattery.
> A friend and conscience are as one
> In tempest, cold, and thunder,
> Safeguard your conscience for your friends!

"I love him," Lukyanov would say of Gorbachev. "I love him, I can't change him, though, speaking openly, I know his weaknesses, his shortcomings. . . . Of all the people who made perestroika, I alone stayed next to Gorbachev, the rest left, from the left and right. . . ."

But that was later, when Lukyanov was in jail charged with treason.

As Bush was arriving in the Soviet Union for the summit in the last few days of July, *Moscow News* had asked me to write a short article about the U.S. reaction to what was going on in the Soviet Union. I used the opportunity to say that as long as Gorbachev was surrounded by anti-Western reactionaries, there would be no end to Washington's caution about providing aid and investment. "It's a mystery to the West why Gorbachev's circle is still stocked with so many aides and professionals so seemingly at odds with reform," I

wrote. "For every Aleksandr Yakovlev—a figure who has transformed his own vision of the world—there are, it seems, at least a dozen Pavlovs."

I was only repeating what I had heard a thousand times, but who was listening in the Kremlin? I went around with Michael Dobbs and a couple of visiting editors to see some of Gorbachev's closest advisers: the apparatchik-liberals like Andrei Grachev, Yevgeny Primakov, and Georgi Shakhnazarov. We asked about "A Word to the People" and other dark signs, and they explained them away. "Such is the atmosphere," Grachev said, but he didn't seem particularly worried, and neither did the others. In contrast, Yeltsin's top adviser, Gennadi Burbulis, told us that Moscow resembled a "political minefield."

"We tread through it very lightly," he said with a waxen smile.

And, as if to underscore his point and my own, some of Pugo's men slaughtered eight Lithuanian border police during the Bush visit. Pugo denied any knowledge of the incident. He just had no idea.

Gorbachev was humiliated. "It's hard to say what has happened," he told the press, with the American president sitting next to him.

In the meantime, Kryuchkov had tapped Gorbachev's phones and everyone with even the remotest access to the president—even Raisa Gorbacheva's hairdresser. The eavesdropping logs had Gorbachev as "110," Raisa as "111," and dozens of other codes. Kryuchkov could tolerate the president no longer. "Gorbachev is not reacting adequately to events," the KGB chief said repeatedly to his fellow conspirators.

Maybe it was the weather that confused everyone, the bright sun and cool wind that duped one into thinking that soon all was going to be just fine. Or maybe it was the news that Lazar Kaganovich, Stalin's last surviving lieutenant, had dropped dead.

For nearly four years I had been trying to meet Kaganovich, all to no avail. "I see no one," he said over the phone in a voice like worn leather. He had been duped once. A Soviet pensioner, pretending friendship, had come by to talk, and the old and lonely man had let him in, answered his questions. He never suspected his remarks would be published in *Sovetskaya Kultura.* In that conversation, Kaganovich made no apologies for his life, and described the reform of the Stalinist state in a tone of wan disgust. He thought it incredible that people could still blame Stalin for the rotten state of the country.

"Stalin died thirty-five years ago!" he said. And besides, how could they attack a man who "saved the country from fascism"?

Kaganovich complained about his health, his heart attacks, his sleepless

nights. But one thing, he said, kept him going: "Socialism will be victorious. Of this I am sure." It was outrageous, he said, that we were letting Hungary and Poland and the rest "return to a bourgeois line." Here, in the Soviet Union, such a reversal was impossible.

"I believe in the strength of our party," Kaganovich said. "And socialism will be victorious. This is for sure."

Even in death, Lazar Moiseyevich managed to insult his country's dignity. In the 1930s, the secret police used to bring the bodies for cremation to the Donskoi Monastery. At the height of the purges, as many as one thousand victims were cremated there every day. And now Kaganovich, who oversaw much of this industry, was going to be cremated at Donskoi.

While I was off doing summit business, my friend Masha Lipman managed to sneak into Kaganovich's apartment and had a long talk with the old man's nurse. The poor women smelled as if she'd downed at least a bottle of vodka. The apartment was like the library of a ghost, shelves packed with dusty volumes of Communist Party proceedings from long ago.

At Donskoi, Kaganovich's mourners did not seem much interested in the man's victims. They crowded around a dilapidated bus as it pulled onto the grounds, the long, ribbon-covered coffin laid out in the rear end. Kaganovich's daughter, Maya, an old woman herself, led the relatives into the chapel. Before the eulogy, someone opened the coffin lid to reveal the face of Stalin's loyal henchman: black suit, flabby neck, long nose, a fine gray mustache, a huge and withered corpse. The mourners listened as they heard the brief eulogy lauding the great man's construction of the Moscow subway. No one mentioned that he had played a leading role in collectivization. When the eulogy was over, the coffin somehow sank below floor level and automatic doors closed over it. The furnace, I was told, was downstairs. Soon Kaganovich would be a handful of ash.

Outside, afterward, Kaganovich's nephew Leonid told me, "History is still being debated. But what is evil? You must understand the times he lived in." Besides the family, there were about a hundred Stalinists there to bury their last great hero. People were weeping. "He was a man who never changed his mind," said Kira Korniyenkova, one of the Stalinists in town I knew best. "He was a great Marxist-Leninist." Another mourner told me, through his tears, that this was a great man, but "if it were Gorbachev laid out dead here today, I wouldn't lay down a single flower, I can tell you that."

As we left the monastery, Masha and I saw Ales Adamovich. A few years before, Adamovich had been sued by the Stalinist lawyer Ivan Shekhovtsov for slander. It was Adamovich who had warned Gorbachev in the Congress

of the generals who would one day commit bloodshed and wipe the evidence on his suit. He could not resist going to the funeral of Lazar Kaganovich. "Stalin and Hitler and Nero: I think Kaganovich fits into the list," he told me. "This represents the fall of Stalinism. So who will be next to die? The Communist Party itself?" I'd never met a man at a funeral in a better mood.

Maybe what made the men of the regime seem so vulnerable that summer was that they had long ago lost the Mystery.

The Mystery—the theological notion that the acts and purposes of the deity are unknowable—was always a critical part of the pseudo-theology of the atheist state. Stalin must have gotten the idea during his failed career in the seminary. One of the keys to his own mystery was to stay out of sight; hence, a pockmarked mediocrity becomes a god. For decades, the Thursday-morning meetings of the Politburo were more mysterious than sessions of the College of Cardinals; transfers of power were more difficult to decipher in the Kremlin than in the Vatican. The catechism language of *Vremya,* the iconic posters of the great leaders, all added to the Mystery. And now it was all but gone. Now we learned from the press the details of the Lenin Mausoleum; it turned out that there were other floors beneath the holy of holies, and on one of them there was the gymnasium for the guards and a bathroom and buffet for visiting luminaries; beneath that there was a "control room" which carefully monitored the temperature and deterioration of Vladimir Ilyich. Yeltsin's memoir, *Against the Grain,* became an underground best-seller precisely because it hacked away at the Mystery. He revealed what the mighty talked about in private, their petty greed, their weakness. He described for all Gorbachev's taste for luxury, his marble bathrooms and swimming pools.

One morning, *Komsomolskaya Pravda* ran a story about a woman who had worked for many years as a seamstress in the secret tailor shop the KGB maintained for the use of the country's highest leaders. Klava Lyubeshkina stitched suits for everyone, from the entombed corpse of Lenin ("every eighteen months the cloth begins to lose its original splendor") to Gorbachev. "The tailor dummies of the Politburo members were kept in special closets which nobody except us, the cutters and tailors, dared ever to touch," she told the paper. "We always worked behind closed doors and surrounded by armed guards. . . . Two or three times a year a KGB specialist would go abroad, usually to Scotland or Austria, to buy material for the suits."

The secret police had opened the shop in 1938, the height of the purges. Klava saw her customers only on *Vremya* and referred to them, mysteriously, as "units." She was devoted. She would watch the leaders on television expressly "to see if their suits fit them well or if there were wrinkles." She

remembered how she worked night and day for three days to get ready the gold-embroidered laurel leaves and stars in heavy gold thread for the new defense minister, Marshal Ustinov. She remembered Andrei Gromyko's stinginess ("He always sent in for repairs, never a new suit") and Mikhail Suslov's temper tantrums when the fit was not quite right.

Klava's sense of the Mystery ended one day when three men in white smocks attacked her, twisted her arms behind her back, and dragged her off to a psychiatric clinic. The KGB had mistaken her for a dissident. Klava asked to be released, saying that she was making a suit for Yuri Andropov which had been left "unattended" at the studio. The agents let her use the phone and she was able to tell her colleagues where she was. Soon the KGB released her. For the "moral damage" committed, the state awarded Klava a Japanese watch. Just before she retired in 1987, she had the pleasure of making a suit for Gorbachev. The new Soviet leader rewarded her with a box of chocolates.

In her old age, Klava received a poverty-level pension of 100 rubles a month. She wrote the Kremlin for more but got nothing. The Bolsheviks, however, could not be counted as unfeeling men. In 1991, Kryuchkov mailed all the seamstresses cards wishing them well on International Women's Day. Klava, for her part, took her pleasure in revealing her trove of secrets from the Kremlin sweatshop to the twenty-five million readers of *Komsomolskaya Pravda.* "We worked there for so long in silence," she said, "and all along we wanted to reveal the mystery."

Most of the apparatchiks who still came to work at the Central Committee that summer were tired and old and deeply worried. They were hanging on, hoping to get another year on the gravy train. The smart ones had all become businessmen.

Arkady Volsky had been a loyal servant to the Party. He was an aide to Andropov, a captain of socialist industry, an adviser to Gorbachev. And he knew what was coming. So Volsky and some of his semiliberal and ultra-clever friends started to take a look around at the new world. They saw how the Young Communist League, once the incubator of rising ideologues, had become the Harvard Business School of the new culture, turning out entrepreneurs who moved quickly into everything from video-game concessions to computer sales to publishing. With access to government connections, extraordinary tax breaks, and hundreds of millions of rubles in Party funds, Komsomol leaders set up huge commercial banks that began to dominate the Soviet financial scene. Some of the older liberals in the Party were cashing in, too. Svyatoslav Fyodorov, an internationally known ophthalmologist and

member of the Central Committee until 1990, set up a modern, independent clinic and made a fortune. When Prime Minister Pavlov visited Fyodorov's clinic and demanded 80 percent of the clinic's hard currency earnings, Fyodorov told him, "Fuck off."

"The political fight for power now is the fight for property," Fyodorov told *Komsomolskaya Pravda.* "If people get property, they will have power. If not, they will forever remain hired hands."

Volsky and an experienced factory manager named Aleksandr Vladislavlev started the Scientific Industrial Union. The idea was that they would act as fixers between potential foreign investors and the existing enterprises in the Soviet Union. As if to make sure that everyone understood the kind of connections he had within the Party and the world of Soviet industry, Volsky rented office space for 750,000 rubles a year in a building adjacent to the Central Committee. "We're here for the same reason a bank in New York wants to be on Fifth Avenue," Vladislavlev told me. It was brilliant. The union was the place to go for high-powered access. "We link our resources and cheap labor with your brains and technology," Vladislavlev said. "You come to us because we know where the best deals in privatization are." Thirty-nine Soviet industrial associations, such as the Association of Military Factories, paid 10,000 rubles annually to be members. Another two thousand individual enterprises paid a percentage of their profits as dues.

It was a sweet deal, and I wrote an article for the *Post* about the emerging class of Communists-turned-capitalists in the spring. When a couple of my editors came for the Bush summit, I had to find places for them to go, people for them to see. They mentioned they might like to see Arkady Volsky. Why not?

We arrived, three of us, at Volsky's office for what we thought would be an interview about the economy.

"Pleased to meet you," Volsky greeted one editor.

"Pleased to meet you," he said to the next.

And then to me, "Less pleased to meet you."

He glared and flared his nostrils like a bull. This was not going to be easy, I thought. I had no idea why.

For a few minutes, Volsky complained that my article had been unfair, that it made fun of a "normal" process of creating a market economy. But then his complaints took an ugly turn. Volsky noted that I had written that one of his main "konsooltants" was Rodimir Bogdanov, a well-known KGB officer. Through the late stagnation and early glasnost years, Bogdanov was one of the few people visiting foreigners could come to for an interview. What's more, Volsky pointed out, I had written that Seagram's chairman Edgar Bronfman and the real estate and publishing magnate Mortimer Zuck-

erman had met with Bogdanov and other people at the union in hopes of completing possible business deals.

"You are the worst kind of anti-Semite!" Volsky barked. Why had I besmirched the reputation of such a good man as Bogdanov, why had I mentioned two such obviously Jewish names as Bronfman and Zuckerman. "Don't you realize what people will do with this?"

I could not quite tell yet whether Volsky, in his fury, knew that I was Jewish. To be frank, a Malawi tribesman could take one look at me and say, "This man is a Jew." But Volsky was off on a flight.

"This is ridiculous," I said finally. "Don't you realize I'm no different from Zuckerman or Bronfman? Just poorer. Where do you get off lecturing me on anti-Semitism?"

I did not understand what it was all about until Volsky finally said, "Don't you realize what those people up the hill can do with this?"

"Up the hill" from us was Lubyanka, the headquarters of the KGB.

—

Volsky, for all his financial cleverness, for all his guile and connections to the military industrialists, was one of the moderates in the upper echelons of the apparat. He helped found in August, with Yakovlev, Shevardnadze, Popov, and Sobchak, the new Movement for Democratic Reforms. And like the others, he had a sixth sense for what was brewing in the minds of the men who would make the coup. Volsky was a nervous wreck, and he had taken a little bit of it out on me.

The liberals who still had some access to Gorbachev were hopeful about the new alliance with Yeltsin, but they saw ominous signs that summer. They had always known, despite their public assurances, that an open counterrevolution was a possibility. The truth was, Shevardnadze told me, "We have always had difficulties since the very first days of the April plenum in 1985 and the beginning of perestroika. If someone thinks that Pavlov, Kryuchkov, and Yazov's predecessors were more progressive, they are mistaken. There were also very strong conservatives back then. It's important to have at least a general idea of the sort of struggle there was in the political leadership for the 'general line' and for perestroika."

Shevardnadze said that after his resignation as foreign minister in December 1990, he still got calls from his conservative rivals in the leadership on matters of practical politics: how to deal with the Afghans, who was who in the various Western governments. But he said he noticed by about June 1991 that he was no longer being consulted as he had been. He got the sense that a vacuum was growing around him and that his phone was bugged. "A shadow power was forming," Shevardnadze said.

Yakovlev, too, said he watched helplessly as Lukyanov, Kryuchkov, and the rest surrounded Gorbachev with deceptive advice. "These are toadies," Yakovlev told me. "They will look at you with these honest blue eyes and say, 'We're with the people, we're your only saviors, the only ones who love and respect you. And these democrats, they criticize and insult you.' Gradually, it affects a person. Lukyanov would pretend to be a democratic cohort, and then at Politburo sessions he would be a bigger hawk than anyone. Lukyanov would say, 'Suppress them totally! Mercilessly!' He would say, 'You know, Mikhail Sergeyevich, they are aiming at you, they are trying to get you, to overthrow you.' "

In July, just before he left Gorbachev's staff for good, Yakovlev told Gorbachev, "The people around you are rotten. Please, finally, understand this."

"You exaggerate," Gorbachev said.

Shevardnadze and Yakovlev, the two men who had been closest to Gorbachev at the peak of perestroika, now watched helplessly as the storm clouds gathered. "Gorbachev is a man of character. A person with no character could not have started perestroika himself," Shevardnadze wrote in his memoir. "Gorbachev will enter history as a great reformer, a great revolutionary. It was not so easy to begin. But he enjoyed maneuvering too much. . . . Of course, a major politician has to know how to maneuver, but there must be limits. There comes a moment when one has to say that tactical considerations are not the most important thing, that this is my strategy, my stake is with democracy and the democratic forces. And in this, he was too late, my dear friend."

The hints of betrayal were everywhere that summer. Gorbachev's press secretary, Vitaly Ignatenko, picked up little clues of impertinence and overconfidence among the conservatives that worried him. He saw how on August 2, before there was any order from Gorbachev, someone cut off Yakovlev's Kremlin phone lines and government communications systems. Meanwhile, the darling of the apparatchiks, Yegor Ligachev, who had been retired for a year, still had Kremlin phone lines . . . in his apartment.

Ignatenko also said that while he was on vacation in Sochi in the days before the coup, he noticed that Politburo member Oleg Shenin moved into dacha No. 4 on the special compound, a separate personal residence. "He was vacationing not according to his rank," Ignatenko said, "but in a huge dacha which had not been occupied in six years or more. . . . Only the president had the right to his own dacha there, or maybe the prime minister."

For those in the know, the clues were unending. Aleksandr Prokhanov told *Nezavisimaya Gazeta* that the time had come for the "patriotic forces" to seize power "by the throat." Prokhanov said that the movement allying

"Marxist-Leninists, Marxist-Stalinists, Russian Communists, social democratic liberals, extremist pro-fascist organizations, writers, artists, the military industrialists, monarchists, and pagans" was forming fast to prevent the disintegration of the country. "Our nation should have a real leader," he said. "People cannot be left to the mercy of fate at a time like this."

In June, Kryuchkov flew to Havana at the personal invitation of Fidel Castro. According to a report in *Izvestia* months later, Kryuchkov concluded several secret agreements with Castro in which they assured each other that Cuba would remain Communist and in the Soviet sphere of influence—despite the conflicts between the two countries during the Gorbachev era. A few weeks later, Kryuchkov's ally Vice President Gennadi Yanayev sent Castro a letter saying that he should not worry about the situation in Moscow: "Soon there will be a change for the better."

On August 6, after Gorbachev and his family had flown to the Crimea for their summer vacation, Kryuchkov called two of his top aides and told them to write a detailed memorandum analyzing the situation in the country in terms of instituting an immediate state of emergency. The two KGB officials were joined by General Pavel Grachev of the Ministry of Defense. After two days at the KGB's posh recreation and work complex in the village of Mashkino, the working group told Kryuchkov that a state of emergency would be an extremely complicated affair politically and might even cause further disorder in the country.

"But after the Union Treaty is signed it will be too late to institute a state of emergency," Kryuchkov told them.

On August 14, Kryuchkov called the working group together once more and told them to work out documents for a state of emergency. They had no time to lose. By the 16th, a draft of the first declaration of the State Committee for the State of Emergency was on Kryuchkov's desk. At two o'clock that afternoon, Kryuchkov called in his deputy Genii Ageyev and told him to form a group to go to Foros in the Crimea to plan the disconnection of Gorbachev's communication system with the outside world.

In mid-August, Esther and I were preparing to leave Moscow after three and a half years. We were going to miss our friends, our life in Moscow, but there was a vacation to take and a year-old son, Alex, who had not gotten to know his grandparents and countless cousins. It was time. In those first weeks of August, we said good-bye to friends, and during the day I tried to finish up some pieces and interviews that I wanted to do before going home. Aleksandr

Yakovlev, for one, agreed to see me a few days before I left, and I went with Michael Dobbs and Masha Lipman to meet him at his new office at the Moscow City Hall. We talked about many things, especially some of the main events of the previous six years, and at one point we asked if there would be a military coup. He said the reactionary forces were still dangerous, but as for a military coup, well, there was no tradition of it, and besides, the military "can't run anything on its own—including the military."

It was strange, then, that two days later, on the 16th, in his resignation from the Communist Party, Yakovlev issued a statement via the Interfax news wire, saying, "The truth is that the Party leadership, in contradiction to its own declarations, is ridding itself of the democratic wing of the Party and is preparing for social revenge and for a Party and state coup." In view of what was to come, it seemed that Yakovlev had found something out, something specific, on the 15th or 16th. But months later, in a second interview, Yakovlev told me that he knew nothing about the actual planning for the coup. "It's just that there was a certain logic at work, a feeling I had," he said. "It made sense that they would struggle for their power. Without it, they had no future."

On August 17, Shevardnadze told me later, Yakovlev and the other twenty-one leaders of the Movement for Democratic Reforms had met in a closed session and agreed unanimously that a right-wing coup was an imminent threat. "This should have been more than enough warning," Shevardnadze said. "I reprove the president because he could have come to the same conclusion and the coup would have been prevented."

The U.S. government was concerned as well. Intelligence reports only grew more anxious after Baker's meeting with Bessmertnykh in Berlin. In fact, it turned out, according to documents recovered later, that Kryuchkov began holding meetings and drawing up plans for a coup as early as November 1990.

On the 17th, Esther and I went on a picnic in the country with a bunch of our friends and everyone's babies. The kids splashed around at the river's edge and smeared themselves with lunch. We watched the Russians sunbathe, marveling at how you could actually see their winter-pale flesh flame up as quickly as a sheet of paper.

After a while, Masha, Seriozha, and I took a long walk along the river and through the woods, past the dilapidated dachas and the old men in dirty T-shirts working on cars that would never run again, past kids chasing their dogs in the dust.

A few weeks before, the three of us had gone to a meeting of Moscow

Tribune and heard Andrei Nuikin, a popular journalist and activist, say that a coup d'état was "not only possible, but inevitable." Nuikin had been saying this for years, and we left the meeting that day thinking he was slightly off his rocker, like someone who has been poring over the Kennedy assassination just a little too long.

Now, as we walked, I asked Seriozha and Masha what they thought. The most important thing, they said, was that they had decided they would never leave, no matter what happened.

"We have this 'last boat out' policy," Masha said. "And that is that if things go really bad, if there are tanks in the streets and people are starving, if the worst happens, then we'll leave to save the kids. But not before that."

"Besides, a coup would never hold," Seriozha said. "I'd be shocked if they were stupid enough to try it, more shocked if it lasted."

That same afternoon, at a KGB compound outside Moscow known as ABC, Vladimir Kryuchkov convened a meeting of conspirators. It was another of the KGB's sanatoria, with a swimming pool, saunas, a movie theater, and masseuses. Kryuchkov could feel sure that the meeting would be confidential here. The compound was surrounded by guards and high walls. Gorbachev and his more liberal aides, Anatoly Chernyayev and Georgi Shakhnazarov, were all on vacation in the Crimea. And who listened to Shevardnadze or Yakovlev anymore?

Kryuchkov convened the session outdoors, at a picnic table. Present there were Defense Minister Yazov, Prime Minister Pavlov, Politburo chief Oleg Shenin, military industries chief Oleg Baklanov, and presidential chief of staff Valery Boldin. There were assorted snacks on the table, and everyone drank either Russian vodka or imported whiskey.

"The situation is catastrophic," Pavlov said. "The country is facing famine. It is in total chaos. Nobody wants to carry out orders. The harvest is disorganized. Machines are idle because they have no spare parts, no fuel. The only hope is a state of emergency."

Kryuchkov and the others agreed. "I regularly brief Gorbachev on the difficult situation," Kryuchkov said. "But he is not reacting adequately. He cuts me short and changes the subject. He does not trust my information."

This was not the first such meeting of the hard-liners, and these were the familiar complaints. But now the situation had changed, grown more urgent. Gorbachev was planning to return to Moscow to sign the new Union Treaty with Yeltsin and the other republican leaders on August 20. With Kryuchkov as their leader, the conspirators decided they could not wait. They would notify their other allies: Vice President Gennady Yanayev, Interior Minister

Boris Pugo, and Supreme Soviet Chairman Anatoly Lukyanov. Months later Lukyanov ruefully told *The Washington Post* that Gorbachev had surely adopted "antisocialist positions" and that a state of emergency was required to "save the existing order." But, he admitted, the opportunity to succeed had been "hopelessly missed." Yeltsin and the other republican leaders were now too strong, too popular.

Still, the conspirators pressed on. They decided to send a delegation to the Crimea to confront Gorbachev. They would give him an ultimatum: support the state of emergency or step down. Someone suggested that one member of the delegation ought to be Boldin, Gorbachev's chief of staff, his liegeman for more than a decade.

Yazov turned to Boldin and said, *"Et tu, Brute?"*

On his trip home, Yazov recalled later, he felt a fleeting sense of pity for Gorbachev.

"If he had signed the treaty and then gone on vacation," the marshal thought, "everything would have been fine."

AUGUST 18, 1991

The morning after he'd been arrested, Marshal Dmitri Yazov sat in full-dress uniform and answered the first questions of the Russian prosecutor. Yazov said he felt like "an old idiot." He would spend the rest of his life wondering how he could have been so stupid, how he could do something that would bring such dishonor on him and the armed forces that he had served for a half century. The plot was slipshod from the first, he admitted, the product of occasional emotional discussions and then the sudden impulse to head off Gorbachev and the republican leaders before it was too late.

"We were already meeting earlier at various places. We talked about the situation in the country," Yazov said in his slow, slightly doltish voice. "It was unavoidable that we came to the conclusion that the president was to blame. He had distanced himself from the Party. . . . Gorbachev in recent years had been going abroad and often we had no idea in general what he was discussing there. . . . We were just not ready to become greatly dependent on the U.S.A., politically, economically or militarily. . . ."

QUESTION: In what form did you make a decision?

YAZOV: There was no real plan for a plot. We met on Saturday [August 17].

QUESTION: At whose invitation?

YAZOV: Kryuchkov's.

QUESTION: Where did you meet?

YAZOV: At a point in Moscow at the end of Leninski Prospekt—a left turn near the police post, there is a road there. . . . At the end of the working day, Kryuchkov called and said we had to talk. I came. Then Shenin came, then Baklanov. And then it was said: maybe we should go to Gorbachev and speak with him.

QUESTION: Why was there such a hurry? Was it because the Union Treaty was to be signed [on the 20th]?

YAZOV: Of course. We were not happy with this draft and we knew the state would fall apart. . . .

QUESTION: What brought up the idea of an Emergency Committee?

YAZOV: We were in Pavlov's office. Yanayev was there, and at about nine Lukyanov came. He came by plane. He'd been on vacation. Lukyanov said: "I can't be a member of such a committee, I'm chairman of the Supreme Soviet, a legal organ which is ruled by this and that. Naturally, I can do something—I put out an announcement saying that the result of the Union Treaty would be the destruction of the constitution." After that, he left. Yanayev was already rather drunk. . . .

The last good coup operation had been in Poland, in December 1981. On a freezing night between 2:00 and 3:00 A.M., the military and the secret police rounded up thousands of Solidarity activists and sympathizers and locked them up in "internment camps." The military regime secured the borders and then invaded its own country with tanks and troops, cutting up Warsaw and other key areas into carefully patrolled zones. They took over the radio and television stations. Over and over, they broadcast martial music, the national anthem, and the words of the Leader, the declaration of a "state of war." In case anyone missed the point, the newscasters wore army uniforms. All demonstrations, all unions and student organizations were banned, all mail and telephone traffic censored. There was a curfew from 10:00 P.M. to 6:00 A.M. The Military Council told the population that they were acting to prevent a "reactionary coup." They were acting in the name of "national salvation." It was a perfect operation.

Perfect, but nothing new. In a letter dated September 26–27, 1917, Lenin wrote a letter that later became a widely distributed pamphlet called "Marxism and Rebellion." Just a few months from grabbing power, he was clearly obsessed with the need for absolute ruthlessness and efficiency: "To approach a rebellion in a Marxist way," he wrote, "that is, as one would an art, it is necessary not to lose a minute moving loyal battalions to the most important objects, to arrest the government . . . seize the telegraph and telephone.

. . . One cannot at this critical moment remain true to Marxism and not treat rebellion as an art."

The successors to Lenin and Jaruzelski made feeble attempts to ape the old efficiency. From a factory in Pskov, they ordered a quarter million pairs of handcuffs; they ordered the printing of 300,000 arrest forms. Kryuchkov issued secret orders doubling the pay of all KGB men and called them back from vacation to go on alert. He cleared out two floors of Lefortovo Prison and prepared a secret bunker in Lubyanka in case the leaders of the coup needed to find safe refuge. And to keep pace with the times, they would carry out the coup under legal pretenses: a nation in crisis, a president taken ill. They would fill the stores for a few months, drawing on military stockpiles kept in case of war. The people would acquiesce. Hadn't they always?

Gorbachev was resting in splendor. When he came to power in 1985, he built himself a magnificent place to rest, a compound in the Crimean town of Foros that cost the Soviet government an estimated $20 million. He and his family lived in the main house, a three-story structure with a central hall done up in marble and gilt. It was the sort of opulence you see sometimes when a sheik moves into Beverley Hills. There was a hotel for the staff and security guards, a guest house for thirty people, fruit trees, an olive grove, an indoor swimming pool, a movie theater, an elaborate security system, and an escalator to the Black Sea.

It was a wonder that Gorbachev went on his vacation at all. At the worst moments, it was never really safe for him to leave Moscow. The Nina Andreyeva letter in 1988 was published as he was leaving for Yugoslavia. The planning for the Tbilisi massacre of 1989 came when he was in England. The conservatives in the Politburo often made right-wing speeches when Gorbachev was in the Crimea. And now, despite all the warnings and omens, he left Moscow again. He took long walks on the beach with Raisa. He swam, watched movies, read volumes on Russian and Soviet history. His doctors did what they could for his bad back. Gorbachev also took time to write a speech for the Union Treaty signing ceremonies and a long article on the future—an article that even pondered the possibility of a right-wing coup.

Gorbachev has said that he was not naive, he knew well what the conservatives were capable of; but he has also insisted that he had no prior knowledge that there would be a coup, or even a concerted demand for the declaration of a state of emergency. According to phone logs obtained by Cable News Network, Gorbachev talked four times with Kryuchkov on August 18; he also talked with Yanayev, Shenin, Pavlov, and the deputy prime minister,

Vladimir Shcherbakov. Sometime after 2:00 P.M., Yanayev called Gorbachev and asked about meeting him at the airport in Moscow when he returned from vacation the next day. They agreed to see each other then.

Yanayev, who was probably making sure the mark was still in place, was the worst sort of Party nonentity. He was a vain man of small intelligence, a womanizer, and a drunk. I'm not sure it is possible to describe just how hard it is to acquire a reputation as a drunk in Russia. And Yanayev was not merely a drunk, he was a buffoon. On the day he went before the Congress for confirmation as vice president, one of the deputies asked him if he was a healthy man. "My wife has no complaints," Yanayev said and snickered.

At around 4:00 P.M., Georgi Shakhnazarov, one of Gorbachev's last remaining liberal advisers, called to check on details for the trip to Moscow. Then, almost as an afterthought, Shakhnazarov asked Gorbachev about his health. Gorbachev said he was fine except for his chronic back pain.

Gorbachev had worked hard on his speech for the treaty signing, and now he wanted to spend some time with Raisa and their daughter, Irina, son-in-law, Anatoly, and granddaughter, Oksana. But at 4:50, the chief of Gorbachev's security detail told him that they had unexpected visitors, including Yuri Plekhanov, the head of the KGB's Ninth Directorate, the division charged with the security of the leadership.

Gorbachev picked up a phone to find out what this was all about. He had called no meetings and he was not accustomed to unannounced visitors. The line was dead. Then he picked up another, also dead. Gorbachev was stunned. Raisa came in to see what was going on. "Mikhail Sergeyevich has eight or ten telephone operators and all the phones were silent," she said later. "I picked up the receiver and checked it out and all the phones were silent, even that of the commander in chief. We have this phone everywhere—in our country house, in our flat—everywhere. It's under a kind of lid and we do not even remove dust from this phone because we are not supposed to remove the lid. He picked up the receiver on that phone and there was silence there. We knew that was it. There was nothing else we could do."

Before the visitors got inside the house, Gorbachev knew perfectly well something was very wrong. He called his family around him and told them "that anything could follow this." They, in turn, said they were ready to see it through with him "to the end." Later, when she described the scene, Raisa seemed to refer to the murder of the Romanov family after the Bolshevik coup to describe the depths of her own worst fears: "We know our history and its tragic aspects."

"I paced the room and thought," Gorbachev recalled. "Not about myself, but about my family, my granddaughters. I decided: in this situation, it is impossible to value my own skin."

The delegation arrived: Plekhanov, Shenin from the Politburo, Baklanov of the military-industrial complex, Gorbachev's personal assistant, Boldin, and, representing the army, General Varennikov, the head of ground forces. Gorbachev led them to his study.

"Who sent you?" he said.

"The committee," one of them said. "The committee appointed in connection with the emergency."

"Who appointed such a committee? I didn't appoint such a committee, and neither did the Supreme Soviet."

Varennikov told Gorbachev he had little choice. Either go along or resign.

"You are nothing but adventurers and traitors, and you will pay for this. I don't care what happens to you, but you will destroy the country. Only those who want to commit suicide can now suggest a totalitarian regime in the country. You are pushing it to a civil war!"

Gorbachev reminded the delegation that there was to be a signing ceremony of the Union Treaty in Moscow on August 20.

"There will be no signing," Baklanov said, according to Gorbachev. Then Baklanov said, "Yeltsin's been arrested. He'll be arrested. . . . Mikhail Sergeyevich, we demand nothing from you. You'll be here. We'll do all the dirty work for you."

Gorbachev said he would play no part in their "adventure." The delegation continued to press. They gave Gorbachev a list of the members of the State Committee for the State of Emergency (the GKChP). Gorbachev was especially stunned to see the names of Yazov and Kryuchkov. He had plucked Yazov out of obscurity to make him defense minister precisely for the sake of having his own man. And besides, he was not bright enough to be disloyal. Yazov, Aleksandr Yakovlev would say, "is no Spinoza." Kryuchkov, who was perhaps the most forceful and determined of all the plotters, surprised Gorbachev because he had come through the recommendation of their mutual mentor, Yuri Andropov. Gorbachev thought of Kryuchkov as a cultured man, someone who had been abroad, seen something more than the inside of Lubyanka. But as the prosecutor's report on the putsch said, "For Kryuchkov, Gorbachev was a madman. Gorbachev destroyed the system that had given him everything—servile aides, the respect of his foes, and a comfortable, even splendid life-style. Could a person in his right mind get rid of all that?" Time and again, Kryuchkov urged Gorbachev to break up demonstrations, to "show, at last, our strength." And when Gorbachev would refuse, Kryuchkov would tell his friends, "The president is not responding to events."

Boldin was a terrible betrayal, too. He had started working for Gorbachev in 1978 and had his absolute trust. Boldin was the chief of staff. He vetted

every appointment, controlled absolutely the flow of paper to the president's desk. Along with Kryuchkov and Boldin, the other chief plotter was Oleg Baklanov, a figure little known to the public, but one with tremendous power. Baklanov's chief interest in a coup was clear: he wanted to prevent any deterioration of military spending or might. In one speech prepared for the April 1991 plenum of the Central Committee, he wrote that current policy had caused the Soviet Union to "fall practically under the dictate of the United States." According to one of the country's leading weapons scientists, Pyotr Korotkevich, Baklanov "froze" a major plan worked out by specialists in the hierarchy to create a smaller, but professional, army, demilitarize the economy, and reduce military spending by half.

The rest of the list was less surprising. Pavlov and Yanayev were obvious enemies of radical reform, though they were too bumptious, too drunk, to have acted alone. The rest were symbols of the conservative interests. Aleksandr Tizyakov, the president of the Association of State Enterprises, had given Gorbachev an ultimatum the previous December to end strikes and impose economic discipline. "You want to frighten me," Gorbachev had said then. "Well, it won't work." And there was Vasily Starodubtsev, the head of the Union of Collective Farm Chairmen, an ardent opponent of private farming and private property.

Gorbachev tried now to persuade the delegation to take up the question of a state of emergency in the parliament. There could be a full debate. Let the Supreme Soviet decide. "If you go to a state of emergency, what are you going to do the next day?" Gorbachev told them. Varennikov said they were carrying out this mission because the "committee" would not allow "separatists" and "extremists" to dictate the future of the country.

"I've heard all this," Gorbachev said. "Do you think the people are so fatigued that they will just follow any dictator?"

But it was no use. "It was a conversation with deaf mutes," Gorbachev said later. "Their cycle was in motion."

As the delegation was preparing to leave at about 7:30 P.M., Baklanov stuck out his hand to shake hands with Raisa Maksimovna. She looked at him, said nothing, and walked away. The delegation rode back to the Belbek airport. In the front seat, Plekhanov spoke on the radiophone to Foros, giving further instructions on the isolation of the president. In the back, the others spoke in short, disgruntled phrases. They had thought Gorbachev would give in to their demands, and he hadn't On the trip back to Moscow, they began to drink.

—

Raisa, the Gorbachevs' daughter, Irina, and Gorbachev's aide, Anatoly Chernyayev, had waited outside the study until the meeting was over. After the plotters left, Gorbachev looked at Chernyayev and said, "Well, have you guessed?"

"Yes."

Gorbachev described the demands and his replies "in terms I cannot repeat with ladies present." He showed Raisa a list of the conspirators he had copied down, and added at the bottom "Lukyanov . . . ?" He still could not see that his great and loyal friend from college days had turned on him, too.

Gorbachev said he would not go along with a state of emergency or a return to dictatorial rule. "I was always an opponent of such measures," he said later, "not only for moral and political reasons, but because in the history of our country they have always led to the deaths of hundreds, thousands, and millions. . . . And we need to get away from that forever."

Raisa said that it would be best now, if there was anything to discuss, to talk out on the balconies and on the beach, the better to avoid the listening devices that were obviously in place and working.

When they arrived at the Kremlin that evening, Vice President Yanayev and Prime Minister Pavlov (the twin fools of this low comedy) saw Kryuchkov, Boldin, Shenin, Pugo, Yazov, and the rest sitting at a long conference table. Lukyanov called from his car and said he was on the way. No one sat at the head of the table, the president's chair.

"A catastrophe is taking place," Kryuchkov said. There would soon be an armed uprising against the leadership. They were going to take over key points, the television tower at Ostankino, the rail stations, two hotels. They had heavy arms, missile launchers, everything. They must be stopped and there were only a few hours in which to do it. Then Plekhanov chimed in. He and Boldin had just come back from Foros. Gorbachev was ill. "It's either a heart attack or a stroke or something," Boldin said.

Yanayev hesitated. He said he could not sign the document creating the Emergency Committee and making him the new president. Kryuchkov pressed him. "Can't you see?" he said. "If we don't save the harvest, there will be hunger and in a few months the people will be on the streets. There will be a civil war."

Yanayev was smoking one cigarette after another. He said he wanted to wait to meet with Gorbachev before taking action, and besides, he did not feel morally prepared or otherwise qualified to be the president. But the men

around the table kept after him, stressing that Gorbachev was sick, that the situation would be temporary.

INVESTIGATOR: Why did it fall apart?

VALENTIN PAVLOV: Most of those present [at the Kremlin on the 18th] did not understand what the whole thing was about. Emergency measures had been discussed before. They'd been discussed in the spring. So there was nothing unusual about it. But when it came to Gorbachev being sick and no one knowing what was wrong, when it was unclear whether or not he could fulfill his duties, then we hesitated and decided to transfer it to the Supreme Soviet. Yanayev did not want to sign it. He kept saying, "Guys, I do not know what to write. Is he sick or not? It's all hearsay." The rest said, "Take the decision." Whose word did he take? Hard to tell.

Lukyanov arrived late to the meeting carrying a copy of the draft Union Treaty and the Soviet Constitution under his arm. Eventually, after listening to Lukyanov describe how the Supreme Soviet would eventually "legitimize" the state of emergency, Yanayev began to waver.

"Sign, Gennadi Ivanovich," Kryuchkov said.

And finally he did. In his trembling hand, Yanayev signed the documents grabbing power from his president. Then he passed the document around the table. One after the other, Yazov, Pugo, Kryuchkov, Pavlov, and Baklanov put their names to the decree declaring the state of emergency.

Now Aleksandr Bessmertnykh, Shevardnadze's successor as foreign minister, arrived. He had been on vacation and had flown to the meeting having no idea what was going on. Kryuchkov took him into an anteroom.

"Listen, the situation in the country is terrible," Kryuchkov said. "A chaotic situation has emerged. It's a crisis. It's dangerous. People are disappointed. Something should be done, and we decided to do something through emergency measures. We have established a committee, an Emergency Committee, and I would like you to be part of it."

"Is the committee arranged by the instructions of the president?" Bessmertnykh asked.

"No," Kryuchkov said. "He's incapable of functioning now. He's flat on his back at his dacha."

Bessmertnykh asked for a medical report, but Kryuchkov refused. Something was obviously very strange about this, though Bessmertnykh's instincts either were not sharp enough or he saw danger and tried to negotiate a safe course for himself. In the days to come he called in sick and refused to come out publicly against the coup. But at least he turned down Kryuchkov.

"I am not going to be part of this committee and I categorically reject any participation in that," he said.

As they went back to the meeting, Kryuchkov told the others that the foreign minister had refused. Bessmertnykh told the group that their idea would isolate the country, it would bring on sanctions from the West, maybe a grain embargo. The committee seemed glum. They so wanted the appearance of consensus, of legality, before the world and the people.

"We still need a liberal," Kryuchkov said.

"Then the so-called committee began to fall apart and to split," Pavlov told the prosecutors months later. "The whole situation was odd. Bessmertnykh fell sick. I was sort of carried out of the room. I did not think it would end this way. If someone had not decided out of foolishness to bring in the military hardware, nothing at all would have happened."

At one point at the Kremlin meeting, Lukyanov asked what sort of plan had been worked out, what the details of the state of emergency were. In fact, was there a plan?

"Why do you say that?" Yazov said. "We have a plan." But as he told the prosecutors later, Yazov knew there was nothing. "I knew we had nothing except the sketch that we had been absorbed in that Saturday at ABC. This was no plan and I knew very clearly that, in any case, we had no real aim at all."

AUGUST 19, 1991

Ol'var Kakuchaya, the director of *Vremya,* was dead asleep when the phone rang at 1:30 A.M. It was his boss on the line, the head of state television and radio, Leonid Kravchenko.

"Ol'var, what's your address?" Kravchenko said urgently.

"Are you sending someone to me?"

"I want to send a car."

"What for?"

"I'll tell you when you get here."

Can't this wait? Kakuchaya asked.

No, it can't, Kravchenko said. We have an emergency.

The morning show had to be changed—changed drastically. He'd explain when they got to the studios at Ostankino. Kravchenko told Kakuchaya that they needed two newscasters to get ready, one man and one women—or whoever could get to the studios fastest.

The car came for Kakuchaya in no time and brought him to work. Kravchenko called again, this time from his car on the special "Kremlin line."

"We're on the way," Kravchenko said. "Go outside and I'll give you the scripts you need."

"How long will you be?"

"I'll be there in seven minutes."

Kravchenko's car pulled up in the parking lot. He was usually a dapper man, an apparatchik for the television age, but now he seemed absolutely pale. He said that he had just gotten into bed when he was called and told to come immediately to the Central Committee. He was given a stack of documents—the appeals and pronouncements of the Emergency Committee that would begin going out over the air at six that morning. He was told to create an atmosphere on television similar to that on the day of a state funeral: somber, classical music, deadpan announcements.

Kakuchaya took a quick look at the documents. They seemed to have been typed in haste on an ordinary typewriter. And there was Yanayev's signature, a hasty scrawl. Kravchenko told him that soon there would be tanks around the TV tower. No one should go outside. Use the underground tunnels connecting the various buildings to get around. And obey orders.

Gennadi Yanayev, still buzzed from drink, took power at 4:00 A.M. Thirty minutes later, Marshal Yazov dispatched Coded Telegram 8825 ordering heightened alert status for all military units. Soldiers were ordered back from furlough. The Taman Guards, the Dzerzhinsky and Kantemirovskaya mechanized divisions, and several units of the Ryazan Airborne Division would occupy the city of Moscow.

At the Ministry of Defense, Yazov repeated Kryuchkov's elaborate conspiracy theory about an imminent anti-Soviet coup and the need to take the upper hand. "There will be people in the crowd who will throw themselves in front of tanks or throw Molotov cocktails," Yazov warned his commanders. "I want no bloodshed or carnage."

It was a hellish morning for Prime Minister Pavlov. He had stayed up most of the night drinking with Yanayev, and now Kryuchkov was trying to reach him to organize planning sessions at the Kremlin.

At about 7:00 A.M., one of the Kremlin doctors, Dmitri Sakharov, was summoned to Pavlov's dacha and told only that the prime minister was "very unwell."

"Pavlov was drunk," Sakharov testified later. "But this was no ordinary, simple intoxication. He was at the point of hysteria. I proceeded to give him attention."

The barracks of the Kantemirovskaya Mechanized Division in the town of Naro-Fominsk outside Moscow were quiet, and Private Vitaly Chugunov, a young man with wheat-blond hair from the city of Ulyanovsk, was in the middle of a deep, untroubled sleep. These were the last sweet moments before Monday reveille and another week of training. Chugunov had thought he would be among the first generation of Soviet soldiers blessed by the rise of a peaceable kingdom, a country in which a policy of "new thinking" ensured against another Afghanistan, another occupation of Eastern Europe.

Suddenly, an officer burst into Chugunov's barracks, shouting his charges out of bed. There were no complicated explanations, nothing about Gorbachev or a state of emergency. "We all thought it was one of those training alerts, and we quickly got everything ready to go," Chugunov said. Soon he was inside his armored personnel carrier, part of a huge convoy headed for Moscow. Chugunov and his buddies were confused, not quite sure why they were taking the highway north into the city at such a fast clip and churning up the asphalt.

Along the way, Chugunov could see a few people waving at the tanks and the armored personnel carriers; people shouting at them to turn around and go home. Slowly, the young soldiers began to understand, Chugunov fastest of all. His father had been in a tank when the Soviet army invaded Prague in 1968. He'd always told his son how scared he was that day. The commanders had told them that the Czechs would give them boxes of chocolate and the chocolate would have poison inside them. Watch out for poisoned wine, they told them. And then, as his tank rumbled into the city, he heard the insults: "Occupiers!" "Pigs, go home!" Looking out at the road now, Chugunov thought that he was headed for something far worse than his father had ever known.

The coup went on the air at six. The announcers, so obviously nervous and confused, began to read the documents that had been delivered to Kravchenko at the Central Committee:

"We are addressing you at a grave, critical hour for the future of the Motherland and our peoples. A mortal danger has come to loom large over our great Motherland.

"The policy of reforms, launched at Mikhail Gorbachev's initiative and designed as means to ensure the country's dynamic development and the democratization of social life, have entered for several reasons into a blind alley.

". . . All democratic institutions created by the popular will are losing weight and effectiveness right in front of our eyes. This is a result of purposeful actions by those who, grossly violating the fundamental law of the USSR, are in fact staging an unconstitutional coup [!] and striving for unbridled personal dictatorial powers. . . .

"The country is sinking into the quagmire of violence and lawlessness.

"Never before in national history has the propaganda of sex and violence assumed such a scale, threatening the health and lives of future generations. Millions of people are demanding measures against the octopus of crime and glaring immorality."

Yeltsin was eating breakfast at his dacha in the village of Usovo when the calls started coming in. Gennadi Burbulis, Ruslan Khasbulatov, and all the other Russian officials in the smaller dachas in the woods near Yeltsin's quickly gathered round. Yeltsin had gotten some hints from agents in the Russian republican secret service that a coup was coming. With Gorbachev flirting to the end with his own worst enemies, Yeltsin knew that a coup was possible. But until now he hadn't thought it would actually happen. And now he had to act without hesitation.

The Leningrad mayor, Anatoly Sobchak, heard about the coup by phone at his hotel room in Moscow. Tanks were on their way, he was told. Sobchak called his driver, and together they headed out of town at top speed for Yeltsin's dacha. Along the way, they saw armored personnel carriers and tanks. One tank had fallen into a ditch and was burning. Sobchak, like Yeltsin and around seventy other reform politicians, including Aleksandr Yakovlev and Eduard Shevardnadze, were on KGB arrest lists, but so far the secret police had made only a few arrests of some minor officials. Sobchak made it to Usovo untouched.

Sobchak saw that Yeltsin was already determined to do what he could to shore up resistance to the coup. Yeltsin had called the leaders of the biggest republics and was taken aback by their calm, their lack of resolve. They told him they did not have enough information to act. Yeltsin was on his own. As he strapped on a bulletproof vest and then his shirt and suit, Yeltsin said that he and his aides would head for "the White House," the massive Russian parliament building on the Moscow River. Without saying so, they would follow almost precisely the tactics of the Lithuanians in January: use the parliament building as a barricade, an oasis and symbol of democratic resistance, communicate with the outside world by whatever means possible. Yeltsin told his aides to convene immediately a nonstop session of the Russian parliament.

As Yeltsin got into his car, his daughter said, "Papa, keep calm. Everything depends on you."

After following the convoy part of the way to the city to make sure Yeltsin got past the tanks, Sobchak and his driver peeled off for Sheremetyevo Airport to wait for the first flight home to Leningrad. When he got to the waiting lounge, Sobchak saw three bodyguards coming at him. For a moment, he thought he was finished. To the contrary. They were bodyguards from the Russian KGB there to make sure that the mayor caught his plane.

By 9:00 A.M., tanks surrounded Moscow City Hall. Soldiers had taken down the Russian tricolor and replaced it with the red Soviet flag. Tanks were taking positions in all the key points of the city: the TV and radio stations, newspaper offices, Lenin Hills, the White House. A journalist called General Yevgeny Shaposhnikov, the commander of the air force. Shaposhnikov had listened to Yazov's commands and explanations of the coup, but he made no secret to the reporter that he was revolted by what had happened. "Let the sons of bitches comment on what they are going to do with the country," he said.

While Yazov worked at the Ministry of Defense and Kryuchkov at Lubyanka, Yanayev sat in his Kremlin office wondering what it was he was supposed to do.

Yuri Golik, the chairman of the Supreme Soviet committee on legislation, got through the gates of the Kremlin without any problem and went immediately to see Yanayev.

"Is it a putsch?" Golik asked.

"It's a putsch," said Yanayev.

Later, Vadim Bakatin, a member of Gorbachev's Defense Council, also came to see Yanayev. Bakatin, like Golik, was loyal to Gorbachev, and he demanded an explanation. Before he could even work up his temper, Bakatin noticed what bad shape Yanayev was in.

"I've been here since four o'clock in the morning," Yanayev said, pacing, smoking, excitable, bags under his eyes. "I don't know myself what is going on. They came and tried to persuade me for two hours. I didn't agree, but they finally persuaded me."

"Who came?"

"They came."

The Kazakh leader, Nursultan Nazarbayev, called Yanayev, who seemed to be in a daze, drunken or otherwise. "He didn't seem to know what was going on," Nazarbayev told reporters in Alma-Ata, the Kazakh capital, "or why I was calling or even who I was."

Yanayev's desk was stacked with unread documents, many of them months old. Usually he let his aides do all his serious work for him; among those aides was Sergei Bobkov, the son of Filipp Bobkov, Kryuchkov's trusted deputy at the KGB. But while Yanayev was foggy at times, obsessed with love affairs and the bottle, he kept on his desk one document that made it clear that the coup itself was more serious than he was, that the real powers behind it—Kryuchkov, Baklanov, Boldin, and Yazov—knew their history and the methods of the old regime.

REGARDING CERTAIN AXIOMS
OF THE EXTRAORDINARY SITUATION

1. We must not lose the initiative and enter into any kind of negotiations with the public. We have often ended up doing this in an attempt to preserve a democratic facade. As a result, society gradually becomes accustomed to the idea that they can argue with the authorities—and this is the first step toward the next battle.

2. One must not allow even the first manifestations of disloyalty: meetings, hunger strikes, petitions, and information about them. On the contrary, they become, as it were, a permitted form of opposition, after which even more active forms will follow. If you want to proceed with a minimal amount of bloodshed, suppress contradictions at the very beginning.

3. Do not be ashamed of resorting to clearly expressed populism. This is the law of winning support from the masses. Immediately introduce economic measures that are understandable to all—lowering of prices, easing up on alcohol laws, etc.—and the appearance of even a limited variety of products in popular demand. In this situation do not think of economic integrity, the inflation rate, or other consequences.

4. One must not delay in informing the populace about all the details of the crimes of one's political opponent. At first they will avidly search for information. Exactly at this point one must bring down an information storm of exposure, the revelation of guilty groups and syndicates, corruption, and so forth. On other days the information about one's opponent should be given in an ironically humorous key. . . . The information must be graphic and as simple as possible.

5. One must not crack the whip with direct threats; better to start rumors about the strictness of the regime and the control of discipline in production and life, as if there were systematic raids on stores, places of relaxation, and others.

6. One must not be slow in dealing with personnel decisions and reassignments. The population should know who is being punished and for what evident reasons; who is answering to whom for what; and to whom the population should turn with its problems.

Before going to the *Washington Post* bureau on Kutuzovsky Prospekt, where she was working as a translator, Masha Lipman watched the bland declaration of a state of emergency. As she stared at the television her first thoughts were of her children, her six-year-old daughter, Anya, and her sixteen-year-old son, Grisha. She was terrified. Suddenly, these years of promise seemed betrayed. After years of thinking the problem through, Masha and Seriozha had decided against emigration. They'd cast their lot with Moscow. Now all she could think was "Will Anya be indoctrinated as we were? Is it all coming back? Will we emigrate? Should we? Can we?"

Nadezhda Kudinova, a seamstress at a parachute factory on the edge of town, arrived at work. On the way, she had heard some vague rumors on the bus that the newscasters were announcing that Gorbachev had resigned for "health reasons" and that Yanayev and some unpronounceable committee—the "GKChP"—had taken power. It all seemed so vague and unreal. The factory director immediately gathered all the workers and insisted that they all stand by the Emergency Committee, that what the country needed now was stability and discipline in the workplace.

Kudinova looked out the window. There was nothing to see, nothing to hear. On the radio, the announcers repeated the decrees of the committee, over and over again. She and her friends began talking about what they could do, whom to support. At the factory, opinion was split down the middle. Half were outraged. Half thought that maybe life would be better now without Gorbachev. Maybe there would be food in the stores for a change.

Kudinova thought to herself that the workers who were taking sides with the committee were counting on a passive country. As the day went on and she heard that Yeltsin had begun organizing the resistance at the White House, Kudinova brightened. "Maybe I should start writing some leaflets," she thought. On her way home, she saw the tanks, she saw how the tanks had chewed up the road, a violation. She saw the crowd beginning to gather at the White House, and she made a decision. She would protect the president she had voted for just two months before. She had no thought of Mikhail Gorbachev. She went to the White House for Yeltsin, for an independent

Russia. It wasn't about Gorbachev, she thought. Gorbachev had gotten what he deserved.

Yeltsin arrived at the White House at around 10:00 A.M. He and Ruslan Khasbulatov, the chairman of the parliament, and Ivan Silayev, the Russian prime minister, drafted an appeal, "To the Citizens of Russia," denouncing the putsch as a "reactionary unconstitutional coup d'état" and calling for a nationwide strike. Khasbulatov and Vice President Aleksander Rutskoi, a war hero in Afghanistan, began broadcasts from a makeshift radio station inside the parliament building, the White House. Vladimir Bokser, a young pro-democracy politician, organized a phone network of activists to come to defend the White House. Yeltsin dispatched his foreign minister, Andrei Kozyrev, to Paris to seek Western support and establish a Russian government abroad if the resistance was crushed.

"By eleven the depression in the city was beginning to lift just slightly," said Masha Lipman's husband, Seriozha Ivanov. "People riding in the trolleys were laughing at the tanks, mocking them." Children climbed on the tanks and asked the young soldiers how to drive; pretty young women teased the recruits and said that maybe they should all go home and do something more interesting than sitting around on a tank.

Then, just after noon, Yeltsin walked down the front steps of the White House and clambered up on a T-72—Tank No. 110 of the Taman Guards. It was an indelible image that would set the tone for the next three days. As a small crowd of demonstrators and reporters listened, Yeltsin's voice boomed out. "Citizens of Russia," he began. ". . . The legally elected president of the country has been removed from power. . . . We are dealing with a right-wing, reactionary, anti-constitutional coup d'état. . . . Accordingly, we proclaim all decisions and decrees of this committee to be illegal. . . . We appeal to citizens of Russia to give an appropriate rebuff to the putschists and demand a return of the country to normal constitutional development."

Then Konstantin Kobets, a retired general now appointed Russian defense minister by Yeltsin, climbed aboard and addressed not only the citizens, but the soldiers of Russia. "I am the defense minister of Russia," he said, "and not a hand will be raised against the people or the duly elected president of Russia." Kobets had led a battalion during the Prague invasion in 1968, and he said he was not about to repeat his mistakes. He would organize the military resistance and try to convince the officers and troops that they could not, as soldiers or citizens, follow the commands of a junta.

Yeltsin had been criticized in recent months for flirting too much with the military. He had spent much of his campaign in places like the Tula military

bases and, over the objections of many radicals in the parliament, made Rutskoi his vice president. Now he was counting on that relationship to pay dividends. Rutskoi responded instantly and went on the radio: "Comrades! I, an officer of the Soviet armed forces, a colonel, a Hero of the Soviet Union who has walked the battle-torn roads of Afghanistan and knows the horrors of war, call on you, my brother officers, soldiers, and sailors, not to act against your own people, against your fathers, brothers, and sisters."

Outside the White House, the first demonstrators cheered as the gunners in ten tanks of the Taman Guards turned the barrels of their guns away from the parliament. The attackers were now ready to defend the White House.

Private Chugunov sat in his tank, parked in the Lenin Hills. At first there was real fear, he said. People shook their fists and shouted, "Don't shoot your own people! Turn against your officers!" He saw women crying, people brought them food to eat, flowers to stick in their guns, leaflets from the White House, Yeltsin's appeal to the military to obey their oath to the people.

The soldiers unloaded their AK-47s and kept them out of sight. "Why don't we make a U-turn and go home?" they began to say to one another. Chugunov and his friends felt ashamed, and they told the crowds around them they would do nothing to disgrace the names of their fathers, they would not shoot at their own people.

At noon Yeltsin went on the radio: "Soldiers and officers of the army, the KGB, and the troops of the Interior Ministry! Countrymen! The country is faced with the threat of terror. At this difficult hour of decision remember that you have taken an oath to your people, and your weapons cannot be turned against the people. You can erect a throne of bayonets but you cannot sit on it for long. The days of the conspirators are numbered. . . . Clouds of terror and dictatorship are gathering over Russia, but this night will not be eternal and our long-suffering people will find freedom once again, and for good. Soldiers, I believe at this tragic hour you will make the right decision. The honor of Russian arms will not be covered with the blood of the people."

At the White House, a retired lieutenant from the Taman Guards—"Baskakov is my name, here is my tattoo"—took command of Civil Defense Unit No. 34. He was proud to see that it was his boys who were the first to come over to the side of the resistance. Baskakov had quit the Communist Party the year before and he felt that it was his duty "as a Christian" to come to

the barricades. He never said a word to his family, just walked out the door and took the metro to the White House. Baskakov's men, a ragtag outfit of Afghan vets, took command of entrance 22 of the parliament, where key figures, like Shevardnadze and Popov, were going in and out.

Baskakov's men spotted snipers in the windows of the Hotel Mir across the street and near the American embassy. For years, American diplomats had assumed that the KGB used the hotel as a lookout point on the embassy. Baskakov's troops were pathetically armed with black-market pistols, knives, billy clubs, an occasional machine gun. If there was an attack, they'd be cannon fodder, and they knew it. Everyone knew it. It was that combined sense of heroism and fatalism, especially among the kids who had joined the resistance units, that moved Baskakov. "I used to be critical of the young," he said. "But there were bikers, the Rockers, going on reconnaissance missions on their motorcycles across the barricades, giving us news about the troop movements. The young girls that people call prostitutes, they were there giving us food and drink."

The defenders of the White House came slowly: first a few thousand, then ten thousand. By the end of the day there would be around twenty-five thousand. With advice from the military men, they began building barricades, gnarled heaps of scrap: construction rods, concrete blocks, rusted bathtubs, bricks, tree trunks, even cobblestones from a small bridge nearby that had been the site of an anti-czarist uprising in 1905. The strike leader, Anatoly Malikhin, showed up wearing a United Mine Workers Union T-shirt ("United We Stand, Divided We Fall"). He went inside and quickly strapped on a machine gun. Somehow, he said, he had had the feeling it would come to this when the first mines went out on strike two years before.

At the airport in Leningrad, Sobchak's aides were there to meet him. They told him that the Leningrad regional military commander, Viktor Samsonov, had already been on television to announce that the Emergency Committee had taken power from Gorbachev and that a state of emergency had begun. So far, there were no troops into the city. Sobchak told his driver to take him straight to the city's central military command at top speed. Once he was there, Sobchak left his guards downstairs.

"I saw that they were bewildered and confused, and right away I didn't let them open their mouths," Sobchak recounted. "I told them if they moved one finger they would be tried the way the Nazis were tried at Nuremberg. I scolded Samsonov: 'General, remember Tbilisi? You were the only one there who acted as a reasonable man. You remained in the shadows. What are you doing now? You are involved in this gang. This committee is illegal.'

"Why is it illegal?" Samsonov said. "I have an order. I have this coded cable. I can't show it to you. It's a secret."

Sobchak pressed, telling Samsonov to remember how the generals in Tbilisi in April 1989 had also exceeded orders and turned a peaceful demonstration into a bloodbath.

"Why do you raise your voice?" Boris Gidaspov, the Leningrad Party chief, shouted.

"Shut up!" Sobchak said. "Don't you realize that with your presence you are liquidating your own Party?"

For the rest of the meeting, Gidaspov whimpered in his chair, a beaten dog.

Samsonov faced a choice. Yazov and Kryuchkov had appealed to his commitment to empire and discipline. Sobchak, who had the support of the city, appealed to his conscience, his commitment to history. The choice was what the past six years had been all about. And the general found it almost easy. He backed off and ordered his men to stay out of the city. Leningrad, now St. Petersburg again, was saved.

That evening, Sobchak went on the local television show *Fakt* and referred to the conspirators as "former" ministers and as "citizens," the way a Russian prosecutor would refer to the accused.

Samsonov kept getting calls from the conspirators, but he held fast. Sobchak was pleased. "General," he said, "can't you see how these people are just nothing? They will not hold on to power long even if they are able to seize it!"

The leaders of the junta had already failed miserably to follow the prescriptions of Lenin or Jaruzelski. Nearly everyone on their arrest lists was still free and working with the resistance. The editors of a group of liberal papers, including *Moscow News,* had already begun planning a joint underground paper to be called *Obshchaya Gazeta*—"The Common Newspaper"—and the editors at *Nezavisimaya Gazeta* were also putting together a samizdat edition. Opposition radio stations, particularly the Echo of Moscow, would go off the air for a few hours and then return. Telephone, fax, and telex lines at the bureaus of foreign news organizations worked flawlessly. CNN, the BBC, Radio Liberty, and the Voice of America pumped out continuous coverage. Reporters commandeered phone lines inside the White House and called out their reports without a hitch.

At the offices of the key Soviet newspapers, the situation was more complicated. The junta had ordered the shutdown of all the main liberal papers and used the high-circulation Party and government papers to do nothing more

than publish their decrees and spurious reports on how normal the situation was, how calm. *Sovetskaya Rossiya* was enthusiastically cooperative, some of the others less so. At *Izvestia,* there was a war.

Izvestia was one of the most paradoxical institutions in the country. On the one hand, its editor, Nikolai Yefimov, was a shameless sycophant. His patron was the parliament's chairman, Anatoly Lukyanov. Yefimov was only too happy to fulfill the demands of his betters: about half the paper's staff of thirty foreign correspondents were KGB operatives. Although official government censors no longer sat in the editorial offices, Yefimov was more than able to handle the job himself. He was always quick to kill stories that he thought might damage or insult precisely the men now leading the coup d'état. On the other hand, the paper was brimming with talent. Mikhail Berger published some of the sharpest economic pieces in the country. Andrei Illesh wrote a series of articles on the shootdown of Korean Airlines 007 that was more revealing and critical of the Soviet leadership than anything published in the West. The better reporters and editors, the honest ones, despised Yefimov. They thought they had the talent and the resources to report the news far better than even the young renegades over at *Nezavisimaya Gazeta.* If they only could.

At around 1:00 P.M., a fight broke out in the composing room at the *Izvestia* plant on Pushkin Square. A few of the reporters had brought back a copy of Yeltsin's appeal to the people for resistance to the coup, and, with the support of the printers, they had already set it in type for the evening edition. But Yefimov's deputy, Dmitri Mamleyev, demanded that Yeltsin's words not appear.

The printers were furious. Pavel Vichenkov, one of the foremen, shouted, "We voted for Yeltsin! You can publish the statements of the committee, but we insist on Yeltsin's statement going into the paper as well."

"It's not your job to decide what goes into the paper," said Yevgeny Gemanov, one of Yefimov's men. "That's the job of the editors. Your job is to print what you are told to print."

"You can shoot us," a worker, Pavel Bushkov, said, "but we're not going to put this paper out without Yeltsin's statement. We live the life of animals, in poverty, and we don't want our children to live the same way."

Yefimov had missed the start of the battle because he was racing back to Moscow from his vacation house. As soon as he walked through the door, a small group of reporters surrounded him and demanded he publish Yeltsin's statement. Yefimov said there was no way and yanked the metal type from the printing press.

Ordinarily, Yefimov would have had his way. But now the printers, like the Siberian miners or the factory hands of Minsk, said they would sooner quit

than give in. They would sooner destroy the presses than publish *Izvestia* without the appeal of Boris Yeltsin.

Twenty hours late, *Izvestia* appeared on the streets of Moscow and in every city and village of the Soviet Union. The Emergency Committee's proclamations blared out from page one. Yeltsin's appeal to resist the coup was on page two.

It was time for the junta to face the press. An early-evening appearance at the Foreign Ministry press center was part of their strategy to put a face of normalcy on the situation, to create the impression somehow that this was not a putsch but a legal, constitutional transition. This was their chance to compete on the evening news broadcasts of the world, to counter the image of Yeltsin, like Lenin at the Finland Station, rallying the people from the top of a tank.

In the first hours of the coup, Kryuchkov, for one, felt euphoric. There were no strikes, no demonstrations. Radical republican presidents such as Zviad Gamsakhurdia in Georgia made no move to act against the coup. Yanayev, for his part, wandered around his office and the Kremlin hallways. Other men were making the decisions. But this was his moment. At the press conference, he had to convince the people beyond the camera that all was well, that he was in control.

The problem was that Yanayev could not control his own self. He sniffed like a smack addict in need of a fix, and his hands trembled like little wild animals quivering in front of him. He was lost from the start. His answers were transparent lies, his attempt at calm had the brittle ring of hysteria. The reporters, except some of the obvious reactionary plants, showed no fear or respect in their questions. They even laughed at him! Gorbachev had been stripped of his "nuclear football," the case containing the codes. All the codes were now in the hands of the military and the KGB. A junta in control of a vast nuclear power, and they laughed!

About halfway through the disaster, Yanayev called on a twenty-four-year-old reporter from *Nezavisimaya Gazeta,* Tatyana Malkina. Just a year before, Malkina had worked as a low-level researcher at *Moscow News,* rummaging through the clips, doing scut work for the older reporters. Now she was a staffer on the hottest paper in Moscow. She got out of her seat, took the microphone, and fixed her eyes on the half-drunk pretender to power.

"Tell me, please," she said, "do you realize you have carried out a state coup? And which comparison do you find more appropriate—1917 or 1964?" The Bolshevik coup or the overthrow of Nikita Khrushchev?

For an instant, the man who would be king looked at his own wretched hands; he seemed sad, as if he wondered if the shaking would ever stop.

At the Ministry of Defense, Dmitri Yazov watched the press conference with his wife, Emma. She wept as she watched the pathetic spectacle and begged her husband to call Gorbachev and call off the coup.

"Dima, what have you joined?" she said through her tears. "You always laughed at them! Call Gorbachev. . . ."

But the marshal told his wife that was impossible now. The connections had all been severed.

Working out of a war room on the third floor, Yeltsin signed a decree creating a backup shadow government and dispatched a team of twenty-three civilian and military leaders in the Russian government to set it up in a secret headquarters thirty-five miles outside Yeltsin's home city of Sverdlovsk in the Urals.

"The idea was to act in the name of the Russian government if the White House was captured," said Aleksei Yablokov, Yeltsin's environment minister and one of those who went to Sverdlovsk. Working in bunkers thirty feet underground that had been built during the cold war, the Russians began sending an unending series of faxes and telexes calling on local organizations and governments around the Soviet Union to resist the decrees of the junta.

The leader of the Urals Military District was one of the most reactionary generals in the country, Albert Makashov. It had been Makashov who had run against Yeltsin for the presidency on a purely Stalinist platform. Now Makashov was telling his charges to round up any suspicious people, including "cosmopolitans," the old Stalinist code word for Jews. But his troops paid little attention. The passions of the city of Sverdlovsk were with Yeltsin. More than 100,000 people staged a demonstration defying the junta in the main city square. There were no arrests.

Valentin Pavlov convened a meeting of all the government's ministers at 6:00 P.M. Environment Minister Nikolai Vorontsov, the only non-Communist in the group, took notes on the session and read some of them to Masha and me before they came out in the press days later.

"It was a chorus of agreement," said Vorontsov. Every minister but three expressed absolute support for the coup. After Pavlov repeated the tale of the "counterrevolutionaries" with their Stinger missiles and evil intentions, one minister after another rose to say the committee was their last hope. They made little secret that what they wanted most of all was a chance to stay in

power, to hold on to the last sweet scraps of privilege. Vladimir Gusev, the head of the state committee on chemistry and biotechnology, was a typical case, telling his fellow ministers, "If we step back even an iota, we will sacrifice our jobs, our lives. We will not have another chance."

When Pavlov finished the meeting, he spoke with Yazov on the phone. Yazov could tell immediately that the prime minister, whom everyone knew as "Mr. Porky," was drunk again.

"Arrest them all," Pavlov said at one point.

Yazov knew things were going badly. Where was the plan? He was beginning to think that the collapse of the plot would be better than its success. But he pressed on.

The junta, of course, had banned the Russian Republic's new television station. The public would have no chance to see the puckish hosts of the news program *Vesti.* There would only be Central Television, and for news, there would be only *Vremya.* Just like the old days.

Even the best directors and reporters at *Vremya* knew they could not be heroes. They could not take to the airwaves with appeals for resistance. Their entire operation was riddled with informers, agents, and officers of the KGB. It was out of the question. Besides, all the really irreverent people had long ago gone to *Vesti* and the more liberal shows.

But a young *Vremya* reporter named Sergei Medvedev watched the CNN feeds and decided he had to do something. His editors gave him an assignment for the 9:00 P.M. broadcast: film a feature on "Moscow today." The idea, he knew, was to show how calm everything was, how "life is going on as normal." In fact, it was true. Much of Moscow, like nearly all of the rest of the country, did seem normal. People went to work. Some watched television and read the papers and tried to figure out what had happened. There were millions of people who thought the coup might even do some good; and there were millions who could not have cared less. But Medvedev also made sure to fill in the rest of the picture. He got some brief footage of the scenes around the White House: the barricades, the protesters. He even included a clip of Yeltsin on the tank. He handed it over to his editors and hoped for the best.

Yelena Pozdniak, a veteran director at *Vremya,* also decided she would do what she could to preserve, at the very least, a marginal sense of honesty. She got the word from Kravchenko and his deputies that if it was technically possible, she should edit out Yanayev's trembling hands at the press conference, the laughter in the hall, the scoffing reactions of the correspondents. Although that was easy enough to do, Pozdniak thought, "Let them see it

all!" She'd had enough of the lies. In the days of Brezhnev, she had cleaned up the stutters and blurts of the leaders on a nightly basis. Brezhnev had the verbal style of a senile crocodile and required special polishing. "He used to have a favored word, *kompetentnost* ["competency"], to which he always added an extra letter: *kompententnost,*" Pozdniak recalled. "I had to find another speech where he said it correctly and then dub that in so no one would notice." But not this time.

Valentin Lazutkin, Kravchenko's deputy and a semiliberal man, also made his move. On the air, his rebellion would look slight, if not invisible; the broadcast was filled with the proclamations and approved commentaries of the committee. But he put Medvedev's piece on the air and he let the clips of the press conference run, complete with Yanayev's waggling hands.

"People got to see that Yeltsin was alive, that he was free and working, and that meant there was hope," Lazutkin said. The minute *Vremya* went off the air, the calls started coming in: three Politburo members and, worst of all, Boris Pugo, the interior minister.

Pugo was in a rage. "The story on Moscow was treacherous!" he said. "You have given instructions to the people on where to go and what to do. You will answer for this."

Later, Yanayev called, too. He did not seem to know what to talk about, and so Lazutkin politely asked him how he had liked the newscast. "I saw it," Yanayev said. "It was a good, balanced report. It showed everything from different points of view."

"But they said I would be punished for it," Lazutkin said.

"Who are they?" Yanayev asked. "From the Central Committee? Fuck 'em."

Beginning that night, Lazutkin acquired a new friend: a colonel of the KGB. The colonel went wherever Lazutkin went, listened to all his conversations, watched as he made all his decisions.

"Why are you here?" Lazutkin asked.

"For your security," the colonel said.

But soon the KGB man came around. He and Lazutkin exchanged smiles as the coup began to erode. And then they took out the bottle, the eternal equalizer of men.

"Cheers!" the agent said.

"Cheers!" said the man who had shown Big Brother with his pants down.

Lazutkin's son was proud of his father's subtle rebellion, but he could not call him to say so. Sergei Lazutkin was at the White House, on the barricades.

AUGUST 20, 1991

For the three days of the coup, Yeltsin did not sleep. Early on the morning of the 20th, he and his aides looked out the windows and out to the barricades. There were still people outside the White House, about ten thousand or so gathered around portable radios or little campfires. But those inside were nervous. They needed huge crowds. They had to depend on the most undependable thing in the history of Russia: the stubborn, free will of its people.

In the hallways, people milled around, fueled by nerves and rumor. There were middle-aged men armed to the teeth, men who had not held a rifle since the day they left the army. A few hundred young men who worked for new security guard agencies, such as "Bells" and "Aleks," signed up with the Afghan vets. In the corners of offices, under secretaries' desks, there were little mountains of machine guns, grenades, Molotov cocktails. Mstislav Rostropovich, who had played his cello less than two years before in front of the remnants of the Berlin Wall, returned to his homeland now and stood guard near Yeltsin's office for a few hours cradling an AK-47 assault rifle. Some of the best-known "men of the sixties" were coming: Yuri Karyakin, the Dostoevsky scholar; Ales Adamovich. The New Wave politicians were there, too: Sergei Stankevich with his peachy cheeks and leather jacket looking like a student council president trying to be cool; Ilya Zaslavsky, limping urgently from office to office; the constitutional scholar Oleg Rumantsyev and the lawyer Sergei Shakrai hunched over desks, drafting decrees for Yeltsin.

Yeltsin's men seemed to have a pipeline to all the goings-on at the key points of the coup. They had military men calling them with intelligence reports, Russian KGB calling in with information about Kryuchkov. At about the same time, Yazov was at the Ministry of Defense cursing about a lack of active support from the Party, cursing the passive resistance of some of his top generals. One group after another was telling him they were "not prepared" to attack, and he, too, felt that it was all going wrong, that a "lake of blood" would not bring victory but deeper shame.

As traffic picked up out on the streets, Yeltsin's people could see that the crowd around the White House was thickening. With the help of leaflets pasted up in subway stations and bus stops, people heard more about the truth of what was going on and what was needed. Yeltsin called a demonstration for 10:30 A.M.

Standing on the White House balcony above a huge Russian tricolor and behind a bulletproof shield, he showed his combative face and sounded his baritone, warning that the "junta used no restraint in grabbing power and the junta feels itself under no restraint in keeping it."

"Doesn't Yazov have his hands covered in blood from other republics? Hasn't Pugo bloodied his hands in the Baltics and the Caucasus? . . . The [Russian] prosecutors and the Interior Ministry have their orders: whoever fulfills the commands of this illegal committee will be prosecuted!

"The troops have refused to follow these putschists blindly. I believe it is necessary to support these troops and together with them observe a sense of order and discipline. . . . I am convinced that here, in democratic Moscow, aggression of the conservative forces will not win out. Democracy will. And we will stay here as long as it takes for the junta to be brought to justice!"

It was not a brilliant speech, but it gave more than 100,000 people the chance to see the symbol they were risking themselves to protect, whatever his faults and vanities, Yeltsin was now the symbol of democracy, he was the man they had elected—not Gorbachev. Of all the speakers on the White House balcony, it took Yelena Bonner, Sakharov's widow and no friend of Gorbachev, to mention the man who was now languishing in fallen luxury in Foros: "I had my disagreements with Gorbachev," she said, "but he was the president of this country and we cannot allow a bunch of bandits to take over."

Oleg Kalugin, who had eluded arrest by his former colleagues at the KGB, introduced a lieutenant colonel in the secret police who appealed to "Volodya" Kryuchkov to stop the coup which was "about to collapse." The much-loved comic Gennadi Khazanov imitated Gorbachev the way Rich Little used to do Nixon. In his best Gorbachev voice, full of softened *g*'s and grammatical slips, he said, "I feel healthy, but I just can't help thinking that you can't carry off a clean policy with trembling hands."

Then Yevgeny Yevtushenko, the poet of equal parts irreverence and self-promotion, got his chance at the microphone.

> No! Russia will not fall again on her knees for interminable years,
> With us are Pushkin, Tolstoy.
> With us stands the whole awakened people.
> And the Russian parliament, like a wounded marble swan of freedom,
> defended by the people, swims into immortality.

It was far from Yevtushenko's worst, and the crowd loved it. All the same, I preferred the four-liners that were already spreading around Moscow, including:

We're told that order's now assured us,
But the junta's hand can't rest;
They're a little Pinochetist
And just slightly Husseinesque.

In a cool drizzle, I walked down Kutuzovsky Prospekt, across the bridge, and to the White House. I saw a group of men in their twenties, well-dressed Soviet business types, carrying stacks of pizzas from the Pizza Hut down the road. Another delegation of ruble millionaires had been dispatched to McDonald's for further provisions.

I stayed all afternoon and into the night. At 4:00 P.M. there was a rumor that plainclothes KGB agents had gotten into the building and had been caught. Then Yeltsin cut short a phone call with John Major, the British prime minister, saying that tanks were on their way to the White House. There was, it turned out, no such raid in progress. The Kremlin was busy with other things. For one thing, Yanayev contacted Saddam Hussein and promised to restore good relations with Iraq. In all, the coup won support from Hussein, Muammar Qaddafi, and Fidel Castro.

By the early evening, support for the resistance was pouring in over the telex and fax machines. The leaders of Kazakhstan, Ukraine, and other regions, after some hesitation, were speaking out against the junta. Even the Ukrainian KGB chief, General Nikolai Golushko, called to say that he did not support the coup. Just as important, there were pathetic signs of weakness, news that Pavlov had been hospitalized for "high blood pressure." There were rumors that Yazov and Kryuchkov had resigned. Lukyanov, oily to the last, told one of Gorbachev's aides, "I had nothing to do with the putsch." The military leaders supporting the Russian government were growing bolder by the hour. Colonel General Pavel Grachev, commander of the airborne units, kept putting off Varennikov, the ground forces commander who wanted him to get in place for a raid on the White House. Shaposhnikov even ordered his men to be prepared to intercept and shoot down assault helicopters on the way to the White House. Later, Shaposhnikov said that he had even considered the possibility of making a retaliatory air raid on the Kremlin if the conspirators managed to storm the White House.

In the war room, Yeltsin, Kobets, and Rutskoi knew that if there was going to be a raid it would have to come soon, that night. The plotters could see that the crowds around the White House were growing. In the West, some commentators were saying that Moscow had not reacted the way Prague had in 1989, when virtually the entire population was on the streets. True enough. But the Czechs could also rest assured that their leaders were not about to launch a full military attack against them. In Moscow, with fifty thousand

troops in the city, with the Manezh, Red Square, the Ring Road, Lenin Hills, and other points lined with tanks, there were no such assurances. What assurances could there be after Baku, Tbilisi, Vilnius, Riga, and Osh?

On the barricades outside, as people milled around, their feet sloshing in the puddles, there were new rumors every minute, and every rumor went out over the radio. There were self-appointed leaders with megaphones making pronouncements, few of which made any sense, all of which caused even greater nervousness and confusion. Just to stand still in that crowd took some endurance. For a while there was boredom, and then, with the newest rumor, the skin tingled the way it does before you jump from a high board or head, inexorably, into a car accident. I saw one man, a vet in his old jungle fatigues, holding a stick in one hand for protection and a bottle of vodka in the other for bravery. The most reassuring sight was the way the soldiers in their tanks welcomed kids aboard and flirted with the girls. There was hope in that.

And there was real hope in the grit of these people. Along one barricade on Kutuzovsky Prospekt, I talked with a middle-aged woman, Regina Bogachova, who said she would sooner be crushed by a tank than move. "I am ready to die right here, right on this spot. I will not move. I am fifty-five years old and for years nothing but obedience and inertia was pounded into my brain. The Young Pioneers, the Young Communist League, the unions, the Communist Party, all of them taught me not to answer back. To be a good Soviet, a screw in the machine. But Monday morning my friend called me and said, 'Turn on the radio.' I didn't need to. I heard a rumbling and went out on my balcony and saw the tanks rumbling down below, on the Mozhaisk Highway. These monsters! They have always thought they could do anything to us! They have thrown out Gorbachev and now they are threatening a government I helped elect. I will ignore the curfew. I'll let a tank roll over me if I have to. I'll die right here if I have to."

The dramas at the newspaper offices had only heightened.

At *Izvestia,* Yefimov took a call from Yanayev and was told that he should not publish any more of Yeltsin's decrees or any other material not authorized by the junta. Yefimov, of course, wheezed his ready agreement. When one of his deputies told him that he was acting so weakly that "none of us are going to defend you if they put you on trial," Yefimov fired her. He was going to follow the orders of the junta, no matter what.

At *Nezavisimaya Gazeta,* the staff worked day and night gathering material. Especially after the first day, when the junta showed its wavering hand, they were having a blast. This was their moment. Vladimir Todres, a twenty-

five-year-old political reporter, said that he and his friends at the paper saw the coup as the defining event of their generation, the street-level, media-age equivalent of what the Twentieth Party Congress had been for Karpinsky, Gorbachev, and the thaw generation. "For us, the putsch was not a matter of simple politics," Todres said. "Usually we hate politics, to tell you the truth. But this was the Pepsi Generation under threat. Our very existence was in jeopardy. The bikers feared for their motorcycles. The young businessmen worried about their markets. The racketeers even thought about their bottom line and came to defend the White House. Prostitutes, students, scholars, everybody had an interest in this new life, and we were just not willing to give it all up to these old men. And also, it was like being in a great movie. Life and art were all mixed up together. My friends who were abroad were heartbroken, not because they felt fear, but because they felt left out. They couldn't be in the movie."

The journalism part of the movie was splendid. On the first day of the coup, *Nezavisimaya Gazeta*'s editor in chief, Vitaly Tretyakov, had decided not to defy the coup plotters' press ban. His thinking was that a quick, wrong move could endanger the staff and end the paper entirely. Some of the younger reporters were furious, especially when they heard that the printers at *Izvestia* were willing to challenge the ban and work the presses. Tretyakov insisted. But on the 20th, as it became slightly clearer that the coup leaders had neither the will nor the level of organization to mount a full-scale attack on the press as a whole, Tretyakov and the staff put out a photocopied version of *Nezavisimaya Gazeta* with the lead headline "The Feeble Coup: It Is Still Not Over." The edition was filled with news about the putsch from Moscow and the provinces. The few thousand readers in Moscow who managed to find the underground edition learned that the coup was almost completely centered on Moscow. The main problem spots outside Moscow were the Baltic capitals, where troops quickly took up positions at the main television towers and other points, and the region of Tatarstan, where Party leaders calculated that they had a better chance of gaining independence from the Russian Republic if they supported the coup. The attack on Leningrad had stalled, and, despite some early wavering by the republican leaders, Kazakhstan, Ukraine, and other key republics saw almost no visible sign of the coup on the streets. Otherwise, the country was quiet. You could walk for just a few minutes from the very center of Moscow and not know that there was a coup d'état in progress.

But at the center of the coup, the reporters were working the story hard, especially Sergei Parkhomenko and Pavel Felgenhauer, the paper's military correspondent. Felgenhauer stayed in the White House throughout the siege and was in constant contact with the military leaders who planned Yeltsin's

strategy of resistance in their makeshift "war room." Felgenhauer, a bearish man who spoke fluent English, had never set out to be a journalist or a military expert. He had a Ph.D. in biology and had won what he called "a measure of international fame" with his thesis, "RNA Synthesis During the Maturation of Frog Oocytes." He told me, "I quit science because you can't do science anymore in this country. We can't even afford test tubes or food for the frogs. So I became a journalist. I always liked to write."

Felgenhauer had followed military affairs the way some American kids follow baseball. It was all a game, a combination of action and statistics. "Pavel is a kid who likes toy soldiers. He's a gigantic forty-year-old kid who is a genius," Parkhomenko said. "He loved the coup because he got to play soldier and war correspondent all at once."

Parkhomenko could not believe the look of supreme contentment in his colleagues' eyes as they sat in the White House. "As for me, I was terrified," he said after the coup. "I thought I was a dead man. They try to say that it was all nothing, that there was never any danger. But that's ridiculous. It was all a war of nerves, a dangerous telephone war. There were orders and counterorders by phones. When the Russian government found out that a contingent of tanks was being sent, they set up rows of gas canisters so that there would be a huge explosion. Their strategy all along was to maximize the threat of bloodshed, to scare the shit out of the KGB and the putschists by essentially using unarmed people as a shield."

In Foros, Gorbachev listened to his Sony transistor radio. Several times a day, he passed along his demands to his captors: to be freed, to address the people. Raisa told him not to eat the food he was served; eat some of the food given to the guards instead. She was afraid he would be poisoned, shot. "We tried to keep calm," Raisa would say later. "We tried to go through our normal day." But it was impossible, and she, especially, suffered, losing control of one hand—from sheer fright, apparently. Late at night, Gorbachev's son-in-law, Anatoly, set up a videocamera and taped Gorbachev reading what was essentially his last testament, declaring that he had refused the plotters and saying what he stood for.

". . . I have been deprived of my governmental communications, the plane which was here with me, also the helicopters. . . ."

Gorbachev and his son-in-law made four copies of the film and snipped them up into pieces. They thought they could hide them somehow, sneak them out to Moscow.

". . . I am under arrest, and no one is allowed on the grounds of my dacha. . . ."

Gorbachev's aide Chernyayev said maybe he could swim along the shore to freedom and, from there, reach the Russian government. But it was absurd. There was nothing they could do. The battle, now, was elsewhere.

—

The first shots came just before midnight, the distant popping sounds of tracer bullets. Had the storming of the White House begun?

General Kobets knew that if the KGB and military units got past the barricades, they would lose the White House in "not less than fifteen minutes." There were a number of elements still in the Russians' favor. The barricades, organized by the war room, had been built high and strong by the protesters on the street. They might not stop everything—or anything—but they put an element of doubt and chaos into the plotters' blueprints.

Suddenly, tens of thousands of people who had come from all parts of the city to protect the White House began their defiant chant: *"Pozor! Pozor!"* ("Shame! Shame!") And then, *"Rossiya! Rossiya!"*

Until the next morning, few would learn what had happened. Three protesters were killed when they clashed with a tank near the barricades on the Garden Ring Road. Some of the demonstrators set fire to tanks with Molotov cocktails. The smell of burning gasoline in the air did nothing to ease the nerves of the huge crowds defending the White House.

—

Now the coup had produced three martyrs. How many more were to come?

The factory seamstress, Nadezhda Kudinova, took up her position on the barricades across Kutuzovsky Prospekt. She was soaked from the rain, but someone gave her dry socks and shoes. The usually surly administrators across the street at the Ukraine Hotel opened up their rooms for the women on the barricades to sleep in two- and three-hour shifts. All the while, Nadezhda kept her radio tuned to *Echo of Moscow* and listened to Rutskoi and Khasbulatov, who were urging calm—civil disobedience, but calm. Every few minutes there were bulletins about troop movements, the possibility that reconnaissance planes would signal an attack. "We always felt they were there with us," Kudinova said. "They spoke in a special sort of language, in a heightened tone, like the words a man speaks before his death. They spoke to us very candidly, creating a feeling of unity beyond description. We heard them and they heard us."

The women defenders formed the front line of the southern barricade with a handpainted sign: "Soviet Soldiers: Don't Shoot Your Mothers." They were ready to die as heroes of war. "The people in the White House ordered us to step aside, not to jump on the tanks if they came," Kudinova said. "But

we knew that if the tanks came, we would step in front of them. We talked about where we should put the tanks that had defected over to our side, in front of the barricades or behind them. We put them behind the barricades, because if they had been captured, the coup loyalists would have shot their crews dead. They are just young kids, after all."

The plan to storm the White House was brutally simple.

On the afternoon of the 20th, the deputy defense minister, Vladislav Achalov, presided over a planning session for "Operation Thunder," a meeting that included such leading generals as Boris Gromov, Pavel Grachev, Aleksandr Lebed, and Sergei Akhromeyev, Gorbachev's lead military adviser, as well as KGB leaders Genii Ageyev and Viktor Karpukhin, the head of the elite Alpha Group. With the help of airborne and KGB troops, the Alpha Group would storm the parliament, blasting through the doors with grenade launchers, and then they would make their way to the fifth floor to arrest, or kill, Yeltsin. The Beta Group would suppress any resistance while the Wave troops, working with other KGB units, would arrest the other Russian leaders. The tanks would fire shells to deafen and stun the defenders of the White House, and helicopter gunships would provide support and storm the roof and balconies.

The Alpha Group already had a reputation for bloody efficiency. In 1979, they burst into the palace of the Afghan dictator Amin and murdered him on the eve of the Soviet invasion. (This was later described in the Soviet press as the "fraternal invitation of the Afghan peoples.") And it was the Alpha Group that had been the lead unit in Vilnius during the January 1991 massacre.

Although Kryuchkov's intentions were clear, the loyalties and intentions of the KGB as a whole were a muddle. KGB sources were the first to alert the Russian government that Yeltsin was to be arrested as the coup began. They provided the Russian government with crucial information about the communications systems of the Defense Ministry and the KGB itself. *Moscow News* reported later that the KGB gave Yeltsin's team a printing press to publish its leaflets, and retired agents now in private business contributed more than a million rubles to a Russian defense fund. Early in the putsch, middle-rank officers in the KGB drafted a statement denouncing the junta.

Yeltsin's sources in the KGB told him that the Alpha Group would move on the 19th at about 6:00 P.M. But there was dissension in the ranks. After the coup, sources in the KGB told me that the middle and "upper-middle" ranks of both the secret police and the army had no faith in their leaders. They saw them as muddled dinosaurs, not to be trusted. They saw how, time

and again, the leadership conceived its schemes—the war in Afghanistan, the assaults in Tbilisi, Baku, and Vilnius—and then avoided all blame. Gorbachev's aide Aleksandr Yakovlev told me that even such generals as Gromov and Grachev, decorated veterans of the Afghan war, "were working both sides of the street, keeping in close contact with the White House even as they were sitting in on the planning sessions of the coup. They're no democrats, but they refused to have blood on their hands for the sake of such idiots as Kryuchkov and Yazov."

"There is a huge crowd," General Aleksandr Lebed said at the afternoon meeting with Achalov. "They are building barricades. There will be heavy casualties. There are many armed men around the White House."

Yazov arrived and said, "Well, what have we got?"

Achalov said they simply didn't have the force to storm the White House successfully. Yazov told his subordinates to call in more troops, "we can't lose the initiative." But he seemed to let the matter drop.

At a separate planning meeting of the Alpha Group, a senior officer, Anatoly Salayev, got up and said, "They want to smear us in blood. Each of you is free to act according to his conscience. I for one will not storm the White House." In Tbilisi, Baku, and Vilnius, the military and KGB rank and file had seen how they had been used to shed blood, and each time the leading men in power dodged responsibility. They simply would not let it happen again, especially not when it involved killing their own countrymen.

In the meantime, KGB and undercover police agents continued to take photographs and videos of the scene outside and inside the White House. "We filmed everything," Karpukhin told a reporter from *Literaturnaya Gazeta.* "We had agents both among the defenders and inside the parliament. At night, General Lebed and I toured the barricades. They were toys; we could have smashed them easily."

"What was the battle plan?"

"At three A.M. the OMON police troops would clear the square. They would disperse the crowd with tear gas and water cannons. Our units would follow, from the ground and from the air, by using helicopters, grenade launchers, and other special means. . . . Then we would take the building. . . . My boys are practically invulnerable. The whole thing would be over in fifteen minutes. . . . It was all up to me. Thank God I couldn't bring myself to do it. It would have been a bloodbath. I refused."

There were more mundane considerations, too, for the KGB. Like the difficulty of landing helicopters in rainy weather and on a roof that had deliberately been strewn with broken furniture and other debris. Like the problem of air force commander Shaposhnikov, who refused to allow the use of his helicopters for the raid and even threatened an airborne counterattack

against the junta. There was also the threat of an extremely high body count. Anyone on those barricades that night—KGB informers included—knew that there was at the White House a general willingness to die, a refusal to clear the way for an attack. What's more, there was also the possibility of humiliation, even defeat. Yeltsin and some of his aides spent part of the night in an underground bunker sealed by a twenty-inch-thick steel door. The KGB might have wondered what would happen if, at the cost of thousands of lives, they "took" the White House, but could not come away with Yeltsin. According to the prosecutor's report, Generals Grachev and Shaposhnikov agreed that if the Emergency Committee began to storm the White House, they would retaliate and give the order to send bombers over the Kremlin.

—

At 8:00 P.M., the Emergency Committee met at the Kremlin. Yanayev shocked his colleagues, telling them that he had heard "rumors" that the committee was organizing an attack on the White House. He proposed that they announce on television that the rumors were untrue.

There was a silence, witnesses told the Russian prosecutors, and then Yanayev said, "Is there really someone here among us who wants to storm the White House?"

No one answered. When Kryuchkov began to talk about how he was hearing from all over the country that the committee had won massive support, Yanayev said, no, he had been getting telegrams telling him just the opposite. The putschists were hoping to win support by flooding the stores with goods and lowering prices, if only for a few weeks. But it was all a fantasy. The military reserves were not what anyone thought they were. There was just enough to feed the army for a few days.

The coup was unraveling. At 3:00 A.M. on the 21st, Kryuchkov called the White House. He spoke with Yeltsin's closest aide, Gennadi Burbulis.

"It's okay now," the spy chief said. "You can go to sleep."

AUGUST 21, 1991

Thousands of people woke on the barricades that morning happy to be alive. They were still there, and that was something. Most of the talk I heard there was about the death of the three demonstrators on the Garden Ring Road; they pieced together the details of that quick burst of hysteria and gunfire that had killed Dmitri Komar, Ilya Krichevsky, and Vladimir Usov. Most of all, people were exhausted, sore, still nervous, still overstimulated by the

stream of rumors. Some people were still passing around bottles of vodka and Armenian cognac. Nadezhda Kudinova headed for home, satisfied she had done what she had to do. "On the barricades," she said, "there was this incredible feeling of fellowship, which you will never get on a queue or on a trolley where men will never give you a seat. In everyday life, I guess you just don't notice it. But these were extreme circumstances, and somehow this week I saw the profound aspects of human nature. I never knew there were so many kind people in my country."

What Kudinova and the others could not have known was that they had won. The coup, insofar as it had ever really taken hold, had collapsed. The combination of confusion, stupidity, drunkenness, lack of will, miscalculation, and happenstance (the blessed rain!) had all conspired against the committee. And just as a change in consciousness in the people had led to this incredible resistance, one could not rule out that even the conspirators had evolved beyond their ancestors. They had the same Stalinist impulses, but not the core of cruelty, the willingness to flood the city in blood, call it a victory for socialism, and then go off to a midnight screening of *Happy Guys.* They could pick up the pistol, but not always shoot it. They were bullies, and bullies could be called on their bluff.

Already the members of the committee were thinking about the future. Oleg Baklanov was still talking about arresting Yeltsin and his aides. "If we don't get them, they will hang us," he told General Gromov.

At three separate meetings—with Kryuchkov at Lubyanka, with Yazov at the Ministry of Defense, with Yanayev at the Kremlin—the Emergency Committee was making plans to shut it all down.

"We must think now what to do," Yazov told his senior commanders. They responded quickly, voting unanimously to send troops back to their barracks and lift the curfew. Yazov knew that some of these officers had defied him, even provided intelligence to Yeltsin, and so he agreed, saying, magnanimously, "I will not be another Pinochet." Then the generals demanded that Yazov quit the committee, but, for all his reservations, he refused.

"I'm not a boy," he said, as he got up to leave. "I can't act in this manner, joining yesterday and resigning today. . . . I'm sorry I ever got mixed up in this business."

Yeltsin hung up the phone and knew it was over. Kryuchkov had called, suggesting they fly together to Foros. Yeltsin knew well that it might be a ruse, a way for Kryuchkov to flush him from his nest, capture him, and keep

the junta going. But it smacked of desperation. He would stay in Moscow, but he would send Rutskoi, the Russian vice president, and Ivan Silayev, the prime minister.

"We've got the bastards," Yeltsin told Burbulis. "They're on the run."

The retreat began after 11:00 A.M. when the first tanks turned around near Red Square. By 1:00 P.M., huge convoys stormed along the main arteries out of town, endless columns of tanks and personnel carriers chewing up the soft asphalt and heading toward their barracks.

I jumped into a car with Debbie Stewart of the Associated Press, who drove wildly along the tank column. Weaving in and out of the convoy and racing up and down the columns, we saw an amazing display of joy. The armies of Napoleon, Hitler, and other would-be conquerors of Moscow had time and again fled Russia in despair and defeat. These soldiers were retreating in relief and sheer pleasure, as if they had won the victory of an age. The machines made Leninsky Prospekt tremble. I could feel the rumbling at the base of my throat and on the soles of my feet. All along the convoy, the soldiers, most of them eighteen or nineteen years old, smiled and laughed. The worst had not happened. They had not shamed themselves. They had not shot at their brothers and sisters, their mothers and fathers. In gratitude, old women threw bunches of red carnations and white roses at the boys in their tanks. Construction crews stopped work and applauded the parade. The soldiers answered with the thumbs-up and applauded back.

"It's over! We've got our orders!" a commander shouted above the furious din. "Thank God, we're headed home!"

At one point along the retreat, at the huge sign on Leninsky Prospekt declaring "The USSR: Stronghold of Socialism," a man named Sergei Pavlov pulled his Lada over to the side of the road and shouted out his window that he was ready to follow the parade all the way to the barracks. "I'm taking no chances," he said. "I want to make sure the tanks are really leaving."

Thus commenced the "race to Foros," with both Yeltsin's representatives, Vice President Rutskoi and Prime Minister Silayev, and the men of the putsch, Yazov, Baklanov, Tizyakov, and Kryuchkov, flying on separate planes. Lukyanov, in a marvelous touch, took yet another plane, as if to distance himself from all but his own peculiar position. He brought along Vladimir Ivashko, the deputy general secretary of the Party.

And while everyone else was migrating south, Yanayev sat in his office, disheveled, as two of Gorbachev's men came in. The aides had been down the hall working during the entire coup d'état.

"Has everyone been arrested?" Yanayev said, his face twitching.

"Yes," said the former steelworker Veniamin Yarin, in a blatant lie.

Yanayev whined about how the plotters had threatened him with jail and a "tribunal" if he didn't cooperate. He had joined only "to avert bloodshed," he said, meaning his own, not Moscow's.

"Yanayev realized why I was there," Yarin said later. "There was fear in his eyes. . . . And, yes, he was very drunk."

Yanayev stayed in the office all night, and when Yarin returned early the next morning, there were empty bottles all over the floor. Yanayev was awake, but he could no longer recognize Yarin. As Jim Hoagland of *The Washington Post* wrote of the putsch, it began like Dostoevsky and was ending like the Marx Brothers.

On the flight to the Crimea, Rutskoi's men—around fifty troops from the Ryazan officers' school—sat in their seats cleaning their machine guns. One colonel said that if there was a problem at the dacha, "We'll break through anything." But Vadim Bakatin, the liberal interior minister who had been fired as Gorbachev began his shift to the right, spoke up and said the soldiers should stay out of sight and avoid any sort of provocation. "If there's even a single shot, they'll blame it on us when Gorbachev is found dead," Bakatin said. The soldiers agreed to stay on the plane.

When the delegation of Russians arrived in Foros, they were let through the gates, but they saw snipers in the trees and on balconies. They were anxious until the very moment they made it to the door. There was no attack, no trap. Clearly, the KGB guards had been instructed to stand down.

Gorbachev wanted only to see the Russians. He refused to meet with Kryuchkov or Yazov. As he greeted Rutskoi and the rest, Gorbachev looked weary but relieved. He wore a light gray sweater and khaki trousers and was literally trembling with excitement. He kept repeating that there had been a coup against a legitimate president, a commander in chief, that the briefcase with the secret codes had been taken away from him, that it was all a "blasphemy." "There's one thing I want to say," Gorbachev explained. "I made no deals. I maintained a firm position, demanding the immediate summoning of a session of the Congress or the Supreme Soviet. Only they can decide the issue. Otherwise, after any other step, I would have had to finish myself off. There could be no other way out. . . . I was cut off from any communication. The sea was closed off by ships. There were troops all around. It was complete and total isolation."

Bakatin and Yevgeny Primakov, two Gorbachev loyalists who had supported the resistance, told their man several times what a singular role Yeltsin had played and that when Gorbachev returned to Moscow there could be no

more conflicts. Gorbachev promised he would do this. Some of the Russians, none too gently, reminded Gorbachev that the conspirators had all been the president's men. It was true, Gorbachev admitted. "I had complete confidence in the people around me, and I relied on them. My gullibility undermined me. On the one hand, it's probably good to trust people, but not to this extent."

Gorbachev got testy when someone said he had to pass a decree saying that he was reinstated as president. "I never stopped being president!" he said. And as for the charge that he had been critically ill, it was all "nonsense, an absurd pretext." Silayev had brought along two doctors—both heart specialists—but there was clearly no need. Gorbachev, Silayev said, "looked amazingly well." Raisa was quite another story. The Russians were startled as they saw her try to navigate the stairs and come down to greet the Russians. "She was in horrible condition," said one member of the Russian delegation, Vladimir Lysenko. "She wobbled as she walked, but she did make sure to kiss all of us."

"Should we fly home tonight?" Gorbachev finally asked Raisa.

"Yes," she answered softly. "We must fly immediately."

Gorbachev did have a brief meeting with Lukyanov, his old friend from Moscow State University and the Komsomol. Right away, Lukyanov tried to explain his position, how difficult it would have been to convene an immediate emergency session of the Union parliament, how he had tried to fend off the coup.

Gorbachev was having none of it.

"We have known each other for forty years!" he said. "Cut the bullshit! Stop hanging noodles on my ears!"

At the Belbek military airport, the presidential plane, the Ilyushin 62 marked "Sovietsky Soyuz," idled on the tarmac. A half mile away, near some MiG-29 fighter jets, was the smaller Tupolev 134 which Rutskoi had brought from Moscow. The Zil limousines raced between the two planes, trying to make it seem as if Gorbachev had been dropped off at his usual jet. He hadn't. Finally, Gorbachev boarded the Tu-134.

On the runway, Gorbachev approached the state chief of civil aviation and his personal pilot and said, "Please don't have hurt feelings, but I'll be taking the Russian plane. Understand the situation. I'm doing the right thing."

"Let's go," Raisa said, "but only with the Russians."

With the collapse of the coup, the Russian Republic's own news show, *Vesti,* returned to the air at 8:00 P.M.. The lead announcer, Yuri Rostov, who had been thrown off the air by the head of state television, Leonid Kravchenko, could barely contain his glee. He was grinning and on the edge of tears. "Congratulations!" he told us. "The junta is at an end!"

Rostov did not bother with the niceties of objectivity and did little to control his contempt for the men he wryly called "the saviors of our Motherland"—the plotters who had engineered the coup. He also made sure to warn the viewers that Russia "should not repeat one of Gorbachev's greatest mistakes: forgetting that the KGB is the biggest opponent of reform." After going through the stunning news of the day, Rostov delivered the bulletin that may have delighted him most of all, the dismissal of "that man beloved by us and treasured by you TV viewers, Leonid Petrovich Kravchenko."

In the early hours of the morning, Gorbachev sat in the forward cabin of the plane surrounded by his exhausted family. His granddaughter was wrapped in a plaid blanket, and slept on the floor. Rutskoi and Silayev talked quietly with Gorbachev, the better not to wake the others. They opened a bottle of wine and drank to the end of the coup.

Off in the rear cabin, Kryuchkov sat alone, a captive, his head thrown back, his eyes closed, but he was not asleep. He spoke to no one and no one spoke to him. Armed guards watched his every twitch.

When the plane landed in Moscow at Vnukovo Airport, the escort delegation told Gorbachev to wait a bit before coming down the steps until the guards were sure there would be no surprise attack. A guard with a machine gun came out the door first and scanned the airfield. There was nothing, no last trap. The conspirators had nothing left in them. Finally, Gorbachev appeared in the doorframe. He wore a beige windbreaker. His suntan looked, under the circumstances, ridiculous. His face was a cross of pleasure and fear as if he did not know quite what awaited him even now. Behind him was his daughter in her denim miniskirt, Raisa, and his granddaughter clumping sleepily down the stairs. Raisa was dazed, spent.

From the minute Gorbachev got off the plane, people kept telling him that he had returned to a "different city," even a "different country." The "slave mentality" that had plagued poets from Pushkin on was at an end, and Gorbachev seemed to agree. He could not afford to disagree. At least he understood that much.

Gorbachev paused in front of a television camera. Before anyone could ask a question, Yevgeny Primakov said, "No, Mikhail Sergeyevich is tired. The car is ready. We should go."

"No, wait," Gorbachev said. "I want to breathe the air of freedom in Moscow."

Out on the tarmac, the Russian prosecutors arrested Kryuchkov, Yazov, and the industrialist Tizyakov.

"Did the people really see our actions as so terrible?" Kryuchkov said. "Well, now it is the end of the committee."

Sergei Shakhrai, one of Yeltsin's closest legal advisers, said Kryuchkov "lost control of himself when he was detained. He could not control his hands or his facial expressions or recognize his own things. The man could be seen to be in a state of profound depression. . . . Yazov behaved more calmly and was in possession of himself, though he was deathly pale. The first thing he requested was help for his sick wife. . . . Tizyakov was outwardly normal, but you could sense he was bursting with spite. You got the feeling that he was ready simply to bite and tear to pieces anyone who got too close."

The men who had set out to save the empire were now under arrest. An officer of the law took away their shoelaces, belts, and all sharp objects. It was standard procedure.

The conspirators had launched the putsch to save the Soviet empire and their positions in it. Their failure was the finishing blow. No Baltic independence movement, no Russian liberals, had ever done as much to bring it all down. And now Yazov, at least, seemed to know it. "Everything is clear now," he said as they led him into a van with bars on the windows. "I am such an old idiot. I've really fucked up."

PART V

THE TRIAL OF THE OLD REGIME

For two days after the fall of the coup, the dictators of the proletariat and their assistants at Central Committee headquarters ransacked their desks and emptied their safes. They fed one incriminating document after another into the shredding machines. To destroy everything in the archives would have taken months or years, yet there was a chance, at least, that they could eliminate all evidence of the Party's support of the coup and other recent embarrassments.

There was so little time. Thousands of furious demonstrators were shouting up at the windows of the Central Committee, demanding the destruction of the Party, the confiscation of its properties. The same crowds of students, housewives, workers, and intellectuals who had defended the White House now fanned out across the city, toppling the monuments of the regime and carrying signs reading "Smash the KGB!" "Send the Party to Chernobyl!" "Bring the Party to Trial!" But then the shredders began to jam and break, one after another. In their haste, the men of the Party had failed to remove the paper clips.

With the shouts from the street throbbing in their ears, some panicked officials suggested building a huge bonfire in the courtyards. Their juniors, however, advised them that if the demonstrators saw smoke coming from the

Central Committee, they would know what was happening and would storm the building. What could they do? Party workers were already driving truckloads of material away through the hidden tunnels and back exits of the Central Committee building, and even that was not enough. There was so much to destroy and hide! And so now these ashen men—men who had ruled an empire with an inimitable blend of insouciance and banality—began tearing apart documents with their bare hands. They would sooner die of paper cuts than leave the evidence to the hordes.

The Party men, of course, were not interested merely in history's judgment. They refused to leave anything to the masses. To the very end, their serene sense of entitlement guided them. They stole telephones, computers, fax machines, television sets, video recorders, stationery. Anatoly Smirnov, an aide in the Party's International Department, said that his superior, Valentin Falin, gave him 600,000 rubles in cash and told him to stash it in his personal safe. Immediately.

And change the nameplate on my door, Falin ordered. Falin was sure that if he identified himself as a "People's Deputy" rather than as Central Committee secretary he would be immune from future prosecution.

Falin had a great deal to answer for. His office was in charge of dispensing millions from the state purse to "brotherly parties" or terrorist organizations in Greece, Portugal, the United States, Angola—nearly one hundred countries in all, according to the Russian government. He ran the secret workshop within the Central Committee that produced fake passports, beards, and mustaches for operatives on the road. Falin eventually took refuge in Germany, lecturing to the university students of Hamburg.

"Those were awful days for us," Vladimir Ivashko, the deputy general secretary of the Party, told me. "We were all terrified. We were suffering terribly inside the Central Committee. The Party was in the midst of reform, but no one would listen to that! It was terribly unfair!"

Even after he returned from captivity to Moscow following the fall of the August coup, Gorbachev defended the Communist Party. He was its son, its protector, and he would neither abandon nor kill it. At his first press conference after the putsch, Gorbachev spoke earnestly about his allegiance to the "socialist choice" and the Party's "renewal." He told all who would listen that he had returned to a "different country," but he did not seem to know what that meant.

Gorbachev's closest adviser, Aleksandr Yakovlev, grew furious as he watched that mystifying session with the press. For six years, Yakovlev had prodded Gorbachev to abandon the hidebound nomenklatura and join

forces with the urban intelligentsia, the pro-independence forces in the Baltic states—with all those who actually sought a transformation of the old order. But Gorbachev refused, insisting that the party had "begun perestroika and would lead it." Even now, after falling victim to a putsch, Gorbachev failed to see what was right and necessary.

"You have given the worst press conference of your career," Yakovlev told Gorbachev privately. "The Party is dead. Why can't you see that? Talk about its 'renewal' is senseless. It's like offering first aid to a corpse!"

Yeltsin catered even less to the sensibilities of Mikhail Gorbachev. Their personal battle had gone on for so long and contained so many seriocomic incidents that they seemed paired in eternal tension and dependence. Yin and Yang. Punch and Judy. On August 23, at a raucous session of the Russian parliament, Yeltsin clearly had the upper hand, and he used it to flay and humiliate his opponent. He forced Gorbachev to read aloud a transcript of the August 19 Council of Ministers meeting at which all but two of the ministers whom Gorbachev himself had nominated pledged their hearty support of the coup.

Gorbachev looked small and weak, but Yeltsin was not finished. "And now on a lighter note," he said with a jack-o'-lantern grin, "shall we now sign a decree suspending the activities of the Russian Communist Party?"

"What are you doing?" Gorbachev stammered. "I . . . haven't we . . . I haven't read this . . ."

But it was too late. Gorbachev was powerless. And on August 24, he resigned as general secretary of the Communist Party, dissolved its Central Committee, and declared, in essence, an end to the Bolshevik era.

The people of Moscow did not celebrate Gorbachev for his announcement. He could have done no less. Perhaps one day they would come to recognize and revere Gorbachev's contribution, but not now, not yet. Now they celebrated themselves and the ruin of the System. All around the city, young people smeared statues of Old Bolsheviks with graffiti and uprooted them with crowbars or, when necessary, cranes. The Moscow city government sponsored the removal of the huge statue of "Iron" Feliks Dzerzhinsky from the square outside KGB headquarters, thus creating the ultimate image of the regime's demise: the founder of the secret police dangling from a noose as the crowd cheered. Within a few days, the field next to the Tretyakov Gallery had become a Communist mortuary; children climbed on toppled statues of Sverdlov, Dzerzhinsky, and other fallen revolutionaries. The Museum of the Revolution put up a display honoring the resistance to the coup, and the Lenin Museum simply closed down "pending reconstruction."

For a while, the celebration was mixed with the macabre.

Marshal Akhromeyev, Gorbachev's military adviser, was found dead in his office, his neck in a noose, a series of suicide notes laid out neatly on his desk. The first described how he had botched a first attempt: "I am a poor master of preparing my own suicide. The first attempt (at 9:40) didn't work—the cord broke. I'll try with all my strength to do it again." Another letter was addressed to Gorbachev, and in it Akhromeyev explained why he had rushed home from vacation to support the coup; in closing, he asked forgiveness for having broken military regulations. And in a letter to his family, the marshal wrote, "I cannot live when my Fatherland is dying and all that I have made my life's work is being destroyed. My age and all I have done give me the right to leave this life. I struggled to the end."

Investigators arrived at the apartment of Boris Pugo to arrest him for his role in the coup and instead found a revolting scene of carnage. Pugo, dressed in a blue track suit, was dead, a gaping bullet wound in his head; his wife was also shot, but half alive. Pugo's aged father-in-law, in a late stage of dementia, wandered around the small apartment, as if nothing had happened. Pugo left a suicide note for his children and grandchildren: ". . . Forgive me. It was all a mistake. I lived honestly, all my life."

Nikolai Kruchina, a Communist Party official who had administered the finances of the Central Committee, jumped from his apartment window to his death. The newspapers speculated that Kruchina knew better than anyone else about the Party's foreign bank accounts, its funding of foreign Communist parties, its secret squandering of gold reserves and other resources. According to Russian journalists, the official news wire Tass was aware of at least fifteen other suicides but did not report them.

Under arrest, the chief conspirator, the now former chief of the KGB, was cool and unrepentant. "My heart and soul are full of various feelings," Kryuchkov told a reporter for Russian television. "I recall the entirety of my life, the way I lived it, and if I had the chance, I would take the same course. I believe I've never done anything in my life my Motherland could blame me for. If I could turn back the clock five or six days, I might have chosen a different way and I would not be behind bars. I hope the court will pass a fair decision, an optimal judgment, that will allow me to work in conditions of freedom and serve my Motherland, whose interests mean everything to me."

After his plea of innocence failed in the Supreme Soviet, Anatoly Lukyanov also went to jail—isolation cell No. 4 of Matrosskaya Tishina, "Sailor's Rest," one of the most notorious prisons in Moscow. And as he waited for the prosecutors to prepare their case and begin a trial, he turned once more to poetry. He still believed in "the cause," and that the people of the Soviet Union should trust in him. His new theme was self-pity:

Human gratitude! There will be none of that!
Do not wait for it, do not torment or mourn,
All trust is now in ashes,
And there are glib slanders in all the papers,
But I know that there will be rewards,
There will be an honest trial in our souls,
There will be new shoots, like the gifts of spring.

Andrei Karaulov, the cultural editor for *Nezavisimaya Gazeta,* visited Lukyanov and heard him complain about Gorbachev. "I love him. I can't change him, though. Speaking openly, I know his weaknesses, his shortcomings," Lukyanov said. "Of all the people who made perestroika, I alone stayed next to Gorbachev, the rest left, from the left and right. . . . Time will show I was loyal. . . . I will remain a Communist, maybe without a Party membership card, but all the same. . . . I am to blame before the parliament, because this dealt it a blow. These are my children, my pain, my creation. This is very painful. I feel my blame before my mother, who lost her husband, lost her first son, and now is losing me. She is eighty-five and I love her very much. I am to blame before my wife, a great scholar, a corresponding member of the Academy of Medical Sciences, before my daughter . . . I am to blame before my grandson, my greatest pleasure, but to him and to all people I can say that I lived honestly, worked, without complaining, sixteen hours a day. And maybe they will remember some good poetry I wrote. . . . I don't know if I'll write again, but I . . . well, I'll say that my book closes with these words:

" 'And yet, and yet,
I hurried to turn
The final page . . .
I believed in our shining destiny . . .'

"No, no, that's not it. Now . . . now I remember . . .

" 'I believed in our shining destiny,
I never avoided the hard work,
I was ashamed to work poorly . . .
And if . . .' "

But Lukyanov gave up. "I've forgotten it," he said. "I've forgotten. . . ."

—

With time, Gorbachev himself began to admit that he had played a dangerous game with the Party for far too long. In interviews he seemed a kind of political analysand, rambling on, finding moments of self-discovery among the ego, the pride, the self-deception: "Do you think I did not know that the Party's conservative circles, which had united with the military-industrial complex, would make a strike? I knew, and I kept them beside me," he said. "But they procrastinated. They, too, were also afraid that the people would not follow them, and they waited for the people's discontent. . . . I will tell you: if [the conspirators] had acted twelve or eighteen months earlier the way they did in August, it would have come off. It is worth realizing this. . . ."

He was right. Had the leaders of the KGB and the Central Committee wanted in 1988 or 1989 to get rid of Gorbachev and return to an Andropov-style regime of modest reform and bitter discipline, they could have succeeded. At least for a while. But now they had to deal with an elected leader of Russia and tens of thousands of people who now felt themselves to be citizens, empowered. Gorbachev had to admit that he had failed to understand the fury of the hard-line opposition. "I certainly did not think they would go as far as a putsch," he said. "At some point, I misjudged the situation. For all the importance of strategy, it is important in politics to make the right decision at the right moment. It like a battle in war. . . . I should have forged a strong common front with the democrats. . . . I should have realized that earlier, in August 1990. I should have looked for some form of cooperation then, held a roundtable discussion or some other meeting. I missed that opportunity and paid dearly for it."

In early September, Gorbachev assembled the Congress of People's Deputies at the Kremlin for what would be its last session. It would be the last time, in fact, that the Kremlin would function as "the center."

The session itself was an elaborate ruse, a last bit of political theater directed by Mikhail Gorbachev. While the Baltic states, Moldavia (now Moldova), and Georgia already considered themselves independent, the remaining ten republican leaders decided with Gorbachev to dissolve the Congress and create the basis for a new decentralized Union. Gorbachev envisioned the new Union with Moscow retaining some key functions as a coordinator of the common defense and foreign policy. Yeltsin differed and said that the Union presidency would be ceremonial, "something like the Queen of England." What was most remarkable was the way Gorbachev and his newfound allies rammed the interim proposals on a new Union through the Congress, a body, after all, that was packed with Communist Party apparatchiks. Gorbachev was so eager to get what he wanted and finish the

Congress that he promised the deputies that even after the dissolution of the legislature, they would still get salaries and priority access to plane and railway tickets. That was enough to win their votes.

On December 26, 1991, at his dacha in the woods outside Moscow, Mikhail Gorbachev climbed into the backseat of his Zil limousine and headed north toward the Kremlin. Suddenly the Soviet Union was a half-remembered dream and its last general secretary a pensioner. Ukraine's decision to pull out of the negotiations for a new Union finally ended Gorbachev's hopes for a place for himself as its president. Instead, the leaders of Russia, Ukraine, and Byelorussia patched together a sketchy plan for a new commonwealth. There was no role left for "the center." The republican leaders voted on Gorbachev's retirement package.

Now, in Moscow, Gorbachev wanted to take care of some last-minute meetings and clean out his desk before leaving for a few weeks of vacation. The Russian government had promised him a peaceful boxing day before they took up residence. But when Gorbachev arrived at the Kremlin, he saw his nameplate had already been pried off the wall. "Yeltsin, B. N." gleamed brassily in its place. Inside the office, Boris Nikolayevich himself was behind the desk. For days there had been the air of self-pity about Gorbachev, and this petty incident, a gaudy exclamation in the intricate narrative of these revolutionary days, magnified his fury. Never mind Gorbachev's own assaults on Yeltsin over the years. "For me, they have poisoned the air," he complained. "They have humiliated me."

Comeuppance was what it was. In 1987, Gorbachev had dragged Yeltsin from a hospital bed and made him stand before the Moscow city Party organization for hour after hour of denunciations. Yeltsin spent the next several weeks under a doctor's care, suffering from nervous exhaustion. When given the chance to humiliate Gorbachev, Yeltsin grabbed it.

In their last meeting, Gorbachev had promised Yeltsin he would stay away from politics. He would not be an opposition figure. He had, it seemed, no other choice. "Yeltsin had Gorbachev by the balls," said Sergei Grigoriyev, who had been deputy spokesman for Gorbachev. All the KGB, Communist Party, and military archives were now in Yeltsin's hands. KGB officials told me that in the days before and after the coup, secret police workers were dumping crates of documents into underground furnaces, but the few files that did leak after the coup could only have embarrassed Gorbachev. There were documents showing Gorbachev's approval of secret funding of the Polish Communist Party even after Solidarity came to power. Another file showed him maneuvering to prevent the German government from opening

the old East German archives. Yeltsin also came into possession of transcripts of his own phone calls from the days when the Gorbachev government and KGB tried desperately to discredit him. Gorbachev's handwritten notes were in the margins.

Moreover, few believed anymore that Gorbachev was merely an innocent bystander during the worst moments of the perestroika years: the military attacks on peaceful demonstrators in Tbilisi, Vilnius, Riga, and Baku. When his popularity was at its height, he escaped blame. He was out of the country or out of the loop. But now even those closest to him admitted otherwise. "I am sure Gorbachev knew all about what was going on in Vilnius and Riga," said Nikolai Petrakov, who had been Gorbachev's chief economist. Other top-ranking officials, sympathetic to Gorbachev, agreed.

But that was all past, and now Russia faced a great historical moment, an elected president occupying the Kremlin for the first time in the thousand-year history of Russia, the hammer and sickle gone from the flagpole, the regime and empire dissolved. And yet it all had the pallid, made-for-television feel of Washington ceremony. History felt like nothing more than a miserable winter day, the sky as empty and wan as the butcher shops. The Western press corps roamed Red Square in desperate search of passion or comment. "You care, we don't," a fist-faced old woman from the provincial city of Tver told a clutch of reporters. With that the woman stormed off in search of potatoes and milk for her family.

In the afternoon, Gorbachev's press secretary, Andrei Grachev, invited a small group of aides, foreign reporters, and Russian editors to a reception at the Oktyabrskaya Hotel. A farewell party, Grachev billed it, and he could not have chosen a more appropriate stage. For years, the hotel across from the French embassy had been a symbol of the Communist Party's opulence, heavy on the marble and mirrors.

At a few minutes before five o'clock, the reporters and editors stood waiting at the top of the marble stairs for the guest of honor to arrive. By chance, I took my place near Len Karpinsky, who was now the editor in chief of *Moscow News,* and Vitaly Tretyakov, whose *Nezavisimaya Gazeta* was now, with *Izvestia,* the most respected paper in the country. Gorbachev's resignation meant a transition from the intellectual idealists of Karpinsky's generation to a breed of younger men and women like Tretyakov—business neophytes, scholars, hustlers, and, in this case, newspaper editors—who would perhaps build a new world not so much out of the jagged ruins of the old experiment, but on a model, faintly perceived, from the West, from Europe and America. As Gorbachev was leaving center stage, so, too, was Karpinsky. *Moscow News,* which had broken one taboo after another in the first years of perestroika, was a tired paper: still interesting at times, still

honest, but one that spoke to a generation that now seemed, like Gorbachev, exhausted.

"It's good that Gorbachev's leaving now, but I am moved to the core of me," Karpinsky told me. "How can I deny that I have just finished the most important chapter of my life?"

—

In the spring of 1992, Gorbachev toured the United States in the Forbes corporate jet, *The Capitalist Tool.* He saw nothing odd or ironic in this. The crowds tossed garlands at his feet, plutocrats deposited checks in his name. He spent an afternoon with Ronald Reagan drinking wine and eating chocolate-chip cookies. They reminisced about the cold war, long over. It seemed to all the victory tour of the century's last great man.

But in Russia, Gorbachev was unwanted, hated by the Party men he had betrayed and ignored by the democrats he had abandoned. Many were ready to think the worst of him. *Izvestia,* the most authoritative daily in Russia, published a front-page item in May saying that Gorbachev was getting ready to walk out the very doors he had opened. The first and last president of the Soviet Union, *Izvestia* said, had bought a two-story house in Florida "with a lot of land" for $108,350 in a development called Tropical Golf Acres.

In fact, Gorbachev had not bought land abroad and denied any plans to emigrate. "I repeat, for anyone who is still willing to listen," he said, "I have no dacha in California, nor in Geneva, nor in Tibet with tunnels leading to China." And yet some of Gorbachev's closest friends and confidants admitted to me that he was angry and on edge, harboring both terror and grand illusions about his future. "Gorbachev fears he may have to flee the country one day like some kind of Papa Doc Duvalier," said the playwright Mikhail Shatrov, who was helping Gorbachev write his memoirs. "He knows only too well that eleven of the fourteen coup plotters have testified against him, claiming he somehow encouraged the August putsch. Gorbachev knows the situation is unpredictable. At the same time, Gorbachev has delusions of returning to power. Not right away, but someday. But it won't happen. He cannot return to power."

Gorbachev's new base of operations was now a plush building in northern Moscow once known as "the School with No Name." Foreign Communists from nonsocialist countries once came to this institute to learn their ideological catechism. Under Gorbachev, the institute was intended as half think tank and half nonprofit foundation. But it wasn't much of either. Gorbachev was restless and open for anything, it seemed. For a sequel to Wim Wenders's *The Wings of Desire,* he played himself, wandering around a soundstage improvising a soliloquy on Dostoevsky and the state of the world. For

300,000 pounds, he sold the world television rights to his life story to an independent British company, Directors International, promising interviews, archives, and other access for a four-part series.

Naturally, Gorbachev's enemies in the press were prepared to attack him as a carpetbagger. "Those who are responsible for this country's catastrophe and smeared the word 'Communist' are now making a cozy nest for themselves at the expense of ordinary people," wrote *Sovetskaya Rossiya.*

Gorbachev was furious. " 'Yesterday's men' are a vengeful breed," he said in a long interview with *Komsomolskaya Pravda.* "Before, they tried to steer us away from the democratic path, and now they are after me personally. Well, to hell with them! What am I supposed to be afraid of? The firing squad? The courts? I am not going to tolerate accusations coming from people who have spent too much of their time believing in the slogans of the thirties."

Unfortunately, many commentators in Russia and in the West thought it necessary to choose sides, to be "pro-Gorbachev" or "pro-Yeltsin." They failed to see the beauty of what history had provided. Without Gorbachev, the agony of the system might have gone on indefinitely, not forever, surely—there was no money for that—but another ten, twenty, who knows how many years. What would the world look like in that case? But without Yeltsin, Gorbachev might well have dallied more than he did, the radical democrats might never have found a single, strong leader, the coup might have succeeded. As much as they had come to despise each other, Gorbachev and Yeltsin were linked in history.

Some of the best minds in the urban intelligentsia—the constituency that Gorbachev courted and ultimately lost—now regarded their former leader with a certain air of superiority. "His speech is that of an uncultured man. He whips the air," said Leonid Batkin, one of the leaders of the Democratic Russia movement. "Yet he is an outstanding man in his way, a great apparatchik. After Stalin, Gorbachev was the most skillful of all the apparatchiks. But when the time came for a real politician, Gorbachev did one stupid thing after another. He played his great role by yanking the stopper from the bottle. Now, he is not really interesting."

Natalya Ivanova, a literary critic, compared Gorbachev to "the man who gave the orders to begin the fateful experiment at Chernobyl. He wanted to refine the machine, but the machine went out of control and exploded."

And the novelist Viktor Yerofeyev said that Gorbachev was "like Valentina Tereshkova, the first female cosmonaut. She fainted right away and was dangling in orbit but still managed to press the right buttons at the right time just because she was dangling in the exact right place. She took off, she dangled, and she didn't die. That was her triumph. The same with Gorba-

chev. Gorbachev pressed the buttons he needed to and the combination of wrong and right buttons turned out to be just right. That created a metaphysical figure—a divine provident for Russia. Gorbachev guided Russia to its historical fate. He has entered the pantheon of Russian history and gradually he'll come to be seen as that great figure. But not soon. Russians are an ungrateful people."

Even Gorbachev's most sincere critics missed the point of what he was and who he was. Gorbachev was not Andrei Sakharov. He was not a moral prophet or an intellectual giant. He was not even a man of exceptional goodness. Gorbachev, above all, was a politician. He combined a rough sense of decency with a preternatural ability to manipulate a system that had seemed, from the outside, unbendable. If, in the language of the Greek fable, Sakharov was the fox, a man with a singular sense of moral and political ideals, then Gorbachev was the hedgehog, a man capable of deceit and cruelty, a man of shifting values and ideas, but a genius at a nasty game. An irreplaceable man in his moment.

From March 1985, when he began, until June 1989, when he presided over the first elected legislature of the Soviet Union, Gorbachev chipped away at the totalitarian monolith. From there, his personal story became tragic. He was dragged along by events and never seemed able to decide how to maneuver from one day to the next without losing himself entirely. "Watershed moments in history are not particularly pleasant to live through," Gorbachev said many times. "Before you stands a man who has been through a lot."

While he was in Palo Alto in 1992, Gorbachev delivered a speech at Stanford University that echoed that moment in November 1987 when perestroika really began in earnest. It was the seventieth anniversary of the Bolshevik Revolution, and Gorbachev used the occasion to declare the crimes of the Stalin era "unforgivable." At the time, he had to speak in euphemisms, he had to celebrate six ugly incidents to denounce one. But, now, in California, with power long gone, Gorbachev wanted us to feel as though he had always been a democrat, a liberal in his heart. Instead of quoting Lenin endlessly, he referred to Tocqueville, Solovyov, Jefferson, and Berdyaev. He even thanked the dissidents for their "contribution to the intelligentsia and even parts of the Party apparatus."

"Politics is the art of the possible," he said. "Any other approach would be voluntarism. . . . There were failures, mistakes and illusions, but the task was to unfetter the democratic process. . . . I tried to use tactical means to gain time, to give the democratic movement a chance to get stronger. As president, I had powers, including emergency powers, that people tried to push me into using more than once. I simply could not betray myself."

When I returned to Moscow at the end of 1992, the relics of Soviet Communism were passing quietly into the museums of the world and into the flea markets where kitsch is sold. "The Great Utopia," a vast exhibition of early revolutionary art, drew enormous crowds in Amsterdam, Frankfurt, and New York. On the main pedestrian mall in Moscow, the Arbat, young capitalists were conducting a bankruptcy sale of the fallen regime. They sold jackboots, epaulettes, Warsaw Pact compasses, thick tomes on dialectical materialism and scientific Communism. Maps of the Soviet Union were now sold as arch amusements, like bowling shirts or lava lamps. One student I met on the Arbat was making a killing with his stunning array of silk and velvet Communist Party banners. "I buy them cheap from retired apparatchiks," he said. "They dig them out of the closets, and then I sell them for five times the price."

In the triumphant days following the defeat of the coup in August 1991, the newspapers were filled with speculation over what was to become of the Lenin Mausoleum, that transcendent model of Soviet kitsch. Surely Lenin's waxy remains should be given a decent burial. Surely a better use could be found for the neo-cubist tomb on Red Square. A museum? An office building? A Pizza Hut? Boris Yeltsin hinted broadly that he, too, would just as soon put Lenin's corpse in the ground and get on with the new era.

At first, the leading figures of the Communist Party gave Yeltsin little reason to fear. He could afford a sense of irony. A few old apparatchiks gave interviews voicing muted resentment that Yeltsin had "undemocratically" outlawed the Communist Party and seized its properties in a series of three decrees issued in August and November 1991. But their voices were strained, wan, not quite convincing. Viktor Grishin, a former member of the Politburo who had made a feeble attempt to challenge Mikhail Gorbachev for the top Communist Party post in 1985, created a pathetic and fitting symbol of the old order's sorry fate: he dropped dead while waiting in a long line at his local pension office. He was hoping for a raise.

The Russian earthquake, however, for all its drama and ruthless speed, was far from complete. Much of the old regime survived. The smartest of the Communist Party men had long ago hired themselves out as "*biznesmeny*" and "*konsultanty.*" The average apparatchik hardly left his chair. Although the headquarters of the Communist Party's Central Committee had become the headquarters of the Russian government, the personnel inside were much the same. A few weeks after the fall of the coup, one of Yeltsin's aides visited the commandant of the Central Committee, Aleksandr Sokolov, and asked for a copy of its old phonebook. The Yeltsin government needed

experienced bureaucrats. "The result is that most of the same people are sitting in the same offices as they did a year ago," Sokolov told Michael Dobbs of *The Washington Post.* "When we were forming the new structures, we had to hire people from the old structures. Our supporters—the people who came to rallies and street demonstrations—didn't know anything about how to run a country."

In the Russian parliament, the most influential block of deputies was aligned with Civic Union, a band of moderate to conservative collective-farm chairmen, bureaucrats, and provincial bosses. A more reactionary alliance of nationalists and Communist ideologues known as the National Salvation Front controlled another sizable block of votes. The Communists in the Russian legislature never really renounced heir allegiance to the Party. Hard-liners like Sergei Baburin talked of the "renewal" of the "old ideals," and vengeance for the destruction of the Party. The conservative newspaper *Dyen* ("The Day") wrote openly of seizing power, "by any means." Yeltsin could count on the firm support of no more than 25 percent of the deputies in parliament.

Somewhere to the side of the daily political struggles that dominated post-totalitarian Russia, a historical sideshow had begun—a judicial battle over the life, death, and potential resurrection of the Communist Party. After members of the old regime had recovered from the shock of the coup and its humiliating aftermath, a group of thirty-seven Communist deputies petitioned the newly formed Constitutional Court of the Russian Federation in late 1991 for a hearing, declaring that Yeltsin's decrees outlawing the Party were unconstitutional. Wasn't Yeltsin acting as a dictator while pretending to be a democrat? A group of fifty-two anti-Communists—Yeltsin's supporters in the parliament—filed a counterpetition, claiming that the Communist Party was an unconstitutional organization. They agreed with Yeltsin's November 6, 1991, decree that the Party "was never a party" but rather "a special mechanism for the creation and realization of political power."

On May 26, 1992, Valery Zorkin, the chief justice of the new Constitutional Court, decided to try the suits simultaneously. After all, he declared, the issue was the same: was the Communist Party of the Soviet Union a constitutional political party, or something else?

Since late 1987, with the rise of such historical societies as Memorial and the publication in the press of the atrocities of the Stalin era, scholars and human rights activists had wondered if a time would ever come in the Soviet Union for a legal accounting, a Nuremberg-style trial. The mere mention of a trial was revolutionary, for one of the fundamental principles of the Bolsheviks had been to deny the primacy of civil law. Constitutions were written, celebrated in the pages of *Pravda,* and ignored: the Party was above the law.

Or as Lenin put it in 1918, the dictatorship of the proletariat "is unrestricted by law." Within months of taking power, Lenin liquidated the fragile legal system that had been in place since the czarist reforms of 1864 and commenced a system of state terror that was designed to intimidate the population and ensure the survival of the regime. "We must execute not only the guilty," Lenin's commissar of justice, Nikolai Krylenko, said. "Execution of the innocent will impress the masses even more."

Despite their hunger for historical judgment, even some of the best-known democratic activists in the country worried about the wisdom of a trial centered on the Communist Party. With the economy in collapse, with political structures so unsettled and moral questions of responsibility and repentance so painful and raw, where would such a trial lead? "Finally, the time has come now for this reckoning, and for repentance, but our circumstances are so peculiar in Russia that such trials are bound for failure," Arseny Roginsky, one of the founders of Memorial, told me one evening. "Nuremberg was a trial on war crimes, and the criminals were being judged by the victors, the victims of those crimes. Here we must judge ourselves. We judge each other. And who is unsullied? Who was a pure victim of the Party? Who was not complicit? I realize that is not the stated purpose of the Constitutional Court, but those are essential questions."

Such a trial was certain to be hopelessly confused—a political event in which old rivalries and resentments would be at issue. The Communists wanted the forum to charge Gorbachev with the betrayal of the Party and Yeltsin with the collapse of Soviet power. Yeltsin's team wanted to discredit Gorbachev—to take the shine off his historical reputation—and make sure that the old men of the Party had no easy access to building a conservative opposition. What was more, this was, in essence, a Constitutional Court without a constitution. The post-Communist state was still operating under the old Soviet Constitution while waiting for a new one to be written and approved.

Gorbachev, for his part, had become a bitter, deluded man, unable to understand why his fellow Russians would want to do anything but celebrate him. From the first announcement of the trial, he declared unequivocally that he would refuse to testify in court. It offended his dignity, his stature, his sense of propriety. He would not be questioned. In public, in private meetings, and in an interview with me, he wore his resentment like a pistol. "Look," he said, "I am not going to take part in this shitty trial."

The Constitutional Court convened on the morning of July 7, 1992. The courtroom was a remodeled meeting room in a part of the Central Commit-

tee complex that was once the offices of the Party membership committee. Thirteen judges, all but one of whom were former members of the Communist Party, sat at a curved dais in front of the Russian tricolor, the czarist-era flag. They wore long black robes, a strangely elegant and ecclesiastical outfit. The court had bought the fabric from the headquarters of the Russian Orthodox Church, and then Slava Zaitsev, the best-known fashion designer in Moscow, shaped it for judicial purposes. The haphazard mixture of symbols underscored the historical jumble prevalent in the court—the looming presence of the past, the fragility of the future.

Instead of brandishing a gavel to preserve order in the court, Chief Justice Valery Zorkin tapped his pen against a golden plate that dangled before him, gonging the lawyers into silence. Zorkin's task was as complicated as any jurist's in modern times. In a country with such a dubious legal history, he had to invent the procedures and decorum of the Constitutional Court just as he was presiding over what would surely be its most sensational trial for years to come. Zorkin himself had been a member of the Communist Party until October 1991—a fact that initially gave the pro-Communist side some relief—but he did not much romanticize the country's regard for law. "We have always swung from the icon to the ax," he said. "Everyone who came to power tried to make himself into an icon, but then they were cut down by the ax, metaphorically speaking. Every ruler liked to wield state power, but no one really tried to build a rule-of-law state. It is too soon to talk of Russia as a democratic state. Only these first few steps have been taken toward the rule of law."

On that first day of the trial, an angry crowd of pro-Communist demonstrators gathered outside the building. They screamed at the police, demanding to be let in. This was largely the same crowd that staged regular weekend protests outside the Lenin Museum near Red Square. They sold hard-line, neo-Stalinist newspapers and carried such placards as "Gorbachev and Yeltsin: To the Gallows!" Inside, the Communists, who had initiated legal proceedings in the first place, argued, in tones of injury and outrage, that they were "on trial" only because they had had the bad luck to lose power after the coup. One of the first speakers for the Communist side was Viktor Zorkaltsev, a Communist deputy in the Russian parliament, who shifted from ornate respect to high indignation within seconds:

"High court!

"Esteemed chairman!

"The Party that is banned here is the Party that consolidated society and rallied it to battle against fascism, thus ensuring the victory in the Great Patriotic War and sustaining, together with the people, irreplaceable human losses. . . . This does not mean that there have been no mistakes or negative

moments in the Party's activities. There was the dramatic phase of Stalinism in the thirties; there was suppression of dissent in the seventies; and there was the apostasy of the Party elite during the [Gorbachev] period. All of this happened. At the same time everyone knows that there have always been forces within the Party that rose up against these vices. And so it renewed itself, cleansed itself of this scum—sustaining losses, restoring its ranks, maintaining its ideals. And now, once again, this process is interrupted and it is banned at a turning point.

"Having shackled the party, the [democrats] have destroyed the national economy and the Union itself. They have changed the social system. The carving up of Russia has begun. The country has arrived at a dead end. What Hitler, world fascism, and capitalism were not able to accomplish has now become possible after the banning of the Party. The ban on the CPSU is also a signal to other parties: 'Beware! You are next!' And many parties feel this danger. Therefore only those who pathologically hate democracy and do not accept the socialist idea are gloating on this occasion. Thoughtful politicians do not approve of the president's decrees and do not support them. . . ."

And so on. The Party would be shameless to the end. Its members would argue their case on the basis of civil liberties, political pluralism, and the historical record. The Party men said now that the country had triumphed under their rule and gone to ruin in their absence. Such was history as they were prepared to present it in court.

When that high-minded tactic did not seem convincing to the court, or perhaps to themselves, the Communists' tone shifted from mock-heroic to threatening. At one point, another of the Party's representatives, Dmitri Stepanov, said that if Yeltsin's decrees were declared constitutional in court, then the Communists were prepared to use "the same methods" as the members of the August putsch to grab power.

"Emergency committees are nothing out of the ordinary," he said. "We have them all the time." He also defended the "alleged" brutality of the Party by saying that more people are killed in a couple of years in traffic accidents in Russia than were killed by Stalin. And besides, he added, the Party was never as brutal as the U.S. Army: "The Americans mowed down whole villages in Vietnam, whereas in the Baltic states we just exiled people to Siberia."

Sergei Shakhrai, Yeltsin's lead advocate in the Constitutional Court, was also prepared to argue the historical record. Shakhrai, a celebrated jurist in his mid-thirties, had written nearly all of Yeltsin's legal decrees during the siege of the White House. With the help of two other lawyers, Andrei Makarov and Mikhail Fedotov, Shakhrai set out to establish a case against the

Communist Party based on a historical record of dictatorship, deception, and violence.

"The organization that called itself the CPSU was neither a de facto nor a de jure party," Shakhrai said after a court session one day. "According to every canon of the Marxist-Leninist theory of the state and the law, we had a state that called itself the CPSU. There was a particular group of persons who dealt with the government and had a monopoly on the state: the one and a half million people in the Party nomenklatura, several million civil servants, and, finally, the special apparatus of coersion. The KGB was the armed detachment of this organization that called itself the CPSU and it was even used for the physical destruction of dissidents. Essentially we had a regime in which the basic law of the state and society were the rules of the Communist Party."

Among Shakhrai's first witnesses were three well-known political dissidents and former political prisoners: Lev Razgon, a writer who spent more than a decade in forced labor camps under Stalin; Vladimir Bukovsky, who was in the camps under Brezhnev from 1967 until he was finally traded to the West for the Chilean Communist leader Luis Corvalán in 1976; and Gleb Yakunin, a dissident Russian Orthodox priest who was imprisoned and later banished from practicing in Moscow. All three men provided firsthand testimony to the Party's brutality. To supplement the historical record, Richard Pipes, a historian at Harvard University and the author of *Russia Under the Old Regime* and *The Russian Revolution,* submitted into evidence an eighteen-page essay outlining the Communist Party's assumption of absolute state power within three months of the October coup.

"From the point of view of historical science," Pipes wrote, "the so-called party of the Bolsheviks was, of course, not a party, but an organization of a wholly new type, which had some features of a political party: Its structure was without precedent, an organization which was beyond government, which controlled the government and controlled everything, including the country's wealth. It was beyond any outside control. In no sense of the word was it a political 'party,' nor a voluntary social organization. . . . This political organization of an absolutely new type . . . was a precedent for the Fascist party of Mussolini and the Nazi party of Hitler and the countless so-called political parties of a totalitarian character which, beginning in Europe and then spreading throughout the world, established single-party government. . . . Never, in all its years of activity, did the Communist Party consider itself responsible to the law or constitution. It always considered its will and its goals the decisive factor; it always acted willfully, that is, unconstitutionally."

Although the testimony of former political prisoners, legislators, and Western historians was impressive enough, Shakhrai and his team meant to build an even more specific case. As a bureaucratic machine, the Party and the KGB left behind a paper trail of tens of millions of documents. Shakhrai petitioned the Russian government's new committee on the declassification of Party and KGB archives in order to provide documentary, and not merely anecdotal, proof of the way the Communist Party wielded and abused power. "Every kid in school now knows about the horrors perpetrated by the Communist Party, but we want to prove our case legally, with documents, so it cannot be denied," said Andrei Makarov.

When they first considered using the archives, Shakhrai's team had no idea what would be available to them. There was no telling what was lost—the tradition of destroying documents began early on when Lenin is said to have ordered the archive on the Red Terror cleaned out—but tens of millions of papers are now in government hands.

The Shakhrai team, of course, could not possibly hope to read even a fraction of the available documents, but they were able to obtain files describing in painful detail the purges of the 1930s, the repression of dissidents in the 1960s and 1970s, even transcripts of Politburo meetings at which the invasion of Afghanistan was discussed.

During the court's August recess, Shakhrai, Fedotov, and Makarov read through tens of thousands more pages of documents marked *Soversheno Sekretno,* "Top Secret." They were preparing for the climax of the trial scheduled for late September and early October when some of the biggest names of the Gorbachev era were scheduled to testify, Politburo members and Central Committee secretaries known mainly by their grainy portraits and the rumors of their politics and personalities: Yegor Ligachev, Nikolai Ryzhkov, Vladimir Dolgikh, Valentin Falin, Aleksandr Yakovlev, Ivan Polozkov.

Gorbachev, for his part, was still warning the court that he had no intention of testifying, that he would not appear "even if they dragged me there in handcuffs." (For this latter remark, the puckish daily *Nezavismaya Gazeta* published a front-page cartoon featuring Gorbachev being dragged to the court, hands cuffed.) The lawyers on Yeltsin's side certainly wanted to question Gorbachev, mainly to establish the idea that no one was above or beyond the legal system, but they also felt they could do without testimony from him. Mainly, it was the Communists who wanted the opportunity to put their former general secretary on the stand, to lacerate him for what they said was his betrayal of the Party. "Gorbachev had evil plans," Dolgikh said. "He destroyed the Party in 1989. Sure, the Party made mistakes. But the whole world recognized our power. When there was a Party, this country was

not falling apart." Ligachev, who had been the number-two man in the Party from 1985 to 1990, called Gorbachev a "revisionist," the same word Stalin once used like a branding iron on his doomed opponents. "Gorbachev started us on the path of anti-Communism," said Ligachev. "Perestroika lost its way and headed toward bourgeoisism."

After the first few days of the trial in July, most Russian and foreign journalists stayed away. They had more urgent things to do than cover this curious epilogue to the Communist era. There were wars in Abkhazia, Nagorny-Karabakh, and Tajikistan. There were breadlines and no electricity in Armenia. Vast hunks of Russia, from the northern Caucasus to Yakutia, were threatening to break away from Moscow's rule. The crime rate was spiraling almost as quickly as inflation. Shady businessmen were exploiting the new economic chaos and were exporting billions of dollars in capital out of the country. The Russian army was threatening to go to war in Moldova. The West was worried that the republics were still playing politics with the control of nuclear weapons. There were reports of arms deals with Iran and China. In Latvia and Estonia, few of the heroes of the independence movements showed themselves as nasty racists, forcing Russians, Poles, and other non-Balts into the status of second-class citizenship. In anger, Yeltsin put a halt to the withdrawal of troops from the region just weeks after it began.

So, no, the former Soviet Union was not wanting for more urgent issues and tragedies. For most, the trial was an afterthought. But, still, I wanted this last glimpse of the old regime—the last exhausted generation of Communist leaders. I could not resist it. For so many years, Soviets had seen these men as distant antigods, men with rumpled faces and dark fedoras, possessed of immense power, and silent. In the first years of the perestroika era, their unearthly quality faded somewhat as Gorbachev stripped the city of the old ubiquitous portraits and slogans. But they were still accountable to no one, available to no one. By the end of the decade, the press, both foreign and domestic, began to learn more about these elusive shades from their opponents, from rumor, even from actual interviews. But until now, they manipulated interviews the way they did the state. They were perfectly capable of listening to a reporter's question and then reeling off a pompous, hour-long speech, then dismissing the guest, his tea now cold in its china cup. But in court the Party men were nonentities, tired men in bad suits. In the audience, they mumbled angrily during testimony they did not approve of, and, like Baptist parishioners, they barked agreement to urge on their compatriots at the lectern.

On a day when Nikolai Ryzhkov was testifying on his five years as prime minister under Gorbachev, I spent the two-hour afternoon recess with Ivan Polozkov, a Party chieftain from the southern Russian city of Krasnodar

who in 1990 had become the leader of the Russian Communist Party and Ligachev's successor as the conservative "dark prince." At Central Committee meetings in 1990 and 1991, Polozkov had been openly critical of Gorbachev, but even then there was something guarded about his speech. A glimmer of traditional Party discipline, to say nothing of simple desire for self-preservation, prevented him from saying the things he was saying now.

"I am free now," he said, "free now to vent my spleen." Like the other Party men who came to court every day, Polozkov operated on the fuel of resentment. He was, in his mind, a great man made small by the deceptions of Gorbachev, Yeltsin, and the Central Intelligence Agency.

I asked him why he thought the Communist Party and the Soviet system had collapsed with such stunning speed after seeming to all the world to be unconquerable, a monolith of power and strength.

Polozkov's eyes widened, more in surprise than in anger. "They had so much and we . . . we had nothing!" he said.

"What do you mean?" I said. "That the Communist Party had nothing and the opposition had everything?"

"Precisely," Polozkov said, with a satisfied little nod. "We know the CIA financed parties here. You gave them Japanese cameras, German copying machines, money, everything! You had your dissidents who worked for you, the liars, the diplomats, the military double agents. Gorbachev, Yakovlev, Shevardnadze, these men were all yours, too. They were yours! Look at the book contracts they've gotten! Millions! One of our secretaries in the Russian Communist Party, Ivan Antonovich, was in the United States and he was invited to speak at a conference. Shevardnadze was on the bill, too. Shevardnadze spoke first, and then he left. Then Antonovich spoke. Afterward they gave him a souvenir: a copper coffee cup. Someone came up to him from our embassy and said how unfair it was, that Antonovich had only gotten a mug and he spoke in English while Shevardnadze spoke in his bad Russian and got five thousand dollars!

"Look, I understand what it was all about. It was a confrontation of two systems. Reagan called us an 'evil empire' and other Western leaders were judged according to how anti-Soviet they could be. The putsch was just a culmination of this struggle. And I will admit this: so far you have been winning this war. But I want to emphasize—'so far.' Remember this: Napoleon was in Moscow, but France did not defeat us. The Nazis were near Moscow, but look what happened. But I must tell you—and listen carefully—the war is still on and, in the end, you will not be able to endure in this competition with Communism."

I asked Polozkov if he thought that Gorbachev was a paid traitor. He began nodding, rapidly, crazily.

"Look," he said, "who do you think is on Gorbachev's level, historically speaking? What sort of stature do you think he has?"

I said that I'd just read an article in the French press comparing Gorbachev to de Gaulle.

"What?" Polozkov barked. "How can you compare Gorbachev to de Gaulle? Pétain is more like it! He lies like Pétain! He betrayed his country like Pétain! De Gaulle did not bend low before Hitler the way Gorbachev did to the West. It's an insult to our people to compare Gorbachev to de Gaulle. Gorbachev fled the Party like a coward. For his first couple of years, Gorbachev did well. But then he began to travel. He was praised abroad. They celebrated him as a great leader, and this tickled his ambition. He lost a sense of who he was, where he came from. He became vain, always out for his own career. And then they gave a Nobel Prize to a man who destroyed his country with wars and collapse. They made a mockery of that prize."

After talking with Polozkov and several other Communist Party chieftains who came to the small courtroom every day to watch the proceedings, I realized that these men had processed the August coup in their own minds, first as tragedy and now as farce. That is, they were so shaken by the way it changed the world that when they recovered from the shock of losing power, they began to excuse the putsch as a mockery, a nonevent. It simply never happened.

Vladimir Ivashko, the former deputy general secretary of the Party, was typical in the way he regarded the coup as "no coup at all." He had served the Party so long, and so well, he had lived by its myths so thoroughly, that he could not, and would not, think of the "August days" as the study in betrayal and incompetence that they were. "I know these men who are in prison," he said. "I know them as well as one man can know another. They are capable men, the top men in the Party. Honest men. Do you think they are fools? Yeltsin was never arrested. There were tanks, yes, but they never fired. People put flowers in the gun barrels. This is a coup? No, I am sorry. This was a drama, designed to crush the Communist Party and create bourgeois power in Russia.

"In the West, even here, they try to say that the Communist Party was reactionary, that it was against change. Those in power—and I knew them all well—none of them were against change. The discussion was always about the pace of change, about the retention of the Union. The members of the so-called putsch acted in the interest of a native power. To say they acted as opponents of reform is groundless. The Party kept this country together. Look at the Balkans, look at Ireland. Why were we able for so many years—until now—to avoid such conflict? Because there was unanimity from the top to the bottom. The tragedy of Gorbachev and of Yeltsin is that they de-

stroyed the Party mechanisms but created nothing in their place. Nothing will take the place of the Party. Nothing. Never."

I spent the better part of two days watching both sides question Nikolai Ryzhkov, a politician so emotional and prone to personal slights in his time that he was known in the press as "the weeping Bolshevik." In his days as Gorbachev's prime minister, Ryzhkov would choke up and splutter if members of the Supreme Soviet dared question his economic plans or his role in a weapons scandal. Unlike Ligachev or Polozkov, who affected the steely toughness of a regional Party boss, Ryzhkov had a touching vulnerability and righteousness that was his last selling point before his popularity vanished completely by late 1990. His memoir, *Perestroika: A History of Betrayals,* was filled with venom toward Gorbachev, Yakovlev, and Yeltsin.

Uncommonly slender and spry for a Party leader of his seniority, Ryzhkov stood at the witness stand with a studied casualness, his hip cocked, his left hand thrust in his pocket, as he answered the first easy volleys from the Communist side. Then, as Makaraov and Fedotov began to ask questions based on confidential Party documents, he bristled at what his life had come to. He came to attention.

Makarov picked up one bound set of documents after another and seemed to mock Ryzhkov simply with the manner of his question. Makarov was possessed of an elephantine girth and the voice of a field mouse; somehow this queer combination made him seem skeptical, even sarcastic, with no effort at all. He needed only to open his tiny cupid's mouth.

Respected witness, he would say. Here is a document describing secret arms sales to foreign Communist parties using government monies. Here's another specifically setting out the plan to cover up the nuclear accident at Chernobyl. Here the Politburo allocates money to "education." Do political parties usually have educational systems? Respected witness, respected Nikolai Ivanovich, the CPSU supported left-wing parties in capitalist, developed countries. Does that mean we gave succor to capitalist, developed countries? Toward what end?

For a long time Ryzhkov kept his cool and deflected painful questions about the past by saying "that was then" and "the Party was in the process of reform."

"Why did the Party, even after it relinquished its constitutional guarantee of power in 1990, why did it continue to control the government and virtually run public life?" Makarov asked. "Does that indicate to you constitutional, legal behavior?"

Finally, Ryzhkov lost his temper. "I protest these questions!" he said.

"You are asking me questions as if I were a criminal. . . . You are trying to paint me into a corner!"

Ryzhkov's self-image, that of the reasonable moderate surrounded by reactionaries like Polozkov and unconscionable radicals like Gorbachev and Yakovlev, began to appear ridiculous. When transcripts were read to him describing how he voted for one pernicious measure after another, his explanations were weak and absurd.

"Many times I spoke out against a measure," he said, "but when I found myself alone or in the minority, I voted for it."

Chief Justice Zorkin tried to keep the proceedings above emotion and raw political battle, but the effort was doomed. After Makarov had whispered into his microphone the proceedings of yet another Politburo meeting that the Communist Party never imagined would be read aloud, Ryzhkov snapped.

"Secrets are secrets!" he said. "One day soon we'll realize that. There were always secrets! Try and make an American turn himself inside out for you!"

At one point, Makarov swung his bulk in Ryzhkov's direction and said he "worried" whether the "respected Nikolai Ivanovich" wasn't tired.

"You don't have the figure for worrying," the former prime minister said. "You shouldn't worry."

"Well," the lawyer huffed, "at least I don't cry."

—

One night after a long court session, I accepted an invitation from Shakhrai's team to follow them out to their "work dacha" at a government compound in the village of Arkhangelskoye. The compound was one of the Russian government's many spoils of victory. Although most former members of the Communist Party leadership were still living lives of relative splendor even as they pled poverty in court and on television, most of the booty—the vacation homes, the resorts, the limousines—were now in the hands of the state. Yeltsin made his name by mocking the privileges of the Party powerful, but he was now doing a fairly good imitation of Louis XIV. Gorbachev's old arrangement of a cortege of three Zil limousines did not suffice; Yeltsin traveled in a fleet of three or four Mercedes-Benz sedans.

A high gate, a surveillance camera, and an armed guard marked the entrance to the compound. Shakhrai himself was in Austria that day—"buying himself a dacha in Salzburg, no doubt," one of the Party lawyers had cracked—and Fedotov and Makarov had a long night ahead of them to prepare for the next witness, Yegor Ligachev. They seemed unfazed by their twenty-hour workdays. Fedotov, whose reddish beard and bald pate earned him the nickname "Lenin" among his friends, had grown up in what he called

"dissident circles." In the early 1960s, he attended public readings at Pushkin Square and Mayakovsky Square of banned poetry; for his trouble, he was expelled for a while from university. Fedotov was now the Russian government's minister of "intellectual property," presiding over the country's copyright bureaucracy.

If Fedotov was the earnest intellectual of the team, Makarov was its rogue. In 1984, he defended the Soviet president of a Soviet-Swiss bank that went mysteriously bankrupt. "Americans killed the bank, the CIA," Makarov said without malice. "Nine members of the Politburo testified in the case, and so anything I learn now about the Party comes as no surprise." In 1988, Makarov defended Brezhnev's son-in-law Yuri Churbanov. After his marriage to Brezhnev's daughter, Churbanov won a high-ranking post in the Interior Ministry police, a job he rather quickly exploited for its bribe-taking possibilities. On a trip to Uzbekistan, he accepted a suitcase stuffed with a few hundred thousand rubles. Makarov won high marks for his defense, but there was not much he could do for a son-in-law who was on trial as much for his relation to a family in disgrace as for his hunger for gold.

Fedotov led the way into dacha No. 6—the same cabin where Gorbachev's and Yeltsin's advisers had tried to hammer out the abandoned 500 Days economic package in 1990. While dinner was being prepared, Makarov and Fedotov led me to a small study. A desk was stacked high with folders, many of them red and marked "Materials of the Politburo."

"We have to meet for a while," Makarov said. "Why don't you sit down and help yourself."

The hors d'oeuvres he offered were several short stacks of some of the most closely guarded secrets of the 1970s and 1980s in the Soviet Union.

"We've gotten about eighty thousand documents," Fedotov said. "Now there's only around forty million more to go."

"Oh, before we leave you with these things, you might want to hear our performance of the Politburo meeting of August 29, 1985," Makarov said.

The two men began laughing with the anticipation of it, and like an old radio team—Bob and Ray coming to you live from dacha No. 6!—they read their script from one of the documents marked "Top Secret, Sole Copy." Makarov read Gorbachev's lines, giving a fair approximation of Gorbachev's southern accent and grammatical flubs, and Fedotov read the remaining parts. The document was even more fascinating than its bizarre performance.

At that session, the members of the Politburo discussed their strategy options regarding Andrei Sakharov and Yelena Bonner, who were still living in forced internal exile in the closed city of Gorky (its name has since been changed back to the original, Nizhni Novgorod).

Gorbachev says the Politburo has received letters from the Sakharovs and from elsewhere asking that Bonner be allowed to go abroad for medical treatment.

Viktor Chebrikov, chief of the KGB, dominates the discussion and informs the other members of the Politburo that Sakharov "is not in excellent health and now is receiving an oncological exam because he is losing weight." He fails to mention that Sakharov's weight loss was due to a hunger strike which led the KGB to attempt to cram a tube down his throat and feed him.

Another participant, Mikhail Zimyanin, warns that "no decency can be expected of Bonner. She is a beast in a skirt who was appointed by imperialism." They are clearly worried that Bonner, half Jewish and half Armenian, will plead the case for emigration and human rights while in the West. Chebrikov cautions that if they allow Bonner to go to the West for treatment "she may make statements and get awards. . . . But it would look like an act of humanism. . . . Sakharov's behavior is under the huge influence of Bonner and he is always subject to that. . . ."

Gorbachev: "Well, that's what Zionism is!"

Makarov and Fedotov collapsed in laughter.

Later on, over a dinner of broiled chicken and rice, Fedotov said that the two of them had spent hours reading the documents and had been alternately stunned and amused at the banality of the Politburo sessions. Makarov said he hoped that the theaters of Moscow would soon stage the old sessions of the Politburo using the transcripts as scripts.

"When we read these absurd documents we laugh ourselves all the way to the floor," Fedotov said. "But that is only when we are not crushed and despondent. Recently I read a Central Committee document from 1937 that said that the Voronezh secret police, according to the 'regional plan,' repressed in the 'first category' nine thousand people—which means these people were executed. And for no reason, of course. Twenty-nine thousand were repressed in the 'second category'—meaning they were sent to labor camps. The local first secretary, however, writes that there are still more Trotskyites and kulaks who remain 'unrepressed.' He was saying that the plan was fulfilled but the plan was not enough! And so he asked that it be increased by eight thousand. Stalin writes back: 'No, increase by nine thousand!' The sickness of it! It's as if they were playing poker."

"It's true," Makarov said. "Later, we read a document from Marshal Tukhachevsky giving instructions to his men saying if you meet a person on the street and he fails to identify himself immediately . . . shoot him! This is 1921, not the Stalin era. See, the thing to remember about the documents is

not the sensations they provide. It's their routineness, their banality, the way these very ordinary directives ordered the life of the country."

After dinner, I sat at the desk once more leafing through documents that recorded those banalities and, until now, were considered "eyes only": KGB analyses of a school of writers in 1970 known as SMOG; a list of Western correspondents and dissidents at a rally at Pushkin Square on December 5, 1975; copies of private letters sent by Aleksandr Solzhenitsyn and intercepted by the KGB; a KGB dossier on the creation in Krasnodar at School No. 3 of an eighth-grade "Club for the Struggle for Democracy"; a September 1986 Politburo meeting at which the KGB chief, Chebrikov, says that while political prisoners are being released, "they will be watched . . . in connection with prophylactic work"; an analysis by Brezhnev's ideologist Mikhail Suslov of Sakharov's first set of underground essays ("To read this is to become nauseated").

The minutes of a July 12, 1984, Politburo session revealed a truly nauseating spectacle: the leaders of the Party still defending Stalin against Khrushchev's revisionism. At the meeting, the members listen to a report on how Vyacheslav Molotov, Stalin's foreign minister, was "overwhelmed with joy" at the Politburo's decision to restore him to the Party ranks. Molotov had been expelled during Khrushchev's "thaw."

"And let me tell you," says Marshal Dmitri Ustinov, the head of the armed forces. "If it hadn't been for Khrushchev, they never would have been expelled and there never would have been these outrageous actions regarding Stalin. . . . Not a single one of our enemies has inflicted so much misfortune on us as Khrushchev did regarding his policies and his attitude toward Stalin."

Gorbachev, who knew well at the time that he would have to get the support of the conservatives to win the top job once Chernenko finally died, plays a marvelous game, saying that he would support the restoration to Party ranks of Molotov's cohorts, Lazar Kaganovich and Georgi Malenkov. ("Yes, these are elderly people," the Leningrad Party boss, Grigori Romanov, chimes in. "They may die.") But Gorbachev also knows the value of discretion. As for the Molotov rehabilitation, he says, "I think we can do without publicity." Ustinov gets so excited by this little neo-Stalinist wave that he says, "And in connection with the fortieth anniversary of our victory in the Great Patriotic War, shouldn't we rename Volgograd back to Stalingrad?"

"Well," Gorbachev says, "there are pluses and minuses to this."

Even after Chernenko's death and his own assumption of power, Gorbachev offered bones for his reactionary colleagues to gnaw on. At a March 20,

1986, Politburo meeting he suggests changing the name of the icebreaker *Arktika* to *Brezhnev*.

"Yes, let's do it," Ryzhkov says, "but don't announce it on television."

Finally, I lingered over a document that Sovietologists have been waiting to see for years: the transcript of the March 11, 1985, Politburo meeting at which Gorbachev was made general secretary. For years there had been speculation that it was a close vote, that the chief of the Moscow Party organization, the hard-liner Viktor Grishin, challenged Gorbachev, and had it not been for the absence of one or two conservative voters, Grishin might have won. Former Politburo members Geidar Aliyev, Yegor Ligachev, Aleksandr Yakovlev, and Grishin himself, in a brief phone conversation before his death, told me that it was untrue, that the vote was unanimous. But that was never good enough for Sovietology.

Gorbachev opens the fateful meeting with the announcement of Chernenko's death, and Yevgeny Chazov, the minister of health, gives a detailed description of Chernenko's illnesses and final hours. Then, in a move that stunned some of the conservatives, Andrei Gromyko, a top official under every Soviet leader since Stalin, stands up at his place at the table and nominates Gorbachev. First, he provides some ritual words of praise for Chernenko's "historical optimism" and the general "rightness of our theory and practice." And then, in nominating Gorbachev, the baby of the Politburo, Gromyko pays tribute to his man's "indomitable creative energy" and his "attention to people."

"When we look into the future—and for many of us this is hard—we have no right to let the world see a single fissure in our relations," Gromyko says. "There is more than enough speculation on this abroad."

For his part, Viktor Grishin says, "When we heard yesterday about the death of Konstantin Ustinovich, we predetermined to some extent this issue [of the new leadership] when we arranged to approve Mikhail Sergeyevich chairman of the funeral commission." Clearly, Grishin, who had worked with one party ideologist, Richard Kosolapov, to devise a program for his own election, could not have been thrilled that the behind-the-scenes maneuvering had left him powerless and Gorbachev head of the committee in charge of Chernenko's funeral and, now, general secretary. But he did not challenge Gorbachev, and, instead, sings his praises just as loudly as the rest. During Chernenko's illness, Gorbachev had proved a superior politician and Grishin must now swallow his ambition.

Finally, Gorbachev gets up to speak. His performance, even on the page,

is worthy of Machiavelli's demands for a would-be prince. "Our economy needs more dynamism. This dynamism is needed for the development of our foreign policy," he says. "I take all your words with a sense of tremendous excitement and emotion. It is with this sense that I am listening to you, my dear friends.

"We do not need to change policy. It is correct and it is true. It is genuine Leninist politics. We need, however, to speed up, to move forward, to disclose shortcomings and overcome them and realize our shining future. . . . I assure you I will do everything to justify the trust of the Party."

Then he announces a plenum of the Central Committee in a half hour at which the leadership question will be "resolved."

Thus was the last general secretary of the Communist Party elected—with, as the old newspapers would add in parentheses, "prolonged and thunderous applause."

—

The morning after my trip to Arkhangelskoye, I went to court to hear the testimony of Yegor Ligachev, once the second most powerful man in the country. In power, "he was like a locomotive," Ryzhkov recalled, and he certainly looked fit now. Ligachev had just published a memoir titled *Zagadka Gorbacheva* ("The Enigma of Gorbachev"), in which he laid out the conservative case against the last general secretary. Gorbachev, he wrote, "began well" with a gradualist program, but then fell victim to international acclaim, vanity, and the duplicity of the "extremists" in his midst. And instead of reforming the system, Gorbachev started on the road to "antisocialist" thinking. As he had in his memoirs, Ligachev tried in his testimony to portray himself as the last honest man victimized by endless conspiracies to destroy him and the socialist state. He was never an "opponent of perestroika," as he had been portrayed in the press in Russia and abroad, but merely an advocate of gradual change.

The Communist lawyers wanted Ligachev to feel comfortable and lobbed him a few easy leading questions to fuel his soliloquy. The government lawyers were not nearly so accommodating. For their part, they insisted on knowing Ligachev's reaction to a raft of Politburo and Central Committee decisions during his years in power. Once more, Makarov read through the documents:

Respected Yegor Kuzmich, he would say, what of this document dated November 1, 1989, in which the Politburo approves the funding for the construction of a rec room for the Afghan leader and his family? And what of this document that you drew up dictating to the press the rules for the

coverage of the war in Afghanistan? "There will be not more than one report of a death or wound per month among Soviet servicemen."

And what of this document in which the Politburo approves of the creation of a news bureau for *Komsomolskaya Pravda* in Canada and stipulates that the resident correspondent be an officer of the KGB?

"What of it?" Ligachev said. "This is a practice broadly implemented by other countries."

And what of the Politburo decision to create a special military unit of the KGB manned by people "infinitely loyal to the Communist Party of the Soviet Union and the socialist Motherland"? Isn't it curious that the Party, which had allegedly relinquished the one-party system, could still dictate such a policy to a government ministry?

"Well, I am sure there was no ill will intended," Ligachev said.

And what of this document, esteemed Yegor Kuzmich, a Politburo session on March 24, 1987, at which the members agree that permissions given for business trips abroad must be tightened up because, as they say, "we regret that only professional competence is being taken into account and not political concerns"?

"What's wrong with that?" he answered. "That just means that we were not indifferent to how people behaved abroad—moral factors included."

Finally, after a long day at the witness's lectern, Ligachev began to show flashes of why he was feared by the hundreds of men and women working in the Central Committee apparatus. For years he had been the one asking the tough questions, not answering them, and now he, like Ryzhkov, snapped.

"Look," he said, "if we'd taken decisive measures at the beginning, this country would not be on fire as it is today! This war is not only close to Russia, it is entering our own homes. It is here! . . . Mikhail Sergeyevich took decisions only when every last citizen in the country knew they were necessary, when every last apple had ripened and fallen from the tree!"

After a few days of watching the testimony at the Constitutional Court, I found it remarkable that there was hardly any interest at all among the public. The spectators' gallery was nearly empty. Some days there were no more than five or six journalists around. Nearly all the regulars—the true court buffs—were themselves dinosaurs of the Communist Party.

For nearly everyone else, the struggles and pleasures of the present were of far greater concern, for Moscow now, little more than a year after the coup, had become a phantasmagoria, a post-Communist world as painted by Hieronymus Bosch. Younger Muscovites, especially, seemed determined to

rush headlong into some weird, pleasurable, vulgar world of primitive capitalism. In a leap typical of all Russian history, the new economy had bounded from one stage of development to the next, gliding quickly from complete deficit to sensual indulgence, never stopping to solve the mundane problems of subsistence, structure, and property. In the subway stations and the kiosks, you could buy a lace tablecloth, a bottle of Curaçao, Wrigley's spearmint gum, Mars bars, a Public Enemy tape, Swiss chocolate, plastic "marital toys," a Mercedes-Benz hood ornament, American cigarettes, and Estonian pornography.

In the alleyways and restaurants, Moscow was beginning to look like the set of *Once Upon a Time in America.* As the old Communist Party mafia structures withered, more conventional ones took their place. The city was awash with twenty-five-year-old men wearing slick suits and black shirts and announcing their occupation as "a little buying, a little selling." Their molls dressed in spandex and fox. A kiosk owner's failure to pay his weekly protection money usually left him with a kiosk reduced to sticks and broken glass.

As hyperinflation drove the ruble into irrelevance, a system of financial apartheid arrived. The dollar, suffering everywhere else, was supreme in Russia. Every day more foreign business executives arrived at Sheremetyevo Airport, toting their briefcases like pickaxes and pans, hoping to find the new Klondike. In the meantime, they were also the new colonials, hiring servants and snapping up Russian antiques for a song. In the House on the Embankment, the swank home of the nomenklatura a half century ago, the former apartment of Stalin's chief executioner was now occupied by the top executive of McDonald's.

There was no nostalgia or reverence for the old dogma. At the biggest bookstore in the city, the House of Books, I saw a weary sales clerk using a stack of the collected works of V. I. Lenin as a stool while she handed out copies of the latest editions of Agatha Christie and Arthur Hailey. Moscow had become a city of disorientation, so much so that you could easily take a wrong turn into the nineteenth century. A former journalist named Vadim Dormidontov sat in an office at Moscow City Hall and decided which streets and neighborhoods would lose their Soviet-era names and regain their old ones. Lenin Hills was Sparrow Hills once more. The residents of Ustinov Boulevard now lived again on Autumn Boulevard.

While nearly everyone tried to get his bearings in this strange new world, Yeltsin struggled with a hard-line opposition more than willing to exploit the collapse of the economy for its political gain. The coalition of conservatives was often known as the "red and browns," the alliance of former Communist Party bosses and ultranationalists, even neofascists. For Yeltsin, the trial was

a critical front in the battle to stave off the reactionaries. "The so-called red and brown forces are advancing," he said on the eve of the trial. "I would say that today Russia's destiny depends on the Constitutional Court rather than on the president. . . . Any support for the Communists may play into their hands and promote their destructive activity, which may push us into a civil war."

In Moscow now, hardly any politician dared refer to himself as a "democrat," for fear of appearing too Western, too liberal, incompetent. Some of the leaders of the radical reform movement tried to broaden their political appeal by playing, however cautiously, the nationalist card. Sergei Stankevich, the young adviser to Yeltsin, had begun his political career in 1989 as a radical democrat and now referred to himself as a "statist democrat." He wanted a little nationalist shading to broaden his political base. Yeltsin, too, had to emphasize his "national feeling," making fast friends with the hierarchy of the Russian Orthodox Church and refusing to make a deal with the Japanese on the Kuril Islands. Yeltsin realized that it was hard for Russians to lose all the time—lose territory, power, influence—and count it as victory.

But the radical right was not impressed with Yeltsin's guile. He was considered the chief culprit in the fracturing of the Soviet state and the fragmentation of Russia itself. The historian Yuri Afanasyev, a deputy now in the Russian parliament, told me he thought the Russian scene was one of dangerous flux. "The old system will never regain its shape, but all kinds of possibilities exist for the future of Russia," he said. "We could look like South Korea, or, say, Latin America with a taint of Sicily. It is a far from sure thing that we will resemble the developed Western democracies. The pull of the state sector, the authoritarian tug, is still a very dangerous thing. Fascism, in the form of national socialism, is a major threat. And it is finding supporters not only in the lunatic fringe, but in the alleged center. The Russian consciousness has always been flawed by a yearning for expansion and a fear of contraction. Unfortunately the history of Russia is the history of growth. This is a powerful image in the Russian soul, the idea of breadth as wealth, the more the better. But the truth is that such expansion has always depleted Russian power and wealth. Berdyaev was right when he said that Russia was always crippled by its expanse."

To some degree, the Communist Party's myth-making machinery had been replaced by Russian nostalgia for a prerevolutionary utopia that never was. Stanislav Govorukhin's 1992 film *The Russia We Lost* portrayed the last czar—previously considered a dolt and a weakling in Communist propaganda—as a man of great learning, military skill, and compassion. Lenin is a "slit-eyed" fanatic with "pathological obsessions" and, naturally, Jewish forebears. Gorvorukhin told the newspaper *Megapolis-Express* that were

there to be another putsch he would not rush to the White House to defend the popularly elected government as he had during the August coup. "Following a totalitarian regime," he said, "a sea of democracy and freedom is a safe road to fascism." His credo now was the famous declaration of the czarist reformer Pyotr Stolypin to the Russian Duma: "You want great upheavals, but what we need is a great Russia."

Although there were only a half-dozen people in the Moskva Theater when I went to see *The Russia We Lost,* and while the opinion polls did not indicate a great public longing for an overthrow of the Yeltsin government, Moscow seemed filled with demagogues who would be czar. The first to appear on the scene was Vladimir Zhirinovsky, an unabashed neofascist who won six million votes—almost 8 percent of the electorate—in June 1991 when he ran against Yeltsin and four other candidates for the Russian presidency. Just after the coup, I watched Zhirinovsky at a parliamentary session at the Kremlin deliver two hour-long monologues to clumps of fascinated deputies in the corridors. He rambled on, picking up so much speed as he described his imperial ambitions that he showered his listeners, and the television cameras, with little sprays of spit:

"I'll start by squeezing the Baltics and other small nations. I don't care if they are recognized by the UN. I'm not going to invade them or anything. I'll bury radioactive waste along the Lithuanian border and put up powerful fans and blow the stuff across the border at night. I'll turn the fans off during the day. They'll all get radiation sickness. They'll die of it. When they either die out or get down on their knees, I'll stop it. I'm a dictator. What I'm going to do is bad, but it'll be good for Russia. The Slavs are going to get anything they want if I'm elected.

"I will send troops to Afghanistan again, and this time they'll win. . . . I will restore the foreign policy of the czars. . . . I won't make Russians fight. I'll make Uzbeks and Tajiks do the fighting. Russian officers will just give the orders. Like Napoleon. 'Uzbeks, forward to Kabul!' And when the Uzbeks are all dead, it'll be 'Tajiks, forward to Kabul!' The Bashkirs can go to Mongolia, where there's TB and syphilis. The other republics will be Russia's kitchen garden. Russia will be the brains.

"I say it quite plainly: when I come to power, there will be a dictatorship. I will beat the Americans in space. I will surround the planet with our space stations so that they'll be scared of our space weapons. I don't care if they call me a fascist or a Nazi. Workers in Leningrad told me, 'Even if you wear five swastikas, we'll vote for you all the same. You promise a clear plan.' There's nothing like fear to make people work better. The stick, not the carrot. I'll do it all without tanks on the streets. Those who have to be

arrested will be arrested quietly at night. I may have to shoot one hundred thousand people, but the other three hundred million will live peacefully. I have the right to shoot these hundred thousand. I have this right as president."

Despite his surprisingly strong showing in the last Russian presidential race, the vast majority of people believed Zhirinovsky was either mad, an agent of the secret police, or both. But he was not alone in his extremism. Aleksandr Sterligov, a former KGB colonel who promised the "iron hand," was only the latest in a collection of would-be dictators who were hoping the public would grow so disenchanted with the Yeltsin government that it would turn to them.

One afternoon on my trip in the fall of 1992, I visited the grungy editorial offices of *Dyen,* the newspaper that was now one of the leading voices of the hard-right coalition. Just weeks before the August coup, *Dyen* published the infamous "Word to the People," the front-page appeal for a military seizure of power. I met with the author of the appeal and the editor of the paper, Aleksandr Prokhanov, and his deputy, Vladimir Bondarenko. Bondarenko told me he had just returned from the United States, a trip, he said, that was sponsored, in part, by David Duke, the former Nazi and Ku Klux Klansman.

"Perhaps Duke's views are a bit extreme," Bondarenko allowed. "I suppose my views are better compared to those of your Patrick Buchanan."

We talked a long time about the coup, and here, too, the conservatives spoke of the putsch as a shadow play, something that was not what it seemed.

"When people heard about the putsch, most of them said, 'Finally, at last, they are doing what they have to do,' " Bondarenko said. "They did not believe in terror, but they wanted elementary order, the sort of order that states have everywhere. But the leaders of the coup were so stupid. They are to be condemned not because they pulled off a coup, but because they did it so stupidly."

Prokhanov, a performance artist of the right wing, made Bondarenko seem almost rational. "You did it!" he said, pointing at me as the representative American. "You did it! And how do I know? I have friends at Langley, at the State Department, and at the Rand Institute. The general concept was yours—the CIA's. I am sure of it. The process was regulated and designed by your people. The so-called leaders of the coup were pushed forward and then betrayed. They were left to be torn to pieces by the public opinion. They were so stupid to have believed Gorbachev.

"In this whole drama, only the CIA was smart. They alone knew that the Soviet Union would fall apart under the concept of republican sovereignty—an idea they planted in the Baltics and then elsewhere. Do you think East

Germany fell apart on its own? Do you think Poland, Bulgaria, Yugoslavia, and finally the Soviet Union fell apart on their own? The plan of struggle against the Soviet Union has existed ever since World War II."

Prokhanov said he was "elated" on the first morning of the coup and "disgusted" when it collapsed three days later. But he said he was sure that his time would come again. "After a year in which the government has lost trust and the democrats are in a state of collapse, the patriots from the left and the right will come together and the war will continue. And it will be, I assure you, an anti-American movement. There are three ways we can come to power—and we will use any means to do it. First, we can do it in parliament. Second, there can be a split within the government and the liberals lose the support of the army, the new KGB, and there is a gradual drift to the right. Or we can do it through extra-governmental means: strikes, demonstrations, general chaos. In any case, the Yeltsin people should not relax."

—

The trial shoved ahead. Interest dwindled even further. "Society is sick of history," Arseny Roginsky, of the Memorial historical society, told me. "It is too much with us. For people trying to cope with crazy inflation and adjusting to a new economy in which the rich get richer and the poor get poorer, it's a natural psychological situation. People do have some sense that their current troubles are tied to the history of the Party, but it is not always easy to step back and see that."

The only aspect of the trial of the Communist Party that was grabbing any space in the newspapers and on the evening news was the question of Mikhail Gorbachev's refusal to testify. Chief Justice Zorkin insisted from the start that Gorbachev's testimony, as general secretary of the party from March 1985 until August 1991, was essential. In Zorkin's summons, however, Gorbachev saw only the invisible hand of Boris Yeltsin and another attempt to humiliate him. The two men had been playing out their opera of rivalry and unconscious cooperation for so long that Muscovites had wearied of it. As part of his "retirement package," Gorbachev got from Yeltsin a dacha, bodyguards, a pension, and a fine piece of real estate—the former Party institute on Leningrad Prospekt. Gorbachev, for his part, said he would use the institute as a base for research, not political opposition. But détente, such as it was, collapsed quickly. Gorbachev began accusing Yeltsin of running a government not dissimilar to "an insane asylum," and Yeltsin's aides began chipping away at Gorbachev's retirement deal, first taking away his limousine and replacing it with a more modest sedan, then threatening worse. "Soon," one newspaper cracked, "Mikhail Sergeyevich will be going to work on a bicycle."

During the trial, I went to see Gorbachev at his institute, hoping to talk about many things besides the furor over his refusal to testify. There was no chance of that. He had already been fined 100 rubles by the court—around 30 cents at the time—and he knew well that more sanctions were on the way. After he greeted me, he plopped himself down into an armchair, saying with false cheer, "They are running around like mad. They all got into this shit and they don't know what to do now."

Gorbachev was furious, obsessed. I asked a question and he finished his answer forty minutes later, an answer that was part set piece, part harangue. I had spent many hours while living in Moscow listening to Gorbachev at press conferences, summits, interviews, meetings, and he was never one for concision. But now, he seemed at times like Lear raging about plots against his underappreciated self. He truly believed that the court's summons amounted to political persecution of the most heinous sort.

"Even Stalin's sick mind could not have dreamed up anything like this!" Gorbachev said. "To rule that eighteen million Communists be deprived of their citizenship and swept away! Not just simply to deprive them, but sweep them away with a broom. And with their families, we are talking about fifty to seventy million people. Only a lunatic would do this. If you call yourselves democrats, prove it with your deeds. Gorbachev had enough courage always to tell the truth to everyone and endure the pressure. I've got plenty of courage and even now I will not yield.

"What is this, a Constitutional Court? There is no court in the world that can judge history! It is up to history proper to judge history. Historians, scholars, and so on. . . . Will the court go all the way back to the October Revolution, to the Bolsheviks, or even earlier? Will they anathematize it all? Is this the business of the Constitutional Court? Let's analyze what Lenin did to take power. Does this mean that all the countries that cooperated with Soviet Russia, and all the agreements that were made, do they all go . . . pffffft? . . . Is it all rubbish? Unconstitutional? God knows what this all is! You don't have to be too bright to understand what this process is likely to lead to."

Somewhere along the way I managed to ask Gorbachev if he kept in contact with Yeltsin any longer. Gorbachev frowned. He was being ignored. This seemed to him worse than any sanction of the court.

"He never calls me," Gorbachev said. "I called him several times at first, but from his side there has never been a call. Boris Nikolayevich knows everything! We have no relations. What kind of personal relations can there be when his press secretary publishes a statement saying that they will take measures against Gorbachev, that they will put him in his place? What relations can there be? This is ruled out.

"The democrats have failed to use their power. Look at how they struggled for power and how much they promised. There were even statements that the Russian president would lay himself down across the railroad tracks if living standards went down. Well, now they've gone down fifty percent! The tracks must be occupied.

"They have to tell the people how they are going to get through the winter, what there will be to eat, whether there will be any heat, and what will happen to reforms. And they have no answer. They don't know what to say. They need to play for time and they need to find a lightning rod. It's amazing—Yeltsin's team, the Constitutional Court, and the fundamentalists who defended against the August coup are all in this struggle together against Gorbachev. This is phenomenal!"

I left Gorbachev's office thinking that everything about him was outsize: his achievements, his mistakes, and, now, his vanity and bitterness. At one point in his monologue he even passed on a rumor that at the tensest moments of the coup, Yeltsin had been making plans to hide in the American embassy. This was hard, if not impossible, to believe. For all of Yeltsin's shortcomings, it was his courage that won the day in August of 1991. Gorbachev, in suggesting otherwise—especially in such a dark and clumsy way—revealed the depths of his bitterness. He had loved his place in the world—a place he had earned despite all the mistakes—and now, it seemed, it was slipping away, almost gone. He was despised in his own country.

Feeling a little stunned, I left Gorbachev and headed down a flight of stairs to visit the man who had been his closest friend and ally in the leadership, Aleksandr Yakovlev. I told Yakovlev what I had just heard, and he rolled his eyes in amusement and frustration. Yakovlev had always betrayed a certain intellectual condescension for Gorbachev, but he also appreciated his political gifts, his complexity.

I told Yakovlev I had finally seen the transcript of the historic March 11, 1985, Politburo meeting and I was a little surprised that things had gone so easily for Gorbachev. Why had there been no opposition? And had Gorbachev been deceiving the conservatives? Why had they made him general secretary if they knew he would try to change the system?

"There was a preliminary agreement," Yakovlev said. "Everything was agreed on beforehand. Everything was clear. Grishin's entourage prepared a speech, a program for him. Richard Kosolapov, the editor of *Kommunist,* was very active on Grishin's behalf. But that was just in case. In fact, there were no other candidates for this position. Once Gorbachev was made chair-

man of the funeral commission for Chernenko's funeral on March 10, everything was clear.

"But about deception. This was really a question of the inertia of the Communist Party. Every new general secretary got carte blanche at the beginning. A new man would come to the fore and he was supported. You know, let him talk about innovations, about something new, it has to be tolerated, and then he will calm down and everything will go back to normal. Let him talk about democracy and pluralism, but sooner or later we'll all be back together harnessed to the same horsecart. That happened with every newcomer: Khrushchev, Brezhnev, Andropov. And the same destiny was expected of Gorbachev.

"Gorbachev played politics, but he also realized that things had to change. It was impossible to go on living as we were. But when he started changing things, the system resisted those reforms. These changes were hindered by the simple logic of the state. And whether he wanted to or not, Gorbachev had to deal with these contradictions. Like Gorbachev, at the beginning, I believed that in our country, only a revolution from above was possible.

"Even now Gorbachev talks about our 'socialist choice.' . . . But we cannot speak of a socialist choice in this country. Our experience, our 'choice,' is not socialist and never was. We had a slave system here. Who can talk about a socialist choice? Maybe Germany, or Israel, or Spain. But not us. . . . But Gorbachev could not overcome his mentality. In general, this power, the concept of power, acts like a poison on a person."

—

During my talk with Gorbachev, his press aide, Aleksandr Likhotal, had slipped him a note. Gorbachev went silent, read the note quickly, darkened with what seemed to be anger, composed himself, and then picked up the long string of his monologue. I didn't think much of it then. But later that evening, as I watched the evening news show *Vesti,* I realized what the note must have said: for his refusal to appear in court, he was being deprived of his right to travel abroad. He had a trip planned to South Korea and there were more on the schedule. That was a cruel and clever blow. Gorbachev was endlessly applauded abroad; he was treated as one of the great figures of the century. In Moscow, he was punished, mocked, and ignored.

Three days later, the Russian government announced it would take back most of the building it had given Gorbachev as part of his resignation package. On a cool, gray morning, three buses filled with Moscow police officers pulled up to the institute. The police chief, Arkady Murashev, ordered his men to surround the building.

Just minutes later, Gorbachev arrived, in a rage. The press gathered around him on the front steps of the building. "You don't know the pressure that my family and I have endured in the past seven years!" he told the reporters. "But personal matters are not the thing. They are trying to put Gorbachev in his place! The Russian press speculates that Gorbachev is traveling the world looking for a vacation house! There's the rumor that my daughter is in Germany and her husband is to join her there. Or America. And now that he has a daughter settled, Gorbachev is looking for a warm place for himself. Well, they'd be very happy if Gorbachev left the country. They'd probably pay a million for it. But I'm not leaving. . . ."

A few miles away, the Constitutional Court heard its next witness. The tired men of the Communist Party protested their innocence. How could we have been what you charge? they seemed to say. Just look at us. We are plain. We are ordinary. We are nobody now.

A few weeks later, the Constitutional Court of Russia ruled that Communists were free to meet on a local level but the Communist Party, as a national entity, was illegal. The Party's assets and properties remained under the control of the elected government of the Russian Federation. The era that had begun in 1917 with the Bolshevik coup had now ended—in a court of law.

AFTERWORD

The Heart Is Not Yet Joyful

From the first moment that Mikhail Gorbachev began his frenetic tinkering with the Soviet system, time, and the perception of time, lost its normal rhythm. Every year seems like an entire era. So many triumphs, agonies and bitter surprises register on the landscape of the old empire that it is hard to focus on anything more distant than the previous week, much less on that Christmas night in 1991 when Gorbachev signed his resignation papers and the red flag over the Kremlin was lowered for the last time. But even now I cannot forget that time. As Gorbachev was preparing for his departure, I went to the Kremlin to see one of his most loyal aides, Giorgi Shakhnazarov. Like Gorbachev, Shakhnazarov had hoped to reform communism, to rescue the system and drag it into the modern world. That project, the last lingering dream of socialism, turned out to be folly. Now the regime was in ruins and the empire in dissolution. All the talk was of a democracy and a free market; Gorbachev had passed into history and the movers were coming to cart away the boxes.

"How will all these republics survive without Moscow?" Shakhnazarov said. He was a gnomish man—half scholar, half apparatchik—and now he

looked resigned, withered. "What will become of them? What will a republic like Georgia do? Do you think they'll get any oil selling mandarin oranges to Saudi Arabia? And Armenia and Azerbaijan: don't you think they will be at each other's throats?"

Shakhnazarov's desk was bare but for one, single-spaced letter he was leaving behind for the next occupant, "whoever that might turn out to be."

"I'm just letting him know I wish them all luck," Shakhnazarov said. "They're going to need it."

In the more than two years since, Russia and the former Soviet republics have surely not been blessed with anywhere near the amount of luck they have needed. Nor have they always had the wisdom or the means to avoid economic and political disaster. One can only begin to count up the mounting catastrophes in the old Soviet Union: the collapsed economics; the troubling diaspora of twenty-five million Russians in "foreign" lands; the threat of nuclear accidents and ecological ruin; the rise of hard-line Russian nationalists and the astonishing persistence of various Communist parties. In retrospect, Boris Yeltsin wishes that he had acted even more quickly and decisively in the wake of the August coup. While he still had the political support, he should have dissolved parliament and called for elections, thereby avoiding the disastrous two-year-long confrontation with parliament that led to the bloody storming of the White House in October 1993. But history is unforgiving; it does not accommodate the words "if only."

On my last trip to Moscow, toward the end of 1993, everywhere I went, from the central market to the villages outside of town, from newspaper offices to Kremlin anterooms where aides sat dully around, watching music videos, there was a sense of drift, even hopelessness, about political life. "The October events" and then the dispiriting December elections, which brought into the new parliament dozens of ultra-nationalists and Communists, obliterated any shred of triumphalism left over from the defeat of the August coup of 1991. The relatively easy verities of the old political struggle—good versus bad, reformers versus reactionaries, democrats versus Communists—had dissolved into a bitter soup of uncertainty. The December elections confirmed the bitterness of Russians, as nearly 25 percent voted for the ultra-nationalist Vladimir Zhirinovsky, more as a protest against the squalid status quo than as an endorsement of his mad program of aggression abroad and the iron fist at home. Nearly half the electorate did not bother voting.

Much of the opposition to Yeltsin is rooted in one form or another of mythic nostalgia: the Communist nostalgia for the order of Stalin and the supposedly dependable standard of living under Brezhnev; the military nostalgia for the fear the Soviet arsenal once struck in the heart of the Western

enemy; the nationalist nostalgia for empire and higher spiritual purpose. It is natural—all too human—that nostalgia should be such a powerful force of politics now in Russia, just as it was for the Ottomans and the British as they lost their hold on the earth. Empires are not lost happily. Enoch Powell was driven to fits of poetry over the loss of India and even today "neo-Ottomanism" is a powerful force in Turkish politics.

For tens of millions of Russians, the story of their country since Gorbachev's advent in 1985 has been one of unremitting loss and wounded pride. What took decades for the citizens of Constantinople and London to absorb, struck the Russians in an instant. The empire has vanished. That the economy has been dying is obvious to any Western visitor. Less obvious is the Russian's anxiety about his place in the world. The jewels of empire are lost: the beaches of the Crimea, the vineyards of Moldova, the oil fields of Kazakhstan, the ports of Odessa—to say nothing of Prague, Budapest, and Warsaw—are all within foreign lands now. The army is fraught with draft-dodging and erosion. Foreign policy is a road map of retreat. A leading sociologist in Moscow, Yuri Levada recently published a poll in the daily newspaper *Izvestia* showing that only 11 percent of the population believe that Russia is still a great power while two-thirds of the respondents said that the country should regain its lost prestige on the world stage. Between those two statistics is a great longing, a feeling of national loss and anxiety. And that longing, as much as the failing economy, is a lethal weapon in the hands of Yeltsin's political opponents. While Yeltsin and his supporters are trying to create, all at once, a market economy, a democratic political system, and a civil society, his opponents, more often than not, indulge in a politics of loss, a new sort of populism.

Many influential liberals in politics, such as Yeltsin's former adviser Galina Staravoitova, feel that Russia's economic failure and wounded self-esteem are so profound and combustible that the advent of a charismatic authoritarian movement in Russia cannot be ruled out. "One cannot exclude the possibility of a fascist period in Russia," Staravoitova said on the radio station Echo, of Moscow. "We can see too many parallels between Russia's current situation and that of Germany after the Versailles Treaty. A great nation is humiliated, and many of its nationals live outside the country's borders. The disintegration of an empire has taken place at a time when many people still have an imperialist mentality. . . . All this is happening at a time of economic crisis."

In his campaign for parliament, Vladimir Zhirinovsky played on the feelings of humiliation in the post-Great Power era and spoke in a rhetoric of stark simplicity and darkest comedy. Jews, Central Asians, Armenians, and Azerbaijanis should be driven from positions of power; only people with

"kind Russian faces" should appear on Russian television. He declared himself willing "to blow up a few Kuwaiti ports and aircraft plus a few American ships" to defend the old Soviet ally, Iraq. And should the Japanese press their demands for the Kurile Islands, "I would bomb the Japanese. I would sail our large navy around their small island and if they so much as cheeped I would nuke them." As if this were not enough, he promised everything from a magical end to the economic crisis to "love and romance" for the lonely. The pro-reform democrats, for their part, gave Zhirinovsky his opening. They were smug and divided, nearly oblivious to the fact that they were doing nothing to build support for radical economic reforms that have proved painful to millions of people. Zhirinovsky's triumph was a warning. Russia and the world cannot afford a President Zhirinovsky.

If Russia was under any illusions about its being a democratic country, it is no longer. In conversations with Yeltsin's aides, all of them admitted that the illusion of a smooth and swift transfer from a communist dictatorship to a free-market democracy is gone. It turns out that the fall of the old regime, which had been so morally satisfying, has left the new regime in an impossible moral position. The choice is stark: Behave with the manners of a Western democrat and allow the current anarchy to overwhelm Russia, or take "decisive measures" and risk flouting any semblance of civil society. Now the talk is of a transitional regime of "enlightened authoritarianism" or "guided democracy" or some such hybrid that makes no secret of the need for a prolonged concentration of power in the presidency. "The hand of power cannot be totally weak," Yeltsin's legal adviser, Yuri Baturin, told me one afternoon at the Kremlin. "When the use of power was necessary during the October events it was impossible to use it right away because the so-called power ministries—defense, security, police—were hesitating. Had they used their force more quickly, it would have been accomplished sooner, with less blood."

But Yeltsin's advisers also admit that, in trying to restore some degree of order in Russia, there is a constant danger of an imperceptible drift into the traditional habit of iron rule. "Like Gorbachev's perestroika, everything now in the development of democracy is being guided only from above," said Giorgi Satarov, a member of the presidential council. "It is very easy to slip into dictatorship. There are no checks. Monopolistic rule is responsible for checking itself, and this self-restriction has to hold somehow before there are real checks and balances. There can be little steps toward dictatorship, each one seeming small in and of itself, but the trend can drag us into

dictatorship. This can happen. But so far as I know the president and his motives, I do not think he has any intention of becoming a dictator."

There are more than enough people who have called on Yeltsin to become an unabashed autocrat. A poll published recently in *Izvestia* showed that three-quarters of all Muscovites welcomed the brief state of emergency that followed the October events and wanted to see it prolonged indefinitely. But even if Yeltsin were inclined to become the leader of a full-scale authoritarian regime—and he is not—he wouldn't be able to manage it. Although some of his advisers point to South Korea and parts of Latin America as places that built potential democracies under authoritarian rule, the analogy falls flat before Russian realities. Despite the military's decisive role in October 1993, the army has no Latin-American-style ambitions for junta-dom; the generals would much rather win higher wages and other social guarantees than take the upper hand in politics. Nor can Russia rely on an Asian work ethic or efficiency, to say nothing of a democratic political culture—a feature of life in Chile before Pinochet. Russia has to make democracy with Russians.

The truth is that Yeltsin, or any other leader who emerges as his potential successor, has the near impossible task of trying to build a democracy in conditions of social and economic anarchy. Aleksandr Rutskoi and Ruslan Khasbulatov may be in jail after their failed grab for power in October 1993, but theirs is not likely to be the last episode of rebellion or violence. Even those who accept or, at least, are resigned to Yeltsin's notion of transition understand that the anger and disillusion throughout Russian society is growing ever worse. The dulling realities of Soviet society—equality in poverty, the stability of repression—have come unwound, and now Russia is a scene of radical polarization. The fondest wish of the Russian reformers in 1991 was that out of economic change would emerge a huge middle class and a business élite that would become the main constituents for further change. There are no signs of this happening. Instead, Russians have watched with fury and envy as a handful of people have grown rich—gaudily rich—amid growing chaos and criminality. Capitalism in Russia has spawned far more Al Capones than Henry Fords.

There is not a single field of activity, not a single institution, free of the most brutal sort of corruption. Russia has bred a world-class mafia. According to Luciano Violante, chairman of Italy's parliamentary committee of inquiry into the mafia, Russia is now "a kind of strategic capital of organized crime from where all the major operations are launched." He said that Russian mob leaders have held summits with the three main Italian crime organizations from Sicily, Calabria, and Naples to discuss drug money laundering, narcotics trade and even the sale of nuclear material.

Russia, he added, "has become a warehouse and clearing house for the drug market."

The new Russian mobsters, who are into everything from arms sales to banking, have learned to work with former officials in the highest ranks of the Communist Party and the KGB as well as mob bosses abroad. There is also little doubt that the ministries of Yeltsin's government—especially in areas like foreign trade, customs, tax collection and law enforcement—are thoroughly corrupt. According to Yuri Boldyrev, until recently the government's chief investigator, the corruption in state and public institutions now "goes beyond the limits of the imagination." A ten-page report drafted by the police and security ministries and submitted to Yeltsin in 1993 described how senior military officers based for years in the former East Germany have been involved in huge embezzlement schemes. The officers set up their own companies to buy food and liquor, transported as military supplies, and then sold them on the free market in Poland and Russia. Sales were estimated at a hundred million Deutsche marks—fifty-eight million US dollars. In another case, Air Force Major General Vladimir Rodionov and his deputy, Colonel Giorgi Iskrov, were charged with using military aircraft for commercial flights and keeping the proceeds.

Yeltsin has not been averse to admitting what is before the eyes of everyone. According to a report by Victor Yasmann of Radio Liberty, Yeltsin told the heads of the central and regional law enforcement agencies that two-thirds of all commercial and financial enterprises in Russia—and 40 percent of individual businessmen—were engaged in some form of corruption. He said in 1992 that two billion dollars had simply "disappeared" from the budget of the Ministry of Foreign Economic Relations. Even the anti-mafia investigators are suspect. One of the chiefs of the Interior Ministry was arrested in 1993 for taking a one-million-ruble bribe. A subsequent search of his home found another eight hundred and five thousand rubles in cash.

Foreigners trying to do business in Russia have become easy targets. A friend told me about a Westerner who was caught in traffic in Moscow and, as he inched along, lightly touched the bumper of the car ahead of him. A man dressed mainly in jewelry and leather leaped from the car, ran up to the foreigner's window, stuck a revolver in, and said, "Buy my car now or I will kill you!" The foreigner, an experienced resident of Moscow, knew well that this mafioso was not joking. He went home, gathered up all the cash he could find, and bought the car. The following week, the same unfortunate man was traveling to St. Petersburg on the midnight train. Someone drugged him, and when he woke up in the morning all his valuables were gone. Such crimes shock no one in the West, but they are an ominous novelty in Russia.

Law enforcement, too, is a bitter joke. Mobsters at every level have more troops and more powerful weapons than the police. Army officers and recruits, desperate for cash, are only too glad to sell guns, rocket launchers, and grenades to the highest bidder. It is not unknown for members of mafia gangs in southern Russia to use a tank to settle an especially stubborn account. And at a time when nearly everyone is impoverished—including police, jailers, and judges—the likelihood of successful prosecution is minuscule. Vladimir Rushailo, chief of the Moscow police department, said, "Even if we manage to jail an influential member of the mafia, his fellow bandits immediately unleash a campaign pressuring the victims, witnesses, judges, public accessors. And they do this quite freely. Clearly, the criminals are more inventive than the law makers."

Perhaps the constituency that has been most stunned by the course of Russia since the collapse of the old regime is the liberal intelligentsia—the array of writers, artists, academics, and journalists who were at the forefront of the perestroika era. For centuries, Russian intellectuals had been a kind of shadow government, a moral prod to the tsars and, later, the Communist Party. When Pushkin stood up to the tsar, or Sakharov to the General Secretary, they were asserting a belief in the power of truth and the individual against a brutal system. For years, American writers like Philip Roth would return from the Soviet Union and Eastern Europe marveling at the importance of literature there. Roth once remarked that in the West everything is permitted and nothing matters, and in the East nothing is permitted and everything matters. Now in the East everything goes—and the intelligentsia matters less than it ever has.

One afternoon I went to the ramshackle offices of *Znamya* (*The Banner*), which was one of the leading literary and political monthlies in the Gorbachev years, to see the deputy editor Natalya Ivanova. I had been visiting Ivanova as a reporter on and off for six years and had never known her to be so pessimistic. At first I thought it might be the fate of *Znamya* and the other literary magazines. Where once they sold a million or more copies in the late 1980s, none now sells more than eighty thousand or so. Where once the bestseller lists were filled with titles from Solzhenitsyn, Orwell, and Brodsky, they are now litanies of mass-lit.: Dale Carnegie, John Grisham, Latvian sex manuals. Larissa Vasilieva, a Russian pop-historian, has made a fortune with *Kremlin Wives*, a look at the seamy world of political boudoirs in the Communist era. Rex Stout may now be the most popular novelist in the country. "People want a little pleasure," one writer told me. "If they have to read about one more concentration camp, they'll die."

But Ivanova was worried about more than the statistics of culture. It was inevitable, she realized, that once the regime fell, the importance (and outsized popularity) of serious literature would fade. "We can all accept the idea that the only people reading now are the ones who read for nonpolitical reasons," Ivanova said. "Now you see the rise of advice columns, personal ads, Harlequin romances. Well, that's OK. What is unexpected is the general degradation of culture and of the intelligentsia itself. Its dominant position is now held by this new class of so-called businessmen and they have no class at all. This new bourgeoisie is mostly made up of speculators stealing from the country." Ivanova showed me the galley proofs for an article of hers called "Double Suicide." It is an angry piece in which she accuses her fellow artists and thinkers of being more interested in "the course of the dollar than in moral problems," of bowing humbly before a new and vulgar image of what the Leninists once called the "shining future."

Where once the Russian landscape was littered with one kind of propaganda—"We Are Marching Toward Leninism!" etc.—television, radio, and the newspapers are now filled with propaganda of a different sort: advertisements for unaffordable luxuries, fantastic commercials geared toward lives that hardly exist. One minute you are Homo Sovieticus surrounded by the aggressive blandness of communism, the next minute you are watching a Slavic vixen sucking on a maraschino cherry and telling you which casino to visit. There is something profoundly irritating and American about ads for investment funds or "premium" cat food in a country where the vast majority live in poverty. A year or two of exposure to American-style commercials has produced what decades of Communist propaganda could not: genuine indignation on the part of honest people against the excesses of capitalism. But the intelligentsia is bewildered by it all and incapable of providing moral guidance. "They struggled for a new life and it turned out that this life deceived them," Ivanova said sadly.

For the young, there is just no sense, no prestige, in pursuing intellectual life. At Moscow State University, it is suddenly a cinch to gain admission to the humanities department; everyone wants to learn finance. The endless ethereal conversations around the kitchen table, the wonderful no-show jobs at academic institutes, the huge audiences for poetry readings—that world is dwindling. "What we had under Gorbachev and for the years before was like the ecological system in Australia before the English brought their dogs and rabbits," another friend, the political scientist Andrei Kortunov, said. "We had their weird, authentic, original kind of culture. The intellectuals were even a privileged class. But when the English

came with their dogs and rabbits, the ecological system decayed. I suppose we need to go through this period of consumerism and pop culture, just as they are in Poland and Czechoslovakia. The question is whether Russia will ever to be able to preserve even part of the old ecology, its distinctive intellectual character."

One night I took Leonid Radzikhovsky, the journalist, to dinner at the plush Italian restuarant in the Kempinski, a new, German-owned hotel across from the Kremlin. When I asked him about the lost world of the Russian intelligentsia, he betrayed no wistfulness. "I am a cynic maybe, a realist," he said, "but there is no more moral authority in Russia. Russia is a country in the stage of primitive accumulation of capital. Look around you, at this restaurant. What will dinner cost? At least one hundred dollars right? An average Moscow salary for a month. In the nineteenth century there were landlords and peasants and no thought of mixing them. But now everyone thinks he has a right to have dinner at the Kempinski. And everyone wants it. This is *all* anyone thinks about. They don't think about novels or plays or poetry. If it is true that everything in America is about dollars, it is even more true now in Russia. This is a hungry country and it wants to be fed."

A while after returning from Moscow, I traveled up to Cavendish, the small town in Vermont where Aleksandr Solzhenitsyn has lived in exile for eighteen years. When I visited him, he had just finished his life's work, the massive historical novel *The Red Wheel*, and was preparing to return at last, in May 1994, to Russia. The house was filled with packing crates. His wife, Natalia, was frantically trying to find a mover that could ship all their books and papers to Moscow without losing anything. A fax came from Moscow with more troubling news: the roof on their new house on the outskirts of the city was damaged and would have to be repaired at great expense.

"All the same, we can't wait to go home," Natalia Solzhenitsyn said over lunch in the kitchen. "Our minds are already back in Russia. It's as if we are no longer here in this house we have lived in for so long."

There are two adjacent houses on the property, and Natalia led me to the smaller one, where Solzhenitsyn has worked, fourteen and sixteen hours a day, without a day off since the family moved to Cavendish in 1976. He sat at a small table in his study, his face a kind of living photograph of a nineteenth-century man. But while his beard and Asiatic eyes are reminiscent of Dostoevsky, Solzhenitsyn is a man of the Russian twentieth century. He, more than anyone, more even than Sakharov, made it impossible for

the West to ignore any longer the true nature of the Soviet regime. If literature has ever changed the world, his books surely have. *One Day in the Life of Ivan Denisovich* opened the world of the camps up to the people of the Soviet Union in the early sixties, and the three volumes of *The Gulag Archipelago* erased all lingering doubts in the seventies.

We talked for the better part of the day, and Solzhenitsyn spent much of the time criticizing Gorbachev, whom he dismisses for "running in place year after year," and Yeltsin, whom he admires, for letting so many millions of Russians fall far below the poverty line. What was strange to me was that Solzhenitsyn never for an instant betrayed a moment's pleasure in the victory that he, after all, had done so much to bring on: the fall of the Communist regime. "In August 1991, my wife and I were incredibly excited to watch on television as Dzerzhinsky's statue was taken down in front of the KGB. That, of course, was a great moment for us," he said. "But I knew inside that this was not yet true victory. I knew how deeply Communism had penetrated into the fabric of life. And what were we doing? What was Yeltsin doing? Just fighting Khasbulatov and nothing else. We forgot everything and just fought each other. The same even now. All is decay. It's too early to celebrate. Why was I silent for so long about Gorbachev? Well, thank God something did begin, but everything was begun so badly. So what do you do, celebrate or weep? It is too early to celebrate. I just could not have gone over to Moscow in August '91 and had a glass of champagne in front of the White House with Yeltsin. The heart is not yet joyful."

What he hopes for now, he said, was not a new empire, not the resuscitation of a great power, but simply the development of "a normal country." It was time to join in that process. After a life that had reflected the agonies of the old regime—a communist youth, the war, prison, the camps, the battle with the Kremlin, forced exile—now, at the age of seventy-five, he was completing the circle. He had tickets to return home. "Even at the worst times, I knew I would be coming home," he said. "It was crazy. No one believed it. But I knew I would come home to die in Russia."

David Remnick
January 1994

ACKNOWLEDGMENTS

The last generation of foreign reporters in the Soviet Union was the luckiest. We were witnesses to a singular triumphant moment in a tragic century. What's more, we could describe it, we could talk to the players, major and minor, with relatively little fear of jeopardizing anyone's freedom. In the past, journalists, historians, and diplomats writing about Russia and the Soviet Union were always wary about acknowledging their friends and sources. It is with a great sense of relief and promise that I feel freed of that constriction.

During my time in the twilight of the Soviet Union, I had occasion to interview hundreds of people, some repeatedly and for many hours, some for just a little while in a Kremlin corridor or on a park bench. At first there were the old risks. I remember meeting the Ukrainian human rights defender Bogdan Horyn in a park in Lvov, the better not to be overheard or arrested. By the time I was preparing to leave for New York, I was interviewing Bogdan in the independent Ukrainian parliament, of which he was a prominent member. In my source notes, I've listed the interviews that were especially important to this book.

The greatest source of my education in Moscow was the friendship of those who let me and my wife, Esther Fein, and our son, Alex, into their homes and lives. They were much more than sources of information. Masha Lipman, a superb translator and reporter, worked tirelessly for *The Washington Post* and on behalf of this book. I was lucky to count her as a friend and to have her wise counsel, her sharp eye for the fatuous and the absurd. Masha's husband, Seriozha Ivanov, is a friend and guide through the academic and historical forests. The other members of the "gang of four," Masha Volkenshtein and Igor Primakov, were good friends and teachers. Thanks also to Grisha Kosazsky and Lyola Kantor, Judith and Emmanuel Lurye, Eduard Gladkov, Misha and Flora Litvinov, and many others.

The press corps in Moscow was superb, and I want to thank some my friends among them: Frank Clines, Bill Keller and Ann Cooper, Jeff and Gretchen Trimble, Xan and Jane Smiley, Eileen O'Conner and John Bilotta, Jonathan Sanders, Laurie Hays and Fen Montaigne, Marco Politi, and, at the *Post,* Eleanor Randolph, Gary Lee, Fred Hiatt, and Margaret Shapiro. My main running mate and bureau chief at the *Post,* Michael Dobbs, was indispensable, both as a

friend and as a colleague. Lisa Dobbs showed my own family constant friendship just as surely as she showed Moscow the meaning of free enterprise.

A number of scholars, both in the United States and in Russia, were of great help, among them Richard Pipes, Stephen Cohen, Arseny Roginsky, Leonid Batkin, and Natalya Ivanova.

At *The Washington Post*, a raft of editors supported my work in Moscow, and I am especially grateful to Michael Getler, David Ignatius, and the wizard, Jeffrey Frank, for their advice and editing as the copy flowed in. Thanks also to Ben Bradlee, Leonard Downie, Robert Kaiser, Don Graham, and Katharine Graham for giving me one of the best jobs in journalism the century could offer.

At my new home, *The New Yorker*, I am grateful first to Robert Gottlieb and Pat Crow for publishing an early piece of the book, and then to Tina Brown and Rick Hertzberg for making the arrangement permanent.

Barbara Epstein invited me to write for *The New York Review of Books* while I was still in Moscow and has showered me with kindness, superb editing, and Federal Express packages ever since. Barbara, Jeff Frank, Masha Lipman, and Seriozha Ivanov read the manuscript with great care and insight.

I am also grateful to the Council on Foreign Relations for making me its Edward R. Murrow Fellow in 1991–92, which gave me the time, the room, and the quiet in which to work.

At Random House, Jason Epstein's intelligence, wit, and skillet are all matchless. My agent, Kathy Robbins, is the source of endless patience and wise counsel. Early on, Linda Healey also gave me some very good editorial advice.

I received great support from family and friends before, during, and after my time in Moscow. My parents gave me the go-ahead to move to the Motherland. I am in awe of their strength and forever grateful for their unquestioning love and support. My brother, Richard, and sister-in-law, Lisa Fernandez, as well as my grandmother, Miriam Seigel, were just as helpful, and to them much thanks and love. Esther's parents, Miriam and Hyman Fein, let me take their daughter off to a terrifying place for them, and then they visited us there. They are a joy. Steve Fisher helped in the mysteries of the computer.

Eric Lewis and Elise Hoffmann, Richard Brody and Maja Nikolic, Marc Fisher and Jody Goodman, Michael Specter and Alessandra Stanley, and Henry Allen were all friends in deed, even at such a great distance.

My son, Alexander Benjamin, named for great-grandfathers born in the last empire, was a little late getting to the show—he was born smack in the middle of the Twenty-eighth (and final) Congress of the Communist Party—but when he did arrive, he took Moscow by storm.

My greatest thanks are to Esther, who ran off to Russia with me—a strange and wonderful way to begin a marriage. In Moscow, she wrote a string of elegant features and news stories for *The New York Times*, visited some of the stranger corners of the empire, and delighted the competition all the while. Back in New York, she was the manuscript's keenest editor, and its author's sustenance. This book is not only for Esther, it is also very much hers.

NOTES ON SOURCES

My main source of information for this book was personal interviews. Because many of those interviewed speak for themselves in the text, I have not noted them formally here. I also picked over many of my own dispatches in *The Washington Post* from January 1988 to January 1992, as well as longer pieces in *The New York Review of Books* and *The New Yorker.*

While in Moscow, I also gained a great deal from reading, among others, Bill Keller, Francis X. Clines, Esther B. Fein, and Serge Schmemann in *The New York Times* and, especially, Michael Dobbs in the *Post.* Dobbs's reports on Chernobyl, the assault on Lithuania in January 1991, and the August coup, including the battle for control of *Izvestia,* were particularly useful. The following notes mention some supplementary material and sources not self-evident from the text.

PART I

1. THE FOREST COUP

Allen Paul's book on the Katyn massacre is the best so far in English. As the archives open there has been more material than ever coming from Moscow, including evidence that the Gorbachev leadership knew far more than it ever let on to the Polish government. Interviews with Colonel Aleksandr Tretetsky, Yuri Afanasyev, Yegor Ligachev, and Aleksandr Yakovlev were important, as was Tretetsky's interview with the executioner Vladimir Tokaryev, first published in the *Observer,* October 6, 1991, p. 1.

2. A STALINIST CHILDHOOD

Natalya Gorbanevskaya's account of the Red Square demonstration and Pavel Litvinov's speeches, essays, and letters were helpful, but the Litvinov family members were the key sources here.

3. TO BE PRESERVED, FOREVER

Yerofeyev's *Moskva-Petushki*, available in English as *Moscow Circles* (with the author's name transliterated Benedikt Erofeev), is a seminal novel of the Brezhnev, or stagnation, era. The Brodsky trial transcript is available in a number of dissident anthologies. Brodsky's letter to Brezhnev is quoted in *The Washington Post*, July 25, 1972. I interviewed Yurasov several times, and he also gave frequent interviews in the Soviet press. The best article on him in Russian is Viktoriya Chalikova's essay "Arkhivni Yunosha" ("The Young Archivist") in the St. Petersburg–based journal *Neva*, No. 10, 1988.

4. THE RETURN OF HISTORY

Gorbachev's history speech of November 2, 1987, was published in *Pravda*, *Izvestia*, etc., in Russian on November 3, 1987, and in *The New York Times* the next day in English. Both *The Short Course* and *The History of the Communist Party of the Soviet Union* are available in English editions. Yeltsin's *Against the Grain* contains a colorful version of the negotiations over the language of Gorbachev's speech, and his retelling agrees for the most part with accounts given me by Yakovlev, Ligachev, and others.

5. WIDOWS OF REVOLUTION

Stephen F. Cohen's *Bukharin and the Bolshevik Revolution* is still the definitive work on Bukharin. However, there are more negative assessments in Adam Ulam's *The Bolsheviks* and Nekrich and Heller's *Utopia in Power*. Anna Larina Bukharina's memoir will be available in an English edition from Norton in 1993.

6. NINOTCHKA

I've tried to piece together the Nina Andreyeva intrigue through interviews with the main players in the drama, including Nina Andreyeva, Mikhail Shatrov, Yegor Yakovlev, Aleksandr Yakovlev, Viktor Afanasyev, Yevgeny Yevtushenko, Aleksandr Gelman, Len Karpinsky, and Yegor Ligachev. Her article originally appeared in *Sovetskaya Rossiya*, March 13, 1988. Among the more useful articles on the affair are Robert Kaiser's "Red Intrigue: How Gorbachev Outfoxed His Kremlin Rivals" in *The Washington Post*, June 12, 1988; Dev Muraka's "The Foes of Perestroika Sound Off" in *The Nation*, May 21, 1988; and Vladimir Denisov's " 'Krestni Otets' Nini Andreyevoi" ("The Godfather of Nina Andreyeva") in *Rodina*, No. 1, 1991. Ligachev's description of the Andreyeva affair in his memoir is an attempt to paint himself as a victim of an intrigue by Yakovlev and Gorbachev. The BBC documentary series *The Second Russian Revolution* was an excellent source of information on the Andreyeva affair, as well as on other secret deliberations of the Communist Party, including the Politburo's control over information surrounding the Chernobyl nuclear disaster.

7. THE DOCTORS' PLOT AND BEYOND

The Rapoport family was the key source here, as well as Yakov and Natalya Rapoport's memoirs. There are good descriptions of the Doctors' Plot in Salo Baron's history of the Jews in Russia as well as in the Ulam and Volkogonov Stalin biographies and Khrushchev's memoirs.

8. MEMORIAL

I interviewed many of the original and eventual leaders of Memorial. Arseny Roginsky, Yuri Afanasyev, Andrei Sakharov, Leonid Batkin, Nikita Okhotin, and Lev Ponomarev were especially helpful. Roy Medvedev in Moscow and Zhores Medvedev in London both spent many hours describing their early years.

9. WRITTEN ON THE WATER

Aleksandr Milchakov's articles in *Vechernaya Moskva* describe in great detail his search for the remains of gulag victims in Moscow and elsewhere. Among the more useful articles appeared in that paper on June 9, 1990, July 12, 1990, September 28, 1990, October 20, 1990, April 14, 1990, May 17, 1991, August 10, 1990.

PART II

10. MASQUERADE

Jay Leyda's classic *Kino* is by far the best history of the Soviet cinema. So far the literature on Soviet television is relatively thin. Ellen Mickiewicz's book contains useful information on *Vremya* and other early glasnost programs but was a bit early to include the real wave of liberation. Leonid Parfyonov, Eduard Sagalayev, Bella Kurkova, Igor Kirillov, and many other executives and journalists at the main glasnost-era programs were the best sources of information.

Mikhail Gorbachev, understandably, still awaits his biographer, a wait that could take years while scholars gather all the necessary documents, interviews, and material accumulated over his incredible career as the Soviet Union's last leader. In the meantime, he is at work on what his aides say is a serious memoir. So far the memoirs that have appeared, including Gorbachev's *The August Coup,* are thin justifications of policy written in the heat of the political moment. Zhores Medvedev and Michel Tatu wrote early, useful biographies, and journalists such as Christian Schmidt-Haeur, Gerd Ruge, Dusko Doder and Louise Branson, Robert Kaiser and Angus Roxburgh have gathered useful information in their various books. Gail Sheehy's biography contains some interesting information from her own trips to the Stavropol region, but the book is too weighted down by inaccuracies and misunderstandings of Soviet history and politics. Raisa Gorbacheva's memoir, *I Hope,* is sentimental and almost entirely useless, but it

does contain some interesting letters and other glances at life in Stavropol and in the Kremlin. Ligachev and Yeltsin, while ideological opposites, have written the most engaging (if not always truthful) memoirs, while Shevardnadze and Yakovlev have, so far, been hesitant and dry.

11. THE DOUBLE THINKERS

Sakharov's two volumes of memoirs are remarkable, especially the first half of the first volume, in which Andrei Dmitriyevich describes his transformation from a man of science and the system into a dissident.

Len Karpinsky described his strange career to me in a series of interviews. I am also grateful to Stephen Cohen for bringing Karpinsky to the attention of the West by publishing the essay "Words Are Also Deeds" in *An End to Silence* and then an interview with Karpinsky in a book edited by Cohen and Katrina vanden Heuvel, *Voices of Glasnost.*

I interviewed many of the most prominent of the men and women of the Gorbachev generation, including Fyodor Burlatsky, Andrei Sakharov, Lev Timofeyev, Giorgi Shakhnazarov, Vitaly Korotich, Tatyana Zaslavskaya, Abel Aganbegyan, Oleg Bogomolov, Nikolai Shmelyov, Aleksandr Bovin, Mikhail Ulyanov, Giorgi Arbatov, Yegor Yakovlev, Yuri Karyakin, Andrei Bitov, and Sergei Khrushchev.

12. PARTY MEN

Leonard Schapiro's *The Communist Party of the Soviet Union* remains the classic history of the Party, but I also found useful Michael Voslensky's *Nomenklatura,* Konstantin Simis's *USSR: The Corrupt Society,* and, especially, Arkady Vaksberg's *The Soviet Mafia.* Geidar Aliyev, Dinmukhamed Kunayev, Arkady Vaksberg, Lev Timofeyev, Andrei Fyodorov, Yuri Shchekochikin, Dmitri Likhanov, Andrei Karaulov, Arkady Volsky, Telman Gdlyan, Boris Yeltsin, and Yegor Ligachev all provided me with their own versions of what was the Communist Party.

13. POOR FOLK

All the material, except where noted in the text, is based on reporting trips to Turkmenia, the Vologda region of northern Russia, the steel town of Magnitogorsk in the Urals, and the Moscow netherworld. I am grateful to Murray Feshbach at Georgetown University for his work on the question of poverty. Stephen Kotkin's book on Magnitogorsk and John Scott's *Behind the Urals* are complementary portraits of that city and industrialization. Robert Conquest's *The Harvest of Sorrow* is the key—even heroic—work on collectivization. Esther B. Fein's articles on poverty in *The New York Times* (January 29 and August 14, 1989) and *Komsomolskaya Pravda*'s reports on infant mortality in Central Asia (April 25, 1990) and poverty in general (April 19, 1990) were very helpful.

14. THE REVOLUTION UNDERGROUND

Officials at the Red Proletariat machine-tools factory in my neighborhood in Moscow kindly gave me access to the election process there. I received even greater hospitality and access in western Siberia at the Yagunovsko mines and in other mining villages surrounding the city of Kemerovo. Anatoly Shcheglov and Anatoly Malikhin were just a couple of the miners who gave me long interviews and tours of the mining region. I had similar help from miners in Donetsk, Ukraine, in Karaganda, Kazakhstan, and on Sakhalin Island, Russia.

15. POSTCARDS FROM THE EMPIRE

Bogdan Nahaylo and Victor Swoboda's *Soviet Disunion* is a useful primer on the nationalities issue. The works by Helène Carrère d'Encausse anticipating the ethnic crises in the Soviet Union remain invaluable.

16. THE ISLAND

Chekhov's book is available in an excellent English edition, *The Island: A Journey to Sakhalin.* Nikolai Batyukov, Anatoly Kapustin, Vitaly Guly, and Ivan Zhdakayev, a bulldozer driver and deputy in the Supreme Soviet and friend, arranged my trip to Sakhalin and were extraordinarily helpful in describing life and the political transformation on the island. I am also grateful to Bruce Grant, an anthropologist at Rice University, who spent six months working in a fishing collective farm, for his tales of Sakhalin.

17. BREAD AND CIRCUSES

Anatoly Kashpirovsky and Alan Chumak both gave me a series of interviews and I attended their healing sessions. The Byzantine scholar Sergei Ivanov provided the quotation from Agathias.

18. THE LAST GULAG

Elena Chukovskaya, Vadim Borisov, Sergei Zalygin, Natalya Solzhenitsyn, Yegor Ligachev, Aleksandr Yakovlev, Lev Timofeyev, Tatyana Tolstaya, and Viktor Yerofeyev helped me piece together the Solzhenitsyn drama. John Dunlop's *Radio Liberty* report (#407, 1989) was also helpful.

Solzhenitsyn's article "Kak nam obustroit' Rossiya?" first appeared in *Komsomolskaya Pravda,* October 2, 1990. Michael Scammell's biography of Solzhenitsyn is a superb work, and Charles Truehart provides some additional details on Solzhenitsyn's current working life in *The Washington Post,* November 24, 1987.

Before going to Perm-35, I interviewed a number of former political prisoners, including Bogdan Horyn, Vyacheslav Chernovil, Sergei Kovalev, Levon Ter-Petrossian, Sergei Grigoryants, and Lev Timofeyev. Natan Shcharansky's memoir *Fear No Evil* has a fine description of the Perm camps. The researchers at

Helsinki Watch also provided useful details on political prisoners and Perm-35. All the prisoners with whom I spoke at Perm were released in the wake of the fall of the August coup.

PART III

19. "TOMORROW THERE WILL BE A BATTLE"

After his return from Gorky, Sakharov was not quite as available to journalists as he had been in the 1970s. I had one formal interview with him at his apartment and numerous short interviews with him at meetings of Memorial, Moscow Tribune, the Congress of People's Deputies, and other public venues. There are helpful glimpses of Sakharov in many books by dissidents and Western journalists, but Sakharov's own books are the best source: *Memoirs, Moscow and Beyond, Alarm and Hope, My Country and the World, Sakharov Speaks,* and *Reflections on Progress, Peaceful Coexistence, and Intellectual Freedom.*

Yelena Bonner's *Mothers and Daughters* and, especially, *Alone Together* are extremely moving accounts of her life.

Of all the tributes to Sakharov published after his death, the best was a special edition of *Moscow News,* December 17, 1989.

20. LOST ILLUSIONS

Aleksandr Yakovlev's books include *Predisloviye. Obval. Poslesloviye.* ("Preface. Collapse. Afterword."), *Muki Prochiteniya Bitiya* ("The Pain of Perceiving Life"), and *On the Edge of an Abyss: From Truman to Reagan.* The two recent books in Russian include the major speeches and an especially valuable interview first printed in *Komsomolskaya Pravda,* June 5, 1990. Yakovlev's article "Protiv antiistorizma" ("Against Anti-historicism") appeared in *Literaturnaya Gazeta,* October 15, 1972.

My own interviews for this chapter that were the most helpful were with Yakovlev, Vitaly Korotich, Yegor Ligachev, Stanislav Shatalin, Nikolai Petrakov, Arkady Volsky, Eduard Shevardnadze, Anatoly Sobchak, Giorgi Shakhnazarov, Sergei Grigoriyev, Fyodor Burlatsky, Vyacheslav Shostokovsky, and Yuri Afanasyev.

Bill Keller's profile in *The New York Times Magazine,* February 19, 1989, was also helpful.

21. THE OCTOBER REVOLUTION

Ilya Zaslavski gave me free run of the October District, and I was able to sit in on meetings and private planning sessions as well as conduct interviews with his allies and enemies. The mayor of Moscow, Gavriil Popov, was also helpful with an interview on the difficulties of building a municipal government.

Alex Kahn helped guide me through the world of the trade mafia in Leningrad and was able to arrange my meeting with "the Charity Society." I also had useful meetings with young businessmen, legitimate and not, in the Baltic states, Tbilisi, Yerevan, Baku, Leningrad, Perm, and Magnitogorsk.

22. MAY DAY! MAY DAY!

Gavriil Popov, Aleksandr Yakovlev, Yegor Ligachev, and numerous demonstrators gave me their versions of what happened on May Day 1990. I was also able to read the Politburo's anxious analysis of the event in the Party archives during my trip to Moscow in September 1992. Masha Lipman, Masha Volkenshtein, Seriozha Ivanov, Igor Primakov, Alex Kahn, and Kolya Vasyn were especially helpful on the theme of generations.

23. THE MINISTRY OF LOVE

I am grateful to Jeff Trimble of *U.S. News & World Report* for his help on many subjects, and he was especially insightful about the KGB.

24. BLACK SEPTEMBER

Members of Aleksandr Men's family as well as his parishioners were helpful in providing me with interviews and copies of his lectures, sermons, and writings. Andrei Yeryemin, Men's assistant and follower, was especially generous with his time, as were Pavel Men, Gleb Yakunin, Aleksandr Ogorodnikov, Lev Timofeyev, Andrei Bessmertni, Aleksandr Minkin, Maria Tepnina, and Tatyana Sagalayeva. Also useful were *Twentieth Century and Peace,* No. 1, 1991; Andrei Eremin's "In Memory of Aleksandr Men," *Znamya,* No. 9, 1991; Tamara Zhirmunskaya in *Smena,* No. 11, March 1991; and Mikhail Aksyonov-Myerson in *Russkaya Misl,* September 21, 1990.

25. THE TOWER

In reporting on the crackdown and eventual independence in the Baltic states, I am grateful to the staff of the newspaper *Diena* in Riga and a range of politicians and activists in Vilnius, including Vytautas Landsbergis, Arvydas Juozaitis, Romouldas Ozolas, Kazimiera Prunskiene, Algimantis Cekoulis, Justas Paleskis, Vladislav Shved, and Algirdas Brazauskas.

Vitaly Tretyakov, the editor of *Nezavisimaya Gazeta,* gave me free run of the editorial offices there, and the staff, especially Sergei Parkhomenko, Pavel Felgenhauer, and Tatyana Malkina, described the short and brilliant history of the paper.

In Moscow, both sides of the crackdown were available for interviews, if not always completely forthcoming. Eduard Shevardnadze, Stanislav Shatalin, Grigori Yavlinsky, Vitaly Korotich, Ales Adamovich, Aleksandr Yakovlev, Len Karpinsky, Andrei Grachev, and Giorgi Shakhnazarov—all, in their own way,

defenders of reform—talked with me about the tense months leading up to the coup. Nikolai Petrushenko, Viktor Alksnis, Aleksandr Nevzorov, Sergei Akhromeyev, Aleksandr Prokhanov, and other conservatives were, strangely enough, just as helpful.

26. THE GENERAL LINE

Volkogonov's main work so far is *Stalin: Triumph and Tragedy.* The Trotsky biography is available only in Russian; Volkogonov is also at work on a biography of Lenin and a memoir.

Walter Laqueur's *Stalin: The Glasnost Revelations* is a helpful compendium of the recent discoveries about Stalin that have supplemented the standard biographies by Robert Tucker, Adam Ulam, Isaac Deutscher, Roy Medvedev, and Boris Souveraine.

The transcript of the meeting denouncing Volkogonov was published in *Nezavisimaya Gazeta,* June 18, 1991. Nina Tumarkin's "The Great Patriotic War and Myth and Memory," *Atlantic,* June 1991, describes the role of the war as a legitimizing myth in the minds of the older generation.

27. CITIZENS

In Rostov, General Matvei Shaposhnikov described for me his experience at Novocherkassk. Olga Nikitina's "Novocherkassk: Chronicle of a Tragedy," *Don,* Nos. 8 and 9, 1990, is an excellent oral history of the massacre. At the Communist Party archives, I was able to read KGB documents on the Novocherkassk affair made available only in 1992. Solzhenitsyn's account in the third volume of *The Gulag Archipelago* has stood up well despite the appearance of new materials.

Robert Conquest's *Kolyma: The Arctic Death Camps* is the best historical compendium so far on the camps of the Soviet far east, but I was told that a number of scholars are now beginning work in the Kolyma region on more complete histories.

PART IV

For this account of the August coup, I depended largely on my own experience and the reports from the *Post* by Fred Hiatt, Margaret Shapiro, and, especially, Michael Dobbs.

I am also grateful for having had the chance to read the reports by *The New York Times, The Wall Street Journal, The Boston Globe,* the *Los Angeles Times, Nezavisimaya Gazeta, Komsomolskaya Pravda, Literaturnaya Gazeta, Izvestia, Argumenti i Fakti, Ogonyok,* and *Stolitsa.* A useful compendium of press reports from Russia and the other republics on the coup is *Korichnyevii Putsch Krasnikh*

Avgust '91, published in 1991 by Tekst. The Russian, Moscow, and "main" television channels also carried helpful interviews, especially in the three or four days after the fall of the coup.

Eventually, the best history of the August coup will come out of the dozens of volumes of testimony assembled by the Russian prosecutors. As I write, a year and a half after the coup, there has been no trial though one is scheduled for Spring 1993. The testimony and "inside" workings of the coup in my account come from the prosecutors' attempt to select the highlights from the still-closed investigation; in most cases, these details checked out with other published reports in the Western and Russian press.

Stuart Loory and Ann Imse's CNN album of photographs and reports, *Seven Days That Shook the World,* is based largely on the network's excellent coverage. The BBC series *The Second Russian Revolution* also has excellent interviews with Gorbachev, Yeltsin, and other key players.

Sobchak, Yakovlev, Gorbachev, Shevardnadze, Ryzhkov, and Bakatin were useful in their books, since each had his own angle of vision in this Roshomon tale.

Karaulov's interviews with Yanayev, Lukyanov, and other players in the coup for *Nezavisimaya Gazeta* will soon be published as part of a book. But perhaps the most revealing interview was Yuri Shchekochikin's talk in the October 2, 1991, issue of *Literaturnaya Gazeta* with Pyotr Korotkevich, a top missile scientist in the military industry, who described Baklanov as a conspirator of dark genius.

PART V

THE TRIAL OF THE OLD REGIME

This section came out of an article on the trial of the Communist Party I wrote for *The New Yorker*'s November 30, 1991, issue and an article on Gorbachev's trip across America for *Vanity Fair*'s August 1991 issue.

INTERVIEWS

In one way or another, hundreds of interviews, long and short, helped me with this book. The "ordinary people" I spoke with for this book are usually cited by name in the text only. What follows is a list of those interviews with public or semipublic figures who were especially helpful. The list seems chockablock with "legislators," "historians," "activists," and, God help us, "journalists." But such were the times. In Moscow, Leningrad, and the Baltic states, especially, these people were at the center of public life. There were times when the Congress of

People's Deputies seemed, in part, like a joint convention of political hacks and the faculty club. That is changing now as a class of professional politicians evolves. Rather than list just the names, I have given some short indication of who these people were during the perestroika period and the immediate aftermath of the failed August coup of 1991. My thanks to all of them.

Tengiz Abuladze (filmmaker)
Ales Adamovich (writer, legislator)
Viktor Afanasyev (editor, *Pravda*)
Yuri Afanasyev (historian, legislator)
Abel Aganbegyan (economist, adviser to Gorbachev)
Marshal Sergei Akhromeyev (military adviser to Gorbachev)
Vasily Aksyonov (novelist)
Yuz Aleshkovsky (novelist)
Abdulfaz Aliyev (Uzbek nationalist)
Geidar Aliyev (former Politburo member)
Colonel Viktor Alksnis (leader of Soyuz faction)
Anatoly Anayev (editor, *Oktyabr*)
Nina Andreyeva (neo-Stalinist, chemistry teacher)
Anton Antonov-Ovsenko (historian)
Giorgi Arbatov (government adviser, Americanist)
Tatyana Baeva (participant Red Square demonstration, 1968)
Grigori Baklanov (editor, *Znamya*)
Dmitri Barshevsky (filmmaker)
Leonid Batkin (historian, legislator)
Zoya Belayeva (television journalist)
Valentin Berezhkov (Stalin's translator)
Andrei Bessmertni (Christian activist)
Andrei Bitov (novelist)
Mikhail Bocharov (economic adviser to Yeltsin, legislator)
Oleg Bogomolov (sociologist, legislator)
Larisa Bogoraz (human rights activist)
Aleksei Boiko (legislator)
Yuri Boldyrev (legislator)
Vadim Borisov (subeditor, *Novy Mir*)
Artyom Borovik (journalist, *Ogonyok, Top Secret*)
Aleksandr Bovin (commentator, *Izvestia*)
Algirdas Brazauskas (former Lithuanian Party chief)
Joseph Brodsky (poet)
Gennadi Burbulis (adviser to Yeltsin)
Aleksandr Burdansky (Stalin's grandson)
Fyodor Burlatsky (journalist, playwright)
Shaun Burns (U.S. diplomat)
Algimantis Cekoulis (Lithuanian journalist, legislator)

Giorgi Chanturia (Georgian nationalist)
Yelena Chekalova (student, Memorial activist)
Yuri Chernichenko (writer, agriculture expert)
Vyacheslav Chernovil (former political prisoner, mayor of Lvov)
Micah Chlenov (Jewish activist)
Lydia Chukovskaya (writer, human rights activist)
Yelena Chukovskaya (writer, human rights activist)
Alan Chumak (faith healer)
Ivan Drach (leader of Rukh, Ukrainian activist)
Major Nikolai Dronin (military investigator)
Yevgeny Dzugashvili (Stalin's grandson)
Nikolai Efimov (former editor, *Izvestia*)
Yakov Ettinger (Memorial leader)
Mikhail Fedotov (lawyer)
Pavel Felgenhauer (journalist, *Nezavisimaya Gazeta*)
Vladimir Fromin (editor, *Komsomolskaya Pravda*)
Thomas Gamkhrelidze (literary scholar, Georgia)
Zviad Gamsakhurdia (former Georgian president)
Mikhail Gefter (historian)
Aleksandr Gelman (playwright, former member Central Committee)
Boris Gidaspov (former Leningrad Party chief)
Lev Ginzburg (music critic)
Lydia Ginzburg (literary critic)
Eduard Gladkov (photographer)
Vitaly Goldansky (physicist)
Vitaly Goldovitch (prisoner, Perm-35)
Andrei Golitsyn (monarchist)
Mikhail Gorbachev (president, general secretary of CPSU)
Anatoly Gorbunovs (Latvian government leader)
Andrei Grachev (former Gorbachev aide)
Daniil Granin (novelist)
Sergei Grigoriyev (former Gorbachev aide)
Sergei Grigoryants (journalist, activist)
Boris Grushin (sociologist)
Igor Gryazin (Estonian activist, legislator)
Nikolai Gubenko (actor, director, former minister of culture)
Vitaly Guly (journalist, Sakhalin Island)
Father Ivan Hel (priest, Lvov)
John Hewko (American-Ukrainian, government legal adviser)
Bogdan Horyn (former political prisoner, Ukrainian legislator)
Mikhail Horyn (former political prisoner, Ukrainian legislator)
Edward Lee Howard (former CIA; alleged defector to KGB)
Sergei Ivanov (police official, Interior Ministry)
Sergei Ivanov (historian)

Natalya Ivanova (literary critic)
Dainas Ivans (Latvian nationalist and leader)
Vladimir Ivashko (deputy general secretary, CPSU)
Arvydas Juozaitis (Lithuanian legislator)
Janis Jurkens (Latvian activist and foreign minister)
Genrikh Joffe (historian)
Nadezhda Joffe (camp survivor)
Boris Kagarlitsky (Moscow Popular Front)
Alex Kahn (music critic)
Sandra Kalniete (Latvian government leader)
Oleg Kalugin (former KGB general)
Anatoly Kapustin (legislator, Sakhalin Island)
Andrei Karaulov (journalist, *Nezavisimaya Gazeta*)
Len Karpinsky (journalist, *Moscow News*)
Yuri Karyakin (literary historian, legislator)
Anatoly Kashpirovsky (faith healer)
Tikhon Khrennikov (head of composers' union)
Igor Kirillov (former news anchor, *Vremya*)
Yuri Kiselyov (activist for the disabled)
Vladimir Klushin (husband of Nina Andreyeva)
Rudolf Kolchanov (Gorbachev college friend; journalist, *Trud*)
Igor Kon (sociologist; sexologist)
Kira Korniyenkova (neo-Stalinist)
Vitaly Korotich (journalist, *Ogonyok;* poet)
Andrei Kortunov (academic, foreign policy expert)
Sergei Kovalev (human rights activist, legislator)
Andrei Kozyrev (Russian foreign minister)
Dmitri Krupnikov (Latvian nationalist)
Gregory Krupnikov (Latvian nationalist)
Mikhail Kubrin (October District politician)
Yuri Kukushkin (historian, Moscow State University)
Dinmukhamed Kunayev (Communist Party chief, Kazakhstan)
Stanislav Kunayev (editor, *Nash Sovremenik*)
Bella Kurkova (television journalist, legislator)
Vytautas Landsbergis (Lithuanian president)
Anna Larina (widow of Nikolai Bukharin)
Yuri Laryonov (October District politician)
Mikhail Leontyev (journalist, *Nezavisimaya Gazeta*)
Yuri Levada (sociologist, pollster; Gorbachev college friend)
Yegor Ligachev (former Politburo member)
Dmitri Likhachev (literary scholar; camp survivor, legislator)
Dmitri Likhanov (journalist, *Ogonyok, Top Secret*)
Masha Lipman (translator)
Endel Lippmaa (Estonian nationalist)

Vladislav Listyev (television journalist, game-show host)
Mikhail Litvinov (Pavel Litvinov's father)
Pavel Litvinov (human rights activist, teacher)
Flora Litvinova (Pavel Litvinov's mother)
Judith Lurye (Jewish activist, now in Israel)
Vladimir Lysenko (Russian legislator)
Aleksandr Lyubimov (television journalist)
Igor Malashenko (Central Committee staff, adviser to Gorbachev)
Anatoly Malikhin (coal miner, strike leader)
Tatyana Malkina (journalist, *Nezavisimaya Gazeta*)
Sergei Matayev (journalist, Alma-Ata)
Roy Medvedev (historian, legislator)
Zhores Medvedev (biologist, historian)
Pavel Men (brother of Father Aleksandr Men)
Lennart Meri (Estonian activist, former foreign minister)
Andrannik Migranyan (political scientist)
Aleksandr Milchakov (historian, Memorial activist)
Aleksandr Minkin (journalist)
Viktor Morozov (actor, director, Lvov)
Arkady Murashev (legislator, Moscow police chief)
Aleksandr Nevzorov (television journalist)
Olga Nikitina (journalist, Rostov)
Nodar Notadze (Georgian nationalist)
Andrei Nuikin (journalist)
Aleksandr Ogorodnikov (Christian activist)
Nikita Okhotin (Memorial activist)
Lieutenant Colonel Nikolai Osin (commandant, Perm-35 camp)
Anya Ostapchuk (journalist)
Romouldas Ozolas (legislator, Lithuania)
Justas Paleckis (legislator, Lithuania)
Leonid Parfyonov (television journalist)
Sergei Parkhomenko (journalist, *Nezavisimaya Gazeta*)
Dmitro Pavlichko (legislator, Ukraine)
Janis Peters (poet, legislator, Latvia)
Nikolai Petrakov (economist, adviser to Gorbachev)
Colonel Nikolai Petrushenko (Soyuz faction leader)
Aleksandr Podrabinek (human rights activist, editor, *Express-Khronika*)
Ivan Polozkov (chairman, Russian Communist Party)
Mikhail Poltaranin (adviser to Yeltsin)
Grigori Pomerants (philosopher)
Lev Ponomarev (Memorial activist, legislator)
Gavriil Popov (economist, mayor of Moscow)
Igor Primakov (seismologist)
Yevgeny Primakov (adviser to Gorbachev)

Aleksandr Prokhanov (editor, *Dyen*)
Kazimiera Prunskiene (prime minister of Lithuania)
Andres Raid (television journalist, Estonia)
Yakov Rapoport (survivor of the Doctors' Plot)
Natalya Rapoport (biologist)
Vika Rapoport (set designer, now in Israel)
Lev Razgon (camp survivor, writer, Memorial activist)
Oleg Rumyantsyev (author of Russian constitution, legislator)
Anatoly Rybakov (novelist)
Yuri Rybakov (writer, Russian nationalist)
Nikolai Ryzhkov (Politburo member, prime minister)
Yuri Ryzhov (legislator, Russian ambassador to France)
Eduard Sagalayev (television executive)
Roald Sagdeyev (physicist)
Andrei Sakharov (physicist, human rights campaigner)
Mohammad Sali (Uzbek activist)
Yuri Samodurov (Memorial activist)
Vasily Selyunin (economist)
Julian Semyonov (detective writer, editor)
Igor Shafarevich (mathematician, Russian nationalist)
Giorgi Shakhnazarov (adviser to Gorbachev)
Tofik Shakhverdiyev (filmmaker)
General Matvei Shaposhnikov (retired army general)
Stanislav Shatalin (economist, adviser to Gorbachev)
Mikhail Shatrov (playwright)
Anatoly Shcheglov (miner)
Yuri Shchekochikin (journalist, *Literaturnaya Gazeta*)
Yuri Shcherbak (environmentalist, doctor, legislator, Ukraine)
Ivan Shekhovtsov (neo-Stalinist, lawyer)
Eldar Shengalaya (filmmaker, legislator, Georgia)
Eduard Shevardnadze (former Soviet foreign minister)
Nikolai Shishlin (Central Committe staff)
Nikolai Shmelyov (novelist, economist)
Vyacheslav Shostokovsky (former rector, Higher Party School)
Vladislav Shved (hard-liner, Lithuanian Communist Party)
Yuri Sigov (journalist, *Argumenti i Fakti*)
Olga Sliozberg-Adamova (camp survivor)
Anatoly Sobchak (mayor of Leningrad)
Natalya Solzhenitsyn (wife of Aleksandr Isayevich)
Sergei Stankevich (legislator, deputy mayor, Moscow)
Galina Starovoitova (legislator)
Vladislav Starkov (editor, *Argumenti i Fakti*)
Olzhas Suliemenov (legislator, poet, Kazakhstan)
Boris Sulim (Magadan Party activist)

Maria Tepnina (friend of Father Aleksandr Men)
Levon Ter-Petrossian (president of Armenia)
Lev Timofeyev (former political prisoner, journalist)
Tatyana Tolstaya (short-story writer)
Nikita Tolstoi (physicist, legislator)
Yelena Tregubova (Memorial activist)
Colonel Aleksandr Tretetsky (military investigator)
Vitaly Tretyakov (editor, founder, *Nezavisimaya Gazeta*)
Artyom Troitsky (rock critic)
Aleksandr Tsipko (Central Committee staff, historian)
Mikhail Ulyanov (actor, director)
Arkady Vaksberg (journalist, *Literaturnaya Gazeta*)
Kolya Vasyn (rock and roll pioneer, Leningrad)
Trivimi Velliste (Estonian nationalist)
Akhmuhammed Vilsaparov (journalist, activist, Ashkhabad)
Masha Volkenshtein (sociologist, pollster)
Colonel General Dmitri Volkogonov (historian, adviser to Yeltsin)
Arkady Volsky (adviser to Andropov, Gorbachev; industrialist)
Ulo Vooglaid (legislator, Estonia)
Andrei Voznesensky (poet)
Aleksei Yablokov (environmentalist, adviser to Yeltsin)
Aleksandr Yakovlev (chief adviser to Gorbachev)
Vladimir Yakovlev (editor, *Commersant*)
Yegor Yakovlev (editor, *Moscow News*)
Father Gleb Yakunin (former political prisoner, legislator)
Grigori Yavlinsky (economist, adviser to Gorbachev and Yeltsin)
Boris Yeltsin (president of Russia)
Viktor Yerofeyev (novelist)
Andrei Yeryemin (former aide to Father Aleksandr Men)
Arnold Yeryomenko (human rights activist, Magadan)
Yevgeny Yevtushenko (poet, legislator)
Dmitri Yurasov (archivist, Memorial activist)
Igor Zakharov (journalist, *Nezavisimaya Gazeta*)
Sergei Zalygin (editor, *Novy Mir*)
Tatyana Zaslavskaya (sociologist)
Ilya Zaslavsky (leader of October Region, Moscow)
Ivan Zhdakayev (legislator, Sakhalin Island)
Tatyana Ziman (refusenik)
Samuel Zivs (deputy head of the Soviet Anti-Zionist Committee)

BIBLIOGRAPHY

Afanasyev, Yuri, ed. *Inogo ne dano* (There Is No Alternative). Moscow: Progress, 1988.

Arbatov, Georgi. *The System: An Insider's Life in Soviet Politics.* New York: Times Books, 1992.

Arendt, Hannah. *The Origins of Totalitarianism.* New York: Harcourt Brace Jovanovich, 1951.

Aslund, Anders. *Gorbachev's Struggle for Economic Reform.* Ithaca: Cornell University Press, 1989.

Babyonyshev, Alexander, ed. *On Sakharov.* New York: Knopf, 1982.

Bakatin, Vadim. *Izbavleniye ot KGB* (Deliverance from the KGB). Moscow: Progress, 1992.

Baron, Salo. *The Russian Jew Under Tsars and Soviets.* New York: Macmillan, 1976.

Berlin, Isaiah. *Russian Thinkers.* New York: Viking, 1978.

Beschloss, Michael, and Strobe Talbott. *At the Highest Levels.* Boston: Little, Brown, 1993.

Bialer, Seweryn. *The Soviet Paradox.* New York: Knopf, 1986.

Billington, James. *Russia Transformed: Breakthrough to Hope.* New York: Free Press, 1992.

Bonner, Yelena. *Alone Together.* New York: Knopf, 1986.

———. *Mothers and Daughters.* New York: Knopf, 1992.

Brodsky, Joseph. *Less Than One.* New York: Farrar Straus Giroux, 1986.

Brumberg, Abraham, ed. *Chronicle of a Revolution.* New York: Pantheon, 1990.

———. *In Quest of Justice.* New York: Praeger, 1970.

Bukharina, Anna Larina. *Nezabivayemoe* (Unforgettable). Moscow: Novosti, 1990.

Carrère d'Encausse, Helène. *L'empire éclate.* Paris: Flammarion, 1978.

———. *The End of the Soviet Empire.* New York: Basic Books, 1993.

Carswell, John. *The Exile: A Life of Ivy Litvinov.* London: Faber & Faber, 1983.

Chekhov, Anton. *The Island: A Journey to Sakhalin.* London: Century, 1987.

Cohen, Stephen F. *Bukharin and the Bolshevik Revolution.* New York: Knopf, 1974.

———, ed. *An End to Silence: Uncensored Opinion in the Soviet Union.* New York: W. W. Norton, 1982.
———, and Katrina vanden Heuvel. *Voices of Glasnost.* New York: W. W. Norton, 1989.
Conquest, Robert. *The Great Terror.* New York: Macmillan, 1968.
———. *The Harvest of Sorrow.* New York: Oxford University Press, 1986.
———. *Kolyma: The Arctic Death Camps.* New York: Viking, 1978.
Davies, R. W. *Soviet History in the Gorbachev Revolution.* Bloomington: Indiana University Press, 1989.
Erofeev, Benedikt. *Moscow Circles.* New York and London: Writers and Readers Cooperative.
Garton Ash, Timothy. *The Uses of Adversity.* New York: Random House, 1989.
Ginzburg, Eugenia. *Journey into the Whirlwind.* New York: Harcourt Brace Jovanovich, 1967.
———. *The Magic Lantern.* New York: Random House, 1990.
Gorbachev, Mikhail. *Perestroika.* New York: Harper & Row, 1987.
———. *The August Coup: The Truth and the Lesson.* New York: HarperCollins, 1991.
———. *Dekabr'-'91: Moya Pozitsiya* (December '91: My position). Moscow: Novosti, 1991.
Gorbachev, Raisa. *I Hope.* New York: HarperCollins, 1991.
Gorbanevskaya, Natalya. *Red Square at Noon.* New York: Penguin, 1970.
Havel, Vaclav. *Letters to Olga.* New York: Knopf, 1989.
Heller, Mikhail. *Cogs in the Wheel: The Formation of Soviet Man.* New York: Knopf, 1988.
———, and Aleksandr Nekrich. *Utopia in Power.* New York: Summit, 1986.
Hosking, Geoffrey. *The Awakening of the Soviet Union.* Cambridge, Mass.: Harvard University Press, 1990.
Kaiser, Robert. *Why Gorbachev Happened.* New York: Simon & Schuster, 1991.
Karaulov, Andrei. *Vokrug Kremlya* (Around the Kremlin). Moscow: Novosti, 1990.
Khrushchev, Nikita. *Khrushchev Remembers.* Boston: Little, Brown, 1970.
Korotich, Vitaly. *Zal Ozhidaniya* (The waiting room). New York: Liberty, 1991.
Kotkin, Stephen. *Steeltown, USSR.* Berkeley: University of California Press, 1991.
Laqueur, Walter. *The Long Road to Freedom: Russia and Glasnost.* New York: Scribner's, 1989.
———. Stalin: *The Glasnost Revelations.* New York: Scribner's, 1991.
Lewin, Moshe. *The Gorbachev Phenomenon.* Berkeley: University of California Press, 1988.
Leyda, Jay. *Kino: A History of the Russian and Soviet Film.* New York: Macmillan, 1960.
Ligachev, Yegor. *Inside Gorbachev's Kremlin.* New York: Pantheon, 1993.

———. *Izbranniye, rechi i stat'i* (Works, speeches, and articles). Moscow: Political Literature Publishers, 1989.

Likhachev, Dmitri. *Reflections on Russia.* Boulder, Colo.: Westview, 1991.

Litvinov, Pavel. *The Demonstration in Pushkin Square.* London: Harvill Press, 1969.

Mandelstam, Nadezhda. *Hope Against Hope.* New York: Atheneum, 1970.

———. *Hope Abandoned.* New York: Atheneum, 1972.

Medvedev, Grigori. *The Truth About Chernobyl.* New York: Basic Books, 1991.

Medvedev, Roy. *Let History Judge.* Rev. ed. New York: Columbia University Press, 1989.

———. *All Stalin's Men.* Garden City, N.Y.: Anchor Books, 1985.

———, and Giulietto Chiesa. *Time of Change.* New York: Pantheon, 1989.

Medvedev, Zhores. *Gorbachev.* New York: W. W. Norton, 1987.

Mickiewicz, Ellen. *Split Signals: Television and Politics in the Soviet Union.* New York: Oxford University Press, 1988.

Nahaylo, Bogdan, and Victor Swoboda. *Soviet Disunion: A History of the Nationalities Problem in the USSR.* New York: Free Press, 1990.

Nove, Alec. *Glasnost in Action: Cultural Renaissance in Russia.* Boston: Unwin Hyman, 1989.

Okhotin, Nikita, Arseny Roginsky, et al., ed. *Zven'ya* (Links). Moscow: Feniks, 1990.

Paul, Allen. *Katyn: The Untold Story of Stalin's Polish Massacre.* New York: Scribner's, 1991.

Pipes, Richard. *The Russian Revolution.* New York: Knopf, 1991.

———. *Russia Under the Old Regime.* New York: Scribner's, 1974.

Rapoport, Yakov. *Na Rubezhe Dvukh Epokh: Delo Vrachei 1953 Goda.* (On the edge of two epochs: The Doctors' Plot of 1953). Moscow: Kniga, 1988.

Reddaway, Peter, ed. *Uncensored Russia: Protest and Dissent in the Soviet Union.* New York: American Heritage Press, 1972.

Reed, John. *Ten Days That Shook the World.* London: Boni & Liveright, 1919.

Roxburgh, Angus. *The Second Russian Revolution.* London: BBC Books, 1991.

Ryzhkov, Nikolai. *Perestroika: Istoriya Predatelstv* (Perestroika: A history of betrayals). Moscow: Novosti, 1992.

Sakharov, Andrei. *Memoirs.* New York: Knopf, 1990.

Scammell, Michael. *Solzhenitsyn.* New York: W. W. Norton, 1984.

Schapiro, Leonard. *The Communist Party of the Soviet Union.* New York: Knopf, 1960.

———. *Russian Studies.* New York: Viking, 1986.

Scott, John. *Behind the Urals: An American Worker in Russia's City of Steel.* London: Martin, Secher and Wanburg, 1943.

Shalamov, Varlam. *Kolyma Tales.* New York: W. W. Norton, 1982.

Sharansky, Natan. *Fear No Evil.* New York: Random House, 1988.

Shcherbak, Yuri. *Chernobyl.* London: Macmillan, 1989.

Shenis, Zinovy. *Maxim Litvinov.* Moscow: Progress, 1990.
Shevardnadze, Eduard. *The Future Belongs to Freedom.* New York: Free Press, 1991.
Shlapentokh, Vladimir. *Soviet Intellectuals and Political Power: The Post-Stalin Era.* Princeton: Princeton University Press, 1990.
Shtepps, Konstantin. *Russian Historians and the State.* New Brunswick, N.J.: Rutgers University Press, 1962.
Simis, Konstantin. *USSR: The Corrupt Society.* New York: Simon & Schuster, 1982.
Smith, Hedrick. *The New Russians.* New York: Random House, 1990.
Sobchak, Anatoly. *For a New Russia.* New York: Free Press, 1991.
Solzhenitsyn, Aleksandr. *The Gulag Archipelago.* 3 vols. New York: Harper & Row.
Stepankov, Valentin, and Yevgeny Lisov. *Kremlyevski Zagovor* (The Kremlin Plot). Moscow: Ogonyok, 1992.
Tarasulo, Isaac, ed. *Gorbachev and Glasnost: Viewpoints from the Soviet Press.* Wilmington, Del.: SR Books, 1989.
Timofeyev, Lev, ed. *The Anti-Communist Manifesto.* Bellevue, Wash.: Free Enterprise Press, 1990.
Tsipko, Aleksandr. *Is Stalinism Really Dead?* New York: HarperCollins, 1990.
Tucker, Robert C. *Stalin in Power.* New York: W. W. Norton, 1990.
Vaksberg, Arkady. *The Soviet Mafia.* New York: St. Martin's Press, 1991.
Volkogonov, Dmitri. *Stalin: Triumph and Tragedy.* Edited and translated by Harold Shukman. New York: Grove Weidenfeld, 1991.
———. *Trotskii.* 2 vols. Moscow: Novosti, 1992.
Voslensky, Michael. *Nomenklatura.* Garden City, N.Y.: Doubleday, 1984.
Yakovlev, Aleksandr. *Muki Prochteniya Bitiya* (The pain of perceiving life). Moscow: Novosti, 1991.
———. *Predisloviye. Obval. Poslesloviye.* (Preface. Collapse. Afterword). Moscow: Novosti, 1992.
———. *On the Edge of an Abyss: From Truman to Reagan: The Doctrines and Realities of the Nuclear Age.* Translated by Yuri Samsovov. Moscow: Progress, 1985.
Yeltsin, Boris. *Against the Grain.* New York: Summit, 1990.
Yerofeyev, Venedikt. See Erofeev, Benedikt.
Zaslavskaya, Tatyana. *The Second Socialist Revolution.* Bloomington: Indiana University Press, 1990.

INDEX

Abayev, Aba, 204–5
Abayeva, Elshe, 204
Abuladze, Tengiz, 42–46, 389
Achalov, Vladislav, 482, 483
Adamovich, Ales, 108, 129, 131, 374–75, 442–43, 475
Adylov, Akhmadzhan, 186
Afanasyev, Aleksandr, 328
Afanasyev, Viktor, 72
Afanasyev, Yuri, 29, 30, 39, 46, 61, 85, 113–16, 118, 126, 129, 132, 136, 179, 222, 281–82, 288, 302, 303, 330, 345, 363, 374, 422, 523
  metamorphosis of, 113, 114–15
  in Vilnius, 388–89
  "We Are Moving to the Side of Dictatorship," 379
  youth of, 113–14
Afghanistan, 39, 59, 79, 117, 234, 335, 510, 520–21, 524
"Against Anti-Historicism" (Yakovlev), 294
Against the Grain (Yeltsin), 194, 195, 443
Aganbegyan, Abel, 168
Agathias, 256
Ageyev, Genii, 448, 482
Akhmatova, Anna, 29, 59, 117–18, 265, 344
Akhromeyev, Sergei, 76, 374, 384, 401–2, 410, 482
  suicide of, 496
Aksyonov, Vasily, 18, 121, 367
Aleksandr I, 361
Aleksandrov, Anatoly, 244
Aleksandr Show, 392
Aleksanyan, Vladimir, 315, 318
Aleshkovsky, Yuz, 367
Alexy II, Patriarch, 427
Alik (homeless person), 201–2
Alisa, 312–14, 321
Alisovna, Valentina, 228–29
Aliyev, Geidar, 180–83, 190, 193, 194, 196, 325, 385, 519
Alksnis, Viktor, 385–87, 393, 396, 399, 422
Alksnis, Yakov, 385
Alliluyeva, Nadezhda, 127–28
Alliluyeva, Svetlana, 128, 405
All-Union Conference of Marxist Historians, 37
Alma-Ata, 235
Ambartsumov, Yevgeny, 173
Andreyeva, Nina, 77–84, 131, 400, 410
  anti-Semitism of, 75, 83
  childhood of, 81–82
  letter written by, 72–77, 79, 84, 85, 86, 105, 116, 360, 376, 453
Andropov, Yuri, 62, 168, 191–92, 193, 194, 199, 276, 298, 342, 355, 399, 418, 440, 444, 455, 498, 529
  death of, 192
  Gorbachev as protégé of, 62–63, 191–92
Annayev, Khummet, 208

anti-Semitism, 86–100, 129, 171, 321–22, 384, 435, 446
of Andreyeva, 75, 83
"Blood Accusation" and, 94
Doctors' Plot and, 91–92, 96–98, 99
Pamyat and, 86, 89–90, 93, 358, 364, 370
Antonovich, Ivan, 512
apparatchiks, 172, 183, 215, 498
Aquarium, 336
Arbatov, Georgi, 168
archives, 106
of Communist Party, 510, 514, 515
of KGB, 115, 408, 499, 510
Lenin and, 510
of Supreme Court, 35, 46
Arendt, Hannah, 101
Argumenti i Fakti, 281, 376
Armenia, x, 89, 129, 236, 369, 420, 427, 511
Army, U.S., 508
arrests, *see* purges, Stalinist
ARTO, 319–20
Ashkhabad, 204–9
Astor, Lady, 128
Astor, Lord, 346
atheism, 198, 360, 361
Atmoda, 380
atomic bomb, *see* nuclear power and weapons
August coup (1991), ix-x, xi, 3, 7–8, 48, 49, 62, 70, 173, 183, 360, 366–67, 373–75, 376, 384–85, 404, 434–41, 446–48, 449–90, 512, 513, 524, 525, 526, 528
Communist Party trial and, 507, 508
fall of, 485–90, 493–94, 504
Gorbachev and, 3, 85, 436–37, 439, 440, 441, 446–48, 450–51, 452, 453–57, 458, 461, 462, 465–66, 468, 471, 472, 476, 480–81, 487–88, 489–90, 494, 495, 498, 501, 502
Gorbachev's press conference following, 494–95
incriminating documents and, 493–94, 499–500
massacre sites and, 3, 8, 9
suicides following, 496
theft and, 494
Yeltsin and, x, 49, 366, 455, 462–63, 465, 466–67, 470–71, 472, 473, 474, 475–76, 477, 478, 479–80, 482, 484, 485–86, 487, 502, 513
Azerbaijan, 89, 181, 236, 369

Baburin, Sergei, 505
Bakatin, Vadim, 385, 427, 463, 487
Baker, James A., III, x, 436–37, 449
Bakharden, 206, 207, 208
Baklanov, Oleg, 435, 456, 458, 464, 485, 486
in coup, 450, 452, 455, 456
Balliyeva, Aino, 206
Baltic states, x, xi, 39, 149, 216–17, 235, 236–39, 243, 244, 369, 372–73, 374, 386, 388, 394, 396, 401, 420, 427, 439, 495, 498, 508, 511, 524, 525
Estonia, x, 51, 89, 234, 235, 236, 237, 239, 369, 511
Latvia, x, 51, 234, 235, 236, 237, 239, 369, 391, 511
Lithuania, x, 22, 51, 234, 235, 236–39, 301, 302, 369, 387–93, 394–96, 438, 524
Molotov-Ribbentrop Pact and, 51, 235, 236, 237, 239, 243, 401
baseball, 338–40
Basilashvili, Oleg, 427
Baskakov, 467–68
Batkin, Leonid, 29–30, 116, 502
Battle of Stalingrad, The, 293
Batyukov, Nikolai, 248–49
Behind the Urals (Scott), 213
Beilis, Mendel, 94
Belarus, x
Belov, Vasily, 337
Berdyaev, Nikolai, 164, 523
Berger, Mikhail, 470
Beria, Lavrenty, 44, 342, 435
Berlin, 240–41
Berzin, Reingold, 424–25
Bessmertni, Andrei, 363–64
Bessmertnykh, Aleksandr, 375, 436–37, 449, 458–59
Bezrukov, Vyacheslav, 148
Bierman, Wolf, 240

birth control, 225–26, 252
birth rate, 206
Black Hundreds, 89
"Black Hundreds and the Red Hundreds, The," 439
Blinkov, Nikolai, 217–18
Blokhin (executioner), 5–7
Blucher, V. K., 426
Bobkov, Filipp, 177, 379, 464
Bobkov, Sergei, 464
Bogachova, Regina, 478
Bogatyryov, Vladimir, 339
Bogdanov, Aleksandr, 37, 424, 425
Bogdanov, Rodimir, 445–46
Bogolyubov, Klavdy, 192
Bogomolov, Oleg, 168
Bogoraz, Larisa, 18, 19, 163, 164
Bokser, Vladimir, 466
Boldin, Valery, 8, 450, 451, 455–56, 457, 464
Bolsheviks, Bolshevism, 37, 39, 62, 68, 95, 143, 409, 505, 509, 530
  church and, 361, 362
  end of, 495
  propaganda films on, 42
bomzhi (homeless), 199, 200–202, 203
Bondarchuk, Viktor, 251
Bondarenko, Vladimir, 525
Bondarev, Yuri, 337, 439
Bonner, Yelena, 162, 163, 165, 282, 285–86, 287, 288–89, 476, 516–17
Book Review, 265, 266, 267
Boren, David, 422
Borisov, Vadim, 267, 268
Borovik, Artyom, 59–60
Borovik, Genrikh, 59
Bovin, Aleksandr, 168, 173
Brazauskas, Algirdas, 301
Brezhnev, Leonid, 11, 31, 44, 45, 82, 110, 131, 135, 149, 195, 199, 233, 238, 258, 276, 287, 324, 330, 331, 333, 335, 342, 355, 357, 363, 401, 474, 516, 529
  Aliyev and, 182
  autobiography of, 33
  Brodsky's letter to, 27–28
  corruption under, 183, 186–88, 191, 193, 194, 317–18
  cotton scam and, 186–87
  death of, 191
  Gorbachev and, 193, 253
  Khrushchev overthrown by, 27, 38, 174
  political humor and, 147
  Prague Spring and, 18, 19
  Solzhenitsyn's letter to, 369
  Stalinist politics of, 18, 38–39, 109, 114, 174, 175
  television appearances of, 144, 146
  Yakovlev and, 293–94
bribery, 184–86, 193–94, 196, 215, 310, 317–18, 319, 516
Brodsky, Joseph, 27–28, 59, 70, 90, 203, 330
  trial of, 27
Bronfman, Edgar, 445–46
Brovin, Gennadi, 194
Bryuchanov, Viktor, 245
Buchanan, Patrick, 525
Budapest, 342
Bukharin, Nikolai, 38, 62, 63–69, 72, 125, 138, 152, 399, 405, 407
  Andreyeva on, 78, 79
  letter of, 65–66, 68
  trial of, 66–67, 126
Bukovsky, Vladimir, 270, 271, 509
Bulgakov, Mikhail, 265, 363
Bunin, Ivan, 424
Burbulis, Gennadi, 441, 462, 484
Burdansky, Aleksandr, 134
Burdzhalov, Eduard, 41
Burlatsky, Fyodor, 168, 174–75
Burn, The (Aksyonov), 121
Burov, Sergei, 140
Bush, George, 182, 237, 386, 388, 436, 438, 440, 445, 437
Bushkov, Pavel, 470
businessmen, 196–97, 500, 511
Byelorussia, 245, 499
Byzantine Church, 361

camps, *see* labor camps
Cancer Ward, The (Solzhenitsyn), 266, 355
Capitalist Tool, The, 501
Carnegie, Dale, 376

Carter, Gary, 339
Castro, Fidel, 49, 448, 477
Caucasus, x, xi
Ceauşescu, Nicolae, 49, 302, 327
Cekoulis, Algimantis, 388
censorship, 27, 32, 174–75, 193, 265, 267, 380, 392, 397, 470
Central Asia, x, xi, 369
  Kirgizia, 369
  Tajikistan, 369, 511, 524
  Turkmenia, 206, 207, 208–9, 223, 369
  Uzbekistan, 39, 58, 186–87, 369, 524
Central Committee, 4, 181, 222, 495, 496, 498, 504, 510, 517
Central Intelligence Agency (CIA), 348–49, 351–52, 353, 512, 516, 525
Central Television, 473
Chagall, Marc, 90
Chagin, Boris, 112
Chaika, Yekaterina, 153
Charity Society, 316–17
Chas Pik, 396
Chazov, Yevgeny, 519
Chebrikov, Viktor, 192, 221, 297, 342, 517, 518
Chegodayev, Dmitri, 320, 322
Chekalova, Yelena, 260
Chekhov, Anton, 249–50
Chernayev, Anatoly, 168
Chernenko, Konstantin, 45, 63, 191, 192, 199, 336, 355, 518, 519, 529
Chernichenko, Yuri, 116
Chernobyl, nuclear accident at, 90, 244–47, 502, 514
Chernovil, Vyacheslav, 270, 328
Chernyayev, Anatoly, 450, 457, 481
Chevengur (Platonov), 59
Chikin, Valentin, 73, 74, 75, 76
children, 205, 206, 330–31, 333
  indoctrination of, 16, 17, 31–32, 33, 37–38, 40
  as informers, 14–16
China, People's Republic of, 511
Chkheidze, Rezo, 44
Chopich, Vladimir, 139
Christ the Savior, 11
Chugunov, Vitaly, 461, 467
Chukovskaya, Lydia, 28–29, 265, 344
Chukovskaya, Yelena, 28, 29, 264, 265, 266, 363
Chukovsky, Kornei, 28, 264
Chumak, Alan, 259
Churbanov, Yuri, 193–94, 516
churches, 7, 11, 211, 360, 361
CIA (Central Intelligence Agency), 348–49, 351–52, 353, 512, 516, 525
Ciurlionis, Mikalojus, 238
Civic Union, 505
coal miners, 21, 25, 102, 203, 223–33, 252–54, 322, 412–14, 468
Cohen, Stephen, 63, 67, 68–69
Collected Works (Solzhenitsyn), 268
collective farms, *see* farms
collectivization campaign, 7, 11, 38, 39, 47, 51, 54, 63, 79, 108, 130, 149, 152, 184, 210, 211, 212, 213, 291, 400
Communism, xi, 145, 209
  relics of, 504
  rites of, 25
Communist Party, xi, 31, 96, 115, 178, 216, 526, 529
  archives of, 510, 514, 515
  banning of, 438, 495, 505, 508
  Central Committee of, 4, 181, 222, 495, 496, 498, 504, 510, 517
  Constitutions and, 505, 506, 509
  decline of, 7–8
  elections rigged by, 219–20, 252
  finances of, 496, 514
  Gorbachev and, 36, 37, 85, 149, 154, 195, 303, 494–95
  Gorbachev's resignation as general secretary of, 495, 499, 529
  history controlled by, 4, 7–8, 36–39, 115, 136
  ideological divisions within, 176, 178–79
  legal system and, 505–6, 507, 509, 510
  as mafia, 124, 181–82, 183–94, 202, 320, 376, 522; *see also* corruption
  mass quitting of, 377
  New Man and, 31
  Newspeak of, 49, 60, 107, 383
  post-coup survival of, 504–5

ruled illegal, 530
sale of positions and awards in, 184, 187
trial of, 505–11, 513, 514–15, 520–21, 522–23, 526, 527, 528, 529, 530
Yeltsin and, 194, 195–96, 433, 434, 438, 443, 495, 505, 508, 515
concentration camps, *see* labor camps
Congress of People's Deputies, 216–23, 388, 498–99
Conquest, Robert, 17, 59, 404
conscience, intellectual, 174
Constitutional Assembly, 39, 71
Constitutional Court of the Russian Federation, 505
Communist Party on trial at, 505–11, 513, 514–15, 520–21, 522–23, 526, 527, 528, 529, 530
Conversations with Stalin (Djilas), 405
cooperative businesses, 196
corruption, 180–82, 183–94, 196–97, 246, 316–20
Andropov and, 191
under Brezhnev, 183, 186–88, 191, 193, 194, 317–18
bribery, 184–86, 193–94, 196, 215, 310, 317–18, 319
Communist Party mafia and, 124, 181–82, 183–94, 202, 320, 376, 522
Gorbachev and, 181, 193–94
protection rackets and, 316–17, 522
Corvalán, Luis, 509
Cosmic Academy of Sciences, 104
cotton, 186–87, 205, 206, 207, 243
coup, *see* August coup
crime, x, 316, 319, 511
see also corruption
Crimean Tatars, 57–58
Crowe, William, 374
Culture and Life, 41
Czechoslovakia, 5, 18–20, 39, 51, 158, 159, 175, 176, 241–42

Daily Telegraph, 199
Daniel, Irina, 92
Daniel, Yuli, 17, 92, 293
Danielets, Anton, 315–16
Danilov, Viktor, 38, 108
Darkness at Noon (Koestler), 67
Davies, Joseph, 128
Davitashvili, Dzhuna, 258
Death of Elvis, 392
de Gaulle, Charles, 513
democracy, democratization, ix, x, xi, 77, 41, 120, 125, 148
elections and, 216–20, 221, 252
Democratic Initiative, 120, 123–24
Democratic Perestroika, 48
Democratic Russia, 325
demonstrations, 56–58, 236, 302–3, 420–22, 500
Communist Party trial and, 507
Democratic Initiative, 123–24
against invasion of Czechoslovakia, 18–20
KGB and, 19, 20–21, 57–58, 416, 421, 422
May Day, 326–29
Memorial, 117–18, 120
in Vilnius, 387–90, 414, 419, 421
Denisov, Vladimir, 73–74, 76
Deryabin, Anatoly, 202–3
Deutscher, Isaac, 404, 405
Dictator of Conscience (Shatrov), 62
Diena, 373
Directors International, 502
Dispatches (Herr), 60
dissident(s), 28, 61, 92, 107, 114, 168, 175, 176, 177, 178, 293–94, 304, 331, 333, 335, 415, 419, 508, 509, 510, 512, 516
historical works by, 38–39
in KGB, 354
religious, 362–63
Roy Medvedev and, 110
Sakharov and, 163, 164, 167
samizdat and, 17, 31, 59, 123
Stalinists as, 126
Vremya as, 146
Yeltsin as, 195
see also intellectuals, intelligentsia
Djilas, Milovan, 183, 405
Djugashvili, Yevgeny, 134–36
Dobbs, Michael, 388, 441, 449, 505
Dobrodzhanu, Alexander, 139
Doctors' Plot, 91–92, 96–98, 99

Doctor Zhivago (Pasternak), 59, 90, 265
Dolgikh, Vladimir, 510
Donskoi, Gennadi, 156
Donskoi Monastery, 137–38, 442
Dormidontov, Vadim, 522
Dostoevsky, Fyodor, 198
Dovzhenko, Aleksandr, 42
Doyagin, Kostya, 225
Dronin, Nikolai, 270, 275–76
Druzhba Narodov, 92
Dubček, Alexander, 18, 19–20, 62, 159, 241, 242
Dudintsev, Vladimir, 42
Duke, David, 525
Dyen, 376, 435, 505, 525
Dzerzhinsky, Feliks, 342, 344, 345, 495
Dzhanselidze, Nana, 42

Eastern Europe, 234–35, 242–43, 303
Echo of Moscow, 421, 469, 481
economy, x, 24–25, 173, 199, 506, 511, 522, 526
  500 Days plan and, 359–60, 371, 437, 516
  mafia and, 185; *see also* corruption
education, 514
  see also schools
Eisenstein, Sergei, 42
elections, 216–20, 221, 252
Elizabeth II, Queen of England, 346
Estonia, x, 51, 89, 234, 235, 236, 237, 239, 369, 511
Eveni people, 102–3
Exhibition of Economic Achievements, 203–4
"Exhibit of Poor-Quality Goods, The," 204
Express-Khronika, 57, 105

Face of Hatred, The (Korotich), 168
Fainberg, Viktor, 19
Fakt, 469
Falin, Valentin, 234, 235, 402, 403, 494, 510
Falkovich, Oleg, 319–20
farms, 25, 125, 152, 206, 208, 209–12, 250
  Chernobyl and, 245
fascism, 508, 509, 523, 524
Fateyev, Gennadi, 154
February Revolution, 41, 95, 302
Federal Bureau of Investigation (FBI), 348, 352
Fedotov, Mikhail, 508, 510, 514, 515–17
Felgenhauer, Pavel, 479–80
feudal socialism, 205
Field of Miracles, 392
Fifth Wheel, The, 392, 397
Filatov, Viktor, 435
files, 27
Filmmakers' Union, 29, 45, 77, 164
films, 42, 45, 143
  Gorbachev in, 501
  propaganda, 42, 143
  Repentance, 42–46, 48, 389
First Circle, The (Solzhenitsyn), 17, 266
fish, 25, 249
500 Days plan, 359–60, 371, 437, 516
flea markets, 504
Fleig, Leo, 138
Fomin, Vladimir, 416
Foner, Eric, 243
Forbes, 501
Foreign Affairs, 15
Frankel, Max, 355
funerals, 184–85
Fyodorov, Andrei, 185–86
Fyodorov, Svyatoslav, 444–45

Galich, Aleksandr, 18–19, 333, 358
Galkin, Dmitri, 214
Gamsakhurdia, Zviad, 270, 471
gangsters, 316–17
  see also corruption
Gaponyuk, Vladimir, 228
gay culture, 337
Gdlyan, Telman, 194
Gefter, Mikhail, 38, 39, 108, 116, 125, 163
Gelman, Aleksandr, 76–77
Gemanov, Yevgeny, 470
Georgia, x, 369, 420, 427, 498
Gerasimov, Gennadi, 68, 243
German Democratic Republic (East Germany), 240–41, 499–500, 525–26

Germany, Nazi, 36, 75, 79, 134, 186, 238, 509, 512
  Great Patriotic War against, 213, 400–404, 507
  massacres blamed on, 4
  Molotov-Ribbentrop Pact and, 51, 235, 236, 237, 239, 243, 401
Gezentsevei, Ilya, 312, 321
Gibbon, Edward, 256
Gidaspov, Boris, 395, 469
Ginzburg, Yevgenia, 121, 122
Gladkov, Edik, 206, 207, 209, 210
Gladskoi, Boris, 156
glasnost, 42, 54, 55, 59, 92, 116, 148, 148, 215, 216, 249, 264–65, 267, 308, 310, 328, 392, 401, 405
  Khrushchev's thaw vs., 178, 376
  nationalist hatreds and, 89, 90
  Ogzibirlik activists and, 207
  poverty and, 203–4
  Yakovlev and, 297
Glasnost, 311, 313
Glazunov, Ilya, 349
Glory to Christ, 238
Godfather, The, 183
Godlya, 102–3
Goering, Hermann Wilhelm, 11
Goglidze, General, 121
Goldovitch, Vitaly, 274–75
Golik, Yuri, 463
Golubyev, Viktor, 247
Golushko, Nikolai, 477
Good Evening Moscow, 343
Gorbachev, Mikhail, xi, 58–59, 66, 105, 127, 129, 135, 187, 200, 208, 217, 233, 257, 273, 306, 308, 330, 346, 379, 380, 426–29, 438, 499–503, 525, 526–30
  Adamovich's warning to, 374–75, 442–43
  Afanasyev's letters to, 115
  Akhromeyev and, 496
  Aliyev and, 180
  Andreyeva letter and, 74–75, 76, 78, 84–85, 116, 360, 453
  as Andropov's protégé, 62–63, 191–92
  Baltic states and, 237, 372–73
  Berlin visit of, 240
  boyhood girlfriend of, 155–58
  Brezhnev and, 193, 253
  Chernobyl and, 246
  Communist Party and, 36, 37, 85, 149, 154, 195, 303, 494–95
  Congress of People's Deputies and, 216, 221, 222
  corruption and, 181, 193–94
  coup and, 3, 85, 436–37, 439, 440, 441, 446–48, 450–51, 452, 453–57, 458, 461, 462, 465–66, 468, 471, 472, 476, 480–81, 487–88, 489–90, 494, 495, 498, 501, 502
  criticisms of, 502–4
  demonstrations banned by, 420–21, 422
  dual nature of, 60–61, 167–68, 173–74
  500 Days plan and, 359–60, 371, 437, 516
  made general secretary, 519–20, 528–29
  glasnost policy of, *see* glasnost
  grandfathers of, 148–49
  Grigoryants and, 311
  history and, 36, 37, 41, 46, 61–62, 71, 108, 266, 399, 401
  history speech of, 4, 9, 41, 46, 47–51, 52, 54, 58, 60–61, 63–64, 92–93, 106, 115, 148, 149
  image of, 143, 146–48, 503
  Karpinsky on, 173–74
  Kashpirovsky compared with, 260
  KGB and, 194, 345, 356
  Khrushchev and, 62
  Kryuchkov and, 441
  Kunayev and, 190
  and Lieberman's denunciation, 97
  Ligachev and, 75
  Lithuania and, 235, 301, 302, 387, 388, 389, 391, 394–95, 396
  Lukyanov and, 497
  luxury appreciated by, 194, 195, 222, 443, 453, 515
  May Day and, 324, 325, 326, 327, 328, 329
  Memorial and, 118–19

Gorbachev, Mikhail (*cont.*)
military and, 403–4, 421, 440
Moscow News and, 377
at Moscow State University, 158–60
multiparty system and, 301, 302, 303
nationalities question and, 60, 235–36, 237, 238, 239
new Union proposals and, 498–99
Nobel Prize won by, 371, 437, 513
nuclear codes and, 471
Pavlov and, 429, 441
people around, 85, 426, 440–41, 447, 488
Perestroika, 116
perestroika policy of, *see* perestroika
Poland and, 4–5, 234, 387, 499
in Politburo transcript, 516–17
political humor and, 147–48
political rise of, 45, 143, 148, 160, 192–93, 195, 253
Polozkov on, 512–13
post-coup press conference of, 494–95
power consolidated by, 192–93
as reformer, 29, 41, 46, 54, 125, 144, 152, 159, 161, 164, 169, 176, 178, 182, 216, 267, 337, 359, 363, 366, 371, 381, 387, 398, 461, 498, 511, 520, 529
rehabilitation and, 304
Repentance and, 45
resignation of, 495, 499, 529
rightward swing of, 323, 371, 398, 399, 487
Roy Medvedev and, 109, 112
Ryzhkov and, 514, 515
Sakhalin Island and, 251
Sakharov and, 117, 131, 162–63, 164, 280–82, 283–84, 285, 287
secret documents and, 499–500
self-deception of, 60–61
Shatrov's play and, 71, 72
Shevardnadze on, 420
socialism and, 36, 47, 49, 50, 51, 61–62, 63, 149–50, 400, 494, 529
Solzhenitsyn's works and, 267–68, 369–71
Soyuz faction and, 385
Stalin and, 48, 49, 50, 149, 154, 159, 160–61, 503
on Stalinism, 36, 48, 50
Stanford speech of, 503
strikes and, 223, 224, 413, 414
student brigades and, 294
suits made for, 443, 444
Tarasov and, 314
television appearances of, 146–47, 221, 502
Tereshkova compared with, 502–3
Treaty of the Union and, 439–40, 450
and trial of Communist Party, 506, 510–11, 526–27
U.S. toured by, 501
Yakovlev and, 290, 291, 294–95, 296, 298–99, 303, 494–95
Yakunin and, 362
Yeltsin and, 49, 147, 194, 195, 196, 359, 389–90, 413, 420, 421, 426, 427–28, 434, 438, 495, 499–500, 502, 506, 527
youth of, 37, 113, 150, 151, 152–54, 155–61
Gorbachev, Raisa, 129, 146, 155, 158, 160, 194, 222, 301, 441, 480
Brezhnev family and, 193
coup and, 453, 454, 456, 457, 488, 489
Gorbacheva, Maria, 152
Gorbanevskaya, Natalya, 19, 107
Gori, 127, 132
Gorlov, Georgi, 152
Gorodentsov, Yevgeny, 313
Govorukhin, Stanislav, 523–24
Grachev, Andrei, 441, 500
Grachev, Pavel, 448, 477, 482, 483, 484
Granin, Daniil, 108
graves, mass, 137–40
Great Patriotic War (World War II), 90, 213, 400–401, 507
Volkogonov's book on, 400–404
Great Soviet Encyclopedia, 32, 34
Great Terror, The (Conquest), 17
"Great Utopia, The," 504
Grebenshikov, Boris, 336
Grigoriyev, Sergei, 499
Grigoryants, Sergei, 270, 311
Grishin, Viktor, 181, 192, 504, 519, 528

Gromov, Boris, 422, 438, 482, 483, 485
Gromyko, Andrei, 192, 193, 200, 444, 519
Grossman, Vasily, 265
Gulag Archipelago, The (Solzhenitsyn), 7, 38, 39, 61, 107, 266, 267, 268, 269, 368, 414, 424
Gulf War, 388, 435
Guly, Vitaly, 251–52
Gusev, Vladimir, 473

Havel, Olga, 241–42
Havel, Václav, 241–42
health care, 205–6, 226, 231
  Kashpirovsky's séances and, 256–58, 259–63
Heart of a Dog (Bulgakov), 265
Heller, Mikhail, 300
Hemingway, Ernest, 60
Herr, Michael, 59–60
Herzen, Aleksandr, 164
Higher Party School, 4
Historical Archives Institute, 29, 33–34, 35, 46, 61, 115, 363
history, 24, 101, 114, 235
  Andreyeva's view of, 82–83
  anti-Semitism and, *see* anti-Semitism
  archives and, *see* archives
  Communist Party control of, 4, 7–8, 36–39, 115, 136
  dissidents' studies of, 38–39
  Gorbachev and, 36, 37, 41, 46, 61–62, 71, 108, 266, 399, 401
  Gorbachev's speech on, 4, 9, 41, 46, 47–51, 52, 54, 58, 60–61, 63–64, 92–93, 106, 115, 148, 149
  and indoctrination of children, 16, 17, 31–32, 33, 37–38, 40
  KGB and, 7, 38, 106, 107, 115
  Korniyenkova's view of, 132–33
  massacre sites and, 3–9
  Memorial and, *see* Memorial
  return of, xi, 4, 7, 36–51, 113
  Shekhovtsov's slander suits and, 129–31
  Stalin's control of, 37–38
  Yurasov's research and, 30–35, 46–47
History of the Communist Party, 38
Hitler, Adolf, 11, 48, 58, 82, 213, 401, 508, 509, 513
Hoagland, Jim, 487
Hobson, Valerie, 346
Holocaust, 105
homelessness, 199, 200–202
Honecker, Erich, 49, 240, 241, 302
Hope Against Hope (Mandelstam), ix
Horyn, Bogdan and Mikhail, 244, 270
Hospital on the Edge of Town, 392
House of Scholars, 164
House on the Embankment, The (Trifonov), 170
Howard, Edward Lee, 348–54
Howard, Lee, 353–54
Howard, Mary, 352
"How Can We Revitalize Russia" (Solzhenitsyn), 367, 368–71
How to Find Work in America, 337
How to Find Work in Europe, 337
How to Win Friends and Influence People (Carnegie), 376
Humanité, 36
humor, political, 147–48
Hungary, 18, 191
Hussein, Saddam, 388, 435, 477

Ignatenko, Vitaly, 447
Ignatiev, S. D., 91
Illarion, Metropolitan, 335
Illesh, Andrei, 470
industrialization campaign, 47, 63, 184, 400
infant mortality, 199, 203, 204, 205, 207, 208
Initiative Group for the Defense of the Rights of Invalids, 56
Inogo ne dano ("There Is No Other Way"), 116–17, 125
Installation, 166–67
Institute of Marxism-Leninism, 131
Institute of World Economy and International Relations (IMEMO), 295
intellectual conscience, 174
intellectuals, intelligentsia, 17, 28, 29, 46, 59, 95, 176, 178, 233, 333–34, 335, 336, 363, 495

intellectuals, intelligentsia (*cont.*)
anti-Semitic, 87
Communist Party, 238
Gorbachev criticized by, 502
Roy Medvedev and, 110
Sakharov and, 163
Western, Stalin admired by, 128
see also dissident
Interfax, 376
International Life, 356
Interregional Group, 164, 282
Iran, 511
Iraq, 477
Island, The (Chekhov), 249
"It's Absurd to Hesitate Before an Open Door" (Karpinsky), 178
Ivan IV (the Terrible), 361, 406
Ivanov, Nikolai, 194
Ivanov, Sergei, 25, 39
Ivanov, Seriozha, 331, 332–35, 421, 449, 450, 465, 466
Ivanov, Yevgeny, 345–47
Ivanova, Natalya, 363, 439, 502
Ivashko, Vladimir, 486, 494, 513–14
Izvestia, 65, 117, 173, 175, 267, 285, 334, 338, 376, 381, 448, 500, 501
coup and, 470–71, 478, 479

Jablonskis, Jonas, 238
Jakes, Milos, 49
Jaruzelski, Wojciech, 5, 49, 302, 387, 453
Jews, 83, 86, 88–89, 95, 129, 131, 332, 361, 523
emigration of, 91, 99–100
Holocaust and, 105
see also anti-Semitism
Joffe, Genrikh, 38, 40–41
John, Elton, 337
Johnson, Lyndon B., 329
Journey into the Whirlwind (Ginzburg), 121

Kaganovich, Lazar, 10–13, 34, 126, 441–43, 518
death of, 441, 442
Kaganovich, Mikhail, 34
Kahn, Alex, 314, 316, 331, 336
Kakabadze, Shota, 322
Kakuchaya, Ol'var, 459–60
Kalinin, massacres at, 3–9, 51
Kalinin, Roman, 337
Kalitnikovsky Cemetery, 137, 138
Kalnikov, Leonid, 225, 227
Kalugin, Ludmila, 355
Kalugin, Oleg, 354–56, 476
Kamarov, Yuri, 210
Kamenev, Lev, 405
Kantor, Karl, 171
Kapital, Das (Marx), 195
Kapustin, Anatoly, 252–55
Karaganda, 102
Karagodina, Yuliya, 155–58
Karasev, Yuri, 187
Karaulov, Andrei, 378, 379, 382, 497
Karaulov, Natasha, 378
Karbainov, General, 348
Karpinsky, Len, 30, 116, 169–79, 241, 267, 329–30, 376, 377, 378, 379, 380, 383, 389, 390, 500, 501
Karpinsky, Vyacheslav, 169, 170, 171–72
Karpov, Vladimir, 268
Karpova, Tamara, 425
Karpukhin, Viktor, 482, 483
Karpychev, Anatoly, 420
Karsokos, Vitya, 200
Karyakin, Yuri, 29, 108, 168, 173, 179, 220–21, 283, 475
Kashpirovsky, Anatoly, 256–58, 259–63, 360, 392
Katyn, massacres at, 3, 4, 5, 51, 115
Kazakhstan, x, 188, 190
Kazbeg, Aleksandr, 127
Keeler, Christine, 345, 346, 347
Kemerovo, 21
KGB, 24, 59, 112, 137, 192, 195, 220, 221, 233, 274, 276, 313, 331, 341–56, 376, 379, 382, 399, 400, 410, 414, 445, 446, 464, 468, 509, 518, 521, 526
Aleksandr Men and, 357, 362, 363, 364
Aliyev and, 180, 182
Alpha Group of, 482, 483

Andropov as head of, 62, 191
anti-Semitism and, 86, 88
archives of, 115, 408, 499, 510
beauty queen selected by, 343–44
businesses and, 196, 319
Communist mafia and, 183
Communist Party trial and, 510
coup and, 7, 8, 366, 436, 437, 440, 441, 448, 450, 453, 454, 462, 463, 471, 473, 475, 477, 480, 481, 482–84, 487, 489, 498
Democratic Initiative and, 123, 124
demonstrations and, 19, 20–21, 57–58, 416, 421, 422
Gorbachev and, 194, 345, 356
Gorbachev's image and, 146
Gorbachev's mother and, 152
history and, 7, 38, 106, 107, 115
Howard's defection to, 348–54
Izvestia and, 470
Jews arrested and killed by, 91
Kalinin massacre and, 4
Kalugin and, 354–56, 476
Kryuchkov as head of, 196, 342, 343, 345, 354, 359
Len Karpinsky and, 177, 178
in Lithuania, 387, 389
Litvinov family and, 14, 16, 19, 20–21
massacre sites and, 7–9
Medvedev brothers and, 109, 110
Milchakov and, 139
Nevzorov and, 393–94, 396
Remnick and, 151, 154–55, 189, 206–7, 343–44, 345–46
Roginsky and, 107–8
Sakhalin and, 250, 251
Sakharovs and, 162, 163, 164, 285, 517
Shaposhnikov and, 418
tailor shop and, 443, 444
Tarasov and, 314–15
Valentin Lazutkin and, 474
Vremya and, 473
Yeltsin and, 499, 500
Khamara, Stepan, 270
Khasbulatov, Ruslan, 462, 466, 481
Khazanov, Gennadi, 476
Khrushchev, Nikita, 18, 31, 34, 45, 47, 67, 80, 98, 119, 173, 183, 265, 324, 330, 332, 399, 401, 529
Maksim Litvinov and, 15
Novocherkassk rebellion and, 416, 417
overthrow of, 27, 38, 62, 174
Stalin denounced by, 32, 41, 48, 50, 68, 82, 91, 109, 114, 160, 168, 174, 292
television appearances of, 144, 145
thaw under, 17, 32, 38, 41, 42, 61, 62, 70, 92, 168, 178, 376, 518
Khudyakov, Sergei, 218
Kirgizia, 369
Kirichenko, Yuri, 205–6
Kirillov, Igor, 144–45
Kirillov, Yuri, 217–19, 220
Kirov, Sergei, 91, 405
Kiselyov, Yuri, 56–58
Klebko, Aleksandr, 204
Klimov, Elem, 45, 116, 118
Klushin, Vladimir, 79, 80, 84
Klyamkin, Igor, 400
Kobets, Konstantin, 466, 477, 481
Kochetov, A. F., 402
Koestler, Arthur, 66–67
Kogan, Yevgeny, 429
Kokorin, Valery, 223
Kolbin, Gennadi, 190, 235
Kolchanov, Rudolf, 158, 159–60, 161
Kolpakov, Viktor, 224
Kolyma, 37, 102, 120, 121, 250, 269, 422, 423, 424–25
Aleksandr Medvedev at, 111–12
Kolyma Tales (Shalamov), 7
Komar, Dmitri, 484
Kommersant, 314, 319, 376, 390
Kommunist, 113, 115, 173, 528
Komsomol (Young Communist League), 33, 130, 315, 444
Afanasyev in, 113, 114
Gorbachev in, 154, 155, 160, 173
Komsomolskaya Pravda, 174–75, 202, 336, 343, 344, 366, 367, 376, 377, 443, 444, 445, 502, 521
Kongurov, Pyotr, 224
Kontinent, 311

Kopelev, Lev, 17–18, 294
Korniyenkova, Kira, 131–33, 442
Korotich, Vitaly, 76, 108, 129, 131, 168, 222, 267, 282, 296, 374
Korotkevich, Pyotr, 456
Kosikh, Yuri, 269
Kosolapov, Richard, 322, 519, 528
Kostava, Merab, 270
Kosygin, Aleksei, 214
Kovalev, Sergei, 270, 273, 286, 288, 345
Kozlov, Frol, 416
Kozyrev, Andrei, 466
Krasnikov, Zhenya, 381
Krasnodar region, 187, 193, 196
Krasnogvardeiskoye, 151, 153–55
Kravchenko, Leonid, 392, 395, 459–60, 473, 489
Krichevsky, Ilya, 484
Kruchina, Nikolai, 496
Krylenko, Nikolai, 506
Kryuchkov, Vladimir, 139, 350, 355–56, 372, 375, 384, 385, 398, 427, 428–29, 446
  arrest of, 490, 496
  Castro and, 448
  in coup, 435, 436, 437, 439–40, 441, 447, 448, 449, 450–51, 452, 453, 455, 456, 457, 458, 459, 460, 463, 464, 469, 471, 475, 476, 477, 482, 483, 484, 485–86, 487, 489, 490, 496
  as KGB head, 196, 342, 343, 345, 354, 359
  Treaty of the Union and, 439–40
Kubrin, Mikhail, 54–56
Kudinova, Nadezhda, 465–66, 481–82, 485
Kukushkin, Yuri, 39–40
Kulakov, Aleksandr, 321
Kulakov, Vadim, 339
Kun, Bela, 95, 138–39
Kunayev, Dinmukhamed, 181, 188–90, 194, 196, 235
Kundera, Milan, 2
Kurbanova, Geral, 208
Kuriyev, Timur, 318
Kurochkin, 415–16
Kuzbass, Day by Day, 224
Kuzmin, Volodya, 160
Kuznetsova, Mariya, 210–11

labor camps, 101–2, 104–5, 107, 108, 111–12, 113, 165, 170, 230, 249–50, 399, 509, 517
  as gulag archipelago, 21, 120, 270, 271
  see also purges, Stalinist
labor unions, 231
Lakontsev, Viktor, 8–9
Landsbergis, Gagrielus, 238
Landsbergis, Vytautas, 237–40, 288, 387, 389, 391, 395, 396, 399, 426
Landsbergis, Vytautas, Sr., 238
Laqueur, Walter, 37
Larin, Yuri (Larina's father), 64
Larin, Yuri (Larina's son), 66, 67–68
Larina, Anna, 64–69, 70
  Stalin's letter from, 67
Laryonov, Yuri, 55–56
Latsis, Otto, 173, 174, 177
Latvia, x, 51, 234, 235, 236, 237, 239, 369, 391, 511
Lauristan, Marju, 222, 236
Lazutkin, Sergei, 474
Lazutkin, Valentin, 474
Lebed, Aleksandr, 482, 483
le Carré, John, 337
Lee, Bill "the Spaceman," 339–40
Lenin, V. I., 4, 39, 40, 45, 47, 50, 51, 54, 61, 63, 64, 65, 79, 81, 95, 104, 113, 116, 127, 130, 136, 163, 192, 211, 231, 266, 301, 308, 330, 338, 344, 377, 399, 400, 523, 527
  archives and, 510
  church and, 361
  Constitutional Assembly and, 39, 71
  essays of, 62
  funeral of, 64
  Gorbachev's image and, 146–47
  legal system and, 506
  "Marxism and Rebellion," 452–53
  paternalism of, 43
  predictions of, 408
  propaganda films and, 42, 143
  remains of, 147, 220–21, 326, 443, 504

Shatrov's play about, 70–73
Solzhenitsyn's critique of, 265, 267
State and Revolution, 62
statue of, 52, 53, 309
Ukraine and, 244
Vyacheslav Karpinsky and, 169, 170, 172
Yakovlev on, 299–300, 303, 304
Leningradsky Rabochy, 79
Lenin in Zurich (Solzhenitsyn), 61, 267
Leninism, 137, 178, 409, 509
Lenin Mausoleum, 325, 326, 327, 330, 443, 504
Lenin Museum, 495, 507
Lenin Steel Works, 213, 214
Leontyev, Mikhail, 380
"Less Than One" (Brodsky), 330
Let History Judge (Medvedev), 38, 108, 109, 112, 137
"Letter to the Soviet Leaders" (Solzhenitsyn), 28, 369
Levada, Yuri, 171
Levin, Mikhail, 17
Levit, Aleksandr, 332
Lieberman, Vladimir, 97
Life, 60
Life and Fate (Grossman), 265
Ligachev, Yegor, 7, 48–49, 71, 73, 75, 76, 77, 84, 85, 125, 147, 187–88, 194, 195, 196, 234, 254, 265, 267, 296, 298, 303, 337, 385, 399, 429, 434, 447, 510, 511, 512, 514, 515, 519
May Day parade and, 327, 328
memoirs of, 520
testimony of, 520–21
Likhachev, Dmitri, 103–5, 108, 288
Likhotal, Aleksandr, 529
Lipitsky, Vasily, 382
Lipman, Masha, 331–32, 333, 334, 421, 442, 449, 450, 465, 466
Literaturnaya Gazeta, 183, 184, 193, 258, 294, 369, 376, 483
Literaturnaya Rossiya, 79, 88, 90
Lithuania, x, 22, 51, 234, 235, 236–39, 301, 302, 369, 387–93, 394–96, 438, 524
Little Land, The (Brezhnev), 33
Little Vera, 335
Litvinov, Flora, 10–11, 12, 13–16, 17, 286
Litvinov, Ivy, 15
Litvinov, Maksim, 10, 14, 15
Litvinov, Maya, 17, 21
Litvinov, Misha, 10, 11–12, 15, 16, 17, 286
Litvinov, Nina, 16
Litvinov, Pavel, 10, 13–19, 20–21, 31, 107, 164
Litvinov family, 14, 31
"Live Not by Lies" (Solzhenitsyn), 33, 177, 266, 392
Lobnoye Mesto, 19
Lolita (Nabokov), 265
Lotman, Yuri, 107
Lubyanka, 138, 342, 343, 446, 453
Lukyanov, Anatoly, 281, 372, 375, 384, 385, 395, 437, 439, 440, 447, 451, 452, 457, 458, 459, 470, 477, 486, 488
imprisonment of, 496–97
poetry of, 496–97
Lurye, Judith, 86
Lysenko, Vladimir, 488
Lyubeshkina, Klava, 443–44

McDonald's, 183, 336, 337, 477, 522
MacLean, Fitzroy, 66, 67
Madyr, Laiosh, 138–39
mafia, 124, 181–82, 183–94, 202, 320, 376, 522
see also corruption
Magadan, 120–25, 188, 422–26
Magnitogorsk, 25, 213–15, 223
Magnitogorsk Worker, 213
Major, John, 477
Makarenko, Anton, 14
Makarov, Andrei, 508, 510, 514, 515–18, 520
Makashov, Albert, 472
Makharadze, Avtandil, 44
Malenkov, Georgi, 518
Malikhin, Anatoly, 231–32, 413–14, 468
Malinovsky, Roman, 95
Malkina, Tatyana, 471

Mamedov, Gamboi, 181
Mamleyev, Dmitri, 470
Mandelstam, Nadezhda, ix, x, xi, 333, 358, 433
Mandelstam, Osip, ix, 63
Mao Zedong, 80, 154
Marchenko, Anatoly, 18, 136, 271, 280
Markov, Dmitri, 153
Markov, Gennadi, 323
Marx, Karl, 63, 116, 134, 195, 298
  Yakovlev on, 304
Marxism, 137, 178, 316, 400, 509
"Marxism and Rebellion" (Lenin), 452–53
Marxist-Leninist Institute, 4
massacres, 3–9, 51, 115
  of Jews, 88
  see also purges, Stalinist
mass graves, 137–40
Mastny, Vojtech, 15
Matlock, Jack, 436, 437
Matreyeva, Zoya, 212
Mayakovsky, Vladimir, 53
May Day, 25, 324–29, 335
Mayorova, Katya, 343–44
Mazenich, Yuri, 323
Mednoye, massacres at, 5, 8–9
Medvedev, Aleksandr, 110–12
Medvedev, Galina, 109
Medvedev, Grigori, 246
Medvedev, Roy, 38, 39, 108–12, 113, 128, 132, 137, 177, 193, 300
Medvedev, Sergei, 473, 474
Medvedev, Vadim, 61, 136, 267, 268
Medvedev, Zhores, 109, 110–12
Megapolis-Express, 376, 523
Mein Kampf (Hitler), 435
Memorial, 105–8, 112–13, 116, 117–19, 120, 125, 129, 131, 136–37, 140, 164, 287, 325, 345, 374, 505, 506, 526
  Milchakov's work in, 137–40
Men, Aleksandr, 357–59, 360, 361–65, 366
Men, Natasha, 358–59
Men, Pavel, 361, 362
Men, Yelena, 361
Mensheviks, 95
Meyerhold, V. E., 34
Meyerovich, Mark, 92
microphones, hidden, 53, 54
Mikhoels, Solomon, 91
Mikoyan, Anastas, 416, 417
Milchakov, Aleksandr, 137–40
military, 500
  Gorbachev and, 403–4, 421, 440
  history and, 7
  Yeltsin and, 466–67
Military Collegium, 138
Military Historical Journal, 401, 435
Military Prosecutor's Office, 3, 5, 9
millionaires, 312–16, 322, 477
Mindlin, Vitaly, 328
miners, 21, 25, 102, 203, 223–33, 252–54, 322, 412–14, 468
Minkin, Aleksandr, 364
Mir Collective Farm, 206
Mirikov, Nikolai, 318–19
Mitkova, Tatyana, 392–93
Mlynar, Zdenek, 158–59
Moiseyev, Mikhail, 402, 404
Moldova (Moldavia), x, 369, 420, 427, 498, 511
Molodaya Gvardiya, 87, 90, 129, 294, 322, 336, 384
Molodoi Kommunist, 172, 203
Molotov, Vyacheslav, 45, 133, 406
  rehabilitation of, 518
Molotov-Ribbentrop Pact, 51, 235, 236, 237, 239, 243, 401
monasteries, 360
moral attitude, 174, 176–77
More Light, 61
Morozov, Pavlik, 14, 15–16
Moscow, 52–53, 158–59, 199–200, 521–22
  homeless in, 200–201
Moscow 2042 (Voinovich), 368
Moscow News, 58, 76, 77, 126, 169, 170, 173, 178, 179, 200, 207–8, 216, 245, 260, 267, 283, 297, 366, 376–77, 379, 380, 382, 389, 390, 392, 393, 440, 469, 471, 482, 500–501
Moscow Tribune, 29–30, 113, 164, 283
Moscow-Volga Canal, 137, 139–40

Moscow Worker, 322
Moskovski Komsomolets, 333, 363
Moskva-Petushki (Yerofeyev), 26–27, 333
Motherland, 321
Movement for Democratic Reforms, 449
Muen Tan Kong, 307
Mukhina, Vera, 203–4
multiparty system, 71, 85, 209, 220, 301–3, 307
Murashev, Arkady, 220, 529
Murashkina, Svetlana, 425
museums, 504
  Lenin, 495, 507
  of the Revolution, 495
  Stalin, 127
music, 335–37
Mussolini, Benito, 509
My Secret Life (Philby), 355
mysticism, 258, 259, 261

Nabokov, Vladimir, 103, 265, 315–16
Napoleon I, Emperor of France, 361, 512
Narashev, Ivan, 233
Nashi, 395–96
Nash Sovremenik, 87, 129, 322, 336, 435
Nation, 213
National Bolshevism, 322
nationalities question, 60, 190, 235–36, 237, 238, 239
  see also anti-Semitism; Baltic states
National Salvation Front, 505
Nazarbayev, Nursultan, 190, 426, 439, 440, 464
Nazi Germany, *see* Germany, Nazi
"Necessity of Perestroika, The" (Sakharov), 117
Nedelin, Mitrofan, 167
Nekrasov, Viktor, 178
Nekrich, Aleksandr, 300
Nenashev, Mikhail, 260
Neues Deutschland, 77
Neva, 136
Nevskoye Vremya, 315
Nevzorov, Aleksandr, 393–94, 395–97
"New Consensus, The" (Leontyev), 380
newspapers, 7, 42, 58–59
Newspeak (Novoyaz), 49, 60, 107, 383
New Times, 342, 345
New York Times, 355, 384, 435
Nezavisimaya Gazeta, 378–83, 389, 390, 392, 447, 497, 500, 510
  coup and, 469, 470, 471, 478–79
Neznansky, Friedrikh, 160
Nicholas I, Czar of Russia, 37
Nietzsche, Friedrich, 162
Nikitina, Valentina, 129
Nineteen Eighty-four (Orwell), 59, 60
Nixon, Richard M., 398
Niyazov, Saparmurad, 207
Nizin, Valentin, 150–51
NKVD, 22, 30, 34, 112, 138, 407
  Kalinin massacre and, 3–4, 5, 6
  slave workers and, 122
nomenklatura, 60, 172–73, 191, 194, 360, 494, 509
Novocherkassk rebellion, 414–19
Novospassky Monastery, 137, 138
Novosti, 346
Novoyaz (Newspeak), 49, 60, 107, 383
Novy Mir, 27, 58, 59, 136, 172, 339
  Solzhenitsyn and, 265, 266–68
nuclear power and weapons, 131, 166–67, 244, 347, 437, 471, 511
  Chernobyl accident and, 90, 244–47, 502, 514
Nuikin, Andrei, 366–67, 450

Obolensky, Aleksandr, 221
Obshchaya Gazeta, 469
October Revolution, 41, 509
Ogden, C. K., 15
Ogonyok, 58, 59, 76, 80, 108, 164, 168, 216, 222, 267, 296, 297, 330, 364, 376, 435
Ogzibirlik, 207
oil, 24, 199, 203
Okhotin, Nikita, 107
Okhudzhava, Bulat, 333
Oleinik, Vladimir, 184
One Day in the Life of Ivan Denisovich (Solzhenitsyn), 27, 42, 172, 265
  theatrical version of, 268–69

120 Minutes, 259
On the Edge of an Abyss (Yakovlev), 295–96
On the Eve of a Great Breakthrough (Latsis), 177
"On the Road to the Premiere" (Karpinsky and Burlatsky), 175
Onward, Onward, Onward (Shatrov), 62, 70–73, 76
Order of Lenin, 184, 187
Orlov, Y. F., 271
Orlova, Raisa, 17
Ortega, Daniel, 49
Orwell, George, 49, 59, 60, 342, 368
Osin, Nikolai, 271–75
Oskin, Viktor, 218
Ostanin, Ilya, 223
Ostapchuk, Anya, 381–82
Overin, Yevgeny, 266
oxygen cocktails, 25, 214–15
Oyupov, Viktor, 215

paintings, 318
Pamyat (historical group), 107
  see also Memorial
Pamyat (nationalist group), 86, 89–90, 93, 358, 364, 370
Parfyonov, Leonid, 146, 260
Paris Match, 332
Parkhomenko, Sergei, 380–81, 382, 383, 479, 480
Pasternak, Boris, 58, 90, 265
Patricide, The (Kazbeg), 127
Pauker, Marcel, 139
Pavlov, Sergei, 486
Pavlov, Valentin, 429, 434, 436, 439, 441, 445, 446, 450, 452, 453, 456, 457, 458, 459, 460, 472–73, 477
Pavlov, Yuri, 274, 275
Penner, John, 138
People's Orthodox Movement, 321
perestroika, xi, 68, 106, 173, 176, 183, 222, 223, 229, 235, 239, 251, 253, 258, 282, 290, 298, 323, 335, 360, 375, 377, 378, 386, 389, 398, 410, 420, 440, 446, 447, 495, 497, 500, 503, 520
  Afanasyev on, 115–16
  conservative reaction against, 76, 77, 78, 79, 82, 85
  Democratic Initiative and, 123–24
  Jews and, 87
  KGB and, 343
  Leninism and, 146–47
  Ligachev on, 511
  Memorial and, 119
  military and, 403–4
  Sakharov and, 117, 164, 165, 167
  Shaposhnikov and, 419
  Solzhenitsyn's essay and, 369–70
  Yakovlev on, 297–98
Perestroika (Gorbachev), 116
Perestroika: A History of Betrayal (Ryzhkov), 514
Perfilyev, I. D., 406
Perm, 269, 270–76, 336
Persian Gulf War, 388, 435
Petrakov, Nikolai, 395, 500
Petrov, Aleksandr, 243
Petrovich, Oleg "the Gypsy," 318
Petrovsky Collective Farm, 245
Petrushenko, Nikolai, 385
Pfeiffer, Michelle, 338
Philby, Kim, 345, 353, 354, 355
Pipes, Richard, 405, 509
Pizza Hut, 477
Platonov, Andrei, 59, 70
plays, 42, 174–75
  Onward, Onward, Onward, 70–73, 76
Plekhanov, Yuri, 454, 455, 456, 457
Pliyev, Issa, 416–17
Podrabinek, Sasha, 57, 58, 105
Poland, 234, 235, 387, 452, 499, 526
  massacres and, 3–9, 115
Politburo, 181, 222, 510, 514, 515
  Gorbachev made general secretary at meeting of, 519–20, 528–29
  transcripts of sessions of, 516–17, 518, 519–20, 521, 528–29
  Yeltsin's ouster from, 108, 194, 195, 297
pollution, 214
Polozkov, Ivan, 196, 510, 511–13, 514, 515
Pomerants, Grigori, 7, 59
Ponomarev, Boris, 173

Ponomarev, Lev, 105–6
Popieluszko, Jerzy, 364
Popkova, Natalya, 215
Popov, Gavriil, 116, 173, 282, 288, 309, 325, 327–28, 378, 422, 436, 446, 468
Possev, 160, 311
poverty, 196, 199–215, 223, 470
  homelessness and, 199, 200–202, 203
poverty line, 202
Pozdniak, Yelena, 473–74
Prague Spring, 5, 18–20, 51, 61, 158, 159, 168, 176, 241, 342, 387
Pravda, 12, 33, 51, 59, 72, 74, 84, 85, 117, 128, 144, 168, 169, 172, 173, 174, 180, 285, 334, 337, 383, 395, 420, 505
Pravdiuk, Viktor, 397
Prigorodni Sovkhoz, 209
Prilukov, Vitaly, 421
Primakov, Igor, 331
Primakov, Yevgeny, 285, 286, 441, 487, 490
prisoners, political, 17, 34, 270–75, 509
  Sakharov and, 163
  see also labor camps
Privalov, Boris, 187
Privolnoye, 150–52, 153, 154, 155, 156
Problems of Peace and Socialism, 168
Profumo, John, 345–46, 347
Prokhanov, Aleksandr, 79, 335, 376, 435, 439, 447–48, 525–26
Prokofiyev, Yuri, 325, 329
property, 181, 209
protection rackets, 316–17, 522
Protexter, Bob, 338, 339
Protocols of the Elders of Zion, The, 90, 435
Pugo, Boris, 173, 179, 384, 385, 392–93, 420, 422, 427, 428, 435, 438, 441, 451, 457, 458, 474, 476
  suicide of, 496
purges, Stalinist, 5, 7, 32, 37, 62, 65, 68, 91–92, 96, 125, 132, 170, 183, 401, 406–7, 422, 423–25, 426, 517
  documents on, 510
  Magadan and, 121–23
  mass graves and, 137–40
  statistics on, 48, 128–29
  Stepanov's defense of, 508
  Yurasov's research on, 30–35, 46–47
  see also collectivization campaign; labor camps; massacres; Memorial
Purification, 131

Qaddafi, Muammar, 477

Rabinovitch, David, 331–32
Rabochaya Tribuna, 304
Rabochoye Slovo, 266
Radek, Karl, 332
Ragimov, Suleiman, 181
Raid, Andres, 239
Rapoport, Natasha, 92–93, 96–97, 98–100
Rapoport, Yakov, 91–92, 93–98, 100
Rashidov, Sharaf, 187, 194
Rasputin, Grigori, 256, 257
Rasputin, Valentin, 337, 383–84, 439
Razgon, Lev, 108, 509
Reagan, Ronald, 33, 295–96, 323, 501, 512
"Red Wheel" novels (Solzhenitsyn), 265, 367
Reflections on Progress, Peaceful Coexistence, and Intellectual Freedom (Sakharov), 167
rehabilitations, 5, 31, 32, 47, 68, 119, 125, 178
religion, 198, 258, 259, 261, 357–58, 360–64
Remmele, Herman, 138
Remnick, Alex, 448
Remnick, Esther, 10, 22, 23, 52, 56, 58, 88–89, 101, 241, 285, 286, 448, 449
Repentance, 42–46, 48, 389
repressions, 80, 130, 510, 517
  rehabilitation and, 5
  see also dissident; purges, Stalinist
Requiem (Akhmatova), 59, 117–18, 265
Respublika, 387
Reznik, Genri, 320
Ribin, Aleksei, 128
Rice-Davies, Mandy, 346
Richard III (Shakespeare), 134
Rivera, Geraldo, 392

Road of Ilyich, 152
rock music, 335–37
Rodionov, Igor, 303, 435
Roginsky, Arseny, 107–8, 132, 506, 526
Romania, 235, 242, 369
Romanov, Grigori, 181, 518
Romanov, G. V., 192
Romanova, Ludmila, 124
Romanov family, 7, 256
Rostov, Yuri, 489
Rostropovich, Mstislav, 475
Rudenko, Vasily, 153
Rumantsyev, Oleg, 475
Rush, Karem, 435
Russia House, 337–38
Russian Orthodox Church, 360, 361, 364, 384, 523
Russian Republic, x, 89, 420, 499
Russian Revolution, The (Pipes), 509
Russian Writers' Union, 88
Russia Under the Old Regime (Pipes), 405, 509
Russia We Lost, The, 523–24
Russky Golos, 304
"Russophobia" (Shafarevich), 87
Rust, Mathias, 403
Rutskoi, Aleksandr, 466, 467, 477, 481, 486, 487, 488, 489
Rybakov, Anatoly, 42, 108
Rykov, Aleksei, 72, 405
Ryzhkov, Nikolai, 48, 425, 426, 427, 510, 519, 520, 521
  testimony of, 511, 514–15

Sagalayev, Eduard, 145–46
Sagaleyeva, Tatyana, 365
Sagdeyev, Roald, 167
Saitmuradov, Guichgeldi, 208
Sajudis, 236–37, 238
Sakhalin Island, 25, 248–55, 260
Sakharov, Andrei, xi, 20, 27, 28, 29, 30, 48, 60, 87, 108, 113, 131, 136, 146, 176, 221, 222, 236, 241, 249, 252, 254–55, 270, 279–89, 293, 300–301, 327, 331, 336, 345, 357, 363, 374, 381, 415, 435, 476, 503, 516–17
  death of, 282–89, 308
  as dissident, 163, 164–65, 167, 168, 175
  on elections, 220
  Gorbachev and, 117, 131, 162–63, 164, 280–82, 283–84, 285, 287
  at Installation, 166–67
  on the KGB, 354
  Nobel Prize won by, 165, 287
  release from exile, 105, 117, 162–64
  Roy Medvedev and, 109
  as scientist, 165
  Stalin's death and, 165–66
  television appearances of, 147
  uniqueness of, 164–65
Sakharov, Dmitri, 460
Sakharov, Efrem, 164–65
Salayev, Anatoly, 483
salmon, 25, 249
samizdat, 17, 31, 59, 123
Samodurov, Yuri, 105, 106
Samsonov, Viktor, 468–69
Satire Theater, 148
Savenko, Yuri, 261
Scammell, Michael, 368
Scandal, 346
Schapiro, Leonard, 404
Schepsi, Fred, 337
schools, 14, 16, 31, 37, 38, 39, 40, 102, 103, 125, 137, 330
Schubert, Herman, 138
Schultke, Fritz, 138
Scientific Industrial Union, 445
Scott, John, 213
secret police, *see* KGB; NKVD
Selyunin, Vasily, 116
Serikov, Yrui, 154
Seroshtanov, Viktor, 215
Sestakauskas, Raimondas, 393
Seventh Feat of Hercules, The, 196
Sex in the Soviet Union, 330
Shachin, Sergei, 338
Shafarevich, Igor, 87
Shakespeare, William, 134
Shakhnazarov, Georgi, 168, 382, 441, 450, 454
Shakhrai, Sergei, 475, 490, 508–10, 515
Shakhverdiyev, Tofik, 126
Shalamov, Varlam, 17, 424

Shaposhnikov, Matvei, 415–19
Shaposhnikov, Yevgeny, 463, 477, 483–84
Shatalin, Stanislav, 359
Shatokhina, Irina, 226
Shatrov, Mikhail, 42, 62, 70–73, 75, 76, 378, 501
Shatunovskaya, Olga, 115
Shaw, George Bernard, 128
Shcharansky, Natan, 88, 270, 271–72
Shcheglov, Anatoly, 230–31, 233, 412–13
Shchekochikhin, Yuri, 376
Shcherbak, Yuri, 245, 247
Shcherbakov, Vladimir, 454
Shcherbina, Boris, 245, 246
Shcherbitsky, Vladimir, 181, 194
Shekhovtsov, Ivan, 129–31, 442
Shenin, Oleg, 447, 450, 452, 453, 455, 457
shestidesyatniki, 61, 168, 389
Shevardnadze, Eduard, 44, 45, 48, 49, 113, 148, 173, 297, 298, 386, 447, 449, 450, 462, 468, 512
  on Gorbachev, 420
  resignation of, 372, 373, 374, 375, 378, 379, 385, 420, 446
Shevchuk, Yuri, 78
Shield, 419
Shmelyov, Nikolai, 29, 173, 179
Short Biography of Stalin, 128
Short Course, The, 33, 38, 40, 50, 114
Shostokovsky, Vyacheslav, 306, 307, 389
Silayev, Ivan, 368, 466, 486, 488, 489
Sinyavsky, Andrei, 17, 92, 293
Sinyeshikova, Kira, 338
600 Seconds, 393, 394, 395, 396
60 Minutes, 60
slave workers, 122
Smena, 184
Smiley, Xan, 199
Smirnov, Anatoly, 494
Sobchak, Anatoly, 37, 220, 288, 309, 375, 394, 446, 462, 463, 468–69
socialism, 85, 115, 137, 168, 182, 523
  feudal, 205
  Gorbachev and, 36, 47, 49, 50, 51, 61–62, 63, 149–50, 400, 494, 529
Sociological Research, 128
Sofia Petrovna (Chukovskaya), 266, 344
Sokolov, Aleksandr, 504–5
Sokolov, Sasha, 367
Solidarity, 5, 234, 452, 499
Solomenko, Yuri, 247
Solomon, Michael, 122
Solomontsev, Mikhail, 178
Solovki camp, 104, 344, 345
Solovyov, Vladimir, 164, 363
Solovyov, Yuri, 302
Solzhenitsyn, Aleksandr, 17, 21, 39, 61, 87, 105, 129, 132, 135, 164, 176–77, 191, 211, 333, 358, 518
  Gulag Archipelago, 7, 38, 39, 61, 107, 266, 267, 268, 269, 368, 414, 424
  "How Can We Revitalize Russia," 367, 368–71
  "Letter to the Soviet Leaders," 28, 369
  "Live Not by Lies," 33, 177, 266, 392
  on Novocherkassk rebellion, 414, 417
  One Day in the Life of Ivan Denisovich, 27, 42, 172, 265, 268–69
  in return from exile, 264, 265–68
Sopiyev, Muratberd, 208–9
Sotheby's, 318
Sovetskaya Kultura, 74, 243, 441
Sovetskaya Rossiya, 322, 376, 470, 502
  Andreyeva's letter in, 72–77, 79, 84, 85, 86, 105, 116, 360, 376, 453
  "A Word to the People" in, 438–49, 441
Sovetsky Sakhalin, 251
Soviet Historical Encyclopedia, 32
Soviet Union, disintegration of, x-xi, 4, 146, 234–47, 256, 498, 499, 500, 511, 525–26
Soviet Writers' Union, 418
Sovlatvia, 122
Soyuz, 375, 385, 429
Spasskaya, 210–11
Speak, Memory (Nabokov), 316
Spooner, Richard, 338, 339
Spy Who Got Away, The (Wise), 351

Sredni, Oleg, 153–54
Stalin, Joseph, 21, 36, 39, 54, 61, 63, 110, 113, 199, 250, 276, 308, 331, 398, 399, 400, 511, 517, 518, 527
  Abuladze's film and, 42–43, 44, 45
  ancestral house of, 127
  Andreyeva on, 74, 75, 79, 80, 81–82
  Baltic states and, 235, 236, 237, 239, 243
  and Bolshevik-Menshevik split, 95
  Bukharin and, 64–65, 66
  church and, 361
  collectivization campaign of, *see* collectivization campaign
  cult of, 16
  death of, 16–17, 24, 31, 38, 41, 81-82, 92, 97, 114, 128, 133, 160, 161, 165–66, 171–72, 230–31, 288, 289, 332, 408, 410, 441
  democracy and, 252
  funeral of, 114, 133, 171
  Gorbachev and, 48, 49, 50, 149, 154, 159, 160–61, 503
  grandchildren of, 134–36
  history controlled by, 37–38
  Kaganovich and, 11, 12
  Khrushchev's denunciation of, 32, 41, 48, 50, 68, 82, 91, 109, 114, 160, 168, 174, 292
  Korniyenkova's admiration for, 131–33
  Larina and, 64–65, 67
  Lazar Kaganovich and, 34
  Lithuanians and, 239
  Maksim Litvinov and, 14, 15
  Moscow-Volga Canal and, 139, 140
  mystery of, 443
  nationalities and, 58
  nickname of, 127
  opinion polls on, 126
  paternalism of, 31, 43, 169–70
  personality cult of, 38, 50, 65, 68, 85, 144, 168, 174, 175, 178, 292, 324, 362
  photographs of, 144
  Polish officers massacred by, 3–4, 115
  portraits of, 128, 154
  propaganda films and, 143
  purges under, *see* purges, Stalinist
  Sakharov's response to death of, 166
  Shatrov's play about, 70–73
  Shekhovtsov's slander suits and, 129–31
  titles referring to, 128, 169
  Volkogonov's biography of, 401, 404–6, 407, 408–9
  Western intellectuals' admiration for, 128
  Yakovlev on, 299–300
Stalin, Yakov, 134
Stalin: Triumph and Tragedy (Volkogonov), 401, 404–6, 407, 408–9
Stalinism, 116, 125–26, 147, 150, 159–60, 204, 233, 409, 410, 507, 508
  Brezhnev's revival of, 18, 38–39, 109, 114, 174, 175
  Gorbachev on, 36, 48, 50
  Khrushchev thaw and, 17
  see also purges, Stalinist
Stalin Is with Us, 126
Stalin Museum, 127
Stampa, 193
Stanford University, 503
Stankevich, Sergei, 220, 378, 388, 389, 475, 523
Starobelsk, massacres at, 3, 4, 5, 8–9, 51
Starodubtsev, Vasily, 438, 456
Starovoitova, Galina, 30
State and Revolution (Lenin), 62
State Committee for the State of Emergency (GKChP), 3
statues and monuments, 53
  of Dzerzhinsky, 344, 345, 495
  of Lenin, 52, 53, 309
  toppling of, 495
Stavropol region, 150, 151, 152, 153, 155, 156, 173, 193
steel, 213–14
Stepanov, Dmitri, 508
Stepanovsky, Gennadi, 384
Sterligov, Aleksandr, 525
Sterligov, German, 312–14
Stewart, Debbie, 486
Stolypin, Pyotr, 524

strikes, workers', 21, 215, 223–25, 229, 231, 232, 233, 252, 254, 281, 322, 412, 413, 414, 416–17, 468
Stus, Vasyl, 271
Sukharev (NKVD driver), 5–6
Sukhov, Leonid, 222, 429
Sulim, Boris, 425–26
Supplication, 42
Supreme Court archives, 35, 46
Suslov, Mikhail, 31, 38, 174, 293, 297, 444, 518
  Len Karpinsky and, 173, 176, 177
Sverdlov, Y. M., 495
Svinarenko, Igor, 314

Tabenkin, Lev, 318
Tajikistan, 369, 511, 524
Tamerlane the Great, 186
Tamm, Igor, 166
Tarasov, Artyom, 314–15
Tass, 76, 88, 259, 284, 285, 356, 376, 421, 496
Tatars, 57–58
Teatr, 147, 381
television, 4, 42, 70, 143–44
  Congress of People's Deputies sessions on, 221–22
  Gorbachev's appearances on, 146–47, 502
  Kashpirovsky's séances on, 256–58, 260–61
  see also Vremya
Television News Service (TSN), 391, 392–93
Tema, 337
Tepnina, Maria, 365
Terekhov, Vyacheslav, 376
Tereshkova, Valentina, 502–3
Ter-Petrossian, Levon, 270
Tessler, Dmitri, 208
Thatcher, Margaret, 192, 346
theater, *see* plays
"There Is No Other Way," 116–17, 125
Thomas, D. M., 117
Tiger Gorge, 187
Tikhonov, Vladimir, 303
Tillich, Paul, 334
Time, 368
Timofeyev, Lev, 163, 197, 268, 269, 270, 271, 274, 285, 286, 289
Timur Society, 14
Tizyakov, Aleksandr, 438, 456, 486
  arrest of, 490
Tochka Zreniya, 313
Todres, Vladimir, 478–79
Tokaryev, Vladimir, 5–6
Tolstaya, Tatyana, 59
Tomsky, Mikhail, 405
Topolov, Vitaly, 253
Top Secret, 376
torture, 34, 186
totalitarianism, 37, 410
trade mafia, *see* mafia
Transcaucasian republics:
  Armenia, x, 89, 129, 236, 369, 420, 427, 511
  Azerbaijan, 89, 181, 236, 369
  Georgia, x, 369, 420, 427, 498
Trapeznikov, Sergei, 38, 39, 40
Treaty of the Union, 439–40, 450
Tree in the Center of Kabul, A (Prokhanov), 439
Tretetsky, Aleksandr, 3, 5, 8–9
Tretyakov, Pyotr, 250, 251
Tretyakov, Vitaly, 377–78, 379–80, 382, 479, 500
Tribunal, The, 148
Trifonov, Pavel, 103
Trifonov, Yuri, 170
Trimble, Jeff, 137
Trotsky, Leon, 38, 39, 68, 75, 300, 405, 409
Trud, 158
Tsipko, Aleksandr, 400
Tucker, Robert C., 404
Tukhachevsky, Mikhail, 385, 426, 517
Tuplin, Aleksei, 213–14
Turchin, Valentin, 289
Turkmenistan, 204, 205, 206, 207, 208–9, 223, 369
Tvardovsky, Aleksandr, 172, 267

Ukraine, x, xi, 39, 243–44, 370, 499
  Chernobyl and, 245
Ulam, Adam, 405
unions, labor, 231

Union Treaty, 450
Unità, L', 342
United Workers' Front, 321
Unity, 321
UPDK, 52
Usmankhodzhaev, Inamzhon, 186
U.S. News & World Report, 137
Usov, Vladimir, 484
Ustinov, Dmitri, 444, 518
Uzbekistan, 39, 58, 369, 524
  cotton scam and, 186–87

Vaksberg, Arkady, 183, 188, 193
Valinsky, Oleg, 215
Varennikov, Valentin, 387, 401, 403, 404, 435, 438, 455, 456, 477
Vasiliyev, Dmitri, 90
Vasiliyev, Grigori, 310, 312
Vasyn, Kolya, 335–36
Vechernaya Moskva, 129, 130, 131, 139
Velliste, Trivimi, 237
Velsapar, Mukhamed, 207–8
Vertov, Dziga, 42
Vesti, 473, 489, 529
Vichenkov, Pavel, 470
Vietnam War, 508
Villas, Pariscop, 37
Vilnius, 22, 236, 238, 301, 387–90, 395, 414, 419, 421, 500
"Visit to the Museum, The" (Nabokov), 103
Vladislavlev, Aleksandr, 445
Vlasov, Yuri, 220, 342–43
Vlasova, Alla, 322
Voinovich, Vladimir, 148, 367, 368
Volkenshtein, Masha, 331
Volkogonov, Anton, 406–7, 408
Volkogonov, Dmitri, 401–11
Volkov, Oleg, 345
Vologda region, 25, 209–10, 211
Volotsky, Iosif, 361
Volsky, Arkady, 62, 191, 444, 445–46
Voronkov, Vyacheslav, 187
Vorontsov, Nikolai, 472
Voroshilov, Kliment, 166–67
Vorotnikov, Vitaly, 283
Votinov, Andrei, 270
Vovsi, Myron, 96
Voznesensky, Andrei, 172
Vremya, 144–47, 221, 304, 376, 391, 392, 394, 395, 443, 473–74
  coup and, 459–60
  Gorbachev on, 146–47
  rituals on, 145–46
Vyshinsky, Andrei, 66
Vzglyad, 193, 392

Walesa, Lech, 231, 241
Wallace, Henry, 121
Wall Street, 307
Ward, Stephen, 346
Washington Post, xi, 13, 52, 234, 250, 311, 331, 348, 445, 451, 465, 487, 505
"We Are Moving to the Side of Dictatorship" (Afanasyev), 379
Wells, H. G., 128
Wenders, Wim, 501
Western culture, 335–40
  Solzhenitsyn's disdain for, 368, 369
White Book, 355
Wilson, Edmund, 199–200
Wings of Desire, 501
Wise, David, 351, 352
Wishing Tree, The, 42
"Words Are Also Deeds" (Karpinsky), 175–76, 177, 178
"Word to the People, A," 438–39, 441, 525
Worker and the Collective Farm Girl (Mukhina), 204
Worker's World, 267
World War II, *see* Great Patriotic War
Writers' Union, 418

Yablokov, Aleksei, 116, 472
Yad Vashem, 105
Yagoda, Genrikh, 139
Yagunovsko, 412–13
Yakir, Pyotr, 164
Yakovenko, Aleksandr, 152
Yakovlev, Aleksandr, 45, 46, 47, 48, 49, 84–85, 143–44, 146, 148, 173, 179, 191, 216, 239–40, 290–300, 301, 303–5, 306, 330, 337, 355, 371, 372, 375, 390, 399, 420, 428,

441, 446, 450, 455, 462, 483, 510, 512, 519, 528
Andreyeva letter and, 75, 76
Brezhnev and, 293–94
Communist Party resignation of, 449
coup and, 447, 495
Gorbachev and, 290, 291, 294–95, 296, 298–99, 303, 494–95
May Day demonstrations and, 327, 329
Yakovlev, Nikolai, 285, 291–92
Yakovlev, Vladimir, 376, 390
Yakovlev, Yegor, 76, 77, 85, 168, 170, 173, 174, 178, 376, 377, 389–90
Ryzhkov and, 514, 515
Yakunin, Gleb, 288, 362–63, 509
Yanayev, Gennady, 173, 375, 448, 450, 452, 453, 454, 456, 457–58, 460, 463–64, 465, 471–72, 473–74, 477, 478, 484, 485, 486–87
Yarin, Veniamin, 487
Yasin, Valery, 273–74
Yasovsky, Konstantin, 218–19
Yavlinsky, Grigori, 359
Yazov, Dmitri, 375, 383, 384, 396, 401, 403–4, 409, 427, 428, 446
arrest of, 490
in coup, 404, 435, 436, 437, 439–40, 450, 451–52, 455, 457, 458, 460, 463, 464, 469, 472, 473, 475, 476, 477, 483, 485, 486, 487, 490
Treaty of the Union and, 439–40
Yazova, Emma, 472
Yefimov, Nikolai, 470, 478
Yefremov, Oleg, 214
Yegorov, A. I., 426
Yeltsin, Boris, x, xi, 108, 119, 125, 233, 240, 288, 303, 306, 308, 310, 325–26, 327, 354, 384, 402, 406, 421, 446, 450, 451, 498, 514, 522–23, 524, 526, 528
childhood of, 433–34
Communist Party activities suspended by, 438, 495, 505, 508
Communist Party membership exam and, 195
Communist Party privileges and, 194, 443, 515
corruption and, 194–95, 196
coup and, x, 49, 366, 455, 462–63, 465, 466–67, 470–71, 472, 473, 474, 475–76, 477, 478, 479–80, 482, 484, 485–86, 487, 502, 513
as dissident, 195
elected to parliament, 309, 420
500 Days plan and, 359
Gorbachev and, 49, 147, 194, 195, 196, 359, 389–90, 413, 420, 421, 426, 427–28, 434, 438, 495, 499–500, 502, 506, 527
Interregional Group and, 281–82
Lenin's remains and, 504
memoir of, 443
military and, 466–67
Pamyat and, 89
Politburo ouster of, 108, 194, 195, 297
Politburo resignation of, 297
presidential election and, 420, 425, 426, 427
resignation of, 48–49
Sakharov and, 282, 283, 286, 287
Treaty of the Union and, 439–40
and trial of Communist Party, 506, 508, 510
U.S. and 437
Yemelyanov, Valery, 90
Yerofeyev, Venedikt "Benny," 26–27, 333
Yerofeyev, Viktor, 502
Yershova, Lesya, 260–61
Yeryemin, Andrei, 358, 364
Yeryomenko, Arnold, 120, 121, 123–25, 423
Yevtushenko, Yevgeny, 72, 93, 131, 168, 172, 174, 284, 476
Yezhov, Nikolai, 34, 342, 406
Young Communist League, *see* Komsomol
young people, 330–31
see also children
Young Pioneers, 14, 16, 31, 130, 231
Yunost, 80, 92
Yurasov, Dmitri "Dima", 29, 30–35, 36, 41, 46–47, 85, 107, 409

Yurasov, Dmitri "Dima" (*cont.*)
manuscript of, 34–35
Yurasov, Ludmila, 31
Yurchenko, Vitaly, 352

Zadornov, Mikhail, 147
Zagadka Gorbacheva (Ligachev), 520
Zaitsev, Slava, 507
Zakharov, Igor, 378, 382–83, 390
Zaltsman, Isaak, 90
Zalygin, Sergei, 267–68
Zamokhov, Anatoly, 211
Zaplatkin, Yuri, 214
Zaslavskaya, Tatyana, 164, 168, 284
Zaslavsky, Ilya, 220, 222, 283–84, 288, 307–12, 316, 320, 321, 322–23, 475
Zemlyachka, R. S., 95
Zhirinovsky, Vladimir, 524–25
Zhokina, Alla, 323
Zhou Enlai, xi
Zimmerman, Mikhail, 262
Zimyanin, Mikhail, 517
Zinoviev, Grigori, 405
Znamya, 58, 59, 70, 73, 439
Zola, Emile, 216
Zorkaltsev, Viktor, 507
Zorkin, Valery, 505, 507, 526
Zuckerman, Mortimer, 445–46

Discover more about our forthcoming books through Penguin's FREE newspaper...

Penguin
Quarterly

It's packed with:

- exciting features
- author interviews
- previews & reviews
- books from your favourite films & TV series
- exclusive competitions & much, much more...

Write off for your free copy today to:
Dept JC
Penguin Books Ltd
FREEPOST
West Drayton
Middlesex
UB7 0BR
NO STAMP REQUIRED

READ MORE IN PENGUIN

In every corner of the world, on every subject under the sun, Penguin represents quality and variety – the very best in publishing today.

For complete information about books available from Penguin – including Puffins, Penguin Classics and Arkana – and how to order them, write to us at the appropriate address below. Please note that for copyright reasons the selection of books varies from country to country.

In the United Kingdom: Please write to *Dept. JC, Penguin Books Ltd, FREEPOST, West Drayton, Middlesex UB7 OBR*

If you have any difficulty in obtaining a title, please send your order with the correct money, plus ten per cent for postage and packaging, to *PO Box No. 11, West Drayton, Middlesex UB7 OBR*

In the United States: Please write to *Penguin USA Inc., 375 Hudson Street, New York, NY 10014*

In Canada: Please write to *Penguin Books Canada Ltd, 10 Alcorn Avenue, Suite 300, Toronto, Ontario M4V 3B2*

In Australia: Please write to *Penguin Books Australia Ltd, 487 Maroondah Highway, Ringwood, Victoria 3134*

In New Zealand: Please write to *Penguin Books (NZ) Ltd,182–190 Wairau Road, Private Bag, Takapuna, Auckland 9*

In India: Please write to *Penguin Books India Pvt Ltd, 706 Eros Apartments, 56 Nehru Place, New Delhi 110 019*

In the Netherlands: Please write to *Penguin Books Netherlands B.V., Keizersgracht 231 NL–1016 DV Amsterdam*

In Germany: Please write to *Penguin Books Deutschland GmbH, Friedrichstrasse 10–12, W–6000 Frankfurt/Main 1*

In Spain: Please write to *Penguin Books S. A., C. San Bernardo 117–6° E–28015 Madrid*

In Italy: Please write to *Penguin Italia s.r.l., Via Felice Casati 20, I–20124 Milano*

In France: Please write to *Penguin France S. A., 17 rue Lejeune, F–31000 Toulouse*

In Japan: Please write to *Penguin Books Japan, Ishikiribashi Building, 2–5–4, Suido, Bunkyo-ku, Tokyo 112*

In Greece: Please write to *Penguin Hellas Ltd, Dimocritou 3, GR–106 71 Athens*

In South Africa: Please write to *Longman Penguin Southern Africa (Pty) Ltd, Private Bag X08, Bertsham 2013*

READ MORE IN PENGUIN

A CHOICE OF NON-FICTION

The Time Out Film Guide Edited by Tom Milne

The definitive, up-to-the minute directory of over 9,500 films – world cinema from classics and silent epics to reissues and the latest releases – assessed by two decades of *Time Out* reviewers. 'In my opinion the best and most comprehensive' – Barry Norman

The Remarkable Expedition Olivia Manning

The events of an extraordinary attempt in 1887 to rescue Emin Pasha, Governor of Equatoria, are recounted here by the author of *The Balkan Trilogy* and *The Levant Trilogy* and vividly reveal unprecedented heights of magnificent folly in the perennial human search for glorious conquest.

Berlin: Coming in From the Cold Ken Smith

'He covers everything from the fate of the ferocious-looking dogs that formerly helped to guard East Germany's borders to the vast Orwellian apparatus that maintained security in the now-defunct German Democratic Republic … a pithy style and an eye for the telling detail' – *Independent*

Cider with Rosie/As I Walked Out one Midsummer Morning
Laurie Lee

Now together in one volume, Laurie Lee's two classic autobiographical works, *Cider with Rosie* and *As I Walked Out One Midsummer Morning*. Together they illustrate Laurie Lee's superb descriptive powers as he conveys the poignancy of a boy's transformation into adulthood.

In the Land of Oz Howard Jacobson

'A wildly funny account of his travels; abounding in sharp characterization, crunching dialogue and self-parody, it actually is a book which makes you laugh out loud on almost every page … sharp, skilful and brilliantly funny' – *Literary Review*

READ MORE IN PENGUIN

A CHOICE OF NON-FICTION

Riding the Iron Rooster Paul Theroux

Travels in old and new China with the author of *The Great Railway Bazaar*. 'Mr Theroux cannot write badly … he is endlessly curious about places and people … and in the course of a year there was almost no train in the whole vast Chinese rail network in which he did not travel' – Ludovic Kennedy

Ninety-two Days Evelyn Waugh

In this fascinating chronicle of a South American journey, Waugh describes the isolated cattle country of Guiana, sparsely populated by an odd collection of visionaries, rogues and ranchers, and records the nightmarish experiences travelling on foot, by horse and by boat through the jungle in Brazil.

The Life of Graham Greene Norman Sherry
Volume One 1904–1939

'Probably the best biography ever of a living author' – Philip French in the *Listener*. Graham Greene has always maintained a discreet distance from his reading public.This volume reconstructs his first thirty-five years to create one of the most revealing literary biographies of the decade.

The Day Gone By Richard Adams

In this enchanting memoir the bestselling author of *Watership Down* tells his life story from his idyllic 1920s childhood spent in Newbury, Berkshire, through public school, Oxford and service in World War Two to his return home and his courtship of the girl he was to marry.

A Turn in the South V. S. Naipaul

'A supremely interesting, even poetic glimpse of a part of America foreigners either neglect or patronize' – *Guardian*. 'An extraordinary panorama' – *Daily Telegraph*. 'A fine book by a fine man, and one to be read with great enjoyment: a book of style, sagacity and wit' – *Sunday Times*

READ MORE IN PENGUIN

HISTORY

The World Since 1945 T. E. Vadney
New edition

From the origins of the post-war world to the collapse of the Soviet Bloc in the late 1980s, this masterly book offers an authoritative yet highly readable one-volume account.

Ecstasies Carlo Ginzburg

This dazzling work of historical detection excavates the essential truth about the witches' Sabbath. 'Ginzburg's learning is prodigious and his journey through two thousand years of Eurasian folklore a *tour de force*' – *Observer*

The Nuremberg Raid Martin Middlebrook

'The best book, whether documentary or fictional, yet written about Bomber Command' – *Economist*. 'Martin Middlebrook's skill at description and reporting lift this book above the many memories that were written shortly after the war' – *The Times*

A History of Christianity Paul Johnson

'Masterly … It is a huge and crowded canvas – a tremendous theme running through twenty centuries of history – a cosmic soap opera involving kings and beggars, philosophers and crackpots, scholars and illiterate exaltés, popes and pilgrims and wild anchorites in the wilderness'– Malcolm Muggeridge

The Penguin History of Greece A. R. Burn

Readable, erudite, enthusiastic and balanced, this one-volume history of Hellas sweeps the reader along from the days of Mycenae and the splendours of Athens to the conquests of Alexander and the final dark decades.

Modern Ireland 1600–1972 R. F. Foster

'Takes its place with the finest historical writing of the twentieth century, whether about Ireland or anywhere else' – Conor Cruise O'Brien in the *Sunday Times*

READ MORE IN PENGUIN

HISTORY

The Guillotine and the Terror Daniel Arasse

'A brilliant and imaginative account of the punitive mentality of the revolution that restores to its cultural history its most forbidding and powerful symbol' – Simon Schama.

The Second World War A J P Taylor

A brilliant and detailed illustrated history, enlivened by all Professor Taylor's customary iconoclasm and wit.

Daily Life in Ancient Rome Jerome Carcopino

This classic study, which includes a bibliography and notes by Professor Rowell, describes the streets, houses and multi-storeyed apartments of the city of over a million inhabitants, the social classes from senators to slaves, and the Roman family and the position of women, causing *The Times Literary Supplement* to hail it as a 'thorough, lively and readable book'.

The Anglo-Saxons Edited by James Campbell

'For anyone who wishes to understand the broad sweep of English history, Anglo-Saxon society is an important and fascinating subject. And Campbell's is an important and fascinating book. It is also a finely produced and, at times, a very beautiful book' – *London Review of Books*

The Making of the English Working Class E. P. Thompson

Probably the most imaginative – and the most famous – post-war work of English social history. 'A magnificent, lucid, angry historian ... E. P. Thompson has performed a revolution of historical perspective' – *The Times*

The Habsburg Monarchy 1809 –1918 A J P Taylor

Dissolved in 1918, the Habsburg Empire 'had a unique character, out of time and out of place'. Scholarly and vividly accessible, this 'very good book indeed' (*Spectator*) elucidates the problems always inherent in the attempt to give peace, stability and a common loyalty to a heterogeneous population.

READ MORE IN PENGUIN

HISTORY

Citizens Simon Schama

The award-winning chronicle of the French Revolution. 'The most marvellous book I have read about the French Revolution in the last fifty years' – Richard Cobb in *The Times*

To the Finland Station Edmund Wilson

In this authoritative work Edmund Wilson, considered by many to be America's greatest twentieth-century critic, turns his attention to Europe's revolutionary traditions, tracing the roots of nationalism, socialism and Marxism as these movements spread across the Continent creating unrest, revolt and widespread social change.

Jasmin's Witch Emmanuel Le Roy Ladurie

An investigation into witchcraft and magic in south-west France during the seventeenth century – a masterpiece of historical detective work by the bestselling author of Montaillou.

Stalin Isaac Deutscher

'The Greatest Genius in History' and the 'Life-Giving Force of socialism'? Or a despot more ruthless than Ivan the Terrible and a revolutionary whose policies facilitated the rise of Nazism? An outstanding biographical study of a revolutionary despot by a great historian.

Aspects of Antiquity M. I. Finley

Profesor M. I. Finley was one of the century's greatest ancient historians; he was also a master of the brief, provocative essay on classical themes. 'He writes with the unmistakable enthusiasm of a man who genuinely wants to communicate his own excitement' – Philip Toynbee in the *Observer*

British Society 1914–1945 John Stevenson

'A major contribution to the *Penguin Social History of Britain*, which will undoubtedly be the standard work for students of modern Britain for many years to come' – *The Times Educational Supplement*

Answers

98. Apples and oranges

The box labelled "apples and oranges". All the labels are wrong, so this is the only box that can't contain both apples and oranges. Once you know which fruit it does contain, you can easily work out the other two boxes by remembering their labels are wrong too.

99. Alien code

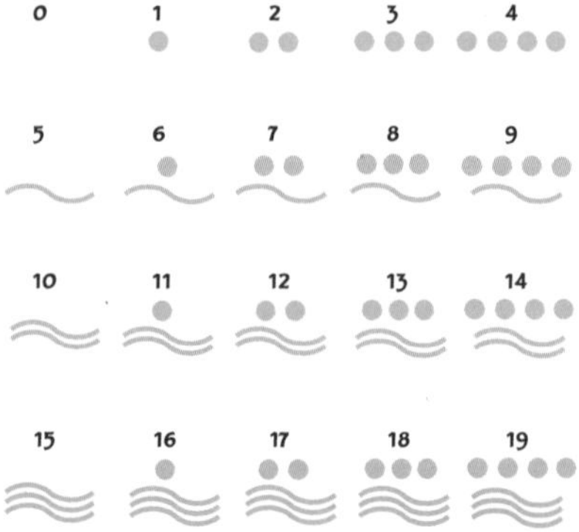

100. Little riddlers

1. The hat, scarf and lumps of coal were part of a snowman that melted because it was a warm day.

2. Two days

3. When you give out the last lollipop, give it inside the bag.

4. An hour and ten minutes is the same as 70 minutes.

5. Friday is the name of his horse.

Written by Simon Tudhope. Designed by Marc Maynard and Ruth Russell. Illustrated by Lizzie Barber and Non Figg.

First published in 2014 by Usborne Publishing Ltd. 83–85 Saffron Hill, London ECIN 8RT, England. Copyright ©2014 Usborne Publishing Ltd. The name Usborne and the devices are Trade Marks of Usborne Publishing Ltd. All rights reserved. No part of this publication may be reproduced, stored in a retrieval system, or transmitted in any form or by any means, electronic, mechanical, photocopying, recording or otherwise, without the prior permission of the publisher. UE. First published in America in 2016.

Answers

91. Robot shootout

c) deliberately miss. Whichever robot he shoots, the other robot will then shoot him. But if he misses he's no longer a threat. Then the robot who fires next will shoot the third robot. This leaves two robots standing, but no shots left.

92. Dolls' parade

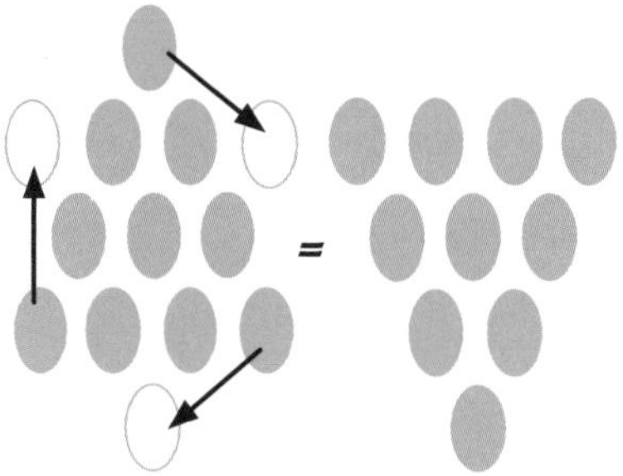

93. Monster munch

Two cookies. Every time Tom gives a monster half of his cookies (one cookie), the monster gives it back.

94. Bridge crossing

16. On the 16th time she steps off the bridge, so she doesn't step backwards.

95. Non-stop pen

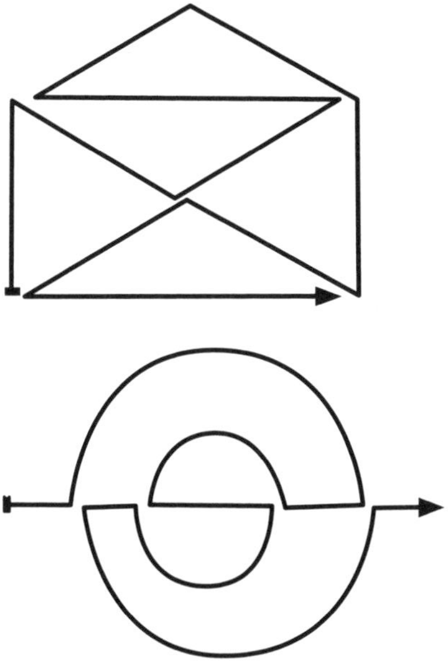

96. On and off

Turn two switches on, then turn one off after about thirty seconds. When you walk into the room, two lightbulbs will be off, but one will still be warm.

97. Hard evidence

1. b and d
2. a and e
3. b and e

Answers

82. Dotty problem

83. Castle code

The bars represent the windows and the arrow represents the type of door.

84. Laundry line-up

C. The pegs are in sequence.

85. Cube in a cube

B

86. Keep it simple!

'For he or she with eyes to see'. Ignore all the punctuation and styles, just write the letters out in a line.

87. Act your age

1. 77. She is only counting $\frac{4}{7}$ of her age. To find her true age, divide her false age by 4 and multiply by 7.
2. 18. He is counting $\frac{9}{7}$ of his age. To find this fake age, divide his real age by 7 and multiply by 9.

88. Arctic explorers

Name	Age	Drink	Food
Ernest	27	Coffee	Beef
Roald	31	Cocoa	Fish
Robert	34	Tea	Beans

89. Boat crossing

They'll both be exactly the same distance from Dublin as they pass each other.

90. Easy peasy

The whole paragraph doesn't contain a single 'e', even though it's the most common letter in the English language.

Answers

72. What's the time?

1 o'clock. The sequence is +2, +3, +2, and so on.

73. Bird's eye view

C

74. Short puzzles

1. E, for Eight. The sequence goes One, Two, Three, Four...
2. WHITE
3. Mary
4. 0% (It will be midnight.)

75. Parrot in a cage

Cage = 5 silver pieces
Parrot = 45 silver pieces

76. Jumbo jumble

Weigh two elephants from different pairs. If one weighs more than the other, it must be from the heavier pair; if they weigh the same, the elephants from the other pair must be heavier.

77. Impossible shapes

A, D, E

78. Tile pattern

A. Each row and column contains one stick of each size, one red oval and one green oval.

79. Salon selection

The stylist who works in the wooden shack. There are only two stylists on the island, so they must cut each other's hair. Therefore, the one with the worse haircut must be the better stylist.

80. Square-eyed

1. 15
2. 25

Each large square adds five new squares to the pattern.

81. Symbol scramble

The sequence is eight symbols long and snakes downwards from the top left corner.

Answers

63. Faulty calculator

64. River crossing

Left shore	On the boat	Right shore
F,R,C		
F,C	R	
F,C		R
C	F	R
C	R	F
R	C	F
R		F, C
	R	F, C
		R,F,C

First you take the rabbit across. Then you take the fox across and bring back the rabbit. Then you take the carrot across and leave it with the fox. Finally, you take the rabbit across.

65. Sudoku

8	3	9	4	7	6	5	1	2
7	2	4	1	3	5	9	6	8
1	6	5	9	8	2	7	4	3
3	5	7	8	6	4	2	9	1
9	1	6	2	5	7	3	8	4
2	4	8	3	1	9	6	7	5
4	7	3	6	2	1	8	5	9
5	9	2	7	4	8	1	3	6
6	8	1	5	9	3	4	2	7

66. Paperboy puzzle

48. The next house number is always double the one before.

67. Cube finder

B

68. Wrong total

24 doesn't divide equally by seven.

69. Age puzzler

Laura is 30. (Her mother is 60.)

70. Tricky triangles

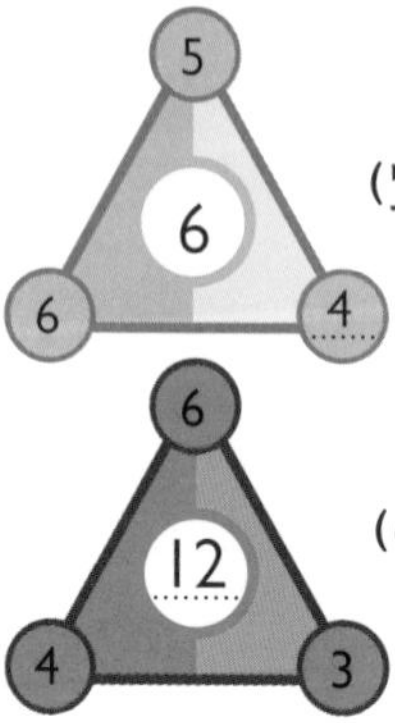

(5 – 4) x 6 = 6

(6 – 3) x 4 = 12

71. In the bay

Name	Owner	Number	Age
Salt Spray	Mick	364	1 year
Merrimack	Joss	109	3 years
Crab's Claw	Seb	238	2 years

Answers

56. Choose carefully

"Which door would the OTHER guard say the treasure is behind?"
It doesn't matter which guard she asks; the answer is always a lie. The lying guard would tell her a lie. The honest guard would tell her what the liar would say, which would be the same lie. So the treasure is always behind the opposite door.

57. Testing tubes

a) 4 hrs and 5 mins.
It would take five minutes of heating to go from one test tube of mixture to two.

58. Art club

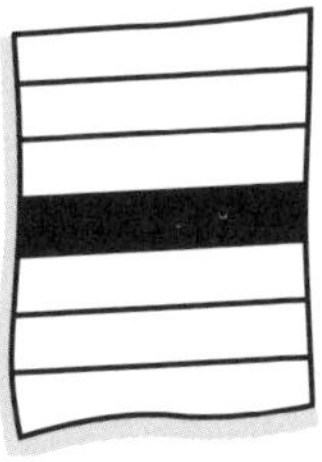

The first picture shows halves, the second shows thirds, the third shows quarters, and so on.

59. Hat puzzler

B. A doesn't shout out, so he must see two different hats. Therefore B knows his hat is not the same as C's.

60. Lollipop pick

B. The lollipops move one place to the right, and the last one becomes the first.

61. Pattern streamers

The streamers follow the sequence 1, 2, 3, 4, 5 ; 2, 3, 4, 5, 1 ; 3, 4, 5, 1, 2, and so on.

62. Planes puzzle

Day 12. 12 is the first number that can be divided exactly by 1, 2, 3 and 4 days.

	1	2	3	4
Day 1	X			
Day 2	X	X		
Day 3	X		X	
Day 4	X	X		X
Day 5	X			
Day 6	X	X	X	
Day 7	X			
Day 8	X	X		X
Day 9	X		X	
Day 10	X	X		
Day 11	X			
Day 12	X	X	X	X

Answers

50. Cryptic grid

51. Symbol sudoku

52. Pattern puzzler

C

53. Tom the cat

Peasant: 4 years
Ship: 2 years
Sultan: 8 years
Age: 16 years old

Add the fractions to get $\frac{7}{8}$. That means the 2 years he's spent in the mayor's house are the other $\frac{1}{8}$. From this you can work out how many years each fraction represents.

54. Detective work

1. b and d
2. a and e
3. c and e

55. Seaside puzzle

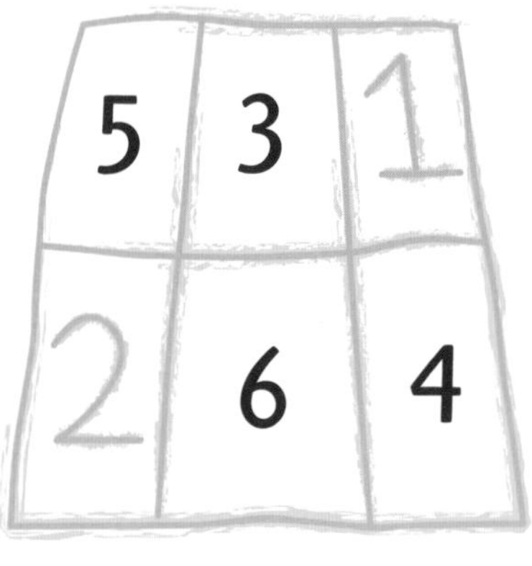

Answers

41. Patchwork pattern

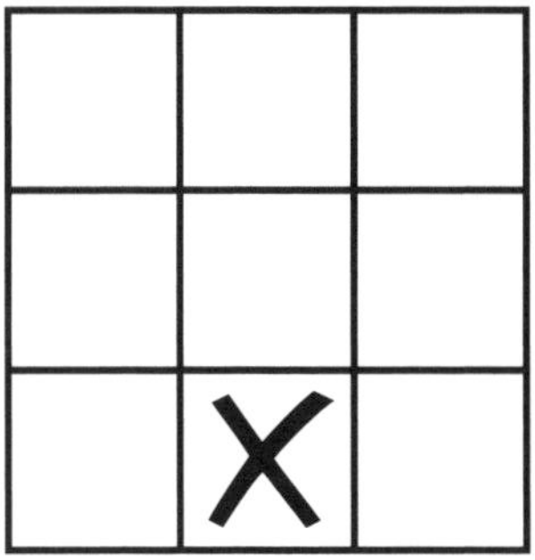

A different square changes places with the middle each time. In square 2, the top middle changes. In square 3, the top right changes. And so on, in a clockwise direction.

42. Prism picker

B, C and F

43. Postage puzzle

32 (top middle)
23 (top right)
33 (middle left)
12 (middle right)
The first number matches the number of butterflies, the second number relates to the background of each stamp.

44. Puzzling print

C

45. See-saw scales

The ball weighs the same as three triangles. The square weighs the same as two triangles.

46. Jester's riddle

Three daughters. One blonde, one brunette, one with red hair.

47. Near miss

He's in a tunnel, or on a bridge.

48. Shape shifter

A

49. Roman riddle

b) three. The password is the number of letters in whatever number the guard says.

Answers

31. Fish in a bowl

B. The fish facing left in the first bowl disappear, and the ones facing right turn around and face left.

32. Hen names

Henny 2, Po 6, Maisie 3, Meg 1, Gina 4, Eggwina 5. The number of letters in their name matches the number of feathers on their wing.

33. Block prints

C

34. Detective school

4. It's the only statement telling the truth about the number of other statements that are false.

35. Cake gobbler

C. The bites on the round cake go around to the right. The bites on the oblong cake go around to the left.

36. Wild West

Day	Cowboy	Horse	Errand
Thursday	Butch	Betsy	Saddle
Friday	Jesse	Dusty	Debt
Saturday	Billy	Red Lady	Dentist

37. Pencils and pens

1

2

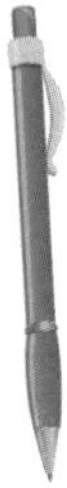

38. Shooting stars

A and F

39. Cuckoo clock

Four seconds. It takes two seconds between each strike.

40. Murder mystery

The wife. Dalia can't be right, because if she is, then Lou would also be right. Since Dalia is wrong, then Sam is wrong, too. That means Anil is correct.

Answers

22. Sudoku

6	9	1	2	7	3	8	5	4
8	4	3	1	5	6	9	2	7
5	2	7	9	8	4	1	3	6
4	6	2	7	9	1	3	8	5
1	5	9	6	3	8	4	7	2
3	7	8	5	4	2	6	1	9
2	8	6	4	1	5	7	9	3
7	1	4	3	2	9	5	6	8
9	3	5	8	6	7	2	4	1

23. Bell ringer

Around to the right. Where the cogs are touching, they turn in opposite directions. Cogs that are connected by a belt turn in the same direction.

24. Breakfast code

A. fried egg

F. two slices of toast

25. Mission to Mars

c) week 11. The total distance the rocket has covered doubles each week. Therefore the week before it arrives on Mars it will be halfway there.

26. Not knots

C

27. Genie's riddle

The third room (the lions would all be dead).

28. Right rectangle

C

Each segment is divided in half vertically.

29. Sequence challenge

3113112221 1A.

Each line describes the line above. For example, '1 A' is described as '1 1 1 A' because you say: "one 1 and one A".

30. Follow the cogs

Right

Touching cogs turn in opposite directions.

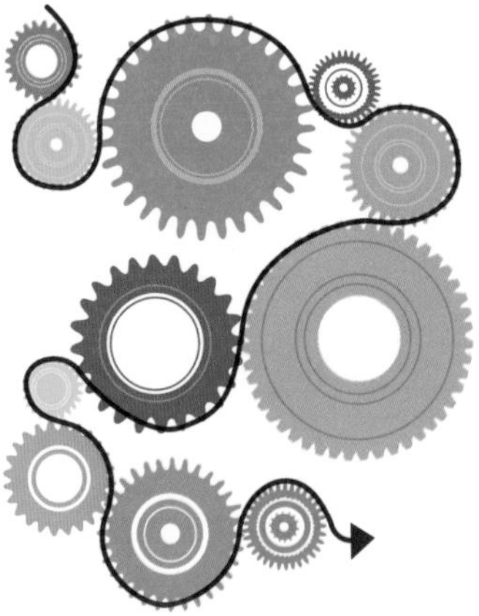

Answers

13. Shapes and numbers

24
Count the number of sides and multiply by four.

14. Which kitten?

Friend	Kitten
Zack	Tiger
Ellie	Shadow
Amy	Rusty
Rico	Sooty

15. Fishy puzzle

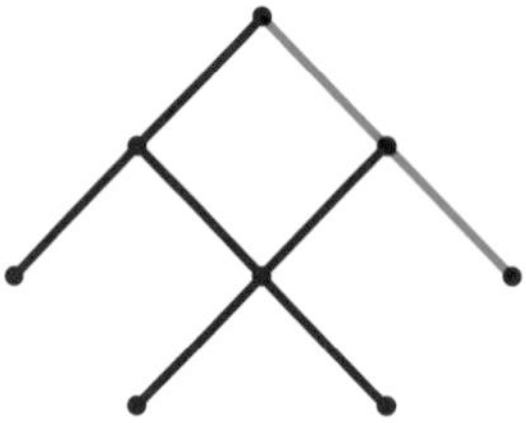

16. Odd pattern out

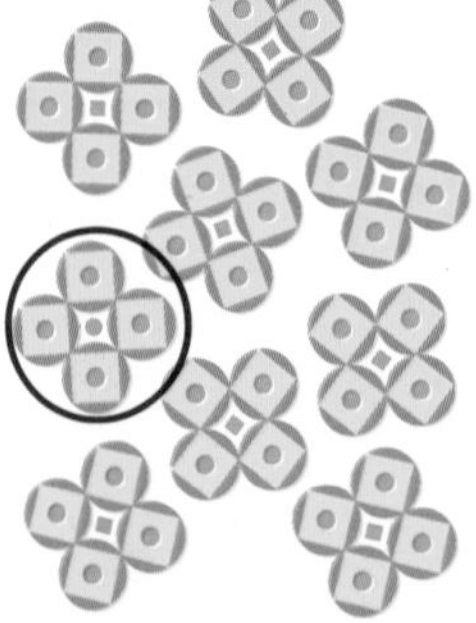

17. Dog toys

	Jojo	Rex	Spot	Bone	Ball	Stick
Ali		✓				✓
Pat			✓	✓		
Riz	✓				✓	

18. Pencil puzzle

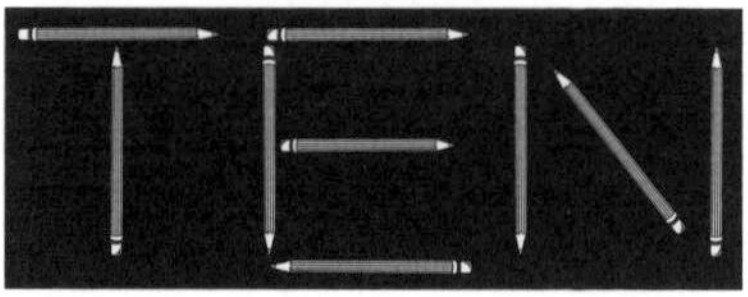

19. The wise son

The younger son rode his brother's horse over the line.

20. Puzzle time

Their hands don't make a right angle (90°).

21. Dots on dice

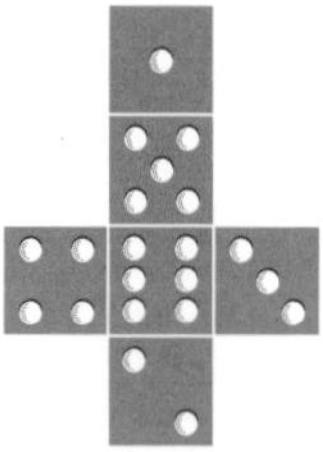

Answers

1. Boat race

Three

2. Lost stone

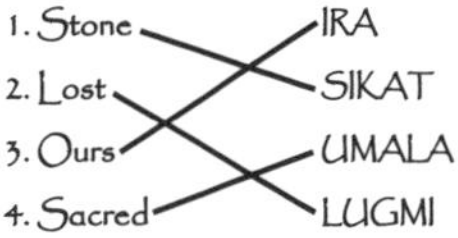

3. Odd one out

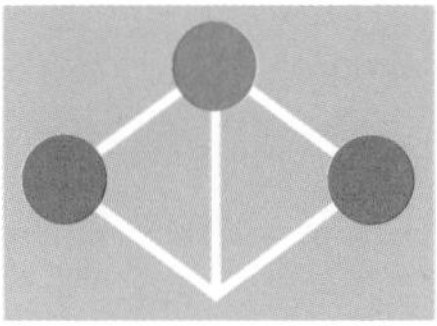

4. Alien weigh-in

1. 40 grobbles. The baby alien's whole weight is made from half its weight, plus 20 grobbles. Therefore those 20 grobbles must be the other half of the whole.
2. 80 grobbles (same logic)

5. Tricky traffic

Car 2 on Wood Lane. All the cars have two windows and purple hubcaps.
Car 3 on Castle Road. All the cars have three windows and hubcaps that match their paint.

6. Toy cube

D

7. Dotty squares

3 dots.
Across: 4+3 = 7, 3+1 = 4, 1+2 = 3
Down: 4–3 = 1, 3–1 = 2, 7–4 = 3

8. Who lives where?

1. Andy and Rose
2. Ray and Mia
3. Mike and Anna

9. Bus driver riddle

He was walking.

10. The jump

She jumped out of a window on the bottom floor.

11. Racing positions

Blue - 1st Yellow - 2nd
Purple - 3rd Red - 4th
Green - 5th

12. Pen puzzle

Little riddlers

Riddle 1. Alesha and her friends are walking across the park on a bright, sunny day. Suddenly they find an old brown hat, a green scarf and some lumps of coal lying on the ground. Why are they not surprised?

Riddle 2. If two people can paint two rooms in two days, how long does it take one person to paint one room?

Riddle 3. There are five lollipops inside a paper bag. How can you give five people a lollipop each, and still have one left inside the bag?

Riddle 4. Every day, trains travel between Trumpington and Gravelly Bottom. They travel on the same track, at the same speed, and there are no stations in between. The 1pm train took 70 minutes to complete the trip, but the 3pm train took an hour and ten minutes. Why?

Riddle 5. How could a cowboy ride into town on Friday, stay three days, and then ride out on Friday?

Alien code

An alien civilization uses number symbols made from dots and wavy lines. Some of them are shown below. Can you fill in the missing symbols?

Apples and oranges

There are three boxes, one filled with apples, one with oranges and one with apples and oranges. But every box is mislabelled. You can pick a box and take one piece of fruit without looking inside. Which one should you choose to find out exactly what's in each box?

Hint: Which box can have only one type of fruit inside?

Answer:..

Hard evidence

In each set of statements, underline the **two** which prove that:

1. Billy didn't rob the bank.

a. Billy said he didn't rob the bank.

b. Billy works at a supermarket in the morning.

c. The getaway driver is Billy's brother.

d. The bank was robbed at 10am.

e. Billy robbed a bank ten years ago.

2. Cathy has eaten a slice of her mother's cake.

a. A slice of cake is missing.

b. Cathy's mother bakes delicious cakes.

c. Cathy has a sweet tooth.

d. The cake was covered in chocolate.

e. Cathy has cake crumbs around her lips.

3. Simon is a werewolf.

a. Simon has very hairy arms.

b. A werewolf ate a yellow canary.

c. Simon never goes out on a full moon.

d. A werewolf was seen near Simon's house.

e. Simon has yellow feathers stuck between his teeth.

On and off

There are three light switches outside a room, and three lightbulbs on the inside. The switches are turned off and the door is closed. You can turn each switch on and off, but only before you open the door. How can you tell which switch controls which bulb when you enter the room?

Hint: There's more than one way to tell if a bulb has been on...

Answer: ....

....

Non-stop pen

Draw these shapes without lifting your pen from the page or going over any line that you've already made.

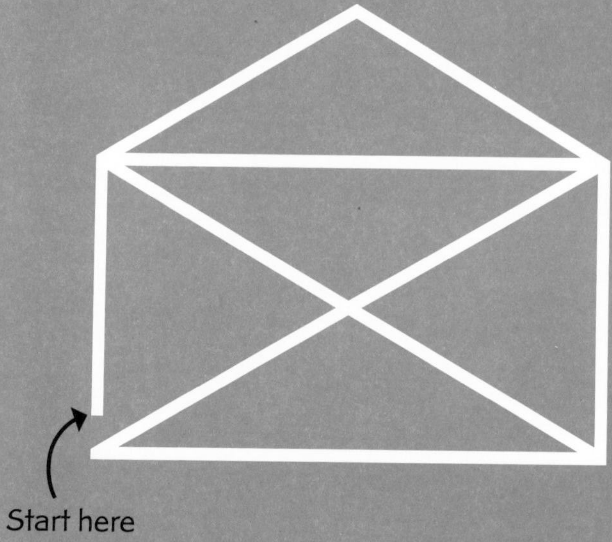

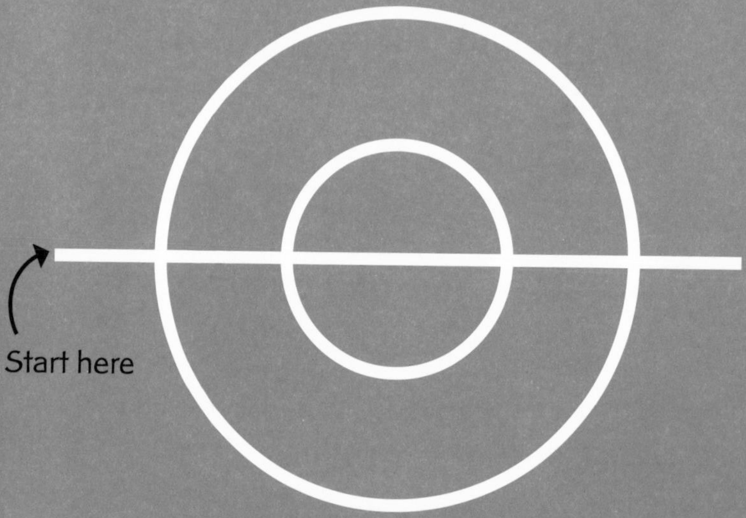

Bridge crossing

Sally has to cross a rope bridge, but she's very nervous. The bridge has 20 planks, and every time she steps forwards five planks, she then steps backwards four planks. How many times must she do this to reach the other side?

Answer: ....

Monster munch

There are five monsters living under Tom's bed. "Feed us cookies!" they howl. "Or we'll gobble you up!" Luckily, they're not as fierce as they sound. The biggest monster sticks out a furry hand, and asks for half of the cookies on Tom's plate. Then it gives one cookie back as a thank-you present. The second-biggest monster does the same thing, then the third, the fourth, and the fifth.

If Tom wants to save two cookies for a midnight snack, what's the fewest number of cookies he can take to bed?

Hint: it's fewer than you think...

Answer: ....

Dolls' parade

Can you move just three of these dolls so that the triangle points down instead of up?

Robot shootout

Three robots are having a shootout: Spike, Razor and Glitch. Their stun guns each have one shot. Glitch is the most accurate, but Spike is quickest on the draw and gets to shoot first. What should he do to have the best chance of surviving?

Hint: The key thing to remember is that each robot only has one shot.

a) shoot Glitch b) shoot Razor c) deliberately miss

89

Boat crossing

A ferry sets out from Dublin for Liverpool. At the same time, a speedboat sets out from Liverpool for Dublin. If the ferry goes at 20 knots and the speedboat goes at 40 knots, which boat is closer to Dublin when they pass?

Answer: ....

90

Easy peasy

This is a most unusual paragraph. How quickly can you find out what's so unusual about it? It looks so ordinary you'd think nothing was wrong with it – and in fact, nothing is wrong with it. It is unusual though. Why? Study it, think about it, and you'll soon find out. You can do it without coaching, don't worry! Just stay calm and it'll dawn on you. Good luck.

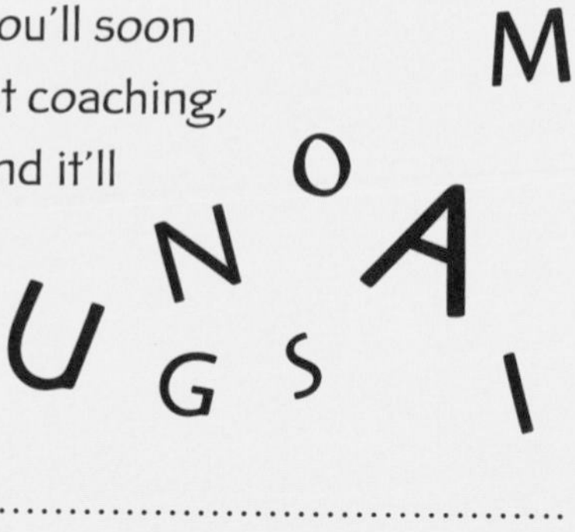

Answer: ....

1. The man who packs the *cocoa* and smoked fish is younger than Robert.

2. The man who packs the coffee, but not the baked beans, is 27 years old.

3. Roald is 31 years old.

4. Ernest didn't pack the tea.

You can use the chart below to keep track of the facts.

	27	31	34	Coffee	Tea	Cocoa	Beef	Fish	Beans
Robert									
Ernest									
Roald									
Beef									
Fish									
Beans									
Coffee									
Tea									
Cocoa									

Arctic explorers

Three explorers are setting out on an Arctic trek. Following the clues on the opposite page, find out the age of each explorer and what food and drink they each pack in their backpacks.

Name	Age	Drink	Food
Ernest			
Roald			
Robert			

Act your age

1. On her birthday, William asks his great aunt Millicent how old she is, and she replies: "Well, young man, I am 44 years old, not counting Saturdays, Sundays or Mondays, because I hate Mondays." What is her real age?

Answer: ....

2. William copies his great aunt's idea, but changes it to make himself sound older than he really is. He calculates his age in nine-day weeks, because he'd like his weekends to be twice as long. If his real age is 14, how old does he say he is?

Answer: ....

Keep it simple!

See if you can find the hidden message on the wall.

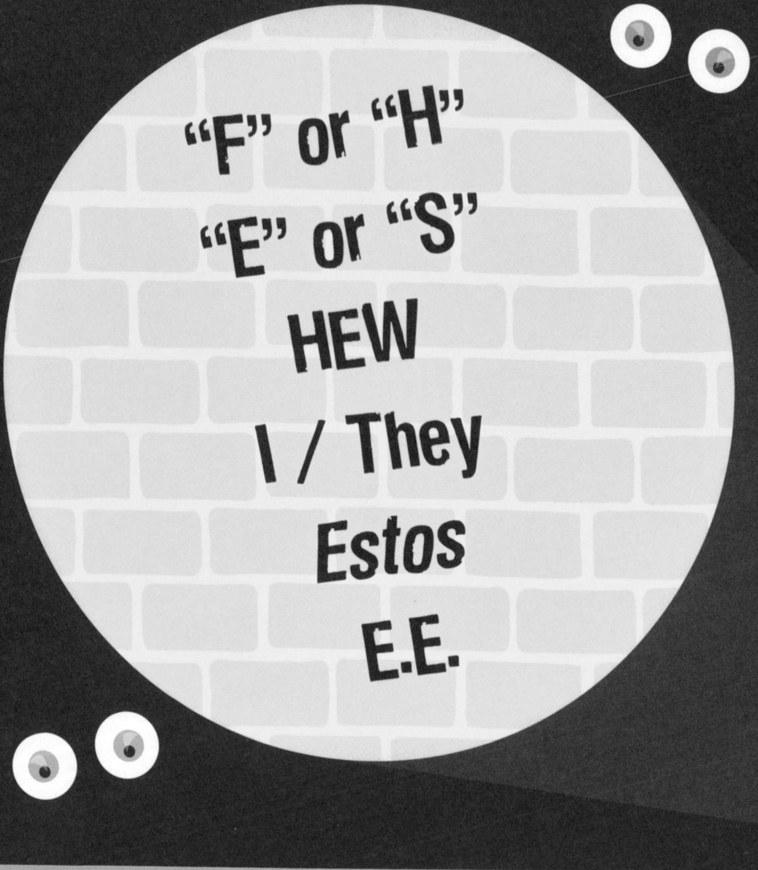

Answer: ....

....

Cube in a cube

Which small cube completes the large cube?

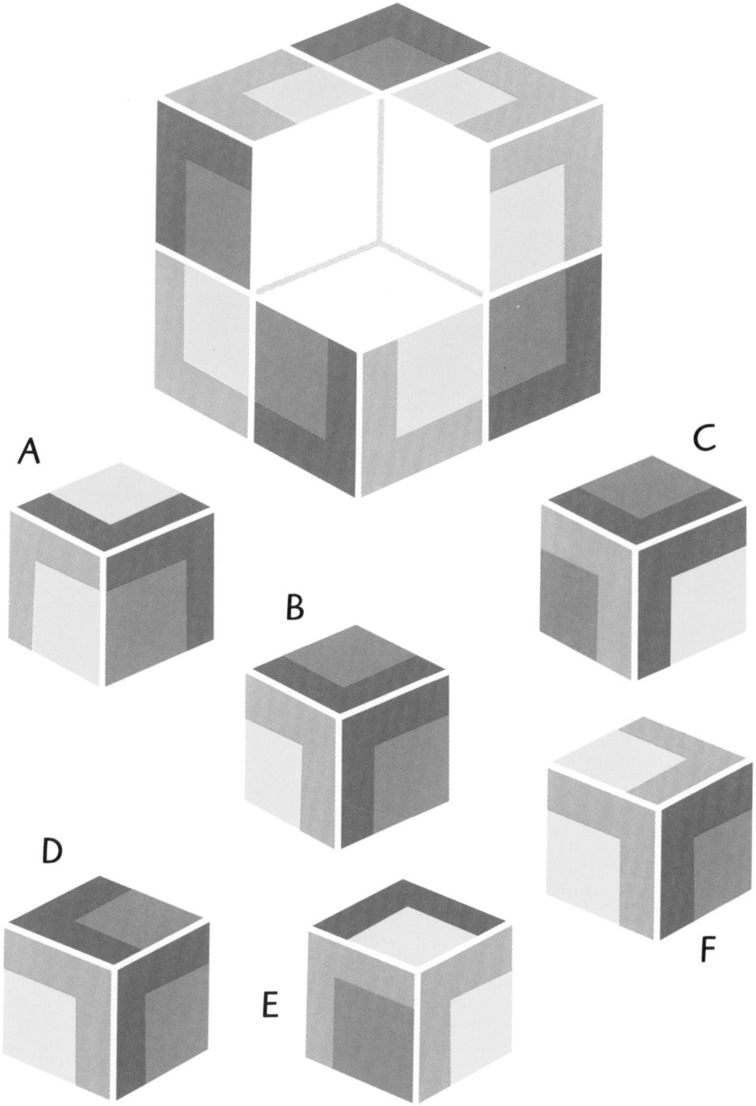

84

Laundry line-up

Look carefully for the sequence on this line, and decide which collection of laundry should be hung up next.

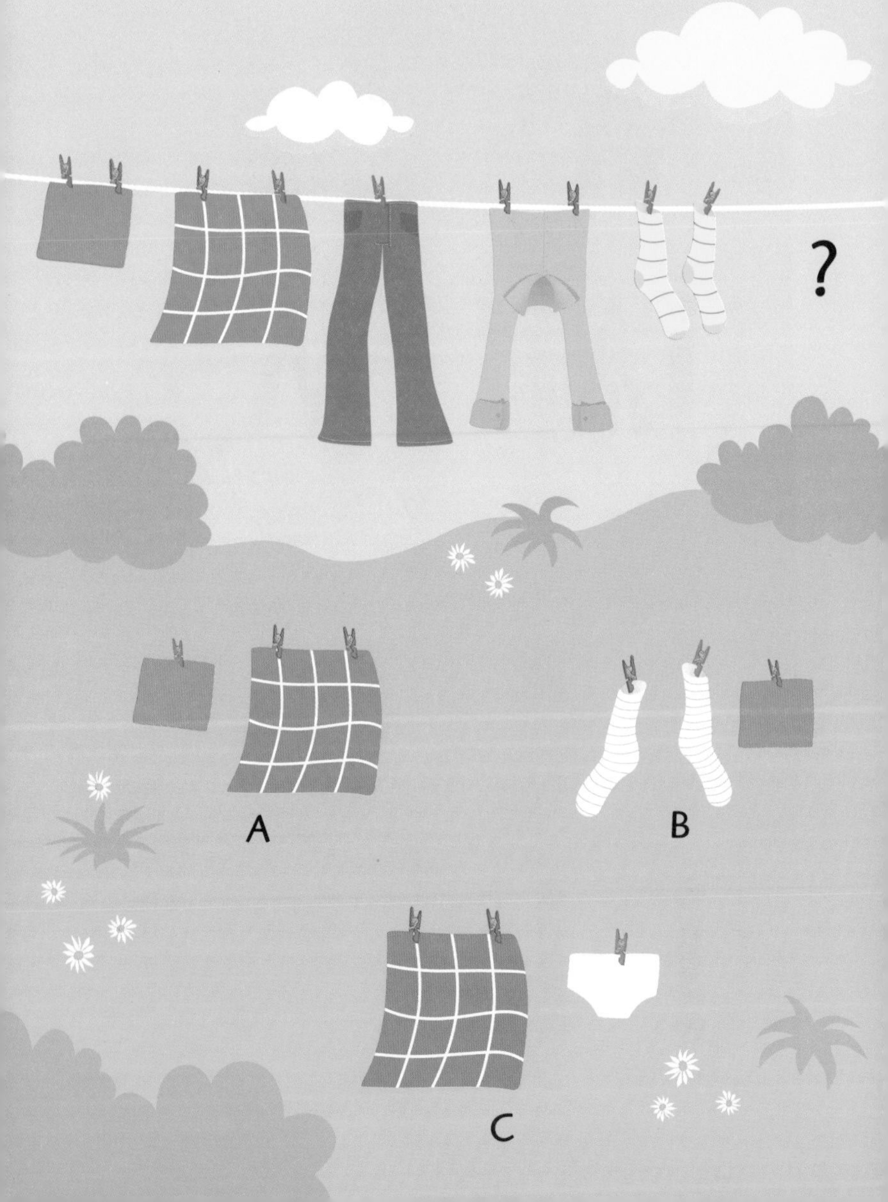

Castle code

The symbols on shields 1, 2 and 3 are related to their castles. Find out how, and draw the correct symbols on shield 4.

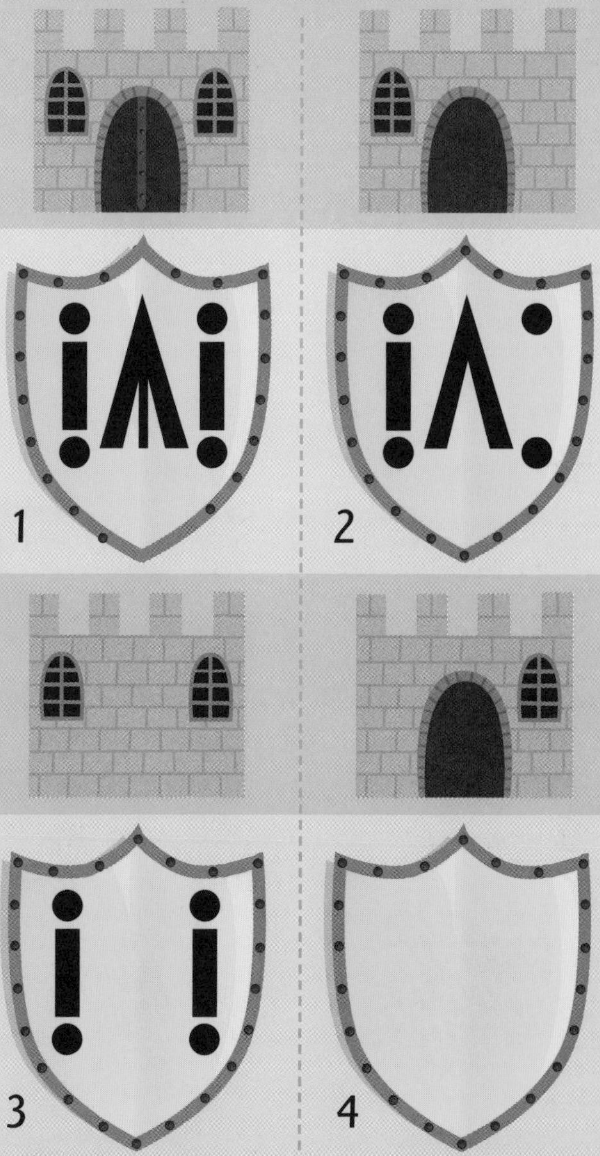

Dotty problem

These four dice show which number is on which side if a dice is rotated while keeping the '3' on top.

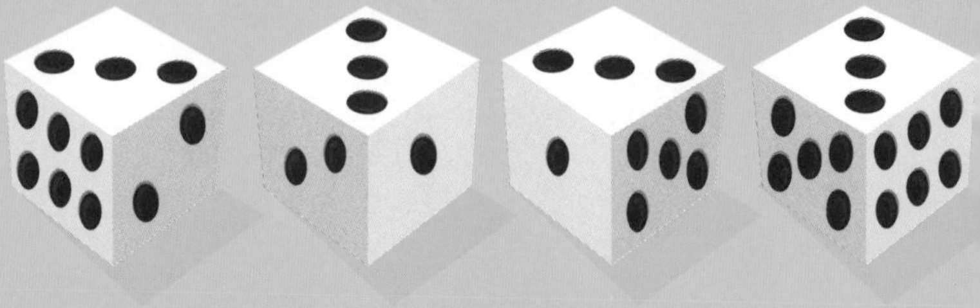

Now the dice are flipped so the '3' is at the bottom, and '4' is on top. Can you fill in the missing dots?

Symbol scramble

Look for the pattern that follows from row to row.
Which three symbols are in the wrong position?

Square-eyed

Look at the pattern below. The blue square forms new squares as it fits around the red square. Then the yellow square fits around the blue square. How many squares are there in total?

1. ....

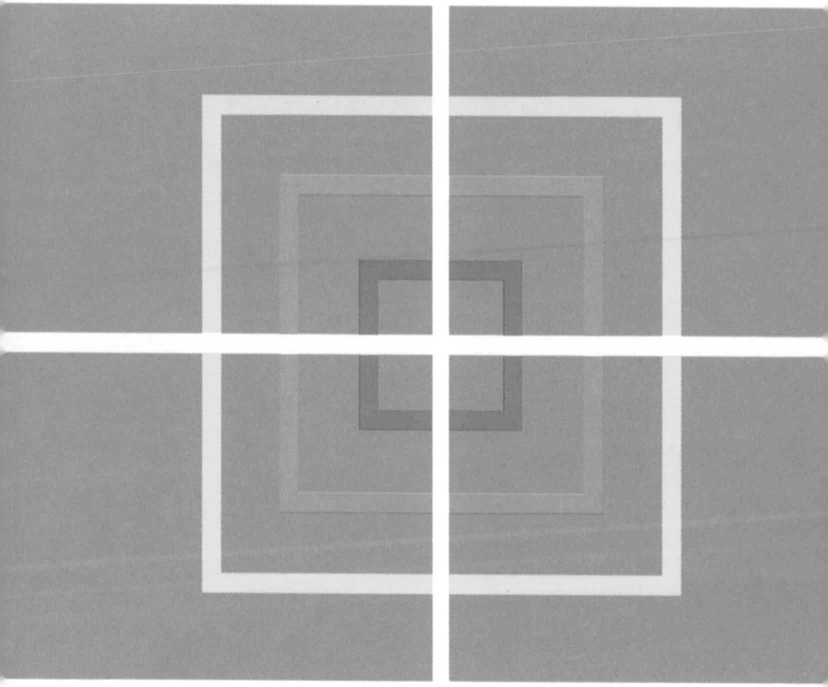

If a larger square were drawn around the yellow square, and an even larger square were drawn around that, how many squares would there be in the new pattern?

2. ....

Salon selection

Minna has moved to a small, remote island. She wants to get her hair cut, and there are two stylists to choose from. One works in a modern salon and has an elegant bob of smooth brown hair. The other works in a wooden shack and has a badly-dyed disaster of a haircut. Which stylist should Minna choose?

Answer: ....

....

Tile pattern

See if you can complete this grid by discovering which is the missing block.

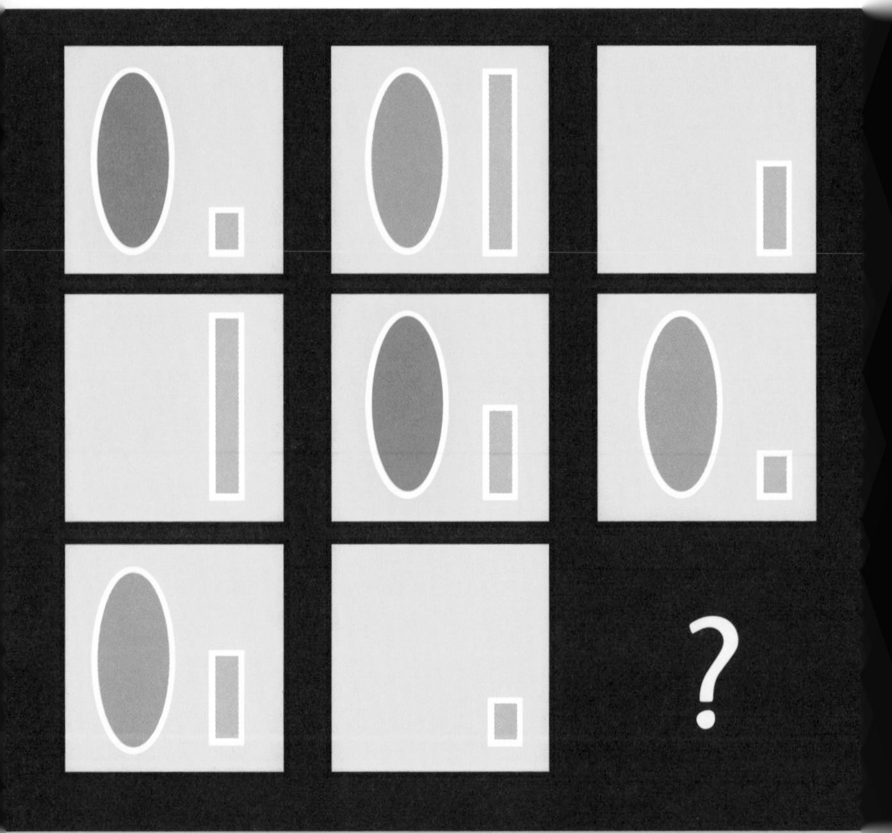

Impossible shapes

Three of the shapes below can be drawn on paper, but cannot exist in real life. Which are they?

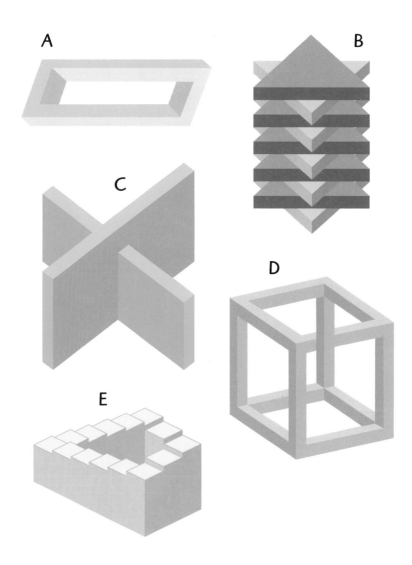

A

B

C

D

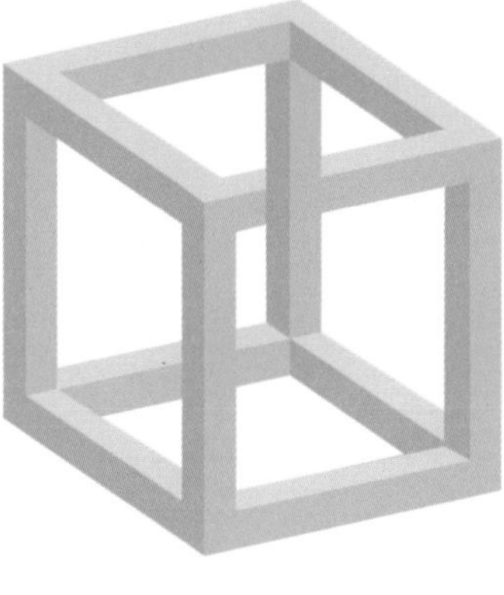

E

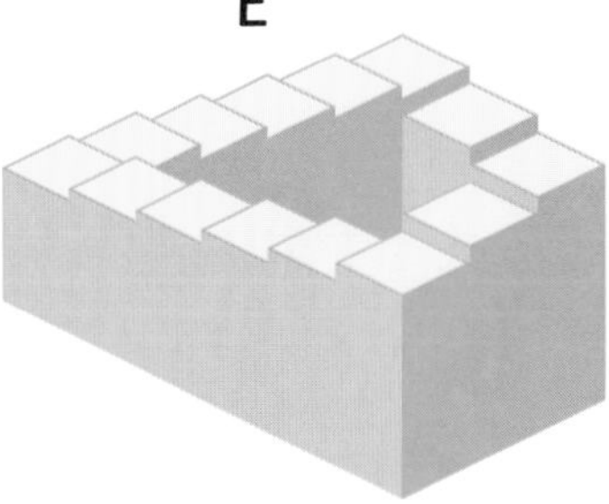

Jumbo jumble

There are three pairs of souvenir elephants. The elephant in each pair weigh the same, but one pair is heavier than the other two. You have some balance scales, but you ca only use them once. How do you find out which pair of elephants is heaviest?

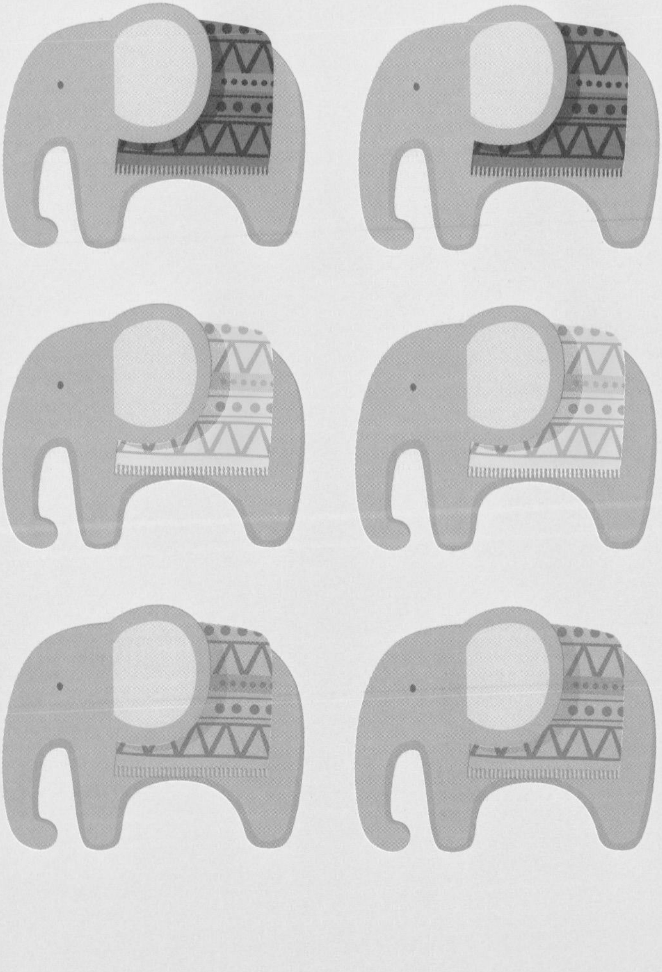

Parrot in a cage

This parrot and cage cost 50 silver pieces. If the parrot costs 40 silver pieces more than the cage, how much does each of them cost? Write your answers on the card below.

Short puzzles

1. What is the next letter in this sequence?

O T T F F S S ?

Answer: ....

2. If a sharp prod can be spelled POKE, and a cape can be spelled CLOAK, how do you spell the white of an egg?

Answer: ....

3. Mary's mother has four children. The first child is called April, the second is called May and the third is called June. What's the name of the fourth child?

Answer: ....

4. At midnight it is raining hard. What are the chances of it being sunny in 72 hours' time, if 0% is no chance, and 100% is a cast-iron certainty?

Answer: ....%

Bird's eye view

Look carefully at the shapes on the board below. Which image would they make if you were looking at them from directly above?

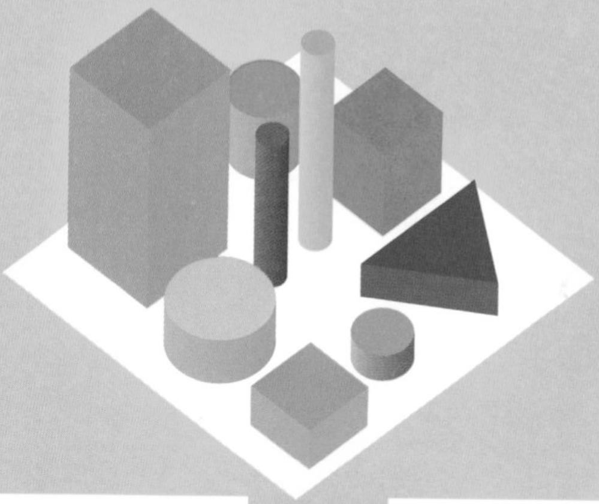

A

B

C

D

What's the time?

Look at the clocks to find out what time the green clock should show, then draw its hands in the correct position.

1

2

3

4

5

6

1. The boat with 109 on its sail is one year older than the Crab's Claw, which is owned by Seb.

2. The owner of the boat that is 3 years old isn't Mick, who has a boat numbered 364.

3. The Salt Spray isn't owned by Joss.

4. The Merrimack is 3 years old.

You can use the chart below to keep track of the facts.

	109	238	364	Joss	Seb	Mick	1 year	2 years	3 years
Salt Spray									
Merrimack									
Crab's Claw									
1 year									
2 years									
3 years									
Joss									
Seb									
Mick									

In the bay

Three boats are docked at a jetty. Following the clues on the opposite page, can you find out the owner of each boat, the number on its sail and its age?

Name	Owner	Number	Age
Salt Spray			
Merrimack			
Crab's Claw			

Tricky triangles

The number in the middle of each triangle is made by doing a calculation with the numbers in each corner. The calculation is the same for all the triangles. Write the missing numbers on the bottom two triangles.

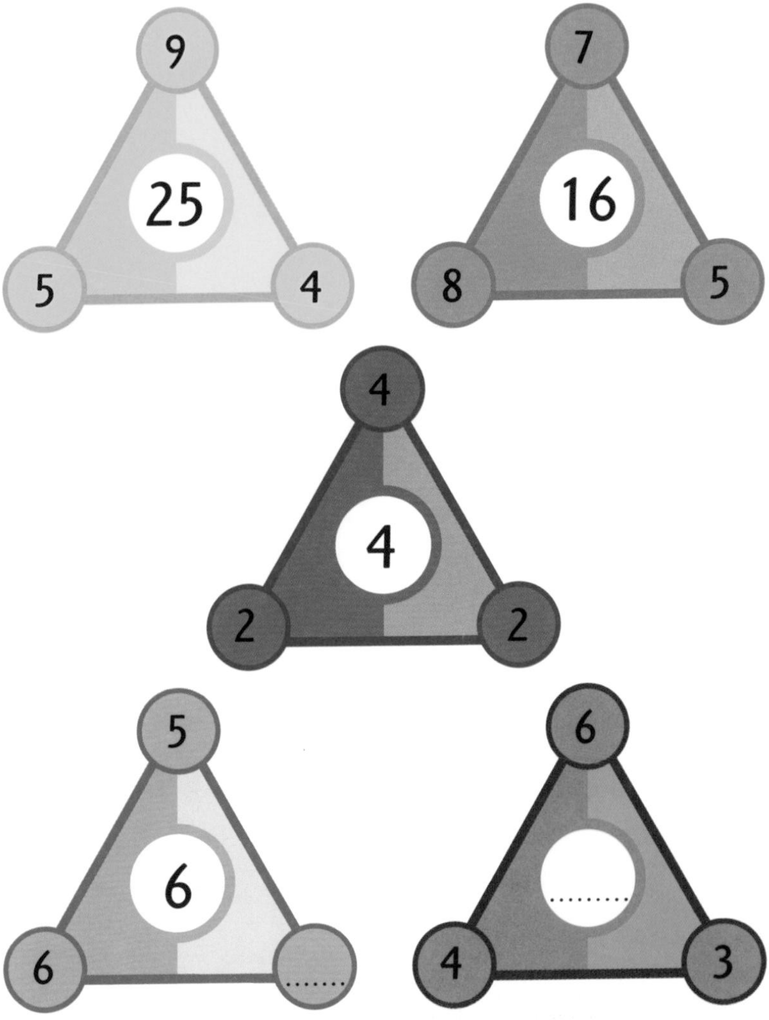

68

Wrong total

Zina and six of her friends are visiting Italy. They all go into a café and choose the same ice cream. The price comes to 24 euros and Zina knows it is wrong, even though she can't remember how much each ice cream cost. Why is this?

Answer: ....

69

Age puzzler

On Laura's 5th birthday, her mother was 35. On her 15th birthday, her mother was 3 times her age. How old is Laura now that her mother is only twice her age?

Answer: ....

Cube finder

This pattern can be folded to make only one of the cubes below. Which one?

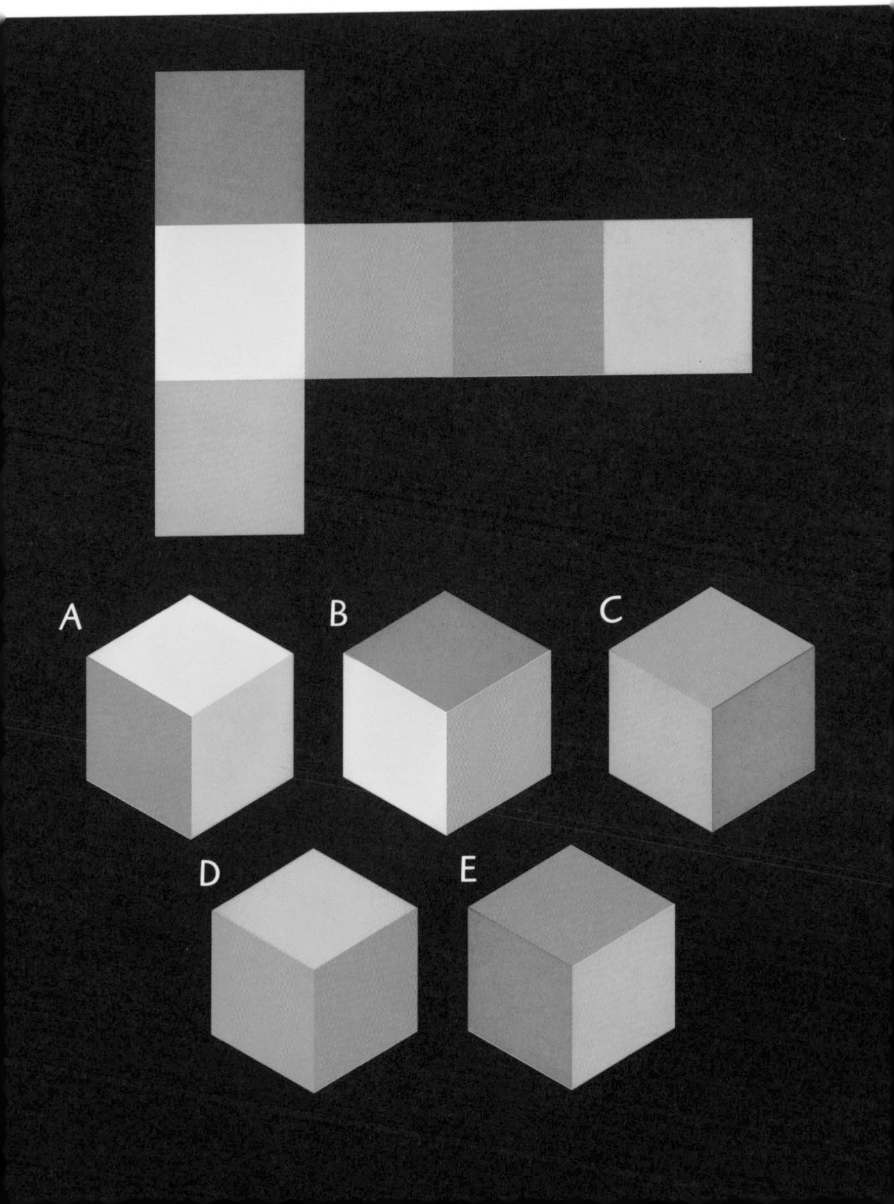

Paperboy puzzle

A paperboy's route goes from orange door, to red door, to purple door, to yellow door. If he continues his route with this pattern, what's the number of the house he'll deliver to next?

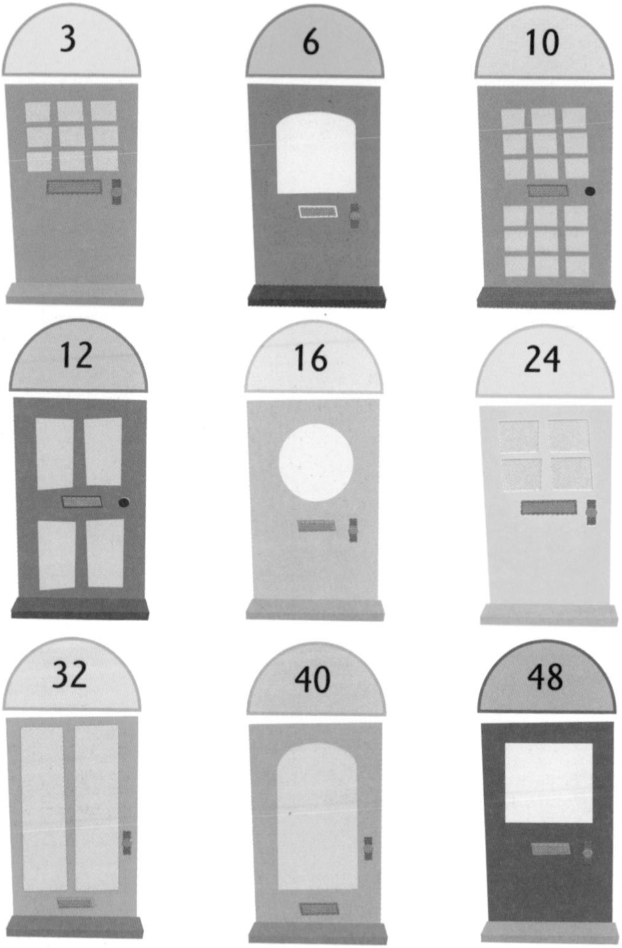

Answer: ....

Sudoku

This grid is made up of nine blocks, each containing nine squares. Fill in the blank squares so that each block contains all the digits 1 to 9. Each digit can only appear once in a row, column or block.

		9	4		6	5		
	2			3			6	
1		5				7		3
3			8		4			1
	1			5			8	
2			3		9			5
4		3				8		9
	9			4			3	
		1	5		3	4		

River crossing

A farmer stands on one side of a river with a fox, a rabbit and a bunch of carrots. She needs to take them across, but can only carry one thing at a time.

If she leaves the fox and rabbit alone together, the fox will eat the rabbit. If she leaves the rabbit and carrots together, the rabbit will eat the carrots. Complete the chart below to find out how she can take them to the other side in the fewest number of crossings.

Left shore	On the boat	Right shore
F,R,C		
F,C	R	
F,C		R
C	F	R

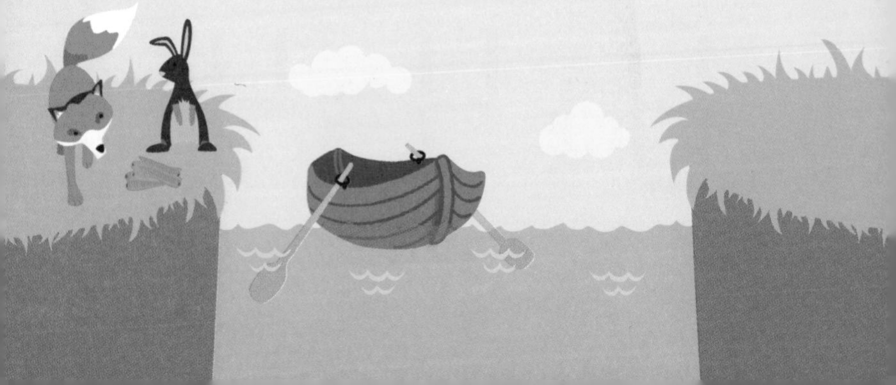

Faulty calculator

The numbers and symbols on the screens below are made up of segments. Correct each calculation in a different way, by moving just one segment to anywhere in the line.

Planes puzzle

Four planes take off from the same airport at the same time.

- The first plane returns to the airport once a day.
- The second plane returns every other day.
- The third plane returns every three days.
- The fourth plane returns every four days.

If they take off on Day 1, which is the next day when all four planes are due back in the airport together?

Answer: ....

Pattern streamers

Find out the sequence then draw the next two patterns below.

Lollipop pick

Which row comes next, A *or* B?

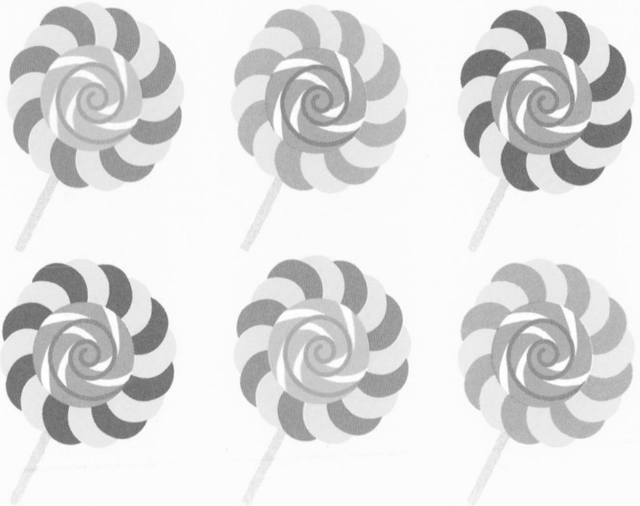

A 

B 

Hat puzzler

A man stands on one side of a solid brick wall, and three men line up, one behind the other, facing the other side. The man at the back sees both men in front of him. The man in the middle sees only the man in front of him. The man in front sees only the wall.

They close their eyes while a hat is placed on each of their heads. They're told two are yellow and two are blue. Then they're asked: "In 30 seconds, can any of you say which hat you're wearing?" They can't move, or talk to each other. Which is the only man who can answer the question?

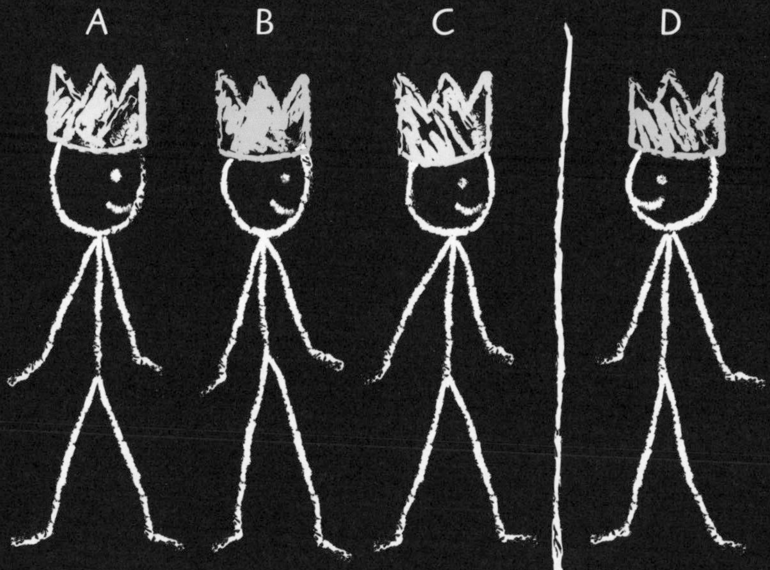

Hint: The man who can answer needs to think about what one of the other men must be seeing.

Answer: ....

Art club

Find out what links all the pictures in this art club display, then choose from the options below and draw the correct design on the blank page.

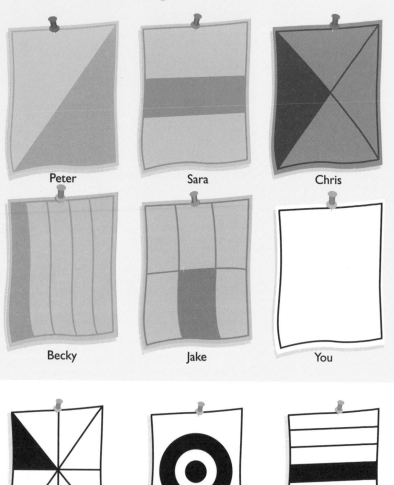

Peter

Sara

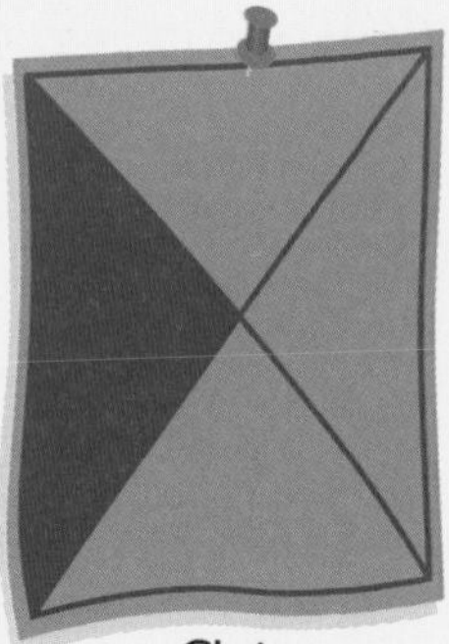

Chris

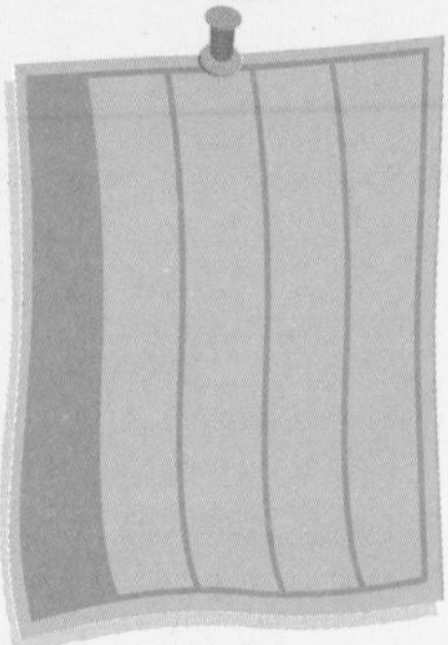

Becky

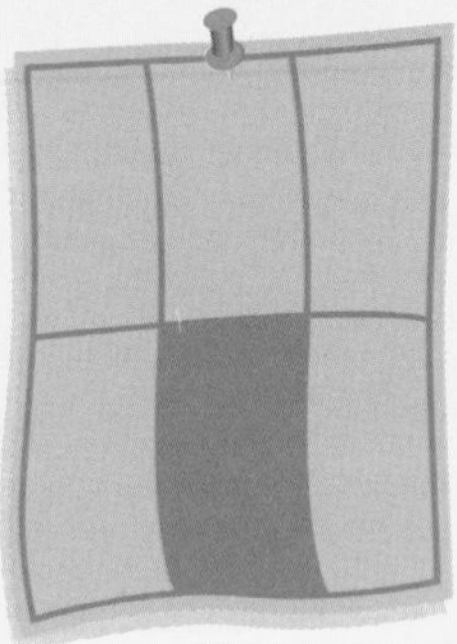

Jake

You

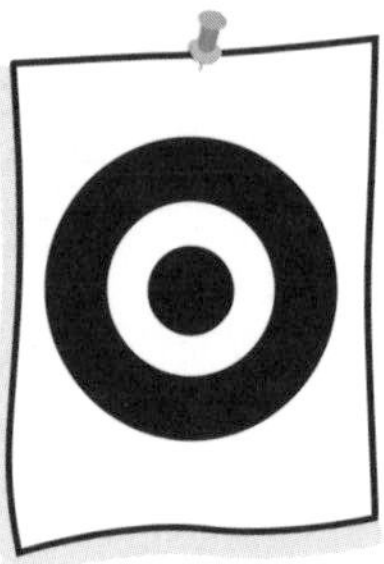

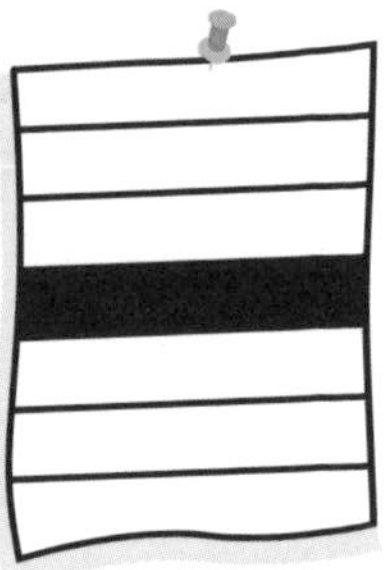

Testing tubes

Boris heats two test tubes, each half-filled with chemical mixture. After five minutes, the liquid doubles in volume and fills each tube. He splits the liquid between four test tubes, heats it for another five minutes and it doubles again. Then he splits it between eight tubes, and so on.

In four hours he makes enough mixture to fill a large barrel. How long would it take if he *only* started out with *one* half-filled test tube?

a) 4 hrs and 5 mins   b) 4 hrs and 30 mins   c) 8 hrs

Choose carefully

A girl finds two identical doors at the end of a secret corridor. Behind one door there are riches beyond her wildest dreams; behind the other there's a pair of sweaty boots. There is a guard at each door. One always tells the truth, and the other always lies, but she doesn't know which is which. Before she picks a door, the girl can choose one guard and ask him one question.

What question should she ask to find the treasure?

Hint: Think of a question that makes the honest guard reply with a lie. Then the reply is a lie whichever guard you ask.

Answer: ....

....

Seaside puzzle

Someone has left a puzzle in the sand. Using the numbers 3 to 6, see if you can fill in the empty squares so that none of the numbers sits in numerical order. For example, 3 couldn't be placed directly above, below or beside 2.

Detective work

In each set of statements, underline the **two** which prove that:

1. A tiger has escaped from the zoo.

a. The tiger enclosure in the zoo is empty.
b. The zoo's only tiger has one ear.
c. The zoo has been closed for the day.
d. There's a one-eared tiger loose in the park.
e. The zoo keepers are all panicking.

2. Edward is a pirate.

a. Edward is a sailor on the Black Dragon.
b. Edward has a parrot.
c. The Black Dragon has red sails.
d. Edward wears an eye patch.
e. The sailors on the Black Dragon steal treasure.

3. The prince fought a giant dragon.

a. The dragon is dead.
b. The prince said he killed the dragon.
c. There's blue blood on the prince's sword and tunic.
d. The prince is known for being very brave.
e. The giant dragon has blue blood.

Tom the cat

Tom the cat has led an eventful life. He spent $\frac{1}{4}$ of it in a peasant's cottage with little food, $\frac{1}{8}$ of it working as a ship's cat, and $\frac{1}{2}$ of it catching rats in a sultan's palace. If he's been living with the mayor of London for the past 2 years, how long did he spend doing each thing?

.... years living in a peasant's house.

.... years working as a ship's cat.

.... years catching rats for the sultan.

Tom is .... years old.

Pattern puzzler

Find the connection between each gift wrap and its tag, then look at the options below and choose the correct tag for the fourth gift wrap.

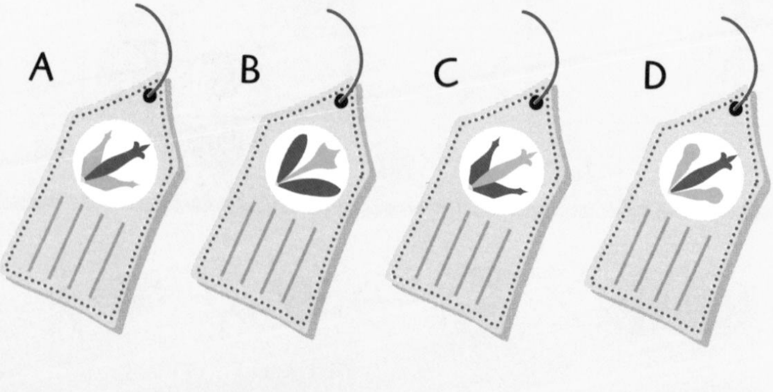

Symbol sudoku

This grid is made up of nine blocks, each containing nine squares. Fill in the blank squares so that each of the nine blocks contains all the symbols at the bottom of this page. Each symbol can only appear once in a row, column or block.

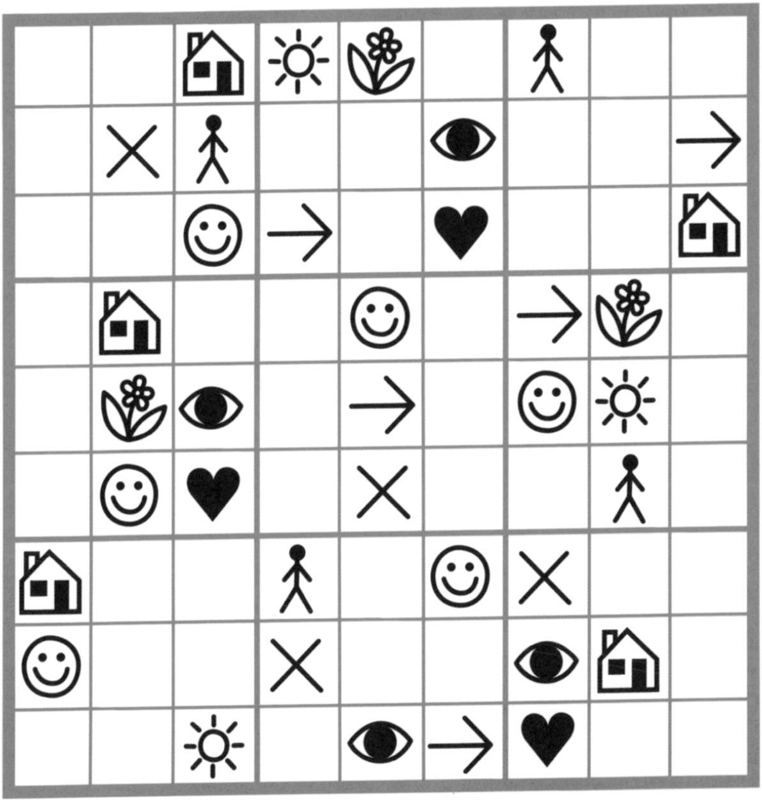

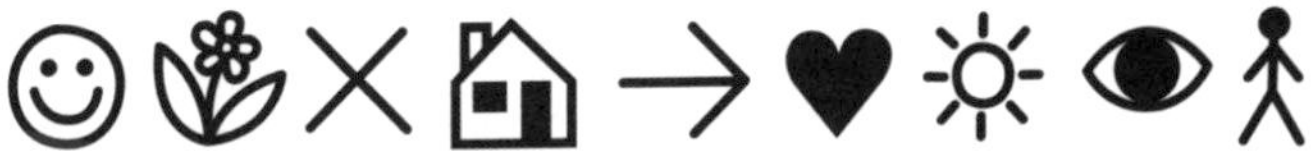

Cryptic grid

See if you can complete this grid by drawing in the missing symbols.

Roman riddle

A man wants to enter the temple but has forgotten the password, so he hides behind a pillar and listens carefully. Soon, another man walks up. The guard looks down at him and says in a gruff voice: "twelve". The man replies "six" and is let in. Then a woman walks up and the guard says "six". She replies "three" and is let in. The man thinks he's heard enough and strides up to the door. The guard says "ten", he says "five", but the guard turns him away. What should he have said?

a) two

b) three

c) four

Shape shifter

Find out the pattern to uncover what comes next.

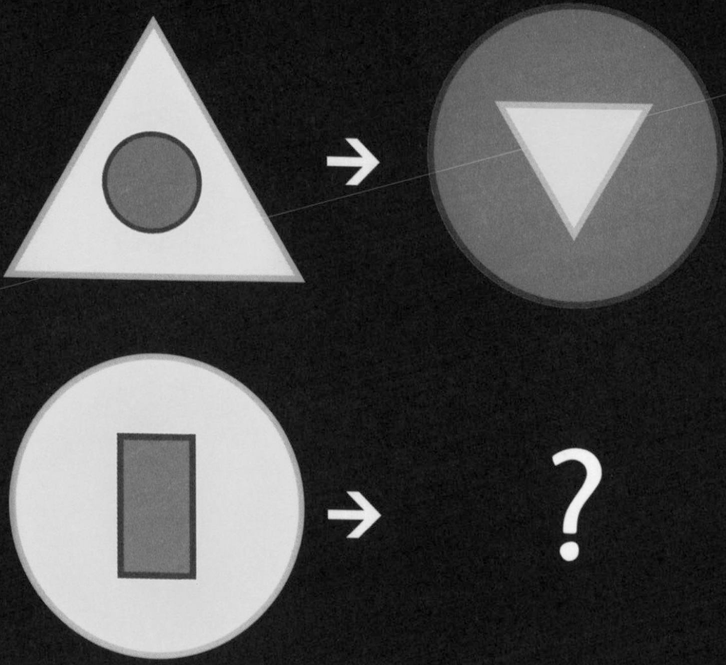

Circle the right answer.

A

B

C

46

Jester's riddle

A jester stands on his head and says: "Everyone calls me a fool, but no one can answer my riddle! Can you? A warty old man has a gaggle of daughters. They're all blonde but two, all brunette but two, and all redheaded but two. How many daughters does the old man have?"

Answer: ....

47

Near miss

Blackberry the rabbit is wandering along a train track, when a train comes speeding towards him. Instead of leaping straight off the track, he bounds along for five seconds then leaps out of the way just in time. Why doesn't he leap off right away?

Answer: ....

....

See-saw scales

The triangle, circle and square each weigh a different amount. The first two scales balance, but the bottom ones don't. Draw a single shape on the left side of the bottom scales that would make them balance.

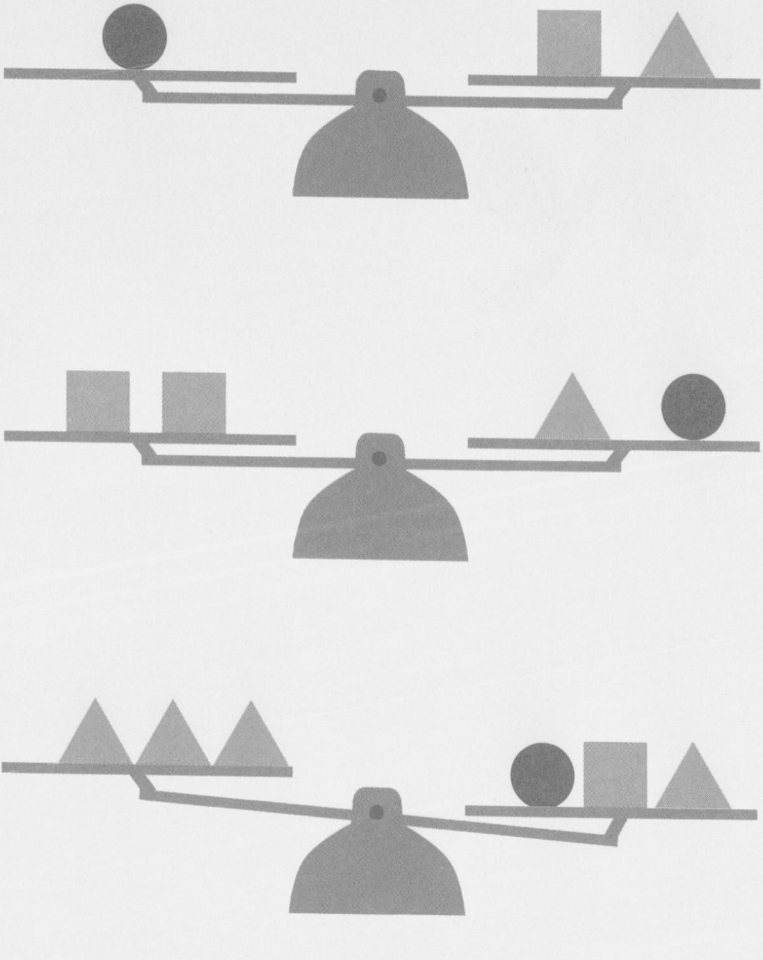

Puzzling print

Only one of the prints below can be made with this potato. Which one?

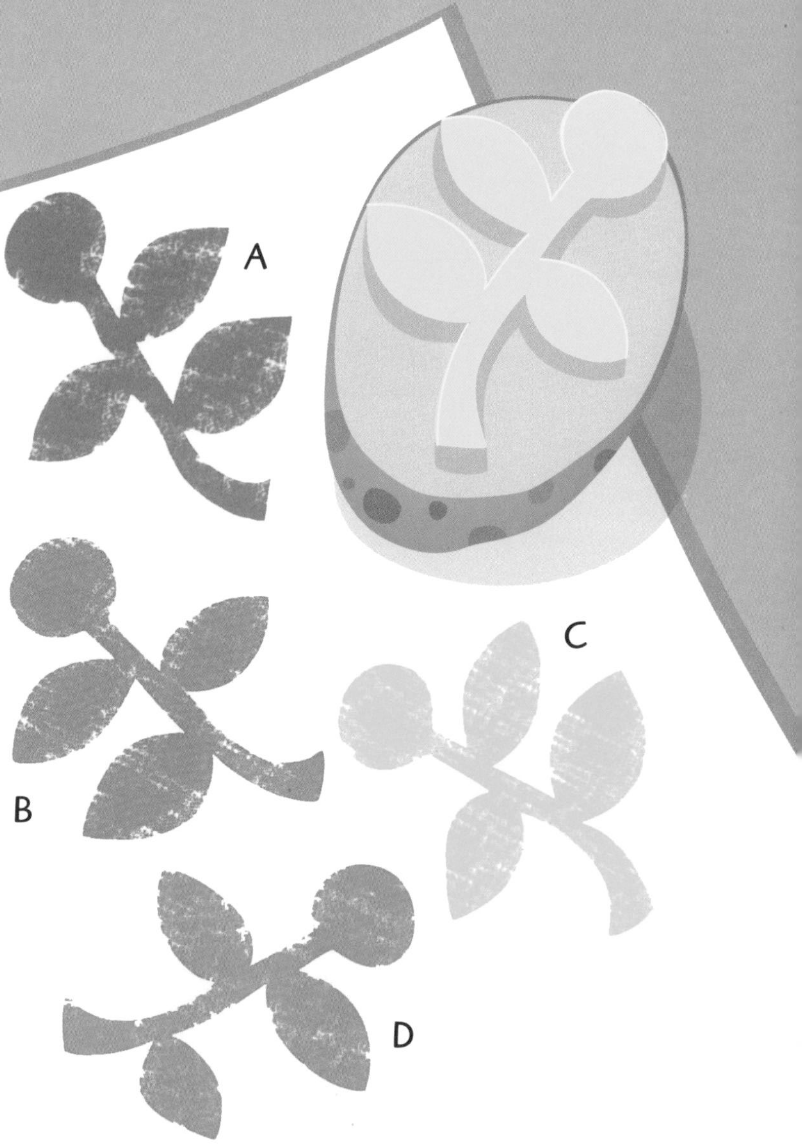

43

Postage puzzle

The prices are missing from *some* of these stamps. Find *out* how they're numbered and fill in the gaps.

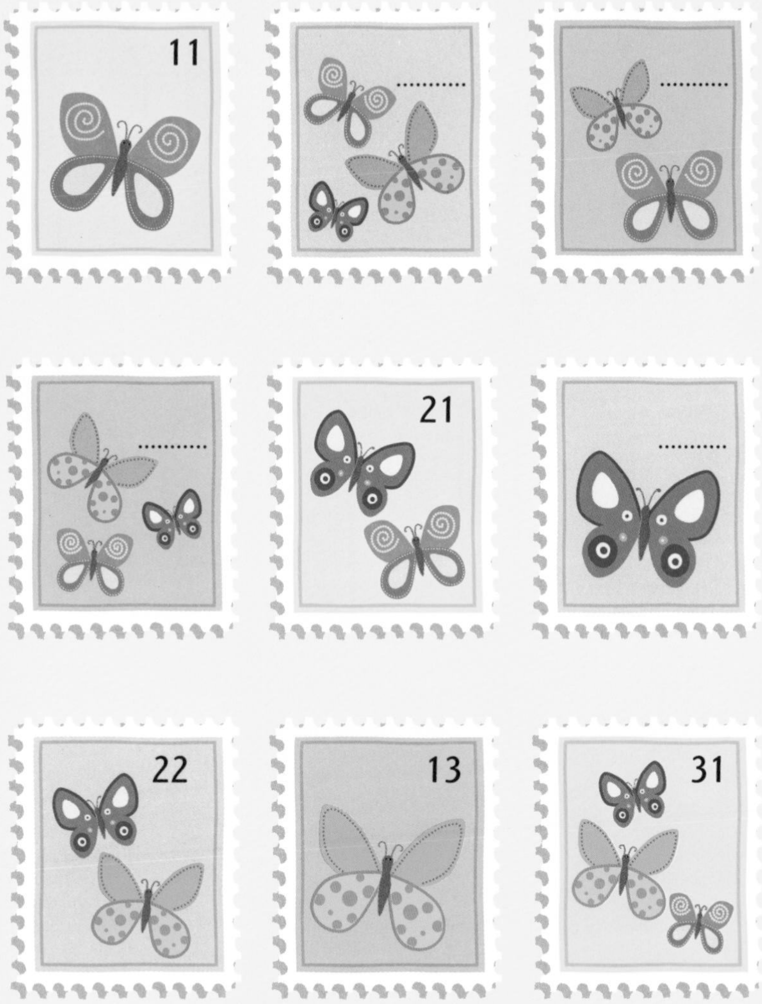

Prism picker

Which three shapes could fold up to make the hexagonal prism in the middle?

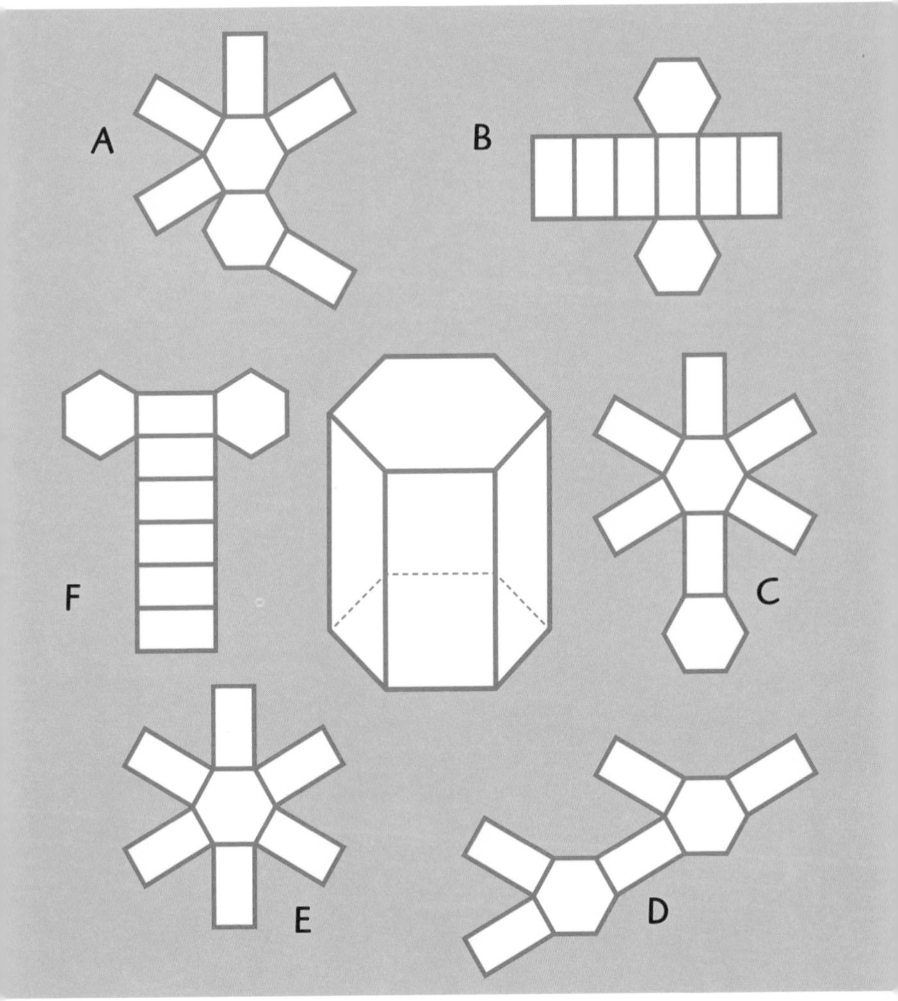

Answer: ....

41

Patchwork pattern

Discover the pattern that links the grids, then mark with an X the position of the orange square in grid 6.

1

2

3

4

5

6

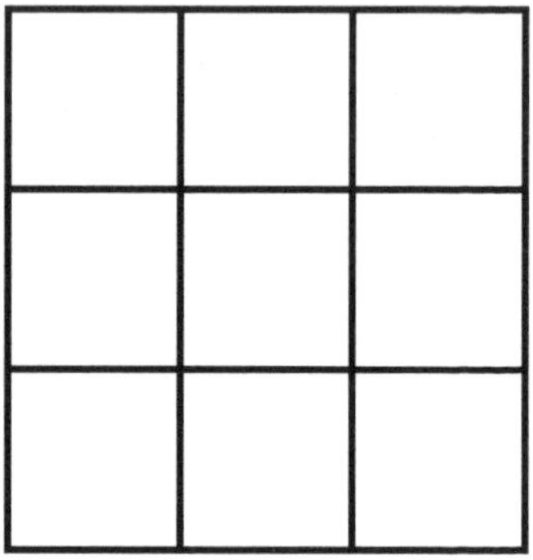

Murder mystery

Four friends are watching a murder mystery movie, set in the criminal underworld.

- Sam thinks the corrupt cop is the murderer.
- Anil is sure that the victim's wife did it.
- Dalia thinks it's either the gangster or the cop.
- Lou is certain that the murderer is the gangster.

If only one of the friends is right, which character is the murderer? Write your answer below.

Answer: ....

Cuckoo clock

If this clock takes two seconds to strike two o'clock, how long will it take to strike three o'clock?

Answer: ....

Shooting stars

Which two of these pictures can be rotated so they match each other exactly?

A

B

C

D

E

F

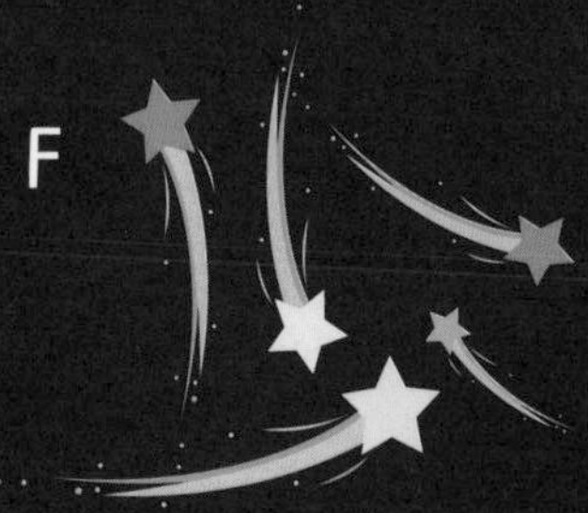

Answer: ....

Pencils and pens

Circle the item that is...

1. ...two to the left *of* the item that's six to the right *of* the item that's *one* to the left *of* the item that's four to the right *of* the item that's directly to the left *of* the black pen.

2. ...two to the left *of* the item that's six to the left *of* the item that's two to the right *of* the item that's three to the right *of* the item that's directly to the left *of* the blue pen?

1. Jesse rode in some time after another cowboy had been to buy a saddle.

2. Betsy carried her owner into town on Thursday.

3. Butch did not go to the dentist.

4. Billy owns Red Lady, and arrived later in the week than the cowboy who was collecting a debt.

5. Dusty was not ridden into town on Saturday.

You can use the chart below to keep track of the facts.

	Billy	Butch	Jesse	Dusty	Betsy	Red Lady	Debt	Dentist	Saddle
Thursday									
Friday									
Saturday									
Debt									
Dentist									
Saddle									
Dusty									
Betsy									
Red Lady									

Wild West

Three cowboys ride into Dodge City. Each cowboy arrives on a different day and has a different errand. Follow the clues on the opposite page to match the cowboy with their horse, and find out when each arrived and where they went. Fill in your answers on the chart below.

Day	Cowboy	Horse	Errand
Thursday			
Friday			
Saturday			

Cake gobbler

What comes next: A, B *or* C?

1

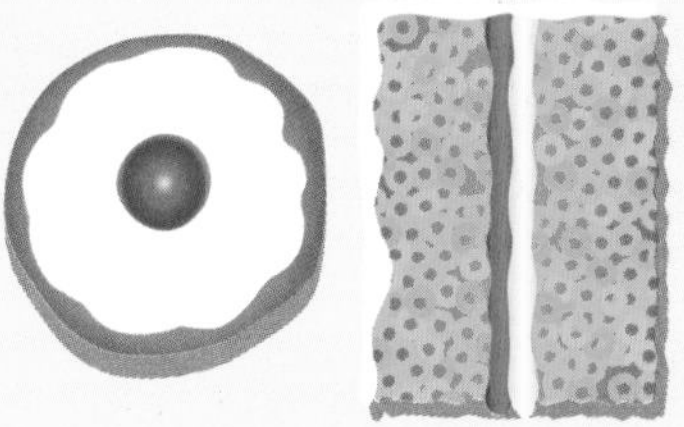

2

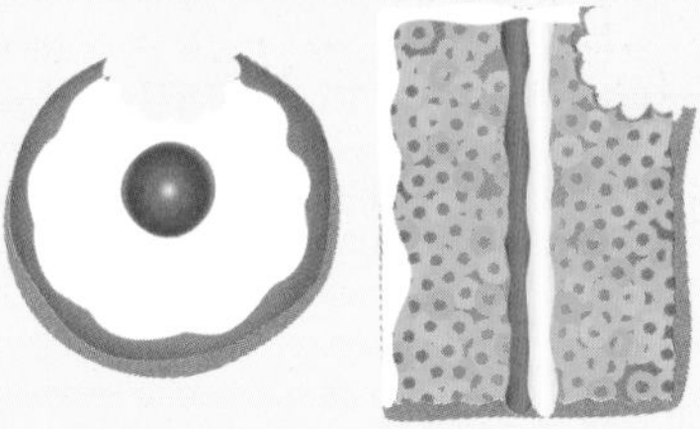

3

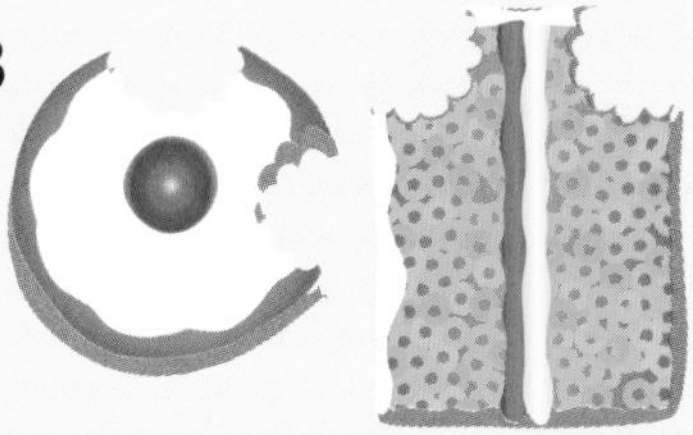

A

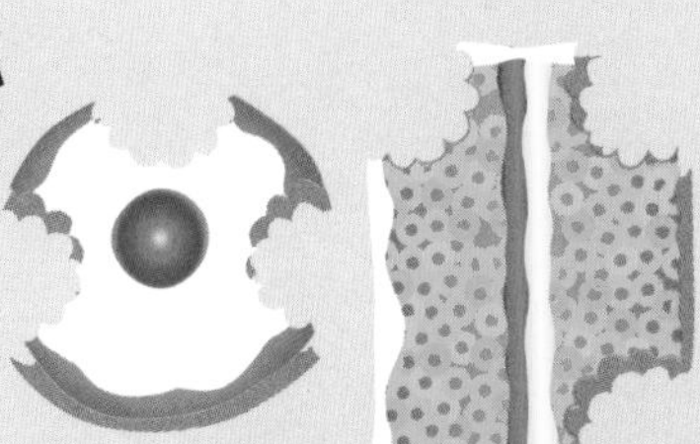

B

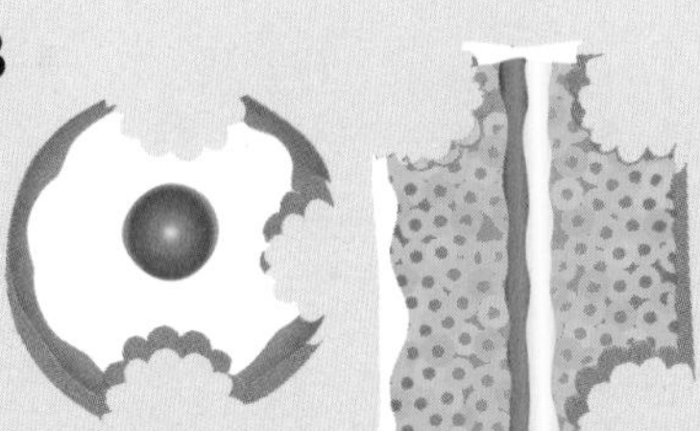

C

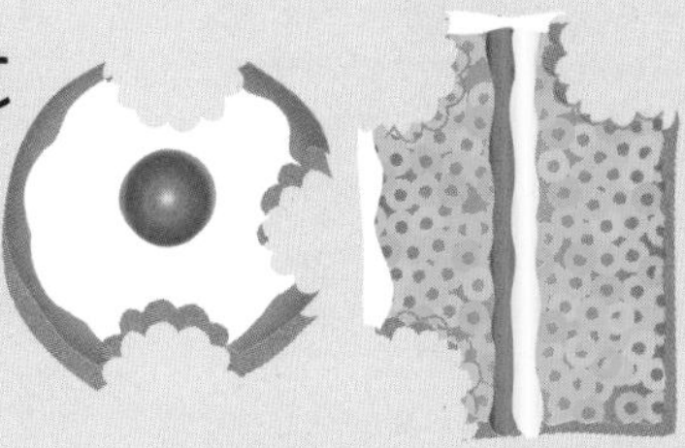

Detective school

Priya wants to be a detective, so her dad sets her a question to test her logic skills. She's given five statements and told only one of them is true. Which one?

CASE 3

A study in logic

1. Exactly one of these statements is false.

2. Exactly two of these statements are false.

3. Exactly three of these statements are false.

4. Exactly four of these statements are false.

5. Exactly five of these statements are false.

Block prints

If this block is turned on its side so the dotted lines are face down, which print will it make?

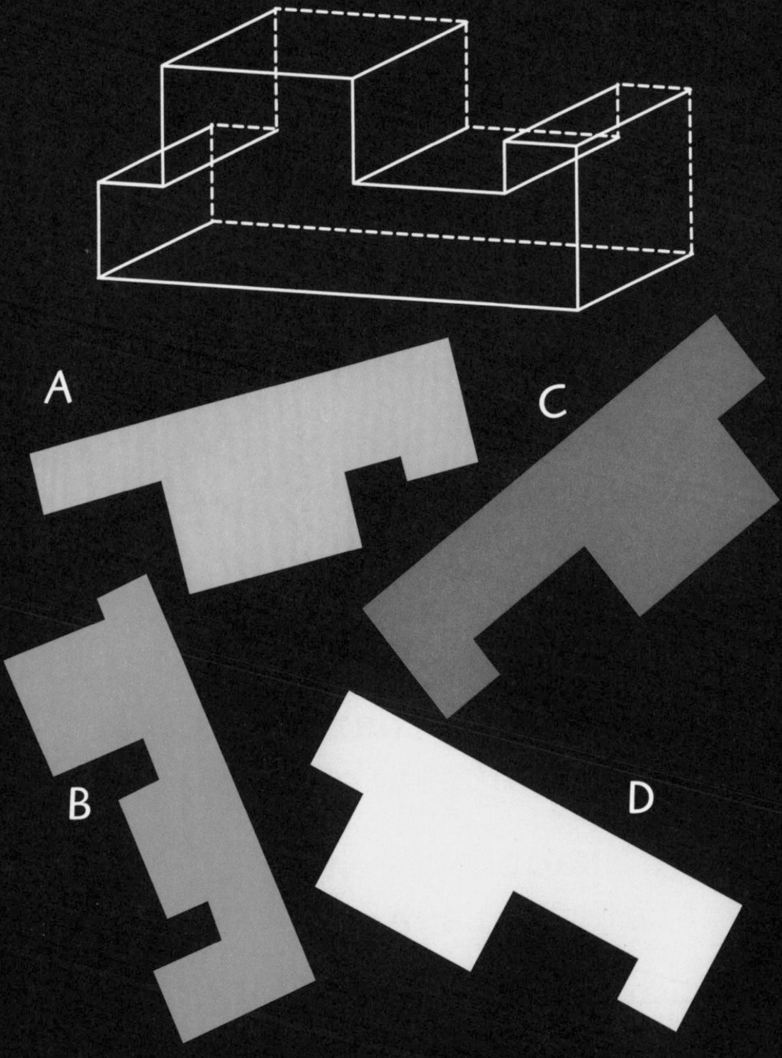

Hen names

Look carefully at the picture and match each hen to its name.

Henny .... Po .... Maisie ....

Meg .... Gina .... Eggwina ....

Fish in a bowl

Find out the relationship between the bowls in row 1, then use the same logic to discover which bowl completes row 2.

Row 1

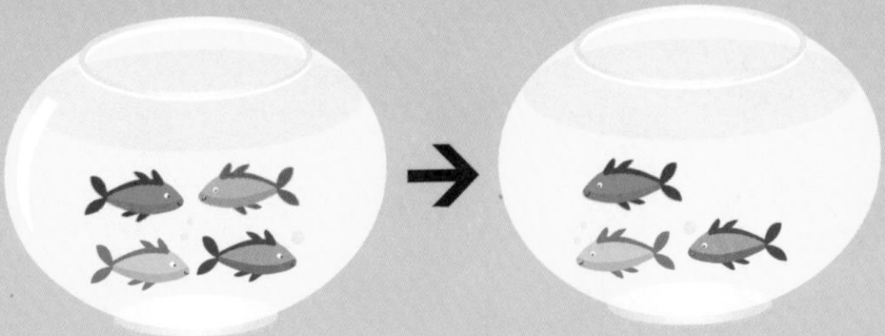

Row 2

Circle the right answer.

A

C

B

Follow the cogs

If the green cog at the top turns around to the right, which way will the red cog at the bottom turn? Use a pen to find out by tracing the movement of each cog.

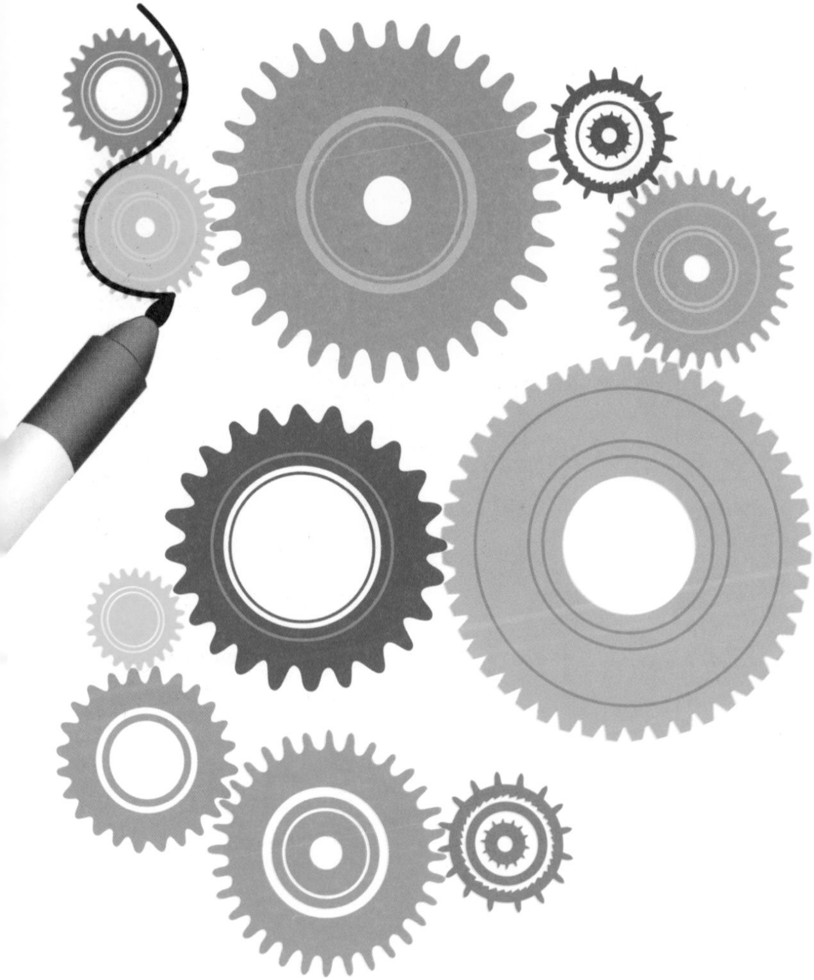

Answer: ....

Sequence challenge

Look at the sequence below, and find out what links each line with the one directly above. Then write the next line in the space provided.

A									
1	A								
1	1	1	A						
3	1	1	A						
1	3	2	1	1	A				
1	1	1	3	1	2	2	1	1	A

Answer: ....

28

Right rectangle

Find out the relationship between the rectangles in row 1, then use the same logic to discover which rectangle completes row 2.

Row 1

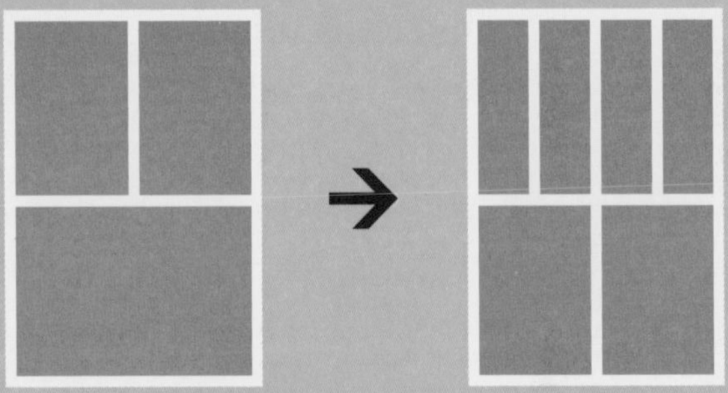

Row 2

Circle the right answer.

A

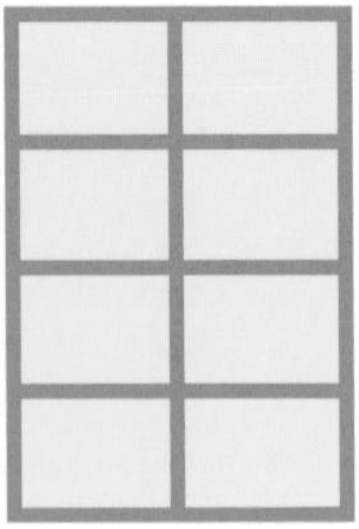

B

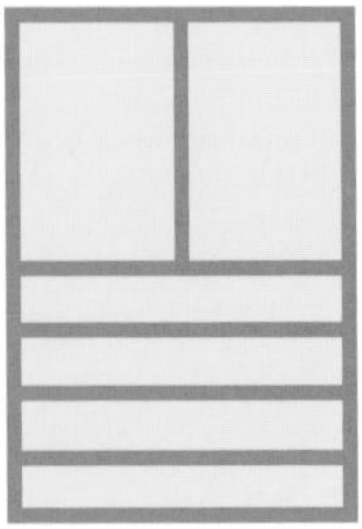

C

Genie's riddle

A sly genie is called from his lamp and says: "I will grant you three wishes, young master, but only if you answer my riddle. There are three rooms set before you, and you must enter one. The first is filled with raging fire, the second with bloodthirsty bandits, the third is filled with lions that haven't eaten in three years. Think carefully, my eager daredevil. Which room should you choose?"

Answer: ....

Not knots

Only one of these ropes would make a knot if you pulled both ends. Which one?

A

B

C

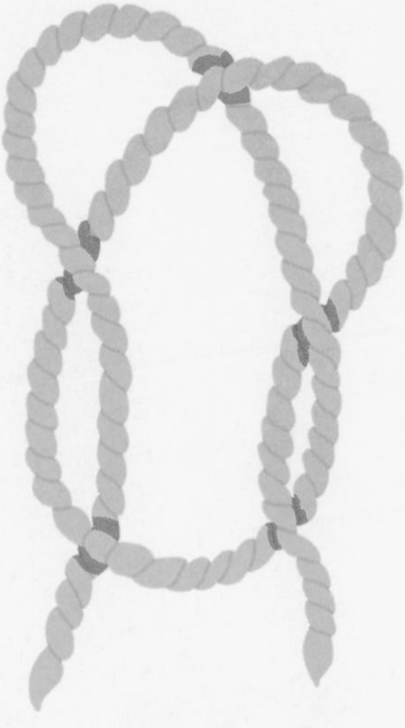

D

Mission to Mars

A rocket blasts off for Mars. By the end of its first week in space, the rocket has left the Earth far behind and is getting faster all the time. In fact, its distance from Earth doubles each week.

If the rocket reaches Mars in week 12, in which week was it halfway there?

a) week 2

b) week 6

c) week 11

Breakfast code

Each letter represents a different type of food. Find out what's what, then draw the right items on the empty plate.

A B

G H

I H

D G

A C

D F

A F

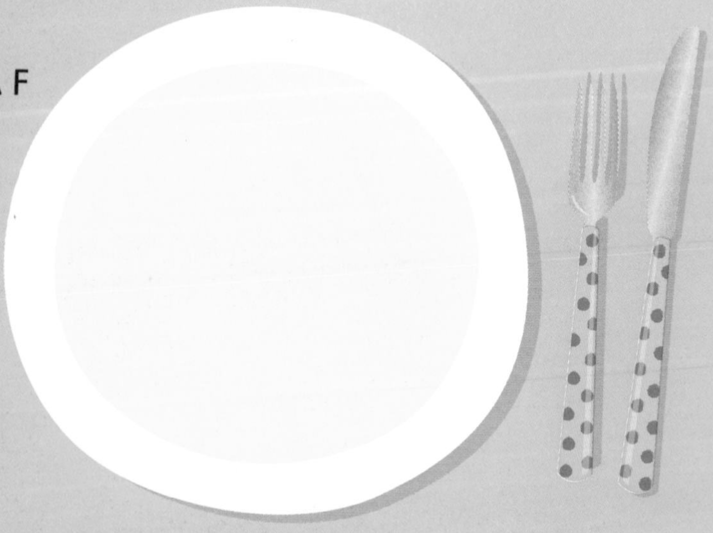

Bell ringer

To strike the bell, should you turn the handle around to the left or right?

Answer: ....

Sudoku

This grid is made up of nine blocks, each containing nine squares. Fill in the blank squares so that each block contains all the digits 1 to 9. Each digit can only appear once in a row, column or block.

		1	2		3	8		
	4			5			2	
5		7				1		6
4			7		1			5
	5			3			7	
3			5		2			9
2		6				7		3
	1			2			6	
		5	8		7	2		

Dots on dice

These four dice show all the numbers that are visible if you turn a dice around while keeping the '6' on top. Look at them carefully and fill in the dots on the net below.

Puzzle time

Which two clocks are the *odd ones out*?

18

Pencil puzzle

Using a pen, cross out six pencils to make ten.

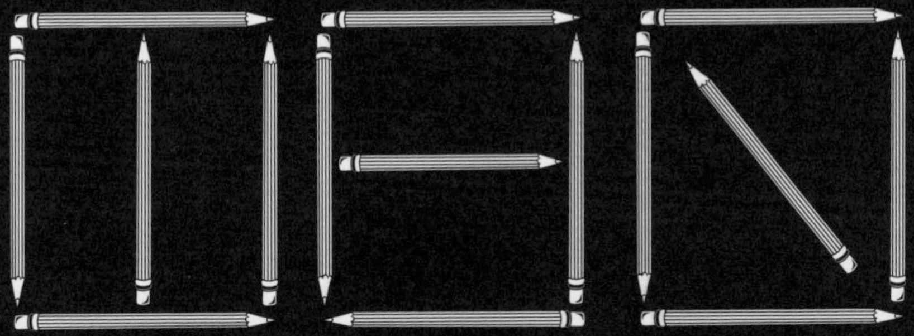

19

The wise son

A dying king wants to leave his kingdom to the wiser of his two sons. He takes them outside for a horse race, but tells them the son whose horse finishes LAST will inherit the realm. The younger son immediately jumps on a horse and rides it over the finish line at top speed. The king leaves him the kingdom. Why?

Dog toys

Three dog owners are playing with their dogs in the park, and each owner has brought a different toy. Follow the clues to find out who owns which dog, and which toy they are playing with. Draw a ✓ in the correct boxes for each person.

Clues:

1. Ali is not playing with the ball.

2. Riz does not own Rex.

3. The person who owns Jojo is playing with the ball.

4. Pat is playing with the bone.

5. The person who is playing with the stick does not own Spot.

	Jojo	Rex	Spot	Bone	Ball	Stick
Ali						
Pat						
Riz						

Odd pattern out

Which is the *odd one out*?

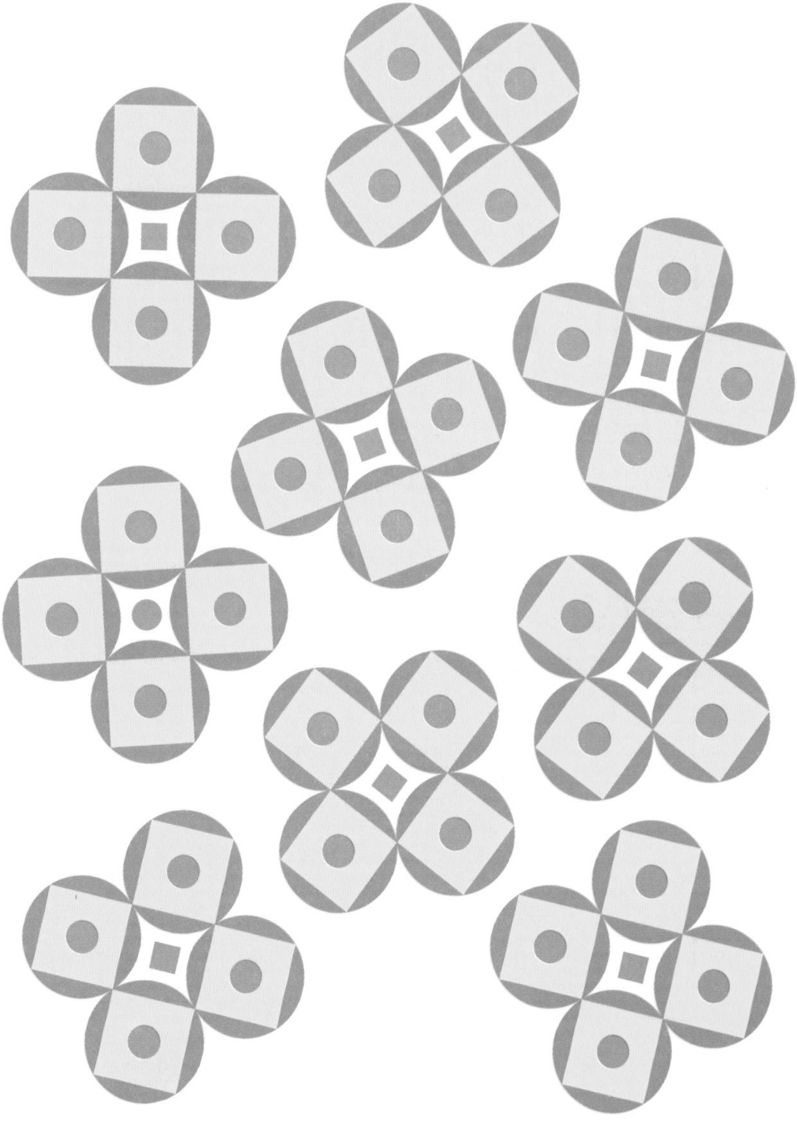

15

Fishy puzzle

Make a copy of this fish, but draw it pointing upwards rather than left, by moving just two of its lines into different positions. The first two lines have been done for you.

Which kitten?

When Joe's cat had kittens, his friends chose one each. There were four kittens:

- Sooty and Shadow were black with pink noses.
- Tiger and Rusty were orange with black noses.
- Sooty and Tiger were nervous.

- Zack didn't want a black kitten.
- Ellie wanted a kitten with a pink nose.
- Amy didn't want a kitten that was nervous.
- Rico had the kitten that neither Amy nor Zack wanted.

Fill in this chart with the name of each person's kitten.

Friend	Kitten
Zack	
Ellie	
Amy	
Rico	

13

Shapes and numbers

Each number is connected to the shape above it. Find out how, then write the missing number under the hexagon.

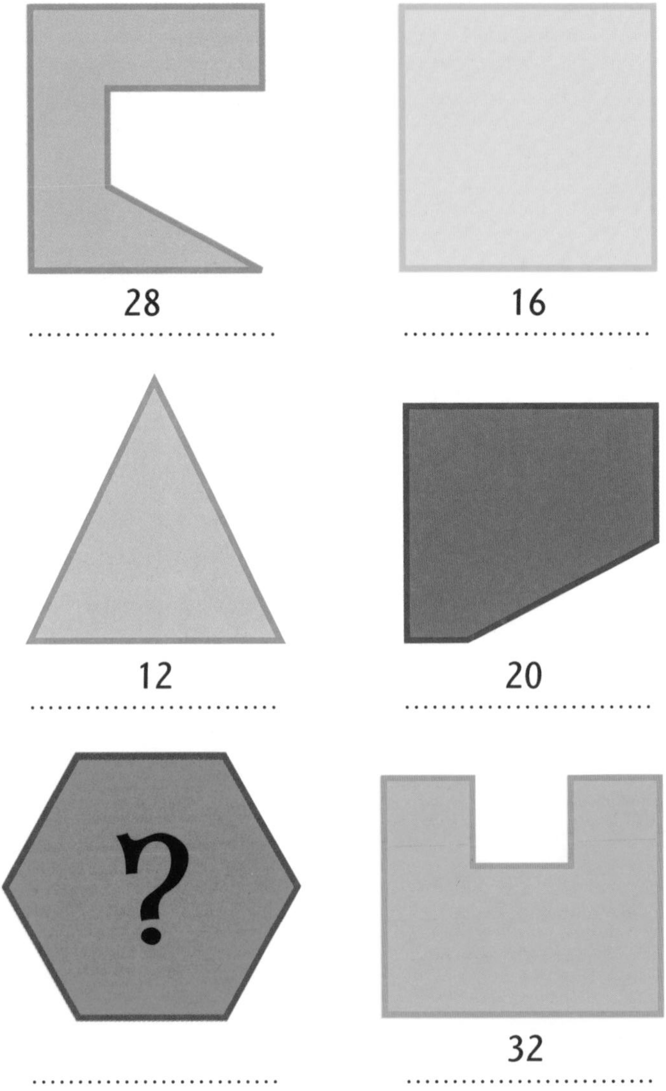

Pen puzzle

Draw this shape without lifting your pen from the page or going over any line that you've already made.

Racing positions

Five cars took part in a race.

- The purple car took third place.
- The yellow car came in before the purple car.
- The red car wasn't last, but it came after the yellow car.
- The green car wasn't first.
- The blue car came in before the yellow car.

Use this information to find out where each car finished and write their positions in the spaces below.

9

Bus driver riddle

A bus driver was heading down a street in Paris. He went past a stop sign without stopping. Then he turned left where there was a sign for 'NO LEFT TURN'. Finally, he went the wrong way down a one-way street. But after all this, no traffic laws had been broken. Why not?

Answer: ....

10

The jump

A girl jumped out of a 20 floor building, landed on her feet and walked away with no injuries. How?

Answer: ....

Who lives where?

There are three houses on this street. Two people live in each house. As you look at the houses...

- ...Mike lives directly to the right of Ray.
- ...Andy lives directly to the left of Mia.
- ...Mia lives directly to the left of Anna.
- ...Rose lives directly to the left of Mia.

Who lives where? Write each person's name under their house.

1...................... 2...................... 3......................

....

Dotty squares

Discover the pattern in the grid and draw the correct number of dots in the blank square.

KU-636-094

LALEH KHADIVI is the author of the Kurdish Trilogy. Her first novel, *The Age of Orphans*, received the Whiting Award for Fiction, the Barnes and Nobles Discover New Writers Award and an Emory Fiction Fellowship, and was followed by the acclaimed *The Walking*. She has also worked as a director, producer and cinematographer of documentary films, and her debut, *900 Women*, premiered at the Human Rights Watch Film Festival. Khadivi lives in northern California and teaches at the University of San Francisco.

A Good Country

Laleh Khadivi

BLOOMSBURY PUBLISHING
LONDON • OXFORD • NEW YORK • NEW DELHI • SYDNEY

BLOOMSBURY PUBLISHING
Bloomsbury Publishing Plc
50 Bedford Square, London, WC1B 3DP, UK

BLOOMSBURY, BLOOMSBURY PUBLISHING and the Diana logo are
trademarks of Bloomsbury Publishing Plc

First published in Great Britain 2017
This edition published 2018

Copyright © Laleh Khadivi, 2017

Laleh Khadivi has asserted her right under the Copyright, Designs
and Patents Act, 1988, to be identified as Author of this work.

Emoji art supplied by EmojiOne.com

This is a work of fiction. Names and characters are the product
of the author's imagination and any resemblance to actual persons, living
or dead, is entirely coincidental.

All rights reserved. No part of this publication may be reproduced or transmitted
in any form or by any means, electronic or mechanical, including photocopying,
recording, or any information storage or retrieval system, without prior permission
in writing from the publishers.

No responsibility for loss caused to any individual or organization acting
on or refraining from action as a result of the material in this publication can be
accepted by Bloomsbury or the author.

A catalogue record for this book is available from the British Library.

ISBN: HB: 978-1-4088-7599-5; TPB: 978-1-4088-7600-8; eBook: 978-1-4088-7601-5;
PB: 978-1-4088-7603-9

2 4 6 8 10 9 7 5 3 1

Typeset by Westchester Publishing Services
Printed and bound in Great Britain by CPI Group (UK) Ltd, Croydon CR0 4YY

FSC www.fsc.org MIX Paper from responsible sources FSC® C020471

To find out more about our authors and books visit www.bloomsbury.com and
sign up for our newsletters

Radical—radık(ə)l

Adj.
Relating to or affecting the fundamental nature of something; far-reaching or thorough

Chemistry
A **radical** (more precisely, a **free radical**) is an atom, molecule, or ion that has unpaired valence electrons. With some exceptions, these unpaired electrons make free radicals highly chemically reactive toward other substances, or even toward themselves

North American, colloquial
Very good, excellent, awesome or impressive

PART I

To Mexico

1

Laguna Beach, California, Fall 2011

THEY TOLD HIM it was the best, there was nothing better. After they started, at twelve and thirteen and fourteen, his friends tried to convince him to try it. *Rez, dude,* they'd say, *it's no big deal. You don't puke. You don't pass out. No one can even tell. It's like daydreaming, like that second just before you fall asleep, but for hours,* they said, for the whole of eighth grade, their eyes glazed with the shine of the newly converted, and by tenth grade they gave up and now, start of junior year, it was habit to make fun of him every time there was occasion, every time they circled up to light and puff and smoke, these friends.

If he wanted, it could have happened last night, or even two weeks ago when Johnson's parents were in L.A. at an industry party and Johnson opened his house to anyone with a six-pack or a girl or a bag of weed. At midnight Rez found them in the laundry room, empty beer bottles and half-smoked cigarettes all over the place, and he sat and drank and talked like everyone else. When it was finally rolled and passed, Rez stood up right before his turn.

I gotta piss, and walked out of the circle.

Bullshit, coughed Johnson, the smoke coming out of his mouth in big clouds.

We all know you can't hang, Rez. Never have. Never will. Those Persians keep a tight leash on their kids . . .

He felt a few laughs at his back but kept going, out of the laundry room, down the hallway, out of the house, and into the backyard, where kids rolled around on the perfect grass, swam half naked in the pool, and ran hand in hand to dark corners. He found a spot by the fence, beside the empty dog crates and gardening tools, and let go, his heart one big pump and burst, pump and burst, as the piss rushed out of him in a long furious stream.

*

He didn't know what he was afraid of. It wasn't like with the girls, a want and a want and a want until everything centered in his crotch and he moved forward without thought, without fear. No, this was different. He wanted it, to be inside the circle, to stay and smoke and laugh and feel whatever it was that was so good, but he couldn't stand the complete unknown. What if I lose it? What if I black out? What if I start crying? What if I get addicted? How much trouble will I be in if Dad finds out? All the trouble. I'll be in all the trouble.

In the dark yard he felt his father about him, a thick outline traced atop his own body. He looked around, shook himself dry, zipped up, and walked back to the house. He moved from room to room, looking, thinking, and tried to bring himself to do all that was being done by the kids in his grade and the sophomores and juniors and seniors above him, and the more he saw, the more he wanted to go home. A girl from chemistry lab caught his arm and pulled him into a doorway and then into a room of people, who saw him and yelled, *Yeah! Rez! Dare! Dare! Dare!* And he drank vodka straight from the bottle up to the count of ten and then stuck his head and hands up Sophia Lim's shirt to feel the smooth mounds and tiny buttons of nipples and wanted badly to suck but did not. When it was over and everyone clapped and yelled and Sophia turned away and tucked in her shirt, Rez walked quickly back outside and threw up in a planter of cacti. He lay down on a lawn chair, shivered, and spat the sour out of his mouth and counted the nine stars above him again and again, until Matthews showed up and said it was time.

Let's go home, man. I'm through with this.

They left without saying good-bye and found Kelly passed out in the back of the Matthewses' SUV, his hoodie backward on his head, face covered, arms crossed like a kind of corpse.

Dude. Get up. This isn't a hotel.

Matthews poked him and pulled the hoodie down and poked him again until Kelly sat up, yawned, and made a face at Rez.

Puked again? Ah, puking. How come the smartest kid in the class is always the stupidest kid at parties? If you would only smoke a little weed, you could keep your liquor down, didn't anyone ever tell you that? My dad told me all about it.

Kelly rambled on and Rez looked out the window and Matthews drove and after a time no one said anything. There was nothing to say, the night had come and gone and Rez still hadn't done it, but he knew he'd have to, soon, if he wanted things to stay as they were. If he wanted things to get better.

Last night at the beach wasn't it either.

The bonfire wouldn't catch and some guys from Santa Ana set up just down the sand and gave them shit.

Hey, faggots! Who's got the tightest pants over there?

Does your mommy know you're out so late?

They ignored the voices and kept trying their fire, and then an older voice shouted from the dark.

No way. No, man, his mommy don't know he's out here 'cause she's at home fucking my brother, her gardener, right now!

Man and *Oh, man* and *That's fucked up* and laughter surrounded them, and Johnson rolled the joint faster, and when it was lit, Matthews took his long deep puff and they passed it fast and smoked fast and again Rez shook his head no.

I'm good.

They left him alone and he worried about the fight coming and the black, gray, brown marks on his face from the guys in the dark and how would he explain that to his father, who would add to it, or take away from it, by calling him a girl or who knows what else? He didn't want his first time to be high and hurting, high and fighting and he waited for his friends to finish their smoke, but they didn't get a chance because the voices came out from the dark again.

Your mommy sure does take a long time, and with a Mexican too!

She must like it. That OC pussy needs a trim!

Rez looked at the eyes of his friends, Peter Matthews, James Johnson, and John Kelly, names of the Bible, apostles, each a right-hand man to Jesus, and he saw them now as one. Hunched over the smoky fireless fire, their shoulder blades spiking up through their thin T-shirts as they sucked at the joint and took the taunts. When it was done, everyone stood up and kicked sand over the two steaming logs that

never caught, and the voices from the darkness stepped in, took the shapes of faces and bodies and walked around them, smiles shining through the murk.

It's cool. It's cool, my brother is done with your moms.

You can go home now.

Don't look so scared!

We ain't gonna waste time with you shrimps anyway.

Yeah, man, stupider than hitting a girl.

The apostles shouted all the way home. High and angry, they were a single voice bellowing through the truck. *My brother knows a guy from Huntington, a senior, skinhead . . . he would fuck them up for sure. Laughton knows how to get a crew together, football guys, they did it once when one of the Asian gangs gave them shit at South Coast,* and on and on with *dude* and *bro* and *fuck 'em* and *wetbacks* until Rez's ears were full and his heart and gut clean with fear. Matthews, who normally drove like the sixteen-year-old stoner with a learner's permit that he was, now sped like an idiot down the 1 and the wide streets of Dana Point. Rez opened the window and let the fast wind hit his face and watched the streets and houses and yards pass by, all asleep, no witness to their aimless rage.

It was going to be today. Not because someone had an open house or there was a party or a girl he wanted to impress, but because everything had come into alignment and finally he didn't care. The recklessness was in him now and it made no difference if he puked, if he said stupid shit, if he got in trouble or addicted and spent the rest of his life begging on the street corner, a shame to his family, he was over it.

The midterm grades were e-mailed that afternoon and Rez forgot. He took the bus home and skated to his door and found his father, at three thirty, on the front steps of the house, a thin piece of paper in his hands, tie loose, eyebrows pushed together. Rez felt his stomach jump and he kicked the skateboard into his hand and dropped his head and ran through the classes. Math. Chemistry. Physics. English. Spanish.

Government. Logic. History, it was history; it had to be history and the quiz on the first Iraq war the night after the bonfire. He took the quiz without studying and thought his GPA would cover it, but now his father was on the steps, which meant a B was printed on that paper and the ceremony would begin.

It started the same way it always started. His father silent and Rez silent and then the first question.

Do you like your life?

Rez knew there was only one right answer.

Yes.

You have enough to eat? Good clothes to wear? A nice school to go to?

Yes, Dad, I forgot the quiz was that day.

It is not important. What is important is that you like your life. You are taken care of. Am I correct?

Rez said nothing, in the script he was to remain silent, and silence was the safest bet, the fastest route to the end. He nodded his head in agreement.

Good. Then I have done my job. And yet you have not done yours.

His father went on, his face set in anger, his mouth opening and closing around the words *ungrateful, punishment, worthless, pathetic, loser,* until Rez swallowed the sobs that came up his throat and tried to blink away tears filling his eyes. The rough sandpaper on his skateboard rubbed against his fingers and he thought of the apostles and how they would laugh if they saw him now, crying, and so he stopped and wiped his face and began to shout.

What did I do? Tell me what I did wrong! I didn't do anything wrong. I got a fucking B. That's all!

His father, surprised but not alarmed, closed his eyes and shook his head.

A disrespect. Your laziness is a disrespect to me, to your mother, to everything I have done for this family.

Rez heard the words, but this time they did not make it all the way down to his heart. He stepped outside himself and saw a boy, nearly as tall as his father, a father, a tyrant without cause, a mass of dark and aimless energy. He saw the boy in a bright light, innocent and right,

and the father, misguided and dim, his only power humiliation. Rez kept shouting until his mother came to the kitchen window, until the squeaky eager yells of an eleventh grader came out, until he was shaking with the words *Fuck you* and *I hate you* and *You are an asshole,* so loudly and with such fury he could not pull back the new bold spirit fast enough, could not push himself back into the body of the boy in time to move out of the line of slaps that sprang from his father's palm onto his soft waiting face.

He skated the two miles to Matthews's house, some of it crying, some of it running. Matthews and Johnson played Xbox and said *What's up?* but didn't look at him. Rez didn't say anything and waited and finally Johnson looked up.

What the fuck, man? You look like a bitch that's just been dumped. Your face is all puffy.

Rez tried to swallow and put his hands in his pockets to keep them from shaking.

Whatever, man. Wanna go to the cove?

They stared at him for a moment and then another moment and Matthews threw his controller on the couch.

Yeah, let's do it. The cove. Today's a good day for the cove.

They picked up Kelly, and when they got to the cove, they walked around it and cleaned up the trash before saying one word. It was an old habit, a leftover from their elementary school beach-cleaning field trips. When Johnson's backpack was filled with pulped cigarette cartons, chip bags, used condoms, and spent lighters, they sat down in a circle. Cool clouds came in from the west, low and to the water, and a damp, icy breeze filled the shallow cove. Rez lifted his face to meet it, to let it press all over the hot prints in the shape of his father's fast hands.

One person pulled out a baggie and the other had the papers and the other had a Zippo and each of them had already done it a dozen times or more and Rez squinted into the cool wind and waited his turn. The joint came by lumpy and crooked and he held it between his fingers and then between his lips and all he felt was fuck. I don't give a fuck. Fuck him. He remembered not to breathe too deep. He didn't want to

choke and didn't want them to laugh. But it was smooth. Smoother than he could understand, and the cold came in with it and he exhaled into the crossed legs of his lap. The apostles looked at him and he nodded without a cough and they smiled one big friend smile.

Yeah, dude. Yeah.

He sat up straight, stretched his back, realigned into another person in another life, and grinned.

Yeah. Totally.

2

The rumors gave him courage. *Dude, that chick Sophia is totally hot for you.* And *Bro, you must tap that ass right away.* Rez laughed but he also looked at her, in class or walking down the hallway, talking to her friends. He always pretended he was looking at something else, someone else, and she always stared back and smiled. He did nothing, and then one morning in chemistry his lab partner, Lila, asked if she could give Sophia Lim his phone number.

What for?

Lila stared at him through her plastic protective eyewear, her eyes big and brown and already laughing.

You know what for.

By the afternoon he had a text.

Hey Rez, this is Sophia. Wanna go to the vista after school? I've got a car.

He read the text ten times as if the sentence were Sophia herself, spread out in front of him, naked, rubbing her nipples and sucking on a red lollipop. That was how it was on the porn he watched, like that and some other ways, any way really, but always and only on the computer. In life he had seen little. A few girls with their shirts off, bikinis he took off in his mind, his mother once in the shower when he rushed to tell her he was a finalist in a statewide chess championship. The possibility of Sophia, her body naked in his hands, pushed through him with such boldness that Rez couldn't think or see or hear for the rest of the day.

Yeah. That sounds cool. I'm down.

They drove the steep and windy roads up to the vista and didn't talk. They listened to Lady Gaga. *Girl pop* the apostles called it and Rez couldn't stand it but didn't say anything because he was too busy

watching her dance as she drove, little shoulder shakes when the beat got faster, and head moves as the music slowed. Her hair was long and black and soft and rolled down her back all the way to her butt. He let himself stare and he let himself wonder: Who is this girl? She was in tenth grade, they had never spoken and had none of the same friends. There was the time at Johnson's party but Rez could not remember it clearly and knew only that it involved vodka and puking, but that couldn't be enough for this invitation, for this ride. He rolled the window down and saw his reflection in the rearview mirror, an eleventh grader with buzzed light brown hair, a square jaw, and green eyes. He once heard one of Matthews's brother's girlfriends say Rez was going to be good-looking when he grew up, but she was a fat girl and most days he still felt like a kid.

They parked in the empty dirt lot between million-dollar homes. The view looked straight down the Laguna cliffs over the expensive beach shacks and Highway 1 and out to the Pacific. The ocean seemed huge from here, as far as you could see, the line of the horizon broken by a few small boats and the shape of Catalina. She turned off the car and snapped down the sun visor, checked her hair, and, satisfied, searched the compartment in her door. She handed him a delicate box of thin wood with elephants painted on it.

Can you roll?

Inside was a small plastic canister of crumbled weed, some papers, and a lighter, all organized in their own sections.

Is this how girls carry their weed?

She laughed.

Plastic baggies are for drug dealers.

He started to roll and she turned back to the mirror and opened her lips to reapply a layer of thick glossy pink lipstick, then she shook her hair out a little bit and looked at him, her whole face, the lips, the eyes, the hair, twinkling somehow.

For the first time since the rumors started Rez didn't look away. He stared at the endless black hair and white skin and the black eyes that turned up with a seductive delight. Her face, her voice, her name,

everything about her was something else, different. She was not familiar like his mother and like the porn he watched but couldn't touch, and as this made him sit back, made the desire center in him, he rolled faster. When it was finished, she took the joint from his hand and the lighter from the box and wrapped her perfect lips around the paper and sucked in the flame slowly. She inhaled and laughed and coughed and smiled and her hair was everywhere and her eyes shone and Rez wanted to jump inside her.

What they did was as much as he'd ever done and it was clear she had done more. She pushed his chair back and slid down in between his legs and took him between her glossy lips and into her warm mouth and Rez felt the world end. His muscles turned to water and his mind evaporated and he was sure it was death, a kind of slow, soft death, and that was all right. He was high and every touch, every lick, opened him up and brought him forth. It had never been like this, not with the porn that jolted and pressured and drew him out in a tense awkward way, not with the few girls in closets and on floors at parties. It may never be like this again, so why live? When she stopped to look up at him with her dark eyes and her open pink mouth, he wanted to push himself in to keep the rhythm going and fuck her mouth the way he had seen it done, but she was in control and she started again and he died again and after a time he let go and came like the happy accidents of his dreams.

Finished, he had nothing to say and she smiled at him and zipped his pants and put herself in the driver's seat, where she took little sips from her water bottle and then fixed her hair and added more lip gloss. She started the car and looked at him with a mischievous smile.

How was that?

Nice. Thanks.

Good.

She drove him to the gates of his neighborhood and he wanted to hop out quick, before his mother or father might see, and she gave him the smile, coy pink lips spread across perfect teeth.

Maybe we can hang out again? I don't have class seventh period.

Yeah. Totally. I'm down.

He walked home and felt himself get hard as he thought about Sophia Lim, and her body, and that she was a bad student with bad

grades and her father was known for gambling in Las Vegas every weekend and gave huge donations to the school every year and they lived in an enormous mansion in Costa Mesa, and even though she was only in tenth grade, she had her own car and it was new. She was a cheerleader. Rez remembered when it was her turn in history, she told Mrs. Heinz her grandparents came to America from Vietnam on a boat with no engine, and Mrs. Heinz said that is impossible and Sophia told her to read her history.

3

He was late for dinner. Not just once, but all the time now. Rez opened the door and found them as they always were at this time of day, around the long teak table—mother, father—Meena and Saladin, in a room with three walls of fine art and one sliding glass door that led to a pool, the water still and steel blue to match the California dusk. Food was set, a meal Rez had eaten all his life, fried eggplant in a stew of onions and tomatoes and beef, buttered rice, fresh greens and radishes. There were the glasses of water, the same knives and forks and spoons as yesterday, the flower piece a bit more dead. None touched their food, none moved, and his father sat at the head of the table, typed into his phone, and said nothing when Rez took his seat. After a few minutes his father put the phone down, lifted and dropped his napkin, and sighed.

Someone has to pay for all this.

Then his father reached for the rice and piled on the stew and ate without talking or looking up. Without appetite Rez watched his mother take her turn and then he scooped the rice onto his plate and then the stew on top and stared at the mound and thought, I have eaten this food, this same stew, these same grains of rice, my whole life. This is the oldest food in the world, and his parents ate it and his parents' parents, and since it was a dish from Iran, maybe the first Iranians, thousands of years ago, ate it too. Rez thought about the apostles and wondered if they ate food from the beginning of time, and what was the beginning of their time? Where did the time of their families start? Ireland? Germany? France? Some mix of all those things that gave them no one old food, no long straight line, no place? Rez had heard his father boast of it. Their place, their line of men and warriors that stretched all the way back to an old village in the oldest mountains. Now Rez sat, stoned out of his mind, at the end of that line, at the teak table and listened to his family chew and sip and swallow and he thought, What does it matter? We are

all animals anyway. He remembered a picture from psych class, a group of chimpanzees sitting around the table, naked, hairy, crouched over and reaching for the dishes with their long ropy arms.

Where is your appetite?

Generally his mother said nothing at dinner. Rez looked at her and she smiled. She knew. How could she know? It was a mistake to smoke so late into the afternoon. He knew it was a bad idea, but when he skipped soccer practice to meet Sophia at Johnson's pool house, he thought about the sex they would have and nothing else. When Sophia showed up and lit the joint, he was still only thinking about sex, and when he got stoned and fucked her, he wasn't thinking about anything, just feeling and being felt and doing with his hands and mouth and tongue what was good. After she left, Rez and Johnson took a swim and Johnson teased him.

I don't think I've ever seen a half-Vietnamese, half-Persian baby before. Have you?

Whatever, dude. It's casual.

Yeah, casual until her father hears about you.

Rez thought about her father and then thought about his own father and then remembered he was late for dinner. He dried and dressed quickly and let Johnson put the Visine drops in because it freaked Rez out to do it and skated home and told himself he was fine, it was wearing off and no one could tell and it was just dinner and then he could say he had a lot of homework and go to his room. He walked into the house and walked straight to the table and sat down and tried not make a big deal but he had never been stoned in his own home and this was not going to be a happy high.

His father looked at Rez and Rez watched as he took a long time to finish his bite, his glasses moving up and down on the bridge of his nose as he chewed, his beard working like a separate animal beneath them. Rez wanted to laugh and tried not to think about the chimpanzees, their jaws chewing in circles, their bony fingers and yellow teeth.

How was soccer practice today?

That was the life his father and mother thought he lived. Chess club from seven thirty to eight fifteen. School. Varsity soccer at three thirty and then home by six. A healthy well-rounded day, nothing of

the distractions that led to the embarrassment of his grade in history a few months ago, nothing of friends or girls. Rez kept his grades high, and when he went to wake and bake with Matthews, Rez finished the chess sets on his phone and sent them in to the teacher in an e-mail. He went to every other soccer practice, showing the coach a forged note about extra hours in chemistry lab. The schedule was, for the first time, his own and everyone left him alone.

Soccer was fine.

And you are not hungry after that running? Are you sick?

The apostles were always talking about hunger, the way weed made them go in search of nachos and ice cream and how they would walk three miles just to eat at Jack in the Box, but Rez never felt it. He smoked and it settled him and the sensation of food, its temperature and textures and smell was too much, disgusting.

No. I ate before. I skipped lunch to study for my math midterm and then ate after school.

He was surprised at the lie, how cleanly it came from him and how much sense it made. His father nodded in approval and dropped his focus back to his plate.

Let's try to get back on schedule tomorrow. It is not good to waste your mother's food. Meena, leave a plate for him in the oven in case he gets hungry later.

He'll be hungry later.

He picked up his spoon and began to eat and wished for his father to ignore him so he could leave the table and sit in his room. The sounds of the knives and forks against the plates went on around him and the time of the dinner passed slowly and Rez did his best to eat and listen to the little talk between his mother and father but could not concentrate because his mind returned to the afternoon and how he had just fucked and smoked and his family, who had known everything about him all his life, knew nothing of him in this moment. They must be full of secrets too. He was sure of it. His powerful father and his silent, dutiful mother. He was certain they left behind empires of lies to come and sit at this dinner table every night and say nothing. Now he had joined them and he let his mouth fill with rice and his mind fill with Sophia Lim and fucking a few hours ago, three times in a pool house, her thin white

body under his and over his and in front of his, and that he had put a finger in her for the first time and that felt like nothing he had ever felt before and how is it that people aren't always fucking? He tried not to look at his mother and father, who had fucked to make him, tried not to think of that, but with all the not and the don't and the looks away, the images only came at him more sharply, razors on his mind until there was nothing left to do. He took the napkin off his lap and stood up.

Thanks, Mom. But I don't feel great. I think I am going to go lie down.

He pushed the chair back from the table. His father caught his arm.

Reza, your face is flush. Meena, go take his temperature, see if we need to call the doctor.

I am ok. Just tired.

They all looked back at him and Rez looked at his reflection in the glass doors that led out to the pool, dark now, and saw an image he had not seen before, his own face, a boy, almost a man, tired, conniving.

4

Laguna Beach, Winter 2012

AT FIRST ONLY the kids with dads or uncles that followed the newspapers and weather channels talked about it. They spoke in a secret jargon that made it *their* news, information for the initiated: code. From the southwest, off the Tahitian shelf, two-minute-long breaks. Double head high! Everyone else just watched it rain and thought: rain. Rain like every winter there was rain, gray and slightly warm and brief. Just enough to wash down a few unsupported slopes and fill the terra-cotta fountain in the backyard. For a few months every year the air became water and the ocean ate up the land. The beaches were covered in sea litter, exoskeletons, long hoses of kelp and faded plastic containers with foreign writing. Rez's mother refused to drive the low stretches of Highway 1 for fear the ocean would, in an instant, flood the road.

What kind of people live so close to the sea? she asked, and then shook her head at the madness battering the shore.

Cool people, Rez muttered as the windshield wipers kept the beat and they waited to cross the rush of sewer water that poured out in front of them.

Last year the rain came and went and Rez didn't know anything about a swell. He hadn't yet surfed and went to the beach like a little kid goes to the beach, with a picnic of chips and grapes, a shovel and a love of jumping in waves. If his little cousins came, he'd build sand castles with them and his aunt would laugh at him. Aren't you too old for that? He liked the water but never swam out past the break, never in the open ocean away from whitewash, never out past where his toes did not easily reach the sand.

This year he was different. A junior at Laguna Prep. He smoked and had been with Sophia more times than he could count and the kids at school were different with him. More people talked to him. Not just the apostles

or the kids in chess club, but other kids, boys who let their hair grow as long as was allowed, who wore caps as soon as they were outside, the juniors and seniors with orange-brown skin from days and days of salt and sun. They looked like kids from commercials; guys from the billboards up and down Highway 1 that showed life as if lived entirely on waves and mountainsides, with hot girls, half naked and wanting.

His father saw a group of them greet Rez through the windshield of the car at carpool one morning. Peace signs and nods and their hair still wet from surfing before school.

Those boys.

His father shook his head.

They will wake up twenty years from now, part-time jobs, divorced, living in shitty apartments, alcoholics, or worse. But now, hey, now life is good. What a waste.

Rez said nothing to his father, but when the guys looked Rez in the eye in the halls and said *What's up?* he said *S'up?* back and pretended it was nothing. He watched them in the courtyard at lunch and during class, where they seemed bored out of their minds, silly with energy that kept them tapping their feet and twitching their pens and laughing at nothing, in some antic state waiting, waiting, waiting for the bell to ring so they could explode onto wheels or water and just be. He saw them in the parking lot too, gathered around their old trucks, hardcore and Beastie Boys playing out just so loud as to keep them from getting a demerit, their blazers tossed onto the ground, their striped school neckties wrapped around their heads like skinny bandannas, shouting back and forth about the swell and what spot they were going to, some girl or two or three, sitting on the hoods or bumper, laughing. He saw them and listened to them and this year he knew that it wasn't enough to smoke or have sex, but to be like that, to be easy and always happy, he had to surf too and so one afternoon he found Matthews and tried out the new tongue.

Let's go to Old Man's. The swell is right.

Matthews didn't say what Rez thought he was going to say, which was *Fool, you don't even know how*. Or *what are you going to do out there? Swim?* No, Matthews looked at him, smiled.

Dope. Killer swell. My brother told me about it. Let's roll.

In an hour they had Kelly and Johnson and without Rez's asking someone lent him a spring wet suit and someone else a longboard and they didn't take him to Old Man's but to a shallow inlet by the Dana Point harbor, a sewage-filled learners' spot none of them had come to since they were four or five. They gave no instructions, just let him paddle, push up, balance, and try to ride. He fell every time but the apostles did not laugh. They waited for him to paddle back to them and one would say *Wait a few extra seconds* or *Paddle harder* or *Push up faster* and Rez would nod and they'd all just sit there and stare at the sea and wait for the next *set*, which was a word Rez didn't know that morning, but understood before he fell asleep that night.

Now he knew all the words. *Swell. Face. Tube. Sucked. Wall. Ripped. Grom. Wash. Turtle.* And this year when the rains came, he was as excited as the rest of them. Girls. Books. Movies. Video games. Nothing came close to the feeling before doing it, the lead in the pit of your stomach and the butterflies in your chest and then the feeling of a wave, the wave that had rolled over thousands of miles of ocean to push you fast fast fast toward land, so fast his hair nearly dried once. And then there was the feeling afterward, the salt caked onto his skin; the tired, blessed state. Hunger and exhaustion. His body understood what was right, fast, dangerous, and safe and his boards got shorter and his friends took him to beaches he'd never heard of, beaches without parking lots, beaches you couldn't even see from the road. He started to care about conditions and the weather because a storm meant a swell and a swell meant epic surf and epic surf meant a hero could grow from your skin.

5

Gonna be epic. So epic. El Niño strikes again.

They were taking rips at Kelly's house, just the two of them passing the bong back and forth, packing it full of herb and passing it back and forth again. The smoke filled the glass tube in a massive way, and when they exhaled, a proper cloud lingered in the air for longer than anyone would have thought. They sat under a yellow-and-black-striped awning and watched it rain into the pool. Kelly lived with his mom and dad and sisters in a huge ranch house in Laguna Niguel. There were horses in a stable and an actual grove of orange trees. The family used to own most of the county, at least that is what Matthews said, and then *they went military.* His dad was a colonel at Pendleton and had been to Afghanistan and Iraq. His brother was at MIT, studying engineering, and his sisters looked like Barbie. Rez liked to walk around the immaculate house and pause at the layers of framed photographs on every polished surface: trips to Washington, handshakes with the first Bush, handshakes with the second Bush, their dad skydiving, Paul standing in a river, an enormous fish hooked on his finger, John on a snowboard at the top of a white mountain. Throw pillows were on all the couches, many of them arranged to highlight the colors of the American flag.

Yeah. My dad says last time it got this big he was in high school, my age. He's been doing curls in the garage every night just to get ready.

Rez let Kelly talk and then he let the silence fall between them, there was no rush. He'd learned when to let a moment go, to wait and let himself fill with certainty and then talk as if he didn't care if anyone heard. It was a new kind of confidence, this waiting, and he felt it more now, a thousand times more than he'd felt it in tenth grade and a million times more than he'd felt it his whole life before when he was just waiting and thinking and quiet.

Baja, man. That is where we should be. The swell is going to be epic.

Kelly stared at him.

What do you know about Baja? You've only really surfed San O's and the Point. Your dad doesn't even know what a surfboard is. Rez, please.

Now he was himself, Rez, and he surfed and fucked and smoked almost as he liked. He no longer cowered before teachers, parents, the world, and when the courage came to him, he didn't tamp it down but let it go, all the way sometimes, and took all the consequences for what they were: inconsequential. He did like Matthews told him, took care of his business, kept Visine in his bag, and looked his father in the face and lied. He lied whenever he needed to, and when it worked, he relaxed and lied again and one bravery led to another and when Johnson told him to say he was studying at his house, Rez did it and they both went to Palm Springs for a rave and took ecstasy and were back in their own beds, still tripping, by six the next morning. He found courage in his success and the next time he told his mom he was staying at Matthews's house to help him with his math homework, and when Rez went directly to the cove to smoke and wakeboard and prank call Alyssa Mathiesson, he didn't even worry about it. Withdraw money he'd won in the debate championship and buy his first eighth instead? Fuck it. Hide the plastic baggie in his sock drawer where his mom could easily find it when she put away his laundry? Fuck it. Tell his dad there were curves on the science quiz, no one scored above an 82, so his 78 was considered an A when it was the same C it had always been? Fuck it. He'd make it up at the end of the semester. The lies came easy, and when he remembered, he tried to be careful, but most of the time he thought fuck it and opened his mouth, closed his mouth, and waited for the moment to pass.

Whatever we get here, it's gonna be twice that down south.

Rez said it like it was his talk, from the center of himself, not from the magazines and movies he pored over every night when he was supposed to be studying. It would be great. He knew it. Because of the Pacific shelf. Because of the curve of the land eastward and in. The waves would be higher by at least a foot and the rides would be longer by a minute. Rez didn't say any of this to Kelly, but Rez knew it and kept quiet like someone who knows more, knows so much he doesn't have to say.

Kelly stared out over the pool and Rez watched the idea occur to him.

Yeah. Baja would be sweet. I mean, anyone who stays here this weekend is a chump. We'd have to get a car. And a few more boards. And get out of school.

Don't stress, man. I've got it all figured out.

Kelly laughed at Rez and took the bong back into his lap.

Oh, do you? Mr. Strictest Parents in America? How are you going to figure it all out?

I got it.

I bet. Kelly lit the darkly packed ash and inhaled whatever was left.

I bet you do, he repeated, exhaled.

Baja. Man, sweet. I should have thought of it.

But you didn't, Rez told himself. I did and now we are going and it will be my trip and the stories that come will be because of me. He took the bong from Kelly.

Yeah, bro, you would have thought of it eventually. It's so obvious.

By Friday they had a truck. Double cab, air-conditioning, a few inches above factory, a little tree air freshener dangling from the rearview mirror. Freddy, one of Matthews's older brothers, a senior who'd dropped surfing to join the varsity football team, charged them twenty dollars a day. For the driver's license with the picture of a red-haired, wide-shouldered, freckled jock that looked just like Peter Matthews but was named Fredrick Matthews, Rez agreed to take his SAT test for him. At first Freddy didn't believe him, didn't think it was possible, but Rez insisted, told him about the math whiz Arash who'd taken the test for Kelly's older brother and no one ever found out and now Paul was a sophomore at MIT. They wrote up an informal contract on the back of Rez's biology study sheet and the license was theirs. For the few days before the trip they practiced calling Peter Freddy but then realized they all called him Matthews anyway and so it didn't matter.

They stocked the truck as they saw fit. Eight boards, five wet suits, two tents, a cooler full of beer and cold cuts and vodka ice cubes Kelly's sister had made them and no other food. No one brought a toothbrush and no one brought a pillow or soap. Their phones were full of music and a half pound of grass sat in the glove compartment next to a cake

of board wax and gas station sunglasses. Rez thought to bring sunblock because he could hear his mother's voice in his head—*You are turning into a Pakistani*—but he liked the new dark of his skin. More important his light brown hair was turning gold and something in his heart jumped every time he saw himself in the mirror.

They left with the calm hearts of good liars. Rez forged a flyer on school stationery about a mandatory, last-minute field trip to Pyramid Lake. He went to the office of Mrs. Bonau and asked if she could find Mr. Francis's yearbook picture for a retirement card the class was making, and when she left her desk to look, Rez took what he wanted of the stationery and a few envelopes and a stamp of the principal's signature he thought might be useful later, if only for a good trade. The heart of prestigious Laguna Prep, all of it at his disposal. The courage was all of him, all through him, and before she came in he gathered himself on the right side of her office and pretended to stare out the window, staring instead at his reflection in the glass of the tall windowpanes, the orange skin and copper hair, the dumb visage of a bored lion.

He chose chemistry because it was his best subject and he wrote out the information in the most succinct and forward manner possible.

> *Unscheduled Field Trip Opportunity for Select Advanced Students.*
>
> *A three-day trip to Pyramid Lake to study the effects of unprecedented rainfall on the phytoplankton and pH levels of the lake.*
>
> *Extra credit awarded to those students who turn in a photo essay on the trip, complete with tables of measurements and synopsis of ecological conditions and hazards.*

Johnson cracked up when he saw it.

Dude. I have a D in chem. My parents are not going to believe some shit about *select students.*

So Rez wrote a separate flyer for each apostle, according to his needs. Johnson got one from the English teacher and Kelly got one from

Coach Sterns about a special orienteering trip for eleventh graders who had excelled in survivalist skills. Matthews didn't need one because his parents had six sons and never noticed if he was around or not. Rez sometimes thought What if I had five brothers? What if I was part of some huge American clan? at Matthews's house, as Rez ate food their cook Blanca made or slept in the pool house the housekeeper kept clean, or laid out on the lawn cut by Amado, the silent old gardener with arms covered in faded tattoos of big-breasted women and fighting cocks. Six sons and rich. No parents. No sisters. No back home that is not here.

Everyone went for it. Rez's mother stayed up late Thursday washing his sleeping bag and sewing the hole in the raincoat he hadn't used since eighth grade. He pretended he needed his father's signature and took the letter to him after dinner on the night before they left. His father read the letter and let out a laugh.

The pH of a lake, as affected by rain? What is this?

It's a field trip, Dad. For the advanced chem students.

Yes, but you and I both know that lake is polluted with runoff. The pH will never be accurate. Here we are spending all this money for the best private school in Orange County and this is the smartest field trip they can come up with?

Rez stood beside the recliner, mesmerized. His father spoke playfully, a light and gentle teasing. Since the last fight there had been the usual seriousness, nothing better, nothing more, and here he was now, joking with Rez as if he too knew the permission-slip joke, the lie of the whole thing. Rez felt the blood go cold in his body and waited for the other side of his father to make himself known, but his father only took the pen and paper and scribbled his name on the line.

Yes, yes. Go. There will be teachers, by law there have to be, eight to one I think, and it will be miserable and wet but you might have a chance to sit next to a girl around a campfire . . . I know why your eyes are dancing. Not for pH, I can promise you that!

Rez stood beside his father and smiled. His father smiled back.

Don't think I don't know . . . I was a young man once too.

Rez took the paper and walked away. A young man. A girl by a fire.

*

They reached San Diego by noon with half a tank of gas and less than twenty miles to the border. They stopped at two In-N-Out drive-throughs and got so full on fries and milk shakes and double cheeseburgers Animal Style they had to smoke again just to stay high. They decided not to stop after Ensenada until they got to the most perfect Mexican beach.

Until the Mexican Pacific licks our toes! Rez shouted like a moron, and this made everyone laugh so hard they didn't notice they were stuck, sweating in bumper-to-bumper border traffic, waiting to be waved across. The high wore off during their wait and they sat quietly and listened to Nas's *Illmatic—Then writing in my book of rhymes / All the words past the margin*—and mouthed the stories about drugs and women and guns and pride and watched the people in the cars next to them, stock-still, heads erect, silent and glassed off. At the first sign announcing the border checkpoint Matthews suggested they hide the weed and they passed the bag around and spoke in serious and knowing tones.

Too big for the glove compartment.

For sure. Under the backseat?

Spare-wheel spot?

Naw, they always look there.

Rez finally opened the toolbox at his feet. Inside Freddy had organized the top shelf with paper clips and scissors and small pincers to hold roaches too tiny to smoke with your fingers. Underneath, in the storage area, rolling papers, a small bong, lighters, a few empty baggies, and small shreds. All of it useless in car repair.

Dude. Perfect.

Rez put the weed with the bong and tucked the whole thing under his seat. At the border they sat up straight and kept responsible, distracted faces as they drove past an empty kiosk with a wooden arm that lifted and lowered automatically; like that, they were in Mexico.

6

Highway 1 continued down and they recognized it and followed the signs. Matthews drove slow down the small, blasted streets of Tijuana. No one said anything about it but they heard Freddy's voice: *Don't even fucking think of stopping in TJ. Don't do it. My truck will get jacked and the cops will arrest you and then ass-fuck you in a Mexican jail. I don't care about your ass. Bring this truck back exactly as I gave it to you.* So they drove on, past the taco vendors and bars that would let them in without IDs and small dark doorways guarded by women, young and old, in spandex skirts and no one said a thing about stopping.

Five minutes out of America and it's like another planet.

Matthews talked to himself. He drove with uncharacteristic tenderness, as if the road were lined with babies, and it made Rez nervous. This was not the Mexican surf trip he'd planned, the city felt like some sort of trap, and he wanted Matthews to drive faster, to get out of town and back to the beach, where everything would look like the magazine pictures of perfect beaches with perfect surf. Kelly pulled his Game Boy out of his bag.

A new planet for sure. A shittier planet.

Kelly pressed buttons, flicked his fingers madly, and small gunshot noises came out of the device. None of them had been to Mexico before and as a rule it would be Kelly to hate it first, to call it names and pretend it was a stupid waste of time. Rez wanted to check his phone and see how long until they were out of the city, at the beaches, surfing, but the battery had died and all they could do was crawl south through the unending town and watch the beggars and old ladies and young fathers move about their afternoon.

Rez looked out the window. It was hard to see at first, the plastic of his sunglasses covered in fingerprints, and the high he'd been working on

since Dana Point had blown up in his head like a balloon, but he tried to keep focus as Tijuana slid past him like an ancient circus. Planets. It wasn't another planet at all, it was this planet, the same planet as San Diego and Laguna Beach and Los Angeles, just more fucked-up. Hydrochloric acid, he thought. Not another planet, just a city sprinkled in hydrochloric acid. In middle school he'd done a report on it in chemistry, drawn to the total anarchy of its composition and the way nothing withstood it, not bone or rock or lead, and now here was a place where everything seemed in some state of decomposition or decay. Up around them on the hillsides tiny shacks clustered together, their paint peeling off and colorful chunks of concrete crumbling into the streets. The sidewalks were chipped and the roads full of potholes. Rez watched a group of girls in school uniforms and white shoes walk into the dark mouth of an old church and he wondered how they stayed so clean. They passed stall after stall of tourist crap, each with a thousand skull statues in a thousand colors, a thousand skeletons drinking a thousand bottles of Corona from their bony hands. The skeletons freaked him out. The way everything looked poor and dirty freaked him out. Nothing at home was so dirty or so poor. Even their maid, Ysenia, lived in a nice apartment compared to this. She had a balcony with flowers that smelled like bananas, and when Rez's mother gave him the check to drop off, he'd always wait a few seconds outside her door just to breathe in the jasmine. Then he'd press the bell and a girl, a few years younger than he was, would answer, take the check, and close the door without a word or a smile.

At an intersection Rez watched a man piss between two parked cars and thought about saying something so they could all laugh together but let it go, his stomach turning at the sight of someone's dick in public. *America is a good place,* he heard his father's voice say. *A good good place.* The shadow was in the car, the long shape of his father sat between him and Johnson, taking up the space with a cool resolve. *We cannot complain. Look at this mess.* His father raised his hand into the air and circled it around. *They don't even have a war here and still they can't keep it clean like we keep our cities and children and grown men clean.*

Who was thinking these thoughts? Rez looked at Johnson staring out the window, his bony shoulders turned away. Was it the weed? The car was quiet and Rez looked at the boys around them and considered they might simply be miniature versions of their fathers, nothing more. Johnson turned.

What?

Nothing.

Rez sat up and tried not to get nauseous from the drive and the sweat and the thoughts. He didn't want to come undone in this place that was coming undone around him. He leaned forward and punched Matthews in the shoulder.

Dude. Whose grandma are you? Do you want to get wet today? Drive faster!

Matthews said nothing, simply lifted a single finger off the steering wheel and pointed in front of them where a man pushed himself down the middle lane of the highway in a wheelchair. Kelly laughed.

Everyone but Kelly stared out the window as Matthews drove carefully around him. The man was skinny. Rez counted seven veins popping out from the man's neck. His head was covered in long white hair but his face was soft and brown and had no certain age to it. He wore sunglasses and a Chicago Bulls jersey and faced forward as his arms pumped up and down to move the chair down the road, two long denim pant legs dragging behind like streamers.

Totally pathetic.

Kelly scoffed and Rez sat back and closed his eyes like he was also bored by Mexico and pretended to sleep when really what he wanted was to stop seeing so he would stop thinking so he could stop the sound of his dad's voice and the nausea, just for a little while. Johnson grunted and laughed.

Yeah. That dude should get a fucking room already.

The meanness of the words shocked Rez. Johnson was not nice like Matthews but he wasn't an ass like Kelly and Rez opened his eyes to see Kelly's wide white palm in the air.

High five to that.

*

The first beach outside Tijuana was a dump. The sand covered in trash and the tiny breaks onshore gray and churning, and Rez felt his heart drop. He convinced them not to stop until K55, the first famous spot, and no one objected and they drove by the ocean for a long time and said nothing. Men and women and children walked together or alone, few in bathing suits, most with enormous plastic cases that looked like luggage or laundry. No one swam. No one lay out. It was a long fifty-five kilometers after an already-long drive and even though James Johnson kept pulling himself up from the seat every half hour to show how much ass sweat he was sitting in, they kept going, each of them waiting for the same sign—a beautiful beach—before they could stop.

A few hours and the sun dropped on their right and the cities turned to small villages that turned to road stops with taco stands, gas stations, and stores that sold garden pots and ceramic birds in cheery colors. The beaches emptied of people and garbage and started to look a little more like California beaches, a little more like the beaches in the magazines Rez had studied before they left. At the sight of the familiar landscape Kelly turned the AC off and Johnson rolled down the windows and Matthews started to drive fast again so when they heard the siren and saw the Nissan SUV, they thought it was for speeding and started yelling. Matthews told everyone to shut up; his brother had given him tips on how to handle this.

Mexican tax time. It's cool. I got it.

The police were exactly like the police from home. Rez tried to find something different about him, but it was all there, the aviators, the uniform, the forearms, the hair, all just like an American cop, maybe a few shades darker. Matthews's voice came steady and willing like it was when he bullshitted in class or talked to a girl he liked.

Yes, officer. Can I help you?

The policeman cocked his head.

Perdón?

Matthews tried to keep his cool but there were no more words between them for so long that everyone got nervous. The policeman took off his glasses.

Otra vez por favor.

We didn't do anything. I was just driving . . . Matthews gestured to the car full of them and their eight surfboards and block of weed and wallets full of money.

Sí. Por supesto.

The policeman pointed to the rolling papers on the dashboard. Matthews shook his head.

Wait. Please wait. Here.

He reached into the back pocket of his shorts and opened the wallet with the crisp bills he'd taken from the ATM this morning. He offered three of his dozen twenties.

The cop stared at the money and then into the car and for a moment Rez could see them as the cop did—four rich kids in a nice truck, young, clueless—and when the cop gave a little smile, Rez felt ashamed. The cop spoke now, this time in near-perfect English.

You were speeding. Fifteen over the limit. Your car smells of *hierba* and here I don't need a warrant to search. Rich kids, boards, suits, nice trucks, they sometimes have trouble on this side of the border. You should be careful. For your convenience, a more substantial payment, and the ticket will be overlooked.

Matthews took another three twenties from the fold and the cop placed the bills in his breast pocket and backed from the car until his hand was on the front of the hood.

Vaya con Dios.

He smacked the hood and Kelly cursed under his breath and Johnson joined him and Rez said nothing, having heard it all before. He kept his mind on the waves and checked the rearview mirror to get a look at Matthews's face and saw he was not pissed at all. His eyes were full of relief. It had always been kindness with Matthews, even in third grade, Matthews was just nice. Nothing else. Rez had watched the boys and girls change, turn onto one of many sides, shift depending on the light and the time and the need, but Matthews was always and only good, a single surface all the way around. Rez relaxed and looked out the window and tried not to hear Kelly talk about wetbacks and illegals and fucking Mexicans and how California should start a war and take Baja, which he was going to call basura from now on.

Basura, you better watch out!

Johnson laughed.

Dude. How did you remember the word for "trash"? That's so fresh.

And that's how it came back, with a laugh, and then they were talking again and everyone knew it was fine because they were rich kids with money to pay off cops and no Mexican prison and no calls home and no damage to Freddy's truck. Now they could just surf and go home and talk about pH levels in Pyramid Lake with their parents and their epic barrels with their friends. Rez felt his gut loosen from all the nerves, and when they turned a curve on the highway, he was the first to see it, the beach, miles long, pristine, at the bottom of a line of short white cliffs. Low in the sky now, the sun reflected off the cliffs so they looked like a kind of pink alabaster or marble or tusk and it didn't matter because it was as he imagined it and they stopped and got out of the truck and stared way out into the sea as the sets came in long and even and glassy and arced, like the grooves in an old record, one after another after another, in just the right rhythm.

They surfed under a soft dusk, the half-moon rising in the east. The water was warmer than they were used to and no one wore a suit. Then they all swam to Matthews, who took a plastic baggie wrapped around a plastic baggie wrapped around a plastic baggie from the key pocket of his shorts, and sat on their boards far from shore and waited for their hands to dry so they could use the lighter and smoke a joint. Then they spread out again, each taking his own slice of sea, and the water turned the same navy as the sky and when Rez paddled out far from the breaks to take a rest, the water grew still and he saw little flecks of stars in the ocean, their shimmer mixed with the easy rolls and laps of the sea. Sandwiched, he thought, folded in, a galaxy above, a galaxy below. This abandon was new to him, new to know his smallness in the scope of everything around.

When they came back to shore, the moon hung on the opposite end of the sky and their skin puckered from the salt. Cool air moved quickly

across the sand and Matthews and Johnson gathered driftwood while Rez and Kelly set up the one small tent, not because they were going to sleep in it but to have something to do, a task to keep the feeling of the ocean inside them until there was a fire to take over. Rez had never slept outside, did not know the pull of stars on dreams, had never woken up with a face covered in dew. He did not mention this to Kelly, who took yearly hunting trips with his dad to a logging forest just outside Yosemite. *There is nothing like shooting a deer,* Kelly once bragged. *You own everything after that shot, the whole world is yours.*

Kelly told endless stories about hunting and guns and fishing and airplanes his father landed on secret lakes and everyone pretended to ignore him, but Rez listened, unbelieving that Kelly's father trusted a sixteen-year-old with a six-inch blade or that he knew how to bleed animals dry by hanging them from trees. My older brother Paul taught me how to do it. And my dad taught him. It's not that big of a deal, Kelly explained when everyone called bullshit. Tonight Kelly set up camp like an expert. With little of Rez's help Kelly put together the tent and pulled out the cooler, arranged the tarp and a few headlamps so that they had a little shelter and a little light. It was as if he'd spent a lifetime living out the back of a truck. Rez tried to help but ended up sitting in the sand and looking around at the nothing that surrounded them, the ocean's even breaks, the sand and water alight under the half-moon, the dark desert that braced against them from the east, and wondered, What have I spent a whole life doing?

They ate the little food they had left over from the In-N-Out in San Diego and drank all the beers. No one talked about hunger or thirst, their exhaustion was so great. They threw their wallets into the glove compartment, locked it, locked the cab of the truck, and took their sleeping bags and towels to the sand and fell off, one after another, silently, slowly, easy with the earth and with the water too, their shoulders sore, their skin tingling from a wind that blew sand across sand.

*

Rez dreamed of swimming, in the open way of an octopus, in constant extension, without confines of air or the stiffness of bones, everything in reach.

The sun woke them and they took their crusty faces and hair and boards directly into a water that welcomed them and made them new again. Rez rode a dozen waves before stopping to see the place by the first real light of day. An empty beach. Behind it a desert of scrub and brush. Every few minutes a car along the highway, no sound, no faces. No power lines. No cities. No signs of life except for their bodies and whatever lived in the dark sea in which they swam. He thought of home, the view from the ocean toward the shore, all roads and parking lots and groomed parks and fast food all the way down the coast. He'd never been to a beach this raw, not even Old Man's in San Onofre, which was far from the highway but right up against the two boobs of a nuclear reactor that hadn't stopped working in forty-five years. He wondered if all the beaches he knew, all the beaches back home, had once been desert too, now dressed up deserts that were made pretty with extra water and gardeners and too many people. Rez circled his feet in the water to turn himself around and paddled back out.

By midday they were in the truck again, shouting over one another about that tube and that wipeout and that ride and no one needed to be better than another because each had had their own glory. They ate at a taco stand on the side of the highway. The woman who served them was young, and pretty, with a little baby nearby so no one looked at her twice, though they did look once. Rez wondered what it would be like, with a mother, a young beautiful mother. All the girls he fantasized about were from school or TV or porn and they all had the same bodies and so he could not imagine it, the small belly, the full chest, the way her legs touched in the middle and then curved far out and tapered at the ankle but the more he thought about it and the longer he watched her chop at the meat with the side of a spatula, the harder he got. He took two Jarritos from the cooler and went to sit down. They were the

only customers and hunger focused them. They ate more than normal and after a while the corners of their mouths and palms were stained red from the chili oil of the carne asada. Kelly looked around and pointed.

Dude. You guys look like melting clowns.

It was funny enough and they laughed because no one cared, no one felt the small self anymore, the one that told them, *I am Kelly and no one else* and *I am Matthews and not Rez* and *I am Rez alone* and on and on, and different by father and mother and sisters and brothers, and instead they sat, exhausted and full, with the one self they shared now on this adventure in and out and in and out of the sea.

After lunch they drove on. Salsipuedes. Shipwrecks. Punta Baja. Isla Todos Santos. Leave If You Can. Drop Point. Rez's Spanish was better than his Farsi and he rolled the words around his mouth and mastered them. The names had a dark thrill to them and he let their mystery call out as he sat in the backseat and listened to Tupac and felt the dry air blow across his naked chest and neck, certain now how he would spend the rest of his life, and then he fell asleep.

When he woke up, they were parked under a grove of palms, the fronds clapping insanely in the wind. Matthews had the driver's seat tilted back as far as he could without hitting Johnson, who had his head against the window and was snoring. Rez unfolded himself from the compacted position he'd slept in and felt pools of sweat in the creases of his body and a spicy unease in his gut. Outside, beyond layers of low dunes, a beach, busier than the one yesterday, with people laid out in pairs and trios, and an ocean, blue and empty except for an enormous rusted ship hull split in two where surfers jutted out fast and to the right.

Apostles.

He tried once and the bodies in the car did not stir. He opened the door and stepped out. Behind him Johnson fell to the side, took up the space Rez left behind, burped and farted and curled into a little ball. Rez slid his borrowed board out from under the others and found a half chunk of wax, covered his board with it, and turned to the beach.

He walked past a group of women and girls having a picnic on a rug of woven plastic threads. Their food did not look appealing and even though he stared not one of the women looked up to notice him. Five or six boys kicked a soccer ball. An old woman, fully dressed, napped on her side, a small dog curled into her chest. When the water hit his toes, he turned his attention to the sea and the rusted monster rising from it. Surfers paddled in just at the edge of the ship's eroded iron ribs and waited for the sets only to ride out quickly, careful to avoid the jagged metal posts. He's seen guys do it at the Venice pier and once in Santa Monica, but he'd never tried. *Fuck it,* he whispered to himself, and his soul lifted and he ran in until the water was hip high and then he started to swim.

The apostles joined him one by one. The swell was perfect and the water was busy. They kept their distance from each other but it was hard to keep space with the other surfers. No one smoked that day, and when Rez caught sight of one of them, their faces folded in with concentration or blank with relief once they had navigated the iron jaws without a scratch, he felt their joy and knew they would return home heroes all.

The last wave of a set rolled and Rez paddled to it, his rhythm matched by the strokes of the surfer next to him, a surfer his age, maybe a few years older, skinny and strong. Rez wanted to swim some space between them and maybe even give him one of the looks surfers in Laguna give that says *Back off* or *This one's mine* or *Go ahead, all yours,* but he let it go. What difference did it make? To the ocean they were all the same, so why not be the same? In any case the wave was coming and they only had a few seconds to turn around and paddle forward and jump up and in those quick seconds Rez hopped up and balanced. He looked over his shoulder to see the guy get barreled, his hands up above his head as if keeping the tube open with the length of his body. When the wave shot them out, they locked eyes, nodded, and swam back to the ship without a word.

*

No one wanted to leave Shipwrecks but a fog came in and one by one they went and sat on the shore, hungry and spent. They rinsed their boards in the whitewash, loaded Matthews's truck, and drove as far south as they needed to find a store with food and water and beer. The food was mostly packaged and the beer was only so cold but a small grill sizzled in the back and the old man who ran the place said Sí sí sí when Rez asked him if he made tacos.

Por supuesto. Tenemos lengua y cabeza. Ricos los dos.

Rez told the apostles.

Tongue and brains. He says they are good.

Kelly doubled over and pretended to vomit.

Come on, man, that's rude.

Matthews hit Rez on the back a few times.

I'll take five of each. I am so hungry I'd eat goat nuts if that was all he had.

Rez gave him a fist bump and they ordered fifteen tacos while Kelly and Johnson ate tostadas and pepitos and something that looked like Mexican Twinkies. They drank beer and sat there for more than an hour and the old man came in and out to give more food and take away empty bags and plates.

No hay cominda en el norte? he joked, and Rez smiled but he didn't translate and no one asked. The bill came to six dollars and they spent four more on beer and a kind of Gatorade drink and then looked out at the night and the dark highway and Rez asked the old man, Hay una playa, para camping? Cerca de aqui?

The old man gave directions to a pullout five minutes down the road.

No hay nadie. Limpia. Seguro.

They drove the short distance and parked in a flat sandy spot where cars had parked before them and Matthews pulled out a six-pack and his sleeping bag and, drunk and tired, they all did the same and stumbled to the sand, where they found a stone circle with usable wood still in it, some new, some only partially black, and Kelly worked to stack and light and relight until there was a fire. Rez threw down his sleeping bag and wanted to say, *This is the shit. This is the best. I am never going back.* But knew he would sound like a pussy and so just lay down and

listened to Kelly tell stories about him and his brother Paul in Lake Tahoe last summer and normally one apostle or another would tell him to shut up but they were asleep and Rez heard the stories in fragments that mixed with his exhaustion and he fell asleep thinking about bears, severed legs, ant piles, long hikes in pathless woods, triggers, steady hands, older brothers, and marked men.

Rez dreamed of a girl from his chess club, Maryam. In the dream she worked at a grocery store and no matter how nicely he asked, she wouldn't give him his change. She laughed and said, *No. Sorry, no change for you.* And then went on punching numbers into her toy register. Behind him a small woman had a basket full of breasts and bras, and when the sun woke him with its early light, Rez shook off the dream that left in him equal parts lust, frustration, and disgust.

The waves at this beach, even and glassy, were the best waves he had ever seen. Rides two or three minutes long. He sat still for as long as it took to clear his head of the beer and the dream, drank what was left of the Gatorade, and when there was no reason to wait any longer, ran to the truck to get a board and paddle out and wash off the sand and sweat and fly through water again.

The first truck he came to looked just like Matthews's truck, but it had long white key marks dragged along the sides and there were no boards on top and the driver's side window had been broken. Sucks for them, Rez thought, and ran up the beach to look for their truck. He jogged a minute and then two and then thought the walk last night was not this long, and there were no other cars parked along the roads and only one pullout. He turned around.

Fuck!

Smashed glass covered the driver's seat and he saw their wallets strewn about, empty of licenses and money and credit cards. In his wallet he found a library card and a Laguna Beach trolley pass.

Fuck.

The boards were gone, all eight, including the two he'd borrowed from Matthews. The cooler, the weed in the toolbox, their phones, and

the pine-tree air freshener, all gone. Rez stopped himself from crying. Why did he want to cry? It wasn't his fault. It was his fault. It wasn't. But it was. The trip was his idea and so this was his fault and even if it wasn't, it would be, they would all remember it as his fault. He pressed the button for the radio to turn on. Nothing. Worse and worse. He didn't walk back to the apostles. He sat instead up against the wheel well and waited.

They got a jump from a delivery guy, his truck covered with pictures of the packaged food they'd bought at the store the night before. When he was done, Rez said, Gracias, and the guy waited for money, a tip, something, and Rez looked back at the truck with broken window and scratches and his pissed-off friends, who walked and kicked the tires and bit their fingernails, and finally the guy said something under his breath and left. Matthews, who accidentally fell asleep with the keys in his board shorts, broke the rest of the driver's-side window with a rock, cleaned the glass off the seat, got in, started the truck, and they all followed. He turned the truck north and gunned the engine and said the same thing he'd been saying for the last two hours.

Three hours to the border. Half a tank of gas. No money. No driver's licenses. We are so fucked.

They flew down the highway and Rez, tired of talking, tired of convincing them he would pay for the boards, pay for a new paint job, pay back the money they'd lost, confess to their parents, said nothing. He just sat there and looked out the window at the perfect waves lapping the perfect empty beaches.

They were mad the moment they saw it and they stayed mad on the drive, erupting, one by one, until the ire was spent. Kelly bitched that his short board was a present from his dad, for his birthday, hand carved by a pro, and there was no way Rez was going to be able to afford another one. Johnson said his credit card had a fifteen-thousand-dollar limit and if it was maxed out, his father was going to shit a brick and how was Rez going to fix that? Matthews, driving Freddy's scratched and shattered truck, said the least, and that made Rez feel the worst,

and the last hour was silence and Rez rolled the window down to watch the desert stream by and wait for the graffiti and garbage of Tijuana.

They sat through Sunday-night border traffic in silence. One hour passed, then another, and finally a third and their car—even in the US RESIDENTS lane—had moved less than a quarter of a mile. They knew they had no identification; no cell phones and no paperwork to show the car belonged to them. When the arguments hit a panicked pitch, Matthews broke his silence to explain his brothers went to TJ for the weekend all the time and always came back without showing anything.

Dude. Look at us. Do any of us look like we are sneaking into the country?

Kelly laughed from the front seat.

Rez does look a little non-gringo.

Everyone turned and looked at Rez, his tan skin and salt-bleached hair.

Kelly turned around and put on a militant face.

If they call you out, you stay behind. Understand? You can call your old-school dad to come and get you. You are not our problem anymore.

Matthews shook his head.

No, dude. Chill. We went in together, we leave together. Shit is fucked but it's not that fucked.

Dusk in Tijuana and the world outside their car, a show of the shitty life, passed by. Women and children and more children and a few men and a girl of ten or eleven, holding a tiny baby, moved slowly through the lines of cars. Rez thought about his father, how his father never wanted to go to Mexico, never wanted to go anywhere. And maybe he was right for that. The shadow that had left Rez alone these last two days was close again, walking leisurely beside the car, lecturing like a teacher on a stage. *America is a good country.* The shadow looked over the chaos of the border and put his hand on the hood. *A good country. We should be grateful. A fair place where even an immigrant like me, no*

papers, no schooling, can succeed. These poor people. And he walked off into the beggars and broken streets, a dark stain in the form of his father, and before Rez could shake the sight of him, they were at the checkpoint and Matthews leaned out the window as if he had just rolled it down.

The border patrol looked like a cop, his uniform green instead of khaki or black, and his face reminded Rez of the PE teacher they had in ninth grade with the thick mustache and almost-long hair.

The patrol looked at Matthews and then in the car at each of their faces and the mess of water bottles and towels.

Good surf?

Yes, sir, Matthews said after the right amount of time. The swell was pretty incredible.

That's what I hear. I've been trying to get in as much as possible at the point over in Ensenada. Where are your boards?

We borrowed some from some buddies we met down there. Didn't want to risk it.

Smart move, son.

Kelly couldn't help himself and leaned over Matthews, and Kelly's voice rushed with ease and confidence and relaxation to talk to the patrol, to someone who was like him, familiar, safe.

My uncle surfs that point. He says it's great even when it's just hip high.

The patrol smiled.

We are indeed blessed. Welcome home, boys. Enjoy those hot showers.

The metal arm of the checkpoint rose up and the truck was through. When they were a few miles across the border, Kelly made Matthews pull off at a gas station and *stop the fucking car* so Kelly could get out and kiss the ground.

Like the pope, Johnson said. Like the pope when he gets off a plane.

Then they were in the stream again, on Highway 5 at night, the fast traffic and bright roads and smooth overpasses to take you from the clean shopping malls and their spotless parking lots to the enormous

grocery stores and back home to the clean toilets and sterile kitchens, the network of invisible sewers gushing under everything and the fair laws over them all, good police who don't fuck with you for no reason and the taxes to pay for some Mexican mother to send her six kids to day care or to help the shitty countries out when an earthquake or hurricane tears up their shitty cities, and laws to make sure that every man can carry a gun but that gun cannot be used against another man in an act of crime, and the honor in that, the honor in sending your kids to schools that make them pledge allegiance so that they can know where they are and who they are with, and when it is time, they can know what they must defend against jackasses from places with no law but fears and from the stupid old shit they believe that hasn't changed in a thousand years when they used to kill each other for fun. They had long passed San Diego and were driving north along the black stretch of scrub desert before Rez realized the talk was not in his head, unspooling in a senseless mass, but coming from Kelly's mouth. John sat in the front and said all of this in the slow, calm voice of a man giving a talk to his friend, like a man, grown and cool and knowing, like the man he turned into every night at the campfire. Rez closed his eyes on the dark America that passed outside and whistled in through his cracked window and tried to feel safe enough to fall asleep.

7

The gas ran out in San Clemente. They coasted down an exit ramp and into an Exxon station, where they pushed the car to a pump and Kelly turned to Rez and smiled.

Close but no cigar. Time to call Daddy.

Rez went to the pay phone and stared at it for a minute. He picked up the heavy receiver and pressed zero and a voice asked what he wanted. He did his best to explain that he wanted to call a number, but couldn't pay.

The voice, a woman, informed him, That is a collect call. I will put you through.

The phone rang three and then four times and Rez waited and heard his mother answer and wanted to hang up. She said yes and then yes and then he heard his father's voice.

Where are you?

In San Clemente. At the Exxon off Pico.

What? The lake is north, why are you so far south . . . ?

Dad can you come pick us up?

Who? Where are the chaperones?

—

Reza?

Yes. Please just come get me.

The line went dead and Rez walked back to the truck but didn't get in. He leaned up against the bumper and waited and thought. There was no precedent. Never had he committed such disobedience. There was the unknown of his father's reaction, the unknown of his punishment, the unknown of how to pay the money back, fix the truck, buy the boards, one hollow wrapped around another hollow around another and he tried not to panic and concentrated instead on the attitude that had helped him these last months as he came home stoned, with the smell

of Sophia's cunt on his fingers, or lied about studying with Matthews or going to soccer practice and going to the cove instead and getting high. Rez took a deep breath and leaned forward: *Fuck it.* He exhaled and inhaled and said it again. Again and again he cultivated the thought and it stopped his knees and hands from shaking, kept him upright and dry eyed. Rez watched the lights of cars stream south to San Diego or north to Los Angeles, and he thought about his father and who punished his father? Another father, his grandfather, an opium addict, military man, too distracted to put the full focus of love or hate on his twelve children, and who punished him? Another man Rez would never know, and on and on back to the first father and the first son and the first disobedience and defiance, and has a boy ever survived untouched? What is the worse he can do? He can't kill me. Anything short of that, fine. But he can't kill me. So fuck it.

The luxury sedan pulled into the station and drove up beside Rez. The apostles hopped out and Kelly whistled.

Nice to see you, Mr. Courdee. You sure did take your time.

The window rolled down and Rez's father, the long face, the glasses, and the mustache, the beard, made no response.

Get in the car, Reza.

No one moved and finally Rez found voice enough to explain they all needed rides. Or money for gas.

Why is that your problem?

His father, logical as ever. Rez looked at his flip-flops and thought, It will be boarding school, military academy. That is what it will be.

But, Dad, our phones and wallets and they don't . . .

Get in the car. They can call their own parents collect. They still have their fingers, don't they?

Rez walked around and opened the passenger door and got in. He heard the sounds behind him, the *No way; no fucking way* and the *You have to be kidding me* and worse than that faded as his father rolled the window up.

*

They drove in the opposite direction of their house. His father turned away from the highway that would have taken Rez to his mother, to his bed, to sleep, and turned instead east down Avenida Pico, where they drove for minutes and then an hour, and then longer, past strip malls lined with gyms and pet-grooming stores and frozen-yogurt shops. At the speed limit they drove away from the endless empty parking lots and gated entrances to neighborhoods with names like Vista Mar and Sunset Villas and Golden Valley, their fountains gaudy with colored lights and Italianate concrete god heads that spouted dirty water from their mouths. The rich ones had a guardhouse with a guard and a flickering television, but as they drove, the guardhouses gave way to simple code boxes and then cheap wooden signs that read DESERT FLOWER, ARROYO HEIGHTS. The stretches of desert were longer and longer now, and the golf courses disappeared and then there was only a single gas station and nothing else for a long time. Rez thought, He can't kill me. He won't. What father kills his own son? They drove on, the streetlamps fewer and fewer, the stars above them more and then many.

In the dark nowhere his father slowed the car and turned right off the road onto the bumpy shoulder and then onto a dirt road. The headlights showed rocks, a few thorny plants, and crushed cans of beer. His father seemed to have a sense of the nowhere and drove easily until they reached an iron cattle gate that said NO TRESPASSING and turned the car off. With the lights of the dash gone, darkness was all around and Rez tried to concentrate on the skin of his hands and knees until his eyes adjusted and all the time he thought, He can't kill me. My mother. The police. He cannot. He won't. It will be bad, the worst, but he can't go all the way. He won't go all the way.

Get out.

His father opened the door and stepped out and Rez did the same. And I can't kill him. No. My mother. The police. Prison. If I had to . . . ? He is taller, stronger. His hands heavier than mine. Bigger. Rez walked around to the front of the car where his father leaned up against the warm hood and stared out into the empty desert night. Whatever mountain the two had been scaling all these years, that hard rock of suspicious and fear and nerves, they now summited and Rez stood beside his father, faced the car, and tried to focus his eyes enough to

catch sight of the road. When he finally saw it, or what he thought was it, he looked at his father, the profile of him in close-up now, an old man, but not completely old, not old in flesh or form, only in relation to Rez. Rez saw his shoulders broad and lean, his mustache and buzzed hair mostly black, his long straight torso thin from the collarbone to the belt. He was a well-made man, and even though his head hung down as if the rocks and scrub held some information, Rez saw now that he was not old, no, but tired, too tired, and a part of Rez stepped down from the summit and gave way. His father spoke.

Is it something you enjoy?

What?

Lying to your father.

No.

And tell me this: Are you afraid of me?

—

Then why did you lie? Whose idea was it? The trip.

Mine.

And the theft, boards, the damage to the car . . .

I said I'd pay for it.

His father lifted his head.

So you have taken your life into your own hands. Tried to trick me into thinking of you as my dutiful, honorable son, while you try to live in your own way. By your own rules.

I thought if I asked you wouldn't let me . . .

Were there drugs?

Yes.

The truth came up from his mouth before he had a chance to catch it, to keep it and think it over and calculate the damage of it. It came out of Rez so quickly he had no moment to prepare for his father's reaction, the head dropping again, and then the tears shook up and out from his convulsing chest and dripped down off his squeezed face onto the dry, dusty ground.

I, a good man, good citizen, honest husband, and responsible father have such filth for a son? How is that possible?

Rez took a step away from the car. He heard an escalation in the question, a change of tone from pitiful to angry, and knew it from the

times before. He took a few more steps back and stopped when he thought he was far enough, when he realized there was nowhere to go. His father looked at him directly.

You must apologize.

I am sorry.

No. You must recognize yourself. Admit to me who you have become. Say, I am an idiot. A filthy idiot who keeps the company of fools.

—

Say it and then it will be done. Say what you are and then I can let you back into the car, the house, the family, because you have named yourself and you will walk with that name for as long as I live beside you.

—

I am a filthy idiot. Say it and let's be done.

—

Reza, my patience is only so long.

No.

And it came in a rush. From stillness to motion in less than a second. His father charged him and before he could move out of the way Rez felt the rocks of the desert digging into his back, into his side, and then into his face as his father's hand pressed down the back of his head as if to drown him in the dirt. The bone behind his eyebrow began to sting and then the bridge of his nose burned too. His father pushed his face into the floor and grunted once for each time he smacked Rez in the back of the head. Tears came and they were not from the pain of the body, which was sharp and unusual and made in part of his father's weight forced onto him, but some older pain, a pain he'd carried since he was four or five, the first pain he could remember and the words that followed then, that first time, followed now, resurrected, the same words in their same ageless plea.

Baba, why are you hurting me? Baba! Why are you hurting me?

8

THE FEVER LASTED five days.

He stayed in his room and sweat and slept and sweat again. His mother brought him watermelon and bowls of herb soup. Rez touched the bruises on his back and they felt small but deep and his whole head throbbed every time he smiled or winced or began to cry. Weary of expression, silent and locked away in his room, he stared at the ceiling, watched television, and avoided the mirror in the bathroom whenever he had to piss or shit. His mother came and went. If he was watching reruns of *Seinfeld* or *The Simpsons*, she would sit on the chair beside his bed and neither of them would laugh or say anything beyond *Are you hungry?* and *No thanks* and *Yes* and *Maybe later.*

His phone died and his laptop battery drained and he made no efforts to connect to anything or anyone beyond the walls of his room. At night when he was too hot to sleep, he stared at those same walls, one and then the other, and saw pro surfers glide down faces of water so high he almost didn't believe they existed. Kelly Slater. Laird Hamilton. Fiji and the North Shore. Tahiti. Injury and glory. Freedom without end. An ocean home. Some part of him believed it, lived in the dream of such possibility, and another part of him saw the photos the same way he saw images of Pluto or the rings of Saturn, awesome but beyond his reach. Beside those hung posters torn from European soccer magazines, players from his favorite teams. Barcelona and Manchester United, teams he adored in middle school when he and his father would shape a whole Sunday around watching the games during European prime time and American dawn. The players, soaked in sweat and in the moment either before or after a goal, moved with composure and full strength. In Rez's time playing soccer he'd felt that once, maybe twice, and usually tried his best at the far distant defensive positions the coaches put him in.

A few Japanimation sketches he'd made of characters from the graphic novels that obsessed him as a boy and a photo of him next to the HOLLYWOOD sign, not smiling. In the empty spaces between his mother had put up the many plaques and ribbons and certificates for chess matches won, math competitions won, science fairs won. The walls talked.

Without sleep Rez looked again and again at the room around him and saw himself as the walls showed him: once a boy, Reza Courdee, with a family, a life of school and games, hobbies and achievements; and now, not yet a man, with dreams of worlds far from this room, this house, and the people who made him. Inside him now the boy began to diminish and he felt emerge the Rez of the apostles and the ocean and the search for pleasure at all cost, the liar and the desperate soul. Or at least that's what he'd thought, these last months until a few days ago when the boy cried and begged into the desert night, *Please please please stop. Please get off me. I was stupid. I am sorry.*

On Saturday morning the fever broke and he sat up in bed and drank orange juice and played backgammon with his mother, who, in her relief at his wellness, joyfully beat him every time. When they heard the footsteps come down the hall, he looked up at his mother's face and she met his gaze but did not move. His father stood on the other side of the door, not knocking, not opening, just shouting.

Reza, come. Let's go for a walk. The morning is a nice one.

The voice was normal and regular as if announcing *Lunch is ready* or *I found my sunglasses.* The footsteps went back down the hall and Rez's mother nodded to him as if to say, *Go, go on, nothing bad will happen.* He stared at her for a second longer and then put on his shorts and a dirty T-shirt and went out to wait at the end of the driveway where he squinted at a sun he hadn't seen in days.

They walked around the neighborhood of manicured yards with bonsai gardens and boulders hauled in from faraway wild rivers now placed decoratively here and there. His father stood straight and walked quickly,

keeping himself a step or two in front of Rez. They approached a woman with two small dogs on two thin rhinestone leashes. She wore cataract glasses and sensible shoes and opened her mouth slightly in a smile and perhaps a greeting, but by the time they passed she reconsidered and looked down at the pavement without even so much as a nod. Rez wondered what they must look like, he and his father, on this morning walk.

They climbed the quiet streets, higher and higher, to the cul-de-sac where the neighborhood ended and the scrub of the hillside began, and there his father stopped and wiped his brow with a kerchief he pulled from his pocket. He was not winded but the day was hot and it was the heat, not the pace, that made Rez feel an uneasiness slip in his gut, the hazy ends of the fever as it crept back into his skin and behind his eyes. Gathered, his father looked off to the horizon and began to speak in Farsi.

The sound of the language had always aggravated Rez and he waited to feel the slight gag in his own throat at the guttural noises and the weird sounds. But today there was nothing. His body had no reaction but for the slightest twinge of pleasure in understanding the words, and the sudden intimacy the language caused between them.

Ok.

His father started up the trail that led to the ridge and Rez followed, the two of them in a line, past the artichoke cacti and sagebrush and the absence of house or man and after a few minutes Rez relaxed and the fever let go a bit and he felt the goodness of movement and breath and his body. Rez lifted and dropped his legs and his father did the same and then the neighborhood was far behind and some sort of uninhabitable dryness spread out in front of them and his father walked into it with direction and purpose. In Farsi his father spoke to the empty land before them.

You are passing through a rough time. That is normal for your age.

The hill tilted and his father slowed to catch his breath and Rez turned off the desire to jog up the hill and get to the top and kept himself quietly behind, in his father's wake.

I was a boy once, and my father was strict. Much more strict than I am and all I wanted was to get away.

They reached a vista that showed the curve of the beach up against the land and Rez saw where the waves came in strong and high and he let himself imagine the cool water on his hot skin and the wind of surfing, the fantastic wind of it that reached them all the way up on this high hill. His father went on.

I wanted to leave Iran, move to America, become my own person. I cannot tell you how impossible that was. I had no money. No plane ticket. No passport even. Just thinking about it was like dreaming. Sometimes, this is how it is for men.

Rez looked at his father and wondered how many selves he carried within him. There was the self that stood on the arid trail and looked toward the Pacific, and another self left behind a boyhood in a rocky place where he had mountain dogs and loved his rifle and wanted nothing more than what was. There must be one more, the one between, the one who left it and made a journey without return, without looking back. Rez thought of his mother, and her selves and the way they all came to the teak dinner table and said nothing of their halves and quarters and ate the food and stared at the still water in the blue pool. He looked back down at the coast. The waves would be fantastic today, he could tell by the breeze.

I am not a perfect man. I should not have hit you. That was not right. Not in a good family. I apologize.

His voice was soft with an unfamiliar tenderness and Rez took a step away from his father and faced the ocean and the breeze that moved through his short hair and tickled his sore face. He waited for the mistrust to fill him but nothing came, and Rez let the wind blow onto and through him.

Those boys, the ones you think are your friends, will always think of you as an outsider, the foreign kid. If you go with them, try to be as they are, I will not be able to help you in that life.

His father looked to the horizon and Rez waited and watched to see what other new tone he would set, what else the old man knew that Rez did not. But his father was silent and the two stood side by side as

a pair of turkey vultures spiraled up a thermal far above them and the ocean twinkled, gold across the surface of its blue. For a moment nothing felt wrong.

In this life, I can help you. That is what I am supposed to do. Help my son become a man. I will promise to respect you. To keep my temper calm. And in return you promise honesty. That is all I ask.

Fifty-six years old and still, when his father asked for something, his face took on the pleading look of a three-year-old. Fifty-six. If Rez made it to fifty-six and told himself the story of this day, he would say that he was tired, his body was tired from sickness and his head from confusion, but on this day his father changed. Rez could not say what exactly changed, or why he wanted so badly to trust it, or why he wasn't full of suspicion that a fist would fly at his face again. Maybe at fifty-six years old he would understand these unknowns, but on that morning he knew only that he was tired, that the wind was warm and the ocean blue and ruffled, that the earth was under his feet and the sky above, and that he stood beside his father as a man with another man, maybe a father, maybe a friend, maybe even a stranger, on a walk across a dry land. The sensation invigorated him and he breathed in the windy air again and again, as if it were food, and nodded and the two men took up their walking, moving up into the hills until another direction was necessary.

9

He moved back to the front row, open notebook, ready pen. The teachers noticed but said nothing. In the hallways Rez kept his head down and didn't answer the *Whassups* or *Hey, bros* that came his way. He spent lunches in a window seat of the library study tower and tried to read and tried to eat but just looked out the window, down and over the quad, where clumps of students talked and laughed, pushed or draped arms around each other. He watched Sophia walk the brick paths from class to class, her shiny black hair sliding from side to side, ear tilted into her phone, plaid skirt rolled up at the waistband, her legs thin and pale, always alone. In chemistry lab Lila told Rez, without his asking, that Sophia had a new boyfriend.

A basketball player from Anaheim High. Varsity. He's got his own apartment behind his parents' house.

That's cool.

She told me she still really wants to be friends with you.

That's cool.

No one called. No one invited him over. He went to school, soccer practice, home for the quiet meal with his mother and father, the hour of television, the two hours of homework, the long shower and the long sleep that ended just after dawn when he woke to do it all again. The drone and habit of this life calmed him and after a few weeks gossip about the trip and the theft died down and when the spring storms finally ended, he thought he had a chance at normal, at forgetting the mess he'd made. The stolen credit cards were maxed out and then reimbursed. The boards were replaced by Matthews's dad's insurance company, and the car got a new paint job and window replacement courtesy of Rez's father, who offered it to the Matthews family. Rez listened to his dad on the phone with Mr. Matthews.

Let us be grateful they all came home safe.

His father repeated it again and then shook his head slowly.

Yes. Yes. Not at all. Sons at this age, well . . . we've all been there.

And after the rains had long dried up and the end of the school year was a few months away and all everyone talked about was prom and graduation and summer, Kelly still wouldn't let it go. He told anyone who would listen that Rez Courdee was a poser who didn't know shit. He said Rez weaseled his way into going on the trip and then made them camp on an empty beach even though they knew it was dangerous. Kelly wanted a public feud, and every time they passed in the hall, Rez felt a knock at his shoulder and heard, *What's up, faker?* If Rez raised his hand in class, Kelly started laughing or sighing, loud enough and long enough that the teachers asked him to leave the room and he'd say, loud enough for everyone to hear, *I'd be skeptical of what Mr. Courdee might say. He's been known to tell a few lies.* And just like that the class and the teacher would stare at Rez as Rez's hand slid down back onto the desk and he forget what exactly he was going to say. In the locker room after soccer Kelly followed Rez pinching his nose and shaking his head and shouting, *Has anyone ever noticed how Persians smell? They have this stinky sort of stink to them . . .* Rez pretended not to hear and quickly covered his body with clothes and tried to think of other things—equations, historic dates in the Nez Perce war, his SAT prep book—to keep himself from hearing Kelly and keep himself from crying or fighting or something worse.

For a while Kelly had a small crew, Johnson and a few other preppie guys with dads from old OC families who did not mix with the new OC families like Rez's. They gave him shit for a month or two and Rez kept a low profile and after a while most people stopped caring. Everyone knew Kelly could be a dick and Rez had no friends now anyway, so what was the point?

Matthews, with the shittiest deal, stayed close. After all it was his brother's truck that was scratched and his brother's license that was stolen and he had to tell Freddy and so suffer the punishments assigned through some internal system of brother justice. For a while Matthews

came to school with long-sleeve shirts and buttoned his collars all the way up and Rez knew underneath the clothes were bruises from punches and pushes but Matthews never mentioned it. When the other apostles weren't around, Matthews asked Rez out to the car to smoke and they'd sit together in the haze and get retro and listen to Pink Floyd or Red Hot Chili Peppers and talk about USC football or the Angels or anything that wasn't surfing or Mexico or otherwise laced with shame.

10

The year ended. Term papers, assemblies, awards, signatures on the inside covers of the yearbook. *Smellyalateralligator. Have a great summer. Seniors rule. Keep it stoked.* Rez didn't take his out of his backpack, and when someone asked him to sign theirs, he'd write his initials and a smiley face and nothing more. In his photo, taken last fall, he had just smoked with the apostles in Kelly's car, and there he was, a black-and-white head and shoulders amid a sea of black-and-white heads and shoulders, a goofy fuck-it-all smile and wild ocean-stiff hair. On a dare from Kelly he wore his tie crooked and tried to cross his eyes. The photographer wouldn't have it and asked him to straighten up. He looked at the photo and tried to recognize himself and saw only a moment, an expression, a collection of feelings and ways, now passed and far from reach.

On the last day of eleventh grade Rez and a handful of other students sat on the stage of the auditorium and waited as the headmaster called out the names of the best and most promising and honorable and other words that made parents smile and clap and pull out their cameras. Rez wore a new pair of shoes and a pressed shirt and let the boredom settle over him. He stared out at the audience, the first ten or twelve rows full of parents, some old and some not old. There were parents who were happy and parents who appeared otherwise. Rez found the face of Joseph Peterson's dad, Old Peterson they called him, tan and fit and well into his sixties, a known stoner who'd inherited money from old OC land holdings and lived in a house that took up an entire ridgetop above Laguna. He flew a little airplane to L.A. every time he wanted to, surfed Mavericks, had courtside tickets for the Lakers, and didn't go to work. His son, Joey, a straight C student and mediocre jock, had taken a photograph in art class that won a prize and now he sat two rows

behind Rez. Old Peterson. He held the left hand of a small Asian woman who looked fifteen years old, his third wife, a woman from China who spoke no English and wore short shorts all the time and covered her mouth when she smiled. She was not smiling now, and her face looked ashy and sullen as it stared into a phone. Beside her, Old Peterson, a man big enough, blond enough, and tan and pleased enough to seem from another species altogether, smiled directly at Rez and winked. Rez sat up straight and shifted his gaze and found his own mother and father, a few rows back, their faces small and somber, empty of elation or surprise. Then he heard his name.

Reza Courdee.

He stood, smoothed out his pants, and walked to receive the certificate and shake the headmaster's hand and take congratulations for proving that he knew more about AP chemistry than any other junior or senior in the state.

A promising senior year lies ahead for that young man.

The headmaster's hand was warm and plump and Rez nodded and walked back to his seat. Next to him another eleventh grader, Arash Dobani, recipient of the presidential honor for academic achievement, the highest prize handed out all year, smiled and flipped his long inky hair back from his eyes.

Nice work, brother, another certificate for the wall. Make Moms proud.

Arash put out his fist and Rez bumped it and Rez smiled at the words and thought about his walls at home and the posters and the prizes and wondered how Arash knew.

Arash leaned to Rez's ear and whispered, You blaze?

Rez looked at Arash, who looked ahead at the parents and teachers in front of them. He too wore a starched oxford shirt and clean shoes. His hair was as long as allowed and his skin was tan and smooth and even over the square bones of his face. He had rolled up his certificate just like Rez had and they sat onstage, homologues of a kind. Rez looked over the parents in the audience, catching the gaze of his mother, who smiled and dabbed at her eyes. His father, who stared at the headmaster with a dropped and flat brow, and then Old Peterson, now looking out the window with the same broad grin.

Yeah. Sometimes.

Sweet. Let's celebrate.

The assembly went on and Rez said no more and then the event was over and everyone stood and clapped and smiled and students walked offstage and Arash stopped Rez.

Let me give you my digits. A few of us are meeting up later. Give a shout when you're done with the family stuff.

Yeah. Cool.

That was the first of it. The seniors threw their huge graduation blow-outs and Rez didn't get invited to any of the parties he'd gone to last year, not Matthews's or Kelly's or any of the volleyball girls', but ended up elsewhere, at parties with grandparents and babies and uncles who spoke no English and smoked cigarette after cigarette on lawn chairs out by the pool. The tables were covered in presents and fat envelopes that stayed sealed and Rez stood in family pictures next to people he'd just met who draped an arm around his shoulder, around his waist. DJs played music from all over the world and he danced with round old aunts who sweated through their silk blouses and smiled up at him coyly. The parties were catered and the families were delirious with pride and even though Rez had only just met these sons and daughters through Arash, in the last two weeks, he was taken in time after time, and he was kissed. At one house, Mila, a friend of Arash's whose older sister was graduating and going to Harvard, he and a few other kids snuck out to a car and got drunk on a handle of vodka they passed around and around until it was empty. They went back to the party and talked to parents and laughed and danced with little cousins and Rez grabbed Elissa Vasquez by the hand and they walked around looking for a place to make out and ended up in a neat small room with a huge silk rug and a framed portrait of Mecca on the wall, just like the photo his mother kept, in miniature, in her coupon-and-bill drawer. He closed the door and they kept going until they found a guest bedroom and he and Elissa did everything he and Sophia had done and it was different and it was just as good.

PART II

To a Brother

11

Laguna Beach, Summer 2012

THAT SUMMER HE was with Arash and his crew, Yuri, Omid, Cyrus, every day. They were guys Rez knew from class or sports or around but had never spoken to, and except for the different names and darker hair and that they preferred chlorinated pools to the ocean, hanging out with them was a lot like last summer with the apostles. Hip-hop all the time, long stoned mornings, fast-food lunches, naps, long stoned afternoons at someone's country club or backyard, evenings at the movies, weekend trips to Vegas, all the same boast and dare and lust talk. No one had jobs and they sat around and smoked the same weed, joint after bong after vape until nothing mattered and everything was all good. Rez stood beside the body of himself as one world of high school male flesh eclipsed another and the revolution of days, nights, wet and dry, traffic and flow, stayed exactly the same.

Except Arash. Arash was different. Before that summer Rez knew nerds and surfers, preppies and jocks. He'd seen goths and gang kids at the In-N-Out trying to get away from the Christian born-agains they'd hung out with last summer at the mall. This was high school; you started out as one thing and ended as something else. They all started out as boys together in the ninth grade and now they were all trying to turn into something like men, and Rez watched as every single kind, regardless of how tough or cool, stumbled before the leap, grew sour, slipped back into babies and cried for their mothers only to swear them off two minutes later. He saw it and knew he did the same and wasn't proud of it but this was the way it was, becoming was a shitty business. And then he met Arash and saw someone not at all in the process of becoming, but who already and completely just was.

The first few weeks everywhere Arash went, Rez went. He had more freedom now. Ever since he'd won the prize his dad didn't press him

about studying and tests, and his mom, glad he wasn't sad anymore, let him come and go with his new friends. And it was easy to do. Arash kept the parties going, the pipes packed, and the friends in circulation, and when Rez walked in, no one stressed and no one gave him shit for being the new kid in the group. Girls were always around and everyone watched TV or swam and talked about college or the Kardashians or some smart gossip and Arash got everyone high and bought takeout and gave rides to whoever needed a ride. He never dipped into a mood, never left anyone out, never switched off the generosity, never talked smack. The one time Yuri tried to cut down people who hung out with Kelly, called them *OC neo-Nazis*, Rez watched and waited to see what Arash would do, but all he said was *Come on, man, why you gotta talk like that? There's no need . . .* And then he'd move the conversation away from the dark place and take the sulking friend for a ride and they'd come back happy and high. He lived in an open house, no questions asked, and always leaned down to kiss both his parents regardless of whether he was coming or going. He loved all parents, all families, and the first time he picked Rez up at his house he came with a large, many-bloomed orchid and a small smile on his smooth tan face.

For the lady of the house.

Rez and his mother both came to the door and she let out a little gasp. Rez rolled his eyes.

That is not from Trader Joe's.

No, Mrs. Courdee. Our family friend has an orchid greenhouse. Rez told me you liked plants.

I like plants? I said that, Reza?

Rez stood behind his mother and shrugged. His mother stared at the tiny faces of the flowers.

It is true. I do like plants. I didn't realize my child noticed. Please come in.

Rez elbowed Arash.

Dude, you could have honked from the curb.

Arash smiled and soon they all leaned up against the marble countertops and drank orange juice while Arash answered her questions about Syria and his family houses in Damascus and Aleppo as Rez's

mom listened and nodded and then told them things about her home in Isfahan and the garden with the blue fountain in the back filled with koi and other details Rez had never heard. All Rez wanted was to leave, to get out of the house. He hadn't smoked all day, hadn't done anything all day, was bored and fidgety and ready to split and go to the show. When he heard the sound of the garage door opening, he cleared his throat.

A, it's almost four, there will be traffic . . .

Please, would you stay for a minute to meet Sal? Reza's father would like to meet this new friend Rez has told us so little about.

Meena did not even look at Rez and kept her smile on their guest as she rinsed green grapes in a colander. When Rez's father walked into the room, Arash stepped toward him, offered a hand and a full name. Rez's father, caught off guard, took the hand and went through the introductions as if Arash were a colleague from the lab. After a long look and a few grapes he started his questions and Arash answered them with a calm politeness that Rez wanted to call out as ass kissing yet could not. Syrian. Born here. Parents, doctor, housewife. Yes, they'd like to meet you too. Two brothers. Both older. One a surgeon. One the president of a tech company, lives in Newport. Stanford. They've contacted me so I am hoping for early admission. Physics. I think, but I might change my mind. My parents say I am at a good age for changing my mind. Rez watched to see what his father made of this perfect son who was not his. His father popped grape after grape.

I have noticed a change in Reza these last months, you must be the source. Nice to see him making some smart decisions about the company he keeps. It hasn't always been that way . . .

Arash. I think it's time. The show . . .

Arash put his empty glass down and nodded respectfully at the parents.

Right. It is getting late.

His father looked at them.

Show? What show?

We are going to the Hollywood Bowl. My parents gave me tickets as an end-of-the-year gift.

Very nice.

Arash did not mention the show was by a famous rapper who had served time in prison and had rebooted his career by pairing with a classical violinist from China.

Go. Go. You boys should go. Traffic will be terrible regardless, but the earlier the better. It is good. Good to relax a little before this next year. Things will be challenging for you as seniors. Much to be accomplished.

Ok, Dad.

Arash thanked Meena for the orange juice and walked to the front door like he'd been to Rez's house a thousand times already. Rez followed him and mumbled his good-byes as his parents smiled and walked with them to Arash's BMW coupe. The engine started and Rez waved and his parents waved and Rez felt like a dork and Arash drove under the speed limit until they were around the corner and up the street, all the way to the vista, where Arash parked and pulled out the bong and passed it to Rez like he did every time Rez got in the car.

Ass kisser.

Come on now, bro. No need to hate. What can I say? I like parents, old-school, old-world parents. So real. Just think of all they've seen in their lives. They were born in another world and now they can watch it on Google maps. So much change for a single soul to see. That has got to take some balls. Respect, man. Gotta respect.

Rez choked on the smoke he held in his lungs, and laughter and smoke exploded all over the car and Arash started to laugh and then they were high and driving and gone.

The afternoon was hot and all around them on Highway 1 cars stopped and drove and stopped and drove. They kept the windows down and drove through Corona del Mar and Newport and up to Huntington and Seal Beach and past the refineries and loading docks in Long Beach. They listened to the Roots and then to MGMT and smoked a skinny joint while they checked out the skinny women jogging by the beach and the women driving SUVs and the women stopping to let their dogs pee on the palm trees planted into the sidewalks. At a stoplight a cop car pulled up beside them and Rez sat stock-still and stopped breathing,

the joint smoking in his lap. Arash kept moving his shoulders to the music and pushed his sunglasses up the bridge of his nose as they slid down. He half sang the words to the song and then the light turned green and they drove on and Rez exhaled and then inhaled and Arash gave him a friendly punch on the shoulder.

Relax, man. You have got to relax. How much herb is it gonna take?

At Artesia and PCH they turned right and drove away from the coast. Within two blocks the fancy facades of the high-rent strip malls turned grimy with liquor stores next to OTBs next to doughnut shops with scratched-up windows, all of it circled by parking lots and empty buildings with faces and figures in bright graffiti on their sides. At a stoplight Rez watched a woman push a stroller full of groceries as she held an umbrella over her head to keep the sun off. Beside her a man held the handlebars of a bike that was loaded, bag upon bag, with glass and plastic bottles. He wore dark sunglasses, no shirt, and a long black cape and walked with a sense of purpose for another world.

Arash turned up the music and they cruised, intersection to intersection, down the streets of Compton, and Rez wiped the sweat from his palms and told himself to sit back and relax. Arash kept singing.

This show is going to be so dope.

Totally.

By the time they turned off Artesia onto a side street the western horizon was behind them and every object cast a long shadow. They drove down the streets of a neighborhood where each house had the same square yellow lawn and each lawn had its own collection of thirsty shrubs and plants. A few houses had Astroturf and a few lawns were overrun by toys and press benches and weights, and a handful had elaborate rock and cacti gardens. They stopped in front of a house that looked just like the rest and Arash got out. He walked toward the door and turned around.

This is the stop I was talking about.

I'm gonna stay in the car.

That's rude, bro. My friend lives here. Come say hello. We'll be quick. You'll like him.

Rez remembered Arash was picking up a half pound from a friend to have at the show. *To sell?* Rez asked. *No. To share,* Arash responded.

Now they were here, all Rez thought about were the movies he'd seen in middle school—*Murder Was the Case, Boyz n the Hood*—films with guns and drug deals and random stupid deaths. He remembered the lyrics of songs about the never-ending war between the Bloods and the Crips and thought about all the spray-painted murals they passed driving in—*RIP RIP RIP, Our Dear Father. Our dear brother. Our dear son*—and he felt the fool in himself, a kid from OC who loved hip-hop, the beats and the hard lyrics and the anger it let pulse through him, anger he felt but did not have the lyrics or the life for. He felt the fear of a kid who had only ever fronted, who acted tough in a soft world but was scared everywhere else.

Dude. You coming or what?

Rez stepped out of the car and got shoulder to shoulder with Arash.

Man, you don't even need this weed. You buy from Yuri's guy and that's from the clinic. Why are we even here?

Are you whining? Relax. We gotta let the dollar circulate, it's the only way.

Arash pressed the beige circle next to the door. A soft dirge played on the other side of the wall.

Arash said that line a lot, talked about money and how it needed to circulate and if it stayed in one place too long it would go stale and curse its owner. That is how he explained it when Rez asked him why he always gave out weed and offered to pay for food. *It all comes back. In Islam, generosity is a big deal. You can't be Muslim without it.* Rez listened for noises in the silent house and thought about all the free weed Arash would pass out to strangers they would meet tonight and how those strangers would turn into friends for a half hour or so and all of it would be so chill, the edge puffed off. Part of him got it and part of him stayed confused and he slouched a little and tried to stand casual but found no way to be normal in the time between doorbell and door answered.

The door opened and an old man in gray sweats with salt-and-pepper hair and a small prayer cap filled the entire doorframe. Arash stepped to him and they embraced in a big silent hug and when they pulled apart the man put his fist out and Arash bumped it.

All good?

Alhamdulillah. All good, Yusef. And you?

No complaints.

The enormous old man looked at Rez and Arash spoke without hurry.

This is my friend Rez. We go to school together.

Salaam alaikum.

Yusef offered no hand, no fist, and kept a downward gaze on Rez's face.

Rez. Short for something? Reza maybe?

Yes.

Hm. It's your name, you can do what you want with it I guess.

He led them into the kitchen and poured out three glasses of orange juice and for the second time that day Rez stood awkwardly with the bright happy liquid in his glass and waited for the moment to pass as Arash played the part of gracious guest. He answered Yusef's questions about school and the mosque and his family and asked his own questions about the same things and they followed Yusef to the living room, where he filled up all the corners of a recliner that did not recline and Rez and Arash sat on the edge of the couch opposite. Arash told him about graduation, about the prize, and Yusef nodded and Rez looked around at the walls of the room, covered in framed photographs of men and women and children. Face after face after face. Soldiers in uniforms. Women holding round babies. A large group, all ages, in matching T-shirts gathered around a beatific old woman in a wheelchair. Rez's eyes stopped on a series of school photos, the same boy, handsome and smiling and large like Yusef. At seventh or eighth grade the photos stopped and Rez looked away and tried to seem interested in the conversation but could not focus because a sinking feeling started in him and didn't stop. Yusef nodded at what Arash said and Arash nodded at what Yusef said and this went on and on.

Well, you heard about Malcolm's new job, data work, or some such. Says he can do it right from his bedroom. I think he got hired because of that program you all did a few summers ago, that computer program down in Irvine where you met. That did change him. Changed his prospects.

He showed a lot of talent for it. More than most of the other kids there.

Yes. Well.

Yusef grew silent and tapped the empty orange juice glass on his knee.

Yes. Well . . . he said you'd be here about now. I'll take you to him.

Arash stood slowly and Rez stood too quickly and they followed the old man down a carpeted hallway with more framed photos, these older and faded, their subjects wearing dated hairstyles and clothes Rez had seen in movies and reruns. They stood before a door with a poster of Tupac on it and Yusef knocked with one knuckle.

Mal? Arash is here.

A voice from inside said, Cool, and Yusef opened the door and walked away down the dim hallway. Arash went in first. The room was small, crammed with a single bed, a desk, turntables, and a laundry hamper. In front of the desk a broad-shouldered man, a few years older than them, sat in an electric wheelchair. The same handsome smiling face as the boy in the photos on the wall, long past eighth grade, shirtless and broad through the chest, a tattoo of a lion spanning from nipple to nipple. Rez tried not to stare and took the few steps he could into the room, bumped the fist that was offered, and took a seat beside Arash on the neatly made bed and tried to untie the knots in his gut.

The door, man.

Malcolm gestured to Rez with a tilt of his chin and Rez stood and closed it and at the sound of its shutting Malcolm wheeled around and let out a loud bright welcome.

What! Is! Up? Arash! Been a long time.

Same old same old. All good. What's new with you?

Same as same. Got into this Anonymous shit online and tricky stuff, change the world from my wheelchair while paying the bills with data entry. Hustle here, hustle there.

Sneeeeaky.

Indeed. And you? What is in the works for nerd boy?

Same nerd stuff. Science, college, the search for a nice girl . . .

Malcolm pressed a single key on the keyboard and music came on, deep bass and the sounds of a young woman's moans.

I hear that.

Malcolm smiled at his pun and Arash made fun of him for the stupid joke and they talked about school and computers and programming and Rez watched Arash, who was, as ever, himself. The same Arash from his kitchen at home, with the crew, with the girls, with their teachers, in the mirror. The only self he had. Across from him, in his wheelchair, Rez saw that Malcolm was a number of different people, all of them flitting around the room, depending on the topic, careful not to land anywhere. Rez focused on Malcolm's face, the hands of the conversation, the posters in the room, anything to keep him from staring at the empty pant legs that dangled from the edge of Malcolm's chair. Rez tried so hard to do something else that he got nervous and nearly started talking. One of Malcolm's many selves noticed and he turned his attention on Rez.

What's your story?

Rez sat forward on the bed.

Nothing. Same as Arash. Laguna Prep. Waiting to graduate and get out, far out.

Malcolm put his hands in the pockets of his pants and sat back, and for a moment they looked at each other, each set of eyes a vector to the next set, Malcolm looking at Rez, Rez looking at Arash for the next words, Arash looking at Malcolm and then breaking the daze.

It's cool, man, he's cool. Good people.

Malcolm took his hand out of his pocket.

A friend of yours is . . .

He let the words fall and turned on his chair and rolled across the thick carpet to the closet, where a dozen or so T-shirts hung, all a shade of navy, all ironed, and the floor was covered in stacks of neatly folded pants. He reached back behind the shirts and Rez felt his insides electrify with fear. He moved himself closer to the edge of the bed, to a window he could punch out if need be as Malcolm rustled in the closet with one hand. He pulled out an object the size and shape of a brick wrapped in black plastic. He rotated the chair and tossed the package at Arash with the other hand. Arash caught it with one hand.

The goods are good. Hindu Cush. Purple Haze. The usual.

I expect nothing less. Should we roll one?

Malcolm shook his head. Nah, man. Not with Yusef home. These are new days.

Got it.

Arash put the brick into his backpack and handed Malcolm a roll of cash and Rez let his veins open with relief and now for some reason he wanted to relax and smoke in this room and pretend he was never scared or playing out blood scenarios in his head, but he also wanted to get out, as fast as possible, before whatever happened to Malcolm could happen to him, as if tragedy were contagious.

In the car Arash tucked the bag under his seat and rolled his window down.

Not much stink for so much weed.

Arash started the car.

Be nice.

Rez didn't say anything.

I buy it as a favor. I like to help him out. These little buys go a long way and I get to pass out free bud. Win-win.

Outside the car the neighborhood switched back to strip malls and gas stations and the lights of Artesia popped on against the orange lines of sunset at the far end of the sky. A blue Malibu pulled up beside them, sparkle in the paint, chrome all over, after-market tires, the two front windows open. The man in the driver's seat looked at them and then leaned over the woman who sat passenger.

You lost?

No. We're good. Thanks.

Arash answered easily while Rez tried to push himself into the leather of the seat but the leather wouldn't give and he tried to look ahead and not think of guns or robbing or drive-bys or his stupid shitty fear and the shitty racism of his father behind him pushing through. At the sound of a woman's voice he craned his head to look over at the car.

She was beautiful, her face one curved feature atop another, all of it full and promising something Rez had not wanted until just that moment. She smiled at him. Behind her the man smiled as well.

You do look lost.

The man leaned over closer to them.

I hope you're not lost. 'Cause . . .

The light changed and neither car moved. Behind them a truck honked twice and Rez jumped in his seat, all his bones shook at once. The woman in the Malibu laughed at him and the man beside her straightened up behind the wheel and gunned the engine. The Malibu fired past them and the woman's pink hair swirled out the open window like cotton candy.

Arash moved at the speed limit and looked over at Rez.

Dude, Rez. You ok? Your face is white. Don't tell me you're a racist Persian because that is dumber than dumb.

No, it's just, you know, Compton and all that stuff about gangs and . . .

Arash shook his head, his face pressed down in frustration.

Rez, we are all in gangs, man. Think about it.

They parked far from the Bowl and took long bong rips before locking the car and walking the mile or so down the residential streets of West Hollywood. Night had come and the sky was an illuminated blue, bright from the day just passed and all the lights turning on and turning up. Not one star looked down on them, at least one that Rez could see. Their seats were dead middle and perfect and the sky turned pink and then salmon and then turquoise and Rez got high and sipped a beer and found himself close to a girl who moved gently to music that was not gentle. He moved closer and she didn't back away and he moved up to her until an arm touched, a thigh touched as if by accident and Rez felt the warm night and the hard music and her close flesh and was amazed how a single moment could push all things together like this.

They danced for most of the show, closer by accident and then closer on purpose. When the show was over, the girl said her name was Mylaa and she and her friends were going to an after-party and did Rez and his friend want to come? Rez and Arash, both close to six feet but still too skinny to be mistaken for any older than high schoolers, said yes and tried to play it cool at the house on a hill above Silver Lake, where they sat at the edge of the pool and smoked joints and gave away

joints and talked to girls who said they were actresses and said *What's up?* to guys in loafers—all of it under the purple night sky.

The apostles would have died for this.

The apostles are just not as lucky as we are. At least not tonight.

A DJ showed up and the party got crowded and Rez found the girl and danced and then took her back to smoke with Arash, who had a crowd around him and talked and listened like he belonged. More people came and went and Arash handed out nuggets of the weed they'd just bought. Rez heard him say something about hospitality and stood there and stared at his friend. This boy unknown to him two months ago, just another kid in the hall, another kid like him, funny name, dark skin, smart and willing, and now here they were in hills above Los Angeles, at the edge of a pool where actresses jumped in and pulled themselves out slowly and Rez saw the unknown boy was replaced by a person and something greater than a person as well.

The party thinned out and a little light came through the eastern part of the sky. The girls had disappeared long ago but Rez didn't mind. They found two deck chairs and some fruit and Arash told him the story of Malcolm.

I met him at a coding conference for high schoolers. He could walk then. He was a computer geek who lived in the hood. And then he was a bystander.

Rez didn't say anything.

First I bought weed from him because I didn't have anywhere else to get it. Then I started to score from him because I knew it helped him out. He's a nice guy. Why shouldn't we be friends? Love thy brother. It is in all the old books.

Yeah. Love thy brother.

Rez said the words and looked at Arash and wondered if he loved him. He sat with the question for a moment and waited to feel an answer. Arash was a good guy. He made Rez feel good, better about himself, about the life around him, about the world he knew and the world he didn't know. Rez liked to be with him, to watch him move from place to place in a single mood, with a single perspective. Maybe not love exactly but he felt something for Arash, something bright, open, possible.

The music had long stopped and the still water of the pool made the quiet dawn even more so.

Time to go.

Let's do it.

They walked around the quiet house and looked for someone to thank but found only sleeping people, in tangles and alone, passed out on couches and beds and floors. Arash put a few nuggets of weed in the key bowl and they walked the hilly streets down back to the car. Rez leaned the passenger seat back and Arash tuned the radio to the BBC. Rez pressed his eyes closed in mock agony.

Dude . . . really . . . what are you? Someone's dad?

It helps me stay awake. You want me to stay awake, don't you?

Rez leaned his head against his shoulder and let the noise of the voices go in and out of his ears . . . *and today, further attacks by a group known as the Islamic State or ISIS or ISIL. Forty-seven killed in Aleppo after serious fighting with Assad-backed militants. In a YouTube video the group has announced their intentions to take over Syria and Iraq in pieces as part of a larger effort to establish a fundamentalist Islamic state in the region. Their trucks, full with devoted jihadis, pulled into Aleppo as the first front, followed by weapons and explosive specialists . . .*

12

Summer passed fast and then it was August and they were almost seniors. They filled the last days as best they could, pool parties and backyard BBQs and other activities without consequence. Rez learned to relax in front of mothers and fathers, to listen sincerely to the broken English of old aunts as they talked about *back home* this and *now we are here* that. He said sincere *hello*s and *good-bye*s and *thank you*s and could do it while stoned. He watched Arash spot people for hotel rooms on their trip to Palm Springs and pay for rounds of golf at the country club in Huntington, where they were the only dark-haired people on the green besides the gardeners. His generosity came and came and came. Paying for a cab home for Omid if he got too trashed. Ordering pizzas when everyone was high and desperate. He listened as Arash told his mother everything—skirt around the drugs and girls, but only just—and Ms. Dobani always winked and smiled knowingly at her son before kissing his head and saying, *As long as your grades are good, go, have fun. We didn't move here for you to spend your days in a box.*

Rez tried it. He stopped sleeping in and woke up early to meet his mother in the kitchen and talk to her as she made breakfast. He forced himself over the fear and told her what club he went to the previous night and the fake ID he used and the half-naked girls dancing on platforms. She stayed quiet but stayed open and he went on and talked about Arash and how none of them had girlfriends yet and he didn't have one but wanted to and after a few weeks she began to tell her own stories of afternoons smoking apple tobacco in the cafés in the north of Tehran and long evenings driving in cars with her sisters and boys from their high school class. Rez could barely believe she'd ever been a teenager. Within the month they were talking, back and forth, story to

story, every morning as she set out the breakfast and his father joined them and they ate together in one long silence.

By the time school started he was nearly a completely different Rez. The only thing that came back to him from the old life was the waves. He thought about surfing every time he drove on Highway 1, every time he stared at the flat cool vista of the sea from a far hilltop, from the balconies of parties held at houses built into cliffs along the coast. When it got really bad, he texted Matthews and they figured out where the swell was best and went out in the water and waited for waves and smoked and talked and rode.

After one easy session at Thalia Street, he dug around in his bag for something to put on his head and saw the hat he'd borrowed from Arash the night before and slipped it over his sand-crusted hair and waited. It had the words SAND NIGGER arced across the top of it. Matthews stared at him.

Really?

Sure. Why not?

First the white boys and now immigrants? I had no idea you were such a social butterfly.

It's sand niggers for me. All day long.

In tenth grade someone had spray-painted the words on Arash's car. Rumor was it was Jeddidah Paxton, whose uncle was just back from two tours in Iraq with PTSD. Bright orange spray paint and big soft capital letters. *SAND NIGGER.* The school couldn't find anyone to punish so they held an assembly about discrimination, which made no difference because Arash, smart about everything, ordered a series of flat-brimmed baseball caps with an image of a camel on the front, and SAND NIGGER written above it in the same font as the Camel cigarettes, except this camel boldly smoked something else. For a while the hats were a hot commodity and everyone in the school, regardless of where they came from, wanted one.

Matthews's face stayed blank and Rez looked back and challenged his stare.

What?

Nothing.

13

Spring 2013

The bombs went off before noon on a Monday and by lunchtime parents swarmed the campus with quick steps and tight eyes. Everyone was confused. There had been explosions before, bombings, public massacres—the Paris subway. Madrid subway. London subway, a kindergarten in Connecticut, a military base in Houston—but they had never canceled school. Except for the first time, in first grade, when the planes crashed the Towers and Rez helped his dad stick American-flag bumper stickers on all their cars.

Rez and Arash went to the student parking lot and sat in the low leather seats of Arash's car and tried to come up with ways to spend their afternoon. Their parents checked in with them and they said everything was fine and that they were going be at the other's house, *studying*, when they knew they were going to just fuck off, play video games at Neema's pool house or go hang out with the girls at the mall. They considered going to Malick's to work out on his fancy exercise equipment or drive up the coast in Omid's new Land Cruiser, just to be in the car on Highway 1, going slow, seeing, being seen. If they had the time, they would drive all the way up to Huntington to hang out with Arash's older cousin Abbas, who made it a point of reminding them Dennis Rodman was his next-door neighbor.

Arash pulled his bag of weed out from under his seat, packed a pipe, and passed it to Rez.

In-N-Out?

Nah.

Hassan's house?

Nope. He's probably still in class. Unless UCI is closed too.

I don't know, man, where do you want to go?

Rez looked up at the clear sky, saw a little wind blow through the palms and oaks, and thought of waves.

How about the cove? I could bring a few boards, call Matthews. Teach you . . .

Arash inhaled and exhaled and said nothing. Rez had mentioned the cove once or twice before and this was always Arash's reaction. Today, as Rez said it and thought about it and knew the apostles were probably already there—no one wasted a half day like this when there was surf—it came to him why Arash never agreed, never wanted to go and check out the waves. Turf. Turf gave Rez the strange fear in his gut as they drove around Compton, made Matthews say *Be careful,* kept the Mexicans hanging out with the Mexicans and the Vietnamese with the Vietnamese and the Indian kids with the other Indian kids. It was like that in all the grades at all the schools, all over the malls and probably in the brick colleges and glass offices and cookie-cutter homes. All on their own turf. With their own clans. Just like in some stupid fifties movie. Turf. Where some people can go and others cannot. Why was that? What for? Rez understood it in the water, in the way the surfers raced new guys off the waves so they could have the best for themselves, to secure your own spot, and the chance at glory. It meant something, Rez knew, but he was getting stoned now and Drake was coming into Rez's head heavy with bass and suggestions of hookups and putdowns, and he could not think any further, so he let go the tangle of thoughts and stared out the window as parents of middle schoolers and freshmen walked across the lacrosse field, arms around the tiny shoulders and enormous backpacks and it all looked so weird to him, cars and parents and kids leaving at this time of day, the sun directly overhead, no shadows for anyone.

A hand smacked the window of the car and Rez and Arash jolted. Knuckles rapped the glass. Peter Matthews stood outside, his face red, tap tap tap. Rez rolled the window down.

Dude, what's your—

It was Boston, the bombing. Kelly's brother was running it, and now he is at the hospital and the police called his mother to say his legs are fucked-up and he might die. The news says it looks like a terrorist attack. Al Qaeda or Taliban or something, they don't know yet and Kelly is freaking out and shouting about fucking up the first sand nigger he

can find . . . He said you, Rez, you and Arash better watch out, that's what he said . . . A lot of people might be dead, the news said it was bad, like really bad, like body parts in the street bad . . . Kelly keeps saying his brother wouldn't even be in fucking Boston if Arash hadn't taken the test that got him into MIT and all cheaters should go to hell and . . . and . . .

Ok. Ok. Ok. Dude. Ok.

You should go. Get off campus . . .

Ok. Chill out. We're going.

Matthews was still talking, his face puffy with excited eyes, as Rez rolled up his window. In less than a minute they were off campus and up the coast to Newport. They didn't listen to music or talk until Arash finally pulled into an empty movie-theater parking lot because his hands and knees were shaking too much to drive. They looked out separate windows.

This is not good. Not good at all.

Rez sat quietly. His friend's fear was new to him and he felt himself grow nervous—about what, he could not say.

14

The brothers left bombs, pressure cookers rigged with nails and screws, on the sidewalk along the race route. Brothers from Chechnya. Their parents arrived in Boston when the younger one was only a few years old. *A bad time to move children already traumatized by war,* the expert psychologist explained to the news anchor. *It is common to find radicalization among adolescents and young adults who experience traumatic dislocations in childhood, some abrupt move across continents or cultures that takes the child from a known environment, often multigenerational and multinurturing to an unknown environment where they must rely solely on the nuclear family, with both mother and father suffering their own transitional difficulties . . .*

Three days after the bombing they were tired of going to the pool, to the mall, to the library but they didn't want to go back to school. Arash called Javad who said *cool* and gave them the key code and told his brother to relax, said he remembered Paul and was sad to hear it. He told them not to worry, the anti-Muslim thing would die out. No one knew where Javad lived and they should chill and make some food or go swimming in the roof pool.

Did you tell him about the test? That you took the SAT for Paul?

He knows.

Arash parked seven blocks away from the house and he and Rez walked down one street after another until they were on the thin street that paralleled the beach and Arash punched in the code and a light flashed green and then they were in a big room with black marble floors and the three glass walls that separated them from the sea.

They left their smokes back in the car and out of boredom Rez searched the fridge for a beer and the freezer for some vodka. Arash shook his head.

He doesn't drink. He's practicing.

The flatscreen went on and on and Rez, exhausted by the roll of images, turned away and looked around at the apartment. It was unbelievably clean. All in good taste—the modern furniture, the marble floors, the framed black-and-white photos of L.A. street scenes: taco trucks, dried-up concrete riverbeds, graffiti. Nothing with a human face in it. Rez tried to remember something about Javad, Arash's oldest brother, twenty-eight, a success by anyone's measurements. Stanford graduate. Invented something to do with SIM cards. Sold his first company at twenty-three for an amount unfathomable to all parents, immigrant and white alike. The last time Rez saw him was when he spoke at their homecoming assembly in tenth grade. He was tall, like Arash, with the same narrow Syrian face and the same symmetrical features that made them look like the icons Rez had learned about in school. Javad's hair and eyes were lighter, brown and green, like Arash's mom's, and he wore the relaxed clothes of a man who didn't have to wear suits. At the assembly he had talked about generosity. About his work with orphanages in Afghanistan and Syria and how at the end of the day money could only do so much, at the end of the day you had to give your heart as well. Rez remembered now: vintage Nikes with nice pants and a chill shirt. Dressed up but not ass kisser. He reminded Rez of Kelly Slater, the pro surfer Rez saw once, signing boards at a competition in Huntington, who had the same calm attractiveness, an attitude of belonging wherever he stood.

So they watched TV for one and then two hours and the never-ending news spun accusations and suspicions and eyewitness accounts around and around. At one point Rez heard a noise like a small cough and looked at Arash and saw that he had started to cry.

Man, it feels like I fucking did it. Like I fucking left those bombs. Like whatever happened to Kelly's brother *is* my fault.

These things happen. You didn't do anything wrong.

Then why do I feel like this?

Rez had nothing in his head, nothing in his mouth. He sat quietly beside his sobbing friend. What could he offer? What could he offer Arash to make him stop hating himself?

Come on, A, let's go for a swim.

I'm good.

Wanna go back to the car and have a smoke?

Sure.

They walked the seven blocks to the car and smoked with the windows down and smelled the salty air and listened to the waves and then went back and punched in the key code a second time and this time they kept the television off and Rez's phone started ringing with text messages from Kelly telling him *Watch the fuck out* and *Justice will be served* and *Sand niggers will be forced to go home. Start packing*... and then a row of emojis: A knife with blood dripping. A pistol. A rifle. A smiley face with a camouflage helmet. Then there were the rumors, texts from Elissa and Sophia and Matthews with news and ideas and questions. *I heard he's dead. Oh my god. They are having a candlelight vigil at the church on Pico tonight. People are saying someone was after Kelly and that is why the bomb was there then... What is going on? What if he is dead?!? OMG OMG.*

Who's texting you?

Arash looked at Rez, his smooth long face all eyes, the eyes all worry.

No one, just my mom.

Next to the sliding glass door was a small table with a wooden backgammon board and they played as the tide came in and the sun dropped and the apartment filled with that gold light you only get at the beach. Rez caught the dice, threw the dice, made his moves, and looked around the house warm with light and design and intention and thought about how he wanted to be, after high school, after college, when his life was his own. Once all he wanted was to play soccer, drafted by a team in the Champions League, live the celebrity-athlete life. Then all he wanted was to surf, to be left alone on one beautiful beach after another, without attachment to family or future, the waves his only challenge. But no matter how he reached for that self, it did not reach back and he grew tired of craving that which did not crave him. Now he sat in this house and saw another kind of life for himself, one in which he would not have to forgo his parents' dreams for him, or forgo the sea. He imagined himself made of one part who he was and one part whom he

wanted to be. He lost another game of backgammon to Arash and kept his thoughts to himself. The front door opened and Javad walked in. He threw his keys in a bowl, came to stand beside them, and put his hand on his brother's shoulder. For a moment they all looked out the window at the ocean, and Javad shook his head in what seemed like appreciation.

Beautiful sunset. Another day passed. Khodarashokr. Praise be to Allah.

15

Events. Events in response to other events. Think about it. Nothing since the big bang has happened without a reason. And even the big bang might have come from something, because of something. One thing makes another thing, and then that thing makes the next thing. Look at these kids. These two brothers, still kids. They don't know themselves yet. They are acting in response, in reaction, passionate reaction to something that set them off, made them commit to violence. They would not be here if the United States had not invaded Iraq in 2003. The United States would not have had the fertile ground for the lie it told about Iraq, weapons of mass destruction, Saddam Hussein, etc., etc., if not for Osama bin Laden and 9/11. Osama bin Laden would not have been able to recruit those men to learn how to fly planes and then crash them into buildings if not for propaganda about the persecution of the global Muslims, Afghanistan after the Russian invasion, Chechnya in the nineties, Bosnian genocides, or any instance of Islam under attack by the West, one culture trying to extinguish another. History is always a story of cause and effect. Those kids—

Javad pointed to the flatscreen that lit up the otherwise dark house where their lives were shown in photos of the brothers as children, in elementary school, on high school field trips, their faces sometimes caught off guard by the camera, sometimes silly and sometimes sad, attractive, dark eyed.

—are just dominoes, knocked down by all the dominoes before them, and today, they have knocked down the dominoes after them whether it is another inspired bomber, another fanatical anti-Islam party in Europe, some war or death, who knows? Only time will tell us.

Javad sat back on the couch and thumbed at his string of beads and Rez sat beside him, a half-eaten piece of pizza on his lap. Rez had

never heard anyone talk like that. Javad spoke as if he understood all of time and all of history and all of the facts and the way they connected and made a web that caught everything. That night Rez watched him as he walked about his well-designed house, parsed the events on the screen, ordered pizza for Rez and Japanese takeout for himself, watered his orchids, entertained the friends who stopped by—nicely dressed men in their early thirties who took off their shoes and embraced their host with an Alhamdullilah—all the while calming Arash with brotherly pats on the back and encouragements to *relax, relax*. The night went on and the house grew quiet and eventually Arash took a sleeping pill and went to the upstairs bedroom. Javad left the television on and turned off all the other lights and they sat with the flickering light and Rez wished he could see the ocean behind the television but there was only darkness and glass.

Why did he take those tests for Paul Kelly?

I dunno. Money maybe.

Arash has money. As much as he wants. Our parents give us generous allowances.

I dunno then. Maybe he wanted . . .

Kelly to like him?

Javad finished the answer and Rez nodded and tried to listen for the sound of the ocean outside, waited for it to enter his ears and calm him with its soothing crash and hush, but he couldn't concentrate enough. Javad made him nervous and Rez had to consider him, this brother, all-knowing, only ten years older than they were, but complete somehow, finished and whole and wise.

What's the brother's name, the one who's trying to kick his ass?

John.

Is he for real?

Rez thought about Kelly and his hunting trips, the guns and the deer hung upside down to drain its blood. The knife he took to Mexico. The family photos and the father in the military uniform.

I dunno. He's probably really angry now. Their family is really tight.

Javad leaned back on the leather couch and put his socked feet up on the coffee table.

Our family is really tight too.

They heard a noise from upstairs. A groan and then a cough and what Rez thought was a small sob. Then it was quiet again. Javad looked at Rez in the half light.

Why aren't you scared?

I didn't do anything. And John Kelly is a dick anyway. Has been for a long time. Maybe I am used to it.

Javad looked at Rez. Rez let him.

What is your family name? Your last name?

Courdee.

You Kurdish?

Nope. American. Born here.

Yes, but your father or maybe your mother, they immigrated.

A long time ago. Before I was born. So I could be born here.

Javad turned off the television and used an app on his phone to turn on the lights. They came on dimly, just enough to shake the edges off the dark.

We are all from somewhere. Like I said before. Events. These next few years are going to be interesting for our part of the world. In many ways I wish I could go back to be there and see the changes, be a part of this big history that is happening. Eighty years ago the Europeans came in and drew all the borders, now the tribes are redrawing them. Interesting times . . . it would be nice to see it for myself, tell my sons one day, *I was there. I saw the reclaiming with my own two eyes . . .*

Upstairs Arash's phone rang and rang. There were some muffled words and then Rez heard Arash's flip-flops slap down the stairs.

Dude, let's go. My mom wants me to come home.

Rez stood up from the couch and walked to the door, where he waited for Javad and Arash to say good-bye first with an embrace and then kisses on both cheeks. Javad came toward Rez and opened both arms. Rez took a step back and put out his hand.

Thanks.

Not a problem. You are welcome anytime. Watch out for my brother.

Will do.

*

On the drive home Arash put on an old Tupac album and they listened to him talk about dying for causes, loving his mama, failures and bitter success. Highway 1 was empty. On either side of them the shops and houses and parks were dark and even the palm trees and bougainvillea bushes had turned off their color and held still in the night.

Your brother's weird.

Why do you say that?

He's just serious, you know. Like really serious and smart.

The music played and they stopped at a light near the beach volleyball courts. A bearded man with wild white hair sat on a bench beside a neat stack of blankets and bags. He held a big-chested dog on a leash and together they looked out at the sea.

He's practicing. He got serious about it in college.

That's crazy.

What's crazy about it?

When Rez got home, the kitchen lights were on but the house was quiet. He saw the television flash and his father, leaned back in the recliner, asleep. Rez went in and turned off the images of the bombing, the faces of victims, the scroll of the death count and stock market openings in Frankfurt and London, and the room went silent. His father did not stir and Rez stared at the sleeping man. Sal Courdee. Head scientist for the Merck labs. MBA from UCLA in pharmaceutical patents. Homeowner. Husband. Father. Juror. Fan of comedies. Rez kept looking. If he stared long enough, could he see Saladin Courdee, fourth of twelve children from a small village in the mountains of Iran? The man who fled a massacre, or so Rez's mother told him once, who came from a line of Kurdish fighters but wanted to be a movie star. Rez looked and saw only an old man, handsome still, but tired, gravity pulling down the flesh on his face. *I am an American. Whatever happened before was before. A long time ago. Those things don't matter now.* His father's face, soft with sleep, said none of those things now but Rez heard their echoes in the silence of the room. He looked a moment longer and searched for himself in the face, for the fathers before and maybe even the sons and

grandsons to come and found only a singular old man. Rez shook his head to break the trance and then exhaustion flooded in, the night behind him now, part dream, part delirium, and he walked to his bedroom and let go into a wide blank sleep.

The next morning his mother drove him to school and they listened to the news and she cried. Three dead—an eight-year-old boy among them—and 264 injured, many single and double amputees. Rez waited impatiently at the stoplights and intersections and counted the corners until they were at the school, where he hopped quickly out of the car to get away from the sounds of her, of the news, of this new reality that gripped them all.

Be careful, Reza joon.

Bye.

Students were everywhere, waiting for the assembly to begin. Rez walked down halls that now felt like tunnels of stares and whispers. He kept his gaze fixed on his shoes until he got to the auditorium and looked for Arash but only found Omid and Yuri at the top of the bleachers. They sat staring at their phones until the headmaster stood up and the students and teachers and staff got quiet and announced that Paul Kelly had just undergone a double leg amputation and was in critical to stable condition, but alive. The auditorium erupted with claps and cheers and Rez saw a lot of the senior girls cry and hug, and some of the teachers do the same. Inside his chest, his breath coiled tightly and he coughed to get air, to open up the pressure that began to wrap around his lungs and heart. The headmaster went on. He spoke now with a gravitas that no one, not the teachers or students, thought him capable of and the audience sat rapt as he carefully dispelled one rumor after another and explained that the chances of Paul's survival were very good and that the family requested privacy during this period and that John Kelly appreciated the calls and messages and hoped to be back at school soon.

It is your friendship that he is coming back to, the headmaster went on. The warm open arms of this school and this community of

classmates. Please let us take these next few days to practice and prepare our best selves so to welcome John and his family back from these trying times.

The headmaster went on and on to explain classes were canceled for the day and students and faculty were to break up into small groups to focus on grief management and healing. Students were required to attend workshops on culture and conflict and engage in a variety of discussions aimed at *bringing together our diverse student body in understanding and compassion.*

Yeah, right, Yuri muttered under his breath. It's gonna get real now.

The headmaster continued in his sincere and hopeful tone.

We must not let these events fracture or divide our community.

Events. That was the word Javad used last night, Rez remembered, Javad's voice calm, the glass house with the ocean just outside. *Events come from the events before them.* Rez thought about the event of the assembly, the event of a man without legs, the event of no John Kelly, the event of no Arash, and wondered what events followed those.

Two days later Arash came back to school, his easy smile gone, dark bags under his eyes. Kelly stayed gone but his crew, Johnson and the rest, did their best to represent, slamming lockers when Rez and Arash walked down the hallway. The crew would wait for the bang to catch everybody's attention and then pretend to cough or sneeze and shout *towelhead, asshole,* or *terrorist* under their breath. Rez and Arash said nothing, did nothing, kept to themselves and their crew, away from games and parties and girls. The girls were the worst for Rez; girls he had known and liked since sixth grade barely made eye contact now, and when they did, their faces were masks of anger or terror. He tried to do as he had done before, keep things normal, sit at the front of class, answer the questions only when no one else could, get high at lunch in Arash's car, and wait for it to pass. There were moments, with Arash, when things got all right, and the two of them talked about music or classes or teachers or weed like nothing happened. One time Rez got to the car late and saw a girl in the passenger seat, where he usually sat, laughing with Arash. He looked through the windshield to make sure

Arash was actually laughing and he was, the big white smile gleaming through the glare.

What's up?

Not much.

Arash passed the joint to the backseat to Rez.

Fatima is making me remember the Eid party when we put toothpaste on the toilet seat and sat outside the bathroom and listened to people freak out. Not nice . . .

But fuuuun. Come on, we were only eight.

Fatima sang the word and then laughed.

Rez knew who she was, but didn't actually know her. He had seen her a million times; she was the same grade and smart and at the edges of Arash's parties, always alone, always on her phone until the party got big and loud and people got lit and then she'd step in and dance and hang with the rest of them. Rez recognized her as hot, her face a pale white circle in the center of an orbit of black curls, the body beneath it petite, bony and fleshy in all the right places, and yet he'd never given it more thought or flirted with her because she was otherwise so cold. Now here she was, sexy and talky and not afraid, rolling the next joint and thinking out loud in that way some people did when they were stoned, her thoughts slicing at him like blades.

This must be really weird for you, Rez. It is Rez, right, not Reza? I remember in middle school it was Reza and then you changed it. Anyway. This must be such a strange time for you. Weren't you, like, close to these guys? Friends with all of them? You and Kelly used to hang out, surf, do all that American-white-boy shit. Didn't you even go to Mexico once? I remember hearing something about a car getting jacked, or something . . . I am guessing you and Peter, James, and John don't chill anymore. Sometimes you just have to pick a side . . .

Rez looked out the window. It was April and the spring rains and swells had come and gone, filling the breaks with surfers and turning the valley and the hillsides green again.

. . . It doesn't seem like you really know, but Arash says you are cool, then you are cool, right, habibi?

She stuck her head in between the two front seats and Rez smelled the scent of her shampoo, something musky and deep, and the smoke

on her breath fresh and grassy, and however much he had turned off to her, stopped listening, tried to ignore her presence in the car and the truth in her questions, his whole body turned on at her closeness. He stared out the window and tried not to see or smell or want her.

On the other hand, Arash thinks everyone's cool. That is why we love him.

She slid back into the seat and Rez heard the sound of a compact opening, then closing, and things being tossed into a purse and a door opening.

See you guys tomorrow, same time, same place.

The door closed and they watched her walk across the parking lot, pulled-up knee socks, blazer, plaid skirt, long thin legs coming out from underneath—her curly black hair bouncing on her shoulders and down her back with a life all its own—Rez felt himself warm, and he shifted in his seat, and looked past her to the dozens of girls in the same blazers and plaid skirts, and the warmth went away. Arash remained still, silent, unmoved.

Dude, A, how long have you had to listen to her?

Our families have been friends since we were babies. There are picture of us naked in bathtubs together. That kind of thing.

Oh, Rez teased, *that* kind of thing.

Arash did not smile. He opened his door and stepped out and Rez did the same and they entered into the stream of students heading out of smoke-filled cars, music-filled cars, food- and makeup-filled cars, gossip- and sex- or almost-sex-filled cars, walking through the parking lot to the sterile halls. A few spaces away Matthews and Johnson tumbled out of Matthews's truck, coughing and laughing, and slung their backpacks over their shoulders. Matthews saw Rez and nodded and Rez nodded back and the afternoon went on, sleepy classrooms, loud bells, notes, and daydreams.

The first day John Kelly came to class Arash left after second period with a note from the school nurse about a migraine. Rez watched as teachers and students and coaches and even Enrique, the high school

janitor, came up to offer John their hands and hugs and sad eyes. Brittany Foster, a girl who missed her entire junior year to model in Europe, walked the halls holding Kelly by the hand, playing with his hair, leaning against him whenever he stood still. Normally this amount of personal physical contact got you a demerit, but no one said anything. Rez passed him in the halls a few times that week and Kelly paid him no attention, made no effort to catch his eye or say a bad thing in his direction. That afternoon Rez texted Arash and said things were cool and the school was chill and if he wanted to come tomorrow, Rez thought it was a good idea. Arash came back and there were a few more teachers keeping their eyes on the hallways between class and a quieter atmosphere in the locker room after gym, but otherwise it was just another day.

And for the next week the days went like days. Class, break, lunch, parking lot, Fatima talking and talking, class, break, study hall, soccer practice, home, dinner, sleep. By Friday Arash relaxed. No one had spray-painted his car. No one had slashed his tires. Kelly hadn't said anything to him and no one had said anything to Kelly. At some point Arash and Kelly even sat near each other in physics lab and Arash leaned over and said he was sorry about what had happened and if there was anything he could do and Rez braced himself for the cold brush, the punch, something, but nothing came and Kelly muttered, *It's cool,* but didn't take his eyes off the board. During Friday's eighth-period study hall Arash and Fatima checked their phones for parties or clubs to go to and Rez sat beside them in the shade of the founder's grove and loved that he had friends, that it was Friday and he was a senior with summer in front of him with nothing on top of it or below it. Just summer and smoking and swimming until it was time to sit in a classroom in Berkeley and learn and learn and learn until he was deemed smart and grown, and what could be better than that?

My friend's sister is throwing a party in Hollywood. Rich kids from Mumbai.

Could be fun.

O'Neil's is always good on a Friday.

I am not hanging out with old white fishermen.

And on and on, nothing of consequence, nothing at stake, just a night ahead, to do with as they wished. Rez plucked pieces of grass out of the lawn, and when the loud voice of the school secretary shouted through the PA and over the quad, he flinched, it was so aggressive, so unexpected.

Could Arash Dobani please come to the main office. Arash to the main office.

Arash looked up from his phone and his face went pale. He stood up from the grass and pushed out the creases in his khakis. From across the lawn Kelly and Johnson started to laugh quietly to themselves. Rez stood up beside Arash.

I'll walk with you.

Fatima stood.

Me too.

As they passed the apostles, Johnson called over loud and taunting, That's right. A Rash. Could we get *A Rash* in the office please? Rez, could you tell your friend a rash the principal needs to see him.

Rez turned in their direction and felt himself solidify, with a hard body and a hard mind and hard eyes. If there was going to be a fight, he felt himself brace to give and to take, a kind of fuck it—physical, of the body and will—he had not experienced before. A sudden necessity to right something with force of flesh. Arash held his forearm.

Dude. Leave it.

Before the period was over Arash had been expelled. The charges—cheating, use of false identification, and forging a state-mandated test—were leveled with evidence from the Kelly family. They showed Arash the closed-circuit camera footage of him going in, showing the Paul Kelly ID, and sitting to take his SAT exam. Arash was in ninth grade, Paul in eleventh, and the test monitor had barely looked at the driver's license that Arash presented before turning on the computer in front of Arash and saying, *Good luck, Paul.* Arash was told to empty his locker and made to stand, with the school guard, as they searched the contents. They escorted him to his car and forced him to sit in the passenger seat until the car was off campus property, and only then did the guard give him the key. Rez and Fatima watched from the parking

lot as the car made a right turn onto PCH, no blinker, moving at far below the speed limit.

That is so fucked-up.

Rez saw his friend drive away and two thoughts punched each other in his brain. *But they are right, but they are wrong. They are wrong. This is wrong. But cheating is wrong. Arash is not wrong.* Until they exhausted themselves and turned into a long-repeating question. *What is wrong? What is wrong here?*

Beside him Fatima kept spitting out short, angry sentences, her voice getting weaker and weaker with each one.

This is so fucked-up. His life is fucked now. His parents are going to freak out. He doesn't deserve this. Paul *asked* him to do it. *Paid* him.

Fatima's face was tense, pulled at the edges, on the verge of cracking open.

You know those guys. Can you please tell me what the hell is going on?

Her wide black eyes were glossy and the smooth surface of her cheeks turned pink and then red. Rez had no words for her, nothing for the kids who shuffled past them and whispered *Oh, shit* and *Where'd he go?*, nothing for his parents later that night as they sat in shock around the dinner table unable to untangle the wrong from the right. Rez shook his head back and forth at Fatima and turned away from her and walked to the edge of the campus and then down PCH to the bus stop to be alone and think about events and the way they led to other events and the events that followed after those.

16

Fatima lived in an eight-bedroom mansion on the high cliffs above Dana Point. Her father dealt some sort of commodity from an office in Irvine. Every morning at dawn a driver picked him up in a limousine with tinted windows, and after midnight the same car and driver brought him back. Between those hours the house hummed like a train station. Fatima, the youngest of three sisters, one in university in Paris, the other in Damascus, was the last child left. The mother's family filled the house. When Rez and Fatima arrived at the door, her grandmother greeted them with a gold-and-alabaster grin and cupped their faces and waited for a kiss. Rez didn't do it at first, unsure whether he was supposed to touch the old woman in her copious black robes, but then Fatima tilted her chin at him and he kissed the thin skin of the old lady's cheek and just like that she called him habibi and moved aside to let him in. Beyond the grandmother was an enormous living room with floor-to-ceiling windows that looked over the cliffs and the ocean. The television spread out like a tapestry across a wall and was only and always on one of two stations, the Home Shopping Network or Al Jazeera. If it was on HSN, then the room was full of women, aunts and cousins, who sat with tea and telephones and ordered whatever struck their fancy. If it was the latter, the room was full of men with tea and telephones who texted people not in the room, not in the country, and spoke little to one another. The men and women came and went separately, peacefully, taking turns with the room and leaving the children and the old people to themselves. Fatima's mother stayed in the kitchen all day and looked over the work of the two Salvadorean cooks while she talked on the phone. Ellie is what everyone called her but Rez called her Mrs. Hassani and she never hung up the phone when he walked in, just nodded at them and then looked back at the cooks and the ledgers in front of her, everything, the talk, the type, in Arabic. She wore colorful

silk headscarves, Hermès or Gucci, pulled back just enough to show her golden hair. Rez wondered why she bothered. She took Fatima's kisses on one cheek and then another and winked at Rez, and when it was time, it was her voice that called *Ok!* in a thick accent that brought everyone together in the dining room to eat and smoke and speak to one another in a language Rez didn't understand. He watched Fatima smile and laugh and listened to her speak in Arabic. She turned to him.

This is how we live. Clan-style.

And made sure to remind everyone who asked that, yes, this was her chemistry tutor and if she planned to pass the AP exam and skip her first year of science in college then she needed to study. *Ok, ok, you know best, habibi,* they all said, and Rez looked back at them and tried to seem honorable, tried to sit and eat like he was intelligent.

They never even opened their books. She had an A- in chemistry, out of laziness more than anything, and after the first awkward session when they spent most of their time on her bed, watching TV, talking about Arash, arguing about this and that, accidentally brushing body parts against each other until the electrical currents in the room fused mouth to mouth and crotch to crotch, and chemistry was never even discussed. They fucked and then went to the balcony attached to her room and smoked and looked over the ocean and the small green-yellow sliver of Laguna Niguel canyon, where coyotes could be seen if the moon was full enough. After the first time they didn't watch television and stayed off the Web and seemed content to press themselves together with a heat born of their deception and then to peel apart and fall asleep or do some other homework or play games on their phones. She always drove him home before eight and his parents left him alone to ride the high and he'd sleep and dream about waves, or mountains from landscapes he had yet to see.

The next day Rez would meet her at lunch, in the parking lot, and go to classes, where they sat together and answered no questions and refused to socialize with anyone who thought what happened to Arash was fair or just. Their silent protest caught no one's attention but it made for loud sessions of sex in the back of her Lexus SUV. Rez thought about her, her thin body, the black hairs against the pale skin of her

arms and thighs, her crazy hair, and wanted her all day long, but kept it to himself until they were naked and together again to fight it all out by fucking with a quiet vengeance.

They tried to visit Arash every afternoon but only made it three or four times a week once he moved up the coast to live at his brother's house on the beach. They'd show up with bags of burgers and half-melted milk shakes and Arash opened the door with his hair messed up and his eyes zoned out from too much sleep or too much TV. The TV was always on. Al Jazeera. BBC. CNN. Anything as long as it was news. If the room didn't have a TV, then the radio was on, tuned to an all-hours news station. The end-of-the-world tone in all the voices of the hourly broadcast annoyed Rez and he waited for the ten or twenty minutes it took for Arash to get distracted by the food or Fatima and then Rez would mute the TV and turn down the radio and Arash always caught him and said, *Hey, man, I was listening to that.*

If the food and the company cheered Arash up enough, Rez could convince him to go to the beach and the three of them threw towels over their shoulders and walked the ten steps off Javad's porch and onto the sand, where they dropped their towels and went into the water. In the water everything was good again. Rez floated and swam around Fatima, who walked in hip-deep water and dragged her fingers behind her. He kept sight of her long back and the way her wet black curls snaked down it. If she turned around and caught him staring, he grew shy and tried to look away before she smiled, the white of her teeth glinting bright like the light off the water. Arash came and went, floated and kicked and splashed and dared Rez to race him in the butterfly or backstroke, strokes neither of them knew how to do, and the circus of their bodies flailing around the shallows broke the tension every time.

They dried out on the warm sand and Rez dug in his feet and watched the seagulls and rolled a jay. Groups of girls, in their twenties or younger, in high school and middle school, walked by in bikinis and every time Arash averted his eyes. Rez watched him to make sure and each time was the same. This is not what Arash had done at pool parties

or on rooftops in Vegas last summer, he gazed as long as the rest of them at an ass, at tits, a waist and hips. Rez offered him a hit and Arash shook his head back and forth.

Nah, man. I am taking a break.

Really? This is the Cush you were always so excited about, Omid got some from his brother. I can get you—

No thanks. I'm good.

Fatima held it between her fingers and took a long pull as if it were a cigarette. After a few minutes it always made her pee and Rez waited to watch her stand and shake the sand off her thighs and ass and walk back to the house, her hips swaying side to side from the uneven footsteps in the sand. Her hair, almost dry now, flew up and over her head in the wind, black coils raging all around her, and Rez kept a hard and steady gaze until Arash said something.

Looks like you two are hanging pretty hard these days.

Arash smiled, slightly, more than he had in weeks.

Yeah. She's cool. It's easy.

I'm glad. I should have guessed she was your speed.

Rez thought about that. Speed? She smoked, she was smart, she had a fast tongue that didn't let anyone get away with anything. Still, the word didn't sit well with him and he stared at the ocean where a few sets of waves crashed in front of them.

Fatima and I are going out tonight. That chick Emma is going to be there. The French exchange student, the one you sat beside in physics. Wanna come with?

Arash picked up fistfuls of sand, held them up, and let it drain through his closed fingers. His profile was as it always was for Rez: straight lines, perfect alignment, no contradiction, no clash.

Thanks. I am going to stay in. Javad is coming home early. It is Friday.

Ok. But there is nothing a little pussy won't—

In an instant Rez felt stupid saying it, it sounded like an old man's word, a word from old rap songs, and before he could finish his tease, Arash interrupted him.

Everything is not about sex. It's not good to think like that. These are our sisters. We have to respect them.

Arash kept his eyes on the horizon in front of them and Rez saw the profile align and set.

And women have to respect themselves too.

The words were sour. The expression was sour. All of it was not Arash, was not normal. Rez held his hands up and moved his torso back.

Wait a minute. What? I am sorry about what happened, but you need to figure out a way to chill out, if it's not girls or herb, then something . . .

Rez watched Fatima's lanky figure walk toward them from the house. Rez nearly got hard just watching her, the long white body in the one-piece with cutouts along the sides and back, the red lips that she never painted and the big black eyes. The turn-on made him feel bad for Arash but Rez was still pissed at him too, for being so sour, for being so serious, for not being nice-guy Arash. Rez stood up and grabbed his towel and flip-flops.

Come on, Fatima, we've got to go. I forgot I had soccer drills this afternoon.

What are you talking about? It's Friday . . .

I forgot. Special spring practice.

Fatima looked at Rez and he looked away from her, one glance and she'd know something was up. She probably knew anyway. She bent down and looked at Arash.

You ok, habibi?

Yeah. I'm good.

Her face warmed and opened toward Arash and she threw a cotton dress over her swimsuit and grabbed her bag and towel off the sand. As they were walking up the steps back to the car, she said nothing and he said nothing until the engine started and the windows were down.

What crawled up your ass and died?

Dude, Arash is going a little kooksters. You should have heard what he said when you were in the bathroom. And what is it with the news, and Syria and all that shit? Do you think his brother is brainwashing him? Is he going to start doing the prayer push-ups now?

She drove and said nothing, did nothing to break open the tension with an answer, one of the soft chatty explanations she had when she told him things that had never crossed his mind.

You've never been back, have you?

Back where?

To where your parents are from.

Oh, come on . . .

Wait, I forgot. That's right. You are *American.* Just a regular American.

She pushed the engine harder and the car sped up.

Please. Give me a break. You are kidding yourself if you really believe that. You can only be American if you turn into one. Which means a new name, a new nose, new skin, new tongue, new everything. Otherwise you are an immigrant, or the child of an immigrant, and this is not your home.

Now the car was going so fast down Highway 1 that the traffic next to them seemed asleep or drowsy as they passed, the drivers staring ahead into the dimness of their sunglasses, necks craned forward. Rez looked out at the streets and the ocean beyond them, a view he had been looking at all his life. He had spent every one of his days on this strip of land next to the sea; it was beautiful and it was home and he hated Fatima for her question, for thinking anything but what he knew was true. They passed the Jack in the Box in Laguna where he and Matthews sat in the drive-through at six A.M. waiting for it to open so they could have something in their stomachs before they surfed. The lady who took their order was always in a good mood. Always greeted them with Buenos dias, guapos.

Give me a break. You, Arash, all your shit. Whatever. You'll never be American because you can't stop being something else. Next thing I know you'll come back from freshman year all covered up like your mom.

And then it was out of his mouth and he couldn't take it back. The words smashed around the car like a trapped bird and Fatima drove even faster. She stared at the road and kept both hands on the wheel and Rez wished she would at least turn to him and see that he was sorry.

She stopped in front of his house and he got out without looking at her or touching her neck or saying good-bye. Later that night he got a text.

What you said about my mom was rude. Check yourself.

Rez wrote out an apology, probably the longest text he'd ever written, then erased it and turned off his phone. He felt bad and went to the living room and watched television with his dad, an old movie, black-and-white, with corny jokes and corny acting.

I used to watch this movie when I was a boy. I must have seen every screening at the tiny theater in our town. I couldn't even imagine it—the men and woman, talking together, going to dinner in fancy restaurants. Everyone with a car. Unbelievable to me as a boy . . .

His father trailed off and Rez didn't hear anything. He thought about Fatima and felt shitty that he had said something so rude. He wasn't a rude person. Even when he hung out with the apostles and they wanted him to be rude and it was cool to be a dick and make fun of other kids, Rez couldn't do it. And now he had, and he'd meant it in the moment and didn't want to mean it ever again. There was no reason to be that way. He wanted to be a better person. A right person. A person in line with the good and the true. A person whose heart would never let him say a hard word about a mother or a friend.

At dinner he watched his mother set down the plates, pick up the plates, wash the plates, in the same gestures she had done all his life. They ate in silence and he thought about Arash's house and Fatima's house and how noisy they were with guests and talk and laughing. It was never like that at his house. Rez's father did not like to entertain and Rez's mother was not allowed to have her own friends. When the family sat together at the table, they did not talk beyond the necessities of the day.

At the end of dinner Rez followed his mother to the kitchen and stood as she cleaned. He wanted to help, her small frame thinner and thinner every year, the lines of exhaustion, once temporary, now permanent, across her face, but he just stood there, and said, Thanks for dinner, and went to his room. He wrote out a simple text to Fatima: *I am sorry. It wasn't right. What I said about your mom.* After fifteen minutes he got a text back: *It's ok.* He put his phone away and thought

of Fatima, her face and the swirls of hair, the puffy lips and wide eyes with their gaze that pulled him to her regardless of where they were, or when. He jacked off and then fell asleep, his whole body soft, expansive, open to whatever came next.

17

They paddled out until it was calm and straddled their boards. No one was in the water, it was the middle of the afternoon on a Wednesday, and the seniors, less than a quarter away from graduation, got half days on Wednesdays because all the acceptances had come in and no one could concentrate anyway. Rez usually went up to see Arash, but Fatima was having her wisdom teeth removed and he didn't want to be alone so he texted Matthews: *Surfy?* Matthews texted back: *You suck. Long boards at old mans?* They spent twenty minutes in Matthews's garage looking through his dad's boards and then twenty minutes in the parking lot at the beach, listening to Queen and getting high. By the time they made the water they realized there was absolutely zero swell, but they didn't care. It was a warm day for spring and their suits fit snug and the sunlight twinkled on top of the water like diamonds.

Maybe we'll see a dolphin.

Maybe you'll turn into a princess.

Rez was so happy to be kidding again, to be joking and laughing and shooting the shit. Matthews paddled his feet around and around until he was rotating in slow circles and Rez whispered, Faster, faster.

The horizon did not change. Nothing came in and they goofed off and caught some whitewash and then paddled back and fucked around some more.

UC Berkeley, not bad. Not as good as USC.

Ah, yes, but my dad isn't on the alumni board. Ahchoo! Nepotism! Rez teased his friend, who laughed. You see, when you get a full ride you don't need someone to chaperone you in.

Matthews shook the water from his hair until he looked like a porcupine.

True that. It's all bullshit in the end. Four years of partying before the real school starts. And it's good you are going up north. I can drive up, hang out in the Bay, surf Mavericks, meet some nerdy girls.

Totally. Where is Kelly going?

Air Force Academy.

No shit.

Shit.

Rez kicked his feet in the water and wished for a wave but everything around was flat. Matthews lay down on his stomach and tilted his head toward Rez.

Is Arash ok?

Yeah. He's ok.

Not going to Stanford?

They withdrew their acceptance. It's standard if someone is accused of cheating.

So what's he gonna do?

Don't know. He listens to the news a lot. And he doesn't puff anymore. And he's going to the mosque with his brother, says it chills him out.

That's weird.

Show some respect, dude. You wouldn't say that if he were going to church.

Maybe I would.

Maybe you would. Everything is weird for a dweeb.

Rez splashed at Matthews with the flat of his hand and Matthews feigned a clumsy fall off his board into the water in a jokey display.

They ate at a taqueria in San Clemente and ordered everything a twenty would pay for, including beer, because the lady behind the counter never carded, even if they did look like unwashed children who had just crawled out of the sea. Rez loved this feeling more than all other feelings, the sand in his hair, the salt still on his skin, the great wash of waves still in his ears. Only the feeling after sex was just as good.

What's up with you and Fatty?

Don't call her that.

She let everyone call her that in middle school. She was so skinny, it was a joke.

Careful, hombre.

All right, all right. Fa. Ti. Ma. You guys serious?

Just hanging.

I always liked her. She was in my ninth-grade English class. Didn't let anyone get away with anything. And then her hair.

Yeah. There is the hair.

Like Beyoncé.

Yup. Like Beyoncé. It's fun.

Everything is all fun from here on out. Senior summer, buddy.

Rez looked at his friend Matthews, who chewed and then downed his beer in clumsy gulps and sighed the sigh of a glad dog, and Rez could not help but love him in that moment. His love was open and flat like the sea had been that day and he thought how strange that their lives should be like this, happy and chill and of such little consequence. Senior summer and all the ease that stretched out beyond it and how could someone take to it like Peter, without a worry, and someone could be like Arash, a ball of nerves, quiet and angry and torn? How is that? Rez lifted his beer to his mouth and drank the two thirds that was left and felt a sudden wild satisfaction, gold and effervescent.

18

The room smelled like shoes. Shoes and feet and men. Rez breathed through his mouth and then after a while he'd forget and breathe normal and in a second the stench filled his whole face and head and he thought he was going to puke. Arash didn't seem to notice, and if he did, it wasn't a thing. It was part of the whole thing, this dank man smell. Rez slipped off his flip-flops and pushed them up against the wall with the other shoes. Did the woman's side smell as bad? His mother's feet didn't smell, and Fatima's feet, the painted toenails with little gemstones, could not smell, it was impossible. And with just the memory of them they were in his mouth, like yesterday, round and slippery and clean, her legs stretched up to his face. He stared at the pile of shoes, inhaled a few times through his mouth, and went and stood beside Arash in line.

The line was long and slow and Rez looked around to keep himself entertained, to keep himself quiet, to keep from saying anything mean or pissy or rude. True, he didn't want to be here, but also true that he was here and knew it was no big deal, just a few hours and then done. Whatev. Ahead of them men bowed and stooped to wash their hands and forearms and elbows. Rez saw them lift the water to the back of their necks, across their faces and temples, into and out of their mouths with forceful spits. They cupped the water and breathed it into their noses and then blew, one nostril and then the other, quick and violent.

Arash stood close. Rez felt Arash's eyes on him.

You know you don't have to do all that.

Yeah. No. It's cool. I was just checking it out.

You only have to wash your hands. Three times. And your face. You took a shower this morning, right?

Yes indeedy.

He had done all Arash asked. Taken a shower. Kept off the smoke for the morning. Didn't fuck. Didn't have Bloody Marys with Fatima

when she picked him up for brunch. He wore khaki pants and a button-down shirt. Skipped a whole Friday at school. He could wash his hands three times if it meant that the thing would be closer to over and they could go to the beach, light a joint, and chill. Arash seemed pleased.

And your intentions, you got them straight?

I do.

Rez lied to his friend. It was not a word in his everyday life. *Intentions.* And the last time he heard it was in a yoga class Sophia dragged him to in eleventh grade. The yoga teacher said it once—*Now before we start, let us all take a moment to set an intention for your practice*—and Rez was so stoned and the room so hot that the teacher transformed from yoga instructor into an isolated voice that butterflied its way around the room, into his ears, and down his throat, void of all literal meaning. At the end of that class she asked them all to hum a long hum—*Now remember your intentions*—and he still had no idea what she was talking about but opened his mouth anyway and let out the same note that vibrated with all of the other notes in the room.

Arash slapped Rez's shoulder a few times with his palm.

Awesome, man. That's awesome. I knew you could do this.

Rez wanted to remind Arash what awesome was. Awesome was what they did on this day last year when they rented out Sloop, the whole restaurant, in Newport and danced until three in the morning and sang "Happy Birthday" every time they smoked a joint or did a line. *That* was awesome. This was just weird. Rez held his friend by the arm and gave him a friendly squeeze. The worse he felt, the better he lied.

Good, man. I am glad you're happy. It's your birthday, you should be happy.

Rez couldn't figure out why he couldn't just let it go. This is what Arash wanted. When Fatima asked him what they could do for his birthday this year, Arash shook his head no to every suggestion. No to the weekend at Joshua Tree with a night in Palm Springs. No to the barhopping in the Dana Point harbor. No to all of it, Arash dropping his head lower and lower with each suggestion.

So what do you want?

My birthday is Friday. I go to mosque on Fridays. I want you guys to come with.

They agreed as if it were nothing, and Fatima borrowed a silk scarf from her mother and they followed his rules, and now, in the preparation room that led to the prayer room, Rez was antsy, his every thought annoyed. But he kept it together and stood beside his friend as they shuffled forward toward the sinks and Arash received the hugs and kisses of men, young and old, who came up to him and said the same words over and over, their faces solemn with happiness.

As-salaam alaikum.

Wa-alaikum salaam.

Today is a great day, brother.

Yes, brother. A great day.

Rez wanted to make a joke about the hugging and kissing, but left it. *Be good,* he heard Fatima remind him as they'd split up into different washrooms and shoe rooms. *This is an experience with someone's beliefs.* One joke was not going to hurt anyone.

Hey, A, how do all these dudes know it's your birthday? Was there some sort of mosque e-mail?

Arash did not laugh. He looked ahead at the sinks and the washing men.

Everyone always greets each other that way. And today there is a guest imam. He is leading the prayer. We are lucky to have him here.

Then it was their turn and Rez watched Arash and copied him and did almost all the same washing that he did except for the nose part and then they dried their hands on clean damp towels and walked toward the entrance to the prayer room, a large doorway closed off by a thick burgundy curtain. Rez took a deep inhale through his mouth and sighed.

May the force be with you.

Arash stopped.

Are you nervous about something?

No. Why?

Because people make stupid jokes when they are nervous.

No, I am good. I was just . . . sorry, man. I am good.

It's ok to be nervous your first time. Just get your intentions straight and everything will be fine.

Rez nodded. This time Arash put his hand on Rez's arm and Rez saw the look of Arash's whole face, a new face, a different face from

the one he had in eleventh grade, the one that sat next to Rez in the assembly and asked him if he blazed. This face now belonged to a young man going in a direction, toward a thing, not yet arrived but determined. Rez tapped his temple.

Intentions. I got 'em right here.

Arash put his hand over his heart in response. His eyes glassed.

It means a lot to me that you came today.

Of course. A birthday is a birthday. It's your day, bro.

Arash patted his heart again and they walked into the room, their bare feet silent on the end-to-end rugs. Rugs everywhere, Rez had never been anyplace with more complicated carpet. Maybe Vegas. The farther they got into the room, the more Rez stared at the carpets and remembered that guy, his father's old friend, the rug seller who lived in Ventura, the widower with the house full of plants. Rugs everywhere. In the kitchen. In the hallway. On the patio and in the bathroom. Rez would sit down in a corner and stare at the patterns and the colors and listen to his father and the rug seller speak in Farsi. They were nice afternoons, no women, just the three of them sitting and talking and drinking tea, the rug seller letting Rez take four or five sugar cubes from the tea tray and then sneaking him a few more. The scent of the tea, the afternoon sun across the rugs in bands of gold, his father's relaxed and happy moods. The memories came back to Rez with such vividness he thought he was stoned. Following Arash, Rez heard his father's voice on their car rides home from the rug seller's house. *He took me in, in the beginning. My life here in America is because of him. My success. You. Your life and success. A good man.*

Arash pointed to a far back wall where a few old men, too old to sit up without support, leaned back against the wall, moved strings of beads through their fingers, crossed and uncrossed their skinny legs.

You can sit there. You don't have to do anything but listen.

I can do that.

Rez waited for Arash to add one of his wisecracks like don't fall asleep or don't fart or something stupid just to keep it lively but Arash just turned around and walked into a gathering of men, a back among backs.

*

The room, enormous, spread out under a single cascading chandelier hung from the center of the ceiling. Rez was glad it was a big room, full of people he didn't know, all facing away from him. He could sit here for an hour and stare at these guys. He could do that. There were all kinds of guys, blond golfy guys, black guys, really black guys, Asian guys, lots of brown Middle Eastern–looking guys like Arash, whom Rez could no longer find in the crowd. They lined up in rows and sat cross-legged or on their calves and kept their eyes closed and their palms up, everything so ordered and quiet Rez was afraid they'd hear his nerves, the jingle of change in his pockets, his quick and cynical heartbeat.

Far ahead, at the front of the room, a little stand with a narrow staircase led to a podium under a miniature minaret. The structure was not unlike the gazebo in Johnson's yard, the same one Rez and Sophia used to make out in after swimming, splinters in their backs, a view of the birds' nests in the beams when she was on top of him. He thought of her, the straight black hair spilling all over him, her ass in his hands, and Rez looked up at the chandelier and down at the lines of men and knew these thoughts were wrong for this room and he took a few breaths and tried to give himself to the experience, to give the experience a chance. He looked around. Everyone here seemed so easy with it. The man next to him offered his hand.

As-salaam alaikum.

Wa-alaikum salaam.

When the words came out of Rez's mouth, they felt dried-up, like fall leaves, and he croaked them again, held the man's soft old hand in his hand and his soft old eyes on his eyes and let himself join for a moment and then unjoin and then he was relaxed, a bit at first, and then a lot, and sat back against the wall and slowly let loose all his tight doubt.

A man in a white turban and pale robes floated the ten steps up to the podium. All rose to their feet and a wind of moving bodies went through the room and Rez felt it, knew it as intention, and he sensed it

move through his skin. Intention filled the room, singular; encompassing; certain; silently impassioned, and Rez stood too.

For one hour all reality of the room—Arash, the brightness of eleven o'clock in May, the glistening crystals of the chandelier, the snakes and gardens woven into the rugs beneath his feet—dissolved and Rez, in bits and pieces, did too. He slowed his heart, and he craned his neck to hear the man who had not started to talk, and it became clear that these were not entirely his choices, that the air in the room changed and he, Rez, no longer controlled what he felt, thought, believed. The skeptical skin shed itself and he stood and sat and listened and breathed and let himself be one among the many.

The imam spoke with a soft voice. His gestures were gentle, and his face, from what Rez could see, kept the expression of a man about to tell a joke, joyful at the coming joy. Rez let the feeling of the room push him forward to hear, and when his mind wandered, the speaker quickly brought it back with a single word.

Brother.

It was the start of most sentences and the end of many. *Brothers, here we are in the beautiful mosque of Anaheim, California. You must be proud of your brothers who have come together to build this . . . with your brothers, for your brothers.* The imam said it again and again. Rez looked around at the men. Are these my brothers? They all kept a presence, open and receiving; a quiet devotion. Rez tried to hold himself back, to observe and not join, but the atmosphere of the room refused to let him sink into heavy, dull emotions, and so he listened and so he let himself hear.

Today I have come to ask you, What is a Muslim in the world?

The room kept still.

It is a man, or woman, who moves with Allah as their guide. Do not let yourself be distracted by the circus around you. The devil has devised many enjoyable and dark temptations, and heaven will slip from your grasp.

The old men beside Rez sat still but did not fall asleep.

Who creates this desire? What drives a man to villainous acts? To jealousy or anger or mean deeds?

The speaker waited.

A distance from God. And how do we come closer to God? To resist the temptations of the devil and become better Muslims? Through service. Service and duty. I have seen so much suffering and death across this Muslim world, over every continent, on every stage of battle and peace, and the only thing that I have seen again and again is an ache for union. A need to reach out across oceans and help our brothers most in need. For if they are sacrificed, if they go to their deaths against the armies that seek to destroy Islam, then who will we commune with, how will Islam keep its rightful place among the men of earth? You must strive to join your brothers.

The speaker paused and the room and positions changed, prayer beads clinked through fingers, backs stretched. The speaker waited and continued but Rez could not follow the words. His thoughts stayed on brothers, how he had always wanted one. A brother to kick it with, a person to be loyal to, without thought or guess. Once he wanted the apostles, but they were not brothers, except maybe for Matthews, and now Arash, who brought him here today, to show him what a brotherhood could be. Arash, who kept to the goodness of his heart; the worse things got, the more Arash kept faith. Arash his brother since the beginning, since that day at the assembly, since that *Nice work, brother.* Rez sighed and a big want carved a hollow in his gut and he stopped his thoughts and turned his face toward the speaker and the soft voice chronicling a harsh message.

It is the age-old call for the union with all belief so Muslims may be victorious in this world. So your children can grow and live without fear. Your lives are beautiful now and for this we must thank Allah. And when Allah comes to ask you for your service, you must be ready. This is the exchange of love, the exchange that is devotion.

Rez was sure that if he had a brother, older or younger, it didn't matter, he would defend him. Yes. He would. That is the meaning of *brother*. The connection between you makes it so. He looked around the room; all the men had stopped their breaths. Their chests stood flat

as boards and their eyes focused and somewhere above them their hearts floated, full of the electricity of new passions. He saw the backs of necks, pillars of blood life, lined up all the way to the front of the room and he saw Arash's neck, skinny and tan, and the part of Rez that had just joined this room rushed to the front of his mind. *Yeah, dude. I'd save your neck. I'd do that. Totally.*

The speaker led them in another set of prayers and the men stood and bowed and muttered and held their elbows and opened up their palms. Rez wished he knew the prayers, could join in with words, drop and lift his body in sync. His voice was dry and small when he repeated the *Allah be with you* and he felt instantly fragile and undone as if some solid thing in him had evaporated and his body had not realigned itself around the new vacancy just yet.

They met on the sidewalk outside, the midday sun bright and their eyes squinting at the Anaheim streets around them. Fatima was pale now, paler than Rez had ever seen her, and she talked with Arash about the feeling of it, using the word *feeling* over and over. She held her scarf, and her hair was damp and flattened from the cover. *That felt so good. So right. I felt my whole body relax listening to him.* Rez watched her talk and it seemed frantic, a little nervous, different from her normal sure self. Rez said only single words: *Awesome. Super. Relaxing.* And stared at the cars and their drivers as they stopped and went at the light on Milva. Men in trucks. Men in Humvees. Men in cheap cars. All alone. On the phone. Smoking. Listening to music. Men in a brotherless world.

They kept talking, Fatima asking questions and Arash answering, and Rez felt nauseated from the emotions, the new chemistry roiling through him vaporous and cold. The sun felt good, the traffic sounded familiar, and he craved the beach and a joint and a moment to forget and return to the knowing solid form he was this morning as he tried to convince Fatima to put the scarf on and take all the rest of her clothes off. *Please. Just for a minute. Arash will never know! Nudity wasn't a*

rule! He felt eyes on him and saw Arash and Fatima staring, saying his name again and again.

Dude, you ok?

Yeah. Just hungry is all. That was so cool. Thanks, man!

Rez smiled like a loon.

Anyone up for lunch? Smoke? Beach?

His friends stared back at him and Rez felt his teeth start to chatter. He lunged forward and hugged Arash, the thin body slumped in its skin.

What do you say, birthday boy? In-N-Out? Newport? A puff?

Arash shook out of the embrace and stepped back from him.

No thanks, man. Another time.

Arash turned around and walked away, and Rez knew Arash was upset but didn't care. Rez's whole body was freezing and his mind jumpy and his teeth chattered in the cage of his mouth. He might care later, when he could get himself together a little bit, but right now he need to leave, warm himself with Fatima or smoke or the beach. They walked to her car and she wouldn't fuck him near the mosque or in the parking lot of the burger stand or behind the rocks at the beach. And eventually Rez let it go and they sat in the sand, a new silence between them, and stared out ahead at the horizon, the dead flat line of the ocean that gave no hint of the life forces beneath.

19

. . . ***Every turning brought*** *the lights of the town more and more completely into view, spreading a great luminous vapor about the dim houses. Emma knelt on the cushions, and her eyes wandered over the dazzling light. She sobbed, called on Leon, sent him tender words and kisses lost in the wind. There was a poor vagabond wretch who wandered the hillside with his stick . . . a mass of rags covered his shoulders . . . in the place of eyelids empty and bloody orbits. The flesh hung in red shreds, and there flowed from it liquids that congealed into green scale down to the nose . . . to speak to you he threw his head back with an idiotic laugh . . . he sang . . . Maids in the warmth of a summer day, dream of love and love always . . .*

Rez fell asleep and the words came to him in shorter and shorter bits. For long stretches the world of the classroom turned black and his mind, gone elsewhere, saw all Emma Bovary saw, the cobblestones, the lush brocade of her dress, the horses and the steam of their breaths. His consciousness gave up, and up and up until he shook himself awake at the sight of the blind man and the bloody orbs of his eyes. No one in the class noticed he had fallen asleep. No one cared. Twenty-four days before graduation, AP English, it surprised Rez anyone was awake at all.

Mr. Josephs front-perched on his desk, one leg on the floor, book at crotch level, and listened as Meegan, the girl reading the passage out loud, went on and on, in love with the sound of her voice, with the wanting of the woman in the story. Only Fatima, in the seat next to Rez, seemed totally awake, awake and angry. He watched her for a few seconds. Her knees pulsed up and down and she shook her head in the angry way girls did right before they were about to get into a fight. Rez thought to tap her shoulder and say *What's up?* but he was too drowsy to get the words together and it didn't matter much, she was pissy now most of the time anyway.

She raised her hand and Mr. Josephs put a finger up in the air to signal one minute or hold on or you know where the bathroom is and wait and Rez wondered if he should follow her when she left and then they could make out in the empty girls' room like they had twice this week when classes were in session and no one was in the halls. Since their visit to the mosque she was insatiable. Her desire to be fucked like a hunger he'd never known in a girl before. Everything up until then had been good and fun and exciting, and when it was awesome, it had been awesome, but he'd always lose himself in his own experience, glad the girl was there but also glad that he was there too, doing it. Now it was different. Now he woke completely awake to Fatima, to her body and its appetite and to the ways in which he could feed it. For the first time in his life he'd gone down, a thing he'd avoided because the talk was always that it turned you into a pussy, that it tasted like shit, but that is not the way it felt to him. He got between her legs, took his time, tried to avoid it but couldn't help but let his mouth go to all the dark places and lock into her, her pleasure deep, infinite in a way that was totally unlike anything he'd ever experienced. The giving just kept going and the taste stayed with him for hours afterward, Rez passing on the smokes and the drinks at the party they were at, to keep that new intoxication at the front of his tongue. Meegan finished reading and Mr. Josephs, blond crew cut, blond eyebrows and eyelashes, looked at Fatima.

Yes, Fatima?

Why is this book still important? I mean why are we still reading it?

Excuse me?

Emma Bovary is a selfish woman who only cares about pretty clothes and having affairs. She makes women seem vain and shallow. Not all women are like that. I mean, this woman has not one moment of generosity. Not one second when it isn't about her. It kind of sucks, to have to read this *Real Housewives of Rural France* stuff . . .

I like her.

Meegan, her book still in front of her, held up a hand of immaculate navy-painted fingernails and spoke, and the whole class looked up

from their doodles and cell phones and daydreams about summer, college, smoking, and fucking.

I think she's a strong woman. Just because she wants more than what Charles, who is pretty pathetic, can give her doesn't mean she's a bad person. I mean, women have been told to grin and bear it since the beginning of time, and here is Emma, finally, who wants something more beautiful, more passionate, than her stupid muddy life. I like her for it. I think she is a great main character.

That brings us to a good question, Mr. Josephs began, about who exactly is the main character in this book. One the one hand Emma transforms, but so too does Charles—

Emma Bovary leaves her two children to go sleep with some guy who gives her nothing. She has absolutely no honor. Not as a mother and not as a woman.

Fatima was not shouting but her normal even-toned voice, the one she used every time she spoke in class, the one that always had the right answer but didn't brag, was gone now. She sounded older. A slight but desperate edge ended each word and Rez thought she might cry. Meegan raised her own voice to match.

Just because she wants more than she has doesn't make her a bad person. She's a dreamer. And I think she's brave.

The class turned their heads, all chins pointed at Fatima. Girl fight. Rez wished it were with another girl so that he could enjoy it instead of worrying about Fatima, who had become so quiet with her mind these last few weeks and so loud with her body. All the time they spent together had to do with sex and he missed their talks about their parents, or being together in the Bay next year, or even the fight between Drake and Jay Z. But he let it go. Girls were weird, he knew this from his mother and the few friends he had in middle school who were girls, and if they sank a little, it was best to be nice to them and leave it alone. He didn't want to fuck up the sex. Across the room Meegan sat, her face pink now in the center of a million blond curls. Meegan the prom queen. Meegan who dated Johnson for a while in ninth grade but wouldn't give it up and Johnson dropped her and she said whatever. Meegan who was going to Princeton next year because that is where her mom went and her dad went and they said she could bring her horse.

Fatima laughed.

There is a difference between being a slut and being brave.

The room made some small shocked noises. Mr. Josephs put down the book he was holding and crossed his arms but said nothing. Rez watched Fatima's smile get bigger and bigger across her face, almost reaching out into her hair. How could she say this? She had put him in her mouth just yesterday. She liked sex. Was this about sex? What was this honor she was talking about? He was not her first. Wait, was he her first? She had been with other guys. He tried to remember who but didn't get the chance because Meegan, of the debate team, of the SUPPORT HILLARY 2008 sticker, already had her own smile on.

I forgot, Fatima. Your culture believes women are most honorable when they are invisible. That makes a lot of sense, doesn't it?

The shocked noises again, this time louder and this time Mr. Josephs spoke up.

Ok. Now we have brought up some worthwhile issues here. Let's try to talk about them through the lens of Flaubert's work—

Wait. Wait. Let me just point out that in your *culture*, Meegan, a woman can't say anything until she shows her tits and legs. Unless she's something to stare at, a woman has no voice here. That's real honorable . . . Fuck this.

Fatima stood and grabbed her bag and walked out of the room with a strong, straight back. The class erupted with *Oh, shits* and *It's ons*. Rez grabbed his bag and stood up and then sat back down and then stood up again and followed her out. Behind him the class erupted and Mr. Josephs's voice tried to reach through it, tried to reach above and over it and tap it down, but there were shouts and the sound of girls' voices, three or four saying, *It's going to be ok, Meegan. It's all right. Fatima is weird, she's always been weird. She doesn't know what she was talking about . . .*

20

IT ONLY TOOK less than one minute to get out of the classroom. He spent a few seconds watching Meegan and then a few seconds to tell his arms and legs, *Get up, get up, go, go find her. Backpack.* By then she was gone. The waxed linoleum floors of the hallways shone under the orange afternoon light and Rez walked past empty lockers and closed classroom doors to the exit that took him to the parking lot, where he could find her, jump in her car, make her feel better. Maybe she'd be crying and they'd fool around a little bit because she looked hot when she cried and then she'd start the engine and let him put his hands between her thighs. The parking lot spread out around him, completely still. Her car not there. Now committed to this exit, Rez started to walk and thought about the bus and the few dollars in his pocket and why not, it was sixth period and this was a good reason to skip the rest of the day. He got on the one bus that went up and down Highway 1, paid his fare, and sat as far away from the other three passengers as possible. It was only two or three miles to her house and he looked out the window at the small waves and enjoyed the view from the big windows.

He got off at the gates of her neighborhood, said *What's up?* to the guard that watched the monitors, and walked up the steep streets that took him to Fatima's house. The gates to the driveway were closed and he looked in and didn't see her car, or many of the cars normally lined up in front of the two-story mahogany doors, and then pulled out his phone.

Where are you?

Javad's.

And the sickness started in his gut. He put the phone in his pocket and walked down the hill back to the bus stop to ride up to Newport. The wait was longer this time and he watched the cars blow by him

and the light turn from orange to a dirty color without a name that led to dusk. A car full of old women all turned their heads and stared at him. Another car, a gardener's beat-up truck, slowed at the sight of him and then stopped and the passenger, a young man just a few years older than Rez, rolled down the window.

A donde vas?

Rez shook his head.

No. Thanks. I'm good. Todo bien. Gracias.

Bueno.

She wasn't crying when she opened the door but her face seemed washed clean, no eyelash stuff or shadow, just the white skin and dark eyes and pink lips. She looked up at him and her eyes said come in, but her body, so alive to him these last weeks, stood back and stayed cold.

Whatsup?

Nothing. I wanted to be with Arash.

That's cool with me.

From behind her Rez heard the low sound of the new Kanye record and then the louder sound of something on the TV, someone with a British accent speaking in flat, evenly paced sentences. Then he heard Javad.

Rez? Come in. Come in. Close the door behind you.

She moved out of the way and Rez took a step toward her and waited for her to meet him and reach up and wrap her arms around his neck so that he'd know everything was all right, but she turned and walked into the living room, where she sat on the couch next to Arash, who watched TV without saying *Hey* or *Whatsup*.

It was not the regular TV. Not a channel from cable. The resolution was strange and the words at a lag and he saw a computer hooked up to the TV screen, a website image small and then large. An imam in a turban, the same imam who'd spoken at the mosque on Arash's birthday, stood in a different little gazebo and spoke passionately. Arash finally looked up at Rez, a thin smile on his face.

Glad you came. Fatima told us what happened. Pretty crazy stuff.

Yeah.

So much for diversity of opinion at Laguna Preparatory Academy. I guess.

Rez turned his face to the television and tried to block out the imam's words and listen to the thin threads of Kanye coming from Javad's bedroom. Another imam took the place of the first and spoke with a thick British accent, which always reminded Rez of the professors in the *Harry Potter* boarding schools, full of wisdom and magic. They filmed this imam in close-up and Rez saw that he was young, not much older than Javad, and that his hairline had sweat on it and his throat occasionally trembled when he spoke.

Brothers, the Prophet would implore you. Defend yourself. All around the world our men, women, and children are slaughtered for their devotions. Muslim men. Muslim women. Muslim children. If we sit aside, our sons will become usurers and our daughters prostitutes, our caliphate a lost dream.

The beach outside the windows of Javad's house was empty and clean and Rez knew if he slid open the glass doors, the wind that came in would be warm and salty and he listened to the imam and wanted to make a joke about his marshmallow turban or his unibrow or something to break the spell in the room and get Arash and Fatima to laugh and follow him outside. Before something funny came to mind, the screen split in four, the imam's face in one quadrant and the other three filled with pictures of women in head scarves on their knees, prostrated over a dead body; dead families in rubble; children's toys spread across a blast site; a father carrying a wounded, bloody head. A group of men in fatigues and turbans being barked at and bitten by dogs. The photos from Abu Ghraib. A mosque with the minaret demolished. The images changed every few seconds and the names of the cities beneath changed too. *Grozny. Mosul. West Bank. Kabul.* The imam kept talking. *Everywhere there are Muslims, there is sorrow.* The screen went dark and then filled with a field of sunflowers blowing gently in an invisible breeze. *For an eternity of peace, we must fight this last fight.* Fatima started to cry. Rez stood up.

Comeeeeeooooonn.

He waited for the room to unbuckle, to open up and agree with him, but they all just looked at him, with near identical expressions, Fatima and Arash and Javad, their sad open faces, on the verge of rage.

Really? You are going to buy into all of this?

No one said anything.

Rez grabbed his backpack and looked at his friends on the couch. Fatima wiped her eyes and Arash stood up. Rez had had enough.

I gotta go.

Whatever you need.

Arash gestured toward the door.

I don't need this bullshit, that's for sure, Rez wanted to say, but kept his mouth shut, afraid the anger would spill out until it turned into what he really felt, which was sorrow. He wanted the old Arash back. The fun life. He didn't want to beg his friend *Why can't you just chill. Like we did? Like it was?* So he kept his mouth closed, but his eyes must have said something because Fatima rose too now and stepped toward him.

I'll walk you out.

She stood behind him and neither of them said anything until they were just outside on the gravel path to the street.

Fatima, what's going on?

You won't understand, you don't get it. I just can't be this way. Not anymore.

What way?

This way. This stupid American way. It has no honor. No kindness. I don't know who I am.

I know who—

Just go. Please.

Fine.

He turned on his heel and kept himself from calling her a name and swallowed a few times, but when the tears came, there was no more blinking, no more wiping them away, and he let his eyes drip and his face stay wet until he was at the bus stop, where he cupped his palms over his eyes and cried.

The bus came and he got on and the driver saw his transfer and Rez went to the back. The only other person was an old lady, elaborate jewels and puffy gold hair and a large black Lab. The dog wore a vest that said SERVICE ANIMAL and the woman wore the dark glasses of the

blind. For all of Rez's low whistles and tongue clicks the dog did not move from his curled position and Rez turned his face to the window to stare at the faint outline of his reflection and then through that, to the just dark sea that told him, by its color, that it was early evening. Where to go? There was nothing at home but thinking and television and his computer, and all of that would remind him of Fatima, so fuck it. He checked his phone. A picture of Mavericks during a swell went bright and then dim. He rode the bus until Laguna and the shops and people walking around, and got off, walking the mile between where he was and Matthews's house, where he would go, smoke a bowl, and kick it until it got dark.

He skipped the front house, skipped Matthews's sulking sisters and his nosy mom, and walked around to the pool house, where the same Kanye record he heard at Javad's now pounded out loudly through the glass of the windows and Rez heard the sound of people laughing. He listened to the song and picked up his pace, around the pool and the gazebo, to the closed French doors of the little house, where he saw two heads on the couch in front of the television and Matthews walking up and down reciting the lyrics of the song, a bong in one hand, a lighter in the other, enjoying the music, performing for no one.

Rez thought about turning around, going home. He hadn't been close to Kelly, in a room that wasn't a classroom, since all the shit happened so he stood on the far side of the pool and looked in. They were hotboxing the pool house, playing on the PlayStation, chillin'. The smell of herb seeped out of the house and Rez thought, Fuck it, and stepped toward the house and all its happy sounds and smells. Matthews hooted.

Hey, Rez!

Matthews, happy Matthews, easy, glad, all balloons and smiles Matthews. Rez bumped his fist and took the bong from him and knew his friend was so high he had forgotten that Kelly and Johnson hated Rez and that Kelly could at any moment bring up Paul or the cheating A Rash and no one could argue with him and his loss and Matthews didn't know it but if Kelly wanted to be an asshole right now and throw a punch or spit on Rez's shoes, no one could say it was wrong or bad or rude.

Johnson said, Whatsup, and Kelly gave Rez a cold, focused look and turned back to the game and smiled as he pressed his controls with zeal and shot and slammed heads against stones and moved his avatar, a blond head in a Kevlar jacket behind the bouncing barrel of his gun.

Rez sat on a stool at the bar and lit the small ball of green and black and ash at the bottom of the bong, sucked at the tube until the water bubbled and the cool gray smoke filled his lungs. He listened to the Kanye and bobbed his head. He listened to the sounds of the game, grunts and screams and bullets and yells. No one talked and Rez closed his eyes and waited for the high to come, to make things lose their edge, to make him feel like it was ok to stay. He felt a punch on his shoulder.

Dude. Did you hear about Meegan and Fatima?

Matthews stood in front of Rez with his phone on and the Twitter feed going.

Yeah. I was there.

Crazy right? Girl-fight city.

Yeah.

The haze cleared and the other two apostles sat on the edge of the couch now and pushed the buttons and moved their bodies in twitches and jolts as if they were in the game, as if their own bodies filled the military garb, their own hearts tucked into the Kevlar, behind the sweating skin. Rez watched the split screen where their two soldiers marched through various alleys and marketplaces, knocking down doors and pushing over stalls of spices and rugs as men in long shirts and turbans protested and women cowered over small children whose eyes peered back through the shawls and robes. A man rushed before Johnson's character and said something in broken English and took a few bills from the hand of the soldier and disappeared back into the maze where he'd come from.

Intel!

Nice, dude.

Johnson got his man to run and soon the split screen was one and the two forms were joined in a single setting, a small dusty road with dark houses on each side. A dog picked through piles of trash and then ran away as the soldiers approached. Rez wondered at the reality of it all, the street, the garbage with flies, the huffs of the fast walking, the

shifting fabric of their uniforms. To what end, all this reality? He was high now and the television was the biggest thing in the room and he wished it were more fake.

Now? Johnson asked Kelly without looking at him.

Yeah. This house. Here.

They both twisted their bodies to the right and their guys turned right and their boots were in the frame, kicking down the door of a house that was otherwise dark and quiet.

We are soldiers of the defense force. Where is the sheikh?

The avatars shouted now, one and then the other, into dark rooms with faint rugs and small-framed pictures of men and women smiling in the dimness. Ahead of them light shot into the hallway from a doorway and they moved toward it and inside a girl, the oldest sister maybe, sat in front of a few other children, the girls all in head scarves, the boys all with shaved heads.

Where is he? Where is the sheikh?

The girl, almost a woman, attractive and tall, shook her head and said something in Arabic. One of the avatars moved forward and used the butt of his gun to pry the children apart from their pile, to separate them to make sure no one was hiding in the midst of their small bodies. Rez felt his heart beat fast, like he'd just done a line instead of taken a hit, and he took a few deep breaths and cleared his throat and then someone in the television coughed loudly and Johnson and Kelly jumped.

Dude!

He's under the floor! Pull back the rug.

Kelly moved his avatar to do it, and as the floor door opened, the girl yelled and threw herself down at the avatar's feet and then the shooting started and Rez closed his eyes and the shooting was loud and the screams pierced louder but loudest was Kelly yelling.

Sheikh and bake, motherfucker! Sheikh and bake!

When Rez opened his eyes, he looked at the TV and saw the girl outside her house, a boy's head in her lap, his body covered with blood. With his own eyes closed, Rez's mind jumped to the TV at Javad's house and he shook his head to get the memory out, to make it change, but it didn't, the image stayed the same. A Muslim girl in a head scarf,

crying. Blood in her lap. The imam's words from Javad's TV slammed Rez's consciousness . . . *the Muslim is the persecuted of the world* . . .

Rez let himself out. No one noticed. Matthews was on the phone and Johnson and Kelly were shouting *Yeah, man* and *Nice* and *So much for the sheikh* and other shit that Rez couldn't hear because he was out the door and across the yard and around the pool, sweat coming off his palms. He loped down Matthews's driveway and heard the voice of Matthews's mom behind him. She stood in the front door with a glass of wine in her hand.

Hey, Rez! How's it going? You ok?

I'm good, he shouted back with a high wave. And she held her glass of wine in one hand and waved with the other.

Say hi to your mom and dad for me!

Will do!

Then he ran. Down through the neighborhood streets toward the highway and then down the crumbling shoulder. When he got tired, he'd jog but the images came back to him and he had to sprint again. First he thought, The game is not real, just a game, a stupid video game. Then he thought: the imam's pictures were not real, the imam was a known and crazy manipulator. Then he thought that Kelly and Johnson were not real but video-game avatars or that Fatima and Arash were not real but simply brainwashed puppets. After a mile or so he could not run any longer and then he didn't know what to know, he did not, in his high head, know what was and what was not.

When he got to the quiet streets of his neighborhood, confusion and exhaustion churned violently in his gut and he stood in the empty kitchen and threw up into it once and then again. When his mom came through the door, she looked at him and rubbed his back and ran the water from the faucet.

Joonam. I'm sorry. They called from school and said you left early. They didn't say you were sick. Some tea . . .

She put her hand on his forehead to take his temperature, just as she had his whole life.

Let's pray this is just a twenty-four-hour bug.

PART III

To a Good Country

21

The morning of graduation the fog was so thick Rez stared into the blank white and tried to imagine the house across the street. Home of Mr. and Mrs. Haas. Retirees. Proud keepers of bonsai trees and Japanese moss gardens. A matched pair, same white hair, same white teeth, same white sneakers. Parents of a famous movie star, a comedian who took only serious roles now and spent most of his time in a bluegrass band. Once or twice a year the son came to visit, always in a new-model European sedan, always in sunglasses, always alone and in a rush. When Rez was younger, smaller, cuter, the couple would see them in their driveway and call, *Come over!* Mrs. Haas always had lemonade and Mr. Haas once put his enormous bony hand on Rez's shoulder and asked if he wanted to see his sports car. Rez was four maybe five, and followed the old man into his tidy garage, where a dusty green piece of metal sat without a hood, the trunk where the engine would be. It looked like a piece of junk. *It's nice,* Rez told Mr. Haas, and Mr. Haas agreed, *Yes. Yes, she is. I thought you might like to see it. All young boys dream about the same things.* After 9/11 the Haases stopped waving. Mrs. Haas would look up at him from under her gardening hat, then turn her eyes back at the ground. Rez mentioned it to his mother. *They're mean now.* Rez's mother just shook her head. *They are old. Sometimes when people get older, they become quieter.*

But this morning they were gone, disappeared. Between his house and theirs a mist so thick Rez let himself pretend there was no house, no Mr. and Mrs. Haas in their old worn beds, backs to each other, their saggy white bodies silent and still. The sound of Matthews's truck rumbled through the fog and Rez picked up his backpack and his board and wished for a clearing, for some visibility and blue sky to calm his nerves, but knew there was no hope, not until one or two o'clock, until after the ceremony with the gowns and the photos and the dumb hats, all of it pressed down and dreary under this dark low ceiling of wet.

*

Then he was high, floating in the salt water at Old Man's, not giving a fuck. The surface was glassy and almost no one was out, and if they were, Rez couldn't see them. A pod of dolphins glided nearby, their fins up and out of the mist, then down and gone again. The idea of a sea, an infinity of width and depth, filled with life he would never know, dropped his shoulders and opened his breath and he paddled out farther and saw the set as it was coming in and got caught under a huge wave just as it crested and crashed and the big weight of the water pushed down and pressed his body to the seafloor so completely that all the nerves of the day pushed out of him. He caught the next one he saw and rode it almost to shore and then went back for another and another until his body and mind were as numb and loose as any ocean fish.

Matthews drove him home. They wore the hoods of their hoodies up and ate breakfast burritos from Santo's and listened to the morning show on the rock station. When they got to Rez's house, he put a fist up and Matthews bumped it.

See you on the other side.

Not if I see you first.

Matthews cleared his throat and then smiled wide.

So. Uh. Not to get sentimental, but I have really loved sharing these past four years of high school with you . . . It's been really . . . special.

Very funny, jackass.

No. Really. You've been like a brother to me, a brother from another mother, but you know, still . . . Matthews was trying not to laugh, was trying to keep a serious emotional face, and Rez felt his own face try to do the same and soon they were both cracking up.

No. Seriously. I got you a gift.

Matthews put his hands into his hoodie pocket and tossed out a baggie that landed in Rez's lap. Caps and stems. Hard to get. Harder to share.

Dude! Score.

I thought we could take a few right before the ceremony, get loopy during all the clapping and speeches and shit and then be nice and trippy for the family stuff after. Say eleven o'clock launch?

Perfect.

Sweet.

Rez jumped out of the truck and grabbed his board and wanted to wave and shout *See ya* to Matthews, but the fog swallowed the truck and it was just Rez, next to the sidewalk, up the steps, into his house.

An alphabetical-order event. Just like the SATs, class photos, roll call. Rez took his seat between Melizza Cales and Emily Custer, girls he only knew from these ordered arrangements. Melizza had changed the spelling of her first name in tenth grade and then changed her hair color and kept an anarchist *A* in her locker and didn't talk to anyone at the school. Emily. Plump Emily. Emily of Christ and church and the cross that rested just above her cleavage. Mousy until junior year and then born-again and part of a young Christ group with its own music and movies and dates and still chunky, but confident now, looked pretty good, called herself a good daughter of God. Goth and born-again, with him in the middle. What would he be called? He thought of a few names, some types, but nothing went together, none of them fit, and he had to stop thinking because the queasy feeling started and he had to concentrate on unwrapping the ginger candy he'd jammed in his pocket so he could focus on the words of the headmaster, who was up at the podium now, talking and gesturing and smiling, a man so clean shaven and pleased he looked like a baby. Rez tried to turn the blah-blah-blah sound into words.

The meaning of ceremony, through time, has been to mark, to denote a moment of significance. To bring together family and friends and teachers and support networks and take a moment to mark an achievement, recognize a transformation. You have seen these fine young adults as babies, as eager elementary school students, as moody middle schoolers, and now as men and woman on the verge of their own lives. Such tremendous changes and more changes to come. Every student before you has read the works of the great Roman poet Ovid. In his timeless collection, *Metamorphoses*, he says . . . everything changes, nothing is extinguished. Try and remember this when they come to you as college seniors with impressive internships in foreign countries, or as doctors

or as parents, and you can remember that they were once on this stage, once in your lap, once a thought in your heart: Everything changes, but nothing is extinguished.

Rez wanted to cry. He also wanted to throw up. The desire to expel from himself some pent-up substance came and went and he held it together. Clapped. Stood. Sat down. Stood up again when they called his name. Walked to the edge of the stage. Held the diploma, shook the hand, posed for the picture, and then slid back to his seat in the flowing long black robes that made him feel like an eel. When it was done, he tossed his cap like the rest but didn't bother to catch it and stayed back, behind a line of tall hedges, for ten, twenty, twenty-five minutes, while the drugs came up in him and he watched life play out before him, suddenly nude and beautiful and tragic.

As it was in the hallways of high school, it was today, and the families gathered in little clumps, everyone segmented out by color or last name or style. He saw a group of younger brothers and sisters stuff catered cookies in their pockets and then run to hide under the long tablecloths. He saw the old ladies with skinny ankles in saggy hose and men with too-tan faces and guts held back by shiny belt buckles. The fog still covered most things and Rez felt everyone and everything as if it were on the verge of death. A small ray of sun opened a hole through the mist and he concentrated on its glow in a far corner of the quad, knew if there were more, he could do this, he could go into the space of the celebration and celebrate. And then there it was, sun like honey to wash over the scene and make everyone fine looking, make all the eyes glint and the teeth shine. Sun to put gold on the leaves of the trees and warmth on the faces. Rez stepped back from the hedge and took a moment to appreciate the magic of life on earth, just enough water, just enough carbon, just enough oxygen, such a crazy precise formula and yet this one planet had it just right and so there was this: families, trees, soil. He started to cry a little and then a lot, full free sobs of joy, and when that was all done, he took a deep breath and shook himself out from top to bottom and then side to side like a wet dog and walked into the crowd of family and friends and happy teachers. Drugs were so

good. The day was so good. All of this was the universe at peace with itself, everything as it should be.

He let the good feeling guide him and he floated from clump to clump, where he hugged kids he'd never said hello to. Their parents shook his hands and he said *Berkeley*, *Yes, sir*, and *Yes, they are very happy*, and *Thank you, same to you.* And on and on around the quad until he came to Sophia Lim's family, the men in designer shoes, the women in impossible heels, the old ladies seated and snacking with the little kids. He grabbed Sophia from behind and she squealed. Her robed body slipped under his grasp and she turned around, saw his face, laughed, and hugged him back.

Rez! Can you believe it? So cool, right?

Very cool. Graduation day. Just like Kanye said it would be.

Watch out for the college dropout!

She laughed and took a step toward him until they were standing close.

I can't believe we made it. I mean, everyone knew you would always make it, Mr. Chess and chemistry whiz and all that. I'm surprised I got through! I stopped going to class all last term . . .

She kept talking and might have said something about next year or tomorrow or remember when, but Rez heard nothing because her lips, a sharp and shiny pink, flashed in front of his eyes and he could only stare at them, think about them, wonder why they winked at him and then grow embarrassed that such a sex organ should be on a woman's face, right in the front, for everyone to see. Sophia, his first. His virginity and childhood lost to her many holes. Gratitude swallowed him and he reached over and gave her another hug.

Thank you so much. So much.

For what?

She giggled.

For everything. You're the best.

Ooooh k. What parties are you going to tonight?

Um. I don't know . . . all of them?

She gave him a kiss on the cheek and he squeezed her hand. Fifty-two bones in each hand. Sophomore bio. He let the hand go and walked on looking for the next person, the next warm brother-sister feeling.

In a far corner of the quad his mother and father sat on white wooden chairs. His people, and he was their person, their only son, and he walked toward them with tears coming up into his face again. They smiled at him and said things people said all day long and he felt their happiness and wrapped his arms around his mother's small narrow frame and the recognition came to him: I lived inside you once. Once you were my home. But he knew it would be crazy to say it so he said nothing and enjoyed the way mushrooms turned the world into an enormous, pulsing, generous truth. He pulled away and reached for his father, once a monster and now, today, meek, but the strong tall body of straight-up-and-down bones and old skin did not give in to the embrace, and that stiffness, the up-and-down, not-bending body made Rez's thoughts snap toward the dark, the desert, pain, and a million stars. He took a few steps back and felt goodwill leak away.

We are proud of you, Rez. Your mother, myself. You have done well.

Thanks.

Should we go? This is over, isn't it? His father looked across the quad.

We have a reservation at the restaurant at one.

It's only noon, Dad. I need to say hello to a few more people. This might be the last time I see them.

His father sat back down in his chair and looked at his phone. His mother smiled at Rez and pushed him back toward the gathered families.

Go. Go, see your friends. We will meet you at the car in half an hour.

He walked through the groups of families and kids and waited for the good feeling to come back but everything had a stain on it now and all the shadows seemed to fall the wrong way. He heard laughter, clapping, and proud deep voices and he turned in their direction and saw Fatima's entire clan of uncles and aunts and other people he could never name, gathered in the dappled light of a tall Japanese maple, joyous. He walked toward them and they took him in with handshakes and knowing nods and shouts of *For you! For you! Our Fatima goes to Stanford. You and your excellent tutoring.* The old woman, Fatima's grandmother, approached him and took his hand in hers. Their eyes met and Rez waited for her to say something but she did not and so he stood and felt her vibrations, the coursing out of something sure and

strong through the soft parchment of her hands and face. When she seemed satisfied, she let go of his hand and Rez bowed his head to her in some Japanese version of thanks that made a girl nearby laugh.

Getting a little emotional, are we?

For the first time in three weeks he heard Fatima's voice, felt her body close. Three weeks and not a phone call or a text, not even a glance in the hallway or at the year-end assemblies. After the first week Rez wrote her a nasty message about how stupid it was to get so involved with an Internet cause and how Arash was turning into a kook. The second week of silence made Rez sad and he walked around low and angry and tried not to listen to too much Beyoncé or Adele. By the third week Matthews convinced him that the summer was full of girls and Rez started to believe him, wipe his mind of the want of one thing and move into the want of many and let himself flirt, hook up if offered, drift. Now she was near him, it all left him—the anger, the sadness, the want for distraction—and he saw her, beautiful in the black robe and high heels, a colorful bouquet held near her face, and all he felt was gratitude. He took her in with both eyes and felt a calm near numbness take over his frazzled tripping nerves. She seemed like a beacon of all good things, and he stood without speaking like a dumb devotee before his guide. She looked back at him, her face alive and warm and curious.

What are you on?

Rez laughed and Fatima moved a few inches closer and he whispered in her ear.

They made out in Mr. Joseph's room and did as much as they could in fifteen minutes. At some point he had her in his mouth and his eyes opened and looked up to see the posters of Whitman, Brontë, Hemingway, Angelou, that Josephs had stapled above the whiteboard and Rez's heart rushed and he thought, Terrific. Terrifying. Terror.

The mushrooms wore off during lunch with his family, and when Fatima picked him up from the restaurant, she brought tabs of ecstasy and soon he was up again, up and flying. She drove him to the parking

lot just above Laguna Cove where every spot had some kind of view of the sea. They laid down the seats in the back, threw a blanket across the flat surface and let themselves go. Three weeks of energy flowed out of one and into the other until they were both empty and full. When Fatima finally sat up she looked out the window and shouted, *Sunset. Holy shit. Sunset. We've been here for six hours!* And they laughed and rolled around against each other's skin until it was dark.

The night was full of parties, each one wilder than the last. Rez enjoyed them like presents, one sweaty dark room of dancing friends, one poolside bonfire, one round of shots after the next. They held hands all night long, entered and exited each party like the couple they never admitted to being. At Haleh Mernissi's house he followed her outside to the pool, where she took off her dress and jumped in and he did the same and underwater they grabbed each other and kissed and slowly sank. They dried off on lawn chairs, her head in his lap.

I miss Arash.

Rez put his hand on her head and tried to keep his thoughts of Arash away. All day long he'd had to do this, turn his thoughts from the empty space where his friend should have been, laughing, making people laugh, giving congrats, getting them, celebrating his next step, to Harvard or Oxford or some other fancy place. Rez tried to guide her away from the empty space of him.

He will find his way. A's a smart guy. And a good guy. He'll figure it out.

Fatima looked up at him, her eyes alive, black planets all their own.

He already has, Rez. He's already figured it out.

He woke in a hotel room, Fatima beside him as a mass of hair and skin, the bedside lamp still on; condom wrappers, Red Bulls, half-smoked joints all over the table and floor. He felt the great freedom of it, waking in a bed with a girl. He stood and walked to the curtains, which he pulled aside just enough to see the sixteenth-floor view down onto the highways of Irvine, the neat business parks and sprawled-out shopping

malls with parking structures that ran up against the strawberry fields where men and women crouched, covered mouths and noses, heads and hands, to pick and pick and pick in the cool morning sun. He let go the curtain and went back to bed. The first day of summer. High school done. Childhood done. Life at home nearly done. His skin shivered at the thrill of it and he pulled the sheets up over his shoulders and put his body next to Fatima until he was hard and she was awake and they were fucking, quietly at first and then loudly, in a hotel room, like adults.

They ate lunch at a fancy place in Corona del Mar where they were the only ones under sixty. The old men stared at Fatima in her cocktail dress and heels and washed-clean face. They stared at Rez too and a few of them smiled. The drugs left them hollow and wanting and though it was long past lunch they ate breakfast and drank champagne and orange juice and coffee. They both wore sunglasses and neither spoke between bites and Rez let Fatima's bare foot travel up and down the inside of his leg.

On the ride home he looked out the window at the waves off Highway 1 and hoped for a swell big enough to call Matthews and work off the hangover with a long session in the water but the waves looked mushy and Rez felt so sleepy that when Fatima started switching stations, a habit that drove him crazy, he almost didn't notice until he did because each station she turned to played a version of the same thing: breaking news, breaking news, breaking news. DJs that normally sounded like jocks or beauty queens were serious and scared and some of them already angry, reading off the bits of information as it came in. *South Coast Plaza, at least four gunmen still loose, a suicide vest discovered, undetonated, people held hostage in stores, security footage showing attackers firing at random in the food court, in department stores, at the carousel. One of Southern California's largest high-end malls . . . At this point, untold dead . . . Surrounding areas shut down for two miles in every direction . . . a live situation.* Around them cars slowed and some pulled over. Fatima drove twenty and then ten and then five miles an hour and whispered, Oh my God, Oh my God, under her breath. She turned to the NPR station, the same one Arash listened to, and the announcer, her voice steady, told them, *This just in, we have confirmation of the identity of two of what seem to be six attackers.*

Fatima stopped the car in the middle of the road and there were the names, a son and daughter of Islam. Rez watched her hands drop off the wheel and into her lap.

Pull over. You've got to pull over. You can't park in the middle of the street.

She started to cry. Rez reached for the wheel.

Here. Just press the gas pedal a little bit. Can you do that?

She shook her head no but her knee moved and Rez steered the car to the shoulder, where others had parked and sat head forward, listening to their radios, fingers on their phones. They were less than twenty miles from it. Twenty miles south and Rez looked around for signs of a massacre and saw traffic lights that still turned colors, an ocean that kept churning, and bougainvillea swaying up and down in the breeze. Fatima was crying and there was *untold* death close by, but otherwise everything was ok, it was going to be ok, like all the other shootings, this would be ok. Rez put a hand on Fatima's thigh.

Stop. Don't.

Her voice was caught in the back of her throat and she didn't clear it so when she spoke it sounded like a growl.

Leave me alone.

It's gonna be ok. This shit happens now. It's the way the world is and it will pass just like the other shootings and bombings. This is just the—

No. No. No. This is not going to *just* pass. We are fucked. At a mall?! What if there were children? This is right here. Here! Where we live!

She stopped and heaved in a breath and wiped her nose.

Maybe it will pass for you, since all you do is try to pass as some white surfer dude . . . maybe everything *just passes for Rez.*

Rez felt her jab in the middle of his chest, and shame like a hot liquid swallowed too fast spread through the middle of him and he moved away from her, considered getting out of the car and then thought about the walk home, the long miles to his door.

Whatever. Just take me home.

She wiped her nose again and started the car. They drove and even though he was too angry to look, he did, every few minutes, to see if she

was still beautiful, to see if he could stop liking her right now, forget about her face and hair and mouth and damn her in his mind, but there she was, wild hair and smooth skin and shiny black eyes. When he couldn't glance at her anymore, he turned his head and looked out the open window at the world of his home. They stopped at a red light and Rez saw the driver beside them, a middle-aged woman with gray in her black hair, younger than his mom, crying, both hands on the wheel. Rez heard the radio in her car . . . *the death toll continues to rise and one gunman, a woman, has been injured by authorities . . . the situation remains dangerous . . . law enforcement encourages all residents to keep away from Costa Mesa, and immediately report any suspicious activity should this be part of a larger attack . . .* The woman stared back at Rez and Rez held still with a singular thought in his brain: Will she know? Do I look it? Can she tell? The woman, her cheeks streaked with makeup and her eyes wet, peered at him and then past him to Fatima and her face hardened and Rez heard her sobs skip and her breath catch and then the glass of her car window rose between them and severed the air.

Fatima dropped him off in front of his house and Rez pushed himself to forget what she'd said, to lean in and kiss her, to comfort her and say something like *It's going to be ok,* but she did not bend to him, did not take her eyes off the road. He tried a last time.

Call me.

—

Last night was fun. With you. I had fun with you.

—

We can have fun this summer. Things will get better and then we move north. Remember? You said you couldn't wait . . .

—

He got out, closed the door on her silence, and opened the door to the house. No one was home and he moved as quietly as he could, grabbed a towel from the laundry room and took it to the edge of the pool and spread it over the green grass beside the blue water and then took off his shirt and his shoes and pants and lay down to bake his worn body until he felt some calm.

22

First it never happened and then it happened all the time. Sometimes once a week, sometimes a few times a day, but it didn't matter because he thought about it every time he left the house and so the summer was fucked. For a few days after the massacre Rez stayed home, like most people, and watched the news, cycle after cycle on all the channels, every few hours a new detail, a bad detail, to capture the attention and keep you glued. Eighty-three dead. The Spanish tile fountain filled with blood and the floating bodies of two security guards. Men and women and children hidden in dressing rooms, restrooms, clothes racks, play structures, air-conditioning vents. Eighty-three dead. Twelve children. Six attackers. Two Yemeni men, two Iraqi women, a brother and sister from Saudi Arabia. Three of them asylum seekers. Three American-born. They all left the same statement on their Twitter accounts. The same sentence with no remorse: *And we will strike at the heart of America's most sacred center, where the sins of usury, vanity, devotion to false gods, collide, where the souls are damned long before we destroy them.* And then a prayer. There were images of the food court, the glass atrium blown off, shards piercing the bodies of the dead, dressing room mirrors streaked with blood, mannequins toppled over and beheaded. Only Fox, and the Internet, showed those images, but everyone talked about them and debate ramped up on values and freedoms and the coming clash of civilizations. Rez thought of the practicing-Muslim families he knew, Omid's, Yuri's, Arash's, Fatima's, and he thought about his own, his mother's prayers when they left the house, the no-pork rule, the undercurrent of devotion from something long-ago believed in practice. Every house was different. Some had prayer rooms, some did not. Some of the women covered, most did not. Some fasted for Ramadan, some did not. Every one of them shopped. Most had been to that same mall because America was the great place where you could worship many things at once, until now. After a few

days even Rez's dad got tired of the news and one afternoon switched the channels until they found a James Bond marathon and the two of them sat easily and then happily through old ideas of danger and fear and courage.

He didn't feel like calling anyone and no one called him. Matthews was on vacation in Hawaii with his family and Arash hadn't answered his phone in weeks and Rez was still angry with Fatima for what she'd said about his being a poser and how it was and wasn't true.

On the third day he wanted to get outside and left around sunset to go for a walk. Old Mr. Haas stood across the street, his hand in tiny scissors trimming a bonsai tree. Rez raised his arm and waved and shouted, *Good afternoon!* And the old man, who always, at least, waved, put a palm up but did not shake it, left it frozen in the air and then pushed the air back as if to say, stay back. Then he put his scissors in his pocket and moved into the shadows of his garage. Because that was the first time and it hadn't really started happening yet and Mr. Haas was an old kook, Rez shrugged it off and kept walking up the street toward the cul-de-sac that led to the trailhead and then up to the sagebrush and cacti.

Then it happened again. And again. In instances big and small. Sometimes nothing more than extra-long stares, the eyes asking, *Mexican? Middle Eastern? Where from? Should I be scared? Are you the same evil?* And Rez forced himself to look back and say hello or smile. As long as they didn't know his name, that was as far as things went. Only when he showed his name did it get serious, his driver's license to buy rolling papers, his debit cards to get a sandwich after pickup soccer or to buy a brick of surf wax at the store across from the ninety-nine steps, that's when the situation would change. Refusal to sell goods or an error in the transaction, or a hard look and then the question, like a cop would ask, in the same right-to-know tone: *Where is this name from?* To which Rez either answered Iran, or kept silent, grabbed his card and left.

This was not the summer he had planned. No pool parties, no beach fires, no hangouts or trips to Vegas, everybody stuck at home because

of the massacre. And the stories like the one about Hassan the day after it happened and how the cops stopped him for a broken taillight and then took him to the INS, where he sat in a refrigerated room with lights that didn't turn off for two days while his parents tried to find him. He posted about it on Twitter but not a lot of people responded. The air was filled with other noises. Everyone on the radio or television or Internet spewed presidential proclamations, acts of Congress, news of local civilian curfews, and then the death count. The death count that kept rising. The mall with the ring of flowers and candles five feet deep outside its modern glass storefronts. A few times Rez thought, How could this be? This is Laguna Beach, where everyone, even the most uptight housewife, learned how to relax, chill, be kind. It was the way. The beach demanded it. The wealth made it possible. He had known nothing else his whole life. But now his whole life included this, and this included going to the car wash with his dad and waiting for the Mexicans and Salvadoreans to hand-dry the car as a man in golf pants walked past and spat down on the ground, casually, on the toe of Rez's father's shoe. His father didn't look down but Rez did and the man walked slowly on, as if blameless. One of the car wash employees brought over a rag and handed it to Rez's dad. *For your shoe.* And walked away. No one said anything after that.

It can't stay this way forever, Rez thought, day in and day out. After the trip he'd come home and find Omid and Hassan at the gazebo in Laguna Beach and they would smoke and watch the tourists from Riverside and Death Valley eat frozen yogurt and buy T-shirts that declared LOVE SAND and CALIFORNIA RIVIERA and everyone would do as before: Relax. Chill. Be kind.

When it was time for the trip, Matthews started the nonstop texts: *Are you ready? Dude are you listo? Can you hear that? It's a Bali girl calling your name . . .* Rez wanted to say more than *Yeah man, let's do this!* but he was tired and stressed. For a month he did a hundred sit-ups and a hundred push-ups every morning and before bed to get in shape for waves he had only ever read about, rides he could not even imagine. He was completely packed a week before his flight and tried not to read

the guidebook to Bali more than once all the way through. Indonesia. An island chain made of volcanic residue, majority-Muslim population, sophisticated craft culture. Every ten minutes he wanted to go up to his mom or dad and tell them how much this meant to him, the ticket and traveler's checks and the emergency insurance card and the new backpack. When his father gave him the envelope with the tickets and the money, he looked away as Rez opened it.

Your mother wanted to get you a watch. I told her this is what the American parents do. Send their children out for a test run. It is a good practice. Maybe you will come to see your place in the world.

Surprised, Rez couldn't hide his joy.

Dude! This is awesome. Indo?! Thanks, Dad. This is great. Really great. I mean, thanks.

At the airport Rez prepared himself for whatever. He shaved closely. Wore the clothes of a traveling surfer and made Matthews promise to watch his back, tell Rez's parents if he got handcuffed or taken away to some little room. *Just call them and tell them to come here, but try not to freak them out.* But nothing happened. They went to the ticket counter and the pretty Singapore Airlines lady looked at their passports and printed their tickets and gave them neon OVERLARGE tags for their boards and said, Have a nice flight. At security a fit man with a gray mustache looked at Rez's passport and then his ticket and then the computer. He asked the nature of his trip and Rez said leisure and the man nodded his head and let grow a faint smile. Sounds good to me.

Then they crammed into seats and were up in the air, up and gone from the problems of the land, and Rez let his body empty of gravity and roam without limit on any axis. He stared out the window at the open ocean, bright and unbordered, and when he felt the thump of Matthews's sleeping head fall on his shoulder, he left it there and thought, This life.

They landed first in Singapore and sat in a daze at a soccer-themed bar, and then Jakarta, where Rez gave himself over to the jet lag as if to a good

dream where the tweaks on reality were a delight, nothing dark or scary, just surprising in a pleasurable way. In all directions the faces were brown, not a white face in the whole city, aside from Matthews and the random backpackers that crossed their path on the busy streets. Open, soft faces smiled at Rez regardless of whether he smiled first. Everywhere young girls and women gathered in groups and laughed, their heads and bodies draped in colorful patterned cloth, unconscious of their beauty. The food was sticky and sweet and salty all together and from suspicion he ate little but craved much more. The two drank beer in small bars where the music was British or French or Jamaican and sometimes local. Rez listened to these new songs and could not find any sounds of anger or confusion in their jaunty notes and he wondered what the words meant but did not ask.

Neither he nor Matthews tried to pretend this wasn't some amazing happier version of the world they had known their whole lives. The women were mostly in head scarves, but for some reason Rez did not recognize them as Muslim, did not hear the muezzin call above the sound of traffic and music and laughter.

Dude. I feel like I'm stoned, or tripping.

Totally.

And that was the extent of it. *Totally.* They spent an entire afternoon in a craft market, sober as donkeys, looking at rugs of woven straw and wooden masks and life-size Buddhas carved out of teak, all of it smooth and fine and with the mark of hands. Rez stared at the masks for hours, their expressions wholly foreign to him, a single face at once conniving and gracious. Another blissed and demonic. Another repulsed and seducing. Eyeballs unique to each mask just as in an actual human face. That night they went to a club the guidebook listed as *hip international* and met a pair of Australian surfers, brothers, headed to West Java, to Cimaja. Matthews was beside himself.

Dude, that's where we are headed!

Rez, thinking of Mexico, kept his mouth shut.

Yeah. Crazy swells. Super-rides. Four, five minutes. No one for miles.

The Australians had done their research, made solid plans. Their skin was orange and their hair near white; when they spoke, their accents made whatever they said sound like a joke.

Heard you have a black prezzie over there in America?

Yup, first one, Matthews said.

Hard to imagine Aussies electing one of our aborigines, toothpick through the nose making laws and all that.

The Aussie brothers laughed and Matthews laughed a little.

Rez heard the top of the comment, and the bottom of it sank through him. He took a step back from the group and the conversation floated to surfing and comparisons of Australia's west coast and America's west coast and after a few more beers and surf talk, Rez liked them too and it was agreed they'd all take off together tomorrow and split the cost of a rental car.

One of the Australians joked, Best avoid the public buses, what with the goats and chickens and all.

And everyone laughed and they drank more cheap Thai beer and danced with a few girls from England. The next day Rez woke up and swallowed fresh juice of a fruit he'd never before seen and went with Matthews and the Australian brothers to rent a jeep with racks and sat in the back as they drove away from the blurred, muted sunrise of the city into the thrumming green countryside. Rez kept the window down and looked out at the scenery for as long as he could; the humid air and lush land quickly sucked up his head and swallowed him into a happy sleep.

Eight days passed as a single day of wet and dry, day and night. The water was warm and the waves perfect, as if designed by a surfer to please surfers. It did not take them long to find weed and a bar and girls from Japan and France and Holland and they had fun and a little sex and epic sessions that started at dawn and went on long after the sun set. Rez walked about with his skin coated in sand and his hair stiff with salt and each day they talked less and less and simply watched as the ocean stretched out its long hollow arms to meet the land, meet the land, meet the land.

On the second-to-last day a jellyfish stung Rez on the outside of his calf and he rode the board in on his stomach and tried to piss on the sting

but no matter how he turned or twisted or bent, there was no way to get to the spot. A vendor of drinks and snacks watched him and laughed. The vendor jutted his head in the direction of the town and said, Cream cream, and Rez said thanks and grabbed his board and walked away from the beach and into the rice fields that led to the streets. The man at the store took a quick look at the wound and put the tube on the counter and said the price in English. Rez pulled money from his board shorts and felt his leg sting and then burn and then light itself on fire and then sting again. He stood outside the store and rubbed the ointment in and took some relief and walked back to the bamboo shack he and Matthews shared with the brothers. A woman was cleaning and his presence did not upset her. She wore a pink headscarf and Nike sneakers and cotton pants that looked like they could belong to a nurse. He sat on the thin couch and drank a beer and waited for her to finish and then took his first shower of the week and put on something other than board shorts and went for a walk.

The town was small and, unlike Jakarta, quiet. The streets had no order to them and he walked down one and up another and bought a bowl of rice and sweet chicken and ate standing and then walked on until he was lost. In a small alley the call to prayer came over him and he saw that he was standing in front of a loudspeaker, laid into a building that looked a lot like the bamboo hut he was staying in, just a little bigger, with a wide doorway that showed a single room covered in rugs. Men and woman walked toward the entrance and left their groceries and strollers and shoes outside and then disappeared into the dim room. Rez followed them.

The room was full and men took up the first ten or fifteen rows of bodies and the woman sat farther toward the back. Rez removed his shoes, washed as he remembered washing with Arash, and took a place near the back beside a wall to watch the men rise and bow and rise and bend and felt himself want to know the movements and join in. The imam was a small round man with a shiny brown face. He took his place and smiled as he spoke, smiled as he gestured. Rez found himself smiling in the midst of the happy room, and though he had no idea

what was being said, he felt a great and easy joy come from the faces and the hands and the breath in the mouths of the people around him. He sat straighter and tried to find a way to interpret such gentleness among humans, such open love. They stood. They bowed. They opened their palms before their faces and kept a humble gaze.

In the shoe area a few men put out their hands and he shook them and the old imam gave him a jolly grin in passing and a few words that sounded familiar to Rez, but were without meaning. A younger man in a thin hoodie came up to him and gave him a fist bump.

Asalaamalalekiem. English?

Yes. From California.

Nice. I surf too.

He was maybe five or six years older than Rez and his eyes flashed with enthusiasm.

We love visitors here. Not many come to mosque.

Rez said nothing.

It is good you are here, brother.

They guy reached around and gave Rez a hug and then a quick wave and walked out the front entrance. Rez stood frozen for a second and felt eyes on him. At the far end of the room was a young girl, her purple head scarf, inlaid with rhinestones, barely covering the masses of black curls that tried to push out from under it. She caught his eye and dropped her head with a demure expression and Rez felt his breath rise, his body warm, his sex stiffen. For a moment he took her as Fatima, the mouth and cheeks and hair, but without the anger and for a moment he saw what she could be, a person in peace. Rez searched the ground for his flip-flops and walked back into the small streets of a million shops and turned the idea around in his head: *So this is Islam? This is the real Islam. I get it, Arash. I get it.* And with a lifted mood and soothed heart he made his way through the rice paddies and to the beach with such an obvious looseness that Matthews teased him.

Did you get a massage?

No.

Are you sure? There is something very post-blow-jobby about you.

Rez laughed. What can I say? High on life, man. Good surf. Good friends. Beautiful place. A guy can't bliss out?

But Matthews was right, the ease he saw in Rez was real and Rez stood before his friend and smiled. Today was different from days before, now he was different, a door, long closed, had opened in him and his soul stepped through.

23

IT WAS MATTHEWS'S idea to wear skirts, blue and green sarongs with block patterns on them. *Why not? They will be so much more comfortable on the plane.* Finally Rez agreed and they dressed for the airport as if for some sort of costume show-and-tell of their summer vacation. The beaches and good food and days of waves had made Rez silly and happy and he and Matthews spent their last night walking around Jakarta buying gifts and acting like they owned the place. They stood in front of a stall selling fabrics and the owner tried to get them to try on the sarongs and they looked around on the streets and saw men wearing thin cotton skirts like it was nothing. Rez and Matthews tried them on over their shorts and the fabric guy shook his head no and laughed. They took off their shorts but kept their boxers on and walked around the city with warm humid air between their legs and did not hide from each other how great it felt.

Women must have felt like this when they put on pants.

Totally.

They went to a bar and then to dinner and then drinking and then to the club where they met two girl backpackers from New Zealand. Matthews bought them all drinks and they drank way too much and went to a noisy outdoor rave and the girls used the open folds of the sarongs to give the boys hand jobs while they danced close.

Now Rez waited in the passport line in America, waiting to be let into the country that was his but he felt too happy and silly and calm for. All around him the travelers from places that were not Indonesia wore bad-fitting gray or black or blue and seemed pushed down by sleepiness and their dark bland lives. He looked at Matthews beside him tinkering on his phone and laughed at his bleached-out hair, colorful skirt, and neon shirt that said COCA-COLA in Indonesian. Matthews stuck

up his middle finger and kept tinkering and Rez knew it would be some time before their souls returned back to their American-born bodies.

Rez whispered to Matthews, Keep it going as long as it lasts.

Totally, dude. There has got to be an Indonesian restaurant somewhere in the OC.

We'll hit it up on the way home.

Right-o.

The line inched forward and Rez opened up his passport out of boredom. The few stamps were mostly European, with one for the family vacation to Canada, but Indo was the wildest place he'd been. He stared at the photo of himself. Ten years old. Pale skin, light brown hair, bangs cut straight across his face. A serious expression. Maybe even scared. Rez knew that kid, knew he wasn't a happy kid, because of his mean dad and his quiet mom. He had a few friends and soccer and his textbooks and video games and those were fun, but the rest was tense. That was the word that came to him as he looked at the picture of the boy. Tense. Rez closed the passport, he couldn't be more different, that kid had no relation to him now and he tried to clear his mind of the ten-year-old's stare and then the passport official gestured to him *come*.

Her nameplate said FENG and she wore exactly no expression on her face. She opened the blue book, ran the first page under the scanner, and stared at her computer. A small beep came from the machine and she pressed a button and looked again at the screen. Then she looked at him. She closed the passport.

Reason for travel?

Leisure.

Length of stay?

Eight days.

How many cities did you travel to?

Umm. Two, I think. Yeah. Two.

Did you travel alone?

No.

Rez gestured over to Matthews, next in line, his sarong and neon-green tank top and dark tan skin and Rez could not help it and laughed.

I traveled with that clown.

Feng did not smile. She did nothing to change her posture or her face. Rez tried to steady himself, to get himself serious, though he could find no good reason for her seriousness.

Sir, I am sorry but I will have to ask you a few more questions. I'd like you to answer as clearly as you can and keep your eyes on me.

As she spoke, a man entered the glass cubicle where she sat. He stood behind her, in the same green outfit the border patrol wore in San Diego, and leaned down toward her computer screen. The two of them had the most stressed faces Rez had seen in days, their whole selves taut and forced and behind all that a little scared.

Ok.

What cities did you visit?

Jakarta. Cimaja.

While you were there, did you visit any schools, religious organizations, nongovernmental organizations? Please list them by name and location.

No. We just surfed.

He did not think of it, the afternoon trip to the mosque, the room of men and woman at prayer. He thought of the waves and the beaches and the soupy rice fields he had to walk through to get there. There were clubs and restaurants and that nice hostel they stayed at in Jakarta. Feng stared at him and then stared at the computer screen. The border patrol guard did the same and then they briefly looked at each other. The guard walked out of the room and came to stand beside Rez. Feng spoke, her face soft now, lenient, even a little kind.

Mr. Courdee, we need to ask a few additional questions.

Rez looked at the guard beside him and the woman behind the glass and felt no panic. His nerves lay somewhere deep below his skin, deep and out of reach. He had done nothing wrong, he was full of the warm sea, and it gave him a luxurious patience from which he could mine no fear. The country he'd left ten days ago was the same as the country he returned to now, but he, Mr. Reza Courdee, was different.

My pleasure.

He and the guard turned their backs to the line and began to walk away.

Behind him Matthews yelled, Hey! Wait! Rez!

And Rez turned around and called back, Chill. Chill. It's all good. Just some questions. Meet me at baggage claim. And don't ding my board!

The guard took him to an elevator, pressed a button without a number next to it, and then inserted a key beside the button, and the big box moved up and then what felt like down and then what Rez was sure was sideways. He looked at the guard and smiled as if to say, *This is cool,* but the guard stared straight ahead with his hands behind his back.

They walked down a long bright hallway where men and a few women sat with clunky large plastic bracelets on their wrists that flashed every few seconds. They looked at him and he looked at them, every last one of their faces a shade of brown all the way from dark tan to near black. There were a few women in hijabs and a few women in tracksuits and a group of men in Mexican soccer jerseys. Santos Laguna. Club León. Cruz Azul. They seemed tired and bored and Rez tried not to look at them too much and kept his mind on the waves and the clouds of Cimaja, the place most opposite this.

They put him in a room with a single chair and a low table. The guard said nothing and left. Rez looked around and eventually sat down in the chair and closed his eyes and when he heard the noise of the door, he opened them again and took a look at the two men who came in. Both tall. Both thin. The asked him if he was who he was and he nodded again, surprised at their formality, their suits, and that there was nowhere for them to sit.

They took turns asking questions from memory and Rez said what he felt to be true. Yes, he was an American citizen. On a surf trip. A graduation present. Berkeley. No political leanings. Not devout. Not his mother or his father. Yes, he knew of the terrorist threat. Yes, he felt it was a threat. Yes, he was worried for the country. No, he had no other plans to leave the United States in the near future. Chemistry.

Then he paused.

Minor in religion if I can find the time.

He didn't know why he said it. The thought had not once crossed his mind, a minor, religion. But something inside of him was roiling, some defiance, some anger that life was going to be hard again, hard

and ugly and tense. He thought of the boy in the passport picture, serious from the pressures of the outside world, and wanted to be other than that, wanted to embody the bright spirit of these last eight days. The men stared at him.

Religion?

Yeah. With everything going on now, it would be good to see what it's all about. Don't you think? Figure out why people are killing each other for it.

The one who did all the talking said nothing and the other left the room and returned seconds later with a small black box.

Retina scanner. Please look into the lens.

A tiny red speck stared back at him and Rez blinked and the machine beeped and the man who held it left the room and the man who stayed walked toward Rez and crouched until his face was at the level of Rez's knees beneath the sarong.

We have no reason to keep you.

Great.

We saw your name, your travel destination, your smart-ass attitude, and thought we'd take a minute to tell you what is at stake. Every day someone with malicious intent for the innocent people of this country walks or flies or drives across our borders.

Ok.

The people you come from, your mother, your father, their families, the people you know at your fancy school, the rich Indian and Lebanese and Syrians just like you, are not the pride of this country.

Ok.

The man stared straight at Rez.

We let you in because we couldn't keep you out and you know that, your parents know it. You feel it every time someone wins the prize instead of you, gets the part in the play, gets into the better college. Gets the promotion. All of this adds up. And your people, who think they are worth a great deal, know that even after making all that money, they are worthless. Their children are worthless, and if this violence continues, their children's children will be worthless too. The American dream will never play all the way out for you. Do you understand?

The man was not wrong. And his speech repeated inside Rez, his voice, his clean-shaven face, his long torso, and his narrow head stamped themselves onto Rez's mind. He sat up in his chair and focused his thoughts on the mosque, the kind glances, and the jolly imam.

Yeah. I am just trying to do my part. Be a good guy. Go to school. Make my parents proud.

The man stared at Rez and between them not a single vibration of belief pulsed. The man stood up and walked out.

By the time Rez got outside, it was dark. He found Matthews sitting on his suitcase smoking bummed cigarettes playing Candy Crush on his phone.

Dude. What the fuck?

Exactly.

You ok?

Fine. They had me confused with one point three billion other people.

Matthews didn't laugh.

Your folks texted me. I told them we were getting dinner in L.A.

Cool. I'm beat. Let's hit it.

They found a shuttle that would take them to Laguna and loaded their gear and Matthews tried to talk to him on the drive, but Rez finally put a hand up and leaned his head on the window.

Dude. I gotta take a snooze. Long day.

. . . **Ok ok ok.** It's not as bad as it was the first week. I mean, I didn't even leave my house. Did you leave?. . . No. No one did. It was just the fam, sitting around, Moms, Dad, Haleh and Darian, watching the news on TV. Not that it changed, but we watched anyway. Dozens killed. Six attackers, one of them Hassan Amajalad. My name is Hassan. That burned for a few days. I thought about having it legally changed, Henry or Harold or Hank, something . . . Go ahead, laugh. I least I am honest about it. You probably thought about it too. Though I don't know, Rez is such a weird name, like *razor* or *reservation* or something, not as easy to fuck with. But Omid, man, with Omid you are fucked. Anyway the first week sucked and now, look, two months later and we are out, sitting at Maryam's Luxe, smoking apple tobacco and talking shit and welcoming home our friend from his fancy surf trip. What's there to complain about? Are you scared? I'm not scared. Things will go back to normal. They always do.

Man, that is bullshit. Who says you are not scared? Your ass drove under the speed limit all the way here. Two months and my sisters still get shit wherever they go. Yesterday Shadi got coffee at Starbucks and some dude yelled at her from his jacked truck, *Scarf head go home!* She just covers her hair. Nothing else, and this asshole didn't even get out of his car. My uncle says the mosque he goes to gets tagged every night and that the FBI and CIA are parked out front, not even hiding . . .

It'll die down. This is America, man. Didn't you listen to anything in civics class? Plurality? Liberty for all? Remember after 9/11, shit was bad, and way more people died and there was a war and still, things got normal again.

This is different. Something about this is different. I mean three miles from here there was a massacre. Not 9/11 bad, but bad. People died because Muslims freaked out. In our hood. All that America and equality and liberty shit goes out the window! I mean, how many checkpoints

do you have to go through to get gas? To go to the mall? How many times do they pull your car aside after they see your license and look you up and then stare at you and treat you like criminal shit? It's not going to go back to normal for a long time. At least around here. We might not have done the deed, but the police can't tell us apart and we are going to be suspects as long as this crazy Islam shit keeps going . . . All that rap music you love, the cops and gangs and injustice, well you in it now . . .

Omid the pessimist. Relax, dude. Stop listening to your dad's conspiracy theories. Smoke more weed. Just look around. A month ago no one was here. Smoking hookahs and Middle Eastern vibes were like a curse. And three months ago you couldn't get in, the line out the door was so long. People are slow, but they want the normal, the good life, the shit money can buy. It's gonna be nice again, just wait.

Indo was nice. Nice all day. Nice all night.

That's right, dude, listen to us, we're here to welcome you back and you haven't said a thing, how was it? What is the state of the rest of the non-freaked-out world?

Sweet. Good surf. Cheap beer. Nice people. Very different. Most of the people were Muslim. Muslims walking around going to mosque, everything peaceful.

—

Dude, that's right, Indo's got more Muslims than anywhere else. Pretty brown girls in head scarves. It's supposed to be really chill.

Yeah. Makes this place seem like a pressure cooker.

I hear that. And the surf was good, right?

Epic.

They give you any shit at the airport?

Nothing I couldn't handle.

And the massages in Bali?

I plead the Fifth.

25

THEN DAYS AND days of nothing to do. A checkup. A trip to the dentist. The occasional session with Matthews, but mostly Rez's phone stayed silent and he spent the days barefoot in the empty house, reading, watching movies, staring at the surface of the blue pool and then swimming in it, the underwater as quiet as his mind.

He thought about college, the month left until he could get on the Amtrak at San Juan Capistrano to sit for fourteen hours until he got to Berkeley, where a welcome van would pick him up and take him to his dorm. New streets. New building. New bed. His parents agreed to let him arrive alone and he imagined the handshaking from his proud father and hugs from his mother and then he'd be on his own, free to live as he liked to live, whatever that meant. He looked up the beaches closest to Berkeley and the surf spots and saw the wild brown waters of Ocean Beach and the mellow tubes in Pacifica and the late-winter monsters at Mavericks and thought, That will be enough. He'd find a friend with a car, go early in the morning before class, smoke a bowl, harmonize with himself as only the ocean allowed, and then go back to school and learn it up.

He spent his days in preparation; went through his clothes, filled garbage bags with T-shirts and old uniforms and pants he didn't like and left them in the laundry room for his mom to take to Goodwill. He took down the posters of surfers and Champions League soccer stars, the prizes from school and the old anime cutouts, and rolled them up and put them in the garage on the shelf beside his artwork from middle and elementary school, pastels of sharks and paintings of spaceships and a papier-mâché mask of his own, much smaller, face. He did not try it on but pushed it aside to make room for the new old stuff

and wondered if these objects, years of things, were the all of him, a person defined by what he had touched.

Rez looked up to the top shelf: a long row of photo albums, thick spiral-bound books with fake leather covers and gilded edges Rez had seen the million times his mother or father pulled a car into the garage, though not once had he actually looked at them.

He pulled one down at random. Photos of the trip to the Grand Canyon, his whole family smiling with terror before the sheer expanse of rock; himself at four years old and crying at the sight of a giant mouse head bending down to embrace him; at the beach, in a hat and thick white sunblock. A few birthdays and a few picnics and his face, round with pale hair and green eyes, unfamiliar to him but for the serious stare. Maybe he had always been that way in the center, the serious boy, and he felt bad for a moment that he'd tried to smoke it away, surf it away, somehow erase the gravity that radiated from deep inside.

He skipped a few albums back and saw his father's friend the rug seller, younger, a full head of hair, and a smooth face. There were pictures of his father at a rug store, rolling rugs and writing out receipts and posing with a family, an older woman and three long-haired daughters. Rez's father stood a head taller than everyone else and his clothes and hair and sunglasses were fashionable and showy and Rez could not even bring himself to laugh, the man in the photo so different from the man who ate and slept and shat in this house. Rez turned the pages to see a series of photos without human subjects. Landscapes of the desert, mountains that looked like Tahoe, the Golden Gate Bridge.

Rez flipped to the back and a thick envelope slipped out from between the last page and the end, covered in Arabic script, airmail stickers, and stamps of another country's bridges and dams and turbaned men. The only things written in English were his father's name, Saladin Courdee, and an address in Westwood, the handwriting careful and shaky across the front. Rez opened the envelope and shook out a single sheet of paper no thicker than onionskin, and half a dozen photographs, black-and-white with scalloped edges, fell out. The letter was in Arabic script and Rez stared at it for a few minutes and understood nothing. From the pictures he understood less. He did not recognize a single person, did not understand their poses or the places they gathered. In

one, a tall man in a military uniform leaned on an old black car, a cigarette in one hand and a half smile across his lips. In another, the same man, same uniform, was on a blanket in what looked like a desert, surrounded by a few men in turbans and a few men in suits. The man again had the lopsided grin and Rez stared at him, his square jaw and light eyes, and saw something familiar. In another photo a woman stood in front of a lake with a few children at the level of her hip and a few at the level of her knees. The woman's hair was uncovered but behind her crouched another woman, surrounded by pots and pans, and her hair was covered and her face sour with some old expression. Rez looked at the children, probably old people now, no one he'd ever met, yet every face familiar. He flipped through to the last photos, the man in the military uniform again, young, younger than Rez thought there were cameras for, his uniform still part of an army's but an older army with tight boots laced up to the knee, stiff wool pants tucked into them. The jacket, the belts, the rifle behind the shoulder, the serious look on his perfect face, and Rez stopped and stared down and saw his own self, the same serious face, neither boy or man, lost to time. The same look, the same concern. He put the photo in his pocket.

He put the rest of the pictures and the letter back into the envelope and the envelope back inside the album and thought about the line of life, from the man in uniform through his bride through to Rez's father and into Rez and then what? And how? He sensed the momentum of it, the whole long unfolding line of fucking and fighting that somehow ended here in this garage, at the Santa Claus with a cotton-ball beard and the badly painted clay balls of the solar system he made in fourth grade, all of it the spinning tail end of something started in a time far before the times of these photographs, in the mountains and rivers of a faraway place where Rez's face already existed in the bones of the faces now long dead, the faces of men and woman who didn't know Reza Courdee, but knew one day he would be.

He heard the garage door open and stepped away from the shelf, and his mom's white SUV pulled in. From inside the sealed car his mom waved. Rez waved back and walked into the house.

How to become a man?

Rez held himself and knew the organ in his hands was not it. He was male but that didn't make him a man. Fatima slept beside him in sheets that tangled around her limbs, black hair flung out around like a dark halo, all woman, no part girl. But how? Because she bled? Because her chest was no longer flat and she didn't giggle? She hadn't had a baby, wasn't married, and yet when the world looked at her, they saw a woman and when it looked at him, they saw a boy.

Fatima rolled from her side to her back and Rez looked at her, the ribs coming into and out of view as she breathed, freckles spread out on her breastbone and shoulders, the neck a strong thin muscular cord, and the head, eyes closed, totally still. He filled his eyes with her as if this were the last time. He looked and looked.

Why did his body jump to her and only her? All the girls before, Sophia and everyone else, never made him feel like this. He wanted their bodies when they were in front of him, offered or teasing his eye, but afterward he forgot about them. It was only Fatima he craved in her absence. When she called him, three weeks after he came back from Bali, nearly two and half months after the massacre, he answered the phone on the first ring and said *Not much* and *Yeah, I can hang* and *Cool.* Then he begged his mom for a ride to Fatima's house. Now the desire had a destination and he focused on that moment with such discipline that when she answered the door in a long loose dress and silk scarf wrapped around her hair, Rez still let out a short sigh of relief, like a man whose plane has landed in a war zone after a turbulent flight. He smiled and said hello and wanted to say thank-you, for asking him over, for letting him back into her, and she took a step away from his attempt at a hug and pulled the door wide, her face a warm open smile.

It is nice to see you, Reza.

You too.

He put his hands in his pockets and took them out again. She stood back from the open door.

Come in.

The house was empty, the whole family gone to a cousin's wedding in Santa Ana, no one back until late. Normally Rez knew what that meant, but now as he watched her move around the kitchen steeping black tea, he tried, with difficulty, to tame himself of any expectation.

They sat outside under an overlarge umbrella and drank the hot tea. Rez took tiny sips of the bitter drink and realized she had never before prepared anything for him, never served him more than a soda tossed from a fridge or a perfectly rolled joint. He drank and kept his eyes on the hummingbirds that came and went from the ornate glass feeder hung from the branch of a nearby Japanese maple. It took some time but they started to talk, and when they did, it was not the talk of adults but also not the conversations they had had as high school kids. Rez did not ask when they were going to smoke, said nothing about how good she looked, and Fatima sat up straight and the drank her tea with patience. She smiled each time she asked him a question and behaved as if the thing that had once banged around her bright pale face had come to land. They sat in the empty garden and Rez felt seriousness between them, becoming them.

How was the trip?

Rez wanted to answer in a few words but talked for a long time and with much excitement about the world he'd found in Indo, a place where Muslims were everywhere and no one, no single life, even the poorest ones, seemed stressed. He told her about his visit to the mosque and how he'd sat there and the way his whole body felt loose with a kind of love.

Sounds nice.

Fatima looked into her teacup. Rez saw the sweat bead around her forehead and lip. He wanted to lick it off. He pushed himself farther back into his seat and adjusted his shorts. He didn't mention what happened at the airport.

Your scarf looks hot. I mean, it looks like it is making you hot. I mean warm. You know what I mean.

She laughed and adjusted the edge of it to cover the stray bits of hair come loose around her face. It wasn't well tied, like the ones the girls in Bali wore, and he wanted to see her hair.

It feels nice. Keeps my hair in one place. Doesn't stick to my neck now.

He knew better than to ask why she was wearing it, what was going on with the outfit and the tea and the invitation.

What have you been up to?

Studying.

Studying? Rez nearly laughed. School is over, Stanford doesn't give summer reading, do they?

No, thank God. I've been studying other things. The Koran, politics.

For what?

For me.

Oh.

Rez tried not to let his mind go back, to the afternoon at Javad's house, the violence on innocent people, the determined imam, the YouTube clips.

And what have you learned?

That there is much much more to learn.

Rez waited.

And I've learned that so much of what we think is important, isn't.

—

It is important to believe in a power bigger than yourself. To pray. To honor your family. To serve. To have a spiritual center. To love.

Love. In six months of sex, long stoned afternoons at the beach, and parties, it was a word she'd never said. Whenever he wanted to say it, he resisted, knowing it was not her language, not even in that way that girls always said, *I love those shoes. I totally love that show. I love that song.* Now here it was, from her lips, *love,* and Rez wanted more of that word, more of her lips, more of more.

She drank the tea and sweat.

I started to cover the day after the attacks. The day after we graduated. My mom wears it and I wanted to do something to show I was with her, with my aunts and cousins and other Muslim women to show

that not all Muslims are terrorists. To challenge anyone who came at us. I am young. This country teaches young women not to be afraid, I am not afraid.

A hummingbird buzzed up to the feeder, extended its beak, buzzed away. Stillness and motion.

It took only one day. Some guy threw a full jar of peanut butter at me in the parking lot of Albertsons and called me a terrorist whore. The jar just missed my head. I called the police, and when they came, they acted like it was my fault. They asked if maybe he dropped the jar by accident. If there were any witnesses. Maybe I cut him off with my cart. Without witnesses there was nothing they could do. Then they told me to be more careful.

She stopped talking and took another sip.

One of the officers said I should be brought in, just to make sure I had no affiliations. The other cop, a Mexican guy, told him to drop it. Then they left. There have been other incidents since. Mostly harassment. But that was the worst.

She put the teacup down and sat back and stared at Rez, her posture still straight, her gaze harder now. Rez waited and she said nothing. He waited a little longer.

Tomorrow I'm going to a new mosque, to begin my studies, to see what I can contribute.

Rez waited for the invitation to join her, waited to see what his heart felt at the thought of it, but she did not ask. Fatima stood and tucked the new loose hairs under her scarf and then put out her hand to him, not with the palm sideways like a handshake, but with the palm up, as an invitation. He placed his hand on hers and they closed fingers and for a minute the garden, the table, the three-tiered fountain, and the million-dollar house swirled as his head went light and his balance gave.

But first I needed to see you. The way we used to. One last time.

He followed her to the bedroom they'd spent countless afternoons in, smoking and fucking and not even pretending to do the chemistry they were supposed to be doing. At first their bodies met in silence, with

intensity; the second time slowly; and the third time with a violence she did not protest. She fell asleep nearly immediately afterward and he sat up beside the smell and sight of her, the woman of her, and thought the thought that wouldn't leave him: how to become a man?

Choices. To make them yourself and then live by them. To know what to do with your own body and mind. A man made choices. A child did not make choices. He thought of the man in the military uniform from the black-and-white photographs. His pleased gaze, in command of his fate. He saw his father, just arrived in America, the man in him beginning to make the decisions that would take him into manhood and now old age. Rez stared at Fatima, who directed the course of her life, regardless of what people thought. He considered himself, and the way he moved in reaction, like a pinball, from one thing to the next, as he was told, as was expected, as made the least friction, and he knew this was the lazy behavior of a scared boy.

He watched her sleep. He watched her sleep and stretch and sleep again and told himself this would not be the last time to see it, her naked body full of him, this body that made him awake to life. No, this would not be the last time. He let this feeling form in him like a strong sense of direction and slowly it became a determination and a decision. To be a man was to be with Fatima, to have the woman of his choice, to make a union with her, see this body without cover, available to him at any time. To be a man he must enter into love.

27

THE PACKET CAME with the rest of the mail and Rez grabbed it off the floor. It was heavy and stamped with the words WELCOME, FRESHMAN across the front and the back. He went to his room, threw it on his bed, and closed the blinds against the heat.

Afternoon today was hotter than yesterday and the day before and probably not as hot as tomorrow and this was late July in SoCal. He should have been at the beach but he liked the cool empty vibe of his house and stayed home, in board shorts, in and out of the pool, reading the old copies of *National Geographic* his father collected before the Internet showed the world at a glance whenever they wanted. Rez fanned out the pieces: magazines and leaflets and flyers and a decal of the university bear. The pictures showed students and teachers and classrooms, lots of grass and lots of backpacks. Rez saw a photo of a clock tower with a great bay behind it and the Golden Gate Bridge in the distance. The water looked steely and flat and Rez wondered where exactly the waves were.

Consent forms. Class offerings. A letter from the head of the chemistry program. Orientation schedule. Social mixers for freshmen. Dorm assignments. Sports clubs. Academic clubs. Student health clubs. *10 Tips for Surviving Your First Month.* Rez wondered, what would kill him the first month? All the images in the pamphlet showed students all around campus, smiling in various versions of the school logo, sweatshirts, shorts, T-shirts, soccer socks. There were no heads in any of the photographs, just artfully shot body parts. The pages were numbered like a *Letterman* countdown: *10. Don't overpack. 9. Attend welcome events. 7. Don't forget where you come from. It is ok to feel a little homesick at first, or to even feel like you've outgrown your home . . . 3. Ask an upperclassman for help. 2. Call home. 1. Keep an open mind.*

Rez gathered the materials and shoved them back into the envelope and threw the whole packet into the bottom drawer of his desk. In three weeks he could look at it again, maybe then it would mean something.

Who doesn't like surprises?

Fatima asked again and again until he finally said, Ok, and when she came to pick him up, he had to talk himself down from horny expectations and just be happy to see her and sit in the closed space of the car with her skin and scent.

Salaam.

Hello to you too.

The last time they hung out she'd brought a picnic and they went to a park and sat in the shade not far from a playground full of blond kids and OC moms. She sat across from him and snacked on grapes and read passages from the Koran out loud to practice her Arabic, to *try out the thoughts*. Rez resisted the sound of them, their order and severity, but after a while he opened his ears and his brain switched to student mode and listened to her slow and faulty Arabic and the translation she did immediately afterward. He wondered about the passages, their odd directives and complete certainty, and considered the feelings they left him with—at once gentle and determined—his mind turned toward them now, curious. Fatima read on.

And forget not your portion of legal enjoyment in this world and do good as Allah has been good to you and seek not mischief in the land.

Rez noticed her scarf, nicely tied, was cleaner around the face now, neater over the head. He'd complimented her on it when she picked him up.

YouTube, Arab girls in the projects in France have their own channel. The girls in France don't mess around.

He saw how much care she put into it, how it was ironed and smooth, and when the wind blew, it fluttered a little but nothing was exposed. She continued to read as if in a kind of musical meditation.

Stand firmly against injustice as witness to Allah even if it be against yourselves or your parents and relatives. It feels like it was

written for me, maybe for all of us. Here we are, in this country suspicious of us, in a world that is trying to make life miserable for Muslims who want to be peaceful and devout. Stand firm. Stand firmly.

On and on it went until the grapes and the chips and the lemonade were gone. Rez absorbed each passage like the solution to a long problem he tried to solve every morning. How to be good. How to trust. How to be a person. The words from the Koran were clues, and when an ant crawled slowly up his flip-flop and his foot, he let it alone and thought of grace. Fatima read and he listened and watched the children play their games on the playground, their souls unconcerned with God, and the words of the old text came through him and he understood them as a call to a devotion complete and without error.

When she dropped him off at his house, Rez said thank-you and wanted to touch her but instead just let his eyes settle into hers for a moment longer and the heat built between them. Rez felt himself light up from the center out to the fingers and toes and Fatima blushed.

Ok. Bye.

Bye.

When he sat for dinner with his parents, he stared at the food, eggplant stew and rice, fresh radishes and mint and green onions, and thought of the perfect symmetry, the crisp and soft, fresh and cooked, and opened himself up to it and to the gratitude he had to his mother and father for providing it. Another kind of heat began to spread, evenly and throughout his form.

This is so good.

His mother looked at him and tilted her head.

Same as it has been all these years.

From the head of the table his father gave a loud, solid laugh.

Yes, but he is just starting to realize how much he will miss it in two weeks! Don't worry, we will visit. I am sure she will bring a cooler full of food.

Rez did not know what he had done to deserve the mother before him, the father, and it broke his heart to imagine himself far from them, detached. He stared at the flat blue water of the pool outside and focused

on the single yellow ginkgo leaf in a slow float across the surface, the water's easy way.

She drove down Highway 1 until they turned into an anonymous strip mall where Rez assumed she was going to run some errand. Nail shop. Dry cleaner. Designer consignment. Walgreens. Sushi restaurant. FedEx. Kinko's.

The surprise is dry cleaning?

Hop out.

He followed her into the Kinko's and waited before the counter as she paid the cashier in cash for an hour on a computer.

What's wrong with your computer? Why the cash? What happened to your card?

Don't worry about it.

The cashier, in his late thirties with soft thin blond hair and crooked shoulders, pointed at the computer farthest away from him and said, Use the headphones if you are going to chat and don't talk too loud. He seemed to have an idea of who they were and what they wanted, which was more than Rez could say.

Fatima woke the screen and logged on to her Skype account with a name he didn't recognize. She scrolled through a list of contacts Rez had never heard of. She clicked on one before he had a chance to read it and the screen went blue and they sat and stared at the reflection of themselves: two people, a pretty girl in a scarf, big cat eyes and pale skin, and a handsome guy, younger than a man but older than a boy, square jaw and close-cut hair. For that instant Rez did not recognize himself or Fatima and saw two strangers, a boy and a girl, waiting. Then the call connected and a guy in a funny hat, with a spotty thin beard, spoke to them and Rez nearly jumped out of his seat.

Dude. A! What's up?!

Light filled Arash's eyes.

Reza, my man! Long time!

And it was him. Arash. The same voice, same happy face, thinner and smaller under the hat. Different costume, but everything else like it was. A sharp sensation went through Rez and he wanted his friend

here right now, to hang with, to fill the hot, empty days with thinking and talking and smoke. Rez remembered the night they went to the Hollywood Bowl show, how fun it was to have a friend like that, how much better college would be with someone he didn't have to explain anything to. Fatima spoke to Arash in Arabic and he spoke back and Rez tried to give them a moment but he was too excited.

Dude, where are you? Where have you been? What's with the beard? It's a little . . . fluffy . . . and not total coverage exactly, but the hat's dope . . .

From wherever he was, Arash laughed and then Rez laughed.

It is good to see you, brother. Looking well. Looking ready.

Where are you, dude?

Arash went quiet for a moment and Rez was about to repeat himself when his friend's face got serious and the voice that responded was deeper.

Brother, I am in the good land. The land of right and wrong. A place I cannot even describe.

Rez looked at his friend and started to see it, in bits and pieces, the truth as it was before him. The clean white shirt, the try at the beard, the Muslim beard, the fundamentalist beard. The beard that proves you believe Islam in all its force as the imam in one of the YouTube videos had said.

Yeah, but, are you, like, ok?

I am well, Rez. Better than well. Don't even think otherwise. You?

Good. College in a few weeks. Gonna be better since Fatima is coming with. Stanford. Her family is really proud. I don't want to brag, but I think my tutoring in AP is really what did it . . .

Arash said nothing, made no gesture with his face or head, and Fatima looked down at her hands, clasped tight in her lap. She did not share in the joke that had always been a joke. On the screen Arash leaned forward, the smile still pasted across his face. The screen unfroze and then he was talking again.

No one can tell the future, my brother. Only Allah knows the way.

Yeah. Well. I know my own way.

There was the defiance again, the defiance Rez had felt the day at Javad's when they watched the imam's talk about Muslims as the

victims and the need to rise up, to fight. Rez wanted nothing to do with it. Fatima placed her hand on his knee.

Remember? The suras I read you? Patience? An open heart?

Rez felt her fingers not as if they were on the outside of his pant leg but as if they were stroking him, keeping him calm and safe and pleased.

He looked at Arash and saw his old friend in new form and took a breath and pulled his roller chair closer to the screen and took another breath.

So then where are you?

In the good land. Building a new country.

Building? Building what?

A country. A community. A homeland where there is no punishment for believing in Allah. Only rewards. I am happy for you and your life, Reza, my brother. I hope that you can be happy for my life as well. Like I said, we are all on the paths set out for us.

Yeah. Well, I wish you were here too. There were good times this summer. Rez lied.

That's good, man. I wish you were here. There is so much to show you. We are going to build beautiful new hospitals, smooth streets without beggars, all the children in schools. I've even got enough engineering under my belt to work on a water-treatment plant. Can you believe it! Work my father wasn't allowed to do until he was thirty-three! I am only eighteen!

Rez smiled at his friend's giddy brags. There he was, just a million pixels in a weird costume, still Arash.

My time is up soon. What a great day to see both of your faces. We need people like you here. But I guess the world needs good people like you everywhere. Rez, stay true. You know how we do.

Arash put his fist up to the camera and in simple reaction Rez did the same and hit the screen with a bump and felt dumb as soon as his knuckles hit the screen. Fatima said a few words in Arabic and Arash listened and said a few words back and Rez looked around at the empty Kinko's and caught the eye of the cashier, who stared at them, his look impatient and suspicious and Rez saw them as they seemed. Two kids, Middle Eastern–looking, talking to a guy on the screen with

a beard. That is all he needed to make a call. Rez took off his headphones and tapped Fatima on the shoulder and tilted his head toward the door. He heard Fatima keep talking, saying good-bye the way they always did at her house or Arash's house with long phrases such as Alhamdulillah and Bismillah again and again until there was the silence and the frozen image of Arash, the cement wall and smiling face.

29

It was hot in the car and it was hot outside. Rez sat in the driver's seat with the windows down and watched men and women come and go to the Jummah prayers and to the small grocery store next to the mosque. Then it was sweltering and he got out and stood beside the car, on the sidewalk, and paced the few feet between parking meters and wondered how it could be so hot in Anaheim. It was only twenty minutes from his house, thirty with traffic, and yet the air, the plants, the dirt, was all desert. He got back in the car, rolled up the windows, and turned on the AC and the radio, and when the car was an icebox and he was still burning up, he knew the heat was inside him, and had been all morning since the beach.

He went because Matthews said it was the best swell of the year and there would be nothing like it at the mushy beaches up north and so why not? Matthews had time for a super quickie, two or three waves before the doctor's appointment he'd already flaked on twice, but he could take Rez and then Rez could stay and bum a ride home. Rez texted. *Fatima can pick me up.* There was a pause and then a ding and Matthews's jokey reply: *Oh I bet she can . . .*

Rez texted her and she told him he'd have to come to mosque with her afterward and wait in the car and he said fine and he and Matthews went into the August ocean with just board shorts and spent an hour so blissed out that he thanked Matthews for the heads-up and thanked the tectonic plates for the way they made the shelf off the coast of California and thanked the ocean herself for the fast, elegant heaves. After he surfed along for what felt like a lifetime, Rez rode a shallow wave in and walked onto the shore and up to his small pile of things.

Next to him a group of guys, still wet, sat together and looked out over the water and he gave a what's-up nod in their direction and a few

of them looked back and a few of them looked away. He took off his leash and his rash guard and heard laughter. First quick and quiet and then big and loud. He stared in the direction of the group of guys and the sounds stopped and Rez grabbed for his towel and wrapped it around him and took off his board shorts and looked around for his jeans, naked and searching, he heard the word *monkey* and then *hairy* and then *Arab*, and then *I didn't know Muslims could swim. All that desert and shit.*

Rez first looked down at his body. Were they talking to him? He had hair on his chest, a thin patch between his nipples, and his shoulders and back were smooth, like a kid's. He looked like most guys his age, and certainly not as hairy as some, or as dark. What were they talking about? He wasn't an Arab. His parents were from Iran. Rez was born here, as American as they were. They didn't know shit. What the fuck?

I hear those guys are hung like camels. Should we check?

The laughs were snickers now, fast and furtive. A few stood up and walked toward him.

Rez grabbed the towel around his waist, clenched it to him, and straightened his body and faced in their direction.

Fuck off.

It's cool, man. It's cool. Just doing a little research. Gotta know your enemy.

They put their palms up in a fake innocence but kept moving toward him.

I mean, you are a population under suspicion here, it's not like we don't have a right to take a look. For national security.

The other two also stood up and Rez did not want to take the chance. There were four of them, enough to do whatever they wanted, and he couldn't stop them. He felt them, behind him, next to him, around him, their thoughts thinking, and their bodies on the verge, and just like the times with his father, he felt his own body, already loose with fear and pain. He held the towel with one hand and grabbed his jeans and board with the other and walked down the beach, and when he was far enough, he turned back to them.

Rez shouted. You deserve what's coming. Fuckers.

He had no idea what he meant, but it got them quiet. The four stood back and didn't move and Rez stomped through the sand, each step sinking a little deeper than the last, until he was at the parking lot, fire in his belly, through his chest, up his neck and into his head. He put his pants on and checked for his wallet and his phone and pulled his shirt over his head and waited.

Fatima asked him what was wrong and he said nothing. She asked again and he said, Nothing, just a wipeout. I wiped out, that's all. And he knew she didn't buy it, and she patted down her white silk scarf and drove with her eyes straight ahead.

On the ride inland Rez said nothing, his body hot and his mind flashing. He thought about himself, his face and body and his features and how they said something that he never said. A few other guys with hair on their shoulders and hair on their backs didn't swim at the pool parties and didn't take off their shirts in front of girls. He wasn't like that. Was it his face? What the fuck did those guys know about faces? He knew he had a strong nose, strong eyebrows, features that did not belong to the pale kids. Sophia looked at him after sex once and said, *You're no Ken doll, thank God.* And didn't understand what it meant.

Can we turn the AC up?

Fatima moved the buttons without saying anything and he knew that soon his silence would piss her off. He tried to calm down, to think of nothing, to breathe and watch the highway and then the streets and the strip malls and whatever else passed by.

After an hour he was crazy with heat and got out and locked the car and went into the grocery store attached to the mosque. It was the middle of prayers and the store was empty; the only action came from the television screen hoisted onto the back wall that was playing the English league soccer play-offs, tiny specks running on an impossibly green pitch. Beneath the flatscreen four or five young men stood with their arms crossed and their necks craned upward in fixed ardor. They were a few years older than him and he liked that they chose English league

finals over Friday prayers. One of them turned around and walked behind the glass deli cases.

Welcome, my brother. What can I get for you today?

My brother. The sound of it landed softly in Rez's ear and he thought, Am I? How so? I can be your brother. Why not? This same face and body that marked him as unbrother at the beach, at the grocery store, with the assholes at the airport meant brother here. His face cooled first, and then his neck and shoulders and chest, and within seconds he was hungry and thirsty.

What's good?

Our combo—kebab, lavash, hummus—can't be beat. Lunch special includes a Coke. Or whatever soda you want.

I'll take it.

A cheer came from the guys gathered at the television and Rez and the server both got distracted by the game.

Unbelievable. We thought for sure they had no chance. Hot sauce?

Sure.

The server was tall and lean with cropped hair and a pencil-thin beard that lined his jaw and reminded Rez of the character from *Aladdin*. The server got to work with the plate as the guys at the end gave each other fist bumps and moved a little to get the blood flowing in their legs again.

You a fan?

Yeah. They're good this year. It's hard not to get behind them.

Exactly.

The server held the plate up and looked at Rez. Rez reached for his wallet and the guy shook his head.

Not today, it's on me. Come sit back here, you can see the TV better.

No. Thanks, but I got it . . . Let me . . .

You are our guest, next time you can pay.

Rez followed him to the back and the circle of guys looked at Rez for a second and nodded quickly and went back to the game. They wore Adidas tracksuits and Ecko hoodies and flat-brimmed caps and Rez sat at the table off to the side and watched and ate the delicious food and felt his body relax for the first time since the sea. After a little while he

started to cheer when they cheered and groan when they groaned and it seemed like he was back with Omid and Arash and everything was fine. When his plate was clean of kebab the server looked over and smiled.

Good, right?

Yeah. Good.

Best in the OC.

The game ended with Arsenal one, Birmingham zero and the guys seemed pleased and checked their phones and lingered around before disappearing through a doorway in the back of the grocery store. Rez checked his phone too. There was a message from Matthews: *How'd it flow this morning. Incredible right? Don't tell me, it was probably ridiculous . . . ok tell me. No don't tell me . . . aaaaaaah.* Matthews was a good guy, it was almost chemically impossible for him not to be a good guy.

Rez walked around the clean well-stocked store and recognized a lot of the products from his mother's kitchen and from Fatima's kitchen. In the pastry section he saw the sweet chickpea cookies in the shape of clovers Fatima served him when she gave him tea. They were good cookies. Weird and crumbly and nutty, but just sweet enough, and he grabbed two boxes to surprise her with. The server was not behind the register and Rez looked to the back of the store at the doorway where the guys had disappeared and he walked toward the sound of their voices laughing and teasing and mixed with a new voice, a British voice young and digital as if from computer speakers.

All right, lads, all right. I knew Birmingham wouldn't take it. I knew tonight was not our night. But still, a lucky win by your dear Arsenal. Lucky is all I'll say.

The guys had gathered around a laptop that showed a young man in a white prayer cap as he grinned and shook his head.

Now isn't it a good thing we are not betting men? Thanks be to Allah for that.

The guys in the grocery laughed and Rez took a step back from the doorway but kept his eyes on the screen. The face of the kid was not familiar to Rez's world—dark skin, thick brows, handsome—but it was recognizable to Rez as likable, as a good guy.

If you keep cheering Birmingham it's always gonna be like this. And we will brag hard, bro. We will brag so hard, one of the guys told the screen, and the rest nodded their heads and snickered.

Ok, ok, now, I didn't call to let you gloat. Ok, sure, gloat, especially since you all look ridiculous, five grown men squeezed around Farouk's dad's laptop in that back room. I called because I feel bad for you blokes. It is hard over there right now, I know it. The massacre at the mall was bad business, but got me thinking.

Don't do that man. You could hurt yourself. The server joked.

No seriously. If it's anything like after the subway bombings here then you are in for it. Bad times to come. The other day I was talking to my imam, just chitchatting about this and that, and I am telling him how hard it is to be a good man in this country. To find a good home, a good wife, a good job. As a black Muslim, you know? Here is my father, in this country thirty years, still on the night shift for the school's cleaning crew. Boss of the cleaning crew, yes, but still on the night shift. My mum same thing, at home, can't get a job, and doesn't complain, says this country has been good to us. Took us in when no one else would. And I am thinking, this is no good country. At best we're third-class citizens. Every day I ride the Tube, people look at me scared, with fear leaking right out of their eyeballs, and I want to shout, *What?!? What do you think I am going to do?* So I tell the imam all this, and I tell him I am falling for this girl, good Muslim girl, also from Nigeria, good family. But I don't want to have a child here, who is going to grow up and be kept down at the same time. The imam is listening and nodding and then he just says this one word to me and my mind starts spinning.

The guys in the grocery store lean forward and wait, and when the guy on-screen doesn't say anything, the server eggs him on.

Ok then, what was it? The word?

Raqqah.

What?

That's just what I said. But I think I said, Excuse me?—because you've got to be polite you know—but I was thinking, What is Raqqah? I thought it was some new kind of prayer, and the imam knows I have no idea and is looking at me like I am an idiot. Then I say ok and he

tells me it is a city in Syria, and a civil war is coming and that Raqqah is going to be the new capital, of a new kind of state, a Muslim caliphate. And I am nodding because I kind of understand him and there are these words between us, like *Muslim* and *capital* and *caliphate* but I have no idea what he is talking about. And then the imam looks at me straight on. Yes, brother, Raqqah, the capital of a country with no borders, a country for the believers, for the devout, for the citizens of Allah. And they need men. Men to move there and start their lives. Men and their wives. There is an open invitation to join in. Simply pack your belief in Allah and show up. There will be jobs, a house for you and your family. Schools for your children, hospitals, Islamic law, a good life. And then he leans forward and his bushy eyebrows lift and he goes, You will know always where you stand because you will always stand in the eyes of God. He went on and on and, man, I thought I was gonna fall asleep but I kept listening, to be polite, you know, and then he gave me some sites to check out and some numbers to Skype if I wanted to know more and I did, so I called them and talked to one bloke in Raqqah and then that's it. He showed me around his apartment, I met his baby, but mostly we talked. He came from Peckham and knew the same life I know and told me, Right away, man, right away you must come here. We are ready for you. The city is not ours yet, we need your help, so come. Come fight and live and thrive in a place where you can be a real man. This caliphate will be a good country, the best country. He was so relaxed. I can't even explain it.

A tall guy in an Adidas jacket spoke up.

Let me get this straight. Syria is on the edge of civil war and you are going to move to a city you've never heard of to join an army that was just invented, to make a country that doesn't exist?

The face on the screen smiled.

Tell me Hussein, what else is there? Night shift on team janitor?

The guys in the room moved listlessly and the server spoke.

There's always a lifetime of watching your team have its ass handed to it on a plate.

The laughs came slowly but with relief and good-byes and the connection was cut. Rez knocked on the door frame and held up the

box of cookies and the server jumped quick and walked him up to the register, his movements nervous for the first time, his talk fast, his eyes down.

Sorry, man, an old friend from London, Khalil. Came here for an exchange year at UCI, prayed here. Incredible footballer. Good guy. That's going to be eight fifty.

He sat in the car with windows down, radio off, the cookies on his lap, and listened to the noise of the street and thought about Khalil and Raqqah. Rez had heard the name of the city, and of the mess in Syria, some ugly civil war that no one in America paid attention to, but didn't absorb it. If Arash were here, he'd know all about it. Rez wondered if Arash was over there, *building*. What if there really was such a place? A new place, where you could be a child of Muslims, in love with a Muslim girl, a place where he himself could become Muslim and so be accepted, taken in, left alone to live a life, among brothers, every day, every year. A place where he didn't have to repeat his dad's shuffle and silence and quiet anger.

The possibility turned slowly in Rez's brain. To be Muslim. Why not be Muslim? He already was, sort of. Even before the thoughts formed themselves completely, the idea of it came with a sudden relaxation. He slumped back in the seat and closed his eyes and felt the calm of the decision made ease into his blood. To pray. To believe. To be silent in the audience of an imam. To have rules and guidelines. To know God. He never had, and just the hint of it opened doors and windows in him such that he was no longer hot. To know God. He opened his eyes and watched the streets of Anaheim, the SUVs and nail shops and mothers pushing strollers with two or three kids inside. To know God. He saw the men cross the street, hands in pockets, eyes on the ground. To know God. The sky above blue with wisps of white clouds, an airplane, a faint moon. To know God. Rez felt his muscles let go their clench as he recognized everything before him as part of a larger picture in which he was inconsequential, as meek as the rest. To know God. He felt the power of the change in his limbs before he'd even given it a full thought in his

mind. Conversion, the base of chemical sciences, the transformation from one state to another.

When Fatima came back, her face flush from the devotions, Rez handed her the cookies and she squealed and opened the box and whispered, My favorite, and then took a bite of the crumbly clover-shaped chickpea treat and he watched the powdered sugar cover her lips and her tongue lick the same lips and he thought of other gifts he wanted to give her that might make her squeal and bite and lick her lips.

Fatima dropped him off. He told his mom he was tired and needed to skip dinner and tried to be tired and slow getting to his room when in truth excitement burned through him like a clean fuel and he wanted to explode through this life and these days with great velocity and get to what came next.

He set up his computer and typed in the word Raqqah and in one instant images of a dusty city with traffic circles and spindly palm trees appeared. More photos: old yellow-white ruins, families picnicking beside a slow brown river, intersections full of motorcycles. He looked at a few maps and couldn't decipher much beyond the river and the city center. The aerial shot reminded him of Sacramento or Stockton, brown land with buildings and a course of water running through it surrounded by a bit of green. Nothing new about it.

He clicked on. The newer images came from news sites, photographs of war, buildings with huge holes through the side of them, ambulances surrounding the scene. There were men in green fatigues, men in street clothes with bandannas over their mouths and then a third kind of man, in black, with the longest beards and the heaviest guns. *Islamist groups vie for the city. Assad and his forces fight on.* He clicked and clicked, to find some definition, some explanation of who fought who and why, but all he saw were headlines that announced the growing strength of an Islamist movement, a residual or amalgam of various Al Qaeda affiliates, their men in black, marching in sparse parades with no crowds, moving down the streets of cities that didn't seem to welcome them or turn them away, life carrying on as usual around them. Most of the rest of the images showed guys, young and masked, at dusty camps, training.

Rez read articles in UK papers from just a few months ago—Raqqah was now a city under a more specific siege: harassment for smoking,

a women stoned in public for adultery, the imposition of taxes on non-Shia families, impossible to pay. In one news clip a body swung from a lamppost. *A city in chaos as state forces, rebel forces, and a new force calling themselves New Country scramble to take advantage of the instability.*

Fuck.

He stared at the uniforms of the Islamist army, new fatigues with old boots, scarves for their faces and foreheads, only their eyeballs available to the camera. *The ambitions of the New Country as outlined on their website are to spread a caliphate to the east and west and south and north . . .*

Fuck.

This was not what he wanted. It was not the peaceful faces at the mosque in Indonesia, or the brotherhood inside the mosque in Anaheim, or Fatima's sweet thoughts about right and wrong. It looked like a gang, no different from the gang at the beach, only more desperate, more violent: men in search of power. He thought of Khalil on Skype and of the guys at the grocery store, pictured them in the black fatigues, soldiers for this new army, and Rez stared at the silver square of his laptop and kept himself from crying but could not keep himself from feeling like an idiot, a fool's fool.

His parents slept, the whole neighborhood slept, and in the quiet after midnight Rez sat at the edge of the pool. The moon was new and sharp and its ivory reflection sliced across the flat navy water. He dipped a foot in to disturb it and watched the white light dance across the ruptured surface and flatten again. He must have typed in the wrong word. Done the wrong search. This could not be it, the land of the good Muslims, the city for the center of Islam, the religion Arash loved, Fatima adored, this could not be the religion of murders and massacres that the Americans said it was. He moved his foot around in the water and thought of earlier that day, at the gas station with Fatima and pumping her gas and feeling the stare of a grandmother outside her SUV, the stare that said *Fuck you* and *Don't kill me* all at the same time.

*

He went inside and opened his computer and sat before the empty search box and waited. He thought of nothing, and then when something came, he just typed it, *How to be a Muslim.* And there they were, instructions. Five steps, ten steps, twelve steps. Fourteen steps with pictures. *Learn about the Five Pillars of Islam—Shahada, Salat, Sawm, Zakat, Hajj. Study the Quran. Align yourself with the one God and the path of your life will never be lonely and will never be dark. Brothers and sisters all over the world will welcome you when you arrive on their doorsteps.*

No corpses, no blades, and no guns. He read through a few quoted passages about generosity, about abstinence, about humility and virtue, and he felt Arash near, heard his voice the night they spent at the party in the Hollywood Hills, on the pool chairs after everyone else had passed out. *It feels good to be good.* He felt Fatima close too, her new calm and confidence, and he read on and followed the thread of sites until he got to YouTube videos where men and woman of all ages sat before cameras and told of their journey to Islam, to the caliphate, to be a part of the new country.

Most spoke Arabic, and many more spoke French. A few spoke German and a few spoke British English. Rez listened to the English testimonials and he got stuck on one, a tall skinny teenager with a faint mustache and patchy beard, who explained that he *answered the call.* He said his years in England had taught him to question himself, the smell of his mother's cooking, his name, and his family's customs until the questions turned into disgust, and he couldn't stand the sight of himself.

So I started doing drugs, you know, marijuana and some coke to fit in, to get by, and this took me further and further from the call. Alhamdulillah, my sister brought me to it, sat me in front of the computer, and told me which imams to watch, showed me what was happening in Raqqah, what was possible for us, if we wanted it. If you are watching this, you are lonely. Like I was, confused. Let me tell you what my life is like now. I have never felt so much respect. Now I have a purpose, first and above all to Allah and to my community and to a future of peace for

all followers. I live in a city where I can make a good living and love a woman who honors me. Before my life was not my own. I lived under so much suspicion I was sure I had done all the evil they suspected me of. Now I am myself.

He went on about the propaganda about the New Country in the media, the violence, the news of radicals and gangs of Muslims. *Rumors. Don't believe them. The western media is full of these rumors to distract us, to stop the rush of believers. This is the only place of peace I have ever known. God willing we will be victorious over the forces of Assad and begin our work to build new roads, new hospitals, new schools, and centers for the elderly. For this we need more brothers, more sisters, more devout hearts.*

Rez watched it again and was about to watch it a third time but his computer chimed and he saw a dialogue box open at the bottom of the screen.

Hello brother. Hello sister. Are you interested in joining the Caliphate? My name is Daoud and I am here to answer your questions and provide you with any guidance you might need.

Rez pulled back. It was like on porn sites or when he hacked into a movie site or got illegal downloads of music: pop-ups, text messages, Gchat sessions with people he'd never met. Those were easy enough to ignore, but this put Rez on edge. He stared at the question mark at the end of the sentence *Are you interested in joining the Caliphate?* Another line popped up beneath it.

As-salaam alaikum. Don't worry brother, I'm not a bot, just checking to see if I can help you out.

Rez paused the video and looked out at the night. The moon dropped to another part of the sky and the pool was still and navy now. He closed the computer and went to sleep.

He had rich dreams. First he was in the ocean, surfing a big day at Old Man's, which was a medium day anywhere else. Other people were in the water but he didn't know any of them and he surfed without competition or aggression. He had the good feeling in him, the dropped-shoulder, slack-jaw sensation of acceptance, of a life at the mercy of

the enormous ocean, much greater, much truer, than his small self. In the warm water he let himself be swallowed, taken in. He paddled around the afternoon sea and watched the sun glint off the water and looked back at the hazy shore, in the dream as it had been so many times in waking life.

He woke clearheaded and hard and ignored his desire and jumped from the bed into the shower and knew the time of thinking, of listening and waiting, was over. He dried his body and took a long look at himself in the mirror. The face they called a monkey yesterday. A face they called brother. A solid face. A face inherited from his father and from the father of his father and maybe even further back. The nose, the eyebrows, the eyes themselves, all part of long look through time, across lands and wars and bodies and oceans and love, and he dressed and put on shoes and left the empty house without knowing the time and walked in the direction of Fatima's house, an hour walk at the least, his body light and ready, quick almost, in these first steps on the path of his own choice.

31

Maybe they enjoyed college. What they learned allowed them a good life.

His father talked and drove, drove and talked, and Rez sat in the back, daydreamed, and ignored him while his mother sat in the front and did the same. They drove the windy roads up the highest hills of Laguna and the voice in the car told them where to turn in a patient and calm voice. His mother had dressed up and his father had put on a tie and Rez wore a clean polo and pants and school shoes but didn't look in the mirror to make sure it all worked.

The house, small and modern and expensive and made entirely of glass, was vaulted high up above the sea. When they stepped into the entryway, the ocean was everywhere beneath and ahead of them, like a new kind of ground. For all his years going to parties at the homes of rich friends, Rez had never felt this high, this much like flying. He waited in the line with his parents to meet the hosts, unable to take his eyes off the living room windows, the ocean huge, the line of the horizon closer somehow, the beams of the sun, long set, aimed up, dim and yellow into the dusky sky, just like a child's drawing. All the surfaces of the house were stone and gray and angular and so were the hosts, architects, in their fifties, clean cashmere and linen, glasses without rims, white white smiles. They welcomed the incoming freshmen and their families with kind handshakes and sincere pauses over the foreign names, which they listened to and repeated before they pointed everyone in the direction of the drinks table, where a man in a crisp black shirt listened and poured and listened and poured.

Rez's father went first, made the introductions, Saladin, but you can call me Sal.

And this is Rez then?

The man looked at Rez with his hand outstretched, his soft eyes buried in the soft face. Rez put out his own hand.

Reza actually.

Please excuse me. Reza. Nice to meet you. Welcome, you and your family should make yourself at home. There are drinks there and a table of hors d'oeuvres in the dining room. Please.

Thanks.

Rez felt his father look at him for a long second and then move toward the drinks table, taking Rez's mother by the elbow.

The families, eight or nine of them, walked around and spoke to each other politely and Rez saw nothing hot about the girls and nothing interesting about the guys, who seemed preppy and a little straitlaced. He walked around behind his parents and overheard conversations and tried to open his eyes wide and friendly or lift his eyebrows or even smile when someone looked at him. The host and hostess, both class of '78, gathered them in the living room, welcomed them, and explained why they were such devoted UC Berkeley alumni: it was responsible for their marriage, for their successful careers, their community of friends. Even though they had no children, their association with the school had given them such fulfilling lives. They were happy to answer any questions about campus life, freshman year, parent involvement, and participation in the Orange County alumni chapter, *when the time comes.* The room laughed politely and a few hands went up. Rez let his eyes wander to the ocean, let his mind drift. The sea was dark now, the sky a little less so above it, and in the far distance a few boats, an oil rig, the outline of Catalina. God's view, he thought, this is how God must see things. But these people aren't God, just rich. He felt himself grow frustrated that money could buy such magnificence, money and not devotion or commitment or a generous heart. His mother coughed gently next to him and he looked at her with the small paper plate neatly on her lap, her few hors d'oeuvres arranged in a line. Why was he thinking about God?

Everyone asked questions, parents and freshmen, about the dorms and the commons and visitors and the Cal Bears and drugs on campus, and Rez grew impatient. Who cares? College was just like high school, except you didn't have to go home every day and your mom didn't cook

for you. It was another controlled environment with expectations, rules, and achievements. His job was the same. Do well. Don't embarrass his family and don't strike out in any way that would draw attention. This exercise in college seemed like a pause, a trick. Rez raised his hand. The old man called on him.

Yes, Reza?

About student life, specifically services for Muslim students on campus. Is there a mosque? Are there halal foods offered? What sort of support is there in case of discrimination, harassment, you know, because of recent events?

It felt good to bring it up, to make the room uncomfortable, and Rez kept his gaze and posture steady as students and parents shifted and throats cleared. Without looking Rez knew his father was staring at him, the heat of the look burning Rez's cheeks and forehead, and he tried to keep from withering. The host admitted he did not know the exact details but was certain all religions were equally supported on campus. His wife spoke up.

As you might know, Cal has one of the most progressive and accepting student bodies in the nation. It is a point of pride.

Yes, Rez replied. Now they all stared at him. His parents, other parents, the students-to-be.

Let me be in touch with student life and I will make sure to e-mail you more information. Does that work for you, Rez?

Reza.

Oh, I'm sorry, yes. Reza.

Rez made sure to draw his lips tight in a face of dissatisfaction and responded in a cheery voice, Thanks. And I'm sure I'll find out more when I get there.

Hell to pay. Rez always liked that phrase, though no one he knew used it. For the rest of the evening he prepared himself: once they were in the car, there would be *hell to pay*. His father would probably drop his mom off and then drive Rez back to that abandoned dirt road in the desert and punish him one last time, for this one last fuck-up. But now they were still stuck at the polite party and Rez's mom was talking to a

tall woman about sculpture classes and she looked as lively and engaged as Rez had ever seen her, and in an instant he knew that if he left, if he went to Raqqah and became a man and started a new life from which he could never return, from which he would forgo the attachment to his mother, it would be all right, she would be sad, but she left her own family too, a long time ago.

They drove home with the classical radio station on and nothing else. When the garage door opened, Rez's father kept the engine on and told Meena to get out. Rez felt the little boy bloom in him and slumped in the backseat with the old fear and reminded himself only ten days more and this would be the last of these times.

They drove south on Highway 1 until they got to an upscale supermarket. His father parked and they went into the store together and Rez watched him buy a six-pack of beer and some pistachios. Then they drove to the parking lot of a construction site, a future luxury hotel with views of the harbor and ocean, and Rez wanted to relax; the beer, the parking lot under bright lights, the proximity to home, read like signs that everything was going to be all right, no great violence would take hold of his father tonight. But his father was not a drinker, and Rez watched him grab the beers and step out of the car and he followed him with suspicion until they both leaned up against the hood with bottles in their hands.

I always wanted to do this.

Do what?

Drink beer with my father. Do something with my father as a man, two men together, instead of a father and his son.

Rez looked at his beer but didn't take a sip. It had been weeks since he'd drunk or smoked.

My father was strict. All the fathers of that world were. In this country you and I are allowed to see each other as people, not just who is in charge and who isn't.

Rez wanted to reject him, reject these words—for the whole of Rez's life this man had been in charge, held the power of the fist, of the word, over the quivering soul of himself as a boy, as a teenager—but he could not, as his father then and his father now were two different people. Since the night in the desert, his father's anger and violence

had recoiled, pulled themselves back like a tongue, and Rez lived with a much meeker man who took the massacre in step, took the demotion at his lab in step, said nothing about Rez's SAT scores or final grades and spent most evenings by himself in front of the classic movie channel, a dreamy look on his long thin face.

You feel good about this next week? College? Moving out?

Yeah. Great.

You feel like yourself?

Sure.

Why did you ask the alumni to call you Reza?

It's my name, isn't it? The one you gave me?

His father looked out over the dark sea and then down into the hole of his beer bottle.

You know that to be a Muslim in this country right now is not something to joke about?

I wasn't joking. A lot of my friends are Muslim.

And they will have a hard time. They are having a hard time.

And it's not fair.

No, it's not. When I came to this country, I saw religion separate people. So many different beliefs, all against each other, and I thought, Why put my kid through this? This is going to make their life harder, not easier. We have Islam in our background, yes, in the way we eat or think sometimes, but it is not who we are. We are people first, then a family, and then Americans. That has served us very well.

Rez kept quiet but his mind moved angry and fast. Has it? Has it served us well? Let you be a man who is spit on at the carwash? In public?

He watched his dad take a long sip. It looked awkward, the way he held the bottle to his mouth, tilted his head far back instead of the bottle. Rez considered his father—maybe he'd never ever seen his true self, through the stress of his American self. Maybe at the rug seller's house where he sat on the floor, comfortable in his skin, tongue, and thoughts, were the only times he let himself relax. Rez felt the anger seep away and his throat and mouth filled with a sudden sadness. For a second he wanted to tell his dad about this other country, where Rez and Arash and Fatima could live among brothers and sisters and make

a state in their image, not at the mercy of money or the laws of people who dismissed them. To be in their own skin.

It's cool, Dad. It's just something I've been thinking about. That's all.

Of course. This is a big change for you. Give it a week, once the classes and assignments start coming and you start soccer and meeting girls and friends, you won't even remember this feeling now, you will be as solid as a rock. We are here and very proud of you. I am very very proud.

Rez imagined himself not in one week but in two, or even three or four, not in college at all, but maybe in a distant desert, arrived in the New Country, welcome citizen with rights and responsibilities, no longer boy, no longer teen, but a good man with Fatima beside him, a good family to come. Rez looked at his father, and his father looked back, eyes warm and generous with love, and Rez had no armor, no argument against, and forced himself to swallow and straighten up and talk.

Yeah, you're right. In a few weeks I'll be fine.

I know it. Beginnings are bumpy. Look at me. I landed in this country and slept on the beach for a week! I took a chance, a single huge chance, and everything turned out fine.

Rez blinked back the liquid in his eyes. For a moment, he was proud of himself too, many years the obedient son, not knowing who he was or where to go until told, now stepping into a new world, a foreign world, the chance at a bravery all his own. Rez took a sip of his beer and stared out at the open lightless sea.

Yeah, you're right.

32

The morning of the mosque visit he showered and dressed in a clean oxford shirt and ironed slacks and his mom asked, What's the occasion? He told her lunch with Fatima's parents and she said, That's nice, and left him alone. Fatima laughed a little when she saw him.

Fancy.

Well. You know . . .

They were both nervous and rode in silence down the 5 past small beach towns and the enormous military base, where Rez saw a line of tanks in the distance, rolling, on a military exercise. They drove through the San Diego suburbs and near the In-N-Out he'd stopped at with the apostles on the way to Mexico all those days ago. Rez felt a shake of embarrassment go through him and tried to change his thoughts and was glad when they pulled up to a clean white building with a blue-tiled roof and a thin spire minaret. The Abu Bakr Masjid. The parking lot was lined with tidy tall palm trees and Fatima circled a few times before she found a spot.

Busy.

Friday prayer.

She adjusted her scarf in the mirror and touched up the little bit of makeup she still wore, mascara, some blush.

Remember, we are cousins. You grew up secular but your parents were born Muslim, they just don't practice. And now you are curious about your religion, about Islam.

That is true.

It is?

Yup.

Her stare was long and flat and without any emotion Rez could easily read.

*

He followed her down clean long hallways and watched as she greeted other women with Salaams and eager smiles. Rez did not recognize this happy public person. In all the years at school he'd never seen her smile in the halls, in class, at the assemblies, and now she glowed openly. All around him men and women did some variation of the same: saw one another, clasped hands, kissed cheeks, greeted each other with love. He stood a few steps away and she did not once introduce him.

At the end of the hallway bright light shone through two separate doorways. Cubbies for shoes lined the walls and the sinks and towels were set up further beyond that. Fatima went to the door on the left and greeted an old black man whose prayer cap covered a bald head.

This is my cousin. He is here to pray with us.

Welcome, my brother. It is a good day. We ask that visitors sit in the back rows.

Ok.

The old man gestured for Rez to enter and he did but when he looked back Fatima was gone. He stretched his neck but there was nothing of her scarf or her shoulders. For a second he panicked, alone in the unknown world of belief, and stood in the entrance to the enormous room and watched men and boys sit down cross-legged and barefoot and quiet. And like the times before, Rez felt their powerful goodwill toward each other, toward him—the stranger—and he found a space against the wall and sat down and let his mind wander.

The imam was young, in a navy suit and green tie, and he spoke like Omid did, as if maybe once all his friends were from Compton. Rez tuned in and out of the lecture about the nature of love and the story of Abraham and where the allegiances of the heart lie when you pledge your life and soul to Allah and thought of Fatima in the room next door, watching the same lecture on the large screen, surrounded by women she liked and maybe even loved.

He found her afterward looking for her shoes. He tapped her shoulder and she beamed at him, clean and energized as if she had just come out of the shower.

So good, right?

Yeah. It was cool.

Something had happened to her during the prayer. The nerves and suspicions were shaken off and now she looked up at him with a ready face and he wanted to hold her cheeks in his hands, bring her fresh lips to his, and take her and take her and take her until the beams shone through him as well. He stepped away from her.

Lunch?

Let's do it.

They ate at a deli next to the mosque. Tables were set up off to one side, girls at some, boys at others. Men and women shopped and ordered kebabs and tabbouleh and drinks and watched Al Jazeera. Fatima and Rez took their food to a table of guys their age and Fatima introduced Rez as her cousin *just visiting* and they made space for him and said *What's up?* and kept on with their conversations about the Lakers or the new *Fast & Furious* movie. The person next to Rez, a little older, with a nice watch and a clean beard, turned to him.

Where are you coming from?

The Bay, Rez lied.

Nice. Mom's side or Dad?

Dad.

Cool. Fatima's awesome. So glad she joined this mosque. Not a lot of new young women come on their own. Good to see a fresh face. And fresh other things, if you . . . you know . . .

The guy looked up from his food as he spoke and Rez followed his stare to the table of women where Fatima sat and laughed and covered her mouth as she practiced some Arabic phrases. Rez looked back at the guy, who turned to him and winked.

She's so lovely. Such a lovely presence.

Rez spoke quickly, I am not sure she wants to stay at this mosque forever. Just trying it out, you know, like me.

That's interesting. See that girl she's talking to? That's my sister. Fatima told her she really likes it here. Wants to settle down in this community. I am hoping my sister will invite her over sometime, meet the rest of the family.

He turned to Rez and smiled, part shyness, part something else. Rez stood up and left his tray of food on the table.

Nice to meet you. I just remembered . . . a phone call . . .

You don't like the food?

No. I just remembered my mom is expecting me to call.

Ok. Well, um, have a good visit.

Yeah. Thanks.

Rez walked to Fatima's table and leaned down toward the place her ear would be inside her headscarf.

I want to talk to the imam.

Why?

I have some questions.

Now?

Yes. I mean, if it's ok?

I am still eating.

I can wait outside.

The women at the table grew quiet and Fatima nodded at him. Ok, just a minute.

Outside she was fast with her words. Dude. What's your problem? Are you fucking with me, with this, for some reason? How I appear matters. You can't just show up because you are curious about my religion . . .

It might be my religion too.

She stopped midword and dropped her head and took a few breaths.

Fine. Let's go.

The imam sat in a small room just off the main prayer room. Up close he looked older than on the podium, and when he took Rez's hand, the grip was stronger than he expected. He was very clean, his skin, his teeth, his hair and clothes. To calm himself Rez imagined him as just another of the guys from lunch and thought about him on the basketball court, throwing bricks at the net. Fatima left them and Rez wiped his wet palms over his slacks and waited for the questions.

Welcome.

Thank you.

The imam smiled and let the room, its single potted palm and dusty burgundy rug and leather-bound books, sit in stillness and silence. Unnerved, Rez waited and the imam waited.

I am interested in Islam. I think I am. I mean, I might want to start practicing.

Yes.

So . . . I thought, what I wanted to know . . .

Your parents? Are they devout?

No. I don't think so. My mom a little, maybe.

A little?

The room got still again and Rez waited.

The imam righted himself and Rez saw that the back of the chair rose high above the height of the imam's head. He reached for a few pamphlets and pushed them across the table.

You must begin at the beginning. Talk to your parents. Read these and then, when you are ready, go be by yourself, turn off your phone, and think about your need for faith. Think with your heart and with your head. The strictures, the lifestyle, the bond with Allah. It's a long road from curiosity to belief.

The kindness never left the imam's face or his voice and yet Rez hated him. As he spoke, all Rez heard was *You're not serious, you are young and foolish and in search of something else.*

The imam stood and offered his hand. Rez stood and shook it. Fuck this guy, he thought. He tried to pull his hand out but the imam held on to it.

If you don't mind me asking, what got you thinking? About Islam, about our *masjid*?

Rez stared at him directly.

Love.

The imam's face did not change but his grip tightened.

That is a good start. The love of Allah is like no other.

33

He typed in the same search, *How to be a Muslim,* and went to the same sites as before and watched all the testimonials he could find. An Australian doctor, the child of Chechen refugees, told of his sense of obligation to join the New Country when it most needed his skill, when the future of the *khalifa* depended on it. *To be Muslim in Australia is to be a second- or third-class citizen. Why should I settle for that? To be a lesser man among men?*

Rez watched two English girls, young from the sound of their voices, who spoke off camera while a still image of a dove showed on-screen. *We were lucky to get out when we did. So many of our girlfriends at school were giving us a hard time for covering, for going to mosque, for not listening to music anymore, and we had to explain: our beliefs are what make us feel respected and useful in the world. We don't have to worry what our bodies look like, our hair, our makeup. A woman is more than her skin here. Here we are the pillars of our households. Our husbands work every day to build the* khalifa *and we work every day to make our homes beautiful, raise our children, make Raqqah a city for the new times.*

A teenager from Germany spoke only in German but his words were translated into English and French subtitles. *This is my apartment, three bedrooms, though I only have two wives. Well, right now I only have two. Let's see what happens in the future. God willing. Here is my kitchen, very modern, my cooler full of food. Here is the room where I keep my guns, a rifle and a pistol, ready when the call comes. Raqqah is a beautiful city and it is the work of every man to defend it.* Rez looked into the teenager's face for some madness, some hint of a craziness for violence, but saw only a young man proud and not at all interested in his own past.

Rez watched and listened and watched and waited for the dialogue box to pop up. Finally it did. The same message and the same name flashed on the screen.

Hello brother. Hello sister. Are you interested in joining the Caliphate? My name is Daoud and I am here to answer your questions and provide you with any guidance you might need.

Rez laid his fingers on the letters.

Hi.

Salaam alaikum.

Salaam.

Who is here?

Reza.

Nice to *meet* you Reza. Where are you?

California.

Great! Northern or Southern?

Southern.

Sweet. I visited L.A. once. Wanted to learn to surf.

Yeah. I surf.

☺

Rez punched in the hang-loose emoticon.

Are you interested in Islam? In our work in Syria?

My parents are Muslim but don't practice, and I've got a Muslim friend, Fatima, and she's very devout now and I wanted to . . .

The box interrupted with a line.

Just a friend? ☺ ♥

Rez left it and waited to see what would come next.

Listen, my brother, I don't know everything but I'll answer as much as I can. Let me just say, first off, your curiosity is a sign that Allah is present within you and that you are trying to return to your original perfect state of being. Step toward your belief and you will step toward perfection, and probably toward Fatima too. ♥ 💍 👰 🤵

Rez stared at the screen.

34

ALL OF IT the same, yet nothing the same. In the days since the assholes at the beach, since the video of Khalil, his chats with Daoud, the nature of time had changed. Rez felt as if he were astride some great wild wave of time that heaved and swelled fast into a tube and then slow until he saw everything in raw epic detail. Whole mornings passed in quick minutes while dinnertimes at the awkward family table stretched out so long he saw neither beginning nor end of them. At night he could only lay his body down for four or five hours before waking up so fueled he had to do fifty push-ups and a hundred sit-ups just to shower without agitation.

He spent the new time differently. He no longer stayed at home in the mornings, watching TV and floating in the pool. Now he ate breakfast with his parents and caught a ride with his father to the main library in Huntington *to get back in the swing of things, you know, get used to staring at books again.* He waved his dad off and then walked around the cool, silent building with his backpack and plugged himself into the most private computer in the public computer lab and did all the things he wanted and needed to do. By the time he let himself be distracted by a piss or a snack, the clock said two thirty or three. His work was never done, but every day he made inroads, read more history, found new sites, connected to better contacts, came up with quicker, cheaper logistics and paved the path out a little farther from where he stood.

He began each day where Daoud told him to, with the Koran. Rez fell into the calm cadence of its calls for generosity, humility, the quiet decorum required to properly follow Allah. He recognized stories from the Old Testament, and new stories for how to be a man, how to be a woman, how to have a family, livestock, money, and honor. Some sites

helped him to think about his conversion, step by step, from the *shahada* to the hadiths, from the best ways to offer prayers to the correct attitudes toward women, food, clothing. Sometimes he read out the phonetic words of the shahada in practice for the day there would be a witness and these words would seal his commitment. He always did so in a whisper, Daoud having reminded him that simply speaking Arabic in public had got people pulled off planes, taken to detention centers.

Then he read history, tried to understand why things were the way they were, why a new country was necessary, vital. He went as far back as the early 1900s, when there were no countries, only dry lands covered in tribes with some loose association to kings and empires, all in service to the one God. What a time that must have been. He remembered the photographs in the garage, his grandfather as a young man among the men of his area, men in turbans with scythes in their loosely bound robes, lives lived on the thick skin of the desert beneath the thin enormous sky.

Then what happened?

He read on. Into the history, the hunger for oil, Europe's keen eyes on the region and the carving that followed, random and haphazard, of tribes into nations, nations into influenced states. He looked at maps that showed random shapes and sizes with their own names and presidents and prime ministers and read of mandatory reeducation programs, tribal language eradication, a tilt toward European customs, the chair, the fork, the necktie.

But then what happened?

The great corruptions, the great rapes of gold and oil and gas and minerals and whatever could be mined or drilled and taken away. Some tried to resist—Mossadegh, Sadat—and came to a quick end. He read on: American support of Israel, American support of the Saudi royal family, and the slow noose of greed threading the neck of the region. And now the modern punishments, just as the imam on YouTube laid them out in Arash's living room: Bosnia, Palestine, Kosovo, places where to be Muslim meant to be a target, to believe in Allah meant a separation, then a discrimination, then a mass slaughter. Rez came to resent his teachers, his life, for not telling him these truths and he read on, hurt head, hurt heart, to find the center chord of

information, a truth he could find and pluck and so feel it resonate in the bones of his new self.

In the encrypted chat rooms Daoud told him what to read, what sites to check out, and who to talk to and Rez would enter and start up conversations with men he'd never meet, kind men with useful information who said the faith had ways for him to turn the anger into action, and explained how they themselves had done it just six months, ten months, one year ago.

And then it was too much. His head was full, he knew what he needed to know, about right and wrong, good and bad, like he knew calculus equations and chemical formulas. His heart, not empty, was not as full as his head and he cast about trying to find passions to lead him. Finally, when he could think of nothing else, when the same idea came to him again and again, he e-mailed Arash.

It took two days but then the name popped up in his in-box next to *hello brother!* In the e-mail there was a quick what's up and instructions on how to get into a video chat room on a site Rez had never heard of, a date and a time. *See you soon! A.*

Rez did as he was told and the next morning, he waited for the library to open and was first inside, first in the computer lab. He logged on with his new fake names and sneaky passwords and soon sat in front of a black screen with a tiny black and white flag waving in the center of it. In his headphones a phone rang and rang and rang. When four or five minutes passed Rez looked around the room and saw the same senior citizens he saw every day and thought about hanging up, then the ringing stopped and Arash popped up. His head was closer to the camera this time and Rez saw his face was thinner, the beard more full. There was a greenish bruise just under his eye and his lips spread beneath it in a large smile.

Rez, dude. Salaam! I was so glad to see your name in my in-box. Thanks be to God. I had a feeling you were going to get in touch.

He sounded different. Rushed. Arash never said things like *I had a feeling.* He didn't say much, usually his manner was so chill it did all the talking for him.

I'm good. Glad you called back. I thought maybe you, well . . . hey. How's it going?

I am not on Mars, dude. Of course I'd get back to you. Was thinking of dropping you a line soon.

Arash didn't move far from the camera and Rez couldn't see what was behind him, what world he was in.

Where you at, dude?

Arash shook his head.

In the good place, the great place, doing the good work. Setting up.

What happened to your face?

A soccer ball. Right to the eye. You know my defense was always crap.

Rez wanted to say what defense? Arash didn't really play soccer. Whenever he went out with Omid or Yuri for a pickup game, Arash sat on the sidelines and read the news on his phone.

Soccer huh? What else are you up to over there? You staying with friends? Family? Beard looks good.

Thanks. I've been combing it.

Arash stroked the hairs under his chin and the grin got even more lopsided.

Yeah. Friends, good friend, I'm staying with some brothers, it's pretty dope. A compound with a pool and gardens and the whole thing.

Yeah?

Yeah. You should come.

And do what?

Build the new country. It's better than I can even describe. Real people. Real respect. Skip college, give yourself an education in truth. Bring Fatima with you.

You sound like an infomercial.

Listen, Rez. It's for real, this place. If you are calling me to check 'cause you are kinda interested that means you are already halfway here. Better than life in the OC by a million. Come, bro, come.

How can I find you?

Get to Raqqah and then just ask around. I am not sure where I will be by then, in terms of digs, but everyone knows everyone here. Come. I am not going anywhere.

Rez could not imagine it. This place. It sounded like camp. His friend's face seemed so present. So ready, skinnier and a little pale, but full of joy, almost too full. Rez leaned forward to speak directly to the speaker in the computer, hoping no one else would hear.

Yeah. I was think . . .

A sharp noise filled the headphones and scratched through Rez's ears. The screen went sideways, cut Arash into a thousand shards, and then went black.

Hello? Arash? Hello?

Nothing. Rez took off his headphones and put them in his backpack and logged out of the computer. It wasn't everything he needed, but it was enough.

By the time he got outside it was early afternoon and Rez went to wait at the bus stop with the Latina maids and nannies and the leather-skinned white guys who made homes out of the caves and park benches up and down the coast, regardless of the season. Rez stood among them and thought about what he had read and seen and about Arash and wondered how different his life would be if he had been born into the skin of a woman in servitude or a man without a way.

35

She let him sit close again. Close enough they touched at the thigh and hip and shoulder, and if Rez wanted to reach for her hand, she let it be held. He wanted to make a joke about how this was the first time they'd held hands but decided against it, so they just sat, side by side, in the gazebo above Laguna Beach and watched the waves and kids and dogs dash in and out of the water's reach.

The new learning rang in his head like loud bells and he wanted to tell her about all he knew, about Islam and the New Country and Arash, but Rez stopped himself, he'd already said so much to her today, now it was better to sit and squeeze her hand.

This ocean is amazing.

She looked at him and smiled. And then laughed a little. And then she laughed a lot.

What?

Nothing.

She laughed more.

He had never heard her laugh like this. Or do anything bubbly and girlish. He'd known Fatima since seventh grade; she'd always been serious about everything—grades, her opinions, even getting high—and now she was relaxed, almost silly.

I just can't believe it. That's all. I mean, this morning I had no idea you were going to show up at my door and tell me you wanted to embrace Islam. Like, what?! . . . It makes me happy, but, come on, it's a little wild, admit it, Rez, a little crazy.

Reza, he corrected her.

Reza, she repeated, and tried not to laugh but started giggling anyway. I mean, Rez Courdee. All-American. Never said a nice thing to a Muslim kid, never recognized his parents were Iranians. Nothing. And now. *Now?!* Wants to become a Muslim and marry me? If I say it

out loud, even if I think about it too much, it sounds crazy. I am not going to think about it.

She took a dramatic breath and got very still, stared out at the sea and got even more still. Rez watched her, worried she would get serious again, get serious and change her mind. Nothing happened for a long time; five and then more minutes went by and he was about to say something and saw she was crying.

Hey. Don't do that. This is all good, right? I want to change my life to be a good Muslim man, a good man in the world and a good husband to you.

I know. It's just weird. Really fast.

It was hard already and Rez hadn't even gotten to the hard part.

What if we left?

And go where?

I dunno. Away. Would that make it easier?

In her stillness he felt her listening.

There is a place for us, in Raqqah, if we want it. An apartment. Jobs. A good life. You are Syrian. It will be like a homecoming. I have already started talking to people.

Raqqah? Syria? In the middle of a war? That's not funny. You *are* crazy! All my family is trying to leave Syria and you want to go there?

I think some good things are going to happen when the fighting stops. I've been talking to people who say a new country is being built there. A fair place for Muslims to live . . .

And I've heard about that group in Raqqah. It's not the Islam I know . . . it is an interpretation, an old Islam and it can be very violent. Very bloody. Why are you even talking about it? This is stupid. You're nervous about college and this is your freak-out.

Rez looked toward the beach. Beyond the first spread of families and picnics, a group of boys took turns with a dragon kite. The tails were many and the nose kept diving down toward the sand until the last minute, when some wind or fast maneuver lifted it back into the sky. He couldn't tell if it was an accident or a trick of skill that got the kite up and flying again.

You know all this is bloody and violent too?

She looked up at the beach.

All what?

These kids, all these families, having fun, driving cars, living in big houses, watching stupid sports games, voting for war in the Middle East every chance they get? How much violence do you think it takes to keep this all so pretty?

He stared at the ocean because he didn't want her face to fuck with his thoughts, with his anger and determination and need.

At least in Raqqah the violence is on the surface. And temporary. At least there we can have a life devoted to something other than lies.

The afternoon light glowed more golden, the laughter of children braided in with the hush and hush of waves. Rez forced himself to see through the beauty of this paradise he'd believed in his whole life. He forced himself to think of pictures of Afghanistan, Abu Ghraib. The bombed-out apartments of Baghdad. Kelly and his maimed brother and their constant threats. The assholes who tried to fight him at the beach.

Arash is there. I talked to him. He invited us. Wants us to join him.

She stayed quiet.

Arash would never do anything on the wrong side, would never match himself with people involved in bad shit. You know that. You've known him your whole life, he's too good for that.

They heard the sound of footsteps on the wooden planks of the gazebo and they turned to find an elderly couple, hands clasped, walking toward the railing. They both wore pressed collared shirts and slacks and white rubber-soled shoes and when they got to the view spot the man took the woman by her shoulders, drew her body close, and kissed her lips. It looked dry and chaste but the woman blushed, her skin flush with color, and the man smiled at her and kissed the top of her forehead and then turned to Rez and Fatima.

Our sixtieth wedding anniversary today! Can you believe it? Sixty years ago I married this woman after proposing to her on that exact same bench. We were probably even your age. Eighteen, nineteen. Made the decision before we knew too much, before we became different people. Best decision of my life. Good times. Good time. Don't you waste this time.

The man smiled as he spoke and joy shone from the pockets of his old face.

36

THERE WAS NO fast *Yes.* No easy *I do.* She asked to see what he saw. Read what he read. Go to the websites that made him think goodness lay at the bottom of the evil.

With some pride Rez introduced her to Daoud in the chat room, quick to mention their engagement and plans to marry.

In Raqqah, God willing. Where the young married couples are blessed. Please direct her to a site run by our sisters. They will give her guidance as to our interpretations and organize the details of her preparation. I will e-mail the address and encryption code.

Rez looked at Fatima to see if she agreed, if it was going to work. She stared at the screen and then at her lap and then at the screen again. A message popped up from Daoud.

The truest unions are under Allah's gaze.

Fatima went down another hole. Even though they went to the library together and sat side-by-side at the public computers, they drifted away into separate worlds, typing, reading, thinking, typing. After a few hours they'd leave and go to the halal deli in Newport to eat and talk and think.

They told me to stop wearing the hijab.

They told me not to grow a beard. To keep my hair short. Not to convert until I was there.

If I take off the hijab, my parents will think it's strange. They'll know something's up.

A few days she skipped the library to stay home, with her mom and grandmother, or to go to the mosque by herself. Rez tried not to worry when this happened, tried not to text her every five minutes and ask if

she was ok; if she was against the idea of the trip; if she still loved him. On these empty afternoons he rode the bus down Highway 1, getting on and off whenever he felt like it or at the beach if it looked nice. He sat on the sand and stared at the sea, the bodies of the people, the sand itself, and when he felt better, he'd get back on the bus and ride a ways until he had to do it again. By the time he got home he felt almost ok with the idea that bothered him most: that she might bail and he might have to go it alone.

Two days before they were supposed to leave to take the train north she texted: *walk?* And he said *sure* and they went down to the San Clemente pier. She wore a bright yellow head scarf and held his hand.

Ok. I am good to go.

Really?

Yes. Really.

Rez tried to pretend he wasn't as happy as he was and kept his eyes ahead of him.

You are sure? What did it?

Positive. Last night my mom and I got our nails done and I asked her about getting married, in passing, you know, casual, like when I should do it and if I had someone in mind did I bring it up now or wait. And she looked at me and laughed like I was crazy and told me I had no choice and when the time came they were going to pick a husband for me. They thought it would be later, after college, maybe after grad school, but ever since I got interested in Islam my dad's been asking around.

Rez felt his brain swim around in his skull, banging against the possibilities. His breath caught and he wanted to stay cool. He looked away from her, out to sea.

What did you say?

I said *Ok, mom.* And now I am saying *Ok, Reza.* Let's go.

Daoud helped him out. They kept in touch nearly all the time, through one of many accounts, Facebook, WhatsApp, Twitter, Instagram. Rez wondered if Daoud ever slept. Rez could reach him at any hour and

never asked where he lived, but now and again Daoud offered stories and still seemed amazed at the turns his own life had taken to get to Allah.

Most of the time they hung out in the virtual space and talked about Rez's travel plans, how he and Fatima were to move about, whom they were to meet and how best to cross the border into Syria. Daoud asked him repeatedly about money, and Rez explained that his parents were to fill his checking account every semester to cover the costs of living at college. *And they won't notice if you withdraw it all at once?* Rez said no, though he wasn't completely sure.

Daoud gave precise instructions on how Rez was to act. *On your flight from LAX to Istanbul, order drinks, sit next to Fatima, be happy. When you get into the city, stay in Taksim, go to clubs, go to bars, don't drink, but be there. Act like a young American tourist. Make sure Fatima does not wear the hijab. On the second day I will arrange for you to meet the smuggler in charge of taking you over the border. He will speak English and look Western. You will follow his instructions from there. Whatever you do in your few days, don't act suspicious and, inshallah, doors will open all the way to Raqqah.*

Like a movie. When he thought about it that way, the coming days terrified him. In the movies guys like Rez always died. When he thought about it as his life, as answering the call of a higher power, as making a choice, he relaxed enough to catch the thrill of it, the covert steps, the disguise of his old self, the company of Fatima as his girlfriend, the secret of her as his wife. The adventure and love and belief and deception mixed into a heady potion and Rez spent hours, alone, drunk on the possibilities and always came back to Daoud's words: *Act normal, act regular, don't let your parents, your friends, suspect anything. All deceptions will be forgiven.*

Rez considered himself from the outside. Rich kid. Freshman at Berkeley. A girlfriend at Stanford. Good little immigrant. Off on a nice start to the American dream: behave and you will earn, earn and you will have a place. He imagined the final scene, the good-bye at the San Juan Capistrano train station, two kids going to college. Proud parents.

Maybe some crying. Hugs. They had behaved and now the next door opened to them. He remembered the words of the agent who interrogated him at LAX: *And your people, who think they are worth a great deal, know that even after making all that money, they are worthless. Their children are worthless, and if this violence continues, their children's children will be worthless too. Does that sound familiar?*

This is how the mind comes to understand the future, by imagination. Rez let his thoughts linger and speed depending on his mood but he could not control the way he felt, brave, renegade, righteous. A single man in control of his fate against the forces that would forever keep him low and scared. And of course the fantasies: Fatima in the hostel room, in the one bed, her body and hair and mouth available to him. He had not mentioned it, not brought it up even as a joke, and practiced his new prayers through these grips of desire. He had only a few Arabic phrases to string together and the rest he had to say in English. Either way, after a while, it always worked.

37

FROM OUTSIDE HE was the same old Rez. He ate dinner with his parents every night, spent the afternoons packing the small shipment to his dorm room and convincing his mother again and again it was a good idea he go up alone.

I just want to have the experience.

You don't want your parents to embarrass you in front of your new friends. You want to pretend you don't have parents.

Even as she tried to joke, sadness leaked through her voice. Rez tried to be annoyed that his mom was worried when in truth he worked hard not to let her quivers shake him too. They organized stacks of sweatshirts and books and toiletries and a few framed photos of them as a family. From his desk drawer she pulled out the black-and-white photo of the uniformed man.

Where did you find this?

In the garage.

Do you know who it is?

Family? Dad's family?

Your grandfather, your dad's dad.

She looked at the picture and then put it back in the desk.

A complicated man. A lot of conflict in his soul. Not happy. Not well.

Stay the same.

Daoud's words scrolled through Rez's head when Matthews texted him.

Rager at my house tonight. One last blast.

Rez responded without thought.

Act normal. Daoud reminded Rez and Fatima it might be hard to keep up their old selves as the departure day came close. *But it is more than important. Any suspicion at this point and you will not be able to leave the country, you will be seen as a suspect and arrested.*

They went together and Rez had to stop himself from saying something about Fatima's loose hair, some compliment or evidence of his arousal. They spent most of their time on the dance floor. Matthews had cleared out all of the furniture from the pool house, and the small room with the bar and kitchen was perfect for crowding with bodies. The lights were off and the windows looking out onto the pool had steamed up and Rez lost himself to the music, old hip-hop, new hip-hop, by Drake and a million different remixes. Some old-school Madonna and Beyoncé and everyone in the room went from being eighteen-year-olds to being twelve-year-olds to seven-year-olds and back again, each song belonging to an age they had all shared.

Rez danced around and next to Fatima and each time he thought, I am dancing with my wife, he felt himself get stiff. She sensed it and teased him, moving her hips and hands against the hard-on and laughing. Eventually he left her alone to go get some water and cool down.

When he found her again, she was outside talking to Matthews. They both had their shoes off and shins in the pool. Matthews had on an

OBEY T-shirt with a block print of André the Giant on it. On his head he wore an extra-large baseball hat that said WORLD'S GREATEST DAD and held beer cans, one over each ear. Rez laughed to himself and then took off all his clothes and did a cannonball just in front of where the two were sitting. When he popped his head up, his friend and his future wife laughed and yelled at him and he swam to the edge and kissed Fatima's foot. She gave him a look he couldn't read.

Nice party, man.

Yeah. That pool house dance party is going to go down in the books. Can you at least agree with me about that, Fatima?

She tried to smile. She and Matthews had been in the middle of something, maybe an argument. Rez saw a serious look in her eyes and the way Matthews was quick with the jokes.

Just a little friendly religious discussion in the middle of a huge party. You know how I roll.

Rez wished he hadn't jumped in the pool. He wanted to be dry and ready to leave.

About what?

Matthews took a long sip from one of the straws that came down from the beer can and hung beside his face.

All I am trying to tell her is that I can't choose one God. Why do I have to? So my parents are Catholics, sort of, doesn't mean I have to be Catholic. I'm too young to be anything. I'm just a guy figuring stuff out, and when I've lived enough, I can decide what I believe.

Yes, but how do you know who you are? How to behave? Fatima asked, the calm in her voice bordering on sadness.

I follow the Golden Rule. I am a nice guy. I don't do shitty things to people. I keep it chill. And I am not in a rush to pick a God for the rest of my life. Who knows how long we will live? Just think about it. When we were born, there was no Internet. Now we can't do anything without it. Maybe tomorrow or twenty years from now, half of us will be living on Mars, and then what is God? All I am saying is no one knows about tomorrow's gods. Not me. Not you. None of us. And I choose not to go backwards, forget the old gods, let's wait and see what comes next.

Matthews looked at Rez with his eyebrows up and an unlit joint he'd just pulled out of his pocket, like a man who'd just won an inconsequential debate, like a joker, like a good soul in love with life. Rez gave his friend one last fist bump and was glad he had to pick up his clothes; he had a reason to look at the ground and keep his eyes to himself as his heart tore and tore and tore.

39

Bricks. That's rare. No one builds with bricks in California because of the earthquakes. Maybe this station was built before the earthquakes, or before they knew that bricks didn't stand up in shakes. Yet this still stands. Maybe there is a sign. Yeah, over there, a historical plaque. *Plaque* is such a great word. Smack lack quack tack. Yup. I was right. Built in 1915 under the watch of the U.S. Western Railway expansion. Mentions nothing about the Chinese slaves that built the railways. That's the way. And then there is the mud-and-straw stucco of the mission. Mission of San Juan Capistrano. Who was Capistrano anyway? Maybe there is another plaque. Yup. Named for Giovanni da Capestrano, a warrior priest from the fifteenth century. Maybe that's who will be in Raqqah, warrior priests . . . Oldest building in California. No mention of all the dead Indians. All the Native people who lived here before the Spanish. Might as well not have existed. Ok. Something else, something else. That family waiting for a train. What else? Weather is nice. Sunny, not too hot, though it is early. I wonder what the surf is doing? We're so close to Doheny . . . not enough time . . . could text Matthews and ask . . .

And this is what Rez did with his mind while he and his mom and dad waited for Fatima and her family to arrive at the train station. He did all he could not to think about the good-byes. Real good-byes for a fake trip. Or maybe the good-byes were fake and the trip was real. Or maybe they were both fake. Or both real. Either way. Either way. Rez tried to make his head fall down the rabbit hole of these digressions, loop endlessly from one unstructured thought to the next, but he was unable. The light of the sun was warm and the day bright and his father gestured to him to come inside the train station.

The stood in front of the counter and read the fares.

Do you have your new ATM card?

Right here.

Ok. Let's see if it works.

They got to the woman in the Amtrak uniform and Rez felt bad that she had to wear something so silly and so he smiled broadly at her and she, with her fifty or so years of life, smiled back.

One-way to Berkeley please.

No. No. Get a round-trip. Just schedule the other half for Thanksgiving. You'll probably save money.

The idea of spending extra money, $120 that could be used in Istanbul, in an emergency, crossing the border, aggravated Rez but saying something was not worth the argument. *Act normal.*

Round-trip please. I just have to make sure I don't lose it.

Well, your name is in the computer, just in case.

Rez looked at his card. Plastic. Where did plastic come from? Petroleum. The chemical makeup of petroleum he remembered from AP chemistry. But why did everything have to be made of plastic? Because it was cheap to manufacture, durable . . . he almost turned to ask his dad but then stopped himself, not wanting to engage in conversation, just wanting to fall away from the reality around him into the spirals of his mind until this last bit of theater was over and he and Fatima were riding north, holding hands, staring at the sea.

Her parents had dressed up. They wore nicer versions of things he saw them in at their home. Her mother's head scarf, a thin lavender sheath, only covered half her hair and draped elegantly down her back. Rez had only met Fatima's father once. Ahmed. His pressed shirt and slacks and shoes looked fresh from a business meeting and Rez shook his fleshy hand and spoke to him for a few minutes. Rez did his best to smile at Fatima's mother when she mentioned she was sure Rez would take good care of her daughter.

Of course.

His own mother was crying now.

I know they will do great.

She'd kept herself from it for as long as she could, until the last possible moment.

We have good children.

That is true. They are good children.

The mothers agreed and used tissue to dab at their eyes. Rez watched Fatima hug her mother and listened to the enormous sobs that shook out of their embrace, tired and long and without shame. Near them on the platform the family of four stared and then tried not to stare, and the fathers cleared their throats and tried to end the show but the women kept on as Rez's own mother stood alone with her face pressed in and down and no one put an arm on her shoulder.

The lights on the platform lit up and bells began to chime and Rez shook his father's hand and then felt the long arms wrap around him and pull him in toward the heart.

We will see you in October. At parents' weekend.

I will be there.

Don't do anything I wouldn't do.

Rez's father's stern face had gone slack and he handed Rez his duffel bag full of Islamic texts and cash and clothes for the desert.

Best of luck.

Thanks, Dad.

Then the train stopped in front of them and Rez and Fatima walked up to the entrance and turned around for a last good-bye to the four faces that had made their faces, to the bodies full with emotion and hope and history and love, before they walked to the opposite side of the train so Fatima could lay her head against the glass of the window and cry.

By the time they were in Newport she had adjusted her head scarf and reapplied her makeup and he had done his best to convince her their decision was right and they sat quietly beside each other with nothing to say. Rez stared out at the dry riverbeds and fenced-in yards with sleeping Rottweilers and sun-bleached swing sets and let the chaos of emotions drain out of them. The conductor came by to check tickets and Rez watched him walk down the aisle, punching a hole in the small cards that signified *paid*, all the way to Berkeley. He stopped at their seats and looked at their tickets and asked them to please stand up and

pull their luggage down from the overhead racks. He slipped on blue plastic gloves and asked again when neither of them moved.

Without your permission I will have to call the U.S. marshal that rides with us. He is legally allowed to search bags. It is easier if I do it.

Fine.

Act normal, Rez remembered.

Under her breath Fatima whispered, *This is bullshit,* and looked away from the conductor. The man, in his late fifties, white hair, pocked and rosy nose, a Californian of many generations probably. Rez watched him unzip Fatima's roller bag and look through the few belongings, jeans, sweatshirts, a hair removal device, bras, lots of bras, scarves, shoes, a few books, a stack of photographs, and a large Koran. He picked up the Koran and leafed through the thin pages.

This your book?

Yes.

The book of your religion?

Yes.

The man stared at Fatima and she stared back, arms across her chest, her breath nearly audible. Rez thought of the books in his bag, not the Koran, but about the Koran, about Islam, and he knew that he would throw them away at the train station in L.A., if they made it that far. The conductor put the objects back and zipped the bag. The train began to slow to the next stop, Orange, and the conductor looked at Rez's duffel, picked it up and moved it up and down to gauge its contents. Then he put it at Rez's feet and hole-punched their tickets.

See that you change trains in L.A for the northbound Coast Starline.

Rez felt Fatima reach for and hold his hand and her hand was cool and soft and ready.

40

They had sex on the plane. The bathroom was small, but big enough for two if he stood behind her, her hair in his mouth and their two faces in the mirror changing and changing. There was nowhere to go so he went in, deeper and deeper, in small movements and watched her watch herself and then watch him and then close her eyes. For a while he stared at her face in pleasure, all the tension of the day, the good-byes, the train ride, LAX, the passport lines, the terminal, the takeoff, sucked down and away and the space between her brows, her lips, opened and her face was a full moon of beauty. He didn't want to come so he looked at himself and when his eyes locked with his reflection—the liar, the escaped son, the convert, the reclaimed—in the mirror his head started to spin with violence. Not the side-to-side spinning of being drunk or getting barreled for too long, but a fast up-and-down dizziness like swallowing his feet or doing a back dive and he blinked and saw himself again in the mirror, a kind of monster covering his face, green and grimacing. His hard-on left him and Fatima opened her eyes.

What's up?

Flying made her nervous; the sex was her idea. They'd held hands during takeoff and the clasped hands became a gentle arm up and down her thigh and then in between her thighs and after the meal and the passengers around them either passed out or were catatonic in front of their televisions, she mentioned it and he agreed and they took turns walking to the bathroom in the middle of the plane, far from the stewardess station. They did not discuss it and Rez wanted to say that it was probably ok, because they were not actually on the ground, on earth, and he wasn't officially Muslim yet, hadn't taken the oath, and this was an exception, a distraction, not an offense. He had this all ready but when he opened the bathroom door, she stood in the small aluminum box completely naked, her pale flesh perked with goose bumps, and he thought, Fuck it.

Reza, you ok?

Rez looked at her face, turned back to him in worry.

Yeah, just got a little light-headed. Give me a second. He took a few deep breaths and ran his hands over his face and then ran them over her back and ass and up and down her legs. Nothing. *Reza. Reza.* The new name. He tried to forget about it or pretend it was no big deal but he kept thinking, Reza had never had sex. Only Rez had. Rez had lived all this life so far, and Reza had done nothing more than buy this plane ticket and lie to his parents. She turned around and sat on the closed toilet and looked at him and he put it in her mouth and the sensation of limpness and arousal and fear, the combination new to him, made him panic and he pulled out and pulled up his pants.

Don't worry about it. We should go back to our seats.

She stood up and hugged him with her naked body.

You're right. That's the right thing to do.

They flew through the night, two or three hundred people in rows, each a universe of histories and desires and fears and futures. Fatima slept, her head resting on a pillow propped up on his shoulder. He looked around at the passengers and their sleep or electronic distraction and tried not to think about what was coming or what had been and let himself be up and aloft in these last hours, unbound.

41

The ice cream here tastes different.

It really does. Sweeter. Or something.

Or. Or. Or.

She teased him and he kept licking trying to find the source of the richness. Eggs? More cream? All he knew about ice cream he'd learned in fourth grade when the class made it as a science experiment about freezing points. He remembered that day in Ms. Motsen's class, the explanation of molecules and how, under cold conditions, they slowed and that slowing was freezing. That night he went home and stared at the contents of his freezer, the mist flowing out toward his face, and tried to understand. Because of the cold the molecules moved slower; time too must then move slower; the freezer is a time machine. Rez explained all of this to his father, who smiled at his son and took the conversation further: *If so, is the oven also a time machine?* They talked science like that until he was in eighth grade, the what-if and how come and this is how, and it was the only time Rez saw his father as a person, a thinker, a curious boy like himself, and not just father of the dinner table, father of the car, hard father of the house.

Hot and cold. Fast and slow. Old and young. The two days in Istanbul split themselves apart like this. When they landed, the two of them still in the center of sleep, they stood in silence in the passport line and they stood alone before the Turkish official who looked once at Rez and once at his passport and then stamped it and called to the next person in line. Rez used printed instructions to get them from the airport to the bus and from the bus to the hostel and everything they passed along the way blurred and creased and failed to catch his eye because it was not real, but some reality buried under the deep confusion of time and space, old and new, Rez and Reza.

*

The hostel was nicer than they expected. Cool in a hot city, tucked into an old stone fortress of some kind, modern rugs and Turkish art. The receptionist was Australian, twenty-five or twenty-six years old and hot with shiny blonde hair and sharp blue eyes and just as with every girl that caught his eyes these last weeks, Rez thought his way into feeling sorry for her and the way she prostituted herself in the short jean skirt and off-shoulder T-shirt and didn't even know her sin.

She took them up to a private room with a double bed and they put down their bags and stared at each other and lay down fully dressed and slept, chaste bodies, chaste minds. Between them the heat had gone and Rez relaxed and gave himself to exhaustion and blank dreams.

They had thirty-six hours before they met the smuggler. They spent their time wandering the tourist neighborhoods of Istanbul, running into people their age, in the same sneakers and T-shirts and trucker caps. Everyone attractive and western and mobile. They e-mailed their parents from a café. Rez typed, *Berkeley is awesome. Foggy in the morning and afternoon, but nice. My room is small but has a good desk and my roommate is from Korea. He seems nice.*

They walked down the Bosporus and bought a deck of cards from a newspaper kiosk and played gin rummy on a park bench. Everywhere they walked, the Hagia Sofia mosque was visible and yet neither of them mentioned it. They joked and laughed and held hands and were happy and then, for no reason, he pulled away, or she did, and they walked apart and kept their thoughts to themselves and complained about the city and the travel and the unknown. On and off. As the day went. She wanted to pray and he reminded her what Daoud had said: *Act regular. Act Western.* And they walked past mosque after mosque and she stared in but said nothing.

At dusk they ate a meal of fried fish and potatoes and green salad ordered from a menu in four languages. They played a game of guessing where people came from by their shoes. They walked down the tourist-filled streets, past clubs blasting electronic dance music and cafés that

spilled out into the streets and bars that played soccer matches on huge flatscreens and Rez wished for a faster way back to their hostel. The city disappointed him, it was neither this nor that, not Muslim and not Western, some nowhere in between.

They lay down in the bed, but did not sleep. Fatima sat up beside him in the dark and together they stared at the little line of light at the edge of the curtain, the night outside loud and bright. He said nothing to her but put his hand on her lower back.

What do you think it will be like?

Rez waited until he felt the answer come to him.

I don't know. Weird, at first, then good. Daoud said they will give us an apartment and then give me a job. They said there are labs, and chemists are needed. And we will be married right after I convert.

What do you think it will be like, to be married?

No answer came to Rez for a long time. He waited and his desire grew, harnessed him, and he sat up and wrapped his body around hers until their breath was the same, in and out, in and out, in and out.

Like this.

They fell asleep in this tangle, and when they woke, the day was already well on its way.

Their meeting was at eleven in a part of the city far from Taksim and Rez showed his Google Maps printout to one cabdriver after another and they all shook their heads and said, No no no, and pointed to the water and the water taxis and then drove away. Rez looked at his maps and saw that the meeting spot, a restaurant named Torkoy, was across the Bosporus, on the Asian side, and he asked the Australian receptionist the best way to get there.

Water taxi and then walking, I suppose. Careful your pockets.

The air and wind and sun on the water taxi ride buoyed Rez and for a moment his worries—about being late, meeting the smuggler, getting

over the border, the new life—left him and he simply sat in the yellow light and soft late-summer wind. The water soothed him most and Fatima put on her sunglasses and tied her hair up and they looked together, in the back of the forty-seat water taxi, like a happy couple on their way.

They arrived on a street busy with stores and stalls and traffic and Rez took Fatima's hand and carried their bags as they started to wind up through the curvy residential streets where nearly all the women wore head scarves and every one stared at the couple as they passed. Fatima took her hand out from his and walked at a distance from him.

The restaurant was a hole in the wall, as was everything else in this neighborhood. Locksmiths and cobblers and butchers and fabric stores all as small as they could be lined the streets, broken up by doorways that looked as if they had not been opened in many years. Above the narrow streets people threaded their laundry lines from building to building, sheets and men's shirts and children's clothes, and at Rez's and Fatima's feet dogs sniffed little bags of trash left on the curb. They stood outside for a moment and stared at the entryway.

You ready?

I am.

Ok. Let's go check it out.

Fatima, I don't think this is for checking out. I think as soon as we walk in and meet this guy, it's done. We go.

Rez stopped himself. In her eyes and voice he saw Fatima pull up the courage to do it. To take these steps into the restaurant. At the back of his mind Rez thought about return, about *in case it doesn't work out* and the ways they would leave. He'd kept a little money in his savings account, in case they needed to get out, get back, but he did not mention it.

Without a smile or a change of voice, Fatima responded, Yes. Ok. Yes.

The smuggler was thin, not much older than Rez, but already bald. He wore a European-league football jersey, sweatpants, and Nikes. He sat

at a table with a cup of tea, punching into a cell phone. When he saw them walk in, he did not stand up and Rez introduced himself and Fatima nodded but said nothing.

Yes. Yes. Sit. You are the Americans?

Yes. For a little bit longer.

There were no laughs and Rez and Fatima pulled out chairs at the table and the smuggler raised his eyebrows at the waiter and soon there were two more glass cups of tea.

Good. I am the man you are looking for. Who is your contact?

Daoud.

Ok. He typed the name into his phone. Rez wondered how far his English went. From the accent and the attitude Rez couldn't tell if he cared about Islam, was concerned with the caliphate.

You have paid him already?

Yes.

But what I see is you have only paid for one.

He kept typing into his phone and Rez waited for him to see that he had paid for two, one price for Fatima to cross and another price for Rez. The man typed more and then looked up.

It says one. One fee.

No. I am sure . . . Can I? Rez gestured to borrow the phone.

You cannot.

I paid for two. I can pay you for two now if you want. Does that help?

If you want to cross.

Rez opened the pocket of his backpack that held his passport, his cash, the pictures his mom had given him to hang in his dorm room. He pulled out four hundred dollars and handed it to the smuggler.

Very good. I am Erdrich. Now my instructions are to take you to the border at Ras al-Ayn. Is that what you are expecting?

Yes.

When we are there, I will not drive you into Syria, but to a safe house where you will find the people who will help you cross.

Yes.

She will have to cover at the safe house.

Yes. We know.

But not until then.

Ok.

The excitement grew through Rez and he found himself trusting the guy more for his abrasiveness.

You have bags?

Just these.

Good. Wait here for an hour. I will come and pick you up. Don't talk to anyone.

The roads that led out of the city were congested and Rez and Fatima sat in the back of the Nissan sedan and sweated and looked out the window at the pulsing city. They said nothing, and when they were finally out and away from the traffic, driving past wheat fields and industrial parks, they fell asleep and woke up in much of the same at a different time of day. The driver did not speak. He drove with one hand and texted with the other and smoked as much as he could. They stopped at a gas station with a restaurant attached and Rez and Fatima went in and stared at a fountain of bubbly milk until the server came by and handed them both cups and poured a ladleful of salty, carbonated yogurt in each. The taste was phenomenal and disgusting at the same time and they drank it and laughed and looked for snacks and the bathroom and Rez felt himself on a road trip like any other he had ever loved being on.

They drove into the evening and at dusk the land around them changed. What was yellow and green turned into the orange of the desert and emptied of plant life. Rocks were everywhere and in the distance jagged dark mountain ranges spread beneath the sky and Rez remembered the pictures of Raqqah, the dusty town center, the one beautiful river, and all the parks alongside. Neither of them asked any questions and the sky turned dark, shade by shade, one degree at a time, as they drove east and Rez thought of them heading into night, into the purple dusk and the navy beyond.

*

The safe house was empty and the driver walked through turning on lights, opening windows, and checking the fridge. There was no furniture but there were rugs and cushions and some flat bread and blocks of feta in the fridge. Each room had a few rugs on the floor and near the electrical outlets tangles of chargers left behind. Rez could not tell how long it had been since someone was here. Two days? Two weeks?

The toilets work. Ok?

Rez didn't know what to say. It was ok. They were four miles from the border and all they had to do was wait.

Yes. Thank you.

The driver took a long inhale from his just-lit cigarette.

For the Islam, yes?

What?

Islam? In Raqqah, yes?

Yes, yes. We are going to Raqqah. For the new country.

The driver looked at Rez and then looked at Fatima.

Ok.

He looked at them again and nodded and let himself out the thick wooden door that he didn't shut behind him and they watched him drive away. Fatima closed the door and took her bag upstairs, and when she came down, her hair was covered and her eyes and cheeks puffy from crying.

Again the night grew dark around them and they could not sleep. They sat up and read the books Fatima had brought and Rez wished he hadn't thrown out his books on Islam at the train station in L.A. Fatima prayed and they pulled out the cards and played and waited for sleep but nothing came. Not too long after midnight the door opened and two men walked in and said, As-salaam alaikum, and Rez and Fatima stood up and greeted them in return.

The two men insisted that they make tea, and they all sat on the floor in the empty living room and drank. One of them wore a long beard

and the other looked like a young guy from Istanbul. They were both good-looking, clean, with bright eyes.

We are glad Daoud and our sisters led you here. It is our honor to help you along on your journey.

Their faces stayed jovial and calm and they spoke with precise words. The English was accented, but not terribly so, and they had many compliments for Rez and Fatima about their decision, about their devotion, about their coming marriage.

No one checked his or her phone and no one left the conversation for anything more than another cup of tea or the bathroom. They asked if Rez or Fatima had any questions and then answered them patiently, saying all the things Rez and Fatima wanted to hear—a nice house, probably in a lab if chemistry is still your expertise, there will be other young families nearby, no, no one from California, and, yes, it is marvelous to be in a place where Islam is prized, you will be among the first families to establish a haven for our beliefs, our type of living, it is a brave thing you do, one that will not be forgotten by the generations after you.

Fatima smiled at Rez and he could tell the fear and sadness had left her. She moved her hand closer to his so that their fingers barely touched and the smugglers talked on and on. By dawn Rez himself relaxed enough that all he wanted was sleep and stood to excuse himself and Fatima stood with him and the men, cross-legged on the ground, told Fatima to sit and she looked at them and Rez. He kept her stare, wondered if she would do it.

Fatima, please. There are a few details we need to discuss with you. Moving a woman across the border is much more difficult than moving a man. There are details, please, we will keep you only a half hour, no more . . .

Fatima sat back down and Rez sat down beside her.

The bearded man smiled broadly.

We are brothers here, please do not worry about her, she is in company as secure as yours.

The man from Istanbul nodded.

Yes, my friend, tomorrow your day will be long, it will be hot and there are difficult portions. It is better you rest. But it is your choice.

Rez looked at them through a head thick with sleep. He took in one face and then the other. The two of them appeared without malice. Strangers in this strange life. He had no energy left for nerves, for suspicion or fear, and wanted more than anything else to erase this world for a time, to draw down into darkness and forget his commitments, his pledges, and his changes and changes of heart. Want of sleep was all of him.

Fatima gave him a gentle nod. I'm good.

Rez looked at her face, its beautiful round moon glow tired and dim. The exhaustion made her soft and willing and the man next to her tilted his head at Rez to gesture up toward the bedrooms.

You sure?

Yes.

Go, my brother. Get your strength. Take a stretch. We will wake you when it is time to go.

The room had a few mattresses strewn across a dusty tile floor. Rez found the one closest to the door so he could hear the talk downstairs. At first he sat up to listen but then he quickly felt himself slump over and then fall onto the bed and into a sleep, heavy and syrupy, over which he had no control.

When he woke, his body was in the same position and covered entirely in sweat. The house made no noises and his limbs did not lift as he ordered them and his thoughts stayed irretrievable somewhere at the bottom of his head. He closed his eyes and fell asleep again. The second time he woke, the sun had moved across the walls and he was alert and afraid. Next to him the bearded man sat and read.

Ok, brother. It is time. Time to go.

Fatima. His first thoughts panicked. Where was she? In all this strangeness he needed to see her, to lock eyes on something familiar. He jolted up and walked out of the room and down to the living room where the tea glasses sat washed and set aside and he knew the house was otherwise empty.

Where did they go?

They left a few hours ago. Hamid took her across first. We never cross with more than one at a time. Especially a woman.

Daoud said we would go together, the whole way. Together.

He is not a smuggler. He is not on the ground in Syria. This is our way.

Daoud told me specifically—

Please. Remember your faith in Allah.

Rez stared at the man with the scraggly beard. He saw now how short he was, how there was a weapon, a small pistol, tucked into the back of his pants. Rez edged into anger. Daoud had mentioned nothing about a separation; assured him they would cross the border together; that she would be beside him the whole way. *As it is with husbands and wives, it will be with you.*

Where is she?

I don't know.

Where will we meet her?

I don't know. That is not up to us. My job is to take you to Raqqah, to deliver you to my commander.

But I am going to Raqqah to get married . . . to become a Muslim and get married . . . and my friend Arash . . . This is what I have arranged.

The man smiled with half his mouth.

Yes, my brother! Well done. And now let us go!

Rez carried his bag and walked alongside the man on small streets and then on the side of a big street and then through the dry land with no streets at all. The man walked ahead a few steps and every now and again sang something in Arabic or whistled. Rez left heavy prints with each step and asked about Fatima again and again. Can you explain, please, why did she have to go ahead? How can I be in touch with her? Who is she with right now?

The man with the beard sometimes answered and sometimes shook his head no. When he did respond it was with a surplus of good cheer that aggravated Rez. Have faith, my brother! Things are not as

bad as they seem! You must trust that Allah will do what is right for you! This is the faith you want, isn't it?

Rez no longer wanted faith. He wanted Fatima beside him and another earth under his feet. They seemed to walk into nowhere, nothing visible ahead of them, and the small town with the safe house was a dot on the horizon behind. Soon exhaustion and thirst took the place of his anger and Rez thought about Allah, about the all-merciful, all-knowing, and with concentration he told himself to believe in it, to believe what he felt among the men in the mosque, among the faces in Bali; the great truth, the great rightness, the great faith. His steps grew lighter and Rez felt that each move forward was a move toward Fatima, toward a life of peace in his soul and body, and a move away from the harsh hatreds and sad empty lives of a world that lived on the surface of itself. He thought of her soft lips, of the soft skin of her hands, of her breasts when she was asleep, and he craved. Allah will provide for me. He remembered Daoud's saying that to him again and again: *Allah will provide.*

It was dark when they reached the fence and Rez, thirsty, his feet sore, looked around for lights of some sort but nothing shone. The man with the beard kicked the bottom of the metal fence with his foot, and when he came to a section that gave to his kick, he crawled down on his hands and knees and motioned for Rez to follow. There was no hurry, no rush, and the man seemed without agitation at all. Rez looked around at the land again, rocks, dry hard earth, this fence, and nothing else. The stars were abundant in the sky, maybe more than he'd ever before seen in his life, and he took this as a sign. He stopped and gazed, let his neck stretch back as far as he could to see the uninterrupted scape, the infinity of depth, and this unknown put Rez in mind of the sea, the great ocean that had breathed beside him his whole life that was now nowhere to be found.

Now, brother. Now is the time. She waits for you on this side, not over there.

Rez dropped to his hands and knees, threw his duffel bag in, and crawled through. When he stood, he looked up and saw this side was

no different, the sky just as infinite, the land as dry. He looked back up to find a constellation, to center himself on something, anything, to remind him he was still on earth, and as he did, the want for the ocean swelled and he desired it now more than anything, more than Fatima, or belief or belonging, a night of surf, the feeling of his board under him, his body lifted and dropped, swaying and swayed, the great unfathomable beneath, rocking him to and fro.

EPILOGUE

Ras al-Ayn, Syria, March 2014

Everything in the right way.

In training they learned how a thing was done. How to stand, the proper way to sit with attention, the way to approach a target in clear daylight, and the best way to attack at night. They learned how to load and aim automatic rifles, took lessons on how to fire, what verses to recite as the bullets flew, and what verses for the moment after they hit their marks. Instructors told them which way to wear their backpacks, their face masks, how best to lace their boots. They studied the knife, how to cut across an earlobe, a thieving hand, a neck. They learned how to lie during an interrogation, deny any previous identity, and look directly at photos of their sisters and say *That is not my sister* and pictures of their fathers and claim *I do not know that man.* They were given cyanide capsules and, as backup, instructions on how to hang themselves with a sheet and what kind of knot to make around their necks when the opportunity presented itself. There were long afternoons of recitation, prayers for the night before the battle, leading up to battle, and just before the capture of women and children. Instructors regularly blindfolded them and then said calmly, Run, before firing live ammunition at their feet and legs while the recruits wet their pants and cried for the mothers they had forsaken. Then the blinders were taken off, and the instructors handed them guns and told them to shoot and run from each other, with points given for accuracy without kill, escape without injury. They ran and fought until their fear reached its zenith and crossed over into a numb courage and only then did the instructors shout, *Stop!* And take the guns from them with assurances: *Don't worry. It will be some time before you are trusted with the work of executioner. For now you are soldiers. Allah will test you first. Everything in the right way.*

*

Months of training and study and prayer and practice, and on this, the morning of his first battle, Reza forgets all he has dutifully learned. He closes his eyes and begins to put himself together, piece by piece.

His name as it is now: Reza al-Alawah.

His age as it is today, the day of his first battle, his first pledge: nineteen.

His God as he believes him: all-powerful, all merciful.

Whoever puts his trust in Allah, He will be enough for him.

There it is. The faith.

Allah does not burden a soul beyond what it can bear.

He tries to do as he has trained, but cannot conjure the dozen faceless virgins in heaven or the lavish feasts of paradise, and thinks only of Fatima; of the skin of her cheeks and the curved dip of her back and her soft mouth. That is what waits for him after this trial. That is what the commanders have promised: first he must prove himself, then he can marry.

The recruits repeat it and beat their chests with a closed fist.

A line of open-bed trucks waits and as many men as can fit are packed in and then four or five more. The bodies touch and everything spreads—fear, smell, sweat—from man to man like electricity. They wait, nervous, in the dark of some hour closer to midnight than morning. Commanders appear, each with a flashlight and a map, and spread out to talk to two groups of trucks at a time.

The city is K.

They point to a dot on the map and then at the mountains around it, the streets into it, and the city center. The commanders identify the seven targets that begin the siege and Reza sees the logic in it, generators, hospitals, the television station, a government building, bridges across the river, and nods with the rest even though his Arabic is not good enough to understand and his thoughts wander and run and sprint to the memories of the graduation party at Matthews's pool house and Fatima's hips locked to his. The reminiscence is an agony, a kind of torture that makes Reza shift from foot to foot, changing his weight,

trying to change the contents of his mind. The commander looks at them one by one and speaks slowly.

Your trucks are the first line. You will enter the target destination. Fire to kill—all civilians, all police, and military—until the site is secure.

Reza looks around the truck. There are no British guys, no Norwegians or French. Not even a German who can speak enough English to translate for him. There have never been any Americans in his camp and he has spent most of these last weeks with a fighter from Pakistan playing game after game of silent, difficult chess. Reza stands now beside a man who won't look at him, a man he has seen in the showers, in the barracks, in the food tent, always quiet except to tell the same story over and over: that he is from Iraq, that his mother and brothers, aunts and two uncles, the dog, and all the pigeons in the coop were killed in a drone strike that missed its mark. Reza does not try to catch his eye. In the truck beside them he spots Fariq, the DJ from Morocco, and tries to get his attention and ask, *What is he saying?* But Fariq's head is bowed, his long beard touches his chest, so Reza pretends to listen to the commander and stares at his feet and tries to pray. The trucks start their engines and a few recruits lean over the edge to throw up and a few, like Reza, stare away from the faces of the other men and either look down to their boots or up at the purple sky and the million stars that slowly fade.

Before the town is too close the trucks veer off onto a gravel grade that takes them down to a dusty low flatland with a thin creek. The drivers follow one another until the trucks form a large circle, and when the engines stop, they shout back to the recruits to stay where they are. An older man and a commander appear from a small mud-and-grass structure and walk to the center of the circle. The commander is familiar; his presence at the training camp, regular and still celebrated. A fighter of the best credentials—Afghanistan, Bosnia, Kosovo, Baghdad, Mosul—he has a megaphone and hands it to the cleric, who begins with a prayer that Reza knows, can recite by heart to readily pledge himself, his heart, body, life, to a God that is great.

The cleric announces, Deal with them in a way that strikes fear in those behind them.

The cleric opens his palms and asks that God find and honor their cause of a state, so a state may thrive, through time and the hearts of mortal men and women who can worship Him without persecution, in the proper way. The cleric is old, calm, and his voice is easy to listen to, sonorous with conviction and a kind of love. Reza's head goes quiet and now he can focus, can commit himself, and brings to mind the image that will not fail him, that has served him every time. Fatima in her head scarf, reading the Koran; the look up, her lashes and black eyes and the golden sun of a California afternoon, the sound of kids playing on the playground in Laguna Niguel, the taste of grapes in his mouth, the dream of their children, one day, laughing nearby. Richness and love. A better family. That is all he wanted. A life made of family and God and love. A life of a joy his own life had never known.

And now this. A mistake.

The cleric sings his joyless song and the sky grows bright and the men around Reza sweat their fear and the order of the day is battle and possibly death and if he can only tie himself to the memory of her, at the other end of this, Reza can pull himself through. But his mind fails him and he can't conjure her in a scarf or on that afternoon and instead has an odd, vivid memory, out of time, out of place: his mother making his bed. His room bright and clean, the familiar small woman straightens the sheets, rights the pillow, flattens down the comforter, and hums to herself, *Good Morning America* on the TV in the background, and the sound of the traffic of Highway 1 streams in the open kitchen windows. The cleric sings and Reza stares down at his black boots and knows that here, at the edge of battle, possibly at the edge of his life, belief has abandoned him and he is undone and, so, damned.

Do not fear death. What is offered in God's paradise is far greater than anything on this dry earth.

The commander speaks now and Reza catches every other word, every odd phrase.

The prophet says, I have been given victory by means of terror. We spread our message by the sword. To build this state for our sons and for the sons of our sons.

Reza looks around at the other men in the truck and sees that most of them twitch a hand or a knee. Some keep their eyes closed and nod their heads and a few keep nobly still. He thinks of the sons he wanted and he thinks of the sons these men desire or have left behind and Reza remembers a comment by a recruit from Lebanon, that the Hezbollah fighters are given pills, an aggressive kind of ecstasy, that turns the mind red and the body into a fast, efficient machine, and Reza wonders why the commanders don't just give them all pills. He would take a pill now in the place of all this talk.

God is great!

Think, brothers, of the wars waged on you. Your fathers taken into slavery by the enemies of Islam, your mothers turned into whores, you yourselves kept in prisons, kept powerless, kept from the glory of our caliphate!

God is great!

This morning K is ours!

God is great!

The recruits scatter slowly through the valley and Reza walks away from them as quickly as possible to walk the cold ground and leave boot prints in the thin frost. He wonders how long they will stay here, tucked away, worrying before battle. Thoughts of Fatima prance nimbly at the far corners of his mind and he finds himself staring at his boot prints pressed through the frost and knows the sun will come up and erase them and day will finally begin. He tries not to let his mind fail him, to loop back to the life he has quietly and slowly cursed these last weeks and months, but pushes toward the dream of her, the sense and smell and sight of her ahead of him like a mirage. A small sparrow hops toward him, its eyes and neck and chest flit and flit with ceaseless tiny energies. Reza stares at the bird and the bird, a silly serious thing, a creation of God, stares back. He tries to remember a simple prayer, to say a blessing for himself. Nothing. He tries to remember Fatima.

Nothing. He closes his eyes against the day and finally it is quiet. The valley. The morning. His mind. Reza looks around and feels it, the passing over and passing through of all fear and all courage until he is left alone, not a convert and not a coward, no hero or martyr, simply the flesh of a man who walks the earth in search of his woman, and maybe his god and maybe a home on the other side of this battle, if it is to be.

The sparrow hops and then jumps up and flies away and behind him as the trucks start their engines and turn their steering wheels in the direction of town. Reza rises, all the fight drained from him now, and jogs to his truck and hops in next to the others, some with green faces, some with darkened eyes, and sits among them and joins them as empty a man as he can be, a man ready to fire the bullets or receive the bullets, a man ready to give himself away and be received by love.

ACKNOWLEDGMENTS

To the people who make books come into the world. As ever, Ellen Levine and Alexa Stark and the stellar team at Trident Media. Anton Mueller and Alexandra Pringle for your support of this trilogy from word one, remarkable editors with lovely long-distance vision. To all at Bloomsbury who put these words before the readers' eyes, managing editor Laura Phillips, and copyeditor Steven Henry Boldt. Many thanks to Payam Nahid for his help with issues of English futbol and to Karl Mendoca for his assistance in finding that last reader.

Motherhood and writing novels are not, by their nature, compatible endeavors and for this story to come to life I relied (heavily at times) on the gracious hearts of family and friends who must be named and celebrated. David Deniger for his support when the book was just a notion and would have stayed such if not for his help sending a then two-year-old to day care. Andre Julien, who received said two-year-old in his warm and nourishing home. Mary Sue and Patrick Kelly for their availability and kindness week after week, year after year. Antara Medina and Diana Montes Ortiz, whose generosity of heart allowed me to exit reality and enter into the world of fiction.

And most urgently my gratitude goes out to the people to whom I return, season after season, for inspiration, support, and love, who mix art and life such that they are one: Muthoni Kiare, Keenan Norris, Joel Tomfohr, Saneta deVouno Powell, Ramona Ausubel, Micheline Marcom, Cristina Garcia—thank you. To Kamran and Fereshteh and Kamyar, who have supported my adventures in fiction year after year.

Timothy: there is no language for my gratitude, without you this book would not be. To Keon and little (for now) Kassra: you keep me dialed to the station of love, thank you.

Also available by Laleh Khadivi

The Age of Orphans

Winner of the Whiting Award for Fiction, the Barnes and Nobles Discover New Writers Award and an Emory Fiction Fellowship

A nine-year-old Kurdish boy plays in his village in the Persian mountains, gazing over the land of his fathers and forefathers. But when messengers from the hills bring whispers of war and rumours that the Shah's army is on the march, he must stand alongside his villagers and fight for their land. Years later, he can only faintly recall the brutal murder of his father and cousins. Orphaned on the battlefield, conscripted and given a new name, Reza is married and has risen up the ranks to become Captain. But he will soon be sent west to Kermanshah, to rule as the Shah's servant in the land of his birth.

'Bold and beautiful . . . Khadivi's language is sensuous and rich'
Financial Times

'Assured and endlessly creative' *Metro*

'Khadivi's debut novel, remarkable for its beautiful and brutal poetry, tells the story of a lost Kurdish child and the history of "this invisible thing called Iran"' *Independent*

Order your copy:
By phone: +44 (0) 1256 302 699
By email: direct@macmillan.co.uk
Delivery is usually 3–5 working days.
Free postage and packaging for orders over £20.
Online: www.bloomsbury.com/bookshop
Prices and availability subject to change without notice.
bloomsbury.com/author/laleh-khadivi

BLOOMSBURY PUBLISHING

Also Available by Laleh Khadivi

The Walking

A haunting novel of the immigrant experience in America, from the author of *The Age of Orphans*

Iran. 1979. The mullahs have come to power and they want everyone to know. Two young Kurdish brothers, Saladin and Ali, are forced to swear their loyalty to the new regime by taking part in a massacre. In the traumatic aftermath of the killing they flee.

For Saladin, the younger, the decision to travel west is exciting. But his euphoria is not enough for the reluctant Ali, who belongs, heart and soul, to the mountain town of his birth. As they cross the treacherous Zagros mountains by foot to Istanbul, to the Azores by freighter and finally as smuggled cargo aboard a plane to Los Angeles, Saladin realises that his dream of a better future can only be fulfilled alone.

'This is a brave and haunting book about displacement and identity' *Independent*

'A strangely distancing style, as though the self-conscious beauty of her prose and the distressing events she writes about are ultimately irreconcilable, which in many ways they are' *Sunday Herald*

'A haunting novel of the immigrant experience in America' *Bookseller*

Order your copy:

By phone: +44 (0) 1256 302 699
By email: direct@macmillan.co.uk
Delivery is usually 3–5 working days.
Free postage and packaging for orders over £20.
Online: www.bloomsbury.com/bookshop
Prices and availability subject to change without notice.
bloomsbury.com/author/laleh-khadivi

BLOOMSBURY PUBLISHING